OLD KILN

JIA PINGWA

TRANSLATED BY

James Trapp, Olivia Milburn
and Christopher Payne

SINOIST

Published by Sinoist Books (an imprint of ACA Publishing Ltd)
London - Beijing

info@alaincharlesasia.com ☎ +44 20 3289 3885
www.sinoistbooks.com

Published by Sinoist Books (an imprint of ACA Publishing Ltd) in
arrangement with People's Literature Publishing House

Author: Jia Pingwa
Translators: James Trapp, Olivia Milburn and Christopher Payne
Editor: David Lammie **Cover Art:** A. Bodrenkova **Proofreader:** Hui Cooper

Original Chinese text © 古炉 (gu lu) 2011,
People's Literature Publishing House, China

ALL RIGHTS RESERVED. NO PART OF THIS PUBLICATION MAY BE REPRODUCED IN MATERIAL FORM, BY ANY MEANS, WHETHER GRAPHIC, ELECTRONIC, MECHANICAL OR OTHER, INCLUDING PHOTOCOPYING OR INFORMATION STORAGE, IN WHOLE OR IN PART, AND MAY NOT BE USED TO PREPARE OTHER PUBLICATIONS WITHOUT WRITTEN PERMISSION FROM THE PUBLISHER.

English Translation text © 2025 ACA Publishing Ltd, London, UK. A catalogue record for *Old Kiln* is available from the National Bibliographic Service of the British Library.

This novel is entirely a work of fiction. The names, characters and incidents portrayed in it are the work of the author's imagination. Any resemblance to actual persons, living or dead, events or localities is entirely coincidental.

Paperback ISBN: 978-1-83890-526-2
eBook ISBN: 978-1-83890-527-9

*Sinoist Books is honoured to be supported using public
funding by Arts Council England.*

OLD KILN

JIA PINGWA

Translated by JAMES TRAPP, OLIVIA MILBURN
and CHRISTOPHER PAYNE

SINOIST BOOKS

PART ONE
WINTER

ONE

SOMEHOW OR OTHER, Inkcap just didn't make the connection. All he had done was climb up the outside of the cupboard to take a sniff at what was on top, and, to his surprise, the oil jar had fallen to the ground.

But that jar was made out of porcelain, it was an antique. Gran said that, ever since she had married and moved to Old Kiln Village, they had always kept their soya bean oil in that jar. It was of a quality that hadn't been fired in the kiln up on the mountain for a hundred years. Inkcap had put a small plank stool on top of the square table he plonked hastily in front of the cupboard and had just scrambled up to the top when the peg in the wall snapped with a sharp crack. He watched helplessly as the jar went tumbling down to become a pile of shards on the floor.

Gran was sitting in the doorway combing her hair, which was still thick but snowy white all over. After a while, she tugged the loose hairs out of the comb, rolled them into a ball and stuffed it into a crack in the wall beside the door frame. There were already quite a few such balls in that crack. Inkcap was waiting until Noisy arrived with the carrying basket on his bicycle and called out from the stone lions in front of the entrance of the village. He planned to exchange the hairballs for some cooking sugar.

"What was that?" Gran asked when she heard the crash.

"The oil jar," Inkcap replied. "It fell off."

With the comb stuck in her hair again, Gran rushed into the house, snatching up a small broom on her way with which to beat Inkcap. She had delivered one blow with the broom when her eye fell on the oil pooling on the floor. She hurriedly tried to scoop it into a dish using a ladle, but it was the wrong utensil for the job. So she used her fingertips instead, wiping the oil off the floor and scraping it off her fingers on the edge of the dish until she couldn't pick up any more. Then she wiped her oily fingertips on Inkcap's lips. He stuck his tongue out and licked up the oil.

"Look at my good oil!" Gran yelled. "Did you break it, you clumsy great brute?"

"I wanted to smell the smell and it just fell off."

"Smell what smell? What are you talking about?"

"There was a special smell," Inkcap protested. "I smelt it."

Inkcap first noticed the smell a few days ago and it was still there now. It was like nothing he had smelt before, weird and coming in sudden wafts. It was a bit like camphor, a bit like rotting peaches, with a whiff of worn shoes and vinegar and maybe even a trace of 666 pesticide powder. It was a bit-of-everything kind of smell. He had tried tracking it down but without success.

"Maybe there's something wrong with your nose," Gran said, tilting his head back to inspect his nasal passages. There didn't appear to be any problem, but Gran did wipe away a bit of snot, then cleaned her fingers on the sole of her shoe.

"I kept smelling a smell," Inkcap said. "I thought it was coming from the wall up there."

Gran glanced round the main room whose walls were chalk-washed to a brilliant white. A picture of Chairman Mao was hanging on the wall above the cupboard but next to it was the broken peg from which the oil jar had been hanging. Gran stared at it distractedly for a moment, then asked, "And did you knock the oil jar when you were smelling your smell?"

"I didn't knock it. It fell by itself."

"Don't get all pig-headed with me, you pig-head!" Gran yelled and began to beat him with the broom again.

Inkcap jumped out of range of the broom, and the two of them proceeded to run in circles around the room. When the broom hit Inkcap on the arse, he tried to ward it off but it hit him on the hand instead. The cat under the table screeched, "Ow! That hurt! Ow! That hurt!" in sympathy, but didn't even squeak when Inkcap kicked it as it got in his way.

"Are you just going to let me keep hitting you and not escape?" Gran exclaimed, at which point, Inkcap did indeed make a break for it out of the door. Gran went after him, still lashing out with the broom but only hitting the ground behind his pounding legs. Even when Inkcap reached the end of the alley, Gran was still impotently beating the frame of the courtyard gates with the broom and making them reverberate.

It hadn't snowed that day, nor was there any wind. The snow that had fallen a few days before had all been swept into the drainage ditches on either side of the alleyway, and snow and mud had been churned together so it made a click-clack sound when you walked on it and your shoes didn't get wet. But icicles were still hanging from the ends of the gullies of the tiled roofs of the courtyard walls, and they dropped from time to time, point first, into the mud or the snowdrifts. Inkcap had short, stumpy legs, which meant he had to swing his arms vigorously if he really wanted to get up speed when he ran. The rubber tree at the mouth of the alleyway, which belonged to Inkcap's family, shook violently. He thought it was him making it shake, but when he stopped in his tracks, the tree kept shaking, sending a creaking noise up into the heavens.

A bunch of people were squatting under the tree: Sprout, Barndoor, Baldy Jin, Sparks and Tag-Along were all there. The skin-stripping heat of summer was long over, and the winter was so cold even the rocks were frozen doubly solid. The men had just delivered a load of piss to the production team to mix in with the night soil and were resting up now and blowing on their hands. Although the sun was still in the sky, it was only the faint red of a slapped arse and the men's breath formed white clouds as they blew, which wreathed in the air like when the lid is lifted off a basket of steamed buns, or when a cow lifts its tail and deposits several dollops of manure on the ground.

Caretaker's wife and Lucky were having a row in front of the mountain gate, probably because Lucky had borrowed one yuan eighty fen from her several months ago. Lucky was claiming he'd repaid it recently and Caretaker's wife was saying he most certainly hadn't. The two of them had been at it for ages without any sign of a resolution. None of the men under the tree intervened to try to settle the argument, mainly because they had no idea how to go about it. In the end, some kid came out and took a shit in the alleyway, and a man somewhere started calling his dog, "Yo! Yo! Yo! Yo!..." Actually, it was Ever-Obedient's family dog that was being called. It was a huge, imposing beast but all the other little curs pricked up their ears and came running, yapping, "He's coming! He's coming!" But their voices were so patchy and excited that they just sounded like a cacophony of barking. Lucky and Caretaker's wife stopped their arguing too. The Shun family dog came padding out, huge-framed and with a coat so shaggy it looked as though it had a large quilt draped over its back. It raised its head at the top of Three Fork Alley and gave a single great "Woof!" The sound was dragged out for a long time, and all the other dogs stopped their yammering and tucked their tails between their legs.

The village was now quiet and the men under the tree felt bored. Some of them smoked and some of them dozed off, or they undid their jackets and began to pinch out the lice from the cotton padding. Baldy Jin was relieving an itch by rubbing his back against the rubber tree and was the first to see the smoke rising from the kitchen of the house halfway down the alley. The blue-grey smoke went straight up at first but then curled and softened like grass in water. He was still a little bleary from sleep, but when Inkcap came running up, shouting his head off, his brain cleared immediately, and he called out, "Inkcap! Hey! Hey! Inkcap!"

Inkcap had something of a reputation in the village. His actual name was Ping'an, meaning "Peace", but the villagers never called him that. They all called him Inkcap, which literally means "Dog Piss Moss". It is the name of a kind of inedible, poisonous mushroom, no bigger than the pad on your index finger, which grows on ground where dogs have pissed. He knew that he had got the nickname because of his small size and because the other villagers walked all over him. To start with, he hated anyone calling him that, but later on, as everyone started using it, he put up with it.

"Hey, Inkcap, has Gran had your hide again?" Baldy Jin asked.

Inkcap didn't like Baldy Jin, so he squinted at him and shouted back, "Baldy Jin! He's a real slaphead! Not a single hair!"

"What did you say?"

"Nothing, Slaphead... I mean Uncle Jin!"

Baldy Jin wasn't just bald. Ever since he had married Half-Stick, he had often complained of lower back pain, and had heard from somewhere that it could be cured with eucommia from the rubber tree. So he had been secretly scraping the bark off Inkcap's family's tree to make an ointment. Inkcap had caught him at it and sworn at him, so he stopped, but he still came and rubbed his back against the tree when the opportunity arose. He was delighted at having forced Inkcap to call him "Uncle" and he rubbed himself against the tree with renewed vigour. Inkcap couldn't help feeling something untoward was going on. The tree was up against a big, hard wall and was going to get hurt. He ran over and tried to push Baldy Jin away.

"Stop rubbing against that tree."

"It's only a tree. It's not like I'm rubbing myself against you!"

"It's my family's tree."

"Yes, and I'm rubbing against it. So what?"

Inkcap couldn't budge Baldy Jin by pushing him, so he rammed him with his head, only succeeding in butting Baldy's trouser belt. Baldy was unperturbed and even ruffled Inkcap's hair, saying, "Aiya! What are we to make of you, Inkcap? If you reckon you're one of those lower-middle peasants turning black in the sun all day, then turn black, why don't you? But you're not a lower-middle peasant, are you? And your eyes bulge. If it was just bulging eyes, it wouldn't be a problem, but you've got a big belly and sticks for legs! Actually, that would be fine too, but what about those bat ears? You could even get away with the bat ears if you weren't so short. Why are you round as a ball and not growing any taller?"

These words just pissed Inkcap off even more, and he used all his strength to pin Baldy Jin's hands against the tree. "Suppose I don't want to grow any more? Did you think of that?"

"You're pretty fierce for a little squirt, aren't you!"

Inkcap ground his teeth in fury so hard it made his ears waggle.

"What's that all about?" Baldy Jin asked. "Are you trying to tell us you want a hat to wear?"

You need to understand that when Baldy Jin mentioned a hat, he wasn't talking about the blue canvas cap he was wearing, nor the button-up-earflap fur hat that Cowbell wore. He meant a political dunce's hat, like the ones reactionary factions were made to wear during the Cultural Revolution. Inkcap hated the mention of hats more than anything else. This was because Old Kiln didn't originally have any of the four standard hostile factions of landlord, rich peasant, counter-revolutionary and Bad Element, but when the Social Education Movement started and Commune Secretary Zhang came to make an inspection, he asked Village Branch Party Secretary Zhu Dagui why a place the size of Old Kiln didn't have any class enemies. Thereupon, Lightkeeper's family were immediately designated "landlords". Lightkeeper's dad was so enraged that his bottled-up fury made his belly swell and he died, and the "landlord hat" was passed on to Lightkeeper. But the shit didn't stop there, and it was discovered that Inkcap's grandfather had been press-ganged by the Kuomintang Army and taken to Taiwan in 1949, so Gran was also classed as having joined Chiang Kai-shek's puppet army. From then on, whenever there was a class struggle in the village, naturally, Lightkeeper and Gran were the targets.

When they were at home, Gran cursed Grandpa: "You God-cursed old devil! It would have been better if you'd been shot outright."

"Does that mean I'm part of the puppet army too, Gran?" Inkcap asked.

"You don't have a hat."

"Do you think they might still give me one to wear?" Inkcap asked anxiously.

"Don't worry, little darling, your gran will wear it."

"What about when you die, Gran?"

Gran cradled him in her arms. "I'm not going to die. Your gran isn't going to die."

Inkcap really believed Gran was going to live forever, and, from then on,

5

Gran kept his head shaved nearly bald, even in cold weather. The whole affair meant he couldn't stand the sight of anyone wearing any kind of hat, and he couldn't bear to hear people talking about hats either.

"You're the one wearing a hat!" Inkcap yelled at Baldy Jin.

Baldy Jin was indeed wearing a hat, though he had just taken it off to scratch his head, dislodging scabs as red as roasted persimmons. Sprout and Sparks sniggered because everyone knew that Baldy Jin had never used to wear a hat because his head was too itchy, but once he married Half-Stick, she made him wear a blue canvas hat, winter and summer. He even wore it in bed because Half-Stick wouldn't let his head touch the pillow without it.

Shame flared into anger in Baldy Jin. "You little shit! I'll rip your tongue out!"

Baldy Jin's fist flew past Inkcap's nose, just as Barndoor snatched him away and pulled him in close. Barndoor had just finished a pipe of tobacco and the dottle he knocked out still contained a kernel of flame as it landed on the upper of his shoe. He stuffed more tobacco into his pipe, but when he picked up the embers, the spark of fire in them had died so he told Inkcap to fetch him a light.

All the villagers were accustomed to sending Inkcap on little errands, and Inkcap was quite used to it. He actually liked it this way because it meant the villagers could say he was a harder worker than Cowbell. He knew that Barndoor had deliberately sent him for a light to get him out of the way and avoid a beating from Baldy Jin. Baldy was clearly intent on bullying him today, so he looked around towards the mountain gate, where he saw that Lucky was smoking a pipe.

Lucky and Caretaker's wife were arguing again. "Stow it, you two, or we'll get the Branch Secretary to stow it for you," Sparks shouted.

"Bet you wouldn't dare," Caretaker's wife yelled back.

"Of course I'd fucking dare!"

Caretaker's wife flopped to her knees at the mountain gate and said, "I swear by the God of Sunlight, all I want is my one yuan eighty fen. May the Five Thunders of Heaven and Earth set fire to me like a matchstick, and may I die a miserable death if I'm lying."

When she'd finished, she stared at Lucky. Lucky immediately fell to his knees too and proclaimed, "There is Heaven above and Earth below, and between them is my conscience. If I haven't paid back that money next time I climb the mountain to cut the grass, may I be battered to a pulp when I slip and roll down the mountainside to my death."

When he had finished, the two of them calmly stood up and went their separate ways.

Lucky came over, pipe in his mouth, with saliva dribbling from its white jade mouthpiece.

Inkcap stood up and went over to meet him, saying, "Why are you taking stupid risks with her like that, Uncle Lucky?"

Lucky just glanced at him and took no notice.

"She said the thunder could strike her down," Inkcap persisted. "Could it really strike her down?"

"What do you think?"

Inkcap's face blushed crimson. He didn't want to offer Lucky a light any more, nor did he want Sprout, Sparks and the others to see him getting all choked up at Lucky's mockery. "Tell Useless to get your light," he said abruptly.

Useless had just crossed the alley, book in hand, reading as he went. He was about to step in a mound of dogshit when Sprout called out, "Watch where you're putting your feet!"

Useless snapped out of his reverie but too late to stop his foot from landing firmly in the dogshit. Everyone standing under the rubber tree gave a shout of laughter. Embarrassed, Useless was about to beat a hasty retreat when he noticed Inkcap in the group and called out to him, "Come here, Inkcap. Come over here."

"Go and find a light," Inkcap replied. "Uncle Barndoor wants you to get him a light."

Useless showed no sign of having heard him and just said, "I taught you your characters. Can you write your name?"

Useless had been to primary school and the more people there were around, the more he liked to show off about having taught Inkcap to write.

"Of course I can," Inkcap said.

"You can, can you? What else can you write? Can you write the characters for 'antonym'?"

Inkcap didn't know what an antonym was.

"If I give you a word, can you tell me what the opposite is?"

"Of course."

"Eat."

"Not eat."

"Revolution."

"Not revolution."

"Go away!" With a look of contempt on his face, Useless aborted the attempted lesson and walked out of the alley.

Why had he stopped? Inkcap didn't understand and nor did the rest of the group. Just at that moment, a bird flew across above them and dropped a dollop of shit, which, aimed or not, landed flush on Inkcap's head. The first to notice the bird flying past was Tag-Along's family dog. It was a tail-less creature that used to pretend to be a wolf at night and crouch on the ridge outside the village to scare people. It came bounding down from the kiln site, and, once it was through the mountain gate, launched itself into the air with a great bark.

Sparks looked up into the sky and exclaimed, "Ha! It's got a fish in its beak!"

Inkcap looked up too, and immediately recognised the bird as the one that lived in the cypress tree in the courtyard of the Kiln God Temple. It had a white tail and a red beak, in which, sure enough, there was a redfish. If the bird had left its cypress tree, it must mean that Goodman had also left the temple to go and diagnose someone. Everyone picked up stones to throw at the bird. Baldy Jin even took off his shoe and threw that, but they all missed.

"There's a lot less redfish in the Zhou River this winter," Baldy Jin said, but no one took any notice of him and his words fell to the ground and faded away.

Useless's brief passage and the bird up in the sky had interrupted the flow of conversation under the rubber tree, and Baldy Jin sat down again to scratch his bald pate. Everything returned to normal and they grew bored again, just looking aimlessly out towards the Zhou River. Fog was rising on the river. The Zhen River Pagoda and the cabins below it had begun to disappear, as had the surface of the river itself. For a while you could see the water, but it didn't seem to be flowing, as if it was covered in sheet glass. A while later, everything had disappeared to leave just an expanse of white. A car drove by on the road beside the river, and a pack of dogs started chasing and snapping at it. Inkcap smelt that smell again.

TWO

INKCAP COULD SMELL THE SMELL EVERYWHERE, in the courtyard, in the alley, even at the kiln site. He could smell it by the spring, in the underbrush, even on humans and dogs. But when he mentioned it, no one believed him. "Oh, that old bullshit. Haven't you got any new crap to talk about?"

They would flick him on the forehead with their fingers, pop-pop poplike they would crack open a gourd to make a ladle. Even Decheng, a wizened old chap who was sitting at a desk in the team headquarters recording the work points, joined in when he heard Inkcap ask Happy, "Hey, Grandpa Happy! Can you smell anything?"

Happy, who was giving Decheng the cattle feed figures, just looked at him suspiciously, and Decheng called Inkcap over. "So you've smelt something weird again, have you?" he asked.

"That's right."

Decheng put a hand underneath his buttocks and let rip a fart. Then he stuck his hand under Inkcap's nose, saying, "So what does that smell like, then?"

Inkcap felt aggrieved because he really could smell that smell. What particularly spooked him, though, was that he had smelt it when he walked past Pockmark's door and, not long after, Pockmark's mother had died. Then he had smelt it in the reed garden on the embankment and, five days later, the Zhou River had flooded. As if that wasn't enough, he had smelt it in the rear courtyard of Big Root's house and one of Big Root's chickens had been taken by a weasel. He had smelt it on Noodle Fish's body, and Noddle Fish's two stepsons, Stonebreaker and Padlock, had got into a vicious fight. When Cowbell got to hear about this, he spread the word around the village. Cowbell believed there was something weird about Inkcap and he kept pestering him about smelling out a rat's nest where there was grain stashed. Last year, Cowbell had found a rat's nest on the embankment at the south entrance of the village and when he dug it out, there was half a *jin* of maize hidden in it. After that, he went digging all over the embankment but never found anything else.

"I can't smell that kind of thing," Inkcap told him. "And even if I could, I wouldn't tell you."

"Ha! In that case," Cowbell said, "you can't have any of my dried persimmons."

Cowbell had two dried persimmons in his pocket and he'd been going to give Inkcap one of them but now he didn't. Inkcap tried to snatch one anyway, and the two of them had a crazy set to in the mouth of the alley. They were locked in each other's arms, wrestling away, when they crashed into the Branch Secretary, sending him tumbling to the ground and knocking his tobacco pouch out of his sleeve.

"Grandpa!" Cowbell squawked in alarm.

"Grandpa!" said Inkcap. "I didn't do it on purpose, Grandpa Secretary!"

"I know you didn't," the Branch Secretary said with a smile. "You wouldn't dare. Have you hurt your nose?"

Inkcap's nose had smashed into the bunch of keys hanging down from the Branch Secretary's belt and was as red as if it had been smeared with chilli juice.

"Aiya! Now Inkcap won't be able to smell anything!"

"What's all this nonsense about smelling things?"

"No, it's true," Cowbell said. "Inkcap really can smell a special smell. Whenever he smells it, something weird happens in the village."

The Branch Secretary became serious. "Your family background is bad enough, Inkcap, so don't go making things worse by spreading crazy stories. You need to be on your best behaviour, and you definitely don't want to cause me trouble."

So Inkcap didn't dare talk about the special smell any more, but that didn't stop him from smelling it occasionally. Now, however, he went to tell the tree because he felt trees were reliable things. If they started growing somewhere, that's where they went on growing forever. They weren't like clouds, which always went chasing after the wind.

"What's going on?" he asked the tree. The tree rustled its leaves at him with a noise like a ghost clapping. He tried asking a pig. He liked pigs better than chickens and dogs. Pigs were silent most of the time and just ambled amiably along. But when the pig heard his question, it kept mum and just creased its forehead into wrinkles like ropes. All Inkcap could do was tell Gran, who immediately took fright. She made a thorough check of his nostrils again, but everything seemed fine. Once, Cowbell had arrived with the black pits of his nostrils streaming with snot, but Inkcap's nose had remained dry and clear. So what exactly was going on with his nose that he kept smelling the smell? Gran said it was probably the cold weather, and once winter had passed, maybe everything would be fine. She may have said that, but from then on, when she made her lucky flower papercuts, she didn't stick them on the windows or on the rice and noodle jars on top of the cupboard, but shoved them in increasing numbers under Inkcap's pillow and thrust them under his bellyband. She also thought that the way flowers and trees bloomed so colourfully was a manifestation of their souls, while human intelligence and ingenuity illustrated their spirit. Even the birds in the air and the pigs, dogs, cattle and cats on the ground were possessed by the gods, so she made more papercuts in their image and muttered incantations over them, begging the gods to protect her grandson.

Even when Inkcap still caught a chance whiff of the smell, he couldn't say anything but just had to keep it bottled up inside him, making him look even more stolid and doltish than ever. The villagers would see him standing around in a daze, either in the long alleyway or under some wall or other. He would be peering at something cautiously, but as soon as he realised someone else was there, he would slink away furtively. Nobody cared much whether he stayed or left, any more than they cared about a stray cat in the alley or the wind blowing through the trees and stubble. But one time, Bash saw Inkcap standing around looking vacant. He grabbed him by his bat ears and asked, "Why the long face, eh?"

Inkcap didn't mind Bash grabbing his ears because it didn't really hurt, and he just replied, "I come from a bad family."

"And that's making you unhappy? Are you happy running errands for everyone, then?"

"I've always done that."

"You don't have a choice! Hey, have you smelt that smell again recently?"

"Nor for the last ten days or so."

"Really? There's going to be a funeral in the village soon, so how come you haven't smelt it?"

"I really haven't!"

Looking disappointed, Bash reached out and tore down a spider's web from a corner of a wall. A spider sitting on the web had a pattern like a ghost mask on its back. When Inkcap looked more closely, he realised it was a type he'd never seen before. Bash broke off one of its legs, then another and the spider gave off a hissing sound. Inkcap couldn't bear to watch any more and jumped to his feet.

Bash was the best-looking and most relaxed man in Old Kiln. He was tall, broad-shouldered, with a fresh face and white teeth, but Inkcap was unhappy with him pulling the legs off the spider. When Inkcap jumped up, he was intending to yank at a clump of Bash's fringe, but Bash was too tall for Inkcap to reach his hair.

"What do you think you're doing?"

"Your hair was hanging over your eyes. You couldn't see what you were doing."

Bash released the spider, rearranged his hair and then turned his gaze slowly onto Inkcap. "Tell, me, how come you can smell that smell? And what do you feel when you do smell it?"

"I feel like my dad's come home."

"Your dad? Do you even know who your dad is?"

"No."

"I don't know either, but I heard that Granny Silkworm went to market in town and came back with you. I'm not sure whether someone gave you to her in town or whether she found you on the way back."

When Inkcap heard this, he felt even more well-disposed towards Bash. He reckoned that Bash really cared about him because no one in the village had ever told him anything like that before. Even Gran said he'd been fished out of the river with a wicker sieve, or that he'd sprung out of a crack in a boulder. Only Bash had said that Gran had carried him home.

Inkcap often thought about his grandfather. At Gran's "struggle session", they said that his grandfather was a Kuomintang officer in Taiwan. But where was Taiwan? And what was a Kuomintang officer? Inkcap simply couldn't imagine what his grandfather was like. He also thought about his mum and dad. Who were they? He had been both ways up and down the Zhou River, to the township of Luozhen, as well as to the villages of Xiahewan and Dongchuan. The people in Luozhen were very like those in Dongchuan and Xiahewan. So what would his mum and dad be like? Inkcap had the random thought that he really hoped his dad wasn't like Lightkeeper. Lightkeeper came from a bad family, and he was too tall and thin. He didn't like him. He wanted his dad to be like Bash. That would be great. As for his mother, who did he want her to be like? Well, not Noodle Fish's shrew of a wife, nor Baldy Jin's wife, who was too full of herself. Awning's wife had a good temperament but there was something wrong with her eyes. She should be like Flower Girl. He liked her smooth skin and soft body, and she was always smiling.

From then on, Inkcap enjoyed Bash's company, except that he couldn't quite figure out his moods. Sometimes Bash would pinch Inkcap's ear and say it was as soft as cotton, and he would be all talk and smiles, but other times, he went cold and wouldn't let Inkcap follow him around.

When Inkcap saw him tidying his box of cobbler's tools, he asked, "Are you really going to go mend shoes?"

"Nobody's going to give me any pocket money if I don't, are they?"

"Are you going back to that little wooden shack of yours?"

"What about it?"

"I'll come with you."

"Are you my tail now?"

"I can run errands for you."

Bash carried his box of tools to a little wooden shack beside the public highway and Inkcap followed him from a certain distance, neither too close nor too far away. Even when Bash picked up a clod of earth and threw it so it broke into pieces at Inkcap's feet, he still didn't go away.

"You're harder to brush off than hot radish stuck to a dog's teeth."

"I'm going to stick to you like that."

Bash finally gave in and laughed. "Ha! All right, all right. You can go and get me a light, then."

All the men of Old Kiln smoked, but while the others smoked pipes, Bash rolled his own cigarettes. Inkcap wasn't very happy about getting a light for Bash. He wasn't happy because he wanted to go to the wooden shack with Bash, but if he went home for some matches, Gran certainly wouldn't let him out again to run wild, and in any case, he didn't want to take their matches out of the house. But he didn't give the real reason when Bash asked him why he didn't want to get him a light. "I'll run any other errand for you, but I won't get you a light."

"Aren't you listening to me?"

"You don't listen to anyone else in the village," he said doggedly. "I know what you're like."

"You've got to listen to me. Let me make this clear, you and me aren't the same. I'm a poor lower-middle peasant and no one can touch me. You? You're from a bad family so you've got to do what you're told. When I tell you to get me a light, I'm educating you. From now on, when you go out, as well as running errands for people, you must always carry a light with you. If anyone wants a cigarette, you can offer them a light. And if you look after them right, they won't give you a hard time despite your background."

"So I'm only there to give people lights now, am I?"

Bash's anger flared up when he saw Inkcap's expression. "You just don't get it, do you, you useless turd."

Inkcap didn't dare say anything in the face of Bash's tongue-lashing, and Bash went on to explain that he wasn't losing face in being a light carrier. "How could a dreggy leftover from the Kuomintang Army lose any more face? That would be like a blowfly complaining that the crapper's got shit on it. Besides, this isn't just about you carrying a light around in case someone wants one. Don't you know, right back in the earliest times, fire was really important to people. In primitive tribes… you know what tribes were? They were when people first grouped together. In primitive tribes, only really important people were made the keepers of the fire."

"Does that mean I can be an important person in Old Kiln, then?"

This made Inkcap very happy. He felt that Bash was different from the others, and this was a really good idea. Starting the next day, every time he went out, whether he was in the alleyways of the village or out in the fields, he began to carry matches with him. He would make his way over to wherever people were gathered together, on the lookout for anyone who looked like they wanted a smoke. As soon as someone started stuffing tobacco in their pipe, he would be there to light it.

From then on, no one took matches with them when they went out. If they wanted a smoke, they would just shout, "Hey, Inkcap, where's my light?"

Inkcap would be there almost before the words were out of their mouth, and if no one else looked like lighting up, he would shout at them, "Why aren't the rest of you smoking?" The problem was that he kept the matchboxes in his inside pocket too long, so they often began to fall apart, and the striking surface wore away so the matches wouldn't light, no matter how hard he tried. In the end, he came up with a cunning trick, which didn't need the striking surface: he would put a matchstick in his ear to warm it up, then, when he took it out, if he struck it hard enough, he could light it on a wall, or even on the sole of his shoe. The others wanted to know what his trick was, but he wouldn't tell them and just kept the lit match cupped in his hands, where it flickered like a frog's beating heart. Keeping it hidden, he would take the burning match to whoever needed a light. Later on still, he even stopped carrying matches when he went out because he felt that they were actually Gran's matches and she had spent good money on them, so he shouldn't be wasteful. He started twisting safety fuses at home, and, when he went out, he lit one and carried the smouldering fuse with him. He made his fuses out of corn silk and when the corn silk at home ran out, he begged more from other households and hung the finished fuses on a peg under the eaves of Gran's house.

Inkcap's relations with the other villagers gradually improved but Bash's behaviour became more and more eccentric. After he had set up his shoe repair business in the little wooden shack at the side of the public highway and had a little cash in his pocket, he went to buy wine at the commission store run by Kaihe's family. He drank until he was half-pissed, and then went and dropped a rock into the lotus pond. He said he wanted to make it grow a tail in the water. Inkcap didn't believe him. How could a rock grow a tail? Of course, it didn't, but it did scare a frog into jumping out of the pond. Bash told Inkcap that the owl is the Sky God, and the frog is the Earth God.

"Why?" Inkcap asked.

"Do you know about Nüwa?"

"No."

"Of course you don't. And I don't suppose you know what the myth says either. In the myth, there was a hole in the sky and water was leaking through it–"

"So it rains because there's a hole in the sky?"

"Nüwa patched up the sky with stones and the frog is a reincarnation of Nüwa."

"Can a frog jump all the way up into the sky?"

"Don't interrupt me when I'm talking, OK? Have you ever seen a fish jump up onto dry land? Well, when a frog is still a tadpole it swims in the water, but when it turns into a frog, then it can jump up onto dry land."

Inkcap could see the logic in this story.

"I think I might have been a frog originally," Bash continued.

Inkcap didn't believe him. "How could you have been a frog? A frog has a big mouth and a big belly. That sounds more like Sparks!"

Sparks just happened to be passing at that moment. "What's that?" he said. "What are you saying? I don't like people gossiping about me behind my back."

"Uncle Sparks, Bash said that the frog is the Earth God and that he himself was a frog originally," Inkcap said.

"You would believe him even if he said he was Bookcase Zhu?" Sparks replied.

"Bookcase Zhu is an old fart," Bash said.

Inkcap stood there, wide-eyed and mouth agape. Bookcase Zhu,

Secretary Zhu, was Old Kiln's branch party secretary and Bash was calling him an old fart?

"That's great, Bash," Sparks said. "In our village, Soupspoon does whatever anyone tells him, but you're completely the opposite."

"So, what about it?"

"Nothing. Cattle Track loves collecting nightsoil and spends all day working out how to collect the whole village's shit, so he's known as Scraper. Now you're mending shoes, I've told everyone to call you Studs."

"Do you think I'm going to keep mending shoes forever?"

"You mend tyres too," Inkcap added helpfully.

Bash gave Inkcap's ears a tug, then said, "Come over here, Sparks. Come on."

He began to undo his belt and pulled something out of his trousers, saying, "Look what I've got growing here."

"It's a mole, isn't it?"

"Have you got one on your balls? Have you seen anyone else with one?"

"What a show-off," Sparks said with a sneer and walked away.

The more pretentious Bash became, the more he was criticised. He became less inclined to socialise with the other villagers, and it was only when he was going to work in the little wooden shack or passing Apricot's family courtyard on his way home from work that he sat down on the stone roller diagonally opposite the gates to have a smoke. There was an elm tree outside the gates which had a bell hanging from it. Apricot's dad was a team leader and he rang the bell three times a day to mark the start of a shift. Sometimes when Bash sat on the roller, the gate would open and Apricot would come out, but sometimes it would open and it would be Apricot's dad, Potful. That's who it was this time.

"What are you doing sitting there?" Potful asked.

"I'm watching the bell in the tree."

"It's a fucking bell. What is there to watch?"

"I'm watching how its sound rises into the air."

"You've been mending shoes for a while now. How come you haven't paid the production team any commission?"

At the mention of the word "commission", Bash stood up and walked away, leaving Potful yelling at him, "Don't be so fucking rude!"

Cowbell told Inkcap not to keep tagging along after Bash because Bash had a bad reputation, but Inkcap replied by pretending to count off on his fingers. "You do the maths," he said. "How many people in the village treat me decently? Only Bash."

Inkcap failed to mention the other reason, which was that Bash was both a poor lower-middle peasant and a good-looking fellow. Goodman Wang always used to tell him, "Some people you meet, you feel immediately well-disposed towards, for no apparent reason. They were your friends in a previous life. Some people you meet, you hate on sight. They were your enemies in a previous life."

Inkcap thought that he and Bash must have had some connection in a previous life. Once he was taking a basket of radishes down to the spring to wash and Bash was going to do the same with his big, black dog. As they passed Baldy Jin's house on the edge of the embankment, Baldy's wife, Half-Stick, was in the courtyard heating water to wash her hair. The gate was open, and she asked, "What are you up to, Bash?"

"I'm going to the spring to wash my dog until it's white."

"Everyone says you're weird. Proper weird. How can you wash a black dog white?"

"Why do you think I can't? Where's Baldy Jin?"

"He's gone to Nanshan to sell some maize. He'll be back today. I've got to wash my hair."

"He's coming back to screw her," Bash told Inkcap, "and her hair's the last thing on his mind!"

Inkcap guffawed, took over leading Bash's dog for him and the two of them made to leave.

Half-Stick called out to them, "Are you going? Don't you want to see how long my hair is? Do you think it's longer than Apricot's?"

"Long on hair, short on wisdom," Bash shot back.

"Ha! You must know Apricot, then!" Half-Stick snorted.

When they got to the spring, Inkcap asked, "Why didn't you say anything when she said that stuff about you and Apricot?"

"What the fuck are you talking about?"

"She'll get people talking about you and Apricot."

"Oh yes? And so what?"

"What do you mean, 'so what'?" Inkcap felt that by ignoring what Half-Stick had said, Bash was just encouraging the gossip. Bash might not be worried about his own reputation, but Apricot was clearly out to make a name for herself.

"Apricot called me 'Uncle'!"

"So what if she did?"

"You can get involved with anyone you like, but not Apricot."

Bash turned to look at Inkcap. "That's my business not yours, so keep your nose out of it."

Then, all of a sudden, he pushed his dog into the spring so that its tail was still on the bank and bubbles were bursting with a plopping noise on the surface of the water. Inkcap was so startled he was rooted to the spot.

Bash pulled the dog out of the water and said quite calmly, "You're not allowed to talk if I'm in a bad mood. So just shut up now and wash the dog."

Inkcap knew you couldn't wash a black dog white, but he went ahead and washed it anyway.

THREE

THE WIND WAS BLOWING that day and when the wind blew, the clouds became playful and frivolous, darting first this way and then that. The trees waved their branches and shouted at the chickens, "Get back to your roost!" and the chickens obediently flocked back to the henhouse from beside the courtyard gates. The trees also called out, "Bring in the washing! Why haven't you brought in the washing?" Gran gathered up the clothes hanging on a line in the courtyard while, at the same time, shouting to Inkcap to secure their stooks of straw.

Their stooks were piled up on the embankment at the south entrance of the village, and the wind had already blown the top off them. Inkcap spent quite a while running about madly, passing several turns of rope around all the stooks and then weighting down the end of each rope with a rock. The wind was still blowing and a haze was forming over the strand that ran along the river below the embankment. It was impeding clear sight of the public highway, but Inkcap could just about make out a vehicle parked up on the road and people moving about. It looked like they were arguing. Their voices were raised but Inkcap could not make out what they were saying, as the wind just blew their words into a confused, indistinct drone.

The wind had blown Sprout's hair into a disorderly haystack, and he, too, was looking towards the public highway with his hands tucked into his sleeves. Soupspoon was carrying a basket of furnace ash to his plot of land and the wind had got in among it. He had tried stamping it down and shielding it with his body, but it had been no use and half the ash was already gone.

Sprout began to laugh. "You could have chosen any time to scatter ash on your field and you picked today!"

"Who knew the wind was going to be this strong?" Soupspoon replied.

"Has Bash been quarrelling again?"

"I'm afraid he's been quarrelling with outsiders this time."

"Well, those outsiders are welcome to the fucker. I wish they'd cart him away."

"What makes you say that?"

"I bumped into him today and I was all friendly. I asked him if he had eaten yet, the usual stuff, and he said no, he hadn't eaten and was I going to feed him? Then the son of a bitch just lost it and started sounding off at me. 'What the fuck's the matter with you?' I said. He wanted to know if I still wanted to fuck him around and I asked if there was anyone else he wanted to have a go at. He said he was thinking about it. What the fuck do you think's the matter with him, Sprout? I said he surely couldn't have any reason to be cursing me out, and he said I was too much of a brown-nosing creep to be worth cursing anyway. Is the man crazy or not? You tell me that, Sprout."

"So you're a brown-nosing creep, are you?" Soupspoon said.

"Whose arse am I supposed to be licking?"

"The Branch Secretary's, of course."

"Aiya, Sprout! The Branch Secretary represents the party in Old Kiln. Don't you follow the party line, then?"

"I do the accounts, don't I?"

"Yeah, sure, but anyone who can use an abacus could do them."

Sprout could see that Soupspoon was getting a bit hot under the collar and he didn't want to antagonise him further, so he called out, "Inkcap, hey Inkcap! Come here."

Since most of what the two men had been saying was lost in the wind, Inkcap hadn't bothered to interrupt, and now he pretended that Sprout's summons had gone the same way. He slid down the slope to the bottom of the embankment.

"Didn't you hear me call?" Sprout demanded. "Where do you think you're going?"

"I'm going to the wooden shack."

"Are you going to help Bash pick a fight, then?"

"I'm going to watch the fun."

Inkcap ran along the earth track by the embankment to the little wooden shack, where he found Bash squaring off with a truck driver. They were really going at it, thumping their chests and so close they were spitting in each other's faces. Of course, Inkcap was on Bash's side and if the two men actually started to fight, he would join in. The first thing he'd do would be to catch hold of the truck driver to give Bash a chance to have a real go at him. But in the end, the two men didn't come to blows, and Inkcap just stood there staring at the truck driver. When the man took a step in front of Bash, Inkcap threw caution to the wind and picked up a clod of earth and threw it at the man's face. But the wind caught it and it never reached its target.

"So you've called for help, have you?" the driver said. "Got all your mates from the village to pile in?"

Bash was pissed off with Inkcap. "What the fuck do you think you're doing?"

"Helping you."

"Did I ask for your help? You can fuck right off."

Apricot called out to Inkcap. What was she doing there? She was sitting on the doorstep of the wooden shack, waving him over. When he got there, he saw that Apricot's family breeding sow was also lying in the doorway.

"What's up with the sow? It doesn't have a pink under-pelt, does it?" Inkcap lifted the pig's tail but it didn't move.

"It's dead," Apricot said.

It was only then that Inkcap noticed a streak of blood on the pig's body, and he hurriedly asked, "How?" He could hear a buzzing noise in his head.

Ever since the public highway from Luozhen first went through the village, the residents of Old Kiln had had trouble adjusting to the speed of the vehicles on it. Often, they would start crossing the road when they thought a car was still a long distance away, only to find it was on top of them before they were even halfway across. Within a year, Cowbell's uncle had been run over and killed, and so had Lightkeeper's nephew. Tag-Along's wife was also run over; she wasn't killed but did lose a leg. Now, disaster had also struck Apricot's family's breeding sow, but what was the animal doing on the public highway in the first place?

Apricot told him that she had been bringing the sow back from the breeding station at Xiahewan and the truck had run the animal over. Inkcap looked at Apricot and Apricot looked at Inkcap. She blinked a couple of times, then looked at Inkcap again only to discover he was still staring at her.

"What's the death stare in aid of, then?" she asked.

"Have you been coming to the shack again?"

"What if I have?"

"Did the two of you cook up a plan to let the sow run loose on the highway?"

"What are you asking me for?"

"Answer my question."

"Why should I?"

"Because I'm your uncle."

"Get you! You're like a pug dog yapping on top of a shitheap. My uncle, my arse! Go and find somewhere else to play."

If Bash berated him, Inkcap accepted it, but he wasn't at all happy to be talked to like this by Apricot. As to whether something was going on between Bash and Apricot, he had seen quite enough to know but chose to turn a blind eye. The villagers, however, were full of ugly gossip, and if Bash and Apricot hadn't heard any of it, Inkcap certainly had and all he wanted to do was warn them. He was unquestionably Apricot's uncle in terms of family seniority, but here she was talking to him like that! When he walked out of the shack again, he saw that Bash was still arguing with the truck driver.

"So you're saying it was my fault?" the truck driver was saying. "Is there a pigsty on the highway, then?"

"No," Bash replied, "there's no pigsty on the highway, but you tell me this, was there a highway on that pig? Well?"

It was a good point, well made, and only Bash could have come up with it. Inkcap applauded it enthusiastically. The wind had begun to drop, and the general miasma was dissipating as Bash stood there, presenting his finely chiselled profile with its distinctive nose and mouth. The other inhabitants of Old Kiln had rather fleshy, round faces like dried persimmons while Bash's features were long and angular. He was still wearing his sunglasses as he squared up to the truck driver, but now he took them off and polished them on the lapel of his jacket and squinted at the other man. Inkcap noticed a beatific smile on his lips.

It was clear from the driver's changed posture that he was beginning to soften his attitude. He let out a long breath through his nose and said, "OK, I can see I'm really in the shit here." He took a bundle of notes out of his inside pocket and began to count them out. He put thirty yuan on the herbal tea stand as reasonable compensation for the pig and then picked the carcass up by its hind legs and slung it into the rear compartment of his truck. He had paid compensation, so the pig was his by right and Bash had nothing more to say on the matter. He did, however, snatch up his trimming knife from his workbench.

"What do you want that for?" the driver asked.

"Not to kill you, at any rate," Bash replied.

He grabbed hold of the pig's tail, there was a dazzling flash, and all Inkcap saw was the tail come free attached to a lump of flesh from its rump.

"Fuck off now! Get out of here! You can have the pig's leash as a bonus."

The driver got into his cab, muttering to himself, and drove away with a roar of the engine.

"Aren't you staying for a cup of tea, lad?" Bash said. Then he gave a great shout of laughter, and, before the truck had even passed the turn-off for Old Kiln, Apricot came out of the shack and Bash swept her up in his arms. She tried to cry out in protest, but no sound emerged because Bash had sealed her mouth with his own.

This sudden, unexpected change of mood caught Inkcap unprepared, and he found himself unable either to turn away or close his eyes. Instead, he grabbed an apron from the cobbler's bench and covered his face with it, exclaiming, "Dirty bastard! Dirty bastard!"

The door to the shack was swaying half open, half shut. Bash had tried to hook it closed with his foot as he carried Apricot inside, but it was a swing door and had swung open again. Inkcap didn't go in but stayed outside beside the tea table listening to the sounds of laughter and objects falling over coming from inside. A thread of water like a snake flowed out of the shack. At this point, ecstatic moans and groans could be heard. Inkcap wanted to encourage the couple to greater heights, so he added his own moans to theirs. The sounds from inside stopped abruptly.

Three people were pulling a flat-bed cart down towards the public highway and you could tell at a glance that they must have come to Old Kiln to buy porcelain. Inkcap was keen to find a distraction, so he made himself think about porcelain. Long, long ago, Old Kiln had been a centre of porcelain manufacture. Those who don't know too much about the area have only heard about the Zhu family kiln in Luozhen, but Old Kiln was in operation before that and when you actually look into it, you discover that the Zhu family were originally an offshoot of the Hei family of Old Kiln. The story is that the Hei family's forbears had come to Old Kiln to set up a kiln and then brought in a nephew called Zhu from Shanxi to teach him the techniques of kiln management. However, the Hei family was in decline, while the Zhu family was growing to the point where two branches of it moved to Luozhen. The centuries-old Hei family was left behind, continuing to dwindle in number and their kiln business declined too, eventually leaving them unable to produce fine porcelain such as pale green and sky blue celadon ware and having to specialise only in an assortment of terracotta jars for storing food and water.

The three men with the cart had reached the Zhen River Pagoda, where they were examining a clump of bamboo which was unusual in the way that it grew twisted as soon as it emerged from the ground. Although Inkcap was seething with resentment over Bash and Apricot, he didn't want these outsiders to witness their goings-on, so he shouted at them, "I'll look after you. I'll look after you." When he went down to greet these potential customers, he saw that the man pulling the cart was a fellow called Rockface.

"Are your kilns firing here?" Rockface asked.

"Are you in the market for porcelain, then?" Inkcap asked in return.

"Only top stuff."

Rockface looked like a monkey as he shaded his eyes with his hand to survey the little basin of the Zhou River. To the south of the river, it is all rocky mountain slopes but to the north, earth ridges form something like the frame of a winnowing basket and in the middle of that basket a mountain rears up and Old Kiln half encircles its base.

"Top stuff," Rockface repeated.

Now, "top stuff" was what the villagers of Old Kiln called a pretty girl, but from the way Rockface used the term, Inkcap knew he had come from a certain mountain valley to buy porcelain, and he was rather contemptuous of him.

"Hey! What do you call that mountain in the middle there?" Rockface asked.

"Middle Mountain," Inkcap replied.

"Sounds right. Are we in Middle Mountain Village then?"

"You've come here to buy porcelain and you don't even know Old Kiln? What's that all about?"

Rockface wasn't the least put out and just looked at Inkcap before abruptly grinning and repeating, "Top stuff."

It was quite clear that this time Rockface was directing his observation at Inkcap himself. Inkcap was not the least bit good-looking and was quite used to people insulting his appearance. He assumed Rockface was being sarcastic, so he just turned away and ignored him. On turning around, he saw that Bash was back sitting on his cobbler's bench in the doorway of the wooden shack. The sunglasses he was wearing made him look like a panda.

Rockface called out "Top stuff" yet again and made his way straight over to watch Bash with some curiosity as he sat there working on a pair of shoes. Beside the cobbler's bench, there was an air pump tethered with a rope, and beside that, a stone-topped table on which stood a porcelain teapot and three teacups. Rockface picked up the teapot and shook it to see if there was any tea in it. There was, so he asked, "How much for a cup of tea?"

"No charge," Bash replied.

Rockface poured himself a cup, but it was cold and unpleasant, so he didn't drink it. His companions, a man and a woman, came over too. Bash noticed that the heels of their shoes were worn down on one side, so he told them to sit down, saying, "Do you want me to mend your shoes? Or your tyres?"

They told him their tyres were fine and they didn't want their shoes fixed. The woman stared at Bash and asked, "Is there something wrong with your eyes?"

Bash took off his sunglasses and put them on the table. This time it was the woman who said, "What about some top stuff then?"

"Top stuff," Rockface repeated.

A cough sounded from inside the wooden shack and Apricot came out.

The woman's gaze slid away from Bash's face and she said, "We're after porcelain."

When Bash put his sunglasses down on the table, Inkcap went over and started fiddling with them.

"Keep your filthy hands to yourself," Bash shouted.

Inkcap put the sunglasses down. He knew Bash was cross because the three newcomers didn't want either their shoes or their tyres mended and that was why he wouldn't let him play with the sunglasses. Determined to curry favour with Bash, he went over to the flatbed cart and tested its tyres. He was hoping to surreptitiously snap off the valve stems so the visitors would have to pay Bash to reinflate the tyres. But Rockface had his eye on him, so he didn't dare try. Instead, he said to Bash, "Why don't you recite the county records for them?"

Quite often, when travellers on the public highway stopped at the wooden shack, Bash would eagerly regale them with the story of Old Kiln, telling them that, from its foundation right through to the Qing dynasty, kilns littered the mountain from top to bottom, and the villagers were all busy firing the vessels. The countryside was constantly lit up by the fires and every spring night, when viewed from afar, the mountain was a flickering, twinkling dome. Inkcap was particularly proud and impressed that Bash knew more about the subject than Useless. Whenever he was reciting this account, he would pace up and down, head held high, and often he would stalk over to stand in front of Inkcap, tilt his head up with a finger and say, "Did you know that?" and Inkcap would always reply, "I don't understand." Bash would always say, "Of course you don't. This is the text of the county records."

But this time, Bash wasn't interested in any of that. "They want to buy porcelain," he said. "Take them to the village."

Inkcap had led potential customers to the village countless times, but on this occasion, he took against Rockface, so, although he did indeed lead the way to the village, he ran ahead of them to show Rockface and the others how fast he could go, despite his short legs. He set an impressive pace and the strangers pulling their cart couldn't keep up.

When you enter the village, the main road runs east to west with countless little alleyways running off it to the north and south. The courtyard walls of all the houses were made of kiln saggars and misfired pots, and the road surface was even more monochrome, as it was laid with columns of roof tiles. Rockface and his companions still kept calling out "Top stuff" over and over again, and Inkcap broke through their voices with a shout of "Customers". The combined racket made the walls echo with a buzzing noise like reverberating bronze.

The leaves of the morning glory at the gates of Awning's home had already fallen, and Inkcap thought it a shame that the newcomers couldn't see it in all its blooming glory. The tentacles of hundreds of twisting stems reached upwards and outwards like skinny snakes. They forced their way up through the thickets of bamboo, and the flowers had huge, trumpet-shaped mouths. You could hear them whistling and thumping away as soon as you saw them. Although the leaves had fallen, the vines were still there like a barbed wire frame and there was a large flock of chickens beneath them, with a black rooster scolding one of the hens: "So you're going to let your rooster fuck with one of my hens, are you? I'll fuck with you all the way up and over that wall!" The two birds kept up their continuous quarrel, scrapping with each other and leaving behind a mess of feathers on the ground. Inkcap shooed them away, but then another hen, with a bright red head, came through the gate crowing, "I've laid an egg!" A big red rooster standing on top of the wall screeched back, "I don't believe you. I don't believe you." "Come and see for yourself, if you don't believe me," the hen squawked back. The rooster stretched out its neck to look down from the top of the wall. Its red comb was so big it couldn't stay upright and drooped to one side, looking like Cowbell's hat which always had one earflap up and one down.

Inkcap looked into the courtyard through the door and saw Awning's wife pick up an egg from the nest of straw on the threshold and rub it against her eye sockets. Her eyelids were always inflamed, and a warm egg was supposed to be a cure. The big red rooster looked on and crowed, "That's the way. That's the way."

Inkcap recognised the rooster as belonging to the Branch Secretary and he asked, "How's your Big?"

"Big" meant "Dad" and was the term the villagers of Old Kiln always used. You're big and I'm little was the thinking, but children were never called "Littles", they were called "Shards".

Inkcap asked the rooster, "How's your Big?" but then thought to himself, How can the Branch Secretary possibly be a rooster's father? As he was pondering this, the Branch Secretary turned into the courtyard from the street. He was talking to Noodle Fish.

The Branch Secretary had his jacket draped over his shoulders and his hands tucked into his shirt sleeves behind his back. This was how he dressed throughout the year. In warm weather he wore a lined, buttoned jacket and when it was cold, he switched to an overcoat with a dog fur collar, under both of which he always wore one or two raw cotton shirts, cinched at the waist with a cloth belt. This was the style of dress adopted by all the branch secretaries in the villages up and down the Zhou River, but the secretary of Old Kiln stood out because of his long-stemmed tobacco pipe which he gesticulated with when he was talking and kept tucked up his sleeve when he was walking around with his hands behind his back. There was a gentle downward slope when you turned the corner into the alleyway and the Branch Secretary was squinting, apparently not looking at Noodle Fish. He used his feet to shuffle a stone in the road over to the bottom of the wall and said, "Have you boiled the maize yet?"

"Yes, the whole forty *jin* of it," Noodle Fish replied.

"I bet the whole lot didn't get boiled. Did you leave a bit behind? Did you build the stove yourself?"

"I did, I did."

Noodle Fish had been directly behind the Branch Secretary and had taken a step back to talk to him. The Secretary had done the same, but without looking where he was going. His foot caught in a rut in the sloping road, but he didn't fall over.

"It's not a problem," Noodle Fish said. "But I've heard other people might have something to say about me being given forty *jin* of maize."

"That's for sure. Bash was hopping about in the village, shouting the odds."

"Have I told you about him and his shoe-and-tyre-repair business? All the plasterers and carpenters pay the village a commission when they go out on a job, but he never does. Have I told you that? Nothing, not a single fen. And now he's trying to put the bite on me!"

"He's welcome to his opinion, but I'm telling you that I, Zhu Dagui, am always fair and above board. From now on, any household that produces a baby gets forty *jin* of maize to make wine with."

"I'll sleep more soundly now you've told me that."

"But you need to know that once the baby is born, you have to invite the whole village for a drink. The harmony of Old Kiln starts with you."

The Branch Secretary's overcoat seemed to slip down a bit, but he just shrugged it back into place and set off again, speeding up a little. Noodle Fish didn't follow him but just stood there, muttering to himself. Meanwhile, Inkcap came running up to the Secretary and said, "Grandpa Secretary, we've got some customers."

The Branch Secretary didn't say anything, but he looked narrowly at the woman and two men coming up behind Inkcap. Then his eyes lit up and he asked, "Do you want to buy some porcelain?"

"Eighty bowls and sixty plates, what's the price?" the woman asked.

"Standard price," the Branch Secretary replied.

"We'll buy more sets if you make it a bit cheaper."

"Do you try and haggle in a department store too?"

"This is a village, not a department store!"

"It's the village you're doing business with, not me, Zhu Dagui, personally."

Inkcap saw that the Branch Secretary had been all smiles up to this point, but with those final words his expression hardened, and he turned down the lefthand alleyway and walked off.

That alleyway was on a gentle slope too and led directly to the mountain gate. The mountain gate in question was the gate of the Kiln God Temple, and from there you could see the doors of the temple itself. In that doorway, there were two cypress trees that were so old they had lost their canopies and their trunks were gnarled and twisted like the gate gods Qin Qiong and Jingde. To the west of the mountain gate was the communal dirt field where the villagers could dig earth for building work. The first dwelling south of the field was a large courtyard house with iron gates. The three main buildings inside were public property, and slanting away from them were three cowsheds. The gate was wide open, and six or seven cows were tied to a row of wooden stakes in the courtyard, with their tails down and their heads facing west.

The Branch Secretary walked on by himself, and the prospective porcelain buyers remained where they were, looking blank. "Keep up, keep up," Inkcap shouted to them as he followed along behind the Secretary.

The big red rooster looking down from the wall followed too. The Branch Secretary walked up the slope, panting uncontrollably, his footsteps getting heavier. There were big gaps between the saggars that made up the courtyard wall, and Inkcap went up to peer through them to see what the people in the courtyard were doing. Then the courtyard door creaked open, and Cattle Track walked out. He noticed the Branch Secretary and said, "Have you eaten, Branch Secretary?"

"Why would I have eaten, it's not lunchtime. Why aren't you at work?"

"I've got the trots."

"Well, eat a lump of garlic, that will bung you up."

"Got the trots?" one of the customers said, not understanding.

"It means his guts are running loose," Inkcap explained.

But how could Cattle Track have the trots when the whole village was constipated?

"Top stuff," the customer said.

The Branch Secretary continued on his way, but his overcoat was still heavy and kept slipping down. He shrugged his shoulders occasionally, while the big red rooster stretched its head forward, dragging its wings back to the ground as if it was wearing a coat too.

The cows in the public courtyard didn't change posture after the arrival of all these people. In fact, they didn't even swing their tails. The Secretary opened the door of the public building. It comprised three rooms, one of which contained a large, square Eight Immortals table and four benches. The walls were adorned with a portrait of Chairman Mao and red silk banners of various sizes. The other two rooms were locked with small padlocks. The Secretary didn't rush to open the padlocks but decided that one of the banners wasn't hanging straight. He walked over and rehung it, then took out his pipe.

"Smoke?" he asked.

"I don't," the customer replied.

The Secretary kicked a bench into position and sat down to smoke by himself. He threw some keys to Inkcap, who unlocked the padlocks to get out the porcelain goods.

On receipt of such an important task, Inkcap straightened his back and felt a little taller. He did, however, regret not having brought his safety fuse, so the Branch Secretary had to strike a match and hold it to the bowl of his pipe, sucking hard on the mouthpiece. Various porcelain goods were piled up head-high in the two rooms. The potential customers cried out in surprise and delight, took out the dishes to see their quality and rapped them solidly, making Inkcap call out repeatedly, "Be careful, be careful!" The Secretary snorted and ordered him out of the room.

Dejectedly, Inkcap left the room, just as Happy carried a bundle of maize stalks into the cowshed from outside and asked him to help chop it up. At that moment a spotted bullock standing next to a wooden stake by the door sneezed violently. The bullock was so thin its bones were sticking out, and the corners of its eyes were covered in flies and mosquitoes. Its sneeze sounded odd.

"Are you laughing at me?" Inkcap asked.

Inkcap twisted his head which then nudged into the bullock's belly. Unexpectedly, all the other cows bellowed and strained at their tethers as they moved in to surround Inkcap. They told him, "Don't hit it, it has bezoars in its guts."

"What are bezoars?" he asked

"Don't you even know that?" the cows asked.

Inkcap didn't know. He looked at the cows' faces, which all had very serious expressions.

"What do you mean by that? Do you really think I don't know?"

He dropped the subject and went to help Happy chop the straw. A pitchfork was lying on the ground, resembling a man with his legs apart. Inkcap used it to feed a forkful of maize straw into the jaws of a guillotine and Happy pulled the blade down, making the cut sections spray out the other side. A foul smell of urine permeated the cowshed, and the vat of mash for the cows was bubbling away making plopping noises on the stove in the corner.

"What were you doing?" Happy asked. "Were the cows giving you orders?"

"I was talking to them."

"Eh?"

"They told me the spotted bullock has bezoars."

Happy's mouth gaped especially wide because he had no teeth left and when he closed it, his pursed lips looked like a baby's arsehole.

"What are bezoars, anyway?" Inkcap asked.

"They're a kind of tumour that grows on the cow's liver. They're used as medicine. They're really expensive. Can the cows really talk to you?"

"They tell me everything." Inkcap fed the guillotine another bundle of straw and thought about saying, Do you think it's only people who can talk? But before he could get the words out, the Branch Secretary called out to him, sounding very impatient.

The Branch Secretary took receipt of payment for the porcelain goods and went to enter the transaction in the ledger, but hard as he scribbled with the pen, there was no ink. He called to Inkcap to go to Soupspoon's house to get more ink.

Soupspoon was a bookkeeper, so he was bound to have some ink. Inkcap hurried over to Soupspoon's house, but Soupspoon wasn't there. His mother was sitting in the courtyard, her hand clutching her chest and her lips a blue-black colour. The whole village knew she had a heart condition, so Inkcap made sure to keep his voice down when he addressed her so she wouldn't be given a fright. He practically whispered to her that the Branch Secretary needed some ink. If she could tell him where the ink was, he would go and get it and take it back to the Secretary. Soupspoon's mother pointed to the counter inside the house, from where Inkcap collected the ink bottle, which didn't have a top, and came back out of the door. Soupspoon's mother stood up to tell him something, but Inkcap didn't want to talk to her any more, so he hunched his back to make himself as inconspicuous as possible and scuttled away. But he stumbled at the entrance of the alley, spilling ink onto the ground. There was less than half a bottle of ink left. Inkcap looked round and saw there was no one around, so he hurriedly used his feet to scuff earth over the spilled ink, then headed back over to Soupspoon's house, where he told Soupspoon's mother, "I'm thirsty, Auntie, is there any water in the barrel?"

"What have you been eating to make you thirsty in this freezing weather?" Soupspoon's mother asked.

Inkcap was already in the kitchen, where he scooped up a ladle of water and poured it into the ink bottle. "Your water's so sweet, Auntie," he said. "Do you put sugar in it?" Then he left.

Inkcap was very pleased with himself for thinking of adding water to the ink. None of the others would have come up with a dodge like that, certainly not Cowbell and not even Useless. He didn't dare break into a trot again but carried the ink bottle very carefully, scared of spilling another drop.

Back in the public office, the Branch Secretary drew some ink up into his pen, but when he wrote the figures down, they were too faint to read.

"Did you get this from Soupspoon's house?" he asked.

"Soupspoon wasn't there," Inkcap replied, "but his mother was. She's sick again."

The Branch Secretary could see that Inkcap was looking guilty and had begun to gnaw his bottom lip.

"Was the ink bottle always this full?"

"Yes, full up."

"Did you trip on the way back?"

"No."

"There are ink spots on your jacket. Are you still saying you didn't trip?"

Inkcap panicked and made a clean breast of it.

"Then fuck off!" the Branch Secretary roared.

Only then did Inkcap realise that adding water to ink would make it unusable. Fuck off! Fuck off! Just get away from the public office! The cows all laughed simultaneously, which made them sneeze. The Branch Secretary hadn't accused him of sabotage, nor had he told him to pay for the ink, so Inkcap didn't harbour a grudge against him. But he did begin to be resentful of himself. He took off his cotton jacket, leaving him wearing only the unlined jacket that had been under it. Ignoring the cold, he set out, heading due east.

FOUR

THERE WAS A MILLSTONE at the eastern end of the village and on the flat stone surface were some fruits from the neem tree.

Old Kiln boasted more than a dozen millstones and roller stones, the oldest of which were the pure bluestone roller stone at the west end of the village and the millstone at the east end. The Branch Secretary often liked to say that the Zhu family ancestors were the envy of people for fifteen *li* up and down the Zhou River during the village's most prosperous years. A feng shui gentleman had examined the physiognomy of one of the Secretary's ancestors, which proved not to be very propitious. He also went to Old Kiln to inspect the geography and said that although the millstone at the east end of the village and the roller stone at the west end were not intended to be decorative, they were precisely situated to represent the Azure Dragon of the Left and the White Tiger of the Right but the village lacked the Vermilion Bird of the South and the Black Tortoise of the North, nor were the existing stones particularly prominent. He also said that he suspected the Zhu family ancestral tomb was sited in a miraculous cave. He suggested they go and have a look at the tomb, but the ancestor said maybe it would be better to wait a while and then go.

When the feng shui gentleman asked why, the ancestor said that his family's radish field was next to the tomb, where some children were stealing radishes to eat. If they were to turn up too suddenly, it would scare the children. The feng shui gentleman sighed expressively. "Oh, then there's no need to go. I know why Old Kiln will thrive."

By this time, the lower stone of the millstone at the west end of the village had been worn down until it was only three fingers thick, and a big rock had been placed on the upper stone to maintain pressure so the whole assembly could still be used. The roller stone at the east end of the village had broken a long time ago, so the neem tree growing next to it dropped its seeds and fruit on the remaining stone surface. Plop, one falls, plop, another one falls and they both bounce around on the stone. One dusk, two years previously, a wolf pack passed across the slope north of the roller stone. Every family shut their courtyard doors. Ever-Obedient, whose house was just north of the roller stone, was messing around with tobacco leaves on the stone surface, pulling the flesh of the leaves off their ribs, one by one. Suddenly, his white-haired dog started barking. The wolf pack passed through Old Kiln once a year. In groups of four or five, they either walked along the rocky strand of the Zhou River to the south or across the sloping land to the north. The villagers yelled and shouted, hoping to make the wolves walk faster and deter them from entering the village. What annoyed the white-haired dog was that the wolves walked so slowly and kept their mouths closed, so they looked like they were smiling. That was why it kept barking.

As soon as the wolf pack passed, the water in the Zhou River rose. No one knew what the connection was between these two events, but two years previously, a month after the wolves had gone, the river was particularly swollen.

As soon as the water rose, all the villagers went to collect firewood. Ever-Obedient took a big fishing bag and stood on the top of the stone pier on the riverbank, catching broken branches and bits of tree bark, as well as watermelons and aubergines. But to save time and salvage more, he failed to transfer his catch up onto the embankment sufficiently quickly. When he went back to his fishing, the water rushed in and washed away all the firewood and fruit he had originally salvaged. Everyone laughed at Ever-Obedient's stupidity, so he moved to the stone pier below the Zhen River Pagoda to try again. This time, he came across a rafter floating at an angle down the river. As he stood in the water, he was tied to the stone pier by a leather rope around his waist. To his amazement, he saw two hands grasping the rafter as a woman was pulled along behind it.

"It's a ghost!" Ever-Obedient exclaimed.

He poked at the woman with his fishing bag, hoping to dislodge her so he could haul in the rafter, but the ghost's hands held tight and couldn't be dislodged. He moved in closer to put his hand over the woman's mouth to check if she was still breathing. She was, so he hugged the rafter to him and towed it to the shore. All the other salvagers rushed to help and started pumping her chest, pinching her and even loading her onto the back of a cow and leading the animal around in circles, until the woman spat out a pool of water and revived. This particular woman was known as Yoyo but, after she revived, she certainly didn't leave, but stayed in Old Kiln. Gran gave her a few bowls of rice to eat and she followed Gran home, calling out, "Granny Ye!"

"Who are you calling?" Gran asked.

"Isn't your family name 爷 [Ye]?" Yoyo asked in return.

"There are two main family names in the village," Gran said. "One is 朱 [Zhu] and the other is 夜 but 夜 isn't pronounced the normal way like 爷 [Ye], it's pronounced Hei."

"Ah!" Yoyo exclaimed. "So, it's Granny Hei!"

"She's not called Granny Hei either," said Inkcap. "Our family name is Zhu and my gran has her own name, it's Can [Silkworm], so everyone in the village calls her Granny Silkworm."

Inkcap didn't like Yoyo. She had a mole on her lower lip of the kind called a "greedy mole" and he hated it that she was eating their food. When she kept coming to the house, he took to sweeping at her feet with a broom, and Gran scolded him for not understanding the rules of hospitality and chased him out with her curses.

Gran wanted to teach Yoyo how to make papercuts but Yoyo didn't want to learn. Instead, she just picked up wastepaper or pretty leaves for Gran to work on. The old lady told Yoyo she wanted to make a match between her and Lightkeeper but Yoyo told her, "The Branch Secretary told Ever-Obedient he should come and seek me out."

Gran immediately shut up and began to cut a persimmon leaf. Persimmon leaves are thick and chunky, and a cow's head appeared on this one, proclaiming, "Ever-Obedient is a good choice. Ever-Obedient is a poor peasant."

Ever-Obedient was in his forties and had never married. The only thing he had raised was his white-haired dog, and when the Branch Secretary urged him to marry Yoyo, he said, "Do you mean I salvaged a wife for myself?"

"That's what it looks like to me. Any way you look at it, she must be your woman."

So Yoyo became an Old Kiln resident. The others stopped treating her like a visitor, and she gradually became the subject of disparaging village gossip. This was because she always cried out during the night, "Ooh! Ooh!"

Cowbell heard a noise when he was walking past Ever-Obedient's gate late one night. He thought it was a wolf howling, so he took to his heels and ran, shouting as he went, "There's a wolf! There's a wolf!" All the village children started wailing and the men rushed out brandishing sharpening steels and iron shovels. Of course, there was no wolf, the noise was Yoyo shouting in her sleep and from then on people lost interest.

With the villagers now blanking her, Yoyo counted for nothing. Sprout mocked her for not being able to roll noodles and for snoring when she slept, and for having the temerity to have enough to eat when others went without. In winter, some members of the production team used to carry loads of urine to mix with the night soil as fertiliser, while others picked cotton on the threshing floor. The cotton flowers were picked at the end of autumn and piled up on the threshing floor. There were still some immature bolls when the flowers were picked, but they dried out after a month on the threshing floor and some cotton could still be extracted from them. Of course, the colour was inferior but it was still white enough, like leftover snow on a woodpile. The cotton-pickers were talking about this and that, setting the world to rights, and the subject turned to Yoyo. Useless's mother pursed her lips and said, "Yelling like that! As if she's the only one who has a man to see to her!"

"You don't have a man to see to you," Half-Stick retorted.

Useless's mother was a widow, but she pretended not to hear and continued, "Everyone has a man, or at least has had one, isn't that right, Pockmark?"

"Ever-Obedient's poor, lame and short of spunk," Pockmark replied.

Everyone laughed uproariously and told Pockmark that he may well have had plenty of spunk himself once, but he'd wasted it by spraying it all up the wall.

When Inkcap got home, Gran wasn't around but there was food warming in the pot. When he had eaten, he decided Gran must have gone to sweep up the leftover stalks and straw from the roadside at the entrance to the village for heating the bed known as a *kang*. But when he went to look, he was surprised to see her picking cotton on the threshing floor. Watching her expression from a distance, he was afraid Gran was going to scold him again, but Stargazer pulled him to one side and said, "Hey, Inkcap, did you break the oil bottle? That'll teach you to watch what you say."

"Fuck you," Inkcap said, turning and walking away.

"Where are you off to?" Stargazer asked.

"To see if Gran will still have a go at me when she sees me."

Stargazer took a handful of beans from inside his jacket and thrust them at Inkcap, saying, "Here's some castor beans. If you haven't got any oil, you can stew some of these. Your gran won't have a go at you then, will she?"

Inkcap gave Stargazer a bow and said, "If you need any errands run, I'll do them for you."

Then he heard Pockmark mocking Ever-Obedient.

Pockmark was a bachelor. His skin was so dark you could almost imagine that the black clothes he always wore had actually been stained by his skin. Others may not have been aware of it, but Inkcap knew that every night, Pockmark went round to Ever-Obedient's house to eavesdrop on what was going on. One bright, moonlit night, Yoyo heard a noise outside the rear window.

"It must be a mouse," Ever-Obedient said.

"Oh and are you going to let the mouse in?" Yoyo asked, laying on her own tremulous moans even thicker.

Pockmark was furious when he heard this, and he tore the tiles off the courtyard wall and flung them into the paddy field beside the embankment. The frogs were so disturbed they didn't stop croaking until dawn.

Gran had picked out half a basket of cotton flowers which were all free of stringy veins and opened at a single tug.

"You and Ever-Obedient are both members of the Zhu family from way back," Gran told Pockmark. "You mustn't bad mouth him."

She was trying to be helpful but Pockmark replied fiercely, "What's that about, then? Are you saying there aren't any class enemies in the Zhu family?"

Gran immediately shut up and didn't say anything more.

Inkcap walked over from beside Stargazer to where Caretaker's wife was sitting, legs outstretched, listening to Gourd's wife teasing her mother-in-law about the way she talked, deliberately hawking drily as though she was about to spit. As Inkcap stepped over her legs she said, "Watch where you're going."

Inkcap was now standing in front of Pockmark. "What did my gran ever do to you?" he demanded.

Pockmark thought it was all a big joke. He stood up with legs apart and leapfrogged over Inkcap's head. He often messed about with Inkcap, who took no notice of him. He didn't take offence but just walked on. Sometimes Pockmark walked behind him, bending his legs so he came down to the same height as Inkcap, sometimes he vaulted over his head. This time, he did the latter, and Inkcap just kept looking at him and repeated, "What did my gran ever do to you?"

Pockmark vaulted him again but this time Inkcap headbutted him right in the balls as he passed overhead.

"What do you think you're doing?" Pockmark exclaimed.

"I'm my grandma's grandson," Inkcap said.

"Her grandson, eh? What kind of grandson exactly? Eh?"

Gran swooped like an eagle and folded Inkcap in her embrace. Someone else called out, "What do you think you're doing pestering kids, Pockmark? Why don't you just mind your own business?"

"You can fucking talk with your background!" Pockmark retorted.

He gathered up the picked cotton, put it in the basket on his back and left. The others on the threshing floor went on talking, and Gourd's wife stuck a cotton flower on top of her mother-in-law's head and told the others to see how pretty she looked.

"Why are you mucking me around, you little devil?" her mother-in-law said, twisting Gourd's wife's ear.

"But you look really pretty with a flower in your hair!" Then she wrapped her mother-in-law's head in her own headscarf, just leaving the cotton flower showing. This time, her mother-in-law didn't move and let her daughter-in-law wrap her head. "Look at you, dressing up your little girl!"

Everyone else began to laugh and Gourd's wife and her mother-in-law joined in.

"I don't dare laugh," the mother-in-law said. "It makes my tummy too hungry."

"When it gets dark, we can go back and make ourselves some dumplings."

"You can't get a fart out of a gourd just by making a hole in it," Flower Girl observed, "but a daughter-in-law can make her mother-in-law happy just by giggling a bit."

"You and your bloody dumplings!" Caretaker's wife said. "Some folk can never afford to eat a single dumpling and you boast about going home and stuffing yourself with them at night. You really know how to sweet talk people, don't you!"

"Real filial piety isn't just a matter of food and drink," Flower Girl said. "Real filial piety means making your old folks happy."

"That's true, that's true," Gran said. Then she ordered Inkcap to carry all the cotton stalks that had been stripped of their flowers to the edge of the threshing floor.

"I'm not being paid to be a porter," Inkcap complained.

"If you're not being paid, don't do it. What's your problem?"

Reluctantly, Inkcap shifted a load of stalks, still inwardly cursing Pockmark. Six Pints' house stood next to the threshing floor, and beside his pigsty stood three locust trees. The pig was rooting around in the earth and had found a radish top that he proceeded to bite into. But it wasn't a radish, it was a section of white plastic piping. The crow perched in the locust tree started to laugh.

"What are you laughing at?" demanded the pig.

"I'm laughing at how black-hearted you are."

"You're the black one! You look like you've just crawled out of a chimney!"

"Takes one to know one."

Inkcap gave the tree a kick and the crow flew away. He thought to himself that Pockmark was another fucking crow.

Did Inkcap really not know where he came from? Well, many years ago, Useless's family's breeding sow gave birth to seven piglets all in one go, one after the other. There they were for all to see. Sometime afterwards, Inkcap and Cowbell squabbled over some mulberries they were eating. When the children of Old Kiln were angry and having a go at each other, they would resort to calling each other's parents' names. Apparently, this was the worst kind of cursing and the most vicious insult. Cowbell's father's name was Wufu, meaning "Five Blessings".

"Your dad's not a blessing, he's a mangy bat," Inkcap taunted.

Of course, Cowbell didn't know Inkcap's name, let alone who his father was, so he shouted, "You're adopted. You don't have a proper dad."

Inkcap didn't know what he meant by this, so he asked Gran.

"Who said that?" Gran asked, and Inkcap told her it was Cowbell.

"I'll pinch his lips for him, the little bastard," she continued.

"But where am I really from?"

"You were salvaged."

"Even piglets come out of the sow's belly, so how come I was salvaged from the river?"

It was only two years later that he learned from village gossip that he was adopted, but no one would tell him where from or why. He gave up asking, but from then on, the doubts over his origins felt like a permanent scar which he didn't want anyone else to see. If others chose to mock him, so be it, but Pockmark in particular was always going on about it. With so many people talking about his background, he suddenly thought of Yoyo. That year when the Zhou River flooded, he had been standing on the embankment and had seen Ever-Obedient fish someone out of the water. He wondered if that was how he had been pulled out of the river too. When Yoyo was being led around the cattle pen on the back of a cow, he took a pair of Apricot's old shoes and followed her until she was taken down from the cow, so he could give her something to put on her feet. She had been barefoot when she was fished out onto the bank.

When Inkcap left the threshing floor, it was a sparrow that led him to the toon tree in front of Ever-Obedient's house. The sparrow was like a piece of gravel, first bouncing along the ground in front of Inkcap, then flicking up into the air over and over when he got close, before landing and bouncing along ahead of him again. The sparrow normally chattered away all the time, but this time it was silent; it just kept flying up and landing, teasing Inkcap all the way to the toon tree in front of Ever-Obedient's house. From his position under the tree, Inkcap could see that the house's door was open, and it was dark inside. He could hear a deep grunting noise coming from somewhere, as though someone was digging a cellar, but there was no one to be seen, only the white-haired dog lying under the eaves.

"Stay where you are, don't come over," the dog said.

"I'm looking for someone," Inkcap said. "Is anyone in?"

Yoyo came out of the house. She had a mouth like a fire-breather with protruding lips and buck teeth, which showed very long and sharp as she gnawed on a radish. The sound of her chomping made the radish seem delicious to Inkcap and he couldn't stop his mouth watering.

"D'you want some?"

"You go on, radish is too spicy for me."

So Yoyo didn't give him the radish but just kept gnawing away herself. At the same time, someone could be heard calling out, "Hello! Hello!"

Inkcap could hear both the sound of her tearing at the radish and also, someone shouting. He worked out it must be Ever-Obedient's voice. Ever-Obedient had lost one of his front teeth, so he whistled when he spoke. Yoyo put the radish down on the windowsill. She reached over to the door frame from where she produced a long-barrelled copper key and made her way towards the outhouse beside the mountain wall. Inkcap suddenly realised that Ever-Obedient was over there having a shit and Yoyo was going to poke the stuff out of his arse.

Apparently, 1965 was the Year of the Snake in the lunar calendar, and both the Dragon and the Snake brought good weather. But although the early summer harvests were good, everyone still had to eat rice husk fried noodles to make sure there was enough to go round. Rice husk fried noodles are noodles made in winter by mixing soft persimmons with stir-fried rice husks and bran, then drying them in the sun. These noodles are tasty enough and easy to swallow, but once they're down there, it's sometimes not so easy to force them out. You have to prise the shit out with the barrel of a key or a stick.

Inkcap snatched the radish from the windowsill and took a delicious bite, which he chewed and swallowed. The dog shouted curses at him and, momentarily taken aback, Inkcap couldn't get his tongue round his mouthful of radish, so he lay on his back to chew.

Yoyo came out of the outhouse, saying, "I told you to shit slowly. You've strained too hard. Have you forgotten you've got piles?" Inkcap still had lumps of radish in his mouth which were getting stuck in his throat, so he squatted down, bending forward and pretending to tie his shoelaces.

Yoyo went back to gnawing on the radish, not noticing that someone else had had a go at it. "Inkcap!" she said suddenly.

Inkcap choked, hurting his chest, but he didn't make a sound.

"Who gave you such an ugly name? Anyway, does this village get any food relief?"

He didn't know what made him do it, but what he answered was, "You were fished out of the river…"

"What's wrong with that? Can't someone fished out of the river have food relief, then?"

"I didn't mean that…I, I… Gran told me I was fished out of the river too, didn't she?"

He thought she would understand what he meant if he put it like that but Yoyo replied, "I'm different from you. I was fished out by Ever-Obedient. I'm the wife of the poor farmer Ever-Obedient now. You're…"

She didn't finish what she was going to say, but the colour of her face changed suddenly as she made choking noises and all that came out was the smell of radish. She still managed to go on, "I heard ages ago that someone was out to get Ever-Obedient. When it comes to dividing the food relief, they're suspicious of me and of my own family's status. What is there for them to investigate? Whether my dad is an out-of-office cadre of the Social Education Movement? Or whether I turned into some kind of water monster that crawled out of the river after I was swept away by the flood?"

"You're even more pissed off than I am, aren't you?"

"I asked around and it seems most of the people in this village came out of their mother's bellies while I was fished out of the river. I guess that makes them so much better than me, doesn't it?"

"Don't take it out on the village. It's the village that took you in."

"It would have been better if they'd left me in the river. If I'd died, I might have been reborn somewhere better."

Inkcap regretted coming to see Yoyo for no good reason. He turned on his heel and left. The alley was on a downward incline and the porcelain tiles piled up in it were glistening. Someone had thrown out some water which had turned to ice, forming a glittering sheet on the surface. He saw a half brick lying in the middle of the road. He aimed a kick at it, but it was frozen fast and stayed solidly in place, sending a shock of pain through his foot. A pig came running down the slope, followed by Lightkeeper's sister-in-law. Her pig had escaped from its pen and the faster she chased it, the faster the pig ran.

"Stop that pig, Inkcap!"

Inkcap stopped the pig.

"Have you and Yoyo been badmouthing the village?" Lightkeeper's sister-in-law asked.

"Not me," Inkcap replied.

"It's OK for Yoyo to do it, but if you start, you'll bring down a heap of trouble on your gran."

"I know that. How did the pig get out?"

The woman beat the pig vigorously, shouting, "Everyone else is being kept on the straight and narrow by hunger, causing no more mischief than a tortoise. What do you think you're doing rearing a pig like this that always wants to get out of its sty and run amok outside? Fuck you! Do you think you've been reborn in the village cadre's house?"

The pig just lay there in silence and Inkcap said, "It's starving too and just wants to find something to eat like the rest of us. What about Almost-There? My older brother Almost-There, couldn't he make the wall higher for you?"

"He's gone into the mountains to exchange his rice for grain."

Old Kiln produced rice that was famous on both sides of the Zhou River. The villagers would thresh the rice and sift out any rotten grains along with the husks, and keep that to make porridge, then take the good rice deep into the South Mountain area to exchange for grain. One kilo of rice was worth one kilo of grain. If you were really lucky, you could get as much as two for one and so have more to eat.

Inkcap was annoyed by this news. "He said he'd tell me the next time he was going, the lying bastard."

"You know your way into the mountains, do you?"

"Of course I do." He straightened himself up, even standing on tiptoe to look taller.

"Would you look at that!" the woman said. "Inkcap's gotten taller. He'll be overtaking Cowbell soon."

But she still pressed down on Inkcap's head, forcing him back down to his original height, which meant he only came up to the level of Almost-There's wife's breasts.

FIVE

As the sun turned Middle Mountain white, the sky behind the mountain became as blue as a bottomless lake. However, half of the bulk of South Mountain, Yijia Ridge in the west and Beacon Tower in the east were still dark. But within the darkness, you could make out the terraced fields and the trees, bare of leaves that grew on them. Most of these trees were persimmons. In winter, persimmon trees are just thick trunks with thin, upward-slanting branches. Goodman Wang had often said that Old Kiln was the most beautiful place on the banks of the Zhou River and pointed out how much the persimmon trees resembled so many Thousand-Hand Guanyins.

Early one morning, Bash was dropping wine bottles onto the road in front of the Zhen River Pagoda, crash, crash, one after another. He considered what Goodman had said and decided that when he described Old Kiln as "beautiful", it was because all he ever saw were Buddhas and bodhisattvas. But when he, Bash, saw beauty in the scenery, it was the actual beauty of the landscape itself. His was a more generous appreciation, something that could be shared with others. But with whom? His mouth opened, but no words came out and he was soon enveloped in a white cloud, as the three steams of breath from his mouth and nose condensed in the cold air. He shivered and tied his padded jacket more tightly around him. This jacket had seen him through several winters, and the outer layer was torn in several places, exposing the cotton padding. Awning had once joshed him, saying that his jacket was showing its lard. Bash had been rather nettled by this remark at the time and it still rankled when he thought about it now, so he smashed another bottle on the road.

Cattle Track, who was out gathering dung, stood on the road some distance away, watching Bash for a while. "Why are you smashing those bottles, Bash?" he asked.

"If I didn't smash any bottles, whose bike and trike tyres do you think I'd get to repair?"

"Well then!"

"What d'you mean, 'well then'? You're collecting dung, aren't you?"

"Why don't you try it?"

"What's the point you trying to collect dung on the highway? Cars don't crap, do they!"

"So how many tyres do you repair in a day?"

"Balls to that. I haven't repaired a single one for the last few days."

"You might as well collect dung, then."

"That's all you know how to do, isn't it?"

Bash smashed another bottle, followed by another and another until he'd smashed seven or eight, then a shard of glass flew up and across the back of his hand, cutting him and drawing blood.

"Fuck that," he cursed and headed back to the little wooden shack.

Cattle Track thought to himself that there really was something pretty weird about Bash. If he thought he was too good for collecting dung, what exactly was he going to do?

"Bash! Bash! Aren't you going to keep smashing bottles?" he called after him.

"I'm going to buy wine," Bash replied.

Crows were cawing everywhere, but when Cattle Track looked on either side of the road, there wasn't a crow in sight. In fact, the birds were perched on the persimmon trees on South Mountain. Countless persimmon branches were reaching up into the air, trying to catch something. But what was it? The clouds? Cloud after cloud floated across from behind the mountain, but the trees didn't catch a single one.

Bash was actually intending to go to the commission store run by Kaihe's family on the east lane of the village. The hunk of pig's rump with the tail was hanging on the back of the door of the shack and he smeared his lips with some pork fat from it when he went out, making them look thick and giving off a faintly rancid aroma.

Old Kiln had needed a commission store and it was Bash who had suggested opening one. But in the end, the Branch Secretary had told Kaihe to run it rather than Bash. That was why Bash had started mending shoes and tyres and had built the little wooden shack for that purpose. The village team leader had seen this as the tail end of capitalism and thought it should be cut off, but the fact was that the village carpenters and masons often went elsewhere to find work. What was more, Big Root was still plaiting straw mats and Dazed-And-Confused was making straw sandals which they took to sell in the market at Xiahewan Village once a week. Bash had long felt aggrieved that he had no place to develop his own talents and thought it was completely unacceptable that his "capitalist tail" should be cut off. The Branch Secretary said it was fine for him to develop his own specialism as long as he paid a commission to the production team. All the village carpenters, masons and bamboo craftsmen paid their commission, but Bash refused.

Bash picked up a bottle of wine and walked down the alley. Almost everyone could see it and smell it. The residents of Old Kiln loved alcohol, but they couldn't afford to drink bottled wine from the consignment store. They only had fermented maize beer, which every family knew how to make. However, in recent years, food had become increasingly scarce, and no one dared even to do that. When they saw that Bash had bought another bottle of wine, people whispered behind his back that it was the tenth bottle he'd bought this year, and that he often went to the Xiahewan market to buy pig's intestines, pig's lungs and pig's trotters to eat. It was even being said that while the other villagers' shit was so light and insubstantial it got blown away by the first breath of wind, if you went to look behind Bash's wooden shack, his shit was there in great lumps, which stuck to the shovel when you scooped them up and stank to high heaven.

Big Root was flattening reeds with a stone roller in the empty space behind his home. "Another bottle of wine, Bash?" he said.

"You want a drink?" Bash replied. "Bring some bean curd round tonight and you can have one."

Big Root blew his nose, spread the reeds out on the ground and ran the roller to and fro to flatten them.

"If I had the money to buy bean curd, don't you think I'd be buying my own wine?" And then he asked, "Does Kaihe give you credit?"

"No one else does, why do you think he would? He wouldn't have a shop if it wasn't for me. He's going to owe me for the rest of his life!"

"Everyone seems to owe you."

"Of course. Do you think Old Kiln would still be so poor if it dared put me in charge of things? Do you believe me?"

"I believe you. I'd believe you if you said you could poke a hole in the sky with a bamboo pole!"

"Are you making fun of me?"

"Let me give you some friendly advice. If you drank less, you'd have more money and you could save it up to start a family and become an ancestor."

"Do you think I can't find a wife and have a baby? Let me tell you, I want a mother-in-law in every village up and down the Zhou River!"

"Have it your way, have it your way," Big Root said, pushing the stone roller aside and spitting contemptuously. "But you're still a stupid fart."

As Lightkeeper came back to the village from the kiln field, a cloud happened to pass overhead. The cloud's shadow cloaked him in a darkness that kept pace with him as he jogged along the base of the alley wall. Bash called out to him, but he made no reply. His older sister had married into a family in the provincial capital, and he was wearing a pair of ankle-length rain boots that his brother-in-law had given him. They were big, heavy boots and he made a clattering noise as he walked.

"Hey, it's you I'm talking to," Bash called out. "What kind of boots did your brother-in-law give you? They're all worn through at the heels."

"I can still wear them, OK."

"If it was me, I'd ask him for a new pair. He's got it made in the city and he's married your older sister. He's already had the best of what's on offer, so why should he begrudge you a new pair of boots?"

From a distance, Big Root called out, "You're always going to hold a grudge against my brother-in-law, aren't you?"

"There's nothing fair about this world," Bash said. "Some clothes are worth wearing and others you can't wait to get rid of. If a piece of clothing doesn't keep me warm, I don't want it."

"Is that all women are to you? Clothes?"

"If they're not clothes, what are they?"

37

"You took his sunglasses, and you cursed him out," Lightkeeper said as he passed.

"What are sunglasses to people like that? They're just a drop in…"

At that moment, Potful walked past carrying a mattock, and Bash forgot about Lightkeeper and smiled at Potful.

"Do you want a drink, Team Leader? Here, take this."

"Do you really think I'm going to touch your wine? What you need to do is pay Soupspoon the commission you owe and pay it now. He'll make you out a bill."

"What commission?"

"Who do you think you're kidding?"

"Sure, the carpenters and masons have to pay up, but do I leave the village when I'm mending shoes and tyres? No, I don't. I set up a stall on the road and there have been lots of accidents. I've always been first on the scene and I've always managed things properly. I've done so many good things for Old Kiln, why should I have to pay any commission?"

"Don't try and muddy the waters. This whole thing has been studied by the Team Committee, so why don't you just pay up?"

"I don't have any money."

"But you can still buy bottles of wine? What are you drinking? Piss?"

"Even if I'm forced to drink piss and it kills me, I still won't pay." He popped the top of the bottle of wine and chugged it down. He immediately began to go red in the face. "I'm not going to pay,' he went on, "and I'll kill myself if anyone tells me to."

He actually made to bang his head against the tree next to him. Big Root rushed over to stop him, saying, "You're a real man of principle!" But he wasn't fast enough and a lump appeared on Bash's head.

Potful left the scene, saying, "The Communist Party won't fall for your tricks. I've made a report to the Branch Secretary."

In the commotion, Big Root had been trying to soothe both sides and eventually managed to make himself heard over the shouting. When Bash raised the bump on his head, Big Root shouted that there was blood, and someone should get some chicken feathers quick so they could use them to stop the bleeding. Inkcap heard the noise from the courtyard of Palace's house, and, ignoring Goodman, ran out to join in the fun.

Inkcap had originally been picking field pumpkins on the land set aside for individual use, but the vines in that particular patch had all withered and died because the fruits had been left on them too long. The Branch Secretary was picking spring onions on his own plot of land, which was next to the one where Inkcap was working, and Inkcap had once again suggested that the Secretary give him some of the work to do for whatever work points might be on offer.

"What can you do?" said the Branch Secretary. "You're not even as tall as the piss bucket! Do you want me to cheat the production team out of their work points?"

Inkcap's thoughts about this were not pretty, and his poor mood continued until after dinner when Gran, who was sitting on the *kang* making flower papercuts, told him to go down to the entrance to the village to gather some persimmon leaves. She said the leaves were good and red and could be cut into beautiful shapes. Inkcap ignored her and went to watch the pig rooting for radishes in the cellar.

The pigsty of Inkcap's house was in the southeast corner of the yard and housed one large pig and one little one. The large pig often put its head up on the wall and looked around so it could jump out when no one was paying attention. When it saw Inkcap sitting on the laundry stone, staring into space, it jumped out of the pen and tiptoed over to root about in the radish cellar. The radishes were all kept in that cellar pit, and they were covered over by a great mound of earth, so the devil only knows how the pig knew they were there. Inkcap gave a grunt and the pig turned to look at him. He beckoned to it, so it ambled over and stood in front of him.

"You're a greedy one, aren't you," Inkcap said.

"Mmm," the pig replied.

Inkcap slapped it on its cucumber-shaped snout and the pig grinned foolishly. He shoved his hand under the pig's belly and the pig collapsed onto the ground, trotters splayed out on either side and grunting comfortably.

"Do you like persimmons?" Gran asked.

"Who brought us persimmons?" Inkcap asked.

"So you can hear me when I mention food," Gran said sharply, "but you're deaf when I ask you to collect persimmon leaves?"

"The pig was rooting up the radishes. I had to take care of it."

He drove the pig back into the sty but then shrilled in alarm, "Gran! Gran! A wolf's snatched the little pig!"

"Nonsense. When did a wolf get into the village?"

"Well, where's the little pig then?"

"I gave it to Iron Bolt's family. This summer, he bought a flail and two piss buckets. I agreed to give him our piglet, but he said it was too small. I said I'd feed it up and give it to him in the autumn. I saw him this morning and he raised the subject, so I sent the pig over to him."

"That's not much of a deal for us after how much we fed it."

"Good deal or bad, if someone's willing to advance us money, we should take it as a favour."

"It's going to feel odd here without it."

"That's what the big pig thinks. Didn't it just escape from the pen!"

"I'm the one who's not going to get used to it."

This little pig first came to Old Kiln when Half-Stick bought it from her aunt in Xiahewan. After she'd got it, she cut off half its tail. Later, Noodle Fish's wife told Gran that the pig had been born with a flat tip to its tail, and a pig with a flat-tipped tail is a wolf's favourite food and is bound to be taken sooner or later. Its tail had been cut off at the earliest opportunity. Noodle Fish's wife told Gran she should give the pig back to Half-Stick, but Gran disagreed, saying she'd bought the pig fair and square so why should she give it back? Besides, with the flat-tipped tail chopped off, no wolf would recognise it for what it was. So they kept the little pig and Inkcap particularly favoured it because it only had half a tail. When the big pig hogged the feeding trough, he chased it away so the little one could eat its fill. It behaved like a dog whenever Inkcap came into the yard, jumping out of the pen, nuzzling his feet with its snout and wagging its stump of a tail. The sight of that stump made Inkcap sad every time he saw it, and he would try to encourage the little pig by saying, "Ai! What a beautiful tail! What a delicate, refined tail!" And now, suddenly, the little pig wasn't there any more. Inkcap really couldn't get used to the thought. He turned and walked out, saying he was going to collect persimmon leaves. But that's not what he did and instead, he made his way to the courtyard gates of Iron Bolt's house.

The courtyard of Iron Bolts' house was locked. Its outside walls were made of bowl saggars and, through the gaps between them, Inkcap could see into the courtyard where the little pig was tied to the windowsill of the main building, lying down flat with its eyes closed. Inkcap gave a cough, and the little pig immediately stood up and twisted its head around to look.

"I'm over here," Inkcap called.

The little pig saw him and tried to run over, but the rope stopped it. Suddenly, it snorted and shrieked at Inkcap, who knew that the little pig was getting angry with him and scolding him. "Why did you give me away? Eh? Eh?"

Inkcap couldn't bring himself to blame Gran so instead he tried to encourage the little pig: "Now you're here, you've got to behave yourself. The farmers in these parts are poor, so this is a good place to be. You must know you're really lucky to be growing up here."

The little pig shrieked again and began to grunt with tears in its eyes. Inkcap couldn't bear it.

"At least we're in the same village and I can keep coming to see you."

Caretaker's wife from the next-door courtyard came out to pour out the dregs from some medicine and saw Inkcap lying on the courtyard wall of Iron Bolt's house.

"What are you doing?" she asked. "They're not at home. Are you planning to go in and steal something?"

"When did I ever steal from anyone?" Inkcap said

"You may not steal, but you hang around with Cowbell, and Cowbell's hands are certainly dirty."

Inkcap decided to take no notice of what she was saying and asked, "Is Uncle Caretaker better yet?"

"It's good of you to ask, Inkcap. The medicine isn't doing any good. I've asked Goodman to come and have a look at him."

"Ah, good. You've asked Goodman to come."

He went into the courtyard and, as he expected, the door to the main building was open. Caretaker was sat on one rush mat and Goodman was sat on another. They were talking together and Inkcap didn't dare disturb them, so he sat on the threshold and listened.

Goodman Wang wasn't originally from Old Kiln. He first became a monk in the Guangren Temple in Luozhen, but the Socialist Education

Movement forced the monks there to return to secular life. The commune then assigned him to live in Old Kiln and he took up residence in the Kiln God Temple. He no longer recited sutras to the Buddha, but he did practise medicine. One thing he did was set bones. Often, when he had no other job on hand, he would sit and practise by smashing a porcelain bottle into pieces, mixing it with bran and putting the mixture into a cloth bag. Then he would reach into the bag and put the bottle back together again. The other thing he did was talk to illnesses. Some diseases can be cured just with words. At first, Inkcap had thought this was really weird, and few other villagers believed in it either. But later on, word got round that Goodman really had cured lots of people of different diseases.

Caretaker's family was well regarded in the village. The courtyard walls of his house were not made of waste saggars but of proper bricks, and even the chimney on the stove was not made of cracked ceramics, but of whole blue tiles. Caretaker put on airs rather, and his relationship with his neighbours was fraught. In fact, even the family members were at odds so the family itself was fragmented and very troubled. Caretaker had a diseased mass in his stomach, and the injections at the Xiahewan Medical Station had done no good. Both Traditional Chinese Medicine and Western medicine at the Luozhen Health Centre had proved ineffective, and his condition was becoming increasingly serious. He wasn't even able to consume half a bowl of rice a day.

Inkcap heard Goodman say, "Wood is restricting Earth in your system. Every day, you see other people making what you think are mistakes, but you don't speak out. Because you hold on to your dark humour, you have gradually become ill. If you want to recover from your illness, you need to change your temperament. If you don't, I cannot guarantee you will continue to live. You have to practise smiling before you talk to people and look for their good points. That way, you can find happiness in your heart, and you will recover."

"You haven't been in Old Kiln for very long, and you don't normally have any contact with us. How do you know what I'm like?" Caretaker asked.

"If it were otherwise," Goodman replied, "how could I possibly talk people through their illness?"

"I've never been to school, and I'm less well educated than Bash and Useless. In fact, I'm not even as clever as Lightkeeper, but I still look down on their abilities. I love to find fault with people."

"This is something I have often studied. Resentment of others is a sea of poison, and the more people blame others, the sadder their hearts become, so that they either get sick or cause trouble. How is that not a sea of poison? Dealing with individuals is hell. If you deal with one element, the others hate that element and if you deal with ten elements, the others all hate those ten elements. If that isn't hell, what is? A well-educated person will blame his faults on his own lack of self-cultivation, while a small-minded person will blame his faults on others. The more he blames others, the sadder his heart becomes. Anger is toxic when it is stored in the heart and is equivalent to feeding oneself poison. Good people do not blame others, and blaming others is the mark of an evil person. A wise person does not get angry, and anger is the mark of a fool. A noble person does not take advantage of people, but an ignoble person does. A noble person does not put on a show of temper, but an ignoble person does. If we compare a person to a cabbage, being angry is like being hit by a gale, being wronged is like getting maggots, and being angry is like being smashed by hail. Do you hear me, Caretaker? Do you hear me?"

"I understand what you're saying," Caretaker said.

But Inkcap hadn't understood. An ant had crawled out of a crack in the stone step and shaken its antennae as if it was saying something, though there was no sound. This had distracted Inkcap from what Goodman was saying. Instead, he watched as dozens of ants lined up and crawled out, all at the same speed, like soldiers drilling.

Caretaker's wife came over, holding two eggs. "Why don't you make some poached eggs for Goodman?" she said. "You want to listen to his talking for free?"

"What's he talking about?" Inkcap asked.

"He's talking about ethical behaviour."

Inkcap had no idea what that might be, but he did know what he was hearing now: people arguing. His ears pricked up and he said, "That sounds like the Team Leader arguing with Bash."

"Bash and Apricot have patched things up," said Caretaker's wife, "so how can he be arguing with Potful? No, that's Big Root's voice. It's Big Root arguing."

Inkcap listened again and what he still heard was Bash and the Team Leader arguing, so he stood up and walked out of the courtyard. Behind him, Goodman was still talking: "If you can admit you are wrong, take advantage of it and retrace your steps."

Inkcap was already in the alley when he saw a dog hurtling along before coming to a sudden halt under a tree.

"Where's the arguing coming from?" Inkcap asked.

The dog stood up on its hind legs and let loose a stream of piss.

Inkcap turned down three alleys and discovered Bash standing on the open ground in front of Big Root's house. A lot of people were standing around, but strangely there was no sign of the Team Leader. Big Root was chattering in whispers with Soupspoon and Sprout, while still keeping an eye on Bash. And what was up with Bash? He could see Inkcap quite clearly, but he ignored him and called to Useless, who had just gone past, to stop.

"What's that book you're reading, Useless?"

Useless held the book up and flashed the cover.

"Is it still that textbook?"

"Do I have to read one book all the way through before I start another?"

"Why wouldn't you? That's what I'm asking."

"Let me test you. On page thirty-seven, Lu Xun names three specialists. What are they?"

"Thinker, writer and something else."

No one else there spoke while Bash and Useless were talking about the book but what Inkcap didn't understand was why Bash seemed so unconcerned when he had just been involved in a quarrel that had brought so many interested spectators. Moreover, what kind of person was it in the book that even Bash couldn't give the right answer? He crept a little closer so he could see what was in the book. It was a photo of an old man.

"When a dog looks at the stars," Useless said, "all it sees is how bright they are."

"I know the answer," Inkcap said. "It's an old man."

Useless and Bash both burst out laughing and laughed so hard they sprayed Inkcap's face with spittle.

SIX

COWBELL CLAPPED HIS HANDS as he sat astride the ridgepole of his house. As soon as he did so, the poplar trees by the gable wall shook, and the leaves slapped against each other, joining in with the applause.

There were taboos in Old Kiln about not planting mulberry trees in front of the gates of houses, as mulberries represent mourning, not planting willows behind the house, for fear of thieves, and not planting poplars beside the gable of a house. The leaves of the trees crackled, like ghosts clapping their hands. The poplar by the gable of Cowbell's house did not actually belong to him. Awning had planted it beside his pigsty, which happened to be next to the gable of Cowbell's place. He heard the trees applauding but pretended not to, and shifted his position but remained astride the ridgepole and spat towards Awning's house.

Cowbell's family home was located directly behind Awning's. Cowbell's house was the taller of the two but Awning was renovating his old place and raising the foundations by one foot. Cowbell's mother, who had died of an illness that year, had also raised the ridge of the house by one foot five inches and had a mirror set into the middle of the ridgepole. Awning's father said it was a ghost mirror deliberately directed at the family house. From then on, a feud developed between the two families. Of course, the Branch Secretary was consulted, and he made the judgement that first, Cowbell's family should take down the mirror and second, Awning's family should give up any further plans to raise their ridgepole, pour out a pot of wine, cook three dishes and bring the two families back together over food and drink. Awning's father drank a cup of wine, Cowbell's father drank a cup of wine, and they left the rest for the Branch Secretary. The Secretary drank until his head spun and his legs became unsteady. He even stumbled as he went out of the door, but he still managed to say, "That's settled, then. As long as I am Branch Secretary, I won't allow social order to deteriorate in Old Kiln Village."

This mediation was praised by Secretary Zhang of the Luozhen Commune, who also brought village cadres from elsewhere to Old Kiln to gain experience. Before Secretary Zhang and his group arrived, the Branch Secretary asked the mason to chisel a stone lion at the south entrance of the village. This statue was very imposing, and the lion had a ball in its mouth. There were also two pairs of old stone lions at the entrance of the Kiln God Temple. All the lions had one foot resting on an embroidered ball, but only the new one had a ball in its mouth. What did it mean? The younger villagers had no idea. Noodle Fish said there had been a story that, after the ancestors settled in Old Kiln, a demon kept coming down from South Mountain to ravage the village. A fairy gave the clan chief a magic pill, saying that if he put it in his mouth, he would turn into a lion that could fight off the demon. But the fairy also said that the clan chief mustn't swallow the pill because, if he did, he would never turn back into a man. Whenever he did want to restore his real form, all he had to do was spit out the pill. So the clan chief put the pill in his mouth and turned into a lion. The monster no longer dared attack the village but nor did it leave South Mountain. The clan leader never spat the pill out, and over time, he actually became a stone lion squatting at the south entrance of the village. Noodle Fish said he heard his grandfather tell this story when he was a child, but he had never seen the stone lion at the south entrance. He didn't know if there had ever been any stone lions at all, or if there were stone lions that were later smashed or moved away. The new stone lion was carved and placed on the roadway just south of the village. The villagers said that this stone lion was the Branch Secretary, or that the Branch Secretary was like a stone lion guarding Old Kiln. Under the instructions of the Branch Secretary, Useless wrote a slogan on the wall at the south entrance which read, "If you are in trouble, ask a party member; if you have a problem, ask the Branch Secretary!"

Bash, who was there at the time, suggested an addition: "Whoever craps it, collects it!"

"Ah, Bash! Are you saying that all troubles come from party members and all problems are caused by the Branch Secretary?"

Everyone stared in astonishment as Bash replied, "When did I say that? When did I ever say that? Did you hear me say that, Inkcap?"

Inkcap didn't know what to say, but Gran said, "Just look at your snotty nose! It's disgusting. Blow your nose."

Inkcap blew his nose and kept on blowing it. Eventually, he went over and wiped the snot off his fingers onto a nearby tree. He didn't dare go back to join the others.

However, the stone lion had only been guarding the entrance to the village for little more than six months when Awning's father died. Ten days later, Cowbell's father died too. The two households' family tombs were not far away, and a flock of white-billed birds and a flock of red-billed birds often perched in the cypresses in the graveyard. These birds began to quarrel as dusk fell so the graveyard was always full of bird shit and feathers. The villagers said that the two flocks were the two enemies who had met again in the underworld but unfortunately, no one had come to mediate between them.

What surprised Inkcap was that after their fathers died, Cowbell and Awning came closer together, although, of course, Cowbell sucked up to

Awning. When Awning caught a fever and the corners of his mouth were ulcerating and his eyes were gummed up with pus, he told Cowbell to go to Soupspoon's house to fetch a bowl of fermented vegetable water. Soupspoon's mother made the best in the village and whenever someone wanted to make pickled cabbage, they always went to her for the starter. That's what Cowbell fetched this time. When Awning asked around for a smoke, Cowbell would beg some tobacco from anyone with a tobacco pouch at their waist, then search out a piece of paper to roll Awning a trumpet-shaped cigarette. Awning also often praised Cowbell's tree-climbing abilities. "Are there any eggs in the nests in those trees?" he asked.

Cowbell shinned up the tree, gripping it with his hands and feet. The people down on the ground called out to him to be careful as he climbed to the topmost branches, where he picked up the eggs in his mouth and reached with both hands to swing from a branch. Inkcap told him not to do this kind of thing but Cowbell replied, "Awning is a commander in the militia and he's got a gun."

"Would he shoot you?" Inkcap asked.

"I want to be a commander in the militia myself, one day."

When he'd got over being mocked, Inkcap went across the alley and watched Cowbell clapping his hands on the ridgepole of the roof. He knew that Cowbell was laughing at him and he got rather annoyed. "Hey, Cowbell! Cowbell! Are you going to put a mirror back on the ridgepole?"

"You watch your filthy mouth and let sleeping dogs lie," Cowbell said.

"Have you got a guilty conscience, then?"

Cowbell laughed grimly, then, when he saw Inkcap preparing to go, he called out, "Why don't you come up here? The persimmons are soft and frost-bitten."

Inkcap stopped in his tracks. In the winter, almost everyone put a sack full of maize stalks on their roof in which to store persimmons. After the winter solstice, the persimmons softened and were made sweet by the frost. Inkcap didn't have a persimmon tree at home, so when Cowbell invited him to eat persimmons, he forgot that he hated him. But he found he couldn't climb up. Cowbell had only built one rafter under the eaves and Inkcap couldn't reach it.

"You'll have to throw me one down," he shouted.

"Give me a smile, then," Cowbell shouted back.

Inkcap grinned up at him and Cowbell dropped a persimmon. Inkcap missed it and it splattered on the ground in a pool of red juice. Cowbell dropped another one and Inkcap caught it, but it still splattered.

Cowbell climbed down from the eaves and squatted, letting Inkcap step on his shoulders, and then he raised himself up. Inkcap began to climb the wall, but he still couldn't reach the eaves from the top of the wall. Cowbell had to get back to the eaves, stretching his hand and pulling Inkcap up. When he squatted, Cowbell's trouser crotch split, exposing his arse.

"You're so clumsy," Cowbell said.

"Put your hat on properly," Inkcap responded, reluctant to admit his weakness.

Cowbell's left ear had been gnawed by rats when he was a baby. In winter his injured ear couldn't stand the cold, so he always pulled the left earflap of his hat down to cover the deformed ear. As soon as Inkcap told him to put his hat on properly, Cowbell felt a sense of inferiority. He straightened his hat, covered his left ear and did not utter another word.

Dunce caps were growing from the trough where the rows of tiles met on the roof and some of them already had white flowers.

"Do you really still want some persimmons?" Cowbell asked.

"You offered," Inkcap replied.

"You can have five."

"Eight!"

"Six is my best offer."

When Cowbell ate persimmons, he held them carefully by the stem and gently bit open the very top with his teeth. With one strong suck, he cleared all of the flesh from inside the fruit and then blew into the skin. The persimmon skin returned to its original shape and was placed on the rows of tiles. He said the persimmon skins were still quite edible after ten days or a fortnight. Inkcap didn't want to leave any skins behind and ate each fruit one bite at a time. The juice flowed down from the corners of his mouth, and he licked it up with his tongue before taking the next bite.

"Spit out the core, spit out the core," Cowbell told him.

But Inkcap didn't spit them out, and he shoved the persimmon stems into the uppers of his shoes when Cowbell wasn't looking. Cowbell went to pull up some of the succulents growing in the tile seams, and Inkcap observed that they shouldn't be flowering in such cold weather.

"Why not?" Cowbell asked. "Aren't you eating my family's persimmons and they shouldn't have fruited yet either?"

"There's no wind today, and the flowers are all asleep," Inkcap said.

"Do flowers actually sleep?"

When Cowbell pulled up one of the plants, the millet-sized flowers scattered like sand. At the same time, all the other flowers on the tiles shrank into themselves, forming tight little balls, as white as if they had been sprinkled with salt.

"How many have you eaten?" Cowbell asked.

"Four. Look, here are the four stems." Inkcap ate two more, never, of course, owning up to the four extra stems stuffed in his shoes.

Down in the alleyway, Noodle Fish's wife walked past carrying a grain trug. She was a wide-hipped woman whose upper and lower body parts didn't seem to belong together, so she looked as though she was going to fall apart when she walked.

"Stonebreaker's mother's arse is so big it'd cover the entire mouth of a vat," Inkcap said.

"A big arse is good for having babies, that's why she's got Stonebreaker and Padlock, and Orchid and Plum Blossom," Cowbell observed.

"With that many children, when she was breastfeeding, did she have two of them lying on one side of her and two on the other?"

"What, you think she was like a sow suckling?"

At that point, Noodle Fish's wife arrived behind the house, so they had to abandon their discussion. Noodle Fish's wife went and knocked on the courtyard gate of Third Aunt's house in the rear alley.

Noodle Fish was not an old resident of Old Kiln. He had moved from Donggou in Yijia, and still had land there. The villagers went to Donggou twice a year to plant and harvest soya beans. It was because of Noodle Fish that Old Kiln had fermented vegetable water and bean curd to eat and had a reputation for them. But when Noodle Fish moved to Old Kiln he was in his thirties and was still single at the age of forty. When Stonebreaker's father died, he left a widow and four children. Life was difficult for them, and Third Aunt acted as matchmaker to bring the two households together. Ten years on, Stonebreaker and his siblings were all grown up and Noodle Fish's hair had turned completely white and he was bent at the waist. Pockmark had a go at Noodle Fish, telling him it really wasn't worth it for him to take on such a huge extra burden. He'd lumbered himself with four extra mouths just to get a wife to spend his days with. But Noodle Fish said, "What nonsense. I planned for those children."

"Are they your children, then?" Pockmark retorted. "Do they call you 'Dad'?"

"Of course they do. What else would they call me?"

"Ha! They just call you 'Dad' because you screwed their mother!"

But both Cowbell and Inkcap knew that Stonebreaker never called Noodle Fish "Dad". Cowbell had fought with Stonebreaker and come off second best because Stonebreaker was the bigger man. So instead, he had tried taunting him: "Fish! Fish! Fishy noodles!" But Stonebreaker hadn't got angry and just replied, "If you want to curse out Old Fishy, go right ahead."

Stonebreaker wasn't particularly tall but he had a big head and a thick waist. He ate three meals a day at home but didn't sleep there. At night, he took his quilt and made up a bed in the cowshed with Happy. He didn't even talk to Noodle Fish if he saw him.

Potful tried to school Stonebreaker: "Where's your fucking conscience gone? If Noodle Fish hadn't brought you up, the four of you would be dead twice over!"

Stonebreaker turned his head away when he heard this.

Noodle Fish's wife took the grain trug into Third Aunt's yard, where the cat lay on its back and yowled. A warty chicken tiptoed over to look, but the cat ignored it and concentrated on yowling and yowling as if it were crying.

"Third Aunt, Third Aunt!" Noodle Fish's wife called out. "You have to lend me some wheat flour."

Third Aunt was sitting spinning on the steps of the main building, and all the spinning was making her ankles itch. She stopped spinning and untied the belt of her trousers and loosened her stockings to search for lice. She had just caught one when she heard Noodle Fish's wife call her. Her hand shook and she lost her grip on the louse. It fell to the ground and disappeared because it was the same colour as the soil.

"Why the hell didn't you knock? Come in, come in."

She took Noodle Fish's wife's hand and said, "Look at your hand! Covered in chilblains and you're not even wearing gloves. It's not New Year or any other festival, so what do you want flour for? Has Noodle Fish caught cold and he wants fresh boiled ginger soup?"

"Stonebreaker's mother-in-law's here."

"Ah! How long for?"

"Till the eleventh or twelfth day of the New Year at least, I'm afraid."

"Everything all right with the foetus?"

"Not entirely. That's why she's come, to have a look."

"That's odd. In the past, there's been no trouble with the births in Old Kiln. It's really strange. Previously, the children born here were all born in order. Why have they all come out sideways in the past five or six years? You should ask Soupspoon's mother to turn it."

"Done that. But she's had a really bad reaction and now she vomits if she eats anything, vomits so hard bile comes out."

"As long as it's been turned, that's the important thing. It doesn't matter how bad the reaction is. Have you made the wine?"

"Yes. You must come and try it when the time comes."

"I wouldn't miss it. But what's up with the Branch Secretary at the moment? Is he still not giving out maize to make wine with? My grandson was born on the sixteenth of August which was one day too late to register him, so he didn't get the next year's rations. My daughter-in-law gave birth at the wrong time, but yours is about to give birth now which is perfect timing. You can get dozens of *jin* of extra maize after the birth. Also, I heard that food relief will be distributed soon. I don't know how people will be ranked this time but your family will definitely get it, won't they?"

"Of course, it's good to be ranked, but I wouldn't mind if I wasn't."

Third Aunt brought a wicker tray full of flour down from the upper room and said, "The light's good out in the yard so you can see the colour of the flour. There wasn't any white maize added when it was being ground. Now you can put the flour in your trug and level it out. Then you must use your hands to lift it and sift it back into the trug to make a tower with the tip showing above the edge."

"That's all fine. I'll bring you some wheat flour in exchange when I've ground it."

She picked up the trug and made her way out with it. Third Aunt went back inside, then came running out again with a handful of castor beans that she gave to Noodle Fish's wife, saying, "I'm sure you haven't got any oil at home, so shell these and fry them up. You don't want people saying there's no oil rings on your food."

Noodle Fish's wife's eyes brimmed with tears as she said, "You always look after me, Third Aunt."

"Why are you crying?" Third Aunt replied. "What is there to cry about? Now, just watch where you are going."

Flower Girl was carrying a basket of pepper leaves and distributing them from house to house. She had various fruits, trees, flowers and plants growing in her yard and there was a row of pepper trees at the base of the courtyard wall. When winter came, all the pepper leaves were picked and stored in the sweet potato cellar. She would then distribute them so everyone could stuff some into steamed maize "nest buns" and eat them with a pot of rice congee. She had just reached Third Aunt's gate when Noodle Fish's wife came out carrying her trug, so she gave Third Aunt some pepper leaves and stuffed some inside the jacket of Noodle Fish's wife.

"Ah!" Third Aunt said delightedly. "What blessings Barndoor must have accumulated in a previous life for Flower Girl to have grown into such a kind-hearted person!"

"There are many people in our family, but none of them are as good as this girl with an outsider's family name," said Noodle Fish's wife.

"Maybe not so good," Flower Girl replied. "I haven't been able to produce a single baby!"

Third Aunt had nothing to offer in response, but Noodle Fish's wife said, "Some women can't have children but maybe you're just leaving it late."

"That's right, that's right," Third Aunt said. "People from Luozhen joke that Old Kiln may have fine mountains and clear springs but our persimmons are sour, our peaches are woody, our daughters are dark and our wives are ugly. They don't know how slender and beautiful some of us are!"

And, so saying, she opened the front of Flower Girl's jacket, exposing the snow-white of her belly. When she looked up and saw Cowbell and Inkcap, she hurriedly put the jacket back in place.

"What are you little pricks looking at?" she said. "Is this something you think you're supposed to see?"

"We aren't looking. We're eating persimmons," Cowbell protested.

"What? Still eating them?" Third Aunt exclaimed. "If you eat all the persimmons, what am I going to mix with the rice husks?"

"Don't stuff 'em!"

"Bullshit! If I don't, where are your fried noodles going to come from? And if you have to go without fried noodles for two or three months, you'll be eating tiles and shitting bricks, won't you!"

Cowbell and Inkcap stopped eating. Cowbells slid down from the rafters in front of the eaves, sliding rather too quickly so he ended up falling over backwards, yelping. Inkcap was too scared to slide down and stayed clinging to the trough where the rows of tiles met.

"Are you all right?" Third Aunt shouted from behind the house.

"I'm... I'm fine," Cowbell replied shakily from the front yard.

"If we adults weren't around, kids would spend every day screwing up," Third Aunt observed. Then she saw Noodle Fish walking past the entrance to the alley carrying a load of dirt. "What are you doing still carting dirt around when we've got guests?"

"I was fertilising the sweet potato plot when I heard we had guests, so I came back. I brought a load of dirt back on my way because the pigsty's already turned into a mud bath."

"What about Stonebreaker and Padlock? Couldn't they have done that?"

"They've got their own stuff to do."

"Ha! And what are you going to do? Slave away until you're just a pile of skin and bone?"

"I eat plenty. I'm just naturally skinny. I could eat a whole pig and not get fat."

He didn't stop to rest but went on his way still carrying his load of dirt.

"You need to take better care of him," Third Aunt told Noodle Fish's wife.

"What can I do? He won't stay still."

"Not even at night?" Flower Girl asked. "He's getting old. You mustn't be so fierce with him."

"I don't care whether he wants that kind of thing or not, I've given up even thinking about it," Noodle Fish's wife said.

"Who are you kidding? After a day's work, when the nights are long and his stomach's empty, the only way he's going to get to sleep is with a bit of that kind of thing!"

"When Stonebreaker's dad was alive," Noodle Fish's wife said, "he loved to fool around, fondling and teasing. But Noodle Fish wants everything at once. He starts on the next thing before he's even finished the first, but once he actually gets his leg over, it's finished before he starts! I just have to think of it as doing my duty as a woman."

"He may have gone half his life without a shag, but you can't just do what he wants," Third Aunt chimed in.

"How can I control him?" Noodle Fish's wife asked.

"If you can't control him, then you have to feed him the right stuff. Cook him a spring onion every evening and that will keep him hard all winter," Flower Girl said.

"You have to be careful not to do him a mischief," Third Aunt added.

The three of them talked for a while. Third Aunt looked down and saw the cat standing at the courtyard gate, smiling and washing its face. She stopped talking and hastily called Cowbell.

Cowbell came running out of the front courtyard. A bruise had come out on his forehead, which was oozing blood and covered with chicken feathers. "What are you talking about?" he asked. "It sounds like you're having fun."

"What are we talking about?" Third Aunt said. "We're talking about how useless you are! You'd better not mess up any more of those persimmons on the roof. If the weather's good tomorrow, I'll help you stuff the skins."

"Is that all?" Cowbell asked.

Third Aunt told Noodle Fish's wife and Flower Girl to leave, saying, "Your legs are still young and strong, go to Soupspoon's wife in Number Three Alley for me and ask her why no one's come with the cloth she asked me to dye for her."

"I couldn't think what was going on with all that crazy shouting. What was that all about?" With a toss of his head, Cowbell went back into the front yard and helped Inkcap down from the roof.

As Inkcap slid from the corner of the eaves towards the top of the gable wall, he smelt the smell again, so he ducked down to look into the yard. He saw a snake crawling out of a crevice in a rock at the base of the gable wall and then slither into another crevice. Snakes sleep through the winter, so it was weird to see this one showing itself. He hadn't seen either its head or its tail, but the body stretched between the two crevices was as red as the red of a red flower.

He didn't tell anyone he had smelt the smell again, and he thought to himself, Where did a snake get finery like that in such a cold place?

SEVEN

THAT EVENING, pus started flowing from Gran's ears. The same had happened at the beginning of the year but they had been cured after she had snake slough powder and Bingboron powder blown into them, so this recurrence was unexpected. As the pus flowed, Gran staunched it with some cotton and then rolled the cotton into balls and stuffed her ears with them to block them completely. She didn't cry out at the pain, but just took some deep breaths and got on with cutting persimmon leaves in the lamplight.

Naturally, Inkcap remembered the red snake he saw in the afternoon. "Do you want me to get some more snake slough powder and Bingboron powder, Gran?" he asked.

"No need," Gran said.

Of course, there was nowhere he could have laid hands on the medicines at that time of night anyway. He stood and watched Gran at work and saw that she was cutting out animal shapes.

Cowbell had always admired Inkcap's ability to understand what the animals and plants were saying, but what he didn't know was that Gran was even better at it. Gran had never mentioned it, nor did she allow Inkcap to talk about it. The villagers knew she was very good with her hands and could capture the likeness of anything she saw, but what they missed completely was that, whenever she was in the village, the gluttonous cats, all the dogs with both straight and curly tails, the production team's few cows, Kaihe's fastidious dairy sheep, even the safflower fish and the thornback fish in the river, the snails and earthworms in the wetland, the butterflies, dragonflies and ladybugs all leapt up and down to embrace her. The reason why these creatures got close to Gran was because they wanted her to capture their image and make papercuts of them.

As Inkcap watched Gran making so many animal papercuts that night, he wasn't sure whether she was doing it to drive away his nightmares or to take her own mind off the pain in her ears. Inkcap stood beside Gran, encouraging her to make a pig. Following a flash of scissor blades, Gran made a pig's head appear on the left-hand side of a persimmon leaf. It was the pig they had just given to Iron Bolt's family.

Inkcap felt a twinge of sorrow when he recognised it and said, "I want a bird. The kind of bird that roosts in the Kiln God Temple."

With another flash of her scissors, Gran produced a hook-beaked, long-tailed bird. One by one the leaf cuts covered the top of the *kang* as if she had been slicing sweet potatoes and laying them out to dry in the wheat field. There was a faint sound from somewhere. Inkcap pricked up his ears and asked, "Who's crying, Gran?"

"It's a wolf."

Inkcap started in alarm. "Isn't it somebody's dog pretending to be a wolf?"

"It's a wolf. The wolves are in the village."

Inkcap could just make out the pack of wolves pass across the low-lying land to the rear. They were wearing simple fur coats and moving with their heads down, and they seemed to be smiling slightly. But there was a sinister aura to the wolves, which made people grimace when discussing them. Inkcap looked out through the window, where it was as black as the bottom of a cauldron. His whole body came out in goosebumps.

"Don't be afraid," Gran said. "Gran's here."

She stood up to go and secure the courtyard gate. Perhaps her legs were a little numb, but, for whatever reason, she stumbled as she got up and had to support herself on the edge of the *kang*. "Give me my crutches."

She had been using the crutches since the beginning of the year. Inkcap handed them to her and thought to himself, Her legs are so thin and dried up, just like two sticks. Do people's legs gradually turn to wood when they get older?

Gran closed the courtyard gate, banishing the sound of the wolves. Then she cut out two lions, similar to the stone lion at the south entrance of the village, and pushed them under Inkcap's pillow to help him sleep.

The next day, Ever-Obedient let it be known that he had got up at night because he needed to piss. His household piss bucket was broken, and he was too cold to use the toilet outside, so he decided to stand on the *kang* to piss through the small lattice window in the gable wall. But through the window, he could make out Noodle Fish sitting on a large roller stone not far away.

"Hey, Noodle Fish," he called out in a low voice. "What are you doing sitting on that stone in the cold? Have Stonebreaker and Padlock been getting at you again?"

When Noodle Fish failed to move, Ever-Obedient continued, "Fuck that for a laugh. You raise them and they treat you like this! Come inside, Noodle Fish."

Noodle Fish stood up. But it wasn't Noodle Fish at all, it was a wolf! It raised its tail, slowly turned around and walked away. The villagers found a bunch of hair like a tuft of grass on the fence next to the Kiln God Temple. At the base of the spirit wall belonging to Awning's house, there was a lump of wolf shit, white, with chicken feathers and broken bones in it. Although the wolf had come into the village, no pigs or chickens were missing, so it seemed likely that it was just passing through with an already full stomach.

At noon, Inkcap picked up half a basket of potatoes and went to the spring to peel them. He passed by Iron Bolt's house and remembered the half-tailed pig. Iron Bolt himself was standing at the gate with a black expression on his face and he ignored Inkcap when he caught sight of him.

"Uncle, that pig of ours, is it all right?"

"Which pig of yours?" Iron Bolt asked, raising his eyebrows.

"The wolf didn't take it, did it?"

"I wish it had taken you!"

Inkcap regretted speaking hastily and saying the wrong thing. Would Iron Bolt have got so cross if he had said, "Has that pig we sent you been behaving itself? Did you know that a wolf got into the village last night?"

He berated himself and determined to think more carefully before opening his mouth in future. When he got to the spring, he found Apricot washing clothes. She was using plant ash to scrub away the layers of dirt, rubbing vigorously, then pounding the clothes with a mallet.

As he was in no hurry, Inkcap decided to strike up a conversation. "So you're washing clothes, are you? Shall I crush some honey locust beans for you to get them clean?"

"No," Apricot replied.

The spring was at the base of the embankment at the east end of the village, and on top of the embankment was Baldy Jin's house. Directly facing the door of the house was a large honey locust tree with the bean pods still hanging down like so many bats.

Baldy Jin picked baskets of pods to sell at the market in Xiahewan Village. His family did not raise chickens. "Why should I raise chickens?" he boasted. "You trade eggs from your piddling chickens for salt, but I've got a honey locust tree!"

That tree was Baldy Jin's money box, and he was very possessive of it and didn't let anyone else pick the bean pods. He had turned against Sprout for this reason and also quarrelled with Apricot over it.

Inkcap looked towards the top of the embankment, wondering if he could bring down a bean pod with a well-aimed potato or whether a pod might, by chance, fall of its own accord.

"Stop watching them," Apricot told him.

"Am I not even allowed to look now?"

"Grow up. And keep your eyes to yourself."

So Inkcap stopped looking and just watched what she was doing.

Apricot continued to scrub her clothes. While other women's buttocks made a triangular shape when they knelt, Apricot's buttocks were very round, and her breasts seemed to be straining against her clothes. Inkcap thought she smelt very fragrant.

"What's that perfume you're wearing?" he asked. "You smell really good."

"It's just my natural perfume."

But Inkcap noticed the little perfume sachet hanging around her neck, and he asked, "Did Bash give you that?"

Apricot used her hand to splash water into Inkcap's face, but Inkcap didn't react.

"Look at me," Apricot demanded.

"I've got water in my eyes."

53

"Well, wipe it away and look at me."

Inkcap rubbed his eyes. "You've got a nose, eyes and mouth. They're all there!"

"Have another look."

"I'm not your mirror."

"Well, you can be my mirror now. I want to know if my eyebrows are messed up."

Apricot's eyebrows were usually as neat as if they had been glued on, with a gap between them. Now, they had spread a bit, but their shape was still a sweeping upward curve like the antennae of a butterfly.

"They're a bit spread out," Inkcap said.

"Does it show badly?"

"What does it matter if they're a bit spread out?"

A voice from the top of the embankment chimed in: "If they're spread out, it means you're a bit loose!"

Apricot and Inkcap both gave a start and looked up at the top of the embankment, where they saw Half-Stick standing under the honey locust tree.

Apricot blushed deeply and said, "That's balls. Why are you talking balls?"

"It's not balls. When peaches are ripe, they should be picked. When I was your age, I was already up the duff. Here, let me give you a bean pod."

Half-Stick threw down a bean pod, but Apricot just packed her clothes back onto her wooden tray and left. She tugged at Inkcap as she went, and he had no choice but to follow. When they reached the alley, Inkcap asked, "What did she mean when she called you 'loose'?"

"Don't you start!" Apricot let go of Inkcap and paid no more attention to him.

"What do you think you're doing dragging me away like that and then just buggering off yourself?"

Inkcap was left standing there aimlessly, holding his basket of potatoes. Two chickens ran past with their heads drawn in, clucking as they went.

"What do you think you're doing, chasing us off like this?" one of them said.

"Commune Secretary Zhang has come to the countryside again," the other said. "You're not going to be wielding your knife, are you?"

Inkcap turned to look down the alley, but he didn't see the Branch Secretary accompanying Secretary Zhang into anyone's house. Secretary Zhang always rode his bicycle to visit the countryside and Inkcap didn't hear the ringing of a bicycle bell either. But he did see Lightkeeper approaching from the western end of the alley. He seemed to have got fatter and was carrying a basket on his back.

"Hey, Lightkeeper," Inkcap called out. "Why didn't you tell me you were going to swap your maize?"

Lightkeeper stopped Inkcap from checking out his basket. "You stay away from me. Just keep away from me."

Inkcap managed to grab a handful of maize, which was the colour of yellow agate. He tossed a kernel into his mouth, bit it, and then threw the others back into the basket, saying, "I'm not going to rob you."

"What about Gran? What about Gran, eh?"

"You leave Gran out of it."

But Lightkeeper took no more notice of Inkcap and hurried over to Inkcap's house, as Inkcap himself went into a privy to have a piss. The villagers disliked him and were suspicious of him, including Apricot, who was family. Even Lightkeeper disliked him and was suspicious of him. Inkcap was very unhappy about this, and he directed a stream of piss straight at a nest of maggots in the cesspit, washing them away. When he came out of the privy, a small group had suddenly gathered in the alley, discussing whether Lightkeeper had been poisoned by lacquer when he exchanged his maize.

Almost-There once went to exchange grain in Xiegou on South Mountain, where he had the good fortune to get two kilos of coarse maize for one kilo of rice. This attracted lots of people, so Lightkeeper let Almost-There go into the mountains a second time and told him to make another trip to Xiegou. On one side of the slope at Xiegou, there were lacquer trees with trunks the circumference of a rice bowl. The villagers collected lacquer from the trees, using knives to make diagonal cuts in the bark. They inserted an iron sheet shaped into a trough underneath the hole for the lacquer sap to flow down. They went to collect the lacquer every three days, so the trees ended up covered in knife marks. This was the first time Lightkeeper had seen a lacquer tree, and when he thought of his own life experience and all the scars he carried, he hugged the tree and burst into tears. In fact, what happened when Lightkeeper hugged the lacquer tree and cried for a while, was that the lacquer juice stuck to him and poisoned him. On the way back from Xiegou, a whole load of red bumps the size of rice grains appeared on his face. By the time he got back to the village, his face was swollen to the size of a basin, and his eyes were narrowed into slits.

Lightkeeper was looking for Gran because she knew how to treat illnesses. For example, if someone had a headache or a brain fever, she could apply pressure to their forehead and insert a needle at the point between their eyebrows. If someone had shoulder pain and couldn't lift their hand, she would use a cupping jar. If none of these remedies worked, she would stand chopsticks in a bowl of clear water to dispel ghosts and evil spirits.

When she saw Lightkeeper's badly swollen face, Gran said, "This needs to be singed with white cypress branches." She called to Inkcap, who was at the gate, to go to the cemetery and cut some cypress branches.

It was only then that Inkcap realised Lightkeeper hadn't suddenly got fat but was suffering from lacquer poisoning. Even though only half the potatoes were peeled, which would earn him a scolding from Gran, he ran into the house to fetch a sickle and went to the cemetery at the bottom of Middle Mountain to collect cypress branches. The cypress trees around his family tombs were too tall and he couldn't reach the branches, so he went to Cowbell's father's grave where the flock of birds on the cypress trees were arguing again with the flock of birds by Awning's father's grave.

Inkcap tied up a bundle of white cypress branches with some rope and hauled it back home. Gran, Lightkeeper and a bunch of others were waiting under the rubber tree, where they set light to the branches. A column of black smoke climbed into the air. Inkcap had never seen black smoke rise so high. It was as if a pillar had been erected, connecting the ground to the sky.

One of the bystanders said, "So they're letting you light fires now, are they? Are you using the smoke to drive off the mosquitoes?"

Inkcap lay down and blew on the flames to stir them up and singed his own eyebrows. Gran told Lightkeeper to walk around the fire, three times to the left, three times to the right and then jump over it. "You must say whatever I say," Gran ordered him.

"I'll say whatever you say," Lightkeeper agreed.

"You are seven," Gran said, the Chinese word for "seven" being a homophone of the word for "lacquer".

"You are seven," Lightkeeper repeated as he jumped over the fire.

"I am eight," Gran said.

Lightkeeper jumped over the fire again, saying, "I am eight."

"Say it by yourself."

Lightkeeper jumped over the fire a third time, saying, "You are seven, I am eight."

Useless was standing by the fire, watching the excitement, and, as the cypress branches gave off their black smoke, he coughed repeatedly. He didn't wear his mask, which was tucked inside his jacket at the third buttonhole, with only the ties showing.

"Why aren't you wearing your mask? Put it on," Inkcap said.

"My hands are dirty," Useless explained.

"Useless never wears his mask," one of the bystanders said. "He likes to imitate the people from Luozhen. It's more elegant."

Useless rolled his eyes. He didn't want to bandy words with these people, so he went away. He was splay-footed and walked like a cat.

Useless headed for the Branch Secretary's house, but he wasn't there. However, he did see the Secretary's son, who worked at Luozhen agricultural machinery station, along with his partner. The partner was wearing a mask, but it was at half-mast with part of it hidden below her collar. Useless turned his back for a moment and pulled his own mask out from inside his jacket.

"Where's the Branch Secretary?" Useless asked.

The son told him that he had accompanied Commune Secretary Zhang to Awning's house, so Useless followed them there. Awning's wife had a fire going in the kitchen, and the smoke was making her eyes water. She didn't notice him, so he didn't say hello. Instead, he sat on the *kang* while the Branch Secretary talked to Secretary Zhang, and Awning held a chicken down with his foot by the entrance, getting ready to kill it. The chicken had already had its neck feathers plucked, but when the knife cut into its neck, it flapped its wings madly, hurting Awning's face and making him let go of it. The bird scuttled off squawking loudly to shelter on top of the courtyard wall. Useless was about to go into the main building when the Branch Secretary stuck his head out of the window, laughing at Awning.

"You can't even kill a chicken!" he said.

"Grandpa Branch Secretary! Grandpa Branch Secretary!" Useless called out. "I've got a new form of class struggle to report to you."

"A Branch Secretary is a Branch Secretary and a Grandpa is a Grandpa. What's this Grandpa Branch Secretary nonsense?" the Branch Secretary reprimanded him.

"What new form?" Secretary Zhang asked.

Useless told him all about Lightkeeper jumping over the fire in front of a load of poor lower-middle peasants and chanting, "You are seven, I am eight."

"Was he saying that poor lower-middle peasants are seven and landlords are eight?" Secretary Zhang asked.

"You're not lying, are you?" the Branch Secretary chipped in.

"Of course I'm not," Useless protested. "He's still at it now."

"Go and tell the little fucker to come here."

Useless was about to go when the Branch Secretary added, "Send Awning, and you kill that chicken."

"I don't dare," Useless protested.

"Just do it!"

Useless made gurgling noises to call the chicken but it stayed on the wall. Useless took a handful of maize from the house to tempt it down but it still didn't budge. He rushed over to catch hold of it, pulling its wings back, and the chicken stopped struggling. The chicken looked at him, and he looked at the chicken. Human eyes and chicken eyes stayed locked together for a long time.

"Bring it over here. Bring it over here," the Branch Secretary ordered.

Useless gave the chicken to the Branch Secretary, and the Branch Secretary stood on the *kang* by the window, facing the chicken front on. He slapped its head twice, stunning it.

"Now I can kill it! Let me kill it!" Useless said excitedly. He took the bird away and wrung its neck so hard that its head came off and the body fell to the ground. But even headless, the chicken could still run, and it bounced over to a pear tree. It ran smack into the tree and finally fell down dead.

"What's your name, young lad?" Secretary Zhang asked.

"I'm called Useless."

"Well, be off with you. This is none of your business."

Useless left, but only as far as the courtyard gate, where he turned to look at Secretary Zhang. But the window was already closed and there was no sign of him.

Not long after, Awning returned and told the Branch Secretary and Secretary Zhang that there was no one left in the alley, just a pile of burned cypress branches. He had asked around and was told that those words had indeed been spoken, but they were just an old charm to drive out lacquer poison, and there was nothing wrong with any of it.

"What more is there to say?" the Branch Secretary told Secretary Zhang. "There's nothing going on in Old Kiln. That little shit Useless is always lying." Then, turning to Awning, he continued, "Go and stew that chicken. If you find any soft-shell eggs inside, fry them up especially for Secretary Zhang."

"No, we'll share them. We'll share them," Secretary Zhang protested.

In fact, when Awning arrived at the foot of the rubber tree, Lightkeeper was still there and the fire remained alight. Awning stepped up and put it out. Gran asked what was going on, and Awning told her about Useless's report. Gran turned and left, and everyone else calmly dispersed. But Lightkeeper didn't leave and just stood there waiting for Useless.

Useless did not, as it happened, go back to the rubber tree. Instead, he went home, where his mother told him to help wring out the washed sheets. They each held one end, alternately twisting and untwisting the sheets and then beating them.

"No need to go at it too hard," his mother said.

"I went to see Commune Secretary Zhang," Useless told her.

"Did you just say you went to see Secretary Zhang?"

"Secretary Zhang has long ears."

"So do all officials," his mother replied. She stepped closer, looked at Useless's ears and gave them a tug.

Inkcap and Cowbell came in carrying bundles of unburned cypress branches and were about to say something when Lightkeeper turned up too.

"Aiya!" Useless's mother exclaimed. "How come your face is so fat?"

"Something I ate," Lightkeeper replied.

"What?"

"A magic handsome pill."

"It's lacquer poisoning," Inkcap volunteered.

Lightkeeper beckoned to Useless, and Useless went over to him. Suddenly, Lightkeeper hugged Useless to him and rubbed him against his face. Useless struggled but couldn't escape. Lightkeeper rubbed himself against both sides of Useless's face, then pushed him away so he ended up sitting on the floor.

"You've been poisoned by lacquer and so has Useless now!" Useless's mother cried. "How can you be so fucking stupid?"

"I'm a class enemy, aren't I?" Lightkeeper said. "Of course I'm stupid."

Useless picked himself up and tried to grab hold of Lightkeeper, but he wasn't tall enough. He didn't dare try anything else, so he ran back into the room to find a mirror and look at his face. Useless's mother sprang forward to grab Lightkeeper by the hair as if she were seizing a bundle of cut grass. Lightkeeper in turn tried to tear at her face. He had already got his fingers into the loose folds of skin on her face and was stretching them. Inkcap and Cowbell rushed to separate them. They put their arms around Useless's mother to protect her, at which point Lightkeeper turned and left.

"What did you think you were doing? Why did you hold onto me, not him?" Useless's mother demanded.

"The production team is doing a piss inspection. They're coming here to check on your family."

When Inkcap and Cowbell came over, they had seen Potful, Sparks and a few others going door-to-door making a piss inspection, but they were still surprised to see that Potful and the rest had actually just arrived at Useless's mother's house.

The production team made regular inspections of the household piss cisterns. One picul of top-grade piss, equivalent to about fifty kilograms, counted for two work points, one picul of second-grade piss counted for one work point and one picul of third-grade piss counted for half a work point. Once the inspection was done, people were sent to collect the piss and mix it with the pig manure from all the household pigsties. Useless's mother didn't make a fuss when Potful, Sparks and the others arrived. She offered them her tobacco box and urged them to have a smoke. "Get your fuse," she prompted Inkcap. "Where's your fuse?"

Inkcap had a rope fuse wrapped around his waist, so he took it out and fished a matchbox from the inside pocket of his padded cotton jacket. There were only three matches in the box, and he couldn't bring himself to use one of them. He asked Useless's mother to light his fuse with her matches, but she told him to use his own. So he took one out of his box, warmed it in his ear to make it certain to strike, then gave it a sharp swipe across the striking surface. It caught immediately and he lit his fuse from it. But, as it turned out, Potful and Sparks didn't smoke any of Useless's mother's tobacco. They stirred the cistern with a pole, looked at the colour of the piss, smelt it and then didn't inspect it any further.

Useless's mother was furious. "What's going on?"

"You've put too much water in your cistern," Potful said.

"Even if it's not the best, can't you make it second grade?"

"It doesn't even make second grade."

Inkcap stayed out of the argument. He had seen a bunch of dried maize silk on the windowsill and went over to take it. Useless's mother turned to look at him.

"What do you think you're doing?" she asked.

"You're not using it. I'm going to take it to make fuses."

"It's still mine even if I'm not using it. Leave it alone."

Inkcap obediently put the maize silk back down. Useless's mother set to again with Potful.

"Tell me, hand on heart, did you add water to the cistern?" Potful asked.

"Who wants a cistern with dry shit and thick piss? Of course I added water. I poured the cooking water in there."

"How many piculs of water are there in a cooking pot to make the piss this clear?"

"What do you think we're eating and drinking that our piss wouldn't be clear by itself?"

Potful didn't reply but just turned to Sparks and said, "Let's go."

Inkcap had already pinched out the fuse and now helped by carrying the long urine-testing ladle.

Useless's mother gave him a shove and said, 'What are you getting mixed up in this for?'

"You're the one doing the mixing, putting that water in your cistern."

"Did you actually see me adding the water?"

"I saw you last night. You poured six or seven loads of water into the cistern."

"What you say you saw is just bullshit. Where's your proof?"

"Gourd's cat was up on that wall," Inkcap said. "If you don't believe me, ask the cat."

Even Potful laughed.

Sparks gestured with his hand and said, "Let's go, let's go, let's go. You've got to follow the sun if you want a suntan."

And with that, they left and made their way out of the alley.

Useless's mother stood there choking with rage. She beckoned to Inkcap. "Come here, Inkcap. Come over here."

Inkcap knew she just wanted to take her anger out on him. He walked over to her until he was about three feet away, then giggled, turned on his heel and ran away. He stopped when he got to the old elm tree at the entrance to Number Three Alley.

Inkcap ran along with his short little arms and legs. He was trembling with glee, like a bee buzzing its wings but unable to fly very fast. He felt that his arms and legs were swinging so violently that, if he'd been in water, he would be stirring up the breakers. But wasn't the air just like water? It was invisible water, so he should be able to raise the wind and that wind would make the leaves of the old elm tree rustle. But there was no wind. He waved his hands but there was still no wind and a snail inched up the wall. The sky above the alley was obscured by interlocking elm branches which made it look like there were cracks in the sun and it was about to split into pieces. Inkcap wanted to curse out Useless's mother. He knew that if he started, his curses would echo loudly through the alley because of the way the walls of every house in Number Three Alley were made out of broken tiles and waste saggers. Everyone sitting in their homes would get to hear about how Useless's mother had added water to her cistern, but then, of course, who didn't add a certain amount of water to their cistern? He suddenly felt bored, stopped cursing and let rip with an enormous fart.

EIGHT

LIGHTKEEPER'S LACQUER POISONING began to subside after three days, but Useless was certainly infected. Although he didn't have it as bad as Lightkeeper, his face was covered in blisters the size of rice grains and had turned red as a monkey's arse. Useless's mother had to ask Gran to come and burn cypress branches and get Useless to jump over the fire. The fire jumping was going to take place in Useless's house and Inkcap went along too. Inkcap was intent on being there but, after Useless's mother let Gran into the house, Useless stopped him at the door.

"I haven't come to look at your lacquer poisoning," Inkcap pleaded. "I've come to learn my characters. Won't you let me in?"

"You're too stupid," Useless said. "I won't teach you."

"I'm not stupid."

"Then let me ask you this. Can you make a sentence?"

"What do you mean, make a sentence?"

"I give you a word and you use it to say something. Take 'love and respect', for example. I can make it into the sentence, 'I love and respect Chairman Mao'."

"I love and respect Chairman Mao too!"

"Who do you think you are? You're not qualified to love and respect Chairman Mao."

Inkcap's head dropped, but he wasn't about to leave; he wanted to make a sentence.

"Hmm, OK... I don't like wearing a hat."

Useless stared at him in astonishment.

"Well, did I do it right?"

Useless's mother was standing in the doorway telling him to hurry up and come inside to jump over the fire.

"No, you made a shit sentence," Useless shouted, shutting the courtyard gate.

While it was no surprise that Inkcap couldn't make a sentence, it was a big blow to him that he wasn't qualified to love and respect Chairman Mao. He was supposed to be watching a joke being played on Useless, but Useless had humiliated him. When he left the gates to Useless's courtyard, Inkcap had no desire to see anyone, not even Cowbell. He withdrew into his shell and made his way to the roller stone at the east end of the village. The stone was as cold as a block of ice and, ice being ice, it almost froze the arse off him.

From there, you could see the river strand in the south of the village. The wheat seedlings on the strand had not yet popped their heads up, but nor was there any bare soil to be seen. The remaining snow was piled up here and there, and someone was shouting. A dog went running up one of the snowbanks, from which a layer of fog was beginning to rise, and it started to bark.

Inkcap straightened up excitedly, recognising the person shouting as Bash and the dog as the white-haired one. Ever-Obedient came out of his courtyard gate and said, "Are there really still some wild rabbits down there?"

"Did the dog start a rabbit?" Inkcap asked.

"Weren't you there?"

"How did Bash get your dog to go with him?"

"He just took him. All the dogs love following Bash."

For several winters now, Bash had been calling other families' dogs to hunt rabbits, and the rabbits seemingly voluntarily and as if by prior arrangement, used to appear on the river strand. This noon, Bash discovered another rabbit on the strand. It was a big rabbit with red fur like a fox. Previously, Bash had hunted rabbits simply by calling whichever dog happened to be on hand, but this time, he specifically brought Ever-Obedient's white-haired dog because he really wanted that rabbit pelt. The red fur would make a nice scarf for Apricot. Bash and the white-haired dog cast around for a while without starting any rabbits. If that was how it was going to be, that was how it was going to be. But then, the rabbit, which had disappeared without trace, suddenly appeared in the distance, standing upright with its front paws swinging as if it was waving. Bash was furious, and so was the white-haired dog. It let out three sharp barks, and a dozen or so dogs from the village ran over. It was like a performance of the opera *The Heaven's Gate Formation* was being re-enacted on the river strand. The rabbit ran ahead pursued by four dogs. Running swiftly, it darted to the south, taking the dogs by surprise. The dogs couldn't make the turn in time and fell to the ground in a tangled heap. A couple, however, then hurled themselves southwards, trying to cut the rabbit off, so the rabbit turned east again. The remaining dogs also made the turn, so the rabbit headed north. There were dogs in every direction now, but the rabbit always managed to escape through the gaps between them.

Inkcap couldn't sit still on the roller stone any longer. He tied his shoelaces and was about to run down to the river strand, when Ever-Obedient called to him, "Tell Bash to set my white-haired dog on the rabbit and when it catches it, he can share the meat with me."

But to Inkcap's surprise, the chase was over by the time he got down to the river strand. The dogs had failed to catch the rabbit, which finally escaped up Yijia Ridge.

Bash was yelling at the white-haired dog, which barked, and then cursed the other dogs. The other dogs stayed silent, then dispersed after taking their scolding.

Bash went back to the shack for a drink of cold water, which gurgled in his throat as he swallowed.

"Cold water's bad for you," Inkcap said. "Do you want a smoke?"

Bash stopped drinking and turned his eyes onto Inkcap, but he didn't say anything about having a smoke. The white-haired dog stood in the doorway again, not making a sound. Its tail was normally erect, standing proud from its rump like a feather duster, but now it was down and tucked firmly between its legs.

"Can I come in? Will you let me in?" it asked.

Inkcap took pity on the dog and told it to come in. It did so and lay down next to Inkcap. When it lay down, its long white hair fluffed up like cotton, and its eyes were firmly fixed on Bash.

"You shouldn't go all out after the rabbit from the start," Inkcap said. "Let it tire itself out, then chase it."

"Who are you talking to?" Bash asked.

"The dog."

"Are you trying to give me a class, you little brat? Do you think I don't know how to hunt rabbits?"

Inkcap laughed. "How can you expect to run wearing a thick padded jacket like that?" he said.

"Come here! Come over here!" Bash shouted.

He was calling the white-haired dog, and when it went over to him, he picked up a pair of scissors to cut off its long coat. The hair on the dog's body was a *zha* long, roughly the length of a handspan, and he cut it off. The hair on its head was so long that it covered its ears. He cut that off too, and the hair fell to the ground in a great white pile. The white-haired dog was far from fat underneath it all, but it had a big frame, and its new appearance revealed it to be very ugly indeed.

"Why have you cut all the hair off someone else's dog?" asked an astounded Inkcap.

"It was too long."

"That long hair made it the king of the dogs!"

"I just wanted to see what it looks like without any hair," Bash said before turning to the dog. "All right, all right. Be off with you."

The white-haired dog turned a somersault and ran out of the door. It frisked around on the highway for a bit, but its tail was still firmly between its legs and now it looked more like a stick than a feather duster.

Bash wasn't the least bit worried about cutting off the fur of someone else's dog. As far as he was concerned, it was just a bit of fun. Like when Caretaker was getting married and Sprout had smeared blacking from the cooking pot all over Caretaker's father's face so he looked like the operatic image of the Song dynasty politician Bao Gong; or the time he was working in the production team when, all of a sudden, Half-Stick, Flower Girl and some other women started giggling and descended on him in a confused mob, undoing their trousers and thrusting his head inside them. But Inkcap wasn't in the mood for messing around, as it might become a question of class struggle if he did. As he watched the dog with a stick for a tail gambolling around, he heard the thornback fish in the Zhou River calling out his name and then making a squeaking noise. When he listened again more carefully, the fish were saying, "Leave now. Leave now."

"I'm going home," said Inkcap as he was about to leave the shack, but Bash stopped him and stuffed the dog hair into a bag to give to Apricot.

"She can use it to stuff a cushion," Bash explained.

Inkcap had no choice but to take the bag back to the village. When he reached Apricot's house, the courtyard gates were locked. He hung the bag on the doorknob, but before he could fix it properly, someone behind him asked what he was doing. Inkcap turned around to find Lightkeeper smiling at him. Lightkeeper had once suffered from facial paralysis, and even after applying a medicinal plaster, his mouth was still a bit crooked, and this became more pronounced when he smiled. Although Inkcap had never been very fond of Lightkeeper, today he didn't find that smile at all unsightly.

"What's that fur in your bag?" Lightkeeper asked.

"What's it got to do with you?"

Lightkeeper took an antique porcelain bottle from his inside pocket and made to give it to Inkcap.

"Why are you giving it to me?" Inkcap asked.

"It's to say thank you. I know you broke your oil bottle."

"You didn't get it from the kiln, did you?"

"You know the kiln can't produce a bottle like this. It's from my house."

Inkcap wanted to talk about whether people like them could love and respect Chairman Mao, but he thought better of it because Lightkeeper had the misfortune to be born under a shooting star and he didn't want the others to see he was friendly with Lightkeeper.

"All right, I'll take it but you need to go away now."

The new bottle didn't have any oil in it, but it was still hung on the new wooden peg that had been hammered into the wall.

That night, Inkcap had a dream. In it, he was sitting under the trees next to the Kiln God Temple. There were elms, persimmon trees, medicine trees, ginkgo trees, pines and tung trees. They were either leaning together with one tree supporting three others; or two trunks grew from the roots of a single tree and those trunks arched away from each other as if they were enemies; or a new iron birch tree, covered in thorns, was already growing out of the hollowed-out body of an old willow where earth had already crumbled into the hollow. He heard the thickest of the three tung trees saying, "I want to leave." These tung trees had all fallen ill, and almost every branch had a fuzzy growth that clumped together like so many birds' nests. After the big tung tree had finished speaking, all the other trees fell silent and their red and yellow leaves began to fall to the ground, first one by one, and then all in a mess together. He wanted to collect some of the red leaves to take back for his grandmother to make papercuts but he found himself buried under their great mass. He started awake and opened his eyes. The cotton jacket and trousers he had put on top of the quilt were covering his head, suffocating him. It was already dawn. Inkcap was still caught up in his dream and confusedly called out to Gran, boasting about how many leaves he had collected. But Gran was not on the *kang*, she was sitting on the doorstep of the main room, combing her hair.

"You've only just woken up and already you're shouting loud enough to wake the dead!"

"I was collecting leaves for you all night," Inkcap explained.

"No wonder you're exhausted."

Inkcap finally woke up properly and wanted to tell Gran about his dream, but someone knocked urgently on the door.

The knocking was so insistent that Inkcap sat bolt upright and said, "They want to hold a meeting about you, Gran!"

"Don't make a sound and I'll go open the gate," Gran said, coming back from the threshold. She hadn't finished combing her hair properly, so she spat on her hand and slicked down the tuft of hair that had sprung up.

Inkcap held his breath in alarm and heard Gran opening the door and then muttering to someone. When she came back, her expression had changed a lot.

"Is it a meeting?" Inkcap asked.

"No, it was Iron Bolt."

"Why was he knocking so urgently?" Inkcap said, breathing a sigh of relief.

"Soupspoon's mother has passed away."

"Is she really dead?"

Soupspoon's mother suffered from chest pains and her skin was blue-tinged all year round, but that was all, so why had she died? Gran told him that Iron Bolt and Big Root were going to the bottom of the mountain to cut down a tree and wanted to know if she could go round to Soupspoon's house to help out.

"Are they going to chop down that thick old tung tree to make a coffin?" Inkcap asked.

"How did you know?" Gran asked.

"I had a dream," Inkcap replied and began to get dressed.

"A dream! Well, it wasn't a good dream, that's for sure. It's cold outside, so have a bit more sleep, then get up and take down the dried sweet potatoes and radishes from the wall of the courtyard to make some bran mash for the pigs."

She finished combing her hair and was about to leave when she asked whether there was a copper coin in the house. As people die, they should carry a copper coin in their mouth.

"Are you going to put our coin in her mouth?" Inkcap asked.

"Have you got any other use for a copper coin?"

"It's on the back windowsill."

Gran went to fetch the coin and suddenly exclaimed, "Sister, why have you upped and died on me like this? You're much younger than me, so why have you gone?"

When Soupspoon's mother died, the residents of Old Kiln, no matter whether they were called Zhu or Hei or any other name, all tucked a bundle of hemp paper under their arm and went round to pay their respects and busy themselves preparing for the funeral. Gran stayed there for most of the day because she knew what should be placed on the altar table, such as the big sacrificial wonton buns, which had to be steamed without cracking, and the sheet noodles that mustn't be dressed with any salt, vinegar, onion or garlic. Then there were the sacrificial dough twists made into the shape of a chrysanthemum flower and deep fried in oil, making sure not to burn them. Not to mention how to wash the body of the deceased, comb their hair, put on make-up, dress them in burial clothes, decide whether to put on five or seven items of unlined cotton clothes and whether all the buttons should be done up or only the third button. These old rules were not widely understood, and as Gran got older, she needed to pass them on to the youngsters. Sprout was going to help Gran, and Gran would teach her as they went along.

While Gran was out, Inkcap took the dried sweet potatoes and radishes off the top of the courtyard wall and made up a few sieves' worth of bran mash. At noon, he went to Soupspoon's house hoping to cadge a decent meal. But the household was at sixes and sevens because they had only borrowed eighty catties of unhulled rice from Kaihe's family to husk in preparation for making rice for the villagers on the day of the funeral. In the days leading up to the funeral, only maize grits soup was made for those who had come to help out. Inkcap saw that the trunk of the tung tree had already been hauled back there and Feng Youliang and Iron Bolt as well as Big Root and Cattle Track were taking turns to cut it into planks using a double-handed saw. The wood was so wet that water came out of it as they sawed. This made the ground treacherous, and Feng Youliang almost lost his footing. He called for Inkcap to shovel on some soil to steady things. Inkcap picked up a basket and went out of the courtyard to collect some soil. Half-Stick and Flower Girl were peeling potatoes there. Half-Stick was wearing short cotton trousers which left her calves and ankles exposed. A red earthworm was crawling across them. When Inkcap got closer, he saw that it wasn't a red earthworm after all but a trail of blood.

"Are you bleeding as well?" he asked.

Half-Stick looked down and cried in alarm, covering the blood with her hand.

"You stupid girl!" Flower Girl exclaimed. "Why didn't you use some cotton pads? Go to the privy and sort yourself out."

Half-Stick ran off to the privy. Inkcap didn't understand what was going on and just watched her go.

"What are you looking at?" Flower Girl demanded.

"Did Baldy Jin hit her?"

'Ah, yes, that's right. You just said, 'Are you bleeding as well?' As well as who?"

"The tung tree is bleeding."

"What do you mean, the tung tree is bleeding?"

"Go and see for yourself. The water coming out where they've sawn it is red."

"Hey, Cattle Track!" Flower Girl shouted. "Is there water coming out of the tree where you've sawn it?"

"Lots of it. Trees give off a fuckload of water in winter."

"Is it red?"

'It's not bleeding, why would it be red?"

"Ha! Less of the bullshit then, Inkcap. Have you got pink eye or something?"

Inkcap shovelled the soil to cushion the ground under the sawhorse. The water on the ground was still bright red, so he stopped talking and thought to himself that maybe he had hurt his eyes. With nothing else to do, he sat down under the gable wall, where a Chinese toon tree was growing. The tree was as thick as the mouth of a bowl, and the whole trunk was slightly red. Why red again? Awning's wife went for a piss behind the gable wall, and he asked her, "Is this toon tree red?"

"Yes. What about it?"

"Ah, nothing."

"You're wrong in the head."

Inkcap thought to himself, Will this Chinese toon follow Soupspoon when the time comes? There are so many trees in Old Kiln, does there have to be one tree to follow each person?

There was a reed mat on the threshold of the main room, and Third Aunt and Noodle Fish's wife were sewing a quilt and a mattress for the encoffining of Soupspoon's mother. Third Aunt had used up the thread on one needle and couldn't thread the new one.

"Why are you sitting there like an idiot? Come and thread a needle for me," Third Aunt told Inkcap. Then she turned back to Noodle Fish's wife, and said, "Why are people so fragile? Soupspoon said his mother was fine last night. He was going to steam some sweet potatoes, but his mother asked him what he was doing and said that if you can save a meal, that's a meal saved and they could eat it tomorrow. This morning he went to his mother's bedroom to empty the pisspot to find her quilt half off the *kang*. He called out to her, 'Mum! Mum! Didn't you cover yourself properly last night?' He went over and saw his mother lying there stiff and not breathing. Ai! She didn't get to eat that meal of sweet potatoes after all!"

"She must have thought she was dozing, just dozing, and would wake up to eat steamed sweet potatoes," Inkcap said.

"What do you know about it?" Third Aunt said. "Why do you think people are still just dozing off when they're dying?"

"When I go to sleep, all I know is that I want to go to sleep, but I don't actually know about it when I do fall asleep," Inkcap observed.

Ignoring Inkcap, Noodle Fish's wife said, "It's better to die. You don't suffer any more. Ouch!" She let out a scream as she poked a needle into her hand and quickly put her finger into her mouth and sucked, her eyes fixed on Third Aunt.

"She didn't want to die," Third Aunt said. "You talked about her, but she didn't like listening to other people."

Noodle Fish's wife turned pale and muttered, "I mean, everyone is going to die. If my sister dies peacefully, that means she has accumulated great virtue. Oh, sister, I couldn't bear to let you die."

"You can leave with a clear conscience now. Don't worry about Soupspoon. He's going to be a model worker. And this time, we'll share the food relief. The Branch Secretary said we will share it with Soupspoon."

"Soupspoon's going to be a model worker?" Inkcap exclaimed. "And he's going to share the food relief?"

"Do you think I'd joke about it?" Third Aunt said.

Inkcap was about to say something else, but Potful shouted at him to take his rope fuse to the cemetery because Lightkeeper, Caretaker and the others wanted to have a smoke there to honour the death of Soupspoon's mother.

Inkcap came back from the cemetery to have lunch with Soupspoon's family. The people who were helping with the work all carried bowls and stood or squatted in the yard eating. The maize grits soup was just the right consistency and when they added boiled soya beans, everyone said it was delicious. The slurping of the soup and the chewing of the beans made for a great din. Inkcap went into the kitchen, where Awning's wife was dishing out the food. She had already served the others, but she didn't serve him.

"I'm hungry," Inkcap said.

"You didn't help with the work, so why should you get to eat?"

"I took my fuse to the cemetery."

Awning's wife began to serve Inkcap under his watchful eye.

"Give the ladle a bit more elbow action and get me some more of those beans!"

"I suppose you'd like me to bring you the pot to fish about in for yourself!"

She carelessly ladled out a bowlful and put it on top of the stove. "Take it away and eat."

Inkcap inspected the bowl and discovered a complete absence of soya beans. He refused to eat and was so aggrieved that he actually gasped and sniffled.

"What's the matter?" Awning's wife said. "You're eating for free and still complaining there's no beans?"

Inkcap threw his chopsticks onto the stovetop and one of them bounced into the pot.

"Hey! Hey! You little prick! You're going to bring a curse on me. Would you dare bring a curse on the Branch Secretary?"

Someone at the courtyard gate was saying, "Why didn't you help, Ever-Obedient?"

"I'm sick," Ever-Obedient replied.

"Why are you still coming to eat with us if you're sick?"

"I'm looking for Inkcap, OK?"

Inkcap was in a temper about this.

"Why are you looking for me?" he asked angrily.

Ever-Obedient was being kept at the kitchen door and shouted back furiously, "Did you cut all the hair off my dog?"

Inkcap's bravado suddenly deserted him and he said, "It wasn't me that did it."

"It wasn't you, eh?" Ever-Obedient said. "Then how come Lightkeeper saw you carrying dog hair around if it wasn't you?"

Ever-Obedient rushed over to grab Inkcap, and, because Inkcap had no hair, grabbed him by the ear instead. Inkcap yelped. The person next to him leapt to his feet and demanded to know what Ever-Obedient thought he was up to. Ever-Obedient told everyone about the beautiful white coat of his dog until Inkcap cut it all off. Now, when the dog returned home, it had no idea what it looked like. As Ever-Obedient's wife was combing her hair in front of the mirror, the dog ran over and saw its reflection. It yelped and fainted dead away. Ever-Obedient's wife put the mirror on top of a cupboard where the dog couldn't see it. But then the dog climbed up on top of the cupboard to have another look and it fell headfirst to the floor. Everyone laughed out loud and commented on how vain his dog was.

"My dog is no ordinary dog," Ever-Obedient boasted. "It's the king of the dogs in Old Kiln. How can it go on living after this?"

His anger flared up again as he spoke, and he pinched Inkcap's ear so hard he was in danger of pinching it right off.

After the body had been taken to the mourning hall in the main building, Gran dressed Soupspoon's mother in burial clothes. According to custom, she should be wearing either five or seven items of clothing but Soupspoon said he didn't have that many to hand and they'd have to make do with three. Gran said she didn't know if three was an appropriate number, but Soupspoon couldn't see the harm. If a family's rich they can use more clothes, and if they're poor they have to use fewer. His family was poor, so there was nothing wrong with dressing his mum in three pieces of clothing, was there? As they were debating the matter, they heard the sound of Ever-Obedient cursing Inkcap out in the courtyard.

Gran rushed outside and saw Ever-Obedient pinching Inkcap's ear until it stretched. She immediately went over and threw her arms around Inkcap, saying, "You've got a heavy hand, Ever-Obedient. What's going on here?"

"He cut off my dog's fur," Ever-Obedient explained.

Gran boxed Inkcap's ears, saying, "Did you cut off that dog's fur?"

"It…" Inkcap stuttered and Gran boxed his ears again.

"Did you cut off that dog's fur?"

"No."

"If you didn't cut it off, say you didn't. Have you told your uncle Ever-Obedient yet that you didn't?" Gran asked, before turning to Ever-Obedient to say that it really wasn't him.

"If it wasn't him, who was it?" Ever-Obedient asked.

Sprout had carried her bowl over to the courtyard gates where she saw the Branch Secretary and his wife coming over from the mouth of the alley. She hurried back inside saying, "Ever-Obedient, pigs and dogs shit and piss on the road all the time, are you going blame Inkcap for that too? You can't just accuse people as you please. Even if the dog has had a haircut, what does that matter? It's still alive and well, isn't it? If the Branch Secretary hears you going on like this, you'll be giving him a hold over Inkcap. He'll make a big thing out of it and say Inkcap is a class enemy indulging in sabotage."

She had barely finished talking when the Branch Secretary entered the courtyard.

"What's going on?" he asked. "What's all the noise about?"

"We're trying to get Ever-Obedient to have something to eat," Sprout replied, "but he just wants to go to the cemetery to pay his respects. Everyone says he's a very good party member."

"He hasn't joined the party yet," the Branch Secretary said.

"I want to join," Ever-Obedient said, "but they won't let me."

"You just have to work a bit harder."

"I do work hard. I do work hard."

"You can't call someone a party member if they're not one," the Branch

Secretary told Sprout. "All party members make a good impression, but not everyone who makes a good impression is a party member."

Ever-Obedient took the opportunity to escape from the courtyard. Gran came out and said to him in a low voice, "Haven't you eaten yet?"

"How could I have eaten?" Ever-Obedient replied.

"Take the lad with you, he's awfully fond of dogs. Tell him to talk to the dog, and who's to say the dog won't be happy again?"

Ever-Obedient didn't say anything, and Gran gave Inkcap a meaningful look.

"Old Uncle Ever-Obedient! Uncle!" Inkcap called out and then left, following on behind Ever-Obedient.

NINE

BACK AT EVER-OBEDIENT'S HOUSE, the white-haired dog refused to eat or drink but just lay listlessly on the ground. At the sight of Inkcap, however, it suddenly started to bark and tried to bite him.

"See how angry it is with you?" Ever-Obedient said.

"It wasn't me who cut your hair," Inkcap said. "Why don't you tell me what's upsetting you?"

The white-haired dog stopped snapping but kept up a low growling sound.

"I know you hate it. Get up, walk around, let me take a look... Oh, what a beautiful haircut! Really beautiful! Who says it's not?"

The white-haired dog took a only few steps and then lay back down on the floor.

"Ugly is ugly, there's no two ways about it," Ever-Obedient said. "The hair will grow back again after winter, won't it?... Get up! Get up! It won't get up."

Ever-Obedient wanted to drive the dog out to the courtyard gate, but it wouldn't go outside. He kicked it in annoyance, and it finally got up and slunk out to the shed where they kept firewood.

"We all have to say he's beautiful. If we keep saying it, he'll start to believe us," Inkcap said.

He went into the firewood shed and murmured something to the dog. Ever-Obedient squatted under a tree, fretting and smoking. Just after eating a potful of food, the white-haired dog came out of the shed and stood at the entrance of the courtyard, barking so loudly it made the alley buzz.

When Inkcap came out of the shed too, Ever-Obedient asked him doubtfully, "What did you say in there? Is everything OK?"

"I tried sweet-talking him to start with," Inkcap said, "but he ignored me, so I gave him an earful instead. 'You are a shit-eating dog,' I told him. 'I was born into a bad family, and I'll stay that way all my life, but I'm still alive, aren't I? So you've lost your fur, is that really going to kill you? Well, go to hell then! There'll still be other dogs in this world, and one of them will be king of Old Kiln!' He was fine after that."

"That dog's got no self-respect," Ever-Obedient said with a laugh. "That's the only kind of language he understands. Take him with you for a few days and finish his education. The way you can talk to dogs, I almost think you must have been whelped by one yourself!"

"It's not that I was born from a dog, but that dogs are born from humans."

Inkcap called the white-haired dog over to him and patted its head as it licked his feet.

"You telling me to take your dog away isn't going to fill my empty stomach, is it?" Inkcap said.

"You cocky little sod, do you actually think I owe you? All right, I'll give you three sweet potatoes."

"That's not enough to cover you pinching my ear! What else have you got that's good to eat?"

"I've got some fried noodles too."

Inkcap didn't want any fried noodles, so he led the dog away, eating the sweet potatoes as he went. On passing Awning's front door, he remembered that Awning's wife hadn't let him finish his meal and got so angry again that he told the white-haired dog to bite one of her chickens. A flock of chickens were scratching for food there, and the white-haired dog pounced on one, holding it down with its paws. Inkcap hurriedly beat the dog off, making it let go of the chicken in a flurry of feathers.

"I told you to bite it, not kill it! Let's go to Cowbell's house, and just make sure you behave yourself."

Cowbell was at home, squatting on the laundry stone and looking towards the corner of the courtyard wall. When he saw Inkcap enter, he sucked his breath and wouldn't let him speak.

"What are you doing?" Inkcap asked.

"I'm not going to let you talk. As soon as you talk, the mice run away."

"Why do you want to keep them?"

"Don't you know that having mice at home proves your family is wealthy? I'm rearing a nest of mice. They'd been stealing grain from Awning's house and storing it in their old nest. I ploughed up that nest and found half a *jin* of grain there!"

"You really need to steal at least a *dou* of grain," Inkcap replied.

As the two of them were talking, the white-haired dog suddenly pounced, and a mouse darted past them like a shadow and scuttled through the door to the main room. Cowbell picked up a broom and hit the dog with it.

"That dog's a real pain in the arse chasing mice like that," he said. "When did Ever-Obedient's dog get so ugly, anyway?"

"Don't call it ugly."

"I'm not insulting anyone else. Can't I even insult a dog now?"

"Ever-Obedient put me in charge of his dog for a few days, so if you insult the dog, you're insulting me."

"Ah, so you're brothers now, are you?"

To the west was Pendulum's house. Pendulum fired ceramic ware at the kiln factory. He had been home half the day and was up in the locust tree by his front gate, lopping off branches. From his perch, he could see into Gourd's privy. Gourd's wife was squatting in there, her buttocks showing like a block of white marble. Pendulum hung his axe on a branch and thought about how unfair the world was; not only was she filial in her attitude to her mother-in-law, but she was very beautiful to boot. When he looked again, he saw she was still squatting there, releasing a veritable Yangtze River of piss.

Just at that moment, Goodman passed underneath the tree and asked, "Why aren't you working at the kilns, Pendulum?"

"I have been." Then he remembered who he was talking to and hastily added, "I asked for time off to cut some branches and build a chicken coop."

"I hear you've had an argument with Palace. It's your fate for the two of you to work together at the kilns, so what have you got to quarrel about?"

"He's a fuckwit."

"Palace may talk too much, but his heart's in the right place and he's not picking on you."

"No one picks on me. I'd beat their head in with a brick if they tried."

"It is not good to be so violent. You should just be honest, Pendulum. I'm going now, so make sure none of the branches you chop down fall on my head."

"You're safe, I'm not chopping at the moment."

Goodman had only taken a couple of steps when, by some ill chance, the axe which was hanging on the tree came loose and fell, brushing past Goodman's back and landing on the ground.

Pendulum hurriedly slid down from the tree to see if he had hurt Goodman. He hadn't. He sank to his knees and said, "That scared the shit out of me. I was worried to death."

Goodman made no reply, but after a while he said, "Let me wipe away the sweat. My head feels like it's been doused in ice water."

Pendulum hurriedly bowed his apologies.

"I'm a lucky man. I almost lost my old life there," Goodman observed. "Good things are bound to come my way, for surely this axe represents good fortune sent down from Heaven."

When he saw that Goodman was laughing, Pendulum began to laugh too.

"You really are a 'good man'! Everything turns out well for you."

"Are not such good outcomes the beginning of the road to Paradise?"

Pendulum offered his pipe, but he didn't have a light. Then he saw Inkcap and Cowbell coming out of the gates of Cowbell's house, and he shouted, "A fuse! A fuse!"

"Is that what you think I'm called? A Fuse?" Inkcap said, taking a fuse over to him

Pendulum was very attentive to Goodman and asked him where he had just been. Goodman told him that he had been with Caretaker's wife, talking to her illness.

"Are you still doing that?" Inkcap asked. "Soupspoon's mother was sick, why didn't you talk her better? She died this morning."

"That's enough from you," Pendulum said. "Illness is illness and fate is fate. No one can change that. You say that Caretaker's wife is sick? Is it serious?"

"It is. She's got tuberculosis."

"That's because she's not filial to her mother-in-law. If she doesn't deserve to be sick, no one does."

"Her mother-in-law and Caretaker are not satisfied with her, and that's why she's ill. I told her that her mother-in-law and her husband are her gods, and if she's not making them happy, she's hurting Heaven. 'You surely know your mother-in-law is a busybody,' I said, 'but she does want you to get better. How can you make trouble for her?' She nodded when I said that, so I knew she was thinking straight again. So I said it was also because she didn't think well of anyone that she had caught tuberculosis and she must show Heaven her remorse. She asked me how to do that. I told her to admit her faults to Heaven and describe how she had neglected her husband, how, in the whole of Old Kiln, only Caretaker has not had clean clothes to wear all year round and how, when he rolls his trousers up, his knees are caked in dirt. She said that she had told Caretaker to wash but he'd said the layer of dirt was lucky and that luck would be lost if he washed it off. So I asked if her house was lucky now, and pointed out that the other households have tasty food to eat but all they have is plain rice! She asked how I knew about this, and I told her I couldn't avoid knowing because Caretaker complained about it to everyone he met, saying it was all his wife's fault and that if you didn't manage to find a decent wife, your life turned to shit. She said she didn't know how he had the nerve to complain. She had fulfilled her duties as a wife every night, but what had he ever brought home as a husband? Hadn't she been asking him all year long for a foot of cloth to make the uppers for shoes?"

"Well, he certainly got his fill of tiger meat!" Pendulum exclaimed.

"What are you talking about?" Inkcap said. "There aren't any tigers around here."

"Tigress, then," Pendulum corrected himself. "Isn't it odd how the women of Old Kiln are all tigresses!"

Goodman Wang laughed. "I reprimanded her," he said, "telling her I had come to talk her out of her illness, but for every sentence I managed to utter, she'd come back with two of her own! 'Go on then,' she said, so I told her she was not considerate of her husband, and she didn't look after her mother-in-law. Did she empty her mother-in-law's pisspot in the morning? Did she give any thought to eating and drinking when her mother-in-law was sick? Or did she pout and look daggers at every meal, making her mother-in-law feel guilty and getting so angry with her that she couldn't digest her food and kept hiccupping and choking? She got upset again and tried to argue with me. I told her to listen to me and do what I said if she wanted to get better. She shut up then, and I told her again to admit her faults to Heaven: how she didn't care about her husband and failed to look after her mother-in-law. The more detail she went into, the better. 'Then, at night,' I told her, 'you can go out and laugh at the sky and release the yin so it won't be controlling you any more.'"

"I can't stand unfilial people," Pendulum said. "Caretaker asked me to help him mend his stove but I wouldn't go. But if Gourd and his wife asked me to help them, I'd go even if the sky started raining knives."

"Quite right," Goodman said. "Society relies on filial piety. There's no point in praying to the gods if you are not filial towards your mother and father. Nor is there any benefit in feng shui if you don't have a true heart. Medicine is useless if you don't put your all into it. And if the time is not right and your luck is out, there's no point in asking for anything. If someone is filial to his own elders, but not to other people's, he will still be respected. But if someone is disrespectful and bad mouths his own elders but not other people's, he will still be despised. Among the ethical, there is mutual love and respect, and each spontaneously fulfils their own Dao. Put simply, fulfilling one's Dao is essential, not optional. Only when parents are entirely compassionate, children filial and siblings dutiful, can we say that the Dao is fulfilled."

Inkcap didn't understand any of what Goodman was saying and didn't want to listen any more. He poked Cowbell in the armpit and Cowbell poked him back. The two of them started pulling faces and mucking around.

"If a person is ugly," Pendulum continued, "they can make up for it by having a good heart. Some people are both good-looking and have a good heart. But Caretaker's wife is ugly and spends all day looking for trouble."

"Isn't this the same as building a house?" Goodman said. "If a house is built properly, it will be beautiful. A beautiful house is well ventilated and sturdy. But if a house is built crooked and misshapen, it will be damp and gloomy."

"Just look at Inkcap!" Pendulum said.

"What about me?" Inkcap flashed back. "I just came from a bad background, and your family are middle peasants. That's not much better."

"I didn't say you're from a bad background, you're the one who cares about that. I mean, it can't have been easy for you to grow up like you are."

"I'm just born ugly," he retorted, "but you've made yourself ugly on purpose."

He kicked the white-haired dog, and the dog yelped, which cut Goodman and Pendulum off short.

"Either listen to what Goodman is teaching us or fuck off, the pair of you."

"You've got my fuse," Inkcap protested.

Pendulum relit his pipe, then hurled the fuse as far away as possible.

Inkcap retrieved his fuse, put it out and wrapped it around his waist. The two of them left the alley.

"He said I care about myself," Inkcap said. "Do I?"

"Yes, you do," Cowbell replied.

"I don't care, I don't care any more."

"If you don't care, that's fine."

They saw a fly carrying a grain of rice flying ahead of them. The fly was swooping up and down with the rice in its mouth, and there was another fly that had landed on a rock and was washing its face.

"What a big grain of rice," the second fly said.

The first fly came to rest on a brick in the wall and dropped the grain of rice. "It's from Dazed-And-Confused's steamed rice."

When it heard this, the fly on the rock buzzed off to Dazed-And-Confused's house.

"There's steamed rice at Dazed-And-Confused's place," Inkcap said.

"Do you think you can smell it just because you were thinking about it?" Cowbell asked.

"It's what that fly said."

"Obviously you're just saying that."

"Dazed-And-Confused really is making steamed rice."

"He only knows how to steam sweet potatoes. How could he be making steamed rice?"

Inkcap ignored Cowbell. His stomach was rumbling so he set off after the fly. Cowbell and the white-haired dog followed him at a run. The fly disappeared out of sight in the blink of an eye, but as soon as they ran into South Bend Alley, they really could smell the rice and it smelt delicious.

The courtyard gates of Dazed-And-Confused's house were shut tight but when they lay down and peered in through the wall of discarded saggars, they saw a straw rope stretched tight and, hanging over it, a piece of dog skin with all the fur rubbed off it, drying in the sun. That was Dazed-And-Confused's bedding. He always showed it off to visitors and once, when Inkcap went to buy straw sandals, he didn't have any ready-made but said he'd make some up on the spot. Inkcap couldn't wait quietly and went over to look at the dog skin bedding on the *kang*.

"So this is your dog skin bedding, is it? Let me have a nap on it," he demanded.

"Go ahead. You'll dream about eating sauced noodles."

Inkcap lay down and did indeed go straight to sleep and start dreaming. But he didn't dream about noodles. Instead, he dreamed that the dog skin rolled up around him and turned him into a dog, a yellow-haired dog. In his dream, he heard himself ask, "Why aren't these clothes gold-coloured, not just yellow?" He ran over to stand in front of Gran, but she didn't recognise him. He kept worrying at the hem of Gran's jacket with his mouth, but she still didn't recognise him and drove him away. So he tried howling. His own howling woke him up and he discovered that he was actually still human. His neck was itchy and sore. When he scratched it, he found three lice there. They were all black. Looking at the dog skin bedding again, he saw four more lice and immediately pulled the bedding off the *kang* and threw it on the ground.

"Your bedding is crawling with lice!" he exclaimed.

"Nonsense," Dazed-And-Confused retorted.

"Doesn't it make you itch?"

Dazed-And-Confused said it didn't. Now it was hung over the rope, drying in the sun. Surely that must be because Dazed-And-Confused had found it impossibly itchy. Inkcap was also sure that the lice would be hopping around everywhere, maybe even taking flight, to escape the sun. But the sight of Dazed-And-Confused sitting there on the threshold, eating steamed white rice, made Inkcap forget there were any lice at all in the dog skin bedding.

The rice in Dazed-And-Confused's bowl was like white jade and silver, and it was giving off clouds of steam that could also be taken for the radiance of the rice. The sun slanted down from the eaves, bright with rainbow colours. There was a bowl of pickled Chinese cabbage on the ground in front of him. He picked up a chopstick-load of pickled cabbage and put it on the rice. Green was green, and white was white. He took a clump of cabbage and rice as big as a wine cup, looked at it and opened his mouth. His mouth was so big that it reached from ear to ear. When the food was introduced into this black hole of a mouth, lips and tongue smacked and slurped together, and he was so enraptured that his eyes were screwed tight shut. Inkcap's mouth was also moving and even if no sound emerged, there was plenty of saliva. Dazed-And-Confused hunched his shoulders and stretched out a leg, replete with comfort and satisfaction. As he started to swallow, his eyes still shut tight, his mouth was puckered like a chicken's arse. Cowbell couldn't bear to look at him.

"Just eat your fucking food," he said, plonking himself down angrily on the ground.

When Cowbell's mother was still alive, whenever she made something delicious to eat, she always served a bowl of it to the old folk who were her neighbours on the left and to the kids who were her neighbours on the right. Cowbell's family were better off than either of these neighbours, but they never bothered to hide their good fortune by skulking behind closed doors to eat. Even when Awning who had borne their family grudge was having sauced noodles, he would take his bowl in front of the spirit wall to eat, lifting the noodles high out of his bowl with his chopsticks, all red and spicy.

"Bring us a lump of seasoned lard," Awning would shout, knowing that this clarified lard was particularly tasty with sauced noodles.

"Good times, Awning," Cowbell's mother would say.

"Great times," Awning would reply. "Too good to describe."

"Have you still got any lard left at your place?" she would ask.

"I butchered two *jin* of meat to get it," Awning would boast.

But the truth was that Awning's wife did not give him a lump of seasoned lard, and all he actually got was a pinch of pickled cabbage.

Remembering his dead mother, Cowbell thought of his neighbours on either side and hated how stingy and ungenerous Dazed-And-Confused was. He pulled Inkcap to one side and asked in a whisper, "How come this old fart can still eat so well?"

"He reared a pig and got allocated twenty kilos of rice heads as feed."

"I'm going to rear a pig too, next spring."

Another fly emerged from the crack in the door with a grain of rice in its mouth.

"Why can't there be a whole swarm of flies?" Cowbell wondered.

He swatted at the fly with his hand, and it fell to the ground, still carrying the grain of rice. It rolled over a couple of times, then flew off leaving the rice behind. Inkcap picked it up and blew on it, getting ready to eat it.

"Don't you mind it's tainted?" Cowbell asked.

"Nope," Inkcap replied.

"Oh! I guess that's because your family's politically tainted too."

"What the fuck are you talking about?" Inkcap said, pinching Cowbell's lips between his fingers.

"I guess it was only a rice fly, not a shit fly," Cowbell said hastily. "Not tainted. Not dirty at all, in fact."

Inkcap let go of Cowbell's lips, but he still didn't put the grain of rice in his mouth. He kneaded it into a lump between two fingers, then smeared it on the wall.

The two of them were still upset with Dazed-And-Confused and wanted to throw a stone into his courtyard to startle him while he was eating. But there were no stones to be found around the gate. They went to a nearby privy to pull a tile down from the top of its wall when they saw a wooden stick in the corner covered in blood and shit. Inkcap yanked Cowbell out of the privy and walked down the alley.

"It's been a long time since he last had steamed rice," Inkcap said. "Let's not scare him, just let him enjoy it. You can get sick if you have a fright when you're eating."

"Yes, let's let him eat," Cowbell agreed. "You never know, he might get some strange illness and not be able to eat again for days."

Strange illnesses were common in Old Kiln. Baldy Jin went bald overnight and developed lots of small red sores. Gran told him to use ginger juice and to mash the green skin of walnuts and pepper seeds together, and apply it to draw the poison out, but none of it worked. Soupspoon's mother had endured heart pain all her life, and Soupspoon himself had asthma. The mere sight of anything cold set him off grunting and gasping so he sounded like he had a pair of bellows in his chest. Lucky's mother couldn't stand up straight from the pain in her back and had been crawling on hands and knees for many years. Six-Pints' father, who had only just turned sixty, could no longer hold his piss in and always had a wad of cotton stuffed into his trousers. Tag-Along's father died from chronic distension of the stomach; when he died, he was so skinny his bones showed through his skin, but his stomach was as big as a toad's. Sprout's uncle was as jaundiced as yellow poster paper and unable to breathe properly. He just lay on the *kang* crying out, "Squeeze me to death. Just squeeze me to death." But who could do that? His family wailed and watched him toss and turn all night until he finally vomited half a basin of blood and closed his eyes for good. Almost all the elderly had stomach problems, and even the Branch Secretary, when he spoke at village meetings, had to keep putting his head to one side to spit out a stream of bile and stomach juices. Three years ago, after Barndoor's father died, almost completely paralysed, a strange thing became apparent: no more than two or three months after someone died, someone else in the village became ill or died. Useless's father quarrelled with his maternal uncle and one day when he was planting seedlings in the fields he fell headlong and never got up again. Later on, it was Caretaker's father who lay paralysed on the *kang* and later on still, Almost-There's wife gave birth to a baby who was just a ball of flesh with no nose and no eyes.

"Let's not put a curse on Dazed-And-Confused," Inkcap said. "Even if we curse others, they still get to eat steamed rice which we're too poor to eat ourselves. Even if they get sick and die tomorrow, they can still get to enjoy delicious food if they become gluttonous ghosts. Besides, if we curse others into getting sick, who can guarantee we're not going to get sick ourselves?"

"People from the other townships and villages all say that our Old Kiln has beautiful landscapes and scenery," Cowbell said. "So why are you so crude? What strange illness are you suffering from? Why don't you get any taller?"

"You have a strange illness, don't you? You've got a hole in your ear."

"That's not an illness. My mum told me I was bitten by a mouse when she was in confinement after I was born."

"And I don't want to get any taller!"

With that, the two of them had a good laugh and Inkcap said, "From now on, let's stop taking the piss out of each other, OK?"

"OK. You hungry? I'm so famished it's like a cat's got its claws in my stomach."

"Talking about food just makes you feel hungry, so let's not. How long do you think the main alleyway in the village is?"

"Never thought about it."

"Think about it now."

"Seven thousand paces."

"Ten thousand."

The two of them paced out the distance, going all the way to the south entrance of the village, then took a rest, leaning on the stone lion.

Clouds were passing across the sky, some in clusters, some pulling others along, some moving on their own but all scudding past from west to east.

Suddenly, Inkcap smelt the smell, while Cowbell was still saying, "I said seven thousand steps, is it seven thousand?"

Inkcap didn't tell him that he had smelt the smell, but instead, when he saw, a long way away on the public highway, three or four people coming in and out of the little wooden shack, he said, "Didn't Bash go and help out at Soupspoon's house?"

"He lives alone, doesn't he?" Cowbell replied. "He's never before helped out with any family's wedding or a funeral. Hey, look at all that lot! Has his business suddenly picked up?"

"Maybe, maybe not," Inkcap said.

TEN

THERE CERTAINLY WAS A REASON for the sudden improvement in Bash's business. Cowbell might not have known what it was, but Inkcap did. However, he had sworn a solemn oath to Bash to keep it to himself and not breathe a word about it.

Every morning when he came out of his old lodgings, Bash would lift weights in front of his door, using a stone doorstop. It weighed more than forty *jin*, and the tendons in his arm stood out with each lift. Inkcap was collecting Bash's piss bucket to take to the private allotment and pour the night-time offering over his ridges of spring onions and, as he came out, he bumped into Barndoor, who was coming back from collecting the night soil.

"Still in training, then Bash?" said Barndoor.

Bash grunted.

"That's a lot of effort for nothing. If a farmer had that kind of strength, he'd use it to hoe his own plot of wheat."

"Go collect your own shit," Bash said.

Barndoor blushed furiously and just spat out as he walked away. "Fucking lapdog pretending he's a wolfdog."

Inkcap thought that Bash really was a wolfdog, and hoping to curry favour with him, he went over and squatted down next to him.

"Can you lift it a hundred times?"

"Wanna see?"

"Sure."

Bash dropped the stone weight to the ground with a thud, left it there, went inside and came out with a quilt draped over his shoulders before setting off for the little wooden shack on the public highway.

Bash was always a bit odd temperamentally, so Inkcap wasn't annoyed by any of this, but he did wonder why Bash had draped himself in the quilt. Was it because he was cold and didn't have a padded cotton jacket? Or was he intending to sleep in the little wooden shack? Inkcap couldn't guess. Wrapped in the quilt, Bash strode like a comet out of the alleyway and when the wind caught the quilt, making it flap around, Inkcap thought it looked very fine, as though Bash was about to take off and fly to the heavens.

Inkcap followed close on Bash's heels. He wanted to say something to him but, for the moment, he didn't know what. Suddenly, he remembered how other people went to South Mountain to exchange rice for coarse maize and he hoped that Bash might take him when he next went. Bash stopped in his tracks and looked at him.

"Do you want to go and exchange some maize?"

"Sure. Let's go to South Mountain."

"Why go that far?"

Inkcap certainly hadn't anticipated that Bash would reveal his secret: if you wanted to exchange fine grain for coarse maize, you could do it in the little wooden shack. Not only could you exchange one *jin* of rice for a *jin* and a half of coarse maize, but you could also buy and sell it. You could sell a *jin* of rice for thirty-five fen, while a *jin* of coarse maize could fetch twenty-two fen. It turned out that the little wooden shack had been in the grain business for a while, and the buying and selling side was proving very successful. There was no pressure to take part; people still brought their bikes and trikes to have a tyre repaired and others came on foot with a basket on their backs or carrying a cloth bag, to have their shoes repaired. Inkcap told Gran the news and suggested they polish some more grain to exchange for coarse maize, but Gran wasn't impressed by his home economics skills.

"Why are you so troublesome?" she said. "Are you going to starve to death if you eat that *jin* and a bit less?"

"I soon will do. If you don't go, I will."

"You wouldn't dare."

"I would!"

Inkcap opened the cupboard to see how much rice was in the basin. This was rice that Gran had put aside, planning to make one meal of rice congee every fortnight. She was especially looking forward to having steamed rice on his birthday. But Inkcap refused to listen to her and was about to make off with the rice. Gran was sitting on the *kang* cutting paper flowers, and she hastily threw the scissors she was holding, meaning to land them on top of the cupboard and give Inkcap a fright. Instead, she hit Inkcap and the scissors struck him in the leg. Inkcap yelped and sat down in a heap. Horrified, Gran rushed over to take a look. The scissors had gone through Inkcap's cotton trousers but hadn't pierced the skin. They had, however, raised a green-black lump. Gran threw herself down and licked the lump, saying that saliva would fix it. Sure enough, the lump dispersed as Gran kept asking, "Does it hurt? Does it hurt?"

Inkcap berated her for throwing the scissors, then, quite deliberately, burst into tears. He kept it up until Gran's face had gone white as a sheet with fright, and then he began to tell her that it was nothing. The more he said it, the more Gran hated herself for losing control. She hugged Inkcap tight and wailed over him.

When Inkcap came home for dinner the next day, Gran had cooked a meal of congee. At noon on the day after that, as soon as he came through the door, his grandmother had already brought a bowl of food and put it on the pot shelf for him. She had also covered another bowl to keep it warm. When Inkcap uncovered it, he saw it was *mi'er* noodles, with wheat noodles crammed in alongside rice in a thick bowl.

"Did the production team give us our share of the food relief this time, Gran?" Inkcap asked.

"What are you talking about? When did we ever get a share?"

"Then how come we're eating so well all the time?"

"The tips of your ears are all dry. Looks like if you don't eat some better food, you'll starve to death."

Of course, Inkcap couldn't see his own ears, but he felt them with his hands and found that they were indeed dry. "They're frozen!" he exclaimed. He started to wolf down the food. He thought it was so delicious that he crammed another mouthful in before swallowing the previous one as if a hand was reaching up out of his throat trying to drag the food down, bowl and all. When he finished the bowl, his head was steaming and as he went to the pot for a refill, he leapt from under the clove tree right up to the top of the steps of the main room, bowl in hand.

"You lunatic!" Gran exclaimed.

Walking past her, Inkcap saw the rice congee with mushy vegetables in her own bowl and noticed that there was only one short noodle strand floating on top, like a little fish. He stopped and stared at her.

"Didn't you have any noodles, Gran?"

"I ate them first."

He went into the kitchen and found only rice congee and vegetables in the pot. He realised that Gran must have scooped up all the rice and noodles for him to eat, so he picked up the bottle of chillies and said, "Let me give you some chillies, Gran."

The chillies had been fried in seasoned oil. He scooped a lump of them into Gran's bowl and then another one. Great oily rings floated to the top and it was too spicy for Gran to eat.

Since then, every time Inkcap ate, he was unhappy if he saw that the rice was thick, and he got annoyed when he saw Gran ladling out any kind of thick food for him again. Gran went back to the old-style thin congee made with so little rice it might as well have been just water. Whenever Inkcap ate, he made sure to make loud purring noises and he smacked his lips when he had finished, saying, "I'm stuffed, just like Lightkeeper's rich old landlord of a dad!"

"Don't mention that man," Gran said.

So Inkcap said he wouldn't and told her instead that he wanted to go to the Branch Secretary's house because there were some old newspapers that his son had brought back from Luozhen and he wanted to see if he could beg some of them off him for Gran to use for her papercuts. He dashed out of the room with Gran calling out to him not to run so fast. "If you keep running like that, you'll use up all the energy you've just got from that food."

Inkcap bumped into lots of people standing around eating from their bowls as he ran down the alley, but it was only Baldy Jin who was always bound to be eating thick noodles, and was certain to ask, "Have you eaten, Inkcap?"

"Yes."

"Open your mouth. Open wide!"

Inkcap opened his mouth.

"There's nothing stuck in your teeth. You're eating thin, mushy rice congee again, aren't you?"

Doesn't thin mushy rice congee count as a meal too? he thought to himself. If you economise a little, you can put aside a bit more grain for the family. As long as you get one meal a day and you're not going hungry, everything's fine. But all he actually said was, "I had some noodles. *Mi'er* noodles."

Inkcap didn't raise the question of exchanging grain again, and if trading was going on in the shack, he made sure not to hang around to watch the fun. Gran had been right and that was the end of the matter concerning grain trading in the small wooden shack.

It was dawn but the sky was still dull and lifeless. The chickens were whispering to each other in the shed, saying that the branch on the left side of the clove tree was getting on very well with the branch on the right side. When it was windy during the day, the two branches pulled themselves close together and stayed that way all night. The chickens' gossiping made the branches separate, and three leaves on the left branch and one leaf on the right branch shyly dropped to the ground.

Inkcap had a stomach ache, which Gran said was because he was constipated. He just needed a good shit and he'd be fine. Inkcap went to the privy and tried to take a shit, but instead of shit, a tangle of creepy-crawlies came out. They hung out of his anus but wouldn't drop. He yelled for Gran, causing the chickens in the shed to cluck crazily.

Gran came over and put her foot on the end of the tangle and said to Inkcap, who was still squatting down, to stand up. Inkcap did as he was told and felt as though a rope was being pulled out of his stomach. When he turned round to look, he saw three roundworms squirming in a tangle on the ground.

"I kept saying I didn't know how you could eat so much without putting a bit more flesh on your bones. Turns out these worms were eating it all."

"You mean these worms were eating my food?" Inkcap was appalled.

"As soon as I can, I'll go to Kaihe's store and get you some Precious Pagoda candy."

Precious Pagoda candy was a kind of anti-worm medicine, with a very sweet taste. Big Root's son had taken it. Inkcap asked him to give him some, but he refused. Now, when Gran said she was going to buy a piece, Inkcap could already feel its sweet taste in his mouth.

"How much does it cost?" he asked, but before Gran could answer, the sound of a gong rang out.

Actually, it wasn't the sound of a real gong. The Branch Secretary was beating an empty steel kerosene drum with a mallet. Every morning, he slung his padded cotton robe around his shoulders and made his rounds of the village. He needed to have a firm grasp of production issues, public security matters and the state of the construction of a village kiln; he had to determine where to plant a tree and whether it should be a locust tree or a tung oil tree; he had to see where puddles formed on rainy days and needed to be filled in; he had to inspect whoever's wall had collapsed and needed to be repaired as soon as possible – not only was the damaged wall itself unsightly, the slogan painted on it couldn't be allowed to go short of three characters.

On this particular morning, he turned towards the village embankment and looked at the swirling white mist flowing south of the public highway.

He had just lit a pipe when the mist began to fade and the more it faded, the lighter the day became. It was as though the scene was covered in a veil that began to unravel from the top of South Mountain, revealing the peaks, cliffs, slopes, depressions and trees in those depressions.

The Branch Secretary was not as cultured and educated as Bash or Useless, but he was still able to express his feelings. "How lovely are the mountains and rivers of our motherland," he declared.

Then he saw a pack of wolves not far away, at the bottom of the embankment. They had come from the direction of Xiahewan. They had originally crossed the embankment heading down Yijia Ridge, but as the Branch Secretary looked at them, they returned his gaze and stopped where they were. He was worried they might be about to raid the village for pigs and chickens, so he ran over to Kaihe's house and asked for an empty kerosene drum to beat. Kaihe's family also began to shout at the tops of their voices, summoning the villagers to come and drive out the wolves.

When the shouting started, Inkcap snatched his trousers and went back into the main room where grandmother and grandson closed the door tight. After a while, Gran realised it wouldn't look good if the others drove the wolves away and she wasn't there. So she took a hammer and made to leave the room. Inkcap wanted to go, too, but Gran wouldn't let him. She went out and locked the courtyard door behind her.

Together, the residents of Old Kiln drove the wolves away. The wolves left streams of white faeces on the edge of the canal on the river strand, then they ran off along the base of Yijia Ridge. At noon, Tag-Along went to the little wooden shack on the highway, where he witnessed rice being exchanged for coarse maize. The ones receiving maize in the exchange were from South Mountain and apparently they had arrived the day before and stayed overnight in the shack. Those taking rice were from the villages of Xiahewan and Xichuan. They had just weighed the rice with a set of scales when Caretaker walked in and said, "Right then, there really is a black market!"

The people from South Mountain, Xiahewan and Xichuan were terrified and wanted to run away, but Bash blocked the door, saying, "What black market? Where?"

"I've caught you red-handed," said Caretaker as he tried to snatch the rice sack. "Are you still going to deny it?"

"What do you think you're doing? That's my food."

"You really have this much food?"

Caretaker left the rice sack but seized the scales. He tried to break the balance rod over his knee but couldn't.

"Don't you break that! If you do, I'll break your neck!"

"Listen, Bash," Caretaker said. "You've been running a black market here for ages. Everyone in the village knows about it. I came here today because the Branch Secretary and the production team leader sent me to investigate. I didn't expect to–"

Bash made a rush to grab the scales and pushed Caretaker to the ground.

"You hit me! You hit me!" Caretaker yelled.

Bash ignored him and told the people from South Mountain, Xiahewan and Xichuan to make themselves scarce. They looked at each other and scattered. Caretaker caught hold of Bash.

"You let them go!" he exclaimed. Then he started shouting once more, "He hit me! Bash hit me!"

"Who set you off again?" Bash asked.

Caretaker stopped shouting.

"I was sent here. And you've let them go!" he whined. "How am I going to explain that when I get back? You've got to come with me and see the Branch Secretary and the production team leader."

"I'll see them when I see them. What are they going to do? Eat me?"

The two of them walked back to the village and arrived at Three Fork Alley. There was no one in sight, in front or behind. Suddenly, Bash pushed Caretaker up against a courtyard wall and slapped him twice across the face. Caretaker had his guard down and his face started to go red from the slaps. He was too stunned to make a sound.

"I didn't hit you just now," Bash said. "If you shout, 'He hit me!' again, I'll have to shut you up."

Of course, Caretaker was too intimidated to call out again and just watched Bash swagger home.

At lunchtime, many of the villagers took their bowls out onto the street to eat. Potful demanded an end to the black market in the wooden shack. Some of the diners put down their bowls, while others kept eating on the move, all calling out to each other to follow Potful and go watch the fun.

Once in the shack, Potful issued Bash with a warning: "The black-market trading has to stop. If we find it's still going on, Old Kiln will report it to the Luozhen Commune. The commune will hold a meeting to criticise you. The Public Security Bureau will get involved and arrest you, and the village will demolish this shack."

Bash was furious. He kicked the door leaf with his foot and shouted, "Go ahead and demolish it, Team Leader Bullshit! Why don't you demolish me at the same time?"

He kicked a hole in the door panel, putting his foot through it so he lost his balance and fell over. He also bumped into the tea caddy on the stone table by the door, which began to sway alarmingly.

"The tea caddy! Watch out for the tea caddy!" Bash yelled, but no one steadied it, and he couldn't reach it himself, so it fell off the table and smashed into pieces. "You'll pay for that caddy one day."

Then he looked around and shouted, "Inkcap! Are you there, Inkcap?"

"I'm here," Inkcap called out from the back of the crowd.

"Call the Branch Secretary. Go and get the Branch Secretary."

Inkcap went straight to the village to find the Branch Secretary. He was in his own yard, getting Ever-Obedient to shave his head and face. There was a lot of loose skin on his face, and Ever-Obedient pulled on his upper lip like a piece of rubber, so half his face shifted to one side. Inkcap explained what was going on in the little wooden shack, but the Branch Secretary just told Ever-Obedient to get ready with his razor.

"It was me who sent Potful there," he explained.

"You can exchange grain at South Mountain," Inkcap complained, "so why not in the little shack here?"

"South Mountain isn't Old Kiln, and I'm not in control there. We're not going to have any capitalism in Old Kiln. I don't want to have a capitalist tail."

"Why?"

"Why? Didn't you chase off those wolves this morning?"

"No, I didn't."

"Should we exterminate wolves when we see them? Of course we should. Can we eliminate wolves completely? Of course we can't. Wolves should be killed but can't be wiped out altogether and that's why they still pass by Old Kiln. All we can do is make sure they don't get into the actual village and drive them from our boundaries. You tell Bash that I've got my eye on him and he should just be a good little boy and get on with mending shoes and not cause me any bother. Go on, off you go and tell him exactly what I just said to you."

Inkcap didn't dare say what he was thinking, but then neither did he go to the little wooden shack.

But, come evening, he simply couldn't stop worrying about it, so he went back to the shack. While he was still quite some distance away, he could hear the sound of arguing coming from inside. It sounded like Bash and Apricot. He thought to himself that Potful and Bash had been angry with each other all day, so what was Apricot doing there? He looked for a place to hide. There were no trees on the roadside, and the grass had all withered. A few dry stems were swaying in the wind, rustling noisily. He sat in a ditch, still as a rock.

He could hear Bash cursing to high heaven and shouting that he was born in the wrong time. Why don't we have landlords and local tyrants now? he was saying. If this were the old society, he would get hold of a gun and go up into the mountains as a bandit! Why don't we go to war? If there was a war on, he would definitely be a hero, advancing from soldier to squad leader, then a company leader, battalion commander, regiment commander, division commander and commander-in-chief. Now Old Kiln was losing him money and the Branch Secretary and production team leader were losing him money too! He said he had looked after lots of traffic accidents on the highway and had used three of his straw mats to transport the bodies. But what if the Branch Secretary and the production team leader had an accident? If he got involved, he would only use half a tattered seat cover and not give it a second thought. Of course, Apricot was upset by all this.

"I don't mind you cursing other people, but please leave my dad out of it."

Really? Inkcap said to himself. She should twist his lips for saying such poisonous things.

He didn't know whether Apricot did indeed twist Bash's lips or not, but she certainly laid into him verbally and Bash cursed her again. There were some banging noises as if someone was being pulled around and had knocked over a stool. The sliding door opened with a swish and was slammed shut again with a bang. This was followed by the sound of a loud slap across someone's face. Inkcap felt his face burning. He didn't know whether Bash had slapped Apricot or Apricot had slapped Bash. He looked up at the door of the small wooden shack and saw that the sky behind appeared to be smeared with ashes. Bash and Apricot were standing in the door, face to face and very close together. Bash was tall, much taller than Apricot, but Apricot's hair was sticking up. Neither moved.

It looked to Inkcap that it was Bash who had slapped Apricot, but Apricot didn't call out or even move, except to push her face into Bash's saying, "Hit me! Go on hit me!"

Inkcap was on the point of leaping out of the ditch and challenging Bash with a stream of invective, demanding to know if he had hit Apricot. But right at that moment, he heard everything that was there in the night, the artemisia, the earth banks, the earthworms crawling out of those banks, the water in the river, the rocks, the thornback fish, even a running rabbit coming to a stop in the distance and turning to look back. They were all furiously condemning Bash.

Why didn't Apricot fight back? Why didn't she walk away? Why did she let Bash hit her like that? Usually, when Inkcap talked to Apricot, she got up his nose or belittled him. But when Bash treated her like this, she didn't retaliate, nor even walk away. Inkcap felt that life was unfair and very hard to understand. So hit her, Bash! Sure enough, Bash slapped her face again, but Apricot still just looked up at him and didn't say a word. Bash raised his hand again, but it stopped in mid-air and that air was filled with the sound of heavy, taut breathing.

Inkcap inched up out of the ditch. The frost had formed a layer of white on his hair and body, and his hands and feet were stiff. He did not approach the small wooden shack but walked silently towards the village. The night clothed Inkcap in darkness and his departure went unnoticed by Bash and Apricot. The clumps of grass plucked at his trousers, and he told himself, Hitting her's OK, but if he does hit her, they won't stay together any more.

Someone in the alley was humming some lines from Qin opera: "His uncle and his second uncle are both his uncles, and the high tables and low stools are all made of wood. The king came out with his arse facing behind him so that his belly could face the front."

It was Potful. Inkcap had no idea that Potful could sing like that.

"Hey, Brother Potful!" he called out, but Potful ignored him as he pissed in a urinal outside a privy.

"Team Leader!" said Inkcap, using Potful's proper title, but he still ignored him, so he went over to take a piss in the same urinal.

"So you've had a piss, then," he said.

Potful's piss gurgled in the urinal.

"You've given it a good shake, then."

Potful tucked his prick back in his trousers and did them up.

"It's the middle of the night. Stop talking crap at me," he said roughly then turned and left.

Inkcap's face burned with shame and anger. He had been going to tell Potful about the row between Bash and Apricot, but not now if that's how he was going to be.

The next day, Soupspoon's mother was buried. Funerals were not much of a spectacle. A lot of deaths had occurred in Old Kiln in recent years, but what Inkcap had cared about was whether a drum and gong troupe would come to play at one. There was a drum and gong troupe in Xiahewan, which cost ten yuan a go to hire. According to the rules, only a married woman could go and hire the troupe, but Soupspoon's older sister's home had caught fire last year. Three rooms had burned down and she was finding life unbearable, so she did not go to hire the troupe. The villagers scolded Soupspoon's sister for being unfilial, and even Inkcap joined in. But the real hope was that the deceased would be buried quickly so they could eat as soon as possible.

Finally, the seating began. A table and eight chairs were placed in the main room, which were the only items of furniture Soupspoon's family owned. They were set out for the Branch Secretary, the production team leader and six other elderly folk. There were no tables for anyone else who came, so they flipped over the baskets in the yard on which to put the dishes and bowls. There were only three baskets, two of which were borrowed from next door, so they cleared the top of a cabinet to lay out the banquet and even used winnowing baskets too. It still wasn't enough.

"Bring a charcoal stove too," Baldy Jin ordered, and Inkcap hurried into the kitchen to find one.

"Anyone who hasn't got a seat, come over here," Baldy Jin called out. "I'll paint you a table. Do you want a round one or a square one?"

"A round one," Thimble and Sprout shouted. "You can get more people on a round one."

"A square one," Inkcap said.

Baldy Jin ended up painting a square table, then asked Inkcap, "What are you doing here?"

"I'm here for the banquet."

"You didn't carry the coffin or decorate the tomb. Why should you come to the banquet?"

"I borrowed the baskets from next door and I carried the firewood to the kitchen."

Baldy Jin ignored Inkcap and proclaimed in the courtyard, "Times are tight for Soupspoon's family. There are only a few seats in the courtyard. Each family choose a representative to take charge and everyone else listen to them. The poor, lower and middle peasants take their seats first."

This annoyed Inkcap, who reached out to erase the painted square table.

"What are you doing?" said Baldy Jin. "What do you think you're doing?"

"I brought out the charcoal stove," Inkcap replied before walking out of the courtyard door.

Cowbell was breaking twigs from a broom outside the door to make chopsticks, and Inkcap told him to follow him. Cowbell said that he wanted to eat, and he would come after he'd finished.

"What is there to eat?" said Inkcap. "It's just rice porridge and a few plates of radish slices. I'll give you scrambled eggs. I've got eggs at home."

"The eggs have been counted," Cowbell replied. "If you take just one, your Gran is bound to notice. You can grab some noodles from the jar. Gran will never be able to tell. Then you can go to my place and make pancakes. I'll come with you."

"All right," Inkcap said, and he led Cowbell away.

"How big shall we make the pancakes? This big?" Cowbell asked, gesturing with his hands.

"No, this big," Inkcap said, gesturing back.

Cowbell thought it was too small and the two of them argued and negotiated over the size of the pancakes as they walked along.

Suddenly, Cowbell said, "Why do I smell tofu?" They reached the door of Kaihe's house. Kaihe regularly ground beans to make tofu to sell in his commission store, his family being the only one in Old Kiln approved to sell the product. As soon as Cowbell mentioned it, Inkcap smelt tofu too. The two of them turned their heads and looked into Kaihe's courtyard, where they saw Bash and Useless eating tofu. They found themselves rooted to the spot.

Useless was celebrating his birthday and had wanted to buy half a *jin* of tofu at Kaihe's house. As he passed by the entrance to Bash's old place, Bash was whitewashing the front wall. He swore as the brush slipped from his hand, splashing him all over with spots of whitewash.

Useless was amazed at the sight of Bash painting his wall and said, "Whitewashing the wall, then?"

"I'll whitewash your mother for you!"

"Are you smartening up your house to get married?"

"Fuck you."

"Bit touchy, aren't you?" Useless said and began to hurry off to Kaihe's house.

"Don't go," Bash called to him.

"I'm just going to Kaihe's house to buy tofu," Useless said, his voice trembling as if he was begging for mercy.

"What am I, a wolf?" Bash said, then grinned and patted Useless on the shoulder. "I'll go with you. I want to buy a pack of cigarettes."

"You smoking ready-mades now?" Useless asked in amazement.

"Are you saying I shouldn't smoke them or I can't afford them?"

"If you can afford them, go ahead and smoke them."

When they arrived at Kaihe's house, Bash bought a nine-*fen* pack of Flock of Sheep brand cigarettes and tore it open on the spot. He gave one each to Kaihe and Useless and lit one himself. Useless could see that Bash's temper was mellowing, so he tried asking again if he was whitewashing his wall because he was going to get married. Bash didn't reply and just kept smoking. Useless asked if it was Apricot, but again Bash kept on smoking.

"Does Bash want to marry Apricot?" Kaihe said, directing the question at Useless. "Is there something going on there? How come I don't know about it?"

"What do you know about anything?" Useless retorted.

Kaihe shook his head like a rattle-drum and looked at Bash, who was still sitting in silence.

"Is that true, Bash? Why don't you say something, or are we too common for you to talk to?"

"It's these fucking cigarettes you sold me," Bash said, taking the cigarette out of his mouth. "They'll burn out if I stop to talk."

"I didn't make them, I bought them in," Kaihe protested.

Bash looked at Useless and asked, "What do you think about Apricot? She any good?"

"Sure," Useless replied. "There's no one better than her in Old Kiln, and no one to match her in Xiahewan either."

"What about Luozhen, the county town and the rest of the province?" Bash asked.

"Ha! Why are you looking in the pot when you've got a full bowl in front of you?"

"I want to make sure I've got the best."

"Brother Bash is nothing if not ambitious," Useless said with an amazed laugh. He bought half a *jin* of tofu, broke off a corner, and split it in two. He ate half of it himself and gave Bash the other half.

Cold tofu is cold tofu and tastes like it. A white residue built up in the two men's mouths and they kept sipping from a bowl of water to wash it away. Useless took a sip, stirred it around with his tongue for a while, then swallowed it and said, "How much tofu can you eat in one go if you really lay into it, Brother Bash?"

"A block. A block of tofu is like a box of tofu, and a box of tofu weighs twenty *jin*."

"You're like a chicken standing on a pile of corn that it can never finish!" Useless said. "Have another lump."

"Fuck you! Don't you believe me?"

"If you can eat a block of tofu, I'll not only pay for it, I'll give you another three yuan."

"Stuff your money."

"I'll give you my pen."

"It's a deal. If I can't eat it all, I'll pay for the tofu. I've got a few books over there and you can have them all, and then I'll kneel down and crawl between your legs."

"There's one condition – you have to eat it on the move, and you have to finish it by the time you reach the door of your little wooden shack, without taking a shit or a piss on the way."

Bash told Kaihe to get out a block of tofu without cutting it. He reached out and broke off a piece and started to eat, saying how delicious it was. His cheeks bulged like balloons, his throat worked as he swallowed and slurping sounds came from his mouth. "Delicious," he said. Turning his head, he saw Inkcap and Cowbell standing outside the gate. He opened his mouth, proudly showing how it was full of white tofu. "Come here, come here," he spluttered.

Inkcap and Cowbell went in, thinking that Bash was going to treat them. They stood in front of the box of tofu, mouths watering, but Bash just told them to carry the box to his shack.

"Just carry it, don't steal any," Useless warned them. "It's a bet."

"Understood," Inkcap said.

The four of them went out together, with Inkcap and Cowbell carrying the box in front, Bash behind them and Useless bringing up the rear. Bash broke off a piece of tofu and ate it, then another. The smell of the tofu was picked up by the birds on the trees, the ants on the ground, as well as the chickens, dogs and pigs. They flew in the air and followed on the ground.

Bash sneezed, spraying out tofu crumbs, so that the birds swooped down and the chickens rushed forward.

"You did that on purpose!" Useless complained.

"Can't I even sneeze out a few crumbs? Somebody must be missing me."

"Apricot's missing you," Useless said.

"She may miss me, but I don't care about her."

Bullshit! Inkcap said to himself. Apricot doesn't miss you.

"Then who are you interested in?" Useless asked.

"Peony." Peony was Lightkeeper's sister.

"Peony!" Inkcap exclaimed.

"Bash went after her before," Useless said, "and he almost got her too."

"What do you mean 'almost'?" said Inkcap.

"If I hadn't despised her high status, she might have had three of my children by now," said Bash.

"Brother Bash sure knows how to brag," Cowbell said.

"Brag?" Bash repeated. But then he just grunted and said with a laugh, "I don't care about Peony any more. Fuck it. Why is it that decent women look down their noses at me but not at others?"

Inkcap knew that he had said this particularly because it was Apricot he was actually talking about. He curled his lip in a sneer.

Bash's anger seemed to have been roused and he began to curse Peony loudly, saying that marrying into the city had changed her ideas of status. Why didn't she just be open about it and let her family exploit the farmers from then on? He also cursed the Branch Secretary's son, asking how such a lumbering idiot of a man could not only find work sponging off the state but also get to marry a teacher from Luozhen!

Everyone else kept quiet as Bash cursed away. The spray of tofu crumbs splattered onto the back of Inkcap's hand. He pretended to wipe his nose while changing hands to hold the box and licked them up. Cowbell sniffed hard, unable to resist the fragrance of the tofu. He stopped and refused to go on.

"Keep walking," Bash ordered.

"My hand hurts."

"Fuck off out of here then," Bash yelled in fury.

Cowbell left immediately but Inkcap couldn't follow him. If it had been anyone else, he would have left long ago, but it was Bash there in front of him eating tofu. And since he couldn't leave, he went on carrying the box by himself. Bash had already eaten half of it, and it was beginning to slow him down. He needed to stop from time to time, staring at a piece of tofu in his hand and gasping for breath before starting to eat again.

In the distance, Tag-Along's wife and child were standing in the doorway of his house.

"I want some tofu," the child wailed.

Tag-Along's wife dragged the girl back inside and almost certainly slapped her arse because a burst of crying was heard shortly afterwards.

Useless had been staring at Bash, saying, "No, no. That won't do. That won't do."

Bash was about to reply, but stopped himself and broke off another piece of tofu. Inkcap put the tofu box down on the ground and waited for Bash to go on eating. He kept his head down because he didn't want to see Bash's mouth. Bash is going to win his bet and Useless will have to cough up the money and his pen, Inkcap reckoned. But then he also thought that if Bash couldn't eat it all, he himself might get to eat what's left. However, Bash swallowed the tofu in his mouth, broke off another piece and set off again. Inkcap picked up the box and followed him.

In this way, they walked all the way to the stone lion at the south entrance of the village. There was only one piece of tofu left in the wooden box, but Bash's face was rigid and his step faltered.

"I'm going to lean on this lion and eat," Bash said, doing just that. He put the last piece in his mouth, but he couldn't swallow it and it looked as though he was about to throw up.

"If you throw up, you lose," Useless said.

Bash stared at Useless. He made a mighty effort to swallow and finally succeeded.

"Open your mouth, open your mouth," Useless demanded.

Bash didn't open his mouth but, instead, fell slowly onto the stone lion and slid down it to lie on the ground. Inkcap wanted to help him up, but Bash said, "Don't even think about it. Don't move me." His voice was no louder than the buzz of a mosquito, and his eyes were fixed. Inkcap and Useless were both panicking.

"He's dying!" Inkcap wailed. "He's eaten himself to death!"

Useless shook his fist in Bash's face, saying, "You are the tiger-slayer, Brother Bash. Stop trying to scare me."

He told Inkcap to run and get someone to help pick Bash up.

Bash was unmarried and Inkcap didn't know who to ask for help. At first, he ran to the door of Apricot's house, but then he remembered that Bash and Apricot had fallen out, and she wasn't the right person to get involved, so he ran on to ask Baldy Jin. Baldy Jin was not in, but Half-Stick was moving a basket of pig bran out of the firewood shed. When she heard what Inkcap wanted, she put down the bran basket to go with him.

"We need to take a door panel," Inkcap said.

Half-Stick took the door panel down with a clatter and told Inkcap to help carry it. Inkcap was too small to help, so Half-Stick picked up the panel on her own and told Inkcap to find someone else to help. Inkcap intended to go and find Sparks but he met Ever-Obedient on the way.

"Ah, you're in a rush. Chasing wolves again?" Ever-Obedient said.

"Bash is about to die from eating tofu."

"What are you on about? How can anyone die from eating? I don't believe it."

Just then, Half-Stick came up with the door panel on her back.

"How much tofu did he eat?" Ever-Obedient asked.

"Twenty *jin*!"

"Why has the stupid fucker pigged out like that?"

Ever-Obedient helped Half-Stick carry the door panel to the entrance of the village, still asking, "Can someone really eat himself to death? I want to be a full ghost too!"

ELEVEN

BASH LAY ON THE *KANG* FOR FOUR DAYS, neither eating nor drinking. He also had such a high fever that even his fingertips were hot. Useless was afraid something bad might still happen, so he came to see to his needs every day. A faint whistle could be heard from outside.

"What's that noise?" Bash asked.

"You're awake, are you?"

"I asked you who's blowing that whistle."

"I don't want to say."

"Tell me!"

"Awning's gathering the militia for training."

Bash raised himself, cleared his throat making a vile stench, then lay back down, his face suffused with a dull red colour.

"Give me the pen. You lost, but you haven't given me the pen yet."

Useless took the pen from his pocket and gave it to Bash, saying, "I didn't want to tell you because it would make you angry. It's only because Awning knows how to fire a rifle, but how many characters can he read?"

"Are you saying I don't know how to fire a rifle?" Bash threw the pen away, so it skittered under the *kang*. Useless bent down to pick it up.

"Of course not," Useless said. "And you're just as good with a pen as you are with a gun."

Useless straightened up and went over to shut the door. Once it was shut, they couldn't hear the sound of the whistle any more.

But Awning was still blowing his whistle out in the alley, blowing it like a cicada in the summer, never running out of breath.

The previous year, the village had received a document from the authorities stating that the international situation was very serious. Apart from the blockade the United States had imposed on China, the Soviet Union might well start an aggressive war. They demanded that everyone become soldiers and stand ready for action. So Old Kiln had formed a militia and had been equipped with a rifle.

Bash was particularly excited. "Are we going to fight? Are we going to fight?" he said excitedly. "Once the fighting starts, I can become a general."

However, he had not been given the chance to compete with Awning for the position of company commander. Awning had a good relationship with the military cadres of the Luozhen Commune, so it was he who had got the post. A few days ago, he had gone to the commune for a training class and, when he got back and learned that Bash was lying sick on his *kang*, he assembled the militia for drill practice. Awning told them that, apart from rifle practice, this session also involved another task. If the Soviet Union invaded China, they would lure them into a trap by letting them come in through Xinjiang.

"Who said that?" asked Sparks.

"Chairman Mao!"

"Why should we let them in? Why not simply fight and drive them out?"

"I just told you that we set a trap and once they're in that trap, we spring it and we have them helpless."

"I don't understand."

"It doesn't matter. You do what Chairman Mao tells you to, whether you understand or not."

"Tell us about it! Tell us about it!" the others demanded.

"The training class I've just come back from was to learn Russian. Every militiaman is required to learn Russian."

By now, everyone was confused.

"Learn Russian?" Sparks exclaimed. "So are we Chinese supposed to speak Russian or Chinese?"

"Russian!"

In fact, Awning only learned two sentences of Russian in the training class. One was "Surrender your gun and we won't kill you" and the other was "We treat our prisoners leniently". Awning couldn't master either of them. The commune's military cadre told him to write down the Russian pronunciation in Chinese, so "We treat our prisoners leniently" became "My sister asked if tadpoles lose their mothers and quite a few surely do". When Russian is spoken as Chinese, with a hard tongue, no matter how hard you try it sounds wrong, so the military cadre had to go over the curled tongue pronunciation again. Sometimes Awning could produce a kind of tremolo, but on other occasions he couldn't get his tongue to roll up and only managed to produce a kind of bubbling, choking sound.

When Awning passed on what he had been taught to the others, he learned from his own experience and, instead of teaching the two sentences straight off, he first tried to teach the curled tongue technique. Being small, Sparks was standing in the front row and got splattered with Awning's spittle as he spluttered through his demonstration. When another coating of saliva landed on him after he had wiped away the first, Sparks couldn't help starting to giggle.

"What's so funny?" Awning demanded.

"Why can't these fucking Russians talk like human beings?"

"Go get Lightkeeper. He learned Russian in middle school. I'll get him to teach everyone."

"I'll go," Inkcap piped up.

Of course, Inkcap wasn't in the militia, but whenever a training session was held, he was always there waiting to one side with his rope fuse. During every break, he went over to light pipes and cigarettes, and then he tried to pick up the rifle. However, it was a long-barrelled rifle and when he lifted it, its butt still rested on the ground.

There was a poplar tree beside the threshing ground whose bark was as white as if it had been whitewashed. Awning pulled him over to under the tree, carved a line with a bayonet at Inkcap's head height, and said, "You keep growing and when you've grown another four fingers, I'll let you join the militia."

But growing those four fingers was easier said than done. At every training session, Inkcap would go over to the tree to measure his height, but it was always the same as the mark Awning had made that first time.

Inkcap went to the kiln yard halfway up Middle Mountain to look for Lightkeeper. There was a mud pond near the kiln, where Winterborn was irrigating pottery clay. Inkcap shouted for Lightkeeper, but he couldn't see him anywhere.

"There's no point shouting," Winterborn said. "He's gone to dig porcelain clay."

Inkcap helped Winterborn irrigate the clay, intending to wait for Lightkeeper. Winterborn was wearing a pair of rubber boots as he trod the mud in the pool and was gasping for breath, which surged out in clouds around his face. Inkcap was intrigued and wanted to have a go himself.

"Let me make some clouds too," he said.

"What are you talking about?"

"If I make some clouds, I can fly up among them."

Winterborn still didn't understand. "'Fly? What are you, a bird? It's too cold for bare feet, but these boots of mine are very big. You'll disappear if you put them on."

In fact, Inkcap had his eyes on a pair of rubber shoes sitting at the entrance of the small house by the pool. They were Lightkeeper's, but Inkcap intended to wear them. So he went over, put them on and started treading the mud in the pool. The muddy water gurgled, and a stream of it splashed up and hit him in the eye. He was so startled, he fell back and sat down in the mud. Just at that moment, Lightkeeper returned, pulling a cart full of porcelain clay.

Lightkeeper cursed Inkcap not just for wearing his rubber shoes but for filling them with muddy water too. He dragged him out of the pool and pulled off the shoes. Inkcap was soaked from the waist down, but he still smiled and told Lightkeeper that Awning wanted him to teach Russian and was taken aback when Lightkeeper didn't make any move to go.

"Awning's showing you a lot of respect, why won't you go?" Inkcap asked.

"I'm not going."

"This business only concerns Lightkeeper," Winterborn said. "It's nothing to do with you, Inkcap. Awning should come and ask him."

"Aiya! Shall I get Awning to ask, then?"

"You listen to me, Inkcap," Lightkeeper said. "A black chicken can't start growing white feathers simply because it goes around with white chickens. The Branch Secretary told me to look after firing the kilns and that's what I'm going to do, as well as I can."

Inkcap felt that Lightkeeper wasn't going to step up to the mark, so he went back down the mountain. On the threshing ground, Awning was no longer teaching Russian and was setting up the target. Inkcap didn't tell him what Lightkeeper had said but just that he couldn't come because he had a sore tongue and couldn't even speak.

"What do you mean he's got a sore tongue?"

"Maybe his teeth thought it was a piece of meat and bit it."

"He bit his tongue on purpose because he doesn't want to come? Fuck him. A class enemy's always going to be a class enemy. Is he still hoping the Soviet revisionists are going to fight their way in?"

"I'll kill him as soon as the war starts," Pockmark said.

Inkcap couldn't bear listening to such ferocity from Pockmark. He heard a sparrow perched beside the threshing ground, chirping away.

"Fuck you," Inkcap shouted and threw a stone at the bird so it quickly flew away.

"I'm not going to learn any more Russian," Awning exclaimed. "When the time comes, if the Soviet revisionists do dare attack us, I'll kill them on sight. Even if they put their hands up to surrender, I'll still kill them."

They started shooting at the target, keeping Inkcap on the edge of the threshing floor and not allowing anyone to walk past. Ever-Obedient's dog arrived.

"They're shooting," Inkcap said to the dog. "Do you want a go?"

The dog stopped and smiled at Inkcap.

"Just look at those two," Pockmark said. "People aren't people any more, and dogs aren't dogs."

Ever-Obedient's dog tensed its arse and let out a fart that was so thick it almost suffocated Pockmark.

"It's saying hello to you," Inkcap said.

Pockmark came over, rolling up his sleeves but then the rifle went off with a bang, startling him so much that he forgot about giving Inkcap a slap.

At the sound of the gun, the birds flew off, and the villagers, as well as the chickens and cats, all kept their distance. Inkcap felt quite at ease for the time being and just lay on his back in the wheat by the threshing ground cuddling Ever-Obedient's dog. He had the whole sky up above him and the sun was like a soft persimmon, slipping smoothly across the sky as though it was about to fall. He opened his mouth, hoping that the sun would fall into his mouth. But what actually fell was a leaf, which, instead of falling straight down from the poplar tree, slid in an oblique circle and covered his left eye. He didn't move and, with his right eye, looked at the shepherd's purse growing in the wheat field. Ha, so, even in weather this cold, the shepherd's purse was putting out young shoots! After the New Year, they could be dug up and boiled in a pot or chopped up and wrapped in steamed buns. But right now, the tender little buds would give you heartburn and it was not a good idea to pick them.

Inkcap undid his jacket and allowed his belly to bask in the sun. His belly seemed to lack any fat, and even Ever-Obedient's dog could see the bones, sinews and blood vessels under his skin. The dog could see the muscles and subcutaneous blood vessels in his flesh. Its long tongue kept licking his belly all over. The tender buds of the shepherd's purse still beckoned to him. The temptation was too great, just like the sight of Flower Girl's nose. At first glance, it looked good, so you couldn't help but take another look and it still looked good. So he reached out and stuffed shepherd's purse into his mouth.

"Look at my belly! Look at my belly!" he told Ever-Obedient's dog.

He thought that through his skin, he could see a green ball inside his belly.

"What are you doing, eating wheat seedlings like a sheep?" the dog asked.

Inkcap sat up suddenly. It wasn't Ever-Obedient's dog talking, it was Half-Stick and she was standing behind him.

"Who's eating wheat seedlings? I'm eating shepherd's purse," he protested.

"Do you really want to be eating the production team's shepherd's purse?" Half-Stick asked, squatting down beside him. "Besides, eating them unwashed will give you a bellyful of roundworms."

Half-Stick was originally from Laoshangou. When she married into Old Kiln, she couldn't spin yarn and didn't know about retting hemp or how to dye cloth because neither cotton nor hemp grew in Laoshangou. She wore long, wide clothes of an ugly grey colour. Now, several years later, she had acquired all those skills and her clothes were decently cut. It was only now, dressed in finer clothes, that her slender waist and long legs were apparent to everyone, but her skin was no longer delicate and white but had turned yellow, like a pancake baked with too much alkali.

Half-Stick always said that Baldy Jin had tricked her. She met him when he took rice to Laoshangou in exchange for potatoes. She was already grown-up and life was hard for her. Baldy Jin boasted that there was white rice in Old Kiln and that the last meal he had eaten was steamed rice and so would the next one be. Every year, he gave her another pile of porcelain goods, so she got divorced, married Baldy and came over to Old Kiln. But as for the meals, three times a day, all they consisted of was sticky rice and grits gruel so thin you could see someone's silhouette through it.

As soon as Half-Stick spoke, Awning turned and looked at her. Inkcap understood that she'd spoken in a loud voice for Awning to hear too, so he shouted, "Brother Awning! Company Commander Brother Awning!"

"What are you calling him for, eh?" Half-Stick said huffily.

"Didn't you come looking for Awning?" Inkcap asked innocently.

"Did I say I did?" She poked Inkcap's forehead with her finger, but her eyes glanced towards Awning.

Awning didn't speak to Inkcap but shouted to Feng Youliang to push the stone roller over. Feng Youliang grunted and did as he was told. Awning bent down and pressed his belly against the roller as it lay flat on the ground. With one great surge of strength, he stood the roller upright. Everyone clapped, Half-Stick included.

"If you haven't trained with stone weights," Awning said, "you'll never be able to lift the roller."

"If Bash practised with stone weights again, could he lift the roller even with his sticks for arms and legs?" Half-Stick asked.

"Sit down," Awning said.

Half-Stick sat on the roller.

"Can I join the militia?" she asked.

"All right, as long as you've got the nerve to use the rifle," Awning replied.

Half-Stick jumped up from the roller and lay down behind the rifle. As she lay down, her buttocks rose in the air. Awning pressed them down, saying, "Lie down properly." Half-Stick lowered her buttocks and her legs stuck out like two roof beams. Awning helped her load the bullets, showed her how to aim with three points along one line and taught her to hold her breath and gently pull the trigger. Awning was still holding her by the hand when she pulled the trigger. There was a crack as the bullet flew out, and both she and the rifle jerked up from the ground like a leaping toad.

The Branch Secretary happened to be coming up from the path by the wheat field, but the gunshot stopped him in his tracks. After surveying the scene for a moment, he called Awning over.

As Awning trotted up to him, the Branch Secretary asked, "Why are you letting women play with the rifle?"

"We have to have female militia. None of the other women in our village dare touch the rifle. She's the only one with the nerve to get close to the fucker."

"It's you that's got a pissing nerve."

"Hey!" Awning protested.

"Do I have to remind you that you're the one who's getting the branch party training? You have to think with your head, not your dick. If you don't, I'm the one who's going to get it in the neck from the authorities."

"No, no. Of course not."

The Branch Secretary's padded cotton coat slipped from his shoulders and Awning helped him readjust it. The Branch Secretary asked what had happened to the Russian class and Awning told him about Lightkeeper not wanting to teach it. The Branch Secretary was furious and ordered that Lightkeeper be summoned again.

"His tongue hurts, does it? How can he eat, then? What nonsense."

Awning called Inkcap over again and the Branch Secretary said, "Go and get him, and tell him it's me who wants him."

When Awning went to the kiln yard to get Lightkeeper, Lightkeeper did come back this time, but his mouth was covered in blood. He stuck out his tongue for the Branch Secretary to inspect, and there was indeed a hole in it.

Inkcap was puzzled. He had made it up when he told Awning that Lightkeeper's tongue was festering. Lightkeeper didn't know anything about it, so how come there really was something wrong with his tongue when Awning went back to fetch him? Inkcap didn't say anything about his doubts. The Branch Secretary could see that Lightkeeper's tongue really was festering and he couldn't speak properly, so he told him to go back to the kiln. Before he left, Lightkeeper turned round and gave Awning a look of sheer hatred. Awning failed to notice this, but Inkcap saw the twin flames in Lightkeeper's eyes.

Six Pints' home stood at the northern end of the threshing ground. Six Pints, who had been gradually wasting away from disease for many years, came out of the door, picked up a broom and watched the target practice for a while.

"Haven't you finished your training yet?" he asked Kaihe.

"Are we stopping you from sweeping the threshing ground?" Kaihe replied.

"My quilt's too thin. I won't be able to cope if I can't light the *kang*."

Inkcap suddenly remembered that he should be sweeping too, so he stopped watching the target practice and hurried home to fetch a broom and basket.

Throughout the winter, almost everyone in Old Kiln kept their *kang* lit. They were reluctant to burn bean stalks and wheat straw, so they took their brooms to the roadside to sweep up the "ground foam". This ground foam was actually grass waste that was collected by sweeping the dead grass over and over with brooms and collecting the resulting stems, roots and soil in baskets. The villagers then took it home, as it was ideal fuel for their *kang*. After sweeping all the places in the village proper that could be swept, people went further and further afield, until they reached the millstone at the western edge of the village, and even continued down the slope below it.

Inkcap couldn't help with the household upkeep, but he could make sure that the *kang* was lit every night to keep Gran warm. He picked up his basket and broom and walked out into the alley, where he saw the sun was sitting just above Yijia Ridge. He could sense the sun jumping, jumping, jumping and then falling out of the sky with a thud. He heaved a sigh then turned his head and saw Bash literally flying past the end of the alley.

Has Bash grown wings? Inkcap was so scared that he almost fainted. He ran to the end of the alley and looked again. It turned out that Bash was wearing his quilt around his shoulders. The quilt was dyed grey and its two corners were being raised by the wind, like black clouds floating in the air. The quilt had rotted away and exposed the cotton filling in several places so as it flickered up and down, the cotton looked like a white stork flitting through the clouds.

"Brother Bash! Brother Bash!" he called out. But Bash didn't stop and the quilt kept inflating in the wind. He grasped its two corners as tightly as he could, but his toes couldn't get a grip when they touched the ground. Inkcap was still shouting for him as Bash tipped forward and almost fell, making the quilt spill all its wind and drop over his head.

"Are you trying to fly up to Heaven, Brother Bash?" Inkcap asked.

"Fly up to Heaven? Ow! Ow! You fly to fucking Heaven if you want!"

"Then let me try it on too."

Inkcap wanted to wear Bash's quilt but Bash wouldn't hand it over.

"Even if you really did grow wings when you put a quilt over your shoulders, you still wouldn't be able to fly since you're just a chicken, and chickens can't fly."

"Why's that then?"

"You're a poor middle peasant, aren't you?"

Inkcap became despondent and looked at Bash as he walked on.

"Are you going to the shack?" he asked. "Do you sleep there at night?"

"I'm going to Xiahewan to see a shadow puppet show."

There was a theatrical troupe in Xiahewan that put on puppet shows during festivals.

"Is there another temple fair in Xiahewan?" Inkcap asked. "I'm going too."

"Fuck the fuck off. You'd even follow me into the crapper when I want a shit, wouldn't you!"

Bash walked on, with Inkcap following, until he arrived at the south entrance of the village. Bash picked up a lump of earth and threw it at Inkcap's feet. The lump burst apart and Inkcap watched anxiously as Bash went down the dirt road by the embankment. His quilt was doing its cloud impression again, floating more gently this time. Just at that moment, a cat padded up silently, with a bell tied around its neck. The bell was ringing, but the cat's steps did not match the sound of the bell.

Inkcap recognised it immediately as the cat belonging to Potful. What was Potful's cat doing walking back along the dirt track from outside the village? Then he thought he'd seen something. He stood at the edge of the slope and looked down. There, sure enough, was Apricot, standing under a persimmon tree. She had a red scarf wrapped around her head so you couldn't see her face, but even from the back, it could only be her. She and Bash walked together away from the bottom of the slope and down the field's dyke.

Inkcap suddenly felt as though he'd been duped. He thought that after the quarrel in the shack, Apricot would never have anything to do with Bash again, but it turned out that they were back on good terms. Apricot!

Oh, Apricot! Do you really think Bash loves you? Don't you have any ambition? Furious with Apricot, Inkcap rushed over to the cat and kicked it to the ground. The cat's four paws were pointing up in the air and it didn't roll back over. It just looked at Inkcap in astonishment.

"Why don't you follow her?" Inkcap asked. "Off you go."

"They won't let me go either," the cat said.

"What do you mean they won't let you go?"

"They're not letting you go, are they?"

Inkcap turned round and was about to leave, when the cat said, "Hey!"

"Haven't you fucked off yet?" Inkcap said.

"You have to help me roll over."

Inkcap flipped the cat back on its feet and it lowered its head and trotted away.

The cat was already back in the village and the sound of its bell could no longer be heard. Inkcap was still standing by the side of the slope, listlessly sweeping up the ground foam again. But the fog was beginning to rise on the Zhou River, and it spread slowly up from the river strand, enveloping his feet. It was a long time since there'd been such a thick fog, and it followed Inkcap as he began to walk back to the alley. He swept at it with his broom, but it kept coming and swallowed up his legs.

"Off you go, then. Let Bash suck you back in. It's no skin off my arse." Inkcap was mindful not to get angry again as he walked past the courtyard walls, getting close to the jars and saggars and peering in through the cracks. He could make out various villagers going about their business: Big Root laying out reed on the steps of his main room, a drip of clear mucus hanging from the tip of his nose; Ever-Obedient lighting a fire in the brazier, using a small tower of corn cobs whose flames looked like gold chrysanthemum petals; Decheng, afflicted by a sore lower back again, leaning to one side and walking sideways; Caretaker in a blind fury, kicking a rush cushion over to the kitchen door, making a chicken jump onto the wall where it dislodged a lump of earth that fell and hit Inkcap on the head.

Inkcap left without daring to make a sound, and by now the fog had already rolled up in front of him, like a grey stone roller. Someone was standing at the corner of the wall, two people in fact, hugging and whispering. Who was it? Inkcap walked over to what turned out to be the outside of the east wall of the courtyard of Bash's old house. He could see two trees, one a Chinese toon tree and the other an elm. They were a little distance apart and, originally, their trunks were as bare as pillars. But the elm had grown a cluster of branches out of its trunk at about the height of a man that spread across towards the toon tree. A branch from the trunk of the toon tree also extended towards the elm tree, causing the two sets of branches to intertwine. Inkcap kicked each tree in turn.

"I thought you were people."

Moving on, he arrived at the screen in front of the courtyard gate of Awning's house. Inkcap couldn't figure out why he hadn't noticed these two trees in normal circumstances. Why did they look like two people in the evening fog? Suddenly, he made the connection with Bash and Apricot. Fuck it! These trees were at it together, just like them!

Inkcap turned round and retraced his steps. He tried to separate the two trees, but they both had thick stems and he couldn't manage it. So he grabbed the bunch of branches growing out of the trunk of the elm tree and twisted so hard they all snapped off. He also tried to break the branch on the trunk of the Chinese toon tree, but he failed. So he forced it towards him and when he let go, it twanged back and forth over and over again. Inkcap was covered in sweat and getting angry. He took his belt from around his waist and used it to tie the branches down against the trunk.

Inkcap felt very pleased with himself. Perhaps, in the future, Bash would no longer seduce Apricot, and Apricot would no longer get entangled with Bash. He walked home and passed by the entrance to Awning's courtyard. How come there was a tree growing in front of the screen wall when none had been before? Inkcap stopped dead in his tracks. It wasn't a tree, it was Lightkeeper, bending over in front of the vine that grew there. Then he straightened up, walked silently away and disappeared without a trace. Inkcap froze, unable to understand why Lightkeeper should have bent down at the entrance of Awning's courtyard because previously he had noticed that every time Lightkeeper went by that gateway, he would spit and walk straight past without stopping. Inkcap moved closer. Everything was fine with the wall and everything was fine with the vine too. The fog covered the ground, making it difficult to see clearly. However, when he caught hold of the vine branches to inspect them, they came away in his hand. Anxiously, he crouched down and touched the vine's roots. They were all broken, cut through with a knife right at the level of the soil. Inkcap was more than a little scared and scurried away. The fog enveloped him and together they rolled off down the alley.

TWELVE

THIRD AUNT AND THIMBLE were still busying themselves at Inkcap's house.

On the way back from the burial of Soupspoon's mother, Thimble begged Third Aunt to help her dye three *zhang* of coarse cloth. Third Aunt was quite ready to help out, but she wanted Thimble to prepare some indigo plant first. Noisy sold the stuff from his peddler's pole but he hadn't been around for several days. Third Aunt suggested smearing the cloth all over with the green mud from the lotus pond, but the colour always came out uneven. The two of them had brought the cloth to ask Gran for advice.

"Have you prayed to the immortals?" Gran asked.

"No," Third Aunt said.

"Well, it's no wonder! You're all over the place, old sister. How can you not pray to the immortals when you're dyeing so much cloth?"

"What immortals?" Thimble asked.

"You youngsters these days don't know about the two immortals, Mei and Ge?"

Gran climbed up the ladder to the roof beam and took down a cloth bag. Inside it were some shoe templates, flower patterns for embroidered pillow covers and a coloured New Year woodblock print. The two ancients standing side by side in the New Year picture were the two alchemists Mei Fu and Ge Hong who were believed to have invented several dyes and pigments. Grandma told Thimble that there used to be a dyeing workshop in Luozhen that contained statues of these two immortals. Nowadays, the supply and marketing cooperatives all sold imported foreign cloth, so there was no dyeing workshop any more. There was no problem dyeing small quantities of the coarse cloth the villagers normally wove in the lotus pond. However, if there was a lot of cloth and you simmered it with dye extracted from the indigo plant, yet didn't pray to the immortals, the colour would often come out uneven. It was a strange and unpredictable thing, rather like steaming flatbreads – everyone knows how to make steamed flatbreads, but if you happen to encounter a demon, then your bread turns out as hard as porcelain.

"You're right," Third Aunt said. "When I took the cloth from Thimble and covered it with mud, I was almost knocked over by a mini whirlwind. I guess it must have been a demon and that's why the cloth came out stripy like a tiger's face."

Gran pasted the New Year picture of the two immortals Mei and Ge onto the wall and poured out a bowl of clean water because she didn't have any incense sticks to burn. The three of them knelt down and kowtowed.

"When we've prayed to the immortals," Gran said, "there's another process to go through. Take the cloth back with Thimble, boil some water and test it with a finger to make sure it's not scalding hot. Add the ash of wild jujube thorns and some pomegranate peel before putting the cloth in. Make sure to soak it thoroughly, then take it out and cover it with the green mud from the lotus pond for three days."

Thimble was overjoyed and complimented Gran on her knowledge.

"Do your ancestors come from Old Kiln, Granny Silkworm?"

"Is Gran's name Silkworm?" Thimble asked.

"Don't you even know your grandmother's name?" Third Aunt exclaimed.

"Usually, I just say 'Gran this' and 'Gran that'. Who uses names? I don't even know my father's name either!"

"It's true," Third Aunt said. "Even if the children in this village know their grandparents' names, they certainly don't any further back. You're all so concerned about keeping your family line going, but how can you do that if you don't know anything beyond two generations?"

"That's not what we're talking about," Gran said.

"Yes, you're right," Third Aunt said. "From now on, we'll always come and ask you, Granny Silkworm, if there's anything that doesn't come out right."

"You're just messing with me now," Gran said. "Those clothes of Palace, the ones that are all blackish-grey and greyish-black, did you give them to someone else to dye?"

"I dyed them myself."

"Go and tell Palace that if he has any more of that cloth, he should dye it again just as I've just told you."

"You mustn't tell anyone called Hei about this," Thimble said.

"That's really petty of you, trying to make sure you're the only one with pretty clothes."

They heard the sound of wailing coming from outside the courtyard. It was long and drawn out, like a sheep baa-ing. The three of them stopped talking and listened.

"That's Stargazer's mum. She's quarrelled with her daughter-in-law again," Third Aunt said.

"Everyone called Hei is like that," Thimble said. "Baldy Jin is a jerk and Dazed-And-Confused is a troublemaker. Tag-Along is honest enough, but he's such a stiff you couldn't get a fart out if you shoved three knitting needles into him. Almost-There is always looking to take advantage, while Bash is as much dog as he is human and he's a wandering ghost."

"That mother-in-law and daughter-in-law have been at it every day," Gran said.

"The more they argue, the poorer they get," Third Aunt observed.

"I've always said that there isn't a single normal person among that Hei lot," Thimble said. "Stargazer's fierce enough when he's out and about, but he's pussy-whipped at home."

"She's going to get ill wailing like that in this weather and getting too much cold air in her lungs," Gran said. "Let's go and have a word with her."

The three of them went over to Stargazer's house. Stargazer's mother was in tears, sitting on a rock at the entrance of the courtyard, and quite a crowd had gathered to watch the fun. She seemed to recover her strength and she turned and shouted back through the courtyard gate, "You've had three bowls already! How many more do you want? The pig is squealing with hunger in its pen and I haven't got enough to feed it."

"What three bowls?" her daughter-in-law yelled back from inside the courtyard. "You've stuffed yourself with food and so has your son, but I shifted a dozen or more loads of soil for the pigsty and all I had was two bowls of watery congee. When I went to get another bowlful, you took the pot away and washed it, then gave what was left of the rice to the pig. Now I've married into your family, don't I count for as much as the pig?"

"No, you don't," Stargazer's mother shouted back. "If we raise a pig for a year, we can sell it for decent money, but what use are you? You've been in the family for a good few years now and haven't produced so much as a cat or a dog by way of children."

"Are you saying that's my fault? Why don't you go and ask your son about it? If the seed's all shrivelled, you're not going to get anything growing in the field. If it's grandchildren you're after, I'll go and find myself a secret lover and give birth to a whole bedful!"

"You fucking little shit," Stargazer's mother yelled.

"You're the fucking shit," her daughter-in-law yelled back.

"How dare you swear at me like that. Your mother has a son, too, and he's got married, so does that daughter-in-law curse her like you're doing me? Damn you, Hemp Leaf. What kind of daughter did you whelp that you let her swear at me like that?"

"You need to shut up a bit," a bystander called out. "You really need to shut up a bit."

Stargazer's mother began to wail again, her hands and feet flailing wildly.

"You need to shut up, Stargazer's Mum," Barndoor said. "What kind of talk is that? Is it because you've got so many people watching you? Do you think you can make out you've won when you've actually lost?"

"You heard her," the daughter-in-law shouted. "Where else in Old Kiln are you going to find such a ridiculous old woman?"

"She may be ridiculous but she's still your mother-in-law," Barndoor reminded her.

"Who's ridiculous? What do you mean by that?" Stargazer's mother protested.

"All right, all right. You're not ridiculous," Barndoor said. "You're pure as they come. Not a stain on your character."

At this point, Goodman Wang appeared. "Goodman! Goodman!" Barndoor called out. "It's good you've arrived. There's something wrong with the whole family here. Can't you do something about it?"

"If they haven't invited me, there's nothing I can do to help."

"I told Stargazer to fetch you to come and talk his wife out of her illness, but he said that was all just superstition."

"So he's not a believer, then. Let me tell you about that superstition. People are harmed by whatever most concerns them. The rich die because of their wealth, and the poor die because of their poverty. Those whose lives revolve around water will be killed by water, and those whose lives revolve around trees will be killed by trees."

"So will I be killed by my daughter-in-law, then?" Stargazer's mother asked.

"Those who hate their daughter-in-law are subject to their daughter-in-law's anger, and those who don't love their mother-in-law are subject to their mother-in-law's anger. To find a way out of this situation should be considered reasonable, but to remain in it should be considered superstition."

"You need to eat if you're going to talk to this illness. I can make you a dish of poached eggs. But if you want money, I don't even have two yuan."

"Don't be stingy, Auntie," Thimble said. "Otherwise, the two of you will just keep bullying each other. You mustn't let your anger turn into a lump in your stomach."

"Don't ask for any money today, Goodman," Barndoor said. "Just talk to both their illnesses."

"Actually, everyone is doing that already," Goodman said. "A man who hits his mother and father, but doesn't hit anyone else, is still hated by everyone and despised by Heaven. A man who is filial to his mother and father, but not to anyone else, is respected by everyone and loved by Heaven."

"You're right," Barndoor said. "Go inside and tell them more about it properly."

He pushed Goodman towards the house and tried to pull Stargazer's mother there too, but the old woman wouldn't get up.

"You need to talk to my daughter-in-law's illness," she said. "Why are you tugging at me?"

"Aren't you going to go inside and make Goodman welcome?" Gran asked. "It's cold and foggy out there. You're not going to sit around just begging to get sick, are you?"

"I don't care if I die," Stargazer's mother said. "It'll make people happy."

She still wouldn't get up and refused to go in through the courtyard gates.

"Hey, you!" Gran said to the daughter-in-law. "Why don't you come out and take your mother-in-law back in? Come on, come and get her."

Stargazer's wife came out and pulled her mother-in-law by the arm.

"Stop yanking at me," Stargazer's mother said, going in through the gates. "Do you think I've forgotten how to walk?"

Laughing and shouting encouragement, the crowd of bystanders broke up.

Amid the chaos of departing footsteps, the ground-hugging fog that was creeping in got kicked up like dust. Someone felt an itch in their throat and coughed. Immediately, everyone else began to cough too. More and thicker fog rolled out from another alley and with it came Inkcap. He was holding the waistband of his trousers in one hand, and a broom and basket in the other. He looked suspiciously at what was going on.

"What time do you call this to be coming home?" Gran demanded.

"I'm back now, aren't I?"

He gave the broom and basket to Gran, then grabbed her jacket and chivvied her along urgently. As soon as he was inside their courtyard, he shut the gate and let his trousers fall around his feet.

"What's the rush?" Gran asked.

She pulled Inkcap's trousers up for him and enquired about his belt. He told her it was broken and then panted out the story of Lightkeeper cutting Awning's family's vine off at the roots with a knife. Gran's expression hardened.

"What nonsense. Did you really see it?"

"I really did. Is this what they call class enemy sabotage?"

Gran put her hand over his mouth.

"You didn't see anything."

"I did see it!"

Gran poked her finger at Inkcap's forehead.

"You didn't see anything," she repeated.

Inkcap took one look at Gran's expression and changed his mind.

"I didn't see anything."

That evening, Inkcap was on his best behaviour. He didn't say anything about Lightkeeper, nor did he mention that he had broken and tangled up the branches of the elm tree and the Chinese toon tree. At dinner, there were no boiled beans in the maize grits soup, not even sweet potatoes, and Inkcap just slurped them up. Iron Bolt's family next door seemed to be drinking, and they were playing a noisy game of "guess-fingers".

"One cup to you. One cup to me."

Whenever a household in the village was having drinks, the hosts told Inkcap to go round inviting people, and when he'd got everyone who was supposed to be invited, he would stand around with his fuse, waiting for anyone who wanted a smoke and needed a light. He would also help identify anyone who was holding back on the wine and would force them to drink. "Say something! Say something!" he would order them and then fill their mouths with wine so that they had to swallow it as soon as they tried to speak. However, the hosts never kept a seat for Inkcap, nor did they let him have a drink, but occasionally, when someone really couldn't drink any more wine, he would say, "Drink it for me, Inkcap!" Inkcap would pick up their cup and drain it. He could drink ten cups without getting drunk. Of course, drinking late into the night, some people did get drunk and then the hosts would call out, "Take him home, Inkcap." Inkcap would lead the man to his door. At first, he would see the man in, and the man's wife would curse him out for letting her husband get so drunk. He got sick of this after a while, so when he now took a drunk home, he would get them to their door, knock on it and then run off as soon as he heard a response from inside.

With the sound of guess-fingers coming from next door, Inkcap began to get agitated. He wondered to himself why, if they were having drinks, he hadn't been asked to go round inviting people. He looked at Gran. She knew exactly what he was thinking but ignored him and began to wipe down the stove top with a cloth. She wiped it and wiped it until it was gleaming.

Finally, Inkcap put down his bowl and said, "Iron Bolt and the others are having drinks."

"Have you had enough to eat? Leave them to their drinking, let's go to sleep."

"My stomach's all sloshing around. I'll piss on the *kang* if I go to sleep too soon."

"Just go to sleep."

The noise from the game was getting louder, and Inkcap felt as though a cat was scratching at his insides. He told Gran he was going to the privy for a piss but instead, he went over to the corner of the courtyard wall, lay in a gap in the jars that made up the wall and looked through to next door. Over at Iron Bolt's house, the door was open, and there was a pottery brazier burning. Iron Bolt and Pockmark were drinking, and the wine was in a porcelain cup, sitting on the rim of the brazier. Each of them had a white radish in one hand and a bundle of pig bristles in the other. The loser took a bite of radish, dipped the pig bristles in the wine, sucked it and then let his opponent suck it too. Inkcap snorted. It was just "I drink, you drink" so what was all that nonsense with the pig bristles? He went back to the house and continued eating the maize grits soup. The sound of the game was still ringing out, like the flapping of the wings of a flock of pigeons flying over Iron Bolt's house. Grandma stopped Inkcap from drinking any more of the slurry, took an egg, and fried it on the stove with an iron ladle.

"Now, get a grip on yourself, eat up and go to bed."

Inkcap didn't get up to piss once that night, and when he woke up and checked both himself and the mattress, nothing was wet. This put him in a good mood until he heard Awning's wife cursing out in the street. She was demanding to know which fucking black-hearted bastard, which pissing lily-livered scum, which gun-toting, knife-wielding cowardly shit made the vicious cowardly attack on her house last night.

"What's happened? Why are you shouting curses this early in the morning?" someone asked.

"I want to know who the fuck it was who cut our morning glory vine off at the roots."

"Oh, I thought someone must have hurt Awning."

"If he had the balls to cut the vine roots, who's to say he wouldn't have hurt Awning if he'd bumped into him?"

Then she began to wail again, and the wailing turned back into cursing, saying that whoever had done that to her vine should die a painful death, should be rolled down from the top of a mountain, should drown in the depths of a river, should catch the plague and die without descendants.

Inkcap threw on his clothes to go outside and watch the fun, but Gran wouldn't let him.

Awning's wife kept the cursing up all morning and it was so bad that even the chickens, cats, pigs and dogs didn't dare make a sound. All the trees trembled in the cold, and their withered leaves dropped one by one. No one dared reply to her or tried to persuade her to stop because it would only make them look guilty. Awning's stomach was rumbling with hunger, so he went over and ordered her back inside. At last, she brushed herself down and left the scene.

Afterwards, everyone in the village was whispering to each other, trying to guess who would cut the vine off at the roots. Its shining leaves and flowers were part of the beautiful scenery of Old Kiln. Why would anyone want to cut its roots? And cut them right through at that? Sure, some villagers were unhappy with Awning, or even hated him, but no one should vent their anger on flowers and trees. Who was it? Who could it be?

Useless nudged Inkcap and asked, "Did you do it?"

"How could you think that?" Inkcap said.

"Even if someone was really angry with Awning, the most they might do is cut off some of the vine, but cutting the roots right through, that's class hatred that is."

Inkcap's face turned ashen.

"But if it's class hatred, why not kill him or set fire to his house?" he said. "Why just cut the roots of his vine? Even if it is class enemies out to destroy things, I'm not the only one in the village from a bad background."

"Are you saying it was Lightkeeper who did it?"

"When did I say that?"

Inkcap forgot about hating Lightkeeper. Now he hated Useless and wanted to take revenge on him.

But what kind of revenge? Inkcap had no idea. That afternoon, he sat under the medicine tree at the west end of the village and watched Ever-Obedient working on the old millstone. The mill had been abandoned for many years, and the upper part of the millstone had been tipped over onto the ground. Ever-Obedient was using a chisel to open up the furrows in the stone. He loved doing pointless tasks like that, and, even more absurdly, he took them very seriously. Inkcap watched him for a while, then heard a chicken somewhere nearby demanding fiercely and accusingly, "Whose egg is this?" He saw the rooster from the Branch Secretary's household coming up from the slope of the earth bank. Its face was crimson, its feet were splayed, and its wings were extended behind it. It was furious.

Feeling there was something weird going on, Inkcap went to the edge of the earth bank to take a look. This was the place where, for hundreds of years, the old kiln yard had dumped its waste porcelain. Originally, garbage had piled up to form one corner of the earth bank, but years of rain erosion had made that corner collapse, revealing a cross-section of bright, shiny porcelain shards. An egg was nestling in the grass at the bottom. Someone's broody hen must have laid an egg out in the wild and the Branch Secretary's rooster had realised that must be from a hen that he hadn't mated with, and he was furious about it. Inkcap half ran, half tumbled down the bank and lost control of where he was going. He tried to dodge but was too late and his foot landed on the egg, smashing it into a puddle of yellow and white soup that got trampled into the soil. Useless and his mother were mowing grass in their private plot in the wheat field under the bank. Useless didn't know that Inkcap had tumbled down the bank on purpose to nab an egg. He thought he had stumbled and fallen, so he laughed uproariously. Inkcap hated him even more for gloating at his misfortune.

He was considering all the balls of straw that were stuffed into the eaves and rear rafters of Useless's house and reckoning he could go and drag some of them out to let the cold wind in. Yes, that wasn't a bad idea, but how many should he remove? If he took just one, they wouldn't notice, but if he took three, that would make it too cold. Useless's mother had asthma, and she might get really ill if she got too cold. He'd just take one. Inkcap made his way to Useless's house on Nanxie Lane.

Useless's family was the only one on Nanxie Lane with the family name Zhu; all the rest were called Hei. There were six or seven persimmon trees in the alley, all of them bare of leaves, and all of them turned black. There had been a frost, and, on the ground, the leftover sprouted maize, rotten paper and an old straw sandal that no one had worn were all damp, limp and falling apart. Inkcap walked around from the gate of Useless's house to the main room and looked at the balls of straw stuffed in the rafters. But the rafters were too high and there was no ladder to get up there, so he was frustrated. As he wound his way back from the rear of the house to the courtyard gate, he couldn't think of any other form of revenge. He kicked the gate leaf hard with his foot, making a clattering noise. He had a sudden inspiration and, looking to see if anyone was about, he felt around the frame of the gate for the key. There it was!

Apart from the foreign locks on the doors of the production team's office, almost all the houses in Old Kiln still used old-fashioned copper locks. Householders locked their doors but didn't carry the key around with them. The accepted place to leave it was on the door frame. Inkcap got hold of the key to Useless's house, which was a straight copper stick with a groove, now polished smooth, and ran off with it to the southeast corner of the village where he threw it into the lotus pond.

Inkcap was delighted with himself. How had he come up with such a brilliant idea? He had also already decided that the next time he saw Lightkeeper, he would ask for some of his dried persimmons because Lightkeeper should thank him for venting his anger for him. Inkcap sat at home through the afternoon, waiting for something to happen. He wanted to see Useless coming home from his private plot and finding he couldn't open the gate. Then he would watch him smash the lock with a stone and lift the gate leaf out of the way and see him start shouting and cursing in the alley. But the alley stayed quiet and peaceful all the way up to dinner. When it was time for dinner, Inkcap took his bowl and ate it in the yard. The soup was so thin you could see the stars reflected in it.

"What a pig. How can you make so much noise?" Gran said.

"The rice is so thin, how am I supposed to slurp it up without making a noise?"

"Add some pickled cabbage, then stir it around and it'll soon thicken up."

Inkcap did as she suggested and walked out of the courtyard, bowl in hand. The alley was empty, almost all the courtyard doors closed, with only a few households still open and spilling out patches of light. A cat padded by, then suddenly hurtled up the courtyard wall. The two sparkling green lights of its eyes disappeared into the darkness. When he got to Nanxie Lane, Inkcap was surprised to see that Useless's family courtyard gate was one of the ones that was open.

Useless was sitting on the step eating a bowl of food. Inkcap could not retreat without being seen, so he had no choice but to go over and pretend to be looking for Inkcap's neighbour, Decheng.

"Decheng! Uncle Decheng!"

Decheng's courtyard gates remained locked.

"What did you have to eat, Inkcap?" Useless asked.

"What do you think?" he grunted back. "Isn't Decheng in?"

"It's his father-in-law's birthday and they've all gone over to Xichuan to celebrate."

"Oh," Inkcap said and just walked away.

That night, Inkcap didn't sleep well. He couldn't figure out how Useless had opened the gate. Did he pry open the lock or did he lift the door leaf off its hinges? Why hadn't Useless been cursing him and complaining?

Weirdly, over the next few days, a constant stream of talk circulated in the village about lost courtyard keys. It seemed that someone in every alley had lost their key. Inkcap was stunned. Was someone else stealing keys and chucking them away?

One day, Gran came back from work around midday and passed by the wall of the Branch Secretary's family courtyard. She picked up a newspaper from the ground and liked the look of it so much that she folded it up and took it home for papercuts. However, when she got to her courtyard door, she couldn't find the key on the doorframe and was so anxious that she kept walking in circles in front of the door. At that moment, Bash and Apricot turned up and, when she saw Gran standing there, Apricot went into a nearby privy and didn't come out.

"What's the matter, Gran?" Bash asked. "Are you a bit confused?"

"I can't find my key."

"So your key's missing too, is it? I'm going over to see the Branch Secretary. Keys have been going missing left right and centre in the village over the last few days. What kind of a Secretary is he, losing control of public safety like this?"

He really did go over to see the Branch Secretary and found him and his wife papering their bedroom walls with newspaper. Old Kiln had an order for the provincial newspaper which was originally pinned up in the public office. However, it took several days for the newspaper to be delivered by the town postman, and, when it did come, only a few villagers could read it. When they went to the office in the evening to record their day's work, the villagers took to tearing strips off the newspaper to use to roll cigarettes. In the end, the Branch Secretary took the old newspapers home, collecting enough of them to paper his walls.

When the courtyard bell rang, he called out, "Who is it?"

"It's me!"

"What does that wandering ghost want with you? Just ignore him," the Branch Secretary's wife said.

"If a thief wants to steal from you, the more you guard against him, the more he'll keep thinking of ways to get around you. If you just go out and greet him and ask him in for a meal, he'll get spooked and leave you alone. This fellow is a persistent bastard. You can get away with ignoring other people, but not him. Go and open the gate."

"Give me a moment," his wife said.

She hurried out into the courtyard and came back with a wicker tray which she laid out. On the tray were little snacks that people had brought them. There were too many for the two of them to eat, so she had put them on the tray and left them out in the sun to dry.

Bash came in and the Branch Secretary told him to sit down. He himself hunkered down on a stool, smoking his water pipe. When he went out, the Branch Secretary always had his long-stemmed pipe tucked up his sleeve, but at home, he preferred the water pipe. He was very particular about how he smoked it. He would rub the tobacco between his fingers to form a small ball, which he pressed into the bowl of the pipe. Then he lifted the bowl in one hand and held a smouldering paper spill to it with the other, wrinkling his mouth and blowing on the spill. It would catch and bloom into fire like a small plum blossom. He then held it to the tobacco and started puffing and snorting as he inhaled the smoke. The noise coming from the pipe's water pot made it sound as if there was a pigeon trapped inside it, cooing at the top of its voice.

Bash didn't sit down. He was worried that if he sat down politely, he wouldn't be able to put his point across with sufficient energy. He started by talking about the state of public security in the village and how there were thieves among them, going around even stealing keys. It certainly wasn't just one thief, but a gang of them. With a snort, the Branch Secretary blew one finished ball of tobacco out of the bowl, rubbed together another one and blew on his paper spill. Bash was talking very agitatedly while stuffing his face at the same time.

"Hey! Hey!" the Branch Secretary shouted.

Bash stopped dead, wondering what he meant by it.

"Are your ears stuffed with dog hair? I'm calling you."

"Are you calling me?" his wife asked from the bedroom.

"Pour Bash a bowl of hot water so he can sip it slowly."

His wife came out of the bedroom with snack crumbs on her lips.

"Oh, it's you, Bash," she said with a smile. "Let your auntie boil some water for you."

"I don't want any," Bash said. He still had his speech to finish, so he continued, "Is this socialism led by the Communist Party? In the past, Old Kiln was a fine, honest, straightforward place but now there are so many thieves there's no hope of catching them."

The Branch Secretary was no longer exhaling through his mouth, but his nose was filled with smoke. Two plumes were swirling around him as Bash circled in front of him, turning this way and that. He exhaled until there was no smoke left.

"Your family are poor peasants, if I remember rightly."

"That's right."

"And is this really what you poor peasants say? That Old Kiln isn't run by the Communist Party but by these reactionary right-leaning elements, the landlords and rich peasants?"

Bash choked to a sudden halt.

"I am here to report the situation to you," he said.

"OK then, report it and don't worry, just tell me what's the matter."

"The keys to Granny Silkworm's house are missing."

"I know about that."

"You know already?"

"I know everything. I even know which bugs and insects are crawling through the streets of Old Kiln. What else is there?"

"Nothing else."

"If that's the case, then go back and see to the rear eaves of your house, a bunch of tiles have fallen off."

Bash left the Branch Secretary's house and went home to check his rear eaves. There was indeed a tile missing. He was taken aback that the

Secretary really did pay such detailed attention to every plant and tree in Old Kiln, but he also thought to himself that he had gone there to give the man a piece of his mind, so how had he managed to turn the tables and end up on top, without me noticing?

Back at his home, the Branch Secretary smoked another water pipe of tobacco and then went out to see if the key to Inkcap's house really was missing. Sure enough, he couldn't open the gate, so he asked, "Could you have left the key somewhere else?"

"Where else would I have put it?" Gran said. "Us old folk always put the key on the door frame."

The Branch Secretary removed one leaf of the gate for her and then went to investigate everyone else in the village who had lost their key. He discovered that the first key to be lost was in Nanxie Lane, then Xiguai Lane, Cross Alley and Three Fork Alley. After that, it went from north to south via Temple Lane and Guaibazi Lane, and then back to the east. The Secretary's expression hardened, and he asked if anyone had lost anything else. Everyone said that they still had all their rice and noodles and that their radishes and potatoes on the shelves under the eaves were untouched too.

The Branch Secretary suddenly realised what had happened. He asked Decheng, who had lost his own key, "How did you open the door after you lost your key?"

"I can't lie. When I couldn't open it, I took the one on the door frame of the Feng family next door and opened it with that."

"You stole my fucking key, you bastard!" Feng Youliang exploded.

"I didn't steal it, I just took it."

"Call it what you like, you still stole it."

"So how did you open *your* door when you couldn't find your key?" the Branch Secretary asked Feng Youliang.

"I took the key from the next door along too. It was only because we'd lost our key."

The Branch Secretary asked the different households one by one, and it turned out to be the case that the keys disappeared one after the other. There were a few times when a family was away so there was a gap of a few days until they got back and took their neighbour's key. And that was the way things went until they reached Inkcap's house.

"So everyone was taking someone else's," the Branch Secretary concluded. "It seems that just one lost key turned the village upside down and put everyone at each other's throats."

He wasn't going to tolerate one key causing all that upheaval. Whoever it was who stole the first key couldn't have done it for money because what was a key worth? It must have been done deliberately to cause trouble. He told someone to fetch Lightkeeper.

Originally, Winterborn's role at the kiln yard was settling the muddy clay and transporting the unfinished vessels, while Pendulum lit the kiln, and Credit and Pillar dug and transported the porcelain clay, cut down trees for firewood and went to Beishaogou to buy coal. Later, after

Lightkeeper left, Winterborn was asked to do all the work, but there was a set tradition of tasks handed down in Lightkeeper's family, which he had passed on to Winterborn, so all Winterborn did was what was called "settling the clay" and "nesting the clay" to make the porcelain forms. Lightkeeper also handed on his leggings and swivel knife and gave him a start with erecting the drying racks for the forms and lighting the pit furnace to bake them. Lightkeeper's forms were always well turned, but he was suspicious that Pendulum had either made the kiln too hot or not hot enough, and every time the kiln was going to be lit, he went over there to adjust the accelerant. Pendulum was not as even-tempered as Winterborn and he became impatient. He quarrelled with Lightkeeper several times, and in the end, he joined forces with Winterborn, Credit and Pillar to limit Lightkeeper's activities because he had no idea of his own incompetence in everything he did. From then on, he was only assigned to fetching the porcelain clay or transporting the coal bought from Xiahewan to the foot of the mountain, and then lugging it to the kiln with a carrying pole.

The Branch Secretary sent someone up the mountain, where they found Lightkeeper darning a leg of his trousers. It had got snagged on the thorns of a mountain laurel when he was pulling the porcelain clay along.

Even so, Pillar still said accusingly, "You only managed two barrow loads and just look at the state the tyre's in!"

"Do you think I did it on purpose?"

"I told you this morning the tyre was flat, and you didn't pump it up, so no wonder it's like this now."

"Class enemies are inherently destructive, surely you knew that."

He drove the sewing needle into his hand and, in his annoyance, he pulled out the thread, tore open the rip in his trouser leg, then tore it apart, piece by piece until it was just so much cotton wadding.

"And who were you trying to impress with that?" Pillar asked.

At that point, the messenger arrived and pulled Lightkeeper to his feet, telling him that the Branch Secretary wanted to see him. So Lightkeeper made his way down the mountain in his uneven-legged trousers.

It was only when Inkcap got back for dinner that he discovered not only was the key to his own house missing, but also that the Branch Secretary was on the warpath and had summoned Lightkeeper. He now bitterly regretted his actions, but he didn't dare admit he was the one who had stolen the first key. Nor could he bear to let Lightkeeper take the blame, so he urged Gran to go to the Branch Secretary's house to see what was going on. Gran was also concerned for Lightkeeper, so she took Inkcap with her and made her way over there. Lightkeeper hadn't arrived yet, so she got a broom and began to sweep the yard. When Lightkeeper did arrive, Gran exclaimed, "Why are you still wearing your trousers when they're in that state? I'll ask the Branch Secretary's wife for some needle and thread to mend them."

"Please let me leave the kiln," Lightkeeper said to the Branch Secretary.

"You don't get to pick and choose. You work wherever you're told to work," the Branch Secretary told him.

"You can't blame me for the porcelain getting burned like that."

"So what's wrong with the kiln?"

"Winterborn's and Pendulum's skill level—"

"They've been handling the kiln just fine. Are you saying it will all go wrong if you leave? Just look at yourself and the state of your trousers. Are you deliberately trying to tarnish the name of socialism and make me lose face at the same time?"

"How can you raise something like this to a matter of principle and make it a two-line struggle?"

"So now you're saying you're so poor you don't have any other trousers to wear, is that it?"

Lightkeeper didn't say anything but just leaned against the crepe myrtle tree in the courtyard. The tree started to tremble, and a few sparrows flew down from under the eaves, chattering incessantly.

The Branch Secretary stamped his foot, and the sparrows flew away.

"I didn't ask you to come because I had no problems," he said. "You're here because there is a problem in the class struggle. Commune Secretary Zhang reminded me that I must maintain revolutionary vigilance even when everything looks good. I still insisted that everything was fine, but how was I to know that things would suddenly start happening? Not long ago, someone cut Awning's vine off at the roots, and now there are these cases of keys being lost one after another. What's going on?"

"There must be a thief."

"And you're saying that's news to you?"

"Yes."

"You need to be honest with me."

"Do I have a history of stealing, then? Is all the pig shit and dog shit mine too?"

"What are you so het up about?"

"Why would I be stealing keys? To use them to dig the shit out of my arse? In that case, why would I need to steal so many? How many arseholes do you think I have?"

"Shut up!" the Branch Secretary roared. "Just shut your mouth, Lightkeeper."

Then he continued more reasonably, "Even if it wasn't you, I still have to investigate, don't I? It's all very odd."

"Let's just keep our cool, shall we, Lightkeeper," Gran said, trying to smooth things over. "If you didn't steal them, you didn't steal them. But if he's going to investigate things, he has to start with us, doesn't he?"

"Even if there's been no destructive behaviour," the Branch Secretary said, "we still have to look into our innermost thoughts to see whether any destructive ideas are lurking there. Now, be off with you."

Gran and Lightkeeper left the Branch Secretary's courtyard and as soon as Lightkeeper was out of the gates, he came across an inchworm, known locally as the "hanging ghost bug". Its silk thread draped over his face. He swiped at it a couple of times before getting free of it, then stamped on the caterpillar that had fallen to the ground, grinding it into the earth.

"Don't be so childish," Gran said. "What had that bug done to you?"

"I'm all out of sorts now."

"And that gets us off the hook, does it?"

Inkcap didn't go back with Gran. Instead, he helped the Branch Secretary's wife carry some baskets of sweet potatoes up from the cellar. When they'd finished, he wanted to talk to the Branch Secretary. He told him that Gran was old and her ears had been leaking pus all year, so she hadn't been able to sleep at night. He went on to say that in the production team, strong labourers could earn ten points in a day, but Gran could only earn six points. Ten points were worth twenty fen, but six points were only worth twelve. How could she support him on twelve fen a day? He said that he wanted to be able to go out to work. He might be small, but he wasn't a little baby pissing in the mud any more. He couldn't carry the manure or plough the land, but he could do other jobs. He could catch and harness the oxen ready for ploughing; he could collect bedding stones for others to build weirs; and he could sweep away the chaff when it was time to winnow grain. He said that if he was allowed to go out to work, the best thing would be for him to earn four work points, but if that wasn't possible, three would do. No one interrupted him while he was speaking. He felt that his thinking was particularly clear, and he was speaking very eloquently. If the Secretary refused to allow him to work, that would mess up everything.

The Branch Secretary looked straight at him and asked, "Who do you say stole the keys?"

"I don't know."

"It wasn't any of the destructive five elements in our village, so who else might it be? Could it be outsiders?"

"I don't know."

The Branch Secretary walked out of the door by himself and, of course, Inkcap followed. The Secretary took long strides and, when Inkcap couldn't keep up, he had to break into a trot, looking up at his companion's broad back. There were lots of people in the alley, all talking about the lost keys.

"Stop talking about the keys," the Branch Secretary ordered. "Is the sky going to fall in just because of a lost key?"

"We've stopped, we've stopped," someone said. "Have you eaten, Master Branch Secretary?"

"It's dinner time. Of course I've eaten."

The Branch Secretary went first to Baldy Jin's house because Half-Stick was an outsider who had married into the village from Laoshangou. Baldy Jin's gate was locked, however, so he went on to Ever-Obedient's house, looking for Yoyo.

At that moment, Inkcap saw a louse on the bald spot on the back of the Branch Secretary's head and called out, "Sir! Master Branch Secretary! You've got a louse on your head!"

The Secretary glared at him and continued walking.

"Sir, Mister Branch Secretary! You've got a louse on your head!" Inkcap repeated.

The Branch Secretary swept his hand round to slap Inkcap resoundingly on the head. Inkcap stopped dead in his tracks, his head numb with the pain. He stopped following and whispered, "Bite him. Go on, bite him."

In the end, Inkcap didn't know what the Branch Secretary said to Yoyo at Ever-Obedient's house, but that evening, Apricot told everyone that he had gone to the commune for a meeting and brought back the relief grain for Old Kiln. The topic of universal interest soon changed from the lost keys to the distribution of relief grain. When Millstone, Sparks and Dazed-And-Confused got to Ever-Obedient's house to test the piss, Yoyo didn't come out of the house at all, but Ever-Obedient overheard them talking about the food relief.

"Will it be divided per person this time?" he asked.

"It was done per person last year," Sparks said, "but I heard that Commune Secretary Zhang criticised that method. It's hardly likely to be done the same way this year, is it?"

"That's good. It's not fair to divide the food per person. Some families have lots of children who don't eat very much. I eat three or four bowls at a sitting. It should be given to those who need it the most."

"It doesn't matter how it's divided, you won't be getting any."

"Why not?"

"The Branch Secretary was round here today, wasn't he?"

The words were hardly out of his mouth before Yoyo came hurtling out of the house. Her eyes were red and puffy as she yelled, "He suspects me of taking those fucking lost keys. Everyone from Old Kiln is as pure as the driven snow, apparently, but all outsiders are crooks and thieves. Oojamaflip isn't married and Wotchamacallit's wife is a villager. I'm the only outsider, so I'm the thief. Isn't that it?"

"It wasn't just you," Sparks said. "The Branch Secretary was looking for Half-Stick too."

"Let me tell you this, and just listen to me. My own family are poor middle peasants and come from three generations of poor middle peasants. You can't dump this bucket of shit on me."

When she had finished, Yoyo's face went ashen, her body twitched, and she fell writhing to the ground. Ever-Obedient was about to rebuke Yoyo and tell her to shut up, but when he saw her lying there, dead to the world, he panicked and shouted, "She's dead!"

Millstone and Sparks rushed forward and actually stuffed Ever-Obedient into his own piss cistern. Luckily the liquid level was quite shallow, and he was able to scramble out. Lips drawn back and wailing, he took Yoyo in his arms and shouted, "Yoyo! Yoyo!" Yoyo's eyes were rolling in their sockets and she was foaming at the mouth, but she didn't make a sound.

"You drove my wife to her death, Sparks!"

"I didn't drive her anywhere. It was the Branch Secretary who came looking for her, not me."

"He may have come looking for her, but that didn't stop her breathing. She even made him two fried eggs. You drove her to it. You drove her to it."

"And how did I do that? Did I hit her, or curse her or strangle her?"

Millstone looked on helplessly, then shoved Sparks, saying, "Go get Granny Silkworm. Now!"

Sparks hared off to Inkcap's house, where he found Gran sitting on the *kang* making papercuts. Without a word, he lifted her onto his back and set off again. When they got there, Gran tried Yoyo's nose and found she was still breathing. She pulled down the clothing that Yoyo had clutched up to her breast, and covered her exposed belly,

"She's fine," Gran said. "Just let her lie quietly and she'll come to in a while."

"Fine? What do you mean she's fine?" said Ever-Obedient. "Look at the foam on her mouth, and you can't even see her pupils they've shrunk so much."

"She's epileptic," Gran said.

Ever-Obedient was stunned by the revelation, as were Millstone, Sparks and Dazed-And-Confused. Epileptic? Was Yoyo epileptic, then? Lots of other illnesses were rife in Old Kiln, but there had never been an epileptic. There was an epileptic man from Luozhen who came to buy porcelain and he had fallen down writhing in spasms when he was carrying away a porcelain jar. Epilepsy could be fatal but it came on suddenly and went away just as quickly. When they heard Gran say it was epilepsy, the three men breathed a sigh of relief because what they were really thinking was that if his wife had epilepsy, then Ever-Obedient's reputation would be as black as if it had been lacquered.

It was Sparks who started the bad-mouthing: "I think I know why she fell for Ever-Obedient now."

"Ha! She wanted him to look after her so she could find a doctor to treat her illness!" Dazed-And-Confused said.

Dazed-And-Confused was a bit younger than Ever-Obedient. He had had his eye on Yoyo too, but she had gone with Ever-Obedient and his feelings about this were not pretty. Ever-Obedient didn't seem to hear what Sparks and Dazed-And-Confused were saying and he turned to Gran.

"Just let her lie here for a while and she'll be fine?"

"That's right," Gran replied.

"The ground's cold, won't she catch a chill?"

He took off his own clothes, intending to put them underneath Yoyo, but he realised they were damp and rather smelly, so he went and fetched a quilt from the house instead. Gran didn't want to let him disturb Yoyo, so he called his dog, and it lay down next to her. Dazed-And-Confused couldn't stand that dog, so he went over and kicked it.

"Let it lie there," Ever-Obedient said. "It'll warm her up."

"Are you going to let it go to sleep?" Dazed-And-Confused asked.

But Gran cut him short and asked Ever-Obedient, "Has she had a fit like this before?"

"Not that I've seen. I never had the money to pay for a doctor when she wanted to see one."

"Maybe you were all the prescription she needed!" Sparks said. "Look how thin you've got."

"Why would she need him when she's got the dog," Dazed-And-Confused said with a leer.

"Be off with you!" Gran said. "Get back to your work."

Millstone gave the other two a shove and they left. Yoyo opened her eyes. Her head was covered in a film of sweat and she gasped for breath as if she'd just dug a whole *mu* of land.

"Fuck the lot of them," she said all of a sudden. "I'm the one who's been wronged."

Ever-Obedient hoisted her onto his back and carried her home. Yoyo was a tall girl and when she was on Ever-Obedient's back, her two feet trailed along the ground.

THIRTEEN

SO WHO ACTUALLY STOLE THE KEY? Pockmark suggested they make an official report. He said that he knew Station Captain Li at the commune police station. Captain Li would call in all the suspects to hang them up and beat them, so it wouldn't take long for the truth to come to light.

"You're a suspect too," the Branch Secretary observed. "Should you be the first to be hanged and beaten, then?"

What he really meant was that, since no evidence could be found to convict anyone, there was no need to cause trouble in Luozhen.

"So we just forget about it, do we?" Pockmark said.

"Who said we should forget about it?" the Branch Secretary replied.

But the truth was that, in his own mind, he had already shelved the matter. As a leader, there are some things you can talk about but not do, and even a few you can do but not talk about, and what did Pockmark know anyway?

The Branch Secretary told Useless to get his limewash and paint a new set of slogans on the walls of the alleyways.

There was a slogan on the gable wall of Ever-Obedient's house that read, "Eat thick when you are busy, drink thin when you are idle". After scraping it off, he started a new slogan, but he was worried that if he just used a ladder to write on the wall, it would come out uneven. So he asked for some newspapers from the Branch Secretary, wrote the characters out first, and then cut them out and pasted them on the wall. He drew around the characters and then blocked them in with limewash. He picked up his bucket and climbed the ladder, getting Yoyo to stand at the bottom to steady it.

Yoyo couldn't read and asked him, "What characters are you writing?"

Useless had little respect for Yoyo and just said, "Grey and white ones."

Yoyo immediately let go of the ladder and Useless hurriedly told her to steady it again.

"It says 'Listen to the party and follow the Branch Secretary. The situation is favourable, and everything is possible'."

"Ah... but there's a thief around," Yoyo said.

"What are you talking about?"

"With all those lost keys, there must be a thief around."

"The Branch Secretary wrote those words. Have you got a problem with them?"

"It was the Branch Secretary who let me stay in Old Kiln. I know when to turn a blind eye."

"Do you know what propaganda is, you uneducated woman? It's positive publicity."

"All right, I am an uneducated woman."

"Then hold the ladder steady and if you do, I'll get you a work point."

Useless's mother appeared with some gloves because she was worried his hands would get frozen when he was painting the slogans. She couldn't read either, but she still told him how well he had written the characters, how firm and even they were.

But when she heard him having a go at Yoyo, she said, "Go a bit easier on her. She's been ill and isn't properly better yet."

Yoyo's epilepsy was a new condition to Old Kiln, and everyone sympathised with her. But in private, they were also discussing how her illness meant she'd have no trouble getting food relief. When Useless's mother said, "She's still not properly better yet", Yoyo did not demur, but went on helping Useless paint the slogan on the gable wall of her house and then followed him to other places to paint more.

By the time he got to Tongzi Lane, Useless's straw sandals were falling apart. When he went into Dazed-And-Confused's place to buy a new pair, he could see that Dazed-And-Confused also couldn't write, nor had he asked anyone to write characters for him either. The couplets on either side of the portrait of Chairman Mao on the wall were actually interlocking circles, neatly arranged by painting around porcelain bowls.

"Take it down," Useless said. "Take it down and I'll write on the wall for you with my limewash."

"No, I don't want it taken down," Dazed-And-Confused said. "The red paper looks really festive stuck up there. Aren't my painted red circles just as good as anything you can write? I'm not going to let you take it down."

"You really are a backward element."

This upset Dazed-And-Confused, and he tried to bundle Useless out of the door, but Useless wouldn't budge. He grabbed hold of the door frame and wouldn't let go. Dazed-And-Confused hammered on Useless's fingers with his fist so that he dropped his brush and tumbled out of the door.

"So, I'm a backward element, am I? Are you trying to set me up for when they share the food relief? What's backward about me? Is it my status? Or are you saying it was me who stole someone's key and then stole their wife?"

He glared at Yoyo as he raved.

"Don't look at me!" Yoyo exclaimed. "I didn't steal any keys, and I'm a poor middle peasant too. It was the Branch Secretary who asked me to help Useless write slogans."

"I haven't got on to you yet," Dazed-And-Confused said. "Haven't you just pretended to be ill so you can get a share of the food relief? And why do you have to do whatever the Branch Secretary tells you to?"

"What d'you mean, 'pretended to be ill'? And what else have I done?" Yoyo's expression hardened as she repeated, "Pretending to be sick! What else have I done?"

Dazed-And-Confused looked at the face in front of him and raised his hand to hit her, but when it fell, it barely touched her. Yoyo began to scream so loudly it frightened Dazed-And-Confused into shutting the gate.

"My brush! What about my brush?" Useless yelled.

Dazed-and-Confused threw the brush over the courtyard wall.

"You and your woman go fuck yourselves," he yelled.

Although it didn't trigger an epileptic attack, after Dazed-And-Confused abused her like that, Yoyo was not her usual self. She kept saying that Dazed-And-Confused was following her.

This annoyed Ever-Obedient so much that he burst out, "How can he be following you?"

"His ghost is following me."

"Dead people have ghosts. How can someone still alive have a ghost?"

"It's a living ghost."

Ever-Obedient had no choice but to keep Yoyo company when she went out, but now she seemed to need less and less sleep. It was all right during the day as he could go around with her, but at night, he slept like the dead while she got up even before first light. She was at a loose end when she woke, so she took the stone roller from outside Big Root's courtyard gates over to outside Iron Bolt's place. However, Big Root needed it to press his reed mats, so, with a great deal of grunting and groaning, he pushed it back over to his house. As he did so, he thought to himself how strong Yoyo must be.

After the last winter, three terraces were cut into the northern plateau and the original road could no longer be used. So the village allocated some labour to build a new road. While the road was under construction, Potful went round summoning everyone to go to work by ringing the bells hanging on trees outside their gates.

Then, just after Yoyo had taken the roller, he went to bang on people's gates shouting, "Come out to work, the food relief is being distributed."

And what with all that, no one got any proper sleep.

When it came to Awning's house, Awning liked to get busy with his wife first thing in the morning and was just climbing on board, when he heard someone outside shouting, "Captain! Captain!"

"Tell them I'm not here," Awning told his wife.

"The captain... isn't... isn't... isn't... here... Ai!...Ai!... Ai!... Ai!"

But Yoyo kept on calling for the captain, saying, "Drill time. Shooting practice. Soviet revisionist aggression."

Awning looked through a chink in the window and when he saw it was Yoyo doing all the shouting, he lost it completely, seized the piss bucket and hurled its contents through a crack in the door.

The ice in the lotus pond grew thicker and thicker, and the male labourers smashed through it to dig out the mud at the bottom. The women then collected the mud and piled it up by the mountain gate, waiting for it to dry to provide soil for the floor of the cow pens. The children cut down the dried-out lotus stems on the ice, and, because there were lots of small holes running through the stems, they lit them and pretended to be smoking long cigarettes. Inkcap lit up a stem and started smoking it. At the first puff, he suddenly smelt the smell. He froze, not daring to speak. But Half-Stick took the lotus stalk and sucked on it. After one puff, she couldn't stop choking and coughing. Yoyo looked at her and laughed. It was a sudden laugh and sounded like popcorn bursting in a popcorn machine. The noise made everyone jump.

"You scared us to death," Half-Stick said, but Yoyo just kept laughing. She laughed so much that she had to lean against the dyke, hugging her top to her so it rode up, exposing the waistband of her red trousers and her belly button above it.

"Yoyo! Yoyo!" Gran shouted.

"What's up?" Yoyo said.

"Your belly button!"

"Mine's an outie. I've heard people say innie's are lucky. Is that right?"

Gran went over to her and pulled her top down. "There are lots of men around–"

"We've all got a belly button," Yoyo said and hooted with laughter.

Everyone exchanged glances, thinking how shameless Yoyo was. Gran went to tell Ever-Obedient that Yoyo's epilepsy had caused brain damage, and it needed to be treated.

"How can I afford a doctor?" Ever-Obedient protested. "Besides, eating the five different grains will not cure every kind of disease, so everything's fine. All she has to do is eat well."

"You think it's only a problem if she doesn't eat, do you?" Gran said. "If you don't have the money to hire a doctor, you can always ask Goodman to talk to her illness."

Ever-Obedient invited Goodman to his house that night. As soon as Goodman came in through the door, Yoyo started talking incessantly, arguing the point about everything, and Goodman just sat listening peacefully without making a sound.

He stayed sitting there until midnight, then said, "Heat some water, Ever-Obedient. Her mouth will be dry and she'll need a drink."

Goodman stood up and left. Ever-Obedient followed him out.

"Why did you leave without saying a word?" he demanded.

"Not saying anything is also part of the treatment."

"So you're just diagnosing, you're not saying you can cure it, then? I'm not paying good money for that or even wasting any eggs on you."

"Do you think I covet money and eggs? I take money and eat eggs simply to get the patient's attention. I'll come back tomorrow."

When he came back the next day, Goodman asked Yoyo, "Do you think there was reason in what you said yesterday? Did it conform to the Dao?"

"Of course there was reason. How could I choose to talk nonsense if there was no reason?" Yoyo replied.

"There are four types of reason," Goodman explained. "Heavenly reason, the reason of the Dao, righteous reason and emotional reason. If you argue about reason without understanding, of course you will fall ill. If you want to recover from your illness, you must admit you are wrong. If you can change your mind, not by arguing right and wrong with others, but by voluntarily admitting your mistakes, then your illness will be cured."

"What do you mean 'arguing right and wrong'?" Yoyo asked.

"I talk about books concerned with virtue every night," Goodman said, "and many villagers come and listen to me. You should come and wait quietly outside the door. When someone enters, you must kowtow and admit your fault. For example, when Ever-Obedient comes in, you must say, 'I am not worthy to be your wife any more'. If Ever-Obedient's brother comes in, you must say, 'I am not worthy of being your sister-in-law any more'. Even if the captain comes in, you should kowtow and say, 'I am not worthy of being a team member any more'."

"I won't say any of that," Yoyo declared. "What crime am I guilty of?"

Goodman was so choked with frustration he couldn't speak, so he stood up and left.

A small group were waiting for Goodman at the gate of the Kiln God Temple. They had an arrangement with him to come every night and listen to him reading from books about virtue. He asked them to wait, saying that he wanted to bring Yoyo over to kowtow to everyone at the door and confess her sins. If she laughed and made them all laugh too, that was fine. Laughter can concentrate the spirit, ensuring sufficient spirit and powerful *qi*. If this activity could make her sweat all over her body, then her illness would be cured. To everyone's surprise, a disconsolate Goodman returned alone, and they asked him why Yoyo wasn't with him.

"She wasn't interested. She's in as much danger as a blind person riding a horse or someone standing at the edge of a precipice in the middle of the night."

Just at that moment, Potful and Soupspoon walked past. Soupspoon had a notebook tucked under his arm. They were deep in conversation but stopped talking when they saw the group standing around.

"They must be going over to the Branch Secretary's house to discuss the distribution of food relief," someone whispered.

Sparks went over to them.

"Are you off to see the Branch Secretary, Captain?" he asked.

"What are all these people doing here?" Potful asked.

"They're listening to Goodman reading books about virtue," Sparks told him.

"So you're reading books about virtue, are you?" Potful asked Goodman. "Has the Branch Secretary given you permission?"

"I haven't heard any objection from him, and silence means acquiescence."

"So what are you saying, that it's better than studying in a village meeting?"

Goodman put his head to one side, smiled and said, "There are hundreds of people in Old Kiln. You are the team leader, but how many of them do you hold in high regard and how many genuinely listen to you?"

Potful was temporarily lost for words.

"You don't teach people," Goodman continued. "You manage them on a daily basis. Are you aware that managing people is like playing with a ball? The harder you strike it, the higher it bounces and, with people, over time, they become enemies, and you lose their trust."

"He's right. He's right," Sparks said. "Just look at what Old Kiln had become."

"And what is that, exactly?" Potful asked scornfully. "Everyone's a crook and each person is a more accomplished liar than the last. If you cheat the land by not planting crops properly, the land won't reward you with a good harvest. We're still in the twelfth month and there's nothing to eat and the winter harvest isn't even finished."

"Man has three natures," Goodman said. "One comes from Heaven, one comes from disposition and one comes from habit. The one from Heaven is pure good with no evil. The one from disposition is pure evil and no good. And the one from habit can be either good or evil…"

Soupspoon dragged Potful away and they walked over to the mountain gate.

"That's how you manage people, is it?" Soupspoon said.

"Talking about their work always riles me up," Potful explained.

As soon as Potful and Soupspoon had gone, Gran asked Goodman, "Is there no way you can talk through Yoyo's illness?"

Goodman admitted that there was nothing he could do and told Gran to try her "standing chopsticks" method. It was already midnight when Gran got back but she immediately fetched some chopsticks and a bowl of water. But try as she might, the chopsticks wouldn't stay upright.

"Is it going to work if she's not here in front of the chopsticks?" Inkcap asked, standing to one side.

"I really can't cure epilepsy," Gran admitted. "But when your grandfather was alive, he told me a folk remedy for the blank stare disease. The blank stare disease and her illness are pretty similar, so I might as well try it on her."

Inkcap asked what kind of remedy it was, and Gran told him she would get some maggots from the piss cistern, wash them, dry them on a stove tile and grind them into powder. Then, she would find some dragon bones and grind them into powder too. The correct proportions were two-thirds maggot powder to one-third dragon powder, and she would administer it with boiled thornback fish soup.

"Maggots?" Inkcap exclaimed. "How can anyone drink that?"

"It's a cure, isn't it! You have to drink it no matter how horrid it is."

To make sure Yoyo didn't know it contained maggots, Gran told Inkcap to prepare the medicine. He got some maggots from the piss cistern and washed them. Then Gran took a sheet of paper and baked it over the fire, before putting the maggots on it to dry and grinding them into a fine powder. That bit didn't take much effort but searching for the dragon bones kept Inkcap busy for a day and a half. These dragon bones were not actually bones from a dragon, but rather animal bones from a ditch behind the kiln. These bones were partially, but not completely, petrified and the villagers called them dragon bones. If anyone had a stomach ache, they would go and dig up a bit of bone and scrape some powder off it to consume. Inkcap and Cowbell went to the ditch to dig and eventually came up with a piece of bone. They scraped it into powder and mixed it with maggot powder.

"Why are we making medicine for Yoyo when she's so nasty to me?" Inkcap complained.

"Don't wash the maggots properly when you wash them. That'll show her," Cowbell suggested.

But the maggots had already been ground into powder, so Inkcap picked a scabby spot off his nose and mixed that in too.

Nothing changed after Yoyo drank the medicine. Useless kept writing slogans and Yoyo continued to tail him with the bucket of limewash. They painted a slogan on the rear wall of the Branch Secretary's house, but Yoyo also painted the wall by the courtyard gate with the limewash. By the time she was halfway through, lots of folk were accusing her of sucking up to the Branch Secretary.

"So what if I am?" she retorted. "Where would I be without him?"

Hearing the commotion, the Branch Secretary came out and sternly reprimanded Yoyo. The wall wasn't at all neatly painted and was as dirty and streaky as a tiger's beard.

The Branch Secretary went to see Gran, and, on hearing she had given Yoyo some medicine, he asked why it hadn't worked.

"Just give her family some food relief to treat her illness," Inkcap interjected from beside Gran.

The Branch Secretary's expression darkened.

"Is that your idea or did someone else put it in your head?" he demanded.

"It's my idea," Inkcap insisted.

Grandma pushed him aside.

"Be off with you. This is none of your business."

"We've only got a little food relief and everyone in the village is getting so greedy and envious. Let me have another proper look at it," the Branch Secretary said.

Gran and Ever-Obedient tried the "standing chopsticks" spell again to exorcise demons and ghosts. That involved filling a bowl with water, wetting three chopsticks and trying to make them stand upright in the bowl.

"Is it because Yoyo's illness has affected the ghost? Or is it Yoyo's dad?" Gran muttered. "You drowned, didn't you, Yoyo's dad? Have you come back to haunt your daughter? Just stand still if it's you."

But the chopsticks still wouldn't stand up, so Gran continued, "So who is this ghost, if it's not you? Is it a ghost from one of the dead from the village? Is it Cowbell's dad?"

But still, the chopsticks wouldn't stay upright. Gran tried five different ghosts, one after the other, with the same result.

"Could it be Dazed-And-Confused's mum?" Ever-Obedient asked. "Dazed-And-Confused has always had an interest in Yoyo. Could it be his mother's ghost?"

"If it's you, Dazed-And-Confused's mum," Gran said, "then stand still."

No sooner had she uttered these words, than the chopsticks stayed upright.

Ever-Obedient's face hardened and he said, "Dazed-And-Confused is a bad person, and you are an evil ghost. I helped shovel the earth onto your grave at your funeral but now you've come back to haunt my wife."

"If it's really you, you must leave. Go! If you go, Ever-Obedient will burn a hundred sheets of joss paper for you. If you don't, I'll take a knife to you."

With the chopsticks still standing upright, Gran took a chopping knife and banged it down. The chopsticks fell to the ground, and Gran took the bowl over and threw the water out onto the steps outside the door.

As he watched the whole process of the chopstick exorcism, Inkcap found himself very scared of rousing any ghosts. Indeed, even during the day when he passed the cemetery at the base of Middle Mountain, he would keep his eyes fixed on it and spit profusely as Gran had once said that ghosts were afraid of saliva. If he didn't spit, he would touch the stubble on his head because touching your hair released yang energy, and that would keep the ghosts at bay. Normally he both spat and touched his stubble. He couldn't see for himself if he had any yang energy on his head, but when he touched it, he heard a cracking, slapping noise.

The day was over and as darkness fell, Inkcap walked alone down the alley. When he saw a figure in the distance, he wondered whether it was a ghost. Sticking close to the wall and ducking behind a tree, he stared fixedly at it. It was only when the figure arrived in front of him and he discovered that it was one of his fellow villagers, that he finally relaxed. But then, after just a few steps, his suspicions returned: was this person, whoever it was, someone dressed as a ghost?

He stopped again and asked, "Is that you, Uncle Big Root?"

Big Root just kept walking, his hands tucked into his sleeves, but he turned his head to say, "Who else is it if it's not me?"

"You're not a ghost, then?"

"You're the ghost."

"I thought ghosts might be haunting the alley now it's dark."

"Ghosts eat shit, so you often find them in privies. Stamp your feet when you go into one and the ghosts will run away."

Big Root was an honest sort and wouldn't lie, so Inkcap believed him. Even so, he held his piss in and didn't dare go into the privy. He ran home and slammed the door as soon as he was through it.

"What's the matter?" Gran asked. "What's the matter?"

Inkcap told her there were ghosts in the village, but instead of asking him what kind of ghosts, Gran made him stand still, then picked up a pinch of earth from the ground and sprinkled it on his head.

"Where are the paper flowers I laid out for you?" she asked.

From then on, more paper flowers started to appear in Inkcap's pockets and Gran also told him to give some more to Yoyo. Yoyo didn't seem to be afraid of ghosts, but Inkcap was increasingly convinced there were ghosts in the village. Looking at the trees, pigs, dogs, chickens and cats, the birds in the sky, the mice on the ground, and even the rocks, he felt that they must all be reincarnations of the village dead. Conversely, when he looked at the villagers, he felt they must be the reincarnations of all the dead trees, oxen, frogs, eagles, cows, dogs, pigs and chickens.

Inkcap told Bash about these confused thoughts. Bash had nails in his mouth and a shoe in his hand but he dropped the shoe and took the nails out of his mouth.

"Did your gran put all that in your head?" he asked.

"What? Why?"

"It's superstition."

Inkcap immediately thought he'd better not get Gran involved in anything.

"I thought of it myself," he said hastily.

"How can a useless little prick like you think up something like that? So what do you think I was reincarnated from?"

Inkcap couldn't answer.

Bash was the most handsome man in Old Kiln. He was tall, with an angular face and fair skin. As long as he didn't talk or move around, and just sat there quietly, he looked even more like a teacher than the teachers at Luozhen School. But when he moved around and opened his mouth, there was a wave of seminal energy and evil power that could stop people in their tracks.

Bash glared at Inkcap and said, "So what was I reincarnated from, eh?"

Inkcap suddenly thought of a bear, so he said, "Ah, a polar bear."

"We've got wolves and foxes here, but where are the polar bears? Have you ever seen a polar bear?"

Inkcap had never seen a polar bear, but Soupspoon's mother had once told him a story of a white bear, saying that when she was a child, there was a white bear on South Mountain. This bear could stand upright, walk and laugh, and often turned into a young man. Many women were attracted to this handsome young man and went up to talk to him. He caught hold of the women and laughed uproariously. As he laughed, he turned back into a bear and ate them. So the women who lived on South Mountain generally didn't dare go out. If they wanted to go up the mountain to tap for lacquer or collect acorns, they put bamboo tubes on their arms. If they were caught by the white bear, they could slip their arms out of the bamboo tubes and escape when the bear started to laugh. Inkcap thought that Bash was the reincarnation of a white bear, and that Apricot was infatuated with him. Moreover, Soupspoon's mother said that the white bear had poor eyesight, and its nickname was Blind White. Bash always wore dark glasses, and his eyesight was also bad.

"There used to be a white bear, and you're its reincarnation," Inkcap said.

It seemed likely that Bash was going to beat Inkcap up, but unexpectedly, he burst into gales of laughter that went on and on.

"The white bear laughed just like that," Inkcap ventured.

"Go get the mirror from the windowsill, Inkcap," Bash said.

Inkcap fetched the mirror, and Bash looked into it as he asked, "How old is Soupspoon's mother?"

"She's in her seventies already."

Bash twisted his waist to show off how strong and sturdy he was round the middle. Then he took a step forward and roared a few times.

"Soupspoon's mother said she heard there was a white bear on South Mountain when she was a child. She hasn't seen a white bear for more than seventy years because it takes that long for another white bear to be born."

Once Bash acknowledged that he was the reincarnation of a white bear, he really wanted to make himself look like one. When he walked, he swung his arms behind his back, and he no longer went at any great pace but strode with his legs wide apart. He used to say, "Huh? What?", but now he would growl "Oh?" in a low, surly voice. When he laughed, he would throw his head back and guffaw in a way that many people found rather scary. Inkcap was even more intimidated by Bash than before. But the more intimidated he became, the friendlier Bash was towards him and the more interested Bash became in deciding for the whole village who was a reincarnation of what. For example, the Branch Secretary always wore his coat draped over his shoulders and, when he was not busy, walked very slowly, with lowered eyebrows and downcast eyes. The corners of his mouth were deep pits and his cheeks bulged, and when he was eating, his whole face was set into vigorous motion. However, when his eyes were open and his mouth was opened wide, he seemed particularly powerful, so he must be the reincarnation of a tiger.

Sparks had protruding eyes and a square mouth that could accommodate a fist, so he was a toad tadpole. Half-Stick's waist was so thin it shimmied when she walked, so she must have been a water snake. Noodle Fish had a round, clean-shaven face, and the wrinkles on his forehead looked like they'd been carved with a knife, so he must have been a pig. Soupspoon sat like a sack of potatoes and always felt tired. When people were talking about things that had nothing to do with him, he wilted like a frostbitten flower, but once the talk turned to something he was interested in, his eyes would fly open, especially if he was talking to Flower Girl, Half-Stick, Apricot and the others. The more he talked, the more animated he became, and the young women were quite exhausted by the time he stopped. Soupspoon was very attractive to women when he talked to them, so he was an old fox.

Pockmark's eyes were always darting here and there and his voice cracked, so he had been a wolf. Barndoor must have been a tree, probably a walnut tree. Ever-Obedient was reincarnated from a knot in an elm tree. Dazed-And-Confused must have been a dog, and a blind dog at that. Useless had been a snake, but a different kind of snake from Half-Stick. His was a snake slithering into the grass or a crack in a wall, dressed in gorgeous colours. This kind of snake can't keep its flickering tongue still and is capable of squeezing you to death. However, when its head is pinned down and it is lifted by its tail, its bones break one by one, like a grass rope. His mother was a chicken. Cowbell's ear had been bitten by a mouse and mice like to nibble potatoes, but he wasn't a potato. He was definitely a monkey! Potful was an ox, with a big nose and always shouting. Awning was as stubborn as they come, like a donkey, like a cow, like a dog, like a wolf, and yet not like any of them. Sprout talked a lot, and except when she was eating and sleeping, her mouth never stopped. She had been a toad. But no, a toad has a big belly, and that was not her. Ah yes, that was it, she was reincarnated from a sparrow.

They were very proud of themselves every time they decided on an animal, and the more they decided, the more pleased with themselves they were, until they became truly arrogant and went around the place shouting the odds.

"You really were an inkcap mushroom, Inkcap," Bash declared.

"I was a tiger," Inkcap insisted.

"Balls. OK then, you were a mouse."

"No I wasn't."

"Nothing wrong with having been a mouse, mice are good. Mice get to eat whatever we are eating. Although everyone yells at them and hits them if they go out on the street, when there was an earthquake five years ago, on the very next day, the mice were all over the alleys. And when the Zhou River flooded last year, the mice climbed the trees on top of the embankment. Mice are very clever little creatures."

"But mice have sharp front teeth," Inkcap protested. "I've got a mouthful of broken teeth, so how can I be a mouse?"

In the end, Bash couldn't figure out what Inkcap was reincarnated from.

"You were fished out of the river, and you've got sticking-out lips, so maybe you were a fish."

Inkcap's heart missed a beat as he hoped Bash wouldn't make the link between his origins and Yoyo's.

"I wasn't anything," he said hastily.

"It hasn't been easy for you, growing up like this," Bash admitted. "Maybe you were a stone that fell from the sky?"

Inkcap thought for a moment about whether or not he had been a rock. Lightkeeper was a rock, but he was a rock from a privy, wasn't he!

"Then I was a meteorite."

To make doubly sure of their verdicts, they walked through the village alleyways, passing one house after another. Either Bash said "Cow!" or whatever, or they passed on to the next house and Inkcap would call out, "Chicken scratching for food!"

"You've been to the provincial capital, haven't you?" Inkcap said. "Is the zoo there like this?"

"We've got more animals here in Old Kiln!" Bash replied.

In Pianxi Alley, Iron Bolt's second uncle was on his haunches. He was holding an old bowl filled with potatoes boiled in thin rice congee. The potatoes hadn't been cut up, so he picked them out and put them in his mouth whole. His eyes were as big as eggs and as he chewed, a bulge appeared first in his left cheek and then in his right. After a bit, he choked and beat himself on the chest with his fist.

"Slow down, no one's going to steal it," Bash said.

The lump in Second Uncle's throat finally disappeared. He smiled and ducked his head to drink the rice congee, slurping loudly.

"Another pig," Bash observed.

Second Uncle drank the bowl dry, licked his lips, and when he saw Bash and Inkcap walking away, he said, "If I'm a pig, that's fine with me. Pigs are lucky."

Bash started talking to Half-Stick at the side of the alley. Half-Stick was squeezing honey locust pods with a clamping stick. They had already determined that she was the reincarnation of a snake and now, as she pinched the pods, her waist seemed to become even more slender and Inkcap could see the smooth white of her belly and the red cloth belt below it.

"You look busy, sister-in-law," Bash said.

"What's this 'sister-in-law' crap?" Half-Stick demanded. "I'm younger than you. Just how old do you think I am?"

"I call Baldy Jin 'older brother', so of course I call you 'sister-in-law'. What's your zodiac animal?" Bash asked, trying to work out her age.

"I'm a snake."

Bash winked at Inkcap. "A snake, are you?"

"If you don't believe me, just look at my legs."

With that, she lifted the legs of her trousers and the skin of her ankle was indeed patterned like snakeskin.

"So do you want any of these pods? I can give you some if you like."

"I don't want any," Bash said.

"I've got a pile of rotten shoes in my room. You can have them. You could still use the soles."

"I don't want any of your tatty old shoes."

"What do you mean?"

"I don't want your rotten soles."

"The only thing you want is Apricot, isn't it!" Half-Stick said tartly.

Bash tugged at Inkcap and the two of them walked away while Half-Stick went on, "It's only 'cause she's young, isn't it? When I was young, my skin was better than hers. It was pure white, tinged with red, like a boiled egg that's been peeled and rolled in a box of rouge. Come on Bash, come and have a sit down inside if you've got nothing else to do."

As they turned the corner, Inkcap told Bash, "She fancies you."

"I just don't know which of them would be best for me," Bash sighed.

When they looked up, Lucky's mother was standing on the gentle slope up ahead of them waiting for someone. She was bent at the waist with her hands held in front of her chest, drooping limply from her wrists. She reminded Inkcap of another animal but he couldn't pin down which one for the moment.

"Who are you waiting for, auntie?"

"I'm waiting for Lucky," Lucky's mother said. "He went to sell some porcelain in town, and I don't know why he isn't back yet. They're allocating the food relief this afternoon. Why isn't he back yet?"

"Who said that about the food relief?" Bash asked.

"Potful knew all about it. And the Branch Secretary told Lucky to go and sell porcelain today, so he went. Do you think he was deliberately getting Lucky out of the way so we don't get our share?"

"Impossible," Bash reassured her. "It's not up to the cadres to choose who they like. There's a group of people in the office drawing up a list."

As he was talking, Pockmark met them on his bicycle, with Sparks riding pillion. Pockmark was teaching Sparks to sing Qin opera.

"If you take one step forward and two steps back, it means you haven't left at all. Now, you sing!" Bash instructed Sparks.

"One step forward and two steps back means you haven't left at all," Sparks sang back.

"If you eat one *dou* of rice and shit out ten *sheng* of shit, that means you're shitting too much," Pockmark sang.

"If you eat one *dou* of rice and shit out ten *sheng* of shit, that means you're shitting too much," Sparks sang back.

"Here come the wolf and the toad," Inkcap said.

"Bash! Bash!" Pockmark shouted, sending the bike hurtling over towards Bash and Inkcap and almost hitting Inkcap with the front wheel. Pockmark was still astride the bike when Bash picked up a length of straw rope from the ground and threw it at the wheels. The rope caught in the chain and the bike toppled over. As it fell, Pockmark's feet touched the ground and he was able to keep his balance, but Sparks rolled off from his perch.

Inkcap was annoyed by the near miss with the front wheel but didn't dare curse Pockmark, so he swore at Sparks instead. "Great fall! I fucking told you to be careful on that bike and what did you fucking do? Great work!"

Sparks had had the wits knocked out of him by the fall and was lying still, face down on the ground. His arms were spread out in front and his legs splayed behind him.

"A toad! A toad!" Inkcap crowed.

"He was talking and singing when he was sitting on the back of the bike. Do you think the fall jolted him back to his original form?"

This bicycle didn't belong to Pockmark, it was actually Awning's. He was the only person in Old Kiln who owned one like it. Awning had wrapped the forks, struts, handlebars and even the back seat with strips of red and green plastic. There were a few folk in Old Kiln who knew how to ride a bike, but Awning never lent his to anyone except the Branch

Secretary when he wanted to go to a meeting at the Luozhen Commune. He rode it out of the village and through the lanes and alleys. It made a crisp, whirring noise like Apricot's sewing machine, but more subtle and refined. Chickens took flight when they saw it and dogs burst into a run. Even when the wheels ran over someone's grain-drying mat, they didn't get upset when they saw who it was and just said, "Wow! Just look at that bike!"

"Why would Awning lend you his bike?" Bash asked Pockmark.

"Why wouldn't he lend it to me, just because he doesn't lend it to anyone else."

"Are you going to town to hear some announcement from the high-ups?"

"Nope, that's not it. I had a message from Chief Li at the police station asking me to go for a drink."

"Yeah, right. A drink of piss."

"I know you don't believe me, but look at this." He lifted his coat out of the way to reveal an electric torch hanging from his belt.

"Take it off and show me."

Pockmark got off the bike and raised the torch, pointing it straight at Inkcap, dazzling him. There weren't any torches in Old Kiln. Secretary Zhang of the Luozhen Commune, Director Wu Gan and Director Li carried such things in their pockets when they came to Old Kiln on inspection visits. At night, when they were prowling the alleys, they shone them on anyone they saw. Sometimes they caught a pig in the beams of their torches, freezing the animal to the spot. The same thing happened with people too. Bash had never used an electric torch before.

"Why did he give you a torch?" he asked, grabbing it.

"I sent him a basket of carrots to celebrate his son's one-month birthday."

Bash pocketed the torch, tugged at Sparks to come with him and set off down the alley.

"I'll just borrow it for a few days," Bash said.

Pockmark didn't want to give it up, but Bash had snatched it away from him and made off with it, leaving Pockmark helpless. Inkcap started chuckling.

"What are you laughing at, you useless little prick?" Pockmark yelled.

"I'm laughing... I'm laughing at her," Inkcap improvised, pointing at Yoyo who happened to be standing in the mouth of the alley opposite.

The only thing Pockmark could think of doing was to bully Inkcap, so he flexed his legs and leap-frogged over his head. Then he got back on the bike and rode away.

A patch of grey cloud was being pulled along like a curtain. Ah, wouldn't it be good if it could turn the sky black. But the cloud just stopped once it was over the village. Yoyo waved to Inkcap to come over.

Inkcap didn't move.

"Come here. I've got something to tell you."

Inkcap flapped his hand as a wasp flew up from under his feet. What was a wasp doing there when the weather was so cold?

"Why don't you come when I call you?" Yoyo said.

Inkcap carried on down the alley. He heard the wasp buzzing and buzzing, telling Yoyo the reason why Inkcap was ignoring her.

FOURTEEN

IN THE AFTERNOON, Potful rang the bell on the tree. A single ring was to call people out to work while continuous ringing meant that the workers' meeting was about to begin.

Gran was driving the pig back into its pen. It had jumped over the wall the day before and got into the radish cellar in the corner of the yard. It had already been beaten for the act, but it didn't remember the beating, only the radishes, so it had done the same thing again. Gran heard the bell as she was driving the pig back and it made her heart beat faster and faster. She called for Inkcap to take over with the pig and went into the house to comb her hair.

The residents dashed to get changed whenever there was a village meeting. Gran and Lightkeeper knew they couldn't miss the meeting but really didn't want to be there either. Gran knew she was either going to be criticised or made to stand in front of the audience, but even so, she had to comb her hair. Inkcap drove the pig back into the pen and wedged a horizontal bar across the top of the wall. He saw Gran sitting on the doorstep with a basin of water in front of her, dipping her comb into it to comb her hair.

"What's the point in doing that?" he asked. "At your age, why do you still–"

"Even if I was two hundred, I'd still be a woman," Gran retorted.

When Inkcap told her that the meeting was not about class struggle but about how to share out the food relief, Gran asked him how he knew, and he told her about the nonsense with Lucky's mother that morning.

"That bell sounds urgent," Gran said with a cry of alarm.

Then she went back to slowly combing her hair before stuffing a clump of it she unwound from the comb into the crack in the wall.

"Why's it been so long since we last saw Noisy?" she asked.

In the yard of the public office, Happy had tethered all the cows in the shed but hadn't had time to shovel up the cow shit. Pretty much the whole population of Old Kiln had come, and they were all looking for something to sit on. Some of them took a handful of straw to use as cushions, and Happy went round with a face like thunder, snatching it back. Inevitably, there was a frank exchange of views between the two parties. As soon as Gran arrived, she stood in front of the table, behind which the Branch Secretary sat smoking a cigarette. Two streams of smoke came out of his nostrils, like elephant tusks.

"Where's Lightkeeper?" he asked.

"Isn't he here yet?" Gran said. "He won't be long."

"You don't need to stand there today. Go and find somewhere to sit down."

Gran hesitated and Third Aunt said, "The Branch Secretary told you to sit down, didn't he? Come on, come and sit next to me."

Gran sat down next to Third Aunt, and Flower Girl, who was sitting behind them, tugged at Gran's collar. She was stitching the sole of a cloth shoe, but she stopped and took out a papercut flower she had done herself, and showed it to Gran.

The Branch Secretary was still smoking and tusks kept appearing intermittently from his nostrils. All the other men were smoking, too, as if they were trying to start fires in their stomachs, but the fires weren't catching and only giving off smoke. The smoke was forming strange shapes that shifted constantly until finally coalescing into a continuous mass that flowed over the heads of the assembled like water. The sun was already falling below the tiled roof of the office building so that the steps under the eaves were half black and half white. Gradually, even the Branch Secretary became a yin and yang figure, with his front half in the light and his back in shadow. Even so, he still delayed opening the meeting.

When everyone had finished smoking, they began whispering to each other. Ever-Obedient and his dog were squatting off to one side. He hated the cold and was tucked up in his padded cotton jacket, cuddling his dog, which he had tied to himself with a length of hemp rope. Even so, the dog kept looking around for Inkcap.

Yoyo came walking down the slope from the mountain gate. Her eyes were red-rimmed and bloodshot, but she was munching on some sweet potato slices she had in her pocket as she walked. Inkcap caught sight of her as soon as she reached the entrance of the courtyard and was about to turn and go when she called out his name. He pretended not to hear and went to sit with Barndoor and Feng Youliang. Feng Youliang was explaining things to Barndoor, and Inkcap understood the gist of what he was saying. It turned out that the relief rations had been brought to the village ages ago, but the distribution plan had not been finalised. After the incident of the lost keys, it was the Branch Secretary's opinion that anyone who had lost their key and stolen someone else's should not get a share of the grain. However, the production team leader felt that, since the original culprit had not been found, that meant that everyone was potentially guilty and they couldn't deprive so many needy households of the relief rations, as they would not be able to survive.

"So what's the final decision?" Feng Youliang asked.

"I don't know," Barndoor replied. "Us outsiders don't have any cadre to represent us."

Feng Youliang was Useless's next-door neighbour and Useless had taken his key when he lost his own. Feng Youliang had then taken his other neighbour's key.

"Maybe it was Useless who lost his own key and was the first to steal someone else's, starting the chain reaction. He's at the bottom of the whole disaster," Feng Youliang said, his eyes fixed on Useless, who was sitting not far away in front of him.

Useless turned round to look. Feng Youliang hurriedly covered his words with a cough and Useless turned back to face the front. Feng Youliang started to chatter away to Barndoor again.

Useless was sitting with Soupspoon and both of them were wearing face masks. Soupspoon's mask was so dirty you couldn't tell it had once been white. Pockmark came over and plonked himself down, raising a miniature dust storm.

"Is your asthma bad again, Useless?" he asked.

Useless was not only wearing a mask but had also put a new lined jacket on top of his padded one.

"You're throwing up dirt like a donkey having a dust bath," he complained.

"Let me see if there are any lice," Pockmark said, flicking open Useless's new jacket.

Useless stood up and went over to sit under the legs of the table. Meanwhile, Feng Youliang was still talking to Barndoor: "I'm going to kick off if Useless gets given a share."

Barndoor kept puffing away furiously at his cigarette, so Feng Youliang continued, "I didn't get a share last year and I just put up with it, but I'm not going to take it this year. Everyone called Zhu and Hei in Old Kiln gets a share, but all of us with an outsider family name are easy targets for them to rip off."

Barndoor was still concentrating on his cigarette and Feng Youliang kept on at him: "I'm talking to you. Why don't you say something?"

"What kind of tobacco do you call this?" Barndoor shot back. "Why won't it light properly?"

The non-smokers were on one side of the courtyard, while, on the other, Awning called out, "Inkcap! Where's Inkcap?"

"I'm here."

"We haven't got a light over here," Awning went on. "Go get us one."

Of course, Inkcap had brought his rope fuse with him when he came to the meeting, so he went over to where Awning was and gave everyone a light. The Branch Secretary banged his pipe on the table: Bang! Bang! Bang! Everyone knew that the meeting was starting and they fell silent. The Branch Secretary called Useless over and told him to check if anyone was missing. Useless stood up and looked around for a while.

"Why don't you take off your mask and put on a cow muzzle for me?" the Branch Secretary said, and everyone laughed.

"My face is cold," Useless replied but he still took off his mask. "Where's Inkcap? Inkcap!"

Inkcap knew quite well that Useless was upset about being ridiculed and was deliberately trying to take it out on him in turn. Useless knew he was there – he'd seen him arrive – so he was just pretending to ask. He didn't reply.

But then the Branch Secretary said, "Why isn't Inkcap here?"

"I am," Inkcap said, standing up.

"Why don't you stand up when the Branch Secretary calls you?" Useless demanded.

"I am standing up!" Inkcap protested, and it was only when everyone burst out laughing that he realised that Useless was making fun of his short stature.

The Branch Secretary finally opened the meeting. He said that, as all those assembled knew, it was being held to decide how to divide the food relief. Everyone did indeed know that, and they had been looking forward to it for so long that their eyes were bleeding with anticipation.

"Judging by how many of you are here today, I can be pretty sure you do already know."

Everyone was also pretty sure that he was going to go on to say, as he had done in previous years, that the food relief came to them all from the Communist Party and that, if they were still living in the old society, no one would care if they starved to death. In the eighteenth year of the Republic of China, thousands of miles of barren earth and thousands of villages were sunk in depression. People wanted to eat dogs when they saw them, and dogs wanted to eat people.

In Old Kiln, 132 people had died and forty-seven households had been wiped out. How had Awning's grandfather died? At the age of sixty-two, he had died in the course of a day spent digging a pit in the low ground at the rear of the village. He had succumbed to starvation and fallen headfirst into the pit. And how did Iron Bolt's aunt pass away? She was still young at the time but had fainted from hunger in the wheat field, and barking dogs gnawed her flesh to the bone. Decheng's second uncle had gone mad after eating flesh from human corpses. He wanted to eat everything he saw and went around biting people until the villagers had had enough and beat him to death with sticks.

Now that they were in a better society, they were given food relief every year. So whenever they drank water, they should remember its source and repay the kindness; they should never forget Chairman Mao and the Communist Party. To everyone's surprise, however, that was not what the Branch Secretary said on this occasion. What he did talk about was the lost keys.

He said that, for generations, the atmosphere in Old Kiln had been excellent. Apart from during a few serious famine years, no one locked their doors at night and no one got robbed on the road. When people went into the mountains to gather firewood or help tap lacquer trees, or went to bring back coal from Beishaogou, if one of their straw sandals broke, they would leave the other unbroken one by the roadside so someone else could use it if needed. In the autumn, every household left their grain outside in winnowing baskets under the eaves. Chicken coops were left unsecured and so were pigsties. At the end of the working day, shovels, hoes, sickles and rakes were just left at the door or simply thrown on the ground.

"Let's all consider this," the Branch secretary continued. "I have been in this post for ten years. What has ever been lost in this village? Who has ever stolen anything?"

"I've never stolen a thing," everyone cried out.

"So no one has ever stolen a corncob or a persimmon?" Pockmark interjected. "No one's ever stolen Baldy Jin's honey locust pods or Barndoor's peaches and apricots? Is that what you're all saying?"

"You always have to be the one to make a fuss and stand out, don't you, Pockmark. Just so everyone knows who you are," the Branch Secretary said. "Yes, sure, people have taken a couple of corncobs, or a few sweet potatoes from the production team, or a handful of peaches and apricots from their neighbour, but that's all just to get a little taste of something fresh."

"He's right," someone shouted. "Pockmark carries nightsoil for a living, and he never steals any of that to eat!"

"I'm not just talking about food," Pockmark continued. "What about stealing people too? Didn't Number Three Zhang steal Number Four Li's wife? Don't women steal other women's men? Don't fathers-in-law steal their daughters-in-law?"

"Shut your dirty fucking mouth, Pockmark!" The Branch Secretary imposed himself on the conversation by banging the table as he spoke.

Pockmark shut up and sat down, but not before he had muttered, "Is anyone still claiming there's no thieving going on?"

"That's that prick Pockmark for you," came a voice, and the whole meeting burst out laughing.

"Stop laughing," the Branch Secretary shouted, banging the table again. "And stop talking out of turn."

He returned to his opening remarks, saying that Old Kiln had always been a place of kindness and consideration, and where the world was a simple place. But recently, keys had been going missing one after another. Why would anyone steal keys? You can't eat them or drink them. Nor had he heard of anyone losing anything else. It was obvious that someone was deliberately causing trouble, upsetting neighbours, causing panic, tarnishing socialism and giving him a pain in the neck as Secretary. He spoke very seriously, and in absolute silence. Then, when he had finished, he stared at the audience in turn and they stared back at him, afraid that his gaze would panic them and make them look guilty. But right at that moment, the Branch Secretary ducked his head to one side and spat out a mouthful of acid reflux.

"The Secretary's stomach trouble's back," Potful shouted to Gourd. "Have you got any hot water over there?"

"Why would I have hot water in a cattle pen?"

"No need," the Branch Secretary said with a wave of his hand. Then he continued, "Why did I talk about the missing keys before commenting on the food relief? Because they reminded me that there will always be new situations and new problems in the class struggle and that is a warning one should never take lightly at any time. If the country can give us food relief every year, we must show our love for the people's communes and production teams. Old Kiln has always been the red flag village in Luozhen, and we must hold on to that flag and never let its colour fade. Let me say this one thing, here and now – I, Zhu Dagui, will not spare anyone who smears the reputation of this village, nor can they expect to get a single grain of food relief."

The floor was then given to Potful, who began to talk about the specific distribution plan for the food relief. He stated that the previous year the distribution had been averaged out across the whole population, with everyone getting the same share, so it had been done purely on a per capita basis. However, although every family had their own difficulties, ten fingers are not all the same length. Some families had specific and expensive demands on their money, such as recovering from a fire, building a house, getting over an illness or arranging weddings and funerals. Some families had a lot of men with large appetites, while others couldn't organise themselves properly or plan their days. On that basis, distributing the food relief per capita would not be appropriate. Last year, the village cadres had held a meeting to allocate the relief, and everyone had a lot to say about it. Based on that experience and the lessons learned, this year everyone would be properly evaluated, and food relief would go to the families that needed it the most. There would be a full discussion, in which everyone could have their say on who deserved how much.

When he spoke these words, you could hear a pin drop in the courtyard and it stayed that way for the time it would take to smoke a pipe of tobacco, disturbed only by the sound of the cows chewing their cud in the nearby cattle pen and the swish of their tails. Inkcap kept his eyes on the faces of everyone at the meeting, and they all looked to him like either persimmons or potatoes.

Suddenly someone coughed, and then others joined in.

"What's the matter? Normally, you lot won't shut up," the Branch Secretary said. "Why doesn't anyone say something? Why are you coughing? Have you all got chicken feathers in your throats?"

"What's that shit you're smoking?" Half-Stick asked Sparks. "It's making me choke."

"Don't sit there, then," Sparks retorted. "If you were at home on your *kang*, you wouldn't be choking."

"If I wasn't here, you think you'd have it all for yourself, don't you?"

"Even if you stay here, you're still not going to get anything."

"Why not? Why not?"

"Stand up, Sparks," the Branch Secretary ordered. "You speak first."

"I don't have anything to say."

"Normally, you never shut up," the Branch Secretary observed tartly, "but now it's something serious, you've got nothing."

Inkcap shoved Sparks, but however hard he tried, Sparks wouldn't budge, so he farted instead. Everyone heard it and wanted to laugh but didn't dare.

"Did you have garlic for lunch?" Cowbell asked.

"Try again," Inkcap said, squeezing out another one.

"If you keep talking, Inkcap, you have to be the first to speak," Pockmark said, and this time everyone did laugh.

"What's going on?" the Branch Secretary demanded. "What's all this nonsense?"

The courtyard fell silent again, but no one got up to speak. The sweet potato slices Yoyo was eating were too hard, and it made a loud noise when she snapped off a piece with her teeth. Ever-Obedient threw his cigarette packet at her, and she stopped eating.

"No one's speaking because their stomachs are all busy doing the sums," Lucky said. "So which households should we choose? Families with lots of children should come first. Children are nothing but open mouths and if they don't get enough at a meal, they just wail and moan. All the children in our village have got big heads and slim waists."

Lucky had a lot of children and, that morning, he had been beating his son out in the alley, cursing him for eating so much without ever having enough to fill his bottomless belly. Before Lucky had finished speaking, Stonebreaker piped up, "I agree with what Uncle Lucky said."

"Your daughter-in-law should have given birth ages ago," Sprout chipped in. "Is she waiting for the food relief?"

"That's childbirth for you. Do you really think the baby's not coming out because I won't let it? Have you not had any children yourself?"

In fact, Sprout didn't have any children which was a source of great dissatisfaction to her mother-in-law, and she was a bit uneasy about Stonebreaker bringing it up in this manner.

"No, I haven't had a baby before. So what? There are lots of women here who haven't. You can't play off someone else's weakness just because you're about to give birth."

She looked at Flower Girl for support, but Flower Girl didn't say a word.

"What kind of shit are you talking?" Barndoor demanded.

"Oh, so I'm going too far, am I?" Sprout said indignantly. "Attacking someone without slapping them in the face and criticising them without showing up their faults? So what if your wife's having a baby? You've already made off with several dozen *jin* of grain from the production team and now you want another share?"

Noodle Fish stood up to say something, but his lips just flapped and nothing came out. Instead, his wife said, "That *jin* of grain is for making wine with. I hope their liver and guts rot if anyone eats a single grain of them."

"The way I see it," Cowbell said, "families with lots of children shouldn't get a share. It should go to the able-bodied labour force. They're the ones who do the real work. The piss buckets are never off their shoulders, and they need a lot to eat. Children get the same share as grown-ups but they eat much less, so their households never go short."

"Doesn't everyone who's born, grow up?" Lucky protested. "Doesn't every grown-up start out as a child? Are you saying that because they can't go out to work to earn a living, children shouldn't get anything to eat and should be left to starve to death?"

When the two of them had had their say, they sat down, huffing and puffing, and didn't speak again.

"If anyone has any further opinions, speak up now," the Branch Secretary said.

The courtyard fell silent again, except for the sound of the cows sneezing and laughing.

Then Millstone stood up and pronounced, "I've got a way of doing it."

Millstone had a walleye, so when you thought he was looking at you, he was actually looking at the person next to you. Now he was speaking to the Branch Secretary, but his eyes appeared to be elsewhere. He was very excited, and his neck was flushed. He seemed to need a smoke to calm down, but the hand he was trying to light his pipe with was trembling too much.

"There's no rush, Millstone," Almost-There reassured him, steadying Millstone's pipe with his hand. Millstone got it going but didn't draw on it.

"So, here's my thinking. Suppose someone's given a share, then everyone will have their eyes on the cake thinking that if you take a bite, that's one less bite for me. That way simply stokes up jealousy and it's a real bone of contention. So why don't we just draw a circle and everyone inside it gets a share and anyone outside it doesn't?"

The villagers thought that sounded like a really good idea.

"All right, then," the Branch Secretary said. "We'll use this exclusion method and see who won't get a share this time."

The courtyard fell silent again.

"Why go to all that trouble?" Pockmark said. "Why don't we just let the cadres decide?"

"I specifically said this time everyone was going to make the decision together," Potful objected. "Why have you dragged us back to that?"

"Draw lots, then. Draw lots to find out who's who," Pockmark said.

"Stop fucking around," Potful exploded.

Pockmark stood up, slapping the dust off his backside. "I'm going for a piss," he said. Then, as he was leaving, he called out to Almost-There, "Are you coming for one too?"

"Yes, I'm coming," Almost-There called back.

The two of them walked out, followed by three or four others who also needed a piss because they'd had thin rice congee for lunch.

"Are you going or not?" Sparks asked Barndoor.

"This is no time to go for a piss," Barndoor barked. "Hold it in."

"Yes, yes, yes. You're right. You're right. If I go for a piss now, the rest of you will share things out between you. I'll just be pissing away twenty or thirty *jin* of grain."

"Millstone," the Branch Secretary said. "You suggested this exclusion method, so you must have had some idea of how to go about it. Go on, tell us."

"How to go about it, eh?" Millstone mused. "Well, I don't think criminals should get a share."

"We don't have any criminals in the village," the Branch Secretary replied testily. "Stop messing about and get to the point."

"All right, then. First of all, the Four Bad Elements are excluded."

Inkcap gave a yelp.

"What are you shouting about?" the Branch Secretary demanded.

"Cowbell poked me in the arse."

Cowbell was miles away from Inkcap and certainly hadn't poked him in the arse, but Inkcap was concentrating on Millstone's exclusion categories, as he was quite sure that both his household and Lightkeeper's were going to be excluded. They had never got any food relief in the past, but at the beginning of the meeting, the Branch Secretary had asked whether he was there or not and that had made him dream that this time his family might be awarded some. Then along came Millstone, who knocked them out of the reckoning once again. As soon as the Branch Secretary reprimanded him, Inkcap went quiet, but he could no longer just sit there and listen to the debate about how to share out the food relief. Turning around to look at the mountain gate, he saw a dog wandering past aimlessly; it was Tag-Along's tailless dog. Ah! Another dog was following it, a curly-haired dog. There was no dog in Old Kiln with a tight-curled tail like that, so Inkcap thought it must be some kind of exotic wild dog. He moved over next to Tag-Along's wife and poked her in the back with his finger.

Tag-Along's wife had half a leg missing but she was still the fattest person in the village. She put on weight just by drinking water, and she snored as soon as her head touched the pillow. When he was out and about, Tag-Along always complained that his wife took up half the *kang* when she was sleeping. She hadn't got any food relief the previous year because she was so overweight, but ten days or so ago, she had put it about that if her family didn't get any this year, she was going to hang herself in the doorway of the public office. She didn't react when Inkcap poked her, so he did it again.

Her eyes stayed fixed on Millstone's mouth as she whispered, "Stop poking me. I'm listening to Millstone's exclusions."

"You're so fat, you're bound to be excluded," Inkcap said.

"Fuck off out of it. What do you mean by that? How am I fat? This is fluid retention."

Not wanting to dig himself any further into trouble, Inkcap didn't dare ask her whether the wild dog actually belonged to her and her family, so he turned to Cowbell and said, "There's a wild dog in the village."

"Where?"

"Let's go and have a look."

Inkcap uncurled himself like a cat and left, making as if he was going for a piss. Cowbell followed him out.

Inkcap and Cowbell watched from below the mountain gate as the two dogs entered the forest next to the Kiln God Temple one after the other, and then they chased after them. At the entrance to the temple, Goodman was bringing water back from the spring. He didn't use a carrying pole to transport it but carried a bucket using both hands, which made walking a bit awkward. The villagers speculated that Goodman knew how to do magic and could conjure up a little ghost to carry his sedan chair at night, so Inkcap reckoned that he didn't use a carrying pole because the same little ghost must carry the bucket, right? But he, Inkcap, just couldn't see it.

"Ah, you're fetching water," Inkcap observed.

"That's right."

"And you don't need a carrying pole?"

"That's right."

"Is there any such thing as ghosts in this world?"

Goodman just grunted. Inkcap got the impression that Goodman didn't really want to talk to him, so he shut up. When they reached the temple, Inkcap looked up into the forest again. The two dogs were entangled there. Tag-Along's bitch was standing quietly while the wild dog mounted it from behind, hugging the bitch's body with its front legs. One of its hind legs was anchored on the ground while the other scrabbled against a tree trunk, making its whole body shake.

"What are they doing?" Inkcap asked.

"Haven't you seen two dogs mating before?" Cowbell asked in astonishment.

"Is that what they're doing?" The sight seemed to annoy Inkcap. "Let's break them up."

"Watching people screwing is bad luck and the same goes for dogs," Cowbell said as he led him back down the gentle slope from the Kiln God Temple.

After they came out of the meeting, Bash, Gourd and Stargazer went behind a heap of straw at the bottom of the same slope to piss, competing to see who could piss the highest. Inkcap told Bash that there was a wild dog in the woods, and it was mating with Tag-Along's bitch.

"What?" Bash exclaimed, clearly wanting to go have a look.

"They're sharing out the food relief. I don't dare waste any more time here," Stargazer protested.

"Let them. We're going to go eat dog meat."

The five of them ran hooting and hollering up the slope, crashing through the fences of anyone who had a vegetable patch behind the temple. Bash picked up a stick to use as a club and so did Stargazer, but when Inkcap went to do the same, he picked up a rock instead. Inside the wood, the two dogs were still locked together.

"Are they fucking all the way to Old Kiln?" Bash said, then led the charge over towards them.

When the wild dog realised there were people there, it twisted round and ran away. Unfortunately, its prick was still stuck inside the bitch underneath it, and the poor creature was dragged along with it. They couldn't run properly locked together like that and they tumbled to the ground. The wild dog stared at Bash with bloodshot eyes, baring its fangs and scrabbling with its claws. Bash hit the wild dog with his stick, and the wild dog leapt into the air, taking the bitch with it, then falling back to the ground. Bash pressed down on the wild dog's back with his hand.

"Nice and fat," he told Inkcap. "Do you fancy some dog meat?"

"The bitch belongs to Tag-Along's family," Inkcap said.

"We don't eat bitches," Bash replied.

Then he hit the wild dog again to separate the two of them, but even though the wild dog ran east and the bitch ran west, they still couldn't pull themselves apart.

"This dog's balls are all in a lump, they're locked tight," Stargazer said.

He levered his stick in under the dog's testicles and pushed it through, telling Gourd to pick up the other end. But even then, the two dogs stayed connected. Their barking had lost its ferocity and tears were flowing from their eyes.

"Forget it," Bash decided. "Find a rope and tie the wild dog to a tree. He can go soft in his own time and then they can separate."

Cowbell went over and pulled a kudzu vine off a fence and used that to tie up the wild dog. Bash slapped it a few times, saying, "So you dare to come to Old Kiln, do you?"

He told Inkcap and Cowbell to stand guard, while he, Stargazer and Gourd went back to the meeting, promising to come back and kill the dog once the meeting was over.

As soon as they left, Cowbell asked, "What does dog meat taste like? Have you ever tried it?"

"No."

"I bet it's delicious." He smacked his lips, his mouth watering.

There was a sudden loud noise, and when they looked, the two dogs had separated. The bitch took one look at Inkcap and Cowbell, then turned and ran away. Meanwhile, the wild dog was struggling hard, and the knots in the kudzu vine were loosening a little. It jumped up but couldn't stand. One leg was paralysed, its left eye was bleeding, and the blood was gurgling out like a spring. Inkcap and Cowbell hurried over to tighten the vine and Inkcap heard the wild dog say, "Let me go. Let me go."

"How can I? I want to eat meat."

The wild dog barked low and pitifully, and Inkcap went cold all over.

"I shouldn't have told Bash about you, but how can I let you go now? I don't dare let you go."

"Are you talking to the dog?" Cowbell asked.

"It's talking to me."

"It's talking to you?"

"It's so pitiful."

"It is pitiful."

"So shall we let it go, then?"

"Let it go?"

Inkcap went to untie the kudzu. The wild dog stayed motionless on the ground for a long time, then stood up, shook itself and rubbed its head first against Inkcap's legs, and then against Cowbell's.

"If you want to get away," Inkcap told the dog, "go quickly and never come to Old Kiln again."

The wild dog left, dragging its broken leg behind it. It crashed into a tree and fell but got up again and bounded to the entrance of the village. When it was beside the millstone, it looked back at Inkcap and Cowbell, then walked down the dirt field and disappeared.

"No more meat, then," Cowbell said.

"No more meat."

The two of them took to their heels and ran out of the forest. They didn't go back to the meeting but ran up the slope of Middle Mountain until they reached the white-barked pine at the top.

"When Bash asks," Inkcap said, "we say the wild dog broke the vine and ran away. We can't tell the truth."

"If we don't tell the truth, Bash will beat us up," Cowbell said.

"If he beats us, he beats us, you can't betray us."

"I won't betray us."

FIFTEEN

AFTER BASH TIED UP THE WILD DOG IN THE FOREST, he returned to the meeting, only to find it had just finished. Millstone's elimination method had been approved by the vast majority of attendees. First, it excluded the Four Bad Elements, and then it excluded those who had built new houses and renovated courtyard walls and doors. Every household in the village had small or run-down houses, and those who were able to build new houses and or carry out renovations had to do so for themselves. Also excluded were children under the age of one who were born before the thirtieth day of the fifth lunar month, because, according to the regulations, such children had already been given autumn rations. Then there were those who had sold a pig or whose pig had piglets. All pigs had land allocated for their feed, and anyone like that would definitely either be well-off already or about to become so. Also excluded was anyone who had had a death in the family in the past year because the production team would not collect anything from that family's private plot for three years. Even after all these exclusions, a large number of households remained outside the exclusion circle, and many different opinions were aired about how to decide who should get more and who should get less.

In the end, the Branch Secretary thought things through again and decided that everyone included in the distribution would have their share allocated equally on a per capita basis. However, Soupspoon calculated that the average individual ration would then be less than five *jin* of grain. Millstone suggested that, since five *jin* per person simply wasn't enough, they would have to make some more exclusions. In that regard, some people said they should only include those who were present at the meeting and anyone absent should be excluded. If they couldn't be bothered to come in the first place or had left early, surely that showed they weren't taking the food relief seriously in the first place. Everyone shouted their agreement. Yoyo, who was just about to leave to go to the privy, sat down again and then got up and walked out of the courtyard, calling loudly for Flower Girl.

Flower Girl saw Noisy pushing his grocery cart past the mountain gate and ran to see if there were any thimbles or threads. Just as she fitted a thimble on her thumb, she heard Yoyo shouting for her at the top of her voice, so she ran back into the courtyard, leaving Noisy shouting excitedly in her wake, "I've got more top-notch stuff for you."

Flower Girl ignored him and kept running crazily, her two huge breasts jiggling away. In the end, those present were left on the list, but those missing included Bash, Sparks, Cowbell, Gourd, Stargazer, Pillar, Almost-There, Ever-Obedient and others. Everyone on the list would receive ten *jin*, which meant that an average household would get thirty to forty *jin* in total.

When Bash got back to the courtyard, Happy was clearing away the table and taking it back into the office.

"Is the meeting over?" Bash asked. "I didn't think it would finish before midnight. Why did it break up?"

"Because you ran off, you ran yourself out of a share of the grain."

The Branch Secretary was shrugging his coat onto his shoulders and tucking his pipe up his sleeve, preparatory to leaving.

"Why am I left out then?" Bash demanded. "What is it about me that means I don't get anything?"

"Everyone agreed it. Ask them," the Branch Secretary replied.

"The meeting was still going on," said Potful, who hadn't left yet. "Where did you run off to like that? You don't do things properly yourself, but you still expect the village cadres to come running to your door to give you your share, do you?"

"I went for a crap. Is that OK or am I supposed to suffocate in my own shit? What is this so-called evaluation method? It's a conspiracy. Of course, it's a fucking conspiracy."

"What's your problem? What are you shouting the odds about?" the Branch Secretary said.

"I'm going to sue you."

"Sue me? Pah! If you want to get a share, first you'd better pay the production team the money you owe them. Have you paid them a single fen in commission for all the shoes and tyres you've mended?"

"Have all those carpenters and bricklayers paid up?"

"Some have paid, some are still short. I've made it quite clear that anyone who wants a share of the food relief has to pay up in full first thing tomorrow morning. As for those who don't, even if the rest of the village has given them a share, I will overturn that personally and make sure they don't get a single grain."

As Potful was still trying to argue Bash's case, the Branch Secretary told him, "Drop it, Potful, you're just wasting your breath. What's decided is decided and anyone who doesn't like it can go sue."

Bash calculated to himself that he owed twenty-two yuan and forty-five fen, but he only had ten yuan and fifteen fen to his name. Where could he find so much money? Looking in on the forest at the bottom of Middle Mountain, he found that not only had the wild dog he had tied up gone missing, but so had Inkcap and Cowbell. He exploded into angry curses. He didn't curse anyone by name, but identified a lump of earth in front of him as Branch Secretary Zhu Dagui. He cursed it and stamped on it until it disintegrated. Then he decided a rock was Potful, so he swore at that and kicked it away. He kicked it so hard his shoes went flying. As he walked over to collect them, he kicked barefoot at a clump of dried cypresses, which he made stand in for Inkcap and Cowbell because it was them he now blamed for his absence when the rules were being decided. Pah! Everyone was holding him back. Everyone was plotting against him. Kick! Kick! Kick! Kick! A tree branch caught in his padded cotton jacket and tore a gaping hole in the outside covering. It's just a hole, Bash thought to himself. He didn't bother trying to close it up or tidy the ragged cloth and simply left the cotton padding exposed.

Goodman Wang from the Kiln God Temple stood in his doorway, watching the scene unfold. When Bash came over from the path beside the fence, he said, "What's happened this time, Bash?"

"Take no notice, I'm just a bit irritable."

Goodman sighed and said nothing more. At the mountain gate, Ever-Obedient's wife picked up a broom intending to go and sweep up the dried grass and other detritus from the road to the Kiln God Temple, but Goodman waved her to one side to make way for Bash. The woman ignored him, so when Bash arrived, he bumped into the broom and even barged into her, turning her around.

Bash passed the entrance of Noodle Fish's courtyard just as he had picked up a jar of wine and was about to come out. He stopped in his tracks to protect the jar but some of its contents still spilled out.

"What have you been up to, Bash?" Noodle Fish asked. "Why are your clothes all torn like that?"

Bash's face went pale with anger, but he didn't say a word as he walked over.

"Are you sick?" Noodle Fish persisted.

"You're the one who's sick," Bash snapped back.

"Oh yes? And what's wrong with me?"

But by then, Bash had caught a sniff of something and stopped.

"What's in your jar?" he asked.

"It's some wine I've made. It's fresh out of the fermenting bucket. I'm taking it over for the Branch Secretary to have the first taste."

"Has the baby been born, then?"

"Not yet, but it won't be long."

"The Branch Secretary gave you thirty *jin* of grain, so you're giving him the first batch of the new wine as a mark of filial respect?"

"The Branch Secretary has always taken care of us. Do you think we don't know how to behave in return?"

"I fed Stonebreaker a lot of good lines when I was matchmaking for him, so why don't you give me a drink too?"

"Come into the courtyard and I'll pour you a cup."

"I want some of that first batch."

"I told you, the first batch is going to the Branch Secretary."

"I want the stuff in that jar. What if I pay for it?" Bash said, snatching the jar away from Noodle Fish.

"But... but..." Noodle Fish protested feebly.

Bash pulled out a banknote and threw it on the ground. By chance, a gust of wind picked up the note and stuck it to Noodle Fish's face. He peeled it off and looked at it: it was a two yuan note.

"That wine isn't for sale. Not even for this much."

But Bash was already disappearing into the distance.

Bash didn't go back to his old lodgings but made for the little wooden shack by the highway. There, he downed the jar of wine and fell to the ground, dead drunk. After dinner, Noodle Fish began to feel uneasy about the whole affair and went to give the two yuan back to Bash. When he got to the shack, Bash was lying motionless in a muddy puddle. After Noodle Fish had been shouting at him for ages, he came to and Noodle Fish showed him the money before stuffing it into Bash's pocket. Bash just mumbled drunkenly. Noodle Fish was worried that the money might get lost or that Bash wouldn't remember him returning it, so he closed the shack's door and ran back to the village to find Apricot.

When he got back to the shack with Apricot, he showed her the two yuan he had given back.

"You have to look after him and make sure his head is kept up, so he doesn't suffocate."

Apricot wiped Bash's face and helped him onto the *kang*. Noodle Fish wanted to go, but Apricot wasn't keen.

"You can't leave me here alone," she said. "If you must, then get hold of Inkcap so he can stay here with Bash overnight."

Noodle Fish went back to the village, thinking that Apricot had just been talking for effect, but he still went and found Inkcap.

As soon as Inkcap arrived, Bash was able to sit up, although he had a thumping headache. Apricot made him some thin soup. Inkcap got in quickly with his explanation that he and Cowbell hadn't stayed put and that the wild dog had escaped from the vine rope by itself. Bash swore at him for screwing things up. The real shame of it was that if you ate wild dog meat when you drank Noodle Fish's first-batch wine, you wouldn't get drunk. Inkcap had already heard from Gran that Bash hadn't been given a share of the food relief, so he didn't dare mention the meeting.

To his surprise, Bash himself raised the subject. "They want me to pay more than twenty yuan. What kind of a deal is that if it only gets me ten *jin* of grain?"

"That's not how it works," Apricot protested. "Haven't you owed the production team that money for ages?"

"They've set the commission rate so high. For them, making money is as easy as sweeping up leaves."

"What are you shouting at me for? Setting a high commission rate is a way of restricting business on the side. It's the capitalist tail. Insisting on mending shoes without paying up is ruining your reputation."

"Who wants a reputation? And what reputation do I have anyway? If you've got no money, you've got no money."

They locked horns like this until Apricot was too angry to stay and look after him any more, and she made for the door. Bash snatched up the pillow from the *kang* and hurled it at her, yelling, "Fuck off, then. And don't come back."

When Apricot got home, Potful wasn't there. She looked at her mother's memorial tablet hanging over the cupboard and at the small photograph of her in a bottom corner of it. Tears welled up in her eyes. Mother, oh mother! When you were alive, you protected your daughter from everything. But now, that living person had been transformed into a piece of paper on the plaque, and when Apricot felt wronged, she wept for her. Her tears flowed for a while until she felt an itching sensation on the back of her neck. Looking round, she saw that it was the leaves from a pot of henna on top of the cupboard, brushing against her. Apricot was growing a potted henna plant which, in the winter, she took outside in the morning and brought back inside at night, and it was still in bloom. But she didn't have the heart to pick the flower petals and dye her nails any more. Instead, she went rummaging through the chest and cupboard until she finally located fifty yuan hidden in a cloth bag at the bottom of the chest. She took out twenty-two yuan and was still licking her fingers and counting the notes when her father came back.

When Potful asked what she was doing with the money, Apricot told him she wanted to lend it to Bash so he could pay the production team. Potful exploded with fury. He grabbed the money and slapped Apricot's face. He had already heard the rumours among the villagers and now when he saw Apricot actually stealing the household savings to give to Bash, anger flooded through him.

"What kind of creature is he?" he said. "He's ignorant. He's a rake and a wastrel. He's supposed to be a farmer but he doesn't act like one. He's an ordinary village cur pretending to be a wolf. Why are you fooling around with him? Even if you don't care about losing face, I do."

"What face am I losing by talking to him? Is Bash a rich landlord or part of some anti-revolutionary faction?"

"Stop yelling at me. Do you want to feed all those wagging tongues out there?"

Apricot flung the window open.

"What is it you don't want them to hear?" she demanded. "So what if I go over to his place? Those gossips can choke on their own tongues, and if their lips get too loose, they can get them pounded back into shape with a pestle and mortar."

Potful tried to drag Apricot away from the window, but she wouldn't budge, so he slapped her round the face a few more times and she began to weep and wail.

Naturally, the neighbours knew all about it when things kicked off in Potful's household and they stood in their own courtyards listening to the fun. Half-Stick pretended to want to borrow a sieve from Third Aunt's house.

"Are you using your sieve, Third Aunt? Who's the captain arguing with?"

"I can't tell. I don't hear very well."

"Can you tell if it's Apricot? Why would Apricot be sounding off at her dad?"

"Don't all kids talk back to their parents when they get a bit older?"

"Too true. Too true. You can't keep a grown girl at home forever and if Apricot is fine with Bash, that's all there is to it. Potful is too strict with her."

"Have you fed the pigs yet?" Third Aunt asked suddenly.

"Not yet."

"Then go and do it now and be quick about it. My pigs are all grunting with hunger."

Half-Stick wanted to say more but she could vaguely make out someone coming down the alley, so she held her tongue.

The person approaching was Inkcap. He had hung around a bit after Apricot left the little wooden shack, before returning to the village and finally making his way over to Three Fork Alley. When he heard Apricot's crying, he approached the entrance to Potful's courtyard but stopped, afraid of being noticed. He went into a privy diagonally opposite to listen. The privy was suffocatingly close and smelly, so he lay on top of the wall to be able to breathe. Unfortunately, the earth of the wall was crumbling and it gave way, so he slipped back down into the privy. One foot went straight into the pit and the bottom of his shoe got covered in shit. Even so, he didn't come out and slip quietly back home until Apricot's house was silent.

When Gran saw Inkcap coming back so late, with one shoe covered in shit, she asked him where he had been. Inkcap told her about what had been going on in Potful's household, and she sighed. Inkcap wanted Gran to either try to talk Potful round or to tell him a few home truths about Apricot.

"There's an ox-heart persimmon in the pot if you want it," said Gran.

Every night for dinner, Gran either boiled up some shredded radish with salt and spices for him or heated some water to cook an ox-heart persimmon. But he had no appetite that night and he told her so.

"If you don't want to eat, go to sleep," Gran said.

The two of them went to bed. For half the night, Gran kept tossing and turning at one end of the *kang* while Inkcap did the same at the other, as rats scuttled carelessly along the roof beam above them. Eventually, three of the rats started fighting each other, biting and squeaking, and then there was a thud.

"A rat's fallen off the beam," Inkcap said.

"Yes, a rat's fallen down," Gran said.

"I didn't know we had so many rats in the house."

"It's good to have rats."

"Why's that?"

"If we didn't have rats, we'd starve to death. Now, why are you still awake? If you can't go to sleep, go and have a piss so you don't wet the *kang* again."

Inkcap didn't reply. He vaguely felt as if a rat was standing in front of him.

"Go away, I want to sleep."

"You go away," the rat replied

"This is my house."

"It's my house!" the rat insisted.

"Who are you?" Inkcap asked, feeling that something strange was going on.

"I'm you."

How could it be me? Inkcap thought to himself in annoyance. It's so old and small and it's got a beard.

He reached out and pulled at the rat's beard, pulling one hair, then another. He reached for yet another but he wasn't sure if he had pulled it out or not as he fell asleep.

The next morning, the men of Old Kiln were digging mud in the lotus pond, while the women were hoeing the wheat field in the low ground at the rear of the village. Gran got up early to go out to work but didn't wake Inkcap. In fact, Inkcap did wake up when Gran got up, but he found himself pissing on the *kang* and didn't dare speak up. He used his body warmth to dry out the mattress and it took half the morning before it was done. He was just having a stretch outside the door when Gourd's mother came out of East Bend Lane with her grandson on her shoulder, and pressing right behind her like a mad woman was Flower Girl.

"Quick! Go and tell Awning to get on his bike," Flower Girl shouted at him.

"What's the matter?"

"The kid's got an abacus bead stuck in his throat. We have to get him into town."

At that moment, Gourd's mother's legs gave way as she ran, and she fell to her knees. Flower Girl took the child from her and ran down the alley with the child on her shoulders. Inkcap hurried over to Awning's house but found the gate locked, so he turned and ran back again. He thought that if they couldn't use the bike, he could go to the highway and get Bash to stop a car. But as he hurtled up East Alley, in the distance he saw Gourd's mother and Flower Girl sitting on the ground.

It transpired that, after Gourd and his wife went to work in the morning, Gourd's mother was left in charge of their child. She wanted to get on with her spinning, so she gave the boy a handful of abacus beads to play with. Not knowing it was dangerous, the child tried to eat one of the beads and it got stuck in his throat. Gourd's mother tried to prise the bead out but couldn't get at it. The child was choking and turning blue, so she snatched him up in a panic and set off running, not really knowing where she was going. As Flower Girl ran along East Alley, carrying the child, he called out to her to stop running.

"You'll die if I stop," Flower Girl panted back. "Let's find the Branch Secretary. He'll think of something."

She ran on a few steps, then thought to herself, How come the child's talking?

She held the kid out in front of her and asked, "Did you just talk?"

"No."

"No? What do you mean?"

"The bead's gone."

Flower Girl hurriedly opened the child's mouth.

"Did you swallow it?"

"It got spat out."

Flower Girl couldn't see any bead on the ground at her feet, so she told Gourd's mother to look on the road behind them. Sure enough, there was an abacus bead on the road, which had been dislodged as Flower Girl was running along with the child on her back. The two women sat on the ground and laughed until they couldn't laugh any more.

It felt like there was thunder and lightning in the air and it was about to rain, but not a drop of rain fell. Inkcap watched them all go home and lost interest. Then he thought it was time he went to see Bash, as he didn't know whether he had sobered up and was awake yet.

Bash was fully awake, his torn padded cotton jacket had been patched, and he was wearing his sunglasses. However, he wasn't mending any shoes and didn't even have his tools laid out. Instead, he was pacing back and forth in the room like a caged animal.

As soon as Inkcap arrived, Bash asked him, "Did you come to my place last night?"

"Don't you remember? Me and Apricot helped you onto the *kang*, washed your face and made you some soup. Are you sure you don't remember?"

"I was drunk, wasn't I? So you all just left me?"

"You told Apricot to fuck off."

"I told her to fuck off, and she did?"

"What else was she supposed to do?"

"Whatever I said, she should have stayed."

"Just who do you think you are?"

"I'm her Night-Time Bash."

"Hmm."

"What are you hmm-ing about?"

"Apricot is so beautiful–"

"And is she the only beautiful girl in the world?"

"Her dad's the production team leader."

"That's why I want her."

Inkcap made for the door.

"Stop where you are!" Bash yelled.

Inkcap didn't stop so Bash grabbed hold of him as if he was catching a chicken. Inkcap struggled hard but couldn't get away. Bash shoved his big nose right up against Inkcap's little one, his eyes bulging.

"Have I got it wrong? Eh? Eh?" he yelled. "I got drunk, but she didn't get drunk with me? I was lying here and she just buggered off and left me, the bitch?"

Inkcap was being squeezed so hard he could hardly breathe.

"You're crushing me. I'll be as flat as a dried persimmon. Don't you know that she went back to steal a whole load of money from her dad so you could pay off what you owe? Her dad beat her all night for it? Are you telling me you don't know that?"

Inkcap was telling Bash the truth about Apricot being beaten and cursed at by her father as a warning to Bash that he wasn't in her good books, and he had better stop taking things out on her.

Bash just stood there, staring in amazement.

"Apricot tried to steal money for me, and he beat her really hard?"

"That's right. He beat her all night. He used a stool and broke one of its legs."

The hair on Bash's head seemed to stand on end. He grabbed the stick which he kept over the door to fight off burglars.

"Come with me, Inkcap. Follow me," he called out, setting off for the village as if he were on fire.

It was a windy lunchtime, and the wind was sidelining the sun. The broken shards of porcelain in the alley were all shiny, and the leaves on the trees were fluttering and making the shards shimmer. Bash walked ahead with his stick in hand, and there seemed to be a light coming out of the top of his head, like a cockscomb, like a flame, flicking and flickering, and steam was coming from his mouth and nose, trailing behind him like a flowing white beard. Inkcap had never seen Bash so riled up before. He was more than a little scared, so he ducked behind a tree and ran away. Bash made his way over to Potful's house, but the door was closed. He kicked it open, shouting, "Potful! Potful Zhu! Come out here!"

Potful had just brought a basket of sprouting potatoes up from the cellar and was sitting at the kitchen door, pulling out the sprouts. When he saw Bash kick open the door, he was aghast and stood up.

"What are you doing?" he shouted.

"Did you beat Apricot?"

"What the fuck's it got to do with you if I did?"

"I'm here today to tell you, once and for all, that from now on I'm recognising you as my father-in-law and if–"

"Fuck your 'ifs'. You recognise me as your father-in-law? Get over yourself. Apricot will die of old age as a spinster before she ever goes with you."

"We've already slept together. Are you still going to stop her?"

Potful threw the basket of potatoes at Bash, hitting his body and knocking the sunglasses off his face. They didn't break, so he bent down to pick them up, but, as he did so, he slipped on one of the potatoes. He scrambled up, saying, "Just remember, Potful, you started all this today."

"It wasn't just me. You came over here with a stick to beat me with, didn't you? Go on then, beat me."

Potful was short and stocky, rather like a stone roller, and he had a shovel in his hand. Bash raised his stick but didn't dare swing it at Potful, so he went crazy, swiping at the potatoes on the floor. Potful hit Bash full on the arse with the shovel, making him stumble. As he tried to launch a second blow, Bash picked himself up and ran away.

This incident caused a sensation in Old Kiln but that sensation wasn't about how angry Potful was or how he beat Bash with a shovel. No, the discussion was all about the fact that Bash and Apricot were on such good terms and that Bash had personally said that he had already slept with Apricot. How dare a crook like Bash sleep with Apricot? And just how brainless was Apricot? A flower bud can only bloom once, so why had she let herself be plucked by someone like Bash?

For the next three days, Potful didn't go outside but just slept. So no one rang the work bell, and the crows dripped a thin line of white shit across it. Bash, on the other hand, went to see Sprout and asked her why she couldn't get along with him. Sprout was the leader of the women's team.

"Have I even talked to you in all these years?" she asked him. "If you want to have a quarrel, I simply haven't got the time."

"Then why did you say at the food relief evaluation meeting that I shouldn't get a share?"

"Who told you that?"

"Walls have ears. Did you say it or not?"

"I didn't. The last thing I like doing is messing around with what's right and what's wrong. But since you've asked me, go and speak to Sparks."

"So it was Sparks who originally said it, was it?"

"I didn't say that. I just told you to go and ask him."

Bash went off to look for Sparks who he found trying and failing to light a fire in his house. The smoke was making tears run down his face.

When he saw Bash coming, Sparks said, "I heard that Potful broke your leg. How come you're still running around?"

"Sparks, was it you who first said at the food relief meeting that I shouldn't get a share? Did you say that?"

"I said it. So what? Big Root said that you live well and have meat to eat, and I said that if you had meat to eat, why would you be worried about a little grain."

Bash turned on his heel to leave.

"Can you light my fire for me?" Sparks asked.

"Forget that, but I am going to set that fucker on fire!" Bash roared.

He went over to Big Root's house where Big Root was using the threshing roller in front of his gate and asking his son to help turn the grain stalks. The boy's face was blue from the cold, and he really didn't want to help, so Big Root was scolding him. Although his son was turning the stalks, he wasn't doing a very neat job and Big Root got so angry he jumped off the roller and began to beat him.

"When did you ever see me eating meat?" Bash said.

"What?" Big Root replied. "What's going on? It's nothing to do with me if you eat meat or not."

"If it's nothing to do with you, why did you say at the food relief meeting that I had meat to eat and shouldn't get a share?"

"Did I say that?"

"Yes, you did. How dare you talk nonsense and then deny it, you old prick."

"My dear nephew, if you have something to say, please don't hold back. Let me think, did I say that? Oh, I know. I said I heard Half-Stick say she saw you eating meat. That's right. Half-Stick told everyone in the village. Now, what do you want me for?"

"Did Half-Stick really say that?" Bash asked.

"Yes, she did. If you want to see her, go look for her. By the way, is your *kang* mat rotten? If it is, you can bring it here and I'll fix it for you. Dog's Bollocks! Dog's Bollocks! Where the fuck are you?"

Big Root yelled for his son, who was now in the courtyard. Big Root rushed in as if to grab his son by the ears and drag him out but, instead, he slammed the door as soon as he was through it. Bash gave the gate a kick and then went on to Baldy Jin's house.

Baldy Jin wasn't there, and Half-Stick was chasing a chicken to feel up its backside to see if it was about to lay any eggs. The chicken flew up onto the courtyard wall and then out of the courtyard altogether. Half-Stick ran out after it, coming face to face with Bash, who had one foot on the chicken's tail, holding it down.

"Aiya!" she exclaimed. "How did you know I was chasing that chicken? Quickly, have a feel up its arse to see if there are any eggs."

Bash lifted his foot and let the chicken go, saying, "I'll feel up your arse!"

"What are you saying?" Half-Stick said with a grin. "In broad daylight too!"

"What were you talking about? When did you ever see me eating meat?"

"You? Eat meat?" Half-Stick was still grinning. "Whose meat do you want to eat? You be careful or Baldy Jin will beat you up."

Bash was still looking daggers. "You said at the food relief meeting that I shouldn't get a share."

"So? You ran off when they were allocating the rations and you ran so well, you ran yourself out of a share. Baldy Jin saw you at it, running off so fast and never coming back. You did us out of a share too."

"All I asked you was when did you ever see me eating meat?"

"How could I have seen you when you eat your meat behind closed doors?"

"So did you tell everyone that I eat meat?"

"Who said I did?"

"It was Big Root, wasn't it," Bash said. "You told Big Root."

"I didn't say you eat meat, I said you eat tofu. That's what Sprout told me herself. But you're not stupid, so you came looking for me, not Sprout. Did you think I'd be easy to bully because I come from Laoshangou?"

"Who's bullying you? Why am I being falsely accused of bullying you, for no good reason? If you're not getting a share, you're not getting a share and that's all there is to it. But anyone who says I eat meat had better be sure that it's their fucking bones I'll be gnawing!"

He was about to leave but Half-Stick held him back, saying that they needed to see Sprout together to confirm that it was Sprout who had told her about him eating tofu. Half-Stick dragged Bash by his lapels all the way back over to Sprout's house, jabbering away the entire time.

"Yes, I said it," Sprout confirmed. "I said you eat tofu. What do you have to say about it?"

"Sure," Bash replied, "when it comes to eating tofu, I ate twenty *jin* of it. What about it?"

"Well then, why have you come chasing after me about eating tofu? Are you saying I'm talking nonsense now? Is that why you've come looking for me?"

"I want to know why I didn't get a share of the food relief."

"What's that got to do with me? I'm only interested in the question of you eating tofu or not."

"Of course you've eaten tofu," Half-Stick broke in. "You ate twenty *jin* of it and it almost killed you, or is that still a secret? What do you want from me?"

"What do you want from me?" the two women shouted in unison.

"What the fuck's going on here? It's obvious I'm being cheated out of a share of the food relief, but no one's taking responsibility for it."

He felt an itch on his nose and when he put his hand up to it, he discovered a boil on its tip. By that evening, the corners of his mouth had sores on them, and his eyes were red-rimmed and bloodshot. He ran out alone into the alleyway and howled like a wolf.

Every household in the village could hear the howling. Gran was sitting on the *kang* making papercut flowers, muttering about how Bash was getting weirder and weirder.

"Gran," Inkcap said, "do you think he is a good person?"

"How can you tell whether a person is good or bad?" Gran replied. "Everything else in the world is easy to recognise, except for these lumps of flesh we call people."

As for how Bash treated Apricot, she continued, it was fine to start with when he fed her steamed buns, but not so good when he kept stuffing them in her mouth when she was full. He was extremely capricious, and you never knew which was his true face. Whoever it was who told him about Potful beating Apricot, they succeeded in setting the whole village on edge.

"It was me who told him," Inkcap admitted.

"You told him? Do you think a pile of shit doesn't stink so you have to stir it up with a stick?"

She got crosser and crosser as she spoke, and she pinched Inkcap's lips.

"It must be because your mother was such a nosey gossip that you're so cross-grained and contentious."

Inkcap kept trying to convince her that all he had wanted to do was warn Bash off.

"You can reason with Bash," Gran said, "but you can't intimidate him. What did you think you were doing?"

When she left for work the next day, she locked Inkcap in the house and kept him there for several days. In the end, Bash sent Cowbell with a message for Inkcap telling him to come over to his place. Cowbell lay down under the back window to deliver the message and Inkcap crawled out of the same window and made his way to the little wooden shack.

The door of the shack was locked. Inkcap was confused. Why would Bash call him over and not be there himself? As he turned to leave, he heard a cat saying, "Fantastic! Fantastic!" At the same time, there was a noise like an ox ploughing a paddy field. He peered in through a crack in the door and saw four bare feet sticking out from under the quilt on the *kang*. One pair was pointing up and the other was pointing down, and the toes were all tensed. He didn't quite make out what was going on for a moment, but the cat was underneath the *kang* pulling hard on the overhanging quilt with its claws until it pulled it right off. The two intertwined naked bodies on the *kang* were Bash and Apricot.

Inkcap's brain was in turmoil. He understood exactly what was going on, but he stood there, rooted to the spot, unable to drag himself away. Bash's buttocks were raised like a pestle pounding a mortar and he was making a sound like gnashing teeth, while Apricot screamed as if she was being murdered. Her screams got louder and louder until, suddenly, the middle of the *kang* collapsed, and her body disappeared leaving her legs sticking up in the air. At that point, Inkcap turned and fled. He ran past the little wooden shack, skirted the Zhen River Pagoda and went to sit on a rock beside the river.

Inkcap had never experienced anything like this before. He remembered what Cowbell had said about how unlucky it was for anyone who encountered such a situation, and that made him angry. The thornback fish in the river were groaning out their own name again, and the Zhen River Pagoda seemed to be leaning at such an alarming angle, it was a wonder it hadn't toppled over. Then, suddenly, the little wooden shack collapsed.

I'm not going to rescue anyone either, Inkcap told himself.

He didn't know how long after it was, but he found himself listening to the door of the shack creaking open and Bash shouting his name: "Inkcap! Inkcap!" He didn't reply until Bash appeared from behind the pagoda and called him over. He followed Bash back to the wooden shack, which was in a terrible state. He saw Apricot walking towards the village. She was normally very steady on her feet, but now she was weaving all over the place. The cat was following on behind. The bedding on the *kang* was rolled up but there was a gaping hole in the middle of it. He looked at the door again, wondering how it could have been locked on the outside when there were people inside, but then he realised that there was a big crack in it so you could close it from the inside and reach through to lock it on the outside.

"Did you see it all?" Bash asked him.

"All what?"

"If you saw it, you saw it. Are you going to tell the rest of the village?"

"No."

"Well, then?"

"There's no point in me worrying over what kind of people you and

Apricot are, and there was no point in me breaking off the branches of the elm tree outside your courtyard wall."

"So that was you, was it?"

"Yes, it was me. Are you going to beat me up?"

"I'm going to buy you a bowl of steamed rice."

Inkcap couldn't believe his good fortune.

"You're going to give me some steamed rice?" he exclaimed, then watched as Bash did indeed bring over a porcelain dish a little under half full of rice grains.

Bash poured all the rice into an earthenware basin, rinsed it with some water, poured it into a cooking pot and began to light the stove. Once Inkcap had made sure that it really was rice, the thought of it made him forget all his troubles and humiliations. He went straight to the back of the room to collect a bundle of dried stalks and helped Bash feed the fire.

"If there's anything in this room you want, take it," Bash said.

Inkcap couldn't believe his ears.

"If you give me that bundle of maize silks, I can make fuses out of them."

"Anything else?"

"What's up with you? Why are you being so nice to me?"

"I owe you for tipping me off."

Plucking up courage, Inkcap said, "I want your sunglasses."

"You can fuck right off with that. You can't have them. I can't sleep at night if I'm not wearing them."

"Then give me that pig's tail."

"You can't have that either. We're going to be eating it in a while."

"Then there's nothing else I want."

Even so, he took a pencil that was lying on the table and put it in his pocket. It was the pencil Bash used to draw the outline of his customer's feet on the leather when he was mending shoes.

The steamed rice was ready, but there was only one bowl in the little wooden shack. Inkcap got a water ladle and told Bash to put the rice in that. But Bash told him not to be in such a rush. He filled the one rice bowl with all the rice, then chopped up the pig's tail that was hanging on the back of the door, breaking it down into small pieces. He rendered off some of the fat in a wok then added the rice to stir fry the whole lot together.

"If you're going to eat," Bash said, "eat well!"

The two polished off the fried rice. Inkcap ate sitting on the bench. His legs were too short, and his feet couldn't touch the ground. He ate so much that he could move his head but not his body. At first, he couldn't get off the bench, but he eventually managed to slide down from it and, of his own accord, went to fetch water from the river to wash the pot. He retched as if about to throw up and quickly covered his mouth with his hand.

"Have you finished, then?" Bash asked.

"Don't talk to me, or I'll throw up."

"There's no bet this time. If you need to throw up, just do it."

"I hate throwing up."

Inkcap covered his mouth again and stopped talking.

SIXTEEN

INKCAP KEPT GOING without throwing up even a single grain of rice. As he walked back to the village, the sun fell below the ridge of Cowbell's house and sat itself under the screen at the entrance to Awning's courtyard. After lunch, everyone started feeding their pigs. The pig food was made of bean leaves and bran soaked in swill. After taking a few mouthfuls, the pig would look up at its owner standing by the wall of the pigsty. The owner would pinch three fingers worth of bran from a gourd ladle they were holding and scatter it in the trough. The pig would take a few mouthfuls and lift its head again. The owner would hit the pig on the head with his mash stick and scold it: "You're such a greedy sow!" It was like scolding a wife or a child, both annoyed and pitying. Finally, they would sprinkle all the bran into the trough to encourage the pig to gain weight faster.

Barndoor actually jumped into his pigsty, and ran his hand along the animal's spine, which was sticking out, sharp as a knife. "Why don't you put on weight?" he exclaimed.

Stargazer was cleaning out another pigsty with a shovel. "Well, Barndoor," he observed, "people these days don't have a conscience, so why would a pig show any over how it eats?"

"How come Baldy Jin's pig is growing so fast?" Barndoor asked. "It was bought in on the same day as mine, but it's already a head bigger."

"It's got a good frame to build on," Stargazer pointed out. "The ones we bought in are both pimply creatures. You need to check the mothers when you buy piglets. If we rear pigs again next year, we'll go into Luozhen to buy them. Almost-There's piglets may be cheaper, but he won't sell them to us."

Awning's wife was combing her pig's hair, but because she refused to feed it bran, it had grown a velvety red undercoat.

"Did you hear that Stonebreaker has sold his pig?" Awning's wife asked Stargazer.

"If he didn't, how would he be able to afford a baby?" Stargazer replied.

"I thought he was going to kill it to feed the guests after the baby's born," Barndoor said.

"That's wild talk. How could he afford to?" Awning's wife said as she turned to Stargazer. "What grade did he sell it at?"

"Third grade," Stargazer replied, "but it almost failed the examination. Noodle Fish had to do a lot of fast talking with that lot at the purchasing station, and they only reluctantly agreed. The trouble was it shat a hill and pissed a lake when it was being weighed and it missed the weight division by five or six *jin*."

"It really wasn't being very cooperative, was it?" Awning's wife said.

Inkcap arrived on the scene.

"Your pig must be really warm wearing that red velvet coat," he said mischievously.

Awning's wife shot him a look, too angry to reply.

"You watch your mouth, Inkcap," Barndoor said sternly.

"This pig's a lot smarter than you!" said Awning's wife, finding her voice. "Just look how tatty and ripped that padded jacket of yours is. Are you off to Bash's place again?"

"Why would I be?"

"When tadpoles follow big fish, they have to be careful not to get left behind in the wake."

"Bash is doing just fine."

The pig stopped eating again. At a casual glance, it seemed to be listening to Inkcap. Awning's wife beat it with her mash stick saying, "OK, don't eat for me, then. That's just great if you won't fucking eat for me."

Inkcap wrinkled his nose as he smelt something. Hah! Yes, it was that smell again.

"Stop it! Stop wrinkling your nose at me," Awning's wife complained.

Inkcap didn't let on he had smelt the smell again and just went home.

As Inkcap was leaving, some bad news reached the pig feeders: Stonebreaker's wife was having a difficult labour.

It started with Noodle Fish's wife dragging Gran down the alley. Gran had bound feet and although they had later been unwrapped, they were deformed and had calluses, so she couldn't run fast no matter how hard she tried.

As Ever-Obedient passed by carrying water from the spring, he called out, "Hey, Granny Silkworm, have you been called up to the front line?"

As soon as the words were out, he remembered what had happened with Inkcap's grandfather in the Autumn Campaign of 1947. Back then, the reeds and the mulberry grass on the river embankment were in bloom and the wind was blowing the flowers across the Zhou River in a layer of red mist. A Kuomintang troop passed through the village, and it was then that Inkcap's grandfather had been pressganged into their army. He had been dragging Gran down ever since.

Ever-Obedient changed the expression he had used to, "Have the wolves got in?"

Gran really hadn't minded Ever-Obedient's impetuous turn of phrase and just said, "Quick. Put me on your back and carry me to Stonebreaker's house, fast as you can. His wife's having a difficult labour."

Ever-Obedient put down his water buckets and carried Gran at a run to Stonebreaker's house. By the time he got back, the news was all round the village.

When they heard the news, the people feeding their pigs stopped feeding them and those washing their pots and pans stopped washing their pots and pans. They all ran clattering down the alley towards Stonebreaker's house. When he'd finished eating, Useless sneaked into the east building where he slept and closed the door. He always felt uncomfortable and on edge after meals, and the only remedy was to have a quiet wank. He knew it was bad for his health, but he couldn't control himself. As soon as he looked at the woman in the New Year picture pasted on the wall, he shot his load.

Out in the yard, his mother called out, "Stonebreaker's wife is giving birth, Useless. Are you coming?"

"No," he shouted through the window, then whispered to himself, "I didn't have anything to do with it, so why should I go?"

"I hear it's a difficult birth," his mother shouted back.

"Ah!" Useless said, but by the time he opened the door, his mother was already out of the courtyard. He stood at the gate, thinking to himself that Stonebreaker was two years older than him, and his wife was already giving birth. He hadn't even settled on a potential partner yet, so what did it matter to him if it was a difficult birth? He grinned to himself, then saw the Branch Secretary coming over.

"Hey, Useless!" the Branch Secretary shouted. "The characters in the slogan on the rear gable wall of Palace's house aren't properly finished off. Why haven't you done something about it?"

"That's because the wall was collapsing," Useless replied. "I told him to fix it first, but he hasn't done anything yet."

"Isn't he part of this village? Why hasn't he fixed it up?"

"The first time I told him to do it, he said he couldn't because of the militia training."

"How long can a job like that take? He seems to have time to play chess all night with Pockmark."

"Exactly. When I tried again with him, he said it would cost money and he didn't have any."

"How much does some water from the spring and some mud from the ground cost?"

"Exactly."

"You just tell him from me that he must fix it tomorrow and stop tarnishing the image of Old Kiln."

Awning's wife ran down the alley and saw the Branch Secretary. She stopped and said, "What's the problem, Branch Secretary? Why does everyone have such difficulty having a baby in Old Kiln?"

"Why don't you give your hair a comb?" the Branch Secretary replied. "All you young people have hair like a hen roost!"

Awning's wife spat in her hands and used them to flatten her hair.

"Now, what was that you just said?" the Branch Secretary asked.

"First Stonebreaker's wife started saying 'The baby's coming, the baby's coming!' and it didn't come. Then, a couple of weeks later she said that the melon stalk would drop off when the melon was ripe and the baby would be born when it was ready. And now she's having a difficult labour."

"Is that so?" the Branch Secretary said, looking stern.

"Don't you know about this?" Awning's wife asked in amazement. "How can you not know about something like this?"

"I agree, it's ridiculous that no one came and told me about such an important matter."

The two of them set off for Stonebreaker's house.

There were a lot of people standing in the courtyard of Noodle Fish's house. Stonebreaker's wife's room was in the western annex. Its door was closed, and Stonebreaker was standing outside. Inside the room, his wife was screaming like a stuck pig. She kept cursing Stonebreaker, saying that it was his fault she was suffering like this.

"I want to die, Stonebreaker! You're going to suffer in Hell for hurting me like this, Stonebreaker."

Stonebreaker stood facing the room roaring, "What the fuck are you yelling about? Do you think you're the only wife who's ever given birth?"

Gran came out. "She's in pain," she said. "What does it matter if she curses a bit? What are you yelling about anyway?"

Some of the others dragged Stonebreaker away and out of the courtyard.

"The Branch Secretary is here! The Branch Secretary is here!" someone called from outside the courtyard.

"The Branch Secretary can't solve this problem," Baldy Jin said from inside the courtyard.

"The Branch Secretary's here!" Pockmark called out. "Can the baby come out to say hello?"

Sprout punched Pockmark on the back.

"Let's be off," Pockmark went on, unabashed. "She may be having a baby but she's not giving us a grandchild!"

The Branch Secretary came into the courtyard, and Noodle Fish leapt up to get his cigarette box, shouting to Inkcap to get his fuse. No reply came from Inkcap, but the Branch Secretary brushed it aside with a wave of his hand. Then he saw Third Aunt coming out of the kitchen with a basin of water to take over to the annex.

"Didn't I hear that the foetus is in the right position? Why's she still having such difficulty?" he asked.

"That's right," Third Aunt said. "I came over when her belly first began to hurt and everything looked fine. But when her waters broke, the first thing to come out was a hand, so I immediately asked Granny Silkworm to come over."

"Why don't you take her into town?" the Branch Secretary said, by which he meant going to the township health centre for a caesarean section. Seven or eight children in Old Kiln had already been delivered that way, to the point where people from Xichuan and Dongchuan Village in Xiahewan were openly rude about the wives of Old Kiln who had scars across their bellies.

"If it can come out the natural way, it should come out the natural way," Third Aunt said. "I don't think things will get to the point of it not coming out, but the mother's going to suffer a bit."

"If things don't work out, send someone to tell me and I will arrange for the flat-bed barrow to be ready to take them to town," the Branch Secretary instructed. Then he turned to the crowd in the yard and said, "It is good that everyone cares, and it's fine to come and have a look, but you mustn't all crowd in the courtyard. This afternoon, everyone who is building the eighteen-acre weir at the embankment will go back to work on it. Sparks! You and Winterborn get the barrow ready, just in case."

"And if we don't go to work?" Spark said.

"Do you want the work points?" the Branch Secretary asked pointedly in return.

"Let's go, let's all go," said Baldy Jin. "There's no point in us being here."

"Oh no?" Pockmark broke in. "I've been listening all the time and didn't I hear Stonebreaker's wife cursing me out."

"And since when has your mouth been pure as driven snow?" Sprout retorted.

Everyone laughed, and almost all the men left the courtyard. The women were still chattering away under the peach tree in the yard, and Palace's wife was breaking off a peach branch. She snapped it into small sections, tucked one section inside her top and did the same for all the other women there.

"Peach wood sticks can ward off evil spirits," she said. "You won't have any trouble giving birth in future."

She gave a stick to Half-Stick, but she didn't want it.

"Life can be really scary," Sparks' wife said. "It's so difficult to give birth now. How have you ever seen it so difficult before? Stonebreaker's mother gave birth to Stonebreaker and his three brothers, and it was as easy as taking a dump."

"Why is your man called 'Sparks'?" Palace's wife asked.

"It's because his mother was cooking at the stove when she gave birth to the baby. She saw to the baby and kept on cooking the food."

They all chuckled and left the courtyard in ones and twos.

As Noodle Fish escorted the Branch Secretary out, the Secretary said to him, "Get the wine ready. All the villagers will come and drink the baby's health when it's born. Are there any dishes to go with the wine?"

"I'll make up some pickled cabbage and some seasoned radish," Noodle Fish said.

"Just pickled cabbage and seasoned radish? I can tell you aren't in charge of the food here! Cook up some tofu too. Do you have money? If not, I'll lend it to you."

The Branch Secretary gave Noodle Fish five yuan. The people outside the courtyard saw him do it and said to each other, "Right! Let's come and drink the wine and eat that tofu tonight!"

Noodle Fish saw that time was already getting on, so he put the five yuan in the crown of his hat and went to Kaihe's place to buy the tofu. On his way back, he ran past Millstone's house and remembered that Millstone had an Eight Immortals table, so he went in and borrowed it. He carried the table on his head and the basket of tofu in his hands. As soon as he entered the courtyard, he saw his wife crying under the peach tree.

"As long as the mother is well, there's no need to cry," Third Aunt comforted her. "Hurry up and boil some water to make some eggs for the new mother."

Noodle Fish's wife nodded and went over to the house, still crying, to pick up the eggs, but she ignored Noodle Fish. He felt something was wrong and put down the table.

"What's the matter?" he asked Third Aunt.

"Oh, the baby was born, but it wasn't breathing."

Noodle Fish stumbled and almost dropped the basket of tofu.

"Is it dead?"

"Not so loud!" Third Aunt chided him. "It was a blue baby and didn't even cry when I slapped its buttocks. I thought the amniotic fluid had choked it, so I cleared out its mouth. Gran's got it under a cover now."

Noodle Fish looked towards the kitchen, but Third Aunt wouldn't let him go.

According to the custom of Old Kiln, they did not follow the practice of nearby villages of throwing stillborn babies into a piss bucket or wrapping them in a straw sack and throwing them onto the river strand. Instead, the villagers believed that the child was possessed by a ghost and should be put under a wicker cover with a lit fire. Gran had used this method in the past, and, while most of the babies died, there were two or three times when they actually came back to life. Noodle Fish, Third Aunt, Flower Girl and Sprout stopped talking and looked at the kitchen door to see if the baby was crying. The sky was dark but not completely black and the wind still swept low across the ground, but the straw on the roofs of the buildings in the courtyard was still swaying rhythmically, and the birds from the top of Middle Mountain flew fluttering like leaves in the sky above Old Kiln Temple. They fanned out over the village, passing over the courtyard of Noodle Fish's house, slanting down to land on the roof, but then flying away.

Gran came out of the kitchen with a pale face and whispered, "It's hopeless, Noodle Fish. This baby should never have come to your house. When it's dark, wrap it in a bundle of straw and take it away."

Tears flowed silently down Noodle Fish's cheeks. His wife took an egg from the cupboard, but her legs were too weak to walk on, and she sat back down on the doorstep of the main room.

"Don't let Noodle Fish go," Third Aunt said. "I'll go with Flower Girl."

They walked over to a corner of the courtyard to collect some straw, then went into the kitchen to wrap up the baby. As they went out of the courtyard gate, Third Aunt called across to Noodle Fish's wife, "As long as the mother is all right, do we have to worry about her not being able to have another baby? After all, doesn't every gourd vine have a few barren flowers?"

People began to arrive in the alley. They came to drink fermented wine and eat tofu, radish and vegetables. As soon as they found out that the baby had miscarried, they went on past the gate, but Noodle Fish stopped them, saying, "I made this wine for everyone, and we can't drink it all here. Let me give you some to take home and drink there."

Everyone took a small porcelain jar of wine, saying that it didn't really seem right to be drinking it. They still took it away with them, though.

The people who took the wine away made it known to others that the baby had miscarried, and this deterred many from wanting to go on to visit. The Branch Secretary soon learned about the situation and told

Soupspoon, "You go door to door and tell everyone to collect some wine. The baby may have miscarried, but everyone should still show concern for it. The amount of wine that gets taken away is a reflection of the spirit of Old Kiln."

As a result, everyone went to collect a small porcelain jar, and Noodle Fish made sure they all got some. The bottom of the jar was clearly visible when he tapped the rim with a wooden ladle.

"It's gone. It's all gone," he said. But in the end, a last half ladleful was scooped out. Noodle Fish himself drank it and immediately started choking. Man and jar fell to the ground together.

None of the women wanted to drink their household's share of the wine, so the men suggested going to Sparks' house. His wife enjoyed the noise and excitement, and Sparks enjoyed his wine. After drinking for a while, the men got a little over-excited. They almost forgot about the death of Stonebreaker's baby and started shouting and fighting. It was Awning who was the first to suggest drinking over at Sparks' house. He picked up a jar and took a swig while shouting, "Palace, Millstone, Stargazer, Baldy Jin, you lot bring the wine over to Sparks' place!"

As Millstone left, his wife chased after him, shouting, "Get a communal hotpot going. Don't just booze yourselves stupid until you start chucking up blood. And throw in a radish for Millstone to soak up the wine so he doesn't end up with cats scratching out his stomach lining."

When Baldy Jin came out, Half-Stick followed him.

"Where do you think you're going?" Baldy Jin asked. "You're not telling me someone's wife is having a drinking party?"

"Do you think only men have mouths to fill? If none of the women of Old Kiln drink wine, then I'll start the tradition right here."

Baldy Jin walked on, and Half-Stick followed him. He gave her a shove and she shoved him back. In the end, there was nothing for it but for him to go back home and fetch out a bowl of wine for Half-Stick.

"Drink up, then," he said grudgingly.

Instead of drinking, Half-Stick leaned against the door and turned to Awning.

"Hey, Awning. How many *liang* of wine can you drink at a sitting?"

"How many *liang*? How many *jin* more like!"

"All right then. You come round after I've made my wine next year, and we'll see who can out-drink who."

"Won't you be having a child next year?" Stargazer asked.

"And how's that going to stop me making my wine? What kind of kid do you think I'm going to have, a little Baldy Jin?"

Everyone laughed and Baldy Jin looked crestfallen. He pushed his wife back through the courtyard gates and pulled them shut on her.

As the four men walked past the gate of Almost-There's house, Awning shouted, "Hey, Almost-There! Bring your wine over to Sparks' house for a party."

The light in Almost-There's window went out, and there was total silence.

"There's no point shouting," Baldy Jin said. "That skinflint won't join in. He's keeping his wine for the New Year."

In the end, more than twenty people made their way to Sparks' house and each of them poured the wine they had brought into a big porcelain bowl. It was settled that no one could hold any back, and they would drink it all that evening. They were not allowed to leave until it was all gone. Inkcap came over as soon as he heard the news, bringing his rope fuse with him, of course.

"You run faster than anyone else in the village if there's a whiff of food in the air," Sparks' wife commented.

She set him to washing radishes while she shredded two plates of radish and soaked two plates of pickled cabbage in brine.

As soon as Baldy Jin arrived, he asked, "Did you bring any wine, Inkcap?"

"I don't drink."

"You may not, but other people do. Go and get your household's wine."

Inkcap had no option but to do as he was told. On the way back, he decided to try some of the wine for himself. Of course, he wasn't used to it, and after two mouthfuls, his stomach was on fire. He cursed Baldy Jin and anyone else who was going to drink his family's wine that night, calling them pigs and dogs. When he'd finished cursing, he still wasn't satisfied, so he spat into the wine jar.

The wine lasted until the cock crowed three times, and the smell of it filled the air. The three pigeons that lived in a nest in the elm tree outside the courtyard kept flying up and down restlessly. Inkcap was not allowed to drink at the table. He always had to stand by and refill cups as the need arose. He was also responsible for monitoring who had not finished the wine in their cup and who was taking the wine into their mouth then secretly spitting it out under their feet. Whoever he exposed would automatically curse Inkcap for being a blind little bastard.

"I'm just doing what Uncle Awning told me to," was Inkcap's invariable response.

Awning himself was already tongue-tied with drink, but he still pointed at Baldy Jin, ordering him to drink up. Suddenly, he stuttered out, "Hey! Meilibadoushim, keburangshim!"

"What are you talking about?" Baldy Jin asked.

"You're still in the militia, aren't you? That's Russian."

"Well, sir, if the Soviets do invade, I'm sure they'll be terrified when they hear that."

Everyone laughed and Sparks asked, "Why haven't you been at the training recently, Awning?"

"What training? The training's tomorrow."

"Well, then. When are you going to get the gun so we can go hunting on South Mountain? If we don't bag any wild boar or gazelle, we might still get some pheasants."

"Stop teasing him, Sparks," Millstone said. "There are strict rules about using the gun and we don't want Awning to make any kind of mistake."

"Mistake? What mistake? I'm Awning and I don't make mistakes. Tell Baldy Jin to drink up. If he doesn't, I'll dismiss him. Militia regulations."

"Drink up! Drink up!" Baldy Jin shouted. "I don't usually get to drink when I want to. Let's the two of us play guess-fingers."

"If you want," Awning replied, "but put your hat on so I don't have to look at your bald head."

Baldy Jin lost his temper and wouldn't drink. Then Millstone challenged him, and, still furious, he lost five rounds in a row. He deliberately made his hand shake when he was holding his wine cup. Inkcap glared at him and asked if he was trying to shake the wine out of his cup.

Baldy Jin hurriedly changed the subject: "Why are the pigeons making such a din outside? Is there an eagle?"

"The smell of the wine is keeping them awake," Inkcap said.

"I think it's you who's been sniffing the wine," Baldy Jin said. "Come on, drink this cup for me."

Inkcap went to do as he was asked.

"No substitutions," Awning shouted. He tried to jump up and snatch the cup from Inkcap's hand, but he suddenly retched and vomited all over the boy. Inkcap screamed, then looked at Stargazer and Sparks, begging them to hurry up and help him take Awning out into the yard to throw up again.

"No need, no need," Awning said. "How could such a small amount of wine ever make me drunk enough for that?"

As he walked to the door, he turned around and stared at Inkcap. Inkcap thought he must have done something wrong and hurriedly said, "I don't think you're drunk."

Awning didn't respond, but what he eventually stuttered out was, "Why… why… why haven't we seen Bash? Why hasn't Bash brought any wine?"

Sparks and Millstone realised that he had a point. They hadn't seen Bash or his wine all night.

"He lives alone, doesn't he? I expect he didn't hear the news out in that wooden shack," Millstone said. "Inkcap, you're always over there. Didn't you tell him?"

Inkcap gave a stifled yell, realising he had neglected his duty.

"Hurry up and ask him to pick up the wine at Stonebreaker's house," Sparks said. "He's the last person we should have forgotten."

Inkcap gave everyone a light again, then left, swinging his fuse to keep it alight.

Seven or eight dogs were standing around outside the courtyard, drawn there by the smell of the wine.

"Off you go. Off you go," Inkcap ordered. "That lot are hardened drinkers and they're not going to throw up for you, however drunk they get."

He told Ever-Obedient's family dog to go with him. It didn't really want to, and it muttered and grumbled all the way.

As soon as Awning went into the courtyard, he decided he wanted to go for a piss, but he stumbled over the laundry stone and vomited all over it. Then Millstone came out to throw up too.

"You really know how to make a mess, don't you!" Sparks shouted at them from inside the room. "Why are you throwing it up when you just got it safely in your bellies?"

He pushed open the door of the main room, so a patch of white light spilled out.

"Big Root! Big Root! Can you lay out a fresh mat in the doorway?"

With a gurgling sound, a spray of vomit spurted from his mouth. The dogs outside the courtyard pushed the gate open and squeezed in through it.

When Inkcap reached the little wooden shack on the highway, he found the door locked. As it was still daytime, he reckoned that Bash must have locked himself inside with Apricot. He banged on the door and shouted, but nothing stirred. Peering in through the crack in the door, he found it was too dark to see, but there was still no movement.

The thornback fish in the river were calling out their name again: "Ang-er-chi—Ang-er-chi..."

PART TWO
SPRING

春

SEVENTEEN

Moss had grown all over the stone lion at the south entrance of the village, so it was effectively dressed in a coat of green and brown. Throughout the winter, it was clothed entirely in black, with patches of white spots. Now, the moss had come back to life and the lion had changed into new clothes, but Bash had still not returned.

As soon as Bash left, he flew like a bird. By the end of the twelfth lunar month, and even after the New Year was over, there was still no news. On New Year's Eve and on the fifteenth day of the first lunar month, in the cemetery at the base of Middle Mountain, there were lights in front of every grave mound, but Bash's mother's grave was in darkness.

Inkcap and Cowbell sat under the stone lion and looked up. The wind was blowing a single cloud across the sky, leaving no trace behind it until it finally disappeared over Yijia Ridge.

"Will Bash starve to death out there?" Inkcap asked.

"Impossible," Cowbell replied. "He might not have any food stamps or letters of introduction, but he's not the kind of person to sit around drowning in his own piss if he's in trouble."

"Will he be arrested as a fugitive?"

"Oh, if he's got his wits about him, he'll make for Xinjiang."

Inkcap didn't know about Xinjiang, but Cowbell did. He had heard from people in Xiahewan that Xinjiang was vast and sparsely populated, and fugitives went there to pick cotton. North to south, with vast areas of cotton to be picked, the area was guarded by only a single watchdog lying in the dust.

The day was getting warmer, and it was already time for the noon break. The women ran back home to cook, and the chimneys in all the houses started smoking away. The plumes of smoke coalesced above the village, obscuring the tree canopies so that their trunks seemed to have become supporting pillars for the sky, which was now very close to the ground. The men relaxed, their limp bodies suddenly appeared shorter, and none of them went home. They gathered at the entrance of Three Fork Alley to gossip. They were sharper-tongued than the women, mocking anyone worse off than themselves and hating those who appeared to have a better life. Caretaker's wife shouted from her door, calling Caretaker back for lunch, but that just seemed to make him furious.

"Why can't you bring my food out to me here?"

Caretaker's wife came out carrying an old bowl full of rice and, one after another, the wives of Palace, Tag-Along, Stargazer, Iron Bolt and Pillar followed suit. Cowbell wanted to go home to make his own lunch, so, after parting from Inkcap, he gathered an armful of dried stalks from the straw pile and made his way back. He went outside and squatted at the base of the gable wall, peeling potatoes and singing:

> *Ninety-nine and eighty-one, the children of the poor stand against the wall in the sun;*
> *The sun may keep them warm, but their bellies still ache with hunger.*

He might as well have starved to death for all the notice anyone took of him. Those with their own bowl just got on with eating and drinking. They all stopped talking as they ate the first half of their meal. They opened their mouths wider and wider, thrusting them right into their bowls and slurping away. Halfway through the bowl, they were breathing hard and their heads were steaming. They shifted their posture and resumed talking. Once again, the subject of their conversation was Bash. Ah, Bash! The bastard hadn't seemed like much when he was out and about in Old Kiln, but as soon as he left, the village felt empty.

"Let's just get on with our lunch," Palace said. "Who knows what he's up to this time."

"Having nothing to eat is the pits," Feng Youliang said. "You're better off staying at home than going out to work."

"You're often out building houses and tombs for people," Palace observed, "and you get paid for it, so how come you still say that?"

"Making money's hard work," Feng Youliang replied. "Who do you know who's living comfortably but still likes going out to work?"

"Wasn't Bash living comfortably enough?" Palace asked.

"He wasn't as comfortable as you," Feng Youliang retorted.

"I've got parents and children to look after. And a lot of mouths to feed. Once he'd fed himself, his whole household was full and you're saying I'm more comfortable than him?"

"You really don't understand Bash, do you," Feng Youliang said.

"Not understand him? I'll still understand him when he's just a pile of ashes!"

Pockmark snorted and got up and moved away.

"What are you snorting about?" Palace asked. "Have you just swallowed some chicken feathers?"

"You don't know what you're talking about," Pockmark sniffed.

"Ah!" Sparks chipped in. "Someone selling flour always looks down on someone selling quicklime."

"I don't look down on Bash. You're the ones talking about him. But who knows why he left."

"He got Apricot up the duff. What else could he do except run?" Pockmark said.

"That's fucking nonsense," said Feng Youliang.

Pockmark was about to say something, but he stopped himself and buried his head in his bowl.

Apricot wandered over. She picked a handful of spring onion leaves from her personal plot and walked on slowly and deliberately, as if she was trying to kill ants as she went along.

"Ah! So Potful can still only manage some thin gruel with spring onion leaves," Sparks said.

"Everyone has stomach trouble sometimes, but why has he been sick for so long? And it's getting worse," Feng Youliang observed.

"That's because he's so angry, isn't it," Sparks said.

"Why's he still so angry now that Bash has gone?" Palace asked.

He threw a glance at Apricot, whose breasts and backside were definitely bigger than before but whose waist was still slender.

"You really are talking bollocks, Pockmark," he commented.

"Are you going to look at the neem tree?" Pockmark asked.

"Why?" said Palace. "What's wrong with the neem tree?"

"Someone's slashed it with a knife, three times."

"Who did that? Why?"

"You're saying you don't know?" Pockmark shot back, then called for Inkcap.

Inkcap was eating from an old bowl. It was bigger than his head and too heavy at the base, so he had curled his left arm under it as though he was about to put it on his shoulder. He didn't go over to the group standing at the entrance of Three Fork Alley but walked on down the alley drinking his congee. Whenever he came to a tree, he picked up some rice with his chopsticks and rested it on a branch, saying, "Here's a mouthful for you." All the trees in the alley got some rice and Inkcap looked back at them, thinking that now they had their rice, the flowers would bloom particularly brightly and all the ones that bore fruit would have a particularly heavy crop.

He heard Pockmark call him, but he didn't answer.

"Have you been to the neem tree, Inkcap?" Pockmark asked again.

"Eh?"

"Are there any scars on the neem tree?"

"What?"

In normal circumstances, Inkcap would have gone back to the neem tree to see what had happened, but because it was Pockmark asking, he didn't want to, nor did he want to know why there might be scars on it. He carried his bowl back home because he still had to go to Middle Mountain after dinner.

As soon as Inkcap had got up that day, which happened to be the second day of the second lunar month, Gran cooked an egg and some thick soup for Inkcap. After dinner, he had to go to Middle Mountain to pick moxa leaves. These were stuffed into the door and window frames to stop snakes, cockroaches and scorpions coming into the house. When he got home after collecting all the moxa leaves from the shady, low-lying places, he found Third Aunt and Flower Girl in the house, talking to Gran.

"Such an evil thing," Gran was saying. "That kind of talk is sure to harm Apricot. Who said it?"

"Barndoor heard it in the village," Flower Girl said. "You know what he's like. He hears a whole load of stuff that makes him mad, and he comes back and tells it all to me. Oh Gran, is it really possible? Can neem seeds cause a miscarriage?"

"Yes, all right, it is possible," Third Aunt said. "But just because Apricot collected some neem seeds doesn't necessarily mean she used them for that, does it?"

"They're saying Potful went there at night to take his anger out on the tree and slashed it three times with a knife," Flower Girl said.

"Is that so?" Third Aunt said. "Has Apricot ever come to see you, Gran?"

"After her mother died, she came to see me the first time she got her period. Didn't you see her then? Other than that, why would she come to see me... Who's there?"

Inkcap had been listening in something of a daze, but couldn't hear the women very clearly. As soon as Grandma shouted out, he hurriedly stamped his feet in the yard and said, "It's me, Grandma. I've brought the moxa leaves."

Inkcap put moxa leaves in the door and in the windows. With the remainder, he inserted some in the doors and windows of the neighbours on either side. He felt that the only people in the village who treated him well were Cowbell and Bash, so he took a handful of moxa leaves and first went to Cowbell's house. When he found that Cowbell wasn't there, he wedged some of the leaves in the crack of the door and ran onto the little wooden shack. It was only when he reached the entrance to the village that he remembered Bash wasn't around any more. He stood there for a while, then threw the moxa leaves down the embankment.

There was a millstone a little way down the road to the west of the embankment. It wasn't as big as the one at the western end of the village, but it had been in constant use, and even now Useless was harnessing up a bull to grind black beans. Black beans are the best fodder for cows, and, originally, it had been Happy who did all the grinding, but a lot of people were suspicious of the practice. They said that if the stockman both ground the feed and fed the cows himself, how could anyone know how much he ground and how much he actually fed? They were even saying that eating black beans made you fart more, and Happy did fart a lot. So in the end, they took the job away from Happy and gave it to Useless.

The bull that Useless led out of the cowshed was white with black spots, and it was so thin it resembled a cowskin draped over a frame that could be pulled off with a single tug. At first, Useless helped push the grinding rod, but then he stopped and sat on the edge of the millstone reading a book, as the bull moved slower and slower.

"Why are you walking so slowly?" said Useless. "Do you think you're going to the slaughterhouse?"

The bull actually stopped moving and stood there, loosing a stream of shit. Useless jumped down and hit it really hard with his whip, yelling, "Fucking animal! I bet you're one of the Four Bad Elements among bulls."

Inkcap saw Useless grinding the beans, but he didn't say hello, as he was afraid Useless would use the fact that he was teaching him characters as leverage to get him to help with the grinding. But when he heard Useless scolding the bull as one of the four bovine Bad Elements, he couldn't resist getting involved.

"So," he said, "you just sit there and let the animal do all the work, eh?"

The bull moo-ed at Inkcap.

"Oh, so you're talking to Inkcap now, are you?" Useless yelled and whipped the bull again.

Goodman Wang walked up from the base of the embankment with a double-pocketed cloth bag slung over his shoulder.

"Hey! Hey!" he called out. "Stop that. I know that bull well. It has a bad liver."

"Maybe so," Useless replied, "but Happy's still quite content to let me do all the work grinding the beans, and he's sure to have something to say about it if I don't do a good job."

Then, addressing Goodman directly, he said, "Your special thing is talking to illnesses, isn't it? Why don't you do that with this bull? Isn't there some saying about playing a lute to an ox? Well, you can talk illness to a bull, can't you!" Delighted with himself, he chuckled at his own witticism.

Goodman didn't take offence, but simply said, "The Branch Secretary won't let me treat it. Its liver disease is caused by bezoars, and the Branch Secretary wants to get his hands on them when the time comes. They're a really expensive medicine."

"If you want your bezoars, you can have your bezoars," Useless said. "But if I want the bull to pull the millstone, it will pull the millstone."

With that, he whipped the bull again.

Inkcap rushed over to grab the whip, but he couldn't catch hold of Useless, so he snatched the book he had been reading instead.

"If you hit the bull again, I'll rip this book to pieces," he shouted.

"Listen to me, Useless," Goodman said. "Some time ago, I left the temple to live in Xigouchuan. There was a thief about in the village at the time and they couldn't catch him. Instead, they arrested an innocent man and beat him until he would say any old nonsense. He insisted that I knew who the thief was, so they arrested me and gave me a good beating too. I didn't blame anyone, nor was I angry. It was only later when I found I could talk to illnesses that I realised something. When I was in the temple, the abbot told me to drive the cart that was transporting the bricks and tiles for the construction work at the temple. I beat the draft animals when we were on the road. I beat them really hard. It was then I realised that sins committed in the bodily realm must be paid for in the bodily realm."

Inkcap threw the book back down onto the millstone and looked at Goodman.

"When will Useless get beaten in return, then?" he asked.

"You're the one who'll get beaten!" Useless exclaimed. "You're the one who has committed a sin, otherwise why would you be a part of the Four Bad Elements?"

That one sentence knocked the stuffing out of Inkcap. He looked at Goodman, but Goodman remained silent as he pulled Inkcap away with him.

Inkcap kept his head down as they went, and he had trouble keeping up with Goodman because his legs were so short. Ai! He was always doing something in the heat of the moment, and then people would always drag up his background. He was like a maize seedling just beginning to stretch out its arms and legs when a sudden hailstorm smashes it to the ground. Crops that have been hit by a hailstorm never grow very tall, and he hadn't grown very tall because he was always being knocked back by someone. The sun began to shift towards the west, moving his shadow from behind him to in front of him. The shadow was so short and ugly that it angered even him, so he tried to stamp on it. But the shadow kept jumping forward and he could never catch it.

"Please be happy, Inkcap," Goodman said.

"How can I be happy when people keep humiliating me?"

"When others bully you, they take away your bad karma. Isn't that a good thing? Let me give you something."

Goodman took out a small, round mirror from his cloth bag and gave it to Inkcap. Inkcap looked into the mirror and saw a sorrowful face.

"Smile," Goodman said and then a smiling face appeared in the mirror. "If you smile in the mirror every day, the mirror will always give you back a smiling face."

"So it's me inside and outside the mirror?" Inkcap asked.

"You're giving yourself a smiling face."

Inkcap laughed and offered to carry Goodman's bag for him, but Goodman wouldn't let him. The two of them walked to the middle of Crosswise Alley, where Noodle Fish was sitting on a stone at the foot of a wall, smoking a ready-made cigarette, his face wet with tears.

"Didn't you go and fetch the soil for the cowshed floor today, Uncle Noodle Fish?"

Noodle Fish just looked at Inkcap with the tears still running down his face.

"Hey, you're still smoking ready-mades! Why are you still buying them?"

"Enough. Enough. If you want to destroy this family, just get on with it." Noodle Fish drew fiercely on his cigarette, choking and coughing repeatedly.

"What's this? What's this?" Goodman asked with a smile. "Who's making Noodle Fish so angry?"

Noodle Fish grasped Goodman's hand and said, "Oh! Oh! What sin did I commit? I have such a large family and if I don't put steamed buns on the table, what will they have to eat? If I don't do the work in the family plot, no one else will do it. If I don't do something, it just doesn't get done. Even if I do actually do it and don't die of exhaustion, the house is in an uproar all day long until dark. Stonebreaker and his wife are clamouring to split up. Let them. Their lives may be better for it. My two stepsons use shovels when they eat and scrape the pot clean right to the bottom. They even steal money from the house and go to Kaihe's place to eat tofu. He came to me yesterday to ask me to settle my account and said that Padlock was over at his place asking to buy ready-made cigarettes on credit. What do you think of these days we are living in?"

"Aren't you always telling people that the children all acknowledge you as their stepfather?" Goodman said.

"Everything was fine before, but now, who knows? Just what is going on?"

"Will you listen to what I have to say?"

"You can talk to illnesses, can't you? Tell me what illness my household is suffering from."

"Because you are mean to the poor, all the poor ghosts have been reincarnated into your house."

Noodle Fish opened his mouth to reply.

"Don't interrupt me!" Goodman snapped. "Just listen. Back when you weren't in charge of the wheat field, people worked through the night there and got a meal of mixed noodles for their work. That summer when you were in charge, you decided that it cost too much, so you changed it to two *jin* of sweet potatoes each. You need vegetable soup to go with steamed sweet potatoes, but you even thought the soup was too expensive, so you skimped on that by not adding either the chillis or the salt that always goes into it. Wouldn't anyone consider that cheating the poor?"

"Aiya! I saved money for the production team, didn't I?"

"When you make wine in the twelfth lunar month, there are village regulations about how much to make and how much each person gets, aren't there? Are you telling me you didn't secretly keep some back for yourself?"

"It was only one jar. Do you know everything?"

"The jar of wine you sold to Ever-Obedient during the Spring Festival was originally priced at twenty fen a *jin*, but you sold it for twenty-five and watered it down with a ladleful of water. When you sell onions, garlic or carrots, your scales don't give true weight. Because you are afraid of poverty yourself, you are mean to the poor. That's why the poor ghosts seek you out. There's no point you asking who's done this to you, you've done it to yourself."

After hearing what Goodman had to say, Noodle Fish stopped smoking and went into his courtyard, still crying.

Inkcap felt sorry for him and when he saw the pack of cigarettes still lying on the stone where he had been sitting, he poked it in through a crack in the courtyard door.

"Why did you say that to him?" Inkcap asked Goodman.

"If someone feels wronged when something happens to them, it is because they do not understand the nature of cause and effect."

"Cause and effect? What's that?"

He didn't understand what Goodman was saying and watery snot began to run from his nose. He sniffed it back in, but it just started to flow out again. He wiped it away with his hand, but then couldn't find anywhere to wipe his hand clean.

"If you sow melon seeds, you harvest melons," Goodman explained. "If you sow bean seeds, you harvest beans. It's the same with people. If you honoured the Buddha with flowers in your previous life, your present life will be a good one. If you stole other people's lamps in your previous life, your eyesight will be bad in your present one. If you fought with pigs for their bran in your previous life, your face will be pockmarked in your present one."

"Oh," Inkcap exclaimed. "Pockmark must have fought with pigs for their bran! But how come a man could do such a thing?"

"He must have been a beggar in his previous life," Goodman explained. "Beggars fight with pigs for their bran, don't they? From the nature you have in this life, you can tell what you did in your previous life. If you have a Fire nature, you must have been an official. If you have a Water nature, you must have been a businessman. If you have a Wood nature, you must have been a worker. And if you have an Earth nature, you must have been a farmer."

Goodman was chock-full of ancient lore and once he got going, he didn't stop. It was like pouring out a sack of walnuts.

"Master Goodman! Master Goodman!" Inkcap called out in an attempt to make him stop, but he just went on.

"There is foolish fire in the nature of cows and yin wood in the nature of dogs, so those are the forms they take, and those are the sufferings they endure. If they could change their nature, they could escape the cruel life of dumb animals."

Inkcap still couldn't find anywhere to wipe the watery snot off his hands, so he patted Goodman's cloth bag and wiped the rest of it off on that.

"What did you call me?" Goodman said. "If you're going to call me 'Master', don't put 'Goodman' after it."

"Master, I don't care about my past life or my present life. What I want to ask you, is what I can be in the future."

"Oh? And what do you think that might be?"

"I think I'm just like the others. We are all going to be poor, lower-middle peasants."

Goodman looked at him in silence.

"Why don't you say something?" Inkcap pleaded.

"You need the Branch Secretary for that kind of thing."

Inkcap felt very discouraged. Goodman's words were of no practical help. If you don't believe him, just leave, Inkcap told himself, and that's what he did.

"Alas, this child's heart is empty," Goodman said from behind him.

"Why wouldn't it be?" Inkcap said without looking back.

"If there are heavenly principles in your nature, your heavenly destiny will not be empty," Goodman continued. "If there is reason in your heart, your earthly fate will not be empty. If there is sense in your body, your yin fate will not be empty. People encompass the spirit of all things, so all things hope to transform into people. Unfortunately, when people get lost, they have to transform back into things, which is why the human cycle is endless. If people are deluded or fretful, they cannot join the cycle and cannot become human again, and if they are unreasonable, their hearts cannot be redeemed. If they are dissatisfied or ignorant, they cannot redeem themselves. If things are not empty and affairs are not pure, purpose cannot be redeemed. You must do one thing and do it to the end, you must find a path and follow it to the end. You can move forwards but never backwards. If you can avoid being ensnared in the world's net, then you can redeem your destiny. When you meet adversity, if you can happily accept it as what must be, then all will be fine. If you can't accept it and feel resentful in your heart, even though it passes on this occasion, adversity will always return in the future."

The only phrase that Inkcap understood and latched onto in all of that was "what must be", so he said, "We're all just ordinary folk here in Old Kiln, so why should Useless be a good element and me a bad one?"

"I haven't explained it clearly to you. No, I haven't explained it clearly."

"Then what should I do?"

"You must think of yourself as a puppy."

"I... don't... want... to!"

As Inkcap ran out of the alley, he heard Goodman say, "Child, there is no such thing in this world as a cloak of invisibility."

EIGHTEEN

GOODMAN HADN'T INTENDED TO SAY ANYTHING about invisibility cloaks, but the idea lodged itself in Inkcap's head, ringing like a bell and setting him thinking. He went home and fell asleep, still thinking about invisibility cloaks. Wouldn't it be great if there really was such a thing! He could go wherever he pleased. For example, he wanted to go to Apricot's house. Did she have a miscarriage after drinking soup made with neem seeds? If they had made up the drug there, they would have poured out the dregs at the base of the courtyard wall. One look would tell him. Or he could go to the Branch Secretary's place. He had once watched his wife through a crack in the gate as she laid out snacks on a mat in the courtyard to dry in the sun. Now he wanted to go straight in, stand next to the mat and count the snacks, one by one. The Branch Secretary and his wife wouldn't be able to see him, nor would their son. Not even the pigs or chickens would be able to see him. He also wanted to sit under the crepe myrtle tree at the Branch Secretary's house, watching who came bringing gifts. Had Awning ever brought a gift? Or Almost-There? Big Root Hei and Barndoor Bai certainly had. Feng Youliang and Barndoor Bai were outsiders and would want to suck up to the Branch Secretary; moreover, they were carpenters and builders, so how could they go out and earn an honest living without being on very good terms with him? As far away as Bash was from the Branch Secretary, that was how close those two were. Winterborn and Pillar had definitely brought gifts. Pillar was so stupid, how else could he have got a job at the kiln site? A hundred per cent, Useless had too! Inkcap had seen Useless give leeks and pumpkins, so who was going to believe he hadn't given snacks as well? Yes, that was it, he would put on the cloak of invisibility and go to Useless's house. Useless could put on a good front when he was out and about and was invariably polite. People like him were always good-tempered outside but cursed and swore at home. Useless and his mother were so stingy they'd never willingly give the Branch Secretary any snacks and if they were forced to, they'd certainly put a curse on them so the Secretary got a stomach ache after eating them. Oh yes, and he wanted to go to Baldy Jin's house and Pockmark's, and, fuck me, wouldn't it be great to go when they were eating so he could spit in their food or slap them round the face. They wouldn't be able to see him so they would think it was a ghost. And that ghost would slap them about, three times a day. Pockmark was really tall, so he'd have to stand on a stool to reach his pissing face.

Half asleep, Inkcap swung his hand out from under the quilt, knocking over the kerosene lamp hanging on the wall by the *kang* with a bang. Gran wasn't asleep but was cutting her paper patterns in the lamplight. When the lamp fell on the *kang*, she was quick to pick up the fuel tank. Inkcap woke up and went to light a match to relight the lamp. The kerosene had spilled onto the padded jacket that was covering the quilt. Gran was annoyed she couldn't wipe it up, so she yanked Inkcap's leg and twisted it. Inkcap fell back, face down on the *kang*, and she spanked his exposed buttocks. Inkcap knew he had done something bad again, so he didn't say anything and let her spank him. She spanked him until his arse turned red.

When she was out of breath, she stopped hitting him and asked, "Were you dreaming?"

"I was dreaming I was fighting someone," Inkcap lied.

"Do you always fight with people in your dreams? Who can you beat and who beats you up when you have these fights?"

Gran's anger flared again and she hauled Inkcap off the *kang* and onto his feet. Standing up, he was pretty much the same height as when he was sitting down.

"I told you to be a good boy and stay indoors, but you couldn't even manage one whole day. You want to go and pick fights with people instead. Why can't I talk any sense into you?"

"I'm not a baby any more, and I can't stand being cooped up."

"You still need to stay in, even if you don't like it. When are you ever going to grow up and calm down a bit?"

"You want me to be an old fuddy-duddy, don't you? Do you want me to look like a rat, growing whiskers on my chin while I'm still young?"

That made Gran laugh, and she pinched his lips affectionately. She covered him with the quilt and then went to find some alkali powder to get the oil stains out of the jacket.

Inkcap wasn't annoyed with Gran and, after all, he had hit Pockmark hadn't he! As the sun came up, he took the piss bucket and splashed its contents over the wheat seedlings in their private plot. Before the seedlings had begun to revive, a rabbit ran past and Inkcap shouted excitedly, "A rabbit! A rabbit!" The rabbit leapt into the air, curving its body like a bow, hurdled the irrigation channel and ran off.

Pockmark was scattering ash in a field not far away and when Inkcap saw him, he told himself, I hit you! And sure enough, when he looked, he saw that the left side of Pockmark's face was swollen.

"Who hit you in the face?" Inkcap asked.

"I've got a toothache. What do you mean, who hit me? The person in Old Kiln who could hit me hasn't been born yet."

"There are two people who can hit you."

"And who are they?"

"Bash has hit you before."

"He's gone, hasn't he? He might as well be dead. Who else is there?"

"Someone wearing an invisibility cloak."

"What invisibility cloak?

Inkcap didn't say anything else but just picked up his bucket and walked away, head held high.

It started raining at noon, and the spring rain was as precious as oil. The wheat seedlings in the field suddenly stood up and regained their spirits. It was lucky that Inkcap had watered his plot with piss that morning. Although the rain wasn't heavy, it continued to fall until evening. Most of the villagers wore straw hats or coir raincoats, but Inkcap didn't own a raincoat. What he did have was a green plastic sheet with two corners sewn together, which covered him from head to foot. He thought how strange it was that he had hit Pockmark in his dream last night, and today, Pockmark's face was all swollen. He had better go and see if there was anything different at the homes of Useless and the Branch Secretary. He walked along the alley and no one paid him any attention. Noodle Fish, who had been weeping and wailing the day before yesterday, was now using a shovel to divert water from the eaves into his piss cistern. He glanced across at him and started shovelling again without saying a word. Cowbell was clearly visible standing at his courtyard gate, and he didn't speak either. Why did they not see him when they looked at him? Was he wearing an invisibility cloak? Could this plastic sheet be making him invisible? Inkcap suddenly felt that that must be what was going on. But why didn't this plastic sheet make him invisible before? Had it only acquired this special power after he had had his dream?

Inkcap's sense of excitement rose as he made his way to Useless's house, but the courtyard gate was locked. He couldn't carry out his plan, so he kicked the gate, leaving a muddy footprint on one of its panels. At this point, a group of people came out of the alley, including the Branch Secretary, Millstone, Awning and a fat, dark-skinned man. Inkcap didn't run away but just stood under the courtyard wall. He suddenly wanted to piss and thought to himself, They can't see me!

But then Awning yelled at him, "Hey! What do you think you're doing?"

Inkcap didn't reply and kept on pissing.

Awning came over and kicked him, saying, "Commune Secretary Zhang is here, and you're pissing in the alley?"

"Could you see it was me pissing?"

"Yeah, of course, if that's really you, Inkcap! Now fuck off out of here."

It was only then that Inkcap realised that the plastic sheet didn't make him invisible. It was simply that Noodle Fish and Cowbell had ignored him on purpose.

The production team loved to hold meetings on rainy days, and as expected, they held one that evening. Even Potful went. Apricot helped him to a long stool in the public room, but he lay on it rather than sit down. Only the Branch Secretary spoke throughout the whole meeting. He said that in the afternoon, Commune Secretary Zhang came and led an inspection of the village. He fully affirmed and praised the work of Old Kiln and emphasised the need to strengthen militia training and learn from the village of Dazhai in building terraces. Secretary Zhang had first come to the village office and then went to the old Kiln God Temple. When he asked who lived in the temple, he was told that Goodman lived there. He ordered Goodman to leave the temple and return to secular life. Why should he be living in such a huge space when the village office was so small and cramped? He also said that all the tables, chairs and benches in the office should be replaced. The Branch Secretary said that this was the leader criticising them but also showing his concern for them. He went on to say that he had some good news to pass on, that the commune had received a target allocation of ten new tractors. The leader had not originally considered giving any to Old Kiln, but given the excellent work the village had done in such primitive conditions, it was to be allocated a quota. The Branch Secretary also said that, at the end of his visit, the leader had asked him if he had any problems or difficulties. He had told the leader that there were none: Old Kiln was a red flag village and its residents had high political awareness and great enthusiasm for their work. They loved the community like their own homes and lived in harmony. However, he also told the meeting that he had concealed one thing, and that was the matter of Bash. He had originally been going to report his disappearance but changed his mind because Bash had been gone for so long. If he had gone off mending shoes and tyres without official permission, that would be a reflection of the fact that Old Kiln had not yet succeeded in cutting off its capitalist tail; and if he had gone out begging for food, that was a stain on the village's socialist reputation.

It took five pipes worth of time for the Branch Secretary to say all this, and everyone thought that the meeting must now be over. However, the Branch Secretary went on to announce four more decisions. First, the militia must conduct intensive training every ten days. Second, the eighteen *mu* of terraced fields on the rear slope of Middle Mountain had to be repaired before the wheat harvest. Third, the village office was to be moved to the Kiln God Temple, and the two public office buildings were to go on open sale. Once the price was determined, everyone in Old Kiln, except for the Four Bad Elements, could apply to purchase them. Once in receipt of the proceeds of the sale, the village needed to buy a tractor and two more flat-bed barrows for the kiln, and to buy furniture for the new office. Fourth, Goodman was to move out of the Kiln God Temple and live in the Mountain God Temple on top of Middle Mountain, which was close to the kiln. In future, Goodman would go to work in the kiln.

Old Kiln received new decisions every spring, but this year's were more significant, unexpected and urgent than in the past. Three days later, Goodman moved to the Mountain God Temple, and work started on the terraced fields on the rear slope of Middle Mountain, under the supervision of Millstone. The new public office was much better suited to the job, as the Kiln God Temple was a quadrangle courtyard. There were five rooms in the north and three rooms in the middle to serve as offices. On each side, there were three storage bins made from woven willow withies which held a reserve of a hundred kilograms of rice and a hundred kilograms of grain for the production team. This grain was held in readiness for emergencies caused by natural and man-made disasters, and they were only to be used as a last resort. There were also five jars containing various types of seeds and black beans used to make quality cattle feed. As for the two side annexes to the main hall, the east annex was piled high with fired porcelain goods, while the west one was filled with communal ploughs, ropes, wooden shovels, forks, rakes, some wooden rafters and bamboo poles, as well as flags, gongs, drums and fuses for community celebrations during the Chinese New Year.

No one had anything much to say about all this, except that there was a lot of discussion about the sale of the public office. Why sell it? Was it just to buy a tractor and flat-bed barrows and to replace office furniture? Who was going to buy it? No family in Old Kiln was short of accommodation. Bash's old lodgings were run down and dilapidated, so he might have been in the market, but he wasn't here any more, and who else was there? It seemed that no one wanted to buy a house. The Branch Secretary must have been well aware of the situation, so why did he make this decision?

Inkcap and Cowbell gave no thought to these questions, as all they were worried about was going out to work. So they went to see the Branch Secretary again and said that since there was work to be done on the terraces on the east slope of Middle Mountain, they should be allowed to join in to earn work points. The Branch Secretary finally agreed but stipulated that Cowbell was worth four work points a day, but Inkcap merited only three. Cowbell had grown a little taller since the Spring Festival, but Inkcap was still the same size. On the terrace construction site, Millstone, Barndoor and Baldy Jin were building the stone terrace walls. Big stones were to be excavated from the mountains and the small stones used to fill in the gaps, known as slurry stones, were to be gathered by Cowbell and Inkcap from the roadside and in the fields. Inkcap wasn't very strong, so he had trouble carrying the baskets of slurry stones. Grunting and groaning, he took one to Baldy Jin who poured the stones into the gap between the big stones with a loud clatter.

"Why don't you use a bigger basket?" he complained. "It takes you half a day to bring just a tiny number of stones. What the fuck do you think we're doing here, filling teeth?"

Inkcap mustered all his strength to collect some more slurry stones until the pads of his fingers were bleeding and he ran until the uppers of his shoes were torn and coming away from the soles. Baldy Jin urged him on and so did Millstone and even Barndoor. They swore at both Inkcap and Cowbell for not being able to do better and told them not to bother coming to work if they could mess up such an easy job as this.

The two boys were so tired that they took turns going to a secluded spot to have a rest while taking a piss and a shit. When they'd finished, they'd pelt their shit with stones. "That's for you, Baldy Jin!" they would shout. "That's for you, Millstone! That's for you Barndoor!"

Useless took his bucket of limewash and painted slogans on a blank wall in the village. Yoyo was still helping to steady his ladder, but the characters he painted seemed different from before. Inkcap walked past the wall just as Yoyo went off to the privy.

"Hey, Useless!" he said. "Your characters used to be all square. Why are they slanting now?"

"It's official script, isn't it."

"If it's official, shouldn't it be standing up straight not falling over?"

"That's not what it means, but since you can't write, I can't very well explain it to you."

Inkcap stopped talking about characters and said, "Your writing is easy work, but building terraces is knackering."

"Those who work hard with their minds will govern, and those who work hard with their hands will be governed by others," Useless said.

"What do you mean?" Inkcap asked.

"You get what you deserve."

"Oh, I didn't take the Branch Secretary any snacks, so I deserve it."

"Well, write it down. Write it down."

Of course, Inkcap couldn't write, so he grinned at Useless and said, "You talk to the Branch Secretary for me and get him to let me hold the ladder for you. I'm bound to do it better than Yoyo, and I can run errands for you too."

"Is that so?"

"Yes, it is. It is."

"Come over here and I'll let you know."

Inkcap went over and stood at the bottom of the ladder, while, up above him, Useless plied his brush and the limewash dripped all over Inkcap.

"Nope, I don't want you," Useless said.

"I'll knock you off that fucking ladder," said Inkcap, walking away.

In the end, the Branch Secretary realised that Cowbell and Inkcap were of no use on the terraced field construction site, so he sent them to work at the kiln. The people there were not as bad-tempered as Millstone and Baldy Jin, and they were assigned to Winterborn and Pillar. They ran around doing odd jobs. They were very much in favour of the Branch Secretary, who they thought could do no wrong. They would have been even more in favour of him if he had stopped Useless from writing slogans.

At the kiln site, Goodman helped Winterborn sift the clay. Most of the time, he kept his head down and got on with his work. But as soon as he took a break and someone asked him about their illness, he became a different person and words flooded out of him.

"It's a good thing his mouth is made out of flesh," Cowbell told Inkcap. "If it was made of wood or stone, it would have worn away ten times over by now."

"I've never seen him read a book, so how come he knows so much?" Inkcap asked.

They thought Goodman was an extraordinary person and couldn't understand how someone like him came to be living in Old Kiln. They liked to stay close to him but were careful not to overdo it.

After working at the kiln for three days, during a rest period on the fourth day, Goodman put a basin of water on the top of the hot kiln. The water soon heated up and, while he washed his hair, Inkcap and Cowbell secretly ran up to the Mountain God Temple on the top of Middle Mountain to see the treasures it contained. The door of the temple was already rotten, and a picket gate had been constructed out of maize stalks, but it wasn't even locked and opened at a push. Inside, the temple was very small. There was a new *kang*, a stove, a window, a table in front of the window, and three jars for storing grain and other miscellaneous items. Otherwise, there was only room for two round meditation cushions and a brazier.

"Wow!" Inkcap exclaimed. "The mountain god can't be very tall."

There was no statue of the god in the Mountain God Temple, and there were no murals on the walls.

"How do you know the mountain god isn't very tall?" Cowbell asked.

"The temple's so small, isn't it?"

They were searching around on the *kang* and in the jars, hoping to find something to eat, such as walnuts, persimmons or sweet potato slices, but they came away empty-handed. Cowbell went to root around in the corner near the stove.

"I'm going to sit on the cushions," Inkcap said.

Goodman was able to sit on them with his legs crossed so his feet rested on his thighs, but Inkcap couldn't manage that.

"Hey!" Cowbell exclaimed. "Eggs! Let's take them back and cook them on top of the kiln."

But Inkcap cried out as sharply as if he had been stung by a scorpion: "Hey, the flower! The flower!"

"The cunning old sod, hiding his eggs there! How many should we take?" Cowbell asked.

"Are there more than a dozen?"

"No, only six."

As he carried two of the eggs over, Cowbell saw that Inkcap had squeezed his head into a narrow gap and was looking out the door and was still exclaiming, "The flower! The flower!"

Cowbell looked out too and asked, "What flower?"

"It changed into a bird and flew away."

Looking at the birds wheeling and turning in the sky, Cowbell recognised them as the red-beaked, white-tailed flock that used to roost at the Kiln God Temple. He tapped Inkcap on the head and asked, "Don't you recognise those birds? Flowers? Flowers? What nonsense are you filling your head with?"

Inkcap wasn't sure he could believe his eyes. Had the dozen or so flowers he had seen so clearly on the tree suddenly turned into birds? Did that mean that all birds were transformed from flowers?

When they brought the eggs to the kiln, they also took an earthenware basin, filled it with water and placed it on the top of the kiln.

"If you were going to take them, you should have taken more, so you could cook one each for everyone here," was all Goodman said.

He kept on washing his head and didn't pay any more attention to the two lads.

Inkcap laughed uneasily and said, "Master Goodman, sir, we just wanted to see what your eggs taste of."

"They taste of chicken farts," Goodman replied.

"Hee hee! You only have six eggs left, can we really take some more?"

"Someone will bring some more in a while."

The birds appeared again on the wooden poles by the kiln, forming a line, stretching their necks, singing together and then suddenly flying down the mountain. Once again, Inkcap saw that when the birds landed and didn't move, they looked like flowers, and only when they flew up again did they become birds. A moment later, the birds flew off again, but this time they didn't stop on the wooden poles by the kiln. One by one, they flew up the mountain and perched on the branches of the white-barked pine.

Cowbell was boiling the eggs. Winterborn was filling the mud pool with water, muttering curses at someone, and Lightkeeper was looking miserable as he shovelled coal. After a few strokes of the shovel, he banged it hard on a rock. Pillar was fixing the earth-moving barrow by tying the back plate back on with some wire.

"Mind what you're doing with that shovel," warned Pillar. "That belongs to the production team."

Goodman finished washing his head and went off to transport the pottery forms. He smiled broadly at Inkcap and when Inkcap saw how his eyes simultaneously narrowed and lengthened, he felt he should smile back, so he did.

On the path below the kiln, he caught up with Kaihe who was holding some eggs wrapped in a towel and shouting, "Goodman! Goodman!"

Winterborn hurried over from the mud pond.

"What do you want Goodman for?"

"To talk to an illness, of course. What else would I want him for?"

"'Why are there so many illnesses about?" Winterborn complained. "Goodman hardly gets any work done at the kiln because someone or another is always calling for him."

"No one likes illnesses," Kaihe said. "My wife had heart pains during the New Year holiday. She tried traditional Chinese medicine and Western medicine, but nothing worked. When she was ill, it was me who had to do the shopping and make the tofu–"

"You need to spend some of your money, Kaihe," Winterborn said. "Those who've made a lot of money forget their responsibilities."

"I might take that from someone else, Winterborn," Kaihe said tartly, "but not from you."

Inkcap and Cowbell came running down from the kiln. Goodman had said that someone was going to bring him some eggs, and there he was! Cowbell took the towel package from Kaihe and said, "You live well, Goodman. Do you have eggs to eat every day?" He opened the package and exclaimed, "Why are there only four?"

"My chickens only laid four," Kaihe replied.

"Why didn't you bring some tofu as well?"

Kaihe just laughed.

"You said everyone at the kiln was going to have one," Cowbell said to Goodman, "so I'd better go and cook these."

Of course, Inkcap was happy about having eggs to eat, but what he really admired was the holiness of Goodman's character.

"How did you know someone was bringing eggs?" he asked.

"Ask your grandmother. No one else can make papercuts like her. How is she able to cut whatever pattern she likes?"

Inkcap didn't think there was anything particularly holy about Gran.

"Teach me to talk to illnesses," he said.

"You want to learn too?"

Goodman didn't promise to teach Inkcap, but nor did he say that he wouldn't. He patted the dirt off his body and was about to go down the mountain with Kaihe.

Pillar was not happy about this. "There you go off down the mountain again," he said. "How can I give you work points for this?"

"Let him go, let him go," Winterborn said. "He's going to talk to someone's illness not idle about. I won't eat my boiled egg, you can have two."

So Goodman left with Kaihe.

"Ah!" Inkcap exclaimed. "So all along, the reason you lot didn't have any objections to Goodman coming to work at the kiln was because you wanted the eggs."

"Why would he be so generous with eggs when he leads such a frugal life himself," Winterborn said.

"I know," Inkcap replied. "Do you think the reason he won't teach me is because I would want a share of the eggs?"

After the eggs had been boiling for a while, Pillar walked to the top of the kiln to see if they were cooked. He took one from the pan of water, peeled it and ate it. Then he did the same with another one. He squared his shoulders, took a third one out of the pan and peeled that one too. The egg was white and tender.

Pillar suddenly raised his hand and said, "Goodman was once a monk. Anyone who eats this egg will never find a wife, so I'm throwing it away."

Try as they might, Inkcap and Cowbell couldn't see what Pillar had done with the egg, but as soon as they turned around, they saw the bulge in Pillar's cheek and realised they had been tricked. The two of them rushed over to take the egg out of Pillar's mouth. Pillar was so big, they couldn't hold him down, so Inkcap tickled his armpits. When Pillar laughed, the egg stuck in his throat so he couldn't breathe, and his face turned blue.

"He's going to die!" Cowbell yelled.

He and Inkcap broke into a run but Winterborn shouted to them from below the kiln, "Slap his back! Slap his back!"

They got hold of Pillar and slapped him on the back. He made a gagging noise and his eyes lit up again.

"Serves you right for trying to take advantage," Inkcap said.

"Slap me some more," Pillar demanded.

Inkcap slapped him some more, then stopped when he saw a figure coming down from the mountain along the highway. The person had his chest thrown out and his broad shoulders were pulled back. "Can you see who that is?" Inkcap asked Cowbell.

"It's Bash, isn't it?"

"Slap me! Slap me!" Pillar was still yelling.

"It is Bash!" Inkcap confirmed, smashing Pillar hard with his fist.

"Ouch! Ouch!" Pillar yelped, as Cowbell and Inkcap disappeared down the mountain as quickly as if they had been snatched up by the wind.

NINETEEN

IF BASH HAD NEVER COME BACK and had not wanted anyone to know what he was up to on the outside, then, as far as the villagers were concerned, he would have been like Lightkeeper's older sister: someone who had sloughed off their farmer's skin and gone on to live the good life. But now, Bash had returned.

Wasn't Bash a capable fellow? Didn't he have all the essential abilities? So why had he come back? Many people wouldn't laugh at him openly but did mock him in private. He went back to live in his little wooden shack on the highway, mending shoes and tyres, but apart from Inkcap and Cowbell, no one went to welcome him home. However, the Branch Secretary, at least, was in a good mood, as he opened his courtyard door and waited for Bash to visit. He took down the string of tobacco leaves hanging on the wall, unravelled them, and laid them one by one on the damp ground next to a bucket. He stripped out the ribs and snipped the leaves into thin strips with scissors. These he sprayed with wine and dripped with sesame oil, before nestling them carefully in his tobacco box.

He was thinking, If domestic pigs escape from their pen and run off, they don't become wild boars when they're up on the mountain, do they? Bash will come and report to me about what he got up to out there over the past few months. When he has reported, I will definitely make a review. Now, how should I reprimand him? I will crush him under a barrage of words.

In that respect, the Branch Secretary was well-acquainted with the necessary rhetorical devices. Now, his tobacco was neatly nestled in the tobacco box and he had sat in his chair with his copper water pipe for three days in a row, but there was not even the ghost of a sign of Bash.

There was another matter that set the villagers' tongues wagging over those three days and that was Awning sawing the right handlebar off his bicycle. Normally, Awning didn't lend his bicycle to anyone, but people who wanted to go to Luozhen for whatever reason were always pestering him to borrow it. On this particular day, it was Pockmark and Baldy Jin who came to ask. Awning didn't want to lend them the bike, Baldy Jin said something Awning took exception to and the two of them began to squabble. In a fit of anger, Awning used a small hacksaw to cut off the right handlebar. Because he was left-handed and very strong, he could push the bike, mount it and ride it, all with just his left hand, but anyone else would find it impossible. Sawing off the right-hand handlebar put paid to the idea of anyone ever borrowing the bike again.

On the same day, Soupspoon was drying some maize on a mat outside his house and all his neighbours' chickens came over to steal it. He exploded out of his door and drove them off, but as soon as he went back inside, they came running straight back. He was so angry that he grabbed an axe and was about to throw it. But he was worried that it might kill one of the chickens, so he came up with a ruse. He tied a length of thread around a kernel of maize, wrapped the thread around a small wooden stick and put the kernel down in front of the drying mat. Sure enough, a hen came to eat the maize and swallowed it down so it was followed into its stomach by the thread. Eventually, the little wooden stick got lodged sideways in the hen's mouth and it was unable either to swallow it down or spit it out. It flapped its wings like crazy and left. One of his neighbours scolded Soupspoon for being so fucking stupid as to come up with such a damaging trick. As they were exchanging views, Bash came out of the alley. Soupspoon saw him and ignored him, as did his neighbours.

"What I did to that chicken is nothing compared with what Awning did," Soupspoon said.

"Awning sawed the handlebar off his own bicycle," his neighbour said, "but you're trapping someone else's chicken!"

"So why did you let your chickens come over here when you could see I was drying my grain? At least my little trick will stop anyone else doing that."

At that point, Bash walked past and, as soon as he was gone, Soupspoon and his neighbour stopped going on about chickens and started talking about Bash again.

The Bash they saw now was not at all unkempt or dressed in tatty clothes. He was still thin and dark-complexioned and wore dark glasses, but he was dressed in a four-pocket Mao suit. It had the faded grey colour that comes from multiple washings and the collar and cuffs were frayed, so it certainly wasn't new, but it was the kind of thing only city folk wore. Did that mean Bash had been to the city? If he had, the only people he knew there were Lightkeeper's sister and her husband, so was the Mao suit one of Lightkeeper's brother-in-law's cast-offs?

When it came to speculating about Bash's Mao suit, Inkcap firmly denied that it came from that source, as Lightkeeper himself wore an old Mao suit given to him by his brother-in-law, and it was collarless, whereas the collar of Bash's jacket was like the one worn by Commune Secretary Zhang. It was made of foreign cloth and was particularly white in colour. Hearing what Inkcap had to say on the subject, Useless called him into his courtyard for questioning. Useless's mother was holding a hen and pulling a thread out of its mouth. Inkcap realised it must have been Useless's chicken that was snared by Soupspoon and he wanted to laugh, but he didn't dare.

"You're very close to Bash," Useless said. "Has he told you what he was doing while he was out there?"

"No."

"Has he told you why he came back?"

"No."

As soon as Useless's mother had pulled the thread out of the chicken, it flew up onto the courtyard wall, fell off and flew up again.

"Are you still trying to fly?" she scolded it. "Do you really think you can? You can't even get past the courtyard wall. What do you think you are? An eagle? Or a phoenix?"

On the morning of the fourth day of his return, Bash went up Middle Mountain.

Inkcap and Cowbell were picking locust flowers from the trees beside the road, halfway up the mountain. All the locust flowers in the village had been picked and mixed with flour to make a steamed snack known as *caimaifan*, and only the ones on the mountain road were left. There were always wasps in that particular locust tree grove, and their nests looked like gourds made out of mud. Few dared to go there, and even the workers in the kiln field ran past on tiptoe, constantly looking round them. But Cowbell had his greedy eyes on the locust flowers and persuaded Inkcap to go with him. He took a handful of hemp stalks with him, saying that if they encountered any wasps, he would use them to make a torch. However, when they got to the locust tree grove, they didn't dare go in after all and instead stuck to collecting flowers from the trees by the roadside. Bash came over to see what they were doing.

"Here are some locust flowers for you, Older Brother Bash," said Inkcap.

"I don't eat *maifan*," Bash told him.

"Why not? Don't you have the flour to mix the flowers with?" Cowbell asked.

Inkcap knew that Bash had no food in the shack when he came back, so he made disparaging noises to try to stop Cowbell from upsetting Bash. But Cowbell persisted.

"Why did you leave without a word, Older Brother Bash?"

"I was starving. Why wouldn't I just leave?"

"Then why have you come back?"

"I would have starved to death, wouldn't I?"

In a fury, Bash lashed out with his foot at the locust tree, so hard that it shook. Cowbell hurriedly grabbed hold of a branch and swung himself up into the air. A flock of red-billed, white-tailed birds flew down from the white-barked pine on top of the mountain, circled above their heads, and then flew back to their tree again.

"Are you going up the mountain to see Goodman, Older Brother Bash?" Inkcap suddenly broke in.

"How did you know?"

"I know everything, don't I!" Inkcap was very pleased with himself and he wanted to tell Bash why, but Bash didn't let him and just turned away and headed up the mountain.

Bash didn't ask Inkcap to go with him, but he didn't tell him not to either, so Inkcap knew that he actually did want him to follow. He forgot about Cowbell and the locust flowers and tagged on behind Bash like a tail.

Goodman was cooking maize grits rice congee as the sun streamed in through the window, turning the room half black and half white. He was walking around the room, so he too kept turning from black to white or remaining half and half when he stopped on the dividing line between the two. The soup was bubbling in the pot and the plopping of the bubbles as they burst sounded like croaking frogs. He knew that someone was coming to see him, but he hadn't expected it to be Bash. Bash did not call out Goodman's name or stamp his feet or cough. He just went straight into the building where he took off his Mao jacket and hung it on the door made of bundled corn stalks. This indicated that he did not want anyone to come in, and that included Inkcap, who was close on his heels. Inkcap's interest was piqued, and he waited under the white-barked pine tree. It was when Bash took off his jacket that Inkcap discovered that what had looked like a white shirt under the jacket turned out to be just a collar. He was very disappointed by the revelation.

Goodman stayed sitting in front of the stove and didn't get up. He told Bash he could sit down on one of the cushions, or, if he took off his shoes, on the *kang*.

"You are the thoroughbred of Old Kiln," he told him. "You are the eagle on the banks of the Zhou River. Why have you come to see me?"

Bash said he had come for instruction about what fate held in store for him. He had been living a good-for-nothing life here in the village and had left in a fit of anger. But the more he went out into the world, the more chaotic his feelings became. He said he had gone to the county town first to meet his classmates. They were now the kind of folk who went to restaurants, wore watches and leather shoes, and rode bicycles to work. And after work, the young couples even went for an evening stroll along the river! Later on, he had gone to the provincial capital and met up with Lightkeeper's sister and her husband. Their life was even better. They sat in chairs with springs, read books as thick as bricks, ate their meals at the table and bathed once a day. Just what the hell was going on? He had been no worse in school than them. He and Lightkeeper's sister got on fine, but he still thought of her as a class above. Goodman smiled without saying anything, and his silent smile made the wrinkles appear on his face.

"Are you mocking me too?" Bash said. "I couldn't stay at a hotel while I was out there because I didn't have a letter of introduction, and I couldn't go to a restaurant because I didn't have any food tickets. I just had to rely on mending shoes, eating whatever I could lay my hands on and sleeping wherever I was when night fell. Now I'm back, the first thing I've done is come to see you. I haven't talked about this to anyone except you, Goodman. And all you can do is mock me?"

Goodman kept on smiling. "I'm not mocking you. And I will never tell another soul about what you have told me today."

"You said I was a thoroughbred, but where is the open grassland for a thoroughbred to gallop? You said I was an eagle, but where are the open skies for an eagle to soar? Is this my destiny, then? To be a farmer in Old Kiln and be downtrodden all my life? You understand yin and yang, Goodman, and if you understand that, you can pray people better. Cure me, Goodman. Pray me better and change my fate. Change my fate."

"I don't know how to do that," Goodman replied." I only talk to illnesses, and you have an illness."

Bash really was ill. A patch of broken red pustules had appeared on his forehead. He had already squeezed them but only managed to squeeze out a little pus. Now he didn't dare touch them. He was also constipated. He had eaten without shitting properly for three days, with only little pellets like sheep droppings coming out. He sprayed saliva when he breathed out, the corners of his mouth were ulcerated, and his teeth hurt.

"I am ill," Bash admitted. "My body burns like it's on fire. When I sleep on the *kang* at night, I'm afraid the quilt will catch fire. My teeth have been hurting for ages. When they hurt, it feels like my mouth is crammed full of horses' teeth."

"Don't worry, Bash," Goodman said. "You need to treat your illness first. This illness is so severe that it can't be cured with just one or two treatments. You haven't eaten, have you? You will eat with me today. Do you need another bowl of water? You can have it here."

Goodman stood up and pulled Bash over to sit on the *kang*. He added an extra ladle of water to the pot and sat in front of the stove to light the fire.

"Now then, Bash," he said, "there's a cigarette box on the *kang*, so you have a smoke and listen to me."

He began to talk and what he said was not directly concerned with Bash at all. He just stared at the stove where the fire was crackling away.

This is what he said: "When a person falls into a sea of suffering, it is difficult for him to get out of it without someone who can swim to save him. When I save people, I not only save their lives but also their essence. Saving people's lives is temporary and is still bound by cause and effect. Saving their essence is eternal. Once you save someone's essence, you break the cycle forever. When a person's essence is rescued from a sea of suffering and landed safely on the other shore, it will never fall back in again."

"People are easily confused," he went on, "and often take falsehood as truth, which is called an inability to see through things. That's why they get angry with others when they are told they are wrong. In fact, it is they themselves who cannot see through things and if they could only penetrate the worldly, they would be sure to laugh. When I first realised there were no good people in the world, I was so angry, my anger made me suffer from tuberculosis for twelve years, and it almost killed me. It was only later that I began to study books about goodness and learned to talk to illnesses that I realised my anger was wrong, and I confessed my faults to the heavens and took responsibility for them. My tuberculosis healed overnight, and I immediately emerged from Hell.

"People have to recognise that there is virtue in reversal. You should not talk of suffering a loss because it is certain that you owed the other party. If everyone feels sorry for you, you will live a long life. If I am beaten and cursed for no reason, it is because I am at fault. I have to repay what is due and be grateful. If I had not been beaten and scolded, how would my sins have been redeemed? Even the small-minded man has his good points, for he is the one who squeezes the good out of people and helps you from the opposite side, just as Yue Fei was helped by Qin Hui, and Guan Gong was helped by Cao Cao. So how can you not be grateful to him? The Dao is formed in adversity and bad comes out of good. Just consider that meat is fragrant but stinks when it goes off, while cabbage has no fragrance and does not stink when it goes bad. Fruit does not spoil when it is green, but when it is ripe, it is very close to spoiling. The same is true in human affairs."

"Refining human nature is what we call learning," Goodman continued. "You should practise it among relatives and friends, and once you've done that, you won't be afraid of anything you encounter. This is like bricks and tiles that become strong after being refined. Those that are not refined are like adobe, which melts when exposed to water. Ordinary people cannot learn the Dao, and their illness lies in their desire to be superior and hatred of being inferior. They do not realise that high places are dangerous but low places are safe. It's like digging a well – you don't choose a high place to dig, because the lower you go, the more water you will find. The same is true in human affairs. You need to fill in the deficiencies at the bottom. If others don't want it, you can pick it up yourself. If others don't do it, you can do it yourself. If others dislike it, don't be disgusted by it yourself. This is the same as the way water raises everything from underneath. Do not seek knowledge from others, do not rely on your own strengths, do not speak of your own achievements, and in doing so you will gain everyone's respect. That is the true Dao.

"To understand the Dao, one must first understand one's own Dao, then the Dao of one's family, then the Dao of everyone else, and finally examine the Dao of all things. If there are things you don't know, ask and answer yourself, and gradually you can come to understand. This is called asking the heavens. When I left the temple, I asked myself why people do what they do. I answered: to make a living. Why do they make a living? To feed people. Why do they feed people? Because that is to follow the Dao. I thought about it very carefully and realised that I had got it all wrong and had not been following the Dao at all. Only then did I wake up to the need to understand the Dao of being a man, of being a woman, of being a father, of being a son, of being a couple, of being a relative or a neighbour, of being a member of the village, and of being a cadre. That is called the fundamental Dao."

Goodman smelt that the rice was cooked and put out the fire. He stood up to serve the meal, only to see that Bash had fallen asleep on the *kang*. A mouse was perched on the lid of the porcelain pot at the corner of the *kang*, its long tail hanging over the edge and its eyes as bright as if they had been touched in with paint.

"And all that time, I've been lecturing to a mouse!" Goodman sighed, then shook Bash by the foot. "Wake up. Wake up. I'm still going to feed you."

"I wasn't asleep," Bash said. "My head was a bit heavy and I just stretched out."

"So you heard me talking to your illness then?"

Bash opened his eyes wide, and his face took on a fierce expression.

"You said you could talk to illnesses. Is this how you go about it? You just talk a load of nonsense as if my illness means nothing to you? I came here for you to pray me better. I trusted you, and all you can come up with is that load of tripe. Are you trying to make a fool out of me?"

Goodman was momentarily stunned.

"I'm not trying to make a fool out of you."

"Do you think I'm not going to pay you? Is that what it is?"

Bash put his hand in his pocket, counted out five yuan and slapped the coins down on the stove.

"Alas," Goodman sighed. "The world may kneel down and burn incense to ask the Buddha for blessings, life and wealth, but who knows what the Buddha really is?"

"I want you to pray me better," Bash insisted.

"How can I do that? There is no point in honouring the gods if you are unfilial to your parents. There is no point in making friends if you are unfaithful to your brothers. There is no point in consulting feng shui if your heart is not true. There is no point in taking medicine if you are not willing to make the effort. There is no point asking for things if your luck is bad."

"I want you to pray me better," Bash insisted.

"Ah! Same old Bash," Goodman laughed.

Then he pulled Bash's head towards him and muttered something in his ear.

"Is that going to cure me, then?"

Goodman stuffed the money back into Bash's pocket, but Bash retrieved it and slapped the coins back down on the stove, saying, "You have to take this because that way I won't owe you anything."

Then he slipped out of the door.

It was only when Goodman went to stand in the doorway that he realised Inkcap was outside.

"If Bash doesn't want to eat the rice now it's ready," he said, "what about you, Inkcap?"

"I'll eat it!"

Inkcap went inside, took the lid off the pot and saw a thin glutinous rice congee. He dipped a ladle into it and took a mouthful. It was scalding hot, but he still managed to say, in a low voice, "So you can pray people better. How did you manage it for him?"

"Before she died, Stargazer's mother was always sick and not long for this world. When others were still wearing un-lined clothes around the tenth day of the eighth month, she was wearing a padded cotton jacket. I told her I couldn't talk her illness away, and she asked me to pray it better. I told her she had to go up to the mountain to pray to the mountain god. She did as I said and went every day for a year. Her health improved and she lived another three years. Why did I make her worship the mountain god? Well, it raised her spirits and with her going up the mountain every day for a year, how could her health not slowly improve? Do you understand now?"

"No, I don't," Inkcap said.

"Are you coming, Inkcap?" Bash shouted from under the white-barked pine where he was standing.

"I'm off," Inkcap said.

The rice was still too hot to eat, so Goodman took half a carrot from the chopping board and gave it to Inkcap. He took it and left.

As Bash and Inkcap walked down the mountainside, Lightkeeper was pulling a cartload of clay up from the bottom of the slope.

Lightkeeper noticed the Mao suit Bash was wearing and asked, "Did you find my brother-in-law?"

"Ah!" Bash said.

"Didn't he give you anything for me?"

"No."

"Well, don't go looking for him in future."

"You're you and he's him," Bash retorted.

He waited for Lightkeeper to go past with his cart, then said, "That's a laugh, him telling me what to do. I need a piss."

He undid his trousers and started to piss as high as he could.

"You do what I tell you from now on, Inkcap," he said.

Inkcap had heard that Bash had a mole on his prick but he didn't dare look.

"Yes," he said.

"Just listen to me, and you'll do well out of it in the future."

"So did you find Lightkeeper's brother-in-law? Did he give you this Mao suit?"

"Don't listen to what you shouldn't be hearing, and don't say what shouldn't be said. Heaven is deaf and Earth is mute."

Inkcap stopped talking, but he couldn't keep it up.

"Did he only give you a collar to go inside the jacket?"

"You know shit. This is called a false collar."

Inkcap had learned something new.

Bash shook his prick vigorously and tucked it back into his trousers, saying, "Wrap it three times around your waist, drag it eight *zhang* along the ground and try and take a fucking crow out on the wing!"

Inkcap's mouth twitched.

"Wait for me by the cowshed this evening," Bash said, then he strode away so fast, Inkcap couldn't keep up with him any more.

Inkcap had no idea what Bash was up to at the cowshed. The sky was getting dark and every child in the village had had its last shit of the day. "Yo! Yo! Yo!" The sound of someone calling dogs rang out, and all the dogs cheered and ran into the alley. Ever-Obedient's dog showed up, yelping and bumping into Inkcap. It was the dog that had had its fur cut off and even though it had all grown back by now, the creature still liked to play around with Inkcap, so it jumped at him, wagging its tail vigorously.

"I don't have time," Inkcap said, and he made his way straight to the cowshed.

There didn't seem to be anyone in the cowshed, so he called out, "Grandpa Happy! Grandpa Happy!"

A rough voice from behind the feed trough at the north of the shed told him to shut up. It was Bash who had pushed the trough to one side and was bent over digging out the earth with a mattock.

"Has Grandpa Happy gone home for dinner? What are you digging for?" Inkcap asked.

"Stop talking and shovel that earth to one side."

The soil under the feed trough was soft enough, but as Bash dug, he hit a large stone. He took the stone out and kept digging until he had a large pit more than three *chi* deep. The moon climbed out from behind the mountain, then rested on the ridgepole of Bash's old lodgings next door. The cows became restless and frisky and came over to the edge of the pit, where they kicked at the excavated soil with their hooves. Although they were all tied to pillars with nose ropes, they still attempted to use their heads to nudge Inkcap. He tried several times to keep shovelling but had to keep ducking away because he didn't dare get too close to the cows.

"Hit them with a stick," Bash said.

A pickaxe handle swung past Inkcap and hit a bull between its hind legs. Inkcap recognised the spotted bull with bezoars as it bellowed in shock. After that, it lay down on the edge of the pit. Bash kept hitting it, but it wouldn't budge. He grabbed the nose-ring rope, threw it over the crossbeam, and pulled hard. As the cow's neck was stretched, it got to its feet with beads of sweat like beans rolling down its back.

"Don't pull any more," Inkcap said. "It's got bezoars. You might pull it to death."

"If it dies, there'll be beef to eat," Bash said.

He dug down another *chi*, then exclaimed, "Fuck Goodman! It was him who told me to do this."

It was only then that Inkcap realised all this digging was Goodman's way of praying Bash better.

"Did Goodman tell you to dig?"

"He said there's a stone tablet under the feed trough and I should set it up in front of the temple gate. So where is the bloody thing?"

"Did he say what the stone tablet was?"

Bash set to digging with his pick again and dug up a soft object the size of a basin.

"Is it meat?" he wondered out loud.

"Can you dig meat out of the ground?" Inkcap asked.

Bash hauled the thing out of the pit and it was indeed a lump of meat. How could there be meat in the field?

"Am I dreaming?" Inkcap asked.

"What kind of dream would that be?"

Inkcap poked the meat vigorously and found it could move.

"It's alive!" he exclaimed. "What kind of animal is it?"

Bash dipped his head to have a look. It was alive and it was an animal of some kind, but animals have noses, eyes and mouths. This animal had none of them and was just a soft lump of flesh. Spookily, Happy chose that moment to appear.

Happy had been quietly eating his dinner at home, when he suddenly began to panic. Had he put out all the fires for heating water? Were all the cows tied up by their nose rings? He put down his bowl and went back to the cowshed.

Inkcap heard a noise below the temple gate. He turned his head and listened again. It was the sound of Happy's footsteps, and they were coming towards the cowshed.

"I have to piss," Inkcap said, and he ducked into the shadow of the gable of the cattle pen. When Happy and Bash began to argue, he slipped away.

Happy untied the cow's nose-ring rope from the crossbeam and demanded in a loud voice why there was such a big hole under the feed trough. Had the Branch Secretary asked him to dig it? Or was it the captain of the production team?

"Are you trying to make the cowshed collapse so you can take all the cows home with you?" Happy asked.

Bash sounded calm at first and asked Happy not to raise his voice. He said he was excavating a stone tablet. Once he'd got it out, he would fill in the hole and restore the cow trough to its original position.

"How can there be a stone tablet under the cowshed?"

"It must be there," Bash said. "Goodman wouldn't dare mess me around."

"And is Goodman the Branch Secretary? Can he back up what he says?"

"This is important to me. Don't kick up a fuss."

"It may be good for you but it isn't good for the production team. This is their cowshed. No one can simply come along and dig it up as they please and make off with the cattle."

"Why are you being so difficult? I've told you what it's all about, so get out of the way and don't make me lose my temper."

"Go ahead and lose it. I'm already so angry it's leaking out my arsehole! You can't dig here."

With that, Happy jumped into the pit.

Bash pulled at him, but he wouldn't budge. That was when Bash really lost his temper and, in a flash, he seized hold of Happy and had his arms and legs pinioned so he couldn't move.

"Are you going to hit me?" Happy squealed.

"No," Bash replied, and with a grunt, he threw Happy out of the pit like a basket of soil. Happy lay on the ground for a while, then leapt up and ran off, saying he was going to see the Branch Secretary. Suddenly the alley was filled with his shouts: "Bash has trashed the cowshed! Bash has trashed the cowshed!"

Bash dug out a few more shovelfuls, but still couldn't find the stone tablet. The village dogs began to snap at him, so he picked up the pickaxe handle and shouted for Inkcap a couple of times. He swore at him when he didn't reply, then stumbled over something. It was the lump of flesh he had dug up. He found a dung basket in the cowshed, stuffed the lump into it and carried it away.

Happy ran over to the Branch Secretary's house to make his complaint but the Secretary wasn't there as he had gone over to the commune for a meeting. Happy's cries, which made it sound as though someone was being murdered, brought lots of people running towards the cowshed, and they were amazed to see a large hole dug in the floor. Some of them said the cowshed was common property, so anyone who wanted to dig it up was free to do so. Others said that if Bash had a problem with the Branch Secretary, he couldn't just take it out on common property. If he dug a hole today, who was to say he wouldn't make off with the roof tiles tomorrow? Of course, there were also people who defended Bash, saying that if he had really wanted to do some damage, he could have taken a knife to the cattle or, if not that, he could have chopped down the pillars that supported the cowshed. Then the talk shifted from digging up tablets to Goodman. He had said that there was a stone tablet under the feed trough. Was there really a stone tablet there? Some said that Goodman was an unusual person whose predictions often came true, while others said he was unhappy about being moved out of the Kiln God Temple and was using Bash to take revenge. Because the Branch Secretary was not in the village, and Potful was too sick to come out, everyone was bandying their own opinion about, until they eventually lost interest and set to together to fill in the pit. Then they moved the feed trough back into place.

It was then that Yoyo suddenly said, "This public office isn't at all bad. I wonder if they've fixed the price yet."

As soon as she spoke, everyone fell silent.

Under the moonlight, the top of the public office's gable wall cast two long, black shadows across the courtyard, dividing it into three patches of white.

"Are you going to buy it, then?" Sparks asked.

"Your poor brother Ever-Obedient couldn't afford it even if he sold his own bones!" Yoyo told him.

"Hey!" Sparks said. "Bash had the nerve to dig a hole in the cowshed. Do you think he wants to buy the public office and the cowshed together?"

"He ought to buy it, but can he afford it?" Barndoor said.

"The way I see it," Yoyo said, "no one in Old Kiln can afford it, and the buildings will fall apart if they're not lived in. I expect they'll be turned over to cows in the future, so the whole courtyard will be filled with cattle pens and cowsheds."

"There is someone who can afford it," Sparks said.

"Who's that?" Ever-Obedient asked.

"How about the Branch Secretary? Would he want to buy it, though?"

Everyone thought about it for a while and realised that it was a possibility. Although the Branch Secretary had a courtyard house, the old couple lived in the main building, the east annex was the kitchen, and the west annex was given over to their son when he came back to stay from the Luozhen agricultural machinery station. But both the east and west buildings were so shallow there was no room to turn round once you were inside. The son got engaged last year and if he got married, could the east and west annexes be used as the newlyweds' quarters?

"Ah!" Old Faithful said.

"Ah! Ah! Ah! Ah! Ah!" Big Root, Baldy Jin, Caretaker, Iron Bolt and Feng Youliang all said together.

"I didn't want to say it, but you lot seemed blind to the possibility," Sparks said. "The Branch Secretary always looks ahead. He probably had the idea of moving the public office to the Kiln God Temple when his son got engaged. Commune Secretary Zhang said it was too spacious for Goodman to live in. That's the reason the public office is being moved to the Kiln God Temple."

"Then it's a conspiracy, isn't it?" Baldy Jin said.

"Leave it," Useless said. "It's all just guesswork."

"Admit it," Sparks said. "It's obvious, isn't it?"

"It's hard for the Branch Secretary to find housing too," Useless pleaded.

"Not as difficult as it is for Bash," Sparks said. "His old lodgings are about to collapse."

"We're talking about a house for sale here," Useless insisted, "not free housing."

"I've got a gut feeling," Sparks said.

"What do you mean?" Useless said. "Whose guts are you feeling?"

"My guts!" Sparks sneered. "Who the fuck's guts do you think?"

Everyone else tried to get them to stop as their conversation descended into insults.

"Enough! Enough! This is a public building. Anyone can buy it, and it doesn't matter how much for because the money isn't going to be divided between our households. Let's all go back to sleep."

Barndoor slapped his buttocks and left, to be followed by Feng Youliang, Big Root, Ever-Obedient and everyone else.

TWENTY

BASH'S FAILED ATTEMPT TO DIG UP THE STONE TABLET caused quite a stir in Old Kiln. It was impossible for him to try again, and he became increasingly angry and annoyed at everything he saw. Soupspoon was grooming his dog at his courtyard gate. When he saw Bash carrying a load of gravel, he asked what he was doing.

"Washing stones," Bash replied.

"Washing stones? Are you crazy?"

"No, are *you* crazy?" Bash shot back.

"All right. All right. I'm crazy," Soupspoon said. "I've got a tear in both my shoes. Can you mend them for me?"

"No."

"Not even if I pay you?"

"No."

Soupspoon's dog rolled over and bit Bash.

Bash kicked the dog so it rolled back over.

"Did you just bite me? Now I'm going to bite you!"

He went back to the wooden shack where he found Apricot's family cat stretched out in the doorway, waiting for Apricot. He combed his hair in anticipation of Apricot's arrival, but after waiting for a long time with no sign of her, he messed up his hair again and carried the basin containing the lump of flesh over to the door, thinking to himself, You've got no eyes, ears or mouth, so what exactly are you?

A warm wind blew down from Yijia Ridge, causing the grass on the roadside to stretch their leaves upwards, and making the wings of the little grey moths climbing the trees flap, so they turned yellow and pink. The sparrows flew from the Zhen River Pagoda to the river embankment. They did not look like they were flying but bore a greater resemblance to stones being thrown. Maybe they were not sparrows after all, but really were stones, stones that took to the air in the spring. Bash felt sleepy and wanted to yawn. Aaah! He did yawn once and then several times in succession.

A bicycle was weaving along the road towards him, catching him mid-yawn. The cyclist was an old man. He stopped at the door to get his tyres pumped up. Suddenly he saw the soft lump of flesh and asked, "Where did you get this?"

"I dug it up," Bash replied.

"Where?"

"Out of the earth."

"Is it for sale?"

"Yes."

He looked at the man, who was all beard from the nose down, with no visible mouth. Although he had already said it was for sale, he continued, "If you know what it is, you can buy it."

"Are you testing me? It's a *taisui*, isn't it?" said the man, referring to a rare aggregate of fungus, mould and bacterium used widely in traditional Chinese medicine.

"A *taisui*?" Bash pricked up his ears. He had heard of *taisui* but thought they were just a myth. So they were a real thing, after all! "This is a *taisui*?"

"Didn't you know?" the old man asked.

"Of course, I knew. I dug it up, didn't I?"

"You mustn't disturb the earth on top of a *taisui*, but you've dared dig it up. You're quite something!"

Although Bash was secretly alarmed, he said boastfully, "Can't you see that for yourself?"

The old man regarded Bash and said, "You look OK, so I reckon you can control it. If you can't control this thing, it will bring disaster down on you, but if you can control it, it will bring you good luck. What do you want for it?"

"Your eyes."

"What do you mean, 'my eyes'?"

"I mean I just want you to look at it, no money involved."

"How do I know I can take someone like you at your word?"

"That's rich coming from you! You haven't even got a mouth!"

"What do you think this is?" the old man said, parting his beard.

He gave a laugh and then told Bash, "The water from a *taisui* like this is very nourishing, and if you eat the flesh, it will get rid of diseases, strengthen the body and prolong life."

As he spoke, he lowered his head to drink a few mouthfuls from the basin and dipped his fingers into the water to rinse his eyes with. Seeing the old man's enthusiasm, Bash fetched a small earthenware pot from the house and half-filled it with the water for the old man to take away with him.

Bash had never thought he could dig up a *taisui*, this amazing object with so many beneficial effects. He remembered all the stories about immortals pretending to be white-bearded old men or toothless old women giving people stones that turned into gold. Was this old man actually an immortal who wanted to bring him enlightenment? He immediately felt better and had the impulse to talk to the cat.

"Stand up," he ordered.

The cat stayed lying where it was. Bash lifted its front paws to make it stand, but as soon as he let go, it flopped back down.

"You're just a piece of shit, lying there on the ground."

That evening, Bash drank half a bowl of *taisui* water. When dawn broke the next day, there was no more crud in the corners of his eyes, and his forehead and nose were now populated with far fewer red pimples. He began to believe what the old man had said and treasured his *taisui*. He called Inkcap over and gave him some of the water, telling him it would make him grow a head taller. Inkcap didn't think it tasted anything special, but he still leaned against the door and asked Bash to draw a line on the door panel to see how much he might grow over the next fortnight.

Bash went down to the river to wash some rice and told Inkcap to dig the ash out of the stove in the small wooden shack. Inkcap dug for a while and then used some chopsticks to poke the *taisui*. It moved when he prodded it. Inkcap thought to himself that if drinking *taisui* water could make him grow a head taller, its flesh might make him grow even more. He couldn't stop himself from cutting an egg-sized lump out of it with a knife. It was like tofu and didn't bleed. He tucked the lump safely and secretly inside his jacket. When Bash came back from washing the rice, Inkcap said he was going home.

"Why the rush?" Bash asked. "Are you stealing from me?"

"What have you got for me to steal?" Inkcap shot back.

Bash looked at the *kang*, and his torch was still there. He looked at the stove, and his sunglasses were still sitting there. He smiled and said, "How can you mock me for being poor, Inkcap? Yijia Ridge is mine, and the Zhou River is mine too. You just wait and see."

Inkcap made sure his jacket was firmly tucked in and left, saying as he went, "I'll wait. You can give me a piece of cloud from Yijia Ridge when the time comes."

He wanted to laugh but didn't dare. He broke into a trot, farting as he went.

He rushed excitedly to the village entrance where he found Gran. She had nothing else to do and liked to hang out there. The pus in her ears had got worse, preventing her from hearing clearly what others said, so didn't speak very much herself. In the evening, she watched the clouds and mist on Yijia Ridge stack up, one by one, like a succession of white trees or like smoke rising from a simmering fire. She was watching a cat sneak out from under the wheat grass, its body impossibly elongated. She was watching the cows coming back from ploughing the fields as they trotted past the alley, their hind legs stretching like a man jumping over rocks in a river. Inkcap knew Gran was collecting ideas for her papercuts, so he caught a snake in the weeds in the field, held it by the tail and shook it so it hung straight down. He let Gran look at the snake's body, telling her that it was a lighter green than Apricot's green dress, but with more of a jade tone.

"Drop it! Drop it!" Gran pleaded.

Inkcap could see how happy Gran was so he had no compunction about telling her a fib, saying that Cowbell had begged him to go and spend the night with him. Gran agreed but reminded him that when night fell and they went to sleep, they should wake themselves up to go for a piss because if both of them pissed the *kang*, the *kang* would collapse.

They cooked the *taisui* flesh at Cowbell's house. It wasn't particularly tasty and was rather like cooked mushrooms. But in the middle of the night, both of them felt hot in their stomachs and their mouths and tongues were dry. They drank a ladle of cold water but did not fall asleep again.

The next day, Inkcap was worried that Bash would find out that the *taisui* was missing a piece of flesh and would come and beat him, but there was no sign of him. Whenever he saw anyone, Inkcap told them that Bash had dug up a *taisui*, which could cure illnesses. He wanted to go back to the shack but he didn't dare.

At noon, some people went to the east slope of Middle Mountain to build terraces, and some went to work on the weir in the lotus pond. The weir frequently collapsed in winter, and it was necessary to shore it up with mud shovelled from the pond. The water in the pool was still a little cold and the workers were barefoot in the water, so, every so often, they hurried out of the water and sat in the wheat field by the pool, smoking cigarettes and talking. The women were digging out grass in the wheat field. When they saw that the men who were shovelling mud in the pool had stopped, they stopped too, took shoe soles from inside their tops to mend, and shouted for Dazed-And-Confused. As soon as he heard his name, Dazed-And-Confused came running over. He was a well set-up fellow, but lazy and liked to hang around with the women, and the women liked to joke around with him. Flower Girl mended her shoes for a while but ran out of thread. She looked at the trousers Third Aunt was wearing.

"How did you dye those?" she asked. "The colour is so even."

But Third Aunt was distracted and said, "Aiya! I can't dawdle here any longer. It took me all morning just to clear a few plots of grass."

"The men are all slackers," Yoyo said. "They want us women to do all the work."

Third Aunt picked up her basket and mattock and made her way back to the wheat field, where she found Pockmark lying on his back looking up at the sky.

"What are you doing sleeping here?" she asked.

"If I wasn't here, how would I get any work points?"

"You've got a nerve, playing the system like this."

"Why didn't you tell me some people haven't come?"

"Like who?"

"Can you see Bash anywhere?"

Not far away on the dirt road, a few women were idly talking to Dazed-And-Confused. Suddenly, they surrounded him and started to beat him. He kept giggling as they hit him. But then they overwhelmed him, undid his belt, twisted his arms behind his back and tied his hands together with the belt. They shoved his head into the crotch of his trousers and told him to get up. They lifted him up and put him on the kerbside saying, "Don't move. If you move again, we'll roll you into the ditch."

Watching the commotion, Baldy Jin said, "Dazed-And-Confused loves this kind of thing."

Third Aunt was weeding away by herself. She worked for a while before stopping and saying to Soupspoon, "The Branch Secretary and production team leader aren't here, so how come you've done so much work on the weir this morning?"

"Hungry men work harder, don't they?"

"How come you've always got more than enough energy when it's your own plot you're working on?"

Inkcap and Cowbell didn't go into the pond to shovel mud. Their legs were short, and the muddy water came up to their thighs as soon as they stepped in. All they did was stand on the side of the weir helping the men doing the construction. As soon as Inkcap saw Dazed-And-Confused having his head stuffed into his crotch – this was something the villagers often did during breaks and it was usually the women doing it to Dazed-And-Confused – he perked up and ran over.

"Does it smell nice down there?" he asked.

Third Aunt grabbed hold of him and said, "Stop trying to stir things up. Go and shovel some mud."

"I only get three work points a day."

"With everyone skiving like this, the day's not going to go very well is it?" Third Aunt said to Soupspoon.

"How should it go, then?"

"If you divvied up the land by family and household, you wouldn't get any slacking, would you?"

Soupspoon clamped his hand over Third Aunt's mouth.

"Don't let anyone hear you say that."

Then he changed the subject and asked Inkcap, "Where's Bash? Has he gone to help level the soil in the terraced fields?"

"He's looking after his *taisui*."

"Bash has a *taisui*?" Soupspoon exclaimed.

Inkcap had told several villagers that Bash had a *taisui*, but no one took him seriously and thought it was just Inkcap talking nonsense again. But when he said it now, it caught the attention of the idlers in the wheat field, but they still didn't really believe it.

"Why are you behaving like dumb animals?" Inkcap asked.

"You're the dumb animal!" Baldy Jin jeered.

Inkcap was so angry that he clenched his hands into fists and his lips turned blue.

"Hey, kid!" Third Aunt said. "Why are you so angry?"

"Why won't they believe me?" Inkcap wailed.

"You think quite a bit of yourself, don't you? I believe you. I believe you."

Everyone now believed Inkcap and their expressions changed. Five years before, when the Zhou River flooded, someone discovered a *taisui* in the waters. No one dared move it and everyone ran away. When they plucked up the courage to go back and have a look, it was gone. Now Bash actually had a *taisui* that he was keeping at his home. Fuck it! Why did this kind of thing always happen to Bash? But then again, who else would dare keep such a thing at home? The workers put down their farm tools and made their way from the wheat field to the small wooden shack on the highway to see this rarity for themselves. Pockmark wanted to go too. He leapt up from the wheat field and ran off. As he did so, he started a pheasant which flew up in panic, dropped down, flew up and dropped down again. It flew up and fell, then flew up and fell again. He simultaneously shouted for his dog and kept driving the pheasant.

Bash went to bed late, drank some more *taisui* water and fell asleep. His trousers were off and he was naked on the *kang*, but he still wore his sunglasses. Visitors knocked on his door, but he didn't wake up. They poked him with a stick through his back window, and when that did finally wake him up, someone asked, "Do you always wear your sunglasses when you're asleep, Bash?"

Bash put his trousers on and opened the door.

"I can't go to sleep without them," he explained.

Inkcap looked at the *taisui* in its basin and, to his astonishment, saw that the flesh had grown back where he had stolen his chunk the night before, leaving no trace. So the *taisui* could do that too! Did that mean eating it could also heal wounds? However, he didn't dare say anything.

When Bash saw so many visitors to the little wooden shack – something that had never happened since he built the place – he took full advantage of the situation to show off his treasure. He used a stick to open up every part of it for them to see and even scooped up some of the water in a ladle for them to drink, but no one dared try it.

"It tastes really good," Inkcap said, taking the first drink, and after that everyone else rushed forward and smacked their lips after drinking, saying, "It's magic water!" They all wanted more but Bash wouldn't let them. He said he was no longer going to mend shoes and would instead be selling *taisui* water at the side of the high road. It would cost five fen a mouthful.

Just as Bash was boasting about his plans, Awning rode up from the highway with the Branch Secretary on his bicycle. At first, the Branch Secretary didn't want Awning to stop, but not only was there such a crowd at the door to the little wooden shack, Inkcap also stepped out into the middle of the road to stop the bicycle, saying, "Mr Branch Secretary, sir, come and try the magic water."

The Branch Secretary was forced to get off the bicycle and he addressed Inkcap sternly: "What kind of water is this? Do you think I've never drunk water from the Zhou River before?"

"It's *taisui* water," Inkcap said. "Bash has got a *taisui*."

"Where did he get a *taisui* from?"

"He dug it up. He dug it up out of the ground."

The Branch Secretary didn't approach the little wooden shack but asked, "He dug up a *taisui* even though no one dares even disturb the earth above one? Why is no one working today?"

"The weir on the lotus pond is finished," Soupspoon said.

"And does it reach all the way to the highway?"

The Branch Secretary was clearly furious, and everyone turned grey with fear. Someone dashed towards the lotus pond, and then everyone started running after him. Inkcap was still saying "Mr Branch Secretary, sir... sir..." as the Branch Secretary strode away determinedly with his hands clasped behind his back.

As soon as the Branch Secretary got home, Soupspoon arrived to report on the excavation at the cowshed and the villagers' discussions about the disposal of the public office when they went to fill in the pit. He was unsure of himself as he spoke, and the Branch Secretary sat in a chair with his eyes closed. Soupspoon thought he was asleep and waved his hand in front of his face.

"I am awake," the Branch Secretary said.

Soupspoon continued his report, saying that Bash had dug up the *taisui* while searching for a stone tablet. How could he be permitted to keep it at home? It was evil and unlucky and came from the devil. What did he think he was doing with it? He had found it when he was digging a pit and that was what had set the villagers off, saying all sorts of stuff about the sale of the public office. What kind of pit was he digging? He was digging a pit to trap you, Branch Secretary, a pit to trap our collective interests, a pit for the foundations of socialism! The Branch Secretary's eyes were still closed, and he hadn't moved a muscle. Soupspoon didn't say anything more. The Branch Secretary's wife carried a bamboo basket over to the threshold and Soupspoon went over to help her.

"Go on," said the Branch Secretary.

Soupspoon bent down and sat on a small stool in front of the Branch Secretary. He said that Noodle Fish had told everyone that the reason Bash had dug the pit was because Goodman had told him to. The Branch Secretary opened his eyes.

"It was Goodman's idea?"

"Yes, that's right."

"What else?"

"Nothing else."

"Be off with you, then."

The Branch Secretary closed his eyes again.

That afternoon, the work bell rang but it wasn't Potful ringing it. He was still lying on his *kang*. It was the Branch Secretary, and he was ringing it rapidly and urgently.

After feeding the pig, Gran picked up a piece of paper in the alley. She took it back home and ironed it flat on the table. As soon as the bell started ringing so urgently, her entire body began to tremble. She supported herself on the table with her hand thinking she could stop the trembling, but to her surprise, it only got worse. It felt as though she was shaking bits of flesh off her bones.

Inkcap came in from outside and Gran asked, "Can you hear the bell?"

"It's not a struggle meeting, it's a study session."

"Then why's it ringing so urgently? Who told you?"

"Pockmark's out in the alley telling everyone."

Gran went straight to the public office but when she got there, she encountered a large group sitting in the courtyard in front of the office. According to existing regulations in Old Kiln, no matter whether it was a struggle meeting or a study session, Gran had to stand at the front, so she made her way to the steps of the office. The rainwater falling from the eaves had worn a series of pits in the earth in front of the steps. Gran usually stood in the eighteenth pit, but now, Lightkeeper was standing in the seventeenth pit and Goodman was in the eighteenth.

Goodman had a slight stoop and his head naturally hung down as he stood there. He saw ants crawling out from the cracks in the stones on the steps. They were yellow ants, with big heads and thin waists. They formed a neat line and climbed onto his shoes and then onto his trouser legs.

"Step forward, you. Step forward," the Branch Secretary said.

Goodman stepped forward, and an ant fell off his shoe. The ant never knew it was climbing a shoe, and it never knew why the earth shook so it fell off. It scrambled back to its feet and rubbed its face vigorously with its antennae, still uncomprehending. Goodman was afraid of stepping on the ant, so he twisted his feet away from it, almost falling down in the process, and took an extra step forward. Sitting in front of him was Baldy Jin. Baldy had taken his hat off, revealing a few extra pustules on his head. Three of them were broken and oozing with some kind of sticky substance.

"Have you been eating meat over the last few days?" Goodman whispered.

Baldy Jin rolled his eyes and said, "Yes, I caught a pheasant a few days ago, and got a cat yesterday. Who knows where the cat came from, but its meat tasted sour."

"You should observe the food taboos."

"If I try observing the taboos when I'm already starving, I'll end up so hungry I'd want to eat a dead baby if I saw one."

"You should become a vegetarian. Being a vegetarian benefits your cycle of reincarnation. If you avoid eating a certain category of things, you separate yourself from that category. If you don't eat meat, you will separate yourself from the animals and beasts."

"And now, because I ate meat, I'm just an animal, am I? Is that why you're reprimanding me?"

"I'm just talking to your illness."

Gran tugged at Goodman's jacket from behind. Meanwhile, the Branch Secretary, who didn't miss anything of what was going, called out, "Guo Baixuan!"

The villagers all called him Goodman, but his real name was Guo Baixuan.

Goodman turned and said, "I'm here."

"Why have you come here?"

"I have come here to stand."

"If you've come here to stand, then stand up straight."

Goodman stood up straight without replying.

Lightkeeper, who was very tall and slim, shot a sidelong look at the cowshed and Goodman followed his gaze. The pit had been filled in, and the new soil was obvious. The cows were standing with their heads facing east and their tails down. Only the spotted bull with bezoars was still lying down.

Inkcap arrived late. He had been stopped by Bash and stayed with him under the temple gate for a long time before they made their way to the public office. When the Branch Secretary had ordered Goodman to the meeting from the kiln, Bash guessed that he too would be summoned to stand in front of the villagers, so he forced Inkcap to keep him company and deliberately went on chatting and joking with him, while all the time being alert to what was going on. But no one called Bash to stand up front. In fact, no one even took the slightest notice of him. They simply brushed past him without a flicker. Even Apricot just glanced at him and hurriedly walked away.

Inkcap called softly after her, "Apricot! Apricot!"

Apricot had not seen Bash since he got back. She kept on saying that Bash would come looking for her, but he didn't. She took the gamble that if he didn't visit her, she wouldn't go to see him either. When Bash dug up the *taisui* and the villagers went to drink *taisui* water the next day, Inkcap told Apricot about it. But Apricot just said, "Where is he, then? What's wrong with his legs?" and she didn't go. Now, when Inkcap called softly to her, she just set off at an angle towards the public office. He saw that she couldn't walk properly any more. Her arms and legs were stiff, and she almost fell as she crossed a slight dip. Even so, the ends of her pigtails were tied with flowers made of handkerchiefs. Inkcap had no idea why Apricot was like this. He looked at Bash, who grimaced, and he grimaced back.

Potful didn't come to the meeting as it seemed he simply wasn't up to it.

Millstone stood at the door of the office shouting, "Are you all here? Are you all here? Is everybody here? This is a study meeting."

These words were obviously directed at Bash because he was the only adult still outside the courtyard. He let Inkcap go ahead of him and the two of them walked in.

The Branch Secretary remained sitting behind the table, stuffing his pipe with tobacco from his pouch. He seemed to be filling it continuously, but he never took it out to smoke it. From the door of the public office to the courtyard gate, the ground was full of people, but the meeting didn't start for a long time. Someone would chirp or chatter; or someone farted, and A scolded B for farting and B accused A of being the culprit; or a child being held by someone pissed, and the piss slithered along the ground like a snake; then someone stepped in the piss and turned on the child's mother, and the child's mother made a show of scolding the child so the accuser would lose face, while all the time, the child was crying.

Millstone was trying to reprimand the crowd: "Is this a meeting or a temple fair? Get the children out of here. Get them out."

Pockmark and Soupspoon were sitting together, and Pockmark said, "If Potful's not here, you should be the one greeting people. What does that Millstone think he's doing, standing there?"

"I'm too lazy to do that," Soupspoon replied.

Dazed-And-Confused began to drive the children out of the courtyard. Some of them didn't want to go, and they held onto the frame of the courtyard gate with both hands. Dazed-And-Confused prised their fingers apart and the children taunted him: "Dazed! Dazed!"

"Fuck that," Dazed-And-Confused said.

The Branch Secretary finally finished filling his pipe. He put it on the table and coughed.

The Branch Secretary coughing was his way of announcing the meeting had started. The courtyard gate creaked shut, a sneeze issued from the cowshed, and no one spoke again.

The Branch Secretary told Useless to read from the newspaper. It contained a long editorial. After reading that, he read the provincial statement and the county statement on implementing the spirit of the provincial statement, as well as the Luozhen Commune statement on implementing the spirit of the county statement. Useless put the newspaper down on the edge of the table and when he wasn't paying attention, Baldy Jin pulled it off and folded it up to put it in the crown of his hat.

"That's the newspaper!" said Tag-Along, who was sitting next to him.

"It's useless now it's been read out," Baldy Jin said.

"The Branch Secretary will want it back when the meeting's over."

Baldy Jin didn't put the paper in his hat but behind his back, and waited until the end of the meeting so he could take it home if the Branch Secretary didn't say anything about wanting it back. Inkcap saw what he'd done and hooked the newspaper away with a stick. But Cowbell, who was sitting side-on to him, put out a hand and stopped him.

"Give it to me!" Inkcap demanded.

"Is it for your Gran?"

"I'll tell her to cut you out a lion."

Cowbell lifted his hand and Inkcap took the paper. He folded it again and stuffed it in his jacket pocket. Useless was still reading out documents. He read very fluently, not failing to recognise occasional characters or stumbling over the rhythm of a sentence as the Branch Secretary did. It was possible that he wanted to show what an advanced level he had reached, as he read faster and faster. The audience looked at those two lips of his, the short upper one and the long lower one, flashing open and closed, and they thought of the thornback fish in the Zhou River swallowing their food.

"Useless has read so much without a single slip," Big Root whispered.

"He's got a mouth that's sharp as a knife," Decheng said.

They turned to look at Useless's mother, who knew that people were looking at her with envy, but she didn't respond. Instead, she remained motionless and stared at her son, saying, "What a long document!"

Useless's face was covered in sweat from the effort of all that reading. Under the table, his right leg was resting on his left and was swaying in time to the sound of his voice as if marking the rhythm. This rhythmic swaying was making the audience sleepy and although they hadn't actually dozed off or ended up whispering into each other's ears, they were finding it difficult to stay sitting upright. And when they did finally relax, they flopped down one after the other like a pile of dung slipping out of a cow's arse.

After he had read all the newspapers and documents, Useless looked up and said, "Finished."

"Well, sit down if you've finished," the Branch Secretary said.

Useless sat back down at the corner of the table and the Branch Secretary said, "'That's all for today's study. Millstone, check who hasn't shown up. From today onwards, for all study sessions, the work points for all attendees are increased from five to eight. Anyone who doesn't attend will be docked five points."

The courtyard immediately regained its energy. Sparks fancied a smoke and called out to Inkcap for his fuse. Inkcap had brought his fuse to the meeting, but when he saw so many people already smoking, he put it out.

When he heard Sparks shouting for him, he re-lit it and ran around lighting everyone's pipes and cigarettes. Millstone stood up to count the size of the crowd and said there were five missing.

"Have you counted me?" Inkcap asked.

"Oh, I forgot about you. What are you running around for? Sit down," Millstone barked.

Inkcap sat down, the Branch Secretary coughed, and at the same time, another sneeze issued from the cowshed. Everyone quieted down again.

The Branch Secretary began to speak. He had to give a speech after every study meeting, and his tone was very flat. He said that since last year, the revolutionary situation in Old Kiln was good, and the production situation was also good. A hundred and eighty *mu* of terraced fields had been built, they had opened five miles of irrigation ditches, large and small, and had fired twelve kiln-loads of porcelain. Although four old people had died in the village and a baby had miscarried, three new women had been married. No pigs, dogs or cats had suffered from infectious disease. Apart from the loss of the keys, there were no other thefts. The commune police had come five times in total, but on no occasion was it to investigate a crime or arrest a criminal. The commune and the county had awarded five certificates to the village, one as a model public security village, one as an advanced militia organisation village, one for the red flag of Dazhai in agriculture, one for the branch party and one for the Branch Secretary personally. However, when the Branch Secretary got to this point, he stopped and began to put away his pipe and tobacco pouch. The courtyard was completely silent because the Branch Secretary always talked about the positive revolutionary production situation at the beginning of his speech. It had become a kind of rule and a set pattern that what he would say next was the real reason the meeting had been called. However, many of the audience had no idea what it was the Branch Secretary was going to talk about. They could see that Goodman was standing together with Lightkeeper and Gran, so Goodman must have done something wrong. Was it something to do with telling Bash to dig a hole? But if it was about digging the hole and Bash was still sitting down, then Goodman must have done something else, and something very serious at that.

The Branch Secretary did indeed talk about Goodman. "When I last went to the commune for a meeting," he said, "the commune delivered a document from the province. This document is a confidential document, pointing out that there is a bad trend in society. Some people are dissatisfied with socialism, the leadership of the Communist Party and the cadres of the Communist Party. This is especially the case in some big cities. We are a very long way from any big cities, and quite a distance even from the county seat and Luozhen. However, when the wind blows outside the mountains, dust will fall on Old Kiln. When there are dark clouds in the sky, rain falls in Old Kiln too. I realised why the village lost its keys last winter. That was actually a raindrop from those dark clouds falling here in Old Kiln. And in the two or three days when I was away at the commune, something else happened here. What happened was down to Guo Baixuan.

So today, Guo Baixuan stands here to go back to school and to receive an education. Everyone knows that Guo Baixuan moved to Old Kiln after returning to secular life. Returning to secular life is in accordance with the policy of the Communist Party and with the instruction of Commune Secretary Zhang, for how can the new society still allow such things from the old society to remain? Everyone has to work, and no one can just sit there and expect to be fed. After Guo Baixuan arrived in Old Kiln, he lived in the Kiln God Temple. He should be grateful to the vast number of poor and lower-middle peasants in Old Kiln for allowing him to live in such spacious accommodation, and he should actively reform through labour and reshape his muscles and bones. However, what Guo Baixuan did was turn the Old Kiln Temple back into a temple.

"Happiness is given to us by the Communist Party. The vastness of Heaven and Earth is not as great as the kindness of the Communist Party, and the kindness of a great mother is not as great as that of Chairman Mao. Why should Guo Baixuan not have been moved out of the Kiln God Temple after he turned it back into a temple? Which is greater in this world, the Buddha or the Communist Party? I believe the Communist Party is greater. The Communist Party has overthrown the Buddha, and where is the power of Buddhism now? The Communist Party has not lost a single hair! Of course, he was unhappy about being made to move out, pretending to be a ghost, spreading rumours and disrupting society. A simple mountain farmer may not have much learning, but he surely knows better than to instigate others to dig pits in cowsheds! And who is to say such a person as Guo Baixuan might not want to go even further and burn the cowshed down or poison the yoke cattle? In addition, some people are talking nonsense about the clearing out of the public office. It makes me very angry to hear this. Is this how poor and middle peasants should talk? It is all influenced by Guo Baixuan. As for why we are selling the public office, didn't we already make it clear that we need to buy a flat-bed barrow for the kiln and a walking tractor to sell porcelain goods in town? What is wrong with any of that? The question of the public office may seem to be different from digging holes in the cowshed, but they are actually the same thing. The chain of events reflects a new trend in the class struggle. We must be vigilant, be sensible and stamp out any sparks that are not conducive to socialism as soon as they are discovered. We cannot let them catch light or begin to smoke."

By the time the Branch Secretary had finished, he had spoken for as long as it takes to eat two full meals, and the crowd had been shifting position as they sat on the ground, their tailbones getting sorer and sorer. Of course, some of them had to go to the privy, and they stood up, patting the soil off their buttocks and coughing here and there. Inkcap was curious. He felt that there wasn't usually that much coughing. Taking great care, he turned his head to see who hadn't coughed yet. Interestingly, as soon as he looked at someone, they coughed, and the sound became louder. But Useless and Dazed-And-Confused didn't cough. Useless put on his mask as soon as the dust was stirred up and Dazed-And-Confused just sat there muttering and eating fried noodles. Dazed-And-Confused must have been reincarnated from a hungry ghost as his pockets were full of fried noodles and he would pull out a handful from time to time and shove it into his mouth. When Inkcap went out to pee, he caught a seven-star ladybird on the privy wall and took it back to the courtyard in his hand so he could play with it. When it flapped its wings in a bid to fly away, he covered it with his hand and then suddenly released it. He wanted it to fly into Useless's ear because if it made his ear itch, Useless would definitely cough. But the ladybird flew away and out of the courtyard gate. As for Dazed-And-Confused, he suddenly stopped talking and seemed to have gone mad, unable to move.

Almost-There, who was sitting next to him, asked, "'What's up with you?"

Dazed-And-Confused remained motionless, his mouth open and not breathing. Everyone looked at him and even the Branch Secretary stopped talking and said, "Dazed-And-Confused, you look like you need to sneeze. Go outside and do it."

Dazed-And-Confused stood up and went out but still couldn't get the sneeze out.

"Look at the sun," Gran said. "You'll sneeze if you look at the sun."

Dazed-And-Confused looked up at the sun and... Ahhhh-choo! A great sneeze rang out like thunder in an explosion of snot, tears and even the remaining fried noodles he had in his mouth. Everyone wanted to laugh but the Branch Secretary coughed, and no one did. Dazed-And-Confused tried to rejoin the meeting but Millstone pushed him away and wouldn't let him in.

"All right, then, but don't take away my work points."

He left the courtyard and sneezed three times in a row.

The meeting finally broke up and everyone crowded at the entrance of the courtyard. Bash told Inkcap to go with him again, but Inkcap had to wait for Gran. Gran, Lightkeeper and Goodman had to wait until everyone had left before they could leave themselves.

Gourd's wife also stayed behind and whispered to Goodman, "If I'd known you were going to be criticised today, I would rather have gone without work points than come. Don't be angry, no one will laugh at you. Is there anyone in Old Kiln over the last ten years or so who hasn't criticised someone or been criticised themselves? Lightkeeper and his dad have long been targets. Six Pints' grandfather was a middle peasant and he was criticised for not taking an active part in society. Old Faithful's father was criticised for causing a fire by smoking while harvesting wheat. Caretaker's mother was criticised for not wanting to cut down her family's trees to make steel during the Great Leap Forward. Thimble's father was criticised for making complaints at the beginning of the period of 'learning from Dazhai'. As for the Branch Secretary and Potful, the Four Clean-Ups Movement allowed the people from the commune to investigate them left, right and centre!"

"I know," Goodman said. "But don't say any more, the Branch Secretary is looking this way."

"I've not said anything that isn't true."

Even so, Goodman moved away and sat on the threshold, massaging his legs. Now he had stopped standing, his legs began to tremble, and the trembling only got worse when he started massaging them.

"Just look at these legs, Lightkeeper," he said. "Trees do better than this! Trees stand all year round without trembling, but just look at them!"

"You're simply not used to it," Lightkeeper replied. "They won't shake after you've had to stand there a few times."

"You mean it's going to happen again?"

"Once you've stood up there once, you have a criminal record. You were just looking for trouble, weren't you? Why did you put that idea into Bash's head?"

"He's bored," Goodman said. "If I hadn't given him a safety valve, he might have exploded. I'd heard that a stone tablet from the village was used to cover the pit when the cowshed was being built. I told him the tablet might be in the cowshed and if he found it there and set it up again, that might prove to be a good thing. How was I to know he was going to dig such a deep hole?"

"The Zhu clan's family motto is engraved on that tablet," Six Pints told him.

"You really do know how to mess people around, don't you?" Lightkeeper said.

"So are you going to get me in trouble with trumped-up accusations?" Goodman asked.

"You heard what the Branch Secretary said," Lightkeeper replied.

"Did I?"

"Weren't you listening when you were standing there?"

"When I was standing there, I was thinking that this standing was all right because it was better than kneeling. The Branch Secretary accused me of pretending to be a god and playing the devil. Well, I can't play the devil, so I have to pretend to be a god. As for him, if he isn't lecturing people he's shouting at them or even cursing and beating them. He is angry, that makes others angry and that anger is the devil. If I can pretend to be a god, and I see someone in the wrong, then I just laugh. Happiness is divine and when the god is present, nothing can hurt me."

"You'd better make sure you massage those legs well, you're going to need them," Lightkeeper said.

Then he walked out of the courtyard gate.

In the end, only Goodman and Gran were left in the yard. Gran bent down, picked up the bricks that had been used as seats and put them in a corner. Inkcap told her off for wasting her energy, but she replied, "Are you saying I should leave it all for Grandpa Happy to do?"

Bash was still standing outside the courtyard gate. After everyone had gone, he came back in and said to Goodman, "Ai! I've brought all this down on your head."

"What does this have to do with you?" Goodman replied. "I made the dumpling skins myself, mixed the stuffing myself, wrapped the dumplings myself. I know myself."

Bash didn't say anything else and kicked a feed rack in the cowshed. Happy glared at Bash, but Bash ignored him and just urged Inkcap to leave with him.

Inkcap was asking Gran, "Have you got back pain, Gran?"

"Where don't I have pain? Where are you off to now?"

"Brother Bash has *taisui* water at his place. I'll go and get some for you, and your back will feel better."

Happy was still standing there, so angry that he had gone red in the face.

"We're going now," Goodman said. "Lock the gate and have a good laugh. Look up to the heavens and have a good laugh. Then you won't be tortured by all the negative energy any more."

Inkcap followed Bash to the little wooden shack. Bash seemed to have forgotten about collecting some *taisui* water for Gran and he took out a bottle of wine and sat down to drink it. He drank hard, and didn't even offer any to Inkcap, who watched three empty bottles pile up in the corner of the room. He wondered where Bash had got the wine from and thought, Did he bring me over here just to watch him drink?

Very soon, the whole shack stank of alcohol and Inkcap wrinkled his nose.

"Stop breathing it in," Bash ordered him.

"Why?"

"I didn't fork out good money on this wine for you to suck in the fumes."

"Fucking miser," Inkcap said.

He watched Bash drink two fingers of wine at a gulp and asked, "Did you make a lot of money when you left the village?"

"Of course."

"What's it like out there?"

"Do you want to go too? I'll take you with me next time."

"Are you leaving again?"

Bash glared, his nostrils dilated, as if he was quarrelling with someone.

"Why wouldn't I?" he said.

Inkcap was taken aback, and before he could regain his composure, Bash pulled him over, picked up the bottle and poured some wine into his mouth. Inkcap took a lovely swallow, and another, then choked, but Bash kept pouring. When he did let him go, Inkcap was unsteady on his feet and he almost sat down on the ground.

Bash hooted with laughter, like an owl.

"You're drunk!" Inkcap said.

"You're drunk!" Bash replied.

Inkcap took out the small mirror Goodman had given him and looked at his reflection. His face was as red as Guan Gong on the opera stage.

"Go and drop the wine bottles in front of the pagoda. They'll fall onto the road," Bash said.

"You mean they'll fall onto the road and puncture someone's tyre."

"And if they puncture his fucking tyre, I can then mend it, can't I?"

Inkcap unsteadily picked up four empty wine bottles and was about to go out. He felt he had grown taller all of a sudden. He had never been so tall before, and he even ducked his head when passing through the door. The fog had risen again in the evening, and the whole wheat field was like a pot of boiling water shrouded in white steam. The fog grew legs and climbed onto the road, and the road seemed to soften. He smashed three wine bottles, but his head began to swim terribly as he dropped the fourth.

As the crash of the fourth empty wine bottle rang out, Inkcap heard another smashing sound. When he turned to look, on the dirt road up from the village he could make out the shadowy figures of Apricot and Potful, who was leaning on a crutch. Apricot picked up something on the ground, but Potful snatched it from her. Another smashing sound followed and Apricot began to wail.

"Are you trying to find some other fucking way to be rid of me?" Potful said to her. "What is it? Drinking water? Drinking piss? Drinking poison?"

He raised his crutch to hit Apricot but fell over.

Inkcap was worried that with all the commotion, Bash was about to rush out of the shack to grab Apricot. If he stood still and did nothing, there might be a real fight. He didn't know who to side with, Bash or Potful. He waited for a long time, and Apricot had been beaten and cursed all over the village, but Bash had not yet come out. He went back into the shack where he found Bash sitting inside the door, his face as black as thunder.

"Potful is beating up Apricot," Inkcap said.

Bash didn't say a word.

"Apricot must have been coming to find you."

Bash still didn't say a word.

Inkcap began to get annoyed.

"I'm not going to let you get back with Apricot. You'll only fuck her around again. You stirred up a shitload of trouble for her when you ran off, and now you're back, you haven't even been to see her."

"So what if I don't see her?"

He was so fierce, Inkcap thought he might be about to eat him, but he was happy even so. That's fine, he thought to himself. He's finally given up on her.

"She's just the daughter of a production team captain, isn't she? What's so special about that? Do you think I can't find another woman? If I can't find a country girl, I'll find one in the city."

Inkcap reckoned that, even if Bash had given up on Apricot, that was no reason to bad-mouth her, so he still wanted to stand up for her.

"Find a city girl, eh? Well, you go right ahead and do that. Where exactly are you going to find one?"

"You just wait."

From out on the highway came the sound of footsteps and someone pushing a bicycle. Bash said it was the sound of business and told Inkcap to fetch a basin of water so they were ready to mend the tyre. Inkcap picked up the porcelain basin but dropped it.

Bash gave a start of alarm and said, "So you're still all fired up, are you, you little prick?"

"What do you think?"

Inkcap turned on his heel and went back to the village.

"Come back here!" Bash yelled.

But Inkcap was already gone, and he heard the man pushing the bicycle say, "Just look at him! He's an odd one, isn't he?"

TWENTY-ONE

THE PRICE OF THE PUBLIC OFFICE was soon announced, and it was three hundred yuan. The Branch Secretary bought it. This outcome was no more than the villagers expected, but they said nothing. The money was used to buy two flat-bed barrows for the kiln site, to replace the desks and chairs in the production team headquarters and to buy a tractor. There was only one yuan and eighty-three fen left. Soupspoon listed the accounts in detail, copied them on a piece of red paper and pasted them on the gate post. Inkcap couldn't stop thinking about that piece of red paper, but he didn't dare tear it down. He waited for the wind to peel it off, then snatched it up and pressed it under the mat on the *kang*. Gran used it to cut out twelve cows. That was the exact number of cows in the cowshed, and each papercut looked just like one of the cows. Inkcap pressed the papercuts under his pillow. At night, he dreamed of cows fighting.

On waking up, he said to Gran, "They brought back the tractor they bought yesterday afternoon. Didn't you go to see it?"

"I saw it, the monstrous lump of iron," Gran replied.

"Pockmark says there'll be no more cows in the future, and everything will be done by tractors."

"You shouldn't be calling him Pockmark, you should call him 'Older Brother'."

"I told you, he's not here. Does that mean there won't be any cow shit to collect?"

"You worry too much. Now, go and have a piss and get to sleep."

When Inkcap got up to have a piss in the piss bucket, he heard the village dogs, barking and snapping.

The dogs were snapping at the tractor. The machine couldn't get into the courtyard of the Kiln God Temple, so it had stopped at the gate. When Ever-Obedient's dog caught sight of the great iron lump, it rushed towards it, and then retreated, asking, "What's this? What's this?" When all the other dogs saw that Ever-Obedient's dog didn't know what the thing was, they went up and bit it, then retreated in fear, howling, "What is it? What is it?" The racket went on all night.

All this kept many of the villagers awake and as they lay in bed, they wondered who was going to drive the tractor. There were too many capable candidates in Old Kiln, and they all thought they were the best qualified. So for several days, they were constantly asking each other for news and doing each other down. When Sprout came back from picking shepherd's purse on the field ridges, she saw Half-Stick sitting at the entrance of Three Fork Alley stitching shoes.

"Are you sitting there to show off your skills?" she asked. "What's so great about your shoes? Is the spacing so even or are the stitches really so fine?"

"Can you see who's running over to the Branch Secretary's house? I can't make out who they are."

"Oh," said Sprout. "And does your husband want to drive the tractor too?"

"Yes, he does. He was asking me whether to send the Branch Secretary a gift or not. I said not, so we can find out just how honest and straight-dealing he really is."

While they were talking, Pillar approached them. He was hugging something to his chest and took a step or two back when he saw Half-Stick talking to Sprout, but then went over to them again.

"Here's another one," Half-Stick whispered.

She deliberately stretched her legs out to block Pillar's way.

"Hey! Just get on with your mending," Pillar exclaimed, stepping over Half-Stick's legs.

"Where are you off to?" Half-Stick asked.

"Old Faithful's house."

Old Faithful's house was next door to the Branch Secretary's.

"There's an idea!" Half-Stick said. "Let's go and see Old Faithful's wife, Melons Ying."

"I'm going to lay some foundations and mix up the adobe," Pillar said.

"Is that so? And do you need a package of titbits to do that?"

"What titbits, you stupid woman?"

"Let go with your hands and we'll see."

Pillar clutched his hands tighter to his chest and turned and left.

"Hey! I thought you were going to lay some foundations."

"If I want to lay foundations, I will, and if I don't, I won't. What the fuck's it got to do with you, you stupid woman?"

Whoever was going to drive the tractor not only had to learn how to, as soon as possible, but they also had to be able to sell the porcelain and know how to keep clean accounts. With Half-Stick making mischief the way she was, the only people who dared to put themselves forward were Useless, Pockmark, Bash, Baldy Jin and Lucky. The Party Secretary hummed and hawed and eventually chose Baldy Jin.

"I didn't give the Branch Secretary any titbits, not even a spring onion. He is a good Branch Secretary," Baldy Jin asserted.

He also suggested to the Branch Secretary that Lucky could be his assistant, but the Branch Secretary appointed Stonebreaker and instructed him to take charge of the accounts.

After that, Baldy Jin began to learn to drive the tractor in the wheat field. Half-Stick always wanted to go with him, and she sat on the tractor frame, directing him this way and that.

"Who's driving this thing, you or me?" Baldy Jin complained.

"Well, it's not me," Half-Stick said, "'cos you're driving like an old fart."

One dawn, Baldy Jin was still asleep, so Half-Stick took a bucket to fill the tractor with water. It was still dark, but yes! There was a man standing next to the machine. Half-Stick saw that it was Lucky and asked him what he was doing.

"Collecting shit," he told her.

"Tractor shit?" Half-Stick asked.

Lucky shouldered his carrying pole and piss buckets and went off to the marshy ground at the rear of the village. Just at that moment, the wolf pack was also passing through the same area. The animals at the front had already gone past, while the one at the rear was sitting on the roadside in front of a mound of earth, howling mournfully and sounding just like an old woman wailing.

Lucky felt there was something odd going on and walked over to ask, "Hey! Who are you? What's the matter? Why are you wailing like that before the sun's even up?"

The wolf turned around, with a serious expression that morphed into a sudden grin, and it swished its tail across the ground. It was only then that Lucky realised it was a wolf. He tried to turn and flee but he was so frightened he didn't know where to go and ended up running in circles. As chance would have it, as he swung round and round, the piss buckets swung with him and emptied themselves. The shit splashed out like a meteor hammer. The wolf ran away, streaked with a thin stream of shit, and Lucky pissed himself.

In the middle of the morning, Six Pints, who lived next to the threshing ground, went to Soupspoon's house to collect an earthenware pot in which to make up some medicine. The village had only one such pot suitable for simmering Chinese medicine, and it had been bought by the Branch Secretary. Anyone who used this medicine pot was not allowed to give it back afterwards, as doing so was tantamount to giving back the disease the medicine was treating. If anyone got sick again and needed to make up more medicine, the pot couldn't be sent back either for the same reason. A member of the sick person's family had to collect it. When Six Pints went to Soupspoon's house to collect the pot, he saw lots of people painting white-grey circles on the walls of their pigsties, so on his way back, he asked Baldy Jin, who was driving the tractor, "Hey, Baldy Jin, were there wolves in the village again last night?"

"So what if there were? You're not reincarnated from a pig are you, so why are you afraid of wolves?"

As Six Pints went inside to boil up the medicine, he thought to himself, Fuck you, Baldy Jin. You're the reincarnation of a pig and a wolf!

When he went out again, he had to paint some circles on his own pigsty and by the time he got to the threshing ground, there was no sign of Baldy Jin or the tractor, and the rain had begun to clatter down.

The rain fell fiercely, not like spring rain at all. When the raindrops hit the ground, they turned to smoke, and the threshing ground immediately became covered in that smoke. Then the smoke dissipated and there were puddles, rippling with a dense hammering of raindrops, like dancing nails. The village bell rang with them, the gong was being struck by them, copper basins and iron pot lids were ringing out, and seven or eight rough voices were shouting for everyone to go to the kiln to move the clay forms. On the dirt road from the village entrance to the mountainside, people were running up with ropes, and the kiln site was like a pot of muddy porridge. The forms drying at the kiln site could be carried into empty caves and sheds in their frames. Those who couldn't lift a whole frame could carry one or two pieces in their arms, or take off their clothes to cover them. Some people were shouting that it was one thing for it to rain, but what the fuck was it doing raining so fiercely without any kind of warning or shift in the weather beforehand? Others fell over as they ran and were roundly cursed: "Fuck your trousers, just make sure the forms aren't broken. Hurry up! Hurry up!"

The rain was getting heavier and heavier, and the clay forms were now being piled up at random. The ones on top were distorted by the rain, and the ones below were splashed and twisted out of shape from above. A pile that was half the height of a man groaned and subsided. Immediately someone shouted, "We can't move any more, we can't move any more, where's the straw? Bring the straw." People brought straw and waterproof sheets to cover those few piles that hadn't subsided, then they scattered to take shelter in the caves and under the eaves of the sheds.

Pillar was still out in the rain, looking for undamaged forms among the collapsed piles, and when he couldn't extract them, he stamped on them like a madman, turning them back into mud, and splattering it everywhere.

"Hey, Pillar! Why don't you come in from the rain?" Barndoor shouted, but Pillar ignored him.

"I thought it would rain today as soon as I heard about the wolves," Big Root said. "Nine times out of ten over the last few years, it's rained when the wolves came. But I never expected it to rain so hard."

"So many forms have been broken," Barndoor said. "It's at least a fortnight's work."

"I've wasted ten days' work," Dazed-And-Confused complained. "That's no work points for two weeks."

Pillar turned to look at them. In the rain, his hair and clothes were sticking to him, and his ribs were clearly visible.

"Where do work points come into it?" he said. "If it rains, it rains. Where do work points come into it? You shit what you eat, don't you? What have you eaten?"

"Why are you so stingy?" Dazed-And-Confused asked. "Aren't I allowed to say anything?"

"If you haven't got anything useful to say, just keep quiet," Pillar retorted.

"Well, I have said it. What are you going to do about it? Slap me round the mouth?"

Barndoor tried to talk him round, but couldn't, and just then, Big Root rushed onto the roof of the kiln, shouting, "The Branch Secretary! The Branch Secretary!"

Up on top of the kiln, the Branch Secretary and Winterborn were looking to see if the water was going to get into the interior of the kiln.

The Branch Secretary looked very solemn and called out, "What's all the shouting about? Why bother with the arguing, why don't you just go straight to fighting and be done with it?"

All went silent and the Branch Secretary continued, "Look at all these forms getting soaked and being ruined! Do you think shouting and fighting is going to stop them being spoiled? If you're going to go on like that, we might as well let the whole village go to rack and ruin and be done with it!"

Everyone came out into the rain from the doorways of the caves and from under the eaves of the sheds, hoping to save more forms. But the rain was now falling straight down, stiff and hard as steel rods, and they were forced back to their shelters.

Suddenly, the sound of wailing rose from the village at the foot of the mountain, and someone shouted at the top of their voice, "It's collapsed! It's collapsed!"

Everyone ran out into the rain again and stood in the field, looking at the village.

"Hey, Lucky!" Sprout said. "That's your wife, isn't it? Looks like your courtyard wall has collapsed."

Then Palace cried out, "Ai! Half of my pigsty wall has collapsed. I hope the whole lot doesn't come down."

He ran back down towards the village, and as soon as he went, the others began to worry about their own homes and followed in a rush. The backs of Old Faithful's shoes were worn through and he couldn't run in them. He squatted down and looped a straw rope under the soles and tied them onto his feet.

"Leave some rope for me!" Soupspoon shouted.

His foot slipped and he knocked Old Faithful to the ground, leaving him dazed. Running down the slope, he tripped over his own feet and couldn't stop himself as he banged into Old Faithful.

"What's your fucking hurry?" said a furious Old Faithful.

At the kiln site, Awning was carrying the soaking wet firewood for the kiln into the shed. When he looked back, he saw that the Branch Secretary and Winterborn were still clearing the gutters on the roof of the kiln. Bash ran over to help him carry the firewood.

"What are you running for, for fuck's sake?" said Awning. "Has the war started?"

There were splashes of mud on Bash's sunglasses. He took them off and wiped them. When they were clean, he put them on again.

"War would be fine by me," he said. "The Soviet revisionists are always talking about attacking China, so bring it on!"

Awning glanced at the roof of the kiln and lowered his voice: "You're talking nonsense, Bash. You surely can't be serious about wanting the Soviet revisionists to invade us."

"Why not? That way at least we can see who's got a backbone and who hasn't."

"You're right. Just look how fast that lot ran away. There's only us few party members who stayed behind."

"I'm not a party member," Bash reminded him.

"Sure, you're a bit rough," Awning said, "but there's no hiding your true quality, Bash. If you just changed your bad ways, you'd be sure to be made a party member. I'd even recommend you myself!"

"Really?" Bash said. He laughed abruptly and walked off down the mountain by himself.

Awning tried to call him back a few times, but Bash had already disappeared. The mud on Awning's straw sandals had clumped together into two big lumps. The harder he brought his feet down trying to shake the mud off, the stickier the lumps got. In the end, they were too big and too sticky, and he simply couldn't move so he untied the straw ropes, slipped his feet out and walked off barefoot.

In fact, nothing major had occurred in the village, except for a one-*zhang*-long section in the backyard wall of Lucky's house that collapsed. It transpired that, as Baldy Jin drove the tractor from the village to the highway, he passed the backyard of Lucky's house and the tractor knocked into some of the bricks at the corner of the wall. Lucky didn't know anything about it, and Baldy Jin simply didn't care. When it rained, water poured into the cracks, and the wall collapsed. Rather than trapping Lucky's wife when it collapsed, it trapped the family sow, which gave birth to piglets prematurely. Lucky's wife wept inconsolably. Lucky held the five piglets in his arms and wiped them down with some old cotton wadding.

"Stop your fucking crying and go and make some congee for the piglets," said Lucky

In the end, when the congee was ready, three of the piglets opened their mouths to eat and two didn't.

Lucky's wife began to cry again and said, "What the hell's wrong with you? You don't get to drive the tractor, a wolf scares you so much that you piss yourself and now even the pigs have turned against me! A piglet's worth five yuan, now we've lost all that money just like that."

Lucky was so angry that he threw the dead piglets into the piss cistern.

When Bash came back from the kiln, he didn't go straight to the little wooden shack but went back to his former lodgings instead. Two rafters on the east and west rear eaves of the old house had long since rotted, and some boards and tiles had fallen off. The rain had soaked half of the wall, and water was seeping continuously into the house.

"If you're going to fall down, just get on with it and fall down," Bash said.

But despite uttering these words, he set up a ladder to get access to the roof, covered the wall with a blanket of straw and found a waterproof sheet to protect the exposed rafter heads. While he was busy working, somebody was talking in the yard next door. It was the Branch Secretary's wife and son wearing straw hats and discussing the newly purchased public office:

how to seal up the door and open a new one; how to replace the sash window with a diamond-pattern lattice one; how to strip off the old wall covering and redo it with limewash. A woman was standing next to the Branch Secretary's son. She was quite short and had two braids that were so long they rested on her buttocks. She said that the steps needed to be rebuilt and made wider so that they wouldn't trip when going in and out at night, and she also said that a wall should be built to separate the cattle pen and shed so that the smell of cow shit was kept where it should be. Bash thought to himself that this must be the Branch Secretary's future daughter-in-law, and he was surprised to discover that she was such a midget of a girl. He looked back down to concentrate on wrapping the rafter heads but then asked himself how a titch like that had wormed her way into the Branch Secretary's family. He turned to look back at the yard next door. The woman flicked her braid, and the end of it just caught the pen in the top pocket of the Branch Secretary's son's jacket. The son ducked away, and the woman screamed, saying that her hair was being pulled out. She raised her fist and hit him, but he just giggled. Bash suddenly realised that the Branch Secretary had put the public office up for sale just so he could buy it for his son when he got married. His anger surged up until it filled him completely.

There was an old elm tree in the yard next door which had five large branches. Three of them grew upwards, another stretched towards the cowshed, and the last one extended diagonally, almost crushing the courtyard wall. The Branch Secretary's son was saying, "Do you see this elm tree? The five branches are our five children who are going to pass their exams all the way to the top. You're going to give us five sons!"

Bash didn't want to hear what the woman had to say to that, so he finished wrapping the rafter heads and climbed down. Back on the ground, he fetched a saw from the house, climbed up to the top of the courtyard wall and sawed off the branch that extended over it.

Next door noticed the movement as soon as he started, and the Branch Secretary's wife called out, "Hey! What do you think you're doing there, Bash?"

"I'm sawing off this branch," Bash shouted back.

"That tree is growing in my courtyard, isn't it?"

"It's invading my airspace."

Bash finished cutting off the branch, which fell into his yard. He picked it up and threw it over the wall. Then the argument broke out in earnest.

At the first sign of a commotion, lots of the villagers came running over, first to watch the excitement and then to have a go at Bash. He opened his courtyard gate and sat down on a bench in the yard, wearing a straw hat and sunglasses.

"If people don't offend me, I won't offend them," he said. "If they start something, I will retaliate."

"Are you saying my family are Soviet revisionists?" the Branch Secretary's wife shouted back. "Bash! Bash! When did we ever do anything to you to make you treat us like this?"

Hair unpinned, she threw herself towards the interior of the courtyard, only to be restrained by the onlookers.

"How can you talk like this?" she said accusingly. "And how can you saw the branch off a tree that's only giving you shade and shelter from the rain? Trees are just like people. How would you get on if someone cut off one of your arms or legs?"

"Auntie! Auntie!" Awning's wife said. "Don't get so het up. He isn't the one who got to buy the public office, so just allow him to let off a bit of steam."

"Do you think I'm interested in that place?" Bash asked derisively. "What am I, a cow? Why would I want to share the same yard with a cattle shed?"

"Are you having a go at me? Are you saying I'm a cow?"

"Maybe I'm a cow! That would mean I get up earlier than a rooster, eat less than a pig and am cheaper to look after than a dog. So yes, maybe I am a cow, then."

Awning had been waiting in silence outside the courtyard, but he was spurred into action by these words. He went in, saying, "What are you shouting the odds about, Bash? Do you think you're behaving reasonably here? 'If people don't offend me, I won't offend them. If they start something, I will retaliate.' Isn't that the anti-revisionist slogan you were just quoting? Well, who has offended you?"

"The tree was violating my airspace," Bash said.

"Airspace?" Awning replied. "The sky is the Communist Party's sky, and the earth is socialism's earth. What airspace do you own? Let me tell you, the Branch Secretary is already very angry. He hasn't come here today, but he's an important man with a lot of clout, so why are you kicking up this fuss?"

"If the Branch Secretary is so angry, why don't you push off and look after him?" Bash said, shoving Awning out of the courtyard and shutting the gate.

"That's right. Shut the gate. That's really going to help," Awning said as soon as the gate closed.

Then he turned on his wife and said, "Haven't you said enough? Just go home."

The onlookers in the alley shook their heads and discussed what a loner Bash had become. Only Awning dared get close to him, but when Awning sent his own wife away, quite a few of the others left too. But some stayed to see if the Branch Secretary really was going to come or not. If he did, things would get even livelier.

In among the crowd, Cowbell whispered to Inkcap, "Do you want to eat some meat?"

"I'll eat you!"

"I'm serious. But if you don't want to, forget it."

Cowbell turned and left. Inkcap ran after him asking, "What meat? Have you caught another wild dog, or a cat?"

Cowbell's voice sank to a whisper: "I pulled two dead piglets out of Lucky's piss cistern and Pockmark's skinning them over at my place now."

Inkcap followed Cowbell over to his house.

Cowbell's courtyard gate was locked, so he opened it and locked it again when they were inside. He did the same with the door to the main building. Just as he had said, Pockmark was skinning the two piglets and in fact he had already finished. The piglets' skins were no bigger than rabbit pelts. When Inkcap looked at one of the piglet's faces, its eyes were still open.

"It's staring at me!" he exclaimed.

"Is that going to stop you eating it?" Pockmark scoffed.

Cowbell came over with a knife and gouged out the piglet's eyes saying, "If you don't want to watch, go and light a fire."

Inkcap couldn't bear to look at Pockmark, but he didn't say anything and just went over to load firewood into the stove and light it. Pockmark complained to Cowbell about him bringing Inkcap, and that made Inkcap even more uncomfortable.

"You eat the meat and I'll just have soup," he offered.

Pockmark cut up the skinned piglets on the chopping board, and Inkcap whispered to Cowbell, "Why did you get Pockmark involved? Couldn't you have skinned them yourself?"

"It was his idea in the first place, so I had to. Besides, if there's any trouble, he can take care of it for us."

As the meat cooked in the pot, the aroma soon spread everywhere. Pockmark made Cowbell close all the windows in the main building, and Inkcap went out into the courtyard to see if he could smell anything. He couldn't, but lots of birds started flying into the courtyard and some of them were trying to burrow in past the rafters under the eaves. They couldn't get in, so they started screeching and shitting on the wall below the eaves.

Inkcap knew the birds were cursing him, so he told them, "I'll give you some bones later."

A cat crawled onto the courtyard wall, purring. Inkcap picked up a broken straw hat and threw it at the cat, saying, "It's not for you."

Back in the house, after the meat had been cooking for a while, Pockmark lifted the lid off the pot, took out a lump of meat, twisted off a piece and ate it.

"Well, it's not done yet."

After a while, he took out another piece and ate it, saying, "It'll still be a while."

"Why do you keep eating it, then?" Cowbell asked.

"I'm checking whether it's done or not."

"At this rate, you'll have finished it before it is."

Cowbell took a piece of meat on the bone for himself and chewed on it. The meat wasn't in fact cooked, and he couldn't bite it into pieces, so he swallowed the meat whole, took out the bone and gave it to Inkcap to gnaw on. Inkcap threw the bone away without gnawing on it, and all the birds suddenly swooped down. One of them caught the bone, flew away with it, but dropped it mid-air. Three birds flying below the first bird caught the bone before it hit the ground and flew out of the yard together. All the other birds followed them.

The door of the main building stayed closed for an hour and when it did open, Pockmark came out with a contented look on his face, followed by Cowbell and Inkcap, who both had grease stains around their mouths. Cowbell buried the gnawed bones in a basin in the corner of the courtyard wall and said he was really thirsty. He scooped up half a ladle of water from the bucket and asked Pockmark, "Do you want some?"

"Do you want to give yourself the runs and waste all that food you've just eaten?" Pockmark said.

After that, Cowbell didn't dare drink any water.

"They were too small. They were gone before we even started," he complained.

"They were pigs, not cows!" Inkcap replied.

"Maybe next time it rains," Pockmark said, "the cowshed will collapse. That would be even better."

Pockmark opened the courtyard door and left, and as soon as he was gone, Inkcap cursed him for being a thief who had taken all the best meat. He and Cowbell went out through the courtyard gate and walked through the village alleyways. They didn't have any particular purpose in mind but just went for a snoop around. The rain subsided, and the air seemed sweet to the taste, as if it was full of sugar. All the leaves were emerald green, and there were snails crawling up the walls on both sides of the alleys, leaving bright silver trails behind them. After their soaking by the rain, the tile pines on the roofs bloomed into a carpet of small flowers, so they looked as if they had been sprinkled with salt. And wow! Just look at the old vines that still covered the screen wall in front of Awning's courtyard like a barbed wire fence. The new seedlings growing out of the soil were already half as tall as the old vines, and dozens of branches were crawling up among them. Inkcap took a stick and poked one of these branches, which curled itself round the stick.

"What does this look like?" Inkcap asked.

"It looks like a human finger," Cowbell said.

"It looks like a tongue," Inkcap insisted.

As they argued, Inkcap looked up and saw Lucky, standing with arms folded, under the rubber tree by Inkcap's house. Inkcap hurriedly pulled Cowbell towards Crosswise Alley, but Lucky shouted at them to come over to him.

"We've been found out," Cowbell whispered without moving his head.

"I'll never own up," Inkcap said.

The two of them just looked at each other as Lucky asked, "Did you eat my piglets?"

"No," Cowbell said.

"Open your mouth," Lucky demanded.

Inkcap snorted and two thick streams of snot tears came out of his nose. Lucky decided not to look in their mouths.

"Fuck it," he said. "I threw the dead piglets into the cistern, but then I thought I could still eat them. I went to fish them out, but they'd gone."

Cowbell and Inkcap hurried away, and in the distance, they could hear Lucky's wife shouting and cursing, "Listen to me, whoever stole my meat, I hope your fucking lips and tongues rot away and your guts bung up and you have no arsehole! Oh, oh, oh! You ate my meat! Ooooh!"

For several days after being cursed by Lucky's wife, Inkcap actually felt there was something wrong with his stomach. It didn't hurt much, but he kept feeling the need to shit, but when he got to the privy, he found he couldn't go.

"Have you got the runs?" Gran asked.

"It's nothing," Inkcap insisted.

"If it's nothing, stop drooping around. I've collected a basket of ash from the stove, and you can go and scatter it on the potato seedlings in our plot."

Inkcap had picked up the basket and was out of the door while Gran was still explaining how to heap some of the ash around each seedling and then cover it over with earth. While he was packing wood ash around the seedlings in their private plot, in Noodle Fish's plot next door, Stonebreaker's brother Padlock was taking a dump. He and Decheng had been supervising the village irrigation ditches when he was caught short. He ran over to his own family's private plot and when he had finished, he stayed squatting and squinted along the black line that separated the two plots.

"Hey!" he said. "Why are your potato seedlings growing into our plot?"

"That's not possible," Inkcap said.

"Look for yourself. There's a bend in the middle."

Inkcap looked and there were some irregularities in the dividing line between the two plots, and two potato seedlings were right up against it.

"What's going on here?" Inkcap asked. "I've heard that this whole field belonged to my family before Liberation."

"What's that?" Padlock exclaimed. "What are you talking about? Are you trying to turn the world on its head?"

In normal circumstances, Inkcap enjoyed going to Noodle Fish's house because the old couple were good to him. But he didn't like Stonebreaker or Padlock. In fact, although Stonebreaker was very cold towards him, he had never cursed him or hit him. However, and he didn't know why, whenever he saw the compact features and pigeon-toed stance of Stonebreaker and Padlock, he found himself disliking the two brothers.

Now he had let his mouth run away with him and Padlock had grown very serious. He regretted having misspoken and hurriedly said, "That's not what I meant."

"What did you mean, then?" Padlock demanded. "What exactly did you mean?"

"I got it wrong, OK?"

"I'm telling you now, Inkcap, you better not say that again."

Inkcap was chastened. "You won't tell the Branch Secretary, will you?"

"I'll let you off this time because our two families know each other so well."

"Please don't tell Gran either."

"Then you just pull up those two potato seedlings for me."

"It would be a shame to do that now they've already grown so big. Let's wait till they've fruited then I'll remember to dig up the potatoes and give them to you."

"I told you to pull them up!" Padlock said.

So there was nothing else for it but for Inkcap to pull up the two seedlings and only then did Padlock leave satisfied.

As Inkcap watched Padlock walk away, he could feel the anger gurgling away in his belly. Then it coalesced and jumped from his belly to his upper abdomen and from there to his heart. He cursed the potato seedlings as he pulled them up. "Who said you could go over there? Who said you could go over there?"

The seedlings were fresh and plump when he pulled them up but they immediately drooped their heads as though they were frostbitten. But Inkcap did not throw them away. He transplanted them into his own plot, and they immediately revived. As the bundle of anger inside him subsided, Inkcap's belly began to feel uncomfortable. He walked out of the family plot and headed towards the wooden shack on the highway. He wanted to drink *taisui* water. Drinking *taisui* water might make his stomach feel better.

The *taisui* water had already developed a miraculous reputation, and Bash wanted to stop every vehicle that passed along the highway so he could tell their drivers about it. Some of them were curious enough to pay a few fen for half a bowlful. Inkcap drank three mouthfuls, rubbed his stomach and belched a few times. Bash could smell the food Inkcap had eaten and asked him what delicacy it was that had made his stomach so uncomfortable. Inkcap didn't dare tell the truth and said that Padlock had made him so angry his belly hurt.

"Don't take any notice of him," Bash said. "He learned from when he was a little boy to feel cheated if he doesn't have the upper hand."

When Bash said this, Inkcap couldn't help thinking to himself that what Bash had done to the branch of that tree in the courtyard of the public office was just the same as how Padlock had behaved. So he didn't say any more about the business with Padlock. He scooped up another ladleful of water and drank it.

"You're not going to charge me for drinking your water, are you?"

"Go ahead and drink as much as you want as long as it makes your stomach better," Bash said. "Maybe you'll grow taller too and no one will bully you any more."

"It would be great if drinking it could change your status," Inkcap said.

Seeing how dark it already was outside, he helped Bash by moving the stools back into the shack from outside the doorway, along with various old tyres and the air pump. As he watched Inkcap working away, Bash said, "Have you seen Apricot over the last couple of days?"

"You're not in her good books at the moment. What do you want with her?"

"That's what I'm asking you."

Hearing Bash's pleading tone, Inkcap became serious himself: "What exactly are you asking?"

"Is she OK?"

"Not really."

"So it's not helping that I'm ignoring her?"

"She's got a lot sicker, and she cries whenever she's alone."

"Women are always fucking crying."

Gran waited for Inkcap to take the ash to scatter on the potato seedlings, then went back inside to eat. She waited and waited but there was no sign of him coming back. When she realised that he must have gone off somewhere, she stood on the embankment at the entrance to the village and shouted, "Hellooo... Ping'an! Hellooo... Ping'an!"

When the residents of Old Kiln called someone, they drew out the first sound as long as possible, and then the last part was the content of the call. That way, the sound really travelled a long way.

Flower Girl was bringing water up from the spring and asked, "Who are you calling, Granny Silkworm?"

"Ping'an! It's dinner time and there's no sign of him."

"Who's Ping'an?"

"How many people in the village do you know called Ping'an?"

Flower Girl suddenly realised who she was talking about and laughed. "All the ones I know are called Inkcap! So he has a formal name, does he?"

"Yes, my baby boy has a formal name."

"What for? He's fine just being Inkcap, isn't he?"

"It's just that if everyone keeps calling him Inkcap, he'll never grow any taller."

As the two of them were talking, Awning came running over, sweating profusely but not saying anything. Flower Girl and Gran exchanged glances, thinking this was all rather strange. Awning ran on a few steps, then turned back and said, "Give me a drink of water."

He sprawled down beside the bucket, choking as he drank.

"What do you think you're doing, gulping it down like that when you're so hot?"

"There's something wrong with me," Awning said. "I've got to go and see Goodman."

And with that, he ran off again.

On top of his normal work, Awning led a militia group for target practice in the threshing ground and also to practise their infantry crawl. Sometimes at night, however, they would go to the ravine on South Mountain with Pockmark and Sparks to hunt pheasants, blow up foxes and smoke out badgers. The rumour in the village was that they would often then shut themselves in and feast off the game they caught.

As Awning left, still clearly burning up, Flower Girl asked, "What's happened? Has the gun gone off and injured someone?"

"This place is evil. I don't dare say anything," Gran replied.

"Or has Goodman done something wrong again?"

Gran immediately fell silent, turned on her heel and went home.

Once she was sitting back in her courtyard, Gran's heart was racing, and her hands began to tremble. She was worried about Goodman, thinking that being made to stand in that meeting could have built up resentments in him and he might have been talking wildly. She took a ladle and went over to the dilapidated tank at the base of the courtyard wall, intending to scoop up some water to sluice out the pig's feed trough. On the way, she saw her chickens jumping one by one up onto the vine trellis in the corner. She waved her ladle and clucked at them to get them to come down.

But the chickens wouldn't cooperate. They had perfectly good nests in the henhouse, but they always slept on the vine trellis as soon as it got dark and were as uncontrollable as Inkcap himself. Last spring, one of her chickens went missing, but she didn't say anything. Later on, another one disappeared but she still didn't say anything. But Inkcap found a lot of chicken feathers floating in the piss cistern at Pockmark's house. Inkcap spent several sleepless nights hiding in a window recess, waiting. Sure enough, he eventually heard a noise in the middle of the night. It was Pockmark holding a pole with a small wooden perch nailed to it. He stretched the pole out under a chicken's body and gently moved it. The chicken obediently stood on the wooden perch and Inkcap was about to shout out when Gran put her hand over his mouth. She couldn't let Pockmark steal the chicken, but she also knew they couldn't shout out. If they did, Pockmark would definitely say that she was trying to frame him, and she would be put at a disadvantage. So in the end, she coughed once and then another three times. Pockmark let the chicken go and disappeared. From then on, she always chivvied the chickens down from the trellis and made sure they were safe in the henhouse.

Gran called the chickens, but they refused to come down, so she vented her anger at them on Inkcap when he came back.

"What time do you call this?" she said.

"I scattered the ash all right," Inkcap said, "but Bash called me. He wanted to ask about Apricot."

"So he called you and you just went, did you? Do you think your brother Potful isn't seriously ill, then?"

"I didn't tell him anything."

Gran said nothing more, but she was still furious.

Inkcap massaged her solar plexus and said, "Don't be cross, Gran. If you smile, you'll stop being cross."

Gran wouldn't smile, so he tried again.

"Please smile. Go on, please smile."

In the end, Gran chuckled, and the chickens clucked away on the vine trellis.

"Did you hear about anything happening in the village last night?" Gran asked.

"Somebody ate Lucky's dead piglets."

"Who was it? Who would eat dead piglets that had been thrown into a piss cistern?"

"There aren't many who would. Only Pockmark, Stonebreaker and Dazed-And-Confused."

"Shut your mouth," Gran said. "Do you have any proof?"

"It's what some villagers are saying."

"Let others say what they like. You just make sure you keep your mouth shut when you're out there."

Inkcap called to the chickens, "Come down. Come down all of you."

One by one, the chickens came down from the trellis.

Gran went to scoop up some water from the dilapidated tank, but Inkcap told her not to.

"Don't disturb the water in there, just leave it, and, come spring, there'll be fish and shrimp in there."

"That's nonsense. You haven't put any fish fry in there, so where are all those fish and shrimp going to come from?"

"No one ever put fish fry in the lotus pond," Inkcap persisted, "so how come there are fish and shrimp in there, and mayflies and tadpoles too?"

As they were talking, Ever-Obedient's dog started barking further down the alleyway. It was a wild, disordered sound without any rhythm to it. It alarmed Gran, who became flustered and just watched as, instead of scooping water out of the tank, Inkcap actually added some fresh water from the bucket in the kitchen.

"Are you sure there's nothing going on in the village?" Gran asked. "You shouldn't be adding any water if you're really hoping that tank's going to grow you some fish and shrimps."

"No, nothing's going on," Inkcap assured her. "That water can grow anything it wants."

"If that's the case, how can there be nothing going on in the village?"

TWENTY-TWO

THERE WAS INDEED something going on in the village.

During the day, Baldy Jin and Stonebreaker drove the tractor to deliver a batch of porcelain goods to Luozhen's supply and marketing cooperative. They originally intended to go straight back to Old Kiln, but Baldy Jin went to the township's agricultural machinery station to ask the Branch Secretary's son if he wanted a lift back to the village. Stonebreaker hadn't thought Baldy Jin could be so considerate.

"Do you think your sister-in-law would have married me if I wasn't?" Baldy Jin said.

"Then why does she spend all day quarrelling with you? Is it because it was only when she got to Old Kiln and had a proper look around that she realised there were a lot of people richer and better off than you?"

"That's as may be," Baldy Jin retorted, "but I'm not the one sleeping by myself on the *kang* at night, am I?"

"But with you, it's what's called sharing the same bed with different dreams, isn't it?" Stonebreaker hit back.

"I don't care who she's thinking about. As long as she's underneath me, I'm the one getting the better end of the bargain. And I suppose everything's sweetness and light in your household, isn't it?"

"What do you mean by that?"

"I'm sure your dad treats you all really well."

"He's not my dad. My dad's dead."

Baldy Jin had nothing more to say after that.

As the tractor drove down Two-Way Street, Stonebreaker decided he wanted some driving practice, but he hadn't gone more than a hundred yards when a bicycle suddenly appeared on a side street up ahead.

He panicked and began to shout, "Get out the way! Get out the way! Get out the way! Get out the way!"

The female cyclist was so agitated that the bike was twisting and turning all over the place. Stonebreaker was also terrified and just sat there, jabbing at the brakes. Baldy Jin, who was sitting on the edge of the rear compartment, yanked to the left on the handrail and there was a grinding noise as the tractor overturned in a small ditch by the roadside.

Baldy Jin scrambled up and shouted, "Stonebreaker! Stonebreaker!" The tractor was upside down in the ditch, its wheels facing the sky and still spinning, but there was no sign of Stonebreaker. Baldy Jin hurried to open the cab and found Stonebreaker being crushed into the bottom of it.

"Am I alive?" Stonebreaker asked.

"Yes," Baldy Jin told him.

Stonebreaker touched his crotch and, once he was reassured his dick was still there, said, "Hurry up and pull me out."

"You weren't supposed to drive the thing, but you insisted, and look what a fucking pig's ear you made of it!"

Baldy Jin pulled him out, but as soon as Stonebreaker stood up, he fell straight back down as he discovered one of his legs was broken. Baldy Jin ran to find the Branch Secretary's son. The two of them carried Stonebreaker to the township medical station. The doctor said that the leg was broken and there was nothing that could be done for it. He gave Stonebreaker a few painkillers and told him to go home and cut a hole in a bed board to shit and piss through and lie there to recuperate.

"Some medical station! It can treat piddling little diseases but leaves it to Goodman to set bones."

He stopped a car on the highway and asked the driver to take a message to the Branch Secretary when he passed by Old Kiln. When the Branch Secretary heard the news, he told Awning to take Goodman to Luozhen on a bicycle.

Goodman went straight to the Branch Secretary's son's work unit and kneaded Stonebreaker's bones until there was a cracking noise. Stonebreaker yelled in pain.

"It's not as bad as childbirth," Goodman chided him.

Stonebreaker didn't want to hear about childbirth. "My wife hasn't given birth yet," he retorted. "You just wait till she does, then you'll fucking see something!"

Goodman remained unruffled and ordered him to straighten his leg.

Sweat rolled down Stonebreaker's face as he tried to straighten his leg but couldn't. Suddenly, Goodman brought his fist down on the broken leg and Stonebreaker passed out.

"What was that? What are you doing?" Awning exclaimed in alarm.

"The bones were broken, and it was difficult to bring them together, but they're fine now," Goodman explained as he started to knead the leg again and continued for the time it took to smoke two cigarettes.

Stonebreaker came to but didn't yell any more.

"Does it still hurt?" Awning asked.

"Not now," Stonebreaker replied.

Goodman put short wooden sticks on the leg and bound them in place with strips of cloth.

"I remember you, Goodman," Stonebreaker said. "You were standing at the front at the last meeting and I showed you up for closing your eyes and taking a nap. Now you're taking your revenge by causing me more pain!"

"Well, you can criticise me again in ten days when you stand up, can't you," Goodman said.

"Ten days?" Stonebreaker exclaimed and began to wail again. But he also told Baldy Jin, "You can be my witness that I was injured in the course of doing my public duty, so I must get work points for the ten days I'm laid up."

"Fuck me!" Baldy Jin exclaimed. "I wondered what you were wailing about, and it turns out to be your pissing work points! You may not be able to do without them, but you've got to put the fucking days in to get them."

The Branch Secretary's son came over and said they could spend the night in the spare room there, and he went off to put together some food for them. Baldy Jin thanked him effusively but said to Goodman, "Where are you going to stay?"

"We can all squeeze in together," Goodman suggested.

"We can't all fit in this one bed," Baldy Jin exclaimed. "I'll register you for a bed at the township inn. It's a communal bed there, always crowded and lively, and you're a talkative sort."

"Oh, OK," Goodman agreed and Baldy Jin left.

With Baldy Jin gone, Stonebreaker lay on the bed letting his eyes wander round the room. It wasn't large but it was very clean. The walls were papered with newspapers and New Year pictures. There was a sewing machine, a radio and shelves filled with enamel items: enamel bowls, enamel boxes and enamel thermos flasks.

"This is their spare house," Stonebreaker said. "There's a clock and a bicycle in another room. The bed is covered with a Pacific Ocean brand bedsheet, there are pillowcases on the pillows and silk handkerchiefs on the pillowcases. We may all be human beings together, but just look at the life they're living."

"To live a good life, the five elements must be in their set positions," Goodman said.

"What are the five elements?"

"In a family, the grandparents occupy the Earth position, and Earth controls vitality. Grandparents should always emphasise the strong points of the family, and that is called encouragement. But if they never display equanimity and find fault in others, that is called discouragement. The father occupies the Fire position in the south, and the mother is in the Water position in the north. The father is like the sun shining on the whole family, and the mother assists the father. When the family environment is not good, he is considered incompetent, and if there is anything unjust in the family situation, he must admit it. If a father is unable to hold their position, frustration will lead them either to beat their children or scold their wife. Fire will suppress Metal, and there will either be accidents around the house or someone in the family will get sick. If the eldest son occupies the Wood position in the east, he must be able to stand firm and relish hard work. If there is something he cannot do at home, he may blame himself, but he must not feel aggrieved. The other children occupy the Metal position in the west, and Metal controls relationships. They must have the best interests of the whole family in mind, be conciliatory when encountering problems and resolve those problems. If they spread gossip, it will hurt feelings and bring ruin on the family. If the head of the family is in charge of the fate of the whole family but is not secure in his position and the overall situation is not going well, and he beats and scolds his wife and children, then Fire will overcome Metal. If the person in the Metal position is angry but does not dare voice it, he will blame his elders, saying, 'It is because of your incompetence that we are so angry. We will not be able to survive this day.' When Metal overcomes Wood, the person in the Wood position has refused to admit that he was not able to maintain it and complains that his elders had left him no property, and even if he worked himself to death, it would be to no avail. He complains to his grandfather that once again Wood is overcoming Earth, and this is more than his grandfather can bear. He blames his daughter-in-law for giving birth to a no-good son who has no respect for his elders and who brings out his grandfather's own faults. Then, when Earth drives out Water, the woman of the house has nowhere to vent her anger so she turns on her elders saying, 'Look at you, you are so unreasonable and you always look down on our family.' And finally, when Water suppresses Fire, that will inevitably destroy the family."

Stonebreaker listened as Goodman started talking, but after it had gone on for a while, he wanted to sit up. Goodman told him not to move and said he would get a pillow to support him. Then Stonebreaker coughed, and before Goodman could fetch a dustpan, he spat the phlegm out onto the floor.

As Goodman went to get a broom instead, Stonebreaker said, "Why don't you just rub it into the ground with your feet? What do you need a broom for?"

"I know that the workers here really hate it when people do that," Goodman said.

Then Stonebreaker wanted to piss and he told Goodman to go and get a piss pot from the privy. When he'd finished, he told Goodman to scratch his back.

"You don't ask for much, do you!" Goodman said. "Now let me tell you how the five elements of the family can be in harmony with each other. As a parent, you should always tell your wife and children about the virtues of your ancestors and the good points of the elderly. This is Fire producing Earth. As a grandparent, you shouldn't meddle in things. Do something with your grandchildren if you want to, but let them play if you don't. Teach them to be filial and tell them the good points of their parents. This is Earth producing Metal. When children play happily, parents feel happy. This is Metal producing Water. When the housewife takes care of the housework with enthusiasm and pays careful attention to the food, drink and clothing of the people who go out to work, that is Water producing Wood. Those who work are comforted and work more diligently. This is Wood producing Fire. When the whole household is harmonious, the family will naturally be complete. When the five elements are fully expanded, they are omnipresent. People in the Earth position will remain steadfast, while those in the Metal position will have all their emotions reconciled. For example, if an older brother orders one thing to be done, and a father calls for another, they should immediately agree, and then decide which thing to do first. If a father calls for something to be done first, he should explain the reason to the older brother before doing it. Thus, the loving relationship is complete. People in the Water position need to be able to handle everything, so they must pay attention to household items such as firewood, rice, oil, salt, and all the people coming and going in the household. If something goes wrong, people in the Water position will take the blame on themselves. People in the Wood position must be able to take the lead, and if there is any work that is not done at home, they will take the blame on themselves. People in the Fire position need to be level-headed. When they go to the homes of relatives and friends, they do not go looking for favours, but to find explanations. They should study the way to get things done with relatives and friends. When they find explanations, they will pass them on to their family members. If someone in the family is unreasonable, the person in the Fire position will take the blame on themself. These are the five elements of family ethics that everyone should follow."

Goodman was talking very energetically, and Stonebreaker encouraged him to drink some water. Goodman misunderstood and asked him if he wanted a drink.

"No, you should drink some water," Stonebreaker said. "You have flecks of foam at the corners of your mouth."

"I don't want a drink," Goodman replied.

"Have you finished talking, then? I've broken my leg and want you to massage the bones, but all you've done is mutter on and on."

"I am talking to your illness for you."

"I've only broken my leg, what illness have I got?"

"A broken leg is a broken leg, but there is a reason for it."

"Are you saying I deserve it? That it serves me right I broke it?"

Goodman didn't reply and just looked at the door. The door framed the outside world into a tall, empty rectangle. A chicken's head appeared in the left-hand side of the rectangle, then the body and tail, as the chicken passed silently by and disappeared when it reached the right-hand side of the door frame. After a while, a chicken's head appeared on the right-hand side, followed by the body and tail, silently walking towards the left-hand side. Then the chicken took flight, flapped away and disappeared. Baldy Jin's feet appeared in the doorway. The front section of one of his sandals was broken.

As soon as Baldy Jin returned, he went to another of the Branch Secretary's son's houses. After a while, the Branch Secretary's son brought a bowl of rice congee and a plate of pickled vegetables. He put them down on the table and told Goodman he should eat. Goodman didn't refuse. He filled a bowl and ate it, saying, "Eat up, you lot."

But the Party Secretary's son didn't eat, and neither did Baldy Jin or Stonebreaker. Goodman asked why they weren't eating but then he remembered that the three of them were close friends and must have better food to eat elsewhere. Not wanting to keep them from their meal, he bolted down a second bowl and made his way to the hotel to sleep.

Goodman grew more and more amused as he walked along. He was remembering the saying that lucky people are large-minded and unlucky people are big-headed. They had given him food to eat but then hurried him on his way with no show of fellow feeling, and he wondered which of the two they were.

The next day, all the villagers knew about the incident with Stonebreaker's leg. When he got back to the village, Gran took three eggs and went to pay him a visit. She asked Inkcap to go with her, but he didn't want to. After Gran had left, Inkcap thought to himself, If your brother hadn't made me pull up those potato seedlings, things might not have come to you breaking your leg. He decided to go and have a good laugh at Stonebreaker's expense. Lots of people were in the courtyard of Noodle Fish's house, including Goodman and the Branch Secretary. Goodman had brought his bag of traditional remedies and said that if the patient took five doses of his preparation, the bones would knit much faster. Unfortunately, Luozhen's traditional medicine shop didn't have any "tiger beetles" so they would have to find some for themselves.

As soon as Inkcap arrived, he saw Padlock.

"I knew you'd be coming," said Padlock.

"How did you know that?" Inkcap asked.

"Because you've come to laugh at our family."

Inkcap was temporarily put out by the comment and didn't know how to respond. Then, when he heard Goodman say there were no tiger beetles, he turned around and asked, "What's a tiger beetle? Where can I find them?"

"It's just a dustpan roach,'" Goodman told him. "There are five in a prescription."

"If it's just a dustpan roach, why do you give it a fancy name like 'tiger beetle'?" Inkcap asked.

"You've got the job of finding some dustpan roaches, Inkcap," the Branch Secretary announced.

Dustpan roaches can only be found in damp places, but Inkcap said it would be easy because he had them at home. One night three years ago, he had pissed his bed. He had thin congee every night and could drink three bowls of it, but it made his belly bulge uncomfortably, so Gran only allowed him to have two. Even then she had to wake him up three times during the night so he could get up to piss, and he had always already pissed the bed by the time she woke him the first time. What happened was that he would dream he was bursting for a piss but couldn't find anywhere to go because there were people wherever he looked. Eventually, he would find a secluded spot and tell himself that it was OK to piss at last. Of course, the result was that he pissed the *kang*. On this particular occasion, Gran was taking advantage of the moonlight at the window to stitch the soles of her shoes. When she prodded him awake and found that the mattress was already wet, she scolded him for having a broken bladder. She'd only managed to put in ten lines of stitches on one shoe and he'd pissed the *kang* already! She lit the lamp and told him to remove the wet mattress and replace it with a dry one. In the lamplight, he saw dustpan roaches skittering around everywhere on the floor at the base of the *kang*. He was so frightened that he screamed. He jumped off the *kang* and tried to stamp on the roaches with his bare feet, but by then they had all disappeared.

Now, when Inkcap looked for dustpan roaches at home, he couldn't find any. He moved the water bucket and looked under the chopping board, but still no roaches. He lifted the cellar cover and went into the cellar. There were sweet potatoes and potatoes. He found one roach, but it scuttled into the pile of sweet potatoes. He exhausted himself pulling out the vegetables one by one and eventually caught it. That was it! One dustpan roach! He went to Iron Bolt's house next door to look for more and found two in the cellar. When he arrived at Useless's house, Useless wasn't there. He didn't find any roaches in the cellar, but he did come across a jar that was half full of millet.

"Hey! You've still got some millet, have you?" he exclaimed.

"What millet?" Useless's mother protested. "There's something wrong with your eyes. That's millet bran."

"It's millet all right," Inkcap shot back. "Do you think I don't know millet when I see it?"

The woman's expression hardened as she spat back, "That millet was saved grain by grain from our own mouths, so don't go spreading stories about it."

How could Inkcap not say something? At mealtimes every day, people took their bowls out into the alley to eat, and all those old bowls held was thin rice congee. One person would claim to be eating clouds, referring to the reflection of the clouds on the surface of the congee. When he blew on it, ripples spread across both the congee and the clouds. Another person would say, "I'm fishing for birds today!" It was the reflection of birds in the congee, but those birds were always shitting and not laying any eggs.

Useless's mother also carried an old bowl, but she never had any food in it. Instead, she would raise her chopsticks in front of someone else's bowl and say, "Let me try yours! Hmm, this slurry water is a bit old, isn't it?"

Then she would poke her chopsticks into someone else's bowl and say, "Ah, so you're on shredded radish today. It's so salty it would kill a salt merchant!"

Whenever Dazed-And-Confused saw her coming, he would stir his vegetables into his congee, avoid looking at her, ignore anything she said, put his head down and shove his mouth deep into his bowl and keep it there. Useless's mother tried to make herself look as pitifully old and poor as possible, but there was half a jar of millet hidden in the cellar. Inkcap wanted to expose her so that at least no one would let her taste their food again.

Inkcap went to the cellar in Barndoor's house to look for dustpan roaches. Barndoor was not at home either. Flower Girl was beating starched clothes on the stone in the yard.

"Why are you looking for dustpan roaches?" she asked.

"Don't you know about Stonebreaker's broken leg? Traditional medicine always needs something to set it working."

"Why are all these accidents happening to this family, one after another? And why do they use dustpan roaches to set the medicine working?"

"If you cut a dustpan roach in half and leave it overnight, it will grow back together," Inkcap said. "In medicine, you add whatever it is you need to supplement."

"How does a little brat like you know all this?" Flower Girl asked as she gathered up her washing. Then she let Inkcap go down into the cellar, saying, "You should eat lots of bamboo, it might make you grow faster."

In addition to the sweet potatoes and radishes in the cellar of Flower Girl's house, there were also three large pumpkins and a basket of pepper leaves, which was more than could be found in Inkcap's house.

When Inkcap told her that there was millet in Useless's family cellar, Flower Girl said, "They have to get by one way or another."

Inkcap had no reply to that. They caught five dustpan roaches in Flower Girl's cellar and Inkcap said happily, "Did you find out about Stonebreaker's broken leg early and keep them there specially?"

"Is the reason you don't grow any taller so that you don't have to wear a Four Bad Elements hat?"

This was the first time Inkcap had heard anyone talk about his height like that, and he couldn't help thinking she was right. It was only then that he realised the benefits of being small and began not to feel inferior because of his size.

"You're really nice, sister-in-law," Inkcap said.

"What do you mean?"

"You've grown up really pretty."

"You're just saying that."

"No, you have. Show me your profile."

Flower Girl turned side-on to Inkcap.

"Look how high your nose is!" he exclaimed.

He raised the kerosene lamp to look at her and noticed another dustpan roach on the wall of the cellar. As he swayed towards it, he dropped the lamp which went out and kerosene poured out onto the floor. "Aiyo Aiyo!" he wailed as he groped around on the floor, and his hand found the puddle of kerosene.

"It's nothing. Don't worry about it," Flower Girl told him.

She pulled him over to the entrance shaft of the cellar where the opening above them provided a little light. However, it wasn't enough for them to make out the footholds in the wall of the shaft so they couldn't climb out.

"I'll give you a bunk up," Flower Girl said and, without further explanation, she tried to push Inkcap up into the shaft.

"You're so heavy!" she grunted.

Indeed, he was so heavy she couldn't lift him even using both hands, so she had to hug him to her and shove him upwards. As she did so, her breasts bulged, soft and yielding against Inkcap, who was so discomfited he actually shrank away from her.

"Grab the edge of the hatch. Go on, grab it."

Inkcap did as he was told and hauled himself out of the cellar, followed by Flower Girl. Inkcap blushed furiously and didn't dare look at her.

"I'm so stupid. I spilled all your kerosene."

"What's spilled is spilled," she said. "Have you got the dustpan roaches safe?"

"They're inside my jacket."

"Stonebreaker got injured when he was doing public work, so he gets work points for it. The Branch Secretary ordered you to find the dustpan roaches to activate the medicine, so you need to tell him to give you some work points too."

"I don't care if he does or he doesn't."

"What kind of talk is that? If you don't make the effort now, how are you going to afford to look after yourself and Granny Silkworm when she's older?"

Before lunch, Inkcap decided not to give the twenty-one dustpan roaches he had collected directly to Stonebreaker. Instead, he would hand them over to the Branch Secretary, and he was just making his way over to the Secretary's house when the man himself set out for Noodle Fish's place, carrying a clay jar.

"Why have you brought the roaches here?" the Branch Secretary asked.

Inkcap hesitated, hoping for some words of praise, but none were forthcoming and all he got was a gracious smile. At least that smile indicated to

Inkcap that he was in the Branch Secretary's good books, so he happily tagged along with him on his way to Noodle Fish's house. In the alley, Useless's mother was clearly angry with someone, and she walked past with a face like thunder. Suddenly, when she saw the Branch Secretary, her expression relaxed, and she said, "Oh, Party Secretary, you've put on weight!"

"I've had a stomach ache these last few days and been bringing up acid. How can I have put on weight?"

"No, you definitely have," Useless's mother insisted. "It makes you look prosperous. What are you up to?"

"I'm taking medicine to Stonebreaker."

"Oh, do you have to take it in person?"

"I have to show my concern, don't I?"

"Of course, of course. And as soon as you deliver it, your stomach trouble will be cured."

"Oh!" the Branch Secretary exclaimed in sudden alarm. "I can't give him this jar. Stonebreaker's wife has to come and get it. I was in such a rush, I forgot."

"Couldn't Inkcap take it rather than Stonebreaker's wife having to come and get it?"

"Won't that make me ill?" Inkcap asked in alarm.

"What if it does? You'll be doing it for the Branch Secretary."

Inkcap really hated Useless's mother for sticking her oar in, but he still took the medicine jar from the Branch Secretary's hands and plonked it on his head, wearing it like a steel helmet.

"And I suppose a curse now will bring ten years of prosperity," he declared.

When they arrived at Stonebreaker's house, Noodle Fish was cleaning a turtle in the courtyard. The residents of Old Kiln didn't generally eat turtle, and only used it to make soup when someone was sick, just like women in confinement making pig's trotter soup to bring down their milk.

"I've brought you the medicine jar," Inkcap said, and he set about helping to make a fire to simmer the medicine.

The Branch Secretary asked Noodle Fish about Stonebreaker's injury, and then came over and smoked a cigarette as he watched Inkcap simmering the medicine. He instructed him not to use hard firewood but to use wheat straw so the medicine would cook slowly over a gentle flame. The medicinal herbs were all dried and had to be boiled slowly to release their beneficial properties. Inkcap obeyed the instructions to the letter.

"In this village we have Bash and Pockmark, and neither of those fuckers for know how to take advice," the Branch Secretary said, "but Inkcap here is willing to learn."

"Inkcap's a good lad," Noodle Fish said. "He could teach our kids, couldn't he!"

Inkcap was delighted. He took a small stool over to the Branch Secretary and said, "Please sit down, Master."

The Branch Secretary stirred up the medicine in the jar with chopsticks to see what ingredients it contained. Inkcap recognised Chinese goldthread and reed root among them.

"It's strange, isn't it?" Inkcap said. "Reed roots are sweet, and goldthread is bitter but they both grow out of the ground. Why are they different? Where does the sweetness come from? Where does the bitterness come from?"

And starting from there, he went on to wonder why there were red flowers and white flowers, and why some beans were black and some yellow when they were all beans.

"Everything is there in the soil," Noodle Fish said. "Just like there are poor and lower-middle peasants in Old Kiln, there are also the Four Bad Elements."

As Noodle Fish finished talking, he saw Inkcap freeze and added hastily, "Ah, no, no, I'm just letting my mouth run away with me and talking nonsense."

He took the cleaned turtle into the kitchen and called Inkcap over.

"I wasn't talking about you. Please don't take it to heart."

"I don't mind," Inkcap said firmly. "I'm not one of the Four Bad Elements anyway."

Noodle Fish was cutting the head off the turtle with a knife when the Branch Secretary came in and said, "No need for that."

He placed the turtle in a pot of cold water, put the lid on and told Noodle Fish to light the fire in the stove. Inkcap thought this was rather odd because whenever they'd cooked turtle in the past, they always cut the head off and the turtle sometimes managed to stay alive. The last time, Cowbell had chopped the head off and it had fallen onto the ground under the chopping block. He picked it up to throw to the cat, but the head had bitten him on the finger. It kept its jaws clamped shut and would only let go if there was a clap of thunder from the heavens. There was no thunder that day, so Cowbell put his foot on the turtle's head and pulled his finger free at the cost of a flap of skin. This time, when the Branch Secretary failed to chop off the turtle's head or put a stone on the lid of the pot, Inkcap didn't say anything but waited for a while in case the turtle flipped around in the pot, pushed off the lid and jumped out. Meanwhile, the herbs in the medicine jar kept gurgling away, but the turtle in the iron pot stayed silent.

Finally, Inkcap asked, "Master, why isn't the turtle moving?"

"Why would it move? If you put it in cold water and heat it slowly, it won't notice it is boiling to death."

"Oh."

The Branch Secretary was smiling. His face was wrinkled, and he had a big nose. When he smiled, the wrinkles spread out around his nose.

"So, Inkcap, am I a good master?"

"Yes, you are."

"How am I a good master?"

"Other people bully me, but you don't."

"If you are not from a good family background, you have to be humble and not cause trouble. Just be a good boy and I will treat you well."

"I am a good boy and I've been looking for dustpan roaches today, so please give me some work points."

The Branch Secretary knocked him on the head with the bowl of his pipe. Clonk, he knocked him once, and a bump appeared on his head. Bang, he knocked him again, and another bump appeared. But Inkcap didn't try to dodge, and he didn't complain about the pain. Then the courtyard door creaked, and Useless came in, carrying a lotus root. There was a slip of paper on the lotus root with characters on it. Inkcap hated Useless for arriving so inopportunely. The Branch Secretary was about to agree to give him work points, but Useless distracted him.

Inkcap looked at the lotus root and asked, "Is there writing on that paper?"

Useless ignored him and said to Noodle Fish, "You have to accept this lotus root. It is a mark of my good wishes. I also wrote a few words to Stonebreaker, which I'll read to you: 'You are hard-working, brave and strong, and you are made of special stuff. You were gloriously injured for the sake of our rich and beautiful village of Old Kiln. I want to express my condolences to you and wish you a speedy recovery. With my best regards, Useless Zhu.'"

"Oh, so you want Stonebreaker to know this is a gift from you, do you?"

"Didn't you understand what I just said? You're an uneducated lout!"

"You need to get rid of the sentence about 'made of special stuff'. That's only used to describe communists. Stonebreaker is not a party member, so how can he be made of special stuff?"

Useless was taken aback.

"But that's just my description of him," he protested.

"Description or not, take it out."

"If he was made of special stuff, he wouldn't have broken his leg," Inkcap chipped in.

This was too much for Useless. "Are you really that fucking naïve?" he shouted.

The Branch Secretary turned around and took the lid off the iron pot. The turtle was lying quietly on the bottom, so he replaced the lid. Useless took out his pen and scribbled out the offending sentence in his note.

"There are some other things I want to report to you," he told the Branch Secretary.

"What are they, then?"

"First, it was Goodman who broke Stonebreaker's leg. How can that be allowed?"

"But it's Goodman who is setting the bones," Inkcap protested.

"He's taking advantage of that to get his revenge," Useless insisted.

"I don't want to hear any more of that," the Branch Secretary said. "What else?"

"Decheng was stung by a bee. There was a honeycomb on the back eaves of his house. When he went to take it down, he got stung inside his mouth and it swelled up like a pig's snout. Yoyo got sick too. She was carrying a piss bucket and collapsed to the ground unconscious. Sprout and her mother-in-law have quarrelled. Sprout was eating in secret and hiding some of their cooked rice behind the saucepan lids. That set the two of them off–"

"Those are trifling matters," said the Branch Secretary. "Is there anything else?"

"Yes," Useless persisted, "Bash and Baldy Jin had a quarrel too. Baldy went to Bash and asked for some *taisui* water for Stonebreaker, but Bash refused to give him any. He told Baldy that if someone didn't know how to drive a tractor, he shouldn't drive one. Baldy was responsible for breaking a man's leg and now he was asking for *taisui* water! What was that all about?"

The discussion was getting so noisy that people started gathering around to watch.

"All right, all right. So there's a problem here," the Branch Secretary said. "I'll get the team captain to see what's going on."

"Bash is a real handful," Useless said. "You'll have to go yourself."

"Are you really saying the team captain can't handle this?"

Useless left the scene.

Inkcap went on simmering the medicine, and its smell filled the courtyard. As night began to fall, the fog rose again in the village, spreading through the alleyways and pouring in through the courtyard gates. The Branch Secretary poked the turtle with some chopsticks, and it was indeed cooked through without any fuss or commotion, so he lifted out the turtle's shell.

"I'll give you a turtle egg, Inkcap," the Branch Secretary said, picking one up and giving it to him.

Useless returned at that moment, panting heavily. Inkcap deliberately waved the turtle egg in front of him and stuffed it into his own mouth.

"The team captain's not well, and also because of what's been going on with Apricot, he couldn't handle the situation. Bash and Baldy Jin have started fighting!"

"Damn it," the Branch Secretary exclaimed. "Get Awning to go too. Two hooligans together should be able to handle another two hooligans."

Useless turned to go, but the Branch Secretary called him back, saying, "Do you have any of that red paint left?"

"Yes, I've still got some."

"The affairs of this village are like a pond full of water hyacinths. As soon as you get on top of one, another one pops up. Tomorrow, you can paint some more slogans around the village."

"All right."

"And forget about taking Awning with you. If those two daft pricks, Bash and Baldy, get going with each other, things will really kick off. I'll have to go myself."

"You're right," Useless said. "Otherwise, someone might get killed."

The Branch Secretary put his tobacco pouch in his sleeve, draped his coat over his shoulders and left with Useless. Meanwhile, Noodle Fish strained the medicinal and tasted it. It was terribly bitter. He took it to the house to give Stonebreaker a dose. Stonebreaker drank it while lying on the *kang* and said, "Thank you, Inkcap."

"Why are you thanking me?"

"You're a better person than Lightkeeper. You don't seem like someone with a bad background."

"Really?"

"Sure," Stonebreaker said. "He's got landlord blood in his veins. You're different from him."

When Inkcap left Noodle Fish's house, the fog in the alley was rolling in, but it was more like a cartwheel than a stone roller. He ran away, ahead of the cartwheel, and when he stumbled and fell, the cartwheel followed and ran over him. It didn't hurt, but it did feel as though he had been crushed flat, as flat as a noodle. Suddenly, he smelt a smell in his nose and mouth, the kind of smell he hadn't smelt for a long time.

TWENTY-THREE

IT WAS NO LONGER ANYTHING SPECIAL TO INKCAP if he suddenly smelt that smell. Once he'd smelt it, he'd smelt it, and that was that for him, but if Cowbell was with him at the time, either working or climbing trees or listening to the grunting of the thornback fish in the Zhou River, then he would always ask, "Did you just smell that smell?" This was because every time Inkcap smelt it, something happened in the village. But this could be coincidence, or it could be some distant, chance connection after the event. Even if the coincidence was repeated several times, that could still be the case, and as a result, Cowbell constantly disparaged Inkcap for being reincarnated from all the unlucky creatures like dogs, rats, crows and owls. So now, Inkcap often replied that he hadn't smelt anything, but this always made Cowbell suspicious. However, since Inkcap first smelt the smell after Stonebreaker broke his leg, he smelt it for several days in a row, and this made him feel uncomfortable, nervous and even rather scared.

On the morning of the tenth day of the first lunar month, Inkcap and Gran went to their private plot. The sky was as clean as a washed slab of bluestone, and the clouds were as white as could be, standing out individually against the blue. As they passed the entrance to Awning's courtyard, the morning glory on the screen wall was in full bloom. The colour of a single morning glory flower was not as bright as the rose on the wall of Flower Girl's courtyard, but with hundreds of flowers blooming together, the effect was as red as a fire and as bright as flame. People actually felt hot when they got close, and their faces and hands and even their clothes turned red. Inkcap stood under the screen wall and breathed in deeply with his mouth and nose wide open. He stood stock still as he inhaled, then rubbed his nose in confusion and inhaled again. His face stiffened.

"What's wrong with you?" Gran asked.

"I smelt it."

"Morning glory has a strong smell."

"It's *that* kind of smell."

"What kind of smell?"

"The kind of smell I've smelt before. I've been smelling it for the last few days."

Gran led Inkcap away from the screen to stand under the gable of Cowbell's house. The newly risen sun printed their shadows onto the wall.

"Can you still smell it?" Gran asked.

Inkcap grunted in the affirmative.

"Is there something wrong with your nose?" Gran asked, bending down to inspect him. There were no scabs and no mucus; everything was fine.

"You should stop thinking about it all the time," she said.

"But I can smell it."

Gran looked at Inkcap and pinched his nose.

"Will you buy me a mask?"

Gran couldn't buy Inkcap a mask. For one thing, she didn't want to spend the money and for another, how could Inkcap have a mask like Useless's? When they got home, Gran took a leather bag down from the rafters. It contained several pieces of red and yellow paper she had tucked away specially. These papers were only used to cut window grilles during the Chinese New Year. Now she cut five paper patterns for Inkcap, in the shape of a snake, a scorpion, a toad, a gecko and a centipede. Inkcap knew these were the five poisons and kept them safely in his pocket.

Although he had the five poison papercuts to protect him, he was still worried about what might happen in the village. He hated himself for having the kind of nose he did. When he lit the stove, he got ash on his nose, but he wouldn't wipe it off. When he looked in the mirror, he told his nose, "You're the cause of all this, so I'm fucked if I'm going to clean you."

However, on this occasion, no one in the village died and no one's illness got any worse. In fact, for many days, there were no fights or quarrels. The only change was that Bash started to drive the walking tractor.

To the villagers' surprise, after Baldy Jin and Bash had their fight, the Branch Secretary didn't punish Bash but actually asked him to drive the tractor instead of Baldy. What was that about? Was the Branch Secretary showing his broad-minded nature, disregarding past grievances and employing individuals according to their talents, or was he showing how soft he was and how much he was afraid of Bash?

Baldy Jin said to Soupspoon, "It breaks my heart that we've let ourselves come to this."

"Let me tell you this," Soupspoon said. "If someone can annoy you, they will annoy you, if they can't, they won't. But if they can't annoy you, they will still keep trying, so you have to turn the tables on them and behave nicely and show them respect. Then your life will settle down."

"What do you mean?"

"Do you really not understand? Well, if you don't, you don't."

"We'll have to see about that, won't we," Baldy Jin said. "From now on, this village is going to be a village of devils and monsters."

Inkcap didn't like the sound of that, but even so, he was the first to congratulate Bash, as he hoped that Bash would take him with him when he went to Luozhen to sell porcelain. But Bash had a new assistant in the form of Sprout, and Sprout firmly refused to let Bash take Inkcap along with them. So he had to hang around with Cowbell and go up to the kiln to see Goodman when the opportunity presented itself.

Goodman didn't know how to mix and apply glaze, how to roll out the mud to make forms, or how to light a fire in a kiln. He did odd jobs, transporting rocks to where others were crushing them, carrying clay for those who were making forms, and when the kiln was lit, Pillar told him to watch the kiln guardian through the observation window. Once, he went to check and said that the kiln guardian had fallen over. Pillar came running over to look but saw that the object was still standing so he cursed Goodman out for being an idiot. But Goodman had no regrets. Whenever he had some free time, he was either talking to people's illnesses or squeezing broken porcelain vases back together again in a sack of wheat bran.

Inkcap and Cowbell went back to see Goodman, who was chopping firewood at the time.

"If you'll pinch a porcelain vase back together for us, we'll chop that firewood," they offered.

"I'd rather talk to you about illness," Goodman replied. "Did you know Thimble's mother-in-law is ill? Do you want to know how I can cure her?"

"I'd rather watch you mend that vase than listen to you talking about illness," Inkcap insisted.

So Goodman agreed to do what they wanted. He picked up his cloth bag full of porcelain shards and wheat bran, put his hands inside and squeezed.

Goodman reached out and grasped Inkcap's arm, which was as thin as a stalk of hemp.

"Let me knead it for you," Goodman said.

Neither Inkcap nor Cowbell dared let Goodman knead their bones for fear of him breaking them.

"If you crush Inkcap's bones when you knead them, can you knead a new Inkcap back together again?" Cowbell asked.

"Surely!"

"That's good," Cowbell said. "If you let him knead you properly, Inkcap, he can knead you back together to be like me."

"I don't want to be like you," Inkcap protested. "Your eyes are too small, and your ears have got notches in them."

"But at least I'm a poor, lower-middle peasant!"

Inkcap ignored Cowbell and turned to Goodman. "Are people and their bones all the same?" he asked.

"You have one less bone than Lightkeeper."

"Does that mean I'm less important than him? I should be better. He has to stand during meetings, but I can sit down."

"He has a 'rebel bone' and you don't," Goodman said.

"What's one of them?"

"It's a bone that sticks out at the back of the head."

"Ha!" Cowbell said. "You're not even as good as Lightkeeper. At least he can rebel if he's bullied, but you just have to stand and take it."

Inkcap felt the back of his skull and found that it was flat. This made him both angry and depressed, so he kicked a wooden pole that happened to be next to him. The pole was supporting some washing as they dried and it tilted over, sending the clothes tumbling onto the floor.

Inkcap suddenly burst out, "I'm wearing an invisibility cloak."

"An invisibility cloak? What's that?"

This was a new one on Cowbell and that pleased Inkcap.

"Do you really want to know?"

"What do you think?"

Inkcap waved his hand airily. "Well, I'm not going to tell you."

Lightkeeper came out of a disused kiln at the east end of the kiln field and stood there stretching. He had long arms and legs and was so thin that he looked like he was jointed together using wooden sticks. You could hear the wooden joints cracking as he stretched. When Inkcap and Cowbell looked at him, they could see he had a protruding forehead and a sticking-out bump at the back of his head. They looked at each other and laughed.

"Don't laugh at me, and make sure you chop the firewood properly," Lightkeeper ordered them.

Lightkeeper did manual labour at the kiln site. Whenever he had free time, he would go into the disused kiln chamber he had fixed up. No one else was allowed in. He would put a broom on top of the half-open door with a sack of ash balanced on it. If anyone tried to push the door open and go in, the broom and the sack of ash would topple down and cover them in ash from head to toe. So what was Lightkeeper doing in that cave? Pendulum said he was wrong in the head. He was actually mixing glaze, either by pouring the glaze slurry into a pot and shaking it or by sticking his mouth into the liquid and blowing until it foamed. He knew he was never going to be allowed to do any of the technical work making bowls and jars, but all he dreamed of was making blue-and-white porcelain.

Lightkeeper had told Inkcap and Cowbell to chop firewood, but, in fact, they had already chopped a whole load. This kind of mindless work had originally been done by Lightkeeper, but when Goodman arrived, he had told him to get on with it. Now Cowbell and Inkcap were doing it, Lightkeeper took delight in bossing them around. Lightkeeper stretched and went off to the privy.

"It's a good thing he's a class enemy," Cowbell said. "If he were a cadre, or even just a poor or lower-middle peasant, he'd be even bossier than the Branch Secretary."

"I hope he can't shit today, or shits blood if he does," Inkcap said.

The two of them winked at each other and almost simultaneously set off for Lightkeeper's disused kiln. When they got to the door, they looked to see if there was a broom and a sack of ash on the door panel. There wasn't, so they went in. They wanted to mess Lightkeeper around so they deliberately mixed up the order in which he had laid out all his dishes and jars. They saw some pieces of paper on the table under the window and took them away.

"If any are covered in writing, we shouldn't take them," Inkcap said.

243

"No," Cowbell corrected him. "We can't take the blank paper, but once it's been written on, it's wastepaper and we can take it for Goodman to roll cigarettes with."

Inkcap took a few more pieces of blank paper and stuffed them into his pocket to give to Gran. As they were leaving the cave, they saw a pair of cloth shoes behind the door. There were insoles in the shoes, and the insoles were embroidered with actual individual portraits. Putting a human face on an insole was something completely new to Old Kiln.

"He's fucking skilful," Inkcap exclaimed. "He can spin thread, make clothes and do embroidery."

"This all means he wants to trample people underfoot," Cowbell said. "He's going to trample over us poor and lower-middle peasants."

"If that's true," Inkcap replied, "then it's more than his life's worth."

He took out the insoles, turned them over and replaced them. Then he took them out again and tucked them inside his jacket.

After they left Lightkeeper's cave, Cowbell gave Goodman a handful of sheets of paper, and Inkcap went over to the working kiln and shoved the insoles into the flames.

"What's that you're burning?" Cowbell asked.

"Just a handful of firewood," Inkcap replied.

Goodman looked at the paper he'd been given and exclaimed, "These are the notes Lightkeeper has written on the porcelain firing process. How dare you take them?"

"What process?" Cowbell asked.

Goodman began to read them out: "This process is divided into seventy-two steps, with two steps forming one set. The first set is prospecting and ore burning, which means that after discovering the veins of petuntse rock, they burn them with firewood, then pour water over them. If cracks appear, and the cracks are fine, uniform and form a network, excavations can proceed. The second set is transportation and crushing, which means transporting the porcelain stone and smashing it into fist-sized pieces with a hammer. The third group is grinding and soaking, which involves using a mill or stone mortar to grind the porcelain stone into powder, then soaking it in a pond and raking out the residue. After settling, the thick mud at the bottom turns into a slurry. The fourth set is cleaning and forming. This means that the clean and washed mud is cooled for a while, then rolled into a ball, put into a wooden box mould and flattened, and then taken out of the mould to make a brick-like block. The fifth set is ash burning for glaze preparation, which means that a pure blue-white glaze cannot be attained without ash. Fern leaves and limestone rocks are stacked and burned, and the ash is washed and mixed with water. The resultant glaze slurry must be thick and evenly textured. The sixth set is refining clay and firing saggars. The porcelain forms have to be put in protective saggars before going into the kiln. The clay used for the saggars does not need to be too fine. They are dried for a while and fired once in the kiln. The seventh set is saggar inspection and storing, which means that after the saggars are fired, they must be measured for size, height, depth, thickness and weight, to ensure they comply with the specifications. The eighth set is melting without washing, which means that the brick blocks must be pulped in a large vat without being completely dissolved, all impurities must be removed, and the resultant thick slurry must be poured into buckets and transported to the clay room in that state. The ninth set is shovelling and tamping the clay, which involves putting the mud on a large stone slab and pounding it firmly with a shovel, making it into the shape of the character 口, and continuously beating it to form it into the character 田, then trampling it with bare feet. The tenth set making a clay form, which involves kneading the mud evenly to expel the air, sitting on the wheel frame and rotating the wheel, pressing the mud with both hands, bending, stretching and pulling it back together according to the correct technique to achieve the desired rounded shape. The eleventh set is…"

Goodman stopped reading the full text. "There are lots of them," he said. "I'll just read the titles. The eleventh set is repairing and finalising. The twelfth set is scraping down and printing the blanks. The thirteenth set is keying the blank to accept the glaze. The fourteenth set is cutting the blanks and connecting them. The fifteenth set is raising the blanks and drying them. The sixteenth set is making a slip glaze and applying it by blowing. The seventeenth set is dipping and pouring the glaze. The eighteenth set is mixing and applying the glaze manually. The nineteenth set is washing down and replenishing the glaze. The twentieth set involves lightly painting with diluted pigment. The twenty-first set is moulding and carving patterns. The twenty-second set is transporting and selecting the forms. The twenty-third set is repairing the saggars and loading the forms. The twenty-fourth set is stacking the saggars and preparing the kiln. The twenty-fifth set is selecting the firewood and firing the kiln. The twenty-sixth set is opening the kiln and arranging the baskets. The twenty-seventh set is mixing the mud and replastering the kiln. The twenty-eighth set is inspecting the colour and selecting the porcelain. And the twenty-ninth is weighing the material and assessing the colour."

Inkcap and Cowbell had no idea what a complex process it was to make porcelain. They were listening attentively when a voice came from above them: "Have you finished reading?"

"Not yet. There are thirty-six sets," Goodman said before he suddenly felt something wasn't right.

When he looked up, he saw Lightkeeper standing behind him.

"I didn't take it," he said hastily. Inkcap and Cowbell had already taken to their heels.

"The little fuckers are still at their thieving, are they?"

"Is this your own summary?"

"It was told to me by Master Fu at the Luozhen kiln. I wrote it down and added some of my own experiences, such as the way of using moulds to make the clay bricks which I call '*baibu*'. I also put together a few tips on trampling the clay. Then there are the saggars which often break due to repeated use. I used charred bamboo strips as hoops to reinforce them.

There are also the glaze formulas. Do you know how many formulas there are?"

Goodman admitted that he didn't, adding, "You're quite something, Lightkeeper!"

"Am I fuck," Lightkeeper said. "How come they can make blue-and-white porcelain in Luozhen and we can't, no matter how hard we try?"

"I'm sure with your acumen, you'll manage it."

"Who's going to let me? Even if the Branch Secretary were to call me a treasure, the rest of the villagers are still going to treat me like a broken tile. And do you think the Secretary will make a treasure out of a broken tile?"

"You need to break the ice with the villagers," Goodman advised him. "You don't say a word all day and go around with that hangdog expression on your face."

"I suppose you'd keep smiling when they beat you! They could sell you, and you'd help them count the money! Who do you think I am? Inkcap?"

Lightkeeper retrieved his papers and returned to his cave. Goodman called after him but he didn't reply.

Even though Inkcap had run away, he still admired Lightkeeper and felt that recently, the villagers had been using various tricks to cheat him on his work points. Lightkeeper was putting in a lot of effort over the firing of the porcelain. So a few days later, Inkcap went back to the kiln site to talk to Lightkeeper, but yet again, Lightkeeper wouldn't say anything about the business, kept his hangdog look with his eyes half-closed and refused to pay Inkcap any attention at all. Then one day, nearly all the villagers went up the mountain to help move the fired porcelain goods down to the Kiln God Temple. The irrigation ditch behind the temple was full of water at the time, so wooden boards were laid across it and Inkcap and Lightkeeper carried basketfuls of porcelain across them. Once dozens of bowls had come down and been carried across, Lightkeeper stopped and put a stone under the wooden plank. The Branch Secretary was the last to come down from the kiln along with a few others. He crossed the wooden plank first and, as he stepped on it, it slid away from under his feet. He stumbled and fell into the ditch, covering himself from head to toe in mud and water. After reaching the village, he concluded that it must have been Inkcap who played the prank on him, and he scolded him for it.

"I didn't do it," Inkcap told him.

"If it wasn't you, what grown-up could have done such a thing?"

Inkcap wanted to tell him it was Lightkeeper, but he didn't. In the end, he admitted that he had done it, saying that he wanted Cowbell to fall into the ditch. The Branch Secretary slapped him round the ears.

Inkcap felt aggrieved and went back to tell Gran what had happened.

"That's Lightkeeper for you. He's certainly capable enough in this work, but he's not exactly what you'd call reliable."

"Is he really a class enemy like people say?"

"Alas, he wasn't like this before."

"Is he sick?"

"Yes, he's sick."

Inkcap sat down at the courtyard gate, wondering what kind of illness Lightkeeper had and how he could be someone he admired but couldn't bring himself to like. Of course, he thought of Bash. How strange the world was! But if he was talking about evil, Lightkeeper was certainly more evil than Bash. Moreover, Bash cursed him and beat him, but he would still rather be with Bash than get along with Lightkeeper. The wind was gathering strength and the leaves from all the trees in the lane blew down into the courtyard and swirled around. They lined up like people standing in a circle. They floated, spinning up from the ground, idly shrinking into a single strand, then rising into the sky, twisting into a rope.

"Why are you sitting there in a daze?" Gran called out from inside the house. "Bring me the ladder. Why is there a row of tiles missing from the courtyard wall?"

"I haven't seen Bash for ages," was all Inkcap said.

The rope suddenly disappeared straight upwards, as if it was being hauled into the sky.

TWENTY-FOUR

INKCAP WAS FINALLY ABLE TO GO TO LUOZHEN WITH BASH. He was grateful to Bash for the opportunity and even more grateful to Sprout.

Like Flower Girl, Sprout had not given birth after she got married but Flower Girl was considered beautiful, like a flower on a pumpkin vine. However, the more brightly such a flower blooms, the more barren the plant becomes. Sprout, on the other hand, had long legs and small buttocks, which the villagers said was not a good body shape for giving birth. Flower Girl had neither child nor mother-in-law so was able to live a comfortable life, but Sprout's mother-in-law grumbled all day long about wanting a grandson, and Sprout had no status in her own home. No matter how diligent and filial she was, she never caught a break. Since the twelfth lunar month, her mother-in-law had been grumbling ever more fiercely and she had been losing weight by the day. At first, she thought it was because her food and drink were no good, but later she cooked up some thick rice and was able to eat three or four bowls at a sitting but still she kept growing thinner; so thin in fact that there was nothing of her.

The production team arranged to carry nightsoil over to the family's private plot to fertilise the sweet potato patch. She could no longer carry the nightsoil herself, so she started to use a hoe to load it into baskets for everyone else. But after standing there for a short time, she knelt down, still shovelling away with her hoe, and fainted dead away. Gran immediately pinched the acupuncture point on her upper lip and gave her some soup, telling her that she was ill. Not many people in Old Kiln suffered from this kind of illness; Lucky's grandfather had had it, and he had only got better by drinking water spring onion soup. Water spring onions are not the same as spring onions; they look similar but are actually a type of wild grass that grows near water. Gran explained to Sprout how to make the soup by cutting the water spring onion into two-finger-long sections every morning, tying them into knots as you would do ordinary spring onions, and boiling them in a pot for an hour. You then poached two eggs, and when they were cooked, you removed the water spring onion knots. You ate the eggs and drank the soup together every day for two months.

"This sounds like a rich person's illness," Sprout's mother-in-law said.

"You are a rich person," Sprout replied.

"Rich person, my arse! And will I be rich when I'm dead and a ghost?"

Sprout had still been smiling, but a black look spread over her face when she heard this.

"You mustn't talk nonsense," Gran said hurriedly. "Let Sprout gather some water spring onions for you." And as she pushed Sprout away, she continued in a whisper, "Don't say anything. You have to be as filial as possible while she has this illness."

Sprout huffed and puffed a bit, but then she calmed down and went off to dig up some water spring onions. On the way, she met Stargazer and Dazed-And-Confused.

"Is your mother-in-law better?" Stargazer asked.

"I'm going to dig up some water spring onions," she told him.

"There's no medicine that'll be of any use. She'll only get better when you have a baby."

Sprout hated other people talking about her having a baby, so she snapped, "What baby? A baby Dazed-And-Confused?"

"Are you saying you're going to give me a little Dazed-And-Confused?" Dazed-And-Confused asked.

"It would come out with four legs if I did," Sprout retorted, turning on her heel and walking away.

Dazed-And-Confused had to think about that for a while and finally worked out that only animal babies had four legs and that Sprout had been cursing him out.

"I wouldn't want anything you produced," he shouted after her, "even if you could, you barren sow!"

An infuriated Sprout cursed as she picked the plants on the riverbank. She kicked out at the rocks by the river, kicking one so hard she drew blood from one of her toes. The water spring onions on the bank were all very small and she threw away the few she had gathered. She decided to go and look for some in the reed garden and finally found a clump. She picked a dozen or so and decided to go home and plant them in their yard. She left the reed garden and went for a rest on the riverbank, still cursing Stargazer and Dazed-And-Confused.

It was noon, the sun was red, and the riverbank was entirely deserted. Birds were chirping and making strange noises in the reed garden. Noodle Fish went to the bottom of the mountain on the other side of the river to dig for black garlic. You soaked the heads of garlic in water for three days to reduce their numbing strength and then you could cook them in a pot. He was just crossing the river on his way home when he noticed someone in the distance, sitting on the strand, but he didn't take any further notice. But when he emerged on the other side of the river, he saw the same person lying on the beach, driving their head into the sand bank, shouting: "Ai! Ai!" The person kept on doing it as if there was some force holding their head and pushing it. As he got closer, he realised it was Sprout. Her nose, ears and mouth were full of sand, and she was unconscious. Noodle Fish slapped her several times until she came to. He asked her what was wrong, and she said she didn't know.

For several days, Sprout seemed to be suffering from a serious illness. Her neck was so weak that she couldn't hold her head up. The villagers said it must be the work of a ghost. Sprout went to the kiln to talk to Goodman about her illness. Inkcap happened to be there when she was complaining about her symptoms. When he saw how she looked, he realised she couldn't possibly go to Luozhen to sell porcelain, so he ran down the mountain to find Bash. Bash then took him to see the Branch Secretary.

The Branch Secretary's gums were inflamed, and half of his face was swollen. He was pacing wildly around the room in pain. When Bash told him about Sprout being possessed by a ghost, he reprimanded him, saying that people will always fall ill and if Sprout was sick, she was sick, so why bring ghosts into it? What evil spirits were there in Old Kiln, anyway? He had a fever and a toothache, but was he possessed? As soon as Inkcap heard that the Branch Secretary was afflicted, he went to pick some leaves from the walnut tree outside the courtyard gate. He crushed them a little in his hand and told the Branch Secretary to put them in the waistband of his trousers. Then he went to Barndoor's house to find some pepper seeds, telling the Secretary that stuffing them between his teeth would relieve the pain.

As soon as Inkcap had gone, the Branch Secretary asked, "Why's that little runt being so attentive? What's going on?"

Bash told him that Sprout was ill and couldn't go to Luozhen, so he wanted Inkcap to go with him.

The Branch Secretary thought about it for a while and asked, "Is he up to it?"

"He's small all right, but he's very careful and has a good memory. If we put him in charge of the money, no one will ever think he'd be trusted with cash, so no one will ever think of robbing him either."

"I'm thinking about his family background," the Branch Secretary said.

"This isn't something he could cock up even if he wanted to," Bash said.

So the Branch Secretary agreed, but he went on to say, "You've been to Luozhen lots of times in the past, haven't you? There aren't any problems going on, are there?"

"What kind of problems?"

"Well, the Commune Secretary sent someone with a message…" But then he stopped, before continuing, "No, it's nothing. It's nothing."

His words left Bash puzzled for the rest of the day.

Inkcap brought back the pepper seeds and learned that the Branch Secretary had agreed to let him go and sell the porcelain. He bounced up and down with joy and said, "I kowtow to you, Mr Branch Secretary, sir!"

"I'm not over happy about this, but I'll let you go. Just make sure you keep on the straight and narrow. If anything goes wrong, I'll haul you back here right away and hold a meeting about you."

Inkcap nodded like a chicken pecking corn and tried to stuff the pepper seeds between the Branch Secretary's teeth. The Branch Secretary said he would do it himself, but Inkcap insisted.

"You're a persistent little bastard, aren't you! Give them here."

Inkcap handed over the seeds.

That afternoon, Inkcap helped Bash load the truck. He loaded more than two hundred bowls and six large jars. He drove the walking tractor over to the door of Bash's shack. Bash made it clear that they would be setting off for Luozhen as soon as he woke the next day.

"Are you sure it's safe to leave the goods here overnight?" Inkcap asked.

"It's fine," Bash assured him.

"And you'll take responsibility if anything happens?"

"Are you my manager now?"

Even so, Bash did unload the porcelain goods and put them in the shack. Not only was Inkcap going into town to sell porcelain, but Bash had also taken his advice! He was excited and keen to tell Cowbell all about it. He met Apricot on his way back and couldn't help calling out to her rather nervously.

Apricot was coming back from her private plot with some spinach she had picked. The roots of the spinach were very red, and the leaves were a vibrant green.

She stopped and said, "If you want to talk to me, just watch your tongue."

"Do you have any food stamps at home? Can you lend me four *liang* worth?"

"What do you want food stamps for?"

"I'm going to Luozhen to sell porcelain. I'll have to go to a restaurant there for lunch, won't I?"

"And you're going to sell porcelain?"

"That's right."

"Why do you need to go to a restaurant? You can just take some buckwheat buns with you... Who else is going?"

"Bash, of course. Who do you think?"

"I know he's been told to go and sell the porcelain, but that's not a daily thing. The rest of the time he's just driving around on the tractor. He never spends any time at home."

Third Aunt was standing at the mouth of the alley, looking at them.

"Apricot!" she called out. "That lad's come. What are you doing hanging around out here? You should be going home."

"If he's here, that's up to him," Apricot replied.

"You should stop answering back to your elders, you wretched girl. Just do what I say and go home."

"I've still got some things I want to tell Inkcap."

"And what would those be?"

"None of your business."

250

Third Aunt shot Inkcap a look urging him to be on his way, but he played dumb and stayed put.

"You inconsiderate little prick!" Third Aunt was clearly exasperated.

"Who's she talking about?" Inkcap asked Apricot.

"Tell Bash that my dad's had a matchmaker looking for a husband for me. It's a fellow from Xiahewan."

"What kind of husband are you looking for?"

Apricot just turned and walked away.

Inkcap didn't pass the news on to Bash. He felt that since Apricot and Bash had fallen out and made a clean break of it, what was there to tell? Why be mean and go looking to cause trouble? He hadn't slept well the previous night, and he had heard the cock crow three times. He decided to have a little nap before leaving but he didn't anticipate falling fast asleep. When he woke up, he saw the sun shining through the window and he was furious with Gran for not waking him much earlier. She made him some rice congee, but he didn't eat it. Instead, he snatched up a few sweet potato flour and buckwheat buns, stuffed them in a cloth bag and ran off towards the road. As he went out of the courtyard gate, he turned back, grabbed his rope fuse and hung it around his neck.

"Why do you want that if you're going into town?" Gran asked.

"You wouldn't understand," he snapped back.

By the time he got to the little wooden shack, Bash had already loaded the jars onto the tractor, so Inkcap hurried to fetch the bowls. The cat was standing in a corner of the *kang* and called to him. Inkcap looked at the cat. It was washing its face.

Oh, he thought to himself. Even the cat is washing its face. How can I go into Luozhen without washing my own?

He picked up a hand towel that was hanging on the wall, found that it was already wet and wiped his face with it. The cat miaowed at him.

"What's that? You want to come too?" Inkcap asked the cat, and it miaowed back at him.

"Let's take the cat with us," he shouted out of the door.

He didn't get an answer and instead heard Bash calling him, "Hey! Come out here. Come out here."

Inkcap went outside with a stack of bowls. Bash was standing out on the road, talking to a young man.

Inkcap didn't recognise the fellow. He had a long face and long teeth. He was wandering around, bending down to pick jasmine flowers on the roadside, and turned around when he heard someone call out.

"Hello there," Bash said. "Are you from Xiahewan?"

"Do you know me?" the young man asked.

"Are you here to meet Apricot?"

"Who are you?"

"It doesn't matter who you're meeting," Bash said. "I'll tell you this for free. Apricot has already slept with me."

Inkcap was furious. He knew this must be the lad Third Aunt had mentioned, but how did Bash know that? Had Apricot come up here to tell

251

him last night? Or did he hear it from someone else? It didn't matter either way, he wasn't going to just stand around and let Bash bad-mouth Apricot like that. He put down the stack of bowls and advanced on Bash and the young man, chest puffed up like a fighting cock. Inkcap didn't reckon that the young man would take Bash's nonsense lightly and would definitely start something with him. So when they started to fight, he would join in. He would charge Bash with his head and keep pushing even if Bash beat his head till it bled.

However, the young man paused for a moment and just stood there, still asking, "Who are you? Who are you?"

"My name is Hei. Bash Hei. That's what you can call me. Bash Hei."

"That's all just bullshit. Just bullshit," the young man said, as he turned and walked away.

But Bash wasn't done yet.

"She's got a red birthmark on her arse…"

Inkcap swung the bag of buckwheat buns, hitting Bash on the shoulder.

Bash caught hold of the bag and glared at Inkcap. "What's this, Inkcap? Are you going to play the wild beast now?"

Inkcap launched himself again, leading with his head and thumping into Bash's midriff so that Bash slumped to the ground. Inkcap turned around and walked off towards the village. He kept walking, without breaking into a run because he wasn't afraid of Bash chasing after him. Every step was full of fury and if he hadn't had a shaved head, every single hair on his scalp would have been standing up.

Bash stayed sitting on the ground, making no move to get up. He opened the bag with the buns in it and said, "Hey! These buns are black. They're overcooked."

Even so, he broke off a piece and ate it, calling after Inkcap, "Aren't you coming to town, then?"

Inkcap stopped, thought for a moment and turned back. He couldn't pass up the opportunity of going to Luozhen. He went into the shack and started shifting the bowls again, one by one. When all the bowls had been moved, he said, "Why wouldn't I go? The Branch Secretary has sent me, so why wouldn't I go?"

Bash stood up, took out another piece of black bun then put it back into the cloth bag. He tried to give the bag back to Inkcap, but Inkcap ignored him. Bash hung the bag on the tractor trailer and chuckled. Let him laugh, Inkcap thought. He just sat in the trailer. He didn't say, "Let's go!" He didn't even look at Bash, although his eyes were wide open. Bash laughed again and the tractor set off.

The tractor pulled out onto the bridge under Yijia Ridge, and Old Kiln disappeared from view.

"Are you still cross with me, Inkcap?" Bash asked.

Inkcap continued to ignore him.

"So you're still angry, you little prick."

"You've been mucking Apricot around, so of course I'm angry. If you can't get along with her any more, why don't you just let her take up with someone else?"

"Because she doesn't want to."

"Bullshit. Did she tell you that?"

"That's none of your business, you little prick."

"Did she come looking for you last night?" Inkcap persisted, but Bash didn't reply.

"Why don't you say something?"

"I did say something. You're the one who's not replying."

Inkcap tugged at Bash's arm, and the tractor swerved as it crossed the bridge.

"Don't do that or you'll have us over," Bash protested.

Inkcap stopped tugging and Bash continued, "We had a fight. She told me her dad had found a partner for her, and when I said that was fine with me, she cursed me for being a vicious fucking ingrate and accused me of still laughing at her. She cursed me, so I slapped her face, and she kicked me back."

Inkcap stopped tugging at Bash's arm and sat quietly in the trailer. He couldn't understand why Apricot had still gone looking for Bash, or why she had sworn at him for saying he was OK with her having another partner. Was it because he was too young to understand what was going on between the two of them?

He fell silent for a while, then asked, "Are you really a vicious ingrate?"

Bash turned to look at him and repeated, "Am I really a vicious ingrate?"

"Vicious ingrate! Vicious ingrate!" Inkcap chanted.

Bash began to laugh, but the laughter came out in staccato bursts like bullets shot out of his belly by the jolting of the tractor.

Inkcap was staggered by the size of Luozhen. Just how much bigger than Old Kiln was it? Seven times bigger? No. It was literally ten or even twenty times bigger. The pedestrians looked like ants, and the tractor's horn was blaring non-stop.

They almost rammed a man carrying a cage and he turned and swore at them: "Watch where you're going, you idiots! You could have fucking killed me. You know what you're going to do now? You're going to get out of that fucking tractor and apologise."

Inkcap wanted to jump down and give him what for, but Bash said, "Sit tight. We really will run him over and squash him, and let's see what he wants us to do then!"

On arriving at the town supply and marketing cooperative, they unloaded the bowls and jars and handed them over. They put the money they collected in the cloth bag with the sweet potato and buckwheat buns, and Inkcap kept it hugged tightly to his chest.

"Do you want to eat?" Bash asked.

"There's no water here," Inkcap replied. "Let's wait till we're somewhere where there's some water to help wash the buns down or we'll choke on them."

"If you want to eat, we'll go to a restaurant. What do you need water for?"

"Are we really going to a restaurant? Don't forget the money in this bag belongs to the village."

"You mean I have to fork out my own money to eat?"

The tractor pulled up at the door of a restaurant. Bash jumped down, smoothed his hair, adjusted his sunglasses and walked straight into the establishment. He sat down at a table and when the waitress came over, he said, "Hey, girl, do you have one-*chi*-long carp here?"

When the waitress said that they didn't, he asked, "How about a five-*jin* roasted chicken?"

"No," the waitress said again.

"Don't you have anything? What about *dalaowan*, then?"

"Yes, we've got *dalaowan*."

"Then bring us two big bowls of your best noodle broth."

The waitress looked at him blankly and said, "But we only sell noodles here, not–"

"Not what? Just get a move on."

The waitress didn't argue and did indeed come back with two big bowls of noodle broth. Bash took a bun out of Inkcap's bag, broke it apart and put it in the soup.

When Inkcap didn't move, Bash said, "Why aren't you soaking any? Go on, put some in to soak."

The waitress was astonished and just kept muttering "best noodle broth" as she watched them emptying their bowls clean by soaking up the soup with buckwheat buns.

After leaving the restaurant, Bash drove the tractor around the town to give Inkcap a good look at it. Inkcap was still thinking about what had happened at the restaurant.

"How come you're still so full of yourself when all we had was broth back there?" he said.

"What's the problem with broth? Is there anything shameful about drinking broth? If you're going to hang around with me, you need to follow my lead and stand up for yourself."

This was the first time Inkcap had seen how Bash behaved outside the village. He was even more masterful.

"I'll never learn to act like that," he said.

"Why not?"

"Because I'm from a bad background."

"That's balls."

Behind the new street they were driving down was an old street, with old houses on its north and south sides. Although it was clear enough that each house belonged to a different family, the east gable of one house was also the west gable of the next one, forming a continuous, interdependent row. At some stage, one of the houses had tilted towards the east, so that all the houses now tilted in that direction too, until you reached the theatre at the very end of the row, which remained upright.

Inkcap thought to himself, If that theatre is ever demolished, all the houses on the north side of the street will fall down.

The walls of the houses facing the street were made of wooden boards that slotted into wooden grooves, top and bottom. In the morning, the boards could be removed one by one and then replaced in the same way in the evening. Inkcap thought they looked really good and remembered that there were lanes and alleys in Old Kiln too, but none of them were like this. Bash told him that the wooden-fronted houses were used as shops and said why didn't they open a shop themselves? Inkcap had had the same thought. As they drove down the street, they saw that the shops were full of customers coming and going, both men and women. Many of the men wore four-pocket uniform jackets and hardly any of the women had their hair in large braids. Mostly, it was cut to shoulder length, so the hair draped around their heads and swayed as they walked.

"These town women are really pretty, aren't they?" Bash said.

"Not as pretty as Apricot," Inkcap replied.

"If a phoenix from Old Kiln flew into town, it would immediately become a sparrow," Bash declared.

"Why are you still doing down Apricot?" Inkcap asked, and he began to ignore Bash again.

The tractor turned onto another street, where a large group of people were advancing from the west end. They looked like students and were holding red flags, carrying banners and shouting slogans. Inkcap had never seen anything like it before.

"Is there a wedding going on?" he asked. "Actually, it doesn't really look like a wedding. Is it some kind of folk theatre?"

"They're from the township high school. They're having a sports meet."

Inkcap was shouting and shouting, and Bash asked him what he thought he was doing.

"It's such fun," he said.

"Well, don't shout like that, or people will laugh at you."

As the procession moved down the street, everybody began to follow. The steps in front of the houses were crowded with people, stretching their necks like chickens to look at what was going on. The grocery stalls laid out in front of the shops got knocked over, so their owners began to shout and push and shove until, inevitably, a fight broke out.

"It's not a sports meet," Bash said. "Did you see the words on that banner?"

"I can't read," Inkcap reminded him.

"It said, 'Long Live the Cultural Revolution!' I know what cultural means and I know about revolutions, but I don't know what it means when you put the two together."

As he was still puzzling over the words, the marchers surged forward with a roar, like a river in spate. Bash stood on the tractor and looked ahead, but he couldn't hold his position any longer and got squeezed off his perch.

"Whose walking tractor is this?" someone shouted. "Move it. Get it out of the way, quick."

Bash pushed the tractor to the side of the road but that still wasn't enough, and six or seven people helped shift the trailer too. By the time he'd got everything sorted, Inkcap was nowhere to be seen.

Inkcap got buried in the crowd as the parade swept by. He was so scared that he was sweating all over as he searched for Bash. He couldn't find him, so he had no choice but to go with the flow. His interest grew as he walked. People raised their arms in unison, so he raised his arms too, but he only shouted out "Long live Chairman Mao" after the crowd had already done so. Some of the students looked at him and said, "All shout together! All shout together!" So he caught up with the rhythm. As soon as the main body of the procession had passed, a large crowd, both adults and children, followed closely behind. Inkcap joined in too. The main body of students was very neat and organised, but those following behind were much less so and Inkcap wasn't very happy with them as he was trying to match the pace of the students. He walked almost half the length of the street. The numbers were continuing to grow, and the street was filling up as if it had been flooded. Now, Inkcap couldn't see the crowd properly any more, but he could make out their legs which were as densely packed as a forest. The students quickened their pace, fast and neat. Inkcap's steps were too small to keep up, and he soon had to break into a trot. Several students turned around and asked him if he was from the primary school. He didn't know how to answer and just said that he could keep up with them. The students told him that all the primary school students were parading on campus.

"The same, the same," Inkcap said.

The students didn't understand what he meant, so they ignored him. He followed them along that first street, passed into the old street and then turned onto the new street. When they arrived there, Inkcap realised that Bash wasn't with them. Pah! If Bash was supposed to be so fucking good at everything, why the fuck couldn't he even keep up with a pissing march? Inkcap was contemplating how he would boast about his own abilities to Bash, and even how he would show off to Cowbell when he next saw him. But as he was having these thoughts, his pace slowed and the person behind stepped on the heel of his shoe. When he took his next step, his shoe fell off.

"My shoe! My shoe!" Inkcap shouted into the crowd. He saw his shoe under the feet of the mass of people behind him. Someone stepped on it and kicked it to the side of the road. He elongated himself like a cat and crawled out from under the forest of legs, only having to actually crawl through two pairs. He got knocked over, and someone stepped on his foot, then another and another and another. A woman was shouting, "Don't push. Don't push. You're trampling on people." Those behind used their bodies to block others coming on from behind them.

Inkcap finally tumbled out to the side of the road and heard someone swearing at him, "Whose child is this, eh? What are you pissing around at? Fuck off! Go on, fuck off out of it!"

At least Inkcap's shoes weren't torn, but his feet were bruised and the nail on one of his little toes was missing.

Almost three hours later, with the sun no longer shining on the streets, the parade was over but there was still a lot of noisy activity. Bash drove the tractor along all the streets and finally found Inkcap sitting under the wall of a house. His face was covered with sweat. His right foot was bare and there were chicken feathers stuck on his exposed little toe.

Bash was more than a little angry.

"I told you not to go running around like a mad thing. And what did you do? You ran around like a fucking mad thing and got yourself lost."

"I was marching. I was marching with them."

"And did you have any idea what they were doing when you followed them?"

"No, what were they doing?"

"The township middle school elected five student representatives to go to Beijing. Chairman Mao is going to receive them in Tiananmen Square, so the school held a parade to celebrate."

"Oh."

"I graduated too bloody long ago, otherwise I would definitely have been one of the representatives they chose."

Their clothes were soaked with sweat and still clung to their bodies even when they undid the buttons. Bash drove the tractor back to Old Kiln while Inkcap sat in the trailer boasting about how he had been in the parade. He finished by saying, "There were so many people! What a beautiful trip it was today."

"You call a little trip around Luozhen beautiful? That lot are going to Tiananmen in Beijing."

"Oh? What kind of gate is Tiananmen?"

"Don't you know anything? It's a big tower."

"Ah! Does Chairman Mao live at the top of it?"

"That's right."

"Why does Chairman Mao want to meet those students?"

Bash didn't answer. He didn't know why Chairman Mao wanted to see the students. Inkcap looked up at the sky. It was full of clouds, but they were in pieces, like tiles, and all the tiles were red. He knew that if there were red clouds in the sky, it would be good weather the next day.

"Why does Chairman Mao only want to see students? Surely it should be someone like the Branch Secretary who goes."

"Have you got the bag?" Bash asked suddenly.

"Yes, it's fine. It's tied really tight to my belt."

As soon as he said that, his nose smelt that smell again. He rubbed his nose vigorously, but he could still smell it. His heart lurched. He thought that there must be something wrong with his nose. He always smelt that smell when he was particularly happy about something.

"It's so annoying," he said

"What's annoying?" Bash asked. "Me?"

257

"My nose."

"What's wrong with your nose?"

Inkcap did not say that he kept smelling that smell. He just said that his nose was itchy.

TWENTY-FIVE

WHEN INKCAP GOT HOME, he rinsed his nose with vinegar, but it didn't make any difference so he twisted some cotton into strips and stuffed them up his nostrils. But they always stuck out when he did that and looked like two great big drops of snot hanging from his nose. He took them out and, instead, hung the perfumed bag Gran had given him last Dragon's Head Festival around his neck. Whenever he smelt the smell, he put the bag up to his nose and sniffed it.

He started waking up early every day and washing his face.

"Oh, so my little boy does know how to wash his face!" Gran exclaimed.

"I want to go into town," Inkcap said.

Luozhen had become his favourite place to visit, but unfortunately, he couldn't go there every day. In addition to delivering goods to the supply and marketing cooperative on a regular basis, the retail market was held every day in the lunar calendar month with a three, a six or a nine in it, and it was up to Bash to decide whether to go or not.

"You conned me into washing my face and I still don't get to go," Inkcap would complain. "What's that all about?"

On the occasions when he did go, he didn't chance upon any more student demonstrations, but instead, classes had stopped and the students were out pasting up big-character posters or debating on the street. Soupspoon, Palace, Half-Stick and even Useless's mother were known in Old Kiln for their way with words, but they were nothing compared with this lot. The students of Luozhen had tongues as sharp as razors. What Inkcap loved most was watching the debates. They began with two groups of people standing together before their representatives went up to the table in turn to talk. If one side wasn't trying to eclipse the other with the force of their argument, then the other was attacking the first at its weakest point. Participants were literally foaming at the mouth, waving their arms and stamping their feet. After a while, the people at the table kept snatching away the loudspeaker from each other, while those below it started arguing, three against five, ten against eight, like roosters and eagles fighting, and the crowd became chaotic, like a whirlpool in a river. Inkcap was tossed to and fro in that whirlpool, and he found himself listening to a student with a very loud voice. It turned out that he got quieter as he went along and he often ended up swallowing his own words. Inkcap found this all very interesting. When he got closer, he discovered that the student actually had a stutter, and Inkcap worried that he might choke and not get his words out. When he did begin to talk again haltingly, Inkcap felt as though his own breathing had gone ragged. Then, he went to watch another student. This bastard had very thin lips and talked so fast he hardly had time to catch his breath. The person next to him applauded and called out "Very good!" so Inkcap did the same. But someone else started swearing at him, "What's so fucking good about it, you little shit?" so he shut up and stole a glance at the big-character posters on the walls. One lot of posters was pasted up on a wall, only to be swiftly torn down and replaced by another. Inkcap marvelled at the amount of paper there was in Luozhen, and he thought of his gran, but he didn't dare tear up any of the discarded posters. He waited for others to tear them up, and let the wind blow the shredded paper under the steps at the side of the street. Then he hurriedly gathered the paper and shoved it inside his jacket.

During this time, Gran cut out a lot of paper patterns. Inkcap boasted to her that he was going to put a layer of paper three fingers high under the mat on the *kang*. But then, the Branch Secretary announced that he was going to stop selling porcelain goods.

The Branch Secretary made this decision after two meetings with Commune Secretary Zhang in Luozhen. The reason was that the township was in chaos. Although the supply and marketing cooperative was still purchasing, the quantity that could be purchased was reduced, and the retail sales were almost nil. It was important to follow Secretary Zhang's instructions to keep a close eye on how the current situation developed and to carefully monitor the Four Bad Elements in each village. Of course, what the Branch Secretary didn't say out loud was that Bash was a hooligan and Inkcap came from such a bad background. If those two caused trouble out there, it would be his responsibility.

No longer selling porcelain goods wasn't going to stop Bash from going to Luozhen. He still went whenever he liked but he did limit Inkcap's trips. Inkcap was in a state of constant agitation and visited the little wooden shack every day. Sometimes Bash was there and sometimes he wasn't; if he wasn't, then he was bound to be going to Luozhen. Inkcap sat at the door of the shack and waited until dark when Bash would come back, either driving the tractor or hitching a lift, and tell him about the amazing goings-on in town.

Students began to appear along the highway. They were walking in groups of four or five, all carrying backpacks which had small flags on them saying that they were going to Yan'an, Jinggangshan and Mao Zedong's hometown of Shaoshan in Hunan. These were sacred sites of the Revolution. The student pilgrims often had to sit down and rest at the door of the shack, and Bash served them herbal tea and repaired their shoes for free. The only other thing he did was ask them where they came from and where they were going. These students from the big city were more neatly dressed than the ones from Luozhen, had lighter complexions and spoke with a different accent. They talked about the Cultural Revolution that had already happened in the city, which was about destroying the old and establishing the new and sweeping away all "ox demons and snake spirits", by which they meant getting rid of anything that wasn't aligned with the proletariat. They said Chairman Mao had already met with students several times in Tiananmen Square. The first batch of students he met were selected by the schools and were known as "royalists", but now they were all "rebels" and Mao Zedong's Red Guards. These students were so eloquent that even Bash was dumbfounded, and Inkcap and Cowbell, who also came running over, were even more astounded. They couldn't comprehend what the students were saying, but when they thought about how these people could just shoulder their packs and go where they pleased, they were green with envy. In particular, some students wore small bronze medals featuring Chairman Mao's portrait. When Inkcap and Cowbell made to touch them, the students recoiled and said, "Don't touch! This is a Chairman Mao badge."

The badges looked really good on the students' chests, and Inkcap tried to win them over by offering them a drink of *taisui* water. He asked them if they could give him one of the badges, but they refused. Meanwhile, Bash stared at the hats the students were wearing. They were grass green military caps; even though they didn't have a five-pointed star as a cap badge, they were definitely military caps, and the students looked so majestic wearing them. He had been pretty fond of his own blue cloth cap, which he had padded out with paper to give it an angular shape, but compared with the military caps, it just looked ridiculous, so he stopped wearing it.

The yellow, sand-laden wind had been blowing for most of a fortnight and the layer of fallen catkins floated up in thin clouds whenever anyone approached, swirling and teasing around them. Now they had fallen into the lotus pond and the wheat field, so the field looked as though it was covered in a layer of snow. Under the walnut tree, Tag-Along's little boy was collecting bugs. His pockets were already full, and he was holding more in his hands.

"Why are you catching so many caterpillars?" Stargazer's mother asked.

But when she got closer, she saw that they weren't caterpillars at all, but the fluffy white hairs from inside walnut shells. Stargazer's mother laughed but then began to cough continuously. The wind was giving everyone in Old Kiln red noses and a constant scratchiness in their throats. When Stargazer's mother started to cough, it spread to everyone else. It was a dry cough and no one could expel any phlegm from their throat.

During this period, the wolves passed by again but did not enter the village. It was a fox that came in instead. The fox's fur was so beautiful that people wanted to hunt the animal for it, and Awning and Sparks knocked up some home-made explosive pellets. Sparks' father-in-law was the acknowledged master of blowing up foxes on the southern reaches of the riverbank. Sparks had been shown how to wrap the explosive pellets and he had taught Awning too. He mixed broken porcelain shards in with the gunpowder and then wrapped the result into individual balls using chicken skin. A handful of chicken feathers were stuck into the balls which were then placed on the dirt road that led from the low-lying ground at the rear of the village to the roller stone. But the fox was too cunning for them. It actually took the balls gently in its mouth and moved them to a different place to bury them. As a result, when Awning and Sparks went to retrieve the balls, they couldn't find them. They had to search them out meticulously so that humans, cows, dogs and other animals didn't step on them by mistake.

News came from Dongchuan Village that a leopard was eating its dogs. It was reported that four dogs were taken one after the other. Dogs' heads and tails were found in the wheat field. At first, no one knew what kind of thing could eat a dog like that. Then, that night, a leopard entered the village and bit a cow. The cow and the leopard fought all night long. The leopard rammed its head into the cow's neck, and one of the cow's front legs got stuffed into the leopard's mouth. They were evenly matched, pushing each other first one way and then another. In the end, neither could draw breath but neither was willing to ease off as they stood there bracing themselves with their hind legs. This went on until dawn, when villagers found them, still locked together but both dead. The news threw the residents of Old Kiln into a panic. If there could be a leopard in Dongchuan, wasn't one bound to come to Old Kiln too? Yes, this might have been a solitary leopard, and now it was dead, but who could guarantee that it was the only one? And then there was also the fox that didn't get blown up. Happy didn't dare go home at night, so he slept in the cowshed and placed a copper washbasin next to the door, ready to bang it to raise the alarm if a leopard or fox came in.

Inkcap still ran off towards the highway, with his pockets stuffed with dried chillis for the students who were so tired, they were dozing off as they walked. He once saw a student eating a spring onion and its spiciness clearly revived him. Inkcap couldn't bring himself to pull up his own onions, so he took chillis instead. Spring onions are spicy on the tongue, he told himself, garlic is spicy in your heart, but only chilli spice goes deep and gets you on the way in and the way out! He took a bite out of one himself as he contemplated matters, and some of the students came over to ask for one too. It wasn't long before all the other students were clamouring for one. Inkcap was very pleased with himself.

"Hey, Inkcap," Useless called to him, "has this leopard business got to you? Are you running away?"

"If you lot are running towards the highway, why shouldn't I?" Inkcap said indignantly.

"We're all of good standing," Pockmark said. "The leopard wouldn't dare bite us."

"And I'm not," Inkcap shot back, "so I'm far too lowly for any leopard to bother with."

Yoyo went down to the highway too but didn't say anything. She simply stood there staring at people in a reverie. Inkcap thought she was dozing off and waved his hand in front of her, but her eyes were open, and she just ignored him.

"What are you thinking about?" Inkcap asked.

Ever-Obedient rushed over, shouting to Yoyo to go home.

"He's afraid his wife's going to join them and run away too," Awning said.

Inkcap dragged a student over to stand in front of Yoyo.

"How old are you?" Yoyo asked.

"Thirteen," the student replied.

"Where are you going?"

"Wherever we like."

"Look at him," Yoyo said to Inkcap. "He's about the same age as you and he's got the whole world at his feet while you're stuck here in Old Kiln!"

Ever-Obedient came over and pulled at Yoyo's arm, saying, "You'd better go back too, Inkcap. Now!"

But Inkcap had seen a student flying a kite, so he ignored Ever-Obedient and ran off to watch the kite. Other students were holding red flags or had small red flags on their backpacks. The kite-flier tied lots of triangular red flags to his kite and sent it soaring into the sky. Inkcap shoved himself forward to help tug on the kite string, but the student wouldn't let him. Well, if he wouldn't let him so be it, Inkcap would just have to follow him.

Ever-Obedient was shouting to him, "Inkcap! Inkcap! Your father joined a march back then. What do you think you're doing joining one yourself?"

But Inkcap refused to leave and watched the kite fly higher and higher, further and further, until, at last, it disappeared, leaving only a cloud that came to a halt over the ridgepole of the beacon tower.

It was getting dark, and one by one, the villagers of Old Kiln were heading home from the highway. Only Inkcap stayed put, waiting for more students, but when no more showed up, he too trudged back. The fish in the Zhou River were not screaming that night, but the clouds in the sky were skudding past in a thin layer, like sand blown by the wind on the river strand. The Yangshan Mountains in the south were now dark and so was Yijia Ridge in the west and Beacon Tower in the east. Later, the flowing clouds grew darker and darker, until the whole basin of land turned into the yawning mouth of an overturned cooking pot. The dirt road from the highway to the village was lined with wheat fields on both sides, and there was still some light among the shadows. The wheat had begun to bloom, so was it the pollen that made the wheat fields seem a little brighter? But as the wind blew across Inkcap's body, all it did was set up an itch in his throat that made him cough. There was a whirlpool in the middle of the wheat field and its vortex moved across the wheat, making the whole field sway. Birds and insects were crawling and chirping in there and making a kind of gasping sound. Inkcap had never been afraid of the dark and would happily burrow into it wherever he found it. But now he thought of wolves, leopards and foxes, and the excitement he felt during the afternoon turned into fear, and his scalp crawled. Run! Run as fast as you can! Inkcap ran away on his short legs, rolling like a ball and yelping as he went. As he ran from the dirt road to the slope by the embankment, he was surprised to find that, right in front of him, behind him, even to his left and right, there were wild rabbits running, frogs jumping, bugs with round wings and insects with long, narrow wings flying and even a cat and a dog bounding alongside him. The dog was Ever-Obedient's dog, and the cat was Third Aunt's cat. What were they doing there? Inkcap stopped yelping, slowed down and walked back into the village. As he stood at the entrance of his courtyard, he realised that the rabbits and frogs had disappeared and so had the flying insects and even the cat and the dog. The grass in the tile troughs of the courtyard buildings was shaking and swaying, and because it was still green and not dry, it was making a mellow, coppery sound. He felt as if he were dreaming.

Gran was sitting on the *kang*, cutting out paper patterns, and when she heard the courtyard door, she didn't scold Inkcap for coming back so late. She just said, "There's food in the pot. Build up the fire if it's cold."

Then she went back to her paper cutting. As usual, the meal was shredded radish soup, which is good for soothing one's stomach before going to sleep. Inkcap had one bowl, then added some chillis and chopped spring onion to another and ate that too. He fetched the piss bucket from inside the privy and placed it outside the door of the small building, then climbed onto the *kang* to sleep.

"Why are you being so good today, going to bed as soon as you got back?" Gran asked.

"So you've been busy with your papercuts, then," Inkcap said, ignoring the question.

"I've done a lot tonight."

She cut out another lion and held it up to see if it looked like the stone lion at the entrance of the village.

"Were you up at the highway again?" Gran asked.

"There were a lot of people there."

"They're all just getting on with their own business. Aren't you embarrassed tagging along behind them?"

Inkcap was going to say something but thought better of it.

"Look at all these papercuts I've made for you to play with, and yet you still can't stay at home but keep running off out there," Gran complained.

There were several dozen different types of animal she had cut out on the *kang* and the windowsill. She wanted to cut out every kind of animal she had ever seen and also those she had never seen but had imagined how they looked. But Inkcap had no interest in any of them that night and just burrowed into the covers without making a sound.

"Are you asleep?" Gran asked.

Inkcap wasn't asleep. He was still thinking about the student's kite and the cloud he saw when the kite was out of sight. He was also thinking about all those things that were drawing him along and following him as he ran back to the village. And whose cat was that making its mating call, that intensely annoying noise that sounded like someone wailing? Gradually, though, it seemed to him that the wailing had some inherent character and he even began to enjoy it. He fell asleep listening to a cat's mating call. Then he seemed to find himself complaining about Gran making radish soup again. She was always moaning at him for pissing the bed, but how was he supposed to keep it in after drinking all that soup? Then Gran said let's make dumplings, and they really did make some dumplings. Dumplings! Think of that, dumplings! That was so interesting! So interesting that Inkcap actually turned into a dumpling! Scary! Every pig, cow, dog and cat that Gran had cut out, along with the lions, tigers, horses and sheep too, they were all alive. But even so, none of them ate any of the others, and none of them was afraid of being eaten, either. They were messing about in the courtyard. He played hide-and-seek with them but they were all too stupid and he could find their hiding places far too easily. When he wanted to hide from them, he burrowed into a rock and none of them could find him. But then he felt that hiding in a rock was boring, so he came out of the laundry stone and was quickly found.

"If I had an invisibility cloak, I could run around anywhere," he said, "and you wouldn't be able to see me at all."

What next? The chicken wanted to give him its feather hat, the cat took off its skin to give it to him, and the pig removed its shoes. "These are for you," it said and what it took off turned out to be a pair of leather shoes. Inkcap was delighted. He took off his clothes to wear these new ones he'd been given, but before he had a chance to put them on, it turned out that the chicken, the cat and the pig couldn't find where he was. "Inkcap! Inkcap!" they called. How annoying, he said to himself. Do people become unrecognisable when they take off their clothes? He looked at his own naked body and saw that it was just a dumpling with its skin removed. He was just a ball of shredded radish!

Inkcap laughed out loud, and Gran said, "Stop kicking. Stop kicking."

Inkcap opened his eyes to discover that it was already dawn, and Gran was still working with her papercuts. After cutting them out all night, she was now pasting the patterns onto a piece of homespun cloth that was two *zhang* in length and covered the entire surface of the *kang*. Inkcap stayed under the quilt, not daring to move for fear he might wrinkle the cloth and the patterns on it. But just at that moment, he felt the *kang* move, and there was a sudden flash underneath him.

"Gran! Gran! The *kang* is moving!"

Gran was frozen into immobility. She stopped pasting her papercuts and looked at the iron ring on the door of the small room. There had been an earthquake three years previously, and the iron ring had shaken and rung out noisily. Was this another earthquake? Gran looked at the iron ring, but it didn't move. The oil lamp on the windowsill jumped a little and went out as the oil burned dry.

"It didn't move," Gran said.

"It did move! It did!" Inkcap insisted.

He felt that the movement was like a fish breathing, or a cow sighing, or like pickled cabbage bubbling away as it fermented in a vat of brine. Gran took the quilt off the *kang* and put her ear to the rammed earth.

"Oh, the earth is moving," she said.

"The earth is moving?" Inkcap repeated.

"The earth is moving."

"If the earth is moving, isn't that an earthquake?"

"No, this isn't an earthquake. It's the earth's *qi* rushing upwards."

Gran was very surprised. The earth's *qi* only rushes up at the beginning of spring. It was almost the wheat harvest now, so why was the earth's *qi* so strong?

Inkcap kept looking at her and asked, "Is the earth moving a good thing?"

"Yes. Everything grows faster when the earth moves."

"Then I'll grow taller too!"

After he got up, Inkcap stood by the door and measured his height. It seemed to him that he hadn't grown past the line he had drawn before, so he was still definitely on the short side. This upset him and he moped around the yard. Gran knew he wanted to go out again, but she dismissed the idea and asked him to sweep the yard instead. Inkcap picked up the broom and had begun to sweep the yard in a desultory fashion when a loud thump sounded in the distance.

"Hey, Gran!" Inkcap exclaimed. "Has Awning finally managed to blow up the fox?"

"Get on with your sweeping and do it properly. What do you think you're doing? Drawing a beard on a tiger?"

"Last time, the explosives didn't go off and the fox hid all the pellets. Do you think they've got it this time?"

"Sweep the yard clean, then you can go and see."

Awning had indeed blown up the fox. Last time, the fox hid the pellets on the dirt road in the low-lying ground at the rear of the village. This time, Awning put them in a thatched shelter under the earth bank in the west of the village. The fox thought it had nosed out a chicken and went ahead and bit the pellet. It exploded, causing the fox to pass out. Hearing the noise, Awning came running to find the fox was still unconscious with its whole mouth blown away. The villagers of Old Kiln ate breakfast late and had just put down their bowls to go and feed the pigs. When they heard that Awning had blown up the fox, they all went to see. Many of them rushed to the stone lion at the entrance of the village and helped Awning finish off the fox, which had by now regained consciousness, by strangling it with a rope. They all praised the quality of the animal's fur.

Noisy, the peddler, had been resting in Xiahewan the night before. He arrived in Old Kiln on his bicycle early in the morning and bumped into Bash on the road. When they heard that Awning had blown up the fox, the two of them rushed over. As soon as Noisy saw the quality of the fur, he started bargaining with Awning. Awning went high, Noisy went low, and everyone else fanned the flames. There was a continuous stream of students on the highway again, singing songs as they marched.

"Since you can't agree," Bash said, "give it to me to sell. I'll hang it up in my doorway."

He lifted the fox's head. Its mouth was missing and half of its face was dripping blood. No one could bear to look at it and they shouted at Bash, "Don't lift the head like that, it's too scary."

"Is the tongue still there?" Bash wondered.

He started to pull the tongue out but stopped, leaving his hand covered with blood. He wiped it off on the stone lion.

"If we let you sell it," Sparks said, "you'll still give me and Awning the money, won't you?"

"It's just a fox, isn't it?" Bash replied, wiping his still bloody hand on the stone lion's eyes so they were both now red.

"I'm sure Bash wouldn't be stingy," Awning said. But what he didn't say was that Bash could sell the fox.

Instead, he said to Noisy, "You go to lots of different places. What's the state of things out there?"

"The students in Luozhen aren't going to classes any more," Noisy said. "The government officials are still going to work but they're behaving as if they're deaf. There are so many people coming in from the province and county that there's a constant hubbub in the streets. I don't know what's going on."

Everyone was listening to what Noisy had to say when suddenly someone whispered, "The Branch Secretary is here!"

Noisy immediately packed up his bicycle and said to Awning, "If you want to sell it, sell it to me. If you don't, I'll make myself scarce. The Branch Secretary doesn't want me coming to Old Kiln."

"Then off you go, off you go," Awning said.

Just as Noisy was about to leave, the Branch Secretary had a sharp word with him: "Why are you messing around here? There's a consignment shop in Old Kiln, so why are you trying to wheedle money out of people?"

As Noisy pushed his bicycle away, the Branch Secretary said to Awning, "Did you blow up the fox, then?"

"I did," Awning said. "Why don't I make you a vest out of the pelt?"

"I don't want it. Stargazer's mother has been coughing all year and can't bear the cold. Give it to her."

Someone standing nearby said, "Awning won't give it to anybody who's got anything to do with Stargazer."

"Why not?" someone else asked.

The first speaker went over and whispered in the other's ear and he immediately burst out laughing.

"So you're stirring things up again are you?" the Branch Secretary said. "What are you lot doing here when you should be at work? Get on and harvest the wheat. The threshing ground hasn't been levelled and none of the rollers, pitchforks and shovels have been tidied away. Awning, you go and tell Millstone to call everyone to work. Tell him that no one should be wandering out of the village."

The Branch Secretary bent down and noticed the stone lion's eyes.

"Who painted these? What does it mean?"

Bash admitted that he had done it and added, "It doesn't mean anything."

"This guards the good luck of our village," the Branch Secretary said. "We have to look after it."

Bash picked up a handful of grass and wiped the lion with it, but the more he wiped, the dirtier it became. He scooped up some earth and tried using that, but only succeeded in blanking out the lion's eyes completely.

For more than ten days afterwards, students appeared on the highway in increasing numbers, but everyone in Old Kiln was hard at it. After the threshing floor was levelled, water was poured onto it, and it was rolled over and over until it was firm and shiny. The old ropes on the wooden tools and circular baskets in the Kiln God Temple were removed and new ropes were tied tightly onto them. Everyone was grinding sickles, and even Happy in the cattle pen asked Useless to grind black beans and started fattening up the cattle. Inkcap could no longer go running off to the highway during the day and instead had to go to the little wooden shack in the evening. Bash had already let some students stay there overnight, and he and Inkcap listened to stories about the outside world until the small hours.

TWENTY-SIX

THE WHEAT WAS RIPE WHEN IT SAID IT WAS RIPE, and that started with the cuckoos calling. This bird's call sounded like its name, but Inkcap had no idea what it looked like. He heard the call as he was making his way home from the highway one night and searched for the bird in a willow tree, but it fluttered off and perched on the embankment of the wheat field, still singing. The same song came from three other embankments and the four calls rose and fell in response to each other. Inkcap felt he should call out his name too, so he gave tongue, lengthening the sound, "Inkcaaap!" The birds immediately responded, "It's ripe, it's ready to cut!" Inkcap kept changing the cadence of his call and the birds did the same with theirs.

They were still shrieking out their song as they entered the village. Dazed-And-Confused, who was carrying a basket full of barley stalks on his back, yelled back at them, "That's right, you little prick, shout as much as you like. Everyone knows I cut the wheat before it was fucking ripe!"

The grain in the private plots ripened before the grain in the production team's field, and the barley ripened before the wheat. Dazed-And-Confused was the first person to harvest the barley. He had long ago run out of food, so he harvested it when it had only just set its kernels, which meant they were too soft to put under the roller stone. In fact, he didn't even dare beat them with a chain and had to rub them between his hands to separate the kernels from the chaff. He then fried them off in a wok and crushed them into flour with a roller to make barley pancakes. The villagers badmouthed him behind his back saying that, even when he didn't have enough to eat, he still had vegetable soup at every meal, and when he did have supplies for a while, he ate and drank with gay abandon. It really was true that the more he ate, the poorer he became and the poorer he became, the more he ate. What a blind pig he was! They all urged him to wait until the barley was ripe before harvesting it, but his only response was to start digging up his potatoes before they were properly grown and eating them.

Before things got really busy with the wheat harvest, Half-Stick made sure to weave a length of homespun cloth on her loom and she sat in her courtyard weaving away. The warp was pinned into the ground by a dozen or so wooden pegs. The loaded shuttles of various coloured threads were arranged on small wooden sticks stuck in the ground on either side of the yard, and then the threads were pulled back and forth and hung on the wooden pegs when not in use. Half-Stick was having trouble matching the colours of the threads, so she asked Gran to help her, and Gran trotted back and forth in the sunshine. Her feet had been bound when she was young, but they were untied later on. Her feet were neither big nor small, but her toes were deformed. She had calluses on her heels, and she bounced as she trotted so it looked like she was running across hot coals.

Half-Stick laughed and said, "I bet you kicked it up in the *shehuo* when you were young, Granny Silkworm!"

"Are you making fun of an old woman's stiff joints? I'll have you know that, when I was young, I played the Lotus Flower Demon Woman. I was reckoned to give the best performance in the festival at Old Kiln."

"Anyone can see how pretty you must have been when you were young, Gran," Half-Stick said, moving a bench over so Gran could have a rest.

"What are you doing working the loom at this time?" Gran asked.

"We're about to get busy with the harvest. If I don't do it now, I'll never get round to it."

"The wheat is growing well this year, but I don't think it'll be ready for harvest for another fortnight."

"That may well be. It seems to be ripening later than it used to, and everyone's eyes are bleeding with the wait."

"Much better they put up with bleeding eyes than do what Dazed-And-Confused does! Where's your other half?" Gran asked, referring to Baldy Jin.

"He's gone to see the fun over at Bash's place."

"How does he have so much free time at this time of year?"

"Didn't you say there are a lot of people on the highway, Gran? How come they aren't at home harvesting their wheat?"

"They're city folk, aren't they."

"What's going on in the city that they're all running away from it?"

"I don't know."

Happy passed by the gate of the courtyard, leading his grandnephew. The grandnephew saw the warp threads in the yard and stopped to look at them.

Gran went over and flicked the little boy's willy saying, "Hey, where's it gone?"

"It's still there!" the boy said.

"Come and see, Half-Stick," Gran said. "Just one look at this little prick and you know it's Millstone's boy. The two of them came out of the same mould!"

"Hey, Granny Silkworm!" Happy said. "Are you doing the weaving here?"

"What did you say?"

"Are you helping Half-Stick with the weaving?"

"I'm giving her a hand. Why aren't you over at the cowshed?"

"I've fed the cows. Lucky wants to go to Xiahewan, and I'm taking my grandnephew over to his grandmother's house."

"Hey!" Gran said. "The harvest will be in soon, tell his grandmother to give her grandson some *hulianmo*."

Hulianmo is a kind of large pan bread which uncles give to their nephews when the harvest is in.

"You're right," Happy said. "That's how it should be done."

Gran laughed and said, "Great nephews and grandsons are like dogs at the door. As soon as they've eaten, they're off."

Half-Stick sighed.

"Why are you sighing?" Gran asked.

"My poor boy doesn't get to eat either his grandmother's or his great uncle's *hulianmo*."

Gran changed the subject and asked Happy, "Is everything all right with the cows?"

"Everything's fine, except that spotted bull can't stand up any more."

"If it can't stand up," Half-Stick said, "you might as well slaughter it early. If you just wait for it to die, its flesh will be all dried out."

Happy's expression darkened as he said, "You're talking nonsense."

He stormed out of the courtyard, taking his grandnephew with him.

"Don't you dare say that!" Gran scolded Half-stick. "That bull has worked all its life for us people. Who has the right to say it should be slaughtered? That would be a crime."

"It was just a casual remark," Half-Stick said, "and he went off on one at me! Animals are just animals, after all. I save my sympathy for people when they're sick. Last night, I gave Potful six eggs."

"I haven't visited him in a few days," Gran said. "Hasn't his illness turned the corner yet?"

"Not yet. Tell me, how can a man strong enough to kill a tiger just collapse like this from a little illness?"

"We're just coming up to the busiest time for farmers," Gran said. "Quite apart from the production team, how can he harvest the crops on his family's private plot?"

When they'd finished with the weaving, Gran headed for home but turned off to go to Potful's house to see what was going on. She met Apricot in the lane and saw that she had lost weight too. She was holding a few strips of paper mulberry tree bark that had been soaked in the spring.

"Hi, Gran."

"Have you fixed all the household stuff?" Gran asked.

"Some of it's still loose. I've just soaked some more bark so I can tie it up properly."

"Is your dad still ill?"

Apricot nodded.

"You need to work hard for your dad and make sure he doesn't tire himself out. So when it's time to harvest your private plot, make sure you get Ping'an to help."

Apricot grunted her agreement. Then they saw Big Root's wife walking past down the middle of the alley with a young lad who was keeping his head down. Big Root's wife was clearly issuing instructions to the lad and eventually sent him off out of the alley and came over herself.

"Do you think Almost-There's family is big enough or not?" she asked Gran.

"What's up with Almost-There?" Gran responded.

"His family is high status enough but his brothers can't find themselves wives..."

"Almost-There's status isn't very good," Gran said. "Lightkeeper's is a landlord family. Even though there's only one head of the family and the property got divided up long ago, Almost-There is still a middle peasant."

"So Lightkeeper's family history is still having its effect, is it?" Big Root's wife said. "Almost-There's brothers can't find wives and his younger sister Two-Pair is no spring chicken and is still not married. I found her a family from Houpoling, whose status wasn't great either and both sides seemed quite happy with things. But then Two-Pair changed her mind and asked me to take some garlic to the other family's house to break off the marriage. I didn't go. But today, the young man came over here and was going to help them harvest the wheat. As soon as I walked in with that fellow, Two-Pair's face fell and she started cooking something for him. When the food was served, there were three sweet potato flour balls in his bowl! He knew he was being told to get out, so he put down the bowl and left. Well, that's that, I suppose, but who can Two-Pair possibly marry now? Can she still marry into a family of good standing?"

Big Root's wife fell silent in mid-flow and then she changed tack: "I'm not saying that if your family's status is no good, you'll never find a wife to marry into it or be able to marry out of it. If Two-Pair was as clever as Inkcap, then she'd be able to talk her way past people's suspicions, but none of the family can hold a candle to Inkcap."

"So you say, but it doesn't make any difference. My grandson has no intention of getting married anytime in the future."

Big Root's wife was telling the truth, but Gran was uncomfortable hearing it. Although Inkcap was still young, he really would have to face up to getting married in the future. Gran regretted that dawn twelve years ago when she first hugged Inkcap to her breast. Back then, she had never thought that so much could happen. She didn't go to see Potful after all but went home. The courtyard was quiet, and Inkcap wasn't there. As she left home earlier in the day, she had told Inkcap to fix the bottom of the piss bucket, which was leaking. It needed to be taken out and repaired. Then waste cotton could be used to plug the seams in the base, using an awl to push it in bit by bit. Finally, it could be smeared with *baibantu* clay to finish the job off. Inkcap had done all this and done it pretty well. The repaired bucket was hung up under the eaves to dry, but Inkcap himself had stayed at home as he was told. He had disappeared without a trace but, somehow,

Gran wasn't upset with him. Instead, she suddenly began to resent someone else. She couldn't see him distinctly, but what she did remember was that he liked to sit on a stool and drink water, making the same slurping sound as if he were eating. She looked at the pear tree in the yard, which he planted that year, and said to herself, I smacked your arse, and you ran off. Now you are harming me and my grandson. She hit the pear tree with a mallet, and the leaves fell to the ground.

In fact, Inkcap wasn't gone long. After repairing the piss bucket, he had sat watching a bird that was perched on the courtyard wall. He recognised it as one of the birds that followed Goodman around. Those birds had never flown over to his house before, so what was this one doing sitting on the courtyard wall now?

He pursed his lips and gave the bird a few chirrups, saying, "Are you looking for me?"

"No, I am I am I am!" the bird replied.

"Is that a no?"

"Yes," the bird said.

"You mean you are looking for me?"

"No, I am I am I am!"

"You can't even communicate properly. What do you mean, yes or no?"

The bird gave up trying to talk to Inkcap in Inkcap's language and switched to its own: "Zha!"

"So what are you doing sitting there?" Inkcap demanded.

He went back inside for a few kernels of grain which he scattered in the courtyard. But the bird still didn't fly down.

At that moment, Cowbell bellowed from outside the courtyard, "Inkcap! Inkcap!"

Cowbell had found a snake on the screen wall of Awning's house. The morning glory was in full crimson bloom, like hundreds of little trumpets playing to the sky. The buzzing of swarms of bees provided the sound of those little trumpets. A snake was crawling along in the tile trough under the flowers. There was a fist-sized lump in its belly, and it was crawling very slowly. Cowbell knew that this was a snake that had swallowed a rat and he poked at it with a tree branch. The snake was still crawling very slowly, swinging its tail, and got stuck trying to crawl over a tile. If he poked it again, it would fall down. Cowbell went to fetch Inkcap. The two of them ran back, and the snake was still there, just beginning to spit out the rat. It had eaten too much because snakes never know when they are full. Cowbell watched for a while as the snake expelled the rat, after which it suddenly became more agile and shot away into the water hole at the base of the Awning's courtyard wall.

"Why did I chase it away?" Cowbell exclaimed. "That skin could cover the *erhu!*"

He took his branch and poked it into the water hole. Awning's wife came back from the fields and asked what he was doing. She took the stick and threw it over the courtyard wall. Inkcap explained that the snake had swallowed a rat and they had made it spit it out. They showed her the vomited rat, which had a mangled head, no nose and no ears. Awning's wife scolded them for messing around with a dead rat and asked whether they were going to throw it into her yard. Then she kicked them and told them to fuck right off and stop being so annoying.

Inkcap and Cowbell carried the dead rat to the roller stone in the east of the village. Cowbell said that kindness was never repaid, and that he felt sorry for that branch which Awning's wife had thrown into the courtyard to be used as firewood.

"She took away your stick and let the snake get into her yard to bite her!" Inkcap said.

"I hope it bites her in the crotch!"

East of the soil bank was the embankment, and the wheat field under the embankment was a sea of yellow, shining with a golden light. Flocks of sparrows were swooping down in black clouds, then suddenly soaring again. As it happened, there was a scarecrow standing in the wheat field and Cowbell was curious to see how well it was coping, so he ran down to take a look. When he got there, he found masses of edible thistles growing on the field banks and he pulled them out.

Meanwhile, Inkcap stood in front of the scarecrow and exclaimed, "Who made this?"

"It was Soupspoon and Useless made it yesterday, wasn't it?" Cowbell said.

On closer inspection, it turned out that the scarecrow's face was made of paper pasted onto a broken sieve, and it was painted to look like Inkcap.

Cowbell chuckled and said, "Does that mean you can scare off the birds?"

"I'm not even wearing a hat! I'll get soaked in the rain and burn in the sun," Inkcap said.

"What kind of hat do you want? A Four Bad Elements hat?"

Inkcap immediately realised why the scarecrow was painted with his face. It was because his bad status would scare off the birds, wasn't it? He wanted to tear down the painted face but found he couldn't reach it.

"They didn't paint any other fucker's face, they had to paint mine! Give me a bunk up and I'll tear it down."

But Cowbell didn't lift him.

"Why do you want to tear it down?"

"Because they're bullying me again about my bad status."

"That's not it," Cowbell said. "Otherwise, why didn't they draw Lightkeeper's face? Maybe it's because you're ugly enough to scare off the sparrows."

"So now I'm ugly, am I?" Inkcap yelled.

He jumped up and tore off part of the face, then jumped again and tore off some more, and jumped a final time and tore off the rest.

"The Branch Secretary's coming," Cowbell shouted.

The two of them ran down from the field bank, which was reached by a path running diagonally from the highway. That was also the point where the road turned at the foot of Yijia Ridge. They ran until they were out of breath.

"Where's the Branch Secretary?" Inkcap asked.

"I was fooling with you," Cowbell told him.

The wheat on both sides suddenly opened and closed in the wind, releasing a wonderful fragrance. Inkcap wasn't happy about Cowbell tricking him, but he was roused by the smell of the wheat and became very excited. He pulled up three edible thistles on the bank and saw five or six more in front of him.

"There's always a silver lining," he said. "Look at these delicious wild vegetables I've picked."

When he turned around, Cowbell was sitting there eating wheat. He picked up a handful of wheat grains, rubbed them in his hands, blew off the chaff and stuffed them into his mouth.

"Hey! Are you eating the production team's wheat?"

"Why don't you have some too? No one will know."

"I'm not going to eat it."

"Aren't you hungry?"

"I don't dare."

"There's nothing wrong with my status, I'm not scared."

Inkcap suddenly leapt over to him, exclaiming, "We're all members of the production team. If you can eat it, I can too!"

He picked up a handful of wheat ears, plucked the grains, rubbed off the chaff and ate them. The wheat kernels were soft and a little sticky. The two of them stretched their necks and swallowed, leaving the white juice flowing from the corners of their mouths.

"Tastes good, doesn't it?" Cowbell said.

"Tastes good," Inkcap agreed.

But a voice thundered at them, "Spit that wheat out, you little fuckers!"

Inkcap and Cowbell fell to the ground in terror, unable to stand up again. The person started laughing. When Inkcap looked up, he saw Bash standing a little distance away.

"I only ate a handful," he said.

"Go on eating if you want to. Ha! Look how I scared you! It's a big field, let's see how much you can eat."

Inkcap smiled brightly in the sunshine. Cowbell also tried to ingratiate himself with Bash by giving him the edible thistles Inkcap had picked, but Bash didn't want them.

"I was just thinking I needed to find a couple of people, and here you two are! If you want to eat more, go ahead. When you're full, I'll tell you something."

"I'll get a stomach ache if I eat any more."

"Good. Then follow me."

Inkcap and Cowbell had no idea where Bash wanted them to go or what they were going to do, but they still followed him obediently. When they reached the side of the highway, Bash squatted down and told them to do the same in the wheat field. There weren't many cars on the highway, but from time to time they saw students carrying backpacks and holding small flags.

"What are you up to?" Inkcap asked.

"Snatching a military cap," Bash replied.

"Snatching a military cap?"

"Snatching a military cap."

"Eh?"

"One of those military caps will definitely suit me."

Inkcap turned to leave, but Bash held him back.

"I don't dare," Inkcap said.

"But you do dare eat the production team's wheat? If you two don't do what I tell you, I'll hand you both over to the Branch Secretary."

"You shouldn't scare us like this, Brother Bash."

"There's nothing scary about it," Bash said. "Snatching a military cap is nothing. I just love wearing a cap. When I've snatched mine, I'll snatch a couple for you two as well. How about that?"

Inkcap and Cowbell stopped resisting.

Bash told Inkcap to sit on the kerb up ahead and Cowbell to station himself down the road a bit. He explained that if a student came along the road wearing a military hat, Inkcap should cough loudly. Cowbell was to pay close attention and if there was no one else around when he heard Inkcap's cough, he should respond by coughing too.

"What if I can't cough?" Inkcap asked.

"You have to cough," Bash told him.

Inkcap and Cowbell set off in their different directions, and Bash stayed squatting in the wheat field.

Inkcap was still very uneasy about the whole thing, so he shouted out from the side of the road, "There aren't any wolves, OK!"

If a wolf pack passed by Old Kiln during the night, this was what the villagers shouted to reassure each other.

Inkcap hadn't intended to call out but Cowbell called back, "There aren't any wolves, OK!"

Bash was so angry that he threw a stone at both Inkcap and Cowbell. There was no more noise from either direction after that.

A group of students turned up, very much a team, all wearing military caps and walking down the road in a dignified fashion, not making a sound. Three more students showed up, and one of them was a woman wearing a military hat. Inkcap still didn't cough. The sun was giving him a headache, so he pulled up some grass and made a disc out of it to wear on his head. At that moment, a solitary student finally walked over from the road. He was tall, and the yellow school bag he was carrying had short straps and was tightly wrapped around his body. He was wearing a military cap, which must have been washed many times as the green had almost turned to white. He also held a small flag in his hand. Inkcap coughed, not very loudly, then coughed again. Further down the highway, Cowbell coughed too, and Bash emerged from the wheat field. The road was raised above the field, so he stood at the edge of the road and waved to the student. The student walked over to the side of the road, bent down and asked if Bash had been calling him. Without warning, Bash jumped up and snatched at the student's cap. The student recoiled in shock, but the cap stayed on his head. As Inkcap watched, he thought to himself that Bash had failed to grab the cap and that he wouldn't be able to get his hands on it now unless he climbed up onto the highway. But then Bash pounced like a wolf, his belly pressed against the side of the road and his arms wrapped around one of the student's legs. The student fell over and was dragged towards the wheat field. The student tried to get some purchase on the ground with the flagstaff he was holding but failed to do so. He grabbed at the grass on the roadside, but it just came away. Then, the two men disappeared and were marked only by a patch of swaying wheat. Inkcap became nervous and could see that Cowbell was also standing up in the distance, dumbfounded.

Suddenly, Bash shouted, "Come here! Come quick!"

Inkcap didn't move, despite how loudly his heart was beating, but Cowbell ran past him.

Inkcap ran over too and saw Bash and the student locked together and rolling around in the wheat field. First, the student was on top of Bash, then Bash was on top of the student.

"I only want your cap," Bash shouted.

"Why should I give you my cap?" the student shouted back.

"It's easy for you city folks to get caps."

"I'm wearing this cap for the Revolution."

"You're a revolutionary, and I'm a revolutionary too," Bash insisted.

"I had to swap ten badges to get it," the student told him.

Bash then noticed that the student had two small badges on his chest, both with Chairman Mao on them. He pulled the student tight to him and made to grab the cap again. The student held onto the cap with both hands and kicked out hard with his feet. Several times, the student seemed to be about to get the better of Bash, and Bash called out to Cowbell to grab hold of the student's legs. Cowbell did as he was instructed, immobilising the student, but the student grabbed hold of his cap with his right hand and beat Bash around his face with his left, making Bash's nose bleed.

Bash wiped his nose and said, "Just remember, you started this bloodshed."

He punched the student in the face, and the student fell flat, all the resistance knocked out of him. Bash snatched the cap and put it on his head. At the same time, he grabbed one of the Chairman Mao badges from the student's chest, in the process making two small rips in the student's jacket. The student turned over and tried to grab the badge, but Bash threw it to Cowbell.

"Get out of here," Bash told him.

Then Bash ran along the field's earth bank and disappeared from sight. Cowbell didn't manage to catch the badge when Bash threw it, and when he saw Bash running away, he dashed off into the wheat field too.

The student stood up and began to wail. After a while, he got back up onto the highway, where he saw Inkcap off in the distance. He shook his fist, staring at Inkcap, and asked, "Where is this place?"

"Old Kiln Village," Inkcap told him.

"I'll remember that. I'll be back."

"Ha! Get you! Why don't you just get lost and be quick about it!"

The student wiped the blood off his face and disappeared from the highway at some speed.

Bash and Cowbell emerged from the wheat field. Bash's nose was a little swollen, but he was wearing his sunglasses and the faded military cap. Like a rider's clothes matching his horse's saddle, the military cap and sunglasses sat really well together. The combination made Bash look unique and majestic.

"Look at Brother Bash!" Cowbell exclaimed.

"He doesn't look like someone from Old Kiln any more," Inkcap said.

Bash straightened his shoulders and walked up and down the road a few times, taking long, stiff-legged strides.

"Listen up you two. We can join the students in their 'Great Link-Up' if we get the chance. They're free to travel wherever they like. I can take you with me."

They began to look for the Chairman Mao badge in the wheat field. They searched one patch several times but couldn't find it, so they expanded the search area, parting the wheat stalks one by one. Finally, they found it. It was only as big as a fingernail and was made of copper. It showed Chairman Mao's head, with a golden circle of light behind it.

"Goodman once said that everyone's head shines with light," Inkcap said. "For some people it's only small but for others it can be really big. Look how much Chairman Mao shines!"

"Didn't you see the slogans in town?" Bash asked. "Chairman Mao is the sun, so of course he shines really bright."

But Inkcap couldn't read any slogans, of course, so he took the badge from Bash and said, "You've got the cap, so this badge is mine and Cowbell's. That's only fair."

Bash snatched the badge back and said, "I called for you just now, so why didn't you come?"

"I can't fight anyone," Inkcap said.

"Every bit of wind helps when you're trying to blow a lamp out with your farts, but where were you when it mattered? I'm not going to let you have it yet."

He gave it to Cowbell instead, which made Inkcap very cross. Why should Cowbell have it and not him? "That's not fair."

"And when have you seen anything fair in this world?" Bash said. "When has Old Kiln ever been fair to me? I'm not giving it to you as a punishment for being so passive."

Inkcap sat down on the ground, pouting in dissatisfaction. Bash and Cowbell were already up on the highway and they shouted to him to come with them, but he wouldn't move. When they were a long way away, he began to sob.

TWENTY-SEVEN

Bash's military cap didn't just make Inkcap envious, but Awning, Pockmark and Useless as well. They asked him where he got it, and Bash said it was a gift from a student he had connections with. Awning went to Luozhen and met with the commune's foundation militia. They didn't give him a military cap but he did receive a military belt. Awning was the commander of the militia company, but the company's rifle was stored in a cabinet after training and could not be taken out just as anyone pleased. But now that he had a military belt fastened around his waist, Awning carried the gun slung over his shoulder whenever he went out, and this created a very strong impression. Although the weather was hot, it was relatively cool in the morning and evening and most people were still wearing padded cotton jackets before the change in season.

As Awning walked past, Half-Stick suddenly appeared under the elm tree. She was leading a cow.

"Ah!" she said. "So Bash is wearing a military cap and Awning has got a military belt!"

"It's not a real military cap, it just looks like one," Awning said.

Half-Stick dropped the cow's leading rein, went over and tugged at Awning's belt.

"So your wife won't let you change seasons yet. You're only going to make an energetic impression when that belt is round some thinner clothes."

As she looked at Awning, her eyes appeared as bright and shiny as shards of glass.

"What do you mean by energetic?" Awning asked.

Then there was a sneeze from somewhere, and Half-Stick stopped tugging at the belt. When she looked behind her, she saw it was the cow that was sneezing.

She picked up the reins again and said, "I'm going to hitch up the cow and roll the threshing ground."

Awning reached out his hand and Half-Stick walked over to him. He patted the cow's rump, which was firm and rounded.

Awning went home with the gun on his back. He took off his padded cotton jacket, revealing a shirt underneath that was so tatty it had sleeves but no lapels.

"Where's my *jia ao*?" he called to his wife, referring to his lightly padded jacket.

His wife was bent over washing her hair on the steps. "I've just washed it for you," she said.

"Who asked you to wash it? What am I supposed to wear?"

"What's the worry? You're not going back into town, are you?"

His wife's buttocks were sticking out, and her hip bones protruded in a kind of triangle. Awning grunted discontentedly, rummaged through his cupboards, put on a white cloth gown, fastened his belt and slung the gun on his back. His wife raised her head and looked at him as he left the courtyard.

"Are you trying to catch cold?" she said.

Of course, Awning did catch cold that afternoon, giving him a headache and a runny nose. The Branch Secretary had gone to Luozhen again two days previously. Before leaving, he told Awning to sort out the merchandise. When he had finished that job, Awning refastened his belt, slung the rifle back over his shoulder and walked around the village. He continued to have a headache and a runny nose but he kept going without a rest.

When Pockmark saw him, he said, "There's no militia training because of the harvest, so why are you carrying that rifle?"

"We're about to get busy. We must suppress the class enemies. We can't let them sabotage us."

"What you need is a Mauser pistol hanging on your belt," Pockmark said.

"I've got something else hanging there!" Awning replied, shaking his crotch at Pockmark.

"Ah!" Pockmark said with a grin. "Firing blanks, then?"

"Oh, they're not blanks," Awning shot back. "I've just got nothing to fire them at! Massage my head for me."

Pockmark massaged his head and Awning continued, "My head aches so badly I must have bumped into a ghost."

Pockmark went on massaging his head while muttering, "Ghost! Ghost! Awning's got nothing to shoot his load at and you're giving him a headache! Awning must have his head shoved up your fucking arse and that's why it's aching!"

Awning shoved Pockmark aside, so Pockmark laughed and said, "All right, all right, no more massage, and to help you prevent that sabotage, I'll keep a watch on the Four Bad Elements for you too."

In fact, the only person Pockmark could throw his weight around with was Inkcap. So before Inkcap had even finished his lunch, Pockmark was outside insisting that he must root out the grass on the threshing ground.

"In his absence, didn't the Branch Secretary tell Uncle Awning to arrange everything?"

"So? Why shouldn't I arrange things for you?"

Gran shoved Inkcap out of the door to go to the threshing ground.

In winter and spring, half of the wheat field was ploughed and planted with spinach. The spinach field had been levelled a few days before, while Big Root had flattened the reeds and Iron Bolt had worked the adobe mud in the other half of the field. The militia had kicked up the soil and trampled all over it during their training, and there were potholes and weeds everywhere. They had to fill in the potholes and pull up the weeds and grasses. A cow was dragging the roller, flattening the ground over and over. Inkcap and a group of others were hoeing the grass. He got a weird feeling when he saw Pockmark wearing a Chairman Mao badge on his chest, and blurted out, "How come you've got one…"

He just managed to stop himself adding the word "too" and changed it to "one of those".

"Why shouldn't I have one?" Pockmark demanded.

"Let me see it."

"You have to kowtow to me first."

Inkcap hesitated until Cowbell ran over from the other end of the field and pulled him away, saying, "Why should you kowtow to him?"

"I'll kowtow to Chairman Mao!" Inkcap said.

"The fucker snatched my badge!"

It was only then that Inkcap realised the absence of a badge on Cowbell's chest, and he noticed chicken feathers stuck to his forehead.

"Did you know Awning has a military belt too?" Cowbell said. "It looks really good when it's fastened round his waist."

"I've heard about it."

"Awning let me put it on. That's more than Bash ever did. He won't let us wear his cap. Do you want to go to the Kiln God Temple? Awning's over there, and I'll ask him to let you wear the belt too."

The two of them took advantage of the work almost being finished in the field and sneaked away to the Kiln God Temple.

Inside the temple, a group of people were unloading miscellaneous items in one of the annexes and preparing to store the first of the wheat there when it was harvested. When Inkcap and Cowbell arrived, they discovered that Awning had turned around and gone home as soon as he arrived because his head was aching so badly. However, just at that moment, Bash arrived.

"Why have you only just got here?" Iron Bolt asked.

"If I didn't come, I'd lose my work points, wouldn't I?"

"Don't get smart with me, Bash. Not when I was so welcoming to you."

"Oh yes, and how's that?"

"I opened the temple door for you when I saw you in the distance."

Bash just laughed, but turned to Inkcap and asked, "Why wasn't it you who opened the door for me?"

"If you want someone to open the door for you, it should be Cowbell. I'd only get punished if I did it."

"Still holding a grudge then are you, you little prick?" Bash said.

He patted Inkcap on the head, which really annoyed Inkcap so he headbutted Bash's hand. When Bash patted him again, he headbutted his hand again.

"If Inkcap didn't have any ears, he'd be as round as a ball," Iron Bolt observed.

"So the more I pat him, the taller he'll get," Bash said.

Inkcap quite liked the sound of that because it meant Bash understood him, so he stopped hating him.

A grain store made of stone slabs had to be built in the annex room. Darkness fell before it was finished, and everyone had to go home for dinner. They were going to come back to finish the job after they'd eaten, and they left Inkcap to guard the furniture.

"You're always making me late for dinner," Inkcap complained. "I'm not going to be your watchman."

"If you don't do it, who will?" Iron Bolt said.

Inkcap changed tack. "I'm scared of all the paintings of bull heads and horses on the walls."

Bash asked Cowbell to stay with Inkcap and took the electric torch from his belt, saying he could turn it on if he got frightened.

As soon as the others left, Inkcap and Cowbell fought over shining the torch, first one then the other. After a while, Cowbell turned it off completely.

"Why aren't you shining it?" Inkcap asked.

"It uses up the batteries."

"Shine it! Shine it! Keep it on and we'll use up all his batteries for him!"

They turned the torch on and put it on the ground in the middle of the courtyard. They wanted to see how high the light could reach. Good God, just look how high it goes! A solid pillar of white light. Right up to the stars! Great clouds of flying insects swarmed in, circling the beam of light. More and more of them came so it looked as though they weren't flying any more, but were being lifted, layer by layer. The boys switched off the torch and all the insects fell to the ground, landing on their heads and on their backs. The two of them thought it was great fun, so they kept turning the torch on and off. They messed around for a long time, but finally left the switch turned on.

"Do you think someone could climb up this pillar of light, Cowbell?" Inkcap asked.

"No," Cowbell said.

"Wouldn't it be great if you could, though? You could reach the stars!"

Then the torch went out. They fiddled with it, but the batteries were dead, and the light was gone. Inkcap and Cowbell were surrounded by darkness, suddenly blind.

The Branch Secretary walked back to Old Kiln from Luozhen in the dark. Naturally, he was concerned about the wheat harvest, so he went first to the threshing ground to inspect it and then moved on to the field on the rear slope where the wheat ripened first. A man was smoking on the edge of the field and his pipe was flashing red then black. The Branch Secretary asked who was there.

The man came closer, then exclaimed, "You're back, Branch Secretary!"

It was Dazed-And-Confused.

The Branch Secretary could tell that Dazed-And-Confused's hands and feet were filthy and he asked him, "What are you doing here so late?" In the gloom, his gaze fixed on Dazed-And-Confused's waist.

"I'm not stealing wheat," Dazed-And-Confused said blearily.

He was wearing a belt, but he took it off to reveal that he was naked from the waist up under his padded cotton jacket. What the Branch Secretary didn't notice was that his trouser legs were tied at the bottom, and he had a heavy bag stuffed down them. The Branch Secretary reprimanded him and told him to smoke further away from the wheat field.

The grain was ripe now, and heaven forbid it should catch fire. Dazed-And-Confused said he had been so excited about the harvest that he hadn't been able to sleep for the last two days. He had come out to see which field would be harvested first but it was so open and exposed there that he was afraid of ghosts. So he had stopped to smoke a pipe to settle his nerves, then he had put it out carefully. The Branch Secretary asked how the village porcelain production had been going over the last two days and Dazed-And-Confused told him that the team captain was ill and only able to come out to walk about a bit before he had to go back to his *kang*. Their lifeline had been that Awning took charge of the situation, but he had only said that the wheat should be harvested, starting with this field on the next day, but he hadn't organised anything beyond that and all he had done was put on a wide leather belt and strut round the village.

"It's very dark and overcast tonight," the Branch Secretary said. "Supposing it rains tomorrow, where will the wheat be stored after it's harvested? Has the Kiln God Temple been cleared?"

"I don't know," Dazed-And-Confused admitted. "Won't Awning have arranged it?"

"That's something for Potful—"

"Potful's sick, isn't he?"

"What's this nonsense you're talking?" the Branch Secretary said. "Go home and get some sleep."

After Dazed-And-Confused went home to sleep, the Branch Secretary went directly from the rear slope to Awning's house. Awning was sweating under a quilt on the *kang*. His wife and Goodman were talking at the foot of the *kang*. As soon as the Branch Secretary came in, Goodman stood up and said he was leaving.

"Did you come to talk to Awning's illness?" the Branch Secretary asked.

"Awning has a cold," Goodman said. "I cupped him and loosened the skin along his spine."

"Don't leave, I've got something to say to you later."

"All right, I'll sit in the kitchen while you two talk."

"You can stay here, we only want to discuss production matters."

Goodman sat down again and picked up a bunch of chives that was lying by the door. Awning had already got up from the *kang*, and his face was red with fever.

"How did you catch a cold at this time of year?" the Branch Secretary asked. "Sit down if you can, lie down if you can't."

"I'm fine," Awning said.

The two of them discussed the heavy workload ahead.

"If Potful is sick," the Branch Secretary began, "you'll have to take on the team captain's responsibilities for us, and we'll seize food from the dragon's mouth without making any mistakes."

"It can't be done, I'm afraid," Awning said. "The commune's military officials have said we can't relax preparations for war even when we're busy with farming matters, and we can't stop militia training."

"Let's get busy over the next few days and if Potful is still sick, then we'll choose a new team leader," the Branch Secretary said.

Awning nodded and asked the Branch Secretary what kind of meeting he had attended up in town. It must have been something important for the meeting to be held at such a busy time. The Branch Secretary glanced at Goodman, who was sorting the chives.

"You've been listening!"

"No, I haven't. I haven't been listening to anything I shouldn't."

"If I want you to listen to anything, I'll tell you in advance."

"Ah!"

The Branch Secretary told Awning about the instructions Commune Secretary Zhang had made to the county party committee, in which he said that there was a major situation in play at the moment. The city, and indeed the whole county, was in chaos. Students no longer went to class, factories were in such an uproar that no one went to work and the masses wanted a great cultural revolution.

"Oh! Won't the Soviet Union take advantage of the chaos to invade?" Awning asked.

"You're right. There must not be chaos," the Branch Secretary declared.

"No, there mustn't. This sky is the sky of the Communist Party, and this land is the land of the Communist Party. Whether it is a great cultural revolution or a small cultural revolution, the Communist Party can surely handle it, can't it?"

"Of course it can. That is why the instructions emphasised leadership at all levels. The party organisations of the production teams of the county communes must lead this cultural revolution correctly and cannot deviate from the proletarian revolutionary line."

"Every day there are students from the Great Link-Up on the highway," Awning said. "What are they linking up? What is this Cultural Revolution all about?"

"It's just a movement," the Branch Secretary said.

"Another movement?"

"Movements are no problem, we're used to movements. In any movement there are always ox demons and snake spirits that emerge, but once they're exposed, the Communist Party can deal with them. Are there any movements in Old Kiln?"

"I haven't seen anything unusual, but Bash isn't working very well. He spends all day greeting the students from the Great Link-Up on the highway. Oh, and he's also wearing a military cap that belongs to a Link-Up student. Who knows what he'll turn into if he keeps wearing that."

"He's the one I'm most worried about," the Branch Secretary said before suddenly cocking his head to listen to something.

"Who's that talking?" he asked.

Awning cocked his head and listened and so did Goodman and Awning's wife.

"It's the cuckoos," Goodman said.

The cuckoos were having a conversation. There was one in the wheat field at the south entrance of the village saying, "It's ripe, it's ready! Hoo!" Another was in the elm tree of Six Pints' house by the threshing ground replying, "Hoo! It's ripe, it's ready!" Even though they were a long way apart, the two birds could still talk to each other.

"Tell me the truth, Awning. Will we have disturbances in Old Kiln too?"

"I can't say for sure," Awning replied, "but if there's going to be trouble, let's go through the possible causes one by one. Stonebreaker's family kicks up a fuss all day long, but he doesn't have the ability to cause bother in the village. Big Root, Feng Youliang and Barndoor are all outsiders and they may be unhappy with the Hei and Zhu clans, but they are all craftsmen and their problem is with the commission they have to pay the village cadres and how it should be less for work they do outside the village. Baldy Jin and Sparks are capable of cutting up rough with anyone, but neither will start anything themselves. They are like blind dogs who bark a few times and then lose interest. Dazed-And-Confused doesn't count for anything. Iron Bolt, Lucky and Tag-Along will protect their households, but what else are they capable of? Needless to say, Ever-Obedient, Soupspoon and Millstone all have their own little schemes, but they'd never take them far enough to cause real trouble. It's Bash and Pockmark we have to worry about. They have no parents or children, and they get about a lot. We need to put our minds to finding more things for them to do. If they're kept busy and can't leave the village, I don't think there will be any trouble from them."

"Do you know why I stopped the porcelain sales?" the Branch Secretary said. "It was so Bash didn't get to leave the village but could earn work points honestly here."

"It's all 'out of sight, out of mind' with him. When he ran off in the past, he didn't have a letter of introduction or food stamps, and he came back here, didn't he? Once there are no longer any Link-Up students on the highway, he'll be fine."

"Isn't there anything we can do about the Link-Up students?" the Branch Secretary asked.

"Ah, well, the instructions from county level are that we should lead the movement appropriately," Awning replied. "Why don't they just go ahead and restrict the Link-Up students?"

"I don't know."

"So how are we supposed to avoid chaos here?"

"I don't know."

The two men lapsed into a suffocating silence.

A cockerel with a big lumpy crest walked in through the patch of light at the door. It didn't make a noise, but just opened its eyes wide and looked at the Branch Secretary.

"Why hasn't this little fucker gone to roost yet?" Awning said. "Ah, Branch Secretary, have you eaten? Would you like some poached eggs?"

"I'm not hungry," the Branch Secretary replied.

"Go and make some poached eggs. The Branch Secretary has just got back from town. How could he have eaten?"

Awning's wife went to the kitchen, and Goodman went with her, saying, "I'll help you."

In the kitchen, Awning's wife said, "Did you hear what they said, Goodman?"

"Yes."

"Is there really going to be chaos?"

"There already is. The day before yesterday, someone invited me to go to Xiahewan to talk to an illness, and there was a lot of chaos about."

"We have a good life, so why is there chaos?"

"The five elements are in chaos."

"All you ever talk about is the five elements."

"The world has five elements, the nation has five elements, the family has five elements, the sexual realm has five elements, and the emotional realm has five elements. In my opinion, the reason for the chaos out there now is that the five elements of the country are in chaos. These elements are education, agriculture, industry, commerce and officialdom, which are the heart, liver, spleen, lungs and kidneys of the country. The worker occupies the Wood position and is responsible for construction. He works carefully and the finished product is solid. This is his heavenly destiny. Cutting corners and not being practical are his yin destiny. The official occupies the Fire position, presides over etiquette, leads by example, touches people with his virtues and transforms custom into beauty. This is his heavenly destiny. Corruption and perversion of the law and disregard for the national economy and people's livelihoods, are his yin destiny. The farmer occupies the Earth position and focuses on production. Deep ploughing to increase production and support the country and the population is his heavenly destiny. Being lazy, greedy and dishonest, and not working uncultivated land are his yin destiny. The educator occupies the Metal position and to be a role model to others, to be virtuous, to teach others, to be filial before you learn to be fraternal are his heavenly destiny. To be perfunctory, only to talk but not to put into practice and to lead other's children astray are his yin destiny. The merchant occupies the Water position and mainly focuses on the operation of goods and services – benefiting the country and providing genuine goods at honest prices are his heavenly destiny. Only seeking profit and providing counterfeit goods are his yin destiny. If people follow the principles of nature and do their best, no matter what profession they are in, all things will be equal, and each profession will follow its own way. If one person or occupation looks down on another, that is bad luck and the country's vitality will surely be depleted. If everyone sticks to his own position and fulfils his duties, progress will be smooth, and the country will be governed as it should be. When expounding on the Dao, we must focus on ourselves. First, let's talk about what kind of profession we are in. In the past, did we mainly follow our heavenly destiny or our yin destiny? What is true for a country is also true for a village."

"Aiya, Goodman!" Awning's wife said. "Are you giving me your endorsement, then?"

"Let us rather say I am giving you a lesson, but I cannot explain the sun and the moon to a frog at the bottom of a well!" Goodman replied.

"Are you reprimanding me?"

"I am not reprimanding you, I am just concerned."

"The Branch Secretary is so worried, he has come out in a great boil on his forehead. Why don't you instruct him?"

"He is the Branch Secretary. If he is willing to let me talk, I will instruct him. If I were to go and seek him out, if I am lucky he will just think I am talking nonsense but if I am unlucky, he will think I am an ox monster and a snake spirit who is out to destroy things."

The poached eggs were ready, and Awning's wife was putting them into a bowl, but Goodman made to leave.

"There's one for you."

"No, no. There's no need for me to eat here."

"If you're not going to eat, why don't you at least sit down for a while, and then you can help Awning relax."

"It's better that I leave now. Please don't make a fuss, I'll just leave quietly. Awning has already broken out in a fever and after all that talking, it will probably be for the best."

And with that, he really did leave.

Awning's wife took the bowl of eggs into the main room. She looked out at the sky above the courtyard. It was still dark and overcast, and she couldn't make out the seven stars of the Big Dipper.

TWENTY-EIGHT

AFTER TOILING AWAY FOR SEVERAL DAYS, everyone was so tired they had already shed several layers of skin. Most of the wheat in the field was cut, and sheaves of it had been brought back and piled up beside the threshing ground, where they were spread out, one by one, to dry in the sun. Cows were harnessed to the stone roller that was used to crush the wheat. The first passage of the roller threw up the straw, while the grain was gathered together using wooden battens. The process was repeated two or three more times until the grain was piled up like a tomb mound. The women went home to cook, while the men stayed put waiting for some wind so they could start the winnowing.

It remained still for an hour, so the men went home to eat. After they'd finished, they went back to the threshing ground, but there was still no wind. When Inkcap was cutting wheat in the field, he and Cowbell were responsible for tying the cut wheat into sheaves for the adults to carry back, and then they picked up the discarded wheat ears from amid the stubble. Back at the threshing ground, he and Cowbell went to the cowshed to fetch the cows, led them over and hitched them up to the rollers. Ever-Obedient and Millstone gave the order for the cows to start crushing the grain. The cows often had to shit, so the two lads stood at the edge of the threshing ground, Inkcap with a bamboo kitchen skimmer and Cowbell with a gourd ladle. Every time one of the cows raised its tail to drop a load, Ever-Obedient or Millstone shouted, "Pick up the shit!" and Cowbell would trot over to pick it up. The next time they shouted the instruction, it would be Inkcap who went and positioned his bamboo skimmer under the cow's arse. He would follow behind the cow as it walked on and sometimes he caught the manure and sometimes it fell in the wheat so he had to scoop it up with his hands and throw it off the threshing floor.

Nobody could see anything wrong with this and all they said was, "What's so dirty about cow dung anyway?"

Of course, Inkcap didn't think there was any problem either, and he just wiped his hands with some straw and said, "If someone gave me a steamed bun now, I'd take it without wiping my hands again."

"I like your thinking," Ever-Obedient said.

As the wind still hadn't come, everyone was sitting or lying under the trees at the side of the field in random groups, talking about this and that, and generally setting the world to rights. When the adults were talking, Cowbell interjected a few times. Nobody took any notice, but he kept trying until he got into a fight with Tag-Along, who hit him round the head. Inkcap took note and listened without interrupting. But listening was boring, so he just lay there and looked at the wheat sheaves piled up beside the threshing floor, waiting to be untied.

Some of the sheaves were piled up in clusters with two sheaves in one and three in another and one standing apart, alone. Inkcap had always reckoned that pigs, dogs, chickens and cats all talked to each other, and that birds talked to each other on the trees, and the trees conversed too. What he hadn't known was that the wheat sheaves were at it too. He couldn't understand what their rustling voices were saying, but from their expressions, he could see that the wheat sheaf that was standing apart was scolding one of the sheaves in the cluster of two, as it seemed that it had originally been together with the solitary sheaf but had now gone over and formed a group with the other one. The single sheaf was now throwing sparrows at the cluster of two sheaves, first one, then another, while the cluster of three sheaves fell about laughing at them.

Inkcap wanted to watch the argument as it developed but someone shouted, "Inkcap! I need a light. I need a light."

Although Inkcap was, of course, carrying his rope fuse, because they were in the wheat field, he hadn't lit it yet. Now he was being called, he did light it and ran from person to person lighting their pipes and cigarettes.

After a while, someone else shouted, "What about the water, Inkcap? Where's the water?"

Inkcap took a bucket to the spring to fetch water. The spring water in Old Kiln was very good quality and could be drunk without being boiled, winter and summer. But even when he brought the water, there was still someone who piped up, "Who said they wanted bamboo leaf tea? Who was it?"

Inkcap felt that both fire and water were his responsibility, and he knew that he was doing everyone a real service at this time. So he stayed alert and kept his patience, even though he realised they were deliberately trying to provoke him by telling him to fetch bamboo leaves.

"If you want bamboo leaves, I'll go and get them for you," he said.

Cowbell wasn't happy about this, and he whispered to Inkcap, "What's with all this hard-working shit? Are you trying to show me up?"

That was exactly what Inkcap was trying to do, and he trotted off to a spot behind Barndoor's house where there was a clump of bamboo.

However, Awning was getting worried and told Dazed-And-Confused to throw a few shovelfuls of grain up in the air to see if it might be possible to start winnowing. Dazed-And-Confused tried it, but the grains and the chaff just went up together and came back down together, so winnowing was out of the question. The sun shifted the shadow of the tree, and the people under the tree moved with it.

"The treetops aren't moving," Feng Youliang said. "We'll have to beg for some wind."

They all agreed. In previous years, when there was drought or when there was no wind and either no wheat could be grown or none could be winnowed, it was Barndoor's father who did the begging, but he was dead now. Potful had been taught by Barndoor's dad, but he was sick at the moment, so Awning told Soupspoon and Lucky to go and carry Potful back to the threshing ground. As he was being carried, Potful felt embarrassed to have been lying on his *kang* on such a busy and important day. He kept slapping his legs, saying they weren't his legs any more. When he saw the threshing ground, he couldn't help protesting about how the wheat sheaves had been put at the east end of the field. That was low-lying ground! What would happen to them if it rained? And why were there only two rollers? Even if they weren't able to start winnowing, they could at least stack the rolled stalks! Why were they just sitting around waiting for the wind?

"You're right, of course," Awning said, "but I'm really keen to get some wind now, so please can you beg for it?"

Potful said that Barndoor's father had taught him to beg for rain but had never taught him to beg for wind.

"If you can beg for rain, you can surely beg for wind too."

"I can give it a try," Potful said. "I need to find a third-generation Holy Boy."

Everyone started counting on their fingers and found that there was not a single Hei family member in Old Kiln who had passed the name on through a generation and, although there were many households with the surname Zhu, there weren't any with three generations of continuity. There were ones with two generations, but after that, either the family had already died out, or the children had already married or were too young.

"Inkcap's a Holy Boy! Fetch Inkcap!" Sprout said.

"But can we actually say Inkcap has a direct line through three generations?" Pockmark asked.

"Do you know who his father and his grandfather are? There might not be a direct line through three generations at all," Baldy Jin said.

"Yes, but it's not certain there isn't," Pockmark snapped back.

"You're stubborn as a mule, aren't you?" Baldy Jin said. "What does it matter? It's just a ritual. Do you really think the heavens can tell the difference?"

"Would you dare deceive the heavens?" Barndoor said.

In the end, Inkcap did act as the Holy Boy. Potful told him to stand in the middle of the threshing ground and then said, "Holy Boy!"

Inkcap stayed silent and Potful told him, "You have to reply when I call out 'Holy Boy'!"

"But I'm Inkcap."

"You're a Holy Boy now."

"He can't be a Holy Boy. How can he be a Holy Boy if he comes from a bad background?" Pockmark protested from the sidelines.

"Have you ever seen the rain from Heaven pass over and not fall on the private plots of the Four Bad Elements?" Sprout reasoned.

From the centre of the field, Inkcap said, "Ah! I am the Holy Boy. Call me again."

"Holy Boy!" Potful called out again.

"Hey!" Inkcap responded loudly.

In fact, Inkcap understood very well that it was the Holy Boy who begged the wind to come, and he expressly wanted everyone in the wheat field to know that he was now a Holy Boy. He looked towards the edge of the field, searching for Cowbell, who had his arms open and was hunting for lice. Cowbell felt his luck was out that day and was jealous of Inkcap, so he didn't look at him. Clumps of red clouds were following each other across the sky, layered like the petals of roses in bloom. The trees were full of birds, which were not there to eat the grain, but just to sing. There were dogs too, including Ever-Obedient's dog, Sparks' dog and Lucky's dog. They were laughing and wagging their tails. There was also a ladybird, flapping its wings very fast and flying overhead like a tiny shooting star. Shooting stars must also have wings when they streak across the night sky, but they flap them so fast they become invisible.

"Stop twisting your head round and look at the wooden mallet," Potful shouted.

A spot in the centre of the threshing ground had been swept clear, where there was a wooden mallet, sprinkled with salt, and sitting on the head of the mallet was a porcelain bowl with three sticks of incense standing inside it. People were helping Potful light the incense, and Inkcap lay on the ground to see if the salt on the mallet had dissolved. A ladybird had landed on the cuff of his jacket. He kept watching the salt, which still did not dissolve, but the sun made his scalp hurt. He didn't mind the pain, except that it turned into an itch as if there was wheat chaff in his clothes and crepe myrtle bark on his neck. He couldn't stand the itch, so he scratched his head with one hand.

"Don't move," Potful shouted.

Inkcap stopped moving. Potful sat down and began to mutter incantations. In the sunlight, his face was as white as if it was made of papier mâché. Sweat flowed from his forehead to his nose, and then to his chin.

Drops formed on his chin and fell one by one. Inkcap couldn't make out what Potful was saying. His scalp no longer hurt or itched, but it felt very tight, as if it had been coated with mud. His knees were hurting but he kept reminding himself not to move. He had no trouser legs cushioning his knees, nor was there any flesh on them so it was just bone in contact with the ground, like kneeling on an iron plate or a bed of nails. The salt was slowly dissolving. Sweat from his forehead flowed into his eyes and his vision was blurred as he looked at Iron Bolt holding the mallet.

At last, Inkcap said, "The salt is gone."

Potful stopped mumbling, looked at the mallet and repeated, "The salt is gone."

The people on the threshing ground started shouting, all the dogs were barking too, and the birds flew up from the trees with a clattering noise and flashed downwards like a single flickering sheet.

"The birds are eating the wheat! Scare them off," Potful yelled.

Everyone got hold of brooms, rakes and shovels and chased the birds back into the air. They didn't try to land again but floated off in the same flickering sheet.

"Stand up, Holy Boy," Potful ordered.

But Inkpen couldn't stand up by himself, so Barndoor went over, picked him up and carried him over to put him down in the shade of a tree. Inkcap lay there on his stomach, like a toad.

In the middle of the afternoon, clouds did indeed begin to appear in the sky. They covered the sun and mist gathered on Yijia Ridge. If that white mist wasn't formed by the wind it was formed by the rain, but either way, the wind had arrived. The question was whether it would bring the rain with it. In the end, thank heavens, the rain did not fall and the wind was not too strong. It blew gently, just in time to winnow the wheat. The men stood in a line and tossed the wheat grains high in the air with their wooden shovels, almost high enough to touch the sky.

They seemed to be saying, "Offer the wheat to the heavens! Offer the wheat to the heavens!"

The grains fell back from the sky, like rain, as if the heavens were saying, "Leave the wheat for the people! Leave the wheat for the people!"

The chaff floated sideways, the grains fell vertically, and the pile of wheat grew bigger and bigger. The workers were covered in sweat, and the chaff stuck to them, turning their faces and necks bright red. The women covered their heads with headscarves while the men stripped off to the waist. Dazed-And-Confused's tendons were standing out and his belly was so thin you could see the mess of innards inside.

"Where does your food go?" Half-Stick asked.

"I'm only this thin because I don't get any food," Dazed-And-Confused complained.

"But the production team shares out all the grain using the same steelyard, so who are you saying gets more than you? Just look at Ever-Obedient! He's older than you, and he's not a bag of bones."

"He gets to eat Yoyo! Who do I get to eat?"

"Who do you want to eat?"

"He gets to eat his own hand," someone said, and everyone guffawed.

Dazed-And-Confused didn't even try to respond but went over to the water bucket to get a drink. Bash was already at the bucket, gulping mouthful after mouthful from a gourd ladle.

"Hey, Bash!" Dazed-And-Confused said. "What are you doing still wearing a cap in this heat? Have you turned into Baldy Jin?"

"If I've got it, why wouldn't I wear it?" Bash answered coldly.

Dazed-And-Confused picked up the bucket and gulped from it like a cow at a water trough, until he choked to a stop.

It wasn't until after dark that all the winnowing was finally done, and everyone was so hungry that the skin of their bellies was pressed up against their spines. But they still had to think about what they were going to do the next day. Should they first harvest the wheat in the eighteen *mu* of land, or should they carry the wheat already harvested from the river foreshore back to the village and start grinding it? Who would stand guard over the wheat from the foreshore and at the threshing ground? Who was responsible for watching the grain that had already been collected? Should the bran be piled up beside the threshing floor or should it be taken directly to the cattle pen to be stored as cattlefeed? All these things had to be decided. Awning said he had discussed it with Millstone, and Dazed-And-Confused and Tag-Along were to spend the night at the threshing ground. Now everybody was to go home to eat and when they'd finished, they could call it a day.

Cowbell came over, shook Inkcap and said, "Do your knees still hurt? Do you think being a Holy Boy will get people on your side? I wouldn't have gone and knelt there if they'd asked me."

"Don't shake me," Inkcap pleaded. "I see stars when you shake me... Hey! Have you got the balls to guard the wheat on the river foreshore tonight? If you want to, we can go and talk to Awning."

"There are ghosts on the foreshore," Cowbell said. "Sprout is happy enough to bury her head in the sand there during the day, but she's scared of it at night."

Inkcap took Goodman to one side and whispered to him, "I want to ask you something."

"What is it?"

"Do you think there's such a thing as ghosts?"

"Yes."

"Where are they?"

"Do you want to see a ghost? If you do, I'll show you one when the time's right."

"If there really are ghosts, how can I see one?"

"If you sit at a crossroads in the middle of the night, wrap your feet with white paper, put a piece of white paper on your head, put a piece of turf on the paper, and light a stick of incense stuck in the turf, a ghost will soon turn up."

To start with, Inkcap had thought Goodman was just trying to scare him, and he hadn't expected him to take him so seriously. Inkcap was frightened, so he went over to tell Cowbell he wasn't going to ask for permission to go to the foreshore to guard the cut wheat that night. But Cowbell wasn't there. He was off in the distance where he had started an argument with Pockmark. Cowbell saw the badge Pockmark was wearing and had grabbed it and tried to run away. Pockmark caught him and snatched the badge back. Cowbell said that the badge was his, and he cursed Pockmark to hell and back.

Pockmark slapped his face and said, "If you curse me like that again, I'll rip your tongue out."

The bystanders pulled Cowbell away.

Pockmark looked as though nothing had happened, and he turned to Iron Bolt and said, "Tonight we need to go to the foreshore to guard the cut wheat. How about you get a bottle of wine?"

Inkcap did not comfort Cowbell but smiled smugly at him. He gathered up the fuse from under the tree at the side of the threshing ground and picked up the bucket. When he emptied the remaining water from the bucket, he caught sight of Dazed-And-Confused, who said that he was off home early to cook dinner. As he left, Dazed-And-Confused walked through the pile of wheat grain, stomping his feet as he went so that his shoes were buried in the grain. He wobbled his way out of the threshing ground. Inkcap knew that Dazed-And-Confused was stealing the production team's wheat by allowing so much grain to settle in his large shoes.

"Ai! Ai!" Inkcap yelped but stopped when everyone looked at him.

"What's that noise about?" Sparks asked.

"A firefly!" Inkcap replied excitedly.

There was indeed a firefly and soon there were countless numbers of them, all flying with their own lamps to light their way. Inwardly cursing Dazed-And-Confused, Inkcap swatted violently with his hand, knocking a firefly to the ground. He caught three in a row, then he went over to the pumpkin vine growing up the wall of Six Pints' privy near the threshing ground and picked a pumpkin flower. He put the three fireflies inside it to make a lantern, which glowed red and pink. Six Pints' house blocked the light of the rising moon. There was a kerosene lamp hanging on the wooden pole in the middle of the threshing ground, but the light didn't reach very far so it was very dark in the privy. Inkcap was carrying his flower lantern. He felt that the people in the threshing ground wouldn't be able to see him, but they could certainly see the flower lantern. They would be wondering why a bunch of bright lights were hanging so carefree in the sky.

Unfortunately, no one actually looked towards the privy at Six Pints' house.

The people on the threshing ground began to gather up the crushed wheat straw and put it into two piles. They were so tired that their mouths were hanging open pitifully, like hooked fish being pulled out of the river. When Inkcap went back to the threshing ground, he found that almost everyone who was taking a rest had ignored the stone rollers at the edge of the threshing ground in favour of the piles of wheat straw they had collected, and they had lain down and stretched out on the straw. Third Aunt sat down, scratched her waist and put a handful of wheat grains into her waistband. The older women wore trousers and had tied string around the ends of the legs so that nothing would leak out if it was tucked into their waistbands. Even Third Aunt was at it! Inkcap was very surprised and reckoned that everyone must be stealing wheat grain from the production team. He was glad he had not given their game away when Dazed-And-Confused left.

Everybody was waiting for Dazed-And-Confused and Tag-Along to arrive after finishing their meal, and they cursed the fuckers for staying at home stuffing themselves with delicacies and not hurrying back. Gran had spent the whole afternoon bent over a broom sweeping up the chaff on the threshing ground and her back ached fiercely when she stopped to rest, so she got Inkcap to pummel her back.

As he did so, Inkcap whispered to her, "They're all stealing grain, Gran."

Gran pinched his lips shut.

"Really stealing!" Inkcap insisted.

Gran put her hand over his mouth to shut him up.

Inkcap didn't say any more about the matter, but he was still unhappy about it: why were they all stealing wheat from the production team? He had thought these people were usually self-serving enough in their behaviour, but they actually turned out to be thieves! How could he expose their thieving ways and put a stop to them without them knowing it was his doing? He was turning over several ideas in his head, but he couldn't settle on anything.

When Dazed-And-Confused and Tag-Along finally arrived, everyone started jeering at them.

"Hey, Tag-Along, are you so late because you've been screwing your wife again?"

"She's sprained her foot as you all bloody well know," Tag-Along protested.

"She doesn't need her foot to do what you two were doing! Own up. You really were at it weren't you?"

"So what if I was? It perks me up after a hard day, doesn't it."

Everyone pounced on him and slapped him around a bit until he beat a retreat.

Then they turned their attention to Dazed-And-Confused.

"At least he's got a wife. What were you up to that kept you so long?"

"I had to go for a shit after I'd eaten."

"So you went for shit as soon as you'd eaten, did you? It must have been a turd as long as a well rope!"

This little session of chaffing and teasing restored spirits, and the workers started to drift home. Inkcap and Gran were the last to leave and they looked down the dark alley where they saw the others walking slowly and cautiously but laughing and joking as they went.

Inkcap's anger welled up in him again and you could hear it in his voice as he shouted, "The wolves are back!"

When the people in front heard that, they broke into a run, kicking and barging each other in their panic. Some of them stumbled and some of them yelled, "Shoes! Shoes! My shoes!"

They scrabbled crazily around on the ground trying to find their shoes, then went on running, whether they had found them or not.

Even Gran was alarmed and fell flat on her arse, calling out, "Ping'an! Ping'an!"

Inkcap exclaimed in alarm and hurried over to help her up, whispering, "There aren't any wolves. That was just me."

In the dark, Gran put her hand over his mouth and exclaimed bitterly, "You! You! Ach! You..."

Inkcap could hardly breathe under Gran's hand, but inside he was laughing to himself: Thieves! Thieves! That will teach you to steal wheat.

He was telling himself that the next morning, the Branch Secretary or Awning and the others would see all the grain that had been dropped in the alley, and they would investigate what was going on. Then the fun would start!

But the next morning, neither the Branch Secretary nor Awning saw the wheat grains scattered in the alley. They didn't walk down that alley at all, and there was no discussion in the village. When Inkcap got to the alley himself, he saw dozens of chickens pecking the ground. They were in great spirits and chatting away as they pecked. Even so, Inkcap was still smiling when he felt an itch on his neck. He smacked his hand there and a mosquito flew away. What were mosquitoes doing here so early? When he inspected his hand, he saw a little pool of blood on his palm. It turned out that two mosquitoes had bitten him on the neck, and he had killed one of them.

The mosquito that had flown away settled on a wall and said, "That's your blood you swatted."

TWENTY-NINE

AFTER ALL THE WHEAT IN THE LOCAL AREA was harvested and milled, the lanes and alleys in Old Kiln were suddenly deserted. The villagers were sleeping on their *kangs,* cuddling their pillows. From time to time, long drawn-out sounds could be heard through windows, which seemed likely to be the result of a release of fatigue from the chest and from the muscles and bones after a long day's work. All this time, chickens, pigs, cats and dogs came and went merrily. Previously, chickens were kept with chickens and dogs were kept with dogs, but now they broke all the rules and crossed all boundaries. They reported to each other that the bitch belonging to Gourd's family had given birth to a litter of six pups, so they all ran to the gate of the Gourd family courtyard. The courtyard door was always closed, and they just gathered there talking. Decheng's family dog found a bone under the willow tree in front of the Branch Secretary's house. This bone must have been thrown away by the Branch Secretary after he had finished the meat his son had brought back from the town. He gnawed it for a long time and was reluctant to throw it away. He wanted to take it to the Gourd family's bitch, but when he saw so much commotion outside the courtyard gate, he was reluctant to go.

Big Root's cat said, "Your old lady has given birth to six babies for you!"

But Decheng's dog turned tail and left. The chickens, pigs, cats and dogs were astonished by his departure. They grew angry and scolded the dog, saying that he had no sense of responsibility. What a coward to be frightened by the need to provide for six puppies and run away like that! Ever-Obedient's dog naturally felt that Decheng's dog had to be taught a lesson and chased him all the way home. The chickens, pigs, cats and dogs there at the time got hold of the bone but none of them were ready to give it a gnaw. They put it under the stone at the gate of the Gourd family courtyard and left it for the new mother. Several chickens agreed to give some eggs as well. Lots of the cats got ready to go and catch fish in the lotus pond, but Almost-There's pig had already turned round and brought back a cabbage root that it had dug out from under the gable of Cowbell's house with its long snout. It mocked the others for thinking that a dog would want to eat eggs and fish.

The chickens, pigs, cats and dogs enjoyed two relaxed days before the villagers started to gather in the lanes and alleys. Inevitably, when they did get back together, they began to gossip, as they would have gone crazy if they didn't get things off their chest. Then there was the news that Old Kiln was going to have to choose a new production team leader. Many had their eye on the job. Pockmark suddenly became very active, and entirely off his own bat, he picked up a plough and a jar of water and said he was off to plough the fields.

When he bumped into Awning, he said, "Hey Awning! I'll put my hand up for you when they're choosing the new team captain. How about it?"

"I couldn't think of taking the job, I'm already busy enough as captain of the militia company."

"So who do you think will get it?"

"It has to be the choice of the people."

"Choice is choice, but your opinion is important. The team captain has to be someone who is in good health, who can do whatever it takes to keep a lid on things."

"What about Bash?"

"Impossible! Why would you choose your own rival?"

"We're not rivals."

"Just because you don't treat him as a rival doesn't mean that's not how he'll treat you."

"And I suppose I couldn't possibly choose you, eh?"

Pockmark chuckled. "If you really did want to choose me, I'd have to give it careful consideration."

While Pockmark and Awning were talking, a group was gathering not far away. They, too, were discussing the choice of team captain. Some said it should be Bash while others said that was impossible. Those against the idea said that Bash was an ambitious chancer, not a farmer, while those who supported him did so precisely because he was ambitious, and said that if he was made captain, it would also stop him running off again. It would be like tethering an ox to a hitching post. Those who objected said that it was Bash who had made Potful so angry he had become ill in the first place, and if Bash was made team captain it would certainly hasten Potful's death. Later on, Sparks and Millstone came under discussion, and someone said that Sparks was OK but also simple-minded and bad-tempered. Millstone was ambivalent about Sparks, but at least he was genuine team captain material.

As they were talking, Millstone and his uncle, Happy, came over. Someone said, "Hey, Millstone, are we going to plough that hundred and eighty *mu* of land on the riverbank next?"

"I'm not sure," Millstone replied.

Three or four people immediately exclaimed, "Aren't you about to become the team captain?"

"Don't say that. How could I be team captain?"

"Do it for us. We'll choose you when the time comes."

When Pockmark heard this, he hurled the water jar he was carrying to the ground. The crash alerted everyone to the fact Pockmark was standing not far away.

"Why can't you be more careful?" Sprout said.

"So what if I've broken it, I've got others," Pockmark retorted. "What's it to you anyway?"

Sprout lost interest and didn't pursue the matter.

"Harness a cow for me," Pockmark shouted to Inkcap, who was somewhere in the middle of the crowd. "Harness up that red bullock."

"The red bullock kicks," Inkcap said. "I don't dare."

"That wasn't a request," Pockmark snapped.

So Inkcap went off to the cowshed to harness the red bullock.

The red bullock kicked Inkcap during the ploughing, which made him feel furious and really hard-done-by. Pockmark looked at Inkcap's leg and saw there was a bruise on it.

"At least the skin's not broken," Pockmark said. "There's something I want to ask you, Inkcap, and you have to tell me the truth. Did anyone in the village say anything about me?"

Inkcap knew exactly what he was asking.

"Yes, they did. They said you are always bullying me."

"Very funny, you little prick. Now, out with it. What did the villagers say about me? Did they say anything about me being team captain?"

"Isn't Millstone going to be team captain?"

"How could an incompetent little runt like that be team captain?"

Inkcap particularly hated it when anyone brought up either size or status, so he didn't reply. A gadfly landed on the cow's rump. Inkcap waved his hand to shoo it away, but the gadfly flew up and landed on his back, stinging him through his clothes. The sting was as painful as having a raw chilli shoved up his arsehole, a real burning pain.

Over the following days, Pockmark had to pass by the Branch Secretary's courtyard gate every day on the way to work, and he always shouted at the top of his voice for everyone else to hurry up and come out to work.

"You must have had an early breakfast, Pockmark," the Branch Secretary said from inside his courtyard.

Pockmark went in and said, "Where is everybody? They should be hard at it by now."

He went on to ask the Branch Secretary a lot of questions, and the Branch Secretary gave him a lot of answers, but he didn't say anything about choosing a new team captain. Pockmark repeated this routine several times, but when the Branch Secretary still didn't say anything about the team captaincy, he gave up on it. He felt that if he wanted to be team captain, his biggest obstacle was probably Millstone. One day, Director Wang from the town police station went to Old Kiln for a security inspection. Pockmark knew Director Wang, so he invited him to his home and then rode off on Director Wang's bicycle to buy some wine at Six Pints' consignment store. Whenever he saw anyone, he made sure to tell them that Director Wang had come to see him. As they were drinking, he asked Director Wang to suggest to the Branch Secretary that he should be team captain.

"I can suggest that you become a public security officer," Director Wang said, "but I can't say anything about team captain. How is your standing in the village?"

"The Branch Secretary has the final say on matters in the village," Pockmark said.

Director Wang didn't pursue the subject further and the two of them set to playing guess-fingers. After Director Wang left, Pockmark wandered in and out of the house, feeling disappointed and confused. Ever-Obedient's dog was looking for food in the alley. On arriving outside Pockmark's courtyard, it saw a rat burrowing into the drain hole at the courtyard gate. The dog got really interested and reached into the drain hole with its paws to dig the rat out. The rat darted out of the drain hole and ran into the courtyard. The dog ran in after it, still hoping to catch it. Pockmark was suddenly enraged. He shut the gate and hit the dog with a stick. There was a burst of confused noise as man and dog became entangled and fell to the floor locked together. In the end, the dog bit Pockmark in the leg and Pockmark returned the favour on the dog's hind leg, leaving him with a mouthful of dog hair. The dog leapt over the courtyard wall and ran away.

When the dog jumped down off the courtyard wall, Inkcap was making his way to the little wooden shack on the highway. As he passed Pockmark's place, he heard shouting and cursing and saw Ever-Obedient's dog jump the wall. He knew that Pockmark was in a rage, so he didn't dare open his mouth but hurriedly made himself scarce, taking the dog with him.

Three days before, Bash had given Inkcap the Chairman Mao badge. Inkcap was overjoyed.

"Why are you so nice to me, Brother Bash?"

"There's something even better," Bash said, and he gave Inkcap the key to the little wooden shack.

Inkcap asked why, and Bash told him that he would be going to Luozhen more often over the next few days and he wanted Inkcap to come and take care of the shack.

Inkcap thought there was something odd about the plan and said, "The village is about to choose a new team captain and you're going away? Isn't this just like the last time when they were deciding the food relief? Are you trying to blow yourself up again?"

"I was originally planning to go for the job," Bash said, "but now I've changed my mind. As long as that man is still Branch Secretary, what's the point in me being team captain? Old Kiln is a shallow pond, and I am a dragon! What kind of wind and waves can I stir up here?"

"You're from Old Kiln and you can't even be team captain here!" Inkcap said. "What do you think you're going to do anywhere else?"

"Take a plate and go to the river and scoop me up some water."

"Scoop up water with a plate?" Inkcap echoed incredulously. "I'll take a basin, or if there's no basin, at least give me a bowl."

"Sure, I know that a bowl holds water better than a plate, but you can put vegetables and stir-fry on a plate. It's the same with people. Now my time has come, do I, Bash Hei, really still want to be team captain here or am I a plate not an Old Kiln bowl?"

Inkcap stared at Bash.

"What are you staring at? Don't you recognise me any more?"

"I can't work out what you're saying."

"Ha! You wouldn't be Inkcap if you could. You just concentrate on looking after this place for me."

"If I say I'll look after it, I'll look after it. Are we still selling *taisui* water?"

"Yes."

"And can I cut pieces off the *taisui* to eat?"

"Who would dare eat it?"

"I would."

"Then go ahead if you dare."

Over the next three days, Inkcap went to the little wooden shack whenever he had a spare moment. He sold several bowls of *taisui* water, but no one dared eat the flesh. When he cut a piece off and stewed it for himself, he didn't tell Cowbell.

Before the team captain was chosen, a tragedy occurred in Old Kiln: Happy died after eating two bowls of *laomian* noodles.

Happy had never been with a woman in his life and lived with his nephew Millstone. Although money was tight and life wasn't easy, uncle and nephew got along well with each other. Happy often told people in the cowshed that his nephew's wife had made him the gown he was wearing as soon as the weather warmed up. He would take off his shoes to show them off, saying that he got two pairs of shoes a year, and they all had hand-stitched soles. He also boasted that whenever he went home to eat, he was given sweetcorn glutinous rice noodles, and his nephew's wife would always fill him a big bowl first, and then fish out another chopsticks' worth of noodles to add to it. Since there weren't enough noodles left, she would add some pickled vegetables to the pot for Millstone and then fill his bowl with them and what was left of the noodles. She herself would just drink the leftover broth. He was always praising his nephew's wife, and the villagers laughed at him about it, saying that his niece was a randy little madam who kept Happy's *kang* warm when Millstone was away. They teased him about being a sad old man who'd fallen for his nephew's wife. In fact, Happy took this in good part; he was rather flattered that they thought he was up to it.

After the harvest, the food at home improved. One lunchtime, Millstone's wife rolled out the noodle dough, but once it was rolled out, she didn't cut it into the triangle shapes the villagers liked, but used the rolling pin as a guide to cut it into long strips, which she laid out in clumps on the chopping board. Then she went to pick spicy green chillis from a tree that grew in a corner of the courtyard and also pulled up a spring onion. She chopped the chillis and the onion together and told her neighbour Stargazer to call her uncle back for lunch on his way past the cowshed. Then she lit the fire under the wok.

Happy bumped into Noodle Fish on his way home. Noodle Fish stopped him and began to tell him all about what was going on in his household. Once he got going there seemed to be no stopping him, but Happy interrupted him. "I'm on my way home for lunch, brother, and the womenfolk are busy cooking my noodles. When lunch is over, come and find me at the cowshed and you can talk till the sun goes down."

"What a lucky man you are," Noodle Fish said, and he let Happy go on his way. Happy walked into his alley and saw smoke coming from his chimney. As the black smoke rose above the treetops, it took on a bluish translucent tinge, like the clouds. Ever-Obedient's dog lay in the middle of the road barking at him, and he ignored it. He tried to walk round it to the left, but the dog moved to block him; he tried skirting it to the right, but the dog blocked him again.

"Get out of the way, you useless creature," Happy said. "Are you blind?"

"Woof! Woof! Woof-a-woof! Woof!"

Happy didn't understand what the dog was trying to say and made to go on his way. So the dog bit him. Enraged, Happy picked up a rock but the dog ran away.

When Happy got home, the noodles were just done. He said he would eat them with Millstone when he got back but his nephew's wife told him that she didn't know when he'd be back, so Happy should go ahead and eat first. Happy began to eat. He had an enormous appetite and ate out of a basin instead of a bowl. He had filled his basin with noodles, given them a good mix and gone outside to eat by the courtyard gate.

Half-Stick happened by and said, "You've got a good appetite, uncle, if you can eat that whole basinful."

"I wouldn't be much of a man if I couldn't," Happy retorted.

"Aiya! Are those *laomian*? It's your lucky day."

"Yes indeed, Half-Stick. It is my lucky day."

Millstone came home, took a bowlful for himself and sat on the edge of the *kang* to eat. Only then did his wife serve herself, saying, "Do you like this recipe?"

"It's good," Millstone said. "The chillis are great."

"Well, in future, come home at lunchtime, no matter how busy you are."

"She's right," Happy called out from the gateway. "Noodle Fish stopped me on my way back to talk about his family, but I wouldn't listen. I said that, even if the sky was falling in, I wasn't going to be late for my lunch."

"All right, all right," Millstone agreed.

Then, halfway through his own bowl, Millstone noticed that his wife didn't have any noodles in her bowl, only the broth.

"Can't you get enough noodles for yourself too? It's not like there's no wheat left after the harvest."

"As long as you and your uncle are eating well, that's all that matters. You're out there working hard and it would be an insult to you if I sat at home eating *laomian*."

There was a sudden crash.

"What was that?" Millstone's wife exclaimed. "Has someone dropped their bowl?"

Millstone took his bowl outside to see what was going on by the courtyard gate. He saw his uncle lying on the ground, with the basin broken into three pieces by his feet.

"Uncle! Uncle!" Millstone cried out in distress.

Happy was foaming at the mouth as he lay there unconscious. Millstone called to his wife who was so frightened she had begun to cry.

"Go fetch the Branch Secretary," Millstone ordered her.

When the Branch Secretary arrived, lots of the neighbours had gathered around, some pinching Happy's *renzhong* acupressure point between the nose and upper lip and others staunching the blood flowing from his brow.

"This illness came on very suddenly and violently," the Branch Secretary said. "Go to the township health centre and get them to send someone to come and see him. And get Bash. Get Bash!"

Someone standing next to him said, "Bash has been in Luozhen for the past few days."

"Well fuck him, then. Is the walking tractor here?"

"Yes," someone confirmed.

"Then get Baldy Jin to take him. Quick!"

Millstone's wife went into the house, rolled up the quilt on the *kang*, took it out and spread it on the ground. She got some of the others to put Happy on the quilt while she kept moaning, "Uncle, Uncle, Uncle! What's wrong with you, Uncle?"

"I guess you'll need me for this one," Baldy Jin said as he came running up.

The Branch Secretary glared at him so he shut up and drove the walking tractor over. Happy was a large-framed man and as soon as he had been lifted crosswise onto the trailer, Millstone went inside the house and came out with a square piece of stone to put under his head.

"What kind of pillow do you call that?" the Branch Secretary said.

"My uncle always sleeps on a stone pillow," Millstone explained. "He says the coolness of the stone is kind on the eyes, and the more you lie on it the softer it gets."

"How can a stone get softer as you lie on it?" the Branch Secretary said. "Get a proper cotton pillow."

Millstone went into the house and brought out his and his wife's double pillow. There were grease marks from their heads on it and he wanted to wipe it clean. Then his stomach cramped, and for a moment, his face went white, his lips trembled and his whole body felt so weak that he had to sit on the ground.

"Is Millstone not right either?" people asked.

As she came hurrying up to help him, Millstone's wife leaned against the frame of the gate and said, "I feel dizzy too!"

She closed her eyes, afraid to move. Everyone panicked and said, mouths agape, "Ai! Ai! What should we do?"

"That's enough Ai Ai-ing," the Branch Secretary said. "There's something odd happening here. Take them all to Luozhen."

Millstone and his wife were helped onto the trailer, and the tractor took off for town with a sudden lurch.

When they arrived at the township health centre, the doctor examined the patients and found that Happy had already passed away. Millstone fainted as soon as he entered the health centre, but after some treatment, he slowly opened his eyes. The doctor said it was food poisoning. He gave Millstone and his wife enemas and pumped out their stomachs, but even so, they struggled for a long time. In the end, however, they both recovered. The health centre wanted Millstone to stay in hospital for a few days to have some injections, but he simply couldn't do it. He bought a mat and a white rooster out on the street and transported his uncle's body back to Old Kiln.

So much for Happy. He had eaten dozens of basins of *laomian*, and then all of a sudden, he had died. How can human life be so fragile? The doctor said it was food poisoning, but where did the poison come from? Old Kiln was in shock. No one had heard of such a thing happening in the village for generations. Millstone's family set up a mourning hall and started building coffins and tombs. However, the Branch Secretary refused permission for the burial and reported the case to the police station. Director Wang quickly brought over three people to investigate. It was determined that it was a case of murder by poison using rat poison. They needed a dog to go to Millstone's house to taste the pickled vegetables in the jar, the water in the bucket, the salt in the urn and the wheat noodles, rice, barley noodles, bean noodles, rice husks and fried noodles in their various storage jars.

"I say Ever-Obedient's dog should do it," Cowbell said.

Ever-Obedient kicked Cowbell.

"You want my dog to go, do you? Why not send your pig?"

"We'll try it with a chicken," the Branch Secretary decided. "A chicken isn't as valuable as a dog."

Millstone chose one of his own chickens that wasn't laying any eggs and set it to eat the different foods, one by one. The chicken ate very quickly, and when it had finished, it flew up onto the courtyard wall and perched there, clucking. Director Wang wanted it to test the leftover food in the wok a second time. Inkcap called to the chicken to come down from the wall, but it wouldn't.

"Come down," Inkcap said.

"Cluck."

"It's fine," Inkap assured the bird.

"Cluck, cluck, cluck?"

"It's fine. It really is fine."

The chicken came down from the courtyard wall, and Inkcap was about to catch it when Ever-Obedient's dog rushed in from the courtyard door, grabbed it by the neck, and dragged it away like a weasel with a field mouse. Inkcap drove the dog out of the courtyard, and it dropped the chicken and barked at him. Inkcap and the dog began talking to each other.

Everyone in the yard was stunned. "What kind of mischief-making little imp are you?" said Pockmark. "What did you say to that dog?"

Inkcap ran out of the courtyard, picked up a stick of firewood and threw it at the chicken. The chicken flapped around on the ground before he caught it and carried it over to the stove top to make it keep eating. The chicken ate a beakful of something or other, then stood inside the wok and scratched up a piece of noodle with its claws as if it were an earthworm. With a twist of its neck, it swallowed the noodle, flew down from the wok and started scratching around on the dusty floor under the stove. Outside the courtyard gate, Ever-Obedient's dog barked even more fiercely than before and began to whine.

Inkcap came back in and said, "The dog says we shouldn't be using the chicken to taste the food."

"If we can't use the chicken," Pockmark said, "why don't you do it yourself?"

The chicken continued to strut about, zigzagging around the courtyard.

"It's fine. It's fine," the Branch Secretary said. "There's no poison in the leftover food."

But just then, the chicken began to stagger, as if drunk, and the onlookers gave it some space. It started to climb over the kitchen threshold, fell back once, tried once more and fell back again. Finally, it collapsed with a gurgling sound and died.

The only possible conclusion was that the food in the wok had been poisoned. Whoever the poisoner was, they hadn't put the rat poison into the water bucket, the flour jar or vegetable pot, but directly into the wok or onto the rolled-out noodles. After coming to this conclusion and taking stock of the situation, Millstone's wife said that no one else came to the house between the time she was cooking and the time they ate, and not even the chickens or dogs had entered the courtyard. An inspection of the layout of the property showed that the kitchen door opened directly onto the courtyard, but that there was a window in the wall behind the chopping board that opened onto the alley outside. That window was still open. This clearly showed that the poisoner had poured the poison from the window onto the noodles which were laid out on the chopping board. Now, the officers from the police station had to investigate who the poisoner could be, so they left Millstone, his wife and the Branch Secretary, and everyone else dispersed. The Branch Secretary told Inkcap to throw the dead chicken into the piss cistern.

Inkcap picked up the chicken and walked out of the courtyard, shouting, "Remember this, everyone. This chicken has been poisoned. If anyone takes it out of the piss cistern and eats it, they will only have themselves to blame when it kills them."

Inkcap didn't throw the dead chicken into the piss cistern because he thought the place was too dirty. The chicken had died to solve the poisoning case and should be buried somewhere clean. There was a clump of alfalfa on the way to the kiln, and Inkcap dug a hole there to bury the chicken, then piled a small mound of soil on top.

He made a promise to the chicken, saying, "It was the poisoned noodles that killed Master Happy and you. When the criminal is caught and executed, I will cut two lumps of flesh off him and make an offering of one lump on Master Happy's grave and the other on yours."

As he was talking, a spider scuttled over and stopped at the grave. "Where did you come from, spider?" said Inkcap. "And why are you just standing there?"

But the spider didn't say a word. Inkcap sensed that the spider knew exactly what was going on, and the chicken was using the spider to tell him that it had heard what he said.

After burying the chicken, Inkcap felt uncomfortable for a few days. He thought about the chicken flying onto the courtyard wall, and him still telling it that everything was fine. How could it have been fine? He was trying to get the chicken to test for poison, so why did he trick it by saying it was fine? From then on, whenever Inkcap saw any chickens, dogs, pigs or cats, he no longer chased them or teased them. And as for the snakes, ants, snails, earthworms, frogs and caterpillars that crawled on the ground, and the birds, butterflies and dragonflies flying in the air, there was no more stamping and shooting with slingshots. When he was free, he played with them and talked to them, so that wherever he went, there were always lots of chickens and dogs. When he was taking a break from working in the fields, butterflies and dragonflies would fly to him while he lay resting on the ground. Cowbell was very confused by this and asked Inkcap if there was any trick to attracting these creatures, but Inkcap didn't tell him.

The men from the police station stayed in Old Kiln for seven days but couldn't find any clues. The villagers were in a panic and the Branch Secretary was hugely embarrassed. Accidents happened one after another and this made him feel very depressed.

"Have I lost control of the village?" he asked Awning.

"It's not your fault," Awning reassured him.

"This is the kind of destruction caused by class enemies. It's definitely the work of class enemies," the Branch Secretary concluded.

He and Awning weighed up the villagers one by one. No one could surely be a poisoner, but it seemed that suspicion still hung over everyone.

The Four Bad Elements were brought together for intensive re-education over the next two days. In fact, the only people who went to the Kiln God Temple during that time were Lightkeeper and Gran.

"Are there only two categories of the Four Bad Elements in Old Kiln?" Director Wang asked.

"To be honest," the Branch Secretary said, "even these two are not true Bad Elements. Lightkeeper was a landlord, and Granny Silkworm's husband was a member of the puppet army that went to Taiwan before Liberation."

"Is this Granny Silkworm the one they all call Gran?" Director Wang asked.

"She is old and the villagers have always called her that," the Branch Secretary told him.

"If you are that old, surely you can't be a class enemy any more."

"Right. Right. From now on, the villagers must call her just Silkworm or Inkcap's grandmother."

"There have been too few examples of the Four Bad Elements, and that's why this case has happened," Director Wang pronounced.

"There's one other person who has been sent for re-education in the past. He should also come here now," the Branch Secretary told him.

So an order was sent to fetch Goodman for re-education.

With no Happy in the cowshed any more, Dazed-And-Confused was ordered to feed the cows for the time being. The cows had no appetite, so he beat them with whips and sticks. He beat them with whatever came to hand, and the cows kept bellowing in complaint.

Director Wang explained the correct policies to Lightkeeper, Gran and Goodman, and tried to intimidate them, but the three of them said they were innocent and provided individual and material evidence of what they had been doing that day. Director Wang gave up and came out to reprimand Dazed-And-Confused for the way he was looking after the cattle and making them bellow all the time. He himself took a leather belt into the cowshed to beat the cattle with and he whipped the spotted bull until it collapsed to the ground.

Lightkeeper, Gran and Goodman demonstrated that none of them had the time to commit the crime, so they were let go. One household after another confirmed who had and who hadn't bought rat poison, but the result was that all the families had bought some because it was harvest time and every house had grain in it. The rats and mice came to investigate, and even weasels too. Almost-There's household alone had lost three chickens that had only been out of the nest for three days before being taken by weasels at night. The case could not be solved.

The officers from the police station had to keep eating their meals with different households and when they went to Pockmark's house, Pockmark asked, "Has there been any progress with the case yet?"

"No, no progress," Director Wang admitted.

"Could it be someone from another village?"

"I'm from another village! Do you think it's me?"

Later on, Pockmark was heard to say, "That great tub of lard will never solve a case like this."

Even if the case could not be solved, Happy needed to be buried because the body had turned black the next day, and after being left lying for so many days, the blood had pooled under the corpse and the smell was very strong. The burial was hurriedly arranged. The Branch Secretary made it compulsory for the whole village to attend. Normally, the family of the dead person would provide the food and drink, and everyone else would help. But because of the way Happy died, this rule was waived so, on the day of the burial, Millstone didn't cook for the village.

Before the burial, of course, Gran had to wash Happy's face and put on the burial clothes. She dipped a piece of cotton cloth in water and wiped the blood from the corners of the corpse's mouth but as soon as she did so, a piece of skin fell off. She decided to stop wiping, and instead just used her cloth to dab some water a few times on the forehead and cheeks. His burial clothes consisted of three unlined gowns and three padded cotton ones. Gran couldn't put on the first unlined gown because Happy's belly was as swollen as if it had been inflated with a pump down the windpipe. Even after a long struggle, the gown remained unfastened. Obviously, the other two unlined gowns and three padded ones couldn't be put on either so they were just used to cover the body. When the body was put in the coffin, Gran didn't dare help because when it was moved, a black liquid that was like blood but wasn't blood, that was like pus but wasn't pus, flowed out, soaking through the shrouds.

"Why are you so pitiful, Happy?" Gran asked.

In the end, they wrapped the body in a white cloth and lifted it in by the four corners. But the body wouldn't fit in the coffin, so Gran used plant ash covered in hemp paper to protect herself and pushed down one arm, making the other arm pop out again. That arm was bent and hard like a forked firestick. Sprout and Flower Girl were so scared they couldn't watch.

Barndoor reprimanded Millstone, who was standing beside him. "You should straighten the body out as soon as someone dies, but you couldn't be bothered. Now look at it!"

"Do you think this doesn't pain me? Do you think this doesn't pain me?" Millstone cried out as he rushed over to the coffin.

"Make sure you don't let any tears fall on your uncle, or he'll be lost in the underworld. Massage his arm. Massage his arm," she ordered him while muttering to herself, "Happy! Happy! Put your arms down. You have been wronged. The police are solving the case. This case can be solved."

As soon as she said this, Millstone chimed in, "Uncle! Uncle! You must show your spirit and put the murderer into a trance so he gives himself away and we can catch them. Uncle!"

Happy's arms gradually relaxed and, still with great difficulty, they were eventually stuffed back into the coffin. The coffin lid was closed, nails were driven in, and the lifting poles were tied on with ropes. Millstone and his wife burned incense and paper money, then lay down in front of the coffin and wailed. Awning yelled the order to lift the coffin at a group of sturdy labourers, and they trotted away, carrying the coffin to the cemetery.

Bash came back from Luozhen on the day of Happy's burial. He had heard about the murder while he was still in town. He and Happy had quarrelled the previous year over digging up the stone tablet, and he didn't want to go back at first. But when he thought about someone in Old Kiln poisoning Happy, he felt he had to return to see what had happened. Carrying coffins is a task for strong men and when people saw that Bash was back, they wanted him to help carry Happy's coffin.

Inkcap walked to the little wooden shack to fetch Bash. As soon as he went out of the gate, a group of dogs and cats fell in behind him. When he arrived at the shack, he saw a stranger sitting inside, but no sign of Bash.

When the man saw Inkcap, he exclaimed, "It's you!"

"Who are you?" Inkcap asked.

"Don't you recognise me? You were there when that bloke snatched my military cap."

When Inkcap looked again, he saw that it was indeed the student who had been robbed of his military cap that day. Inkcap hurtled back outside and the dogs and cats rushed at the door, blocking the man in and making a lot of noise.

Running onto the road, Inkcap bumped into Bash, who was just emerging after taking a dump in the bamboo thicket behind the pagoda and was still holding up his trousers.

"Don't go in," Inkcap told him. "That student is looking for us."

But Bash laughed. "Yes, it is that student. I met him in town and brought him back specially."

"Didn't he recognise you?"

"No good deal is made without a fight. We're friends now."

He took Inkcap back into the hut, and the man said, "Bit of a surprise for you, eh? But you told me this was Old Kiln and I said I would remember that and return one day. And here I am!"

The man stretched out his hand and Inkcap saw that it had six fingers.

"My name is Huang Shengsheng," the man said.

"Hey, you've got six fingers!" Inkcap exclaimed.

Huang Shengsheng didn't take offence and just said, "Six fingers can point the way for the country all the better!"

The two of them shook hands. Huang Shengsheng had a grip like a pair of pliers, and it hurt Inkcap.

So this was Six Fingers Huang, Huang Shengsheng. He was still as thin as when they had first met, wearing a military cap on his head and with three, not two, Chairman Mao badges on his chest. He took one off and gave it to Inkcap, who suddenly decided that Huang Shengsheng was a good person and he became very welcoming. Inkcap asked all sorts of questions over and over. It wasn't until a distant shout sounded from the village that he remembered he was there to ask Bash to carry Happy's coffin. He hurriedly told Bash, but Bash said he wouldn't go, and he wouldn't let Inkcap go either. He told Inkcap to take a bucket down to the river to fetch water and then bring some firewood so they could start cooking. When Inkcap reached the river strand, he turned around and saw that the coffin bearers had already walked from the lane to the lower slopes of Middle Mountain. Just at that moment, a cow ran on the embankment beside the village, followed by a second and then a third. Dazed-And-Confused appeared, shouting and cracking a whip, as more cows ran out. The cows stood on the embankment stretching out their necks and bellowing, long and loud. Inkcap threw away the bucket, knelt down and kowtowed towards Middle Mountain.

PART THREE
SUMMER

夏

THIRTY

Huang Shengsheng stayed in the shack for three days. From then on, he became a frequent visitor to Old Kiln. He was very well-informed and eloquent. Bash could stay up all night and sit on the *kang* listening to him. Inkcap also went to hear what he had to say several times.

On one occasion, he patted Huang Shengsheng's stomach and said, "How can your belly be so flat when it's got so many words in it?"

"They're not words," Huang Shengsheng said. "They're revolutionary vocabulary!"

But Inkcap didn't understand the new revolutionary vocabulary, he just thought how much more impressive this man was than Useless. He listened to Huang Shengsheng for a while, then scooped up a bowl of water and handed it to him to drink. After a while, he got out Bash's fried noodles. There was no congee to mix the fried noodles into clumps, so he told Huang Shengsheng to eat them dry. Huang Shengsheng kept choking on the noodles when he tried to talk through them.

Everyone in Old Kiln knew Huang Shengsheng, and he became as familiar a sight as Noisy arriving on his bicycle to geld pigs or sell groceries. Even Useless, Awning, Sparks and Pockmark greeted him, gave him cigarettes and invited him into their homes.

One day, Useless asked Huang Shengsheng, "What's the name of your combat team?"

"It's called The Independent Single Spark Ignites the Prairie Fire Combat Team."

Useless wondered why it was called "Independent", while next to him, Sparks asked, "A single spark, eh? Like sparks that fly out of a furnace?"

Useless chortled, but Sparks pursued his line of thought: "But what fucking use is a spark when it's put out by the first puff of wind?"

"You really are a sad sap, aren't you," Useless said.

"Sad sap, am I? What about you? Do I have any less to eat than you, or fewer clothes to wear?"

"It's one of Chairman Mao's sayings: 'A single spark can start a prairie fire'," Useless explained.

"But what does 'Independent' mean?" Sparks insisted. "Does your combat team have nothing to do with anyone else?"

"It means I'm the only one in it," Huang Shengsheng said.

"So you're the only one in it," Sparks mused. "Is that why you come to Old Kiln so often? Because it's easy for just one of you to get food and drink?"

"Do you think I need to come here to cadge food and drink? I am a liaison officer sent from the county town to Luozhen. I am a spark, and this spark has landed on the dry wood in Old Kiln that needs to catch light."

"Catch light? Do you want to burn down the village?" Sparks exclaimed.

"It's like playing a lute to a cow," Useless said mockingly.

"Are you calling me a cow? Fuck you and your cow!"

As soon as Sparks' mood changed, Useless shut up and pulled Huang

Shengsheng away. Sparks had little regard for Huang Shengsheng and he thought that Useless was all mouth, so it was no big deal that Huang seemed to get along with him. He went to his private plot to pick a handful of green peppers before walking over to the Branch Secretary's house.

The Branch Secretary was worried that not only was there no team captain in Old Kiln yet, but also the poisoning case remained unsolved. What was even more annoying was that a stranger kept coming to the village. He was very good with words, but the Branch Secretary couldn't figure out the whole deal with this fellow. After Sparks arrived, they discussed Huang Shengsheng once more.

"Is he here again?" the Branch Secretary asked.

"He's here again," Sparks replied.

"Why does he keep coming to Old Kiln?"

"It doesn't really matter. What can he do?"

"Is he still living at Bash's place?"

"Bash loves having others eat his food, so let him eat. When he's finished all the food, he'll drink the wind and fart himself out of there."

"I must take a look at him," the Branch Secretary concluded.

The Branch Secretary shouldered his coat, put his pipe up his sleeve and went to the little wooden shack on the highway. This was the first time he had been there. A man was sitting on the edge of the *kang* with big eyes and thick black eyebrows that almost met in the middle. If you just looked at him from the nose up, he was definitely tough-looking and handsome, but his mouth was shaped like a fire-breather and his teeth were uneven, which made the whole person appear ugly. How could such a man get the better of Bash?

Huang Shengsheng was frothing at the mouth as he spoke when he suddenly said, "You're the Branch Secretary of Old Kiln?"

"I am."

"Why do the village Branch Secretaries on both sides of the Zhou River dress like that?"

The Secretary didn't know how to answer, so he just gave a dry laugh.

"I guess it's me you've come to see, right?" Huang Shengsheng said. "Do you want to know who I am? I'll tell you. I am a student in the graduating class of the county high school. Do you want to know what I'm doing here? I am fanning the flames. What kind of wind is blowing? The wind of the Proletarian Cultural Revolution. What kind of fire is burning? The flames of the Proletarian Cultural Revolution. The Cultural Revolution is already raging elsewhere, but Old Kiln is still a dead spot. I am here to eliminate this dead spot."

Huang Shengsheng spoke rapidly and urgently, like a sudden outburst of torrential rain, and he stopped the Branch Secretary dead in his tracks.

The Branch Secretary knew nothing of all this, as he was used to talking about "class struggle" and "learning to farm like Dazhai". He couldn't possibly match Huang Shengsheng's fluency in the new vocabulary.

"Young fellow–"

"I am a soldier of Chairman Mao's Red Guard and a warrior of the Cultural Revolution!"

"You may be a soldier of the Red Guard, you may be a warrior, but–"

"'But' is not in a word in the dictionary of the Cultural Revolution."

"Old Kiln has a first-class party organisation. I am the Branch Party Secretary, and I will guard this place for the party. Commune Secretary Zhang told me... Oh, do you know Secretary Zhang?"

"Zhang Dezhang, you mean? Big Pockmark Zhang? Have you seen him recently?"

The Branch Secretary hesitated before saying, no, he hadn't.

"Let me give you some advice," Huang Shengsheng said. "Big Pockmark Zhang is a hero who keeps up with current affairs. He has actively participated in the Cultural Revolution in Luozhen. You must make sure you keep up with things too."

"Yes, yes. You're right," the Branch Secretary said.

He took off his coat and hung it on a nail on the wall, but it fell to the floor. It turned out it wasn't a nail at all, but a fly.

"Give me a fan, Bash," he ordered. "Don't you have a fan here?"

Bash didn't have a fan, so he gave the Branch Secretary a straw hat that was covering a basin on the floor. The Branch Secretary saw a fleshy heap of something in the basin and asked, "Is this the *taisui* you've been looking after?"

"Yes, I'll scoop out a bowl of water for you."

"Just give me some and I'll take it home to drink later."

Bash filled an empty wine bottle.

"Is this water really drinkable?" the Branch Secretary asked as he took the bottle and left.

That afternoon, the Branch Secretary's son came back from the township agricultural machinery station, bringing his fiancée, a large box and a bundle wrapped in a sheet. Soupspoon saw them first and speculated that they would only be coming back together with so much stuff if the Branch Secretary was arranging for them to get married. If that was so, he thought, then the couple would be setting up home in the public office that the Branch Secretary had bought, so it would definitely need some repairs and sprucing up. He went to talk to Barndoor about it, and the two took the initiative to go to the Branch Secretary's house that night to discuss the repairs. But the Branch Secretary must have been busy talking to his son, and when they knocked on the door, there was no reply.

The next day, the Branch Secretary got up very early and walked around the village with his hands behind his back. He met Cattle Track, who was returning from collecting manure outside the village.

"Branch Secretary," Cattle Track said, "the fifty *mu* of land on the back slope have collapsed. Should we take some stones up there to shore it up?"

"Yes, yes, shore it up. Get some people to shore it up."

"But I'm not the team captain. How can I get people to do the work?"

"You must know we don't have a team captain at the moment."

"How can a village this big not have a team captain? It's like a beehive without a queen."

"What do you mean by that? Am I no longer Branch Secretary?"

"I didn't mean you," Cattle Track said hastily. "I was just thinking of the team captain..."

"We will decide on a team captain just as soon as the poisoning case is solved," the Branch Secretary reassured him.

But the poisoning case remained steadfastly unsolved, and Director Wang and his men were getting ready to withdraw. They reimbursed the households that had fed them in the form of food stamps and cash and then, as they passed by Bash's old lodgings, they saw there were a lot of people inside. Director Wang had heard about Huang Shengsheng, so he went in to have a look, but it was Pockmark who met him.

"Are you leaving?" Pockmark asked. "The case hasn't been solved."

"You could think about withdrawing the case," Director Wang suggested. "Is that fellow with the mouth like a cucumber Huang Shengsheng?"

"Yes," Pockmark replied. "That's the six-fingered little bastard. But, yes, since the case can't be broken, why waste any more time on it? After all, it was Happy who died, not the Branch Secretary!"

"Everyone has their destiny," Director Wang said. "Which life is not precious? It can't have been easy for Huang Shengsheng to grow up like that."

"The little fucker certainly has a mouth on him! There's nothing in the world he doesn't know about. I thought the Branch Secretary was a great speaker, but now I know that all he's done is parrot the same few sentences over and over for the last ten years."

The Branch Secretary had not expected Director Wang and his men to leave. He had originally wanted to solve the case, or, if it couldn't be solved, to get Director Wang to help choose a team leader everyone was happy with so that the chaotic situation in the village could be resolved. After Director Wang left, the Branch Secretary listened to what his son had to say. His son told him about the situation in Luozhen where Commune Secretary Zhang was not involved in the Cultural Revolution as Huang Shengsheng had said he was. Instead, he had been given an injection and some traditional Chinese medicine at the town health centre on the pretext of his having high blood pressure. He became a lot less full of himself, put all of his affairs on hold and retired to his courtyard where he stayed, not coming out at all, saying first that he had a stomach ache and then adding back pain for good measure.

During this time, Tag-Along's little boy developed a high fever, and his whole body was burning up, leaving his family in panic.

Tag-Along had three daughters and no son. He had made himself ill with his desire for a son and became both paranoid and irascible. At home, he cursed his wife for being poor soil in which he had sown wheat, but she had grown grass seedlings. Out and about, he loved to argue, picking a quarrel with someone every few days. He also developed a condition that made him hiccup continuously. He had been quite popular beforehand, but later he was widely shunned. Finally, his wife called in Goodman.

Tag-Along took him by the hand and said, "The villagers are bullying me. I feel like I'm a dead ghost because I have no son."

"There is a son in your destiny," Goodman said, "but if you stay as angry as you are now, you will not have that son."

"Please help me," Tag-Along begged. "How can I have a son?"

"I need to explain some basic principles to you."

"I don't want you to talk about principles. The Branch Secretary is always holding meetings to talk about principles. I've listened to party principles and socialist principles until my ears have calluses."

"Then I will tell you about human relations."

"What are human relations?"

"Human relations are the three cardinal principles and five constant principles. Filial piety is the foundation. Filial piety gives rise to monarch and minister, father and son, husband and wife, brother and kin. These are the building blocks of society. Let me give you an example. If you smoke, you will have tobacco, so you need a pipe and bowl. If you have a pipe and bowl, you need a tobacco box, so you need to equip yourself with a table on which to put the tobacco box and pipe and bowl. If you have a table, you need to equip yourself with four stools. So it is with society. Society is a place where the gods take their proper places, where each person follows their own path and responsibilities, and the world is at peace."

"You're talking about principles again. All I am asking is how do I have a son?"

"All right, all right. I will tell you how to have a son. After dinner, you must gather your whole family together and talk about your lack of filial piety in the past, about the mistakes you made, about how you got angry and how you offended your wife and your elders. You must say what are you unwilling to do and what are you dissatisfied with. The more detailed you are, the better."

"I can do that," Tag-Along said.

After dinner, the whole family gathered together and invited him to sit next to the ancestral shrine. He knelt down and talked about the quarrels he had with his family members in the past and how he had offended them by throwing dishes and bowls. He talked for as long as it would take to smoke two pipes of tobacco.

"If you still have a conscience, you must know how to admit your mistakes," he declared in a loud voice. "If there is anything you can't remember, I will speak for you, and you listen."

As he spoke about his past transgressions, he kowtowed with each confession, weeping bitterly. Then he began to vomit. At first, he vomited sputum, then something like thick congee and then thick lumps. Finally, he vomited green water, and the retching sound stopped.

Goodman took up his instructions again: "You have done a good job at home, but that is not enough. For three months, you must carry your dog down to the spring to wash its fur every day. Whenever you meet someone in the village, you must ask after the health of their elders. You must ask if their children are behaving themselves, and you must offer to help with anything you can."

"Very well," Tag-Along said, "I will wash my dog for three months. If I meet people, I will talk to them as people, and if I meet ghosts, I will talk to them as ghosts."

Tag-Along did just as he promised, washing his dog every day and being polite to everyone. He was like a different person, and his wife did indeed fall pregnant and give birth to a son.

The son's health was delicate, and now he had a high fever that wouldn't go away. Drinking ginger soup didn't suppress the fever, nor did bleeding him from his brow. Tag-Along called in Goodman again, who massaged the child's joints.

"You are mollycoddling the boy," he said. "You are afraid that anything you do will cause him harm. A child is like a grass seedling growing in the soil. The wind that blows and the rain that falls actually make it stronger."

"He has been spoiled," Tag-Along admitted, "but he's our only son, and we don't want anything bad to happen to him."

"Then you need to find him a *ganda* so that he can take some of the *ganda*'s spirit."

So Tag-Along and his wife arranged to find their son his *ganda*. According to ancient custom, the way to do this was to get up early in the morning and sit next to a big rock that looks like a tiger's mouth, lay out delicious food and wine, and the first person to come along would be the child's *ganda*. There was no big stone in the shape of a tiger's mouth in Old Kiln, but the big millstone at the west end of the village was the white tiger in the *feng shui* of the village. Tag-Along's wife set up a small table there early in the morning. On the table was a plate of fried tofu with shredded radish and a plate of hot and sour potato shreds, along with a small copper pot of wine. She lit two candles and waited for someone to show up. By chance, Inkcap appeared, carrying a swallow's nest on his head.

Many birds came to Inkcap's courtyard every day. They would fly over the yard and then land on the broom that always stood against the wall in one corner. They made the broom look like a tree, bursting with flowers and fruit. At dawn, the sparrows would call, "Get up! Get up!" They couldn't stand it if Inkcap didn't get up, and would peck at the window lattice making a loud clattering noise. When the sun came out, grey magpies and pigeons arrived, along with the old stork from the riverbank. Once, the old stork flew over without landing and dropped a fish into the yard. Inkcap didn't like fish, and the other villagers generally didn't eat it either. He gave it to the cat, which ate it greedily. Inkcap always hoped that the swallows would turn up, but they never did. Apparently, three years ago, some swallows built a nest under the eaves of the courtyard gate and lived there for a spring and a summer. It was Baldy Jin who scared them away. He had told Gran to go to a meeting. She was slow to get up because she had to comb her hair, and he shouted at her too loudly. The swallows never came back. Although Inkcap knew that the old swallows might never return, he wondered why new ones didn't come looking. Was it because they disliked their family's high status, or did they not know that there was already a nest under the eaves of the courtyard gate? He had taken the nest down carefully and inspected it; it was made of straw and mud and was very delicate. He placed the nest on the wall of the courtyard, but the swallows still didn't come. He also tried using string to tie the nest to a branch of the tree in the yard, but the swallows still didn't fly in.

"Swallows build their own nests," Gran said. "They won't bother about that old one."

"The swallows will come," Inkcap insisted.

"OK, OK, the swallows will come."

Gran didn't want Inkcap to be disappointed, so she made a papercut of a swallow and put it in the nest.

That night, she said, "Go to sleep. The swallow will be here in the morning."

Inkcap went to look at the nest early the next morning, but it was still empty. He picked it up and walked down various alleys, then made his way down to the bottom of the embankment outside the village. When he was tired of carrying the nest, he thought of putting it on his head, but it kept falling off. So he made a loop of straw and tied the nest onto his head with that. Then Cowbell came running up. Inkcap wanted to ignore him because he was afraid Cowbell would be too noisy and the swallows wouldn't come.

"I've got something important to tell you. Will you listen? They are going to Luozhen for a meeting. Are you going too?"

"What meeting?" Inkcap asked.

Cowbell told him that Bash, Pockmark and Stonebreaker were going with Huang Shengsheng to attend a Cultural Revolution meeting. He had asked to join them but they didn't want him to, so he was asking if Inkcap wanted to go.

"Of course I want to go, I want to go a lot," Inkcap said. "I'd better go to the shack to find Bash."

"They think I'm too young," Cowbell said. "Do you reckon they'll let you go?"

They talked it over and decided to take the lane from the west end of the village to the road at the foot of Yijia Ridge to wait for Bash and Pockmark's group. Since they'd already be halfway to Luozhen, even if the others didn't want them, they wouldn't have much choice. The two of them made their way to the west end of the village.

"Why do you have a bird's nest on your head?" Cowbell asked.

"I'm trying to attract swallows," Inkcap told him.

"Attract swallows? You don't think a swallow will come if you simply put a nest on your head, do you? Besides, do you really want to have a bird's nest on your head when you get to Luozhen?"

Inkcap looked for a place to hide the nest so he could collect it when he came back from town. While he was looking around, Cowbell mentioned that he was wearing straw sandals and they wouldn't stand up to the long walk to Luozhen. He asked Inkcap to lend him a pair of cloth shoes.

Inkcap refused, so Cowbell said, "You've got Gran to make your shoes and you still won't lend me a pair?"

"Do you think it's easy for Gran to make my shoes?"

"Well, if you won't lend me a pair, I'm not going."

Inkcap was furious. The little bastard didn't really want him to go to Luozhen with him, he just wanted his shoes.

"I'm not going either," Inkcap said and he continued on his way to the west of the village with the swallow's nest on his head.

Inkcap hadn't expected to bump into Tag-Along's wife and son in front of the millstone. He walked over and said, "Ooh, why such tasty food so early in the morning?"

He reached out and pinched some shredded potato from the plate and put it in his mouth. Tag-Along's wife only had one leg and was overweight, but she still managed to leap up.

"Why did it have to be Inkcap?" she exclaimed.

"That's me. What about it, didn't you recognise me?"

He turned to leave but Inkcap's wife pulled him back. He resisted and she tried to snatch the swallow's nest from his head, shouting, "Xianü! Xianü!"

"Xianü?" Inkcap repeated, mulling over the literal meaning of the word. "What blind woman?"

"The child's name is Xianü," Tag-Along's wife explained.

Inkcap looked at Xianü. He was thin and dark-complexioned but had big eyes and round cheeks. He was wearing a floral-patterned dress and had his hair in braids like garlic sprouts. Inkcap knew that there was a custom in the village to dress a sickly boy child as a girl.

All he said was, "Don't touch the swallow's nest."

"You have to stop, you're the child's *ganda* now. Xianü, give your *ganda* a big kowtow."

But Xianü didn't move and asked, "Is he my *ganda*?"

"Of course he's your *ganda*. Whoever you first bump into is your *ganda*. It doesn't matter whether it's Inkcap or a dog or a pig, they're still your *ganda*."

Inkcap had heard his Gran talk about *ganda* but he'd never encountered the custom before. And now, to his surprise, he was one!

"That won't do," he said hurriedly. "I can't be his *ganda*."

"You can, you can. It will help you avoid evil things happening to you."

Inkcap wasn't happy about any of this.

"Just look at me! How can I?"

"You're a fine, healthy *ganda*," Tag-Along's wife said. "Xianü! Kowtow quickly. Give him a big kowtow."

Xianü walked over and lay on the ground, kowtowing to Inkcap.

Inkcap kept on refusing as he turned to look towards the little wooden shack on the highway. Bash was standing in the door with Pockmark and Stonebreaker. It appeared as though Soupspoon was there too. They left the shack and set off. After a while, a truck drove along and they all stood in the middle of the road to stop it. The truck pulled up and they clambered into the back. The truck drove away again.

Inkcap stamped his feet in frustration, crying out, "It's all over! It's all over!"

"It's not all over yet," Tag-Along's wife said. "Your baby kowtowed to you, so sit down and eat some food and drink some wine."

So Inkcap sat on the ground in front of the small table and began to eat and drink. He seemed to be very angry and refused to let Tag-Along's wife and Xianü sit with him. He picked up the plate and put it up his mouth. He quickly finished it off. He tried a couple of sips of wine but couldn't drink it.

"The wine has to be finished," Tag-Along's wife said. "If you get drunk, I'll carry you home."

So Inkcap polished off the wine too.

Inkcap was drunk, but he refused to let Tag-Along's wife give him a piggyback. Instead, Xianü walked in front of him and he walked behind, holding Xianü's shoulders, all the way from the big millstone back to the alley where Tag-Along lived. Tag-Along's wife told the householders in the alley that her family's Xianü had found his *ganda* and from now on he would look after him and Xianü would be strong and live a long life.

"Who is this *ganda*?" Half-Stick asked.

"Inkcap," Tag-Along's wife told her.

Half-Stick bent down, looked at Inkcap and said, "Ah, so this is Xianü's *ganda*!" Then she collapsed to the ground, laughing fit to burst.

"That little fucker Inkcap has all the luck, getting such a fine meal so early in the morning," Baldy Jin complained. "I usually head west of the village first thing to collect manure. So why did I decide to go to the north today? Pah!"

"Even if you had gone to the west first, it wouldn't have made any difference," Sparks said. "Being a kid's *ganda* is a whole heap of trouble. Do you think Tag-Along would have let you in for that?... Hey, Inkcap, what use does Xianü think a little runt like you is going to be as a *ganda*? How can you protect him?"

Inkcap's head was swimming and when he heard what Sparks said, he began to sway and rock back and forward on his heels.

"Even standing on tiptoe, you only came up to the top of your mother's trousers," Baldy Jin said. "She had to set up a stool for you to suck at her tit!"

Inkcap was so angry that he bent back a small poplar tree by the roadside, and let it go so that it snapped back and hit Baldy Jin, knocking his hat off and revealing a head covered in angry red sores.

However, what Inkcap didn't expect was that when he finally turned into Three Fork Alley, supporting himself on Xianü's shoulders, a swallow flew over their heads. While Half-Stick, Baldy Jin and Sparks were rubbishing him, the swallow flew up high, but when they left, it swooped down low again.

Before Inkcap noticed it, Xianü called out, "A swallow!"

Inkcap saw it too. He stopped dead in astonishment and his eyes lit up.
"Swallow! Swallow!" he cried out.

The swallow flew down and settled on the nest. It didn't lie down but stood there calling loudly.

"I want it! I want it!" Xianü shouted, jumping up to try to catch it.

Inkcap used his body to protect the bird and stop the child from getting his hands on it.

"You're his *ganda*," Tag-Along's wife shouted at him, "and you won't even give him a little bird?"

"This is a swallow," Inkcap told her. Then, ignoring both her and the boy, he walked back home, head held high, while the swallow kept calling.

As soon as he got home, he took down the nest and the swallow flew onto the courtyard wall. The bird watched him tie the nest back together under the eaves of the courtyard gate and then flew into it.

"Gran! Gran!" Inkcap shouted. "Look! It's gone in!"

"Who's gone in?" Gran asked from where she was sitting on the *kang* mending clothes.

She pushed open the window and saw the swallow lying in its nest. She was equally astonished and asked, "Where did you catch it?"

"I called it down."

"So you really did use the nest to attract a swallow!"

"I said I could and that's just what I did."

"Look how happy you are!" Gran exclaimed as he ran into the house. "Now, come and thread a needle for me."

But Inkcap couldn't thread the needle.

"What's up with your eyesight all of a sudden?" Gran asked.

"My head's swimming," Inkcap said.

Then he climbed onto the *kang* and fell asleep.

Gran threaded the needle for herself and got on with her mending. When she saw the sky suddenly go dark and rain begin to fall, making the ground outside look like a pockmarked face, she ran to the embankment at the mouth of the alley, where the family's straw pile was stored. She picked up a bundle of wheat straw, afraid it would get too wet to burn in the stove. There were lots of people standing there holding bundles of their own straw, but the rain was too heavy. They couldn't take the straw back home, and all they could do was stand under a tree to shelter from the rain. To everyone's surprise, someone arrived in the village wanting to buy porcelain goods. They had brought a flatbed trolley over to the tree and asked where to buy the porcelain. Some of the people said they'd have to find Bash, but others said that Bash had gone to Luozhen, and they would need to fetch Dazed-And-Confused, who was feeding the cattle. He would probably have the key to the Kiln God Temple.

'Why is Old Kiln paralysed like this?" the prospective purchaser said. "I've brought money to your door and no one can be bothered with it?"

He went over to the cowshed, and soon Dazed-And-Confused could be heard shouting towards Middle Mountain, "Hey, Lightkeeper! Lightkeeper! Oi, Lightkeeper!"

Everyone ignored him and went on talking about how Gourd's family pig had farrowed again. The mother pig was feeding four piglets but had also actually been feeding the little puppy from Stargazer's family. Did it think the puppy was just another piglet? From puppies feeding on sow's milk, they moved on to Inkcap being recognised as Xianü's *ganda*.

"Hey, Granny Silkworm," someone said, "does that mean Xianü's going to call you Great Gran?"

Gran thought that was quite funny, so she laughed and said, "The rain's easing up a bit. Let's go home."

The group dispersed and everything they'd said disappeared with them.

Grandma went back to her room, where Inkcap was still asleep. She woke him up and caught the smell of alcohol on his breath. Her heart gave a lurch and she said, "They're all saying Tag-Along's little boy found his *ganda* today. Is that you they're talking about?"

"Mmm," Inkcap grunted in agreement.

"Good God! Why you?" Gran exclaimed in consternation. "Just so you can bring disaster crashing down on the child?"

"What disaster?"

"Just think about *ganda*, so what's the problem?"

Gran slapped him round the head and said, "That's as may be, but now I've got to put together ten eggs and a *jin* of cotton for you to give the child."

"What do I need to do that for?"

"If you've been chosen as a *ganda*, then there are things you've got to do. Or did you think you just got to eat and drink for free?"

"Well, that's a bit of bad luck, then."

"Don't call it bad luck. If you call it bad luck, that bad luck will rebound on you. Just look at the miserable expression on your face! Goodman gave you a mirror, didn't he? Take a look at yourself."

Inkcap fished the mirror out of his pocket and smiled into it.

"In future," Gran said, "try not to climb too high or sink too low. If someone's having a fight, don't go and watch. Keep your wits about you and behave when you're out and about, don't get rushed or flustered, and make things easy for us."

"Why's that?" Inkcap asked as he got ready to go out with the eggs and cotton.

"Xianü isn't a very healthy child," Gran replied. "Now you've been chosen as his *ganda*, you have to take on his misfortunes and illnesses."

"Then I won't be his *ganda*," Inkcap declared, and he didn't take the eggs and cotton over to Tag-Along's house.

In the end, it was his resentment at not being able to go to Luozhen that had caused all this.

THIRTY-ONE

Bash and the others stayed in Luozhen for almost the whole day because Chairman Mao issued new instructions in Beijing, and the township organised a celebration rally of thirty to forty thousand people. Firecrackers exploded, gongs and drums were beaten, and red flags were waved. The men from Old Kiln had never seen or experienced a celebration on this scale before. It was all too easy for them to get swept up in such a huge event and they just followed the crowd and kept on going, yelling and jumping up and down, too carried away to stop.

"Have you gone crazy?" Huang Shengsheng asked.

"Yes! We're crazy! Crazy!" Bash said.

Stonebreaker, Pockmark and Soupspoon all joined in yelling, "Crazy! Crazy!"

But they soon began to feel rather embarrassed, and Bash said, "Ai! What's come over us?"

"You must have revolution in your blood to get so excited," Huang Shengsheng said.

"When I saw the students in the Great Link-Up on the highway," Stonebreaker said, "I thought all this stuff was far beyond my horizons. I never thought I would find the Great Cultural Revolution here, right next to me."

By now, Bash was regretting that he hadn't brought even more people from Old Kiln to join in the event.

After the great assembly was over, they had originally intended to go straight back to Old Kiln, but Huang Shengsheng wanted to take Bash to meet someone. Bash told the others to go back into town and have a look around. They could meet up at sundown at the top of North Street. Bash followed Huang Shengsheng to a large courtyard facing the street where they encountered a man somewhat older than them, wearing a four-pocket jacket. He appeared to be a state cadre and was directing a group of locals to burn things in the courtyard. What they were burning was a vast pile of old books and paintings, standing screens with brocade curtains, wooden caskets, instrument boxes, top hats, old photos, decorative hat boxes, shadow puppets, dragon robes and dragon-embroidered stage boots, phoenix crowns and rainbow cloaks. The fire was so strong that no one could get close.

"Does everything here get burned?" Bash asked.

"They're smashing the Four Olds and establishing the Four News," Huang Shengsheng explained.

He took Bash over to meet the older man. As soon as the fellow saw Bash, he went over and took off Bash's sunglasses, saying, "Why are you still wearing these?"

Bash was taken aback.

"They're just sunglasses," he replied.

"I know they're sunglasses," the man said. "Only the bourgeoisie wears such things."

This was the first time Bash had met someone who dared remove his sunglasses. He looked at the man and the man looked at him. Huang Shengsheng thought Bash was going to start a fight, so he hurried over to intervene, but Bash threw his sunglasses onto the fire and was even about to add the torch tied to his belt. The man stopped him, saying that the torch wasn't capitalist, so he could keep it to light the way.

"What's your name?" the man asked.

"My name is Bash Hei."

The man reached out his hand and said, "We are comrades in arms."

However, Bash still didn't know the man's name as Huang Shengsheng had only introduced him as coming from the county and having recently been to Beijing. When Huang and the man started talking off to one side, Bash still felt a bit intimidated and didn't approach them. Huang Shengsheng seemed to be enquiring about the situation in Beijing. The man was saying that the Cultural Revolution had entered a new stage, and the proletarian command had shattered the bourgeois command. Bash wondered if there were two headquarters in Beijing. Looking up at the man, he found that the man was also looking at him, so he dropped his gaze and flipped through a book that was as thick as a brick. He recognised it as a copy of the Kangxi Dictionary and threw it onto the fire. After around the time it takes to smoke three pipes of tobacco, Huang Shengsheng came over and led Bash out of the courtyard. Bash asked what they had discussed, and Huang Shengsheng said he had learned about the revolutionary situation in Beijing.

"How can Beijing have two command centres?" Bash asked.

"Ah, yes," Huang Shengsheng said. "One is the proletarian headquarters, led by Chairman Mao who is our great leader and commander. The other is the bourgeois headquarters led by Liu Shaoqi. For a long time, Liu Shaoqi isolated and undermined Chairman Mao and controlled the central government. That's why Chairman Mao launched the Cultural Revolution to regain power."

"Can Chairman Mao still regain power?" Bash asked.

"He definitely will seize it back."

"So why did you still launch the Cultural Revolution?"

What did he just say? Huang Shengsheng was so stunned, he took the hat off his head and put it back on again.

"I can't explain the affairs of the Party Central Committee clearly, nor can anyone here. You don't need to understand, all you need to do is remember that Chairman Mao is our great leader and commander-in-chief. Chairman Mao asked us to carry out the Cultural Revolution, and we will carry it out. Don't you like movements?"

"I love movements," Bash said.

As the two of them chatted, an old man came over and bowed to them.

"'What do you think you are doing?" Huang Shengsheng said. "What do you think you are doing?"

"Please spare something for me. Please spare something."

He was just a beggar. Huang Shengsheng stamped his feet and roared, driving the old man away.

Stonebreaker and the others wandered the streets for a while, then Pockmark went off on his own. He ate a bowl of *hele* buckwheat noodles in a restaurant before going to the police station to find Director Wang. Director Wang greeted him warmly as an old acquaintance and wanted to buy him a drink. Of course, Pockmark couldn't let Director Wang spend money on him, so he went out onto the street to buy the wine himself and he bumped into Stonebreaker again. Stonebreaker and Soupspoon had also separated, Stonebreaker having gone off in search of a cold fern root noodle stall, but he had turned down two streets with no luck so far. The noodles in a restaurant cost eight cents a bowl, and he only had five cents. There was an outdoor wok stove set up at the entrance to the restaurant with three bowls of unsold noodles on it. They had been there for such a long time that the noodles on top had gone hard. He closed his eyes and walked away quickly. But after walking for a hundred metres or so, he couldn't help but go back. He passed by the door of the restaurant and looked inside again. The noodles there were adorned with chopped spring onions. Just as he turned to leave, he saw Pockmark coming over with a bottle of wine.

"What are you doing here?" Pockmark asked.

"Nothing," Stonebreaker said. "You've bought some wine!"

"You're right," Pockmark said. "I got invited for food and wine, but I kept refusing. Director Wang wasn't having any of that, and in the end he took out some money and told me to go out and buy some wine."

"I didn't know you were so tight with Director Wang."

"I don't want to boast, but even the Branch Secretary isn't as close to him as I am. Where's Bash?"

"He's with Huang Shengsheng's mates. It seems they want him to join their combat unit."

"So is Bash a revolutionary, then?" Pockmark said. "Do you think he's being suckered in by Huang Shengsheng?"

"Do you think someone like Bash would fall for that?"

"I can't figure it out. Why has Bash gone so overboard with Huang Shengsheng? When I went to Director Wang's place, he gave me food and wine. What has Huang Shengsheng bought for you? Not even a bowl of water, I bet."

"No, you're right."

"See? You need to work out who your friends are," Pockmark observed, taking the wine away with him.

Pockmark and Director Wang drank half the bottle, and both of them were a little drunk. Pockmark took off his shoes, rolled up his trouser legs and knelt on his stool. He picked up his wine cup and addressed Director Wang but he didn't call him "Director" any more.

"Drink up, Brother Wang. Drink up."

"I'm the director and I'm still at work. I don't dare drink any more. You drink instead."

"You said it, you're the director, so who are you afraid of? Drink up, Brother Wang!"

Director Wang drank half a cup, and Pockmark drained a whole cup. He even turned the cup to demonstrate there wasn't any left.

"You've got a better head for drink than me," Director Wang said. "That's my lot. I'll get drunk if I have any more."

"If you get drunk, you get drunk."

Pockmark groped at some radishes in the bamboo basket next to him. There were several in the basket, so they gnawed away at them while they drank. When the radishes were almost all gone, Pockmark reached into a cardboard box next to the radish basket and took out an egg.

"There aren't any radishes left. I'm going to have an egg."

"My wife's about to go into confinement. I just bought those eggs to take home this evening," Director Wang said.

"Brother Wang! Are you telling your brother he can't have an egg?" Pockmark exclaimed.

"No, go ahead. Go ahead."

"Brother Wang is too kind. I don't mind if I do."

Pockmark picked up the egg, but he lost his grip and it fell to the ground and smashed. He bent down to pick up the egg, but he couldn't get hold of the yolk and white. There were threads of raw egg dripping from his hands. He sucked at every finger and said, "The case still hasn't made any progress, has it, Brother Wang? It's nothing to do with me, is it? It's those three useless fucking officers from the police station. They can't even solve a simple case like this."

"Stop talking nonsense," Director Wang said. "You've had too much to drink."

"Didn't you all just bugger off, then?"

"Them leaving the village doesn't mean the case is dropped."

Pockmark laughed. "Ha ha, Brother Wang is just trying to save face. The case has been dropped, why not just leave it at that?"

Director Wang was growing a little impatient. "You don't understand anything about solving a case. If the case seems to have been dropped, it will lull the culprit into a false sense of security."

"Ah! So dropping the case is just a ruse, then. Have you found any clues?"

"Yes," Director Wang said smoothly.

Pockmark stopped drinking, looked at Director Wang, got up and closed the door, then closed the window. "Take my advice, Brother Wang," he said, "and don't investigate any further. There's no point. I can tell you it was me."

"What? You're drunk. You're drunk."

"I'm not drunk. I did it," Pockmark insisted.

"How could you have done it?" Director Wang said. "Who's going to believe you? How did you do it?"

"Just think about it. Who would have wanted to harm Happy? The real target was Millstone. Old Kiln has to choose a new team captain. Originally, the job was mine, but then Millstone came along halfway through. I'd been using rat poison that day and as I passed by the kitchen window of his house, I saw the noodles on the chopping board inside, so I put some poison on them. Who could have known it would do for Happy?

That rat poison had been sitting in a corner of my house for a year. I've never seen it kill any rats. I didn't think it was any good. At most, it might make someone feel ill and throw up. Who knew…"

Director Wang's heart skipped a beat. He dashed to get the hot water bottle from the table and said, "Drink some of this. No, wait a minute, I'll make you a cup of tea."

"I don't want a drink, but if you insist, I'll have cold water. Brother Wang, just tell your superiors that you can't discover the culprit, then the case will be dropped completely."

Director Wang sat back and said, "Well, Brother, since you've told me, what is there to investigate any more, anyway? Drink up, Brother Wang. I'll have a drink with you."

Pockmark clinked his glass too hard and half the wine spilled out. He drank what was left in the glass. Then he put his head down, stuck out his tongue and lapped up the spilled wine from the table.

"You can insult anything you like," he said, "but you mustn't insult good wine."

"Yes, yes, absolutely," Director Wang agreed.

He poured another glass for Pockmark and got him to drink it up, then said he'd be back as soon as he'd been to the privy. He looked for some paper on the bed, and when he couldn't find any, he tore a page off a calendar on the wall and went out of the door of the living quarters.

He went straight to the police station and told the guard to shut the gate and lock it. He also ordered three policemen to guard the walls of the east and west courtyards. Then he called the leaders of the County Public Security Bureau to report that the poisoning and murder case had been solved. The culprit was at the Luozhen Police Station, so he should be arrested immediately and interrogated. Finally, he requested to be transferred, saying that he had been in Luozhen long enough. Once the case was solved, too many acquaintances were involved, and it would be difficult to carry out any work in the future. He hoped to be transferred to another police station as soon as possible. Then he went back to the living quarters where he found Pockmark lying on the table. There was filthy vomit all over the floor under the table.

"Oh, brother," Director Wang said.

Pockmark was asleep, so he went over and loosened Pockmark's belt. Then he sat down, poured himself a glass of wine and drank it.

Bash and the others waited ages for Pockmark at the street corner, but there was no sign of him. Stonebreaker said that Pockmark had gone to the police station to have a drink with Director Wang. Bash was jealous and refused to wait any longer.

"What the fuck," he said. "We all came together, but he went off to curry favour with Director Wang!"

It was almost evening by the time they got back to the little wooden shack. The Zhen River Pagoda was full of water birds, and the fish in the river were calling their names again. In the village far away, the tiled roofs showed through the green of the trees. Here they were dark grey, there they were flat, here again they were slanted, staggered and scattered, and there, order was restored. Ah! The chimneys were all giving off smoke. The strands of smoke stretched upwards like birch trees among the elms, willows, locust trees and toons until they had enveloped them all, and the whole village seemed once again to be wrapped in clouds. Perhaps it was because the smoke made them feel hungry and then they thought how good it would be to have soup noodles when they got home, that Stonebreaker suddenly declared that his mother's noodles were the best in the world and Soupspoon said that was impossible because his mother's were the best! Huang Shengsheng sniggered at their arguing.

"That bugger Useless didn't come with us," Bash reflected. "Let's get him to recite a Tang poem."

Huang Shengsheng was intrigued by Bash mentioning Tang poetry and asked, "So you like poetry, do you?"

"Yes, I do. Just look at the scenery of Old Kiln, it's like something from a Tang poem. And listen. There's a cock crowing too."

Sure enough, one long crow was followed by lots of shorter ones, sharp and loud, with the dogs joining in as well. The rough, short noises spat at each other until the mooing of a cow joined in. It was low and deep, and it drowned out the cocks' crowing and the dogs' barking. Coincidentally, the thick grey clouds on Yijia Ridge chose that moment to split open, releasing a red glow that spread all over and shone directly on Middle Mountain. The white pine on the top of the mountain had been transformed into a red pine.

"Beautiful," Bash said. "Look how beautiful it is. I always used to say that the mountains and rivers of our ancestral land were beautiful, except for Xiahewan and Old Kiln. I never thought our village could be so lovely."

Huang Shengsheng looked disdainfully at the scenery and said, "What's so beautiful about this? The Revolution is beautiful."

"Yes, the Revolution will be more beautiful."

As Bash and Huang Shengsheng stood on the highway sighing, Lightkeeper came down from the foggy Middle Mountain. He had got the porcelain buyer to purchase six newly fired urns at the kiln site and he was now taking the proceeds, carefully tucked inside his jacket, to hand over to Potful. He knew that Potful was seriously ill and had already resigned as team captain, but he still insisted on giving the money to him rather than to the Branch Secretary or Bash. Potful had bullied him, held him back and generally mistreated him when he was captain and now he wanted the chance to gloat over Potful's misfortune. After the rain, the road surface in the alley had already dried out, but the dirt track up at the kiln site was still muddy. He wore his old high-top rubber tube shoes, and the mud had stuck to them in two big clumps. He didn't bother scraping them off and went straight into the courtyard of Potful's house.

The yard was silent, and a chicken was sleeping in each of the doorways to the main room and the kitchen.

"Captain! Captain!" Lightkeeper shouted.

"What are you shouting about?" said Apricot, emerging from the kitchen.

"I'm looking for the captain."

"Don't you know he's really ill and hasn't been captain for ages?"

"But Uncle Potful has been captain for more than ten years, how can he not be the captain? Won't the sky fall in?"

"I told you all about it, didn't I? Anyway, what's the big deal now?"

"I heard that the captain is sick. What's wrong with him? I need to see for myself."

Apricot looked down and said, "Thank you for your kindness. He's just gone to sleep, so now's not a good time."

"Aren't I good enough to see him, then?"

"How can you say that?"

But then Potful's voice was heard from inside the house: "Let him come in. Let him come in."

Apricot led Lightkeeper to the main room and opened the door. The room was in darkness. As soon as he stepped across the threshold, Lightkeeper stumbled and almost fell.

"Your feet are covered in mud and you didn't even wipe them," Apricot complained.

High steps led up to all the houses in Old Kiln, but the thresholds were very low. When building a property, the householders always made sure that the threshold was low because they believed it would accumulate wealth and good fortune for them. Although every householder wiped the mud and dirt off their shoes when they went in, it built up into a small mound which they never shovelled away because it represented a mound of blessings.

"Oh, look how high your mound of blessings is!" Lightkeeper said.

Apricot didn't respond but pulled back the door curtain of the small room on the left side of the house. Inside was a large *kang*, on which Potful was lying. A lit kerosene lamp was attached to the wall at the head of the *kang*, and a stick of firewood was leaning against the wall under the lamp. When Potful got sick of lying there for so long, he would use a knife to scrape wood shavings off the stick and light some home-cured tobacco on the top of the lamp. As soon as Lightkeeper came in, Potful tried his best to get up, but he couldn't manage it, so he simply lay back and said, "It's about time you came, Lightkeeper."

"I didn't believe it when people told me you were ill. How can a man who could kill a tiger be sick?"

"That's exactly why you should have come. To have a good laugh at Potful reduced to this state."

With that, he turned away to face the wall.

"Ah, yes, well, ah, someone came to buy porcelain today. Normally Bash would have taken care of it, but he'd disappeared without trace. So I did the business and I've brought the proceeds to hand them over to you."

Potful stayed facing the wall and didn't reply. Lightkeeper put the money on the edge of the *kang*, saying, "That Bash fellow is so unreliable."

"That's enough," said Apricot. "How much more torture do you want to inflict?"

She picked up the money, stuffed it into Lightkeeper's hands and pushed him out of the door.

As Lightkeeper emerged from the house and was halfway out of the courtyard, he heard Potful cursing him from the *kang*: "Lightkeeper! Lightkeeper! You really are a class enemy. You want me to die but I'm not going to die. I won't die!"

"Hey, Apricot, your dad's still in good voice, then."

Apricot slammed the courtyard door on him with a crash.

Lightkeeper walked along the alley, coughing loudly until he finally hawked up a large blob of phlegm. He was thinking of going to Barndoor's place to get some pepper leaves so he could go home and make a pepper leaf pancake to eat that evening. There was a small hole in the sole of one of his rubber tube shoes, and water had seeped in that afternoon. The sticky mud on the sole had dried out and rubbed off, but the water was making a loud sloshing noise in the shoe when he walked. He felt there was a kind of rhythm to the noise, so he marched in step as he made his way to the field in front of Barndoor's house. There he found that Noisy had turned up, pushing his bicycle, and was talking to Flower Girl at the courtyard gate.

"No," Flower Girl was saying, "I don't want to. Besides, Barndoor isn't here, so I can't. Anyway, I'm not going to eat that disgusting thing."

Noisy was holding something wrapped in castor leaves, which, when he unwrapped it, turned out to be a testicle from a gelded pig.

"You sure you don't want it?" Noisy asked. "It's really delicious. And even if you don't want to eat it, you can make a thong out of it for a pounding stick. It's really strong. I brought it all this way specially for you."

"Do you want to stay and eat?" Flower girl asked Noisy. "My sister and her baby are inside. Why don't you come in and sit down?"

"I won't go in," Noisy said, "but don't leave just yet. Come over here for a moment."

Flower Girl was already halfway through the courtyard gate, but she turned, pursed her lips and gave a little squeak.

Lightkeeper had heard that Flower Girl and Noisy were on good terms with each other, but he hadn't expected them to be quite so friendly. He dashed behind an elm tree at the side of the field, sucked up a mouthful of saliva and spat twice in disgust. He changed his mind about going to beg some pepper leaves off Flower Girl and turned to make his way to his private plot to pick some spring onion leaves instead.

He actually had two private plots, one on the river strand beside the highway, and the other on the rear slope. But before he'd got anywhere, Bash shouted to him from the door of his shack: "Hey, Lightkeeper! Come over here."

Lightkeeper looked at Bash without moving.

"I'm talking to you," Bash said.

"What's the matter?" Lightkeeper asked.

"What's the matter? Does there have to be something the matter for me to call you?"

"I expect you're going to criticise me, aren't you?"

"What's with the attitude if you know you're going to be criticised anyway?"

"I haven't done anything wrong. Do you really want to criticise me? If so, you'll have to do it at a meeting. I won't accept anyone's criticism except at a meeting."

"Well, that's some big talk, Lightkeeper!"

Lightkeeper was unable to respond, his thoughts were all over the place.

"Given what you have to say for yourself, Lightkeeper, let me tell you, the Cultural Revolution has already begun."

"What Cultural Revolution?"

"It means revolution. It means the dictatorship of the proletariat. It means movement—"

"Haven't I been hearing the same thing for decades?"

"It's different this time. This time it's culture at the forefront. You come from an educated family, don't you? Early tomorrow morning, you should take the initiative to hand over all the old books, paintings and antiques in your family at the old stone gate, otherwise you'll become the target of the Revolution."

"If I have to hand them over, I will. After all, a dead pig is no longer afraid of being scalded by boiling water."

"That's fine, then. Off you go."

But Lightkeeper didn't leave. He said he had sold some porcelain and asked if he should give the money to Bash or the Branch Secretary.

"Leave it with me, of course," Bash said.

Lightkeeper took out the roll of notes, licked his fingers, counted it and handed it to Bash, saying, "Count it yourself too."

But Bash didn't count the money and just put it in his pocket.

"Give me a receipt."

"Don't be so bloody-minded. No wonder you get criticised."

Bash wouldn't give him a receipt but Lightkeeper kept insisting on one. Bash cursed him for not knowing when to quit and told him to fuck off.

Lightkeeper took the cursing and left. He was no longer in any mood to pick spring onions, let alone go home and make pancakes. It was already dark as he made his way back to the village but, as he passed Bash's old lodgings, he saw that the walls were half collapsed and that a piece of cow hair felt was covering the eaves and rafters. He hated the weather for not raining harder so the whole place would collapse. If Bash was not a poor lower-middle peasant, and if he, Lightkeeper, was not from a landlord background, then Bash wouldn't be so arrogant towards everyone and he wouldn't be getting in his face. He could feel the hate inside him; he hated his father and he hated himself.

"Wah! Wah! Wah!" he moaned. "What a fucking life."

A goose belonging to Six Pints' family was standing next to him. Six Pints' cousin had come from Dongchuangou to visit him when he was ill.

He didn't have anything to give as a gift, so he brought a goose. It happened to be the only goose in Old Kiln. Six Pints didn't slaughter the goose so it was left to wander the village, its white feathers dirty and soiled. It was waddling back home, swaying its backside, when it heard Lightkeeper saying, "Wah! Wah Wah!"

"Do you speak goose?" it asked.

Of course, Lightkeeper didn't understand and just kept his head down, repeating, "What a fucking life."

The goose didn't know that Lightkeeper was talking about his own life, so it pecked him on the arse.

THIRTY-TWO

IT WAS STILL DARK WHEN INKCAP WOKE UP and realised that he had drunk too much wine. For him, drinking too much wine did not mean he fell into a drugged sleep and failed to wake up, but that he went to sleep for a while and then woke up, muzzy-headed. He fell asleep again, and woke up again. When he got dressed and went to stand in the courtyard, he saw more than a dozen stars in the sky shining like sparks and falling towards the top of Middle Mountain. He suddenly remembered something and looked at the nest under the eaves of the courtyard gate. The swallow was still asleep.

"Get up," Inkcap said. "I'm already up, so why aren't you?"

A little swallow's head poked out of the nest and said, "Oh!"

Then it went back to sleep. Inkcap was going to call out to it again, but he saw that the rope he had used to tie the nest on the eaves was covered in mud, and the walls of the nest seemed to be much taller than yesterday. He realised that the swallow had been working all night, so he kept quiet and sat down inside the gate. A gust of wind blew in through the doorway, snapping at the spinning wheel that stood there like a whip. Inkcap shouted for Gran but there was no reply. Then he vaguely remembered that Gran had said she wanted to grind some beans for flour. Had she gone off to the millstone early?

In addition to the big millstone at the east end of the village, there were also two smaller ones. One was in the field outside the gable wall of Almost-There's house, and the other was in Three Fork Alley. So as not to delay the work of the production team, the villagers always found spare moments to grind grain, so the millstones were constantly in use. The night before, Gran had wanted to grind some beans for flour, but the two rollers were being used with another two households waiting to use them ahead of her. So she had got up that morning before first light and had shaken the sleeping Inkcap on her way out, to try to make him get up.

"What for?" he had asked blearily.

"To push the millstone, of course."

"What for?"

"That's a pissing stupid question. What d'you think you'll eat if you don't?"

There was no job Inkcap hated more than pushing the roller. Moreover, when Gran was doing the milling, every time he thought they'd finished, she'd want another go, then another and another until the bran was so fine you could blow it off your hand with one puff. Even then she wanted another turn of the millstone or push of the roller. There had never been a single occasion when Inkcap hadn't snapped back at Gran during the milling or grinding process. When Gran saw that he wasn't going to wake up properly, she told him that she would go on ahead and he should join her as soon as he was up. He just grunted in reply and went back to sleep.

Now, Inkcap looked at the swallow in the nest and said, "It's all right for you, sleeping there. I've got to go and push a bloody roller."

But then he saw Gran walking back. Her hair was only loosely tied in a bun and a lock fell behind her left ear. She closed the gate as soon as she entered the courtyard.

"I think I must be seeing things," Gran said.

"What's the matter?"

"Why are a bunch of people pushing over the stone lion at the south entrance of the village?"

"Pushing over the stone lion? Who'd dare push over a sodding great thing like that?"

"I saw them quite clearly. It's already toppled right over. Bash smashed the ball in the lion's mouth too."

"I'll take a look."

Gran grabbed hold of him and said, "Be a good boy and just stay in the courtyard. With all those others going around the village destroying things, do you want to add your name to the charge sheet?"

Grandmother and grandson were sitting in the courtyard, watching the sky gradually clear. They vaguely heard the sound of some smashing, but they couldn't figure out what it was. Inkcap knew that Bash had gone to town yesterday. Why did he push the stone lion over when he came back? Who was he arguing with now? And even if he was arguing with someone, there was no point in pushing over the stone lion, was there? Inkcap promised Gran that he wouldn't go out, but that didn't stop him from setting up a ladder to climb up to the roof. From the roof, he could see what was going on outside. Just as he got the ladder up to the eaves, there was a loud knock on the courtyard gate. Gran waved Inkcap down from the ladder and sent him inside to lie down on the *kang*. Only then did she open the gate and Third Aunt came in.

"Have you been out yet, Granny Silkworm?" Third Aunt asked.

"I've only just got up and I haven't even combed my hair yet. What's going on?"

"Bash has gone crazy."

"I know Yoyo has epilepsy, but I've never heard Bash have any kind of madness."

"He and a bunch of others were out early and pasted a piece of white paper on the mountain gate. Is Old Kiln going into mourning? The stone lion at the entrance of the village has had its mouth smashed in, all the carvings of people and horses on the mountain gate have had their heads knocked off, and now they're going from house to house collecting anything old and saying they're going to burn them all under the mountain gate. That fucker Bash has gone crazy. He's turned into a bandit."

"Is that really happening? What about the Branch Secretary? Is he still asleep?"

"I don't know."

When Third Aunt had finished talking, she left. Gran stood in the yard feeling flustered, but she didn't dare go out. She was also afraid that Inkcap would go too, so in the end she didn't go off to grind any beans. She pricked up her ears, listening out carefully for anyone shouting for the production team to go to work, but no one did, so she stayed in the gateway and started spinning.

The thread wasn't fine enough, it was bobbly and it kept breaking. She just about managed to spin a ball of yarn and then the village dogs started to bark, a non-stop barrage of short, sharp yaps. But none of the dogs came into the alley in front of her house, so she opened the door just as Dazed-And-Confused walked past carrying a ladder. The ladder was too long, and he knocked down a tile from the courtyard wall when he shifted it from one shoulder to the other.

"Watch what you're doing," Gran said.

"Are you still spinning?" Dazed-And-Confused asked. "What are you spinning for? Why haven't you gone out to see the fun?"

Gran pretended not to know what he was talking about and said, "Why are you carting a ladder around this early?"

Dazed-And-Confused chuckled and said, "I'm setting a ladder up to the sky! That fuckwit Feng Youliang is always joking that there's nothing in my house except stuff for making straw sandals. Well, he's an old middle peasant, isn't he? He's got lots of stuff in his house, and now I'm going to find out just how much."

By now he had already walked past Gran, but he turned around and asked, "Have you handed in your Four Olds yet?"

"What are they?"

"Everything from the old society is part of the Four Olds. You need to hand it all in."

"Why would I have anything from the old society? I came out of the old society myself–"

"I know you were criticised ages ago. What I'm talking about now is things that were used in the old days, like land deeds, account books, that kind of thing."

Gran suddenly turned pale and said, "Don't you dare try and set me up, Dazed-And-Confused. People are going to go to jail and be executed over this kind of stuff. Stop trying to scare me."

"I'm not trying to scare you, I just wanted to ask if you had anything you wanted me to take away. Otherwise, someone might come to search the house."

"I really don't have anything."

"Really? Think carefully. There must be some old things."

"This house is an old house, and this tree is an old tree. Oh, and this laundry stone is old too. Take it away."

Dazed-And-Confused put down his ladder and went in to fetch the laundry stone. Gran was trembling all over. He was a big, strong fellow and he bent down and picked up the stone and walked heavily out of the courtyard with it.

"Mind you don't crush your feet," Gran called out in alarm.

In fact, Dazed-And-Confused didn't have a firm grip on the stone and it slipped out of his hands. Fortunately, it missed his feet, but it did make a big dent in the ground in the courtyard.

"Just this stone, then?" Dazed-And-Confused asked.

"Why have you come here so early to take my stuff away, Dazed-And-Confused?" Gran asked.

"Bash and the others haven't been here yet, so why shouldn't I break some Four Olds for them? Why shouldn't I, eh? I'm a poor peasant, from three generations of poor peasants, so why shouldn't I go to the house of one of the Four Bad Elements and help smash the Four Olds?"

Gran pursed her lips, straightened her back and gave a big sigh.

"Ping'an! Ping'an!" she called out. "Take Uncle Dazed-And-Confused inside. See what Four Olds you can find and let him take them away."

But no sound came from inside the house. Gran shouted again, "Ping'an! Are you deaf? Ping'an!"

Still no reply. Gran went into the house. There was no sign of Inkcap on the *kang*. The window in the back wall of the house was open, and Inkcap must have climbed out of it at some point.

Dazed-And-Confused followed her in.

"Inkcap's not here. You tricked me in here saying he was. Don't think you can mess me around because I'm not Bash."

"Forget about just the people in this village, I respect every wooden stake here! I have no idea where Inkcap's got to. Do you think I'm trying to trick you? Look for yourself. Take what you want."

Dazed-And-Confused looked around the house. There were three rooms in total, the main one and two smaller side rooms to the east and west. In the east one was the *kang* where the grandmother and her grandson slept. The *kang* took up half of the space. At the end of the kang was a wooden shelf with a white wooden box on it. It was covered in tattered bedding. There was a brazier in front of the *kang* which was lit in winter to keep them warm and taken out in summer. The hole in the middle of the brazier stand had a wooden cover to turn it into a low table. There was a piss bucket in the corner, which hadn't been emptied. Coming out of the east room, there was a loom in the middle of the main room, and three pottery storage vats in the corner that held more tattered cotton covers and bran. Wooden pegs were fixed to the wall above the urns, hanging from which was a hoe, a dustpan, a sieve, a domed wicker cover, a flail, a noodle-sifting basket, and two finely woven baskets and one coarse one. A wooden cabinet stood against the north wall, which held food and clothing. In the middle of the cabinet top, there was a folding table screen.

Its glass was engraved with plum blossoms, orchids, bamboo and chrysanthemums and inside, there was a paper plaque with the words "In honour of our deceased father and deceased mother" written on it. Above the screen, a portrait of Chairman Mao was pasted to the wall. One corner had peeled away and was pinned back with a needle. While Dazed-and-Confused was still looking around, Gran sat on the edge of the *kang* in the side room. A thick layer of papercuts was stored underneath the *kang* mat, and she was worried that Dazed-And-Confused would take them out and trample on them. She shifted her buttocks to sit more firmly on the mat, then saw that the ties on her trouser legs were loose. When she bent over to retie them, she folded over her waistband and found a louse. She picked it out and squeezed it. Then she turned to Dazed-And-Confused.

"You're a poor peasant," she said. "Take a good look at this home of one of the Four Bad Elements, and tell me what things are Four Olds."

"Are there any old books or paintings?"

"I made the papercuts in the windows three years ago. Do they count as old paintings?"

Dazed-And-Confused went over and poked at a windowpane.

"Do you have any old clothes? Inkcap's father was a puppet soldier. Do you have any Kuomintang uniforms?"

"Do you really not know, or are you just playing dumb? We haven't seen hide nor hair of Ping'an's father since he joined the army. It was only seven years later that we found out he had gone to Taiwan. So what military uniforms are you talking about?"

"So I'm not even allowed to ask, am I? Are you going to have the same attitude when the Branch Secretary comes?"

"Well, go on and take a look for yourself."

Dazed-And-Confused rummaged through the porcelain jars on either side of the cabinet top. They were filled with various types of beans and salted chillis. He found a pack of *liguo* candy in another porcelain jar and asked, "What's this, then?"

"Don't you know *liguo* candy when you see it? I sold my hair and bought it for my little boy. Go on, try some, if you're not afraid it's poisoned."

"I will, then," Dazed-And-Confused said, taking a piece and popping it in his mouth.

"This is a Four Old," he said, picking up the screen. He tucked it under his arm and made to leave the house. Grandma hurled herself after him saying it was an ancestor tablet and who didn't have an ancestor tablet? Why was he taking it away?

"Who has an ancestor tablet in an old screen like this?" Dazed-And-Confused asked.

"You little bastard. You've fucked off, haven't you? Where have you fucked off to?"

Dazed-And-Confused turned around.

"Are you cursing me?" he asked.

"I'm cursing my grandson. Ping'an! Ping'an! Where the fuck are you, you wretched child?"

While Gran was spinning in the gateway, Inkcap had slipped out through the back window. There was no one at the southern entrance of the village. The stone lion had indeed been pushed over, half of its upper jaw was smashed off, and the ball was missing from inside its mouth. He ran to the mountain gate where all the carvings of people and horses had their heads knocked off and a piece of white paper had been pasted up. There were characters, big and little, written on the paper. A small crowd had gathered at the site, comprising Bash, Stonebreaker, Huang Shengsheng, Baldy Jin, Tag-Along and Lucky. Their hair was messed up and their eyes were red, as if they hadn't slept all night.

Bash was giving instructions on how to assemble a ladder and when Tag-Along had finished doing so, he stretched out his hand to Stonebreaker and said, "Look at my hand! Just look at my hand! This hand has stayed up all night and it's turned into a chicken claw. Where's all the flesh? Where's all the flesh gone?"

"I haven't dozed off once," Stonebreaker said. "I've been working on the Revolution for three days and three nights."

Bash climbed up the ladder and pasted another sheet of white paper at the top of the mountain gate. Useless, who happened to be around too, looked up and shouted, "Wrong. That's wrong."

Bash held up a brush dipped in paste and asked, "'What's wrong?"

"The fifth character in the third line is wrong."

The paste dripped down from the brush and into Bash's sleeve. He gave his arm a shake and said, "What exactly is it that's wrong? Oops!"

He had shaken the paste straight into Useless's face. Useless gave a little scream and rubbed at it. He turned around to Inkcap, who was standing right next to him and said, "It's wrong, isn't it? The traditional character has a left falling stroke but the simplified form doesn't, does it?"

"What kind of characters are they on the paper?" Inkcap asked.

"Black ones," Useless replied and then ignored Inkcap.

A fire was lit under the big medicine tree in front of the mountain gate. Huang Shengsheng and Iron Bolt were tearing up old books and paintings collected from many different houses and throwing them onto the fire, while at the same time directing Cowbell to climb to the top corner of the mountain gate with a hammer to smash the relief carvings up there.

"I'll give you a chance too," Huang Shengsheng said to Inkcap. "Go up there and smash 'Wang Xiang Lies on the Ice' and 'Guo Ju Buries his Child'."

Inkcap had heard about Wang Xiang and Guo Ju in the classic text *The Twenty-Four Paragons of Filial Piety*, but he didn't know that the words were carved on the mountain gate.

"I can't climb up there," Inkcap said.

"Of course you can't. The only thing you can do is eat!" Baldy Jin said. "Come here and tend the fire. Come and tend the fire."

So Inkcap went and tended the fire.

Inkcap picked up a stick to try to separate the objects in the fire so they would burn completely. He saw a painting that had already burned to white ash, but the white ash still showed the picture intact. Wow! It was a painting of Old Kiln, complete with Mount Yang, Yijia Ridge and the beacon tower. The basin of land it stood in was very round, with Middle Mountain in the centre and a cluster of houses at the base of the mountain. Inkcap wanted to find his own house but couldn't. Bash pasted the last piece of white paper and came over to stir the fire.

"Let me have a go at it," he said. "What are you looking at?"

"I can see what this painting was of."

Soupspoon, who was squatting at the base of the tree, said, "That's the illustrated map of Old Kiln I handed in, along with the 'Eight Landscapes' paintings."

"What about the Eight Landscapes?" Bash asked.

"I've already told Baldy Jin, my dad put those pictures up on the roof beams with his own hands. When I took them down, all eight had been gnawed by mice until they were a total mess. Only this one was left in decent condition."

Bash threw a book onto the fire with great force, causing a gust of air that made the beautiful white image of Old Kiln expand and fly up, but as it did so, the colour changed, turning it into a cloud of black butterflies taking wing.

Lightkeeper was clutching a pile of books and carrying a pair of large wood frame lanterns. He stood there and asked, "Who's keeping the register?"

"What register?" Useless asked. "Do you want someone to write you a receipt?"

"That's not what I mean. I mean that I'm handing these things in now and I don't want anyone saying, later on, that I didn't hand anything in."

"You can never trust these poor, lower-middle peasants," Useless said.

He took the books and looked at them one by one, reading out their titles.

"*The Romance of the Three Kingdoms.*" That got thrown on the fire.

"*The Romance of the Gods.* So you even had this one!" That too got thrown on the fire.

He went through six or seven books in the same manner, reading out the title and throwing them on the fire until he came to one that had lost its cover.

"What this?" he asked.

"Oh, that one," Lightkeeper said. "That's *A Thousand and One Nights*. It was written by a foreigner."

"A foreign book, eh? Does that mean you're a foreign collaborator, then?"

More than a dozen books were thrown onto the fire, which grew in intensity. Inkcap kept trying to use his stick to stir it up, and the flames burned his eyelashes.

"Is that the lot, then?" Useless asked.

"Those were all books left behind by my sister and my brother-in-law. I've brought them all," Lightkeeper said.

"I don't think so."

"What do you mean?"

"I've seen a big, thick book in your house, thicker than a brick."

"There was one, but I used it to roll cigarettes and it's all gone now. If you don't believe me, you can go and search."

"We certainly will. There are lots of nice things in your old landlord house."

"Not nice things," Bash said. "Four Olds things."

"Yes, you're right. The old landlord's house is full of the Four Olds."

"Hey, tell me, I want to know," Lightkeeper said. "Why are you confiscating these things now?"

"Ai! Are you interrogating me?" Useless said. "Is that really what you want to ask?"

"You know this is the Cultural Revolution, don't you?" Stonebreaker lectured him.

"I know, I know."

"If you know," Baldy Jin said, "then tell us what other Four Olds you've got."

"Well, there used to be a lot of them," Lightkeeper said, "but they were all divided up during the land reform. Let me think about it. Ah, Lucky's family got a pair of old chairs with carved flowers on the backs. Sparks' dad got a pair of gauze-covered lanterns. The gauze had a picture of the Eight Immortals Crossing the Sea on it. And there was a white copper water pipe. Potful got a *xiapei* shawl and a silver necklace, and Awning's family got a single cabinet and a four-compartment cabinet. Big Root's family were given a pair of camphor wood boxes and Dazed-And-Confused got my grandfather's felt top hat."

Dazed-And-Confused had come over carrying a screen. He stopped to listen and burst out, "That was a fucking useless hat. I boiled whenever I wore it. In the end, I tore it up and used it as stuffing for my mattress."

Huang Shengsheng had been directing Cowbell at the mountain gate, but he stopped and turned to Lightkeeper.

"So this is the member of the landlord faction, is it?" he said.

"My dad was a member," Lightkeeper replied, "but I'm not."

Huang Shengsheng was having none of that and yelled at him, "Then how do you remember so clearly your family's property being divided between the poor and middle peasants? Hah! Hasn't the time come to settle the accounts once and for all and even tip the scales the other way? I think we may have to put you back on the register. Come on, come on, come on, I'll do it right now."

But Lightkeeper ignored him and turned and left. Huang Shengsheng watched his retreating figure and shouted after him, "Why don't you come back here? Come and see how I'm going to deal with you. Are all the class enemies in Old Kiln so arrogant?"

Then he turned on Dazed-And-Confused and said, "Lightkeeper said you disrespected his family's top hat. You shouldn't have taken that lying down. You should have told him where to go and that you'd do what you liked with his top hat."

"I was all agitated and I didn't think what I was saying," Dazed-And-Confused replied.

"If you don't think about what you're saying, you won't think about what you're doing either," Huang Shengsheng said disparagingly.

Dazed-And-Confused picked up a clod of earth and hurled it towards Lightkeeper. Lightkeeper had already turned the corner, so the earth just hit the wall.

"Very impressive! Playing it tough when he isn't here any more," Huang Shengsheng said. "Go and take the ladder to the Kiln God Temple and scrape all the monsters and ghosts off the walls."

Dazed-And-Confused threw the screen he had brought onto the pile of antiques, then shouldered the ladder. However, he didn't leave.

"Comrade Huang is the commander in charge of destroying the Four Olds in Old Kiln, and we must obey him," Bash said.

Dazed-And-Confused turned round and headed off to the Kiln God Temple, but he underestimated the length of the ladder and the end of it bumped into Baldy Jin.

"Watch where you're going," Baldy Jin exclaimed.

"He's got his eyes in his arse," Inkcap said.

There was a small hole worn in the seat of Dazed-And-Confused's trousers, and when he bent over, you could see the dirty black of his arsehole looking back out at you. The comment annoyed Dazed-And-Confused, who lowered the front of the ladder and shoved it at Inkcap so he fell on his backside.

"Get up, Inkcap," Bash shouted, "and take all these Four Olds to the Kiln God Temple."

Inkcap's buttocks hurt and he couldn't get up, so Cowbell came over to pull him to his feet.

"I'm fine," Inkcap said. "I'm just checking to see if anyone's dropped any money."

Everything that could be burned was burned, and what couldn't was piled into the Kiln God Temple. Inkcap and Cowbell formed a team but after they had made a few chaotic trips, Inkcap suddenly felt there was something familiar about a particular table screen. He picked it up and looked at it. He saw scratches on the back that he had made with his own fingernails. He tried to work out how their table screen had come to be handed in. Had Gran done it? He looked around, but there was no sign of her. He guessed it must have been Dazed-And-Confused who brought it just now, and he gritted his teeth in hatred of the man. He clutched the screen, picked up a pair of candlesticks, a round, brimless "melon skin" hat and one of Lightkeeper's wood frame lanterns and headed towards the Kiln God Temple. He went into the fenced field next to the temple, where Noodle Fish was using a bucket of piss to water his cabbages.

"What are you up to?" Noodle Fish asked. "Is this more land reform?"

"It's a cultural revolution," Inkcap replied. "Didn't Lightkeeper tell you about it?"

"What kind of revolution? Why didn't the Branch Secretary call a meeting? Is Bash at the bottom of this?"

"Yes, it's Bash all right. He's got culture, hasn't he!"

"Where's Stonebreaker?"

"Your Stonebreaker's right in the middle of it."

"Well, I sure as fuck didn't tell him he could go. What's he doing running along after Bash?"

Noodle Fish picked up his bucket and left. Inkcap wanted to put the screen in the empty piss bucket and get Noodle Fish to take it back to his house, but he was afraid that Noodle Fish talked too much, so he changed his mind. When Noodle Fish left, he stuffed the screen in among the cabbages and then straightened up and took the other things over to the Kiln God Temple.

After returning from the temple, Inkcap went back to the mountain gate to keep moving things. He found himself carrying a chair that used to belong to Lightkeeper but was acquired by Lucky's family during the land reform. Lucky was actually given a pair of chairs, but one had been broken into pieces three years ago, and the one Inkcap was carrying had a broken leg. The chair was on Inkcap's back but it kept hitting the ground, impeding his progress. He turned the chair upside down and pressed his head against the seat. He saw people coming out of all the alleyways and craning their necks to look in his direction. He couldn't understand why they didn't come to help move things along until a pig came running up and attacked his trouser legs with its cucumber-shaped mouth. When he looked down, Inkcap saw that the pig was the one they had given to Iron Bolt's family. He hadn't seen it for ages. The pig was skinny, and it had grown much longer in the body. He immediately put down the chair and stroked the pig's stubby tail with his hand.

"What are you doing here?" he asked.

"I sneaked out."

"How did you dare?"

"There aren't any wolves in the daytime."

"Stop slacking, Inkcap!" Baldy Jin shouted. "Keep moving that stuff."

"I was having a chat with this pig," Inkcap protested.

"Having a chat? Are you a pig, too, now?"

"He may not be a pig now," Inkcap told the pig, "but Baldy Jin certainly was one in his last life. Go home. Hurry up and go home."

He stood up, put the chair back on his head and went on his way. Then he heard a grunting noise and turned back to look. As the pig ran past Baldy Jin, it took a chomp at his leg. It didn't actually connect, but it gave Baldy Jin a fright and made him jump out of the way. The pig ran off.

Inkcap fell to the ground and let loose a fart. Only he knew that it wasn't really a fart but a laugh.

THIRTY-THREE

BASH AND THE OTHERS were smashing up the Four Olds in Old Kiln, and no one came out to oppose them. The principle seemed to be clear: if Bash had been acting in secret, that would be down to him as an individual and his propensity for causing damage, but for him to be doing it openly meant there must be something, or someone, behind him. And if there was something behind him, then, based on past experience, this was another movement. And whenever a movement comes along, you have to keep your wits about you and follow it, otherwise you'll come a cropper. It's like when a strong wind starts blowing, all the plants and grasses have to drop into a crouch. Or, to put it another way, just face it, is there really any way to avoid wearing padded cotton clothes in winter?

Barndoor went to Decheng's house early in the morning to repair his stove. It had been newly installed that spring, but then relatives from Xiahetan and Xichuan kept coming to visit and, of course, they always had to eat. Decheng began to suspect that the stove was positioned wrongly, so he got Barndoor to come back and correct it. Barndoor had finished with the stove and was climbing up to see to the chimney, when Flower Girl came running in to ask him to hurry home. She told him that Bash had led a bunch of people over to the west of the village and they were shouting for him to hand over his Four Olds.

"Who is this Four Olds person?" Barndoor asked.

"It means old as in antique things," Flower Girl explained.

"How can an antique have four olds?"

"How should I know? I do know that Lucky handed over a chair, Almost-There came up with a silver necklace and–"

"Have you given them everything?"

"Bash says you have to do it. Anyone who doesn't hand their stuff over is a non-revolutionary and a counter-revolutionary."

Barndoor was worried and hurried home, leaving the work on the chimney half-done. He took an old vase, which usually held a feather duster, down from his cupboard and carried it out into the courtyard. He also brought out an old-fashioned shoehorn and a mosquito net. He felt this still wasn't enough, so he added a carved *ruyi* sceptre made out of *jichi* wood that had been passed down through several generations. He hoped that by taking these things out straight away and letting people cart them off, he could stop them rummaging through his chests and cupboards. However, no one came for a while, so he took *ruyi* sceptre back inside to hide it. He couldn't think of anywhere to put it until Flower Girl suggested that, if he didn't light the *kang*, he could hide it in there. Just as he did so, there was a knock on the courtyard gate.

Barndoor hurriedly finished stashing away the sceptre and ran out, shouting, "Who is it? Who's there?"

It turned out to be Noisy, who was momentarily taken aback when he saw that it was Barndoor who opened the gate.

"Ah, Barndoor!" he exclaimed.

He rummaged in his right pocket for a cigarette, took out a dirty handkerchief, put it back again, rummaged some more and came up with a handful of loose change.

"What are you looking for?" Barndoor asked.

"I was looking for a cigarette for you," Noisy said.

"You know I don't smoke."

"Didn't you go out to work today?"

"No, the production team stayed home."

Noisy recovered himself and his leg twitched, which it often did.

"Why's there such a fuss going on? Is someone having a wedding or a funeral or something?" he asked.

"I'm told they're smashing the Four Olds," Barndoor told him. Then he glanced out of the gate and went on, "You've travelled all over the county, Noisy. Tell me, are other places doing the same thing?"

"Oh yes, but I hadn't expected it to have reached as deep into the countryside as Old Kiln. I thought they were raiding Pockmark's house."

"Pockmark's so poor his bare balls bang against the edge of his *kang*. What Four Olds could he have?"

"Of course they raided his house. He's the poisoner."

Barndoor let Noisy into the courtyard, and Noisy took a look around. There was no sign of Flower Girl, but he guessed she was in the house, so he coughed a couple of times. Barndoor pulled up a stool for Noisy to sit down, then did a doubletake.

"What did you just say? What was that about Pockmark?"

"Didn't you know? Pockmark's the poisoner."

Understanding suddenly dawned on Barndoor. "So the case is solved, then?"

Noisy told him how he had heard about Pockmark's arrest in Luozhen. Barndoor's first thought was to tell the Branch Secretary.

Barndoor called Flower Girl, but she didn't come out immediately. When she did, her hair was neatly combed.

"Have you been combing your hair in there?" Barndoor asked.

"Oh, Noisy's here," she said. "Did you bring me that awl?"

"I've got it here."

"Pockmark's been arrested," Barndoor told her. "It was him who poisoned Uncle Happy."

"I'd guessed it was him."

"That was clever of you. Why didn't you tell me before?"

"Director Wang had a talk with me, and I told him it was probably Pockmark who did it. He didn't want to hurt Uncle Happy. It was Millstone he was after, but Happy was the one he got, so Happy died for Millstone. Director Wang didn't believe me."

"All right, all right, so you're the clever girl! I'm going to go find the Branch Secretary. You stay here and gather up the Four Olds. Give them this stuff if they come for it."

"But this shoehorn is made of white copper! I'm not going to give that up. Why can't we give them your wooden *ruyi* sceptre?"

"What are you talking about? What *ruyi* sceptre?"

Flower Girl went quiet.

As soon as Barndoor had gone, Noisy poked Flower Girl in the side.

"Don't do that. I'm holding a vase," Flower Girl said.

But Noisy still put his arms around her waist and said urgently, "Give us a kiss. Go on, give us a kiss."

They heard footsteps outside the courtyard gate. Barndoor came back in, saying, "Come with me to tell the Branch Secretary, Noisy. He won't believe me if I tell him Pockmark's been arrested, so we'd better go together."

Noisy held back and refused to go. Flower Girl took the awl out of his basket and said, "Why don't we have something to eat?"

"How can we think about eating?" Barndoor said. "With something this big, we've got to tell the Branch Secretary as soon as possible."

As the two men left, Flower Girl leaned against the gate post and said, "It's fine if you don't want to eat them now. I'll keep my buns warm in the steamer basket."

The Branch Secretary always made a pot of strong tea when he got up in the morning. This had been his habit for almost twenty years. There wasn't any tradition of tea-drinking in Old Kiln and if people did want tea, they just put some bamboo leaves in hot water. It was only the Branch Secretary who drank aged jasmine tea and, unusually, he had his own special process for making it. He had an empty tin can fitted with a wire handle to serve as a boiling pot. He added tea leaves to the water and boiled them over the fire until just two or three mouthfuls were left to pour out. He only considered the tea ready to drink if chopsticks began to disintegrate when dipped into it. You could get all the energy you needed for the day from just two or three sips of this tea, and if you happened to miss drinking it for a day, your legs would feel too heavy to lift. He had just finished his tea when his son came back with water from the spring. He said that Bash and his gang were kicking up a fuss about the Four Olds, so he started to get dressed. His son asked what he was doing.

"I'm going to have a look. Why didn't you think to tell me about something this big?"

"Bash must be copying the example of Luozhen," his son said. "Are you just going to let him make trouble?"

"Do we not still need order? I'm still alive and in the village, and they dare behave like this? And Stonebreaker too? Huh! When his wife gave birth, I even got the production team to send them grain to brew wine, to keep the whole village happy. And now he's confiscating things and smashing them up, throwing people's hearts into chaos."

"Luozhen is in chaos," his son said, "and Secretary Zhang doesn't even care, so why should you?"

"That's balls. This isn't some great affair of the Communist Party."

"This is the Cultural Revolution. Chairman Mao has ordered the Cultural Revolution. How is it not a great affair of the Communist Party? If it does turn out that they are in the wrong, then the Communist Party will come out and see to them. But what if you turn out to be the one who's got it wrong? What will happen to you?"

The Branch Secretary saw some sense in what his son was saying, but he was still unwilling to accept it.

"They are definitely going to be in the wrong, so let them be exposed. What the fuck did that bastard Bash think he was doing smashing up the stone lion? I put it there during the land reform. He even smashed the ball in the lion's mouth. Does he just want me to stop protecting Old Kiln, or does he want to take charge of the village himself?"

While the two men were talking, someone called out to the Branch Secretary. It sounded like Tag-Along.

"No matter how angry you are, Dad," his son said, "you just have to accept it in front of everyone for the moment."

The Branch Secretary said nothing, let out a long breath and reached for a towel, which he tied around his head. "Tell anyone who comes that I'm sick," he said.

His son opened the door and led Tag-Along into the main room. The Branch Secretary was sitting on the *kang* with a towel on his head and Tag-Along told him what was going on with Bash and his gang smashing the stone lion and tearing the figures of men and horses off the mountain gate. They were also demanding that every family hand over their Four Olds. Just what was going on? The Branch Secretary didn't say anything.

"My father is seriously ill," his son said, "and he doesn't know about any of this. Bash is not a village cadre or village elder and he's not from a progressive faction either. Even if he takes part in movements, it is not his turn to be leader."

"So is there a cultural revolution?" the Branch Secretary asked.

"Just how much culture does Bash have?" Tag-Along said. "He doesn't have a drop of culture in him, and he wants to make a cultural revolution?"

"Let him. Let him kick up a ruckus," the Branch Secretary said.

The Branch Secretary's son winked at his father, who said, "Hey, Tag-Along, I hear your boy's found his *ganda*."

"Yes," Tag-Along told him. "It's Inkcap."

"If Inkcap can be a *ganda*, you might as well just let Bash go on the rampage."

"I think Bash has ambitions," Tag-Along said.

"What ambitions are those?"

"I think he's got the bit between his teeth and wants to be team leader."

The Branch Secretary laughed. "Just listen to yourself! Just listen!"

Then he fell silent, picked up his water pipe and smoked two bowlfuls until he made himself break out coughing.

"You're sick, Dad. Don't smoke so much."

The Branch Secretary just grunted, then stopped pretending to be ill and huffed and puffed away at his pipe, then huffed and puffed some more. Just at that moment, Barndoor and Noisy knocked on the door. The Branch Secretary's son went over and opened it.

"Is this more about smashing the Four Olds? If it is, then keep it to yourselves, he's ill."

"This is much bigger than smashing the Four Olds," Barndoor said. "They've solved the poisoning case, and it was Pockmark who did it! He's already been arrested."

"What was that, Barndoor?" the Branch Secretary asked from the *kang*. "Come in and tell me."

Barndoor and Noisy entered the room and told him about Pockmark's arrest. The Branch Secretary put down his pipe and laughed loudly.

"Excellent! Excellent!" he said.

No one could see what was excellent about it, so the Branch Secretary told Tag-Along, "Go and get Millstone. How many people wanted to be team captain? Only Pockmark and Millstone. Pockmark poisoned Millstone to stop him from being captain, but now he's been arrested, that only leaves Millstone, doesn't it?"

"Everyone will choose Millstone, for sure," Tag-Along said.

"There's no need for anyone to choose," the Branch Secretary said. "I'll appoint him straightaway myself."

As soon as the news of Pockmark's arrest spread, the villagers cursed him viciously. First, someone planted two muddy footprints on the courtyard gate of his home. They were on the upper half of the gate, so whoever it was, must have taken a running jump at it. Then the lock on the gate got twisted, the bolt fell off, and although no one actually went inside, a pile of human shit was dumped on the threshold. Millstone and his wife hastily rolled out a batch of noodles, served up a bowlful, mixed in some seasoned oil, and garnished it with a spinach plant complete with carefully washed roots just like an offering of cold noodles at the ancestral tomb at the Qingming Festival. They took the bowl to Happy's grave as a way of telling their uncle that the case had finally been solved, and the murderer would pay with his life. Pockmark was sure to be convicted and shot in rapid time. After telling their uncle the news, the two of them ate the bowl of noodles themselves. They left the cemetery at the foot of the slope without exchanging a word and walked to the large roller stone in the east of the village.

Only then did Millstone's wife speak: "You didn't say what you thought of the noodles just now."

"I ate them, but I didn't really taste them."

"They didn't seem to have any flavour. I don't know why they were so bland."

"Ah, that was because my uncle's ghost had eaten them."

He was going to say more, but at that point, they saw Stargazer, Feng Youliang's daughter-in-law, Old Faithful and Pendulum coming down the dirt road next to the embankment, each carrying three or four large cabbages in their arms.

Stargazer threw Millstone a cabbage and said, "This one's for you."

"Why?" Millstone asked.

"It's from Pockmark's private plot. He's not coming back so we might as well pick his cabbages and eat them."

"Then I don't want it, it's too hateful."

"Just pretend it's his bones when you're tucking in," Stargazer suggested.

But Millstone took the cabbage, put it on the ground, and chopped at it like a madman, using his hand like a machete. With his five fingers held tightly together, the edge of his hand became so sharp he cut the whole cabbage in half in one go. He kept chopping and chopping until the cabbage was just a pile of shreds that flew everywhere.

Pockmark came from an old family. His father had opened a porcelain shop in Luozhen and there was a stone plaque set into the courtyard gate of the family home that was engraved with the words "Senior Family". When Bash learned that Pockmark had been arrested, he decided that the plaque was one of the Four Olds, so he and Baldy Jin used a steel hammer drill to pry it off the gate and smash it.

As they did so, Gourd observed, "A stone slab like that would have been good for smashing down adobe!"

"Absolutely," Sprout said. "That bastard did a lot of harm, so we're going to do a lot of harm to his house."

"Not just his house," Bash said. "All the Four Olds in the village."

"All of them?"

Bash didn't reply but picked up an eight-pound sledgehammer and set off down the alley with Baldy Jin. They cast long shadows as they reached the entrance of the Three Fork Alley, where they came across a small carved ornamental stone. Bash walked over and swung the hammer at the stone, but the hammer just bounced back off it, making him stagger back a few steps.

"Are you going to smash this too?" Sprout asked from behind him.

"This is a monument to the old society," Bash said. "It's got an engraving of Mount Tai to drive away evil spirits. Let's see if it can drive this away."

He swung the hammer again and it broke the stone in two.

That evening, Millstone became captain of the production team. The Branch Secretary recorded on a piece of red paper that after extensive consultation with community members and study by the Branch Party Secretariat, Millstone had been duly appointed production team captain. He posted it on the door of the Kiln God Temple, then took down the bell from the elm tree outside Potful's house and hung it on the persimmon tree in front of Millstone's house.

Millstone was an expert farmer and when the rice planting in Old Kiln was nearly over, with half of the seedlings in the ground, he arranged for some of the villagers to finish planting the last of them and sent the rest of the workforce to the bottom of Yijia Ridge to clear the water channel. This channel was the reason Old Kiln could grow rice in the bend of the river. The entrance to it was at the foot of Yijia Ridge and there was a stone weir in the river to raise the level and facilitate the diversion of the water. But from the winter of the previous year to the summer of this one, several landslips had occurred on Yijia Ridge, and earth and rocks were blocking a section of the channel. Although a temporary linking channel had been dug alongside it, the new channel was only small and had limited flow. With the Branch Secretary's approval, Millstone decided to clear the original, blocked channel. To guard against further landslips from the ridge once the channel had been cleared, the northern section of the weir had to be raised and more stones transported from the base of the mountain opposite the Zhou River. It took two days to move the stones because Bash and his gang didn't come to do the heavy lifting and everyone else only seemed able to work slowly and inefficiently. Those who should be lifting the big stones only lifted little ones and others who could have carried three loads only carried one. The only thing they did well was moan incessantly.

Millstone hadn't asked Bash and his gang to come and do the work. His thinking was that, if he went to Bash, an argument would ensue and if Bash and his cronies didn't end up coming, he would lose face as the new team captain. However, he was determined to lead the team in doing a decent job. If Bash and his lot didn't come, it would affect everyone else's enthusiasm for the task, so he raised the number of work points to be allocated. He went to the foot of the mountain on the other side of the Zhou River to make an inspection and numbered each stone according to its size and weight. Whoever could lift these stones into the channel would be rewarded with work points according to the number on the stone. Millstone asked Useless to go with him to mark up the numbers, but Useless didn't want to. He said he had to keep on smashing the Four Olds, and only he could tell which items came into those categories.

"And does smashing the Four Olds satisfy hunger and thirst?" said Millstone. "If the channels aren't repaired properly and the rice seedlings aren't planted, you'll end up eating bricks and shitting slag."

"Then you explain it to Bash," Useless said.

"Why should I? Who's the team captain, him or me?"

Useless relented and went with Millstone to mark the stones with numbers in red paint. As Millstone had anticipated, the work rate increased, and more rocks were moved in one afternoon than had been shifted in the previous two days.

As soon as Useless left, Stonebreaker and Baldy Jin began to panic. Sure, it was great fun to watch other people's belongings being confiscated, burned and smashed as Four Olds, but there weren't any work points for it. What was more, the people who were carrying the stones could put in for two or three times more work points per day than before. Bash sought out Millstone and requested that the men who were smashing the Four Olds should have their work points recorded too. Millstone refused. He said that he was the only team captain, and it was the team captain's job to lead the team members in farm work. Anyone who performed farm work would have their work points recorded and anyone who didn't, wouldn't. Millstone was stubborn and not particularly good with words, but, no matter what Bash said, he kept insisting that he was only interested in farming, and that was that. Bash was furious and went to see the Branch

Secretary demanding to know why he had appointed such an unsuitable team leader.

The Branch Secretary kept his temper. He smiled and asked Bash, "If you go through the list of all the villagers, who else could be team captain? Pockmark is such a troublemaker he's ended up in prison!"

"Why are you talking about Pockmark?" Bash demanded.

"Oh, no reason. You said Millstone shouldn't be team leader, and I was just using Pockmark as an example."

"All right, then, if you want to make Millstone team leader, go ahead. But you just leave the village and take a look around. Everyone else is carrying out the Cultural Revolution, but in Old Kiln you're the one suppressing true cultural revolution."

"Ah, Bash," the Branch Secretary said. "You should examine your conscience. Have I really tried to stop you smashing the Four Olds? Has Millstone? The mountain gate belongs to the whole village and you have knocked off all the statues from it. You have smashed the mouth of the stone lion at the south entrance of the village. You have scraped the paintings off the walls at the Kiln God Temple. You have smashed the Mount Tai stone and burned antiques taken from every family in the village. Have I opposed you in any of this? Could you have done any of it without my support? You'd be swamped by all the opposition in the village. There's only a handful of you lot. You'd be no match for the villagers. They'd beat you to death with their bare fists."

"And whose fists would those be?" Bash retorted. "Chairman Mao called for the Cultural Revolution, and I'll kill anyone who raises a fist to me."

"Yes, indeed. As long as Chairman Mao calls for it, of course we will carry it out. As Branch Secretary, am I not a gun in the hands of the Chairman? I will shoot wherever he points me."

"I'm afraid your old gun is out of bullets."

"Not necessarily, my young friend, not necessarily," the Branch Secretary said, with a laugh.

He shouted down to the lower house, "Wife! Wife! Use two more ladles of water today to make rice for Bash. And bring out the big bowls. Let's see who can eat more, the old man or the youngster!"

But there was no answer from down below. The Secretary's wife was chasing a chicken that had got up onto the roof of the lower house. She had chased it into the yard and up the wall and there were chicken feathers everywhere.

Bash was trying to play hardball, but the Branch Secretary just absorbed it like a bag of cotton and Bash couldn't get the better of him until, in the end, he forced his hand, by saying, "I've got nothing else to say, but just let me ask you this: will the men smashing the Four Olds get work points? If not, then they'll stop doing it and the Cultural Revolution in Old Kiln will be a dead duck. Then I'll go to Luozhen to file a complaint. If I can't file it there, I'll go to the county town."

"Oh, I'm really scared!" the Branch Secretary said. "And what exactly will you accuse me of? No one has ever said it's my responsibility to give work points to people who smash the Four Olds. Has anyone starved in Old Kiln? But if you stop to think about it, if work points are given to anyone who smashes the Four Olds, who's going to want to keep carrying the stones to repair the channel? Your enthusiasm reminds me of someone, young man."

"Who?"

"Me! I was a big noise in the land reform, just like you are now."

"And you still won't give us work points for smashing the Four Olds?"

"If there are going to be work points for smashing the Four Olds, the irrigation channel has to be repaired as well. Think of it as killing two birds with one stone. As Branch Secretary, I have to look at the bigger picture. How about this? I'll allocate work points for two people to smash the Four Olds. Let's say you're one of them, who's the other?"

"Only two?"

"Two to start with. We can gradually increase the number according to circumstances."

"Useless, then. You can trust Useless. And Inkcap's handy about the place so you can make him my assistant."

"Inkcap's from a bad background. I don't want to cause trouble for you."

As soon as Bash left, the Branch Secretary closed the door and yelled, "Who the hell does that bastard think he is, questioning my judgement?"

"Are you going to let him cut loose again?" his son said pleadingly. "Won't people come looking for you if you do?"

"Ai! There isn't room in Old Kiln for the both of us."

He walked over to the portrait of Chairman Mao, lit three sticks of incense and murmured, "Chairman Mao, Chairman Mao. If you want to see this Cultural Revolution through, why didn't you tell the branch officials lower down the chain first? Just look at that bastard Bash. Is he the right sort to carry out a revolution?"

"But Dad... Dad..."

"Bring me a bowl of vegetable noodles," the Branch Secretary said. "I'm all on edge."

His son filled a bowl and he drank it down, tears streaming down his face as he sat there.

Over the next few days, the people involved in transporting stones to repair the irrigation channel wore straw sandals and tied pads on their shoulders. Awning had a pair of shoulder pads made of badger pelt, but Stargazer and Iron Bolt had nothing, and their clothes were worn through at the shoulders. They each cut a hole in the centre of a piece of dog skin and put it around their neck. Those involved in smashing the Four Olds got on with their smashing. The weather was already very warm, but Bash was still wearing his military cap and Useless was neatly dressed, with a mask hanging around his neck with the mask itself stuffed into the third buttonhole of his thin padded jacket. Bash strode purposefully while Useless pattered along behind him in small, quick steps that made his trousers creak.

"Take that mask off. What do you think it makes you look like? We're carrying out a revolution here!"

"But I don't have a military cap."

"Maybe not, but I can give you a Chairman Mao badge to wear."

So Useless removed the mask and asked Bash for the badge. Bash told him he didn't have one just at that moment, but he'd give him the one Inkcap had when he got it back off him.

Inkcap didn't know that Bash had requested him to help smash the Four Olds and he was feeling very envious and resentful of Useless. When Bash asked him for the Chairman Mao badge, he was very unwilling to give it back.

"Useless is a revolutionary now," Bash told him, "so he should wear the Chairman Mao badge."

"If he's a revolutionary, why can't I be one too?"

"You come from a bad background, don't you?"

Inkcap gasped. The reason he had been so devoted to Bash was that, while others bullied him, Bash didn't, but now he could see that Bash too thought he came from a bad background. He suddenly grew angry, even angrier than when Baldy Jin and Pockmark had made fun of him. He tore the Chairman Mao badge off his chest, threw it to the ground, turned on his heel and walked away.

Bash was stunned by his behaviour and shouted, "How dare you throw Chairman Mao away, you little prick."

But when Bash went over to collect the badge, Inkcap turned around, snatched it up again and ran off.

Inkcap vowed never to visit the shack again or anywhere near Bash. Huh, he can go wherever he likes, but if he wants me to go and smash the Four Olds, I'll go and carry stones with Cowbell instead, he thought to himself.

Other people could carry large stones, but he and Cowbell could only manage the small ones. When they were crossing the river, the riverbed in the shallow water was covered with slippy rocks which made it easy for them to lose their footing if they weren't careful. When they reached the channel, although the water wasn't flowing too fast and didn't even come up to the knees of the adults, Inkcap was soaked up to his belly. The stones didn't feel heavy to them in the water, but once they were out of the water, their legs became unsteady and started to tremble.

Even Half-Stick laughed at their expense. "Are you having trouble lifting such a small stone? Even I could carry it on my back."

Inkcap had a knack for catching turtles with his feet. There was a patch of muddy sand in the strand on the north side of the river where there were a lot of small holes in the sand with bubbles coming out of them. He knew how to recognise which holes had turtles under them, and he used his feet to catch them. He felt with his toes, and when he felt a hard shell, he would flip out a turtle.

Dazed-And-Confused didn't carry stones in his arms like the others but used a basket on his back. When he saw the turtle Inkcap had fished out, he said, "If you give me that turtle, I'll carry a stone for you."

"Really?" Inkcap replied. "Come over here and I'll give it to you."

Dazed-And-Confused went over to him, but Inkcap lifted the turtle in his hand, said "Fuck you!" and threw it into the river.

After two days of carrying stones, Inkcap and Cowbell had hardly earned any work points. When Inkcap fell asleep, it was as though he was paralysed under a pile of mud. He didn't wake up once during the night but kept on pissing the bed. Gran didn't want him carrying stones, but if he didn't, how was he going to earn any work points? So he came up with an idea. He didn't know any characters, but he could recognise numbers. He discovered that Useless had used too much paint when painting numbers on the stones, so it hadn't dried properly, and he could still wipe it off a few days later. So when Dazed-And-Confused was resting on the riverbank after carrying a stone across, without him noticing, Inkcap used a blade of grass to change the number 10 into a 6 by rubbing out the 1 and adding a stroke to the 0.

When Dazed-And-Confused had carried the stone onto the weir he said doubtfully, "Am I going mad? I'm sure this was a ten-pointer so how has it become only a six?"

"In your eyes," Soupspoon said, "everything in the village should be yours."

"Oh yes?" Dazed-And-Confused snapped back. "And does that include your old woman?"

The two of them started to fight.

After they'd stitched up Dazed-And-Confused, Inkcap and Cowbell changed the stone they were carrying from a 3 to an 8 and took it to the weir to be checked.

"How can such a small stone be an eight-pointer?" Yoyo asked.

"Are you saying what's written on it is wrong?" Inkcap asked.

"Maybe you split a bigger stone in two?"

"Could you do that?" Inkcap asked innocently.

"Dazed-And-Confused has been known to."

But when a close inspection revealed no trace of the stone having been split, Inkcap and Cowbell got their eight points.

Inkcap was so pleased with himself, he started to change the numbers on every stone they carried. He changed 2 points to 6, and 6 points to 8. He congratulated himself on how smart he was. But then he added a 1 to a stone that was marked as a 4, making it 14, and they carried it over to be checked. Yoyo was very suspicious and called Millstone over.

"How can you have any fucking room for doubt?" Millstone exploded. "You know how big a potato is and how big a pumpkin is, don't you? Who carried it over?"

Yoyo told him it was Inkcap and Cowbell. The two lads were playing with a dog not far away at the bottom of the cliff. It was Ever-Obedient's dog and when it started lifting its leg to piss, Inkcap and Cowbell decided they wanted to piss too, and they had a competition to see who could piss the higher. Inkcap was the clear winner as he could actually stick out his tongue and taste his own salty piss.

"Come over here," Millstone called to Inkcap.

Inkcap went over and Millstone slapped him round the head. Then he called Cowbelll over too, but Cowbell ran away. Millstone slapped Inkcap again, saying, "You can have his one too."

THIRTY-FOUR

AFTER FINISHING HIS MEAL, Pendulum went to the kiln site and on his way passed by the entrance of the Kiln God Temple. Bash was chiselling away at the name plaque on the temple door, which was made up of several bricks. But he couldn't shift it.

"What are you up to, Bash?" Pendulum asked.

"Stop squinting at me."

Since childhood, Pendulum hadn't been able to move one of his eyes. If you put up a finger and told him to look straight at it, he couldn't see it. What he saw was the tree next to you. The only way he could see your finger was to look slantwise at it. He was now looking slantwise at Bash as he chiselled away at the plaque.

"How dare you take your chisel to that?" he said.

"It's got the character for 'god' in it so it must be feudal," Bash said.

"Firing the kiln relies on the gods."

"Gods? What gods?"

"Last Spring Festival, Yoyo didn't pay her respects to the gods on New Year's Eve. She put some dumplings on to boil first thing on New Year's Day, and there's no doubt they were proper dumplings, but what came out of the pot were radish dough twists."

"And did you see that for yourself?"

"Yoyo told me about it."

"Yoyo's sick. How can you possibly believe that crazy talk?"

"With the last kiln-load of bowls I fired, Lightkeeper insisted on taking charge of the fire and the stupid fucker didn't go to light incense at the Kiln God Temple. Half the bowls misfired."

"You actually let Lightkeeper take charge of the fire? Sounds like you wanted those bowls to misfire."

"You're a crazy man, Bash. Aren't you even afraid of the gods?"

"Oh yes? Is it crazy of me only to acknowledge Chairman Mao?"

Bash went back to chiselling away at the plaque, but he still couldn't shift it. He told Useless to climb a ladder and smash it with the head of an axe.

"That's right, smash away and smash the gods away! If all the porcelain misfires, that will be down to you lot. Smash away if you're not afraid of the retribution of the gods."

Bash just laughed and said, "Hey, Useless! Have you ever suffered the retribution of the gods?"

"No, but then I'm not the one with a squint."

Pendulum gasped in outrage, then shouted, "Branch Secretary! Hey!... Branch Secretary!"

His shout was as piercing as a shattering vase. There was no reply from Old Kiln but the three characters "Kiln God Temple" were smashed as the bricks fell to the ground. Huang Shengsheng came out of the temple and went to look at the confiscated Four Olds piled up in the west chamber.

"Why does a village this size have so few things?" he asked Bash.

"It may be big, but it's poor," Bash told him. "Before Liberation, there was only one landlord. I'm afraid there won't be any more Four Olds."

"The reason why Old Kiln got its name is because there is a kiln producing porcelain for sale. With a trade like that, pretty well every household must have something."

"We're going round household by household, making the well-off families hand things over."

"You can't rely on them," Huang Shengsheng said. "You have to go into the houses and search. All feudal, capitalist and revisionist items must be confiscated. If it proves difficult, then you must arrest the worst offenders. You have to kill the chicken to show the monkeys you're serious."

"Lightkeeper's the best example of an old villain."

That morning, Huang Shengsheng and Useless went to Lightkeeper's house to order him to keep handing stuff over. Lightkeeper really did have nothing more to give them, so he pointed to a piss pot under the cabinet and said, "If it's Four Olds you're after, there's a good one. Awning's father wanted it during the land reform, but when my father told him it was a piss pot, he didn't take it."

Huang Shengsheng smashed the pot with a kick and said, "What else is old or antique here?"

"The moon is old, Middle Mountain is old and the lice on my body are practically antiques."

"So you still think you can joke around with me, do you?"

He told Useless to take Lightkeeper to the mountain gate to hold a meeting. But Useless found three porcelain vases and a pile of porcelain shards on a shelf in a cupboard on the wall of the little house.

"Are these Four Olds?" he asked

When he took the vases down to inspect them, they all had the words "Made in the reign of Qianlong" on the bottom. Lightkeeper rushed over and snatched the vases back, cradling them in his arms.

"These are old blue-and-white sample bottles," he said. "I bought them in Luozhen for a lot of money. I want to use them to research how we can produce blue-and-white vases in Old Kiln. The Branch Secretary knows all about it."

"That's a laugh," Huang Shengsheng said. "It's not for someone of your rotten status to do this kind of research. There must be some poor lower or middle peasant who can do it instead."

"I seem to remember the Branch Secretary mentioning this," Useless said.

"Even if they are for research," Huang Shengsheng said, "you can't keep this blue-and-white porcelain in your home. It should be kept in the public office."

"If it was kept there, it would either get broken or lost," Lightkeeper retorted.

"Just who do you think you are?" Useless demanded, going over to snatch the vases back.

Lightkeeper wouldn't let go, so Huang Shengsheng broke his fingers and took the vases away.

Gran was required to attend the criticism meeting for Lightkeeper as part of her continuing punishment, but Goodman, who arrived early, was unsure if he was under punishment too. Instead of sitting in the crowd, he stood to one side, waiting for someone to tell him. But no one did. He stayed there for a while before going over to stand next to Gran, saying he thought he'd better keep taking his punishment too.

"Last time you had to stand here," she whispered to him, "it was because of Bash, but this time it's Bash who's in charge. Do you still think you need to stand here?"

Goodman was about to move, when Huang Shengsheng said, "You just stay there. Smashing the Four Olds isn't only about collecting antiques, but also about smashing the Four Olds in your head. I've heard you spend all day talking about feudalism, so in future, you will have to take special care to rectify that. For now, stay put."

So, once again, Goodman found himself standing next to Gran.

Only a few people came to the criticism meeting. Everyone else had been busy transporting rocks and rebuilding the channel for many days, and they all wanted to have a rest. Bash didn't seek out Millstone, and Millstone didn't ring the bell on the tree in front of his house. Instead, Dazed-And-Confused picked out a copper washbasin from the pile of Four Olds when he arrived, banged on it, making a loud clanging noise, and shouted towards the village, "A meeting's being held. A criticism and struggle meeting."

Third Aunt came out and asked, "Aren't we repairing the channel today?"

"We should have held this meeting ages ago," Dazed-And-Confused said. "If we don't hold it now, everyone will be too exhausted."

He banged the washbasin again. Tag-Along saw him and said, "That's my copper washbasin. Why are you beating it about like that?"

"I've already confiscated it as a Four Old, so it's not yours any more."

Clang! He hit it again, denting it, and Tag-Along hit him. As soon as the fight started, a crowd came to watch the fun, and no one tried to break it up. Dazed-And-Confused pulled Tag-Along's hair and Tag-Along scratched Dazed-And-Confused's face. Dazed-And-Confused grabbed Tag-Along by the balls and Tag-Along fell to the ground screaming. A person in the crowd shouted, "Someone's going to get killed" and ran off to fetch the Branch Secretary. As soon as the Branch Secretary arrived, the two parties stopped fighting.

"Go on fighting, why don't you?" the Branch Secretary said. "Continue fighting and turn Old Kiln into a pile of crap."

"You're the Branch Secretary," Third Aunt observed, "and Old Kiln is already a pile of crap. Don't you care?"

"If there's a wind blowing in the courtyard, I can close the doors and windows, but what can I do about a wind out in the fields?" the Branch Secretary replied opaquely.

"I was calling the criticism and struggle meeting, Branch Secretary," Dazed-And-Confused said, "and Tag-Along wouldn't let me start it."

"Every time you open your mouth, you can't help lying," Tag-Along protested. "What do you mean I wouldn't let you start the meeting? I thought you were going to break my family's copper washbasin."

"What kind of a Four Old is a copper washbasin?" the Branch Secretary exclaimed. "A washbasin is for washing your face in. How can you wash your face if you hand it in? Don't you care about your face any more?"

He took the basin out of Dazed-And-Confused's hands and threw it back to Tag-Along.

"But... but..." Dazed-And-Confused protested.

"If you like summoning people so much," the Branch Secretary told him, "I'll give you a gong."

With that, he turned and left, followed by Dazed-And-Confused. The Branch Secretary had the drums and gongs for festival celebrations stored at his house, and he gave Dazed-And-Confused one of the gongs. Dazed-And-Confused took it and set off down the alley, banging it. This time, the noise was so loud that all the sparrows flew off in a black cloud up the Zhou River embankment.

During the criticism and struggle meeting, Bash talked about how dishonest Lightkeeper was. He clearly had some old porcelain vases at home but refused to hand them over. He was also going around spouting arrogant nonsense. The reason why the collection of Four Olds in Old Kiln was not proceeding smoothly, and there was even resistance to it and confrontation, was down to Lightkeeper's influence. In every movement, there were always people who would thrust themselves forward and act as nay-sayers, and Lightkeeper was one such clown. However, this movement was different from others. This was the Cultural Revolution, not just some piddling little revolution. To anyone who dared stand in the way, he and his men were Wu Song, the tiger-slayer! They would kick away anyone who dared to be a stumbling block. They would smash the old world and build the new world.

"That can't be right, Bash," Sprout said. "Didn't Liberation in 1949 smash the old world? We're already a new society, so how can it have become the old world again?"

"Who told you that?" Huang Shengsheng said. "Smash the old world! Build a new world! That is what Chairman Mao has said. Is Bash wrong, then? Is Chairman Mao wrong?"

"Ah! Then I was wrong," Sprout admitted.

"Are you a poor peasant?" Huang Shengsheng asked.

"I'm just a farmhand, poorer than a poor peasant."

"Comrades, commune members," Hung Shengsheng declared. "The poor and lower-middle peasants must have the class consciousness appropriate to their status. Regarding the Cultural Revolution, we must follow both what we understand and what we cannot understand. Now, let Lightkeeper explain himself."

"I will confess," Lightkeeper said.

He closed his eyes and began to criticise himself, saying that he had not studied hard or reformed well. He had handed over some Four Olds and hidden others. He was guilty and in the wrong. His sin was so heinous that it was unforgivable. He must honestly reform himself and start a new life. He had to become a proper human being again. Inkcap sat down and listened, feeling that Lightkeeper was definitely more eloquent than Bash, and spoke smoothly with hardly any stumbles.

"Lightkeeper always says the same thing," Iron Bolt said. "My ears are numb from hearing it."

Lightkeeper kept his eyes closed and said, "Being honest and transforming myself into a new person is now my life work."

This annoyed Iron Bolt, who burst out, "Open your eyes. If you keep your eyes closed, you look like a student reciting a text by rote."

Lightkeeper opened his eyes and looked at Iron Bolt, and Iron Bolt looked at him. Their eyes locked, but Iron Bolt couldn't out-stare Lightkeeper and he was the first to look away, saying to Useless, "You criticise him, Useless. Lightkeeper thinks he's educated."

"His little bit of education is no education at all, is it?" Useless said.

He went on to criticise Lightkeeper by showing how reactionary and opposed to smashing the Four Olds it was for him to say the moon was old, Middle Mountain was old and that even his lice were antiques. As soon as Useless started to speak, Inkcap got up and went for a piss.

Decheng was squatting in the privy, straining away without success. His lower back was hurting too, but he stayed squatting, his head pressed against the privy wall. His head was drenched with sweat.

When he saw Inkcap, he said, "Hurry up and get me a stick of firewood."

"Have you been eating dry fried noodles again? Why are you still eating them when you've already been given proper food?"

"Shut up and get me a stick."

Inkcap waited until he'd had his piss before going off to look for a stick. When he brought one back, he was going to help Decheng dig the shit out of his arsehole, but Decheng cursed him for taking so long, so instead of helping him, Inkcap threw the stick away and left. When he emerged from the privy, several children were playing in the mud and Xianü came flitting over to him like a butterfly, calling out, "*Ganda! Ganda!*"

Inkcap sat back down in the crowd at the meeting and tried to hide.

Useless had finished criticising Lightkeeper, and Bash formally introduced Huang Shengsheng, saying that the Cultural Revolution was happening all over the country. Everyone had seen the people walking along the highway all day long. Huang Shengsheng had come to Old Kiln as a representative of the Great Link-Up of the Cultural Revolution to help them join in too.

"How big an official is he?" Yoyo asked.

"How big an official?" Bash repeated. "You have no idea. It's like Secretary Zhang from Luozhen coming here. It's like a county cadre visiting our village in the countryside."

"Oh," Yoyo said. "Then we must make sure to look after Comrade Huang's food and accommodation."

"Of course, he will still stay at my place and eat there for the time being," Bash said. "And in the future, each family can take it in turn to feed him."

This provoked urgent chattering. Bash hushed the noise and asked them all to applaud Huang Shengsheng and invite him to speak. Huang Shengsheng himself clapped his hands a dozen or more times and began to speak. He spoke with a strong accent and kept waving his arms. He talked about the Cultural Revolution. He said it was a revolution that started with the smashing of the Four Olds. And what was revolution? Revolution was not treating guests to dinner, writing articles or being gentle, courteous and thrifty. Revolution was the elimination of one class by another. Everything old in Old Kiln that should be handed in, must be handed in and everything that should be confiscated, must be confiscated. Let all the class enemies, ghosts and spirits start wailing and spending their days in fear. However, the collection of the Four Olds in Old Kiln had not yet gone far enough. There were still things to be brought in and the Kiln God Temple still had to be demolished. No, wait. It could no longer be called the Kiln God Temple. It should be called the village office building. The roof of the village office building had to be demolished. What was the use of the dragon up there on the ridge pole? What was the use of those carvings of phoenixes? Dragons and phoenixes were things that belonged to feudalism, so they must all be smashed.

Cowbell was sitting next to Inkcap, chomping away on slices of sweet potato. He was afraid that other people could hear him, so he broke the slices into pieces in his pocket. After a while, he took to stuffing a slice into his mouth without chewing it. He waited till it had been softened by his saliva before swallowing it. He had given Inkcap three slices but Inkcap had already finished them off and wanted more. Cowbell refused.

As Huang Shengsheng was saying that he wanted to smash the dragon and phoenix on the roof of the Kiln God Temple, Cowbell whispered, "There's a dragon on Awning's house, so that'll have to be smashed now too."

"That's good," Inkcap said. "His house won't block your feng shui any more. Give me another slice."

"You want more? You've already had three."

"Don't be so stingy," Inkcap said, starting to rummage in Cowbell's pocket.

Cowbell twisted round and said urgently, "Don't move! Huang Shengsheng is staring at you."

When Inkcap looked, Huang Shengsheng had indeed stopped talking and was staring at him. He grasped the sweet potato slices in his hand and stopped moving.

"There's a meeting going on! What do you think you're doing?" Huang Shengsheng shouted at him.

"I'm bursting. Can I go out to piss?" Inkcap responded.

"You've just been to the privy and now you need to go again?" Baldy Jin said. "Is there something wrong with your bladder?"

"I'll pee right here if you don't believe me," Inkcap said.

"Go! Go!" Sprout said. "The kid's congee's too thin and he can't hold his piss in."

Inkcap left the meeting and gave his sweet potato slices to a delighted Xianü.

"Am I a good *ganda*, then?" Inkcap asked

"Good *ganda!*" Xianü said.

"Call me *ganda!*"

"*Ganda!*" Xianü shouted, and Inkcap immediately clapped his hand over the child's mouth.

Inkcap told Xianü to go on playing. Then he stood there and tried to decide whether his body wanted him to piss or not, and his body seemed to be telling him there was nothing to come out. Out of the blue, he saw a swallow flying in front of him. It was his swallow. It flew down, then up and down again. He knew the swallow was teasing him, so he followed it back towards his house. There was a gong propped up on the wall of the privy in the alley. He coughed and Dazed-And-Confused came out of the privy.

Dazed-And-Confused walked around the village a few times beating the gong, and then he went to the door of Potful's house. He beat the gong louder, and Apricot came out.

"Don't you know he's seriously ill?" she said. "Are you trying to kill him?"

"We're holding a meeting. Everybody's got to be there."

Apricot was not at all happy when she heard about the meeting and asked, "What kind of meeting?"

"A criticism meeting. It was Bash's idea. You've got to go."

Apricot wanted to spit on Dazed-And-Confused, but she just said, "My dad hasn't been eating well these last few days. I went up the mountain to gather some fern roots to make jelly. I'll go along later."

As soon as Dazed-And-Confused had left, Apricot strained the fern root paste into a pot and boiled it, cursing Dazed-And-Confused in a low voice for disturbing her. After she'd simmered the liquid for a while, she put it into several bowls to cool down. Then she went to water the henna plants in the corner of the courtyard and didn't go to the meeting. However, when the meeting started, Dazed-And-Confused glanced around the venue and found that Apricot wasn't there. He knew she was making jelly at home, but he didn't know whether it was ready or not, so he went back to her house. She had just watered the flowers.

"Why didn't you go?" Dazed-And-Confused asked.

355

"My dad hasn't eaten yet."

"Didn't you say you were going to make a batch of jelly for your dad, or were you lying about that so you didn't have to go to the meeting?"

Then he went into the kitchen, and sure enough, he noticed several bowls on the pot shelf, and they were filled with jelly. He tested it with a finger.

"It's not set yet," Apricot said.

"It is set," Dazed-And-Confused said, "and this meeting is very important. Bash has already spoken and Huang Shengsheng is talking now but you still don't want to go!"

"You're just after some jelly for yourself."

"Of course I am. Fern roots are hard to find these days."

"You can have some. I'll give you it in a bowl to take away."

But Dazed-And-Confused said he didn't need a bowl and just poured the jelly into his gong. Apricot slammed a bowl into the gong and told him to go away as far and as fast as possible. He used a knife to cut the lump of jelly into a few pieces, poured vinegar onto them, smeared them with a layer of chilli sauce, and left. When he got to the courtyard gate, he took two stiff straws from the broom leaning there to use as chopsticks, and started eating as he walked. He felt the need to go to the privy, so he put the gong on the wall of the privy, just as Inkcap arrived on the scene.

As soon as Dazed-And-Confused came out of the privy, he picked up the gong and said, "Ah, Inkcap, do you want some jelly?"

"You've just eaten it all in the privy, what is there left?" Inkcap replied.

He thought Dazed-And-Confused was trying to trick him, but when he saw there was still some jelly in the gong, he said, "I'll have some!"

Dazed-And-Confused gave Inkcap a lump of jelly, but Inkcap saw a bit of shit on his fingers and said, "Look at your hands! Your hands!"

Dazed-And-Confused became agitated when he looked, but he immediately put his fingers in his mouth and licked them. "Chilli sauce," he said. "Chilli sauce."

Inkcap didn't eat any jelly, but turned round and threw up with a loud splashing noise.

After the criticism meeting, the villagers became nervous. They buried or hid anything they hadn't handed over and which might be considered Four Olds. During the land reform, Stargazer's family handed over a plaque to Lightkeeper's family. The plaque was made of good wood and had many characters on it. It had been hanging in the main room of his house but now he took it down, turned it over and used it as a chopping board. After his father died, Barndoor erected a stele in front of the grave. He followed the agricultural example of Dazhai in levelling the land but his family's cemetery happened to be on that particular plot, so he had to knock down the stele in the process. In fact, Barndoor secretly moved the stele back to his house, hoping that, at some time in the future, he might be able to rebuild the tomb and re-erect it. Now, under cover of darkness, he laid the stele flat on the steps of his house. But even then, he decided that wasn't good enough, and he buried it deep under the roses at the foot of the courtyard wall.

Noodle Fish had a copper hotpot that was left to him by his father. He said that when his family were well-off in the past, there were always coals in the stove in the middle of the hotpot, and they put slices of meat, tofu, fine noodles and red radish in the soup trough surrounding it. The stew was very fragrant, but he hadn't tasted it in the last seven or eight years.

Stonebreaker rummaged through the boxes they had at home and asked, "Don't we have a hotpot?"

"What hotpot?" Noodle Fish replied.

"I'm sure I remember one."

"No, absolutely not."

In fact, the hotpot was hidden up on a roof beam. Because he was afraid that Stonebreaker might find it up there one day, he waited until his brother wasn't around and propped a ladder against the beam to retrieve it. Unfortunately, the ladder slipped, and he fell to the floor, leaving him with a sore tailbone for several days.

"Stonebreaker's a thief," he told his wife. "Take the hotpot and shove it in the chicken coop."

"What do we need a hotpot for now?" his wife asked. "Why are you keeping it?"

"If we hand it in, people will think it's the kind of thing a landlord has. If it's known that I have a hotpot at home, won't it mean my status gets reassessed?"

So the hotpot was stuffed into the chicken coop.

As a young woman, Gran had such magnificent long hair that she had to stand on a stool to comb it. When she put her hair up, she would use a silver hairpin to keep it in place. She had kept that silver hairpin and was reluctant to hand it over, so she wrapped it in paper and shoved it into the crack in the wall by the door. Noisy happened to bump into Inkcap in the village and asked if there were any nests of Gran's coppery, silvery hair to exchange for *liguo* candy. Inkcap said that there were, and a group of villagers went back to his house. When he took the nests of hair out from the crack in the wall, he accidentally split open the paper package. The news that there was a silver hairpin inside spread around the village immediately, and Useless came around to confiscate it.

As soon as the hairpin was gone, Inkcap said, "There's a wide wood panel carved all over with flowers at Dazed-And-Confused's house. Why hasn't he handed it in?"

Bash went round to Dazed-And-Confused's house to inspect it. It turned out to be a decorative panel originally from the Zhu family's ancestral hall. It was currently being used as a cupboard shelf to hold jars of rice and noodles. Dazed-And-Confused handed it over, and immediately fingered some other villagers, saying that when the Zhu family ancestral hall was demolished the year before, Baldy Jin took an incense burner, Tag-Along's father took a fruit offering plate and Sprout's mother-in-law took a cast-iron oil lamp. Useless went to collect all these objects, but the fruit offering plate and iron oil lamp had been thrown away somewhere and could not be found.

When Baldy Jin heard that Dazed-And-Confused had reported that he had taken an incense burner from the Zhu family ancestral hall, he cursed out loud, saying that he was being framed. It was nonsense to say he'd taken an incense burner. But he did go on to say that there were more than a dozen families in the village who still had Four Olds. These included Soupspoon, Potful, Big Root and the Branch Secretary. Useless himself didn't dare go to these homes to recover the stuff, so he made a list to give to Bash. The contents of that list soon became common knowledge. As Bash and Huang Shengsheng were discussing how to collect everything, Useless passed on three more lists of names, saying he had got the information from several different people in the village.

"Isn't it odd?" Bash said. "Everyone says they don't have anything but when it comes down to it, they all have loads of stuff!"

"The waters of Old Kiln run very deep," Useless observed.

Bash wanted to get things straight in his head, so he called in Baldy Jin and went through the names of more than a dozen families who had been informed on, one by one.

"I've also been told your family has some silver coins," he said. "Is it true?"

"How could I have any silver coins?" Baldy Jin protested. "I bet someone's trying to get back at me for informing on them."

"Tell me about the Four Olds you've found in these dozen or so households," Bash said. "Have you seen them with your own eyes? Heard them with your own ears?"

"Actually, I just guessed they might have them," Baldy Jin admitted.

"You guessed?" Bash repeated in astonishment.

"If you stir up the mud at the bottom of a pond, you don't know what might swim up."

Bash stared at him for a very long time.

"What, then?" Baldy Jin asked.

"Here's what you have to do," Bash told him. "You and Useless make up some reporting boxes and hang one at the gate of the public office, one on the mountain gate and one on the willow tree in Three Fork Alley."

Once Baldy Jin had left, Bash said to Huang Shengsheng, "That Baldy Jin's a piece of work."

"Just let him get on with it," Huang Shengsheng replied. "The Revolution needs people like him."

However, they decided between themselves that although they would keep talking about confiscating the Four Olds, they wouldn't actually take any more in. Besides, it was quite likely there was little else to be found in Old Kiln, so they started investigating how best to go about smashing all the different tilework ornaments on the roofs of the houses. Most of the houses in the village had these special ornaments on their tile ridges, and they very definitely belonged in the category of Four Olds. So Bash led Huang Shengsheng on a tour of inspection of the alleyways.

They made a round trip taking in three alleys and then, in the distance, Bash saw someone disappearing under the willow tree at the entrance of Three Fork Alley. When he and Huang Shengsheng got closer, they saw that a report box had been nailed to the willow tree and, on entering the alley, they found a group of people there discussing something. They immediately dispersed. Only Awning and Sparks remained, playing chess. Bash and Huang Shengsheng walked over, and Bash coughed loudly and spat out a mouthful of phlegm onto the courtyard wall.

Awning lowered his head and said, "How about moving your horse?"

"Sure, I'll move it in a square," Sparks replied.

"Then my cannon will cross the mountain and blow up your horse."

"Oh! Then I won't move my horse."

"You can't take back a move in chess."

"You always do, so why shouldn't I?"

Awning knocked over the pieces and said, "I'm not playing any more. You don't play fair."

"Have you two fallen out, then?" Bash asked.

"Who doesn't play fair?" Sparks replied.

"You don't play fair."

"No, you don't play fair."

The two men cursed each other, ignoring Bash and Huang Shengsheng, and walked off towards the mouth of the alley. Bash looked a little concerned.

"Those two are thick as thieves," he said. "They haven't really fallen out."

"Is that so?" Huang Shengsheng mused. And sure enough, before the pair of them reached the end of the alley, something was said between them, and they started to laugh. Bash's ears turned red.

A courtyard gate creaked open, and Gourd walked out. When he looked up and saw Bash and Huang Shengsheng in front of him, it was too late for him to retreat. He smiled and said, "Bash! Comrade Huang! Have you eaten?"

"What are you up to?" Bash asked.

"I was thinking about where there might be Four Olds. Come on. Follow me."

He led the two men into his yard. His mother was sitting on the bed in the upper room when she heard the door to the courtyard.

"Who's there?" she asked.

She said it once in a loud voice, then repeated it more quietly: "Who's there?"

Gourd didn't answer but pointed something out to Bash and asked if the loom by the door was a Four Old. He also took down a baby carriage that was hanging on the wall in a corner. It was covered in dust but still moved freely. It was silent when pulled backwards but creaked like a frog when it was pushed. Huang Shengsheng hadn't heard anything like it before.

"It sounds like the gong they use to clear the road," he said.

He gave it a push, and to his surprise, the wheels fell off.

"I bought this in town when my son was born," Gourd said.

"If you want to hand it in, just go over to the public office," Bash told him.

"Who's there?" Gourd's mother asked from the *kang*.

"It's Bash," Gourd told her.

"Ah, Bash. Why don't you come in and sit down?" she called.

But Bash and Huang Shengsheng had already left the courtyard, and she was left there, repeating in a low voice, "Ah, Bash. Why don't you come in and sit down?"

Over at the threshing ground, Six Pints' wife handed over to the public office a pair of embroidered shoes and her husband's greasy, round "sweet potato skin" cap, and then she went to the top of Middle Mountain to ask for Goodman's help.

Two days before, Six Pints' illness was a little better and he was able to go outside. Useless and Dazed-And-Confused went to his house to collect his Four Olds. They saw a picture frame on the wall. It was very finely crafted and carved with flowers, and it contained a photograph.

"Who's this?" Useless asked.

"My father," Six Pints told him.

"Is he still wearing a long robe and a mandarin jacket? Aren't you from a poor peasant family?"

"My father enjoyed good times when that was taken, and even smoked opium, but within seven or eight years the family fortunes were ruined," Six Pints explained.

"Oh!" Useless said, and he took the picture down from the wall.

"My father! What about my father?"

Useless snatched the photo out of the frame and shoved it into a crack in the wall.

"There, your father's still on your wall," he said and went off carrying the frame.

Six Pints was so angry he fell ill. Already suffering from kidney disease, he now stamped around the house cursing everyone in sight. He was, by nature, someone who loved cleanliness and if there was even a speck of spit or phlegm on the bed cover, it had to be washed immediately. Now his piss and shit were all over the *kang* and no one else could stay in the house. That was why Six Pints' wife called in Goodman.

Goodman had gone to Six Pints' house the night before. As soon as he entered the courtyard, Six Pints shouted from the west room, "Who's making that noise? I don't like it. Please go away."

Goodman told Six Pints' wife that the patient had offended an evil spirit, and that spirit had taken him over. But he, Goodman, was full of righteousness and the evil spirit would not be able to tolerate his presence. With that, he went into the west room and said, "I preach goodness and persuade people to do good deeds. Why don't you want to listen?"

He went on to dispute with the evil spirit residing in Six Pints. The evil spirit prevaricated in every possible way and said that he was a great immortal.

"If you are a great immortal," Goodman said, "you shouldn't be causing this whole family such distress. Are you not transgressing by doing so?"

Six Pints was still unconvinced. Goodman surveyed his appearance and said, "Could it be that you were a prison guard in a previous life, and persecuted people to death? How else could you end up in such a state?"

Six Pints laughed but refused to answer. Goodman tried again and again, yet the evil spirit remained stubborn.

That night, Goodman had a dream. He dreamed about a hedgehog crouching on a household altar to the Kitchen God. He felt very discomfited when he woke up. Six Pints' wife had asked him to visit again, so he went and talked about what he had seen in his dream with her.

To their surprise, Six Pints exclaimed, "That's me!"

"If that's so, you have to leave," Goodman said. "You are finished. Great Immortal, you are supposed to help people and benefit them, so why do you do evil and harm people?"

The evil spirit said, "What you don't know is that when they farmed their land, they killed all my children and grandchildren, so I came to destroy them to resolve the hatred in my heart."

"It is better to quash hatred than nurture it," Goodman said. "The most important thing in cultivating the Dao is to get rid of hatred. The Buddha became a Buddha when his brother King Li had his limbs cut off, and he did not harbour any hatred. Even though you follow the Dao, you still have to break away from the animal realm. If you nurture hatred in your heart again, aren't you afraid of falling into Hell?"

He urged the evil spirit to return to the mountains, to purify its heart, follow its better nature and purge its hatred. Then, he told it, you can escape from the world of men.

"We know that if we fulfil our filial and fraternal duties, we will achieve positive results."

The evil spirit agreed to leave and begged Goodman to escort him. Goodman agreed to the request and said, "People are born in the three realms, and you are born in the two realms. How are you able to deceive and bewilder them?"

"If the human heart is righteous," the evil spirit said, "we don't dare approach it. Although people are born in the three realms, if they frequently lose their temper when they encounter problems, their spirit will be lost. This means they have lost one of the realms and if they are selfish too, they will lose another realm. When they are left with only the corporeal realm, that is when we dare oppress them."

"How is it you are able to speak?" Goodman asked.

"We have to borrow people's yang energy, secretly breathe into their mouths while they are sleeping and then drink their Heavenly River Water. Only then can we speak with a human voice."

"What is Heavenly River Water?"

"It is the saliva that flows out of people's mouths," the evil spirit explained.

"Go away now."

Six Pints lay peacefully on the *kang*.

Six Pints' wife had remained at his side throughout the ordeal. At first, she was so frightened, she had goosebumps all over her body. Then she asked Goodman fearfully, "Is this what's called *tong shuo*?"

"This isn't *tong shuo*," Goodman said. "*Tong shuo* is a way for the souls of the dead to express their grievances through the living. This is possession."

"Six Pints has kidney disease," his wife said, "and he hasn't been out of the village for a year. It was just that Useless came here collecting Four Olds and everything went wrong when he got angry."

"That could be when he was possessed."

"I know dead people can turn into ghosts, but can the living turn into ghosts too?"

"That is a living ghost."

Goodman did not accept Six Pints' wife's money, nor did he eat her poached eggs. Before leaving, he warned her, "Don't mention the illness to outsiders, and most of all, don't mention evil spirits. Otherwise, I will be criticised again."

"I know that," Six Pints' wife said, "but that bastard Useless made Six Pints sick. He took our photo frame. Do you think I should go and get it back?"

"If he took it, then it's gone. It's happening to every household in the village, it's not only you. You just have to put up with it."

Six Pints' wife was very grateful to Goodman and was determined to escort him home. The two of them walked to the mountain gate, where people were burning more Four Olds. They tried to avoid Useless but couldn't, and he demanded to know what Goodman was doing.

"You've been engaging in feudal superstition and talking to people's illnesses, haven't you?"

"No, I haven't," Goodman said.

"Talking to what illness?" Six Pints' wife asked. "Just let the ill die."

Useless glared at her and said to Goodman, "You haven't handed over your Four Olds yet."

"That's what I'm doing now."

He brought out two books with yellowed paper from inside his jacket and handed them over, admitting that he had read them in the past.

"Is that all?" Useless asked.

"Yes, that's all."

"What else have you got in there?" Useless said, as he could still see a bulge in Goodman's jacket.

He went over and patted Goodman down. He found two more handwritten books. He looked at one of them and saw that it was called "Wang Fengyi's Twelve-Character Primer". He flipped it open at the first page, which read:

You should know there are twelve characters, which are: 性 (nature), 心 (heart), 身 (body), 木 (wood), 火 (fire), 土 (earth), 金 (metal), 水 (water), 志 (will), 意 (purpose), 心 (heart) and 身 (body). The three realms of 性 (nature), 心

(heart) and 身 (body) represent the origin of human beings and are the natural laws of the human world. 木 (wood), 火 (fire), 土 (earth), 金 (metal) and 水 (water) are the five elements from which humans are made, and this conforms with those laws. The four great realms of 志 (will), 意 (purpose), 心 (heart) and 身 (body) are the way for people to travel the world and for them to transcend it. Only when you grasp these twelve words can you attain full understanding. When the three realms of nature, mind and body are unified, the five elements rotate in a circle, the four major realms are positioned correctly and the body assumes its proper form.

No matter how educated Useless was, he couldn't understand anything like this.

"Who is Wang Fengyi?" he asked.

"Wang Dashan [Big Mountain]," Goodman replied.

"I don't care how big or small he is," Useless said, "who is he to you?"

"Wang Dashan lived in the Qing dynasty," Goodman explained. "He herded cattle when he was a child and became a labourer when he grew up. He was very filial from childhood and worked faithfully. At the age of thirty-five, he performed an act of bravery for the sake of justice and risked his life to save his friends. He could see the light of day in the middle of the night and understood the Dao. From this, he talked to illness, urged goodness, saved people and transformed the world. He lived for forty years."

"I only asked who he was. By talking so much, you were clearly taking advantage of the situation to play the Ox God and Snake Demon."

He threw the book onto the fire where it stiffened and rolled around in the flames like a captive pheasant. Then it stopped rolling, but the pages of the book turned over and over as if flipped by an invisible hand. A stream of green smoke spread upwards until it reached the top of the medicine tree, and then dissipated from the bottom up until it disappeared at the top of the tree. Useless looked at the second handwritten book and read out, "Yu Family Bone-Setting".

"It's pronounced 'She'," Goodman explained. "It's the same as She Taijun in *The Generals of the Yang Family*."

"Do you think I don't know the difference between 'Yu' and 'She'?" Useless grumbled.

"It's a book about bone-setting. It's the book I used when I set Stonebreaker's leg." Then he shouted, "Hey, Stonebreaker! Come over here and be my witness."

Stonebreaker was standing in the doorway of the Kiln God Temple. He walked over, looked at the book and said, "This isn't a Four Old."

He took the book from Useless's hand and gave it to Goodman.

"So can I go now?" Goodman asked.

"Yes, be off with you," Stonebreaker replied.

But then another voice said, "Stay where you are!"

The speaker was Bash. He had been in the office, checking reports from the boxes. He came out and stretched. He sneezed and wondered if he had caught a cold.

From the doorway, Huang Shengsheng said, "If you sneeze once, someone is thinking about you. If you sneeze twice, someone is cursing you. And three times means you have a cold. Someone's thinking about you!"

"Who's that, I wonder," Bash said with a laugh that turned to a yell when he noticed Goodman at the gate.

When Bash saw Goodman, he remembered about digging the pit at the cowshed. He wanted to ask Goodman if it was true about there being a stone tablet under the cattle trough, or if had he been playing a trick on him.

"That I cannot say," Goodman replied.

"Why can't you say? You were the one urging me on, weren't you?"

"I don't dare."

"Does that mean there really is a stone tablet under the cattle trough?"

"Do you want me to become an Ox God and a Snake Spirit, Bash?"

"Answer the question!"

Bash grabbed hold of Goodman, called for assistance and set off for the cattle shed where he started digging under the cattle trough again. This time he actually unearthed a stone tablet. Written on it was the story of how the ancestor surnamed Zhu came to Old Kiln to take refuge with his uncle surnamed Hei and how things gradually developed from there. This period of history was often talked about by the villagers after dinner, and now there was proper evidence. Bash looked around at the old three-building public office that now belonged to the Branch Secretary.

"This tablet is a Four Old," he told Goodman. "Are there any others buried somewhere?"

For himself, he hoped that there were. If there was one buried under the courtyard or the threshold of the old public building, then he could legitimately dig it up.

"I don't know anything about that," Goodman said.

"You don't?"

"I don't."

Bash hit the steps of the old office with a hoe, breaking off a corner of stone.

THIRTY-FIVE

NEWS SPREAD QUICKLY about the stone tablet dug up from underneath the cattle trough, and it made people realise that Bash had been quite justified in digging there before. Reports of the inscription on the tablet made members of the Zhu clan think it must have come from their former ancestral hall, but when they came to see it, it had already been smashed. They were very unhappy about this, but they couldn't voice their displeasure because the tablet was unquestionably a Four Old. They just had to accept that, for whatever reason it had been smashed, smashed it was.

After the stone tablet had been destroyed, work began smashing the roof ornaments. Old Kiln had one main lane and ten small lanes. The villagers called Hei were concentrated in the east of the village and on Three Fork Alley, while the Zhu contingent were mainly to be found in the west of the village in Willow Alley, Guaiba Alley and Crosswise Alley. The other miscellaneous family names such as Bai, Li, Liu, Wang and Fan were scattered across the village.

"Let's start with Lightkeeper's house," Bash suggested.

It was the obvious choice. It used to have three layers of courtyard: a front one, a narrower middle one and a rear one, but by this stage they had been divided by three short alleys and were all inhabited by families called Hei. The buildings there had upswept roof ridges and flying eaves, which were decorated with various brick and wood carvings and clay sculptures. The Branch Secretary was already Branch Secretary at the time of the land reform and Sparks was a member of the land reform committee. Bash's father had been notified that he was to receive the three houses belonging to Lightkeeper's family, but, at the last moment, the notification was altered, and the houses were given to Sparks' father. Bash still remembered the scene. His father was so angry his face turned blue. Lightkeeper now lived in the three-room house at the end of the alley that was all that was left him after the property was divided up. Bash said they would start their ornament demolition from there, but in fact, Lightkeeper's house didn't have much in the way of decoration, and what he was really after were the brickwork carvings on Sparks' house. They were the really ostentatious ones.

Bash, Huang Shengsheng, Useless and Baldy Jin armed themselves with hoes, hammers and rakes, and Dazed-And-Confused came running up after they had already set out with a roller rod in his hand. He said this was by far the best tool for the job as there was no need to climb up the walls, you could just poke things off the roof with it and they would fall and smash themselves on the ground. Of course, there was nothing Lightkeeper could say to protest, and when they told him to fetch a ladder, he even carried it over himself, set it up against the eaves and held it steady for them as they climbed the rungs. The brick carvings on the roof ridge were quickly torn apart and smashed, and the brick carvings with auspicious characters on the ventilation window on the gable wall were also smashed. When the gang was leaving, they saw a wooden plaque set into the roof of the courtyard gate, with writing on it.

"What does that say, Useless?" Dazed-And-Confused asked.

"It says 'With righteousness and great virtue, blessings are passed down to future generations,'" Useless told him.

"Are we supposed to think Lightkeeper's house is a golden pond flowing with dazzling light, then?" Bash asked derisively.

"That's not the kind of light it's talking about."

"What light? Where?" Dazed-And-Confused asked.

He poked at the plaque with his rolling rod but couldn't dislodge it, so he pulled up a table to stand on and tried again.

"Poke away," Lightkeeper said. "But be careful the gatehouse doesn't fall in on you."

Bash stopped Dazed-And-Confused in his attempts and said that just obliterating the characters would be good enough. So Dazed-And-Confused chopped away at the four characters with an axe until they didn't look like characters any more. Then they continued their demolition work across the houses, which were all connected, jumping from roof to roof while the residents of the houses they were attacking, young and old alike, stood there shouting.

"Don't smash the whole ridge pole or the rain will get in."

There was a great chorus of wailing.

A dragon head was positioned at one end of the roof of Sparks' house and a fishtail at the other, both made of plaster. Useless tried pulling them apart with his hands to start with.

"Who made these?" he asked.

"Barndoor's grandad," Bash told him. "I've heard that he and twelve apprentices made all these houses in the village."

"Barndoor's a builder too, isn't he?" Useless said. "He's not as skilled as his grandad was. This fish-turning-into-a-dragon's really good."

"What does it matter whether you think it's good or not? There's nothing good about anything to do with feudalism," Huang Shengsheng said sternly.

Bash swung his pickaxe, breaking off the dragon's head so it rolled down the tile gulley and fell into the courtyard. Sparks' wife and parents-in-law were standing in the courtyard. His wife wailed, his father-in-law smoked pipe after pipe, and his mother-in-law wailed even louder.

"What are you wailing about?" the father-in-law scolded his wife.

"I'm wailing at the sight of what they've done to my beautiful house. What kind of man are you? A man with no balls, that what."

Her husband lunged at her, but she fended him off and the two of them grappled with each other. Sparks' wife ran off to find Sparks.

Sparks was still repairing the water channel at the foot of Yijia Ridge when his wife ran up to say that Bash and his gang were smashing the roof of their house. Sparks snatched up a pole and marched off, looking very fierce.

"Watch what you say to them and don't get into a fight," his wife warned.

"They're smashing up my house and you want me to be nice to them? I'll beat up anyone who dares touch my house."

"Then don't go. They're smashing up our roof, not our family. They're checking things one by one and only smashing whatever should be smashed. I just want you to go back to check they don't make any holes in the roof that will let the rain in. I know you, you're a hooligan who leads with his fists and will beat up anyone who gets in your way."

She took the pole away from him and clung to his legs.

"All right, all right. I'll just go and see what's going on," Sparks said.

It was a fine day but a patch of dark cloud was heading over Yijia Ridge. Sparks followed the cloud, tracking it as if he was its shadow. He ran to his house. Its roof ridge was already smashed in, and the gang had moved on to Stargazer's house at the near end of the same alley.

Stargazer was coughing so hard he was almost breathless and when he saw Sparks he gasped out, "Sp... Sp... Sp... Sparks! They've smashed it! Smashed it!"

Sparks' wife was right behind him and he said, "Yes, they have. They're smashing all the Four Olds."

"When you build a house," Stargazer said, "you have to have a ridge, and if you have a ridge, there have to be weights on the ridge to anchor it down. Now they've smashed all those decorations that were anchoring the ridge, can you even call it a house any more?"

From up on the roof, Dazed-And-Confused called down, "What do you mean by that? My house only has three rows of tiles anchoring its ridge and you used to make fun of me for living in a coffin, not a house. Well, you're not making fun of me now, are you?"

"This is a revolution, Dazed-And-Confused, not an opportunity for you to take your anger out on others," Useless said, and Dazed-And-Confused shut up.

"Let them smash away if they must, Stargazer," Sparks said. "Smashing the roof ridge is better than burning the whole house down."

"He's right," Useless said, before turning to Stargazer. "You know Bash, don't you, Stargazer?"

"I know Bash."

"But I bet you don't know about the Ba Wang, the Overlord he shares part of his name with. Have you seen any plays? Well, in those plays, Ba Wang led his troops into Xianyang and burned down the Qin dynasty's A Fang Palace."

"You mean you're burning things too?" Stargazer asked. "Are you going to burn down these houses?"

Up on the roof, Baldy Jin smashed off a large piece of brickwork carved in the form of a peony flower from a corner of the ridge and threw it down.

"Look, Stargazer," he said. "This is still a perfectly good piece of brick. Put it in the corner of the yard and later you can use it to build a pigsty."

But Stargazer picked up a stone plinth and smashed it down on the peony carving, then he smashed it again and again until the pieces were the size of his fist.

"What kind of an attitude is that?" Baldy Jin said. "Are you unhappy about something?"

"How could I be unhappy?" Stargazer replied. "What have I got to be unhappy about? I'm overjoyed!"

He went back to smashing the brickwork until it was nothing but powder. Baldy Jin called out to Huang Shengsheng, who came running across the roofs of the other houses and the people below could hear the crash, crash, crash of the tiles under his feet.

"Count them, Baldy," Sparks shouted.

"Count what?"

"Count how many tiles he's breaking by treading on them, and then get Stargazer in to repair them."

"What are you talking about?"

"By all means smash the Four Olds if that's what you've got to do, but do those roof tiles count? Who told you to walk all over other people's tiles? Was it the Cultural Revolution? Did Chairman Mao tell you to tramp all over them? Eh?"

"Why are you being so fierce, Sparks?" Baldy Jin asked. "When we smash the Four Olds we aren't treading on tiles, we are walking on clouds! So what if we break a few tiles? So what?"

He lifted a pile of tiles and dropped them with a clatter.

"Are you looking for a fight?" Sparks roared. "Give me that pole! Give me that pole!"

His wife, who was still holding the pole, refused to hand it over, so he picked up a hammer from a corner of the courtyard and was about to throw it up at the roof. Stargazer and his wife rushed over to grab hold of him.

"Sparks! Sparks!" they shouted, but he still hurled himself forward. So his wife picked up a basin of water from the steps and poured it over him. Then she collapsed to the ground and wept loudly. It stopped Sparks in his tracks, and Stargazer and his own family pushed him through the courtyard gate and out of the alley.

Sparks was so angry that he went to see Millstone.

"I know all about this," said Millstone, "but what do you want me to do? What can I do? This is the Cultural Revolution."

"This Cultural Revolution seems to have the surname Hei!"

Millstone considered the comment and realised that almost all the people smashing the Four Olds were indeed called Hei.

"Oh," he said.

"Oh, what? You're the captain of the production team, aren't you? You're the fucking team captain, but you let people called Hei lord it over people called Zhu?"

"You think I want to be team captain? The Branch Secretary told me to take the job. There's fuck all I can do about this as team captain."

Millstone was an honest and straightforward man, but he tended to get tongue-tied when he became agitated. He slapped himself around the face and said he wasn't going to do the job any more. On seeing him like this, Sparks softened his approach and said, "If you quit now, there won't be anyone to look after the interests of all the people called Zhu in Old Kiln. They'll end up being wiped out by the Hei mob."

"What do you think we should do?" Millstone asked.

"The Hei families have got their Cultural Revolution, so why can't us Zhus have one too? They've smashed up our houses, so we should get ourselves organised and smash up theirs. It's not as though we don't have the people to do it. You need to take responsibility for this."

Millstone hesitated again and said, "I'll go and find the old captain. He may be sick, but he has a clear head. He's been dealing with the Hei mob for more than ten years. I'll ask his advice."

A small delegation arrived at Potful's house, and Potful broke out in a sweat when he heard them.

"This is nothing to do with my dad," Apricot said. "He's sick. What do you want from him?"

"Your surname is Zhu, isn't it, Apricot?" Sparks said. "And you were involved with Bash, weren't you? How can he be acting like this? I think it's all your fault. He's taking revenge on everyone called Zhu."

"You're just thrashing around looking for a scapegoat," said Apricot. "What the hell does this have to do with me? You tried to have a go at Bash and when you couldn't, you came to have a go at me. Is that it?"

"You don't know what you're talking about," Millstone said furiously. "Get out of my sight."

Apricot went to sit in the kitchen and wept, crying for her mother with every sob. Potful then told Millstone to carry him on his back to see the Branch Secretary. Potful was a big man and by this time was just a dead weight. Once Millstone had him on his back, he couldn't move, and the same thing happened when Sparks tried. In the end, they took down a door panel and used that to carry him to see the Branch Secretary. Apricot couldn't stop thinking about Potful and followed on behind.

Halfway there, they passed Awning's house where Awning and his wife were smearing mud over their spirit wall and were already up to the screen's roof.

"Ah! Is our old team leader not well? Are you taking him to the hospital?" Awning asked.

"I'm fine," Potful said from the door panel.

"Are you plastering over your spirit wall?" Millstone asked.

"It just needs a bit of repair. It's got cracks, and if I don't plaster it, it will collapse."

"I don't think it's cracks you're worried about," Sparks said. "You're worried it's going to get smashed up as a Four Old. That screen's got carved brickwork bats on top of it."

"No, no. Not at all, not at all."

"Awning," Sparks said, "you're the captain of the militia. Are you plastering over that screen because you're weak or because you're scared?"

"What else can I do? The Cultural Revolution's arrived, hasn't it? Ai! Why are you carrying the old team leader on a door panel like that?"

"We're going to see the Branch Secretary. And if he washes his hands of the matter, the way things are going, us Zhus are going to be smashed by the Heis."

"I'm coming with you," Awning declared.

So the delegation went on to the Branch Secretary's house, where they were joined by others who had caught wind of what was going on. Inkcap and Cowbell had been following Bash and his gang as they smashed the ridges of the houses. When they got to the third house, Xianü came running over to ask Inkcap for more sweet potato slices.

"You had some a while ago," Inkcap said. "Why do you always home in on me like a sow on a root cellar?"

"You're his *ganda*, aren't you," Cowbell said.

"I can offer you this title of mine. Go home and get some sweet potato slices for Xianü."

Cowbell was about to leave when an animal head was knocked off the ridge. It contained a bird's nest with three chicks inside. Useless flung the chicks down to the ground. One chick died, and two survived. The two lads picked them up intending to look after them, and went to the lotus pond to find them a few small worms. The sky was getting dark by then, and the knot of people hurried on towards the Branch Secretary's house. The sky was tumbling noisily from behind South Mountain, first seeming to drive them onwards and then covering them like black gauze.

"What are they going to do?" Cowbell asked.

"They're filing a complaint with the Branch Secretary against everyone called Hei," Inkcap told him.

"If they want to sue the people who are smashing up their roofs, why are they going after people called Hei?"

"Haven't you noticed that all the families who've had their roofs smashed are called Zhu? Can't you see that everyone here who's come to complain has the same name?"

"Do you think they'll win?"

"Do you want them to or not?"

"It'll be fun if they do."

"Then let's help with the fun."

Inkcap swung his rope fuse around vigorously, hoping that the group would see him and let him and Cowbell go along with them. But they didn't see him, or if they did, they ignored him and had no intention of letting him and Cowbell join in.

"Have a shit for me," Inkcap told Xianü.

"I don't need a shit."

"Have one for me anyway, and I'll give you some sweet potato slices."

Xianü squatted down with his open crotch trousers parted and Inkcap emitted a prolonged shout, "Yo... Yo... Yo!'"

Ever-Obedient's dog woke up at the sound with a sneeze and came running over, followed by all the other dogs. Its hair had grown back and it was now a majestic-looking creature, and the other dogs looked on as it ate Xianü's shit and then licked the little boy's arse.

"Right, now," Inkcap said to the animal. "Take all the other dogs over to the Branch Secretary's house."

"Are you going too?" the dog asked. "I won't go if you're not."

"I'm going."

"Good, then," the dog said.

All Cowbell could make out was Inkcap barking and Ever-Obedient's dog barking back at him, so he laughed and said, "Are you two going to bite each other next?"

Inkcap ignored him and took Xianü over to the Branch Secretary's house. Cowbell followed them and saw that Ever-Obedient's dog was also heading in the same direction, leading more than a dozen dogs. More and more dogs came, then chickens and cats, all kicking up a racket and setting the alleys a-buzz.

A crowd had already gathered when they arrived at the gate of the Branch Secretary's house. The dogs spread out in a row under the tree in front of the door. They were all lying down, with their front legs outstretched and their heads held high. Inkcap and Cowbell tried to squeeze in through the gate. Inkcap was allowed in, but Cowbell was pushed out.

"What are you doing here?" someone asked.

"Why can't I come in?" Cowbell demanded.

"Your name is Hei. You can't come in if your name is Hei."

"Branch Secretary! Branch Secretary!... Master!" Cowbell yelled.

The courtyard was also full of people, with the Branch Secretary standing in the middle. He was looking confident and unconcerned. No matter how loudly Sparks and Millstone cursed and complained, he just smiled and looked around.

"This courtyard is very small. Guests will have to find their own place to sit."

"There are too many people for you to greet them all," Sparks said.

"There are indeed but why are the dogs barking so fiercely?"

"All the dogs in the village are here too," Inkcap told him.

Millstone tried to drag him away, saying, "This is none of your business. Go and find somewhere else to play."

"I earn work points. I'm a member of the village community. I'm not playing at anything."

The Branch Secretary laughed and said, "Did I hear Cowbell calling me? Is Cowbell here too? Let him in."

Cowbell came in carrying the two fledglings, which he handed over to Inkcap.

"I personally smashed the landscapes, human figures, birds and animals carved on my own house a long time ago," the Branch Secretary said. "Who has been smashing the carvings on the ridge of your houses?"

"It was Bash and Baldy Jin," Cowbell told him.

"From what I've seen, it isn't just households called Zhu who've had their roofs smashed. Haven't they done Cowbell's house too?"

"Bash only smashed the mirror on Cowbell's roof," Sparks' wife said. "That's nothing. Do you know what the ridge of Awning's house looked like after they'd finished?"

"It was smashed to pieces," Awning's wife confirmed.

"It needed to be smashed," Cowbell said. "It was built so high, it blocked the feng shui of my house."

"What feng shui?" the Branch Secretary asked. "Feng shui is part of the Four Olds."

Someone, he didn't know who, pulled Cowbell away from behind. By this time, the dogs outside the yard were barking one after another.

"I'm only the team captain and I can't control them," Millstone complained, "but you're Branch Secretary, surely you can do something? If you don't, I'm not going to be team captain any more. I simply can't do it."

"Don't go resigning on me," the Branch Secretary said. "For now, you must take control of production."

"Why the fuck should I do that? I'm not going to give work points to people for smashing the Four Olds. You can do that if you want. It's not just Bash and Useless smashing houses, Dazed-And-Confused and Baldy Jin are at it too. If people are going to get work points for smashing things, they might as well smash everything. People called Hei will smash the houses of people called Zhu, and the Zhus will do the same to the Heis!"

"That's what you think, is it?" the Branch Secretary said. "Well, stop messing me around. You're disturbing the dogs and chickens."

"They're already disturbed, Branch Secretary. You can see the dogs outside. When have you ever had dozens of dogs swarming around your door before?"

"The birds will be here soon too," Inkcap whispered to Cowbell.

"Bullshit," Cowbell replied.

"Go and fetch the swallow from the nest above the Branch Secretary's door, and I'll get all the birds to come here."

There was a swallow's nest in front of the door of the main building of the Branch Secretary's house that had a swallow living in it.

"You're just bragging," Cowbell said.

Even so, under the cover of all the people milling around, he upturned a basket and put it by the door. He climbed onto the basket and felt around in the nest for the swallow. The swallow didn't move so he was able to catch it and pull it out. Inkcap murmured a few words to the bird, and it flew away when Cowbell threw it up into the air.

The Branch Secretary was still talking to Millstone.

"I know all about this kind of thing, Millstone. I've been Branch Secretary for more than ten years, and I've never been afraid of anything, but I am afraid of disunity between the Zhus, the Heis and the other families in Old Kiln. We've had such a long time of stability, how come these two clans have become enemies now? Our ancestors were uncle and nephew, and now we are all members of the People's Commune. What good will it do us to fight each other in our own nest?"

"This is all Bash's doing," Potful said. "What the hell's going on? Sure, he used to be a thorn in our side and a bit of a poser, but we could always get the better of him. But now it's all turned into a bucket of shit which the maggots come crawling out of as soon as the weather warms up."

"Dough doesn't rise without leaven," the Branch Secretary said. "I think it's that Huang fellow who's stirring things up here."

"He's a fucking pain in the arse," Sparks said. "What does he think he's doing, eating and drinking and causing trouble in Old Kiln?"

"Who invited him? Does he have a letter of introduction?" Millstone asked.

"No, no letter of introduction just a fucking big mouth that's made for rabble-rousing," Awning said.

"Inkcap! Inkcap!" the Branch Secretary shouted.

"Why haven't the birds come?" Cowbell asked.

Inkcap looked up to the sky, which was dark and gloomy, without a trace of wind.

"Inkcap!" the Branch Secretary shouted again.

"He's calling you," Cowbell said.

"Here I am," Inkcap responded hastily.

He took out his rope fuse and gave it to the Branch Secretary.

"Did I ask for a light? Go and get Bash. I want a word with him."

As soon as Inkcap left the courtyard, a flock of birds flew over. First were the swallows, led by the one from Inkcap's house, followed closely by pigeons, orioles, larks, grey finches and rosefinches, but there was no sign of the red-billed, white-tailed birds that roosted on the white-bark pine by the Mountain God Temple. The birds flew around for a while, then landed on the tiles of the main house and the east and west buildings. People looked up in amazement. Suddenly, a cloud of gravel materialised in mid-air and hurtled down towards the ground. The crowd scattered, yelling, and even Millstone dragged the Branch Secretary away to shelter under the eaves. When the yard was empty and the gravel landed, it turned out to be a flock of bullfinches. Normal Bullfinches never plummet to the ground like that when they land, but this flock were grey verging on black in colour and as small as quail eggs.

THIRTY-SIX

INKCAP RAN AROUND THE VILLAGE looking for Bash without success and ended up drenched in sweat. Tag-Along, who was sitting under a tree making straw sandals, called to him, and he went over. The work at the channel construction site had stopped, and there was nothing for Tag-Along to do, so he had taken his sandal rake contraption over to the tree to plait sandals. The shade of the tree kept moving with the sun, so he moved with it and had already worked his way from one side to the other.

"What's going on?" he asked. "I'm sweating so much, it feels like I've got sieve holes all over my body. Why are you running around like a madman? Aren't you boiling?"

"Nope," Inkcap said. "If you smear a bit of spit over the tip of your prick, then you don't get hot inside."

Tag-Along stared at Inkcap as though he thought he was having him on. Inkcap kept his expression neutral and didn't smile. He felt that as he was Xianü's *ganda* he was effectively part of Tag-Along's family, like older brother and younger brother.

"It's true. Try it for yourself."

Tag-Along spat on his finger and shoved it inside his trousers to smear it on the tip of his penis. Sure enough, he immediately felt cooler.

"Everyone's gone to the Branch Secretary's house to lay a complaint," Inkcap said. "Why aren't you there?"

"What would be the point of that? When the sky falls in, there's always someone taller than you to hold it up. What good would I be?"

"Well, have you seen Bash, then?"

"One minute you're going to the Branch Secretary's place and the next you're looking for Bash. If there's shit between your buttocks, Inkcap, you don't rub it in both directions... You know I'm talking about you there, don't you?"

"Yes, I know. It was the Branch Secretary who sent me to look for Bash."

"I saw him leading Goodman into Useless's house."

"But Goodman hasn't done anything wrong. Why was he taking him there?"

After Huang Shengsheng had smashed the ridge of Almost-There's house, he jumped off the courtyard wall and sprained his ankle on landing. Useless took him to his house and Bash called in Goodman for him. Of course, Goodman came as soon as he was called. He checked the injury and said that no bones were broken. He applied a hot towel to the ankle and told the patient to rest up for half a day and he'd be fine. Useless's mother boiled some more water, and Goodman soaked the towels for Huang Shengsheng's ankle in a copper washbasin until they were hot, then swapped them over. Huang Shengsheng's leg was hurting, but it didn't affect his mouth and he talked incessantly with Useless. There were several people in the room, including Baldy Jin, Dazed-And-Confused and Stonebreaker. Bash was washing his face, splashing the water out of the washbasin until it was only half full. He then told Stonebreaker to scoop up some water with a ladle and pour it over his head. He didn't say anything after Inkcap left; Baldy Jin, Dazed-And-Confused and Stonebreaker didn't talk to him, and he didn't want to talk to them. He just stood to one side, watching the lips of Huang Shengsheng and Useless, and thinking it was a good thing they weren't made of clay tiles, otherwise they would have worn away long ago.

"There are five river basins on the entire eighty *li* of the Zhou River," Useless said. "Some of them are beautiful and some of them are prosperous, but only the one at Old Kiln is both beautiful and prosperous."

"Impossible," Huang Shengsheng replied. "You haven't even been to the provincial capital. You are like the frog in the well. You don't know what wealth is, and you don't know what beauty is."

"Where are you from, then?"

"The north of the county."

"Ah! Well, you know us folk here are called South Mountain monkeys and your lot up there are called North Mountain wolves. Have you ever been to Huanghualing? Huanghualing is a watershed. The water from the north flows to the Yellow River, and the water from the south flows to the Yangtze. Old Kiln is a Yangtze River basin. If you stand in the Zhou River and have a piss, your piss will flow all the way to Shanghai."

"Impossible! Do you even know where Shanghai is?"

Of course, Useless had never been to Shanghai, so he said defensively, "I've been up north where you come from. The houses there have high walls, short eaves and black tiles. There are no bricks or clay sculptures on the roof ridges, and they are all painted with whitewash. Our houses here are more durable."

"I wouldn't say that," Huang Shengsheng protested.

"They're certainly much better to look at."

"Only because of the brickwork and pottery sculptures, and they're Four Olds, aren't they? What's so attractive about the houses when those are all smashed up? They're like a person's face with the eyes, eyebrows and nose missing. And a face with those missing is just like a gourd or a naked bollock."

"Weren't you the one who told me to smash them, then?"

"It wasn't me who wanted them smashed, though, it was the Cultural Revolution. So there's nothing more to be said, is there?"

"You're not going to get the better of him, Useless," his mother said. "He can beat you every time, even if he only uses half his mouth. Never mind, I'll make you some rice dumplings in soup."

"My mum makes the world's best rice dumplings in soup," Useless declared.

"Nonsense," Huang Shengsheng said. "My mum makes the best."

Useless's face lost its animation as he said, "Eat what you like, then. Eat what you like."

"Soya beans," Huang Shengsheng declared. "Stew up some soya beans if you have any. Soya beans..."

Huang Shengsheng stopped in mid-sentence and looked at the darkened window above the door lintel. Three sparrows were perched on the window frame, chattering away.

"They're saying someone's bragging," Inkcap broke in. "Are they right?"

Everyone laughed and Stonebreaker said, "We've all heard the story about the thin bamboo pole. On top of the pole is a huge bowl, inside the bowl is a cattle pen, inside the cattle pen are two big bulls and the bulls are fighting each other."

Inkcap thought Stonebreaker was mocking him and insisted that he had accurately understood what the sparrows were saying. But Huang Shengsheng hissed at everyone to stop talking. He grabbed a broom and swung it hard. A sparrow fell from its perch. Inkcap rushed over to pick it up. It wasn't dead and had started flapping its wings.

"Not bad," Useless said. "I once caught a fly with one swipe of my hand."

"I bet you didn't," Huang Shengsheng said scornfully. "You couldn't even bring a sparrow down for me. Bring that one over here. Bring it over!"

Inkcap gave him the bird and he immediately shoved a stick up its bottom and cooked it over the fire, just like the villagers of Old Kiln did with corn-on-the-cob. The sparrow was still moving as its feathers charred and blackened. Huang Shengsheng kept turning it until it was black all over and giving off steam. Then he picked it up by the stick and started gnawing away. Everyone was dumbfounded. Goodman stopped changing the wet towel on Huang Shengsheng's ankle and Inkcap cried out.

"What's the matter?" Huang Shengsheng said. "Don't you eat sparrow meat? It's delicious."

He kept turning the stick round and round, gnawing at it quickly and carefully, showing the teeth in his fire-breather's mouth. In no time at all, the sparrow was gone, leaving only a messy lump of innards. Goodman stopped his work with the towels and went off to the privy, and even Stonebreaker and Baldy Jin left the room tight-lipped.

"Find me a bamboo leaf so I can pick my teeth, Inkcap," Huang Shengsheng ordered.

Inkcap gestured to Bash.

"What's up?" Bash asked.

Inkcap dragged him out the door.

"Surely Huang Shengsheng can't be human if he eats sparrows like that," Inkcap said.

"I've never seen anyone eat like it," Bash admitted. "Now, what's going on?"

"The Branch Secretary told me to come and get you."

"Go back and tell him I'm busy."

"Even though he wants to see you, you're still busy?"

"Why shouldn't I be busy just because he wants to see me?"

Inkcap failed to talk Bash round and was too scared to go back and report his failure. However, Bash did go to see the Branch Secretary that night. He chose to go that late to remind the Branch Secretary that he wasn't at his beck and call and would only go when it was convenient. He didn't ask the Branch Secretary what was wrong, he just said the village had to solve the problem of Huang Shengsheng's food. Bash could no longer afford to keep feeding him at his place, so different village families should take it in turn like they did with the town and county cadres when they visited the countryside. If that couldn't be worked out, then the village would have to give him some supplies of food and he would cook for Huang Shengsheng at his place. The village didn't have to worry about providing firewood. The Branch Secretary wouldn't agree to this, saying there was no precedent for such an arrangement. When cadres from the town or county went to the countryside, official documentation was issued in advance. Huang Shengsheng didn't have any such documents when he came to Old Kiln. If he was given meals or a food allocation, then anyone could come along and ask for the same. Food was scarce and expensive, so he didn't dare break the law or party discipline in this way. Bash's attitude hardened and he started arguing back, even slamming the table with his fist. No one had ever dared slam the table in front of the Branch Secretary before. Even last time, when he stopped Bash from digging a hole in the cattle shed, Bash hadn't dared do such a thing.

"Are you slamming the table at me?" the Branch Secretary said in outrage.

"What option do I have? If Huang Shengsheng starves to death in Old Kiln, you will bear the consequences."

The Branch Secretary laughed and softened his tone. "Bash, Huang Shengsheng has been eating your food for several days now and you can't afford it any longer, so how do you expect others to afford it either? If you were Branch Secretary and I asked you to provide food for someone from another village, how would you handle it? As for you, Bash, you don't go out to join the production team if you don't feel like it. You mend shoes as you please and don't pay the commission. Do I give you a hard time over it? No. I let you off because, after all, you are from Old Kiln. But is Huang Shengsheng from Old Kiln? I don't object to him carrying out the Cultural Revolution, and I've accepted whatever he's done. But now you're smashing the Four Olds and the villagers are in uproar, and you still want me to look after his food? I simply don't have the power to do that. Or we can hold a community members' meeting tomorrow. If the members say I should take charge of his food allocation, I will arrange to do so. What do you think?"

"Let's hold a meeting, then, and I will give a speech."

"Very well, very well. I will convene the meeting, but I won't speak."

After seeing Bash off, the Branch Secretary went to Potful's house, where he told Apricot to go and fetch Millstone and Sparks. He told them about Bash's request to allocate families to feed Huang Shengsheng and hand out food to him. Potful, Millstone and Sparks were all outraged.

"Fuck it! He's been smashing the roofs of everyone called Zhu, no one's got on his case and now he wants you to feed him too?"

"What Sparks means is that there is no need to hold a meeting tomorrow. As Branch Secretary, you're being too soft."

"How can you allow such a meeting? If Bash fans the flames there, even though there are lots of Zhus to object, there are still plenty of Heis too, and most of them haven't had their houses smashed up."

"What are we supposed to do if the proposal is approved?"

"None of this is because I've gone soft," the Branch Secretary pleaded. "When have I ever been soft? But how can I get tough with Bash? He's not married and has neither parents nor children, while I am Branch Secretary and I have a responsibility to take care of the whole village."

Everyone fell silent for a while.

Potful sat on the *kang* but couldn't keep it up and had to lie down.

"If that's how things are," he said, "what else is there to say? Let's just wait for the meeting tomorrow."

"Then why did you get me here?" Millstone asked. "This room is as hot as a steamer basket. I'm going to sleep at the threshing ground."

He knocked his pipe out on the sole of his shoe, wrapped his tobacco pouch around the stem of the pipe and got ready to leave.

"If you're going, let's all go," Sparks said. "Those Zhu folk are soft as persimmons and they deserve to be squashed."

"Who are you calling a soft persimmon?" Millstone asked.

"The Branch Secretary is a soft persimmon, and you're softer than him. You're so soft, you've almost disintegrated."

"And you're really tough, are you? You're only tough behind closed doors. You weren't so tough yesterday when that lot were smashing up your house, were you?"

"My wife had me so tight round the legs, I couldn't fucking move, could I?" Sparks said. "Otherwise–"

"What's the point in you two quarrelling?" the Branch Secretary said. "Why don't you sit down and discuss things? Do you really want to leave, Millstone?"

Millstone didn't say anything. He untied the pouch from his pipe and loaded the bowl with tobacco. He went over to the kerosene lamp on the wall by the *kang* to get a light, but the bowl of the pipe knocked out the wick. The room went dark, and the moonlight shone in through the window onto the *kang* in a square of white. Potful shouted to Apricot to bring the matches. Apricot was sitting in her room in the lower part of the house, stitching the soles of her shoes. She took Potful the matches.

"I've been thinking about it," the Branch Secretary said out of the darkness. "If we just list whose houses have been smashed up and whose haven't, the Hei clan may well side with Bash, but if we start talking about allocating families to feed Huang Shengsheng and giving him supplies, then that is taking food out of everyone's mouth and I'm not at all sure they'll be willing to go along with it."

"Hmm, yes," Potful said.

"And you think we can force him out like that?" Sparks asked.

Apricot struck a match and relit the kerosene lamp.

"Who's this you've plucked up the courage to force out?" she asked.

"What do you mean?" Sparks said.

"The reason Master Branch Secretary couldn't do it was because he couldn't see any way it could be done. Isn't that so?"

"You've been keeping your eyes open and your mouth closed, Apricot," the Branch Secretary said. "Have you got something in mind?"

"What idea can she possibly have when things have already gone this far?" Sparks said with a dismissive grunt.

Apricot had heard enough.

"Why don't you think before you open your mouth?" she snapped.

"I didn't make Potful sick, did I?" Sparks retorted. "It was only when your dad stopped being team leader that Bash began to run riot. And if Bash hadn't gone off on one, do you think we'd have that Huang Shengsheng fellow here now?"

"Ooh, listen to you! How fierce you are! If you're that fierce, why don't you see Bash off yourself? If he cuts up rough, you just cut up rough right back."

"Shut your mouth," Potful interjected. "What do you think you're doing here anyway?"

Apricot left the room. She didn't go back to stitching her shoes but sat on the steps outside the door of the main room. The sky was full of stars and one of them flew over the village, shining brightly. It was followed by another. Why didn't one of them fall on Old Kiln, into this very courtyard?

"Can you force him out?" Millstone asked. "How?"

"I'll find some other pretext tomorrow and start something with Bash and Huang Shengsheng," said Sparks. "When the blood starts flowing, you come out and take charge, Branch Secretary."

"I won't take charge," the Branch Secretary said.

"What do you mean you won't take charge?" Sparks asked in astonishment.

"Why don't you simply beat him to a standstill, then throw him out of the village?"

Sparks just stared in stunned silence but Millstone said, "I get it!"

He stood up to go.

"What do you get?" Sparks asked.

"I'll go and find Awning. We need Awning for this."

"Go with Millstone, Sparks," said the Branch Secretary, "and listen to what he has to say."

Still bemused, Sparks stood up and left with Millstone.

Apricot was sitting on the steps with her legs stretched out in front of her. She didn't pull them in when Sparks ran up.

"I'm not trying to say you're right or wrong, Apricot," Sparks said, leaning over her. "I'm just frustrated. I can't seem to get to talk about Bash and that Huang fellow properly because every time I mention them, I lose my head."

Apricot snorted in disbelief.

Millstone and Sparks left the courtyard muttering to each other, but Apricot heard them talking to Palace outside.

"Not asleep yet, Palace?" Millstone said.

'It's too stuffy inside," Palace replied. "I'm going to the threshing ground to sleep."

"Forget about sleep," Sparks said. "Come and make a tour of the village households with us."

"Are you checking household registrations?"

"We're holding a membership meeting tomorrow to resolve the matter of that Huang person," Sparks told him.

"Is this the Cultural Revolution?"

"Did you know that Huang is going to have to share everyone's rations, go to each house in turn to eat his meals and there won't be any food tickets or payment? He needs to eat three square meals a day."

"What's the deal with that? We don't even have enough to eat ourselves. Is he our grandson that we have to provide food for him?"

"That's right, that's right," Millstone said. "Everyone needs to rise up and throw him out."

"Palace," Sparks said, "I'm going to start a fight with him, and I'll need your help."

"Surely you're big and tough enough to handle it yourself. I can just be there as back-up if you need me."

"No, no, he can't do it by himself," Sparks said.

Apricot stood up to shout after Palace to stop, but their footsteps were already receding into the distance. A cat crept out from under the tree in the courtyard towards the entrance. Apricot was startled by its sudden appearance. She couldn't figure out whose cat it was or when it had entered her courtyard.

"Apricot! Apricot!" Potful called from the main room.

"What?"

"Rustle up some food. The Branch Secretary hasn't had any dinner, and we've still got some talking to do."

"Ah!"

Apricot was adding water to the pot in the kitchen when her heart suddenly gave a lurch. She knew Millstone and Sparks were out that night soliciting support from various households, and that Sparks was intentionally going to start a ruckus at the meeting the next day. If Bash and Huang Shengsheng didn't fight back, verbally or physically, everything would be fine, but if they did, all hell would break loose. Not only would Huang Shengsheng be driven out of Old Kiln, but he and Bash might even end up in a bloody heap on the ground. She scooped a whole bucket of water into the pot as she thought about this and, after reaching her conclusions, she scooped up some more, growing increasingly angry with Bash. Why had he brought Huang Shengsheng to Old Kiln and then spent all his time plotting with him at the expense of paying her any attention? She knew Bash had been lying dormant for too long and would certainly take off in a big way when offered the opportunity. But could he possibly fly so high with Huang Shengsheng, smashing the mountain gate, smashing the stone lion and smashing so many roofs without provoking public anger? Well, if he got thrown out on his ear, so be it. He deserved it. She went to fetch a noodle ladle and scooped up maize grits from a jar. She wanted to make grits congee with boiled potatoes, but now she couldn't find the noodle ladle. She looked in the pot, but it wasn't there, so she went back to the jar but couldn't find it there either. She was so perturbed that she actually left the kitchen and went to look in the main house. Only then did she realise that she was holding the noodle ladle in her hand.

"It's all your fault," she hissed, hating Bash but at the same time worrying that the villagers would beat up Huang Shengsheng and throw him out of the village. Bash was bound to leap to his defence and might well get beaten up too. Even if he wasn't beaten, with Huang Shengsheng gone, Bash would lose all his support and followers. He would be like a dog without its tail or a chicken without its wings, an object of slander and ridicule to the villagers. It was such a shame. Bash was like a bell that could only ring out in the open, not buried in the ground. But who else truly understood this? Apricot had no heart for cooking any more. She put the maize grits down on the pot shelf, wrote a note and slipped out of the courtyard. She urgently needed to find Inkcap.

Inkcap's courtyard door was open, and a light was still on in the house, but Apricot couldn't bring herself to go in. She was afraid that whatever Gran might ask her, she wouldn't be able to answer. So she stood in the dark, wondering what to do with herself when Inkcap appeared at the courtyard gate with a straw sleeping mat and a cover.

Gran had stayed up in the house and was saying querulously, "It's not that hot. Supposing there's a wolf? Make sure you run away."

"There's lots of people over at the threshing ground," Inkcap reassured her.

"What kind of wild animal do you think you are? Why can't you stay in the house? It gets cold after midnight. Make sure you keep your stomach covered."

"I know, I know."

Inkcap had already walked out of the courtyard gate, but then he turned around and went back in. He took his rope fuse that was hanging on the gable wall and lit it. Then he walked back into the alley, swinging the fuse in a circle. Apricot tiptoed swiftly behind and called out to him as they reached the top of the alley.

Inkcap was so startled he actually jumped a few paces forward, but then he came to a stop.

"Who's there?"

"I thought you weren't afraid of anything," Apricot said, "but you're carrying that fuse to scare away ghosts, aren't you?"

When Inkcap saw it was her, he said, "The ghosts don't scare me, but you did!"

"Are you going to the threshing ground to sleep?"

"How did you know?"

"Do you think I don't know what you're thinking?"

Inkcap was intrigued. "So what am I thinking?"

"You want to find Bash."

"Wrong."

In fact, Inkcap was thinking about how he had just been sleeping on the mat on the *kang* and, in the heat, his sweat had left an imprint of a human figure on the mat. That figure was the Inkcap who was still sleeping, while he was the other one who had come outside. But he didn't share this idea with Apricot. Instead, he said, "I'm not looking for Bash. He's definitely not sleeping on the threshing ground. He's only being friendly with Useless because of the Cultural Revolution."

"Well, you can go and give him this now," she said, thrusting a note at Inkcap.

"Pass on a message for you? No, I won't."

"Why not?"

"You two aren't together any more. What have you got to write to him about? Aren't you ashamed?"

"You know shit about it. You have to go."

Inkcap softened and said, "What does the letter say?"

"Did I write it to you?"

"If you still want to get back together with him, I won't take it. I have to take responsibility for you."

381

"You take responsibility for me? Do you even know what that means? Anyway, I'm cursing him in that letter, so go."

"You should call me Uncle Inkcap."

"All right, Uncle Inkcap, just make sure no one sees you. But if you hoodwink me by stopping me halfway, think again. Be careful, now."

Inkcap twirled his fuse and left.

Inkcap walked around the threshing ground, where a lot of villagers were sleeping. Sure enough, he saw no sign of Bash, but Millstone was whispering away to some of the others. As soon as Inkcap approached, Millstone stopped talking.

Inkcap spread out his sleeping mat, but Feng Youliang told him, "Sleep over there."

"I'm sleeping with you," Inkcap said. "In case there are any wolves."

"No wolf's going to eat you," Feng Youliang said, hurling Inkcap's sleeping mat away.

Inkcap picked up the mat and took it to the north of the threshing ground, where he laid it out among the three rollers, thinking they might hide him if the wolves came. Seeing that no one paid him any attention, he quietly left the threshing floor and went to the little wooden shack.

As he walked along the dirt road under the embankment, the frogs in the paddy fields on both sides were croaking his name.

"Don't shout it like that," Inkcap said and stamped his foot.

The frogs stopped croaking but that just made Inkcap afraid there might be a wolf up ahead. He looked around and there was no sign of any greenish light anywhere close by or in the distance so he knew there would be no wolves that night. But what about ghosts? A ghost could suddenly come out of the water, grab his head and push it under. Ghosts were afraid of fire, so he whirled the rope fuse vigorously above his head. Then he remembered Apricot's letter to Bash. Was it really cursing him? What kind of curses? He tripped over and lost one of his shoes. His shoe! Where was it? He turned around and searched for it on the ground. He was afraid and yearned to hear the frogs again.

"Croak! Croak!" he shouted.

The frogs burst out delighted croaking again. Inkcap finally found his shoe and put it on, then ran towards the highway as if his life depended on it.

The lamp was lit in the shack and only Bash and Huang Shengsheng were inside when Inkcap arrived. Huang Shengsheng had already fallen asleep, and Bash was washing his military hat in a basin. Bash looked at the note and his expression suddenly changed.

"Huang Shengsheng! Get up, get up!"

"Are you going to get your own back on Apricot?" Inkcap asked.

"What are you talking about?"

"I know Apricot is cursing you in that note. Don't tell Huang Shengsheng about her."

"All right," Bash said. "You go back now and in future, you can carry our notes between us."

"Just how cheap do you think you can get me?"

So Bash scooped up a jar of water from the *taisui* basin for him to drink and said, "I'm in your debt, OK?"

Inkcap drank the *taisui* water and went back to the threshing ground, where he fell into a deep sleep.

The next day, almost everyone gathered on the field in front of the village gate. Millstone and Sparks were set for action, but Bash and Huang Shengsheng were nowhere to be seen.

"Where's this Huang fellow of yours?" Sparks asked Useless.

"What do you mean 'of mine'? You should be calling him 'Old Kiln's Huang Shengsheng'."

"Is he really from Old Kiln?" Sparks replied indignantly. "Is there anyone called Huang in the household register of Old Kiln?"

Useless made no reply, so Sparks went on to ask, "Have all the houses belonging to members of the Zhu clan in the village been smashed?"

"There are two left," Useless said. "What? Do you really think it's only the Zhu houses that have been smashed? Are the Four Olds differentiated between people called Zhu and people called Hei?"

"So why haven't you smashed Bash's family house?" Sparks demanded.

"What do you mean by that?"

"Oh, nothing in particular. You smash what you want to, we'll smash what we want to and between us, we'll smash the whole of Old Kiln to pieces!"

"Be careful what you say, Sparks," Useless cautioned him. "This is the Cultural Revolution you're talking about."

"Well, I don't know how I should be talking. I don't care how cultural or revolutionary it is, I'm telling you this. It doesn't matter whose house you want to smash next, I will take a torch to your house. You and your widowed mother are the only two people in your family. If it comes to a fight, I'm pretty sure I can beat you."

"It's none of my doing," Useless stammered. "I'm only taking orders from Huang Shengsheng."

"Well, go and find the bastard and tell him to come to this meeting. Now!"

Useless went to fetch Huang Shengsheng, but the door of the little wooden shack was locked. Huang Shengsheng wasn't there, and there was no sign of Bash either.

The meeting broke up before it even started, and Old Kiln survived. As soon as peace was restored, there was the sound of the work bell ringing out, of Big Root rolling reeds at the threshing ground, of a child yelling at a dog after taking a shit, of a rooster chasing a hen in the alley, of the hen lying down, unable to escape, and of the rooster treading the hen and then crowing about its success. Goodman brought a bucket of water from the spring, spilling it all the way.

Third Aunt met Noodle Fish in the alley and asked, "What about the Cultural Revolution?"

"I'm afraid there isn't going to be one," he told her.

So the residents who had had their roof ridges smashed began to rebuild their houses. Although the brickwork carvings, wood carvings and clay sculptures couldn't be restored, they set about repairing the tiles. Sparks was at the public office first thing to retrieve the pair of old candlesticks that had been confiscated from his house. Later, the others followed suit, and everything was gone by the end of the morning. Some people went to stir up the ash pile under the mountain gate, but there was nothing to be retrieved so they all cursed and swore loudly.

THIRTY-SEVEN

IT HADN'T RAINED FOR A FEW DAYS, and the dogs were quietly lying in the shade with their tongues hanging out.

The only sound came from the cicadas in the trees: "It's hot. It's hot."

The men couldn't keep their tops on any longer, and they even started sticking leaves of field mint on their foreheads and putting circlets of walnut leaves in the waistbands of their trousers. Gran went to Third Aunt's house to ask for some medicinal powder to treat her three chickens, which had some kind of parasite that was making them lose their feathers, leaving their necks and backsides bald. When she went into Third Aunt's courtyard, she bumped into Iron Bolt's mother, stripped to the waist and carrying her grandson on her back. The child was making a fuss, moaning and whining, so Third Aunt flipped Iron Bolt's mother's saggy, depleted breasts over her shoulder and onto her back so the child could chew on their nipples. She herself took her top off and began to chase a chicken all over the yard.

"Look at you two!" Gran exclaimed. "You really must be boiling."

"I'm in my own courtyard," Third Aunt protested loudly. "I haven't gone out like this. I may be old, but I haven't lost all shame."

"Why are you shouting like that?" Iron Bolt's mother asked.

"Her ears aren't good. If you talk too quietly, she doesn't hear you."

Iron Bolt's mother shouted, "Are your ears still inflamed then, Gran?"

"Pus comes out of them when it's hot," Gran told her.

"You need to look after them properly or you'll go deaf."

"I wouldn't mind. Things are much simpler if you can't hear anything."

As they were talking, they heard footsteps outside the courtyard. Gran hurried to shut the gate and she noticed Inkcap running down the alley.

"You've been in the river again!" she shouted at him. "How come a river ghost didn't get you?"

Inkcap was holding some pieces of hemp paper.

"I didn't go in. You told me not to."

"Come over here," Gran ordered.

Inkcap went over to her, and she ran her fingernails down his bare spine. Several white marks appeared immediately.

"You said you didn't go in the water. These marks wouldn't be here if you didn't."

"Old Faithful told me to catch some thornback fish for the Branch Secretary, but I only went in for a moment."

"Old Faithful's mother's rheumatism was so bad she couldn't stand up straight," Iron Bolt's mother said, "but you never saw him collecting wild honeycomb for a plaster to put on her back. And now he's sending thornback fish to the Branch Secretary?"

"Thornback fish is really strong smelling. Is it any good to eat?" Third Aunt asked.

"It's to make medicine," Inkcap said.

Gran saw a flea jumping around on her foot, but it disappeared in the blink of an eye.

"There are fleas in your yard," she said. "So the Branch Secretary isn't better yet?"

"Don't you know that strong-smelling fish can cure diseases? It's far too smelly to cook and eat."

Third Aunt surveyed the alley, which looked soft in the sunshine, with wisps of white steam rising and shimmering in the sunlight like grass growing in water.

In the end, Third Aunt didn't catch the chicken. The chicken didn't want to be caught. Third Aunt shoved her fingers up its backside every day, fishing for eggs but it was too hot for there to be any that day. When the bird escaped, it ran from the front alley to the back alley, and then over to East Alley.

The Branch Secretary took the medicine jar and poured out the dregs at the mouth of the alley. Almost-There was with him and asked, "Is the Branch Secretary better now?"

The Branch Secretary said he was. Almost-There came over and scuffed his foot over the dregs.

"Kick the dregs away and you'll never get sick again," he said.

The Branch Secretary didn't reply but placed the medicine jar on the rear windowsill of the house and walked along the alley. He was still wearing a black coat, and the white shirt underneath was freshly laundered. His hands were behind his back, and he held his pipe in his right hand, with the long stem tucked up his sleeve. At the foot of the mountain gate, the ash had been shovelled into two piles to be used as fertiliser. Noodle Fish was there, scolding a dog. It was Ever-Obedient's dog, and it was chasing a rat along Crosswise Alley.

"Keep your nose out of things," shouted Noodle Fish.

The dog stopped and turned to glare at him, and the rat disappeared into a crack in a stone at the base of a wall. Noodle Fish stamped his feet to scare the dog away, but the dog didn't move. When the Branch Secretary came over, it ran away.

"That dog's a snob," Noodle Fish said. "Have you eaten yet, Branch Secretary?"

"No. You're welcome to treat me."

Noodle Fish laughed and the Branch Secretary said, "I'm sorry I startled you. Do you know where Stonebreaker is? Is his wife still not pregnant?"

"It's difficult for me to ask something like that, but it doesn't look as if she is."

"You need to get a grip on Stonebreaker, and not let him run around all night without coming home."

Noodle Fish blushed.

"Stonebreaker is a bad lot, Branch Secretary, you–"

"What do you mean, a bad lot? Compared with Pockmark, he's a fine young man, isn't he?"

Noodle Fish grew more nervous and began sweating.

"Branch Secretary, I'll talk to his mother about this…"

The Branch Secretary was staring at the gentle slope by the Kiln God Temple, where Lightkeeper was coming down the road. He was wondering if the reason Lightkeeper had seen him and not tried to avoid him was because he was looking for him. But he stopped looking at Lightkeeper and said, "Never mind, Noodle Fish. Aren't you re-laying the floor of your pigsty today? Look at the sky. It's a beautiful day for it."

Lightkeeper had indeed come looking for the Branch Secretary. He told him that while other individuals had recovered their confiscated items from the Kiln God Temple, when he went to get his pair of gauze-covered lanterns and blue-and-white bottles, none of them was there. Dazed-and-Confused told him they'd been confiscated.

"Other people get their things back, but my family doesn't," Lightkeeper complained. "Isn't there a policy for this?"

"There should be," the Branch Secretary said.

"Policies should be written for people like us. Well, it's fine if all the books are burned and I don't want those lanterns any more, but I have to have those three blue-and-white porcelain vases. I need them for reference when I'm firing the kiln."

"You've been going on about firing blue-and-white porcelain for years now. Why haven't you been able to manage it yet?"

"I can't get the colour consistent. Besides, even though they don't have the expertise, Pendulum and Winterborn are in charge of firing the kiln and all they let me do is transport the porcelain clay."

The Branch Secretary became serious. "My instructions are that you keep transporting porcelain clay," he said. "At the kiln site, upgrading is the first order of the day and firing porcelain comes second."

Lightkeeper suddenly felt deflated.

"If you want to study the vases, you can go to the Kiln God Temple to examine them."

"Isn't it the Cultural Revolution any more, then?"

"Whether it is still the Cultural Revolution or not, it's all the same to you."

With that, the Branch Secretary shrugged his black coat back onto his shoulders and turned away. He knew that Lightkeeper was still standing there, but he didn't look back and walked on to the entrance of the village. Inkcap and Gran were looking at the stone lion and making a papercut.

Gran had taken the medicinal powder Third Aunt had given her back home and smeared it on the chickens. Inkcap gave Gran the hemp paper, saying it was from the Branch Secretary so that she could make a papercut of the stone lion for him and stick it on the gate. Gran was quite taken aback. She didn't know why the Branch Secretary should want her to cut a stone lion just like that. It was not something that had ever happened before. Of course, Gran had to do what the Branch Secretary said, so, despite the sun's heat, she and Inkcap had gone to the entrance of the village.

The body of the stone lion was huge and clumsy. The carved stone patterns had become covered with moss over the years. Now the moss was green with yellow and white patches mixed in, which made the lion look as though it was growing fish scales. Unfortunately, half of the mouth was smashed, and the stone ball was gone from inside it. Gran walked around the stone lion, looking for the best angle for her papercut. When she put her head to one side, pus flowed out of her ears. She just sat there, letting Inkcap mop it up with leaves while she went on cutting. She couldn't cut as she pleased because she was under orders from the Branch Secretary, but once she put scissors to paper, she found herself carried away by them. She took a deep breath, her nose and mouth scalded by the heat of the day, but she also smelt the refreshing smell of the maize and rice seedlings growing in the fields by the entrance to the village. There was a mixture of soil, vegetation, chicken droppings and cow dung, moist and spicy. The hind legs, rump and waist of the lion were the first to appear.

"It's coming! It's coming!" Inkcap exclaimed.

Inkcap had seen cows giving birth to calves and this was just the same. Except once the calf had its hind legs and buttocks out, the person delivering it would pull on its hind legs and plop! The calf would come out in a gush of water.

But Gran stopped cutting and asked, "What's coming?"

"A lion's being born," Inkcap said.

"Does that make me a lioness?"

The two of them bounced up and down on the steaming ground, laughing uproariously.

Just as the lion papercut was finished, the Branch Secretary arrived. He looked at it and said, "Where's the lion's mouth?"

"The mouth is broken off," Gran said. "Don't you want the papercut to be the same as the stone lion?"

"This is no good. You've cut out the lion without a mouth? Cut it again, cut it again. You need to give it a mouth and there has to be a ball inside it. Do you know what that ball is?"

"It's one of those decorated balls," Inkcap piped up.

"That's something you kick around with your feet. Why would you want to put that in its mouth? It's a medicine pill."

"A pill?" Inkcap echoed doubtfully.

"You don't understand, but your gran knows," the Branch Secretary said.

Gran, of course, did understand. There was a folk legend about the lion erected at the entrance of the village. It said that, a long time ago, a monster was born in the mountains and it often came out to attack people and livestock. A certain man in the village was determined to go out and learn the necessary skills to eliminate this evil. One night an old man with a white beard came to his house. After questioning him, the old man saw that the other man was firm in his intentions, so he took out two spherical pills and told him, "Since you are determined, I will give you two pills. When the monster comes, take the first pill. It will turn you into a lion and you can eat the monster in one bite. After that, you take the second pill, and you will return to your human form."

With that, the old man disappeared.

One day, the monster reappeared. The man took the first pill and instantly turned into a mighty lion and rushed towards the monster. The monster was so frightened it fled back to the forest and never dared come out again. When the man put the second pill into his mouth and was about to swallow it, he suddenly thought that if he changed back into his human form, what would he do if the monster came back again to wreak havoc? In order to be able to quell the monster, he decided not to swallow the pill and stayed as he was. He stood at the entrance of the village, guarding it, and he slowly turned into a stone lion, still holding the second pill in his mouth.

Gran told Inkcap the story, adding that she didn't know if there had been a stone lion outside Old Kiln before this one. Maybe there had been, and it was destroyed for whatever reason. Anyway, when she married into Old Kiln, she was told the legend of the stone lion but never saw one. It was only in the year of land reform that the Branch Secretary had someone carve this stone lion and put it there. As she told Inkcap the story, it was clear she understood why the Branch Secretary had ordered her to make a papercut of the lion. Inkcap also understood why Bash had broken the stone lion's mouth when he started smashing the Four Olds.

As Gran was cutting out the new paper lion, the Branch Secretary was walking down the path from the embankment onto the river strand. The rice seedlings planted there were already green and about four fingers tall, while the seedlings planted in the rice field had not yet recovered their colour and were yellow and wilting. He smoked a pipe down on the strand and then climbed back up the embankment. Gran had already finished the papercut of a fierce lion complete with a pill in its mouth. The Branch Secretary was satisfied and put the papercut in the pocket of his white shirt. He pressed it carefully and went off to Millstone's house.

He was worried that the rice seedlings were late taking on colour, and so was Millstone. The fields needed water. The irrigation channel was repaired, but the water flow was not substantial. They arranged for the labourers to improve the stone weir in the river at the entrance of the channel to raise the water level to ensure that enough water could flow in to irrigate the fields, day and night. The irrigation process needed an expert to oversee it and Millstone had been thinking hard about who to appoint. First, he had considered Noodle Fish, but his eyesight wasn't good enough. It was fine during the day but not at night, and Millstone was afraid he wouldn't be up to the job. Then he considered Dazed-And-Confused, but following Happy's death, he had become careless when feeding the cattle. He was either too early or too late, and the floor of the cattle pen was not well cushioned with soil, so there was mud everywhere. In the end, Millstone decided to let Noodle Fish take over the cattle-feeding duties and tell Dazed-And-Confused to supervise the watering of the rice fields. But when he discussed the plan with Dazed-And-Confused, he didn't want to do it. He said he was too sleepy and, if he took the job on, he couldn't guarantee he wouldn't doze off and let the irrigation channel overflow.

"You don't seem to have any trouble mucking around making those grass sandals of yours all night," Millstone protested. "Why don't you doze off then?"

"I make a bit of cash out of them," Dazed-And-Confused said, "and I like money."

"So now you're getting on a bit, you don't sleep because you love money and are afraid of dying, is that it?"

"I may not sleep that much, but I do love dozing."

"I'll send you Inkcap. If you get sleepy, he can wake you up."

Dazed-And-Confused still wasn't happy about the idea and he asked Millstone to send Inkcap with someone else first because he was very fond of the cattle and wanted to feed them for a few more days. Three days, just three days would do. So in the end, Millstone sent Soupspoon and Inkcap to supervise the irrigation of the rice fields, just to start with.

Inkcap and Soupspoon didn't have much to say to each other, and the day passed mainly in silence. When night came, Inkcap asked Cowbell to keep him company while Soupspoon took a straw door curtain with him to go and sleep on the road between the rice fields and the lotus pond. After his mother died, Soupspoon suffered from panic attacks and he often collapsed. He always let Inkcap do the running around to check the water flow, clear out the channel in this field and block the flow in that one.

"I'm exhausted," Inkcap said.

"It's because your little baby legs are so weak," Soupspoon replied.

Inkcap was so angry that he sat down and stopped work too.

"You little prick," Soupspoon said. "How come you didn't get tired when you were running around after Bash all the time? Why won't you take orders from me like that?"

"Well, why don't you come and do the work with me instead of letting me do it all on my own?"

"I've not been in good health recently, and I'm not eating properly–"

"Does the sight of your own shit spoil your appetite, then?"

Soupspoon snatched off his shoe and threw it at Inkcap, but Inkcap dodged and the shoe fell into the water.

Even after this altercation, Inkcap didn't leave, but actually fished Soupspoon's shoe from the water and gave it back to him.

"All right, all right," said Inkcap. "You can sleep on your straw curtain as long as you tell me some jokes."

But Soupspoon wasn't the kind of person who told jokes, and when he went to lie on his door curtain he just went to sleep. He looked like a somnolent pig, but unfortunately, he could no longer sleep soundly. He woke up in a panic and decided that it must have been Inkcap and Cowbell talking too loudly that had disturbed him.

Inkcap and Cowbell lowered their voices.

"Why did you come here on water-watch with Soupspoon?" Cowbell asked.

"He's only doing it for two more days, then Dazed-And-Confused's taking over."

"That lazy hound."

Soupspoon, who had been asleep on his curtain, found that his arse had slipped into the muddy water of the rice field and the feeling of liquid splashing around him had made him want to shit. He snatched up a lotus leaf, spread it out on his straw curtain and shat on it. When finished, he picked up the leaf carefully and flung it into the rice field, leaving a foul smell blowing on the wind.

"You should have wrapped it up and taken it back for your private plot," Cowbell told him.

On the third day, Inkcap reported back to Millstone that Soupspoon only wanted to sleep all night, so instead of getting him to supervise the irrigation, Millstone would do better to send himself, Inkcap and Cowbell.

"Dazed-And-Confused will be going tomorrow," Millstone told him.

But he had no way of knowing that, that very afternoon, the sick bullock in the cowshed was finally going to die.

Inkcap didn't know about the dead bullock. It died in the afternoon, and Millstone asked Barndoor to butcher it. Barndoor knew that the animal had a bezoar, so he cut open the belly and carefully removed it. Lots of people came to see what the bezoar looked like now the old bullock had died.

"How sad for this poor beast. It had endured a life of toil but even in death it has made others rich," Barndoor said.

"Bezoars come from cattle with liver disease," Baldy Jin said. "Do you think Noodle Fish has set aside some money for Stonebreaker in the same way?"

Everyone looked at Noodle Fish, who was carrying his ladder and holding a hammer and a wooden prong, getting ready to skin the bullock and nail the hide to the wall. When he heard what Baldy Jin said, he didn't respond but just bent down to tie his straw sandals onto his feet. The sandals were so old and rotten that they had no heels left, so he had to strap them onto his feet with straw rope.

Barndoor's hands were covered in blood, and he wiped them warningly across Baldy Jin's mouth, saying, "Don't go there."

But Noodle Fish ignored them all and said, "It would be good if my liver could grow a bezoar."

As the hide was peeled off the carcass, a large amount of black blood pooled on the left side of the bull's rib cage. This could only mean that the animal had been beaten. Who had beaten it like that? It could well have been beaten to death.

Millstone went over to look and shouted at Dazed-And-Confused, "How did this bullock die?"

"I fed it in the morning, and it was lying on the ground and couldn't get up. After lunch, I was putting earth down in the pen and it still just lay there. I told it to get up but then, when I looked, I saw it was dead."

"So what's the deal with all that blood?" Millstone asked.

"I don't know."

"You fed this animal and you still say you don't know? Did you hit it?"

"It kept lying there and wouldn't get up to eat, so I used a stick to persuade it to get up, didn't I?"

"You beat it with a stick, and you killed it. You should be dead, not the animal!"

"You can't talk to me like that. I'm your senior, and you should be calling me Uncle. You can't talk to me like that."

Millstone lost his temper too.

"You're a fool. Get out, get out now, and never come back to the cowshed."

"You can't do that. I was appointed by the Branch Secretary. You can't send me away."

Millstone rushed into the rammed earth house next to the cattle pen, threw out a shabby quilt that Dazed-And-Confused kept in the room, and then hurled it even further away. A shoe rake used for making straw sandals bounced out onto the stones outside the courtyard gate, breaking three of its teeth. Dazed-And-Confused hurled himself forward to fight Millstone, using his favoured method of grabbing for his opponent's testicles. But as soon as he lowered his head to attack, Millstone kicked him away.

Even though Millstone was the team captain, he really went for Dazed-And-Confused. The onlookers pulled Dazed-And-Confused away, but he kept struggling to get back in the fight.

"Do you really think you can fight Millstone?" Baldy Jin said. "Take your quilt and shoe rake and go home. Go home now."

He escorted Dazed-And-Confused back home, with Dazed-and-Confused carrying his quilt and shoe rake.

"So what if I beat the bullock?" said Dazed-And-Confused. "It deserved to die anyway. I only hit it a couple of times, how could that have killed it? And what about Millstone? He almost kicked me to death himself!"

"In the end, it was sick, and it wasn't going to live long anyway. Now it's dead, it just means there's meat to eat."

"Too right. And who doesn't like meat? I bet Millstone does."

But Dazed-And-Confused didn't go home. Instead, he tried to get Baldy Jin to go with him to the Branch Secretary's house to file a complaint against Millstone, saying he had kicked him in the balls, that he couldn't get it up now, and that he would never have any descendants.

"You don't even have a wife, so even if you could get it up, you still wouldn't have any children or grandchildren."

Dazed-And-Confused cursed Baldy Jin again, and Baldy Jin just smiled.

"You go if you want to," he said and walked away.

Cowbell stayed with the slaughtered beast and was a very active participant in the skinning process. When Barndoor started to peel back the skin, he went over to help pull it off the legs, but a lot of people were already there and they didn't let him join in. So he pulled at the tail instead. The bull's left eye was still open, bright as a bronze bell, and the right eye was closed. The eyelid was decomposing, but there was a yellow mark under the eye. He knew that this was from the beast's tears, so he reached out to press on the left eye, hoping to shut the eyelid. But it wouldn't close and the eye kept staring at him. He slapped at a fly that had settled there, took the small straw hat off Barndoor's head and put it over the beast's face.

"What are you doing?" Barndoor asked.

"It's looking at me."

"Go get its pizzle."

It was only then that Cowbell saw the great length of pizzle still inside the beast's abdomen. They cut it off, and Baldy Jin took it to hang on a pillar in the cowshed. Several women had already arrived with large pots on their backs and were preparing to light the stove to boil water.

"What's that thing?" they asked.

"It's something nice that men have too," Baldy Jin told them.

"Only men have it, not women?"

"Sometimes women have it too, and sometimes they don't."

The men all laughed.

"Stop talking nonsense," Noodle Fish said. "Hang that thing in a cool place and let it dry in the shade so we can make it into rope for the rollers."

"It would be a shame to waste it making rope," Useless broke in. "I'll take it for the Branch Secretary to steep in some wine."

"That's a clever thought, Useless," Baldy Jin said.

"The cleverer people are, the less hair they usually have," Useless said. "How could I have a clever thought with a head of hair like mine?"

Before anybody could say anything, and out of nowhere, Ever-Obedient's dog rushed over and grabbed the pizzle. It had arrived with its master, but no one had paid it any attention. It was only when it snatched the pizzle that everyone reacted and yelled in alarm. By then, the dog had already run out of the courtyard. They chased after it, carrying sticks to beat it with. In their excitement, they took off their shoes to throw at it but by now the dog had run along the slope in front of the mountain gate and no one could catch up with it. Only Cowbell kept up the chase.

He drove it to the west entrance of the village and then down the dirt bank, but he still couldn't catch it. Even though the dog ate the pizzle, Cowbell wasn't cross with it and instead felt rather exhilarated. He didn't go back to the cowshed but went straight to the rice field to see Inkcap.

Inkcap had filled the channel from one weir, so he blocked the entrance and opened the flow across the other one. Cowbell ran across and told Inkcap about the dead bullock.

"Which one was it?" Inkcap asked.

"The one with the bezoar."

Inkcap gave a little cry.

"Are you happy about that, then?"

"When I woke up in the morning, my mouth was watering, but I didn't expect to be in for such a treat. Have you ever eaten beef?"

"No."

"I haven't eaten it either, but I've heard it's delicious and chewy. The more you chew, the more you want to eat."

Because of the heat and the tempting shade of the tree, Soupspoon was lying naked on his back on his straw curtain under the willow in the far field. Inkcap told Cowbell to keep his voice down lest Soupspoon overhear them.

"But if they share out the beef, everyone will get some anyway," Cowbell pointed out.

"I just don't want him to know in advance."

At that moment, Soupspoon screamed, scrambled up and started jumping up and down. The two lads ran over, to discover that a bee had stung his prick, which by now was already as red and swollen as a carrot.

"Oh!" said Inkcap. "That's a really weird place to get stung."

"Quick. Blow some snot out of your nose," Soupspoon yelled.

Putting snot on a bee sting helps relieve the pain, so Soupspoon blew his own nose first and wiped the snot on his prick, then did the same with the snot Inkcap and Cowbell managed to produce.

"Why don't you lie on your stomach, then you won't get stung down there," Inkcap said.

"I only lie on my stomach when my wife's underneath me. I'm not on top of her now, am I?"

"I've often heard people say that a man who's about to die lies with his prick pointing up in the air."

He wiped a handful of thick snot over Soupspoon's prick, covering the tops of his thighs too.

"Where the fuck did that bee come from?" Soupspoon continued. "And why the fuck did it have to sting me?"

Honeybees die after they've stung someone and, sure enough, when he looked, Inkcap found a dead bee on the ground. It was yellow, and its body was short and fat. It was certainly not one of the wild bees from the locust tree forest on Middle Mountain.

"This is one of Cattle Track's domestic bees," Inkcap said.

Soupspoon went over to have a look.

"Fuck that Cattle Track," he said. "Lots of people in Old Kiln have a bit of rheumatism, but Cattle Track's mother has to have it so bad that she has joint pain all over her body. Her legs are deformed from it, and she doesn't have a single straight finger left on her hands."

Cattle Track's uncle, who lived in Xiahewan, had brought him over a beehive. Of course, the bees made honey, some of which Cattle Track's mother gave Inkcap to eat, but to treat her rheumatism, she herself had to catch three bees a day and let them sting her. Not just anywhere either, but where it really hurt. Soupspoon cursed Cattle

Track for not closing the beehive properly and allowing the bee to sting him.

"Bees collect nectar from flowers, why would it be looking in your stinky old crotch?" Inkcap said.

"Bees are one of the Four Bad Elements," Soupspoon snapped, as he put on his clothes and headed for home. "Make sure you look after the irrigation properly."

Inkcap and Cowbell were preoccupied with the slaughtering and butchering of the bull. They didn't know if the process had been completed, nor when the meat was going to be divided up. However, they didn't dare delay watering the rice fields as the sky was getting dark, so they let the water into the largest rice field and then ran off towards the cowshed. But when they got there, the door was locked.

"Didn't they slaughter it here?" Inkcap asked.

"Of course they did, but maybe they took it somewhere else to butcher it," Cowbell told him. "Is there anyone in the courtyard?"

"If there were, the gate might be closed, but that's locked too."

The two of them felt deflated.

"Surely they're going to share the meat out among the community," Cowbell said.

They walked away dejectedly, but then Inkcap exclaimed, "Hey! I can smell meat."

They both wrinkled their noses and sniffed. It was definitely the smell of meat. Cowbell climbed up onto the courtyard wall from the wall of the privy, and from up there, he saw lights on in the three-roomed house that the Branch Secretary had bought, and several people inside shovelling pieces of cooked meat into their mouths.

Cowbell slid back down and said, "They're eating it in secret. Let's climb over the wall and see if they dare refuse to give us some too."

"I don't dare."

"Don't you want to eat?"

"Of course I do. But my background is no good."

At this point, they heard footsteps in the yard. The two of them knelt in the privy, not making a sound. Then they saw the courtyard door being pulled open. A hand stretched in through the gap to open the lock, and then the door opened.

"You're such an idiot, Baldy Jin," someone said. "You even locked the door."

"If the door was just closed, wouldn't it be obvious there was someone inside?" Baldy Jin said, burping as he spoke.

The other voice spoke again. It was Awning.

"Don't burp like that or everyone will know you've been eating meat."

"There isn't much meat on a bull's head. If you really want to eat your fill, even a leg isn't enough. Why didn't we have a few mouthfuls of stewed beef? No one's going to look inside our bellies."

The last ones to emerge were the Branch Secretary and Barndoor. The

Branch Secretary had a lump of meat in his hand and Barndoor was thrusting something else at him.

"What's this?" the Branch Secretary asked.

"Just take it," Barndoor said.

The Branch Secretary accepted it and said to Millstone, "All right, I'll take my portion home first. You go and tell the community members we're sharing out the meat. I'll tell everyone that when they are eating their beef, they should think about this bullock. It toiled away all its life, ploughing the land and has even given us meat to eat now it's dead."

Millstone grunted his agreement.

"Tidy the place up," the Branch Secretary continued, "and don't let anyone see there's been a fire lit. It might make them suspicious."

The Branch Secretary left and so did Millstone. Barndoor opened the courtyard gate and went in to fetch a kerosene lamp which he hung on a pillar in the cowshed.

"What about the balance rod?" Awning asked. "Where is it?"

Inkcap and Cowbell came out of the privy and tiptoed along the alley.

"I never thought we'd get to eat beef," Inkcap said.

"I've always said that the village cadres serve the people, but now it turns out the fuckers are stealing our meat," Cowbell replied.

"I could never dare say that."

"Well, no one's going to stop me saying it."

"I'll just say I didn't see anything."

"You're from a bad background, so you couldn't give evidence anyway."

Cowbell sniffed at Inkcap.

"Why do you stink like that? Have you trodden in some shit?"

Inkcap looked down at his shoes and saw that was exactly what had happened, so he rubbed it off on the ground.

"How much do you think each person will get?"

"Don't worry about that, it'll be shared out soon, and we'll eat ours the same night. Have you got any radishes at home?"

"What do you need radishes for?"

"Cut beef into shreds and fry them together with shredded radish. The radish blends with the meat and tastes like beef too."

Millstone rang the bell in front of his gate.

The ringing of the bell wasn't loud, but everyone heard it like a clap of thunder rolling across the sky. The alley was alive, and the children in their courtyards cheered, some shouting for their dads and some for their grandads, and everyone appeared to be in awe of the occasion. It seemed as though they had been listening out, just waiting for the bell to ring, and they all came out of their houses with basins in their hands. By the afternoon, the entire village knew that the bullock was dead and was being butchered, and they ran to see it. Later, Millstone said they still had to cut up the meat and wash it. He told them to go home and wait until the meat was shared out in the evening. Now they were standing around in the alleyways, excitedly banging the pots with their hands, and talking about how much meat each person would get.

Inkcap trotted home, and as soon as he was in the courtyard, he shouted, "Gran! Gran! They're going to share out the beef."

But Gran didn't seem to be there. Damp firewood was smouldering inside the house to smoke out mosquitoes. The smoke choked Inkcap and he sneezed several times. He took the earthenware basin from on top of the cabinet cover, but he decided it was too small, so he changed it for a larger one. It was then he saw Gran sitting on the edge of the *kang* in the side room.

"Gran," he called out. "They're going to share out the beef."

Gran still didn't say anything. Inkcap went closer and saw that she was crying.

"Look how happy it's making you," Gran said. "You'd be happy even if your gran had died."

Inkcap stood and stared at her. She must have known that the bullock was dead and that the beef was going to be shared out, and he didn't understand why she was saying this. But she had said it, and now she looked at Inkcap and took him in her arms.

"That's fine if there's beef to be had," she said. "You go and get our share and bring it back here. I'll stew it up for you."

"Cowbell said it's best fried with shredded radish. Can we give him a radish?"

"Sure, sure."

Inkcap took the earthenware basin to the old public office. The courtyard was full of people, and insects were swarming around the kerosene lamp in a black cloud. Millstone was marking off the name of every head of household and as he marked each one, he looked over at Awning who was cutting up the meat. When the meat was cut, he handed it over to Barndoor to be weighed. Everyone got three taels of meat and if it was underweight, Awning added some liver, heart or tripe. If it was overweight, he cut some off. Once-Upon-A-Time had a large family, so, in addition to the meat, Awning added some pieces of leaf tripe.

"Why have you given me so much leaf tripe?" Once-Upon-A-Time complained.

"It goes well with the meat and offal," Awning told him.

"Why didn't Half-Stick get leaf tripe?"

"Where are your eyes? Can't you see I got a bone?" Half-Stick snapped back.

"What are you kicking a fuss up about?"

"How's it kicking up a fuss if I'm not getting my fair share?"

Awning wasn't having any of that kind of talk, and he put down his knife and said, "If you're so obsessed with being fair, you come and do it. Come on."

"Let Awning do it," people shouted. "Let Awning do it."

"Everyone's watching me," Awning said, "so how could I get away with not being fair?"

Cattle Track shoved Once-Upon-A-Time to one side, and the courtyard returned to its former state of lively discussion.

"How am I supposed to cook three taels of meat for one person?" someone asked. "Once it's done, it'll just about fill the gaps between my teeth."

"Well, you've got rubbish teeth anyway, so just don't eat it," came the reply.

"Anyway, how come there's so little meat from a whole animal?" the first man said. "It would have been better if it was that big black bull."

"Bullshit," said Millstone, overhearing the conversation. "If you want to kill off all the production team's cattle, you can do the ploughing yourself."

"Yeah," everyone shouted. "Just shut up."

The man shut up and peace was restored.

Soupspoon arrived, limping as he walked and immediately several people started gossiping.

"I heard Soupspoon got stung by a bee."

When Soupspoon saw Cattle Track, he demanded, "I want compensation from you, Cattle Track."

"What the hell for?"

"Hadn't we better ask Soupspoon's wife if she's willing to or not?" said the man next to Cattle Track. "Huichun! Huichun!"

Soupspoon's wife was called Huichun, and a chorus of voices shouted her name.

"Huichun isn't here," Yoyo said.

"If Huichun isn't here to say either way, do you think we can let Cattle Track stand in for Soupspoon?"

Ever-Obedient pulled Yoyo away.

"That fucker's talking bollocks. You'd best stay out of it."

But when it came to Ever-Obedient's turn to get his share of the meat, Barndoor reduced the weight on the balance rod.

"What's going on?" Ever-Obedient said. "Is that rod showing its age and can't keep it up any more?"

"You should know all about that," someone said.

Ever-Obedient ignored the comment and just said to Awning, "Give me some more. How about some tongue?"

"You're not getting any tongue," Barndoor said. "Your dog snatched the pizzle. That pizzle weighed a lot, so you should be satisfied with what you've been given."

But Ever-Obedient was far from satisfied. The people behind him pushed him away, but he shoved his way back again and said to Barndoor, "If the dog ate it, that doesn't mean we ate it too."

"Is it your dog or not?" Barndoor said.

"Just because we've got rats in our house," Yoyo said, "are you saying they've eaten the grain in the rest of the village too, so you're still giving us less food? What's that all about? Just because you've been put in charge of the balance rod, you think you can use it to persecute people?"

"I may be nothing special, but what about you?" Barndoor shot back. "You just crawled out of the river."

Yoyo hurled herself forward, saying, "Are you throwing my shortcomings back at me?"

She tried to claw at Barndoor's face. He dodged her but in doing so, the balance rod knocked into the kerosene lamp, which swayed about, making the shadows dance.

"Yoyo's epilepsy," someone called out. "She'll have an attack."

"What's all this shouting?" Millstone roared. "Why are you shouting?"

The crowd fell silent. Millstone cut the bullock's tongue into three pieces and placed one on the pan of the balance rod.

"All right," he said. "Take it, take it."

When it was Cowbell's turn, he was given the bullock's muzzle.

"Is this supposed to be meat?" Cowbell asked.

"What else do you think it is?" Awning asked.

"The boy's on his own," Millstone said. "Give him some more."

Awning took the rest of the tongue, cut off a third and put it in Cowbell's basin without even weighing it.

"We know how to do things fairly," Millstone proclaimed. "We'll make sure to take even more care of the old and the orphans."

Inkcap squeezed his way forward and said, "That's good, then!"

No one seemed to have understood what he meant. There wasn't much meat left in the basket and when Awning tipped it back and forth, the last thing he pulled out was some leaf tripe.

"Is that all there is?" Inkcap asked.

Useless, who was standing behind him, said, "Those at the back who haven't got a proper share are all poor and lower-middle peasants."

"Leaf tripe is delicious," Awning said.

"I want a piece of meat."

Lightkeeper, who was behind Useless, called out, "Cut some decent meat for Inkcap. I want the leaf tripe."

"It's not your turn yet," Millstone told him.

"Am I not a member of the community, then?" Lightkeeper asked.

"We'll come to you last and then talk about it. Let's see if you're still so pig-headed."

Inkcap looked at Lightkeeper but he didn't say anything more. Awning put the leaf tripe onto the pan of the balance rod, but even after it was weighed, Inkcap stayed where he was.

"Why are you still here?" Barndoor asked.

"My gran is an old woman living alone," Inkcap said.

Inkcap was so angry that he pursed his lips and gritted his teeth. He suddenly thought of Bash. Bash might be a non-person now, but he could still protect him. If Bash was still there, Useless wouldn't be so arrogant, or if he was, Inkcap would have at least one person to back him up.

With that in mind, he blurted out, "Bash asked me to take his share of the meat for him… Bash is a poor peasant too."

"What are you talking about?" Awning said. "This bullock has only just died. When did Bash ask you to get the meat on his behalf?"

Inkcap blushed furiously.

"When he left, he said that if the village ever distributed anything, I should collect it on his behalf."

"So you know when he left, do you? Where did he go?"

Inkcap became less confident in his explanation and hesitated before saying, "I don't know. I really don't know. And I'd fucking well like to!"

"He's brought nothing but trouble on Old Kiln, and he still wants a share of the meat? He can have a share of our shit if he wants it. Next."

Inkcap didn't dare say anything more, and he stood aside with his basin of leaf tripe. But he didn't leave. He looked at those who had got their share of the meat, and at the cattle that were still awake in the cowshed and he looked at the knot of men doing the sharing out. The cowhide was spread wide and nailed to the wall, and the bullock's skull, which had been boiled clean, had been placed on the table under the kerosene lamp. Finally, the sharing out was finished. Still there in the courtyard as well as Inkcap were Lightkeeper, Cowbell and Millstone, who were beating away at the bottom of the meat basket, picking out a few shards of bone and sucking the meat off them.

"Is the meat all gone, then?" Lightkeeper asked.

"Yup. Nothing left," Millstone said.

"So there's none for me?"

"I've specially left those bones for you. After you crack them, there'll be so much marrow you could boil a whole pot of radish in it." Then he turned to Cowbell and asked, "Why are you still here?"

"I'm waiting for Inkcap to go home and get a radish."

"What's this, you little prick?" said Millstone, turning to Inkcap. "I was going to get Barndoor to cut off a bit of tongue for you, so what was all that bollocks you were talking?"

"You said you'd take care of me," Inkcap said.

"OK, OK." Millstone picked up the skull and put it into Inkcap's basin. "There's no meat on it, but when you look at it, you feel like you've been eating meat."

THIRTY-EIGHT

IT WAS A SLEEPLESS NIGHT IN OLD KILN. The village was filled with enticing smells and laughter. Every household was building fires to cook the meat. None of the dogs, cats or chickens went into their dens or roosts. They lay at kitchen doors while children rode bamboo poles and broomsticks in horse races along the alleys, kicking up as much noise as they wanted, and making sure their stomachs were empty and ready for a good meal. Inkcap took the basin home and told Gran that he hadn't been given a decent portion of beef. Gran didn't say anything. She just took out the skull and put it on the cabinet cover, then looked at it silently in the lamplight. Inkcap remembered what Millstone had said and imagined the cooked meat from the bull's head, such as the cheeks, nose, ears and tongue, and his mouth really did start to water.

"All the meat has been shared out?" Gran asked.

"Yes."

"Where are the bones?"

"They've been divided up too."

"Is the hide nailed to the wall?"

"It's on the wall of the old public office."

"Oh, so there's only this skull left?"

"That's right."

"Good. That's good. Go and dig a hole in the corner of the courtyard and we'll bury the skull."

Inkcap went and did as he was told, but he didn't understand why Gran wanted to bury the skull in her yard. Why did she say it was good? After he had finished digging the hole, Gran went over and put the skull into it.

"They bullied us, Gran. Did they give us the skull because they wanted us to bury it?"

"That bullock is with us now," Gran replied mysteriously.

After burying the skull, Gran started to cut up the leaf tripe. She was very good with a kitchen knife; she never used a grater to shred potatoes but always used a knife and the shreds were consistently long, thin and even. After the tripe was cut and put back in the basin, Inkcap noticed two rats looking down from the roof beam, their eyes glowing green in the dark. He didn't bother to chase them away but put the basin on the ground under the roof beam, pretending not to have noticed anything. One rat slipped down along the rope of a basket hanging from the roof beam, while the other jumped from the roof beam aiming directly for the basin. But just as it was about to land, Inkcap kicked the basin away, and the rat fell to the ground with a thud. Gran was cutting radish shreds at the table and asked what he was doing. Inkcap didn't try to hit the rat, which staggered to its feet and left through the kitchen door.

"Shall we eat it all at once, Gran, or divide it into several meals?" Inkcap asked.

"What do you think?"

"Let's have one delicious meal."

"OK, go on, eat your fill."

She poured a puddle of oil into the bottom of the wok and, when it was smoking hot, she added the leaf tripe. It sizzled as she stirred it and steam rose from the wok. Then she added some water and three shredded radishes. Next came salt, chilli seeds and fennel.

"It would be good to have some sunflower seeds," Gran said.

"What about some Sichuan pepper? I'll go to Barndoor's place and ask for some."

"You're going to ask for Sichuan pepper in the middle of the night?"

"That's not a problem. Besides, some pepper will make the taste even better."

"Off you go, then. Take them two of our radishes."

Inkcap went and got ten Sichuan peppercorns from Barndoor. On the way back, he passed Cowbell's house. He couldn't resist stopping to find out what Cowbell had done with the bull's muzzle.

"Do you want some Sichuan peppercorns, Cowbell?" he shouted in through the door.

Cowbell came out with his mouth full of water. Only after he had swallowed the water with a gurgling sound did he say, "You almost made me choke. I was just brushing my teeth to get the last scraps of meat."

"I've got some Sichuan peppercorns here."

"I've already eaten everything."

"What do you mean, you've already eaten everything?"

"I didn't even cook it. As soon as I got back, I tried a mouthful of it, followed by a bite of radish and I couldn't stop myself. I ate the whole lot like that."

Inkcap didn't want to tell Cowbell that he himself hadn't eaten yet in case Cowbell followed him home in the hope of more food. So he just said "Ah" and went on his way.

The key thing with stir-fried beef and shredded radish is to fry them until almost all the liquid is gone. Inkcap ate half a bowl first. He wolfed it down as if there was a hand reaching up his throat from his stomach and grabbing every morsel as soon as it was in his mouth.

"Is it tasty?" Gran asked, watching him eat.

"Very."

After finishing the first half bowl, he realised that Gran hadn't eaten any yet, so he filled a bowl for her and another for himself. That emptied the wok and Gran wanted to give Inkcap some of hers, but he refused. The two of them sat facing each other to eat and only then did Inkcap discover which bits were tripe and which were radish.

"This leaf tripe is too chewy for me," Inkcap said.

"Leaf tripe is very stubborn," Gran replied. "You have to chew it very slowly, and the more you chew, the more the flavour comes out."

They took a long time over their bowls of tripe and chewed each bite dozens of times until it slipped down their throats of its own accord. Later, Gran stood up and went to add water to the wok to make soup. When Inkcap went over to fill his bowl with soup, he saw there was still half a bowlful of tripe and radish left in Gran's bowl.

"Why didn't you finish yours?" he asked.

"I'm so full, I can't eat any more. You can have it tomorrow."

Inkcap stood beside the stove and called out to Gran. She brought the earthenware basin over, put Inkcap's bowl in it and covered it with another basin. Then she went out into the yard, shouting at the chickens, "Why aren't you in the coop yet?"

A confusion of footsteps sounded from outside the courtyard gate, and someone called for Awning. Inkcap recognised Sparks' voice.

"Hey, Awning! Have you had any of the meat yet?"

"Yes."

"Did you eat it all?"

"That little pimple of meat? Of course I did."

"There wasn't enough, was there? Come and have a drink. Have a drink at my place."

"How come you've still got some wine?"

"It's the medicinal wine from when I hurt my thigh. Go on, uncork the jar. You've got to have some wine if you've been eating meat. Come on. Come on."

Inkcap gave a sudden exclamation and asked Gran, "Where's my jacket?"

"How should I know?"

"I'm going down to the river."

"Are you going to water the fields?"

When Gran followed Inkcap out into the yard, she saw his jacket hanging on the broom in the corner but Inkcap himself had disappeared.

Inkcap had suddenly remembered that he had switched the water from the irrigation channel into the large rice field, which must have filled up by now. He rushed down to the field, where there was no sign of Soupspoon. The water had overflowed the channel and broken through the weir. It had flowed down onto the river strand below, taking a few rows of rice seedlings from the edge of the field with it. Terrified, Inkcap rushed to shovel mud across the weir to block the flow, but it was too strong. He ran over to the water inlet of the upper channel and shut that off. At that point, Soupspoon arrived.

When he saw what had happened, he said, "You ran off and left the water running?"

"I forgot," Inkcap said.

"Of course you forgot. You were stuffing your face with meat."

"How come you've only just got here if you didn't forget also?"

"You've still got a mouth on you, haven't you? Let me tell you this, if I forget, it's just me forgetting, but if you forget, it's deliberate destruction of property."

The two of them managed to repair the weir, but the seedlings that had been washed away were gone, and as it was at the edge of the field, anyone walking past could see at a glance that they were missing. Inkcap didn't know what to do, but Soupspoon just sat down for a smoke.

"Come and give me a light," he said.

Soupspoon's pipe had a very long stem and to get it going, he had to stick a piece of kindling in the bowl, light it and then suck like mad on the jade mouthpiece. At lunchtime the day before, he had been boasting about the mouthpiece to Inkcap. He said that Useless had told him it was an antique and should have been handed in, but he hadn't done so. Now, he told Inkcap to light it for him.

Inkcap didn't move but asked, "Do you think anyone will notice the missing seedlings?"

"Of course they will, unless they're blind."

"Will the team captain deduct work points?"

"Of course he will. Now, light me up and I'll give you some advice."

Inkcap lit the pipe as tears welled up in his eyes.

"Go to someone's private plot," Soupspoon said, "and take some seedlings from there to fill in the gaps here."

That was certainly one way of sorting it out, but whose plot should he take the seedlings from?

"My family plot is nowhere near the river strand."

"Take them from Lightkeeper's plot. There's no problem with doing that."

So Inkcap took ten bundles of seedlings from Lightkeeper's plot.

When he asked if ten bundles were enough, Soupspoon said he needed thirteen, but Inkcap only took one more.

"'Right, I'm going home now," Soupspoon said. "I hardly got any meat to eat, and my stomach's turning over with hunger. If you shovel some more mud onto the weir, the water won't flow into the field any more. Just remember not to tell anyone about this little incident, and if Lightkeeper kicks up a fuss, keep your mouth shut."

Soupspoon left. Inkcap continued to reinforce the earth on the weir for a while until a crashing noise sounded from the rice field, which made him jump. When he looked around, the rice field with the seedlings sparkled in the moonlight as though it was covered in a layer of broken glass. A few birds flew up but stayed low, so their feet were almost touching the surface of the water. Inkcap wasn't afraid of any birds, but he was scared that there might be wolves on the riverbank. He shouted, but the place seemed even more empty and silent when he stopped. So he didn't stop but kept shouting ever more loudly. He lost count of how many times he shouted but just went on and on, more and more urgently and more and more frequently.

In fact, Inkcap had stopped shouting some time ago and it was now only the frogs in the rice field that were making the noise. Inkcap thought it was just him. As he walked back surrounded by the extraordinary din that sounded like a cacophony of gongs and drums, he felt guilty about Lightkeeper who hadn't got any meat that evening and had had to go home with some bones to smash for their marrow to cook with radishes. Now, he himself had pulled up bundles of rice seedlings from the poor man's private plot. So Inkcap pulled up seedlings from the production team's field and replanted them in Lightkeeper's plot. It was only when he left the weir, and the shouting was still going on, that he realised it was the frogs making all the noise. He remembered standing at his house door one rainy night, pissing under the eaves and mistakenly thinking he was still pissing because of the rain pouring down from the roof. Inkcap laughed as he stood there under the moonlight, then he laughed again.

As he passed Sparks' house, the courtyard gate was closed, and the sound of drinking and people playing guess-fingers was coming from the main room. He could make out the voices of Sparks, Baldy Jin and Millstone. They must have drunk too much wine, as their voices were all over the place and their laughter rolled around like broken thunderclaps. Inkcap was keen to go in and join them, but when he pushed open the gate, he changed his mind. They had all stuffed themselves silly with meat in secret when they were preparing it, and now they were drinking together. He resented the fact that they only gave Lightkeeper some bones and him some leaf tripe. If he went in now, they certainly wouldn't give him any wine, but just use him as their gopher and get him to give a shoulder to anyone who was too drunk to make it home on their own. Inkcap gave a little groan and walked on past Sparks' house.

The alley ran along the embankment and, while the houses in other alleys either directly faced each other or had the front door of one house facing the rear window of another, only in this one did the houses stand in a row along the embankment. The village spring was located at the bottom of the embankment not far from their doors. Just three or four yards east of the honey locust tree there was a zigzag dirt road on the slope, and Baldy Jin had built a privy at the end of it. It contained two boards, and when people squatted on them, their shit fell into the piss cistern built into the slope. Everyone criticised Baldy Jin for building the privy there because, when people went to the spring to fetch water, they often heard the sound of shit splashing into the cistern. Inkcap was walking over the slope very cautiously, afraid of slipping and falling into the cistern, when suddenly someone called out, "Hey! Hey!" He turned around but couldn't see anyone. He was about to move on when the voice called out again and a head popped up from the privy. It was Lightkeeper.

"What are you doing here?" Inkcap asked.

Lightkeeper pulled him inside and whispered, "Don't say anything."

He pushed Inkcap's head down and stared at the courtyard door of Baldy Jin's house. Inkcap couldn't work out what he was doing, so Lightkeeper explained in a whisper that those fuckers had only given him a few bones and he was so angry he didn't even eat the radishes. He had taken a mat to sleep on the threshing ground but the brick he was using as a pillow was so hard it made his head hurt and he had gone back home to get a proper pillow. On his way, he passed by Sparks' house and heard the sound of drinking. He looked in through a crack in the courtyard gate and heard footsteps in the courtyard. He didn't want anyone to see him, so he ducked into the privy. He was expecting it to be Baldy Jin coming out because he had drunk too much and wanted to go home, but it turned out to be Awning. After Awning came out, he closed the gate and looked up into the sky. Lightkeeper looked up too and saw the Plough above them. Awning then looked to his left and right, so he did the same. In the dim moonlight, there was no one to be seen and no wind either. He was expecting Awning to come over to the privy to piss or throw up, so he got ready to cough to warn him it was occupied. In fact, Awning went over to the gate of Baldy Jin's house, picked up a pebble and threw it into the courtyard. After a while, the courtyard door opened a crack, and although Lightkeeper couldn't see the person's face clearly, the voice he heard belonged to Half-Stick. Awning asked if she had poured water on the door hinge, then he squeezed in and the door closed behind him. He, Lightkeeper, had been sitting in the privy watching ever since.

"But Awning was drinking with the others at Sparks' house," Inkcap said. "Why did he go to Baldy Jin's place?"

"What the fuck do you think he went there for?"

"That can't be it. They were all drinking together. Maybe he went to borrow something."

"What takes this long to borrow? And what would he be borrowing in the middle of the night? He's laying his eggs in another bird's nest, isn't he?"

The two squatting boards in the privy were clean enough, but the piss cistern underneath was humming with a hot, sour odour. They could just about put up with the unsanitary conditions, but what they couldn't stand was the mosquitoes, which made their legs itch like crazy. They kept watching the gate, but it stayed closed. A cat came out of the drainage channel under the courtyard door and looked around. Inkcap whistled to it. The cat looked his way and Inkcap whistled again. But the cat just said "Miaowuu" and walked away. In the distance, they could still hear the sound of people playing guess-fingers, and Sparks saying in a loud voice, "Fuck you, Baldy Jin. You can't get away with not drinking. You smashed up my fucking house. Anyone else would hold a grudge against you for three lifetimes, but I invited you for a drink. So you'd better fucking drink and drink properly."

"I am drinking, I am drinking," Baldy Jin protested, spluttering as he spoke. "Besides, it was Huang Shengsheng and Bash's idea to smash the house. I just went along with it to earn work points."

"Yeah, yeah," Sparks said scornfully.

Baldy Jin must have been keeping the wine in his mouth without swallowing it, but under pressure from Sparks, he finally relented.

"Fuck me, that burns! Do you think I can't take it? Come on, I'll drink till I drop. From now on, Sparks, I'll do whatever you want. You tell me to lay out the tables, I'll lay out the tables. You tell me to shut the back door, I'll shut the back door. You tell me to fuck someone, I'll fuck them."

"I'll fuck you," Sparks shot back.

"Steady on, I'm not a woman," Baldy Jin said with a giggle.

"If you really can't drink," Millstone broke in, "don't waste good wine. You can do us that favour at least. Now, that's enough talking. Just shut up."

The noise suddenly stopped. Inkcap couldn't keep quiet any longer and asked, "Why don't you come out now? Why do we care what he does?"

"They're always the ones picking on us, but now this is our chance at last. Of course we should care. Go and call Baldy Jin."

"What for?"

"Go tell him that his wife is calling him."

"I won't do it. That would be asking for a beating."

"All right, it doesn't matter if you don't. Just light my cigarette for me."

Inkcap took out a match and struck it. When he was about to light the cigarette, Lightkeeper flicked out at Inkcap's hand, sending the match bouncing into the privy, setting the grass shack alight. Inkcap hurried to try to put the fire out, but Lightkeeper pulled him away and set off with him down the zigzag path to the spring, then turned off onto another path that led to the threshing ground.

"The whole shack will catch light, won't it?" Inkcap said.

405

"Let it," Lightkeeper replied. "Then Baldy Jin's sure to come out. You lit the fire!"

Inkcap's eyes widened in shock.

"It wasn't me," he protested.

"What do you mean? You struck the match, didn't you?"

Inkcap was really frightened now and was about to burst into tears.

"So what if you started it? What does a thatched privy matter?"

"You're not a good person," Inkcap exclaimed.

"Whoever thought I was? How could I be?"

Lightkeeper wanted Inkcap to sleep with him at the threshing ground, but Inkcap failed to nod off and went home. On his way back, he heard the commotion at Baldy Jin's house.

Inkcap couldn't sleep for the rest of the night either. He was afraid of the other villagers, but he was most afraid of Lightkeeper. He missed Bash more and more. He felt that Bash was the most powerful of the lot. When he smashed the Four Olds, Useless, Baldy Jin and Dazed-And-Confused had all followed him. Millstone, Awning and Sparks might have been unhappy with him, but they didn't matter. All they ever did was curse him when he wasn't there, and Lightkeeper didn't even dare to raise his eyes from the ground when Bash was around. But sadly, Bash had left and never came back. At dawn, Inkcap finally fell asleep, and he didn't wake up until Gran called him when she had finished cooking breakfast. Soupspoon came and scolded him for not going down to the rice fields to check on the water. Inkcap talked him round by saying he'd got the runs after eating beef and drinking cold water. Did he already know how to lie, then? If not, he was a quick learner.

When Inkcap arrived at the river strand, he didn't ask about anything until Soupspoon told him that the previous night, Awning, Baldy Jin, Millstone and some others had been drinking at Sparks' house. In the middle of the party, Awning went over to Baldy Jin's house and got it on with Half-Stick. Baldy Jin had no clue about the affair, but Heaven had other ideas. A meteor fell from the sky and landed on Baldy Jin's thatched privy. The hut caught fire and when Baldy Jin came to put out the fire, he saw Awning coming out of his house. He challenged Awning but Awning said he was so drunk he had gone to the wrong door and swore blind that he hadn't got up to anything with Half-Stick. Baldy Jin wasn't convinced, so he called in the Branch Secretary. It was the Branch Secretary who managed to put a plug in this bubbling volcano.

"Didn't you know about this?" Soupspoon asked.

"No," said Inkcap.

"I thought you knew everything that went on in this village."

"No."

"Oh, so now Bash has gone you don't have anyone to tag along behind any more, is that it?" He twisted Inkcap's ear and said, "From now on, you follow me. Let me hear you say it."

"I won't follow you."

"You little prick. If likes attract, why don't you follow Lightkeeper?"

"I'm not following him either."

Soupspoon twisted Inkcap's ear again, but Inkcap broke free and said, "You've twisted my ear twice now. I won't forget that."

"What are you going to do about it, then? Beat me up?"

"I might not be able to beat you up, but I know someone who can."

"Who?"

"Bash."

Soupspoon laughed. "Pockmark isn't coming back and nor is Bash."

THIRTY-NINE

ALTHOUGH SOUPSPOON SAID that the Branch Secretary had plugged the volcanoes that were Baldy Jin and Awning, in fact, he had done no such thing. When the Branch Secretary was called out in the middle of the night, the two men had a very heated argument. Awning said he hadn't done anything, and Baldy Jin said he must have done. Awning told him he could examine his wife, and Baldy Jin said that would prove as much as going into a field looking for holes after the radishes had been pulled. Awning told him that if he didn't have any proof, he should stop trying to frame him.

"Let's see you drink some old pickle juice, then," Baldy Jin demanded.

The residents of Old Kiln had always believed that you shouldn't drink old pickle juice after having sex, even if you had a raging thirst, or you would develop consumption. Baldy Jin scooped up a large bowl of old pickle juice from the pickle jar, but Awning refused to drink it. Baldy Jin said that proved he was guilty, and he began to wail and howl. The Branch Secretary picked up a lamp and told Awning to follow him into Baldy Jin's firewood store. He ordered Awning to take off his trousers, and when he did so, there was his prick standing to attention. The Branch Secretary stuck a piece of kindling into its opening and pulled out a silk thread. The Branch Secretary's face hardened, and he kicked Awning's arse. Then he carried the lamp out of the storeroom and called Baldy Jin and Useless over to him. He told Useless to give him the pen from his pocket.

"Are you going to interrogate them? I'll take a record," Useless said.

But the Branch Secretary took the pen, pulled the cap off and gave the body of the pen to Baldy Jin. He himself held out the pen cap and told Baldy Jin to insert the pen into it. Bald Jin had no idea what was going on, but he tried to do as he was told. The pen cap shook and he missed. He tried again and the same thing happened.

"Can't you get it in?" the Branch Secretary said. "That's a lot easier than what you have to do when a man and woman come together!"

"If the cap didn't keep moving, I'd get it in."

"So what are you going after Awning for? I bet he couldn't manage it either!" Then he raised his voice to address the assembled company: "There's nothing going on here. Why would there be? Old Kiln is really in a bad way. Aren't you all embarrassed at making trouble like this? Go back to your homes, and don't have any more drunken parties like this. If you've got wine, drink it by yourselves. Wine just makes you hate each other."

With that, he left and went home. The thin jacket he had draped across his back slipped off his shoulders three times on the way.

Even though the Branch Secretary had left, the crowd of onlookers failed to disperse. They had all eaten a lot of meat and were feeling hot all over. They tried to talk Baldy Jin down, saying, "Just forget it. This is the kind of thing that happens when people get drunk."

But Baldy Jin wasn't having it. He jumped to his feet and said to Awning, "You drank my wine then went rushing off to my house, didn't you? Didn't you?"

He looked around and saw a pile of bricks on the ground. Everyone rushed to stop him, but he was too quick and snatched up the bricks. Awning stood his ground. Baldy Jin was no match for Awning and he knew it. Ignoring the others who were trying to take the bricks away from him, he threw them at Awning. Awning caught them easily and put them back down on the ground.

"I was just drunk and ended up on the wrong *kang*. I didn't know who anyone was."

Baldy Jin turned and left. When he got back to his own courtyard, he said to Half-Stick, "That fucker may not have known who anyone was, but you did, didn't you!"

His back began to hurt again as he twisted it turning away, and he leaned against the door frame for support.

The next day, nearly the entire village found that their old ailments had returned. Stargazer's coughing sounded as though he had a pair of bellows lodged in his throat. He coughed so hard that neighbours rushed over to press on the acupuncture point between his nose and mouth and release his *qi*. Old Faithful's wife's goitre was twice as big as usual, and the blood vessels at its surface looked like black-and-purple earthworms wriggling along the ground. The Branch Secretary had a stomach ache and so did Barndoor. Iron Bolt had the runs so badly it wasn't worth his while pulling his trousers back up, and Decheng couldn't stand straight because of the pain in his lower back, so he ended up walking crabwise and banging into trees.

That night, after Sprout had finished eating her share of the beef, she started to hiccup. She thought it was an extended belch, but to her surprise it turned into a hiccupping fit that kept her awake for the rest of the night and continued into the following day. She met Goodman in the alley. He was carrying a basket on his back piled high with firewood. Sprout took the basket from him and put it against the wall in a corner.

"Quickly," she said. "Talk to my illness. It's these hiccups."

"Tell me what's going on with you."

"I'm hiccupping, and it's going to give me a nervous breakdown. Do you think I bumped into a ghost?"

She was hiccupping even as she spoke. Goodman looked at her and asked, "When will you pay back the money you borrowed from me?"

Sprout's eyes opened wide in astonishment. "What money? When did I borrow any money?"

"Are you still hiccupping?"

"What are you talking about? Last time you spoke to my illness, I gave you three yuan and cooked you some eggs. Why are you saying I borrowed money from you? Hey, I've stopped hiccupping!"

"Hiccups are nothing, I just distracted you from them and gave you a surprise."

"Ah! So you were talking to my illness. How much do I owe you this time?"

"I don't want a single fen from you."

"Even if you did, I don't have any money today," Sprout chuckled but then went on to ask why so many people in the village had got sick after eating beef.

"Why? Because they shouldn't have eaten it! That bullock spent its life ploughing the fields for the villagers of Old Kiln. It got sick, but because it had a bezoar, the village didn't try to treat it. Dazed-And-Confused beat it. He beat it to death. It was full of grievances, and the villagers built its grave in their own stomachs. How could those grievances not spread?"

"That sounds really scary. So when it died, we shouldn't have eaten the meat but thrown the body into the piss cistern for fertiliser?"

"Didn't you see how excited the villagers were when the bullock died? If they were allowed to eat the cows in the cowshed, they would all be slaughtered in one night! The world is so heartless. Man drinks his mother's milk when he is little and when he gets older, he relies on his father for support. If he has any ability, he leaves his mother and father to go and look after a wife of his own. We have the production team, which everyone depends on. People who are short of food ask it for food, people who need clothes ask it for clothes, and they think that is their right because it's only when they have used up every last bit of family reserves that a family splits up and people go their separate ways, scattering like baby spiders that have finished eating up their parent."

When Goodman had finished, he went over to pick up the basket of firewood. But when he put his arms into the straps and tried to stand up, he found he couldn't manage it. Sprout went over to help him, but even when he was on his feet, Goodman's strength kept failing him. Suddenly he lost his balance and he went down in a heap, basket and all. There was a burst of giggling from nearby.

The giggles came from Inkcap. On his way home from the rice field, he had picked some wild flowers on the weir. These flowers have very long stems and the peduncles at the top taste very sweet. Inkcap went past Tag-Along's house where the courtyard gate was open. He called out to Xianü as he wanted to give him some of the flowers to eat, but Xianü didn't reply. Diagonally opposite, three pigs were snouting around under a tree. They had dug up a cabbage root and were quarrelling over it. One of them heard Inkcap's shout and came running over. Inkcap recognised it as the pig they had given to Iron Bolt's family.

"Hey, you've grown even more!" he said.

"You never come and see me," the pig complained.

"You're someone else's pig now. If I went to see you, I'd want you back. Do you miss me, then?"

The pig just grunted and lay down next to Inkcap, and Inkcap petted it with one of his hands. He saw that it had an iron collar around its neck with a length of red tether hanging from it.

"Did you break your tether and escape?" he asked.

He took off the length of red rope and tied it in the shape of a flower around the pig's ears. It made it look like a little child, so he put the flowers on it too and said, "Good boy! You have to get up and go now."

The pig rolled over, got up and followed him.

"Don't follow me, go home. Gran is waiting for me."

"I'll go and see Gran too," the pig said.

"All right. But when you've seen her, you have to go home. Gran was talking about you just yesterday."

Inkcap and the pig walked along, one behind the other, and when they met Goodman on the way and saw him fall over with his basket full of firewood, they laughed because he looked so silly.

Goodman stayed sitting on the ground.

"Just look at all the weird things going on in Old Kiln," Sprout said. "Why have you tied a flower on that pig's head, Inkcap?"

"This used to be my pig. We gave it to Iron Bolt's family last winter. It can understand human speech. That's why I gave it the decoration."

"People say you hang around talking to pigs and dogs all day long. Is that really true?" Sprout asked. "Tell it to get out of my way so I can see for myself."

"We seem to have bumped into a bit of a bastard here," Inkcap told the pig. "We'd better get out of his way. You can jump over to that tree."

The pig jumped.

"Ai!" Sprout exclaimed. "Has that pig become a spirit or is it you who aren't human?"

Goodman, on the other hand, just laughed and said, "You're quite something, Inkcap! Pigs are stubborn and have foolish fire in their nature. You have transformed its foolish fire."

"I don't understand what you are saying," Inkcap said.

"It doesn't matter if you don't understand. But I have something to tell you. Come over here and don't let the pig hear."

When Inkcap went over to him, Goodman whispered, "That pig is going to die soon."

"Is that because you're putting a curse on it? It's still young, and it won't be time to kill it until the end of the year."

"This pig died last winter, but it owed your family money, and it paid you off by going to Iron Bolt's family for a year. Don't take it back to your house now or you'll put it in your family's debt again. Would that not just increase its suffering? But you have transformed the foolish fire in its nature, and it has escaped the suffering of the animal world, so you have not wronged this pig."

Inkcap had his doubts about all this, and he looked at the pig with tears streaming down his face.

"Why are you crying, Inkcap?" Goodman asked.

Inkcap didn't take the pig back to his house but turned around and went to Iron Bolt's place. He let the pig into the yard.

"Stay here now and eat a little more each meal. And behave yourself."

The pig tried to follow him out, but Inkcap closed the courtyard gate. On his way home, he kept thinking about what Goodman had said. He didn't know whether the pig would die of illness, be bitten by a wolf or be crushed to death when the wall of the pigsty collapsed. The more he thought about it, the more he wondered whether Goodman was having him on. He told himself, It's nonsense. That Goodman is talking nonsense.

Cowbell stopped him in the lane and said that he was hungry. He hadn't expected to be hungry after eating that beef, but now, if he didn't have meat regularly, he found he missed it. Once he had tasted meat, he craved it. When he saw a chicken, he wanted to eat chicken, when he saw a pig, he wanted to eat pork. Huang Shengsheng ate a sparrow, so why didn't they try it too?

Inkcap was determined not to eat sparrows, but Cowbell's words gave him the idea that he could cut some flesh from the *taisui* at Bash's shack and cook that. He also came up with another idea: once he'd had the *taisui* flesh himself, he could scoop up a ladle of *taisui* water and give it to the pig at Iron Bolt's house. Then the pig wouldn't die as soon as Goodman predicted, would it? Inkcap told Cowbell his idea and Cowbell agreed to give it a go. This emboldened Inkcap. On the way, they discussed various aspects of the plan: which way to go to the shack, where to cook the *taisui* flesh and whether Bash would come back. What would happen if he found that the *taisui* had some flesh cut off it when he got back? However, once they started talking about Bash, they got into an argument.

"I don't care what anyone says, Bash has always been the most capable person in Old Kiln," Inkcap said.

"If he's that capable, why isn't he Branch Secretary," Cowbell shot back. "Why was he driven out of the village?"

"He wasn't driven out, he left of his own accord."

"How do you know he wasn't driven out?"

"Of course I know. It was me who reported to the cadres' meeting that the villagers wanted Huang Shengsheng driven out. Bash went with him of his own accord."

"You reported it? How did you know about the cadres holding a meeting?"

Inkcap clapped his hand over his mouth, regretting what he had just said, and quickly added, "I... I was just trying to trick you."

He didn't dare look at Cowbell but directed his gaze at the flashing points of light reflecting from the porcelain shards in the road surface. Just at that moment, he felt distinctly superior to Cowbell. Cowbell might be a bit taller, and his status might be a little better, but what did he really know?

He knew nothing! Inkcap remembered that night, under the tree out front, when Apricot asked him to go to the little wooden shack to deliver her message. He smiled at the tree, and the tree started to sway in the absence of any wind, and without thinking about it, he kept talking about Apricot.

"Apricot?" Cowbell said.

Inkcap realised he was giving himself away and changed tack by asking, "What do you think of Apricot?"

"She's too fond of sticking her nose in other people's business."

Inkcap didn't like this answer.

"Your business, you mean? I don't care what you say about her to others, but don't talk like that to me."

"Why not?"

"I'm her uncle. I'll..."

Inkcap suddenly stopped and was left with his mouth hanging open, as the very person they were talking about was walking towards them from the porcelain shard road. Apricot saw them and stopped where she was. With the light behind her, her whole body seemed almost transparent.

"Inkcap, you—"

"Call me 'Uncle'."

"Have you seen Goodman?" she continued. "He isn't at the kiln or the Mountain God Temple."

"Call me 'Uncle'," Inkcap insisted.

Apricot's face darkened.

"Stop pissing around. I'm trying to tell you something important."

Inkcap was chastened and told her, "I saw him just now, carrying a basket of firewood. Are you looking for him?"

"I need him to talk to my dad's illness."

"Is it bad again?"

"He hasn't eaten for days. He won't eat any of the things he normally likes. I gave him a share of the beef, but he wouldn't eat that either."

If Potful was so ill he wasn't eating, surely that could prove fatal. Inkcap forgot about going to the little wooden shack and told Cowbell to come with him to look for Goodman. They went to both the kiln and the Mountain God Temple, but there was no sign of him at either. They went back to the village, to Sprout's house, where they saw a basket of firewood in the courtyard gateway. What had happened was that Goodman and Sprout had reached the gate of Sprout's house where they found Stargazer's wife, drooling. She stopped Goodman and asked him to talk to her condition.

"Have you fallen out with your mother-in-law again?" Goodman asked.

"Look at my mouth," Stargazer's wife said. "I've been drooling ever since I ate that beef. Isn't it disgusting?"

So Goodman sat down in Sprout's house again and talked to her illness. But when Inkcap and Cowbell arrived, what he was talking about was not how to cure drooling, but about his own past.

"One day in January, three years before I became a monk," he said, "my family told me that our cow had run away again. I said I could find it. We had bought it from the Bai family, and it must have gone back to its old home. I would go and find it after dinner. So, after we had eaten, I did indeed go to Lao Bai's house and he told me not to worry, the cow was there. He also said that I had arrived at a good time as a virtuous person was living there who talked about good books every day and I should listen to him too. I said I would. That night, the virtuous person told us a story about loyalty, filial piety, righteousness, and the retribution of good and evil, and urged us to learn from it. I felt very happy when I heard this and found it all very interesting. The next day, the Bai family asked someone to take the cow home for me, and I stayed with them to listen to more good books. As it happened, I had been suffering from tuberculosis back then and couldn't do heavy work at home anyway.

"One day, he was talking about the Peking Opera *San Niang Educates Her Children*. He talked about how, when the little master was at school, he was told by his classmates that San Niang was not his biological mother. When he got home from school, he had to recite his lessons as usual in the evening, so he deliberately made a mess of it. San Niang urged him to do better, and he sneered at her, saying, 'You are not my biological mother. If my biological mother were here, I would not have to tolerate your unjust treatment.' This made San Niang so angry that she smashed her loom. Their servant Lao Xuebao heard the quarrel between mother and son, came out to ask what was going on and said to the little master, 'San Niang weaves day and night to support and encourage your education in the hope that you will grow up and honour your ancestors. You should never say such evil things. Hurry up now and ask your mother to punish you.' So the little master knelt in front of San Niang and confessed, 'This child is young and ignorant, and he is disobedient to his mother. Please teach him a lesson and beat him.' But San Niang told him to stand up at once, saying, 'It's me who does not know how to be a proper mother. I should not have taken it personally and lost my temper with you.'

"I found this very strange. Weren't the two of them quarrelling? How had they reconciled like that? I thought about it carefully and worked it out. Of course, these were enlightened people. Enlightened people debate the nature of sin, and fools argue about what has actually happened. I experienced my own sudden enlightenment. I had a brother who was gambling, and I was so angry with him that I was making myself sick. I immediately ran back out into the courtyard, reprimanding myself as I went. Even if it was wrong for others to gamble, was I right to be angry? If my brother was gambling, would making myself sick with anger mean that he stopped? I thought to myself, I must be a fool because I was arguing about what was actually happening. Then I started to weep, and after I had wept for a while, I walked home. As I walked, I thought to myself, How can you be right if you only look at people's faults? How can you be right if you get angry when people are wrong? I went on turning this over and over until I got home. At night, I kept worrying about it until I began to laugh. The next morning, I felt my stomach itching, and when I looked, I saw that many years of sores and ulcers from my tuberculosis had scabbed over overnight, and later I was completely cured."

Goodman stopped at this point and asked Inkcap what he wanted.

"Finish telling the others about your illness first," Inkcap said.

"I have finished."

"You only talked about yourself."

"When I started talking to people's illnesses, I told them that if they could truly repent of their mistakes, they would be cured. This method is derived from my own experience. Now, why are you looking for me?"

"Apricot wants you to talk to her dad's illness."

"Is Potful's condition getting worse, then?" Sprout asked.

Inkcap told them that Potful didn't want to eat anything, and Goodman said, "This man can learn from me in future."

"Why do you say that?" Sprout asked.

"I have been in the same situation myself and almost starved to death. I won't go to Apricot's house, Inkcap. I'll tell you my story and you must listen to it and tell it to Potful, then he will definitely be able to eat again."

"That makes me your disciple," Inkcap said.

"I don't accept disciples," Goodman replied. "Bash isn't here at the moment, but if he was, he would say that me talking to illnesses is one of the Four Olds. If I am going to transgress, I will do so by myself and not drag you into it."

"Didn't Bash himself once get you to talk to his illness?" Inkcap asked.

"There was no Cultural Revolution then."

Goodman continued with his own story. He said that after recovering from his illness, he started farming again during the Qingming Festival.

"While I was working, I was always thinking about the various good books I had heard. There was the *Poem on Training Women* that listed the seven reasons for divorcing a woman. I checked over and over again, and among all the women in our village, counting from the east end to the west end, there was not a single one who didn't commit these seven offences. And when I looked at the men, I found that none of them were filial and loving. This made me feel that living in this dirty world was meaningless and that it would be better to die. Then I thought about how I should die. Hanging was too ugly. If I cut my throat when I hadn't actually done anything wrong, it might provoke speculation after my death. After much thought, I finally figured out a way. If I didn't eat, wouldn't I die of starvation? I started to skip meals. That was at the end of April. When my family found out, they became anxious and tried to persuade me to eat, but I refused to listen. They knew I had a good relationship with Master Guo who taught in the village, so they went to ask him to talk me round. I said to him, 'In this evil world where men are unfilial and ungrateful, and women are unvirtuous, what is the meaning of life? What is the purpose of living at all?' He replied, 'Living is living, what purpose are we looking for?' I said, 'If there is no purpose to it, why should I eat?'

"After five days of starvation, without my realising what was going on, my soul left my body, walking without legs, hovering, fluttering and swaying, not far off the ground, flying freely and nimbly, and in no time, I had already arrived at the county town. It was during the Dragon Boat Festival, and they were slaughtering a pig back at home. Far in the distance, I could faintly hear it squealing. I realised my wandering spirit was just a part of the soul that remained with my body. As soon as I heard the pig squealing, I turned round and went home. When I walked into the courtyard, I saw them busy killing the pig, and I said, 'If you kill it, it will kill you. The cycle will go on endlessly. It is so pitiful.' When I went inside, I saw my own body and smiled to myself, saying, 'So there you are, still the same.' After my soul re-entered my body, I revived. When I opened my eyes and looked at my family, they all appeared very worried. I asked myself what they were worried about. What did they think I was doing asleep there like that? Gradually it dawned on me that it was because I was about to starve myself to death. I asked myself, Who will your parents have to rely on when you die? Are you going to starve to death because of the filth in the world? Do you think that if you starve to death, the world will become a better place? No, I thought. Then I asked myself, So why are you alive? I answered my own question: First out of filial piety to my parents, and then, after they have passed away to try to persuade the world to change its ways for the better. With these thoughts in my head, I asked my family to make me some congee, as I wasn't going to die after all."

Goodman paused, then said, "Do you remember what I have just said, Inkcap?"

"I remember."

"Then tell Potful exactly what I have said. If he is in tune with me and can understand my words, then he will be able to eat. If he can eat, his condition will improve, and in future, you can be my disciple."

"What if he isn't in tune with you and doesn't understand what you're saying?"

"Then there's nothing I can do."

Inkcap and Cowbell went over to Potful's house, but they didn't go in. Instead, they told Apricot to come out and passed on to her what Goodman had said. Inkcap kept asking Cowbell if he had left anything out and Cowbell assured him that he hadn't.

"Do you remember all that?" Inkcap asked Apricot.

"Yes," Apricot assured him.

"Tell your dad exactly what I have said to you," Inkcap instructed her. "If he is in tune with me and can understand my words, then he will be able to eat. If he can eat, his condition will improve."

"How can they be your words?" Cowbell said. "They're Goodman's words."

Inkcap smiled at Apricot but she didn't return the smile. She just said, "Why don't you come inside and sit down?"

Inkcap refused.

"Won't you have a drink of water?"

Again, Inkcap refused.

"You'd better be off, then."

Inkcap dragged Cowbell with him as they left. Once they were out in the alley, Cowbell cursed Apricot for being so stingy after they put themselves out so much for her over something so important. She hadn't even offered them a poached egg, and she hadn't even returned their smiles. Inkcap didn't say anything.

FORTY

AT NOON THE NEXT DAY, Ever-Obedient took over management of the irrigation from Soupspoon. He was very steady and conscientious in his work, and didn't have Inkcap constantly running to and fro, opening and closing the waterflow. But just as Inkcap was singing his praises, Ever-Obedient threw two baskets at him and told him to go to the lotus pond to fish out some duckweed for his pig. Pigs love to eat duckweed, but the production team had already stipulated that no one was allowed to fish for duckweed in the pond because it was too easy to break the lotus stalks when doing so, and breaking a lotus stalk damaged the lotus root too. Inkcap told him he didn't dare do it.

"You may not, but I do," Ever-Obedient said. "My pig grew up eating duckweed."

So Inkcap went to the lotus pond to fetch the duckweed. He was so scared of being recognised, he picked a lotus leaf and put it on his head like a hat. Just as he had filled half a basket with duckweed, Millstone passed by the pond and saw him. Millstone reprimanded him and said he was going to dock him a day's work points as punishment. Inkcap went to Ever-Obedient to complain, but Ever-Obedient just cursed him for being so stupid. Why hadn't he waded into the middle of the pond to fetch the duckweed? That way, if he had heard anyone coming, he could have held his nose and ducked under the water. Inkcap quelled his anger and went home for lunch. He didn't greet his swallow when he saw it and, when he met Apricot again, who was still ignoring him even though she had clearly seen him, he didn't even ask whether Potful had started eating again.

Apricot had already run on past Inkcap's house when she turned and shouted, "Quick! Get Gran for me! Get Gran!"

"Ha!" Inkcap shouted back. "You call her 'Gran' but you can't call me 'Uncle'?"

Apricot burst into tears and, just at that moment, Big Root happened to pass by in the alley. Apricot seized hold of him and hustled him off with her, towards her house.

Gran had already finished cooking when Inkcap got home and was sitting on the steps making papercuts. When she looked up and saw Inkcap's hangdog expression, she said, "There's food in the pot, help yourself."

Inkcap filled himself a bowl of flour porridge with potatoes. Gran had left the potatoes whole, so when he ate them, he had to open his mouth really wide, which made his eyes bulge.

"Did you and Ever-Obedient see to watering the fields?" Gran asked.

Inkcap choked on a potato, unable to breathe, let alone speak.

"Ever-Obedient is OK," she went on before looking up and realising Inkcap hadn't replied. When she saw he was still choking, she hurried over and beat him on the back. The potato stuck in his throat finally went down.

"Why are you bolting your food like that? Who have you been arguing with?"

"OK?" Inkcap echoed in disbelief. "That's rubbish."

He went back to eating his potatoes, the hangdog expression still on his face. Gran returned to her papercuts. "You'll make yourself ill, eating with a face like that," she said.

"If I tell you something, do you promise not to overreact?"

"What?"

Inkcap wanted to tell the whole story about Millstone planning to dock him a day's work points, but he just couldn't get the words out.

"What's up?" Gran asked.

"You have to promise not to get worked up."

"I promise."

"Apricot wants you to go round to her house. Perhaps she's had another row with her dad and made him mad again."

"If that's the case, and Apricot wants someone over there, it could be that her dad's condition has got worse."

"I don't know."

Gran put down her scissors and made to leave but Inkcap said, "You promised not to get excited. Why don't you have something to eat first?"

"You think it's not urgent if someone's ill? Can't you even pass on a simple message?"

Inkcap was very unhappy about what Gran said. He didn't blame Gran, but he did blame Apricot, who really was an interfering busybody like Cowbell had said. Not only had she bad-mouthed Bash and made Potful ill, but every time he met her she made him lose his temper. The clove tree in the corner of the courtyard began to rustle its leaves, but he glared at it and it stopped. He just sat there, holding his bowl, his thoughts in a whirl.

Outside, a man was selling *liguo* candy. The sound of his voice was very faint, as it was coming from the roller stone at the entrance to the village. As soon as Noisy entered the village and passed that roller stone, he always began to cry his wares. But this time, his cries didn't excite Inkcap who remained sitting there like a lump.

"Noisy's here," Gran said as she headed for the gate. Inkcap didn't move. Gran bent to the crack in the wall where she kept her nest of hair and pulled out a clump.

"Don't you want any *liguo* candy?" she asked.

"No," Inkcap replied.

"Look at what a brave boy my grandson is! He doesn't even dare break wind! Come on. Get a move on."

As Gran pushed him out of the door, he snatched up a clump of hair on the way.

Noisy had already moved on from the roller stone along Crosswise

Alley to the patch of rough ground in front of Barndoor's house. The patch contained three stooks of wheat straw, one belonging to Barndoor's family, one to Almost-There's and one to Palace's. Noisy had propped his bicycle up and was standing smoking and staring at Barndoor's courtyard gate.

"Get your *liguo* candy for scrap copper, iron and bundles of hair," he shouted.

Barndoor's gate remained resolutely shut. A cat was crouching, baring its teeth like a tiger.

There was no one around, so Inkcap asked Noisy, "Have you brought any pig's testicles this time?"

Two large bamboo baskets were hanging on the rear rack of Noisy's bicycle. Inside them were black thread, white thread, hairpins, mirrors, combs, bamboo back-scratchers, shoelaces, red hairbands, razors, trouser-leg ties, aprons, face soap and face cream. A cloth bag was hanging in front of the bike which held the *liguo* candy. There was also a piece of iron wire inserted into the handlebar, twisted a few times and with a strip of red cloth wrapped around the top, which announced that Noisy could also castrate pigs.

Inkcap's question about the pig's testicles was quite deliberate because, last time Noisy was in the village, he had wanted to give Flower Girl just such a thing. As he asked, Inkcap was looking at the roses growing on top of Barndoor's wall, where one flower was in vigorous, bright red bloom.

Barndoor's courtyard gate opened, and Flower Girl emerged with a cotton kerchief on her head. When she looked up and saw Noisy and Inkcap together, she went past without giving them a glance but walked on over to the stooks of wheat straw.

Only then did she turn and say, "Hey, Inkcap, what have you stolen from Gran so you can get some candy?"

"It's Gran's hair and I didn't steal it," Inkcap retorted.

Three chickens were pecking away under the wheat stooks. They were raising their heads, scratching away at the straw with their feet and then lowering their heads to peck up the grain.

"I can't have got all the grain out first time," Flower Girl said.

She shooed the chickens away, then knelt down and shook out the straw to winnow it. She repeated the process but there was no wind to help her, so she had to blow at them to separate the few remaining grains.

"Have you got any soap?" she asked Noisy.

"Yes, I've got some here," he replied.

But he didn't give Flower Girl the soap, Instead, he took the ball of hair from Inkcap, and without even checking it, reached into his cloth bag, pulled out a handful of *liguo* candy and gave it to him.

"Is that all?" Inkcap said.

"Just how much do you want?" Noisy exclaimed.

Muttering about how stingy Noisy was, Inkcap took the candy and sat down on the straw to eat it. *Liguo* candy sticks to your teeth, but that means you can't eat it all at once and have to prise bits away with your tongue, so you can enjoy its cloying sweetness for even longer.

"Is it tasty?" Noisy asked from beside the stooks.

"Very," Inkcap replied.

"If you close your eyes and lick it slowly, it's even tastier."

Inkcap just grunted. He knew that Noisy and Flower Girl wanted to talk to each other, and now that was just what they did.

"What are you messing around picking up a few grains of wheat for?" Noisy asked.

This was followed by the sound of straw rustling and Flower Girl saying, "Hey you... Inkcap!"

Inkcap knew she was calling him but he was only interested in eating his candy. After a bit, Noisy turned to look at him and he made sure his eyes were tight shut.

"Are you asleep?" Noisy asked.

He disappeared behind the stook and the rustling of straw sounded again.

"You've got some nerve!" Flower Girl said. "Inkcap..."

"The little prick's asleep," Noisy assured her.

"He may be little but he's a real troublemaker," Flower Girl warned him. "I don't believe he could go to sleep that quickly."

Noisy crept round the stook again and Inkcap made sure he looked fast asleep, with his head tilted to one side and his hands hanging loose. Noisy put another piece of candy in his hand to test whether he really was asleep. Inkcap grabbed it immediately, opened his eyes and said, "Do you think a little piece of candy's going to be enough to get rid of me? Not with what you want to get up to!"

Noisy was stunned into silence, but Flower Girl said, "What do you think he's doing, Inkcap? Come and help me pick up the grain."

But Inkcap didn't help her. Instead, he took another piece of candy from the cloth bag and said, "I'm not going to pick up your wheat, I've got to see Gran."

With that, he left. He didn't even run because he guessed that Noisy wouldn't come after him to snatch back the candy he had taken. He was quite right too.

"Where has Gran gone?" Flower Girl asked.

"She went to Apricot's house," Inkcap told her.

"Has she taken the meat out of Potful's throat?"

"What do you mean? Who takes meat out of someone else's throat?"

"You don't know?" Flower Girl asked.

"I heard that a cow died in your village," Noisy broke in. "Did every family get a share of the meat?"

"Yes, of course they did," Flower Girl said. "Almost all of them ate their share the night before last, but Apricot only fried up their meat for Potful this morning. He had cut the meat into large chunks but Apricot was reluctant to eat them because they looked so chewy. When Potful was about to tuck in, she went to the spring to fetch water and he sat on the *kang* to eat. The meat wasn't cooked through, and the chunk he ate was so big that he had to keep chewing and chewing to try and soften it. In the end, he decided it would be a waste to spit the chunk out, so he swallowed it, and it got stuck in his throat. When Apricot got back with the water, the meat was still stuck, and Potful's face was red. Apricot tried to get the lump out with her fingers but couldn't manage it so she asked Barndoor to help."

Noisy laughed. "How could he still choke on a lump of meat at his age? All he needed was a couple of slaps on the back and he could have swallowed a lump of iron!"

"You don't choke on meat, do you Inkcap?" Flower Girl asked.

"No."

"People do silly things when they're ill," Flower Girl said. "Potful's no spring chicken, and he's captain of the production team. How could he be more greedy at the sight of meat than Inkcap?"

Noisy was still laughing as he said, "If something weird's going to happen, it's bound to happen in Old Kiln. If he thought he was going to choke on a piece of meat, why didn't he just spit it out, cut it into smaller pieces and then eat it?"

Inkcap started to feel the panic rising in him and his right eye began to twitch. He rubbed it with his hand, but it kept on twitching.

"Is my eye twitching because something bad's going to happen?" he asked.

"Perhaps it's been looking at things it shouldn't," Noisy said. "Don't you know, you little prick? People should be like those two old court attendants, Tianlong and Diya, and not look at things they shouldn't look at and not talk about things they shouldn't talk about."

Inkcap glared at Noisy and thought to himself that if Barndoor had gone to help fish out the meat, why had Apricot looked the way she did and told him to call Gran? Could it be that the meat was still stuck?

"What can we do if we can't get it out?" he asked.

"Of course it can be got out," Noisy said. "But if it really can't, then there's nothing to be done. He'll suffocate to death. I'm not going to let that happen to me when I eat meat."

That was indeed what happened, though. The lump of meat was stuck fast, and Potful suffocated to death.

The news spread throughout the village. At first, no one believed it and thought it was a joke. They also said that after Potful got sick, he just wanted to die. He had tried hanging himself with a strand of hair, beating his brains out on a bale of cotton and eating himself to death with sweets but none of that had worked so in the end he'd had to kill himself by eating meat! After it was confirmed that he had indeed suffocated after getting a lump of meat stuck in his throat, everyone ran over to Potful's house, crying, "God, how could this happen? How could this happen?"

Inkcap hurried off and found many villagers standing around Apricot's house and courtyard. The Branch Secretary and Millstone were already discussing the funeral arrangements. According to custom, a person must be buried on the third day after death, but Potful had been as strong as an ox before he became ill and was still young. He hadn't given a single thought to death, so he had not had a coffin or tomb made in advance. After he fell ill, there weren't many other members of the family, and Apricot had never thought her father would die so soon. Father got cross with daughter and daughter got cross with father, and that was how they rubbed along. When Third Aunt had nothing else to do, she came over to pass the time of day with Potful. She had once reminded Apricot that there was a big, thick tung tree in the backyard of Almost-There's house and that Almost-There had said he was going to sell it. Apricot hadn't been particularly interested but Third Aunt said, "If the price is right, you should buy it. After all, your dad's health…"

Apricot wasn't very happy with the suggestion. "My father's a youngster compared with you. Besides, he still hasn't fulfilled all his duties."

"What duties does he have left?" Third Aunt asked. "The kiln sites on Middle Mountain are all finished, aren't they?"

"If my father wasn't team leader, do you think there'd be any kilns at all? He's got dozens of years of being cross with me left."

"You're just a child, aren't you?"

Apricot laughed. "My dad does get dizzy and can't walk properly, but he is not sick inside himself and he can still eat and drink."

But Potful was caught unawares, and it was eating and drinking that killed him. Millstone took the lead and bought Almost-There's tung tree. He told Almost-There to fell it and make a coffin, even though the wood was still fresh, and hadn't been dried and seasoned. He told Tag-Along to take some men and build a tomb on the rear slope where Potful's family cemetery was located. That meant there was no need to check the feng shui. Tag-Along said they needed bricks to build the tomb, and they would have to be bought from Xiahewan Village. It would take them two days to transport the bricks back from Xiahewan. Millstone told Baldy Jin to use the walking tractor and it would only take two trips, so nowhere near two days. Millstone recalculated. No matter how fast he got the coffin made, it would still take three days, and another two days to paint it, so there was no way the body could be buried on the third day. With those extra days and the helpers needing three meals a day, Apricot's food store would be seriously depleted and besides, the weather was so hot, the body couldn't be left out that long.

It was the Branch Secretary who made the final decision. Almost-There's tung tree was not to be felled, and the Branch Secretary would donate the coffin he had already had made for himself to Potful. Also, instead of hauling bricks over from Xiahewan, the tomb could be made using discarded saggars and broken pots and bowls from the kiln. The villagers of Old Kiln had used the same scrap materials to build the walls of the temples, so why not for a tomb? Besides, hadn't Potful's major preoccupation when he was alive been with the kiln site? What could be more fitting than a tomb made of bowls and saggars where his soul could live on in peace?

Millstone sent for Pendulum to come down from the kiln site and asked him if there were any old saggars they could use. Pendulum told him there were some, but not many. The Branch Secretary then said they would demolish the wall of Potful's family courtyard. The courtyard walls were all made of waste saggars, and that was how they settled things.

"You have been in charge here for the last few days," the Branch Secretary told Millstone, "and you're the one responsible for his death. Now the village can't even lay on a proper funeral! Potful was the production team captain, so we've got to do right by him. Besides, the current situation in Old Kiln isn't very healthy, and people are all over the shop. Let's take advantage of this to bring the village together."

"I know you've set an example by giving up your own coffin," Millstone said. "The rest of the funeral must be done properly, no matter what. The old captain may have offended a few people during his lifetime, but I've gone from house to house and asked everyone to come and burn some paper money and told those who can lend a hand to come along."

"That's good," the Branch Secretary said. "My stomach's really playing up. I'm going back for a lie-down. If you need anything, let me know."

But before he left, he went up to the house to see Potful. Potful was still lying on the *kang*, and Third Aunt told Sprout to bring her some water to wash the body.

Apricot was still clinging to her father's body, wailing, "My daddy isn't dead! Daddy! Daddy!"

But her daddy didn't reply. She stretched out, touched his hands under the sheet and cried out that they were still warm. Then she touched his feet and cried out that they were still warm too. Then she wept and cried out again, "My daddy isn't dead. My daddy isn't dead."

Third Aunt reached out and touched Potful's hands too.

"They're so cold they'd freeze your marrow, Apricot!"

Apricot wailed and burst into tears.

"Don't cry, Apricot. Don't cry just yet," Third Aunt said. "Wait till you've burned his paper money, then you can cry. Why don't you do it now?"

Someone had already bought some paper money from Kaihe's consignment store and Inkcap, who was standing at the entrance of the courtyard, snatched the paper money from the man who had bought it and ran over to Apricot. She knelt in front of the *kang* and was about to burn the paper money when Third Aunt said, "Did you pay for that paper money, Inkcap?"

"No."

"Are you out of your mind? It's worthless if you haven't paid for it."

But Inkcap didn't have any real money, so he took back the paper money and asked the people gathered in the courtyard if any of them had any cash. No one did, or at least only five or ten fen, though Barndoor had two yuan.

"The Branch Secretary's got a five yuan note," Gourd said. "With that, you can get some more for Potful."

"Are you still serious about bribing ghosts?" Soupspoon asked. "If paper money's worth that much, a man could become a county magistrate when he's dead!"

Inkcap took no notice of Soupspoon and went to look for the Branch Secretary in the annex. The Branch Secretary was just coming out to go over to the main building. Inkcap asked him for the five yuan note, then he spread the paper money out on the ground and touched each sheet with the five yuan note, counting as he went, "Five, ten, fifteen, twenty..."

He went all the way up to eighty-five before he got his numbers mixed up and stopped counting out loud.

"Why don't you close his mouth?" the Branch Secretary said when he went into the main room and saw Potful's body on the *kang*. He tried to press it shut himself but failed. Third Aunt told him she had been trying all that time to get the lump of meat out, so the mouth had been open and that once the body had stiffened, there was no way of closing it. When the body was on the bier, they could raise the back of his head on the pillow so his face dropped down and it wouldn't be so obvious.

"When are you dressing him in his burial clothes?" the Branch Secretary asked.

'They're not ready yet," Third Aunt told him. "Granny Silkworm is working on them in the west chamber at the moment."

"What about Barndoor? Have you told him to decorate the mourning hall?"

Inkcap brought in the paper funerary money they had bought, and Apricot lit it in front of the *kang*. She broke down and wept after burning only a few sheets and Inkcap burst into tears too.

"Stop crying," the Branch Secretary told him, "and go and tell Useless to write the funerary couplets on white paper for the door and the mourning hall. Then send someone over to my house to pick up the laying-out table. I have a long desk we can use."

Inkcap went outside where people were constructing a "seven-star" stove. Cowbell was helping Youliang mix the mud with some wheat straw. Youliang scolded him for mixing the straw in unevenly.

"You'd better not annoy Cowbell or there'll be no one to finish off the stove when you leave," Soupspoon warned him.

"I'm relying on him," Youliang said, "but just look at him, I wouldn't count on him when I'm dead and feeding the dogs!"

Inkcap went over to Cowbell and told him that the Branch Secretary ordered him to go and fetch Useless, and then he wanted himself, Cowbell and Padlock to go to the Branch Secretary's house to bring back a long desk.

By the east wall of the courtyard, Ever-Obedient and Sparks were beginning to break up the waste saggar. There were five dogs outside the wall, and for some reason they weren't barking but just sitting and watching.

Because Inkcap was so small, when he and Padlock were carrying the long desk, his own legs kept knocking against the desk legs. They turned the desk over and carried it that way. The alley was on a steep slope. Inkcap was at the front holding the edge of the table with both hands behind him, but he couldn't get a firm grip and shouted, "Stop! Let's take a rest. My hands are slipping."

But Padlock kept on pushing from behind, and because Inkcap hadn't yet let go of the desk, he fell to the ground, knocking out one of his front teeth. As he was groping around for his tooth, Padlock complained, "How can a sawn-off little runt like you carry anything?"

Inkcap stopped searching for his tooth.

"Who are you calling a sawn-off little runt?" he said.

"You, you sawn-off little runt!" Padlock yelled back.

Inkcap jumped up and spat in his face. Before he was even fully on his feet, Padlock spat a whole mouthful of phlegm back at him. Luckily, Tag-Along was just passing by and he shouted at Padlock. Inkcap felt that he had lost face in front of a family member, so he jumped to his feet to spit at Padlock again.

"Let's carry it together, Padlock," Tag-Along suggested.

The two men set off with the table and Inkcap's spit didn't reach Padlock, so he took off one of his shoes and hit him on the arse with it. He thought to himself that, in the past, Pockmark had bullied him, but Pockmark bullied everyone, so that was all right. But now Padlock was trying it on, and Padlock was a nobody in the village, and that made Inkcap angry. The sun was directly overhead so his shadow was really small. He tried moving but it made no difference and his shadow stayed small. He looked up and cursed the sun. He couldn't believe he hadn't grown any more, so he went over to the sycamore tree at the roadside on which Awning had measured him that spring and measured himself again. He put his hand across the top of his head and carved the level on the tree.

When he looked, he heard the sycamore tree saying, "You still haven't grown."

"So what?" Inkcap shouted back at the tree as he walked away. "You haven't grown either."

Noodle Fish's and Stonebreaker's wives were on the way back from the lotus pond carrying baskets. Noodle Fish's wife, whose basket was full of duckweed, asked, "Who are you talking to, Inkcap?"

When he saw it was Padlock's mother, he said, "I'm really angry."

"Who are you angry with?"

"I'm angry with you!"

"I haven't done anything to you, why are you angry with me?"

"I'm angry with you for giving birth to that fucking son of yours."

"Who do you think you're swearing at?" Stonebreaker's wife said.

"I'm not swearing at Stonebreaker, I'm swearing at Padlock."

"And who the fuck do you think you are?"

Inkcap stopped swearing.

"So you've been down to the lotus pond, have you? The production team's rules say you can't go into the lotus pond. Is that duckweed you've got there?"

"I stood on the bank," Noodle Fish's wife said. "I didn't go into the pond."

"And what are you yelling at me for?" Stonebreaker's wife said. "I went to dig up some water onions."

Sure enough, her basket was full of water onions, muddy roots and all.

"How can you dig up water onions without going into the water?" Inkcap asked.

At this point, Stonebreaker's wife lost her temper.

"What about you? You went straight into the pond and trampled all the lotus plants. Why don't you go and tell the team captain about that?"

Noodle Fish's wife restrained her daughter-in-law and went over to Inkcap.

"You should stop trying to make mischief. Your sister-in-law is sick, and it was your gran who told her about collecting some water onions to make an invigorating soup. If anyone asks, what excuse do you have for trampling those lotus plants, eh?"

Inkcap had heard that Stonebreaker's wife had got sick after giving birth to her child. He didn't know what the disease was, but she was so thin her eye sockets were sunken in her face and her cheekbones were protruding. When she was talking to him, she had had to sit on a stone by the roadside to rest. He didn't say anything else.

Noodle Fish's wife and daughter-in-law walked to the edge of the threshing ground where Six Pints' wife was standing, listening to their conversation.

"Where have all the people in the village gone?" she asked. "I haven't seen a soul."

"They've all gone to Potful's house, haven't they?" Noodle Fish's wife said. "Why haven't you gone too?"

"I can't leave here."

"Isn't Six Pints better yet?"

"They say it's kidney disease and he has to drink weasel's blood. Some folk over on South Mountain have caught a few weasels but they want three and a half *jin* of rice for each of them. He's already drunk the blood of three and another one was sent to me this morning. I'm so worried that I haven't found anyone to kill it for me. Will you two come and help me do it?"

"I wouldn't dare," Noodle Fish's wife said. "Why not ask Inkcap? He's a bloodthirsty little bastard."

"Look at him!" Six Pints' wife said. "His face is so long you could hang a gourd from it. He probably won't come."

"Just tell him he's in charge and he'll be happy," Noodle Fish's wife said.

Inkcap wondered to himself how she could understand him so well. Then Six Pints' wife called his name. He pretended not to have heard anything of what had been going on and said, "What?"

"Can you kill weasels?"

"I can kill wolves! Do you think I can't deal with a weasel?"

Then he looked up and grinned at Noodle Fish's wife.

"See, I was right," she said. "Look how pleased he is."

"It was your Padlock who bullied me," Inkcap said.

"Ah, so that's what it is," Stonebreaker's wife said. "No wonder he's so cross with us. How did he bully you?"

"He made fun of me being small."

"Then he was wrong. You're so tall you have to duck your head to avoid banging it when you go through doors!"

"You and your big mouth," Noodle Fish's wife said, pulling her daughter-in-law away.

FORTY-ONE

THE WEASEL WAS BEING KEPT IN A SMALL WIRE CAGE. It was the size of a kitten and had yellow fur, the yellow turning almost to brown in the whiskery beard around its mouth, which stuck through the wires of the cage.

"You're not very old," Inkcap told the weasel, "but you have a very long beard."

He tried to pluck the beard but found he couldn't. The weasel's claws scratched at the cage, making a rattling noise.

"Don't damage that beard," Six Pints' wife warned him. "Weasel skins are worth money. I've heard the beard can be used to make writing brushes."

Inkcap opened a small door in the cage and tried to catch the weasel by the neck as soon as its head emerged, but it wouldn't come out. He used a pair of scissors to tease it out, but the weasel bit down on them and kept hold. Inkcap still couldn't pull it out.

"That's not going to work," Six Pints' wife said. "And don't try to grab its neck again. It will bite you if you miss."

"Weasel, weasel!" Inkcap exclaimed. "You look like a rat but you're as fierce as a wolf!"

"A bit like Bash, then," Six Pints said from the *kang*, where he had been lying all this time.

"Bash never did anything to offend you," Inkcap said.

"That's true. I know you and Bash are close, so don't tell him I said that."

"I will tell him."

"Come on now, Inkcap, I was only joking. Do you know what Bash is up to now?"

"The Cultural Revolution."

"He's still busy with that, is he? He burned the couplets in my main room…"

There used to be a couplet hanging on the wall of Six Pints' house. When his father passed away early, Lightkeeper's father wrote a ten-character couplet for the mourning hall which read, "A hard worker throughout his life, full of benevolence and righteousness". When Six Pints' father was buried, everything in the mourning hall should have been burned, but Six Pints' wife said what an excellent couplet it was, and she wanted to hang the two scrolls in the main room of the house as a kind of family motto.

"Others got their confiscated stuff back, but the couplets got burned and don't exist any more," Six Pints said, huffing and puffing as he spoke.

"Just lie back and don't try to talk," his wife told him. "If it's burned, it's burned. If I hadn't insisted on keeping it, it would have been burned anyway, wouldn't it? Besides, I rather think your dead father needs to have that couplet."

She took out a cloth bag and told Inkcap to cut a small hole in it, open the cage next to the hole and let the weasel crawl into the bag so he could start work.

"Is the Cultural Revolution really a cultural revolution?" Six Pints asked. "Why did they burn my couplet?"

His wife told him to stop that kind of talk.

"Bash was wild when he came here. It's no wonder he couldn't stay in Old Kiln any longer."

"I told you not to say anything, but you had to go ahead and say it, didn't you?" his wife scolded him. "Don't you know what's happened to Bash? Li Shuanglin from Xiahewan was pretty wild when he was young, and everyone hated him on sight. Then he went off to join the army. Who could have imagined he would become head of the county's military department? During the land reform, Dagui was running around like crazy, battling landlords and dividing up land, and now he's Branch Secretary. Who knows what the future has in store for Bash?"

"Too right," Inkcap said.

He opened the cloth bag next to the wire cage, and as soon as the weasel crawled into it, he tied the bag tighter and tighter, making it smaller and smaller, and waited for the weasel's head to stick out of the small hole so he could secure around the weasel's neck. But the weasel struggled so hard he couldn't hold it. He pressed it between his knees and told Six Pints' wife to get a knife and cut the weasel's throat. The weasel kept twisting around so she couldn't manage it. Besides, if the weasel's throat was cut like that, all the blood would be spilled and none of it would be caught in a bowl. Inkcap finally came up with the idea of tying the weasel to a board, bag and all, and holding it tight like that. The weasel's body was immobilised, but its head was still weaving around. Inkcap teased it with the scissors again and the weasel clamped its teeth on them, stretching out its neck. Six Pints got off the *kang*, cut its throat with a knife, and the blood flowed out. Six Pints' wife got a small bowl and caught all of it to the last drop. All through this, the weasel kept its jaws clamped on the scissors and broke wind noisily.

The weasel's farts stunk and mixed with the smell of blood, they made Inkcap dizzy. He untied the rope, took the weasel out of the bag and said, "Why did you think you had to go to South Mountain for this? Last year, three of Almost-There's chickens were taken by a weasel. If you give me a chicken, I'll catch one for you."

"Oh yes?" Six Pints said. "You just want to eat chicken."

Six Pints' wife brought the blood for her husband to drink. He took the bowl but couldn't get the blood down.

"You need to drink while it's warm," his wife told him.

Six Pints had a sip and picked several weasel hairs out of his mouth. It almost made him throw up.

His wife snatched the bowl to pick out any remaining weasel hairs, saying, "Don't you dare throw up. Hold it in."

At that moment, the sound of gongs and drums could be heard.

Inkcap pricked up his ears and said, "Hey! What's going on?"

Six Pints' wife offered her husband the bowl of blood.

"Get out, all of you," he said. "I'll drink it when there's no one else around."

Inkcap and Six Pints' wife went over to the door.

"Have they hired a troupe of musicians for Potful?" she asked.

Inkcap knew that musicians were invited to come and play for weddings and funerals, and there was just such a troupe in Xiahewan. Their instruments were good, and they knew how to play them, but the trouble was that it was the son-in-law who had to foot the bill. Apricot was Potful's only child, and she wasn't married yet.

"I heard that Apricot's had a marriage arranged," Six Pints' wife said. "Have her future in-laws paid for the musicians?"

"That arrangement didn't work out," Inkcap told her.

"It didn't work out, eh? So is she still mixed up with Bash?" Then she shouted to her husband, "Have you drunk that blood yet?"

"Yes," Six Pints shouted back.

The two of them went back indoors to find that Six Pints had indeed drunk the blood, and his mouth was ringed with red.

"I can't figure it out," he said. "What does Apricot see in Bash? Or is it just that she slept with him and now feels she can't leave him?"

"Wipe your mouth clean," Inkcap said.

The music was getting louder and louder.

What actually turned up was not a troupe of musicians but a convoy of five trucks. They stopped at the door of the shack on the highway. The people inside the trucks tumbled out like dumplings from a pan and the first person out was Bash, holding a large bundle of white paper under his arm. He rushed about marshalling the others and making sure that, right at the front of the assembly, were the people who were banging drums of all sizes, beating gongs and clashing cymbals. Old Kiln had never experienced such an assault before. The trees shuddered and even the houses seemed to shake. The glass-like surface of the lotus pond was shattered and the frogs leapt up onto the lotus leaves, croaking madly. The Branch Secretary's wife had just cracked some eggs to make poached eggs for her husband, and she threw the eggshells under the tree in front of their courtyard. A handful of chickens were scratching around there, and they suddenly flew up to the wall. The Branch Secretary's wife saw a crowd gathering on the highway, led by Bash, and she hurried back into the courtyard to tell her husband, who was sitting in a chair, eating poached eggs. He choked on hearing the news and looked at his wife in silence.

"Didn't you hear me?" she said. "I said Bash is back."

The Branch Secretary pointed at his chest and his wife came over and beat him on the back.

"Why has he come back?" she asked.

After the Branch Secretary had finally managed to swallow the piece of egg and cleared his gullet, he replied, "He's from Old Kiln, isn't he? Where else was he going to come back to?"

He turned to look and then asked, "Are you sure it's him?"

"Of course it's him. What do you think the drums and gongs are all about?"

"Aren't they the musicians hired for Potful? Go fetch Useless for me."

After his wife left the courtyard, the Branch Secretary sat down in his chair again and finished off the water that his poached eggs had been cooked in.

Useless arrived in a rush.

"What did Bash do when he got back?" the Branch Secretary asked him.

"I don't know."

"Aren't you following him?"

"I follow you, Branch Secretary."

"So you keep saying. Well, if Bash is back, he's back. Go and tell Millstone. If he's come back because he hired the musicians for Potful, no more needs to be said and they can play to their hearts' content outside Potful's mourning hall. If it isn't him who's hired the musicians, then he's come back on his own account with almost a hundred men and still we don't say anything. What we have to do is make sure we give Potful the biggest and best possible funeral."

"I know," Useless replied.

As soon as Useless left, the Branch Secretary closed the courtyard door. Useless didn't pass on what the Branch Secretary had said to Millstone. From the bank at the entrance of the village, he saw that the people on the highway were beginning to come up the dirt road to Old Kiln, so he headed off in that direction too. Dazed-And-Confused had also seen the crowd and dashed over towards the dirt road. He split the crotch of his trousers as he jumped over a ditch, but, unembarrassed, he ran to where Useless was standing.

"Are you trying to break your neck?" Useless said.

Where it crossed the dirt road, the irrigation channel used to be bridged by stone slabs so that trucks could pass over it. When the ground flooded, the channel became blocked. It was Soupspoon and Inkcap who had lifted the stone slabs to clear out the mud, but afterwards they had laid only willow branches across the channel rather than replacing the stone slabs. The willow sticks weren't tied together with ropes, so it was easy to lose your footing on them. Dazed-And-Confused watched as the crowd headed for the channel, then he suddenly set off at a run and picked up two large stones from the roadside. Just as he reached the side of the channel, two men came rushing out of the crowd and flattened him as he bent down to gather up the willow branches. One of them caught hold of Dazed-And-Confused by the head and the other held him round his buttocks. Because the crotch of Dazed-And-Confused's trousers had split, the second man's fingers actually slipped into his arsehole, and he found himself flipped over and pitched into the water of the rice field next to the dirt road.

"What are you doing? What the fuck do you think you're doing?" he yelled.

Useless was so scared he stood rooted to the spot.

Bash ran over, shouting, "What's up? What's going on?"

"He's a capitalist roader. He was trying to make off with public resources," one of the two men said.

Dazed-And-Confused got up from the rice field, dripping wet and covered in mud. He had no idea what a capitalist roader was.

"Bash! Bash! I was just going to steady the branches over the channel, and they beat me up."

"Who told you to steady the willow branches?" Bash asked.

"I was just afraid you lot would slip."

Bash turned to the two men and said, "It's a misunderstanding. He wanted to save us from slipping on the willow branches over the channel."

"But he looks so fierce," one of the men said. "We thought he was going to rob someone or start a fight."

"Right," Dazed-And-Confused said. "If someone looks fierce, he's bound to be fierce too, isn't he?"

The two men grinned at Dazed-And-Confused, and he grinned back at them.

Bash greeted Useless and introduced the two men to him: "These are comrades from the joint headquarters of the county proletarian rebels."

Useless made noises of appreciative acknowledgement. Then he looked at Dazed-And-Confused and said, "You were simply trying to help, weren't you? Don't stop now just because your good intentions came out wrong."

"You don't know about the Federation, do you?" one of the men asked.

"Of course I do, of course I do," Useless exclaimed. "It means now Bash is back, Old Kiln can have the Cultural Revolution."

"You know fuck-all then," the man said.

"I told you Old Kiln was a stagnant backwater," Bash said. "You didn't believe me, but now you can see it for yourselves. This one's called Useless, and he's the face of culture in Old Kiln."

"Not at all, not at all," Useless said hastily.

"Why have you suddenly come over all modest?" Bash said, taking Useless to one side. "The Cultural Revolution has really caught on out there and it's firing on all cylinders, 'brilliant as red flames and white blossoms'."

"I know the passage in the Guo Yu that comes from. I should recite it," Useless said excitedly.

"Trust a little prick like you just to latch onto the quotation," Bash replied. "It's not only the students who are rebelling now, the revolutionary masses are joining in too. There are already two major mass organisations in the county, one is the Proletarian Rebellion Federation Command and the other is the Proletarian Rebellion Federation General Headquarters."

"Are they both proletarian rebellion factions, then?" Useless asked.

"The Federation Command is the real proletarian rebellion faction," Bash told him. "The Federation Headquarters are all royalists."

"What's the difference?"

"I can't explain just now. Today's joint attack on Zhang Dezhang was to mobilise the folk of Old Kiln to rebel."

"You mean Zhang Dezhang, the commune secretary? Secretary Zhang?"

"He is the biggest capitalist roader in a position of authority in our commune."

Useless looked over at the crowd, and there was Zhang Dezhang, wearing a tall paper hat and a wooden sign around his neck that had his name written on it, marked in red ink with a big X.

"Ah, welcome, welcome. You are very welcome," Useless said, turning to the two men who had attacked him.

At noon, the sun was as scorching as an oil furnace, accompanied by a light wind. Far from cooling things down, though, all that did was blow heat at everyone. Bash led his group of outsiders into Old Kiln, handing out leaflets along the way. There had never been so much paper in the village. The residents picked up the leaflets, even though most of them couldn't read. They inspected them again and again, but the characters just looked like swarms of ants, so they tucked them under their arms or folded them to use as insoles for their shoes. Cowbell ran out of Apricot's house and had already picked up a thick stack, but he went on, asking anyone he met for their leaflets too. The adults were unwilling to hand them over, saying that if they took them back home, they could use them to wrap salt and chilli powder. So then he tricked the children who were carrying leaflets. He folded one of his leaflets into a paper box and batted it around on the ground. He watched while they made boxes out of their leaflets and let them play with them for a bit. Then he snatched them all up and ran off.

Bash's people finally gathered on the rough ground in front of the mountain gate. Banners written on white paper were pasted on the gate, and the gongs and drums shook the earth and sky, drowning out Apricot's weeping and wailing and the barking of the village dogs. When the mourners attending the funeral at Apricot's house came out one by one, they saw that Bash was no longer just wearing a military cap, but he had a buff-coloured military uniform as well, and even a pair of buff-coloured military shoes on his feet. He stood for a while under the medicine tree, talking to two men, one tall, one short, constantly gesticulating with his hands and, from time to time, looking up at the sky and laughing. After a while, he went over to greet the villagers who had gathered round.

The villagers seemed a little embarrassed when they saw Bash coming to greet them. They laughed and said, "You're back, then?"

"I'm not some outside cadre," Bash said. "It's not a question of me coming back or not, this is my village. Now, stand closer, everyone, stand closer."

Some of them stepped forward, not knowing what for but not wanting to ask. Huang Shengsheng was there, but they ignored him, or more likely, were too embarrassed to acknowledge him. He didn't seem to take umbrage. He stayed next to Zhang Dezhang, who was trying to hug the big wooden sign to his chest so as to take some of its weight off his neck. Huang Shengsheng kicked Zhang Dezhang's legs, and Zhang's hands dropped to his sides. The villagers started chattering, wondering what crime Zhang Dezhang had committed.

When Inkcap left Six Pints' house, he went over to Apricot's to find out who had hired the troupe of musicians. On reaching the mountain gate, he saw that his guesses had been wrong, and it was Bash who had brought all those people back to Old Kiln. His first thought was that Bash had come back to take revenge. He wanted to go to Apricot's house to tell Millstone to stay put, but when he saw Palace carrying water back from the spring, he asked him to take the message instead, while he himself staggered off, carrying the water over to the mountain gate in place of Palace. He reckoned that all those people must be thirsty, and that Bash was bound to notice him if he took them water. That would mean he didn't have to take the initiative of greeting Bash.

Bash ordered Stonebreaker to get a stool, then told Dazed-And-Confused to tie a big megaphone to a tree. Dazed-And-Confused said there was no need to do that as he could carry it and he was much more nimble and active than a tree. He could walk around with the megaphone on his shoulders. The megaphone was connected to a machine by a cord which he tripped over several times as he walked around. Inkcap trotted past carrying the water, and someone came over to ask for a drink. He put down the bucket for everyone to drink from, but there was only room for a couple of them round the rim.

Someone started scooping up the water with his hands.

"Don't be in such a rush," Inkcap said.

He picked some leaves and began to fold them, one by one, into small spoons.

"Is it sweet enough for you?" he asked. "Old Kiln's spring water is always cool and sweet."

As he expected, Bash came over, bringing the short man with him. Bash even patted Inkcap on the head and said, "This lad has an appetite for rebellion!"

"Oh, I didn't bring any food," Inkcap said. "But I did bring some water."

Bash guffawed.

"Don't worry about it, it's just a figure of speech."

Inkcap still didn't really understand what he was talking about, so he just asked, "Have you come back for good?"

"No one'll dare drive me out this time."

Inkcap was afraid Bash would let it be known that it was him who had warned Bash that the villagers were going to railroad him out of Old Kiln last time, so he hurriedly said, "Have some water."

"What are you so scared of?" Bash asked. "Do you think the Branch Secretary and Millstone are going to come and chase me off again? I hardly think they'll dare this time. Where is the Branch Secretary, anyway? Where is Zhu Dagui? Hasn't he come?"

Inkcap looked at the crowd and said, "I don't see him anywhere."

"Go and fetch him. Just tell him that Zhang Dezhang has made the journey to Old Kiln. Doesn't he want to see his old boss?"

Inkcap didn't want to go, so Bash took off his military cap and put it on Inkcap's head.

"Are you giving it to me?" Inkcap asked.

"The hat goes where I go," Bash said.

"Are you giving it to me?"

"You can wear it for the afternoon."

One afternoon was good enough for Inkcap, and he went off to fetch the Branch Secretary. Halfway there, he readjusted the cap on his head as it was too big, and the brim kept slipping round to the back. Even so, he was tremendously excited. There were no mirrors on the road, not even a pool of water, so he couldn't see what he looked like in a military cap. His swallow had gone down to the lotus pond to find some bugs to eat. Once it was full, it had flown back to perch on the wall of Big Root's courtyard.

Inkcap saw it there and called out, "Look! Look! Can't you see who it is?"

The swallow didn't recognise him and twisted its head down to wipe its beak on its belly,

"You mean you can't recognise me just because I'm wearing a military cap?"

The swallow chirped and took to the air over his head. He and the bird continued on the road to the Branch Secretary's house, one flying in the air and the other walking on the ground.

At his home, the Branch Secretary was wiping his body down with a towel and a basin of water. He asked if there had been an accident with the long desk on the way to the mourning hall and was it still all right to use as a support for the coffin? Inkcap told him that no, everything was fine and the desk had been well protected. It was ready to be used in the mourning hall. But the reason he was there now was because Bash asked him to pass on a message.

"Have you attached yourself to Bash again?" the Branch Secretary asked.

"No, it's him who's attached himself to me."

"Is that right?"

"Yes! Yes, it is!"

"Says you."

Inkcap went quiet. The Branch Secretary threw his towel onto the cabinet cover.

"All right, what's the message? What does he want you to tell me?"

Inkcap repeated Bash's message. As he was talking, he didn't look at the Party Secretary's face because he had discovered that when he lowered his head, he could see himself wearing the military cap in the water in the basin.

He had never worn any sort of cap before, let alone a military cap. He opened his eyes wide, then either kept one eye open and one closed or pursed his lips and wrinkled his nose. He thought that the version of him he saw in the water really wasn't that ugly after all. The Branch Secretary's wife came in to collect the water basin. When she heard what Inkcap had said, she looked at her husband, who slumped down into a chair, his face as grey as if it had been stuffed into a cloth bag. She was immediately worried for him and pulled Inkcap away from the water basin to ask him why Bash had come back, how many people he had brought with him, what he wanted back in Old Kiln, why was the Commune Secretary wearing a paper hat and a placard, and was there going to be some kind of meeting in front of the mountain gate? The questions were so detailed that Inkcap stumbled over his answers and the Branch Secretary's wife had to ask them a couple of times.

"Give me a needle," Inkcap said.

"What do you want a needle for?" the Branch Secretary's wife asked.

"This cap is too big. I want to make a fold in it and use a needle to pin it."

Inkcap hoped the Branch Secretary and his wife would notice his military cap, but they didn't mention it.

The Branch Secretary's wife went into the bedroom to look for a needle, and Inkcap followed her, but she couldn't find one anywhere. She turned out her sewing basket and said, "What is it you want me to look for?"

"A needle."

"Oh, oh. Where's my needle? Where's my needle?"

Inkcap saw a needle pinning a New Year picture to the wall, so he folded up the brim of his hat and pinned it up. When he came out of the bedroom, the Branch Secretary was standing in front of Chairman Mao's portrait in the main room.

"Chairman Mao, Chairman Mao," he murmured, "I have been your Branch Party Secretary for more than ten years. Why don't I know how to act now? Is the Commune Secretary in trouble? What's going on? Chairman Mao, Chairman Mao..."

Inkcap didn't know what to say. The Branch Secretary's wife came out of the bedroom too and said, "Don't go, Husband. Secretary Zhang has already been criticised. You shouldn't go. Inkcap, take a message and tell them that Grandfather is not at home."

"I'll go," the Branch Secretary said. "I have to find out exactly what is going on."

"What should I do if you are criticised too?" the Branch Secretary's wife asked.

"If I'm going to be criticised, I have to know what I am being criticised for."

His wife began to wail and curse. "Bash! Bash! You bastard! Who the fuck do you think you are? How did Old Kiln end up with someone like you?"

"Don't curse or cry," said the Branch Secretary. "No matter what happens to me, don't go to the venue, and don't be seen crying in front of others."

He left with Inkcap, locking the courtyard gate on his way out. He wore his coat draped over his shoulders as usual, and walked so fast that Inkcap couldn't keep up.

As he arrived at the mountain gate, the Branch Secretary stopped on the slope. He saw Zhang Dezhang standing on a stool, as if he had just finished confessing his crimes. He looked as pathetic as a river shrimp, his legs were shaking, and he was sweating cobs. The sweat ran down his face and dripped to the ground.

"Is Zhang Dezhang honest?" Huang Shengsheng shouted.

The crowd of outsiders shouted, "No, dishonest!"

The tall man was sitting at the base of one of the pillars of the mountain gate, his head glistening under the beating sun. He took off his shoes and rubbed the gaps between his toes. Maybe he had athlete's foot. The more he rubbed, the itchier it became. He kept his head down throughout, but when everyone else shouted "Dishonest!" he shouted, "No, dishonest!" too. The people standing around the outside of the circle were the residents of Old Kiln, and they just laughed.

Huang Shengsheng was not amused. "Is he honest or not?" he shouted.

He glared at the villagers, but they still didn't shout back. Bash stood in front of them, raised his hands and said, "Everyone must express their opinion. Is Zhang Dezhang honest or not?"

Again, all the outsiders shouted, "Dishonest!"

Then, Dazed-And-Confused shouted, "Dishonest!"

"Dishonest!" said Useless.

They were then joined by all the villagers of Old Kiln, and once they started shouting, they couldn't stop: "Dishonest! Dishonest!"

Inkcap didn't join in but turned his head to look at Old Faithful's mouth. Two front teeth were missing and his breath leaked out through the gap when he talked. That was why people said he was as sneaky as a rat. Then he looked at Decheng who had lower back pain and couldn't stand up straight. When he shouted, the spittle splashed onto the bald head of Kaihe's uncle.

Kaihe's uncle turned around and said angrily, "Wipe it off."

Kaihe's uncle had short lips, which exposed his gums when he was cross. Decheng wiped the back of Kaihe's uncle's head, then said to Inkcap, "What are you staring at? And why aren't you shouting?"

"Dishonest!" Inkcap shouted.

Huang Shengsheng pressed his hands down, gesturing for silence. When the crowd went quiet, he said, "So, if he's dishonest, what should we do?"

This time, Inkcap didn't know what to do, nor did the villagers. They remained silent and wide-eyed in confusion. The outsiders, on the other hand, shouted in unison, "Implement the dictatorship of the proletariat."

Inkcap was confused about what this meant. Two people came out of the crowd, both tall and well-built, each with a length of hemp rope tied around the waistbands of their trousers. Swishing his rope, one of the men ordered, "Bring the bucket over here. Bring it here."

Inkcap thought he wanted a drink of water, so he went to fetch the bucket from under the medicine tree, but Useless had beaten him to it. The two men dipped their ropes into the bucket, swung them again, and splashes of bright water slashed through the air. Then they grabbed Zhang

Dezhang from the stool, pushed him down to the ground and tied him up. Old Kiln had often held criticism and struggle meetings, and there had certainly been times when those who were criticised had not confessed honestly, but they had never been tied up with hemp ropes. The villagers were truly shocked when Zhang Dezhang was tied up in public. They gave a collective gasp and took a step backwards.

The two men glanced at the crowd, as if they wanted to put on a show. One of them grabbed Zhang Dezhang's arm, wrapped his rope around it and tied Zhang's hands together behind his back. He looped the end of the rope around Zhang's neck and gave it a jerk. Zhang Dezhang gave a whoop of pain and surprise as his head was pulled up and back. He was now immobilised, and the two men lifted him onto the stool. Huang Shengsheng waved his arms and shouted slogans. One after another, the people next to him started beating their drums and gongs in unison. All the outsiders joined in, shouting slogans as they walked past Zhang Dezhang. Each of them stopped and spat at him. Inkcap felt that this slogan-shouting was something new and wanted to join in, but Huang Shengsheng's accent was so strong he couldn't tell what he was shouting.

"What's he saying?" he asked Useless.

"Down with the capitalist-roader Zhang Dezhang!" shouted Useless. "The revolution is never wrong! Rebellion is the correct path!"

Ah! So that's what he's shouting, Inkcap said to himself.

The outsiders lined up and circled Zhang Dezhang.

"Join in. Join in," Huang Shengsheng shouted, and the villagers of Old Kiln joined in.

Although they could hear Useless's slogans, the words were unfamiliar and difficult to pronounce. They just squeaked and yelled, then spat at Zhang Dezhang and walked on. It was Useless's turn to spit. Then it was Dazed-And-Confused's turn. He coughed loudly, bringing up a mouthful of phlegm, which he spat at Zhang's chin. Zhang Dezhang closed his eyes, his face covered with saliva, and a mess of phlegm hanging from his chin.

Lucky was standing behind Inkcap. "Your turn next," he said.

Inkcap stood in front of Zhang Dezhang and spat, but only a few flecks of spittle splashed on the wooden placard.

"Jump up. Jump up and spit," Lucky urged him.

Zhang Dezhang's eyes opened as Inkcap jumped up, but he was too frightened to spit.

The Branch Secretary had been standing there all this time. At some point, he stopped shrugging his coat back onto his shoulders and it fell to the ground. He didn't dare go into the crowd, but he didn't dare walk away either. Only when almost everyone had stopped in front of Zhang Dezhang, shouted slogans at him and spat in his face, did he softly call out Bash's name. Bash could definitely see him, and could definitely hear him, but he simply didn't look in his direction.

A bunch of chickens, both roosters and hens, were standing on the roadside next to the Branch Secretary. One said, "Is that Zhang Dezhang?"

"Look how big his mouth is," another said. "He's eaten a lot of us chickens."

"He's not very fat."

"He was fat before, but he's lost weight."

"Shall we go and beat him up?"

"Not me."

"What are you afraid of? He can't eat us now."

The Branch Secretary couldn't understand what the chickens were chattering away about. His eyes were blurred with sweat as he jumped down and shouted, "Bash! Bash!"

The chickens stirred and seemed to be about to jump off the edge of the road. The Branch Secretary flapped his hand to drive them away. They began to cackle and squawk. He called out to Bash again. Bash finally turned around, drove the chickens away, and said, "Oh, you're here too, are you?"

"I've been here a long time."

"Really? And you didn't say hello to Zhang Dezhang?"

"You seemed to be with all these friends of yours, so I didn't want to interrupt. I'd like to ask you something, Bash. What crime has Secretary Zhang committed?"

"He is a capitalist roader."

"What's that?"

"The Cultural Revolution's in full swing. Those in power are all capitalist roaders."

"Oh, I see. They are all capitalist roaders, are they? Then..."

But Bash walked away. He went to say something to the short man, and then drank some water from the bucket.

The short man came over and asked, "Are you the Branch Secretary of Old Kiln?"

"I am."

"Are you still in post?"

"I am."

"The Cultural Revolution has been going on for a long time now, and you are still keeping control of Old Kiln, trying to turn the village into your own impregnable private kingdom, aren't you?"

The Branch Secretary began sweating again and said, "No, comrade, that's not it at all."

"No? I heard you drove out the rebels?"

"No, there aren't any rebels in Old Kiln."

"Didn't you drive out Huang Shengsheng and Bash?"

"I don't know, comrade. Is Bash a rebel?"

"What do you think? Well, let me tell you this, we of the revolutionary masses of the Proletarian Rebellion Federation Command have paraded Zhang Dezhang through the streets. But we will parade more capitalist roaders again in the future. If this capitalist roader still wants to travel that road, then that is the end of Zhang Dezhang."

"Yes, yes, I see."

"Zhang Dezhang is the leader of you village branch party secretaries. Why don't you go and see him?"

"Yes, I will go. I have to go."

He took two steps, but his legs gave way and he collapsed, exhausted by the heat and the occasion.

FORTY-TWO

THE OUTSIDERS LEFT IN THE AFTERNOON. They escorted Zhang Dezhang to Xiahewan for criticism. Before Bash departed, he left the pen, ink and paper he had brought with him, as well as a flag with the word "rebel" printed on it and several bundles of the book *The Sayings of Chairman Mao*. The flag was raised on the roof of Bash's old residence, where it snapped and cracked happily in the wind. He had originally wanted to make a wooden sign, like the ones that hung on the doors of all the public buildings in Luozhen, but he couldn't find a dry board that was suitably long, so, for the time being, "Old Kiln Proletarian Rebellion Federation Command" was written on the door panel in black ink. Bash had asked Useless to write the characters. Useless said that these words weren't quite suitable, and, properly speaking, it should say, "Old Kiln Branch Command of the County Proletarian Rebellion Federation Command". But Bash insisted on the original wording. He was the founder member, and the first person to join the Old Kiln Proletarian Rebellion Federation Command was Useless.

As soon as Useless joined, he received a copy of the *The Sayings of Chairman Mao*. There used to be several copies in the village, but they were all large, with cardboard covers. This new book was small with a red plastic cover, and the villagers saw it as something of a novelty. As soon as people turned up at the Federation Command, Bash and Useless taught them to sing *The Internationale*. Both of them had learned the song at school, but they hadn't sung it for many years and had forgotten the tune. After Bash learned to sing it again in Luozhen, he taught it to Useless, telling him to teach it to anyone who turned up. None of them could ever learn it, so Useless stopped trying to teach them. Bash was displeased, emphasising the importance of singing, which only served to reinforce Useless's respect and admiration for him. Bash explained that the magic weapon that would allow the Communists to seize power was mastery of both the pen and the gun. The pen meant propaganda, and singing was one of the tools of propaganda. The reason why the Communist Party defeated the Kuomintang was that the Communists could sing and the Kuomintang could not. Throughout history, there has always been an emphasis on singing as a tool to achieve aims. Take the *Book of Songs*, for example. What is the *Book of Songs*? Is it really just a collection of ballads? Or look at how Liu Bang's troops sang at the Battle of Gaixia between Liu Bang and Xiang Yu. It was hearing that singing from all sides that made Xiang Yu commit suicide.

Useless was amazed and asked Bash how he knew all this.

"Do you really think I was driven out of the village?" Bash said. "I went to Luozhen to study."

Useless didn't dare ask what other skills Bash might have learnt. After that, someone actually came specially to teach him how to sing *The Internationale*. When Dazed-And-Confused turned up, he said that after Bash left, the village cadres had bullied him and treated him like a slave. *The Internationale* said that if he was a slave, he should rise up. But no matter how hard Useless tried, he couldn't teach him to sing the actual song. After Dazed-And-Confused joined the Federation, he was followed by Baldy Jin, Stonebreaker, Lucky and Tag-Along. As the news spread, the people who were helping out at Apricot's house began to discuss the benefits of joining up. Would it mean they could smash other people's roof tiles while those people would be prevented from smashing theirs? Someone said that his roof had already been smashed up in any case, so what was the point in joining? Those who had not yet had their roofs attacked began to panic, muttering that everyone who was talking about joining had beefs with the Branch Secretary and the team leader. They were worried that if they did join, wouldn't the Branch Secretary and team leader think that they too were lining up against them?

"I support you, Millstone," one man said.

Millstone was working on the trunk of the felled tung tree at the entrance of the courtyard. After the tree was cut down and it turned out it couldn't be used for the coffin, the trunk still had to be sawn into planks. The stump was propped diagonally across a square table with Millstone up on top and Sparks on the ground below. They were working a saw together.

"If you support me," Millstone said to the man, "why did you go over there just now?"

"I just went to see what all the fuss was about."

Winterborn came over and said, "How come that fucker Tag-Along has joined them? You can't tell anything about anyone any more."

"Are you going to join too, then?" Millstone asked him.

"Have you seen that rabble? Of course I'm not going to join."

"Put a bit of effort in, can you, Sparks?" Millstone called down.

"What do you mean, put some effort in? I'm giving it all I've got. You're so used up, even your balls are shrivelled!"

"Millstone's in a bad mood," Winterborn said. "You'd better watch what you say, Sparks."

"What bad mood?" Millstone snarled.

"Ah yes, there you go, happy as a pig in shit," Winterborn said, taking over the saw from Sparks.

For a moment, no one in the courtyard spoke, and the swish, swish of the saw sounded very loud. Inkcap and Cowbell were reassembling the saggars that had been removed from the courtyard wall.

"You can hear the saw talking," Inkcap said.

"What's it saying?" Cowbell asked.

"What the fucking fuck? What the fucking fuck am I doing?"

When Cowbell listened again, that cursing was exactly what he heard.

At the base of the mountain behind the Kiln God Temple, a small group of men had dug a grave for Potful. When other graves were dug, what came out was yellow sand, but with Potful's, when the diggers reached a depth of around two metres, they hit a layer of red sandstone. When then they tried to dig down into it with their mattocks, all they did was make a white scar in the stone; there was no way to dig it out in lumps. This slowed their progress considerably.

Barndoor was sitting on the edge of the pit, smoking his pipe and holding a set square. He seemed to have a firm grip on it but all of a sudden it fell from his hand and broke into three pieces. Everyone thought this was very strange and said that the feng shui of the grave must be very hard. Soupspoon asked Barndoor if hard feng shui was a good thing or a bad thing.

"Who knows?" Barndoor said. "When that huge grave for Bash's father was dug all those years back, they didn't hit a layer of rock, but it was full of big stones and two mattocks got broken on them. That must have been hard too."

"Ah," Soupspoon said. "So hard feng shui is a good thing, but it throws up bad people in the next generation. Hey, Barndoor, aren't you going to join the Federation?"

"Why haven't you?"

"That Bash never did anything for me, and besides, I don't have anything against the Branch Secretary or the production team leader, so why should I join?"

"So you're the kind of sleazebag who stands on the bank and watches the river rise, are you?"

"Works for me."

"Let me tell you something, Soupspoon. Do you know why you're a nobody in the village despite all your talents? It's because you never show up when you might be needed."

"Do you think Bash is really out to cause trouble?"

As he finished speaking, he went over and reached out for Barndoor's pipe so he could have a smoke. As he did so, he slipped and fell into the grave.

"You shouldn't have mentioned Bash's name when you're digging Potful's grave."

"You're right, you're right," Soupspoon said, his face ashen with fear. "Potful couldn't stand Bash. I won't mention him again."

Throughout that afternoon, one group of villagers were at Apricot's house and another was at Bash's place. Both groups were busy. Bash moved everything back from the little wooden shack and changed the water in the *taisui* basin. Dazed-And-Confused, Useless and Baldy Jin each drank half of the original water from an enamel jar, and then they all stood in front of the old house and looked at the flag on the roof. Bash had a sudden idea and went up to the roof again to take down the flag, saying he would raise it every morning and lower it every night. After he had brought down the flag, he said he ought to build a fence at the mountain gate where big-character posters could be put up. He needed mats and wooden rafters for his fence, so he took the mats off his own *kang* and told Dazed-And-Confused to pull down some rafters from the roof of the cowshed. There were lots of rafters hanging from the beams and as Dazed-And-Confused went to remove them, the parrotbills came squawking down, making the cows in the cowshed bellow.

Noodle Fish, who had just finished giving the cows their water, said, "What the fuck are you doing?"

"Is there something wrong with your eyes?"

"So what are the rafters for?"

"None of your business."

"It's my job to feed the cows in here, so of course it's my business."

Noodle Fish went over to where Dazed-And-Confused was standing on a ladder and tugged at his legs.

"The Federation needs the rafters, OK?" Dazed-And-Confused told him.

"I don't give a toss about the Federation, I only listen to the Branch Secretary and the team leader. If one of them has said you can have the rafters, then that's fine with me. If they haven't, then I don't care who it is, they can't have them."

Dazed-And-Confused came down from the ladder and said, "All right, Noodle Fish, don't worry. You're such a wretched creature, I'm not going to hit you. Go and have a word with Millstone. It won't be long before you're bringing the rafters over to the mountain gate yourself. At least that'll save me a bit of effort."

Noodle Fish did indeed go over to Apricot's house to find Millstone. When Millstone heard what he had to say, he gave him a real talking to.

"What do you need to ask me for? If he said he was going to take a cow, would you let him? If he said he was going to kill you, would you just say 'Go ahead'?"

Then Millstone turned to Sparks and said, "Count everyone and see who's missing. Those who have been out working these last few days and anyone who's involved with the funeral tomorrow will get work points."

Noodle Fish left Apricot's house and went back to the cowshed. Dazed-And-Confused had fallen asleep on the steps of the old public office. Noodle Fish didn't wake him but quietly locked the door of the cowshed and told the sleeping Dazed-And-Confused, "I'm avoiding you because I don't want to annoy you."

Then he went back to Apricot's house to lend a hand.

Bash grew impatient waiting for Dazed-And-Confused to come back with the rafters, so he sent Baldy Jin to go and see what was going on. Baldy Jin met Half-Stick on his way over to the cowshed. Half-Stick was taking one of her household's sieves over to Apricot's house and she asked him to help carry the saggars to the cemetery.

"Can't you see I'm busy?" Baldy Jin huffed.

"Oh yes?" Half-Stick replied. "And is what you're busy with going to keep you in food and drink? The team captain has said that everyone who goes to help out at Apricot's house will get work points."

"So he's using the dead to resist the Revolution now, is he?" Baldy Jin sneered.

As he was speaking, Awning's wife walked past carrying two stools, one on top of the other, heading for Apricot's house. The alley was narrow, and she spat as she passed Baldy Jin. Half-Stick did the same. Baldy Jin's face went ashen with fury. When Awning's wife had gone, he stopped Half-Stick from going on to Apricot's house.

"I'm going to bury Potful, not that good-for-nothing baggage," she protested.

Baldy Jin grabbed her arm so tightly she couldn't pull it away.

"Are you going to see Awning again?" he asked her, arching his eyebrows.

"What if I am?"

Baldy Jin's fury increased but Half-Stick had the measure of him. He was so angry that he punched his chest and stomped off to the cowshed. When he saw Dazed-And-Confused asleep on the steps of the old office, he kicked him awake. The two of them went over to the cowshed to fetch the rafters but found the door was locked. When they went back and told Bash, he stormed off to find the Branch Secretary.

After dinner, the Branch Secretary went to Apricot's house. He had had cupping done on his left and right temples and the back of his neck, leaving purple-black marks. Many of the people there were concerned about his health. He just said that it was hot, and he was a little exhausted but was fine now. He asked how much progress had been made with building the tomb and whether the shroud had been sewn, and then told Millstone that Bash was putting up a big-character poster board and he needed some rafters. He ordered Noodle Fish to collect some and take them over. In addition, he announced that people working at Apricot's house and those over at the mountain gate would be awarded work points.

Millstone disagreed with the decision, and the two men quarrelled.

"You've been a tough nut all your life," Millstone said. "Why have you gone all soft now? If he slaps your left cheek, you'll offer him your right cheek and if he slaps your right cheek, you'll let him slap your left. If he wants to strangle you, you'll suggest he shit and piss on your head too!"

"You've seen the kind of times we're in now, haven't you?" the Branch Secretary replied.

"Fine. Have it your way and just let Old Kiln go to the dogs."

Millstone cursed away for a while, but in the end, he let Noodle Fish go to the cowshed to collect the rafters and transport them to the mountain gate, before sending someone to carry the coffin from the Branch Secretary's house to Apricot's. Then he took Apricot to one side to discuss the burial scheduled for noon the next day. In the morning, she was to make some maize gruel for the villagers' breakfast, and when they returned from the funeral, she had to provide another meal of rice.

"How much rice have you got ready?" he asked.

"I've husked fifty *jin*."

"That's not enough."

"There's nothing I can do about it."

"In that case let's make congee, not boiled rice, and put in lots of red and white radishes. How many radishes have you got?"

"I've got white radishes but no red ones."

"The rice won't have any colour without red radishes. I'll fetch you a basketful."

Apricot began to cry, calling him "Older Brother Millstone. Older Brother Millstone."

"There's no need for that. Your brother Millstone may be a coarse fellow, but he knows how to do the right thing. And I'm not doing it because I'm the production team leader, I want your dad to have a proper send-off. But once that's done, anyone who fancies it can be team leader."

With that, he picked up a basket with shoulder straps and went off to fetch the red radishes.

As Millstone left Apricot's house, Bash arrived.

Bash was holding a stack of paper money under his arm, not the hemp paper he bought from Kaihe's consignment store, but the white glossy paper he brought back from Luozhen. As soon as he entered the short alley leading to Apricot's house, he wailed loudly. It was the custom in Old Kiln that if a mother died, her children should wail loudly, and the younger generations of their family or village would wail according to their seniority. However, if a father died, everyone should wail loudly, regardless of whether they were family or younger generation or not.

Bash roared at the entrance of the alley, "Father! Father!"

As soon as the sound reached Apricot's courtyard, everyone exclaimed, "Who's that? Who would wail like that as soon as they entered the alley?"

Apricot was also taken aback.

"Apricot, we have guests," Third Aunt called out. "Go out there and greet them."

Apricot stepped out of the house and identified the source of the wailing as Bash.

"Good God!" she exclaimed as she turned smartly around and went back to her bedroom.

Sprout shovelled a basketful of ash from the stove and took it out to the courtyard. She hurried back inside.

"It's Bash!" she shouted. "Bash is here!"

A man who carrying cypress seeds to put in the bottom of the coffin said, "Heavens, what's he up to? Do you want him here?"

The sound of Bash's wailing was getting closer and closer, and the talking ceased.

"Should we stop him?" Stargazer asked.

He shouted to Apricot, but there was no reply from her bedroom.

"What do you mean, stop him?" Flower Girl said. "Of course he should come. Can't you hear how sad he sounds?"

Bash came in through the courtyard gate. He was too wrapped up in his wailing to pay any attention to those busying themselves around the yard. The kerosene lamp hanging under the eaves of the main building shone with a bright, white light. Everyone could see that Bash was wearing an even finer military cap than before. It was stuffed with paper to make the front protrude most impressively. He also wore a Chairman Mao badge on his chest. It was a huge badge that seemed to be emitting rays of light under the illumination of the kerosene lamp. He appeared to be in the throes of extreme grief as he staggered theatrically to the mourning hall in the main building. He even staggered when he crossed the threshold. Ever-Obedient, who was standing at the entrance to the mourning hall, took the pile of paper money from him and gave him three sticks of incense from the offering table in return. Bash lit the incense sticks from a candle, raised them high above his head, bowed three times and thrust them into the incense burner. Then he threw himself down at the front of the mourning hall and kowtowed. Ever-Obedient pushed a cushion over towards him with his foot, as a way of suggesting he kneel on it rather than the hard floor. But Bash ignored the cushion and continued to kneel on the floor, kowtowing and wailing. Since Potful had passed away, it had only been Apricot who had wept and wailed with any volume in the mourning hall. Most of the villagers who came to burn paper money and kowtow shed a few tears and sighed a couple of times, but Bash was the only one whose cries could match Apricot's wailing.

"Father! Father!" he said. "Why did you leave me? Why did you leave before I could get back? I miss you. Who can I turn to now? You were such a hard-working and attentive father."

Third Aunt went over to him and said, "Stop crying, Bash. The old captain knows how filial you are. Get up. Get up. Where are the cigarettes, Apricot? Give Bash a cigarette."

Bash stopped wailing and stood up. He blew his nose violently.

Apricot came out of her bedroom, but she didn't bring any cigarettes. She leaned against the bier and began to cry again.

"When did he pass away?" Bash asked.

"Two days ago," Apricot replied.

"Why didn't you tell me?"

"Were you even in the village?"

"Ah, no. I only got back after he was gone. Are all the funeral arrangements in hand?"

"Almost."

The two candles in the hall started to flicker. Third Aunt shielded them with her hands, but they went on flickering.

"Close the courtyard gate," she shouted. "The wind's blowing in. Close the courtyard gate."

"There isn't any wind," Sprout shouted back from the courtyard.

Maybe not, but the candle went out anyway. The main room suddenly went dark, and someone could be heard saying, "Where are the matches? Where are the matches?"

Whoever it was must have kicked over a small stool with a crash as they groped around on the top of the cabinet for the matches. Third Aunt took Bash out of the main room to talk to him.

"The matches are in the niche in the wall," Apricot called out.

No one could find the matches, so they shouted, "Inkcap! Inkcap! We need a light."

Inkcap took out a match from inside his jacket and went over to the main room. When the candles had been relit, Apricot threw herself on Potful's bier and began to wail loudly again.

Bash was trying to talk to the people in the courtyard, but they were busy, and he hardly got a word in. There was nothing for him to do either, so he asked Ever-Obedient when the funeral was to be held the following day. Ever-Obedient said it was the long-standing rule to hold the burial when the sun went down. Bash went on to ask if the ropes, poles and bearers had been arranged.

"There's a set of dragon-head coffin poles in the village," Ever-Obedient told him. "We have two lifting poles and four hanging poles and there are three ropes, so we just need one more rope and we're all set."

Bash noticed Inkcap and told him to go with him to his house where he had a leather rope.

"What have you been doing all this time?" he scolded Inkcap. "Why didn't you come and tell me they needed a rope here?"

That night, few people managed to sleep. Apricot kept vigil on a straw mattress in the mourning hall. The helpers were really tired, so they took turns to take naps on the same mattress. Millstone brought the radishes in a basket on his back, and Sprout and Flower Girl took them down to the spring to wash. As soon as they finished, they heard someone wailing again.

"Are they inviting the family spirits to return?" Sprout asked.

Before burial, family members should always take the spirit tablet of the deceased and burn paper money at the ancestral grave to invite all the spirits back to welcome the newly departed.

"Didn't they do that already yesterday?" Flower Girl replied. "It doesn't sound like Apricot."

The two of them listened carefully again and couldn't help feeling something was wrong. They walked up from the spring and looked at the river strand from a distance. The maize seedlings were already very tall and formed a dark mass in the gloom. The wailing was coming from there.

"Is it a wolf?" Flower Girl asked. "Wolves out in the wild often imitate people wailing."

Sprout's hair suddenly stood on end, and she ran away. Flower Girl ran after her, carrying the two baskets of radishes and calling her name. But Sprout disappeared out of sight and Flower Girl dropped the baskets and screamed. Barndoor and Old Faithful were on their way back from the cemetery carrying hoes. When they heard the shouting, they ran over to find out what was going on. Flower Girl told them that wolves were wailing at the bottom of the embankment.

"Wolves only wail like humans during the day," Barndoor told her. "That's no wolf at this time of night."

Flower Girl was still holding a hand over her heart, shouting that it was jumping out of her chest and that she had left the baskets of radishes on the

445

embankment track. When Barndoor and Old Faithful went to fetch the radishes, sure enough, wails were still coming from the strand below the embankment.

Barndoor listened for a moment then said, "That's Almost-There's dog pretending to be a wolf again."

As soon as he had finished speaking, the wailing stopped and Almost-There's dog came running over to them. Barndoor raised his hoe and started beating it. The dog did a somersault and ran away.

Carrying the radishes, the three of them headed back to Apricot's house. Sprout had already brought a group of people to chase away the wolf. When Barndoor revealed the animal's true identity, they turned on Almost-There, cursing him for the kind of dog he was raising, always trying to trick people. Last time it howled like a wolf and got strung up and beaten for it. Now it's pretending to be someone wailing! As they talked, the sky got darker and darker. Just before dawn, it was pitch black. Everyone was eager to get back for a nap on the straw mattress. They had just sat down in the company of Third Aunt, who was watching over the grain and vegetables in the yard in case rats tried to steal them.

"What's it doing raining?" Third Aunt said.

They went outside again and did indeed see raindrops falling from the sky.

"We're burying Potful," Sprout said. "The dogs are wailing, and the sky is weeping."

But Millstone suddenly got worried. "It can't rain. The road will get slippery, and it'll be hard work getting to the cemetery."

He told Sparks out in the courtyard to set up a canopy, but before he could do anything, the rain stopped, and the sky gradually cleared. Millstone was relieved and went to ring the bell on the tree in front of his house. After ringing it, he shouted down the lane telling every male worker in the village to go and have breakfast at Apricot's house. When they had finished, no one was to leave as they were then going to carry the coffin to the cemetery.

When the people who were sleeping at home got up to go to Apricot's house and walked past the mountain gate, they found that a new panelled fence had been erected there, with several white posters pasted on it. Most of them were illiterate and just stared at the lines of black characters which looked like stick figures doing exercises. Then they asked those who were literate to read them out loud.

What they read was: "Ten Questions. Question One: Is Old Kiln under the leadership of the Communist Party or someone's independent fiefdom? Question Two: Is Old Kiln implementing socialist policy or does it allow individuals to do as they please? Question Three: Why are all the village cadres from the same clan? Are the people with other surnames dead or just stupid? Question Four: Why did the public office of the production team need to be sold? Was it for the collective good or has it been transferred into personal ownership and the money used for buying flat-bed trucks for the landlords? Question Five: How much money was collected in total from the sale of porcelain goods? Why have the accounts never been published? What was the money used for? Question Six: Who arranged for the landlord faction to go to work at the kiln? Was it to undergo reform through labour or to evade it under the guise of firing porcelain goods? Question Seven..."

As the person reading aloud went on, the quieter his voice became, until he finally fell silent.

"What else? What else?" the listeners next to him asked.

"Is this aimed at the Branch Secretary?" the reader wondered aloud before he turned around and left.

After the news spread, more people came running over to the fence, shouting from a distance, "Is there really a big-character poster? Is the Branch Secretary on it?"

The man began to read out loud again and when he got to Question Eight, he said, "Who is this about?"

His audience didn't answer but called out, "Keep reading and see who else it says."

As Millstone was shouting his message down the alleyway, Decheng came to tell him about the big-character poster. Millstone was still shouting, "All workers are to go to Apricot's house. There's grits soup with red beans. When you've eaten, the coffin must be carried to the cemetery."

Even so, people were still running off to read the big-character posters, Awning included.

"Quickly now, Awning," Millstone said, "go and have your breakfast. You're carrying the front end of the coffin."

"I'm going to read the big-character poster," Awning told him.

"What for? Are you looking for trouble?"

"It'll be trouble if I don't look."

Millstone didn't try to stop him but went over to Apricot's house. Only a very few people were in the courtyard.

Feng Youliang, who was chopping radishes to put in the congee pot, stopped chopping and said, "It's come to this, has it? So many years since Liberation and movements have come and gone, one after the other, but I've never seen any big-character posters."

"That fucker Bash will do anything," Sparks said. "He even came here last night to weep and wail. He seemed to think Potful was his own father, but that all stopped this morning."

Youliang took his apron off and wiped his dripping hands on his lapels, then took half a radish from the chopping board and gnawed on it before leaving the courtyard.

Big Root followed him, calling out, "Hey, Padlock! Are you going?"

"Leave me out of it, I've got to light the fire," Padlock shouted back.

"I heard there's something about you on there," Big Root told him.

"What is there to write about me?"

"Something about your share of the grain and making wine for your own family."

"The whole village drank that wine, for fuck's sake. Bash had some of it, for sure. And did he ever pay any commission to the production team? If anyone else failed to pay up, they'd never get away with it but he did, year after year, and nothing happened to him. Who exactly is protecting him?"

"Isn't your brother a member of the Federation now?" Big Root asked. "Didn't he put up the big-character posters himself?"

Padlock didn't reply but just picked up the forked fire stick and walked out of the yard. Millstone couldn't stop the two men, so he called to Jindou to take responsibility for fetching the water.

"What about the water? Why hasn't the water been fetched yet?"

In fact, Jindou was just depositing a load of water outside the courtyard gate but, when he saw Youliang and Padlock going off to see the big-character posters, he threw down the buckets and followed them. Millstone was furious and stood in the yard cursing. Apricot was in the mourning hall, trimming the wicks of the candles with a pair of scissors. One of the candles was weeping wax so badly it had almost collapsed. The wax that flowed down was so thin and watery, like the juice of an overripe watermelon that had been cut open, that she couldn't contain it. She cut the waxed wick short and crushed the softened wax into balls to plug the gaps in the candle. The molten wax burned her fingers.

When she went out into the courtyard, Millstone told her, "Bash has ruined this funeral, Apricot. We can't hold it now. We just can't do it."

Apricot was stunned, her face drooping like a wilted aubergine.

"That bastard Bash had the nerve to come here weeping and wailing, crying so hard his nose ran. But in his heart he was hoping that now your father's dead, he won't be able to get a decent funeral."

A loud, strangled, choking noise emerged from Apricot's throat as she walked out of the courtyard gate.

Apricot was wearing a mourning robe and the white skirts were too long, so it was cinched up and pinned at the waist. On her feet were straw sandals. The white mourning socks were sticking out of the sandals and turning black as they dragged along the ground. When she arrived at the mountain gate, Useless was dipping a brush into a bucket of paste to stick up another big-character poster on the panelled fence. She snatched away the brush and threw the paste all over Useless, splattering Bash's face in the process.

She pointed at Bash and said, "We are burying my father today and you've lured everyone over here. My dad is going to start rotting in there and stinking the house out. Is that what you want?"

Bash didn't wipe the paste from his face, but said, with a little laugh, "It's good that you've come. It means you've finally plucked up the courage to come and see me."

"I just want to ask whether you're going to help bury my dad or stick up your big-character posters?"

"All right, all right. We'll bury him, OK, we'll bury him."

So Apricot really had dared to put on mourning clothes and come and scold Bash in front of everyone. They were all amazed at how obedient Bash was, and it just served to convince them even more that there must have been something going on between the two of them. If not and they were just friends, Apricot wouldn't have dared talk to him like that and Bash wouldn't have taken it from her either. They didn't interrupt and stood watching from a distance.

Yoyo turned up late, so she pulled Ever-Obedient behind the medicine tree and asked quietly if there was anything on the big-character posters about the Branch Secretary giving her a home in Old Kiln.

"I can't read the words myself," Ever-Obedient told her, "but I haven't heard anyone read out anything like that. But if there was, I'd tear up the poster myself."

"There's no need to show off what big balls you've got," Yoyo said.

"It's not like there haven't been any movements in Old Kiln before, or that I haven't been part of them."

Yoyo covered his mouth with her hand. Then she saw Apricot arriving intent on kicking up a fuss, so she walked out from behind the tree.

Baldy Jin tugged at her and said, "What do you think you're doing?"

"There's a war starting there. Haven't any of you lot got anything to say about it?"

"About what?" Baldy Jin said. "It's just family stuff."

"Family stuff?" Yoyo exclaimed. "There's nothing going on between them any more, so how can it be family stuff?"

Bash remained smiling, and he still hadn't wiped the paste off his face, so it was dribbling down his chin.

"If I don't bury your father, who will? Yes, I'll bury him all right. I'll even take on the role of eldest son and smash the dishes for him," he said. Then he turned around and said to everyone, "Go, bury the old team captain."

Everyone took him at his word and started to follow Apricot as she walked away. Leading the procession with her mourning clothes blowing in the wind, she looked like a ghost floating above the ground. Yoyo and Ever-Obedient followed on behind.

"What did he just say?" Yoyo whispered. "Did he say he was going to smash the dishes for the old team captain?"

"If he does, Potful will get so furious he'll come back to life," Ever-Obedient replied.

"You're an idiot. Now Bash has caused this rumpus, he's using it to demonstrate his status to the village."

"That fucker will say anything that suits him."

FORTY-THREE

A HUGE VAT OF MAIZE AND VEGETABLE GRUEL had been prepared for breakfast. It wasn't thick enough to eat with chopsticks but nor was it so watery that you could see the owl decoration at the bottom of your bowl.

An owl had been sitting in the persimmon tree since the night before last. The persimmons on the trees elsewhere were still green, but the ones in the corner of Apricot's courtyard had the grey bloom of ripeness appearing on their skins and there was actually one pinkish-red fruit hanging there, much the same colour as Flower Girl painted her nails. There was widespread amazement that it had turned soft and red so early, some saying there must be a worm inside. When they looked at it more closely, they noticed an owl perched motionless on the branch behind the persimmon. This owl had a human-like face, and the way it had been sitting still for so long really spooked the villagers. For several days, no one dared to chase it away, and no one picked the soft, red persimmon either. Inkcap was eating his congee under the tree and was constantly worried that the owl would fly down and take his food if he didn't eat it quickly. But some people had already finished their first bowl and gone back to the pot for a refill. Inkcap cursed his inability to eat the congee while it was still scalding hot.

Everywhere in the courtyard, on the steps of the main house, under the eaves, next to the pigsty, in the gap in the wall, people were standing or squatting, holding bowls. Their mouths never left the rims of their bowls, chopsticks swiping along the edges of the soup inside, sucking and slurping without a pause. They didn't need to chew the congee or the red beans, but there were slices of radish and whole potatoes in there too. Some of the potatoes were the size of hens' eggs and had to be bitten into pieces. The assembled diners were glaring at each other as if there was hatred in the air. In fact, they weren't actually looking at each other, nor did they hate each other. It was the potatoes in their mouths making them open their eyes wide, and they were glaring because the potatoes were getting stuck in their throats.

"Beat me on the back! Beat me on the back!" Baldy Jin called out.

Ever-Obedient hit Baldy Jin on the back with his fist, so hard that Baldy Jin roared, and half a potato shot out of his mouth.

"You be careful," Flower Girl said. "That's what did for Potful."

"You really think so?" Baldy Jin replied. "I'm not so sure."

The others made disapproving noises so Baldy Jin stopped talking and went to get some more congee, but it was all gone.

The congee was right down to the bottom of the pot. Some people had had three bowls, some two but Inkcap only got one. He fetched a spatula and scraped away at the bottom of the pot, making a screeching noise. The pot had been borrowed from Noodle Fish's house and Noodle Fish's wife told him to stop.

"The bottom of that pot is cracked already. You'll break it if you keep doing that. Didn't you get enough?"

"I only had one bowl," Inkcap told her from the back of the platform on which the pot stood.

Millstone shouted to him to go into the yard to clear up the used bowls. Inkcap heard all right but pretended not to.

Bash was the last to arrive, when the soup was all gone, but he didn't complain. Instead, he was arguing about who would be responsible for moving the coffin from the yard to the bier in the house, who would put the body in the coffin itself, who would then go on ahead to see to digging the grave, and who would come to help carry the coffin. His voice was very loud as he went on to tell Apricot to bring out the box of tobacco so everyone could have a smoke. Those who had pipes filled them and those who didn't took pinches of tobacco and rolled themselves cigarettes.

"The old captain was a big man," Bash pronounced, "and the coffin is made of cypress wood, so it's going to be very heavy. I don't think four men will be enough, we'll need six and another four stand-ins at the ready. Then we'll have to have two more to carry the benches. We'll need the benches in case anyone carrying the coffin has to take a rest."

"Aiya, Bash! I never expected you to handle things so decently and respectfully, especially after the way Potful used to hurt you," Noodle Fish's wife said.

"He never really hurt me but he did beat me and curse me."

"You're not trying to say he didn't do the same to others, are you? Still, he's gone now, and we should find something good to say about him."

"All right, then. His punches and kicks were really kisses, and his curses were him whispering sweet nothings. Have you had enough to eat, sister?"

"Yes, yes. Plenty."

Noodle Fish's wife went out into the courtyard and picked up a handful of discarded chopsticks that were scattered on the ground. She wiped them on her clothes, muttering about those who didn't look after things properly.

She went into the kitchen with the chopsticks. Millstone was still sitting on the stove, holding his bowl. He glared at her and went on eating.

"Are you staring at me?" Noodle Fish's wife demanded.

"No, I've just got big eyes."

"It's hot and Potful's remains are beginning to smell. I need to spray it with wine."

Millstone didn't reply but called out to Cowbell. When Cowbell came in, Millstone said, "Go to Kaihe's store and buy a bottle of wine."

"Where's the money?" Cowbell asked.

"Get it on credit. I'll settle up later."

"Kaihe's a snob. He won't give me credit."

Millstone looked through the doorway and saw Bash saying something first to Lucky and then to Jindou. He patted Jindou on the shoulder.

"What's he up to?" Millstone asked Noodle Fish's wife. "Why's he going around putting on a show like this?"

"Who are you talking about? Bash? He's all right. He's just showing he cares."

"What do you mean he won't give you credit?" Millstone said, turning to Cowbell. "Tell him it's me asking. Pah! You're just too tongue-tied to ask properly. I might as well feed your tongue to the dogs."

He continued to curse Cowbell until the poor lad burst into tears.

Noodle Fish's wife gave a start and shouted at Millstone to get him to stop, but he just kept going: "What are you crying for? Are you that full of piss, eh?"

Then he aimed a kick at Cowbell but missed, and almost kicked out one of the door panels.

The people in the courtyard came running to see what was causing the noise in the kitchen.

"What's going on?" someone asked.

Millstone slammed his rice bowl down on the table and shouted, "I give up. Why the fuck should I care?"

He stormed out of the kitchen and walked over to the courtyard gate, where he saw his wife carrying a bag of maize grits.

"What are you doing here?" he said.

"The pot's empty. I'm bringing more grits to fill it up again."

"Who said you could use your grits? Who's so keen to get their hands on your grits? Take them back. Now!"

Noodle Fish's wife bundled him out of the courtyard, saying, "Why are you getting so angry, Millstone? You're the production team captain, aren't you?"

"Am I fuck! Who actually thinks of me as the team captain?"

When Apricot saw Millstone getting so angry, she stood at the door of the main room, her mouth trembling and unable to speak. She cried when she hugged Gran.

As Millstone stormed out of the courtyard, he was followed by Sparks, Decheng and Cattle Track. Baldy Jin tried to leave as well.

"Where are you going?" Bash asked.

"Everyone in charge seems to have left."

"What about the old captain? Who's left to bury him? That Millstone's no fucking use to anyone."

Bash clapped his hands and said, "Listen up, everyone still in the yard. We're all going to die and we're all going to be buried. If any of you don't want to bury the old captain, just go now. If you all go, I'll carry him to his grave on my back."

When Bash said this, the men who were going to leave stayed silent and didn't budge.

"Don't cry, Apricot. Look, hardly anyone's gone. If no one else leaves, we can get on with the funeral. Inkcap! Inkcap!"

"I'm here."

"Go and get Zhu Dagui. Why isn't he here already? Get Goodman too. He can sing the road-clearing song. We want the funeral to be a solemn affair, so we need Goodman to sing."

"The Branch Secretary is so old, how can you call him by his given name?" Sprout asked.

"Names are for people to be called by, so why shouldn't we use them?"

Sprout wanted to respond but stopped, put her hand to her mouth and left the courtyard. Pillar and Yes'm followed her out.

Inkcap ran off to fetch the Branch Secretary and Goodman. He was sorry to have missed the body being put in the coffin. When he got up that morning, Gran had asked him to go to Middle Mountain and chop down lots of cypress trees, burn them to ashes and then wrap the ashes in funeral paper so they were the shape of bricks. Then they could be placed under the body in the coffin. He had watched Gran preparing the other things for the coffin. Apricot had said that she would put the water pipe in her daddy's coffin as he had liked it so much when he was alive. They had quarrelled so many times about it, but now that Daddy was dead, she wanted him to take his water pipe to the other world, a world where he could suck on his pipe to his heart's content and no one would nag him about it. Apricot had wept as she said this, then pulled out a short-handled duster that she said she wanted put in the coffin too.

"Don't put that duster in there," Gran told her.

"Let Daddy take it. Let him take it," Apricot pleaded. Gran had seen the duster in Apricot's house. It had a walnut-wood handle and the duster part was made up of strips of leather. Inkcap had seen with his own eyes Potful beat Apricot with it, whipping her over and over till it raised bloody weals. Inkcap thought to himself that actually Apricot still hated her father and wanted him to take the duster away with him so it couldn't be used on her any more.

What was it with Apricot? Why hadn't she fainted with grief in her father's mourning hall? After all, it was she who had angered and frustrated her father so much he had become ill. It was she who hadn't cooked the meat well enough so it got stuck in his throat. If she really was a filial daughter, she should not have let Bash enter the house. When he did come, she should have beaten him and cursed him in front of everyone in the mourning hall and told him to confess what he had done to her. But she actually allowed Bash in and let him take care of the funeral.

"I really can't put this duster in the coffin," Gran said. "If he takes anything made of leather with him, he'll come back in his next life as a cow or a horse."

Apricot wept. "Isn't that what he was to the production team?" she said. "Just another beast of burden?"

"He certainly worked like one for them. He restored the kiln single-handed, and everyone knows it," Gran replied. "If he's going to take anything with him, you should give him a piece of porcelain."

She told Inkcap to fetch a porcelain vase and bowl from the chopping board and wash them so they could be put at the head of the bier. But Inkcap hadn't seen for himself how these things had been put in the coffin, nor did he know how the mourners had stood around the coffin wailing and moaning after the body had been put in there. When he finally arrived with Goodman, pouring with sweat, the coffin had already been nailed shut and bound with hemp rope.

"Give Goodman something to eat," Third Aunt said. "Give him something to eat."

She knew quite well there was nothing left in the pot, but she still said it.

"No, no, I'm fine," Goodman said.

"Are you sure? Have you eaten already? Then can we get you some water? Thimble! Fetch some water for Goodman."

Goodman didn't have any water either. He took out two wooden bars from inside his top, lowered his head and walked round and round the coffin, passing behind Apricot who was standing at the top burning paper money. The flames from the burning paper scorched his thin face, but his expression remained solemn and serious. The ash flew into the air like black butterflies, and some of it landed on his bald head. The sweat on his head held it in place so it couldn't fly off again, but nor did it disintegrate. It just stayed there like a black sticking plaster. Inkcap didn't know what a road-clearing song was. There'd not been anything of the kind at a funeral in Old Kiln before. Did the roads of the underworld need to be cleared? But Bash knew that Goodman was from Xiangfan in Hubei, a city that placed a particular emphasis on funeral singing, and that was why he now asked Goodman to sing. Goodman agreed, but kept walking round and round and didn't open his mouth. Apricot continued to add more paper to the fire, crying all the while, her tears dripping to the ground. Inkcap went to the yard to find a stick to help with flipping the burning paper. As soon as he had crossed the threshold, Goodman started singing.

The road-clearing song told its story dynasty to dynasty, starting at the beginning of everything with the Three Sages and Five Emperors. Inkcap couldn't understand a word of it, and even thought that perhaps Goodman was teasing the others. Maybe Goodman couldn't actually remember all the words and was just mumbling along in a monotone as if he had a mouthful of walnuts.

Inkcap brought in the wooden stick and knelt beside Apricot. He brushed away some paper ash and asked, "What's this song about?"

Smack! Smack! Smack! Goodman struck his two wooden bars together and began to chant with great clarity: "What is good about living in this world? As soon as you mention death, you die, and neither your friends nor family will know. When your friends and family find out, you have already crossed the Naihe Bridge." Smack! Smack! Smack! "Ah! How different that bridge in the underworld is from the bridges in the sunlit world. It is three *chi* wide and ten thousand *zhang* high, with dome-headed nails on both sides and lubricating oil down the middle. When a strong wind blows, it sways and sways, and when a light wind blows, it sways and sways. The fortunate dead walk on the bridge, while the unfortunate dead fall off..."

Goodman's voice seemed hoarse and cracked with age, like working a pair of leaky bellows back and forth, or beating a broken gong. The courtyard had fallen utterly silent. Everyone had come in to listen, surprised they had never heard Goodman sing before in all his years in Old Kiln. When he sang, he sang so desolately and tragically. As he sang, he wept, and the listeners wept too. Awning's wife was washing out the big pot, and the pot began to leak, first drop by drop, and then in a continuous stream which soaked the charcoal ash in the stove below it.

Palace was squatting, leaning against the persimmon tree and smoking a cigarette. He felt something strange on his back. He turned around and saw juice oozing out of the scar on the trunk of the tree. The juice was dark red. He picked at the scar and a stream of juice flowed down the trunk, wriggling like an earthworm. No one had trimmed the wicks of the candles on the table in the mourning hall. The molten wax quickly reached the edge of the table, where it continued to flow downwards until it set and hung there like an icicle. Snails were crawling up the walls on both sides of the courtyard gatehouse. There had never been so many snails before. Snail trails were weaving across them, making it look as if the walls themselves were weeping.

"Inkcap is dead!" Cowbell shouted. "Inkcap is dead!"

Inkcap had fallen to the ground under the window. His eyes were closed, and his whole body was twitching. He had lost his wooden stick and wanted to go back into the house. The doorway was crowded with people. He didn't want to crawl through their legs, so he stood under the window. Goodman's singing had made him feel that there was a bridge in front of him. The bridge was three *chi* wide and ten thousand *zhang* high. It was swaying in the wind. He staggered and slipped. He threw himself forward with a cry and fell to the ground. The courtyard erupted into chaos. Third Aunt was the first to run over and pinch him. She kept calling his name and at the same time shouted for someone to hurry up and fetch some water. When it arrived, she opened his mouth and poured it in.

"Is this epilepsy too?" Ever-Obedient asked.

"Just because your wife's epileptic, doesn't mean everyone else has to be," Third Aunt said tartly.

"It's... it's someone else, isn't it?" Ever-Obedient said. "It's Potful trying to say something."

This comment triggered widespread terror. There had been several previous cases in Old Kiln. Perfectly fit people had collapsed into a coma. With their eyes closed, they began to talk in the voice of the deceased, saying things no one outside the family of the deceased knew. Awning hurried over to the privy outside the courtyard. A peach tree stood beside the privy wall and he neatly snapped off a load of twigs from it, then fetched a winnowing basket from the kitchen. He shouted to everyone to get out of his way. Before the winnowing basket had fully covered Inkcap, he began to thrash it with the peach twigs.

"Who are you? Who are you?"

Inkcap didn't speak and still had his eyes closed. The peach twigs on the basket made a sound like firecrackers.

"Is that you, Potful? Our old captain? Potful! Potful! If you have something to say, just say it. Don't you want to die? Don't you want to be buried like this? Did someone anger you so much, you died?"

Apricot was still burning paper money as she listened to what was going on outside. She remained kneeling and kept on doing what she was doing. She thought that in the next world, her dad would no longer be poor and trapped because she had burned so many bundles of paper money for him and used real cash to buy them. But she didn't like hearing what Awning was saying.

"My dad didn't die of anger," she called out.

Awning didn't contradict her but continued to thrash away with the peach tree twigs, saying, "Speak, Potful. Say what you want to say."

Apricot burst into tears as Third Aunt said to Awning, "Is it really Potful? Are you sure it's him?"

Eight years previously, Stonebreaker's father died falling down the slope when he was cutting grass on Yijia Ridge. Five days later, Old Faithful's wife, the woman with the goitre, suddenly began to talk in another person's voice. Normally, her own voice was high and shrill, but now when she spoke, it was in the loud, gruff voice of Stonebreaker's father. The voice said that he was dead and that his wife could marry whomever she wanted and his only worry was his four sons and daughters. That time too, the villagers got a winnowing basket, put it on Old Faithful's wife and beat it with peach twigs. While thrashing away, they shouted at her to get rid of the ghost, but the ghost kept screaming and refused to leave, saying he wanted to speak to Stonebreaker. The villagers called Stonebreaker, and Old Faithful's wife wept. Then, as Stonebreaker's father, she whispered that he had hidden ten yuan in one of his shoes and asked Stonebreaker to go and get it.

"Where is the shoe?" Stonebreaker asked.

"The shoe is in the east corner of the chicken coop," the ghost said.

Stonebreaker didn't believe it, so the villagers told him to go home and have a look. He went back to dig in the chicken coop, and sure enough, there in the east corner, he found an old shoe of his father's with ten yuan inside. When he got back, he kowtowed to the ghost and wailed loudly.

Old Faithful's wife laughed out loud and said, "Time to go."

Suddenly her eyes opened and when they asked her what had just happened, she said she didn't know.

After listening to what Third Aunt said, Awning replied, "Who else can it be if it isn't Potful?"

Then he brandished the peach twigs violently and said, "Are you looking forward to someone coming to express their condolences, Potful, or is there someone who is not welcome?"

Awning's questioning was like the magistrate interrogating a prisoner in a play. Everyone was listening, worried that Inkcap would name someone in Potful's voice, and wondering who it would be. When Potful was alive, he was a man who liked to stir things up. He would cut off his own flesh for someone who was good to him but if he took against you, he was so fierce he could bite through an iron shovel. They all looked towards the main house where Bash was. They had been surprised and confused by Bash's sudden appearance, but they couldn't say anything. But if the ghost said that it didn't want him to come to express his condolences, then there would be some real fun to witness. But Bash didn't seem to be paying the slightest attention to what was going on in the courtyard. When he checked the ropes on the coffin, he felt they weren't tight enough, so he took a stick down from the ceiling of the bedroom to tighten them with. When he pulled it down, it brought a shower of dirt with it, which landed on his back.

"Brush the dirt off me, Thimble," he ordered.

As he did as he was told, Thimble whispered, "Potful's talking through Inkcap!"

"Oh?" Bash said. "So you're superstitious too, are you?"

The stick Bash had taken down was too long and needed to be shortened, so Thimble went to find an axe. Meanwhile, Bash put the stick on the threshold of the bedroom door and stamped on it, breaking it into several pieces. His shoes were on crooked and as he stamped, a bit of the stick flew up and hit him on the forehead, raising a greenish bruise. Everyone in the room fell silent.

Out in the courtyard, Awning was still asking, "What is it, Potful? If you have something to say, say it."

But Inkcap remained silent. His convulsions had stopped and the colour began to return to his ashen face. It was like clouds drifting over a mountain after rain, casting black shadows on the summit. No, it was the shafts of morning sun shining through a lattice window onto the *kang* mat, moving brightly across it, one by one. Inkcap's face turned red from forehead to chin, and he opened his eyes.

"Potful, old captain, what do you have to say?" Awning was asking. "Just say it. Say it."

"I'm Inkcap."

Third Aunt took the peach twigs out of Awning's hand and threw the basket away.

"It's not the dead talking," she said. "Why are you hitting him? Inkcap didn't have enough to eat. He simply got scared when he heard Goodman singing and fainted."

The onlookers breathed a sigh of relief and turned the episode into a joke. They started mocking Awning for grabbing the winnowing basket and peach twigs in such haste. Then they turned their attention to Inkcap, teasing him for not eating enough and panicking everyone. They called out to the people in the kitchen to bring Inkcap a lump of tofu, or he might turn into something else on them. Inkcap was sweating profusely. He thanked them briefly but didn't have the strength to stand up. Third Aunt helped him to the *kang* in Potful's bedroom and settled him to sleep.

The bedding on Potful's *kang* was relatively neat, but the smooth stone he had used as a pillow for decades had become shiny from all the sweat that had seeped out of his head. As Inkcap fell asleep, he noticed that the copper water pipe was no longer in the tobacco tray on the side of the *kang*, but he could still see a tobacco box, matches, a knife, kerosene lamp and a piece of firewood for making wood chips. He felt that Potful was still lying there especially because the wall behind the *kang* where his head had rested was also stained with sweat.

"Just have a good sleep and don't be afraid of Potful," Third Aunt said. "Whoever else he may have held a grudge against, it wasn't you."

A commotion started in the courtyard outside the bedroom. Goodman had stopped singing the road-clearing song and Bash was shouting, "Come and lift the coffin. Only those who the old captain wanted here can stay. If he didn't want you here, you must leave. Come on, come on. Get a move on."

There was a clattering of footsteps, the sound of movement and some shouting. Inkcap wanted to hear what people were saying when they carried the coffin away, but he fell into a daze and went to sleep.

When a person dies, he definitely doesn't think he is dead, because, by the same token, when he's sleeping, he doesn't know when he falls asleep. Inkcap was woken by another burst of noise. He found himself wondering whether the coffin had been carried out yet or whether the funeral procession had set off. He turned over and wanted to get up, but Gran held him down and told him to go on sleeping for a while. He didn't go back to sleep and asked Gran why he had fainted.

"Did you see Potful?" she asked.

He said he did, but Potful hadn't said anything. After that, he didn't know anything else. Gran sighed, folded back his long jacket and looked at the wound on his hip where he had been hit with the peach twigs. She cursed Awning under her breath for not fastening down the winnowing basket properly and for being too heavy-handed with the twigs.

"I told you not to go where there were lots of people," Gran said. "But you refused to listen. Now look at the trouble you've caused. Bash thinks you did it all on purpose, and Awning blames you for deliberately not talking."

Inkcap felt he was being very unfairly treated. "How could I have done it on purpose?" he said.

Gran covered his mouth and did not let him say anything more. She told him that the funeral went off smoothly and nothing unexpected happened, except that the Branch Secretary had turned up in a rush as the funerary procession was setting off. He had felt very out of place in the courtyard, though no one else noticed anything and it was only the Branch Secretary who felt awkward. Someone brought him a stool, but he refused to sit down. His complexion looked awful, and he went on ahead to the cemetery. Now, Potful had been buried and laid to rest. Apart from the men who had stayed behind to seal the tomb, everyone else had returned. Inkcap looked at the tobacco box again. He swallowed the spit in his mouth and hated himself for being sick and falling asleep, and not being able to go to the grave.

At noon, according to the rules, Apricot had to give everyone a meal of rice, which it had been agreed would be "half-and-half" congee. But before the funeral, Millstone had been so angry that he walked away without lending Apricot any rice, so she couldn't make the congee. When the mourners came back, they milled around in the yard. Apricot was in tears and told Third Aunt that, since they couldn't make half-and-half congee, then she should mix the rice and grain grits to make soup.

"We can't do that," Third Aunt said. "If the food's no good, you'll be a laughingstock."

Apricot burst into tears again. Third Aunt went out to talk to Gran, Barndoor and Noodle Fish. They all agreed: you could only eat the food and wear the clothes your family could afford. They'd serve the food that they had, and that was no cause for anyone to laugh.

But then Bash came over and said, "If we're not going to have rice or congee, then we won't have anything at all."

"But we've got to feed them," Noodle Fish said. "It's the custom."

"That's balls. It's the Cultural Revolution now. Customs mean nothing in a revolution. If you want to eat, I'll go fetch my *taisui* and we'll make soup with it. *Taisui* soup is worthy of a grand banquet with three different types of meat."

"That's wonderful," the others said. "As long as you're willing to part with it, then get a move on."

Bash brought the *taisui* over, but he only cut off half of it to chop into cubes the size of diced meat on the chopping board. Then he stewed it in a big, round pot. Everyone knew that Bash had a *taisui* but most had never seen it with their own eyes. Now it was a pile of wheat-coloured lumps of meat on the chopping board, squirming like a living creature, even though it was not. It didn't bleed when it was cut open and was more like aspic than anything else, or like the soft gum that forms on blighted peach trees. But when it was cooking, the smell immediately filled the yard and it was like nothing anyone had smelt before. It was reminiscent of the scent of locust flowers, chestnuts or fresh wheat flour steamed buns, but it didn't fit neatly into any category. It also smelt of grass and of soil dug up in a field after rain, of the beetles that got brought in with the wheat straw, and even the smoky smell of cooking you got out in the alleys when the evening meal was being made. It was all of these things mixed together, and you still couldn't tell what it really was, except that it was something strange and new. The villagers breathed it in deeply through their mouths and noses. Ever-Obedient closed the courtyard gate, shouting that they shouldn't let the fragrance escape. However, by now the village dogs and cats had surrounded the courtyard. Some squeezed in through the cracks in the gate but were promptly kicked out. The scent floated upwards out of the yard so the trees inside and outside the walls, the walls themselves and the roofs were full of birds. Bees flew in, thinking some flowers were in bloom, but there were no flowers. They rose again in swarms and settled on the persimmon tree. It only then became clear that the owl with the human face wasn't there any longer.

When the *taisui* flesh was finally cooked, everyone took a bowl of it, but half of them didn't dare eat it. Legend had it that if the soil over a *taisui* was disturbed, disaster would ensue, so what would happen to them if they ate it? No one knew who to ask. They looked to Goodman, who took half a bowlful in an old, cracked bowl and ate it up. His beard was shaved down to a short stubble that was white as silver, with a fine drop of sweat hanging on each hair.

Dazed-And-Confused quickly followed suit and downed a bowlful, saying, "Eat up. Eat up. If you don't, I'll have it."

He reached out to take Tag-Along's bowl, but Tag-Along clutched it close to his chest and then took a sip.

"Aiya!" he exclaimed. "It doesn't taste of anything."

"What do you mean?" Bash said. "Sour? Spicy? Sweet? It must taste of something."

The tastelessness of the *taisui* flesh and its broth was, in fact, an amazing taste in itself. After carefully finishing his bowl, Tag-Along opened his eyes wide and shook himself all over.

"I feel full of energy," he declared.

Others did the same, exclaiming, "Ah, I'm so full of energy too. It's amazing, really amazing."

One of them jumped up for the sake of it and grabbed the leaves of the persimmon tree. In fact, he jumped so high he didn't just catch hold of the leaves, but of the whole branch. He pulled the branch down and then let it go, so it sprang back up, disturbing the bees. Cowbell finished one bowl and headed for the kitchen to get a refill. But Awning grabbed hold of him in the doorway. He was about to slip away under the restraining arm when Awning twisted one of his protruding ears.

"I want some more," Cowbell protested.

"It's all gone."

"If it's gone, it's gone. Now, let go of my ear before you twist it off."

"That *taisui* broth has given me so much energy, I feel like giving you a good hiding."

At that point, Dazed-And-Confused went out of the courtyard gate, jumping up and down and shouting at his dog. The dog retreated, came back leaping and barking and then retreated again, so the two of them were engaged in a kind of tug-of-war in the alley.

Useless did not get any of the *taisui* broth. After he returned from the cemetery, Bash told him to go and get some copies of *The Sayings of Chairman Mao*. Bash said that now Potful's spirit tablet was on the shelves in Apricot's house, there should be some copies of the Little Red Book too. By the time Useless got back with the books, all the *taisui* was gone. Instead of saying that he was going to put the books in front of Potful's spirit tablet to protect the household, he held them up and asked, "Who wants a Little Red Book?"

Everyone rushed to grab a copy, pushing and shoving each other. Countless hands snatched at the books and Useless tried to tuck them under his arms to protect them. But people grabbed hold of him, pushed him down to the ground and kept him there. He curled into a ball, but his clothes were torn, his hair was messed up, and there was blood on his face, hands and neck.

The press of people on top of him piled up so high he had to yell, "I can't breathe! I can't breathe!"

Iron Bolt kicked out at the backside of the person above him. Words were exchanged, and then they started fighting.

Dazed-And-Confused heard the rumpus from outside in the courtyard and rushed in. He caught hold of Iron Bolt and yelled, "What the fuck's going on? Get up! Get up! You're going to crush Useless to death."

As Bash was standing on the steps of the house, surveying the human pyramid, Soupspoon said, "Is it really eating *taisui* that's driven them mad like this?"

Bash smiled and didn't try to tell him otherwise. He saw the Branch Secretary coming out of the courtyard gate. He had been in the room while everyone was drinking the *taisui* broth. He had installed Potful's spirit tablet and told Apricot to make offerings to it three times a day. Then he had packed away all the things in the mourning hall one by one. He told Apricot to sort out the lengths of black and white gauze, wadded the funerary couplets up into a ball and told Apricot to burn them in front of the spirit tablet.

"Your father can take these with him," he said.

"Go and have some soup now, Branch Secretary," Apricot replied.

But the Branch Secretary didn't pick up a bowl. Instead, he watched Apricot burn the couplets and then, after sitting for a while, he got up and walked towards the courtyard gate.

Bash went over and said, "Didn't you have any soup?"

Gran had a bowl of soup that she was going to give to Inkcap as he lay on the *kang*, so the Branch Secretary took a sip from it.

"Is it good?" Bash asked.

"Yes, yes. Very tasty."

But as he walked out of the courtyard gate, his stomach was in turmoil. He held it in until he was out in the alley and then vomited.

FORTY-FOUR

THREE DAYS AFTER POTFUL'S FUNERAL, a strong wind blew in off the Zhou River. This happened every summer, blowing the seed cases of the reeds and cattails on the river bank up into the air. They swooped like dragons, rising and falling, gathering and scattering. At that time, the kiln site on the mountainside was about to have its last firing of the summer, and the maize in the dry fields was almost waist-high and needed to be fertilised for the first time. The rice in the paddy fields was at the point when insects began to attack it. However, the wind started early that year, almost twenty days early.

The night before, it was far too hot to sleep. Inkcap tried to settle, naked, on a mat in the yard. His feet were resting on the laundry stone, but the stone was too hot and there were mosquitoes about, so he got up and went to threshing ground again to try to sleep. Gran was making papercuts on the *kang* in the house. She had made six, all of which were connected with funerary matters, but, as she kept cutting, she finally made one showing a mouse stealing oil from a lamp. Even she felt there was something strange going on. It seemed that it wasn't her hand directing the scissors, but the other way round.

At this moment the courtyard door creaked, and Gran called out, "Where are you going?"

No response came from the courtyard. She guessed that Inkcap must have gone to sleep at the threshing ground again. He had told her that evening that he wanted to sleep there but she had forbidden it, saying he had recently been very sick, so what did he think he was doing running around like that? She made him sleep in the courtyard.

"Can't you get to sleep in the courtyard?" Gran went on. "I'll burn some cigarettes to stop the mosquitoes biting."

There was still no response from the yard. Gran looked out through the lattice window and saw that the straw mat was still there, but no sign of Inkcap. She went back to her papercuts, but she was too worried to stay sitting there, so she went out into the courtyard. All that could be seen of Inkcap was a sweat stain on the sleeping mat in the shape of a human figure. Muttering curses to herself, she looked up at the dark grey of the night sky. A little further to the west, above Middle Mountain, a star glinted dully.

Inkcap bumped into Third Aunt in the alley. Her grandson was covered in prickly heat and was crying constantly. She was walking around, carrying the naked child on her back, saying, "The wolf will come if you cry again."

The child stopped crying, but it kept slumping down and Third Aunt was so tired she was sweating profusely.

"Hold tight onto your gran's neck with your hands, and I'll hold your feet with mine. Then, if the wolf comes, it can't get you."

The child hugged his gran's neck with one hand and pulled her breast over her shoulder with the other, stuffing it in his mouth. Ever-Obedient and Yoyo walked past, followed by their dog, which was panting with its tongue hanging out.

"Didn't you go to the threshing ground to sleep?"

"No," Ever-Obedient said, "I went to the spring to wash myself. I had to try to get rid of my prickly heat. Why is it so fucking hot?"

He was staring at Third Aunt's bare arms as he spoke, but she didn't try to cover up and just said, "I wish I could peel this skin off."

She rocked the child back and forth, saying, "Is there any milk in my boob for you?"

"You've fed many of the village's children with your milk," Ever-Obedient said.

"I've had it too," Inkcap said.

It was only then that Yoyo noticed Inkcap in the shadows.

"Are you too hot to sleep too, you little squirt?" she asked him.

"Does drinking *taisui* soup make you unbearably hot?"

"It's been hot for the last two days and nights, hasn't it?" Ever-Obedient pointed out.

This shut Inkcap up and he stopped following them and turned off to take another route to the threshing ground.

In the middle of the alley he was walking down was Gourd's house, where a group of people were sitting at the entrance to the courtyard. Gourd's wife was giggling, and it made her sound rather silly. As soon as the dog days of summer arrived, Gourd's mother always felt too hot to sleep, so, every night, she had to come out and sit on the stone outside the courtyard to cool down before going to bed. Gourd's wife had to accompany her and keep her entertained. She also had to put saccharin in a bowl of cold water and take it out into the alley, calling on this person and that to come and have a drink so she could gather more villagers to sit with them. That night, even Goodman was there. Inkcap heard them talking about the sky and the crops in the fields. They even discussed who had joined the Federation, who might or might not join in future, and who was determined not to join.

"Hey, Goodman! Why haven't you joined?" someone asked.

"I'm waiting for you to join," Goodman said.

"You mean you want me to join? Do you think I'm that stupid?"

"Am I that stupid too, then?"

Immediately, three or four others joined in: "Are you really stupid?"

"Yes, he is stupid," Gourd's wife said. "He may be well-educated, but has he done better for himself than Bash or even Useless? What else does he do for the village apart from setting bones and talking to illnesses? And just look at the clothes you've mended for yourself, Goodman! See how big the stitches are! I told you to bring them to me to mend, but you refused. And you wouldn't even let me go to your place to mend them either, would you? As for what you eat, it's the same old vegetable gruel three times a day, isn't it? Why don't you learn to roll your own noodles? You live in the Mountain God Temple but you don't even have a proper door, so you have to pile up bundles of firewood to block the gaps in winter. I don't hear you saying anything useful about anything that's going on in the village either."

Goodman laughed. "Children are always playing hide and seek, but have you ever seen adults playing it? Young people need to be smart, but as they get older, they have to be stupid. It's better to be stupid. I have told many people that Gourd's wife is stupid and they should imitate her stupidity."

"I'm not stupid," Gourd's wife replied indignantly. "I only give you saccharin water to drink so that you'll talk to my mother."

She giggled proudly and everyone burst out laughing.

"You see," Goodman said. "Only a stupid person would say something like that."

Inkcap came forward because he wanted some saccharin water too. But then he heard Gourd's mother yawn and Gourd's wife say, "Are you sleepy, Ma?"

"Yes, I am. You lot go off to your own beds, and I'll go to mine."

"Don't worry about us, you go to bed and we'll do the same. Off you go to your beds, everyone."

"Good idea, let's all go to bed," Goodman said. "See what a good daughter-in-law she is. There should be more like her in Old Kiln."

And with that, the party broke up.

Inkcap was sorry to have missed all the fun outside Gourd's courtyard. He walked alone under the locust trees in Three Fork Alley. From there, if he went east, it led down to the threshing ground and if he went west, he would end up at the Branch Secretary's house.

There was someone in the west alley having a chat inside a courtyard.

The man in the courtyard was saying, "Where are you running off to? Why aren't you in bed with your wife?"

The man outside the courtyard gate said, "It's too fucking hot for any of that kind of thing. I'm all restless but I've got nowhere to go."

"I know somewhere. You could go and sleep with Potful. It sure isn't hot where he is!"

The man outside the courtyard hawked and spat. Inkcap shuddered violently and looked towards the east alley. The courtyard walls of the narrow alley were very high. The entrance to the alley was filled with white flowers and moonlight, but the alley itself was dark. He thought he felt raindrops on his head. He looked up and, sure enough, rain was dripping down onto his face. But it wasn't rain at all, it was the mosquitoes up in the trees, pissing to keep themselves cool. He wiped his face and saw a row of bats hanging from the lowest branches. He wanted to cry out, but no sound emerged. He hesitated, then gave up the idea of going to the threshing ground again and ran back towards his courtyard. The sound of his rapid, ragged footsteps bounced from one wall at the alley's entrance to the other. The echo was so loud that it startled the residents sleeping in the courtyards.

"Whose kid is that?" they asked. "It sounds like a stray cat."

Then they rolled over and went back to sleep.

The night was scorching hot and it didn't rain. At daybreak, Inkcap's nose got stuffed up as he slept in the yard. He grunted and snorted for a bit, then woke up. He found he had wheat straw in his hair, and his body was covered by the torn plastic sheeting from the dilapidated top of the wall. It turned out that the wind had started to blow. By mid-morning, it was shaking even the thickest trees, and their branches waved to and fro in the sky like green clouds. Outside the courtyard, next to the gable wall, there was a tree of heaven, with a branch extending diagonally from under the eaves. The branches of the tree were constantly grinding against the eaves in the wind, making a sound like a saw, and three tiles fell off.

The wind came off the river channel at the foot of Yijia Ridge twenty days early, blowing sand along the river strand. At first, the tips of the reeds and cattails surged around in the clouds of mist, taking on the shapes of various animals, but then they were covered by sand and dust. Waves started to surge in the river, undulating in folds like the belly of an old sow. The thornback fish no longer called out their name, even if there had been anyone to hear them. The dust began to spread across the river basin and form dust devils. Standing on the village embankment, you could see something like a winnowing basket in mid-air, filled with sand, soil, grass, wheat straw, tree leaves and reed stalks. The basket reared up, eliciting screams from those who watched it. Then it suddenly disintegrated, hurling its contents obliquely across the village like a flock of starlings, covering it in sand, soil, grass, wheat straw, tree leaves and reed stalks. Disheartened and coughing repeatedly, the villagers retreated inside, where they covered their doors and slammed their windows shut.

The residents of Old Kiln called this kind of wind a "devil wind", and this one blew all day.

The devil wind scattered the three stooks of wheat straw across the threshing ground. This should have been a signal for Millstone to ring the bell to summon the villagers to restack the straw, but no sound came from it. The rose trellis at the base of Barndoor's courtyard wall collapsed. He tied the branches together with rope, then tied stones to either end of the rope and hung them over the top of the wall. He wondered to himself why they hadn't been called out to work.

Millstone walked past carrying a load of manure, with a bundle of bamboo sticks hanging from the other end of his pole.

"Captain! Captain! Which field is being fertilised today?" Barndoor asked.

"The tomato field," Millstone told him. "And we need the bamboo because the tomato vines have collapsed and need propping up."

"I didn't know the production team had any tomato fields," Barndoor said.

"What about the private plots?"

It was only then that Barndoor realised Millstone was going to his family's private plot.

"So there won't be any work for the production team, then?"

"Fuck, no!" Millstone replied, so vehemently it startled Barndoor into silence.

So it was the community members who were going to have to do the work, then! And they'd have to rely on their work points to buy food. A crowd gathered in the middle of the alley, standing around wondering where to start. Someone said that Millstone had quit his post in disgust and that now the village was like a beehive without a queen. The maize in the dry fields had been buffeted, and the soil needed fertilising and reinforcing. As for the paddy fields, they were full of weevils that had to be eradicated. So the workers spontaneously divided into two groups. The women went to pick weevils, and the men took hoes to the eighteen-*mu* terrace on the rear slope. The work went on for three days. Everyone who could join in did so, and the rest were busy with the Cultural Revolution at Bash's place. But in the evening, when Soupspoon was recording work points in the public office, he gave them to everyone who turned up regardless of what they'd been doing.

Awning stormed out of the public office, slamming the door as he did so and kicking over the bench in the courtyard.

"Fuck them!" he cursed. "If all we think about is the crops, then how can we fully grasp the Revolution? And the Revolution is what is going to provide for our children and grandchildren."

"What if the crops fail, you prick?" Sparks shouted after him. "If the crops fail, then they fail for everyone, don't they?"

Over the next three days, fewer and fewer people went to work in the fields.

Huang Shengsheng reappeared in Old Kiln at noon. He gave Bash a bulging shoulder bag at the entrance of the village. By chance, Inkcap was following a group of women who were heading for the paddy fields to pick out weevils, so Bash asked him to carry the shoulder bag.

"Why do you let that little brat keep hanging around you?" Huang Shengsheng asked.

"He's a hard worker," Bash told him.

"We need to concentrate on retraining people and not just fall back on our old supports."

"Is there a steamed bun in the shoulder bag that I can nick?" Inkcap asked.

"That's enough lip," Bash said. "Just follow me, and do as you're told."

When he opened the shoulder bag, it was full of Chairman Mao lapel badges. Each was the size of a hen's egg and showed the Chairman in military uniform, wearing a military cap, pink-cheeked and smiling.

"Give me one," Inkcap shouted.

"These are only for rebels," Huang Shengsheng said. "Why should you have one?"

"I'm a rebel."

"Oh yes? And who are you rebelling against? Be off with you."

Inkcap was going to get angry, and he was already tired of carrying the shoulder bag. He wouldn't take a badge, even if they gave him one. But then he thought about how Bash sometimes relied on him, so he just gave Huang Shengsheng a filthy look and insisted on having a Chairman Mao badge. Bash took over carrying the shoulder bag himself.

"I can give you one if you want one," he said, "but you have to go to the lotus pond and catch us a fish. Comrade Huang needs building up."

Inkcap took a bamboo basket and went to the lotus pond to catch a fish, but he couldn't find any. Then he went to the hole in the stone weir by the pond because he knew that was a good place to find catfish. After feeling around for a while, he came across something soft and pulled it out, only to find that it was a king ratsnake. So you want some fish, do you, you bastard, he thought to himself. He put the snake in the basket and took it back to Bash.

"I couldn't catch any fish," he said. "Only this snake."

To their surprise, Huang Shengsheng grinned and said that snake meat was better than fish. He promptly chopped off the snake's head, peeled off the skin like preparing a spring onion, and put the body on the rice in the pot to make snake meat rice.

Inkcap was stunned by his reaction and even Bash shouted, "How can we eat this? We can't even eat the rice now. Even the pot stinks."

"You have to eat it," Huang Shengsheng said.

"I've never tried it before."

"The Cultural Revolution has never happened before! If you dare try it, you'll find it's delicious," Huang Shengsheng said and then he turned to Inkcap. "You need to eat it too."

"I won't," Inkcap insisted.

"Then I won't give you a Chairman Mao badge."

If he had to eat it, he had to eat it, so Inkcap stayed on. While Bash and Huang Shengsheng were cooking, he went to look at the dilapidated walls in the west of the courtyard. The courtyard of Bash's old family house used to be a quadrangle courtyard, but the east and west buildings had collapsed at some stage. Most of the salvaged wood had been used to build the little wooden shack on the highway, and the rest had gone to build a firewood store on the east side of the courtyard. The west side had been left to itself and was just broken-down walls. Inkcap found a dozen or so inkcap mushrooms growing at the base of the wall. They were almost identical in shape and size, all two fingers high, white and chubby. They looked as though they would seep water if you touched them, but, in fact, they were soft but resistant, like rubber. Inkcap squatted down, asking himself why the villagers called him after these mushrooms. Was that what he looked like to them? He was rather hurt.

While the rice was still cooking in the main room, Huang Shengsheng sat on the doorstep and pulled out a load of pamphlets for Bash to look at. They were talking about Beijing, the central government and the Cultural Revolution faction. Inkcap took no notice of all that, but he did listen when Bash was asking why all the people around Chairman Mao were capitalist roaders. Huang Shengsheng said that they had long opposed Chairman Mao, attempted to undermine him and seize power, and that was why Chairman Mao had launched the Cultural Revolution.

Bash let out a sigh and said, "It's not easy for Chairman Mao to deal with those who oppose him, is it?"

"But you appreciate the great power of the masses, don't you?"

"How can you be sure of that?"

"I've heard what the rebel factions that have come to the county from Beijing say, and I think it's true."

"Relying on the masses is good enough to mobilise the citizens of Beijing, but what about mobilising the whole country?"

"Don't you love movements?"

"Who doesn't? Everyone is quite used to movements."

"So can't you see what an opportunity this is?"

"When the sky warms up in spring, all the grass in the field takes root and sprouts."

"What kind of grass are you?"

"I am a tree," Bash declared. "I want to grow into a tree."

Inkcap looked at them and thought to himself that he would always be as small as those mushrooms in front of him. He sighed and found some bamboo sticks to block up the entrance in the broken-down wall.

"What are you doing over there?" Bash asked.

"There are some inkcaps growing here."

"So you've found yourself, have you?"

"I'm blocking the way in with bamboo, so no one can come in and pick them."

"Who's going to do that? They're not worth a second glance. No one'll want to eat them."

"Maybe they'll grow into trees."

Bash guffawed. "Sure, just watch them grow. There'll be trees two fingers tall."

The snake meat and rice were done, but the snake didn't soften. The rice, however, turned completely yellow. Huang Shengsheng and Bash ate it, but Inkcap didn't dare, so he didn't get his egg-sized Mao badge either.

Huang Shengsheng left again that night. There was new content on the big-character poster board in Old Kiln, and the walls of the alleys were painted with slogans about overthrowing Liu Shaoqi and Deng Xiaoping. In the days that followed, Bash became even more vigorous and full of energy. He hardly slept and got very tired after a few days and nights constantly on the go. When he said he would take a nap, he just lay down where he was or found somewhere to curl up. In the blink of an eye, he would be snoring away. He only slept in short bursts but always reappeared with renewed energy. He had the occasional whim, such as getting Baldy Jin to cut down some willow twigs and weave a decorative border for the top of the poster board, or picking wildflowers from Middle Mountain to make wreaths, and then inserting lotus flowers into them. Enough lotus flowers were picked from the lotus pond for both sides of the board to be decorated with them. He formulated the aims and programme for the Old Kiln Federation, added the terms and conditions of membership, wrote them all out one by one on pieces of paper and pasted them on the wall of the Federation headquarters. He even ordered a thick notebook with covers made of tung wood and cloth. He called it the "Record of the Events of the Great Old Kiln Village Revolutionary Rebellion" and got Useless to update it in ink every day, then read it out to him. Useless was very fond of adjectives and Bash found the text too convoluted, so he told Useless to study the sentence structures and phrases in the pamphlets.

"Put your heart into it," he said. "These important events must be preserved for the future. When people read them in ten or a hundred years' time, they must still make their blood boil."

After recording what had happened in the village that day, Useless would use any spare moment to run off to the high road. The little wooden shack was more his place than Bash's by then. He collected pamphlets from passersby on the road in the Great Link-Up, and revolutionary and rebel language became increasingly popular in Old Kiln. Even Cowbell and Inkcap could close their eyes and recite phrases such as: "willing to be cut all over"; "daring to pull the emperor off his horse"; "revolution is blameless", "rebellion is justified"; "Sima Zhao's ill intent is known to all"; and "if this can be tolerated, what is left that is intolerable?"

At first, Bash was satisfied with the name of the Old Kiln Village Federation, but then he wanted to come up with something fresher and more resounding because out on the high road, there were often people in the Great Link-Up carrying flags with the names of rebel groups such as "Red Iron Fist", "Golden Cudgel" and "The Bayonet Sees Red". He struggled to come up with a good name for his own group. One day, when they had gone back to the Old Kiln Temple to smash the carved couplet with the green dragon once again, Baldy Jin mentioned a set of brick carvings on the screen wall of Awning's house. They weren't easy to interpret but had something to do with emperors, generals, talented sons and beautiful daughters. Awning had replastered the wall, but wasn't that really an attempt to hide the carvings? This actually made everyone remember that Baldy Jin wanted revenge on Awning, but the fact remained that Awning's screen wall had been replastered and should be smashed.

When they went to smash the screen wall, the morning glory vines on it were in full bloom, and it was covered by the new growth. The flowers were as red as fire. Awning and his wife had no real argument to put up, but they did say that although the carvings were Four Olds, the wall itself wasn't and nor were the flowering vines. They pulled down the vines, peeled off the plaster and let their visitors smash only the brick carvings. One or two people had brought pickaxes and iron hammers but most had come with wooden hammers. These hammers were sawn from a tree burr, into which a hole was drilled so it could be fitted with a wooden handle one *zhang* in length, or about ten feet. The handle was carefully shaved until it was perfectly straight, polished with shards of porcelain and repeatedly wiped with tung seed oil to make it smooth and shiny. Every household in Old Kiln had a wooden hammer. In winter, after ploughing, they were used to smash the lumps in the ground. Also, the production team piled up manure and composted it through the winter. In spring, the manure pile was opened up, and the hammers were needed to break it up into usable lumps. In the end, the brickwork carvings on Awning's screen wall were smashed with pickaxes and iron hammers. The wooden hammers weren't used even though lots of people had brought them. It was these events that gave Bash a brainwave, and he renamed the Old Kiln Village Federation the Old Kiln Village Red Hammer Battle Squad.

After that, the hammers were painted red all over and kept at Bash's house. Whenever there was a meeting or a revolutionary rebel action, everyone carried one, which made for a very commanding spectacle. Bash also had a vision of them wearing military uniforms when they held the wooden hammers, but that was not a realistic proposition and was never implemented.

"One day," he said, "we will all wear yellow military hats, tie a sash around our waists and have rubber shoes on our feet."

One initiative that was practicable was shaving people's heads. To confirm his position as the leader, Bash wanted everyone to have their hair cut like his. But his haircut had been done in Luozhen and as there were no hair clippers in Old Kiln, razor blades had to be used instead. He himself once took off an inch of Useless's hair but managed to make it higher on one side than the other and ended up having to shave it off completely. It looked surprisingly good and everybody else shaved their head too. The shaved heads and hammers went together like steamed black buns and pickled cabbage, and Bash was very proud of his design.

The Red Hammer Battle Squad was called just the Hammerheads by the villagers. It was a proper revolutionary rebel organisation. It had a roster of members and, in addition to the original members, more and more came along afterwards. They had to apply to join and each time a new member was admitted, they had to learn to sing and write their name on a piece of paper, which was then posted on the big-character poster board. From then on, the Hammerheads held activities every day. When the whistle blew, they gathered under the mountain gate, ran in formation, sang songs and shouted slogans from the mountain gate to the millstone in the west of the village. Then they sang and shouted from the millstone in the west to the roller stone in the east of the village, before finally returning to the mountain gate to study Chairman Mao's quotations and read pamphlets, or listen to Bash addressing them.

In the previous basic militia training in Old Kiln, Awning had only led the team in running a few laps of the wheat field, and then they had practised shooting and learned Russian. It was definitely not as impressive as the current Hammerheads. Awning had caught a cold after the brickwork carvings on his screen wall were smashed and he was staying at home.

Sparks went to see him. As soon as he was in the courtyard, he said to Awning's wife, "So the fuckers smashed your screen, did they? How is he?"

"He's caught cold and he's asleep."

Awning heard this as he lay on the *kang*, snot running from his nose, which he didn't wipe away. He waited for Sparks to come in, by which time a long thread of the stuff was hanging down.

"So they still came and smashed your screen even though you plastered it over," Sparks said.

"I'm sick," Awning replied.

"Sick, are you? Millstone's thrown in his hand and doesn't give a toss about anything, and now you're sick! That's just great. Why don't we just let them shit and piss on our heads?"

When Sparks left, Awning was so furious he actually wiped his nose and began pacing around the courtyard. The Hammerheads were running through the village alleys again and passed by Awning's house. Bash didn't blow a whistle or shout "one-two-one-two" like Awning used to do during the militia training. Instead, he called out at the top of his voice, "Shout the slogans as loud as you can. I'll shout the beginning and you finish them off. Then repeat them and make sure you keep the rhythm."

So Bash shouted, "Rebellion is justified!"

"It's justified!" the runners shouted back.

"Revolution is blameless!"

"Blameless! Blameless!"

Awning lay down by a hole in the courtyard wall and looked out, watching the Hammerheads running past shouting arrogantly, leaving the sound of their voices echoing down the alley.

Awning's wife had just finished making some ginger broth for him, and she shouted several times for him to come and drink it. But Awning stayed where he was, lying by the hole in the wall.

"I know you can hear me. Stop pretending you can't."

Awning picked up the bowl of chickenfeed at the bottom of the wall and smashed it, making his wife fall down in surprise at the kitchen door.

"Fuck you and your shouting," he said.

Then he stormed back into the house and sat down on the *kang* again.

The Hammerheads ran down the village alleys once a day, attracting more and more converts. It seemed that if you didn't join, you would fall behind, and if the Revolution stalled, it would be your fault. Whenever they ran past, Inkcap would stop whatever he was doing, even if he was eating his lunch or feeding the pigs, and try to join them. But Gran always shut the courtyard gate and wouldn't let him out. One day, Third Aunt came to borrow a colander to make rice noodles, and the sound of running and chanting could be heard outside. The three of them held their breath and let the sound pass.

"Tag-Along has joined them," Third Aunt said.

"Tag-Along has joined them?" Gran echoed in disbelief.

"And Decheng too."

"Decheng is so thin his bones show through his skin, and the bugger walks around bent-double all the time. How can he run around like that?"

"He's drunk, isn't he," Third Aunt explained.

"Drunk?"

"Just listen. Go on, listen. He's shouting 'Not drunk! Not drunk!' He only says that when he's drunk."

"He's actually saying 'blameless'," Inkcap told her. "As in 'the Revolution is blameless'."

"Inkcap's always following Bash around like he's his tail," Third Aunt observed. "Why's he being such a good boy and staying indoors now?"

"That's the Hammerheads out there," Gran said. "Why would he run around with them? Go and get some potatoes from the root cellar, Inkcap."

But Inkcap didn't go to the cellar to fetch any potatoes. He was busy picking up the household's wooden hammer. But just then, he heard the sound of footsteps in the alley and a voice in front of the walnut tree.

"Did you polish the handle with porcelain shards?" the voice said.

"Sure," came the reply.

"Have you joined up?"

"How can I join up if I don't paint my hammer red?"

"So when are you going to paint it, then?"

"Not until I've finished using it to smash up my old *kang* and taken all the soil down to my private plot. Once it's painted red, I can only use it for revolutionary purposes, not for ordinary work."

Diagonally opposite where this conversation was taking place was the gate to Millstone's courtyard, where the man himself was pounding the adobe that he needed to rebuild the stove base in his kitchen. The old base had been there for more than a decade, so its soil was strong enough to be used as fertiliser. The stove soil that had already been dug out was piled up in the corner of the courtyard, and his wife was beating it with a mallet. The yard was filled with such a pungent smell that the chickens and the dog had already fled and Millstone sneezed and shouted to his wife to stop.

471

She had covered her mouth and nose with a handkerchief but still said, "I'm choking. You should be wearing a handkerchief too."

"Bring the mallet over here. Do you hear me?"

She did as she was told, and Millstone picked up a stone support pier and smashed the mallet with it before going over to the wall and throwing the mallet out into the alley.

Useless was going from house to house with a bucket of red paint, asking if anyone still needed their wooden hammers painted. As he passed along the wall of Millstone's courtyard he looked in through the window where Pockmark had introduced the poison. No one was inside. The hammer that came flying out almost hit him.

"Whose hammer is this?" he yelled.

"Mine," Millstone said from inside the courtyard.

"What do you think you're doing?" Useless asked from the gate.

"What am I doing? I'm smashing up my hammer. Is that OK with you?"

Millstone was bare-shouldered and loosened his belt so he could thrust his hand down his trousers to scratch an itch.

"I'm also scratching my balls," he continued. "Anyone who doesn't like it can bite me."

Useless was lost for words, his thin lips were drained of blood and his face was trembling. Millstone slammed the courtyard gate.

Useless told Bash how many families in Old Kiln had hammers, how many had their hammers painted red and how many still planned to paint them. Of course, he also told Bash what was going on at Millstone's house but Bash just laughed and said, "He's allowed a fit of temper, isn't he? Besides, he's not captain of the production team any more, so it won't affect our revolution, will it? What's going on in Awning's household?"

"I heard he's sick."

"He's a big strong fellow, isn't he? How can he be sick?"

"There is one thing we have to address," Useless said. "No one from the crew up at the kiln has come to join up, and I haven't heard of anyone planning to, either. When I bumped into Pendulum, I asked if any of the others were going to join and he played dumb and pretended not to know what I was talking about. I told him I was talking about joining the Hammerheads, and he just said they were too busy as they had the last firing of the year to see to up at the kiln site."

"They're still firing the kiln, are they? Won't anything they produce be corrupted by the capitalist roaders? Let's go up there tomorrow."

But Bash didn't go to the kiln the next day. Instead, he went to Luozhen and brought back several large boxes of *The Sayings of Chairman Mao*. In the afternoon, he held a meeting under the mountain gate. Before the meeting, Useless asked if he wanted him to go door-to-door to call people to participate, but Bash said there was no need as long as they handed out flyers for the meeting all over the village. When the meeting was held, more than half of the village attended.

"Not a bad test of my prestige!" Bash told Useless.

There was no specific content to the meeting. Bash just led everyone in shouting slogans: "We will defeat Liu Shaoqi and Deng Xiaoping, and then we will defeat Pockmark Zhang and Cripple Cao!" Pockmark Zhang was Zhang Dezhang, and Cripple Cao was county party secretary Cao Yiwei, who had never visited Old Kiln. Bash said that Cao Yiwei was a cripple and he wanted to see Cripple Cao defeated, so everyone shouted, "Down with Cripple Cao!"

At past meetings, they had only shouted "Down with Liu Shaoqi and Deng Xiaoping!" Liu Shaoqi and Deng Xiaoping were far away in Beijing, so the slogans were easy to shout and they just disappeared like the wind. But now they had moved from Beijing to the province, to the county, to the town, and the villagers of Old Kiln were shocked to find themselves shouting about defeating their own local leaders, that they must all be overthrown as capitalist roaders. But this is what Bash took the lead in shouting. Bash was the leader of the Hammerheads, and the Hammerheads were under the direction of the County Federation. With his excellent background, surely Bash must be right about the Revolution. So everyone followed suit and shouted, "Down! Down! Down!"

Who else were they going to overthrow? Would the Branch Secretary be next? Or the captain of the production team? Or the production team's chief cashier and accountant? They all turned to look at Bash, who seemed to be their law-giver and policy-maker, but, under their gaze, Bash stayed silent, his calm unruffled. Ah, they thought, is Bash totting up the score? When the Branch Secretary totted up the score, he used to take out his tobacco pouch, fill his pipe, cough, look around the venue and then speak in a loud voice. But look how different Bash was! He didn't say anything, his face was calm, and he distributed books of quotations from Chairman Mao and Chairman Mao badges.

Starting with the front row of the crowd, the attendees filed up to accept Bash's handouts. When the first person stepped up, Useless said, "This Little Red Book and this badge are for you. Bow first, take them in both hands and then bow again."

The people who followed on did exactly the same and then stepped back. Inkcap and Cowbell were standing at the rear of the venue, so it was a long time before it was their turn. They were worried there weren't enough books and badges, and they wouldn't get any. They tried jumping the queue, but Useless shoved them aside.

"Do you two really think you're included?" Useless said. "You can't even read."

"Loads of that lot can't read either, and they're all included," Inkcap protested.

"Come on up, come on up," Bash said. "Both of you will get your share."

Inkcap took the book of Chairman Mao's quotations and the badge. He pinned the badge to his chest and stuck the book up to his face, as if his face was pressed against a sheet of glass.

"Brother Bash!" he exclaimed.

"What do you want to say?"

"You look like Chairman Mao."

"You're talking nonsense."

Actually, Inkcap didn't believe what he had said, so he corrected himself. "I meant that your face is as red as Chairman Mao's."

"Really?"

Bash turned around and wanted to take a look, but there was no mirror and no water.

"You can't read," Bash told Inkcap, "but you must still respect the Little Red Book when you take it away with you."

"Of course I will respect it."

Everyone who received a copy of the Little Red Book carried it back in both hands, but Inkcap put his on top of his head. He took small steps, being too scared to run. Baldy Jin had got his copy early on and was standing in front of his pigsty, watching his pigs eat.

When he saw Inkcap he said, "Who put that bun on top of the roller?"

Inkcap stopped in his tracks and looked right and left, but couldn't see any steamed bun. It was only then he realised Baldy Jin was teasing him about his appearance.

"If there are any buns, you eat them," he said.

"I was just testing you, you little prick. If you drop that book, it'll be your fault and you'll have done it on purpose."

Inkcap was relieved he hadn't fallen for the trick and went on his way, taking even smaller steps and standing up even straighter.

When he got home, he placed the Little Red Book in front of the ancestral tablet in the central cabinet. Gran moved the tablet aside, took three bricks and placed the book on top of them. She searched everywhere for an incense burner, only to remember using it when she was setting up Potful's mourning. Inkcap went off to Apricot's house to get it.

On the counter in Apricot's house there was not only a Little Red Book, but also a plaster bust of Chairman Mao.

Inkcap found the burner and asked for a few incense sticks from Apricot's house too. Thinking things through on the way back, he couldn't figure it out. Apricot didn't go to the meeting, so how did she come by a copy of the Little Red Book? And what about that huge bust of Chairman Mao?

FORTY-FIVE

MILLSTONE'S HOUSEHOLD DID NOT HAVE A LITTLE RED BOOK, nor did Awning's or Sparks'. In fact, none of the households of the men busy firing the kiln owned a copy.

The devil wind blew down a corner of the bricks drying on the clay field. Fortunately, the rain held off, and Lightkeeper and Pendulum kept a close eye on the pulverised glaze stone. Once the glaze slurry was made, it was sieved and poured into a vat for ageing and then used for white glazes. The loess that the wind hadn't blown away was also mixed with water and sieved, and then aged in another vat to use for black glazes. It had been three days by then and the sunny weather had returned.

Winterborn put the basin of glaze on the clay bricks and dipped them one by one into the glaze. He was very skilled at this job, and even intentionally made a bit of a show of the different actions of oiling, pausing, dipping and lifting. Pillar didn't know how to do that kind of work, but he couldn't stand Winterborn's arrogance, so he took his tobacco pouch and went to the shed door to watch Lightkeeper. Lightkeeper was decorating white porcelain. First, he applied a layer of slip, quickly drew the patterns on it, and then applied a transparent glaze while it was still wet. He was wearing a straw hat, but his face had got sunburned. The skin on his arms was peeling off.

"Don't you want to join the Hammerheads, Lightkeeper?" Pillar asked.

"I want to, but who'd let me?"

"But I don't get why you would, you're of pretty high status… Of course, it's always said that class enemies are responsible for sabotaging things, but I've never seen you do any sabotage."

"Little do you know," Lightkeeper said. "If you weren't here, I'd kick this whole lot down. Do you know why that devil wind blew so hard? It's because I told it to."

Pillar giggled. "They've already handed out all those Little Red Books, but they're no use if you can't read. What they should have been handing out is you!"

Lightkeeper didn't reply. The sweat flowed down from his forehead and into his eyes. He couldn't see anything. He held the form in his hand and said, "Come over here. Come over here."

Pillar went over to him, and he rubbed his eyes on his shoulder until he could see again.

"Now get on with your work," he said.

"Millstone isn't team captain any more," Pillar replied, "and the Branch Secretary is no longer in charge. Where do you think you…"

But Lightkeeper ignored him and went to pick up the carrying boards, getting ready to take the half-finished products from the form-resting room to the kiln.

There were originally seven or eight kilns at the kiln site, but they were all so dilapidated that they were no longer in use. Now there remained only one horseshoe kiln. Pendulum was already there, loading it. Lightkeeper moved the bowl forms to the door of the kiln, put them in the saggars and handed them to Pendulum in the kiln. Pendulum was standing in the middle of the lowest level of the kiln, leaving himself a fifteen-centimetre central passageway, setting the *laoxian* length of clay used to measure temperature and arranging the bowls along the back wall to both ends, and then back to the side of the platform over the furnace. There was an accelerant in the middle of each layer. The saggars were stacked to the full height of the kiln arch, and the two sides met to form a circle of gradually decreasing height.

"Is that all of the clay?" Pendulum asked Lightkeeper.

Lightkeeper looked towards the east of the site, but there was no sign of Goodman.

It took Goodman a long time to transport all the forms of the dishes, bowls and jars, and when he had finished, Pendulum sent him off to the edge of the site to mix more clay. Pillar and Lightkeeper didn't have much to say to each other and their bellies were rumbling, so, to distract himself from his hunger, Pillar went over to have a chat with Goodman about what was going on in the village.

When he saw Goodman mixing the clay, over and over again, muttering to himself incessantly, Pillar told him, "Take a break. Even that fucker Lightkeeper is skiving but you're still hard at it. This clay is only for sealing the furnace platform, do you really need to mix it so thoroughly?"

Goodman stopped mixing and the two of them walked over to the form-drying chamber to cool down.

"Whatever you do, you have to do it well," Goodman said.

"Surely even you can't find the Dao in clay."

"The Dao is always there. It's not something to acquire overnight. It is something that you awaken to gradually. When I was mixing clay just now, I asked myself, Why do I work? To make a living, I answered. Why make a living, I asked. To feed myself, I answered. Why feed yourself, I asked. To practise the Dao, I answered. But when I thought about it carefully, I realised that that Dao was ineffectual, and people were in error. The Dao is the Dao of Heaven. It is in everyone and cannot be separated. People also have their own roots. If you always consider your own roots, you can attain the Dao. It is like a beansprout that must keep on growing upwards and upwards until the beans attain their proper form and size."

"Ha!" Pillar said. "I don't dare to ask you any more questions. Whatever I ask you, you just go off on a whole flight of your own."

"To attain the Dao is to share it with the rest of the world. If you cannot share it, you will be responsible for all the sins of the world."

"Hey, at least let me ask you this. Do you know about the Hammerheads?"

"Of course I do."

"Then what do you think about it?"

"It's all to do with Will, Mind, Heart and Body."

"I don't understand what you mean."

"People often say there are three roads on the bridge to the world beyond. One is gold, one is silver, and the third is the Yellow Spring Road to the underworld. A person with ambition takes the gold road, a person with intention takes the silver road, and a person who actually uses his body and mind to do things takes the road to death and the underworld. People in the realm of Will are like spring, concentrating on nurture and development. People in the realm of Mind are like summer, concentrating on tolerance and cultivation, so that all things can grow and flourish. People in the realm of Heart are like autumn, selfish, focusing on things that benefit themselves and not caring about others, so they become fragmented and in disarray. People in the realm of Body are like winter, only interested in destruction and plunder. I often say that the two realms of Will and Mind build the world, while the realms of Heart and Body destroy it. When seedlings are grown, they can be planted out and grow vigorously. However, in autumn, they become the seeds of weeds and tares. Those seeds fall to the ground first during the harvest, and the land is made barren the following year. The people of the world control the seeds of failure."

"So, Goodman, are you saying that people are all the seeds of weeds and tares? Is that true of the Federation? Is it true of Bash?"

"Whether we are the seeds of weeds and tares depends on whether we use our Will, Mind, Heart or Body. Our Dao depends on which we choose."

"Does that mean Bash cannot succeed?"

"Isn't he successful already?"

"Then I should join the Hammerheads?"

"That's your business."

"I saw ten years ago that that bastard wasn't the kind to keep a low profile. That year, Awning's father and Cowbell's father had argued so violently over the height of the roof Awning's father was building that murder could have been done, and everyone else tried to calm them down. But Bash was out collecting manure and didn't join in. He suddenly threw down his basket of manure and said, 'There must be something special about me!' At the time, no one had any idea what he was talking about. When I consider it now, I think he was showing his contempt for the other villagers. Did you know that he and Apricot have a thing going between them, and Apricot even made her dad sick with anger because of him? Previously, he had wanted to treat Apricot as a goddess, but once he had made contact with the Great Link-Up on the high road, he stopped paying her any attention. I saw her with my own eyes begging him to swallow his pride and go and talk to her father, but he told her, 'From now on, I can't play house with you any more.' And just look at the fuss he's kicked up now, stealing the limelight from Millstone and even the Branch Secretary. That one's an ambitious bastard."

"But is he acting from Will or from Heart?" Goodman asked.

"What do you mean by acting from Heart?"

Goodman was about to reply, but, just at that moment, Lightkeeper called out to ask whether the clay was ready.

Goodman hurried out of the drying chamber to say that the mixing was done, and he quickly and neatly stowed his shovel on the cart and pushed it over to the kiln.

"You took your time with that clay," Pendulum complained. "I shouted to you two or three times and you didn't reply. You thought you'd skive off for a rest and a cool down, didn't you?"

"I was talking to Pillar," Goodman told him.

"What about? What were you talking to him about?" Pendulum asked as he used the mud to fill in the gaps between the pillars at the opening of the furnace platform.

The kiln needed very careful handling, and the only person who really knew what to do was Pendulum. Winterborn and Pillar hadn't yet got the knack of controlling the heat. Lightkeeper wanted to learn, but despite his high status, he was only up to making the forms and handling the glaze. Goodman just did the menial jobs. After the gaps were filled in, Lightkeeper and Goodman spread lumps of coal over the bottom of the firing chamber. In the middle, they built a small pile of wheat straw, hard wood and choice pieces of coal and got the pilot flame ready. Lightkeeper stood on top of the ash channel under the furnace shed and asked Pendulum if he should light the wheat straw for the pilot flame. Pendulum had gone outside for a drink of water when he had finished loading the kiln outside.

"Hold your horses," he said. "That's my job, not yours."

Although his eyes appeared to be looking at the clay pond in the distance, he was actually watching the mouth of the kiln.

"The squint-eyed tosser," Lightkeeper whispered. "It's just lighting a poxy fire, isn't it? He's so full of himself."

"Watch what you say," Goodman warned him. "He's got a quick temper."

"He's only like that because we're such pushovers. It's a shame the gods aren't on our side and all we meet are devils like him."

"The gods help people, but so do devils. Sometimes it's opposites that are most helpful, so keep your temper with him."

"So who else should I be cross with? With myself?" Then Lightkeeper raised his voice and shouted over towards the kiln, "I know what it is. It's because I didn't give you any tobacco, isn't it?"

With that, he went over to the little cave where he slept to get his tobacco box. He fished out a handful of tobacco powder to give to Pendulum.

Pendulum laughed and said, "Everything has its own rules. You're no Bash, so why do you think you have to show off all the time?"

"All right, all right," Lightkeeper replied. "But why don't you take it easy today? I can light the pilot flame and once I've got things going, you can go over and feed the fire. I'm not going to sabotage anything, and I'm certainly not trying to take over your job."

"Do you think you can fire the kiln without paying homage to the kiln god?"

"When did you ever pay homage to the kiln god when you fired it?"

"I didn't use to," Pendulum admitted, "but now I do. I had a dream last night. I dreamed of eating persimmons. I've been worried all day long. We have to pay homage to the kiln god, otherwise the kiln will go out. Do you want to be responsible for that?"

Lightkeeper struck a match and, keeping his head down, went to light Pendulum's cigarette. Once it was going, he kept the match burning and grinned to himself as he thought about throwing it into Pendulum's hair. But he didn't and ended up just blowing the match out.

Goodman pretended not to see what Lightkeeper was doing, and he also ignored their conversation. He was getting hotter and hotter under his straw hat, so he took it off and went bare-headed under the sun. Pillar put on his jacket and came over. He rubbed his hands on his waistband and asked, "Are you sweating?"

"I am."

"What's going on with you? How come you can dry all those pots in the sun but you can't keep yourself dry? You can rub all those pots smooth but the more you rub yourself, the thicker the dirt on your body gets."

He laughed at his own witticism then bent down, picked up Lightkeeper's tobacco box and grabbed a handful of tobacco powder. When Lightkeeper saw what he was doing, he snatched the box back and held it close to his body to keep Pillar from snatching it back.

"It's only some tobacco powder," Pillar protested.

"Maybe so, but it's my tobacco powder."

Pillar lost his temper and yelled at him, "OK, it's yours. What else do you have? Doesn't your home have three courtyards, and don't you have hundreds of *mu* of paddy fields and wheat fields?"

"What have I got?" Lightkeeper said. "I've got this tobacco powder."

"What's all the fuss about?" Winterborn asked as he came over. "It's just a handful of tobacco powder, isn't it? Why's that so precious to you, Pillar? Is it made of gold or silver, Lightkeeper?"

As Pillar was muttering away, Lightkeeper hurled the box to the ground, scattering the tobacco powder. He kicked the dirt and stamped on it, then kicked it again sending up clouds of dirt and powder. Lightkeeper's nerves were clearly jangling as the men choked on the dust and no one spoke again. Goodman put his hat back on his head and craned his neck to look up at his house on the mountaintop. One moment, the white-barked pines were covered in luxuriant foliage and providing sanctuary for countless birds, and the next, all the leaves were gone, leaving only a few dead branches. The clouds tumbled one by one, down towards the Mountain God Temple, like dropped handkerchiefs.

Pendulum finished his pipe, knocked it out on the sole of his shoe and tucked it into his belt. Then he got up and walked down the mountain without another word. Winterborn followed him, then Pillar and finally Lightkeeper, but Goodman stayed where he was.

"Aren't you going to pay homage to the kiln god?" Winterborn asked.

"Should you really be going there to pay homage to the god?" Pillar interjected. "It's the public office now, and everything that used to be in it has been destroyed."

"The temple may be gone," Winterborn said, "but doesn't the god still exist?"

Goodman went with them too.

The gate of the Kiln God Temple was open, and the towering eight-character-couplet brick carvings on the pillars on either side had been smashed. The five men kowtowed to the small ancestral hall next to the east wing of the gate, then to the small ancestral hall next to the west wing, and finally to the Rear Hall, where, because the door was locked, they knelt together on the steps. Pendulum chanted and kowtowed resoundingly, and the others kowtowed too. After three kowtows, Pendulum leaned forward to look through the crack in the doors, but he couldn't make anything out. He angled his head and tried again, but still without success.

"Do you remember the gods that used to be in there?" he asked Winterborn.

"I remember them."

What he remembered was a time ten years ago, when statues of the Earth God and the Mountain God were in the East Hall, and the Ox King and Horse King were enshrined in the West Hall. The former statues were there because pottery was sourced from the mountains, and the latter were included because, in the past, the transportation of the finished products relied on the strength of cattle and horses. In the Main Hall was the tasselled-crowned, dragon-robed image of the principal deity, Yu Shun, the Sage Emperor who made pottery by the riverside. In the east chamber was Taishang Laojun, the Fire Official, and in the west chamber was Ye Gong, the first bowl-maker in Old Kiln. These statues had been destroyed years ago by the Branch Secretary and others.

"What an odd situation," Pendulum said. "Anyone who wants to become a village cadre smashes up the Kiln God Temple. Back then, it was the Branch Secretary and now it's Bash."

"When was Bash ever a village cadre?" Winterborn asked.

"Just look at the way he's setting himself up. Isn't it obvious he's planning to make himself a cadre?"

"Who's going to be the next to smash it? No one's yet said the kiln isn't going to be fired again, have they? Whoever's the next person to become a cadre, they're still going to need you, Pendulum."

"Do you remember that statue of Yu Shun had a chain around his waist?"

"No, I don't remember that."

"There definitely was an iron chain," Pendulum continued. "Legend has it that the Kiln God once turned into a big white snake and slithered out of the temple gate. He got a fair way towards West Alley before the temple watchman caught him."

"I was the temple watchman," Goodman said.

"No, you weren't," Pendulum said. "You just lived there."

"Maybe it's my destiny to be the man who lights the kiln," Goodman chuckled.

Pendulum glared at him, but it had no effect, so he went on, "The temple watchman held on tight to the Kiln God and invited him to return to the temple. The villagers were afraid that the Kiln God who looked after all their needs might go away again, so they tied the statue in place with an iron chain."

"Are you saying that you are now the village's Kiln God, and no one can touch you?" Lightkeeper asked.

"What else does Old Kiln have to fall back on, if it's not the income from the kiln?" Pendulum said. "You need to fall in step with me. What else have people like you got to live off without the kiln?"

Lightkeeper mumbled agreement, but as he walked out of the courtyard gate, he shot a look at Goodman, who followed him out.

"He genuinely thinks he's a god, doesn't he?" Lightkeeper said.

Pendulum seemed to have heard him from in the courtyard because he called out, "What's that you said? Just because you've got a bit of fucking culture and you can read and write a bit, you think that makes you some kind of great master, do you? Well, who asked you to be their master, eh? What you really are is a class enemy."

Pendulum had overseen the whole process: the kiln had been fired, the temperature had reached its optimum point, fusing the *laoxian* indicators, one by one, the furnace had been extinguished and the pots had been hauled out to have the finishing touches put to them. Then, to his astonishment, Bash led his men up to the kiln site and sealed the kiln, once and for all.

The Hammerheads sealed the three-building public office that had been sold. Their excuse was that there was something fishy about a sale that resulted in village cadres converting public buildings into private houses. What was the solution? They should seal them up first and then investigate further and implement their findings. They also checked the accounts of the porcelain sales over the years. Porcelain goods were the only way for the village to make money. How much was sold every year? The accounts had never been made public. Was there corruption involved and if so, who was implicated? The public buildings that were originally just shut down were now sealed, and the porcelain business's accounts were audited. The interests of everyone in the village were involved. Over the years, many people had had their suspicions and opinions but never dared to voice them. Now Bash had taken the initiative, it made people think more favourably of him than when he had been leading his faction to smash roofs, rocks, lions and mountain gates. Secretly, the villagers were both pleased and worried. They were pleased because Bash was now feeling that much stronger and more secure, and he dared to find fault in the Branch Secretary. But they were worried that Zhu Dagui, who has been the Branch Secretary for more than ten years, might not tolerate his behaviour. They talked at night in groups, behind closed doors. They sat around pretending everything was fine during the day, and when they met each other in the street, they would say, "Is there nothing going on in the village?" or "What's going on?" or "Everything's fine if nothing happens". But they still pushed and prodded, never saying anything directly, but always keeping half an eye on the Branch Secretary's house.

The courtyard gate of the Branch Secretary's house was open, and his rooster was lying on the threshold. A group of hens had found an earthworm in the doorway, and two chickens had grabbed one end of it each and stretched it out.

No one had visited the Branch Secretary's house over the last few days, or even passed by the courtyard gate. Decheng was carrying water from the spring and had to pass by the house to get home, so he was forced to make a detour down a small alley. Just as he was about to turn down the alley, he heard a cough and looked up to see a small whirlwind swirling at the gate of the Branch Secretary's house, as if it was dancing. When the Branch Secretary came out of the courtyard gate to take a look, the whirlwind disappeared. Decheng dashed down the little alley, splashing water all the way.

Three days previously, the Branch Secretary's son came back from Luozhen again, but without his fiancée this time. He stayed for three days, and the Branch Secretary didn't go out all that time. Now, as the son was pushing his bicycle noisily down the alley, the Branch Secretary emerged and headed for Bash's house. He was going to seize the initiative by telling Bash that he had no objection to the sealing of the old public office. If the revolutionary masses had doubts about the sale, he didn't have to buy it. At the same time, he brought the account books for the porcelain sales.

"I have brought all these account books," he explained, "and every sale is recorded in detail. I am willing to accept the findings of the audit. I have been Branch Secretary for more than ten years. If the masses have reason to doubt me, I will never oppose them. If problems are uncovered, I will correct them. If there are no problems, I will urge myself to greater efforts in future."

After accepting the keys to the public office and a large number of account books, Bash sat down at his desk and started writing. He didn't call him "Branch Secretary" like last time, or even ask him to sit down. The Branch Secretary stood there, watching Bash write.

After filling half a page, Bash raised his head, and said, "Don't you have anything else to do?"

"No, not at the moment," the Branch Secretary replied.

"Off you go then," Bash said, handing him a stack of leaflets.

The Branch Secretary turned around and walked to the door. He looked back and asked Bash if he could also give him a copy of the Little Red Book. Bash gave him a copy. When the Branch Secretary arrived, he had hung his coat on the door knocker because he was sweating so much. As he left, he forgot to pick it up.

"Put your coat on," Bash ordered.

After the Branch Secretary took his coat, he sat on the stone in the yard and rubbed the mud from between his toes. Bash only glanced at him and said nothing.

As soon as the Branch Secretary left, Bash came out onto the steps and stretched.

"When he went out," Dazed-And-Confused said, "his head didn't brush against the branches of the apple tree. He used to be tall. How come he's shrunk?"

"Is that so?" Bash said.

"Yes, he's definitely shrunk. Did he bring the accounts for the porcelain sales like you asked?"

"I didn't tell him to bring them, but he brought them all the same."

"You sure know what you're doing, Bash."

"Maybe..." Bash started to say, but suddenly he wanted to sneeze. He couldn't get it out and his face contorted.

"Look at the sun," Dazed-And-Confused said. "That'll get it out."

Bash did as he suggested. The sun was hanging in mid-air, its rays spearing off like the spines on a hedgehog.

Bash sneezed violently, splattering Dazed-And-Confused's face with spittle. At the same time, Dazed-And-Confused heard him finish his sentence: "…in the future."

The next day, the Hammerheads went to the kiln and extinguished the fire.

The Branch Secretary had handed over the account ledgers and the keys to the public office, and now the kiln had been sealed. The villagers knew for sure that Old Kiln was no longer the same place, so more people came to join the Hammerheads: join up, write your name in black ink and post it on the big-character poster board. One day, Cowbell's name appeared on the board and now he too had a red wooden hammer.

PART FOUR
AUTUMN

秋

FORTY-SIX

THE HAMMERHEADS WERE SENT TO REVIEW THE BOOKS, Old Kiln's accounts for the number of porcelain goods produced and sold. Unfortunately for the village, they found serious discrepancies. Before now, the numbers had all matched, a certain number of kilns firing, a certain number of items produced, each year had been roughly the same. Except for the previous autumn, when the number produced didn't match the number sold. It begged the question: where was the missing china? And if it had been sold, where was the money? Naturally, the Hammerheads called on the Branch Secretary. His first response was a deflection. The previous year he'd been rather ill with a terrible stomach bug. He'd actually had to leave the village and spend a great deal of time away receiving treatment. Afterwards, he'd attended the county cadres meeting and while he was away, Apricot's father, Potful, had taken care of the village's business, including the kiln accounts.

"As you can see," the Secretary continued, "I really cannot say, I mean, I don't know."

To the Hammerheads, this just wasn't possible. Even if he'd gone to the Agricultural Machinery Station to see a doctor and then attended a higher-level cadre meeting, even if he'd put Potful in charge, he'd already gained a well-earned reputation for being meticulous and shrewd. Would he not have checked the books upon his return? Of course, blaming a dead man was the surest way to bury a problem.

Unsurprisingly, once Apricot got wind of what the Branch Secretary had said, she was furious. Yes, her father had been put in charge of village affairs for the autumn, but he was none too happy about things. Apricot recalled one evening a year ago, her father drunk and angry, was kicking at whatever and whoever he saw – their chickens, the dog, anything that got nearby. She remembered berating her old man for overindulging, to which he retorted he needed to drink. Earlier in the day, some hoity-toity lad from Xiahewan arrived and soon after rolled off with five carts of china, three filled with plates and bowls, another two loaded with jars and urns. Apricot asked him why the man from Xiahewan had bought so much, and the story she remembered was that he'd come on behalf of Commune Secretary Zhang whose mum had passed eighty years of age. That was the first she'd heard of Commune Secretary Zhang being from Xiahewan. This titbit of information aside, Apricot followed up with her dad as to why he was so upset; after all, he'd sold five carts of china. Therein lay the problem and the reason for his anger: the fellow from Xiahewan hadn't paid a penny. A message from the Branch Secretary, who was then in Luozhen, instructed him to hand over the goods gratis. Even if these details given by Apricot proved to be true, the missing porcelain still didn't align with the accounts, never mind that five carts of china was no small amount.

Naturally, the Hammerheads had to call on the Branch Secretary again, had to ascertain one way or the other whether Apricot's tale was true. Although he was not especially keen to go over events he'd already explained, Branch Secretary Zhu did think things over and after what seemed like half a day, he slapped his head and proclaimed, "You know what, I do seem to recall some of this. Good grief, my memory is shot! There was this communique I believe, that is, yes, I remember Commune Secretary Zhang speaking to me about monies to be delivered in the winter, to help Old Kiln repair its drainage ditches. It was to be a few hundred yuan, I think."

"And did he send the money?" Bash interjected.

"There was none forthcoming that winter."

"Why not?"

"That I do not know."

"You don't know," said Bash, his voice growing in anger. "I reckon you're making the whole damn story up just to run one by me."

"No, I... I'm not, it's all true. Everything I said. He never sent the money." His voice was still level.

"Well then, if he didn't send the damned money, why the hell didn't you follow it up?"

Secretary Zhu did the only thing he could, he began to criticise Commune Secretary Zhang. After all, it had recently been proved that Zhang was a capitalist roader, he'd been using his power for personal gain and done grievous harm to Old Kiln, to say nothing, Zhu emphasised, of the torment Zhang afflicted on him personally. Droning on, Bash ceased to listen. Instead, he grabbed a nearby table, dragged it out to the woodshed and instructed Secretary Zhu to write everything down. Then, turning sharply to Baldy Jin, he said, "Go tell his family. If he's not finished writing by lunch, tell them to send his meal here."

Dazed-And-Confused sat in the doorway of the woodshed, watching Secretary Zhu. "Remember, if you need to take a shit or a piss, just let me know, I'll, er, escort you."

Saying this, he knelt and picked up a pile of straw, placing it to one side. Using water, he matted the straw together to begin to make a pair of straw shoes. Of course, he'd not brought any tools with him to do the job properly, so he used his stubby fingers to mould the straw into shape. Once satisfied, he straightened his legs and used small lengths of rope to tie the matted straw to his feet. A makeshift shoe if ever there were one.

It had been customary for Branch Secretary Zhu to stroll about the village, hands clasped behind his back, eyes squinting at this and that, and his feet deftly moving between dips and debris in the alleys, all seemingly without a concern on his face. But Potful had feared the man, and so, too, had the rest of the village. Other times, he'd be home, doing nothing at all, a pan frying up the evening meal, his wife making herself ragged with worry about this and that, and he'd be fine, no trace of concern at all. He'd then inevitably find himself curled up in his armchair, his body tilted, his eyes drooping. Now, even though his mind was occupied with what to write, he felt the same tiredness creep up, his eyes grew heavy, he needed to lie down somewhere, anywhere, even against the pile of straw in this dilapidated old woodshed.

The Hammerheads were out and about, already spreading the story of how the Branch Secretary had allowed five carts of china to be carried off to Xiahewan without getting a single penny for them. Needless to say, the story seemed barely credible to most. When the villagers also heard that Zhu was in his woodshed supposedly writing the whole thing down, some were inclined to go and see for themselves. Unsurprisingly, Dazed-And-Confused was letting no one in, so all they could do was peek inside to see Secretary Zhu inclined against a bundle of straw, writing very little. Their sniggering led Dazed-And-Confused to take a look himself, whereupon he flew into a rage and burst into the shed, yelling as he did, "Asleep? You have the gall to sleep?"

Startled, Secretary Zhu responded nearly as forcefully: "I can barely manage sleep at home in my own bed, you think I'd nod off here?"

His eyes bulged in their sockets, causing Dazed-And-Confused to take a step back. Secretary Zhu straightened himself, taking hold of the paper he'd been given, then noticed the sickle leaning against the shed wall. He stood up, grabbed it, flung it outside and turned back towards the straw. "Is this to be my prison, then?"

"Whether you're a prisoner or not beats me," said Dazed-And-Confused. "All I know is that I'm supposed to sit right here at the doorway and this is where I'll be."

"Is that all? Well let me tell you, it's in your best interests to take a moment and actually think about what you're doing. After all, you wouldn't want me to be sending signals to someone or other, would you?"

"I don't know about that, but I'm pretty sure there's no rope in here for you to hang yourself, there is that." Dazed-And-Confused's retort was quick and sharp.

Secretary Zhu slapped the pen against the table. "You'd like me to die, is that it? Well, sorry to disappoint you, but that's not going to happen. And you want to know why, because I can't die, that's why!"

"You wanna try and prove that?"

As their bickering continued and became increasingly intense, word soon reached Bash who had been busy with Useless compiling the report on Secretary Zhu's "gifting" of five carts of porcelain to a lad who'd come from Xiahewan. They'd already written the big-character poster and so were free to race over to attend to the heated situation. Soon the yard around the woodshed was filled with Hammerheads. On the way over, in fact, Bash had the wits about him to send someone for Lightkeeper and Gran, he'd definitely need their help.

Now turning to the Branch Secretary, he said, "So, have you finished writing?"

"Finished?" came Secretary Zhu's response. "How do you think I'm finished, what with all the racket that fool Dazed-And-Confused is making?"

With the crowd continuing to grow, Dazed-And-Confused tried to explain himself: the Secretary hadn't written a thing, not because of the commotion, but because he'd fallen asleep against the straw. All he'd tried

487

to do was wake him up and get him to write, but the old fellow wouldn't and so their argument ensued.

"And one more thing," Dazed-And-Confused continued, "he said us Hammerheads had imprisoned him here in this woodshed. Can you believe it! He—"

"Whatever you say," said Baldy Jin. "The long and the short of it is this, his mum gave birth to him and now he's a party secretary, right?"

"Ah, but he's Zhu Dagui, and he said... he said us here Hammerheads had imprisoned him, that... that he wants to die, that... that he was looking for a knife, a length of rope, poisonous fertiliser, I swear!"

"Why you little f..." Secretary Zhu's fury prevented him from saying anything more.

"If you haven't written anything," said Bash, "then you haven't written anything. Use your mouth, you can tell everyone else what you did with the china produced in our kilns."

Secretary Zhu scanned the crowd, noticing Lightkeeper and Gran. "A self-criticism session? Here? Now?"

"It's for you to be clear on things," said Bash, raising his voice.

So Branch Secretary Zhu told his story, again lumping much of the blame on the deceased Potful, before finishing with, "And that's about it."

"That's about it?" Bash said. "I'm afraid there's something more, isn't there?"

"Damn right there's more," Dazed-And-Confused blurted out.

"Come now, Secretary Zhu," said Bash, his words dripping with venom. "Surely there's more than this?"

Dazed-And-Confused leapt up from where he'd been sitting, brushing off the dust from his bottom and sending it wafting through the air. He stormed over to stand in front of Secretary Zhu, raised his hand and struck him hard.

Collecting himself from the blow, Secretary Zhu righted himself and said to Bash, "If there's a problem I need to clarify, then I'll certainly do so. But tell me, is it acceptable for Dazed-And-Confused here to hit me?"

"I've not yet given you the full experience of the dictatorship of the proletariat," bellowed Dazed-And-Confused.

"Dazed-And-Confused," said Bash. "Sit down, let him speak."

Dazed-And-Confused seated himself once more to let Branch Secretary Zhu continue.

"I spent all of last night trying to sort out the porcelain account discrepancies, trying to ascertain where the problem arose, and that's when I remembered the lad who had come from Xiahewan, the whole business with the five carts. As I was writing this down, something else occurred to me. At the previous county-wide cadre meeting, a number of villages sent, what shall I say, gifts, I suppose. Xishanbao sent several carts loaded with pumpkins and aubergines, Gongjiatan sent about five hundred *jin* of potatoes, Liujiaping despatched sixty gallons of sesame oil produced in their factory. Finally, Xiahewan sent three hundred newly woven straw hats. Old Kiln had to send something didn't we, we couldn't be the only village not to send a thing. But what to send? I mean, I couldn't take the food out of our mouths and send vegetables and the like, so that only left our china, didn't it?"

Bash was the first to respond. "So I guess this means your position as party secretary has been renewed, has it?"

Bash's words had their desired effect: the villagers who'd gathered around the woodshed tensed, their faces seething with rage. In their minds, Secretary Zhu was an old tiger, a corrupt official, one they'd already reprimanded and struggled against. Was that all that was needed? Call him Branch Secretary Zhu, say he was representing the party? Would that give him the leeway to put one over on everyone? That because they were poor, they wouldn't make a fuss? But he'd given away *their* china, so, so generously to who, someone not even from the village. And what, now he was party secretary again! Corruption, to those gathered, that's what this was, no two ways about it.

Dazed-And-Confused started it. "Down with the embezzler Zhu Dagui!"

The remaining villagers were quick to join in. "Down with Zhu Dagui!"

The echo of the slogan reverberated through the village, alarming most, but attracting them nonetheless, especially those not belonging to the Hammerheads. Bash remained silent during the cacophony, only gesturing to Useless and Baldy Jin to head inside.

Upon their return a few moments later, Bash turned to address the still-chanting crowd: "For a good long while, most of our village cadres have been corrupt, there's little debating that. It was us Hammerheads who took the initiative, we seized the porcelain, the kilns. If we hadn't, how much more do you think they would have embezzled? If they weren't stopped, there'd be little to nothing left of Old Kiln but an empty pit. Our village is led by the Communist Party. That means it's a socialist village. Who runs it, that doesn't matter. All we know is that the man running it has tried to swallow us whole. We need to make him vomit us back up. And not just us, but every damn thing, right till it's only bile he's spewing!

"It's because of this, according to the views of the revolutionary masses of Old Kiln, that the Hammerheads have decided to take back the public housing that was sold, especially since the monies earned from the sale were not put in the village coffers. Instead, said monies will be used to offset the costs of the embezzled china. As for what else Zhu Dagui has misappropriated, that has yet to be made clear, but rest assured, it will be. Thus, until such a confession is forthcoming, Zhu Dagui will remain confined to this here woodshed – what say you all?"

"Yes, agree!" they roared in unison.

"Let's do it!"

"That's how it's done!"

Turning to Secretary Zhu, Bash said, "Clear enough for you?"

Trudging back into the woodshed, Zhu groaned. "Yes, abundantly clear."

By mealtime, almost everyone had departed the courtyard surrounding the woodshed, leaving only Dazed-And-Confused seated at the door. Baldy Jin remained as well, and it was to him that Dazed-And-Confused spoke.

"I can't watch him all by myself. If he hangs himself, swallows fertiliser or whatever, what am I supposed to do? Can you stay with me?"

"If he wants to hang himself, I suggest you give him a rope. Same goes for the fertiliser, let him have it if he wants it. To my mind, I'd rather one more grave than one more corrupt bastard in Old Kiln. Watch him for now, I'll relieve you at dinner, all right?"

"Eh... I reckon I don't need relieving, then. Why don't you just bring me a bowl of whatever you're eating later on?"

Baldy Jin smiled and turned to leave, Dazed-And-Confused calling after him, "Be sure to add salt, I like my food salty."

Dazed-And-Confused remained in the courtyard alone, leaving just Zhu Dagui in the shed. He began to pick at his makeshift straw shoes, adjusting the rope he'd used for straps as it was biting into his flesh. First the left, then the right. Once satisfied, he peeked into the woodshed. Old Zhu was again curled up on the straw. He'd written nothing.

"Fine, if you don't want to write anything, don't. Just make sure you're comfortable since you'll be staying here till you do."

"Dazed-And-Confused, you moron," Zhu began. "I think I need some insecticide."

"What? Really? You want to kill yourself?"

"No, this place is full of bloody fleas."

There was no mistaking it. The woodshed was infested. At first, however, Secretary Zhu had not felt them. Even after lying in the straw, he'd still not sensed anything untoward. But before long, his leg grew itchy, and when he rubbed it, the itch only shifted. Pulling up his trouser leg, he could clearly see the fleas. Swatting them away more forcefully this time, he noticed the swarm on the dirt floor, so many, in fact, it seemed as though an intense sports competition was taking place. That was when he called to Dazed-And-Confused.

Dazed-And-Confused seemed less perturbed by this development. "Now, where do you suppose I'm going to get some insecticide? After all, it's not like they'll eat you whole. I reckon..."

His voice trailed off as he began to feel a tickle on his own legs. Leaping up, he undid his trousers and began to scratch at his legs and crotch. He found fleas, but before he could attack them more vigorously, he heard crying coming from near the main gate. Quickly pulling up his trousers, fixing the button that held them around his waist, he went to greet the Branch Secretary's wife who'd come with his dinner. A side dish, a larger bowl and a pair of chopsticks, neatly tied together with a ribbon.

"Crying," Secretary Zhu began as she moved close to the shed, "what're you crying for? I'm not dead or anything."

She stopped weeping and untied the ribbon holding the dishes. She'd brought his favourite rice soup with dumplings and shaved turnips. The Branch Secretary took hold of the bowl but didn't eat. He only dipped the chopsticks in to lift a single dumpling to his mouth, taking just a bite instead of the whole thing. He chewed slowly before swallowing. Once finished, he placed the remaining half of the dumpling in his mouth. Dazed-And-Confused looked at him enviously, his tongue unconsciously licking his lips, his straw-covered shoes kicking at the dirt. He looked down at his own ragged appearance, then back at the bowl, quick enough to see the remaining dumplings before the Branch Secretary's wife covered the dishes to take them home.

This became a routine. Three times a day the Branch Secretary's wife would visit him, bringing along his meal, always rice, sometimes even chicken. At the same time, Inkcap often found his way to Bash's home, at least the courtyard that surrounded it. It was there he noticed the Branch Secretary doing his daily routine, eating chicken wings and then making his way to the toilet, Dazed-And-Confused close behind as his escort.

"Do you need to follow so closely, Dazed-And-Confused?" Inkcap heard Secretary Zhu once remark. "If I'm here eating these chicken wings, I don't believe anyone in the village will be able to fly!"

Dazed-And-Confused's response was to lift his foot and kick at the back of the Secretary's legs, causing him to crumple to the ground. There, on his knees, Secretary Zhu turned to Dazed-And-Confused, who replied, "Well, if you're stuffing your face with chicken wings, you ought to be able to crouch on your knees just as well."

Inkcap did not have the courage to say anything to either of them. He did, however, intend to speak to the Secretary's wife as she left, curious to find out how things were for her husband, but then he noticed Cowbell squatting on the ground near a thresher and felt he'd better not approach her after all. Instead, he sauntered over to Cowbell.

"What are you at?"

Cowbell pointed towards some nearby willow trees. "Watching those dogs," he replied.

At the base of the trees were a scattering of chicken bones being fought over by several village dogs. The remaining chicken feathers were fluttering about in the kerfuffle, some getting hooked on the thorns of the adjacent wild jujubes, giving them the appearance of flowers.

"You know," Cowbell continued, "old Secretary Zhu's been eating chicken for three days straight. I reckon he's living quite well in that old woodshed."

"His wife must be finding it awful," said Inkcap. "I guess she's killing all her chickens because of him being locked up."

"I reckon we ought to go and nick a few of her chickens for ourselves. I mean, he's just going to eat them all up anyway."

Inkcap would never have thought Cowbell would come up with such a plan. "What? You mean to tell me you've taken to stealing now?"

"If not now, when?"

Together they began to work out how they might not only steal Secretary Zhu's chickens, but also how to divvy up the spoils. They'd each get a wing and a leg, that was easy enough to decide. As for the body,

Cowbell suggested Inkcap take the head and the claws and he'd take the gizzard, the heart and the liver. The intestines could be Inkcap's too.

"Oh," Cowbell continued, "and you can have the arsehole."

As Cowbell rambled on, Inkcap could almost taste the chicken. Already drooling, nearly overcome by thoughts of eating, the last bit of Cowbell's spiel caused Inkcap to interject, "Ah, I don't think the arsehole can be eaten–"

"And why bloody not?"

"My gran says it's poisonous."

"Yeah, but you fight poison with poison, don't you."

"What do you mean by that?"

"Well, your class background is rather high, isn't it? Means you're poisonous, I reckon."

"You dirty fucker!"

"All right, all right, my mistake, just a bad joke. If you don't want the arsehole, I'll take it."

Cowbell's quick apology dispelled Inkcap's ire, and even though he insisted the arsehole was not safe to eat, his good humour returned, and they continued to discuss how they'd split the chicken they planned to steal.

Plans finished, Inkcap asked the most important question: "So, do you have the balls or what?"

"What do you mean? I already saw Baldy Jin nick some of their aubergines and no one paid any mind. The Secretary's wife didn't even say a thing."

Inkcap's lingering hesitation disappeared. "All right, then, before our caper, I'll see Stonebreaker and ask to borrow his torch. I'll get a pole ready too. You can do the deed."

"Why you slippery bastard, eh! Trying to get me to do the dirty work? I'll tell you what, we'll do it together."

Stonebreaker's torch actually belonged to Pockmark. It wasn't all that long ago that Pockmark had left Old Kiln to call on Luozhen's Public Security Bureau. Before departing, and to make sure his home wasn't left empty, he instructed Stonebreaker to stay at his place. The only fly in the ointment turned out to be Pockmark's arrest as soon as he showed up at the Public Security Bureau. That was the last anyone had seen of him, at least until now. Not wishing to be associated with someone who'd been arrested, Stonebreaker decided to leave Pockmark's house. When he left, he took the torch with him, as well as a bag of flour.

Most villagers knew what he'd done, which made it difficult for Stonebreaker to avoid censure. His rebuttal, however, came just as quick, justifying his actions by claiming that since Pockmark had stolen poison and murdered someone with it, his house ought to be picked clean by the rest of them. He never mentioned his intended use of the torch, however, and that was to roam about the village at night, collecting his work points and flashing the damned thing into places he probably shouldn't.

None of this stopped Inkcap from asking to borrow it, however. His need for the torch was real, he told Stonebreaker: his cellar had scorpions in it and the only way to get rid of them was to find them at night with the torch.

"So," said Stonebreaker doubtfully, "you mean to tell me you can't catch them without my torch?"

"That's right, the kerosene lamp just isn't bright enough. Come on, just this once, I'll give you your favourite meal…"

Stonebreaker rarely treated him well and he thought it best not to mention the real reason he wanted the torch, that is, to steal Branch Secretary Zhu's chickens, so he changed tack and said he'd give him some steamed sweet potatoes.

"How many?" said Stonebreaker.

"Two."

"Three and you can borrow the torch."

That evening it rained. A white rain. But it didn't rain everywhere. Some places felt the white rain, other places remained dry. More often than not, little furrows formed. Stranger still was the fact that the rain only fell upon Old Kiln, while beyond its limits, the sun could be seen, shining brightly. Afterwards, a sharp crack followed by a pop was heard reverberating through the sky, then the heat soared, blanching the land white. No one sheltered from the rain, most simply stood where they were, letting the warm soak them. The village dogs frolicked in the rain as well, so too the cats, the mice and the snakes. All manner of creatures seemed to welcome the rain's arrival. But it ceased as soon as it had begun, and the village alleyways were left vacant, meaning there was no sign of mice or snakes anywhere. That just left the flies swarming in the privies.

"It'll be cold tonight," Gran told Inkcap. "Best to sleep early."

But Inkcap wouldn't. Instead, he spent the early evening fashioning a slingshot out of the branches he'd cracked off from the trees near their house. Once the village grew quiet, he walked to the courtyard gate before calling back to his Gran, "I promised to meet Cowbell this evening. I'm to give him the bark I've peeled from them branches, he's going to make his own slingshot."

Without waiting for a reply, he trundled off into the darkness in the direction of Cowbell's home.

Upon meeting up, they set off for Secretary Zhu's home, quietly, stealthily making their way through the alleys and lanes. It never occurred to either of them they'd meet anyone, so when they stumbled upon the Branch Secretary's wife, all three jumped and stared at each other. But only for a moment. No words were exchanged, they simply composed themselves and disappeared into the night. Inkcap and Cowbell both wondered whether she was going to see Secretary Zhu in his woodshed. Neither fathomed the possibility she was going to see Apricot.

In the garden pots around her house, Apricot had planted several balsams, also known as touch-me-nots. In summer, the flowers bathed the front of her home in a beautiful red. When she had nothing else to do, Apricot would often pick the flowers to grind into a paste to colour her nails. The white rain earlier in the day had encouraged her to move the pots inside, and it wasn't until nearly bedtime that she remembered to put them outside again. It was after she'd moved three of the pots to the garden that she spied the Branch Secretary's wife at her gate. The old woman approached quietly. Before even saying hello, she stopped to light a joss stick in remembrance of Potful, placing it in front of his memorial tablet and bowing as she did so. She mumbled his name, too, in betwixt tears. This was the first time since Potful's death that she'd called upon Apricot. It was so late at night. Not surprisingly, Apricot thought it rather strange. The only thing she could be sure of was the pain on the old woman's face. Even the night couldn't hide that.

"Come now," Apricot began, "you mustn't cry like this."

"Apricot, today's your father's birthday."

"Yes, I know. I already offered him a bowl of hand-rolled noodles."

As she spoke, she knew this wasn't the reason for the old lady's visit. "Tell me," she continued, "why have you called so late?"

"My husband, my old man... your Branch Secretary, he's locked up in that blasted woodshed. Tell me, how am I supposed to sleep?"

"He's not been released?"

"And he won't be either... oh Apricot, there's no way I can sleep. I've come to you instead, come to beg–"

"Beg me? You know I'm not involved in what goes on in the village. All I've heard is that if he writes something or other down, he'll be free to go home. Why beg me?"

"Apricot, you know my husband's been toppled, struggled against. In the past, we always had people calling on us, but these past few days, not a sole has visited. I'm here to beg you to help him, you're the only one who can save him. Talk to Bash, get him to feel mercy for my old man, free him. He's so old, he can't remain in the woodshed. In a week to ten days, two weeks tops, he'll be dead."

"But it's the Cultural Revolution, do you think anyone will listen to me?"

"You and Bash... you have a connection. Do you mean to say he wouldn't listen to you?"

Apricot's heart skipped a beat. She worried about what the old woman was saying but did not have the courage to respond.

The Branch Secretary's wife continued, "You're the only one, Apricot."

"Mrs Zhu... if someone else had said these words, I wouldn't be angry, but I can't pretend to be pleased hearing you say this."

"Why not? I'm not speaking falsehoods. Tell me I've not spoken in vain. A man can be fierce, but he cannot resist some pillow talk."

Apricot's face turned red. "Mrs Zhu, you can't speak like this. You're right, I am close to Bash, but what you just said, well, I don't want to hear it, it's disrespectful. You can't just think of me as a pair of worn-out old shoes!"

"So that's how it is? You're stubborn with everyone, including me! Do you think I don't know? I've seen the two of you together–"

"Mrs Zhu, I'm not trying to bad-mouth you, I'm not trying to say anything, but I think it best if you leave." Her eyes took on an extra firmness. "You're in my home, I'm worried that I've brought disgrace on you."

Falling to her knees, Secretary Zhu's wife persisted. "Apricot... please... I beg you!"

Apricot moved away from the older woman. Stumbling, she leant against a cabinet and wept. Finally, when she turned to look at her again, a gust of wind blew through her house and extinguished the kerosene lamp, plunging everything into darkness. The only light that remained was emanating from the joss stick. A tiny, distant star glowing in the immensity of space. She moved to the old woman and lifted her from the ground.

"Go home, please. I'll speak to Bash. I can't promise it'll help, but I'll try."

Satisfied, the old woman began to leave, but in the dark of the night, she could barely see a thing and bumped into the washbasin and the pots filled with pickled vegetables. Fumbling, she opened the gate and quietly closed it behind her. As she did, she could hear Apricot continue to cry, her weeping mixed with the clucking and hiccupping of the nearby chickens.

Apricot didn't sleep that night. Nor did her chickens. But the Branch Secretary's chickens did; they went to sleep early, in fact. The Secretary had quite a number of chickens and a somewhat imposing courtyard fence to not only keep them in, but also give them space to roam. But when evening came, led by the biggest rooster, the chickens would all clamber up the nearby elm tree, one after another, hen following cock to perch, three or four together, on the branches. The villagers would remark on how obedient the chickens were, while others said it was all due to his wife; she'd trained them in a manner to demonstrate their power.

Cowbell carried the pole, with laths attached to the end. Inkcap held the torch to light their way, darting it this way and that, soon frustrating Cowbell, who finally shouted, "Where the hell are you shining that damn light? You're going to light up the whole village!"

At that moment the torch illuminated the elm tree, bathing the perched chickens in a soft glow. Some of them stirred and opened their eyes, but soon shut them again because of the glare. Others remained oblivious to their approach, silent as though dead. Cowbell arched the pole towards the base of one of the branches as Inkcap gave instructions.

"That one, yeah, right there, the hen with the big pimple head."

The pole nudged the sleeping chicken, but the beast only lifted its leg as though trying to get out of reach. Then it shifted again and perched on Cowbell's outstretched pole. Slowly Cowbell lowered it. Inkcap moved the torch in unison. But just before the pole reached the ground, the torch went out. Two hands groped in the dark to seize it.

"Come on," said Cowbell, "another one, let's get another one."

Inkcap had the one hen clasped tightly to his chest as he ran.

Back at home, Cowbell complained vociferously, "We thieved, didn't we? Whether it's one or two doesn't make a difference, does it, we still stole."

"Why can't that be enough? Stealing one will go unnoticed, but more than that, someone's bound to discover them missing don't you think?" Inkcap breathed in deeply through his nose.

"What's the matter with you?"

"That, that smell... I can smell it again."

Every time that particular odour wafted across his nose, something bad would happen. Cowbell grew nervous too.

"You and that damned nose, why are you smelling it now? Wait, wait, maybe you're not smelling anything. Go on, sniff the air again."

Inkcap did as instructed. "It's here, I can smell it."

The two of them froze. Like glazed porcelain hot out of the kiln, neither moved.

"Do you think," Inkcap continued, "do you think something's going to happen?"

Cowbell pinched his nose. It felt like a garlic clove between his fingers. He squeezed harder, seemingly intent on tearing Inkcap's nose off his face. Inkcap just bore it, his face turning red from lack of oxygen. Finally, Cowbell released his fingers.

"Sniff again," he said. "See, go on, can you still smell it?"

The odour was gone.

"There," Cowbell shrieked. "I know what's causing it, it's your own worry. There's nothing out of the ordinary to smell, it's just you. Is something going to happen? Bah, the bullock has died, the captain's dead, the Hammerheads are here, the Secretary's got to write his report, what the hell else could happen? Kill the bird! Now, I want the chicken dead!" Cowbell ripped the hen from Inkcap's hands.

Up until then, the creature had remained silent, but now it began to squawk, flapping its pitiful wings. Its reaction egged Cowbell on.

"Now you make a fuss, are you? Go on, fuss away." He slapped at the bird, dazing it momentarily, causing its eyes to roll over white.

But only for a moment. The hen turned its face to Inkcap, almost pleadingly. Inkcap heard it curse Cowbell – was it asking him to be saved? Inkcap pitied the creature and regretted what they'd done.

"Cowbell... perhaps, perhaps we shouldn't eat it. How about... how about we just set it free in your courtyard, we could let it lay eggs for us, what do you say?"

The chicken seemed to nod its head in agreement.

"When there's meat, who the hell wants eggs?" He stormed inside to get a knife.

"But I can't eat it. I mean, it's begging for mercy, isn't it? Come on, Cowbell."

"If a chicken were able to beg for mercy, then it wouldn't be a chicken to begin with. Here, you hold it while I get a knife."

Inkcap did the opposite, releasing the bird, allowing it to half run and half fly, all to save its life.

"Do you really mean to tell me you don't want any?" Knife in hand, Cowbell lunged towards the bird, chasing it around his home this way and that. From the cabinet, the hen scrambled to the window ledge. From the ledge it leapt into the air, tiny, useless wings fluttering until it landed on the table. From there, it clambered underneath, trying in vain to hide. Soon, the floor was covered with feathers from the beast's frail wings and plump body.

Cowbell was unrelenting. "Go on, fly again, fly dammit."

The chicken did so, but this time crashed into the wall, its long beak bashing the surface, knocking the bird backwards and onto the floor. It repeated the action three more times, shattering its small head. In the end, it ended up in Cowbell's pot, but Inkcap refused to eat any.

"It's your choice," Cowbell bellowed, "but you can't tell anyone I stole the beast."

Inkcap, true to his word, did not partake of its flesh. All he did was sample a bit of the broth, but even that made him ill. Cowbell devoured the bird and as he did, Inkcap couldn't help but think how disgusting his friend looked. Bits of chicken stuck between his teeth, dirty fingers trying to pick the meat out, teeth long like fangs.

"You look like a yellow weasel."

"Say what you will," Cowbell retorted, "but it's not like I was being selfish. I had no choice, you've an upset tummy."

Inkcap left Cowbell's house in the dark. As he meandered home through the village lanes, a wind blew, carrying a voice with it. "What a lousy fucking day."

Now the wind was talking to him, and he had nothing to retort. His face grew raw and hot. The wind was unrelenting.

FORTY-SEVEN

THE NEXT MORNING, no one called on Inkcap to come out and work, so his gran refrained from waking him up. It didn't matter though, as he still rose early, if lazily. Sprout did call on Gran, however, asking to borrow some thread. She also asked for advice on knitting, how to properly warp the thread on the loom before the weft was introduced. Afterwards, she pulled out a pile of paper used for big-character posters and asked Inkcap's gran if she could make some flower papercuts.

"Where's Inkcap got to?" Sprout asked.

"He had a late night doing God only knows what. He's still in bed."

"Was he off with the Hammerheads?"

"What on earth would he be doing with them? No, he was just out with Cowbell."

"You ought to tell him it isn't safe running round at night. I heard Xiahewan's had to deal with some wolves roaming around, several times, in fact, and last night there were weasels about–"

"Was it Six Pints' weasel that got loose?"

"No, not that I heard. It seems it was a weasel that stole into the village from the woods. Looks like it raided the Secretary's chicken coop, at least, that's what his wife is saying."

Inkcap pricked up his ears.

497

"She's full of it," Gran continued. "She's been bringing chickens to her husband, three over the last three days. Tell me now, sounds better if a weasel's come and killed one than her continuing to feed her husband so well, doesn't it? He's still being held in the woodshed, right?"

"Yes... but the Hammerheads aren't the law, can they just hold someone like that?"

"Cluck, cluck, cluck," Gran said in a vain effort to call her hens. "Blast it, still no eggs." Turning towards the coop, she yelled, "You're all just teasing me now, aren't you? Damn creatures. Sprout, are your chickens laying eggs?"

Inkcap wanted to listen in some more, but all he heard was a fit of coughing from Sprout. She finally mumbled, "No... ahem... they've not."

A knock came at the main gate and Inkcap's mind turned to the torch he'd borrowed from Stonebreaker. He had to return it straight away.

Gran noticed Inkcap trying to steal out of the house without so much as a good morning and she became annoyed. "You're a beast, aren't you? You won't even stay in the nest for breakfast."

"The production team's got nothing for me today," came Inkcap's reply.

"Even without the production team calling on you, you still have to tend our family allotment, make sure the corn's growing well. The other families have all fertilised their allotments at least once, and you've not even carried one lump of manure!"

"All right, all right, I'll take a look. Should I pinch a few onions while I'm there?" Before she could answer, he was already out of the door.

His first stop was Stonebreaker's to return the torch. Fortuitously, Stonebreaker didn't mention the sweet potato and so Inkcap felt no need to bring it up. In truth, Stonebreaker's face had a waxing yellow appearance as though he were uneasy about something. When he looked at Inkcap, his only words were, "Have you seen Pockmark?"

"Yeah, I think I have. I reckon he wants his torch back, the bag you lifted too."

Stonebreaker's face blanched. "Where did you see him? Where?"

Inkcap could see the seriousness in Stonebreaker's look. "Where? Why, in prison of course."

"Then you haven't seen him."

"Even if I wanted to, I don't imagine he'll be freed in this lifetime."

"Dammit all! Word came last night to the village, somebody had heard that Pockmark had escaped. Now how the hell did that happen? Do you think the bastard will make his way back to Old Kiln?"

Inkcap was startled by Stonebreaker's ire and thought it best to beat a hasty retreat without saying anything else. As he passed through the village lanes, he could hear everyone talking about the same thing: Pockmark's escape from prison. Inkcap noticed Millstone trudging up along another lane, a pole slung over his shoulder.

Lucky saw him, too, and interrupted Millstone's walk home. "Hey, Millstone, have you heard, that bastard Pockmark's broken out of prison and by all accounts he's heading here. You better be careful over the coming days. And you ought to be carrying something to defend yourself."

"You're talking rubbish, how the hell could he escape? The walls of the prison are too damn high. What, were the guards taking a breather or something?"

"Well, I suppose, it is the Cultural Revolution after all, isn't it," Lucky replied. "Things are a mess, he could've taken advantage of this and made a break for it, couldn't he?"

"You might be right. Shame the bastard was only shot the one time when he was arrested. If he makes his way back to Old Kiln, I'm going use my knife to cut my pound of flesh."

With these words, Millstone stomped off home. There, he deposited the pole he'd used to carry the dug-up earth into the pigsty, then he grabbed his shovel and stormed off in the direction of Pockmark's old house to take a look. The gate was bolted, so Millstone knocked on it with his shovel. No response. The shovel left a mark, but Millstone wasn't bothered. He climbed over the courtyard wall, noticing that one of the eaves had collapsed and a pile of stone tiles lay near the base of the wall. Undeterred, he pried open a window and climbed inside. It was empty. A thick coat of dust blanketed the table, so deep it made the mice footprints easily visible. There were no signs of human presence. The kitchen was in the same state. The stove was covered in dust. The cellar was empty as well. The water container was as dry as a bone.

"The bastard hasn't dared come back. If he does, I'll be the one to put him in the ground!" And with that, he grabbed a stone pestle and flung it at the stove, cracking a stone pot and leaving a large hole in it.

Afterwards, Millstone's eyes seemed forever red, the shovel forever over his shoulder. He didn't wander far from home, only to a nearby set of trees adjacent to the village wall. He'd tap on the wall, chipping it repeatedly. Or he'd drive the shovel up into the trees to loosen leaves. The villagers noted how Millstone's temperament had changed. At the time of Pockmark's arrest, Millstone was not so aggressive. It must have been the past year, with no alternative way to vent his anger, perhaps he wanted to take advantage of the situation to show the Hammerheads what he was capable of.

The Hammerheads also knew about Pockmark's jailbreak, as well as the rage that seemed to be simmering within Millstone. But they did little about it or at least refrained from reacting. The only thing they did do was let the Branch Secretary return home. Upon his release from the woodshed, he draped his black coat over his shoulder and wore a half-smile on his face. His eyes were half-closed, his pace measured and slow as though he had to pause after each step to remember how to proceed. In the evening, the Branch Secretary's wife called on Millstone, and they both went to her house. There, he found Branch Secretary Zhu reclined on his wooden bed sipping bamboo tea along with Goodman. Millstone laid his shovel behind the courtyard gate and walked towards the men.

Secretary Zhu gestured for him to sit down and pulled out his tobacco pouch, saying to Goodman, "Go ahead and say what you have to say, then Millstone can give his take."

Goodman sneezed and coughed up a bit of phlegm. He stood and coughed some more. The more he coughed, the more he couldn't stop.

"Come now," said Secretary Zhu, "you can't handle the smoke?" He gave the tobacco to his wife to take away.

Finally, Goodman's coughing eased and he returned to his seat. He turned to Millstone and said, "Secretary Zhu has asked for my opinion."

"He asked for your opinion?" Millstone replied.

Secretary Zhu's face turned red. "You think I've asked him here to criticise him again?"

"The Secretary told me he shouldn't have sent me to reside in the Mountain God Temple. Now, the old kiln has been transformed into public housing, and although he wants to buy it, he hasn't planned to do so, rather he wants me to speak to Bash, to urge him to move in there."

"What's this nonsense about buying it or not?" Millstone replied. "You want to move in there, what's there to say to Bash? The Hammerheads are a production team, aren't they?"

"Ah, Millstone," the Branch Secretary interjected. "You don't understand the situation. The Hammerheads can treat me however they wish, but it's the Cultural Revolution, right, even our president, Liu Shaoqi, can be toppled. The county and commune secretaries, Cao and Zhang, have both been struggled against, what can I say myself? I've been thinking, as secretary, I've been working at this job, been bleeding for it, for more than a dozen years. I've done some good work, but no doubt I've offended some people too. That old building, I shouldn't buy it, I know, but I'd like Goodman to live in it. On the one hand, it'd show everyone I'm not planning to purchase it, on the other, it's an old adobe building, and if no one lives in it, it'll rot."

"All right, Secretary Zhu," said Goodman. "I need to say something. There's a certain logic in what you're saying, but the higher-ups have to learn from those below that by dividing things into upper and lower, all you're doing is dividing the hearts of the people."

"Yes, I understand, the one at the forefront is the one who leads hearts higher."

"All right, Secretary Zhu," Goodman continued, "not buying the old building is up to you, but I can't live there. I used to have a penchant for calling out others' flaws, encouraging them to take care of themselves, find their own cure, if you will. I had no intention of curing anyone else and certainly not the people, I don't wish to borrow anyone's power..."

Millstone listened closely but when he heard Goodman utter these words, his gaze hardened in an effort to silence the man.

Goodman paused and Secretary Zhu seized the opportunity: "Goodman, to be frank, I wasn't pleased with your actions before. You'd go on about willpower and intention, about the heart and improving oneself, I didn't like that, but you did end up helping some people, so how can I tell you to stop, I'm the party secretary and I want to discuss leadership, polices, but the thoughts of the masses can't be unified. But now I'm not permitted to–"

"What do you mean by that?" said Millstone. "The party is still in charge, who's removed you from your post?"

Secretary Zhu waved his hand. "I'm not permitted, Millstone. What Goodman says is reasonable, I've been secretary for over a dozen years, but in the end, am I not just a peasant? The people raised me here, but I'm not much more than a thatched house built upon a much sturdier structure below."

"It's true I called out people's flaws," said Goodman, "but is that truly going against the party? I've also thought something about this doesn't quite make sense. How can people eat well but still get sick? When they weren't cadres, they spoke ill of me, then when they did become cadres, nothing changed. The former secretary was against it, and now it's the turn of Bash and his ilk to oppose it. Baldy Jin even warned me against committing one of the Four Olds, ethically speaking–"

"Bash is a party cadre?" said Millstone. "What the hell does that say?"

"Come now," Secretary Zhu pleaded. "Let Goodman finish what he wants to say."

"Ah," Goodman continued, "I'm not talking about everyone. What I meant to say is, with this Cultural Revolution, it's a big wind blowing, and with it blows the grass, the trees. You may not wish to hear these words, but I think, in the future, if we take the time, if we learn how things work, if we listen, then we can pull through. I don't mean to bluster and bluff, nor am I trying to invite slander, but a good person, the best kind of person, whatever responsibility they may take on, whatever kind of work they do or position they hold, because of that, they are fulfilling their destiny."

"What destiny are you talking about," Millstone retorted. "What's mine, eh? Secretary Zhu, you insisted during the Cultural Revolution that you wanted me to serve as team leader, but this was only for show, I won't be admitted, but at the same time, they won't let me leave. Isn't it like a wooden knife that can't pierce flesh?"

"At least the Hammerheads aren't hassling you," said the Branch Secretary. "Unlike how they're treating me. And you did quit. This poor old village is paralysed and on the verge of collapse."

"Then it's paralysed," said Millstone, "but who's to blame other than the Hammerheads?"

"Don't get me angry with your words. You will serve as team leader, Millstone, I'll make sure of it. After all, I need you to send me to inspect the water in the fields. Inkcap and Dazed-And-Confused have looked already, one ran off to become a rebel, the other is a waste of sperm that oozed out of a monkey's arse and is of little importance. The field water, however, is a problem. If we don't manage things well, this autumn we'll have to reduce our production quota."

"But I thought you'd been removed from your post," Millstone responded, "and now you want me to serve again as captain. Is that why you called me over here tonight?"

"Yes, it was."

"Then I'll say one more thing, if you want someone to check on the water in the fields, you do it yourself, I'm not getting involved." And with that, he got up to leave.

"All right then, you say you don't want to be involved, but I'm not sure if that's going to be possible and I don't think you can just walk off, can you? Not once since I've come back has anyone paid me a visit. I called you here, and now, before your arse has got warm, you're trying to leave. Are you afraid I'll drag you down, is that it? Sit, we'll ask Auntie to poach some eggs for us. We'll have a rare moment of peace, let's listen to Goodman prattle on." He passed a fan to Millstone and reclined back on the wooden bed. His eyes narrowed. "Goodman, continue, please."

"What was I saying?"

"You were giving us your opinion, your deeper thoughts," the Branch Secretary replied.

Millstone had returned to his seat, but he didn't hear a word Goodman was saying. His eyes were focused solely on the gate. The gate was barely visible in the dark, the steps leading from them blurred at first, then swallowed by the black of the night.

Goodman continued to drone on. "Will, intention, mind and body, these four words, these three worlds, the five elements, they're all the same. They pass through the cosmos together, they're all-encompassing, by studying these, we can deliberate on everything. In ancient times, at the beginning, Man's heart was innocent, it wasn't cluttered by random thoughts, it simply was. Becoming was simply that, becoming. One was connected to everyone and everything, it was the age of creation when Will itself brought forth the world. In the time of Yao and Shun, the time of Heaven teaching man, wells were dug to provide water, Man feared sin, actions were limited. Although there was punishment, Man still knew to be thankful, even if he did not know his own heart. Will was used to make Man, thoughts turned to clothes, to sustenance, aid was provided to each other, people could see happiness, people would bow and make way for others, it was the time of summer.

"When King Wu of Zhou invaded the Shang, deference to others was turned into conquest. King Wen drew his hexagrams, Jiang Taigong taught martial arts and a way beyond sin was devised. The eight trigrams were shattered and Man was free to create the world that came after, the Great Harmony became the small well-being, Man was made from the heart, striving for rules became the norm, the Rites were created to order the world, Man's emotions gradually turned false, decoration became common, people no longer feared sin, fatigue entered the world, people saw enmity, disorder and chaos reign, autumn was upon Man. Till the time of Emperor Qin, who swallowed the six kingdoms and unified all under Heaven, Man's heart sank, strife became common, Man was constructed of the earth, a state of affairs that lasted until the present day, until the advent of materialist civilisation. Progress moved ever forward, the mechanical world was born, development advanced, along with greed and corruption, hatred and sin, but development has continued and will continue until the annihilation of Man itself.

"The saints of all religions have become Taoists, they understand the heavens. The Buddhists speak of the great degeneration, the mappō, the Taoists call the end of times the Doctrine of the Three Ages, Christianity calls it Armageddon, Islam speaks of the great tribulations. However, Heaven is cyclical, out of the worst misfortunes comes great prosperity, winter turns into spring, the path becomes clear and everything flourishes, the end of times becomes the beginning. As the old saying goes, don't rejoice at spring's arrival for there are still forty days of cold weather left to endure. At present, Man is being hurt, not things, for things are valued more than Man. Will is overflowing, intention has shifted, the heart is diminished, the body is being coerced and addictions are rampant, sin is great, the heart suffers…"

Goodman blathered on and on, his eyes closed as though in a trance, as if he were reciting a passage of profound personal importance. He continued until his throat grew raw and he needed water to slake his thirst. His eyes opened, but in the darkness of the courtyard he could see nothing. The kitchen door opened and a beam of light shone through.

The Branch Secretary's wife called out, "You're still rambling on, have you so much to say? It's time for some soup."

Millstone emerged from the kitchen carrying bowls. At what point he'd left them to help the Secretary's wife, Goodman had no idea. Nor did Millstone offer an answer, he only smiled. The Branch Secretary, meanwhile, was silent upon the bed.

His wife leant close. "What are you doing, my dear, feeling sleepy are we?"

The Branch Secretary lifted himself up. "I've been listening, what else? Let's have some soup. Is there an egg or two in each bowl?"

"Two in each," came his wife's reply.

Together, in the dark, the three men ate ravenously.

Outside the courtyard, a dog barked. Millstone hurriedly set down his bowl and moved to grab his shovel. No one spoke. Instead, they trained their ears on the darkness. A moment later, Millstone returned.

"It's only Iron Bolt's and Almost-There's dogs making a racket, nothing to worry about."

"They almost scared me to death," said the Branch Secretary's wife. "I feared the Hammerheads had been monitoring us and were about to burst in."

"And so what if they were?" Secretary Zhu said. "What were we talking about that was counterrevolutionary? More important, Millstone, why on earth did you bring that shovel along with you?"

"To protect myself from that bastard Pockmark."

"Pockmark?"

"Yes, we heard he'd escaped prison and he may be making his way back to Old Kiln."

"Escaped?" the Branch Secretary mumbled. "How can someone on death row escape?" He placed his bowl down on the table, unable to continue eating.

"How could he have not escaped?" the Secretary's wife said. "You're the party secretary and those... men locked you up in a woodshed, didn't they?"

"Don't talk nonsense, dear, there's no place for it here. Seized me? Ha, I'm back home, aren't I?"

"You mean you weren't released because of Apricot..." She stopped short and swallowed. She said no more, but turned and went back into the kitchen. At the same moment, a cat leapt up onto the courtyard wall and began meowing into the night, announcing spring.

FORTY-EIGHT

THE VILLAGE WAS ON HIGH ALERT for any sign of Pockmark returning. Inkcap purposely scattered ashes around the main gate of Pockmark's home, checking periodically for any disturbance, a clear sign that the criminal had returned. He also clipped thorns from the wild jujube trees that grew on the nearby mountain, intending to place them on the top of the courtyard walls surrounding Pockmark's home, expecting that if he didn't go through the gate, he'd try to steal back in the dead of the night by climbing over the walls. Inkcap thought himself very clever, his methods to apprehend Pockmark something Cowbell would never think of, nor anyone else in the village for that matter.

But just as he was about to set off with his sickle and basket, Apricot called out to him. Her face was flushed, her fine-flower jacket tight to her skin, a shovel in her hands. She asked what he was up to, but Inkcap remained quiet.

"Going to collect firewood?" she persisted. "Why bother? It's so sunny and hot out, there are no fires to light. Why don't you help me in my fields?"

Apricot had never spoken to him like this before.

"Why so happy today," he asked.

"Me, happy? What on earth are you talking about? I've just spent the morning crying. Then, after lunch, I took a nap and had a most disturbing dream. My father told me his roof was leaking. I awoke shaking all over – was there a hole, could rain be falling into his resting place?"

"Let's take a look," Inkcap suggested, and on their way to the grave, he tried to comfort her. "You know dreams are the opposite of reality, right?"

"Dreams at night are, but dreams that come to you in the day are when family ghosts appear to make requests on the living."

Apricot hastened her stride, one foot falling quickly after another, unconcerned whether Inkcap was keeping up or not. Even though he tried to maintain her pace, he couldn't. To his eyes, the flower pattern on her jacket transformed into fluttering butterflies.

Once they arrived at the cemetery, they saw Awning off in the distance, squatting near a grave marker.

"You think Awning's here visiting his father too?" asked Inkcap.

Apricot looked for a moment. "Maybe, but his family's plot is more over there at the foot of the mountain… why's he not in training with the militia?"

"Millstone never called anyone to work, so why train? Heh, Apricot, you don't reckon the American imperialists and Soviet revisionists would seize on the chaos of the Cultural Revolution to invade, do you?"

"You don't need to worry about that. If they tried, the Hammerheads would be there to fight back."

Apricot patted the top of his head and as she did so, Inkcap noticed her painted nails, redder than those of Flower Girl.

The grass had grown long on Potful's burial mound. Wild mountain chrysanthemums had also sprouted, blossoming egg-shaped flowers. Inkcap plucked one, but on its own, the flower was unappealing. Altogether, however, was a different story.

Then, seized by the moment, Inkcap called out, "Wow, the chrysanthemums just turned all white, but now they've gone yellow again." He couldn't shake the feeling the flowers were making faces at him.

"You have a nerve to carry on like this at a grave."

Apricot's voice rose sharply before trailing off. She fell to her knees just as quickly as she had yelled at him, her eyes transfixed on a single spot. Inkcap followed her line of vision and saw where the earth had caved in, creating a hole the size of a man's fist. The ground was moist, clear evidence rainwater had been trickling down the slope of the burial mound, falling on Apricot's father, just as she had dreamt. Inkcap couldn't help but feel a tingling sensation: her dream was true. Tears streaming down her face, Apricot had risen from her knees to start shovelling earth into the hole. Inkcap began grabbing mounds of dirt as well, but the hole seemed so deep it took forever to fill. Before they'd finished, Awning walked by.

His face was sullen, his high cheekbones giving him an even fiercer look. He offered no greeting to either of them, nor did he ask what they were doing. Inkcap coughed deliberately, trying to draw Awning's attention. The man's only response was to kick at the ground, causing a small pile of earth to fly briefly through the sky.

"Brother Awning," Inkcap began, "where are you off to?"

"I'm going for a shit. What's it to you?"

"You've come to these graves to, er, take a shit?"

"I shit where I feel like it, but better here than inside the woodshed, no?"

Inkcap was perplexed. Usually, Awning treated him well enough, so what was the reason for his vitriol today? Trying to understand, he asked, "The woodshed? Brother, have you not heard that the Branch Secretary has been released?"

"He's nothing. I'm not going back. There's only death there. I'll die before I let that happen."

Inkcap turned his eyes to Apricot who'd just finished filling in the hole. "Uncle," she said, "what are you talking about, who'd dare try to imprison you?"

Awning ignored her and turned to look at Inkcap. "Sparks' mum fell and broke her leg. The Zhus called on her, why didn't you? If you want, you can come with me now."

Inkcap looked at Apricot. "Go together—"

"I asked you," said Awning, "what are you dawdling for?"

"I'd like Apricot to come too."

"She's not part of the Zhu family, why would she call on them?"

"Apricot's not part of the Zhus?"

"Why would you think she is?"

Apricot leaned on a nearby cypress tree, causing its branches to sway.

"Uncle," she said, "what right have you to run me down, here at my father's grave?"

The cypress bent more as Apricot put her weight against it, nearly touching the ground before she stepped away to fall prostrate on the ground. The tree sprang back up as Apricot cried, her sobs betraying the exhaustion she felt. Inkcap moved to lift her up, but she resisted. He tried again and she swatted his hands away.

"What the hell are you doing?" she said, her voice dripping with venom. "Go on, get out of here, go off with Awning, dammit. When someone wants something from me, it's fine to consider me a Zhu, but when they don't need anything, I'm not. Go on, leave me be."

Awning snorted and turned to leave. Inkcap remained in his spot, unsure whether to stay or leave. He decided on neither. He wouldn't accompany Awning, nor would he help Apricot. Instead, he'd go and cut the wild jujube thorns as planned. That was the safest choice, he thought.

Inkcap walked towards the foot of the mountain, passing several burial mounds, also past where Awning had supposedly released his bowels. There was no evidence in between the graves, but he did notice loosened soil near the marker for Bash's father's resting place. He kicked at the loosened dirt a little and discovered a wooden peg underneath. He had no idea why such a peg would be here, but Awning was a company commander in the militia, he wouldn't just come here without a reason, would he?

After collecting a basketful of thorns, he trudged off to Pockmark's home to ensure the walls surrounding the house were suitably difficult to climb. He then went home, all the while contemplating the significance of the wooden peg he'd found in the ground.

"A wooden peg, you say? What are you talking about?" His gran was noticeably concerned. "Such a marker would curse the family, bring an end to their line, it's an evil marker. Why on earth are you asking about such a thing?"

Inkcap couldn't think of a proper answer and had no desire to tell her the truth. His only response was to mumble and tell her it was nothing but an offhand question.

"What do you mean an offhand question? You know a loose tongue brings nothing but trouble. Remember this, when you're out, be quiet, say as little as possible, and before you do say anything, think first, always, and then only speak if it's really needed. I've told you this before, so you better remember."

"I know, Gran, I know."

"You watch it, all right, don't go getting impatient with me."

"Yes, Gran, I understand, it's all fine. Forget I asked."

That night, Inkcap returned to the mountain and removed the wooden peg Awning had placed in the ground. He went by himself, not daring to call on anyone, certainly not Cowbell, whose mouth was far too loose. Once he'd removed the peg, he made his way to the burial mound of Pockmark's father. There he stamped the peg into the ground, not bothering to even cover it with dirt.

Not long after, Noisy returned to Old Kiln, bringing with him the odds and ends of the village's sewing needs. He also brought Inkcap's favourite sweet, *liguo* candy, as well as the black silk ribbons that Flower Girl so enjoyed. Perhaps more importantly for the village as a whole, he brought news that Pockmark had been re-apprehended by the authorities.

For the next few days, his story was all that could be heard across Old Kiln, with no two retellings the same. One tale had Pockmark escaping from prison and making his way to Cockscomb Mountain. It contained many caves that could serve as hideouts, the only problem would be food, which was how he was captured one night when he had no choice but to sneak into the county capital to steal provisions. The alarm was raised, the authorities arrived and he was taken into custody. Another story had him hiding out on Cockscomb Mountain, again because of its many caves. Now, it must be said that this mountain was once littered with tiny Buddhist statues, the bulk of which had been destroyed as easy targets of the Cultural Revolution. However, the destruction of the statues did not stop some of the villagers from still trekking up into the mountains to burn incense in offering to the Buddha. And this was how Pockmark was discovered: a woman who'd been trying to bear a child for many years sought the help of the divine, crawling into the same cave Pockmark was hiding in. Prostrate on the ground, she begged for a child, begged to be fertile, begged for her man to make her pregnant, and if he didn't, then to send her someone else, and on it went. Pockmark couldn't help but break out in laughter at her requests, his mirth echoing throughout the mountain, causing the woman to really believe spirits resided in its caves. Naturally, she told anyone who would listen. The authorities already suspected Pockmark was hiding somewhere in the network of caves, and the woman's story confirmed it. It wasn't long before they tracked him down. It didn't really matter which story was true, the residents of Old Kiln were simply happy that he was recaptured and wouldn't be reappearing any time soon.

"I already told you," Stonebreaker said confidently. "Pockmark is an idiot, too stupid to make his way back here. While the rest of you were tying yourselves in knots, I was sleeping peacefully as ever."

Padlock was unimpressed. "Listening to him, it sounds as though he's got dysentery, lying in bed shitting his life away."

In fact, Stonebreaker was indeed afflicted with dysentery, and wherever he went, if he went anywhere, his trousers would be stained. Soon, his young wife could be seen down by the river nearly every day, washing the stains as best she could. On one occasion, Baldy Jin happened upon her.

"Yuer, I see you're washing Stonebreaker's trousers again," he said. "You need any honey locust soap to make the job easier?"

"It wouldn't do any good. My husband is like a child when he eats. He can't help but waste it everywhere."

"I reckon he's not wasting food though, is he? To speak the unspeakable, I think you ought to talk to Granny Silkworm, ask her to call his spirit back."

Yuer ceased her cleaning, gathered her soiled laundry and dashed off without a word.

The night of the thirteenth was supposed to be a full moon. Gran latched the door and plopped herself down in the courtyard to mend the soles of their shoes. Inkcap's feet grew continuously. They were like teeth, tearing through his shoes, mulching pair after pair on a monthly basis. Before mending his current pair, Gran rummaged through the house for something he could put on his feet. Finding a pair of shoes she'd made for him the previous year, she got him to try them on, but already suspected they wouldn't fit. At least not without some effort that involved Inkcap not only twisting his feet an unnatural way, but also wetting the old grass to make it more malleable. It worked, but the pain was nearly unbearable.

"Dammit all," said Gran, "how can your feet keep growing when you're still as short as ever? You've no choice, you have to wear them, you'll get used to them. You'll have to."

She proceeded to stitch a pair of new shoes for Inkcap. Unfortunately, the light of the moon was little help, hiding instead behind clouds that had swept in as the day fell. Gran lit a kerosene lamp and tried the best she could to continue working on his shoes. Before she got much done, however, Noodle Fish's wife called round, asking her to pop over. Gran had little choice but to agree. Putting down her needle, she got up to leave, yelling out to Inkcap as she went, "Now don't you go out anywhere tonight, get to bed early."

Inkcap hadn't seen Noodle Fish's wife and so he had no idea where his gran had gone. So he squatted on the hammerstone in the courtyard and waited, the stone still warm from the heat of the day. On nights like these, he would often gaze into the night sky and count the stars, always arriving at different results. Tonight, however, there were no stars to be seen. Where had they gone? he wondered. He rubbed his eyes and stared into the blackness of the night, squinting hard to make stars appear. He hoped to see one or two, perhaps even three. As these thoughts trailed through his mind, one star did break the clouds, followed by a second. Suddenly, more appeared. But when he rubbed his eyes again, they were gone, a dark blanket spread once more across the sky. Would it rain? he wondered. A thought then occurred to him out of the blue, and he lowered his head. There, perched just beside his toes, was the swallow that nested in their doorframe.

"Not sleeping?" Inkcap asked.

"Nor are you," came the swallow's reply.

"I'm waiting for Gran."

"So am I."

"All right, we'll wait for her together. Then, once she's back, we'll head to bed. Say, do you know where she's gone?"

"She went to see Stonebreaker."

Inkcap chuckled. "Don't talk nonsense, couldn't she see Stonebreaker if she went to Noodle Fish's house?"

Inkcap derided the swallow for its silliness, and the crickets in the corner of the courtyard seemed to join in the laughter. At nearly the same moment, however, Inkcap heard his gran's voice drawing near. Two voices, in fact, Gran's and Stonebreaker's. There was a raucous quality to how Gran was speaking. And then he heard her drawl, "Come back, oh ho. Come back."

Stonebreaker joined in, his voice echoing that of a proud rooster. "Come back, oh ho, Come baacck!"

The two voices carried on, each answering the other with the same words, one echoing the other, first near, then far, near, far, closer, closer, fainter, fainter. Inkcap finally understood. Noodle Fish's wife had called on Gran to help with Stonebreaker's condition. She was calling his spirit back. In the whole village, she was the only one who could.

Gran truly was trying to call back Stonebreaker's spirit, holding a lantern, although without a candle inside, as was done in the past. The kerosene lamp didn't burn bright, but it was sufficient to illuminate their way, with Noodle Fish's wife and Stonebreaker trailing behind Inkcap's gran. Gran's eyes were closed, presumably part of the ceremony. When they first left the house, neither spoke a word, as instructed by the older lady. In silence, they made their way to the edge of the village, whereupon they circled eight times in the shape of a lotus flower.

That's when Gran first called out, "Come back, oh ho, come baacck..."

Hearing her voice, Stonebreaker replied, "Come back, oh ho, come baacck!"

The reply made, Gran turned towards the gate of Noodle Fish's home and entered, calling as she did, "Stonebreaker, Stonebreaker!"

Opening his eyes, Stonebreaker responded, "Uh huh."

"Don't open your eyes. Don't do anything, just listen to me, call your name." Gran's voice was stern, foreboding. After a brief pause, she continued, "Stonebreaker, Stonebreaker, come back, oh ho..."

Stonebreaker started to echo her. "Come baa..." then changed abruptly, "I'm baacck." He stood in the doorway, unmoving.

"Take a pinch of earth in your hands, just a pinch," Gran instructed.

Stonebreaker remained still, but Noodle Fish's wife had already bent low to grab a handful of dirt, quickly depositing it on Stonebreaker's head. Suddenly, a gong sounded in the night, clang, clang, clang.

"Something going on with the Hammerheads?" asked Stonebreaker.

"Stamp your feet," said Gran. "Quickly now, stamp."

Stonebreaker complied and Gran continued, "Now, go through the doorway, go on."

Stonebreaker thrust his head in the direction of the alley and the sound of the gong. "What the devil is happening?"

Noodle Fish's wife pushed him through the door and over the threshold, promptly slamming it shut behind him.

Gran had carried the lantern, had called Stonebreaker's spirit back, she'd marched him to the edge of the village, and no one saw them. But all the villagers heard them. Some were in their kitchens tidying away the evening's dishes, some were talking about their livestock while others discussed the children's clothes and the crops in the fields. A few were early to bed with no dinner at all, complaining of empty stomachs. As men spoke of hunger, women rebutted by saying people were no more than millstones and hunger was impossible. There were also villagers standing in doorways in small groups, ruminating on the past six months in Old Kiln, the good and the bad. And to a person, they all heard the summoning of a spirit. Sudden it was, echo it did, causing all their conversations to cease. They looked at each other, eyes asking whose soul had been lost, until a tentative answer came: Stonebreaker? They strained their ears to hear more. Listen. Say nothing. Just listen. Face's blank, expressions like fine-fired porcelain. Were their souls being called back? No breathing. Silence. Then release, a long, satisfied exhale as though they'd just gorged themselves on an impossibly large dinner. Returned. Yes, returned. Clang, clang, clang. The gong sounded once more, bringing everyone to their senses.

The gong startled Inkcap, nearly causing him to fall from his perch on the millstone. The sound of someone running through the alleyway near his home came fast after the gong. He wanted to open the gate to see if he could see who it was, but fear held his hand. He had a pee alongside the door frame, before pushing it open a crack to catch a glimpse of Cowbell.

"Hey, what's happening?" Inkcap asked.

"Useless hasn't told you?" said Cowbell.

"Eh?"

"Oh, that's right, he wouldn't tell you, would he, you're not one of the Hammerheads."

"They've called a meeting?"

"Chairman Mao's given us a new directive. Even at night, we're to cheer on the new slogan."

"What's the new directive?"

"I don't know. You want to come?"

"But I'm not a Hammerhead."

"Well, Chairman Mao's new directive is for the people."

"Does that include me? I'm… you better go quick, my gran will be back soon." Inkcap closed the door softly and returned to his perch on the hammerstone.

Not long after, Gran returned, opening and closing the gate quickly, quietly. She leant against the wall to catch her breath, then spied Inkcap crouched on the hammerstone.

"Why are you still up?"

"I was waiting for you to come home, to finish the soul collection."

"Poor Stonebreaker, his life's been draining away. How did you know I went there to call back his spirit?"

"I heard you."

Moving closer to her grandson, she took hold of his arm and pulled him inside. "To bed, now. And don't be concerned. Should anyone come, don't make a sound, you hear, just sleep."

"You think something's going to happen?"

"The Hammerheads must've heard me too. That explains the sudden clang of the gong–"

"The gong was to announce a new directive from Chairman Mao. It had nothing to do with you."

"And how do you know this?"

"I spoke to Cowbell. He asked me to go, but I didn't."

Gran's expression relaxed and she lowered herself to the edge of the bed.

"Stonebreaker's still a Hammerhead," Inkcap continued. "Pockmark won't be back, I guess that caused him to misplace his soul."

"Stonebreaker's a Hammerhead?"

"From early on."

"Oh..."

Gran, despite being tired, didn't sleep. Instead, she returned to mending her grandson's shoes. The gong continued to clang. Later, rain fell, its pitter-patter echoing through the night.

When the day dawned, Yijia Ridge was dark, a smoke-like colour hanging over the mountains. Above the ridge, however, were billowing white clouds like cotton in the sky. Inkcap rose from bed, collected his piss bucket and walked out towards the outhouse to empty it. The path was drenched from the rain that was still falling. Not heavily, but relentlessly. It seemed to bounce along the puddles that had formed. The flowers on the nearby lilac tree, still in bloom, glistened in the rain. It was as though some spirit had possessed them, giving them an especially lustrous hue that trembled in the wet morning air.

Awning, draped in a raincoat, was speaking to Barndoor: "The fields are ripe with insects, they're like great lumps crawling over our crops, getting heavier and heavier with each bite."

"We should have been out there long ago. If we don't act soon, there'll be nothing left."

Wearing a raincoat similar to Awning's, Barndoor's attention was distracted by Lucky, who was walking towards them. Turning back to Awning, he continued, "Shall we head to the fields?"

"To do what? No one's called us to work, even though work needs doing. I don't get it, we're peasants, we're supposed to be in the fields and yet they tell us to make revolution. What will we end up eating, eh? The shit that blows in the wind?"

"Have you heard Chairman Mao's new directive?" Lucky began as he approached them.

"I heard no gong," Awning answered quickly.

"Well, the gong clanged, how did you not hear it?"

"I don't know, but I didn't."

"You mean to tell me you're not going to follow Chairman Mao's directive? You dare!"

"I've been a poor peasant for many lifetimes, I've been a company commander in the militia. If I didn't hear the gong, I didn't hear it. Are you trying to say I'm some counterrevolutionary?"

"Yes, yes," said Barndoor, interrupting their exchange, "you're a poor peasant and a company commander, and now you're calling on the base to head to the fields to work."

"Fuck it all," said Awning, his voice dripping with ire. "Even the militia is paralysed right now. Shit, some of them joined up with the Hammerheads. Fuck it all, I say, let the Soviet revisionists invade, then the Hammerheads can take them on!"

"You ought to be careful, Awning," said Lucky. "You shouldn't be saying these things. Don't the pesticides you use come from the higher-ups? What'll you do if you don't have any, huh?"

"We've got good kilns here capable of producing lots of china, but we're not doing anything. So tell me, who the hell do you hope will make the pesticides?"

"Oh, what a mess," said Barndoor.

"I told you, you shouldn't be saying these things and yet you keep on. Why? What are you hoping to prove? Come on, I'm off to the fields. And whoever doesn't want to join me, so be it, we can only be responsible for ourselves."

Out of the blue, Inkcap yelled out, "I'll go." But none of them paid him any mind.

Despite the lack of attention, Inkcap still went to the fields to battle the insects. He had no raincoat, having only returned home to collect his straw hat and a length of treated rope that could be used as a mosquito repellent. He didn't wear the hat on his head, however, but kept it in his hand, the mosquito-repellent rope wound about his wrist. As he walked after Awning and the others, he mimicked a town crier and called out through the village what they were intending to do. Some heard his words.

"Has the Captain arranged an exercise? Another, erm, movement?"

"Captain… captain? What are you talking about?"

"Then has Bash taken over agricultural production?"

"I can't speak to that."

"Oh, I understand, it's you, dear Inkcap, you've taken charge of things!"

Although pleased with himself, Inkcap had nothing to say, except to continue calling out to the village as a whole to come to the fields and battle the insects ravaging their crops. Pleased indeed, he swallowed great lungfuls of air so that his chest and stomach swelled. He felt taller than ever before. Looking at the few chickens that seemed to be following him, their feathers wet from the rain and slicked back, made him think of how small and short they were, ugly, in fact, incomparably so. Tromping under a willow tree, he leapt and nearly grabbed a handful of leaves. He *was* tall, he thought. It was then that he saw Sprout approaching in the rain.

"So now," Sprout began, "you really think you're a party cadre, eh?" And he slapped Inkcap on the head, immediately making him small again. Inkcap averted his eyes from the leaves on the tree. They were too high for him, far too high.

At first, there were four or five people in the fields. Then, one by one, more came. The bugs had grown fat on their crops, a few green caterpillars as big as swollen silkworms stuffed on mulberry leaves. They'd gorged themselves, spitting up silk, some even forming cocoons. Near the lotus pond, villagers collected lotus leaves to roll into makeshift pouches to place the caterpillars in. Once filled, the leafy pouches were taken to the edge of the field and smashed with a rock. Green juice oozed from the leaves, and a pungent, assaulting smell hung in the air. An insect massacre.

When Inkcap went to pick the lotus leaves, he found Cowbell in the pond, sorting through the duckweed. Quickly, Cowbell grasped a lotus plant and pulled it from the water, tearing out the seeds to eat. He was holding a piece of straw, which he then used to breathe underwater. Splash, he went under. Inkcap approached stealthily without making a sound. He waited for the straw, the only evidence of Cowbell he could see, to get nearer the edge of the pond. When he did, Inkcap reached out and pinched the straw. Cowbell burst out of the water, gasping.

His eyes fell on Inkcap. "What the fuck, are you trying to kill me?"

"You're not helping in the fields, you're just here to stuff yourself with lotus seeds. Don't you know that's killing future lotus plants?"

"What the fuck are you going on about? You know what, go ahead, call me out, I'm not afraid of you. Besides, no one will give a damn. Decheng just went off with a whole basketful himself."

"No one will care about the damage you're causing?"

"Damage? That's a word only for the likes of you, the black sheep, the Bad Elements." And with that, he flung the lotus seedpod at Inkcap.

Inkcap clasped the seedpod and then smashed it against Cowbell's head. "Get out of there and help!"

"Fuck you. I'm busy. The Hammerheads are heading off to Xiahewan."

"Don't play me for a fool."

Cowbell wasn't lying, the Hammerheads were getting ready to march to Xiahewan. After the kilns were closed, the base of operations for the Hammerheads shifted from Bash's home to the Kiln God Temple. A constant stream of people were coming and going, locals and others from farther away. The base was a hub of activity, barely allowing time for Bash to leave, and so he ended up moving in, as it were. Consequently, he instructed Useless to take up residence in his old home and to use the place as a contact point for the Hammerheads. Whether coming from the main roads or not, so long as they were making revolution like they were, Useless was to greet them and invite them to call on the Hammerheads in their main base. In this manner, the Hammerheads were able to link up with other revolutionary groups across the county and demonstrate to them their commitment to the revolution. In fact, because of their growing profile, young cadres from Xiahewan had invited the Hammerheads to attend a struggle session against Commune Secretary Zhang, hence their preparations to travel.

Red flags flapping in the air, gongs and drums clanging and pounding, the Hammerheads set off down the main route to Xiahewan, a veritable pageant of revolutionary fervour. When Inkcap saw them from the fields, he couldn't help ruing his decision to follow Awning. He also hated and resented Cowbell for telling him nothing beforehand. Hands working mechanically to pick the caterpillars, Inkcap's eyes remained on the Hammerheads.

Beside him, Awning shouted, "To the fields, to the fields! Work to be done in the fields!" Awning then noticed where Inkcap's attention lay, and he lowered his voice to speak to him directly: "Nothing to see there, boy, especially for you."

Inkcap lowered his head and focused on the job at hand, but only for a moment before he wrenched his neck to stare in the direction of the Hammerheads. Awning noticed once more, bent low to scoop up a clump of mud, and proceeded to smear it into Inkcap's face. Blinded, his eyes hurting, Inkcap fell to his knees to find some water to wash his face.

"You'd like to be marching with them, eh?" Awning's question betrayed his anger.

Inkcap couldn't respond. He was too busy trying to wash the mud from his eyes.

"You must understand, Inkcap," Awning continued, "we're the backward element in today's society, us poor peasants. But if you want to go and make revolution, go!"

"No, no, no, I won't."

More and more villagers arrived in the fields. Millstone's entire family came, even the Branch Secretary, who'd been watching the drainage ditches, showed up, his head covered by a straw hat. Inkcap handed him a lotus leaf pouch, but he didn't receive any thanks.

"You're not off to Xiahewan?" said the Secretary.

"I'm not a Hammerhead."

"Oh, I thought you were in with Useless and Cowbell, all Hammerheads."

"They're them, I'm me."

The rain was finally easing, but the fields were wet and sticky. When the villagers walked among the crops, droplets of water clung to their clothes, soon soaking their trousers and upper garments. While this produced a pleasantly cool effect, the wetness, mixed with sweat from the hard work, meant that when the leaves in the field rubbed against their bare arms and legs, they were like miniature saws scraping across their skin. Very painful.

When the villagers finally arrived at the opposite side of the field, they climbed over the weir clasping their lotus leaf pouches to toss them into the shallow pit on the other side. Inkcap enjoyed this part of the day's work most. Lifting the biggest stones he could find, he flung them onto the pouches containing the many, many caterpillars. Noodle Fish regretted not bringing his chickens, as they could have feasted heartily on the caterpillars, so he asked Inkcap to save some of the pouches, intending to bring at least some of them home.

"You're quite the schemer, aren't you?" said Inkcap, and he flung another stone onto the writhing mass of insects. Caught up in the slaughter, Inkcap took to squishing many more caterpillars with his feet.

"You waste of fucking sperm! You really should be with the Hammerheads," Noodle Fish yelled.

"But the Hammerheads, they've got more guts than me. If I were to go, I'm afraid I'd lose my soul."

Noodle Fish caught on straight away, he knew Inkcap was calling out his son, Stonebreaker. "Inkcap, I've got something to say to you, but I'm not sure I should."

"Let me think, you want to remind me of my bad family background."

"No, that's not it."

"Then you want to say how small I am, how short, how ugly."

"No, not that either."

"Go on, then, tell me."

"That you've got leeches all over your legs, on your belly too. Looks like they've been there for most of the day, you're covered in blood."

Inkcap looked at his legs and stomach. The leeches had gorged on him and now resembled the plump caterpillars, some with only half their bodies still visible, the rest under his skin. Inkcap pulled at the creatures, but to no avail. Panic rising, he began to squeal and jump about.

The leeches had found him in the pond. They'd attached themselves to his legs and torso, but unlike mosquitoes that made a person itch, with leeches, he'd felt nothing. Noodle Fish looked at him as he tried vainly to remove the leeches, his expression one of supreme calm.

"Don't pull, you'll tear them in half and never get the part that's already under your skin. You've got to slap at them, that's the only way."

Inkcap did as instructed, slapping at his legs and stomach, beating himself relentlessly. Gradually, the leeches released their hold and tumbled to the ground.

No one really bothered with Inkcap and his battle with the leeches. Nor had they warned him about the risk of going in the water. They'd probably drained him of a pint, who could say? But they did pay attention to the show Inkcap and Noodle Fish were putting on. Their squabbling prompted gossip among the villagers, most of it made at the expense of Noodle Fish, for no one really cared about Inkcap.

Gourd was the first to speak. "Hey, Uncle Noodle Fish, has Stonebreaker gone off to Xiahewan?"

"Since he's not feeling well, I doubt he's gone," came Noodle Fish's reply.

Sparks spoke next. "What? His shitty old arse still bothering him? Pockmark isn't coming back, you know, he won't ever be back, so there's nothing to be afraid of."

"I reckon I'd like to see him back here," Awning added.

"What the devil are you saying?" said Millstone.

"Well, if Pockmark hadn't used that poison, he'd still be in Old Kiln, and like Bash, I'd bet he'd be making revolution too. And as you know, one trough isn't fit for two asses, so I imagine it'd be quite the show."

"One Bash is enough," retorted Millstone. "If we had a Pockmark added into the mix, we'd all be fucked."

Branch Secretary Zhu didn't participate in the gossip, he simply kept working, his body aching badly. Finally, he had to stop. Gesturing to Inkcap, the Secretary urged him to rub his lower back. The other men paused their back and forth, and then Millstone asked Branch Secretary Zhu directly, "Secretary, what do you say?"

"I'm not in charge any more, you don't need to call me Secretary."

"Whatever you say, I'll still use the title. Besides, who doesn't love to hear about someone else stuffing dog fur into their ears, hmm? So, what do you say?"

"If the people of Old Kiln were, shall we say, unable to make a go of it, if a rock were to come into contact with another rock, two equally strong forces thrust together, I should think nothing would happen."

"So," Millstone pondered, "do you mean to say that were Pockmark here, he'd be one of those young revolutionaries?"

"Ah, nothing, nothing, I'm just rambling, not making any sense." And with that, the Branch Secretary lowered his head and went back to work.

Millstone remained where he was for what seemed like forever, the Branch Secretary's words seemingly glueing him to the spot. Then, all of a sudden, he walked over to Awning and the two began a muted conversation that sounded almost like gibberish to the other villagers. Lucky, who'd been quiet until then, stretched his back. Time for a cigarette break.

"Hey, Inkcap," he called out. "I need a light."

After a moment's pause, Lucky ruminated on the scene in front of him. "Ha, you know something, there're a lot of Zhus out here working today, and a lot of other family names too, some more questionable than others, but it makes me think of something, how's it that all of us backward folk are so bloody good at work?"

His words resounded through the field, several villagers raising their heads to look in his direction. While there were many Zhus and other names too, there was not a single Hei representative.

"That's because the Zhus are good people," said Awning. "Count them on your fingers and toes and ask yourself, what kind of people make up the Hammerheads? No one with a backbone among them, I'll wager. They might be able to kick and bite, but they're all lazy bastards who have no idea of real work. They're full of hate, dissatisfied with everything. All they're good at is disobeying orders, and these are not just my words, they're just people of poor quality."

"How did the Cultural Revolution become like the land reform, is it all about getting these kinds of people to make trouble?" asked Sparks.

"Shut it," whispered Awning, "don't bring up the land reform, not with the Secretary here, you'll only aggravate him."

But Branch Secretary Zhu was not the least concerned. He'd already finished filling his pouch full of caterpillars and had walked off to dispose of them.

"The Cultural Revolution is a revolution for everyone," Awning continued, "so doesn't that mean someone else's revolution is also ours? Are we incapable of revolution? From Liberation until now, haven't we become accustomed to revolution?"

Sparks, Lucky and Iron Bolt cried out, "You're right, yes, that makes sense, why can't we? Awning, you were a company commander, why don't we make our own unit? They've got Hammerheads, and we've got mattocks."

The more the villagers cheered, the more excited they became. Watching the scene unfold, Noodle Fish leant close to Inkcap. "Heaven help us, another team. We'll never get rid of these caterpillars."

FORTY-NINE

AFTER THE RAIN STOPPED, the sun seemed to burn in the sky for days, scorching the village. Millstone and Sparks had gathered at Awning's home to go over plans for setting up a new revolutionary unit. Awning's wife, seated near the front door, was threshing wheat to dry in the sun, yelling at the lurking sparrows as she did so. They would soar from tree to tree, diving at intervals to snatch the drying grain. Awning's wife fought them off, finally winning the battle when the sparrows halted their attacks. They did not depart, however, but remained in the trees above the courtyard, chirping incessantly. The words of the men could still be heard over the din of the sparrows. Or perhaps it was the other way around. There were shouts of excitement accompanied by panicked outbursts. The argument dragged on, boiling over repeatedly. When Awning's wife finished her work and swept up the husks, the sparrows finally dispersed, chittering as they did. Soon, every pig, cat, chicken and dog throughout Old Kiln would learn of the men's plans.

The sparrows flew hither and thither, spreading their gossip. The villagers had no idea what had got the birds into such a tizzy, many thinking a flock of sparrowhawks must have flown into Old Kiln, or perhaps a snake or two had slithered into their nests. But Inkcap understood. He knew what they were chirping about, knew this was big news. Knew, too, that he dare not speak to anyone about it. This fear, however, did little to diminish his own curiosity, so he decided to sneak over to Awning's home to find out more. It never crossed his mind he'd see Useless standing in the doorway to Awning's place, but as soon as he did, he scolded the sparrows for spreading gossip. There was no way they could form a new revolutionary unit with Useless there. Or so Inkcap thought.

The sparrows gone, the husks swept, Awning's wife seated herself once more near the door, leaving it open just a little, enough so that she could look in both directions, out to the yard, into the house. The sun seemed nearly white in the sky and the heat rose from the ground in sizzling waves, swaying like the leafy parts of the rice plant. She stared for a moment at the screen wall just outside the main gate. It seemed to shimmer, and she thought she could glimpse the relief sculptures that had been carved into it. But when she blinked, they disappeared again, smashed to pieces. In her heart of hearts, she cursed the Hammerheads.

A moment later, her eyes still shifting back and forth, she thought she heard movement near the gate. "Who's there?" she called out.

Useless pushed the gate open. "Me."

Awning's wife leapt up and moved to block his entry deeper into the courtyard. He was carrying a red bucket filled with paste, and he was going door to door to help the villagers put up posters of Chairman Mao.

"I'm here to help you with this," Useless explained, holding the picture high.

"Oh yes, please do. Chairman Mao's image adorning our door will certainly keep the evil spirits at bay."

"Well now, Chairman Mao isn't here to keep an eye on things, but for you to see him whenever you open the door."

"Oh yes, most definitely, that would be wonderful indeed."

Useless proceeded to affix the likeness of Chairman Mao on the gate, a poster on each side, staring intently at whoever opened the doors.

Awning's wife thought to herself, When the gate is closed, the two images of Chairman Mao will be so close together they'd be able to talk to each other. But when the gate is open, they'd be separated. Turning to Useless, she remarked upon his skill.

"It's nothing, really," he replied bashfully. "I do it gladly. Is Brother Awning in?"

"You still call him Brother? He received orders from the commune militia. He's gone to Luozhen."

"The commune militia called him? He's not fit to receive training for anything."

"I agree, he's a backward old sort, but what was he to do, he had to go."

"Well, Brother Awning is a company commander, that's true."

"Ha, a company commander indeed. Too bad he couldn't protect those reliefs out there though, eh?"

Inside the house, Awning, Millstone and Sparks continued to discuss their new revolutionary unit. They'd settled on the name Red Blades. In the past, a common militia song sang of daggers lopping off the heads of demons. It conveyed the right sort of image. And besides, Hammerhead shafts are made of wood whereas daggers are made of steel, steel comes from iron and iron always conquers wood, just like the Red Blades would overcome the Hammerheads. Their new unit would primarily be made up of Zhus. They were, after all, the most dignified and upstanding residents of Old Kiln. This would also help to distinguish them from the Hammerheads who were, naturally, ugly and repulsive. By now, the arguments they had at the start were finished and they were all rather pleased with themselves. Awning took a bottle of wine from a kitchen cabinet so that they could properly toast their accomplishment. He was about to call out to his wife to prepare some garlic eggs and fried vegetables when he heard her speaking to Useless out by the gate. Discreetly, he pulled the curtain to better conceal their presence, gesturing to Millstone and Sparks to keep quiet. Not until Useless had departed did he pull back the curtain and come out to speak to his wife.

"What did Useless stick to the gate?" asked Awning.

She directed his attention to the smiling image of Chairman Mao. Awning betrayed little reaction, before continuing, "Why the hell did you speak to him for so long? Damn. He's a Zhu, isn't he? And a clerk for the Hammerheads. He's probably run off to speak to the Heis."

"Catch a piglet to see the sow," said Millstone. "I reckon he and his mum are the same, they both go too far. He's duped you because you're too easily distracted, and now he's got a brick on our necks."

"Awning is hard-pressed to see things clearly himself," Awning's wife replied. "Damn, he mistakes sparrow eggs for magpie eggs!"

There was a certain truth to her words, prompting Sparks to cut in to deflect the conversation. "Awning, shall we have that wine, then?"

"Yes, yes, come on, let's toast. After all, what do women really know? Nothing, that's what! And people, well, who really knows anyone else? The Red Blades have begun. If he wants to come, let him."

"On that point," said Millstone, "you're a little mistaken. The Red Blades have begun, true enough, and our aim is to split from them, but he is a Zhu, it's also our job to pull him here. He's just lost his way. Getting him here will help cut the toes off Bash, one by one if necessary. But all this is immaterial, the larger issue is the excuse Little Sister made for you, that you'd been sent to Luozhen. I worry–"

"What did call me? Little Sister? To you, that's Elder Sister or Sister-in-Law at least."

Millstone did not shy from the challenge. "But Awning is several months younger than me. I hardly think–"

"And I'm older than him by three years."

"Oh, I didn't mean... Elder Sister it is."

Awning made no effort to add details to this story, he only looked at his wife menacingly. "What are you on about, woman? Quiet, let him speak. I'll not have you interrupt."

"Well," Millstone continued, "I think we have a problem. The Hammerheads formed to cause a ruckus, to rebel, right, but I haven't seen them gain support from anywhere beyond Old Kiln. So where is their support coming from, the county? True, there is a revolutionary unit in the county seat, but they're divided into two factions. Well, we've got connections to the county too, don't we? Awning, you've met Wu Gan, we've just got to play our cards right. You've got to find out who he's connected to, and if it's to who we need, then we get our support for the Red Blades from there."

"That's right," Sparks yelled. "Brilliant, Millstone!"

"Easy with the praise, Sparks. We've not yet heard Elder Sister's point of view."

"Awning's never taken me seriously, I don't expect you will now. I'll go fix something for you three to eat." And with that, she left for the kitchen.

That evening, Awning set off for Luozhen. He returned the following day, accompanied by Wu Gan. The villagers knew Wu Gan well. He was tall and broad-shouldered, with a stern appearance. He wore the same leather shoes in winter and summer, and was known for his swift kicks when people got out of line. Word of his arrival reached Bash almost immediately. He had no idea why Wu Gan was visiting Old Kiln, so he instructed Useless to shadow the man and his movements.

As he dined at Awning's home, Awning took advantage of the opportunity. "Cadre Wu Gan, sir, a man can be fierce, but he cannot resist some pillow talk."

Wu Gan went to the alleys, holding a roll of leaflets and handing one out to whomever he met. Several women were scrambling for the same leaflet. "These are the revolutionary reports," Awning reminded them. "You take them home and paste them on your walls. They are not to be used to wrap chilli powder or cut out for shoe patterns."

Every villager clamoured for revolution, after all. Near the western entrance of the village, they had also seen Lightkeeper milling some corn. When he'd seen them, he only lowered his head and pushed the millstone harder. Wu Gan, not quite sure who it was that was pushing the millstone, had leant closer to ask Awning if it was Lightkeeper or not. Upon confirmation, Wu Gan walked towards the man and had spoken to him directly, asking his name – Lightkeeper – and giving his own, Commune Cadre Lu Wu Gan. Lightkeeper was surprised Wu Gan knew his name, to which Wu Gan replied that he had heard a description of a man in Old Kiln who fitted Lightkeeper's profile, and figured it must be him. Wu Gan also told him how he'd heard that Lightkeeper could speak Russian, but that he hadn't instructed anyone else in the militia how to do the same. Lightkeeper's excuse was that he would have only taught them wrong and that he didn't wish to be blamed for such an error. Wu Gan's response was to laugh at his impudence, or perhaps his honesty, and walk away.

While Wu Gan may not have thought anything further about the encounter, the incident stayed with Lightkeeper throughout the day. Then, when he later saw Soupspoon, a pickaxe over his shoulder as usual, Lightkeeper asked, "Hey, Soupspoon, are you a Hammerhead?"

"I think you need to check your eyes, this is a pickaxe, not a bloody hammerhead. Tell me, who were you talking to earlier in the day when you were at the millstone?"

"He said his name was Wu Gan."

"And? You didn't ask anything further? Why didn't you ask about the kilns? What are we supposed to do if we've no kilns to make china in?"

"Go and ask him yourself."

Wu Gan had also accompanied Awning past Ever-Obedient's home, encountering their mangy dog as they did so. Normally, the beast would yelp, howl and bark at anyone who came near, but when Wu Gan had walked by, the creature refrained from even making a quiet growl. Rather, it stuck out its tongue and loafed about, circling Ever-Obedient's courtyard much like its namesake. Other houses they walked by were littered with broken earthen bowls, basins and jars, some providing ramps to climb up and peer over the courtyard walls. The walls around Barndoor's house, on the other hand, were tall and sturdy, made with earth and reinforced with plywood. Roses had been planted on the top and were in full bloom, making it look like the wall was on fire. Wu Gan had remarked on their beauty. Awning, knowing that Flower Girl had planted them, called in through the gate to convey the praise given. Moments later, Wu Gan was invited inside.

During Wu Gan's visit, Useless tried in vain to worm his way into the man's good books. Wu Gan, however, failed to recognise him, despite Useless's claims to the contrary.

"But sir," he began, "I'm Useless. Last year when you toured the village with Commune Secretary Zhang, after Branch Secretary Zhu sent the yellow lilies, I recited a classical poem. Don't you remember?"

"Oh, I remember now, yes, you're the one who recited that verse."

Flower Girl had joined the retinue. "Useless is quite the man in town, so to speak. He's the brains of the Hammerheads."

"I'm not, stop it, I'm not."

"Well," continued Flower Girl, "Bash is the man in charge, but Useless is, what, third in line."

"Is that so?" Wu Gan said. "Tell me, how many men are there in the Hammerheads?"

"Nearly the whole village, I reckon."

It was Awning's turn to interject: "I don't think so, not even close."

"I know Barndoor isn't a Hammerhead," Flower Girl added.

"Cultured people all have the same illness," Wu Gan said. "They're prone to bluff and bluster and say very little, isn't that true?"

"But we're working hard to mobilise the masses," Useless countered, "and make Old Kiln as red as it can be."

Wu Gan muttered under his breath before lifting his leather shoes to kick Useless in the arse.

"I say, those shoes must've cost a bundle," was Useless's only reply.

The conversation then took on a more sombre tone, with Wu Gan asking Useless what the Hammerheads had accomplished. Useless, in turn, provided a report. He noted how they'd strived to destroy the Four Olds, starting with the clay sculptures representing old superstitions. They'd shut down the kilns and audited the books. They took control of the temple, buried numerous murals and confiscated every old book and antique in the village. They'd also launched numerous study lessons to go along with more struggle sessions against class enemies than he could count. There were also big-character posters and slogans posted everywhere. Bash, Useless gushed, was something of a revolutionary idealist, he'd wanted them to devise a means by which a huge, colourful tower could be erected in the main crossroads in the village so that revolutionary slogans could be seen from every house and structure in Old Kiln, a sort of testament to the revolutionary zeal of the Hammerheads. Their plans included setting up a Mao Zedong Thought propaganda team and a theatre troupe to perform model operas nearly every day. They also intended to paint all the walls of the village red and ensure that every villager in Old Kiln could recite Chairman Mao's Little Red Book. Wu Gan listened intently, taking notes to properly record the activities of the Hammerheads. Useless watched the senior cadre and couldn't help but feel pleased.

"So," Useless continued, "as you can see, Bash has taken the initiative. His energy has been contagious, I've never seen anything like it. He barely sleeps a wink, his days are filled with work, his nights with talk of his aspirations for the Hammerheads, his vision for the future, so to speak. In all honesty, we often can't keep up and end up falling asleep while listening to him. Then, when we wake, he's already risen or hasn't gone to bed, and has sketched out his plans on paper or whatever flat surface he can find. All for the future of Old Kiln, his plans, that's what they're for. But you know what, he doesn't want to stop with Old Kiln. He says once we're done here, we've got to move on to the next place, to Luozhen and the county capital. We're Chairman Mao's army, we wear the hats, the armbands and have his buttons too. We're the Red Hammerheads, keepers of Chairman Mao's Little Red Book!"

"Oh, I had no idea Bash had become a people's artist."

"He has, sir. His revolutionary ambition shines brighter than anyone's. It's part of every fibre of his being. No one noticed it before, it's only the Great Proletarian Cultural Revolution that has brought it out."

Awning could hold his tongue no longer. "Artistic, bah, he's insane!" And with that, he spun on his heels and marched away. As he noticed the roses on Barndoor's wall, he could hear Useless prattling on.

"If Bash had been born in the city, he'd be a well-renowned artist for sure, surely at the level of Lightkeeper's brother-in-law, if not higher. Artistic ability needs imagination, but other people often regard imagination as insanity. I read that somewhere, in a book. I also remember a famous saying: the artist and insanity walk hand in hand."

"It's a pity," Wu Gan said, "that Bash has never truly had the opportunity to become a real artist."

"So very true," Useless responded. "It's regrettable indeed that he was born in Old Kiln, this small, out-of-the-way village. But if such is our lot, if being born in a backward rural shithole prevents us from becoming artists, then revolutionaries we shall be."

Wu Gan couldn't contain his laughter.

The roses had waylaid Awning, who stopped to stare at them a little more, finally asking, "How have you managed to get them to grow so well when so many of us are jaundiced and little more than skin and bones?"

"It's about how they're looked after," answered Flower Girl. "If you visit them daily, speak to them, they'll flourish. That morning glory on your screen, how did you get it to grow so well?"

"Fuck if I know."

"Then it must be by sin."

"You better look after your roses. I heard what Useless said, they're planning some bloody painted tower in the middle of the village. Wouldn't surprise me if they end up tearing your wall down."

"But these roses are my soul, who'd dare destroy them? I'll fight anyone who tries."

"You can fight? How?"

"Well, whoever wants the fish dead must always contend with the fish that wants to tear the net."

"Ha, ha, you're right there, and all you get is a dead fish and a torn net."

Walking together, Inkcap and Cowbell saw Apricot through her courtyard door as she busily beat her clothes against the laundry stone. She was very methodical, soaking the clothes first in the same hot water that had been used to cook rice, then drying it for what seemed like ages. Once a suitable amount of time had passed, she laid the clothes out flat on the stone before proceeding to pound them as though milling grain. She put great effort into cleaning, using nearly every muscle in her body. Her backside undulated with vigorous movement, and her breasts heaved with each gulp of air.

Cowbell leaned in close to Inkcap. "Heh, I don't think she's wearing a bra."

"Geez, don't bloody stare!"

"How can I not with her pounding her clothes so, so... forcefully? I bet Bash enjoys the sight."

Whether Apricot could hear the boys or not, her expression did not change, but she halted her washing abruptly and closed the courtyard gate. The boys halted their steps, too, pretending to be oblivious to her presence through the gate. They turned their attention to a nearby tree and saw a single leaf that had become detached from its branch. It drifted towards them before settling on the ground. In the alleyway a little farther off, they could see Awning escorting Wu Gan, dropping in on houses on both sides. In some, wives could be seen sweeping and occasionally complaining about the bits of mud being tracked across their courtyards by dirty shoes.

Again, Cowbell leaned in towards Inkcap. "You suppose he'll call on Apricot?"

"Well, I don't think he called on the Secretary, wouldn't that mean he won't call on her either?"

"How's he so freaking tall?" Cowbell said, turning his attention to Wu Gan.

"Soldiers have to be. He's deadly with a pistol too. Last year when he visited the militia, he put them all to shame with his precision, hitting every target in the bull's eye."

"I need a closer look."

"He loves kicking people too."

The two of them walked in the direction of Wu Gan and Awning, but neither dared get too close. Better to keep some distance, they figured. They stopped, finally, outside Barndoor's place, where they discovered something unexpected. Floating in the urinal pit, which was just outside Barndoor's courtyard wall, was a dead cat.

"Sister, sister!" said Cowbell. "Your cat's dead, it's here in the shitter!"

Flower Girl had no idea the two boys were just outside her home, but when Cowbell yelled, her first reaction was to grab a bamboo stick and storm off in their direction, yelling, "Bandits, brigands, you're after my flowers. Thieves!" Then she meowed for her cat, calling for it plaintively. To the surprise of Cowbell and Inkcap, moments later a cat bounded into view.

Inkcap looked at Cowbell and whispered, "Who's stealing her flowers, more likely Noisy's coming for you!" And he withdrew a little from where they stood.

Flower Girl called out once more, "My cat's here, so the one in the urinal isn't mine. That means someone put it there. Who could it be? Inkcap... fish it out, it deserves a proper burial at least."

Inkcap did as instructed. At the same time, Awning began to dig the hole, while Flower Girl urged him repeatedly to dig it deep, otherwise the carcass would rot and there'd be too many maggots.

Wu Gan couldn't help but overhear the commotion. "What the devil is going on?" he asked Useless.

"Here I've been giving you a report and you've not heard a word, have you? Now you're asking me about what's going on outside?"

"Oh, nothing, don't worry about it."

"All right, then, what's say we head over to the Hammerheads' HQ? That way you can relay to us any new directives we're to begin."

"They're burying a dead cat," said Wu Gan, more to himself. Then, stepping into the alleyway, he called out, "Hey, Awning, what are you doing, leaving me here to look at some flowers!"

"Wasn't Useless giving you a report?"

"I've walked through most of Old Kiln now, but the flowers up on that wall, they're the prettiest I've seen. I imagine quite a beauty resides inside."

"Come now, Cadre Lu," Flower Girl responded bashfully. "We've never met, how could you make such certain claims to my supposed beauty?"

Useless rose from where he had been seated, catching a glimpse of Wu Gan's notebook as he did. None of what he had reported had been written down. Instead, the only words he spied were bastard, sonofabitch, local bullies and thugs, lazy rascal, careerist, mental case, crazy fuck. Useless's face burned red. Outside he could see Wu Gan chatting amiably with Flower Girl. His only option was to quietly exit through the rear gate, hopefully unnoticed.

Useless had been humiliated. It never occurred to him that Wu Gan would behave in this manner. Naturally, as soon as he arrived back at the Hammerheads, he began to denounce Wu Gan in front of Bash and anyone else who could hear.

Bash's initial response was to simply mumble under his breath that the situation was deadly serious. Raising his head high then lower until he looked directly at Useless, he said, "Why the hell did you tell him so much?"

"I, I… I was only trying to get his support."

"This Wu Gan, damn, didn't you know he was tight with Pockmark? There's no way he'd visit Old Kiln on his own. Awning had to have invited him. I wouldn't be surprised if they're trying to organise their own revolutionary unit."

"Impossible."

"Why? The Hammerheads are mostly Heis, right, and a few others. I wouldn't put it past those damn Zhus to try to set themselves up against us. And if they do, who's to say the few Zhus that are with us won't up and leave?"

"No… they wouldn't, would they?"

"We'd best make preparations."

Useless couldn't help but feel Bash was overreacting, at least to a degree, but he had to admire the man's intuition and insight, more so after learning later that same night that Awning had established a new revolutionary unit, the Red Blades, headquartered in the old public office. Awning and his men had broken open the locks they'd put on the building not long ago, purposefully shouting, as they did, that they were breaking the old and ushering in the new, taking people's ownership of the old public office. Palace had even been ordered to collect cannons from Secretary Zhu's home and relocate them to their new revolutionary headquarters, the same cannons that were fired for village festivals, or when hailstones had fallen. The significance was not lost on Bash and the Hammerheads, even if, unbeknownst to them, Branch Secretary Zhu had been less than pleased with Palace showing up at his home.

"Secretary, sir, have you found them?"

"Yes, I've located three, but one is useless, the metal's corroded."

"That's all right. But listen, you're an old hand at using these, I reckon you should come with me back to our headquarters. What do you say?"

"I say you're a damn fool. When you go back, tell them I didn't have the cannons. Tell them they were at Apricot's house. Tell them they should get her to come along."

"Sorry, sir, but that's not possible. Apricot has that… connection to Bash, she can't be trusted."

"Then tell them you got the cannons from Ever-Obedient's place."

Palace did as instructed. Later in the night, the cannons sounded. Three times.

After supper, the Red Blades held their first mass meeting. Even though the Hammerheads had confiscated most of the drums and gongs that could be found in Old Kiln, Ever-Obedient still managed to bring a few to the meeting.

Gourd was first to notice the gong. "Say, Ever-Obedient, I heard you could down a full bowl of dried millet in the time it takes for a gong echo to die, is that true?"

"No, I can finish the millet and two bowls of pickled veg as well!"

"You liar. I don't believe you."

"If you don't believe me, then go get a bowl of millet. I'll wait and then prove I can do it–"

"I asked you to ring the bloody gong," Awning yelled. "What the devil are you going on about?"

Ever-Obedient looked to Gourd. "Dare me?"

"I'll give you a dare!" Awning roared.

Ever-Obedient hurriedly clanged the gong.

Throughout the exchange, Inkcap had been nearby, holding onto the cannon, waiting as Sparks filled it with gunpowder. Once finished, Inkcap turned to Awning, excited about the noise they were about to make. Awning, however, had other things in mind. "Go and get your gran, Inkcap, I'd like her here."

"Get my gran?"

"Well, this is a people's meeting, isn't it? She should be here, shouldn't she?"

Alas, Inkcap felt no joy at having to collect his gran, his emotions clear to her when he showed up at home.

"Gran… there's a mass meeting tonight, you've got to come."

"At this hour, with the chickens already brought in and dinner on the stove? You stay here and eat. I'll go and see what's going on."

Inkcap did as he was told, but while eating he cursed Awning, thinking the man was no better than Bash. Then, just as he was finishing his food, Gran reappeared.

"There's no meeting. I don't know where you heard it, but I went to the usual place, and no one was there."

"That's because it's being held in the old public office."

"The old public office? Surely not."

"It's not the Hammerheads, they didn't call the meeting. Awning and Millstone called it, they've formed a new revolutionary unit, the Red Blades. I know they've never been nice to you in the past, but Awning asked me personally to come and collect you. I don't really know what for."

"So they're making revolution too, are they?"

"Isn't everybody?"

Gran sat down and began to rub the corns on her feet. They'd burst while she was walking, and blood was now staining her socks. She rubbed a little more before responding, "Go fetch me my clean shirt, it's hanging on a rope by the back window."

"You want to change your clothes in the dark?"

"I better look my best for this meeting, it's likely my last."

"Why do you say that?"

"Well," she began slowly, "your old gran, like Lightkeeper, or I suppose old Goodman, we've no influence left in this village. If we're being called to a meeting, well, it's best to be prepared. Sooner or later, the Red Blades and the Hammerheads will come to blows, and then there'll be no one left to even consider us."

Inkcap mulled his gran's words over in his mind before replying, "I think that'd be best, wouldn't it? I mean, if there's no one left to be concerned about us, then they won't be bullying us either."

"Perhaps, but you and I, we're not like anyone else, we're still different. Whatever the Red Blades end up doing, whatever the Hammerheads do, the main thing is for you not to follow either of them, you want them to forget you're even here, that's what's best. But, boy, let me tell you something, you're always running about, this way and that, and you shoot your mouth off far too much. Remember what I'm telling you, you want them to forget."

"Here we go again, you're always telling me this."

"See, right there, you can't keep your mouth shut. Are you afraid you'll explode if you keep quiet?"

"And if I did, you'd be without a grandson."

He ran outside and stopped under the apricot tree in their courtyard. "Gran, I'm thirsty, can I have some water?"

She ignored him, busy unbuttoning her jacket.

Inkcap looked at the tree. "You only drink water, right? Me too."

FIFTY

Since most of the Red Blades shared the Zhu family name, one by one, those Zhus who'd been in the Hammerheads withdrew and joined up with the Red Blades instead. Naturally, there were some awkward feelings involved, and some complaining too, questions about why the Red Blades hadn't been formed before now, or why hadn't the Zhus got themselves more organised in the first place. After all, wasn't it the Yangs who were supposed to protect the Song dynasty, not the Zhus?

The Red Blades also had their own board for tacking up big-character posters, but they didn't call them that, they just referred to their posters as propaganda. It was placed near the mountain gate, at Three Fork Alley that stretched through the village. There was an old tree adjacent to the board. Its bark, flowers and leaves had medicinal qualities, but it was so aged and so heavily pruned that it was mostly bare. Even its trunk had been hollowed out and was now filled with bricks and mortar. Three smaller alleys forked out from behind it. One led to Sparks' family home, their door opening to the east and onto the gable that ran the length of the main alley. This was where the propaganda board was placed. Useless had been responsible for emblazoning it with its largest slogan: "The red hammer smashes the old world".

Sometime later, Sparks was discovered shovelling earth on the slogan, and while Useless's mother saw him in the act, his only response was that he was shovelling the earth off his own home's wall, and that was nobody's business but his own. Once he'd finished and the wall was now suitably thick, Sparks proceeded to tack a wooden frame to make the propaganda board clearly distinguishable. Afterwards, whenever any Zhu left the Hammerheads to join the Red Blades, notice was made on the board, welcoming them to the revolutionary unit. This continued over several days, causing Old Kiln to transform into a sizzling frying pan, oil spattering this way and that, raising the overall temperature of the village inhabitants. At mealtimes, people took to holding their bowls and staring out of their courtyard gates into the alleys beyond. Should their eyes fall on a passerby, they would saunter over to them, asking who'd left whom now, who still remained with whom and so on, nattering away and nearly forgetting to eat altogether.

Old Kiln was split into two factions, each claiming to be the revolutionary vanguard, each calling themselves Mao's Red Guards, each fighting the other, like wrists in a vice, both trying to take the lead. In the past, the fifteenth day of the first lunar month was designated as the day to celebrate communal festivities. Troupes of villagers would travel between Old Kiln, Xiahewan, Xichuan and Dongchuan, evaluating and comparing the progress the villages had made over the past year. The Branch Secretary, in his desire to pump himself up, praised and honoured the accomplishments of Old Kiln, separating the villagers into two groups, one naturally filled with members holding the Zhu family name, the other the Heis. Both factions were, unsurprisingly, eager to compete against the other, keen to prove their own acuity and the impotence of their adversary.

Inkcap and Cowbell were perhaps even more anonymous at this time, with no one really paying them any mind whatsoever. This did not stop them, however, from being used as information couriers between the two factions, informing on the plans of the other, such as one faction's plan to perform a scene connected to *Journey to the West*, something about the Monkey King's golden headband and his confrontation with the demoness White Bone Spirit, the other group drawing on the folktale of *Dong Yong and the Seventh Fairy*, or perhaps it was the story of the Cowherd and the Weaving Girl, some heavenly match or other. Neither Inkcap nor Cowbell was especially accurate in relating what the other factions were up to, but it kept them busy enough.

What couldn't be denied was that they were the happiest of all the villagers at this time. Although Cowbell was ostensibly a member of the Hammerheads, meaning he couldn't go anywhere near the Red Blades headquarters, this didn't stop Inkcap from dragging him back and forth to this place and that, following whatever commotion they could find. For his part, Inkcap had forgotten the advice of his gran to stay out of the way, instead choosing to consider all of this part of the holiday festivities. He didn't care if the other villagers hurled insults at him or ran him down, he was like a mosquito buzzing about, not upset about the filth he had to wade through. Such was his lot, wasn't it? And if the happiness he was feeling made him forget his social standing, he knew the humiliation would, if nothing else, keep him grounded.

"You're a bad seed, you are, Inkcap," Useless shouted at him. "How's it you look happier than me?"

"What do you mean, surely I get along with everyone!"

"Pah, what tosh. You're Inkcap, a dwarf, a cripple. You've got rocks for brains, you'd be better off being a millstone pounding grain."

Some people were given to considering themselves more important than they were, while others took the opposite tack and thought very little of themselves, even if it wasn't true. Useless's words did nothing to rile Inkcap, who had begun to resign himself to the fact that the villagers ran him down simply to make themselves feel better rather than believing he was a bad influence. It had taken a while to come to this realisation; for a long time he'd wished he was taller, like Lightkeeper, perhaps, but then he thought what was the point? After all, if he were as tall as Lightkeeper, who'd be able to speak to him face to face? Hence, he'd ceased dreaming about being taller. Nor did he continue to measure himself against the tree that stood guard over the alleyways.

"Ha ha," he replied to Useless, "I might have bricks for brains, and I'm certainly not able to make a wall, but throw some of these bricks in the street and I'll be sure to trip you up! Sure, I might be no better than a laundry stone, but if you're the clothes, I'm sure to pound you silly. In the winter I'll freeze you, in the summer you'll burn. Either way, you'll be dead."

Ever after, Inkcap would gaze fondly at the bricks scattered through the village, the laundry stones, too, thinking they were all his dear friends.

One day, as he was returning from collecting the day's water, he spied a brick on the path. He'd not noticed it before, but on the way back he did, quickly stopping in front of it and laying the water pole and the jugs of water to one side,

"I don't suppose you're here waiting for me deliberately, are you?"

Naturally, no reply came.

But Inkcap persisted. "Ah, so you think you can keep more still than me, eh?" He lifted one of the jugs and tipped some of the water over the brick. He knew the brick couldn't ignore him any more, drenched as it now was. He also knew that the brick was aware he was talking to it. He picked up the brick and placed it on a nearby courtyard wall. As he did so, he spotted Yoyo sauntering towards him.

Yoyo had suffered several epileptic attacks. And even when she wasn't enduring a seizure, simply walking and talking was a strain. She'd actually intended to call on Inkcap's gran, but he told her she wasn't in. She then showed him her newly dyed measure of cloth, wondering what he thought of it. To Inkcap's eyes, it was a mess, as though a dog had chewed it before the dye took, leaving a blotted pattern.

"So, what do you think?"

"Hmm, I think it would be better if it weren't dyed."

"You know your name's up on the propaganda board, right? Have you not gone to see it yet?"

Thinking she was only babbling nonsense, Inkcap replied, "Yeah, that's great, I'm bringing credit to Gran's name."

"Like hell you are."

Inkcap changed his tone somewhat. "You mean my name really is up there?"

"No one told you, I guess, but then again, who would want to? Well, I suppose I would, since I just did."

"What's it there for?"

"Why, do you think you've won something?"

Forgetting the water, Inkcap walked off in the direction of Three Fork Alley and the propaganda board. On the way, he saw a cat toying with a mouse, the tiny creature skittering back and forth before the cat pounced on it. A moment passed. The cat relented and the mouse attempted to scurry away, only to be seized by the cat again. This game tracked all the way down the alley as though the animals were following behind Inkcap. Finally, he intervened, grabbing the mouse by the tail and lifting it high above the malevolent cat. As he did so, he spotted Almost-There standing beside the gate to Sparks' home.

"Hey, Almost-There," he yelled. "I've got a mouse for you to burn."

Setting fire to rodents was a common pastime in Old Kiln. They were a pest, after all, and quite fair game. First, you'd catch one, then douse it in oil and set a match to it. The creature would explode into flame and then it would be released so that the small fireball would scurry this way and that before collapsing. Many villagers took part. But it was better at night, a more vibrant spectacle, as it were.

"Set that mouse on fire, you better be careful they don't do the same to you," Almost-There shot back.

"Who'd dare, I'll fuck him up."

"Fuck him up, eh? A little shit like you? Come on, tell me, do you still need to use a stool to climb into bed?"

Inkcap, the rodent still in his hand, walked past Almost-There without another word. Inside the courtyard of the Red Blades HQ, he saw the board and the white paper pasted to it. Scribbled with black characters, he turned back to Almost-There who'd followed him in.

"What's it say?"

With great effort, Almost-There read, "Declaration. Inkcap has bullied me. How? He forced me into joining the Hammerheads. I state today that I want to remove myself from this forced belonging, I'm no longer a Hammerhead, I'm now a Red Blade. Signed. Cowbell."

The words exploded in Inkcap's mind. He stared hard at the poster, the characters like burning stars in the sky. His hand released the mouse and it fell to the floor. But it didn't dart away.

Inkcap lifted his foot over the creature and said, "You better fucking run."

With that, the mouse beat a hasty retreat. Inkcap's eyes seemed to grow sticky. He looked at Almost-There and asked, "Cowbell wrote this?"

"It seems so."

"It can't be, I mean, Cowbell doesn't know how to write."

"OK, so maybe he didn't write it himself, but it would be easy enough to get someone to write it for him, wouldn't it?"

"When everyone else was enlisting in the Hammerheads, it was Cowbell who told me we should too. I told him to go ahead, but that I wouldn't be accepted, considering my background, so he joined them on his own. And now he says this shit?"

Inkcap reached out to tear the poster down, but Almost-There stopped him. "I wouldn't dare do that, they'll think you're trying to stop the Cultural Revolution. Don't say I didn't warn you, but if you still want to go ahead, wait for me to leave first."

Inkcap turned rigidly and ran through the open gate. His whole body felt as though it were on fire, his face red and burning. Shame. This is what he felt. And the red of that shame turned to black, then to a deep aubergine colour. Cowbell, ah Cowbell. Inkcap couldn't believe it. If all Cowbell had wanted to do was leave the Hammerheads, why the hell did he drag him into it? And not only that, why did he get someone to write that damn poster? Ah, Cowbell. My friend. Goddamn fucker. Returning to his water jugs, Inkcap was relieved no one was about. He picked them up and returned home, barring himself inside for the remainder of the day.

What made matters worse for Inkcap was the response of the Red Blades to Cowbell's declaration. Three new posters were soon affixed to the propaganda board, each welcoming Cowbell's abandonment of the darkness of the Hammerheads and then using that to launch their own attacks, claiming that they were the true representatives of the revolutionary vanguard, that their ranks were made up of the genuine poor and indigent, indeed, eighty per cent of their members belonged to the poor and lower classes of the peasantry, and, most important, no one in their ranks belonged to the Five Black Categories, unlike other supposedly revolutionary units who'd been taking advantage of the Cultural Revolution to make their own, personal gains. Traitors to the party bent on stirring up trouble.

Naturally, none of the posters called the Hammerheads out by name, but Inkcap was a different case altogether. He was, after all, a Bad Element. The grandson of an officer in the puppet Kuomintang Army who were biding their time before launching a counterattack from Taiwan to try to retake the mainland. No doubt Inkcap belonged to several clandestine counterrevolutionary groups. And no doubt they were plotting and scheming, roping in poor dupes like Cowbell, cheating and deceiving, instigating and abetting all kinds of criminal activities, including taking advantage of poor Cowbell, causing him to board the wrong boat, leading him astray. And what was all of this for? For the Kuomintang in Taiwan? The Soviet revisionists? For the traitors within and without? All of the above, for their cause was the downfall of the revolution!

Not long after the Red Blades posters were put up, the Hammerheads followed suit a day later, but they did them two better by hanging five posters instead of three. Also, unlike the Red Blades, the Hammerheads had no qualms about naming who they were struggling against. They blamed the Red Blades for inciting Cowbell to defect, and used his defection to claim the Red Blades were purposefully trying to spread rumours and mislead the villagers. Their evil intent, the Hammerheads claimed, was as plain as the treachery of Sima Zhao. As for Cowbell, he was a turncoat, a changeling, a fair-weather friend if ever there was one. And as for Inkcap, the grandson of a Kuomintang officer, he had no connection to the

Hammerheads, nothing to do with them whatsoever. His allegiance lay with the Red Blades, and what did that say about them? The Hammerheads, they stressed, were a true revolutionary unit, hardened by struggle. The Red Blades were littered with all kinds of Bad Elements, opportunists everyone, all bent on taking advantage of the situation to get what they wanted, to overturn Heaven itself, most likely. They had wolf hearts, cold and calculating. Their existence was intolerable.

The posters hung by the Hammerheads contained more sentences, their words were newer, their vehemence greater. And for this reason, they garnered more curiosity. Unsurprisingly, the Hammerheads were quite pleased with themselves, resulting in Awning berating Soupspoon for not being as capable a writer as Useless evidently was.

"Aren't you supposed to be the most cultured person in Old Kiln?" he said. "How's it you're a worse writer than that bastard Useless?"

Shamed by the attack, Soupspoon launched his own defence. "Listen here, Useless made it to middle school, I only ever got as far as elementary. I'm sure he copied those words too, from some other poster, no way he came up with all of that on his own. And besides, isn't he a Zhu? If you can't get him to switch to the Red Blades, then it's like letting your own dog bite your own arse."

It didn't take long for the entire Zhu clan in Old Kiln to begin badmouthing Useless as a traitor and turncoat. As a result, he scaled back his efforts to paint portraits of Chairman Mao around the village. Some even let loose their dogs to try to bite him. Soon he took to only ever going out with Bash, like a fox acquiring the fierceness of the tiger by walking in its shadow.

Worse off was Inkcap. Both factions had labelled him a Bad Element. The grandson of an officer in the Kuomintang Puppet Army. A class enemy. His previous and at times cheerful energy was gone. He rarely left his room, to say nothing of stepping outside. And when he did go beyond the front door of his house, the heat he felt was unbearable. Even when Gran urged him to go and hang around the village as he used to, Inkcap refused.

"I can't... I'm afraid of... everyone. All they'll do is curse and spit on me."

"But you need to get out, and besides, so long as they don't beat you, let them have their insults, pretend you don't hear them."

"I've got ears, Gran, how do I not hear them?"

"Think of the wind blowing instead."

"But their words won't be the wind."

She moved closer and embraced him, soon feeling his tears moisten her shoulder. He noticed she too had started crying.

"Gran, I'll go out."

As he stepped out beyond his courtyard, he crumpled several leaves together and stuffed them into his ears so he wouldn't hear any sounds. While this worked for his ears, he wasn't sure what to do about his eyes. All he could hope for was that he wouldn't bump into anyone. As luck would have it, the alleyway was deserted, giving him some measure of confidence that things would be all right. Unfortunately, his luck would betray him almost immediately, for under one of the towering trees just beyond the mouth of the alley a group of villagers were busily arguing, and he had no choice but to steal a retreat, hoping they hadn't seen him.

"Back already," said Gran as soon as she saw him trudge through the courtyard gate.

"Swallow called me back."

She knew in her heart that Inkcap had little inclination to venture out again, so she chose not to challenge him. "You know, I thought I heard Swallow calling you too. I think she said something about the wind blowing rather fiercely around the eaves and her being worried about her nest. Perhaps she wants you to help her move it?"

"You heard right, Gran, that's exactly what she asked me to do. How about we do it together?"

"That sounds like a plan."

Together, they moved Swallow's nest to a more sheltered area of the roof. They were careful and precise, making sure not to dislodge a single straw or fibre. As they worked, Swallow perched nearby watching them intently. Once they were finished, the bird lifted itself into the air and up into the nest, singing all the while.

"Gran, do you know the song Swallow is singing?"

"What do you think it is?"

"The sun sets over the western mountains, the soldiers return to camp from target practice, return to camp..."

This was the very same song that Awning and the local militia had sung during training. Now, quite literally, the sun had set over the western mountains, painting the sky a brilliant red.

Gran enjoyed watching Inkcap sing, but she noticed he was soon drenched with sweat. "Inkcap, my boy, I think you need to head to the spring to wash. You can collect some more water for us while you're at it."

His head tilted towards the sky, Inkcap replied, "But Gran, I'm not hot at all, and don't we still have water in the barrel? I'll fetch some tomorrow, OK?"

The following morning, not long after sunrise, Inkcap, still afraid of encountering other villagers, set off to fetch more water. On his way back, just as he reached one of the stone lions that crouched at the corner of the alley, a group of men saddled into view. It was too late to hide. All he could do was lower the water jugs to the ground and bound over into the nearby grass to pretend to be taking a shit. He tried to position himself behind the stone lion, hoping it would block their view of him, but the lion had long since fallen over on its side and was not able to hide him. In a panic, he grabbed some leaves from a castor bean plant and held them over his head. It did little more than prevent him from seeing the oncoming people, but to Inkcap's mind, if he couldn't see them, surely they wouldn't be able to see him.

"Hey Inkcap, what the hell are you doing back there?"

Inkcap didn't dare answer.

"Do you really think that because you can't see us we can't see you? You damn fool."

Pulling the leaves back from his eyes, Inkcap smiled up at them. "I'm trying to poo."

Several voices now rang out. "You dirty fucker, taking a dump on the side of the road."

"But I haven't, look," Inkcap replied as he hastily got to his feet. "I've not been able to drop even one little turd."

A few villagers moved closer to check the accuracy of Inkcap's statement. When they saw nothing on the grass, they turned and kicked him in the rump, each villager, one after the other.

Later in the day, Gran accompanied Inkcap to the riverbank. The area was dense with reeds and cattails, their flowers and leaves like the snow of autumn when the wind took them, lifting them into the sky. On this day, however, there was no wind, and the flowers did not blanket the sky. Rather, they covered the ground, piles of dried and decaying leaves mixed in among the sand of the riverbank. Inkcap's gran bent over to gather the flowers and leaves together. It was like she was sweeping up clouds, if clouds could be swept. Despite the seeming futility of her actions, she did succeed in collecting a fair bundle of dried greenery, which she scooped up and stuffed into a sack she had brought. Inkcap didn't join in the sweeping, spending his time instead transfixed by the scene, its stillness, its erectness, the gurgling sounds of the river just beyond the reeds, the flap of birds' wings, the pattering of clawed feet in the underbrush.

No one in Old Kiln could understand why Inkcap and his gran were at the riverbank, but they agreed it wasn't necessarily a good thing. Surely, they weren't just there collecting the fallen flowers and reeds, they had to be up to something else. They could hear Inkcap and Gran speaking, but their voices were too low to make anything out. What were they doing? It was unfathomable, the villagers thought. After all, why would they be clomping around the riverbank at dusk, they must know the area was haunted. Didn't Sprout wander about here some time ago, didn't she bury her own head in the sand among the reeds? Just why the hell were they there? More confusing still was when Inkcap and Gran left. Instead of returning home, they walked in the direction of the Kiln God Temple, Inkcap being dragged behind his gran, seemingly against his will, his face scrunched up and panicky as though he were being led to a killing field.

Bash, Baldy Jin and Useless were standing beside the gate to the temple as Inkcap and Gran arrived. Coming to a stop in front of them, Gran forced Inkcap to kneel.

"You wasted sperm, you still haven't kowtowed to the Hammerheads. Go on, tell Bash, tell him now, are you a member of the Red Blades?"

"No, no, I'm not, I've… I've got nothing to do with them."

"Why you little shit," Baldy Jin said, "you're a Red Blade and you know it, but still you won't admit the truth."

"No, I really haven't joined them."

"Whose leg are you trying to pull? Your family name's Zhu isn't it? How can you not be a Red Blade?"

"Baldy Jin," Gran interjected, "careful with your words. You know the name of my clan, I'll give you a hint, eh, it's a kind of worm…"

"A kind of worm? Pah! A tiger is nothing more than a big insect, a snake a long insect, so what kind of insect does that make you? A louse? A flea?"

"I'd say we're both, and you, Baldy Jin, squish us under your fingernails all the time. That's why I said you should be careful about what you say, Baldy Jin–"

"All right, all right, Inkcap," said Bash, "if you've not joined the Red Blades, then you haven't. Go on, kowtow and go home. Come on, hurry up and get out of here."

Gran turned to Inkcap. "Do as he says, kowtow… another, show the respect they're due."

Inkcap complied, kowtowing three times before Gran pulled him up and said, "Enough, let's go."

Again, they did not go home. This time, they marched over to the headquarters of the Red Blades. Unlike the Hammerheads, however, the entrance to the Red Blades had been concealed with vegetation, for which Granny Silkworm paid no heed, pushing them aside and calling into the courtyard, "Awning, Awning!"

In response to her holler, Noodle Fish sauntered towards them. "And what are you two doing here?"

"Are there any Red Blades here or what?"

Now it was Awning's turn to saunter out, coming to a halt on the raised deck in front of the courtyard gate. "What do you want?" he asked.

As she had done in front of the Hammerheads, Granny Silkworm pressed her fingers into her grandson's shoulders, forcing him to kneel and perform the kowtow.

"And what the hell is he kowtowing for? Well, if you're going to do it, make it three kowtows at least. Come on now, forehead to the ground."

Gran obeyed, again squeezing hard on Inkcap's shoulder. This time, Inkcap did not even lift his knees from the ground, instead slamming his head three times hard on the dirt.

"There," Granny Silkworm intoned. "Inkcap's admitted his mistake, he's apologised, he never joined the Hammerheads, nor did he urge Cowbell to join them."

"So that's why you've come, is it?"

"Well, wouldn't you? You should see the pain it's caused him. He's been at home crying these past three days, he's not been able to eat. I imagine he's given himself an ulcer."

"An ulcer, eh? You mean the little shit can still get an upset stomach?"

"If I'm telling a lie, may lightning strike me dead."

"All right, all right, go on, get out of here, you've said your piece, we have a meeting to start…" Awning paused before continuing, "Tell me, what's in the sack?"

"Catkin floss, we just picked it at the riverbank. If you want some, that's fine, we can always collect more."

"And just what would I do with it?" With these words, Awning turned away from them and went back inside.

Noodle Fish walked over to where Inkcap was still lying prostrate on the ground. Lifting the boy up, he said, "I reckon your place in the clan is rather high, similar to Awning and Millstone. You've shown up here just because of some posters, why bother?"

"What does one's position in the clan mean in the grand scheme of things? The only thing I know for certain is that I'm not like anyone else."

"Yeah, you are, we're all just people in the end."

Gran said nothing more. She just put her hand on Inkcap's arm and dragged him out through the gate.

As they approached Three-Fork Alley, they spotted a large crowd milling about. Inkcap turned to his gran and said, "There're a lot of people there."

Gran did not respond. Instead, she drove her fingers into Inkcap's back, pressing hard to make sure it hurt. "How's that, eh?" she said. "Run, go on, run."

She raised her hand as if to box his ears, never thinking she'd make contact, but Inkcap didn't run and her hand fell hard against the back of her grandson's skull. He grimaced in pain, unsure what was going on. Instinct took over and he started to run, crying as he did. Receding into the background, he heard Gran's voice.

"You worthless piece of filth, you've still got the gumption to cry? One of these days, I'm going to do you in for sure, you no-good grandson of a traitor son, you hear me? Tell me true, who did you join, the Hammerheads or the Red Blades? Ah, you damnable bad seed, you bring nothing but misfortune and calamity, ruin, that's what you are, ruin, poison, you destroy everything around you, don't you? Ahh!" Her voice trailed off into rapid breathing and her knees buckled, slamming into the ground.

The bystanders had watched the scene unfold, assuming Inkcap had provoked his grandmother's ire, thus deserving the punishment he got. They laughed when she had boxed his ears. But none of them intervened, not until Granny Silkworm collapsed. Soupspoon was the first to walk over towards her.

"He was born useless, you know that Gran, there's nothing for it. What's the point of hitting him?"

"Aiya... what did I do to deserve this, why was I given such a grandson? One moment, he's with the Hammerheads, the next with the Red Blades, he'll follow anyone, like some dumb little dog. Tell me it isn't true."

"Hey, I don't think he's either one, not a Hammerhead or a Red Blade."

"You really think... then what about the posters?"

Soupspoon laughed. "Ah, Gran, he's just an easy target."

"But why him, why?"

"If not him, then who? Who else in Old Kiln is such an easy target?"

"I suppose... when you put it like that, it puts my heart at ease a little, but, but... he's still no better than pig shit, dog shit... just shit."

When she eventually reached home, Inkcap had already sent himself to bed and was sound asleep. She didn't wake him, choosing to let him slumber. That was best, she thought. But Inkcap's sleep was fitful and disturbed. He tossed and turned, entering in and out of consciousness, his mind turning over the events of the day. Gran had taken him to see the Hammerheads, then the Red Blades, forced him to kowtow to both, then she'd berated him in public, smacked him, hard and hate-filled. Was it all an act? Was she just trying to dispel any lingering suspicions? He regretted that despite hiding behind the castor bean leaves, the villagers could still see him. How was it that he couldn't see the others, but they could see him? An invisibility cloak, yes, that's what he wished he had, but what exactly was it? He rose from bed and began rummaging through the wardrobe. Every article of clothing he and Gran owned was in the wardrobe. He took every item out, trying them on.

"Gran," he called out, "hey, Gran, can you see me?"

"Ah, wipe your nose, will you."

Inkcap did as he was told and then changed into a new outfit. Again, he called out, "Gran, what about now, can you see me?"

"Eh, boy, look at your shoes. How did you ruin them again? Do your feet have teeth?"

Inkcap merely exhaled in reply.

"All right," Gran said, "why are you going through every piece of clothing in the house?"

"Gran, if we had just one invisibility cloak, that'd be great."

"Ah, boy, what are you talking about, clothes that make you invisible?"

Inkcap plopped down onto the floor and began to cry.

When morning dawned, Gran was awakened by crying. She lifted her tired frame from the bed and went to check on Inkcap. Still asleep, he was crying, gurgling and spasming all over. Concerned, she leant in and stirred him awake.

"Wake up Inkcap, you're dreaming. Come on, wake up."

His eyes opened slowly and he realised he must have been dreaming. His dream had been so real, and he remembered all of it.

"Who was tormenting you in your dream, boy? You know it was just a dream, nothing to be afraid of. I'm here, no one is going to hurt you."

Inkcap refrained from telling her the details of his dream. He only nodded in response before plunging himself into her bosom, his arms wrapping tight around her. But her breasts had long since dried and offered little comfort.

"There's nothing left, my boy, nor are you the age to nurse."

It hadn't been that long ago, however, when she had gone through the ritual of nursing him, only two years in fact. Despite the absence of milk, Inkcap would hold on tight to her breast, the nipple in his mouth. It was the only way he could sleep. Now, though, her words shocked him back to the present and he released his grip.

"Gran, there's no such thing as an invisibility cloak, is there?"

"An invisibility cloak?"

Her words were as vivid now as in his dream and he lifted his face to look at her. "I hate my grandad."

Granny Silkworm's eyes bulged. Her first reaction was to berate and scold him, but she immediately regretted the impulse. Instead, she pulled him close once more. "And why hate your grandfather? I'm sure he never meant you any harm. No one wants to suffer, but life wouldn't be life without it, everyone has their own pain to endure, and that's the key, endurance. Now listen to what I tell you, when you're next outside, if someone hits your right cheek, give them the left to hit as well. And should someone else strike you, do the same. I guarantee you they won't."

Her advice finished, Granny Silkworm released herself from his grip and pulled her up with him. "Come on now," she said, "out you go."

"But... I don't want to see... them."

"For the rest of your life? Go, you have to. Sure, both the Hammerheads and Red Blades have used your name for their own battles, but you just have to forget it."

He asked the first person he saw if there was any work he could do.

After their work in the fields combatting insect infestation, the soil around the roots of their crops had been heaped high. The cabbage seeds that had been sprinkled over the earth had also begun to sprout. As a result, for the time being at least, there was no farm work to be done, so the villagers decided to go over to South Mountain to cut the grass.

In the past, Inkcap and Cowbell had often participated in this work, with Inkcap's job being to carry one of the large baskets used for collecting the grass. The basket, winched around his shoulders and down to his legs, was so big that from a distance no one could see him, only the basket moving across the pastureland. It was hard work, harder even for Inkcap, who had to pause repeatedly to tamp down the collected grass, sometimes even climbing into the basket itself to push it down with his whole body. When full, the baskets would weigh forty or fifty pounds. Inkcap, naturally enough, did not enjoy the work. Cowbell, on the other hand, was contented, only inasmuch as he didn't really do as instructed. Instead of filling his basket with feed for the animals, he would scrounge around in the undergrowth, picking up wild plumage to stuff in the bottom and give the appearance of fullness without the weight. Now, of course, Inkcap had no desire to work with Cowbell. Instead of calling on him to go into the fields together, as he walked by Cowbell's house, his basket and shovel in hand, he spat and continued onwards.

It wasn't until late in the afternoon that the work was completed. Inkcap had dried snacks with him but had started eating them almost as soon as he left home. Well, not really eating, he thought, more tasting. In the past, Gran usually gave him dried sweet potato slices, but on this occasion, she'd made him sweet potato flat cakes. They were delicious, he thought, and before long he'd eaten nearly all that she had made for him, stuffing his mouth with abandon before realising only one flat cake was left. At the riverbank, he stopped and resisted the urge to finish off his food. He warned himself against overindulgence, then knelt to scoop some water into his mouth. When he raised his head, he spied Lightkeeper in the pasture, cutting grass. His legs were far longer than Inkcap's and his trousers were rolled up almost to the knee.

"Hey, Lightkeeper... brother, you're out here too?"

"What else would I be doing?"

Inkcap removed his trousers, rolled his upper garment up to his chest and walked into the river, calling out as he did, "Oh, there's no work at the kiln, no one's bothered with it, are they? You ought to go to your sister's."

"I have a letter from my sister, she'd rather be here in Old Kiln. The Cultural Revolution is in the city too."

"You mean it's chaos there as well?"

"Even more than in the countryside."

The water didn't reach his chest, but the stones below the surface were soft and slippery and Inkcap staggered a little to the side.

"Just ahead of you, the riverbed dips. You'll go right over your head. Go on, check it out."

"Fuck you."

"Hey, let me ask you something, are you a Hammerhead or what?"

"No, I'm not."

"A Red Blade, then?"

"No. Didn't you hear what happened? My gran just beat me in front of the whole village because of this. Everyone knows I'm not a Hammerhead, nor a Red Blade. Why the hell are you asking?"

"Oh, you thought she'd beat you and that'd be the end of it? Cowbell said you forced him into joining the Hammerheads. Awning genuinely believes you're one of their members. And even if you're not an official member, he reckons your heart leans in their direction. Awning can be a bit hard-hearted, don't you think he'll always hold a grudge against you?"

The thought had never occurred to Inkcap. But Lightkeeper had a point. Things were still rather serious. After a moment's reflection, he asked, "What do you think I should do?"

"Well, listen, and listen good."

"OK."

"Heh, if you'd listened to me before, you wouldn't be in the shit you're in now. But I guess that's beside the point. Awning and Half-Stick have a... close relationship. Baldy Jin is their cuckold. I reckon you need to make them hate each other more, or at least bring that hatred to the surface. Try to get Baldy Jin to be nicer to Cowbell too. If you do that, Awning will end up hating Cowbell and suspect he's only there to spy on him for Baldy Jin."

"How am I supposed to get Baldy Jin to be nice to Cowbell?"

"You'll have to figure that out for yourself."

"But if Awning ends up hating Cowbell, I mean, that might be..."

"Wouldn't that be good for you, though? You'd get to watch the ruckus at least."

Inkcap mulled things over. Lightkeeper's plan was a dark one, and he hated Cowbell, that much was true, but Inkcap didn't want him hurt like this.

Lightkeeper, however, was unrelenting. "So what do you think? It's a good plan, isn't it?"

"Yeah... yeah, it is."

Together, Inkcap and Lightkeeper crossed the river to the other side. Lightkeeper suggested they work together nearer Eight Mile Ditch, where there was more grass. Inkcap, however, declined. "That's all right," he said, "I'll work on cutting the grass round here."

The grass wasn't all that long, but Inkcap did not take a rest, working until the sun angled low in the west, his basket just barely full. He was tired and hungry, and ready to cross back over the river. His stomach, however, suggested another action. He needed to release his bowels. Would pooing make him hungrier? Inkcap admonished his own silliness and squatted down low, his trousers round his ankles. Once finished, he raised himself and pulled up his trousers. At the same moment, his last remaining sweet potato flat cake fell out. While the flat cake wasn't exactly round, it hit the ground and rolled, right in the direction of the pile of shit he'd just left. Thank God, he thought, when the sweet potato cake came to a stop, a hand's length from his own filth. Snatching it up, he scanned the fields. No one was about. No one saw him. No one to laugh at him. The only witnesses were two birds perched in a nearby tree.

"Dirty!" one bird squawked.

"Not dirty!" squawked the other.

"It's not dirty," Inkcap said, "you're just trying to get me to leave it for you." With that, he stuffed the flat cake into his mouth, one, two, three bites and it was gone. "Nothing left," he shouted at them.

Inkcap picked up his basket once more and tromped off in the direction of Old Kiln. After some distance, he stopped to rest against a boulder. He soon spotted Cowbell emerging from an adjacent field, his basket seemingly full of cut grass. Inkcap couldn't help but think he was trying to fool everyone again, his basket filled more with useless feathers than feed for the village animals. He had the impulse to turn his head away but fought against it.

Cowbell called to him first, his voice dripping with pleasantness. Inkcap knew it was an act, that Cowbell was trying overly hard to be nice to him. And so he pretended not to hear. Cowbell called to him again, more pleadingly than the first time. Inkcap's stoicism wilted, and he turned his head in the direction of Cowbell.

"What the hell do you want?"

"I gathered some walnuts, you want a few?" Cowbell wasn't the only villager who would steal walnuts when out harvesting feed.

"Sure, I'll have some."

Inkcap looked at Cowbell's ears. They were misshapen and red as though they'd been nibbled by rats. Inkcap thought they looked more like pig's ears than human ears. "Hey, what's wrong with your ears?" he asked.

"I got stung by wasps. Hurts like hell. Feels like they're on fire."

Inkcap put his hand to his nose, blocked one nostril and then blew into his free hand. Thick mucus discharge covered his hand. He looked at Cowbell and raised the hand towards him. "Here, rub this over your ears, it'll help with the pain and swelling."

Plopping his basket on the ground, Cowbell replied, "I thought it was better to rub wasp stings with piss?"

Without waiting for an answer, Cowbell emptied the contents of the basket, not seeming to care about the inconvenience of having to pack the harvested feed again. Near the bottom, he pulled out four fresh walnut shells and laid them to one side. Then he proceeded to pick up the grass he'd just removed. After refilling his basket, he looked around for a suitable stone to crack the shells to get at the fleshy contents of the walnuts. Finding one, he smashed it against the shells, his fingers quickly staining from the carnage. He passed two of the walnuts to Inkcap, who devoured them without a further word.

Back at the village, Inkcap and Cowbell carried their baskets to the feed barn for weighing. Noodle Fish instructed them to place their baskets on the scales. Jotting down the results, he was surprised. "I must say, Inkcap's basket is usually much heavier than Cowbell's, but not today."

Inkcap paid no mind, instead focusing his attention on Awning and Soupspoon who were nearby playing chess. Inching towards them, he said, "Having a game of chess, eh?"

Awning cast him a glance then returned his attention to the game. "Out cutting the grass, were you?"

"That's right, yes."

"The Hammerheads have posted another poster today. They want the whole village to be painted red. You're not going to help?"

"I'm not a Hammerhead, so nobody came to get me."

"Is that so?" Awning continued playing chess, ignoring Inkcap.

Lightkeeper was right, thought Inkcap. Awning still harboured suspicions about him. His hatred for Cowbell grew. His basket empty, Cowbell had already started to depart, but Inkcap called after him, "Say, you're not going to share the walnuts you picked?"

"What walnuts?" came Cowbell's reply, rather too quickly.

Noodle Fish marched towards Cowbell, grabbing his basket to look inside. "Eh, Cowbell, you dirty cheat, look at all these walnuts you've got. You were weighing down your basket with them, weren't you?" With those words, he placed the basket on the scale again, minus the walnuts. "Not even half as heavy, you little shit."

Cowbell's face burned red. He knew he was caught and there was nothing he could do but share the walnuts he'd gathered. A few to Awning, a few to Soupspoon and some to Noodle Fish. This time, he offered none to Inkcap. Ignored and shamed, Inkcap reached for the walnuts himself, but Cowbell pulled them back. Intense anger rose up in Inkcap. He moved quickly, tackling Cowbell to the ground, yelling as he did, "You lying bastard, why did you tell Awning I forced you into joining the Hammerheads?"

Cowbell kept his mouth shut, more concerned with the physical trashing Inkcap was trying to inflict. Clang! Their heads came together with a loud crack, like the sound of the gong calling the village to some revolutionary action or other. But neither of them called out in pain. Rather, they stepped back, seemingly dazed for a moment.

The battle, however, quickly resumed. A moment later and Inkcap was pinned to the ground. After all, it was no surprise he wasn't as strong as Cowbell. Refusing to concede, Inkcap reached out with his free hand and grabbed hold of one of Cowbell's swollen ears. Cowbell grimaced and pulled back, releasing Inkcap from his grip. The fight seemed to stop.

Awning and Soupspoon, who had already ceased playing chess, exclaimed in unison, "Who'd have thought it? That little shit Inkcap can fight!"

Turning towards them, Inkcap shouted, "I never forced him to join the Hammerheads, he joined them all on his own. He just badmouthed me to make himself come across better." His furore showed no signs of abating.

Awning laughed and tossed his walnut to Inkcap.

FIFTY-ONE

AS MORE AND MORE ZHU CLAN MEMBERS abandoned the Hammerheads, Bash grew increasingly annoyed and angry. To Baldy Jin, he remarked about the forests being large and having birds of all sorts, about nephews being little more than dogs hanging about their uncles' doors, scrounging for scraps then buggering off once they had their fill. The Zhus, he said, were once Heis, long ago, nephews or something, but now they were all dogs, feral and untrustworthy. Of course, for those Zhus who heard Bash's ranting, they couldn't help but retort that he was only cursing himself, the Heis were, after all, one of the six domesticated animals of yore. Besides, Bash, Baldy Jin, Dazed-And-Confused, Old Faithful, Cattle Track, Iron Bolt, Decheng, aren't you all in your supposed positions, the pig, dog, chicken, cat, frog, serpent? It never occurred to anyone that the village pigs, dogs, chickens and cats hardly agreed to these men imposing their names on them, and so subsequently the pigs refrained from eating, the chickens stopped laying eggs, the dogs stopped chasing away the cats, and the cows, feeling left out, began mooing throughout the night.

At first, no one could understand why the animals were acting this way, and so Awning and Millstone called a meeting to discuss options, especially since the cows' incessant mooing was beginning to grate on the villagers. Once at the meeting, Awning directed his ire at Noodle Fish.

"Why the hell aren't you feeding the cows?" he asked.

"But I've been feeding the damn animals," a dejected Noodle Fish replied. "I haven't a clue what's wrong with them."

Out in the courtyard, Sprout was trying in vain to round up her pig, calling out to Tag-Along who was marching over to block the pig's path, but Tag-Along paid her no mind whatsoever. Exasperated, she said, "You're welcome to give it a try. I only hope you can catch the beast."

"Can't you see I'm wearing new clothes?" The clothes might have been new to Tag-Along, but they were far from unworn. Rather they belonged to Huang Shengsheng, handed down to Tag-Along. The jacket he was wearing had a wide collar, the pockets cut at a slant. There were two rows of buttons down the front.

Awning turned to Millstone and said, "Tag-Along certainly looks the part, eh, all dressed up and still looking utterly befuddled. Look, he doesn't even know what to say. He's a Hammerhead, isn't he?"

"Careful, a dog needs little reason to bite."

"Ha ha, not a dog then, a blind old pig instead!"

"Come on now, look at him. His rickety old legs, his bent-over waist, certainly not a pig."

"But that jacket he's wearing, two rows of buttons down the front, don't they remind you of two rows of teats?"

The two men roared with laughter. Meanwhile, Sprout continued to try to rein in her pig. Suddenly confronted by men standing in front of it, the animal squealed as if it were about to be slaughtered. That is until Inkcap appeared. Tugging the pig's ears, he pulled it through the courtyard gate.

Awning heard Sprout yell out after Inkcap, "This damned pig's crazy!"

"I don't know about that," Inkcap replied. "I'd rather think it's us who have treated it unfairly."

"Treated unfairly?"

"I, I... didn't mean you. You've not mistreated it, just a... a figure of speech."

"Hey, Inkcap," Awning called out. "Get your arse over here, now!"

Inkcap walked towards Awning, his head low. Once a little closer, he dared to look at the two men, Awning and Millstone. He was frightened by what he saw, which only made him more nervous.

Awning spoke first. "What did you just say to Sprout?"

"I, I... didn't say nothing."

"In denial, eh? A figure of speech... just what did you mean to say, hmm?"

"It was nothing, nonsense, honest."

"We say the Hammerheads are no better than domesticated animals, pigs, dogs, chickens. You disagree?"

"No, it's not that... I just think the animals mightn't like it. You know, I just don't think they'd want to be used to describe the Hammerheads."

"You trying to say you think the Hammerheads are good people, then?"

"That's not what I said."

"But if they're not dogs, pigs, whatever, then what does that make them? Wild fucking animals?"

Inkcap looked at Awning and saw the man's eyes twitching with fury. Timidly he answered, "But, but... listen, the pigs, the dogs, they're... they're quiet." Inkcap was right. The village was still. No dogs yelped. No pigs squealed. Even the cows had ceased their mooing.

Awning and Millstone looked at each other, both thinking it rather strange. Awning then turned to Inkcap. "Go on, get out of here," he said. "You know who and what you are, make sure you watch your mouth."

"Yes... yes sir. No more nonsense." With those words, Inkcap left the courtyard, guiding the pig out as he did so. Sprout had already turned down the alleyway to her house. A chicken waddled in front, then stopped short and squirted out an egg. It broke upon hitting the ground.

As the days passed, the Red Blades began to outnumber the Hammerheads. Bash ordered Baldy Jin to convene a meeting, but once all its members arrived, there was no sign of Bash. To fill the time as they waited, Useless decided to get the Hammerheads to recite a Chairman Mao poem. He started with the first line, "Amid the growing shades of dusk stand sturdy pines..."

The Hammerheads in attendance repeated, "Amid the growing shades of dusk stand sturdy pines..."

Before Useless could continue with the second line, Iron Bolt asked, "What's this dusk thing in the poem?"

"It just means twilight," Useless said.

"That means it's dinnertime, doesn't it? Why would you want to go and look at pine trees at dinnertime?"

"Oh, for heaven's sake, don't be such a bloody idiot."

"I'm the bloody idiot!" He held back from saying anything further.

"I reckon the dumb fucker ate a turnip instead," Jindou said.

The crowd laughed.

"Comrades," Useless said, raising his voice, "this is Chairman Mao's poem we're reciting, some decorum, please. Now, repeat after me, 'Riotous clouds sweep past, swift and tranquil. Nature has excelled herself in the Fairy Cave, on perilous peaks dwells beauty in her infinite variety.' So, did you get all of that?"

The Hammerheads squinted at each other, then at Useless. "Um, no, not a word. I mean, you only recited it once, how are we supposed to remember it that quickly?"

"Oh, for the love of the heavens, am I preaching to deaf ears?"

"Who are you cursing? Who's deaf now?"

"No education, that's it, isn't it? Let me tell you, you mightn't be able to remember Chairman Mao's poem word for word, but you've got to understand the meaning, yes, he's talking about dusk... dinnertime... and yes he's talking about riotous clouds and watching pine trees, but it's more than that, see. Pine trees, you know what these are, yeah? Well, for China, Chairman Mao's our pine tree. That means we're to look towards him. For Old Kiln, our pine tree is Bash. In the past, Old Kiln looked to Secretary Zhu, but not any longer, Bash is who we're supposed to look towards. And it doesn't matter if everything in the village goes to shit, the Hammerheads, all of us, we're in it till the end, all right, to whatever that end might be."

As Useless's voice reached a crescendo, the audience nodded their heads in approval. Then, suddenly, a sound came at the gate. They turned to see Bash marching in. Birdsong echoed and Bash came to a halt. He didn't recognise the sound but tilted his head towards the sky. His jacket was opened at the collar, exposing his broad chest. His hands were at the small of his back, unlike in the past when he usually held them at his waist or chest. His stomach seemed to bulge. He looked at the bird. It had ceased its chirping. Instead, it released its bowels, a thin, milky line of shit trailed down the eaves of the house before dripping onto the ground. He turned away from the creature and walked towards the inner chamber. His steps were slow and deliberate, but he didn't strike the same image as the Branch Secretary had done in the past. What's more, he held his hands in place, not letting them swing in front or beside him. The look was unappealing. His gait seemed unnatural.

Big Root spoke first: "What's he doing with his hands behind his back like that? If he were a woman, I mean, it might be different, but–"

"Shut your mouth," said Useless. "Chairman Mao walked the same way."

"You've seen Chairman Mao?" asked Jindou.

"No, but Huang Shengsheng has, and he told me."

Bash entered the inner chambers, his hands still behind his back.

"How's he so calm?" Useless wondered, mostly to himself.

No one spoke as Bash seated himself at the table facing the Hammerheads.

"A sense of calm is needed to deal with even the most troubling things," Useless bellowed. "Don't let anyone tell you you're not in the presence of a genius. Let's start."

It was an important meeting for the Hammerheads. Bash analysed the current revolutionary situation in Old Kiln. He considered future initiatives and strategies to advance their revolutionary action. There was no discounting it, there were more Zhus in Old Kiln. The Red Blades were using sheer numbers to pressure the Hammerheads. This wasn't surprising, nor should it be. But revolutionary action was about fighting strength, not about how much cow shit one could shovel. The change in the situation in Old Kiln needed deeper thought. Not about numbers, but about who was behind the Red Blades. To Bash, it was clear. Secretary Zhu was the puppet master. And they all knew what that meant. The capitalist roaders were still on the capitalist road. Secretary Zhu was inciting the Zhus against the Heis. The Hammerhead response was also clear. They had to put further pressure on Secretary Zhu, he had to be brought to heel. This was their first task. Their second was that the reactionaries, the Red Blades, likewise needed to be brought down. To help achieve this second task, Useless would get them started by writing a big-character poster. This would be their first volley. As for the other Hammerheads, they needed to remain confident, their belief in the Hammerheads needed to be unwavering. They are the vanguard of the revolution. There was nothing they couldn't achieve. Their task was to mobilise the masses, go out and speak to everyone not named Zhu, recruit them into their ranks, and if they couldn't get them to join up with the Hammerheads, at least make sure they didn't join the Red Blades.

After the meeting, Cattle Track and Huolian, as well as Feng Youliang and Lightkeeper's cousin, Almost-There, joined the Hammerheads. The influx of new members after many had departed was perhaps surprising, to Barndoor at least. More surprising still was when Baldy Jin made overtures to him about becoming a Hammerhead. Moved by the entreaty, Barndoor raced home to tell Flower Girl all about it.

"Do you know what's happening?" he said. "Everyone is joining the Hammerheads, at least everyone but the Bad Elements in the village. Not being part of them is like not being revolutionary, like you're not committed to the cause. We've got to be Hammerheads, it'd be foolish not to join. Besides, if we're Hammerheads, no one would ever dare bully us."

He pulled from his pocket a five-cent coin and pushed it into Flower Girl's hand. "OK, let's try this. Give it a toss, and if it lands heads up, we'll join the Hammerheads, if it doesn't, we're Red Blades."

Flower Girl, however, simply put the coin in her pocket. "We can't join the Hammerheads, whatever Baldy Jin says, I can't… I won't trust them."

"Then the Red Blades?"

"Nope. Not them either. We're not part of the Zhu clan nor the Heis, they've wanted nothing to do with us, and now… now they're fighting each other, causing a ruckus. It's like the eastern wind trying to push down the western breeze, only for the western breeze to try to do the same to the eastern wind. If we join one, the other will hate us, and vice versa. We'll be bullied either way. So… perhaps it's best to stay outside all of this, don't you think? I mean, why don't we just let them fight over us, making sure never to commit to either, that's how we can show that being neither a Zhu nor a Hei is important."

Flower Girl's take on things was unexpected, but there was a certain logic to it and Barndoor was won over. He returned to where Baldy Jin and the others had held their meeting and declined to join up, only handing the man a carton of cigarettes instead.

In their efforts to improve their overall strength, the Hammerheads compiled a list of all their members and posted it on their big-character poster board. Stonebreaker, however, only requested that Half-Stick Zhang be on the list, leaving off his parents and three siblings. Thinking the request over, Baldy Jin reckoned it was a means to control her, so he readily complied and wrote Half-Stick's name down. Not long after the list was posted, when Half-Stick came upon her name, she scratched it out, which predictably resulted in Baldy Jin flying into a rage, returning home to berate her viciously.

"The chicken follows the cock, the bitch its dog, why the hell did you scratch your name off the list of Hammerheads?"

Carrying a container of swill for her pigs, Half-Stick called back to Baldy Jin, "I'm my own boss. If I don't want to join the Hammerheads, then I won't."

"So it's the Red Blades, I suppose? Awning's a member, isn't he? Suppose you want to run to him again, eh?"

Half-Stick threw the container onto the ground and turned to Baldy Jin.

"You vile little son of bitch, you still want to bring that up? Let me tell you, whoever I'm with is none of your fucking business."

"I'm your man and it's none of my business?"

"Oh really, is that what you're thinking about, Awning crawling into my bed?" She slapped her behind and laughed, making Baldy Jin even angrier.

He looked around for a brick but couldn't see any. All he had on him was the carton of cigarettes, so he pulled them out of his jacket and raised them above his head, yelling as he did, "You fucking bitch, I'm going to fucking kill you!"

Half-Stick grabbed a pile of bowls from the nearby windowsill, still unwashed after she and her child had eaten. She mimicked Baldy Jin and held them aloft, cursing as she did, "Going to kill me are you, smash me with that carton of cigarettes? Go on, try, that's what you're good at. Ever since your mother squeezed you out, all you've done is smash things."

The villagers who had been washing clothes in the stream and had heard the racket, had already come closer to hear more. Now, however, they grew fearful. This was no longer just an argument, real violence could happen, so one of them pushed open the courtyard gate to stop them from hurting each other. As they did so, Baldy Jin flung a packet of matches towards the door, screaming at the same time, "Get out of here, get the fuck out!"

Stunned, or intent on making sure no one got hurt, the villagers stood gaping at the scene. A defeated Baldy Jin turned on his heel and stomped off in the direction of an inner room, slamming the door behind him. Half-Stick went off in the opposite direction, slamming her door behind her as well. From this day onwards, they no longer shared a bed. Baldy Jin slept at the temple HQ of the Hammerheads. If he did go home, he'd only sleep in the summer room, far from Half-Stick. On those occasions, especially if she had nothing to do, Half-Stick barricaded herself in the front room, the door never opening until Baldy Jin was gone.

Useless continued writing posters, thirteen in fact. Nine directly criticised the Branch Secretary. The other four targeted the reactionaries. At the same time, Bash made a special trip to Xiahewan to link up with the Red Guards operating there, learning that they, too, had been confronted with the same situation the Hammerheads had been dealing with in Old Kiln. Naturally, they hit it off and made plans to deal with their respective headaches. First, the Bayonets arrested the Secretary of Xiahewan. Next, they trotted him off to Old Kiln. The Hammerheads did the same, seizing Secretary Zhu almost immediately upon Bash's return to the village. Together, they called a joint struggle session against both men.

Not long ago, both were hailed as revolutionary heroes. Heralded by their superiors and feted with Red paraphernalia, now they wore dunce hats and were spat on, cursed as capitalist roaders and counterrevolutionaries, criticised as embezzlers of public wealth and the main culprits of every counterrevolutionary activity in the region. After the struggle session was complete, Secretary Zhu was forced to wear a black armband. There were no words on it, but everyone knew the meaning: he was a capitalist roader. He could never remove it, and if he did and the transgression was discovered, he would be struggled against once more. All his previous duties, everything he was in charge of, was finished. The only task he was given, the only job permitted, was feeding the cows.

It was Bash who had decided upon the punishment, mostly because the cattle stalls were housed next to their headquarters and this would allow him, Awning, Millstone and Sparks to see Secretary Zhu wearing his humiliation every day. And because it made plain the Red Blades were Secretary Zhu's co-conspirators – they were the counterrevolutionaries.

Every day when he stepped outside, he had to wear the same jacket with the black armband. And even though he would often remove the jacket while feeding the cows, when he went home to eat lunch or then again at the end of the day, he had to make sure to put it back on for all to see. His wife worried greatly. She knew her husband had stomach problems and she feared the strain of rising so early, then working so hard throughout each and every day would make things worse. She had no idea how long they would have to endure such a life, nor did she know how serious his problems might be. A dread hung over her. Might he be arrested at any moment and thrown in prison? Might he take his own life in order to escape? Whenever she bumped into Baldy Jin, she often thought to ask, but she never worked up the courage to do so. It wasn't until she went to the ravine to wash some radishes and came across Useless's mum washing clothes that she mustered the nerve to even speak to someone else.

"Washing clothes, are you?"

"That's what it looks like, so I guess that's what I'm doing," said Useless's mum, her tone neither warm nor cold.

"Would you like a radish?" she asked, handing one to Useless's mum.

"You planning to make pan-fried tofu with shredded radish, or are you preparing filling for dumplings?"

"I'm planning to stew them. After all, eating undercooked radishes can give you stomach problems. Doesn't your uncle have issues with his stomach?"

"My uncle? What uncle? What're you talking about?"

"Oh... I didn't mean anything, it's just that... oh, dammit."

"Ah ha, I know what you're trying to get at, you're talking about the Secretary aren't you?"

"What do you mean, he's no Party Secretary that's for sure! But, but... tell me... do you think he's in serious trouble?"

"I'm afraid to say he is."

Her face turned yellowish, and she dropped the radishes she was holding. Her voice trembled and trailed off. "Oh, why don't you even try to make me feel a little better... can't I even get a comforting word or two... just to ease my soul... why won't anyone try to help?"

Useless's mum picked up the radishes from the ravine after they'd floated down into her sudsy water, tossing them back towards the Branch Secretary's wife. "Speak up, why don't you, you sound like you're chanting something. I couldn't hear clearly."

The Branch Secretary's wife offered no response. She stuffed the radishes soaking wet into her basket and turned to leave. She didn't seem to notice how the basket was making her own trousers wet.

Noodle Fish seemed happy by the Branch Secretary's arrival at the cowshed, expressing his joy at being elevated to a higher position now that the latter was here. The Secretary, however, didn't share in Noodle Fish's euphoria.

"You do know I'm being punished?"

"Feeding the cattle is punishment? Does that mean you punished me by sending me here first?"

The Branch Secretary could only laugh darkly to himself.

When Inkcap found out what the Branch Secretary had been assigned to do, he had to rush home to tell his gran. She was seated at the threshold of their home, shearing leaves she had collected earlier in the day. These would be used as padding to make their clothes warmer. In the past, much of her needle and thread work would have included the use of realgar and mugwort powder, but today, Gran seemed to be in a good mood, using both red cloth and other, perhaps less toxic filler for their clothes. On hearing Inkcap's news, she did not respond as he expected, only acknowledging the information with a nod of her head and a quiet, "Oh". She then noticed her yarn had snapped and proceeded to rethread her needle. Pushing it through the eyelet, she pulled the thread high above her head and finally addressed Inkcap.

"Eh... he's in for a hard time, isn't he?"

Inkcap began to help Gran with her threading, saying as he did, "Who's in for a hard time?"

"Why the Secretary... silly boy."

"Since when did you start caring about him? All these years, he and everyone else in the village have done nothing but bully and persecute us. I reckon we've had a harder time than anyone."

"Ah, my boy, it's not the same. I'm used to it... you should be too... but the Secretary? Well now, he's spent most of his life in front of everyone else, to make him wear that black armband, to force him to tend to the cows, I'm sure he's choking on his own bile. No doubt his stomach problems will get worse."

Inkcap said nothing further. He only finished threading one needle before he walked off pouting. Perhaps the swallow could make him feel a little better? Before he could find the bird, however, he noticed through the crack near their courtyard gate a man dashing past. While he only caught a glimpse of the person, he was sure he saw a head of white hair. Could it be Goodman? No, his hair was black, wasn't it? Could his hair have gone white? Curious to find out, Inkcap abandoned his plans to look for the swallow and instead rushed towards the main gate. To his surprise, the figure he'd seen through the crack was indeed Goodman. The man had reached the end of the alleyway, but there was no mistaking him. The sun was pouring down on him and his hair, all white, seemed to shimmer like silk.

549

Inkcap turned back inside and walked up to where his gran was still sitting. "Have you seen Goodman? His hair's gone white."

"I know."

"When did it happen?"

"I saw him yesterday. He told me that the day before yesterday, that night in fact, his hair went white."

"But how?"

"Perhaps his hair didn't want to be black any longer."

Inkcap wanted to ask more, but Gran stopped him by handing him some of the clothing she'd been stitching. She wanted him to try it on. He did as she instructed but buttoned the jacket unevenly.

Gran seemed not to notice. "It looks nice, doesn't it? I say we give it to Secretary Zhu."

Inkcap didn't understand. He thought she'd been embroidering clothes for him, certainly not for Branch Secretary Zhu. But he couldn't pretend to have misheard her. Nor could he disobey. He gave her one more look and then turned to do as he was told.

"Just make sure no one sees you," were her parting words.

When he arrived at the cowshed, Secretary Zhu and Noodle Fish were busy shovelling manure. There were other people milling about, going in and out of the Red Blades' HQ. There was no way he could give the clothing to Secretary Zhu, at least not without being seen. Strangely, thought Inkcap, Secretary Zhu didn't seem all that pitiable, at least not the way his gran made it seem. In truth, he appeared to be working vigorously, shovelled the shit with gusto, a cigarette perched on his lip, although not lit. Spittle could be seen at the edges of his mouth, but together with Noodle Fish, they appeared quite the team, this despite the obvious shit covering both men's clothes, and even Noodle Fish's face, shit mixing with sweat as he carried bundle after bundle of manure from the cowshed to the adjacent fields that bordered the HQ. Noodle Fish's face, in fact, looked oddly like that of a tuxedo cat, or so thought Inkcap. Even their chatting seemed good-natured.

"Oh, Noodle Fish, my boy," cried out the Branch Secretary. "Look at you, you're filthy. Is that on purpose?"

"You tell me, is it possible to keep clean shovelling shit all day?"

"I reckon the cows are cleaner than you are. Go on now, give yourself a clean for heaven's sake."

Noodle Fish did as he was told, walking over to the nearby washbasin to attempt to clean his face at least. Meanwhile, Secretary Zhu sat down on a stump and reached in his pocket for a match to light his cigarette. Out of habit, Inkcap raced towards him to provide a light, then realised he'd forgotten to bring any matches with him. Noodle Fish, who by now had finished washing his face, obliged and struck a match for Secretary Zhu. He then picked up the Secretary's shovel and continued his shovelling.

"Hey now," Branch Secretary Zhu called to him, "that's my job. Put the shovel down."

"Are you saying I'm not allowed? Didn't I tell you I'm happy you're here, you've made things easier for me. And you know, I reckon you were Secretary for too long, you're just not cut out for this type of work, better if I do it for a bit. Wait a minute, Inkcap, what the hell are you doing standing there? Popping round for a visit? Get over here and take this."

Inkcap ran up and Noodle Fish passed him the shovel.

As he started, Secretary Zhu remarked almost to himself, "Yes, that's how it should be, shovel a while for me."

Secretary Zhu drew deeply on his cigarette, enjoying it immensely. When finished, he tilted his head back and opened his mouth wide, letting out a long sigh of satisfaction. Inkcap recognised the sigh as the same his gran would do in the evenings. It seemed to be her only way to release the pent-up fatigue and stress of the day.

"Tired?" asked Inkcap.

"Just because I sighed doesn't mean I'm tired."

"Is your stomach acting up again?"

"I haven't had heartburn for three days now. This work seems to agree with me."

By lunch, they'd finished shovelling the manure out of the cowshed. Noodle Fish collected some dry dirt to scatter around the shed, then collected the beanstalks they had had to remove in the afternoon. With the morning's work complete, they could go home for lunch. Noodle Fish left first, but Secretary Zhu lingered a while, determined to scrape at least some of the cow dung off the soles of his shoes. Satisfied, if not wholly successful, he picked up his black armband jacket and once more pulled it on before leaving the courtyard. Inkcap followed closely behind. The two of them walked down the alleys and as they neared the Branch Secretary's home, his loyal cock chirped and crowed at his approach. Secretary Zhu acknowledged the creature with a nod, nothing more, and continued his walk home. The cock followed close behind, its neck craned high, its comb flaming red, its wings flapping aggressively. Inkcap hated Secretary Zhu's rooster. Why was it so proud? he wondered. Secretary Zhu wasn't even the party secretary any more. Did it know he shovelled shit all day? Inkcap much preferred the pig that used to walk beside them. It didn't put on airs like the cock.

"You've followed me long enough, boy," Secretary Zhu said, interrupting his thoughts.

"Um... who says I'm following you? I'm not, you know."

"Well, if you're not following me, give me some space, all right?"

"But there's no one around." As he spoke, Inkcap looked in all directions, just to double-check they were alone. Seeing that they were, he pulled out the piece of clothing his gran had stitched and gave it to Secretary Zhu. The Branch Secretary hesitated for a moment and then grabbed it from Inkcap's hands, bundling it under his upper garment. His job done, Inkcap released his own long-satisfied sigh. As he did, the rooster pecked against his feet, evidently angry at him. Inkcap kicked the bird, sending it skittering away. Secretary Zhu continued walking.

"You know... when I was still in charge, I ordered your gran to stitch me one of these. She promised she would, but she never delivered. In the end, Useless, that fucker, ended up giving me one. Padded with cotton."

"Well, you can't say she didn't keep her promise now, can you?"

Branch Secretary Zhu laughed and picked up a broken tile from the ground. He placed it on the wall enclosing the privy and said, "How's your gran's leg?"

"It's all right, I suppose, but her corns still hurt… sometimes she finds it hard to walk around."

"Hmm…"

Inkcap spotted Dazed-And-Confused walking into the alleyway, a bundle of alpine rush in his arms. Inkcap lowered his voice when he said to Secretary Zhu, "Come on, let's walk this way," and he pointed to a lane that trailed off from the alley.

Before taking a step, however, Secretary Zhu made him stop. "No, this way, you go off over there," and he pointed in the opposite direction.

"Well… if you're not leaving, neither am I."

"Why you… go on, get out of here."

Too late, Dazed-And-Confused reached them.

"What are you looking at? Do I have something of yours on me?" said Inkcap.

"Your armband," said Dazed-And-Confused, looking hard at Secretary Zhu. "Why aren't you wearing it?"

"It's on my jacket, here, look."

"Then why aren't you wearing your jacket?"

"It's rather hot, isn't it? I just removed it."

"Are you telling me you put the armband on a jacket you won't wear?"

Secretary Zhu pulled his jacket back on and tried not to pay any more attention to Dazed-And-Confused. He and Inkcap began to walk again down the alleyway.

Dazed-And-Confused, however, wasn't done. "Hey, Inkcap! Why have you not been round to buy more shoes? Everyone else pays fifteen cents a pair, I'll give them to you for twelve."

"That's all right, I don't need your cheap grass shoes any more."

"Why, you wasted bit of sperm, here you are escorting a capitalist running dog round the village. I suppose you've read the big-character poster have you, you idiot? Well, I'll tell you what was written, eh, first there were three targets of criticism and three posters, then five… now eighteen!"

Inkcap had heard more posters had been posted, but since he couldn't read, he hadn't bothered to go and check them out. To his mind, it didn't matter, he knew their main target was the Red Blades. Who else could it be?

The Red Blades had seen how the Hammerheads had struggled against Secretary Zhu, how he'd been forced to wear the black armband, forced to shovel shit. They knew, too, that this was all directed at them. But there was nothing they could do; intervening was out of the question. They watched Useless's posters go up, one after the other. For the first seven, they refrained from taking any action. But there was a limit to their restraint.

For posters eight, nine and ten that went up in the morning, they made sure to tear them down during the night. Naturally, this provoked Bash into a response, but instead of catching the culprits in the act, he simply had Useless quote Chairman Mao's passages on the top and bottom of each poster, on both sides as well. From then on, no one, not even the Red Blades, dared to tear the posters down. The result was Awning detesting Useless even more than before, but he was incapable of contemplating a counterattack.

After Noodle Fish and Secretary Zhu had finished their work, on the other side of the village, in the old apartment compound, Awning, Millstone, Sparks, Padlock and Sprout closed the doors and began a meeting of their own. The roosters milling about in the courtyard crowed the arrival of night. Like the men inside, their crowing was a signal of their hunger. Padlock was the first to complain.

"Starting a meeting without letting us go home first to eat?" he said. "Damn, all that does is make us as hungry as the cocks outside."

"What's the difference?" said Millstone. "Even if we did go home, we'd still have to come back for our meeting. Why don't we just eat here and hold the meeting at the same time?"

Without speaking, Sparks stood up and went outside. A moment later, he returned with some black beans that he'd managed to scrounge. "Look, I've got these beans. I'll boil them up for us to eat."

"Where the hell did you find them?" asked Millstone.

"In the storage shed for the livestock."

"Then we can't eat them."

"Says who? Cows and men aren't all that different, I reckon we can eat them. And you're not our commander either, so why are you sticking your nose into everything? Besides, the Hammerheads took what they wanted over at the temple. Look what they did with the village porcelain. I say we can take what we need."

"And so what? Screw them. They did what they wanted, but if we eat these black beans, how much will be left for the livestock? If we eat everything, what will the cows eat?"

"Go and take a look to see if there's anything else we can eat," said Awning.

"Maybe grass," was Sparks' rather quick retort, but eventually he returned the beans to the livestock shed. In doing so, however, he spotted a shadow crossing the courtyard and called out to see who it was. The men inside heard him yell and rushed outside. Sparks called again, "Who's there? Tell us before you get into even more trouble."

The response was first that of someone or something vomiting, followed by a meow. A second later, from out of the shadows, a large black cat emerged. Its ragged tail was standing stick-straight up into the air.

"That's Useless's fucking cat," yelled Padlock.

Everyone in Old Kiln could identify Useless's cat. Its tail was always erect, exposing its arsehole for all to see. Many would joke that if the cat were a woman, she'd be an easy and inexpensive sell. Useless's mum would say in the animal's defence that it was being revolutionary. A born Hammerhead, as it were.

Shortly after Padlock recognised it as Useless's cat, Awning responded, "If you can't find anything to eat, I say we kill that damn beast."

Easier said than done, however. Frustrated at their inability to catch the animal, Sparks yelled out, "Drive it towards the door. If we get it inside, it'll be easier to catch. Whatever you do, don't let it get to the wall."

Driving it inside, they slammed the door closed. Feeling cornered, the cat darted this way and that, then into a corner. They grabbed baskets to catch the cat but failed. The animal leapt upon the table, strained on its hind legs as though it were about to leap up onto the roof beams.

"It's going for the roof!" Millstone shouted.

Awning reacted first. Picking up a wooden stool, he smashed it against the table. The cat was knocked to the floor amid the ruins of the stool. Padlock took hold of it. Its head had been cut open and blood was seeping out. Still alive, its claws were extended in a last-ditch effort to defend itself. Padlock grabbed it by its waist, fearful its exposed claws would make short work of his face. His jacket, however, was not so safe as the cat flailed about viciously.

"Come on. Someone give me a hand."

No one did, however.

"You can do it. Think of it like a ball, hold it tight and then throw it at the wall. That should finish the job."

The cat, sensing its impending doom, clung to Padlock's arm, stopping him from hurling it at the wall. Its tail, still erect, jabbed at Padlock's face.

Awning began to undo his belt, which was not much more than a rough-hewn piece of rope. He got Millstone to do the same. Once undone, they tied the two belts together, then moved towards Padlock before stringing the rope around the animal's neck,

"Damn beast. Wasted fucking sperm, quite the fight in it. Padlock, there, strangle the creature."

The rope pulled tight around its neck, the cat released its grip on Padlock's arm and dropped to the floor. Padlock stumbled to the nearby bench to catch his breath, watching at the same time the cat trying to breathe.

"Now, toss it in the basin," Awning yelled. "That'll finish its nine lives."

Sparks did as he was instructed. The cat struggled in vain. It gurgled water and thrashed about, but escape was impossible. Before long, it moved no more.

FIFTY-TWO

THE FOLLOWING MORNING, Useless's mum went wandering around Old Kiln in search of her cat. By the wheat field, she bumped into Apricot who was carefully carrying a cup of flour.

"What are you planning on making?" she asked. "Something delicious, I'm sure."

"Dumplings." Apricot's reply was simple and without emotion.

"Oh, didn't I hear something about Bash's... it's not his birthday, is it? Let me think, he was born in the autumn, today's–"

"Don't talk nonsense, these are for Six Pints. He's rather ill and wanted to eat some dumplings. I'm just bringing a cup of flour, that's all."

"He's seriously ill? It's nearly harvest time, you think he'd be able to eat some fresh corn? I guess if he can't, that's all right too. He's been sick these past couple of years, but that's not all bad, is it? At least he's managed to avoid other hardships, his wife as well."

"How can you say such things?"

"It mightn't be nice to hear such things, but that doesn't mean they're not true."

Apricot offered no further comment but continued on her way. Useless's mum called after her, "OK, OK, I won't say anything more. I'll call on him myself, one of these days. But Apricot, tell me, have you seen my cat, you know the one, black all over, its tail always sticking up, like a wing, I suppose. I'm afraid I've lost it."

"Ha, that's impossible!"

"Well, if that were true, why can't I find it?"

"Perhaps it's turned into a tiger!"

By lunch, Useless's mum was near Inkcap's home, more specifically, by the rubber tree that stood in the alleyway. There she found cat skin, nailed to the trunk. Her first thought was to suspect Inkcap, the rascal. He'd likely killed the cat to eat it. Naturally, she went straight to his home and began pounding on the door for him to come out. Inkcap appeared a few moments later and Useless's mum accused him in no uncertain terms of murdering her beloved cat. Inkcap swore on whatever he thought holy that he hadn't killed it, but Useless's mother didn't believe him. Nor did she believe his gran after she came out from inside to defend her grandson. When that, too, proved unpersuasive, Gran pulled Inkcap back inside and left Useless's mum wailing and cursing at them from the other side of the courtyard gate.

While Useless's mother was cursing Inkcap and his gran, Six Pints was in bed trying to eat the dumplings that Apricot had prepared with the flour she'd brought. After two, he couldn't get any more down. All he wanted to do was sleep, but sleep wouldn't come. Useless's mother continued to curse out in the alleyway, her colourful language seeping into his room. Six Pints wondered who had the energy and health to curse like they were doing, finally asking, "Who the hell is that?"

"Useless's mother," came his wife's reply. "Someone's killed and eaten her cat. She reckons it was Inkcap."

She got some cotton balls for Six Pints to stuff in his ears. Before he could do so, however, the alleyway went quiet.

"I guess she's decided to take a rest," Six Pints said, and he closed his eyes to try to sleep. Unfortunately, the verbal assault started again, causing him to swear himself, before fainting.

Everyone in the household was shocked by his sudden loss of

555

consciousness and rushed to his bedside. It took quite some coaxing to awaken him, after which Six Pints' son grabbed his father's walking stick and marched outside to threaten Useless's mother into shutting up. She complied, if reluctantly, but was still furious and picked up stones from the alleyway and flung them at the rubber tree. One, two, three, half a dozen, the stones made great gashes in the bark. Bystanders egged her on, asking if she needed an axe since rocks would hardly bring the tree down. Useless's mother was not amused, and she began hurling insults back at them.

"Laughing at me, are you? You bastards. I know you're all just here to enjoy my misfortune."

Of course, there were some who really did enjoy the ruckus. Awning, Millstone and Sparks were certainly having a laugh, particularly since they were the ones responsible for killing and eating Useless's cat. The meat was sour, they thought, and so too were their farts. Their shit as well. Naturally, they made no effort to explain things and exculpate Inkcap's name. In their mind, this was all a way to get at Useless. In fact, they thought they could exploit the situation even further by taking advantage of Six Pints' worsening health to draw in more of the Zhu clan members. This was a strategy they'd learnt from the Branch Secretary.

Millstone took the initiative, marching over to the expanding crowd to say, "The Zhus have to stick together. They can't give up on another Zhu even if they tried. Six Pints' condition shows this clearly, doesn't it? All the Zhus should be here to show their concern. He's been sick for ages now, his whole family is struggling. All the Zhus should be in this together, every family donate a yuan or two, that'll benefit Six Pints and his family, won't it?"

Millstone's persuasion worked, for not long after, the larger Zhu clan raised just over a hundred yuan. Only Useless's mother chose not to contribute. Somewhat surprised at her refusal, Awning sent Ever-Obedient to find out why.

"We've never done anything like this in the past," she explained. "Is Six Pints really in such a serious situation?"

"Yes, he is."

"I still don't think it necessary. If he's that ill, what's the use of some extra money?"

"That's your response? How can you be so callous? You're all part of the Zhu clan, aren't you? The same family. Certainly closer to them than I am."

"What are you on about? I know some Zhus who've done me no favours at all."

"So does that mean you won't be helping out?"

"When Useless gets back, I'll tell him to find Millstone and give him the cash, all right?" And then she cursed Inkcap once more.

"Damn, your mouth is like a dagger. It's just an old cat."

"Just a cat?" she spat at Ever-Obedient. "Are you sure, what about Inkcap, about the kind of person he is, are you OK with letting him get away with such things? Who's to say one of these days someone won't come by and murder me?"

556

"Did you see Inkcap kill it?"

"If it wasn't him, then who? You know he's always going hungry, nicking food here and there. The little shit will eat anything."

"I already made him rinse his mouth out. There wasn't even the smallest bit of meat in the water. He didn't do it."

"That proves nothing, he could've rinsed his mouth before you asked and already swallowed all the bits of meat stuck between his teeth."

"Ah, it's no good talking to you." Ever-Obedient decided to depart, but a little after leaving her alone, he returned to inform her that Awning had contributed two yuan in Useless's name.

News that Awning had donated two yuan in Useless's name spread like wildfire through Old Kiln. Baldy Jin heard it while he was at Barndoor's house. His teeth had been hurting and he'd sought out Barndoor for some herbal painkiller. As soon as he heard the news, however, he rushed off to find Bash to tell him. Bash took the news in silence, prompting Baldy Jin to probe the situation further.

"Do you reckon Useless has joined up with the rest of the Zhu clan?"

"Well, Useless does call Six Pints his uncle…"

"Their family connection is quite strong, perhaps their revolutionary fervour as well?"

"But Useless wouldn't betray us, I can't believe that."

"Caution is at least warranted. Look at me and my situation with Half-Stick."

After their verbal punch-up, Baldy Jin suspected Half-Stick even more. He knew, or at least believed, that she was continuing to cavort with Awning. Every time he came home, he'd tiptoe into the courtyard and up to the door before violently throwing it open thinking to catch her in the act. Each and every time, however, Awning would not be there. Still suspicious, he'd look behind their wardrobe, check the windows, too, to see if they had been left open. He still didn't find any presence of Awning, to which Half-Stick protested venomously that there never would be anyone to catch.

"I suppose that means he's never been there," Baldy Jin said to Bash. "I guess, too, that she's not afraid of thieves, but I wouldn't say the same about her memories. I still figured she'd be thinking about him, so, so… this once, I asked her, you know, if when we were fucking, did she ever think of him? She told me she hadn't, not at least until I said his name, then, you know what she said, she said I'd given her a good idea! The bitch. I went to hit her then, got into a bit of a row we did, you've seen it."

Bash and the other villagers did indeed see it. Periodically, Baldy Jin would be seen with easily distinguishable scratches on his face. Some would ask him what had happened, if he'd been out in the fields again and got cut up by the grass. Baldy Jin would usually blame it on one of the village cats. Unsurprisingly, Baldy Jin and Half-Stick no longer shared a bed. But that doesn't mean he didn't have his way with his wife from time to time. When the urge fell upon him, he'd attack her violently before restraining her with rope. Then rape her mercilessly, yelling as he did for her to think about Awning. On these occasions, Half-Stick went limp. She couldn't smell his stench, couldn't see him. To all intents and purposes, she was dead. Her body was dead. He was fucking nothing more than a dead animal. The only thought that ran through her mind was that Baldy Jin was a weakling. He had a bad back and was always complaining about his teeth hurting, his face would swell and make him look even more pathetic.

Bash smiled to himself as Baldy Jin went on. But he chose not to engage with the topic directly. Instead, he simply asked, "What's the matter? Teeth causing you problems?"

"Yeah, but I don't know why. They've been killing me for nearly three days."

"Better than Half-Stick winding you up."

"Eh, Bash, come on now, why are you going there, got thoughts on doing the same?"

"You think? I don't know, maybe. The more revolutionary you are, the more you want to do it!"

"So you've–"

"And who would I have done it with, huh? You've got Half-Stick, who's there for me? Just my hand."

"So you torment others and think you can do the same to me. Last night, did you–"

"All right, all right," said Bash, waving his hands rapidly. "Go, you've work to do."

As soon as Baldy Jin departed, Bash instructed Almost-There to go and find Useless. Not long after, Useless arrived with his mother. Bash told Almost-There to keep her company while he spoke privately with Useless. Perhaps unexpectedly, the first thing Bash mentioned was Baldy Jin's take on events. Useless responded by cursing Baldy Jin for his slander. He added that when the Hammerheads were formed, Baldy Jin did not immediately sign up. Yes, he'd tagged along, as it were, but it wasn't until Awning and the others established the Red Blades that Baldy Jin officially put his name in the Hammerheads' register. His reasons were to distinguish himself from Awning more than anything else. So, Useless added, his revolutionary motives were… suspect. Dishonest at least.

"See here," said Bash, "I've let you go on, that should make my stance clear to you, yes? Being suspicious of people isn't much use, and using people isn't suspicious. You and Useless, that's one thing, but your family name is Zhu, are you guilty by association? Are you a counterrevolutionary?"

"That may be… but Apricot, well, she's also a member of the Zhu clan, and you and her–"

"Me and her what?"

"I, I…"

"I'll tell you, you won't bring her name up again."

Useless was unsure of what to say. Finally, he offered a reply, "I didn't mean to… ah, I mean you and her… erm?"

"Useless, let me tell you something. You must remember that today we have the opportunity to accomplish great deeds, and to do great deeds we must have great aspirations. As for women, none of them have control over me, they're all for me to use, just like our horses, something to ride from time to time, nothing more."

Useless was stunned and could only mutter as much to himself as to Bash, "Oh, oh... I..."

"Now, do you have a smoke?"

"Um, I don't smoke, but I can ask Almost-There if he's got any on him."

"Don't smoke? What was I just talking about?" Bash paused. "Oh, I remember. In the early days of the revolution, when the party was first making gains, a lot of the main characters were members of the Nationalists, or at least affiliated with them. They were the larger party in the beginning, right, but they knew there was no way the Nationalists could save the country, that's why they made their move."

"Yes, yes, that makes sense."

"We've done good work together, you and me, but there are things now for me to consider. The Hammerheads, we're a revolutionary organisation, we're not just you and me, we're a unit. I just happen to be the leader, and as leader, well, that means you're my right-hand man, deputy leader, right? So we've got to discuss how we're organised, we need to make a list, establish a chain of command, as it were."

Useless was caught off guard by the change in subject. "Um, Bash, captain, yes, that's better, I won't call you by your name any more, you're our captain, so that's what I'll call you, that or 'sir'. Sir, what's the date?"

"The ninth."

"Here's to our good fortune and the Revolution... onwards and upwards."

While Useless was discussing matters with Bash inside, his mother was outside continuing to curse Inkcap as Almost-There listened on. Almost-There was not the greatest with words, nor was he much of a listener. The only thing he did do was sit quietly beside the old woman, scratching his leg from time to time, then his head, his waist, all over, really.

Finally, Useless's mother challenged him on whether he was listening. "So, am I talking to a rock or a tree?" she said, her voice dripping with anger.

"Um, I don't know, I've... nothing to say."

"Nothing to say, eh? OK, that may be true. But you could at least react to what I've been saying, couldn't you? Your face is just blank." She then heard Useless call to her and she got up to go inside, asking as she did, "You've finished talking about work, have you? Bash, tell me, do you think Inkcap murdered and ate my cat? Are you going to let such a bad apple get away with this?"

Useless stopped his mother from saying anything further. The Hammerheads were a revolutionary organisation, Bash was their captain, her son was his deputy, and they didn't have time to deal with something so trivial. Reading the situation well, Useless's mother ceased going on about her cat, choosing instead to focus on something else.

"So," she said, beginning to smile, "when Awning, Millstone and the rest of them called you nothing more than a disorderly rabble, you decided to name a captain and his deputy? I understand. Useless has been a loyal follower, Bash, you've both achieved revolutionary success. Should Bash become village secretary, does that mean you, my son, will be promoted to team captain?"

Bash laughed before responding, "We can't go to the commune, so does that mean we head to the county capital?"

Their conversation over, Bash went to call on Tag-Along while Useless himself remained at the temple HQ, writing down the record of the day's proceedings. To his mind, it was a day of great significance, and a proper record must be made. His mother stayed by his side, her eyes glued to her son. When she noticed his eyes twitching and blinking rapidly, a look reminiscent of a chicken's sphincter clutching and releasing, she thought he must be getting tired. Then, when she also noticed his legs shaking and jerking this way and that under the table, she could hold her tongue no longer.

"My boy, you're tired. Come on, take a rest, won't you?"

"Mum, I'm recording the day's events. This is important, please, don't bother me."

She said nothing further. All she did was watch as he filled one side of paper, then the other.

Suddenly, a loud, hacking cough echoed in from outside. Useless's mum lifted her head in the direction of the door to see Sparks walking in. This was the first time he'd returned to the temple since the formation of the Hammerheads, its walls now seemingly tattooed with various revolutionary slogans. Two red flags hung on either side of the main door, while squat stone pillars were positioned beneath them; presumably, these were used as stools. Just behind the pillars was a long pole leaning against the wall, from which a number of hammers were hanging. Sparks thought it resembled some fucking loyalty hall to the legendary *Water Margin*; he'd seen a performance of the story once, and the place looked the same.

Useless's mother welcomed him obsequiously, "Oh Sparks, it's you! What's brought you to the headquarters at this hour?"

"Headquarters? What the hell are you talking about, isn't this a temple? Ah, never mind, what's Useless up to? I came for him."

"He's recording the day's events. Would you like to come in?"

"Come in? I'll—"

His accent was thick and almost indecipherable, but before he could say anything further to the old woman, she called out to her son, "Useless, Sparks is here to see you."

Sparks, however, didn't wish to step further into the temple, so Useless abandoned his record-keeping to meet the other man in the courtyard. Together, they walked out through the gate and towards the foot of the nearby Middle Mountain and the trees that nestled there. Sparks sat down on the earth and bade Useless to join him. Before lowering himself down, Useless pulled a handkerchief from his pocket and laid it out on the ground.

"These are new trousers I'm wearing," he explained.

Sparks ignored the statement. "You've heard Six Pints is very ill… worse than ever… why have you not gone to see him?"

"I thought Awning donated some money on my behalf. Are you here for more, then? I suppose I can, yes…" and he reached into his pocket. "May I ask that you give it to him?"

"That's not for me to do," said Sparks, refraining from taking the cash Useless held in his hand. "You need to give it to him yourself."

"All right, I will, but later. You can see I'm busy, been busy these past few days. I've not even had time to eat."

"What tosh! How can a Zhu be working so diligently for a Hei?"

"I know what you're getting at, but I'm just a scribe, nothing more."

"A bloody scribe? Ha! I suppose you just love writing and that's it, eh?"

"Awning's illiterate and I was a… a militia clerk before. Go and ask him how many pieces of paper he's bought, how many pens for me to use. He's had me running this way and that. What am I to him, another Inkcap?"

"Why don't you come with me, then, we'll tell Awning this together. That you're here against your will, as it were, that you're just going through the motions."

"And he'll listen to you?"

"Me and Millstone will tell him together. You come, we'll work it out and, what's more, it'll cut Bash to the quick. After all, you're a Red Blade in your bones, aren't you?"

Useless chuckled. "Sparks, brother, could you draw a pancake-shaped circle on this paper here? Do you know Bash gave me and the others some sesame seed-coated flat cakes, they were small you know, but they were real, and you could eat them. But this here, this is just on paper, it might be bigger, but it's still just paper."

"He gave you a flat cake?"

"That's not all… in fact, I'm deputy commander of the Hammerheads!"

Sparks, stunned into silence, lifted himself from the ground and began to leave. Useless called after him, "Worried, Sparks? Worried?"

"Useless," Sparks called back, "the next Tomb Sweeping Day, don't you dare let any Zhu see you." He stomped out from among the trees, paying no attention to the dried grass he crunched under his feet, the sticky sap on his trousers that seemed to attract all the dirt and dust, covering his legs in filth.

At nearly the same time, Inkcap and Granny Silkworm were walking to Six Pints' house to offer their support, Gran with four eggs tucked away in her jacket as a gift. On the way, they spied Sparks walking out from the wheat field, panting heavily.

"Ah," Inkcap called out, "Brother Sparks!"

Sparks ignored him.

Inkcap whispered to Gran, "Have you ever seen the musical based on the Generals of the Yang Family?"

"Wasn't I the one who sent you off to Xiahewan to watch it?"

"Well, yes, anyway, Sparks was in it. He was the seventh son, Yang Yansi, you know, the one who was pierced by all those arrows shot by the Song General, Pan Renmei was his name I think–"

"You don't say?"

"Yes, well, the arrows, anyway, that's how he was killed, and now, look, Sparks' trousers are shredded just like Yang Yansi's were."

"Oh, don't be silly… and more important, stop talking nonsense. How many times do I have to tell you?"

Despite feeling pleased with his literary reference, Inkcap never thought his display of whimsy would result in Gran preventing him from calling on Six Pints. She was afraid he'd open his mouth and say something he shouldn't. Dejected, he plopped down on the ground while she went on. He was angry, angry at the world around him, even the grass, dried and yellow, jagged and sharp. He pricked his finger, trying to draw blood. But it did little to ease his anger. Just then, a loud crack reverberated from a nearby elm tree, and a crow fell from the leaves. It wriggled on the ground, got back to its feet and stretched its wings. It looked at Inkcap, but despite its best efforts to lift itself from the earth, it failed. Inkcap noticed its wings were missing a number of feathers. Stunned by the scene, he had no time to react when Cowbell leapt from behind the tree, a slingshot in his hand.

"I got it! I got it!" he shouted and went to grab the wounded bird.

Inkcap regained some of his composure and shouted at the crow, "Fly! Come on, hurry up, you've got to get out of here."

The crow seemed to obey and flapped its wings once more. This time it was successful in lifting its wounded form into the sky. Inkcap looked on as it flew unevenly above him.

Having lost his quarry, Cowbell himself took on the appearance of a wounded animal and blamed Inkcap for his failure to help.

Unbowed, Inkcap defended his actions. "I'm sure it did nothing to you, so why'd you try to kill it?"

"It's a crow, their mouths are rotten, they're pests."

"Whose mouth is rotten, hey, whose?"

Failing to understand the verbal jab, Cowbell responded innocently, "Hey, what's wrong with you? Did I say something wrong?"

As the two argued, the crow circled above the elm tree. It appeared unwilling to fly anywhere farther. Spotting it above them, the two boys stopped and stared at the tree. They both saw the nest at the same time, as well as the three baby crows inside, their small heads poking up from behind the rim of the nest. Cowbell closed an eye and aimed his slingshot. Before he could release his shot, however, Inkcap grabbed his hand and the stone inside fell out. Out of the corners of their eyes, Inkcap and Cowbell saw the mother crow land on a branch a little distance from the nest. There it regurgitated the food it had caught for its offspring.

"What the hell is it doing?" Cowbell wondered aloud.

"It's teaching them how to feed."

One of the small crows climbed onto the edge of the nest, flapped its wings and half flew, half jumped to the other branch where the food lay perched. Moments later, the second and the third tiny crow did the same.

The mother crow squawked at her offspring's success. A second later, it screeched, twisted and fell to the ground, dead. Inkcap looked at Cowbell.

"See... You killed it. You and your damn slingshot!"

"I wasn't really trying to... I'm not as good with a slingshot as you, I just wanted to try, I never thought I'd actually hit it." The regret in his voice was apparent and he could see Inkcap's hatred of him. He continued, "You know Six Pints is worse. I suppose a crow in a nearby tree is a bad omen."

Inkcap ignored him and tore off towards Six Pints' home. He'd smelt that same odour again and was terrified. He couldn't get it out of his nose, nor the thought out of his mind that something had happened to Six Pints. But when he arrived outside, Gran's words came back to him. He stopped himself from entering and instead walked over towards the pigsty. Leaning against the wall, he pinched his nose. The smell remained.

A crowd had gathered in the courtyard of Six Pints' house, all of them talking in hushed tones about his condition. In the main room, Six Pints had finally become lucid after nearly half a day of drifting in and out of consciousness.

Seeing him awake, his children rushed to the side of his bed and exclaimed, "Dad, Dad!"

His face was dark and his head, which had never been all that large before, had swelled like a melon. His neck seemed to have elongated and a walnut-sized bulge could be seen under the skin. He looked at his son and daughter and opened his mouth, appearing to want to speak, but no sound could be heard. His wife came close and massaged his chest.

"My husband, my dear husband, I'm here. Whatever you want to say, tell it to me."

Finally, his voice crawled up from his swollen larynx. "Oh my son, my dearest..."

Rubbing tears from the corners of his eyes, Six Pints' son said, "I'm here, too, Dad. I'm listening."

"Dearest... dearest... I must smell foul... but listen, at the corner of the bed... those three stones, they're loose, you can move them, in behind, I... I've squirrelled away some money... we owe Binlai five yuan, Thimble five jiao... Huolian owes us three yuan, Dazed-And-Confused owes us two yuan five and Tag-Along... he's got to give me a basket of potatoes..."

Six Pints' children each grabbed a hand and cried.

"What?" his wife began. "My husband, what are you talking about? You've no need to talk about such things, there's nothing wrong with you, you're fine. Goodman just saw you and said the same, that all you need is rest and you'll soon be up and out of here."

Six Pints started to pull his hand from his daughter's clasp but stopped and clutched her tighter. "Oh my baby girl, I've never once been ashamed of you. Oh, baby girl, let me tell you something, your mum, she's... she's got a temper, something fierce, you know that. Don't be stubborn with her, OK? Listen to what she says and don't pay any attention to things you shouldn't, say only what needs saying and keep the rest to yourself... oh, oh..."

His daughter cried even more than before, tears streaming down her face and neck, soaking her clothes.

Her mother tried to console her. "Come now, dear, don't cry. I think you've cried enough." Looking at her son, her eyes guided him to collect his sister and leave the room. Once gone, she lifted her husband to turn him on his side. His back was even darker than his face and an awful stench rose from the bed. Pus seeped out of his bedsores, and he groaned in discomfort. She tried in vain to clean him up, despite the continued groans he made.

Inkcap despised his nose, but the smell would not leave him. He squeezed it harder, but to no avail. Looking in the direction of Six Pints' house, he saw Goodman step out the door and into the evening air. Before he could take another step, however, a voice from behind called out to him.

"Goodman, Goodman, how could you just look at Six Pints, say a few words of fake encouragement, and then leave?"

"There's nothing more I can do. He's beyond my help."

"What do you mean?"

"Best to get word to the provincial capital and ask for them to send a doctor. Even then... I don't think there's much he could do other than identify what's actually killing him. I don't think there's a treatment, he's just got to endure it. Whatever he wants to eat, give it to him, the same for drink."

"But I heard from someone inside, they said these were your words, that all he had to do was endure this pain and he'd survive."

"What else could I say? I can't say he's got kidney disease, can I? That gangrene has set it and it's killing him. In truth, I've never seen anyone so far gone as he is. My word, his bedsores are huge, as big and bulging as the head of a yellow weasel–"

"Six Pints once drank the blood of a yellow weasel," said Inkcap, who had now drawn near. "Five, in fact, one after the other."

Turning to Inkcap, Goodman asked, "Did he kill them first?"

"Yeah."

"Hmm, I suppose this might be some form of justice being wrought then, eh?"

Inkcap felt a shiver up his spine. He'd killed at least one yellow weasel himself. Did this mean retribution would be waiting for him too?

From inside, a few more people spilled out into the courtyard having overheard the conversation. They each asked after the possibility this was some form of vengeance, if Six Pints was paying for previous transgressions.

"Life is not long," was all Goodman could say. "It's like a single clap of the hands, gone in a flash. Nor does a person take their wife and children into the next world. Their possessions remain here. All there is in this world is karma. We're all connected to everything and everything to us, our good deeds and bad are what follow us into the next life..."

Goodman rambled on but by now Inkcap had tuned out. Partly because he didn't really understand, and partly because he was worried about himself and the fact he'd killed a weasel too. He wanted to ask Goodman about his own personal situation, but Goodman kept droning on and on, much to the astonishment of the villagers in the courtyard.

Finally, Inkcap tugged on Huolian's jacket to ask, "Do you understand what he's saying?"

"Not a word."

"If you don't understand, why do you keep nodding your head?"

"He's talking book stuff, but I understand the gist of it. Do good, and you'll be rewarded with the same. Do bad, and, well, you're fucked."

Inkcap wanted to ask more, but Awning arrived with a great wad of cash. The villagers immediately stepped aside to allow Awning to walk through, saying as he did, "Ah, Goodman. At it again, I see. What are you prattling on about this time?"

"Six Pints' illness."

"Something you've got no clue about, yeah?"

"That's up to you to say. There are those in the village who believe my words, and there are those who don't."

"Well, so long as you're not speaking nonsense. After all, this is the Cultural Revolution. If the Red Blades aren't investigating you, that's not to say the Hammerheads won't."

Awning milled about for a moment longer and then entered the house. Inkcap remained where he was, seated on a stone to one side of Goodman.

Goodman looked at him. "Why aren't you going in?"

"I've… there's something I'd like to ask you."

"Go ahead."

"OK, but make sure you answer in words I can understand."

"And if you understand, does that mean you'll report me?"

"And who would I report you to? I won't, I promise."

"I know, I know. So what is it, ask away."

"I killed one of the weasels for Six Pints."

"I see. So that makes you Inkcap, then."

"But I was Inkcap before I killed it."

"Then do you know why you're Inkcap?"

"Because my grandad's in Taiwan."

"And why do you have such a grandad?"

"You mean that's my fault too?"

"It's your karma. From a previous life."

"Karma from a previous life? What does that mean?"

"Well, I could tell you in detail what that means, but I'm afraid you wouldn't understand. I'll just give you a bit of advice. Whatever bad this life brings you, you've got to be patient and endure it. Understand? And whatever you do, don't complain, don't speak your suffering, endure it, live through it."

Inkcap looked at the man. He wanted to stand but couldn't. His legs seemed to have abandoned him. He couldn't feel them at all. Finally, he said, "My legs… where are my legs?"

FIFTY-THREE

MONTHS HAD PASSED WITHOUT ANY RAIN. It was now so dry that the villagers had taken to craning their necks each night to stare at the sky, desperate to see any sign of rain. But all they saw were crumpled bits of scattered clouds, lonely and separate. Anguish filled the hearts of Old Kiln, worry lived on their lips. Their crops would be doomed. The land was failing, the river had grown thin, little more than a trickle. The fields were arid and there was no water to irrigate. Even the leaves on the trees had turned yellow and began to curl. Feng Youliang, Gourd, Jindou and a few others from clans besides the Zhus and Heis took to calling out in both southerly and northerly directions for rain, asking the wind why no water had come.

Barndoor was there as well, a cigarette perched on his lip, lighter in his hand. "I don't suppose someone's stolen the water, have they?" he said. He looked towards the irrigation ditch, following it off into the dried distance, where he spied a figure that bore a striking resemblance to Dazed-And-Confused.

"There," Barndoor yelled to Lightkeeper, pointing his finger in the direction of the man he assumed was Dazed-And-Confused. "Take a look. Is that Dazed-And-Confused watering his personal plot?"

"Eh? That's worth investigating, I'd say," came Lightkeeper's response.

Barndoor, however, stayed where he was and shouted out to Gourd who was standing on a nearby weir, "Tell me, you dirty cur, if we've barely the energy to manage the Zhus, how are we supposed to look after the Heis as well? Dammit, the whole lousy village, it's us who don't belong to either of those clans who have to do all the fucking work around here. That bastard Dazed-And-Confused told us to drink air and shit blanks while he stole water for his own land!"

Barndoor and Gourd agreed to find Millstone, for despite him not being the man in charge, he knew how to get angry and to do something about it. Unsurprisingly, it took little persuasion to get him to come to the fields to see what was going on, and even less time for him to order Dazed-And-Confused to cease what he was doing.

Dazed-And-Confused, however, wasn't easily persuaded. "And why should I listen to you? I'm not a Red Blade, so you can't order me around, can you."

"So," Millstone responded, "are you saying that the land belonging to the production team also belongs to the Hammerheads?" And with these words, Millstone moved to block the water running into Dazed-And-Confused's small plot of land.

"Block the water! Why you dirty…" and Dazed-And-Confused raised his fist, threatening to strike.

"Yeah, come on then, I dare you." Millstone braced himself.

Dazed-And-Confused moved forwards, prompting Millstone to grab a nearby shovel and swing it wildly, connecting with Dazed-And-Confused's arse.

Surprised by the blow, Dazed-And-Confused cowered and withdrew, then turned to run, yelling as he did, "I'm going to find Bash."

At the Kiln God Temple, Dazed-And-Confused didn't find Bash, but he did come across Useless and Tag-Along, and he gave them an account of how Millstone had assaulted him. He was not, however, prepared for the response as Useless and Tag-Along both scolded him for stealing the water in the first place. In their minds, he got what he deserved.

"But," Dazed-And-Confused stammered, "aren't you two supposed to be Hammerheads?"

"And what," Tag-Along replied, "you thought we'd help you do something wrong because we're Hammerheads?"

"But, but... Bash, let me tell him what happened."

"Talk to our captain," Useless shouted.

"Yeah, that's right, I'm sure he'll have something to say about what happened."

"Our captain is concerned with much larger matters than this," Useless intoned. "Why the fuck would he bother with you? Besides, he's not here, he's gone to town. Important business and all that."

"How's he gone to town again? He goes there every day. Is he meeting someone, is that it? Some little tart?"

Since Xiahewan had become one of the first villages to set itself up as a base for Red Guard activities, it was unsurprising that Dongchuan soon followed suit. So, too, did the villages of Chafang Fork and Wangjiaping, despite the latter being such a shithole that even flies refrained from laying their eggs anywhere near the place. But cooperation among the villages was impossible, each one far too interested in upstaging the other, staring eyeball to eyeball to see who could be Redder. Accordingly, each one tried to link itself to the county capital, to Luozhen and some other large town as a means to fortify their Redder than Red activities. For Bash, this was all very interesting. The manoeuvres, the claims to this and that. In it, he saw opportunity. No longer was he confined to thinking only of Old Kiln. Together with Huang Shengsheng, he now craved to be involved with revolutionary activities far beyond the limits of his home.

This explained his nearly daily absence from Old Kiln, for most mornings he would rise with the cock's crow and head off to the county capital. He was also very strategic about who would accompany him. Sometimes, it would be with Cao Xianqi from Xiahewan, on other occasions, it would be Liu Shengtian from Dongchuan. Together, they'd scheme and plot, prepare and design various means by which each and every village could be properly Red. Their ultimate goal was to ensure that the entire region, regardless of what side of the river they were on, was sufficiently revolutionary. And if a village had already set up its own Red faction, they'd try hard to find faults and then strategise how they, and only they, could fix things. Sometimes, Bash would let Useless and Baldy Jin participate in his planning, Iron Bolt and Tag-Along too. At first, Baldy Jin thought the scheming and plotting was good fun, but later he started to complain that Bash was worrying about trifling matters, to which Bash responded enigmatically, "Great talents only emerge from deep waters."

"Don't you know," Tag-Along added, "our captain can tread on stars and lead a thousand men, that's why he's our captain."

Baldy Jin felt the need to contribute as well, although not without a subtle jibe in reference to his own displeasure: "That may well be true, and perhaps it's just small fry here in Old Kiln, one must set one's sights on bigger things, but what does that all mean for the Hammerheads?"

"Who says I'm not concerned about Old Kiln?" Bash retorted. "Besides, how can we hope to defend Old Kiln if the world outside goes to shit?"

"Ah, it's true," Useless said, "how small fry such as us predict the ambitions of the great!"

"What the hell do you mean?" interrupted Baldy Jin.

"It's an old saying."

Huang Shengsheng laughed. "I bet if we were in Beijing, Bash would be planning to overthrow the government of a small African country!"

For every action the Hammerheads carried out, the Red Blades paid close attention. Each time Bash went off to do whatever, he'd returned with Huang Shengsheng, Cao Xianqi and Liu Shengtian, and they'd scheme and plot as though murder was on their minds. On some occasions, so deep would they go into planning and scheming, they would almost lose themselves in their machinations to be Red. It was also noticed that when Bash brought these outsiders with him, he would return with any manner of strange and rarely seen things: a wireless radio set, a glass light box with Chairman Mao's head emblazoned on the outside surface so that when the candle inside was lit, the Great Helmsman's visage would glow. Another item was a tin box with a loudspeaker attached on top, a type the villagers had seen in Luozhen but was worthless in Old Kiln since there was no supply of electricity to hook the device up to in the first place. This didn't worry Bash, however, as one of his priorities was seeing that Old Kiln got connected to the regional power grid. For now, he told them, just keep the device safe.

But when rumour spread through the village that Bash had gifted the radio set to Apricot and, moreover, had returned to Old Kiln in the middle of the night with the three outsiders, it got people thinking. And when they heard that Bash and the outsiders had gone straight to knock on Apricot's door, despite the hour, and that she had invited them in, the villagers thought something further. And to top it off, when they heard that she had fed them, and because several villagers had seen Apricot earlier in the night picking green chilli peppers from her personal plot, which she likely mashed together with garlic to make the noodles they supposedly ate... well, for the villagers, it could only mean that this late-night visit had been planned in advance, right?

Naturally, Inkcap had heard the story. But to his mind, it couldn't be true. He'd been round the rear of her house more than once and he'd not heard the sound of a radio coming through the window. He'd seen Awning's wife behind the window, too, but he didn't think she'd heard anything either. For a moment, he considered talking to Apricot about it, but decided against the idea. Soon after, the whole affair seemed to disappear without a trace. At any rate, he'd best keep quiet, no point drawing attention to himself and stoking the hatred of both Hammerheads and Red Blades.

In the morning, Noisy again came to Old Kiln.

Inkcap, who was just picking a new piece of *liguo* candy, was startled by Cowbell when he came running over. "Hey there," he said, "enjoying those sweets?"

"Sweet enough, I suppose, but they stick to my teeth. I kind of hate them, actually."

"I've got something to tell you, you'll never believe it."

"If it's about Apricot, I don't care, you're not going to get a sweet out of me."

"This morning," Cowbell said excitedly, "Bash brushed his teeth and his whole mouth foamed white. Never heard something like that before, I'll bet. He brushed his teeth outside his shack and then Useless came around. But, as you might know, Useless doesn't have money to buy toothpaste, all he uses is a bit of salt, no foamy white stuff for him."

"I've heard that already," Inkcap replied.

"You might know about him brushing his teeth, but do you know he only shits out by the lower slope of Middle Mountain?"

"He goes all that way to take a dump?"

"Well," Cowbell replied, "everyone else, if they feel the urge, they don't do it outdoors, do they? But Bash, he wanders into the woods, digs a hole and squats over it. Tag-Along is usually there with him... with a shovel waiting."

"And..."

"You..."

Inkcap seemed distracted by a piece of *liguo* candy that had got stuck to his teeth. Loosening it, he pulled it out, looked it over and then put it back into his mouth. "Nothing."

Nothing Cowbell had said surprised Inkcap. What Bash did wasn't like what anyone else did. If he wanted to take a shit outside, then that's what he wanted. Inkcap didn't see the point of listening to any more of Cowbell's stories. He put his head down and walked away along the alleyway, picking up the torn fragments of a big-character poster as he went. Altogether, he picked up at least five pieces, he reckoned. Then, somewhat unexpectedly, he felt an urge to fall to his knees, and as he did so, he noticed Bash coming in his direction. He was wearing a cotton, round collar undershirt tucked inside the waist of freshly washed and well-worn military trousers. A leather belt cinched the trousers together. On his feet were leather shoes very similar to those worn by Wu Gan. And as usual, his arms were held behind his back. Tag-Along was doing what he did best, tagging along behind Bash, a basket in his arms, an army water canteen slung around his neck.

"Brother Bash," Inkcap began, "it's been days since I've seen you. You're looking something special today."

"It's been days since I've seen you too. How's it you're still a little shit?"

Bash laughed at his own joke as he continued on his way, his buttocks sticking out awkwardly.

"Say now," Inkcap continued, "those leather shoes ought to be heavy, I bet."

"Oh, fucking haemorrhoids are playing up," said Bash as he shifted on his feet.

Inkcap thought of the rumours circulating through the village. "Did you enjoy the green chilli peppers? I hear you ate lots."

"Yeah, lots of them."

Inkcap hadn't believed the story before, but now he had confirmation. He grunted, then belched into the air. His thoughts turned to Apricot. "Hey, usually I wouldn't say anything, but there's something I can't make sense of, I mean, how's it you're able to make the living you have?"

The basket Tag-Along was carrying suddenly felt very heavy and he looked for a place to lean against to rest. Unfortunately, he couldn't find anywhere, no set of steps, no wall, nothing. The only thing he could do was hasten after Bash.

Getting no further response from Bash, Inkcap hurried up beside Tag-Along who in the recent past was essentially Bash's tail but was now more an echo of a tail as the distance between them grew.

"Hey, why the urgency?" said Inkcap. "Rushing off to get a shovel?"

Barely acknowledging Inkcap's presence, Tag-Along only offered a question in reply: "What shovel?"

"Well, you're walking behind him, there's an urgency in your step, so I assumed Brother Bash needs to take a shit, which means you need to get a shovel, doesn't it?"

From in front of them, Bash let out a laugh, a hearty, deep guffaw, then said over his shoulder, "Tag-Along, give Inkcap the water canteen you're carrying, let him hold it awhile."

Inkcap didn't wait for Tag-Along to respond, he simply reached for the canteen, pulling it over the man's shoulder and onto his own. The strap proved to be a little too long, causing the canteen to dangle down to his knees, so he knotted it almost as quickly as he'd pulled it off Tag-Along's shoulder so that now it hung at his waist. Unsatisfied with just the canteen, Inkcap pulled at the basket Tag-Along was carrying, urging him to give that up as well.

"Hey, it's not for you to carry, there are explosives in here," said Tag-Along, his voice betraying a growing exasperation.

"Explosives? What tosh. Explosives can kill, can't they?"

Tag-Along refused to hand over the basket, so Inkcap's desire to follow the two men began to wane. He looked at Bash walking in front, then shifted his eyes to Tag-Along. When Bash's arms swayed back and forth, he decided to copy the motion. When Bash's arse rose and fell with each stride, Inkcap mimicked the movement.

Tag-Along noticed what he was doing and yelled out to Bash, "Captain! This little shit is copying your every movement."

Bash stopped and turned around, but Inkcap was quick to say, "Your stride is impressive, especially the way your arse moves up and down."

Bash looked at the boy and started walking again. Inkcap followed and soon they reached the Kiln God Temple. Once there, Tag-Along set the basket down and to his surprise, Inkcap saw that it did indeed contain explosives, dynamite in fact, neatly arranged and packed in tightly. Inkcap wondered what the Hammerheads were planning. He thought to ask Bash, but before he could do so, the leader of the Hammerheads said, "Yes, dynamite. Later tonight, you'll know why we have it."

That afternoon, a group of outsiders arrived in Old Kiln. They were dressed smartly and carried gongs, drums, *huqins*, flutes and oboes. Inkcap soon realised they were a Mao Artistic Troupe from Luozhen and that they must have been invited by Bash. For many years, Luozhen had been known for its theatre, but never had a troupe come to Old Kiln before. Naturally, it was a big deal. And even though the troupe had already performed in Xiahewan and Dongchuan, since many of the residents of Old Kiln had relatives in these nearby villages, they still invited them to come for the show.

For the past several years, Sparks loved watching theatre shows. Bash, Soupspoon and Apricot also enjoyed the theatre. Indeed, after every show they saw, they'd spend the next few days discussing it, marvelling at the performances and the messages relayed. They would even try to learn some of the songs. Apricot was especially good at singing. Her voice carried well. Unfortunately, the same could not be said for her actions, which were stilted and unnatural. Sparks himself was not bad, his voice had range. It was just his memory that let him down as the words would escape him repeatedly. But his onstage presence, if they were to ever go on stage, was magnificent. He could carry every role exceptionally well, using his body language like a professional. Bash had once expressed his desire to start a troupe in Old Kiln. For Inkcap, he figured this was perhaps why Bash had invited the troupe from Luozhen to pay them a visit.

Inkcap had rarely seen performers like these. He was awestruck by them and did his best to cater to their needs. He made sure they all had stools to sit on, and that there was sufficient spring water for them to slake their thirst – acting, after all, put a terrible strain on the vocal cords. Whenever any of the actors sat to enjoy the water Inkcap had brought, he would steal a look at them, up until the point where one of them raised their head and discovered him staring at them, to which he'd hastily call out, "Hey... oh... look!" And then he gestured to some corner of the courtyard and pretended to see a sparrow or some other bird. To further fabricate the story, he leapt up and cried out to shoo the bird away, gesticulating animatedly. In his haste, however, and because he'd been squatting down, his legs had cramped and he stumbled, losing a shoe.

The actors were amused by the entire scene, fond as they were of Inkcap, and called out to cheer him on. A few walked over to him and patted his head. Another took hold of his arms and lifted them high, then asked how old he was, assuming he was at least five but surprised to find him so helpful. Inkcap knew they were making fun of him, but it didn't matter, he wasn't angry or embarrassed. He responded to the question by saying he was twelve years old, that he'd even earned work points in the village, taken care of the cattle, sowed the fields, harvested the crops, even protected Old Kiln from roaming wolves with his slingshot. In all of these aspects, he was much better than Cowbell.

"And who's Cowbell?" asked one of the actors.

"You don't know, his ears are all scarred, rats got at them once."

Before the discussion could move on, Tag-Along came over. He'd just been with Bash and the troupe's leader discussing the content of the performance, but since he'd had little to offer, he left them to it.

When he saw Inkcap, his first words were, "What the hell are you still doing here?"

Inkcap failed to pay him any attention and continued talking with the actors. Tag-Along seemed to abandon his concern for Inkcap's continued presence and instead called out to Bash to tell him about the positioning of the stage. He worried it might be too dark because of where it was in relation to the mountain beyond the courtyard and the placement of the big-character poster bulletin boards.

"Might we string lanterns along the walls and trees to better light the stage?" suggested Tag-Along.

"We've got gas lanterns, haven't we? Just hang them either side of the bulletin boards."

"Oh, sorry, I forgot all about the gas lanterns. They burn kerosene, right?"

"Dammit, do I have to do everything myself? Go and find Useless, tell him the performance is going to be a big deal, tell him to bring the fans, we've got to put on a proper show."

Tag-Along walked away as instructed and Bash sat down. Before he could relax, however, Tag-Along returned and gestured to Bash. He whispered, "Don't we need to feed the actors? It's nearly dinner, how are we going to manage to feed all of them?"

"You know I'm the boss, right, I'm the man. You figure it out, dammit. I asked you to find Useless, go do that, he'll sort their dinner too."

With Tag-Along finally gone, Bash returned his attention to the courtyard and heard Inkcap going on about Cowbell. He immediately interrupted to admonish the boy: "Mind your mouth, you little shit. Go on, get over there and help with setting up the stage."

Inkcap did as he was told, but as he stood next to the gate, he realised he'd spent too much time competing with Tag-Along for Bash's attention. He'd been so enamoured with the theatre troupe that he'd forgotten his station. If the Red Blades saw him helping out the Hammerheads, what would they think? Fortunately, he'd not seen any of them the whole day, but did that mean they didn't see him?

Useless had sent someone to the market to buy kerosene for the lamps, but regrettably, they'd forgotten to get wicks. He instructed Tag-Along to ask Bash what they should do, but Tag-Along was too scared to do so, worried Bash would fly off the handle again. Two actors had overheard their discussion and volunteered to carry out the task. Relieved, Tag-Along turned to other duties, namely stringing the line to hold up the lamps. Someone was needed to scramble up into the tree to hang the wire. Tag-Along yelled to Inkcap to help, but he was distracted by a commotion that involved Cowbell.

He walked towards the scene and whispered to Cowbell, "You're a Red Blade aren't you, what are you doing here?"

"I'm checking them out, a bit of scouting."

The pride in his voice was unmistakable, so much so in fact that it made Inkcap uncomfortable, causing him to raise his voice. "Cowbell's here. He can climb trees."

Unable to pass up the opportunity to show off, Cowbell tore off his shirt and spat on both his hands, slapping them together in preparation for scaling the trees. Unfortunately for Inkcap, Useless insisted that Inkcap do the climbing. This in itself was not a problem, Inkcap was capable of climbing trees, but he was very slow about it. Making matters worse for Inkcap was the climb down. Every branch and twig seemed to deliberately strike at him, tearing his clothes and leaving his skin scratched and red.

Back on the ground, he spied Cowbell sitting on a nearby stone and walked over to him.

"You should be the one climbing, I reckon," said Inkcap.

"I'm a Red Blade, how could I climb for the Hammerheads?"

Useless also helped Tag-Along to prepare the troupe's dinner. Or rather he suggested that they would arrange for each villager to feed at least one actor, as was custom when party cadres visited Old Kiln; one family, one cadre to feed.

"That won't do," said Tag-Along. "Everyone in the village will be here for the show. The Hammerheads should take care of them, shouldn't they?"

Useless lowered his head to think for a moment before responding, "I guess you're right," and then he turned and shouted for Inkcap.

"They're calling for you," Cowbell whispered to Inkcap.

"I don't think he's ordering me," he said to Cowbell, but in response to Useless, he hollered out disapprovingly, "Eh..."

"You better go and help the Hammerheads, shouldn't you?"

"And... do you see me jumping at their beck and call?" But he did walk over.

"Go and fetch some ears of maize. We'll cook them up for the troupe."

"You know the maize is rather tender right now," Inkcap replied. "If we boil them up, yeah, sure, they'll be fragrant, but they'll make you fart something awful... where am I to fetch them from anyway?"

"From your family's plot, of course."

"What? No way."

"All right, all right, I can see how that scares you. Fine, fine, get them

573

from the production team's field, fifty should do it, everyone can eat two or three, I suppose. As for the farts, what does it matter, no one'll hear."

"The production team's plot. You sure that's OK?"

"It's for a Chairman Mao Art Troupe, how can it not be OK? What's the problem, do you need the consent of the Red Blades, is that it?"

"No, I'm not a Red Blade, I'm not an anybody." Despite his claim, Inkcap remained reluctant to do it. "Can't you get someone else to get the ears of maize?"

"Oh go on, quickly, do as you're told," a bystander interjected. "I don't know why you're hesitating, come on, where's the energy you showed before?"

Inkcap regretted following Bash to the Hammerhead HQ, regretted also that he'd spoken to the actors and that this had caused Bash to order him to help in setting up the stage. But Bash wanting him to fetch ears of maize to feed them, that was another matter. One that caused him to wink at Cowbell as he walked past him. The wink in turn caused Cowbell to follow and soon they were strolling down the alleyway together, Cowbell cursing Useless the entire time.

"That fucking fucker, fuck, fuck, fuck."

"I know what you're saying," said Inkcap.

"Just wait till he asks me to do something for him, I'll fuck him good."

"Well, then, why don't we get the ears of maize together, it'll be your chance."

"All right. He wants what, fifty ears? Let's tell the production team we need fifty-four ears, that way we'll get two each and then, on our way back, we'll stop to eat them ourselves."

As they strode towards the fields, they could see the maize had reached beyond the height of an average man. They could see the kernels were soft and tender, and when they got close enough to touch them, one squeeze confirmed it. Inkcap reached down to grab the ears more firmly, speaking to Cowbell as he did so, "Why are we even giving our maize to outsiders?"

"Well, if you don't, Useless will never forgive you. You'd be fucked for sure."

"Not much choice, then, I guess. But shouldn't we be harvesting the maize from his personal plot instead?"

The idea spoken aloud struck them like lightning. That's exactly what they were going to do, what better way to stick it to Useless? Plan set, they tromped off towards Useless's plot, whereupon they collected fifty-four ears of maize, making sure to drop the extra four off at Cowbell's house before returning to the Hammerheads.

With all fifty ears delivered and boiled, they were soon handed out to the theatre troupe. Bash, Baldy Jin and Useless enjoyed them too. Baldy Jin even remarked to Inkcap on a job well done, the kernels were tender and soft, quite delicious. Inkcap offered no words in reply, he simply nodded and left the temple grounds. On his way, Tag-Along appeared, evidently holding detonators in his hand.

Inkcap couldn't help but notice what he was holding and had to ask, "What have you got them for?"

"Why do you think? I'm going to make a big bang."

"Where?"

"Up your fucking arse, that's where! Ha ha."

Inkcap failed to see the humour and chose to say nothing further. His mind had already turned to other matters, namely enjoying the ears of maize he and Cowbell had got for themselves.

Cowbell had actually been waiting for Inkcap just down the alleyway from the temple. When Inkcap saw him, saw his mouth busily working up and down, he suspected Cowbell had already devoured the maize.

"You've eaten it all, haven't you?"

"No, no, I haven't," Cowbell said. "I just took a bite or two. The rest are at home."

Cowbell pulled a few kernels from his pocket and he pushed them into Inkcap's mouth. "Come on, we've got to go, Awning wants you for something."

Awning was not alone. Millstone and Sparks were there as well. As soon as Inkcap walked up to the main gate, Sparks called out, "I hear you've been with the Hammerheads all afternoon, is that right?"

"Um, yeah, yes, they're planning a show. I went to watch them setting up."

"No one from the village is going," Millstone said. "How much could be going on there, do you think?"

Inkcap refrained from saying more, fearful of how it would be interpreted. Fearful, too, that they were looking for a reason to reprimand him without mercy.

"I imagine the theatre troupe is more about boosting the Hammerheads' morale," suggested Awning. "What do you say to that, Inkcap? If you want to watch a show, Sparks here, he's quite the singer, he can put on something special, play the role of a strict parent, say."

"All he can do is point his finger at people," Inkcap offered.

"You've not seen this, then, have you?" Sparks cut in, his finger directed towards Inkcap.

Awning laughed, and he gestured for Sparks to lower his finger. "Inkcap, let me ask you something, what else did Bash bring with him? Explosives, right? Tell me the truth, I'll know if you're lying."

"Yes, yes, two bundles of dynamite. That's what I saw."

"What's he planning?"

"I... I don't know anything about that. I only saw them pack them away, in the westerly corner of their HQ. After that, I left, they told me I had to fetch some maize."

"Maize?" Millstone said. "It's not ready yet. Why the hell did they ask you to fetch maize?"

"To make dinner for the actors," Inkcap replied. "Useless told me to go... to go to the production team's field, he said I could get it from there, but...

575

but me and Cowbell, we didn't do that, we went to his personal plot instead… we got the maize from there."

"That fucker, wanted to use the production team's maize to feed outsiders?" Changing the subject, Millstone turned to Awning and said, "What about the porcelain at the temple? I think we need to get it quick. Those bastards are likely to try and sell it otherwise."

"All right, Inkcap, you did good. Yeah, good indeed, you took Useless's own maize instead of the village's. But now, I want you to go back there, I want you to find out what they're going to do with that dynamite, whether they plan to use it in the village or not. We need to know."

"No, no, Bash wouldn't have the balls, would he?" Millstone interjected.

"You think? I don't trust the bastard. I reckon he's capable of anything. If he wants to blow something up, the other Hammerheads will follow along. Who's to say they're not planning some show of force? Sparks, how many of those charges do you have for setting in fox burrows?"

"My father-in-law gave me ten."

"You head over to your in-law's place. Whatever charges he has, you get them and bring them here, I'll dig around for some too." Awning paused. "Inkcap, get yourself to the temple, find out what they're doing. Then get back here pronto."

"How… how am I supposed to ask them what they're doing? I don't think they'd tell me in any case."

"He's probably right about that," Sparks offered in reply. "Forget about that, Inkcap can be more useful helping me. I've got to walk to Xiahewan, after all."

"Xiahewan?" said Inkcap. "So we're not going to watch the show?"

"The show? Are you a fucking Hammerhead after all?"

That evening was particularly unlucky for Inkcap. He spent part of it on the road with Sparks, trudging off to Xiahewan and Sparks' in-law's house. Sparks' father-in-law loved hunting, but because the number of wild animals in the mountains had dwindled, and because he'd got older and older, he spent most of his days sitting in his courtyard making charges that looked especially like small chickens. He even went so far as to place meat for bait on the charges themselves. The tactic was plain: the foxes would see the small explosives, smell the meat and then try to eat them. Just as they did, the charge would explode and the fox would be dead. Easy. Naturally, Sparks' father-in-law would then take the carcass, skin it and sell the fur and meat in the market at Luozhen.

Unfortunately, the older man's explosives were rather dear to him, so Sparks ended up having to invent a rather contrived story as to why he needed them before his father-in-law permitted him to take away a single basket of charges. On the way back to Old Kiln, Inkcap remained quiet, as he had been the entire time they spent in Xiahewan. Sparks noticed the silence and the speed by which Inkcap's little legs hurried as though he were anxious to get back to the village.

"I know your legs are far shorter than mine, but why are you trying to walk that much faster? What's the rush?"

"I want to watch the show."

"Watch the show, why you little shit, I'll give you a show. Here, bump into this basket I'm carrying, you'll see something then, I wager, likely King Yan himself!"

Just as he spoke, they'd reached the bridge on the eastern side of the river when they heard a loud and reverberating thump. Sparks came to a halt. "Was that thunder?"

"It's a clear sky, look at the stars, couldn't be thunder."

Neither could explain what had made the sound.

When they reached Awning's place, the clangs and gongs of the performance were audible. Inkcap's spirits lifted, the show was still going on. He placed the sack he'd been carrying on the ground for Sparks and made to rush off to see whatever was left of the troupe's performance. Before he departed, however, Awning told him that prior to the show starting, Bash had set off some of the explosives. The blast had shaken through the village and caused the ground to tremble. Awning cursed him: Bash sure loved making a commotion. Of course, in Awning's mind, Bash's actions were in direct response to the Red Blades firing a cannon to announce their creation as a rival faction to the Hammerheads.

Sparks responded grumpily to the information. "So I went all the way to Xiahewan for nothing?"

"And why do you say that?" Awning retorted. "You brought back the charges, didn't you? We'll use them at our next meeting."

"Then," Inkcap began cautiously, "I can leave... go see the show, yeah?"

"For fuck's sake, yes. Go on, beat it."

The lamps they'd hung up did little to illuminate the stage. This was partly due to the number of mosquitoes encircling each lamp, casting black shadows over the little light that was being shone. A fair number of villagers had gathered to see the performance, but no one was sitting. Those at the back were in fact standing on benches to see the stage better. Dazed-And-Confused stood to the side, trying to maintain order. He was clutching a willow branch that served as his crowd-control tool. If the audience started pushing against each other too much, he'd swing the branch across the back of their legs to get them to stop. Most readily obeyed, although that didn't stop them from swearing at Dazed-And-Confused. There was no way for Inkcap to squirrel his way into the crowd in order to see the stage. But then he realised he didn't need to. He knew where the performers would take their breaks and wait their turn to go on stage. He would at least see the actors in their costumes. He never expected that the way would be blocked and that Cowbell would already be there, straining to look between the chairs that had been placed to prevent the theatregoers from getting too close to the stage.

"So," Inkcap said when their eyes met, "is the maize all cooked?"

"Not yet... say, did you know Goodman is a Hammerhead?"

"What? How can he be a Hammerhead?"

"If he wasn't, how could he be here?"

Inkcap followed Cowbell's line of sight and saw Goodman. He was off to the left of the stage, talking to some of the actors. "Perhaps," Inkcap suggested, "one of the actors is ill?"

"We should go over to check, listen if they're talking about someone being sick or about joining the Hammerheads."

The two boys navigated away from the crowd, then round the back and up to the other side where Goodman had been seen talking to the actors. There were no chairs obstructing their passage on this side and they could move closer, close enough to hear Goodman speaking.

"...The body, the heart and one's inborn nature, these are the three realms that make up existence." Inkcap and Cowbell could only grasp bits and pieces of what Goodman was saying, something about the body responding to all things, something else about learning, a snippet on the mind being the repository of all things. They thought he also mentioned a divine spirit or perhaps it was a principle, then something on why Man was no longer spiritual in the present day. Much of what Goodman was saying was lost on them until he turned to matters a little more straightforward.

"You know that comrade of yours, he's quite the drinker, isn't he? He's eaten a lot and still wants a drink. I don't think you should indulge him, I'm afraid he's going to faint. I told him this, but he didn't listen... got angry with me, in fact. Too stubborn, I guess."

"That's just him," one of the actors replied. "Desheng's his name. No need for you to be upset about his reaction."

"Oh, I'm not angry. I might have been in the past, but not now. I've been giving health advice for about ten years. I've had my fair share of irate villagers cursing me for the advice I give, spitting at me even... it's hard, I won't deny it, I'm trying to help, as I was with your friend, you know, get him to think about what he's doing. It's hard, wounds me deeply when they seem ungrateful. Still, I keep doing what I do. If you think you'll be in Old Kiln for a spell, I could try to speak to him again."

"I don't imagine we'll be here that long," another person said. "Lots to do, you know. In fact, I reckon we'll be off tonight. But we know of your skill. If we need help, we can always come and find you out. Say, I've got a little boy myself, only three years old... seems he's always ill, not sure, to be frank, if he'll make it... Perhaps you could take a look at him?"

"I'd be happy to. Back when I was learning all this, an old grandmother paid a visit, she had her grandson in her arms, holding onto her so tightly. She asked the same question, will he make it? I told her straight, this grandson of yours, you did right by him, you came to me. If you didn't, he'd be gone in no time, but you came to see me. But, I said to her, it's a pity, to her and to her son and his wife, that their effort for this child was wasted, it would have to be written off, the child would live for no more than ten days. I remember she asked why, I said it was because their house was out of order, that they'd lost their ethics, their whole family was topsy turvy, no one performing the roles they should. She didn't understand me at first, told me to better explain, so I asked her, what do your son and daughter-in-law do when they first wake up? Do they clean, start the daily fires, warm the water, make food, and she said no, they usually slept until late. Then she added – and I smiled knowingly at this – she said she was the one who did all the work, and I said, I was being honest, I said to her, that's why your house is out of order, they're unfilial, they're not behaving as they should. That's why her daughter-in-law gave birth to a sickly child, a child, moreover, who kept them up at night. She interrupted me then, I remember, to say that's why she brought her grandson to me in the first place, so I told her to go home, to instruct her son and daughter-in-law to act properly, to be moral and upright, that while this child was doomed, if they mended their ways, they'd soon have a second child and that this one would be fit and healthy.

"She didn't get angry with me. In fact, she did as I told her. She went home with her sickly grandchild and told her son and daughter-in-law everything I had said. They took it well, I learnt later. The daughter took her firstborn home to her mother's place, its condition improved for a bit, but then it got sick again. Her mother didn't want it to die in their home, so she sent her daughter back to her husband's house, and you know what, the child died on the road, on the way back. Why am I telling you all this? Well, in Old Kiln, whichever family lives an ethical life will do well, they'll be healthy, and life will be good. For those who live unethically, well…"

Cowbell turned to Inkcap and asked, "What the fuck is he on about?"

"Beats me. I don't think it means anything, to be honest."

Just as they were about to leave, the chairs shifted and one of the actors who had presumably been listening to Goodman drone on emerged. He didn't notice the boys, or at least he pretended not to. Without saying a word, he disappeared into the darkness.

"I guess he didn't enjoy listening to Goodman, either," laughed Cowbell. "Shit, someone asked about a sick child and then got a whole sermon on living… what… living good I suppose."

"Yeah, but what's he up to over there behind those trees?"

Together, they followed the performer, careful not to make a sound. Apparently, the actor had gone behind the trees to take a piss. He saw the boys almost immediately.

"Oh, sorry, uncle, didn't mean to walk up on you," Inkcap stuttered. "Had to take a wee, eh?"

"What the hell else would I be doing out here?"

"I don't know, I suppose you could be…"

The actor tied his trousers and shouted, "Bugger off you little fuckers."

Just as he yelled at them, a loud sound broke through the night. A boom they actually felt. A red flash accompanied the crack, and Inkcap froze. Like a tree rooted in the ground, he couldn't move.

"Dammit, what the hell is going on?" intoned the performer. "They already set off one batch of explosives at the start of the show… they wouldn't do it again in the middle, would they?"

It was pandemonium. The crowd was in chaos. Those who had been standing on their stools fell off. The flash had caused them to turn their attention towards the alleyway.

Flower Girl's voice was the first to be heard. "Oh no, that's not good, that was an explosion in the village. Something's happened."

And with that, everyone began to jostle and push at each other, unsure what had happened, what might have exploded, whether it came from their home. Some fell and were trampled, but despite their pleas, moans and curses, no one seemed to notice. Others began to run. The stage drums reverberated, gongs clanged, people cried and shouted. Pure pandemonium.

FIFTY-FOUR

THE EXPLOSION HAD HAPPENED AT AWNING'S HOUSE.

Sparks had been carrying the basket holding the explosives, intent on hanging it up in the western part of their compound, across a beam that was strong enough to bear the weight. The hooks had been used to hang seed sacks which themselves could be heavy enough. First, he had to remove the seed sacks in order to hang the basket carrying the charges, placing them on the ground. He lifted the basket of explosives onto the hook and as he did so, a rather large rat came into view, its eyes transfixed on the basket now hanging from the beam. Sparks looked at it critically.

"Afraid it's not for you... no food, you see, this stuff will only blow you to bits."

Verbal remonstrations aside, Sparks felt the hook on which the charges hung was a little too low, perhaps not low enough for critters to reach, but low enough for people to bump their heads. To solve this problem, he grabbed a stool and planned to remove the hook and then place it higher up the beam. Once complete, he'd rehang the basket carrying the explosives. Of course, hanging it proved to be much more difficult now that the hook was much higher up, and in his efforts to hang it properly, one of the charges fell and hit the ground, exploding on contact. While the blast from a single explosive wasn't altogether impressive, it was enough to throw Sparks off the stool. And since he'd yet to hang the basket up, the remaining charges went with him, splattering on the ground, each exploding in turn. Boom, boom, boom!

Hearing the blasts, Awning and Millstone, who'd been enjoying a cigarette together, rushed to the western corner of their HQ, only to see an empty pit in the ground and a reddish plume of smoke floating above it, oddly shaped like a mushroom.

"Sparks! Sparks!" Awning shouted. "Answer me."

No answer came. Awning drew closer to the scene of destruction, lamenting to himself as he noticed another great hole, this one torn in the ceiling of the building. He then spied Sparks. It seemed that the first blast that had thrown him from the stool saved him from the full force of the remaining explosives. He lay slumped on the threshold of the building, his face blackened from the explosion. Awning rushed over and lifted him up. Holding onto the other man, he rubbed his hand across Sparks' ash-covered face. It was still white underneath. His eyes looked fine, and there seemed to be no gaping holes in his flesh. Awning spoke to him in hushed tones, tried to tell him everything was all right. He then attempted to lift him, discovering then that Sparks' right hand was missing the index and middle fingers. His ring finger was bent at an unnatural angle, and the whole hand itself seemed to be attached only precariously to the rest of his arm.

Once they'd moved Sparks to a more comfortable location, they tried to find his detached fingers. Alas, there was no sign of them. And besides, they thought, what would Sparks do with them even if they were found? Realising the futility of continuing their search, they resigned themselves to bringing Sparks to the Luozhen medical facility, despite it being late in the night. The doctor did little more than cut off the remainder of the broken finger and bandage the stump, then sent him on his way with some prescribed painkillers.

Unsurprisingly, the morale of the Red Blades was damaged by the incident. The other villagers believed this was all somehow due to Sparks' carelessness. They were his father-in-law's explosives, after all, and he must have been negligent in handling them. Or inexperienced, some suggested. There were a few questions as to why he'd gone to Xiahewan to get them in the first place, and why he'd brought them to Awning's house, but more discussion was devoted to the size of the blast – it had been so loud – and the damage caused to Awning's house. A hole in the roof? Awning and Millstone offered no explanation. Inkcap said nothing either.

The theatre troupe's performance was ended early, unfortunately. But the fact that Bash had got them to come to Old Kiln in the first place won him the respect of a great number of villagers. The end of the day might have turned out better, he thought to himself, but it had worked out in his favour at least. As a result, Bash walked through the village with his chest pushed out just a little bit extra in the days following that ill-fated night. Of course, his overall routine didn't really change, as he was also seen marching off towards the slopes of Middle Mountain with Tag-Along close behind, shovel in hand.

"Say there, Tag-Along," called one of the villagers, "tell us, why doesn't your captain use a privy like the rest of us?"

"He can't, I suppose, 'cause he's constipated."

'Constipated? It's not like it's spring and we're all eating fried noodles, how can he be constipated?"

"Comrade Huang said that all important men get constipated from time to time."

"I suppose that might be so. But why are you carrying that shovel? Gotta dig another hole for him?"

"Well, after he has his shit, I bury it."

"Damn, like an animal, then. I mean, dogs and other beasts do the same thing, bury their shit when they're done."

"You dare! If he were an animal, he'd be a tiger or a leopard at least."

Bash heard the entire exchange but had refrained from saying anything on the matter. Instead, he simply asked Tag-Along about the theatre troupe and how they were getting on after the unfortunate end to their show.

"All OK, yes, they're fine, no issues whatsoever," Tag-Along offered.

"I think Old Kiln ought to have its own theatre troupe, you know," boasted Bash. "We could enlist the entire village as performers... shame about Sparks, though, with his burned face and missing fingers, I guess he wouldn't make for much of an actor."

Ten days or so later, most of the potatoes in the fields were ready for harvesting. Soon after, each household in Old Kiln would be eating them. In most cases, the potatoes would be boiled until soft and then mashed, no cutting required. They resembled dried chestnuts, pasty and not altogether easy to eat. As a result, the villagers would have to chew like cattle munching cud, causing their eyes to bulge as they broke down the potatoes before swallowing.

"You know," ruminated Half-Stick, "I never thought about it before, at least not before marrying into the village, but the eyes of everyone in Old Kiln are certainly large."

A small group of villagers had gathered by the rubber tree to enjoy their potato mash. Inkcap had brought a small bowl himself and joined them.

Sprout noticed him first and called out, "Say, Inkcap, you're walking even slower today. Afraid you'll spill your mash, are you?"

Inkcap knew Sprout was making fun of him, but he stopped himself from getting angry. "Hey, what's that sound, can you hear it?"

The sound of stone rollers was clearly discernible.

"Aiya," Sprout replied. "I guess that means poor old Padlock's house is still making their mash."

Noodle Fish's family had no wheat flour, so they had potatoes every meal. They'd harvested their maize early on, but the kernels had been too soft so they had no choice but to grind the entire cobs into powdery flour and make their mash out of that.

Every year there were families like Noodle Fish's who couldn't wait for the proper harvest time. Once-Upon-A-Time's family, Jindou's and Huolian's too, they all ended up grinding their maize to make mash. But it was hard work. The millstone was heavy, and the cobs took time to break down. Day and night, the rest of Old Kiln would hear them hard at work.

The Branch Secretary never harvested unready maize. In fact, he had some maize harvested from the previous year, so much so that insects had begun to infiltrate and had moved on from the larva stage to festering, black beetles able to fly. Some were so large that the villagers had taken to calling them corn cows. As a result, when they did ground out the maize, beetle bits were inevitable: a head here, hind legs there, a shell, a wing. At the same time, one of the cows the Secretary had been charged with looking after was about to birth a calve, so he spent his days in the cowshed, unable or at least unwilling to come home. Naturally worried her husband wouldn't be eating anything, his wife prepared bowls of boiled potatoes and delivered them to him. Noodle Fish even wished to contribute a little, offering cornmeal buns his family had made, but the Branch Secretary declined.

"Cornmeal buns? Made from unripe maize, I don't think so..."

"Eh, now," Noodle Fish replied, "better than nothing, these are. Think of them as pickled cabbage if you must."

"That's one way of looking at it, but I'd like to ask, why harvest your maize early?"

"I dunno... but we didn't harvest everything."

The Branch Secretary, bowl in hand, stood up and walked over towards the main building to speak to Millstone. "Millstone, how many families have harvested their maize already, before it was ready?"

"More than half, I'd say."

"You know this'll result in a poor maize harvest."

"And what do you think they should be doing instead?"

"In the past, we always had to be more circumspect, had to make sure we had emergency rations too. You mean to say no one has gone to the town to ask about proper procedure?"

"A sign of the times. Besides, there's no one to ask."

The Branch Secretary couldn't think of a suitable response, so he paused and took a mouthful of his potato mash. After swallowing, he continued the conversation, asking, "The autumn harvest, what arrangements have been made for it?"

"And why are you asking me this?" Millstone answered abruptly. "I'm not the team leader here."

"I know that. And I'm not the Secretary," he said, lowering his head and laughing under his breath. "We're nothing, I guess, nothing at all, but the village's farms, they need all the farmers looking after them, don't they? I mean, come on, if we don't, who will? Bash?"

There was anger and a sense of defeat in Millstone's reply: "I suppose that means we're all dead, the whole fucking village is dead."

"Didn't I hear that the Hammerheads have both a captain and his first lieutenant? A second in command?"

Millstone squinted and stared at the Branch Secretary. "Bash said he was Chairman Mao, but does anyone really recognise him as the Great Helmsman?"

"Wasn't Baldy Jin a group leader before, Iron Bolt too? Don't they both hold the same position with the Hammerheads? After all, who's in charge, the Hammerheads or the production team?"

Millstone lowered his head and exhaled his growing anger.

Noodle Fish walked over and joined the conversation. "Millstone, didn't you say you had no interest in being leader? I don't think anyone removed you from a position of power. I saw the fields, the maize was starting to dry. Sure, those nearer the riverbank were still tender, but not the rest of them. The cabbage, too, is ready, far as I can see. True, lots of families have harvested their personal plots early, but that's because there are difficulties on the horizon. What's more, the production team's harvest isn't all that good, no way their crops will last till spring, so that means there's sure to be hungry mouths in late winter."

Millstone did not acknowledge Noodle Fish's words, he only sat, seemingly deep in thought. Finally, he stood up, announced he was going to eat, and with that, he departed, leaving the two men by themselves.

"You see that," shouted Noodle Fish, "he's taking my advice and going to do something about it."

"Come on, let's just eat. We'll see what happens later," said the Branch Secretary.

"How can we just sit here and eat? If they can't hear the bell tolling for them, then what the hell is the point of it all?"

"Tomorrow. Let's listen tomorrow."

Sure enough, the next morning, a bell rang throughout Old Kiln. It had been quite a long time since anyone in the village had heard this bell, and its clang pierced the air with a degree of urgency. But there wasn't much of an echo, if any echo at all. More like the bell had turned to wood, absorbing the sound instead of reverberating. The clanging continued, elongating and echoing across Old Kiln. More and more villagers stopped what they were doing and looked into the sky as though they were seeing the sound waves spread out over the streets, alleys and courtyards. Barndoor was the first to run towards Millstone's home, shouting as he did, "Captain! Captain!" And then, a little less loudly, he continued, "I heard the bell, official business needs doing. May I ask what it is?"

Millstone never contradicted the title Barndoor gave him, instead answering his question, "Men to the mountain foothills, there are soya beans to harvest. Women to the riverbanks, cabbages need picking."

Bash and Dazed-And-Confused had spent the night at their temple headquarters. When day broke, Bash got up and began to exercise, first lifting a stone dumbbell several times, then proceeding to do push-ups. Dazed-And-Confused looked on in bewilderment. This was his lot, he assumed. He'd been sickly since he was a child. No matter how long he slept, or how well, he would always wake up in something of a daze, hence his nickname. Some mornings would take longer than others, but for the first thirty minutes or so of every day, he'd have to just sit quietly, trying to collect his thoughts and wake his brain. This morning, he was sitting on some nearby steps, listening to Bash exert himself with his morning exercises.

As his senses started to return, he called out, "I don't suppose there's a woman nearby, is there? Is that why you're pushing yourself like that?"

A moment later and he had to look away, disinclined to watch Bash get dressed, brush his teeth and do a few more push-ups. He turned his attention instead to the wall and was surprised to see what he thought was a noodle stuck to it. His eyes went large and focused in, not a noodle, he thought. A snail. He closed his eyes again. Just then, the sound of a bell echoed in the air.

"What the hell is that?" Bash asked.

Dazed-And-Confused remained silent.

Bash stood up and asked again, "What the *hell* is that?"

"What's ringing?" was all Dazed-And-Confused could reply.

Bash kicked at Dazed-And-Confused and said, "It's the village bell, but more important, who the hell is ringing it? Go and find out. Now! Say, where's Baldy Jin?"

"He... he left in the night, I think."

"That sonofabitch... go fetch him and find out who's ringing the bell."

Since the Hammerheads had set up their HQ in the temple, Bash had spent most of his nights there, often alone, which he professed to prefer, except he did like it when the easterly quarters were occupied. The night before, Dazed-And-Confused and Baldy Jin had spent the night in the westerly rooms, but when Baldy awoke in the middle of the night, ostensibly to pee, he discovered his manhood was erect for other reasons. Seeing only Dazed-And-Confused sleeping peacefully near the wall and not his wife, he wondered if he could think of the man otherwise. At that moment, Dazed-And-Confused woke himself and saw the look in Baldy Jin's eyes.

"You're having a laugh, aren't you?" Dazed-And-Confused said. "Use your hand if you must, but do it against the wall."

"You use your fucking hand, I'm leaving," said a furious Baldy Jin, and he stomped off.

That was when he left the Hammerheads' HQ.

Now Bash was telling him to go and collect Baldy Jin. But where? Might he be with Half-Stick, she wasn't much more than a slut, after all. Dazed-And-Confused was, admittedly, still groggy and uncertain of himself. He thought it best to have a piss before doing anything, and it was only then, in the privy, that he began to see things clearly. Pulling up his trousers, he spied Half-Stick walking some distance away. She was carrying a basket of unripe maize and seemed to be in a rush. The up and down of her arse cheeks proved that much at least, thought Dazed-And-Confused. Quite the tramp she was, wasn't she? Dazed-And-Confused called out to her, but she seemed not to hear. Someone did, however, and came running in Dazed-And-Confused's direction.

"Is he up?" Useless asked.

"And who wouldn't be?" came Dazed-And-Confused's rushed reply.

"The captain."

"If by captain you mean Bash, then yes, he's up."

"What do you mean by that? The Hammerheads have their leader, and we all follow him, who the hell else would I be asking for if I'm asking for the captain?"

Dazed-And-Confused didn't quite understand what Useless was getting at. "I said he's up, didn't I, course he is... fucking, fuck."

Useless ignored him and ran towards the temple gate, rapping on it with some degree of force. The idea of Apricot being inside would not leave him. The door, however, did not open, only Bash called out from beyond it.

"If you want to come in, why knock so hard?" he said, and he pulled the door ajar.

Inside was quiet and still, no sign of Apricot. Under his breath, Useless cursed Dazed-And-Confused.

"Who rang that bloody bell?" asked Bash.

"That's why I'm here," Useless responded. "Millstone rang it, he's ordering everyone to the fields to work, just as if he were in charge."

Bash did not reply immediately, his face betraying the thoughts running through his mind.

"I've thought things over," Useless continued, "but I've not said anything. I don't know what he's up to acting the way he is, but I can't help but think Baldy Jin is somehow involved. You don't suppose they've... switched sides, so to speak?"

"Baldy Jin would never."

"I guess you're right, he wouldn't say anything directly to Millstone, but perhaps he said something to Half-Stick who said something to Awning and–"

"Let's wait for Baldy Jin, and then we'll figure out what's going on."

Unfortunately, Dazed-And-Confused, who'd already been sent to find Baldy Jin, discovered no trace of him. It wasn't until later that he knew the reason why: Baldy Jin had heeded Millstone's orders and gone to the fields to harvest the soya beans. He didn't appear at the Hammerheads' headquarters until noon. Naturally, Bash asked him what he'd been up to, to which Baldy Jin replied honestly that he'd been in the fields.

"So that's all it takes?" said Bash. "Someone says jump and you ask how high?"

"But the soya beans were ready for harvesting. If they were left, they'd start to rot."

"Bloody pig brains you've got. Millstone gave up his position ages ago, he's not in charge of squat, so why the hell did you listen to him? Hasn't that crossed your piggish mind?"

"I guess it didn't... it was my old lady who told me to go. The men of the village had work to do, so did the women. I didn't think, I just did."

"You're suppressing the Revolution by carrying out field work," interjected Useless.

Now it was Baldy Jin's turn to become angry. Turning to Useless, he shouted, "What bullshit, you're talking absolute nonsense and smearing my good name."

"You're the one talking nonsense, trying to defend your actions, you're out harvesting the fields, aren't you? Today it was soya beans, tomorrow likely the maize, you're doing what *they* tell you to do, aren't you?"

"Shut up both of you," yelled Bash, and the two men went quiet.

For the remainder of the day and into the early evening, the men and women of the village worked the fields, but Baldy Jin refrained from joining them again. Dazed-And-Confused and Useless did likewise. Most of those from the Hei clan declined to work, in fact. Instead, the Hammerheads rounded up those villagers they could and marched over to urge the Branch Secretary to come out from the cowshed. He obliged and appeared shortly after, his conical dunce hat perched on his head. Without a further word, they took hold of him and together they walked off towards the village centre.

When the Branch Secretary failed to return, Noodle Fish grew worried and went out to see what was going on. He saw him with his dunce cap on, surrounded by Hammerheads. The Secretary was filthy, his trousers covered in shit. Noodle Fish heard him ask in vain if he could be given some time to clean up, but Dazed-And-Confused only cursed him.

"Why? You think you're going to some fancy dinner?" and he reached towards the man's legs, grabbed some of the cow dung and smeared it over the Branch Secretary's face.

Noodle Fish didn't dare say anything. He only returned to the empty compound to wait until everyone outside was gone. Once they were, he left to see the Branch Secretary's wife, she had to be told what was going on.

"Why did they drag him off?" she asked.

"I can't say. At first, I saw them heading to the village centre, but I think they took him out of the village altogether."

"Oh dear, oh dear. You don't suppose they're taking him to prison, do you?" And with that thought in her mind, she began to cry.

"Please, don't cry, you can't, it won't help. You know that, besides, if they're taking him to prison, let's think about him for a minute, what will he eat, for example? Perhaps you should prepare something?"

Noodle Fish was purposefully trying to distract her and it worked, for she immediately raced off to the kitchen to make him something. Unfortunately, much of the kitchen was bare. All she could find were a few eggs, and these she carried off in search of her husband. Noodle Fish followed.

"Mrs Secretary," Noodle Fish said when he noticed her slowing pace. "I don't think you'll catch them. Come this way, we need to take a shortcut."

Together they cut behind the toilets in the direction of the outskirts of Old Kiln. Once they reached the stone lions, they caught sight of the Hammerheads who'd made it to the county road leading to the capital. As they crossed over the irrigation canal, however, the Branch Secretary's wife's legs went soft and she crumpled to the ground, tears streaming down her face.

As the Hammerheads marched past, Apricot was busy speaking to Gran. The previous night, she dreamt she'd seen her dead father. It was as though he were still lying on the bed, looking the same as ever. She asked him what he'd like to eat and he responded that he'd been in the fields all day harvesting string beans, so it only made sense for her to make some food for them, didn't it? Just as she was about to start cooking, she woke up. Her head was pounding, she told Gran, hence she didn't go into the fields the whole day. She just couldn't bear picking cabbages with the way her head hurt. Even after eating a little, the pain remained. That's why she'd come, she didn't know what else to do.

"Tell me," Gran began, "did you often bring him food like that?"

"Um... yes, yes I did. That's odd, isn't it? I remember, too, that he could never actually taste anything."

"But he still ate, and now, in your dreams, he's telling you he wants more, he wants string beans again. Does your plot have any?"

"I tried planting them last year, but they didn't grow very well, so I didn't even try this year."

"I think I've got some here. You take them, go and cook them at home, then make an offering to your father."

"When it's time for us to head to the fields again, make sure you come and get me," Apricot said. Gran nodded her head, before sending Inkcap off to their fields to pick some string beans.

Basket in hand, Inkcap walked towards their plot of land. Suddenly, a group of seemingly panicked chickens appeared out of nowhere and ran in his direction. Feathers fluttered in the air, causing Inkcap to call out to them, "What is it, what's going on? What's wrong?"

A few of the chickens made to respond, their necks stretched as though they were about to take this opportunity to vent all the grievances of their species, but the cacophony of clucks, chirps and squeaks drowned out any semblance of intelligible communication. A second later, Useless's mum appeared waving a stick, murder in her eyes.

"Hey!" Inkcap said. "I mean, I'm sorry, but… but… these chickens aren't yours, what are you doing?"

"These beasts were… copulating in front of my house! I can't believe it, have they no shame? It was… was a veritable orgy! I can't believe it."

"And?"

"And? How would you feel if they did that out front of your house?"

"My house, well, no one comes to my place anyway, I doubt even the chickens would bother." With that, he turned to the chickens and shouted, "Run, get out of here."

As though they understood, the chickens scattered, leaving Useless's mum with barely one to beat. All she could do was fling the stick after them and shout, "This is what happens when public morals suffer, chickens copulate where they please!"

"Damn, what kind of world is this?" Inkcap muttered to himself. "A widow yourself, so not even allowing the chickens to have an orgy?"

As he started to laugh, the Hammerheads appeared and stormed over in his direction. Baldy Jin began the verbal onslaught: "Hey, Inkcap, you little shit, what's your gran doing?"

Inkcap mistakenly thought the Hammerheads were practising a march and so was somewhat confused by the question. "Why do you ask?"

"Bloody fool… didn't you see who was marching in front?"

Inkcap looked at the front of the column and saw the Branch Secretary, a conical hat on his head, shit still smeared over his face. Inkcap didn't say anything further, he only ran home to tell Gran. At first, he couldn't find her, she wasn't in the courtyard. He ran inside, but she wasn't there either. Then he ran into the kitchen, shouting as he did, "It's another public denunciation! A struggle session."

Baldy Jin had followed Inkcap and was now standing outside their courtyard gate, yelling, "Inkcap! Inkcap!"

Inkcap closed the kitchen door and walked out into the courtyard. Apricot followed close behind.

"I told you to get your gran," said Baldy Jin, his voice venomous. "Why the hell did you run?"

"She's not feeling well," Inkcap responded.

"Not feeling well, eh? That's quite clever, isn't it? I suppose you think you're smart."

"It's true, she's sick, she's been vomiting and she's got diarrhoea… she's in the privy right now."

"Well, if she's sick, I guess you'll just have to take her place."

"She really is quite ill," said Apricot. "That's why I'm here. Tell me, what's going on?"

"We're going to Xiahewan, want to come?" Baldy Jin answered quickly.

"And why are you going to Xiahewan?"

Baldy Jin babbled on about what they were doing, Apricot only half listening. As they talked, Inkcap tried to slip away. Unluckily for him, Baldy Jin wasn't as distracted as he seemed.

"Are you trying to leave, you little shit? You want to go somewhere, I'll tell you where, to the front of the fucking queue alongside Zhu Dagui and his shit-smeared face!"

Even if Baldy Jin hadn't said anything, Inkcap thought to himself, he'd still probably end up following the Hammerheads, just to see the hubbub. But standing in place for Gran, that he wasn't entirely keen about. As a result, he hesitated, which only angered Baldy Jin more.

"You won't? Well, if you don't go, your gran'll have to, sick or not."

"If Inkcap is forced into it," Apricot interjected, "then I'll be coming too."

Reluctantly, Inkcap took Gran's place and began to march with the rest of the column of Hammerheads. Not far from home, however, he realised one of his grass-knitted shoes was falling apart. He turned to Baldy Jin and asked if he could return home to fetch a new pair but his request was denied. Baldy Jin simply said he could walk in bare feet instead.

Inkcap didn't let the issue go, however. "Baldy Jin, what's got into you? Before, you were never this rough."

"It's revolution and you're a class enemy. You don't deserve kindness."

Inkcap whimpered quietly to himself, partly because of Baldy Jin's cruelty and partly because Bash, who'd been nearer the front of the march, now slowed his pace to take up the rear. Through increasingly tear-filled eyes, Inkcap cast pleading glances back at Bash. After a few minutes, Bash relented and allowed Inkcap to return home to get new shoes. At least Bash seemed to have left a little room in his heart for Inkcap.

Back at home, Inkcap relayed the details of what was happening to his gran, who was more concerned about her grandson being taken in her stead than what the whole point of it was. Inkcap tried to cheer her up by claiming he was going to be amid a great hullabaloo, but this didn't entirely console his grandmother. To make matters worse, there were no new grass-knitted shoes he could change into, all Gran had was a cloth shoe. She tried to convince him to wear odd ones, but Inkcap refused. He'd keep wearing the rotten one instead, make the Hammerheads lose face, or so he thought. At least they had any number of rotten grass shoes in the house to choose from, such was the way Inkcap got through his footwear. And because his shoe was in such poor condition, he decided to take extra pairs with him, that way he could continually change out of one bad shoe after another. With those shoes slung over his shoulder, he raced back to the waiting Hammerheads. Unfortunately, carrying the extra shoes slowed his pace to the point that by the time he reached the stone lion at the edge of the village, he saw the Branch Secretary's wife seated next to it, crying profusely.

"Mrs Secretary, why are you crying?" Inkcap asked.

"Because your Secretary is being hauled off to prison."

"No, don't say that. I just saw him, he's just marching with the Hammerheads."

"And they're the ones dragging him to prison."

"No, no. They're just going to Xiahewan to show their support. There's been some trouble there, I heard, and the Hammerheads, well, they're just bringing your husband along. Lightkeeper is going too, so am I."

"You're not lying to me, are you?"

"I wouldn't do that."

"But if they're just going to Xiahewan to offer support, why do they need to bring my husband with them?"

"Because he's a capitalist running dog, isn't he? What better way to show revolutionary support than marching a capitalist at the front of the column."

"A what? A capitalist running dog, where did you get such language?" There was anger in her voice, Inkcap could tell. Before he could say anything further, however, she made a lunge for his face. Instinctively, Inkcap recoiled, but this didn't stop her from yelling at him, "How dare you call him that?"

Inkcap couldn't help but feel his words had been misunderstood, and he pulled back further from the woman, raising his voice as he did so, "I'm not talking to you any more, I'm off."

Before he could depart, however, she changed her tone and begged him to take the eggs to her husband. He agreed and turned to go. From behind, he could hear her words, telling him not to eat the eggs himself, they were for the Branch Secretary.

News of the march to Xiahewan spread through Old Kiln, soon reaching members of the Zhu clan. And while Inkcap taking the place of Gran might have been significant to some, neither Awning nor Millstone cared a wit. Rather, they directed their rage to Apricot's decision to accompany the Hammerheads alongside Inkcap. As they raged and shouted expletives, many other members of the Zhu clan lamented about the recent past, about how the village had gone from bad to worse after Potful's death, right up to today and the work in the fields. Others found fault with Apricot, blamed her for not breaking things off with Bash, ultimately concluding that she must be a Hammerhead too. The stories got wilder and wilder, each more outlandish than the previous one. Even Sprout began to have trouble believing what was being said about Apricot, finally coming to her defence by questioning whether she really was a Hammerhead.

"And besides," Sprout said, "who's seen her at their temple headquarters?"

"I've seen her out by the temple gate," said Awning's wife.

"And that's just the road in front, isn't it? Tell me, who hasn't been on that road? Isn't it also the only path she can take to her personal plot? What's she supposed to do, fly?"

Awning's wife did not concede. "And how much work does a personal plot need? I've seen her on that road many times in a single day. I reckon she's seeing Bash a hell of a lot more than tending her land."

"How can you say such a thing? We're all of the same clan—"

"Bullshit. The Zhus might have had influence in the past, but what influence do they have now? In our bowl of soup, I'm sure you'll find Useless's rat shit, Apricot's too. So you tell me, doesn't that spoil the soup?"

That night, the production team distributed the cabbages that had been harvested during the day according to household and the number of family members residing in each. No men by the surname of Hei were there, only their wives and in some cases their children, baskets slung around their shoulders, waiting dutifully for their share. Those of the Zhu clan were given their shares first, then those of any other clans. Finally, the Heis. Millstone's face looked perturbed throughout the entire process, and he cursed quietly to himself that when work needed doing, no one came, but now, look at the greedy bastards, they all showed up to get their mouthfuls. Even the bloody Heis. But he had to give them something, he thought. That would be pushing things too far. The Heis that were there, the wives, the children, none dared speak up, even though Millstone's curses were loud enough to be heard. Nor did they say anything about receiving somewhat smaller portions. All they did was leave as quickly as they could when they got whatever they were going to get. At the end of the day, only a single basket of cabbages remained, two-thirds of which was already earmarked for Half-Stick.

"Anyone left?" Millstone called out.

"Bash's not been given any," answered Sprout.

"Well, then, how about you take it on your way and also some for Half-Stick, everyone deserves their share after all."

Sprout complied, but then a thought occurred to her: "Say, there's someone left. Apricot, she's not been given any."

Millstone stared blankly for a while, then replied, "Do you see any more cabbages lying about, is there anything left? Since there's none, what do you suggest we do, give her our own bones?"

The Hammerheads only returned to Old Kiln after the cock crowed. Quite famished, they scattered in separate directions upon arrival. It wasn't until the next day that Apricot learnt the cabbages had not only been harvested but already distributed among the villagers. She went in search of Millstone.

"So where's my share?" Apricot asked. "You've given some to everyone else, but none to me."

"And where were you when we were sharing them out?" Millstone retorted.

"That doesn't matter, we never needed to attend in person before. I'm still a member of the production brigade, aren't I?"

"But there's none left."

"You mean I've come here for nothing? I remember speaking up and supporting you for a leadership role, and this is how you're going to treat me?"

"Do you remember your dad?"

"What do you mean by that?"

"You know what you got up to yesterday. If your dad learnt of this, he'd turn in his grave I'm sure."

"My family's business is none of yours, so you'll not say anything more on this. I've just a question for you, Bash is one of the five types, yeah, so does that mean I'm to have nothing to do with him?"

"I don't care what you do or who you do it with. You want to be with Bash, go ahead, why don't you go and join the Hammerheads too?"

"I'm not a Hammerhead, but hearing you speak like this does make me want to join them."

"Join. Go on. Marry him while you're at it!"

With nothing left to say, Apricot stormed off, heading directly to the Hammerheads' headquarters.

Thereafter, Apricot made no effort to disguise her visits to the Hammerheads' HQ. The Red Blades no longer cared that she was a Zhu, or that Potful had been her father. They'd taken to hating her as much as they hated Useless, if not more. For her part, Apricot was like a changed woman. It was as though she'd been set free, free of misgivings, free to interact with whomever she liked. She no longer spent her days quietly at home, almost afraid to see anyone. And she no longer needed to sneak around to see Bash.

When Half-Stick bumped into her on one such occasion, she couldn't help but say in a loud voice, "Oh, Apricot! Say now, what have you been eating, you've gained weight!"

"What do you mean? I've been eating the same as everyone else in the village."

"My dear Apricot, if your heart is full, then even water will make you put on weight. Say, Apricot, since I married into Old Kiln, I've never seen you so happy, your face always used to be blotchy, but now it's so much better. You know, I used to say I was the only woman in Old Kiln who could do as she pleased. I didn't think you'd be joining me. I guess that makes us sisters. That means we'll have to call on each other more often."

Despite Half-Stick's apparent warmth, Apricot did not feel the same and declined the invitation to call on her. But she did visit one person more frequently: Flower Girl.

Apricot rather liked Flower Girl. For one, she liked her painted nails, always much brighter and more vivid than Apricot could ever manage. Her polish also lasted far longer. Flower Girl tried to instruct Apricot on how to better paint her own nails, that applying lye water first and then the dye was an effective means to a longer-lasting varnish. It was all about the preparation, and then the layering of polish. A level of care too. When the two walked down the alleyways together, the sunlight reflected brightly off their red polish. Apricot also remarked on Flower Girl's face and how it seemed to shimmer. Her cheeks were perpetually rosy. Apricot envied her long braid and how it hung down to her perfectly rounded buttocks. Her breasts were equally perky, thought Apricot, they seemed to bounce like rabbits when she walked. Naturally, when they talked in this manner, both giggled affectionately, pleased by the growing friendship.

On one occasion when Yoyo saw them, she couldn't help but stare.

Flower Girl saw her and called out, "You're welcome to join us. We're going to the ravine to wash our clothes."

Yoyo's eyes took on a cloudy look, but she did not reply. The women didn't seem to care and continued on their way. Having arrived at the ravine, however, Flower Girl's thoughts returned to Yoyo. "She must have fallen ill again," she said. "How can she not be interested in me?"

"I imagine she hates me," said Apricot.

"Why, what did you do to offend her?"

"What makes you say that? I haven't offended her in any way."

"Old Kiln's a small place, how can one villager pretend not to recognise another?"

At around the same time as the friendship between Flower Girl and Apricot blossomed, Huang Shengsheng returned from Luozhen on a bicycle. Bash was quite enamoured with the contraption and took to pedalling about the village and the fields. So practised had he become in riding it, he could easily lift his hands from the handlebars and continue cycling. He could even perform wheelies. Bash wanted to teach Apricot how to ride, but she was afraid to even try. Bash, of course, would not easily dissuaded and intended to keep at it, wear her down, as it were.

Left by herself after one such rendezvous, Apricot spied Awning's wife walking not too far away. Awning's wife, however, paid her no mind, except to lower her head and spit in Apricot's general direction. When it appeared she was going to spit again, only to be racked by a fit of coughing, Apricot called out, "Aiya, sister, what's the matter? Chicken feather caught in your throat?"

Awning's wife never expected Apricot to speak to her, and she was unable to respond. What she heard next was even more surprising, for Apricot called out to Bash, "I think you'd best get back here, Bash. You've got to teach me to ride."

This time, Bash would take things a little slower. Before Apricot started pedalling herself, Bash would carry her on the rear pannier rack, and only round the village alleyways since they were at least cobbled and a little more level than the lanes that meandered through the fields. This didn't stop the bicycle from bumping and lurching, however, forcing Apricot to plead with Bash to take it slow. Bash, of course, only speeded up. He even released the handlebars to cause Apricot greater panic. Originally, Bash intended to ride out to the fields, but since the wind blew harder in the open countryside, causing his shirt to billow behind him and thump loudly, he turned back towards the alleys of Old Kiln, as much to escape the wind as to avoid having to listen to Apricot scream from behind. When he finally approached the stone lion, he turned down the alleyway that led to the county dirt road, then the sloping path to Ever-Obedient's home. There, they discovered Ever-Obedient's old dog at the head of a pack of three other mongrels and five roosters, all of which chittered or barked, seemingly deep in conversation. As soon as the animals spotted Bash's bicycle, they formed ranks, causing Apricot to call out, "Look! What are they doing?"

Bash did not reply, focusing instead on training a path for the bicycle through the animals. The creatures scattered every which way. Unfortunately, the commotion caused Apricot to lose her grip and tumble off the bicycle. She hit the ground and spun along, carried by her momentum down the sloping lane to the maize field at the bottom.

Bash, oblivious to the fact Apricot had been thrown off, continued to pedal furiously. Down through the lane and along to the county dirt road. Turning in the direction of the highway, he shouted, "I've got the hang of this, haven't I? If this were a car, I'd be hitting the throttle and we'd be off!"

No reply.

"Don't believe me?"

Still no reply.

Bash released one hand from the handlebars and reached behind. All he felt was the empty seat. He turned his head and saw no one. Apricot was not there. Slamming on the brakes, he brought the bicycle to a halt and looked around. There was no sign of Apricot anywhere. He did, however, hear Ever-Obedient's dog barking, and decided to head back. Near the bottom of the lane, adjacent to the field, he discovered Apricot slumped on the ground.

Apricot had lost a shoe. Evidently, one of the dogs had run off with it. Her trousers were ripped, exposing bloody knees. The rip extended up her leg, revealing her bare thighs. Her face was bloody as well, and the crash clearly stunned her. Bash leapt off his bicycle and hastily used the sleeve of his shirt to wipe the blood from her face.

"Can you see me?" he said. "Hey, can you?"

Apricot opened her eyes and spoke groggily, "Yes... yes, I can see you."

Bash noticed her left eye beginning to swell badly. He bundled Apricot up and carried her off to the Luozhen medical clinic. There, she received thirteen stitches and some painkillers. Bash revealed his concern for Apricot, interrogating the doctor as to whether the stitches would keep her cuts together and help her wounds heal. Yes, the doctor replied, somewhat perturbed that the young man was questioning his work.

"Will there be any scars?" Bash asked.

"I would think there will be."

"Oh, her beauty's ruined," Bash lamented as much to the doctor as to himself.

Bash's clear disgust at what had happened to her and her resulting disfigurement seemed of little concern to the doctor, who was ordering Apricot to remain in the hospital to recover. At the same time, back in Old Kiln, Six Pints passed away. Apricot was unable to attend. On the afternoon he was buried, Bash returned to Luozhen to visit Apricot in hospital. By this time, she was able to lift herself out of bed, but her face remained swollen and the stitches above her left eye were far from being ready to be removed. She was rather frightening to look at, or so thought Bash. He betrayed these feelings by refusing to look at her.

"You've put me in quite the state, haven't you?" Apricot said. "Come on, raise your eyes, look at me."

Bash lifted his head and the first thing Apricot noticed was the large pimple on his nose. "Ha, look at that, I guess I'm wearing you out, eh?"

In the days following Six Pints' death, the village owl hooted incessantly night after night. It didn't remain in a single tree but flitted back and forth between the trees throughout Old Kiln. Its voice could be heard nearly everywhere, so the villagers rarely knew in what tree the owl was perched. Even when a villager did discover the creature, they wouldn't dare try to strike it. That would be disrespectful. All they could do was politely call out for it to depart and find another tree in a different corner of the village to rest in.

Gran, however, was fond of the owl. In the evenings, after rounding up the chickens and driving them into their coop, she'd sit on her stone steps and wait for the owl's call. If she didn't hear it, she'd grow flustered. She knew it would sound out eventually, but even when it did, her heart would only become even more flustered.

"Oh, where is it?" she cried out.

"Perhaps it's over in the elm tree?" offered Inkcap.

"No, I think it might be in the chinaberry tree."

Both paused and trained their ears in the direction of the chinaberry tree. A faint hoot seemed to carry on the wind, or so they thought.

"You don't suppose someone else's days are numbered, do you?" wondered Gran. She lit her lamp and pulled out her scissors and paper. A unicorn, she thought, yes, she'd cut out a paper unicorn. Once finished, Gran instructed Inkcap to paste the unicorn opposite the paper visage of Chairman Mao that Useless had hung some time ago. Inkcap complied, quietly collecting his slingshot as he did so and then sneaking out of the main gate.

Inkcap's plan was to track down the village owl. He was afraid of both the Hammerheads and the Red Blades, but he wasn't afraid of the owl. He didn't intend to kill it, only scare it with his slingshot – like an annoying fly that goes quiet and seemingly disappears when someone grabs a flyswatter. He was going to be that flyswatter himself or perhaps owl-swatter? But like the disappearing fly, the owl seemed to realise he was out looking for it with his slingshot, for he couldn't find it anywhere. He checked the elm tree, and nothing. The chinaberry tree was empty too. He cursed to himself and headed home. As he passed Apricot's house, he noticed the gate was closed tight, but the western wall was crumbling. A sour date tree was growing among the fallen bricks, its thorns preventing anyone from climbing into the courtyard. The tree, however, didn't block the view and Inkcap could see inside. He also saw that the tree's leaves were rather dry, but they weren't falling to the ground. He looked a little closer and a swarm of mosquitoes rose up around him, causing him to fall back. As he did, he spotted a chicken milling about. Evidently, no one had rounded it up and driven it back into its coop. If Potful were alive, Inkcap thought, there'd be people in the courtyard along with the chicken. The stone steps were a favourite space for Potful and his friends to enjoy a cigarette. He would regale them with stories about this and that. Inkcap smiled to himself. Potful never needed to burn wood to smoke out the mosquitoes, his cigarettes did that for him. Now, no one called on Potful's home. He himself hadn't visited for ages, thought Inkcap. He breathed in and then called out to the chicken. The bird complied and scurried over. Inkcap looked at it.

"Tell me, have you seen that owl? Do you know where it is?"

"And who are you?" asked the chicken.

Before Inkcap could answer, the sound of crying reached his ears. The sobs were broken and stifled, but crying, nonetheless. It was as though the cries were muffled under a quilt or perhaps a hand was covering their face, but regardless, an image of tears streaming down cheeks appeared in Inkcap's mind, tears flowing this way and that, like ants scurrying across the ground. A sense of urgency grew in Inkcap's heart, and he didn't know what else to do but run home and tell Gran. By this time, she'd already cut out six unicorns and was working on the seventh.

"What?" she said. "Run back and tell Apricot to come over, will you? We can have a chat, help ease her mind, her heart."

"Tell her to come over?" Inkcap said, a degree of surprise in his voice. "None of the Zhus want anything to do with her. Do you think we should?"

"Just because that's how everyone else behaves doesn't mean we have to do the same, does it? Didn't she just go to Xiahewan with you? Wasn't that also for me?"

Inkcap didn't immediately call on Apricot. Instead, he wandered towards the southern part of the village and marvelled to himself at how it was. Gran had told him to be like a mouse and on this evening, he truly felt he was a scurrying rodent, unnoticed but all-seeing. He was enjoying his solitary stroll so much that he didn't want to return home, he wanted to spy on some commotion or other, an argument between villagers, or just some folk having a chinwag while they smoked. But there was nothing. No one was about, no one but Inkcap. Resigned to the quietness of the evening, he finally decided to call on Apricot. As he approached her house, however, a dark shadow flitted across in front of him before disappearing.

"Who's there?"

There was no answer. Was it a neighbour's pig that had got loose? Pigs can be stealthy when they want to, he thought. And it wasn't unheard of for them to sneak out of their pens at night. The year before last, this had happened to Old Faithful. A wolf had found its way into the village, attracted by the roaming pig, most reckoned. The beast ended up biting at the pig's ear, while at the same time whipping its tail hard at its hind quarters. In a clumsy way, it looked as though the pig was following the wolf, or so said some of the villagers who'd seen it. Inkcap worried the same scene was about to unfold when the sound of Ever-Obedient's dog broke the silence. Strangely, it barked only once. Inkcap's eyes fell on the gate of Apricot's house. It was then he noticed the pair of shoes just outside. The shoes were in poor shape, worn and dirty. Inkcap wondered who'd be wearing such a shoddy pair of shoes and realised the shadow he'd seen must have been a person, not a pig. He cursed to himself, felt anger at his own stupidity.

"Who's there?" he quietly called out.

The alley that led to Apricot's house was narrow and long, but in the dark, he could see no movement. Nor did anyone offer a reply. His eyes then fell on the privy that jutted off at an angle at the end of the alleyway. Perhaps whoever it was that had passed him by was hiding out there. Yes, that must be it, he reckoned. But he had no idea who it could be. Then he figured it wouldn't matter, whoever it was would still likely beat him. And yet, he had to know. Thinking quickly, he came upon a strategy to find out who it was. He'd pretend to be walking away by letting his footsteps fall hard and then he'd let them trail off. Moving closer to the privy door, he was about to put his plan into action when the shadow he'd seen earlier scrambled over the privy wall, darting off into the night. Inkcap was able to make out who it was: Cowbell.

His anger rose again, but this time it was directed towards Cowbell and not himself. If it had been anyone else, Inkcap would have made no effort to chase him, but it was Cowbell and he was someone Inkcap couldn't just let get away.

Cowbell ran, slowed and then stopped. Turning, he shouted, "Come on, then, if you want to hit me, let's go. I won't run any more."

There was a pause, before Cowbell shouted again, "Hit me, come on, I won't hit you back."

Inkcap made no attempt to take a swing at Cowbell. Instead, he looked at him in the dark and asked, "What the hell are you doing sneaking around Apricot's house at this hour? Why aren't you home? Were those your dirty, worn shoes outside her door?"

"My shoes aren't worn and dirty."

Inkcap thought things over. "If they aren't yours, then whose are they? Could they be Apricot's? No, impossible, I've never seen her wear shoes like that. They mightn't be yours, but I bet you put them there, didn't you? Just what are you up to? Who told you to put those shoes there?"

"Best not ask me that," Cowbell replied. "You know the Zhu clan is cursing her. If you want to know, ask her."

"Ask her? You think she'd tell me? Am I her uncle or something?"

"When's she ever called you uncle?" Cowbell shot back.

All this was true, thought Inkcap. He couldn't escape the reality that he was nothing to her. Inkcap felt his anger begin to subside. He looked at Cowbell again, and some of his anger returned.

"Whether she's called me uncle or not is no business of yours. You just go and get those shoes away from her door."

"But I've come this far," Cowbell groaned. "Why should I go and collect them? Can't I just leave them where they are?"

"Absolutely not."

"Well, if you want me to get them, you've got to give me your Chairman Mao badge."

Inkcap reluctantly removed the badge from his chest. He hated Cowbell, wanted nothing more than to throw the badge to the ground, force Cowbell to scramble around in the dark looking for it, like a dog pawing at the dirt for a morsel of something to eat. But then he thought some more. No, this is a Chairman Mao badge, he'd best not treat it that way.

FIFTY-FIVE

ALTHOUGH THINGS WERE CHAOTIC, Millstone had arranged for all the maize to be harvested. Unfortunately, the sweet potatoes had been forgotten, and the hemp remained uncut. The same was true of the cotton for it was also left on the lower slopes of the mountain, unpicked. Left untended, the production team's land was starting to seed, so too the personal plots for many of the villagers. The activities of both the Hammerheads and the Red Blades seemed to diminish as well. When the bell calling the villagers out to work rang, members of the Zhu clan complied while the Heis stood at their doors, waiting to see if any other members of their clan decided to comply with the clanging bell and the summons to work.

Should they spot one, they'd call out in derisory tones, "Ah, so you're off to the fields, then? Following the crowd, are you?"

And the response would be, "You can hold grudges all you want, but the land doesn't care, does it?"

Sometimes this would be enough to encourage other Heis to join them. There was truth in what they said. As a result, both factions ended up working the fields, each harvesting what they could, each piling their yield as though in competition to harvest more than the other, each only talking among themselves.

Inkcap worked with neither the Hammerheads nor the Red Blades. Instead, he worked alongside Branch Secretary Zhu, Lightkeeper, his gran and even Goodman, all tilling an area separate from everyone else. However, because he continued to carry his homemade lighter for cigarettes, both factions repeatedly called out to him, and he found himself constantly moving back and forth between the two groups. Neither side seemed to think anything about it; it was, after all, just Inkcap. Little did they suspect that Inkcap kept his ears open as he switched back and forth, this despite the insults they hurled at him, the verbal teasing he endured. In truth, he thought it was all good fun.

Things carried on in this manner until the noon sun shone above them and a member of the Zhu clan called out to their faction that it was time to stop and head home to prepare lunch. Naturally, the words were only meant for the Zhu clan, but the Heis couldn't help but hear and follow suit. Later, when a group of Zhus headed to the sweet potato fields and were seen by the Heis, they too sent a smaller group to plough the sweet potatoes. And so it went.

It didn't matter who ploughed the fields, Inkcap and Cowbell were responsible for harnessing the oxen. This had become a sort of unwritten rule, the two of them tasked with not only harnessing the animals but also leading them out to the fields to wait for the ploughmen to come and do the proper work. The ploughmen were an unsavoury, quick-tempered lot. Always smoking, they'd never greet the two boys with a 'hello', rather they'd look at the harnesses and release a litany of curses. Still, they got on with the work, ploughing the fields with the skill expected of ploughmen, or so thought Inkcap and Cowbell.

Of course, their cursing of the boys was not limited to the shoddiness of their harnessing. For one, they couldn't abide by Inkcap and Cowbell just sitting around while they worked, so they took to forcing them to follow along beside the oxen, as though they were cattle to be driven. Their task was straightforward enough: whatever stubble was ploughed up by the oxen, whatever bits of green plants were churned over, Inkcap and Cowbell had to collect them. They also had to pinch their roots so that they wouldn't grow again. Their final task was to clean what they had picked and place them away from the field for the ploughmen to take home with them once their work was done.

Whether the fields were ploughed deep or shallow depended much on the land itself. Likewise, the speed at which the oxen were driven; the quicker they went, the shallower the plough dug into the ground. But if the plough worked too far into the soil, the oxen expended too much energy and grew tired, causing the ploughmen to curse the animals as harshly, if not more, than when they cursed Inkcap and Cowbell for the supposedly poor harnessing. In truth, the men lumped Inkcap and Cowbell in with the animals, seeing little distinction between them.

On one occasion, after Cowbell gave the reins of an old ox to Cattle Track, the beast chose to wander a little unevenly, causing the reins to become tangled among its legs. When Cowbell climbed under the creature to try to untangle the reins, the ox proceeded to kick at him, frightening Cowbell to such an extent that he refused to climb back under the animal. Cattle Track, blaming Cowbell for causing the problem in the first place by incorrectly harnessing the ox, cursed him to high heaven, going so far back in his litany of abuse to disparage Cowbell's grandfather and father for siring such a worthless son, no use in the fields, no use for anything.

"Wasted sperm, you are," spat Cattle Track, "and nothing more."

Cowbell suspected that Cattle Track thought he was a Red Blade, hence the vitriolic abuse, but said nothing of his suspicions. In fact, he said nothing at all, which perhaps only made Cattle Track even angrier.

"Oh, for heaven's sake," shouted Cattle Track, "if you're that useless, let's see how Inkcap makes out." Turning to the other boy, he yelled, "Inkcap, you little shit, get over here."

Switching places, Inkcap attacked the problem of the reins with vigour. First, he followed the harness from the ox's nose down under its belly, untangling it quickly and without drawing the anger of the animal. Once untangled, he followed along the beast diligently, picking up whatever the turned-over earth revealed. At the same time, he also made sure everyone had a light for their cigarettes. But the gadflies proved to be as attracted to Inkcap's blood as they were to the ox's, and soon Inkcap's skin was marked by red, painful bites. Surprisingly, he persisted, refusing to even utter a complaint.

Once the work was finished, the ploughmen departed, leaving Inkcap and Cowbell alone with the animals. The boys, rather exhausted by now, let the cattle mill about, munching on grass, then led them back to their cowshed. It was then Cowbell and Inkcap let loose their own barrage of curses.

"You dirty fucking backstabber... Little shit... Short-necked cunt... Better off fucking dead..."

And on they went, mimicking what they'd endured at the hands of the ploughmen. When they'd finished, they fell into laughter before deciding to head to the river near the kiln once the oxen were returned to their shed and they were free to do whatever they pleased. The kiln itself had not been lit for what seemed like ages now. Lightkeeper remained there, however, spending his nights at the kiln. Goodman was often there as well, down from his own temple lodgings up the hill to teach Lightkeeper how to handle the porcelain and the cloth bags they needed to be stored in. Inkcap and Cowbell had decided to wander over there after work and listen to Goodman go on about some topic.

However, on arriving at the kiln, they learnt that Lightkeeper and Goodman were not there, that Millstone had given them orders to head over to Tiger Mountain to harvest the black soya beans. This was work that would require three to five days for not only did they have to pick the pods, but they also had to open each one and remove the beans since these were all that Millstone told them to bring back. And since they'd been ordered by Millstone, they could not refuse. Millstone, in fact, had arranged for four men to go, Lightkeeper and Goodman made two, the others being Stargazer and Once-Upon-A-Time. Originally, Millstone had wanted Dazed-And-Confused to go, but he refused, choosing instead to spend his time digging sweet potatoes closer to home.

Both the men and women of Old Kiln worked in the sweet potato fields. The men dug while the women picked the potatoes freed from the soil. In the past, when Dazed-And-Confused was working in the fields, foul, vulgar language spewed out of his mouth, often causing the women to clutch at their breeches in embarrassment. There was a strategy behind his savageness, however, for so embarrassed did everyone become that Dazed-And-Confused would end up doing very little work at all, at least when the women engaged with him. Now, though, no female villager would even dare to say a word to Dazed-And-Confused. Disappointed at how he was being ignored, Dazed-And-Confused thought of other tactics to employ to reduce his workload. Spying a suitably shaped sweet potato, he put his plan into motion, lifting it from the ground, dusting some of the earth from it, and then placing it in his trousers, suggestively positioned.

"Hey," he called to Palace's wife, "what do you make of this?" And he stood straight in front of the woman, the sweet potato standing erect in her direction.

Palace's wife ignored him. She even refrained from lifting her eyes.

"Say now, I'm talking to you, don't just ignore me."

"Sorry, what? I wasn't listening."

"I reckon Palace doesn't have one like this, does he?"

"You'd be surprised at what he has for me. Damn sight thicker than yours, I'll bet." And she picked up her basket of potatoes and turned to leave.

Dazed-And-Confused rushed towards her, pulling at her arm for the slight she'd levied against him. Palace's wife wrenched her arm away but tripped and fell, cursing him as she landed on the ground. "There're no sows here for you to poke, you bastard, so bugger off into the mountains to find some crack to stick your rotten prick into."

Her sharp wit and cutting language made everyone in the field laugh. They all knew Dazed-And-Confused looked after a sow; a sow that had, strangely, never sired a piglet for him. They knew, also, that he often spent his nights in the pigsty, supposedly fearful someone would steal his prized if seemingly barren pig, or that the creature would run off. Odder still was the fact that occasionally, frequently even, villagers would hear the sow moan as though it were getting its fill, and yet, Dazed-And-Confused had no boar. Naturally, no one ever said anything about this to Dazed-And-Confused's face, these were words best kept uttered behind his back, but now Palace's wife had put the stories out into the open and Dazed-And-Confused wasn't about to take things lying down.

Over the next few minutes, he swore at her, and she swore back, each voice increasing in volume. Finally, word of the argument reached Palace, who'd been working in an adjacent field. He rushed to the aid of his wife and like two cocks flashing their combs and crowing loudly to intimidate their opponent, Palace and Dazed-And-Confused came to blows. More wrestling, actually, than an exchange of fists. Their arms entangled, their necks and legs too, each man tried to force the other onto the ground.

Dazed-And-Confused yelled in gasping breaths, "Let's fight... come on... give me your best."

To which Palace replied, "My best... you'll get more than that... you fucking scoundrel."

"Oh yeah... is that all you can do? You fight like an old man."

Freeing himself from Palace's grip, Dazed-And-Confused shifted back and undid his belt, pulling it free to use as a whip. Before he could wield it, however, Palace lunged at him and tackled him to the ground. They rolled and tumbled across the field, but finally Palace seemed to gain the upper hand and pinned Dazed-And-Confused beneath him. By this time, everyone had stopped working, entranced by the wrestling match they'd just seen, and now some took to yelling out, urging Palace to fight on, to bite him if necessary. At the same time, Palace hollered in seeming triumph. But as he did, Dazed-And-Confused managed to wriggle out from underneath, and the delighted bystanders thought round two was about to begin. Some wished to fan the flames so they hooted and hollered again. Others grew worried at the savageness of the confrontation and chose to intervene. They all stopped, however, when Dazed-And-Confused let loose an almost primal scream. That's when they noticed. Palace had in fact bitten him. But since his trousers had fallen down because he'd removed his belt, Palace's teeth had bitten into his penis, breaking flesh and causing him to bleed. He stood cupping his wounded manhood, perhaps thankful it hadn't been bitten clean off.

Amid the commotion, Yoyo watched it all unfold. But now she fell to the ground, her head smacking into the earth. Evidently, her illness had returned.

In Old Kiln, the bite was talked about for days, a source of much mirth and laughter. Retold and told again, it didn't take long for the story to reach Xiahewan and Dongchuan. Unfortunately for the village, however, it only served to reinforce the tawdry reputation of Old Kiln. When Awning and Millstone called on Wu Gan in Luozhen, he even asked them about the tale, wondering if it were true.

"Yes, it's true," replied a somewhat embarrassed Awning.

"Hard to believe, I must say. I mean, sure, curses are fired off during a fight, but to egg someone on to bite their opponent, and then for them to follow through and actually do it... hard to believe. Who did it, anyway? I never heard the names."

Neither Awning nor Millstone answered, reluctant to name Palace as the culprit. After all, he was a Red Blade.

In the past, Dazed-And-Confused had always walked about Old Kiln with his head cocked, a smug look on his face. He'd been afraid of no one. But after having been bitten by Palace, he changed. He'd been cut down, as it were, and should he see Palace, his instinct told him to hide until the other man was no longer in sight. He never walked quite the same way either. There was now a noticeable unevenness to his gait that the villagers assumed was because of what had been bitten. Even when he was called out to work by the production team, he could be seen regularly crossing his legs in discomfort. Ultimately, his work suffered and he was in danger of not being able to contribute much of anything at all. Unsurprisingly, some villagers wondered how he would earn his work points, but Millstone offered a defence.

"I say we still give him something. After all, what would we write for his excuse, that he'd half his cock bitten off?"

There was another, if unintended, consequence of the fight. Whenever the Red Blades held an event, Palace would be there telling his story. He'd become a sort of character from a play or novel. There had been an exchange of blows, he'd hit the fucker in the face, received a couple of counterblows, and then they'd wrestled each other to the ground, and then... then he clamped his teeth down hard. After all, he told everyone, the Red Blades had to have their power taken away from them, and what better way to do it? Laughter would always erupt.

Then someone would ask why he hadn't bitten the whole thing off, end the bastard's line once and for all, to which Palace would reply, "I couldn't, the filthy thing stank too much!"

Laughter again.

Inkcap hated himself for missing the show. Barndoor had dragged him out into the fields that day, had worked him to the bone. Some of the ground had been too hard to plough, so Barndoor made him use a shovel to turn over the earth. By the time word reached him of what was happening and he had raced over to see for himself, the battle had already ended. To his mind, it was another instance of the Hammerheads and Red Blades butting heads, neither could leave the other side alone. His only hope was that Dazed-And-Confused would try to seek revenge, then at least he'd have the chance to see part two of the confrontation. Unfortunately, his hopes were dashed. In the days that followed, Old Kiln was peaceful and quiet. After lunch, he neglected to feed the pigs and wandered through the village alleys. There were no new big-character posters. Nothing had been posted. The only person he saw was Cowbell, who was milling about with seemingly nothing to do. They heard someone in the nearby shitter taking a dump. A few dogs yelped and then three or four of them appeared before running off down an adjacent alleyway.

"Nothing going on?" asked Inkcap.

"What are you on about?" replied Cowbell.

"The Cultural Revolution... it's finished, yeah?"

"What tosh. How can it be finished?"

With a little time before they had to be in the fields, the boys decided to play a game of chess. Cowbell was much more skilled at the game than Inkcap, but this didn't prevent Inkcap from taking a chance. To Cowbell's frustration, however, Inkcap was rather slow and deliberate in his moves, holding onto the pieces, hovering over a spot for what seemed like ages. Then he apparently grew distracted and looked up at the chinaberry tree, its vibrant colours glistening in the morning sun. Finally, Cowbell could stand it no longer.

"Oh, for fuck's sake, make your move. Come on, do it!"

"Strange that none of the leaves from the chinaberry tree have fallen yet, don't you think?" Inkcap wondered aloud.

Cowbell shifted his attention to the tree and as he did so, Inkcap surreptitiously changed the piece he was holding and made a move. When Cowbell returned his attention to the board, he noticed the pieces had shifted and accused Inkcap of cheating. Inkcap refuted the charge forcefully, despite the fact he had indeed cheated, and the two began to argue back and forth.

The ruckus drew the notice of Ever-Obedient who'd been just outside the courtyard where they were playing. He stormed up to the chess table, shouting as he did, "Damn waste of sperm, the two of you. Tell me something useful, have you seen your auntie?"

"Not me," said Inkcap. Then he quietly muttered to himself, "Why the hell is he calling his wife my auntie?"

"No one who came out into the fields this morning has seen her," Ever-Obedient continued. "I even checked the personal allotments, but they said she was at home, but there's no sign of her, even the bloody stove was cold."

"I don't know," said Inkcap.

Ever-Obedient turned pale but said nothing further. Instead, he turned on his heel and marched away, down past the courtyard and onto the dirt road. There, the boys saw him break into a run.

"I wonder what's going on," Inkcap mused. "I don't suppose they're in a big fight?"

"Haven't you heard she's lost her marbles?" Cowbell replied.

"I heard she was sick, but I didn't think much about it."

"Well, this time it's more serious, I guess. I saw her this morning, she looked batshit crazy to me, had a broom in her hand and was sweeping the steps in front of the old Branch Secretary's house. I asked her what she was doing, and she didn't even seem to notice me, she just kept sweeping."

"If you'd seen her, why didn't you tell Ever-Obedient?"

"Because we were playing."

Inkcap looked at the board and in one movement scattered the pieces onto the ground. "I'm done. I'm going down to the river to see what I can see."

While he didn't know what was going on, when Inkcap heard that Yoyo had seemingly disappeared, he thought of the river. He couldn't say why the river came to him then, but he felt he had to go there. Yoyo had originally come from up the river, and he thought that perhaps she no longer wanted to be part of Old Kiln, rather, she wanted to return home. Unfortunately, she wasn't there. There was no sign of her or anyone else, for that matter. Cowbell had accompanied Inkcap, in spite of the argument they had had over the chess game, and the two of them decided to follow the riverbank a little further, searching for any evidence of Yoyo. Cowbell mumbled to himself repeatedly, wondering why he'd come along in the first place and why Inkcap seemed so intent on trying to find Yoyo. As a result, he didn't look for her much, he just followed, turning over the same stones Inkcap did. From time to time, small crabs skittered into the river when they overturned some of the stones and the boys noticed they appeared to be frothing at the mouth.

"Shit, even the crabs have gone crazy," said Cowbell.

Inkcap had seen them too and now concentrated his gaze on one particular crab yet to escape into the river. He saw Cowbell lunge and grab it, then hold it high in the air. A smile came over the boy's face and he pulled off one of its legs. Another leg. Soon, the creature was legless. The crab was reduced to what looked like a swollen red pimple. As Cowbell held the creature in morbid triumph, Inkcap, who'd been revulsed by the act of cruelty, lunged at him, twisting one of his legs backwards. Cowbell yelped in pain and dropped the crab.

"Now you know how it feels, eh? What did it do to you?"

Cowbell wrenched his leg free and spat back at Inkcap, "It's just a lousy crab, what difference does it make to you?"

"Suppose Yoyo's turned into a crab."

"That can happen?"

"And why not?"

"I've changed into a rock before."

"You what? Shit, that's crazy, do it again, again!"

Naturally, Inkcap couldn't, so he tried to explain that he only felt as though he'd turned into a rock before, but this only confused Cowbell more. Inkcap decided there was nothing more to say, he only wanted to continue searching along the riverbank by himself, without Cowbell tagging along.

Leaving Cowbell behind him, Inkcap could hear him call out, "Why are you trying to be so nice to Yoyo when she never said a nice word about you?"

Nearby to where they had been arguing, Apricot was washing clothes. Inkcap could see some of them already laid out on stones to dry in the sun. Apricot always wore something colourful, thought Inkcap, and with her blouses lying in the sun in that way, he couldn't help but think of flowers.

"How come you're not washing your clothes in the spring?" asked Inkcap.

"I wash them wherever I wish, what's it to you?" she replied, her voice cold and unfeeling.

Inkcap swallowed hard. He didn't want to provoke her more, even though he couldn't quite understand what he'd said in the first place to make her angry. He did know she was easy to get a rise out of, but she seemed particularly sensitive now.

He decided to change the subject. "Say, have you seen Ever-Obedient's wife?"

"She's not inclined to pay me any attention, so why the hell would I be concerned about her?"

Still angry. Perhaps even more so. Inkcap decided it best not to say another word. Just then, Cowbell came running up, interjecting himself into their tense exchange.

"But I'm all right, aren't I?"

Leaving together, neither Inkcap nor Cowbell said anything further to Apricot, but when they were some distance away from her, Cowbell said, "Did you see that?"

"See what?"

"Apricot washing military clothes... they have to belong to Bash."

In truth, Inkcap had seen what she was washing but pretended he hadn't. "Shit, you're certainly nosy, aren't you? What difference does it make whose clothes she's washing?"

605

"I heard she's staying at the Hammerheads' headquarters... you think that's true?"

"Who says? I reckon you ought to watch what you're saying."

Inkcap and Cowbell found no trace of Yoyo. Nor did Ever-Obedient, and he looked almost everywhere. Most of the village was distressed by her disappearance. She'd been so good to Ever-Obedient. She'd cooked and cleaned for him, she'd kneaded his back when necessary, even held onto him tightly to help him sleep at night. But now she was gone, without a trace. And everyone wondered how.

"Oh, don't worry, she'll be back," some would say to him, "before you know it, she'll be back. You two are meant for each other."

But this did little to ease his pain and worry. "She's gone," he said, "gone for good, her illness has taken her away."

"Then we won't stop looking, everyone will help, and just wait, she'll come round and return. We have faith in that."

Inkcap, however, had faith in Ever-Obedient's words: her illness had taken her. The only question was where? Then a thought occurred to him: when a goat begins to froth at the mouth, it would usually faint right after. And it wouldn't matter where it was, even in someone's piss pit, it would just collapse right into it. Perhaps the same has happened to Yoyo. Just whose piss pit? With this in mind, Inkcap grabbed one of his many bamboo poles and went from house to house sticking it into their outhouse pits to see if he could find anything solid.

When he arrived at Baldy Jin's, Half-Stick was there to greet him.

"Here to check our outhouse too, are you?" she said.

"Yes, just checking if anything's fallen in."

"You people from Old Kiln, you're a strange lot, you know. None of you put a proper cover over your piss pits, and you dig them so bloody deep, let them fill up, it's disgusting. You also dig them right alongside the alleyways everyone walks down. It's almost too frightening to even take a stroll through the village, especially after the sun goes down."

"You're not from Old Kiln?" Inkcap asked.

"No, I married into this shithole, worse luck for me. What are you looking for anyway?"

"If there's any sign of Ever-Obedient's wife, she's disappeared you know."

Half-Stick let fly a barrage of questions, more to herself than to Inkcap: "Eh? Surely a person wouldn't just fall in and disappear, would they? They're not that deep, are they? And besides, even if they did, wouldn't they be able to crawl out? Ever-Obedient's wife, you say? I don't think they're really married, you know. She was just there when he was in trouble, an emergency care type of thing, I suppose. Does that mean she had to stay with him forever?"

Inkcap offered no reply, he simply walked off to check the other houses. As he surveyed his eighteenth, Bash returned from Luozhen. No one knew that he'd gone, in fact, but evidently he'd been meeting with county leaders about new initiatives. Accompanying him on his return to Old Kiln were two men with rifles slung over their shoulders. As soon as they entered the village, Useless and Baldy Jin rushed up to fall in step with them. But they didn't march to the Hammerheads' HQ, nor did they call for a meeting. There were no clanging bells sounding a new propaganda campaign. Surprisingly to the villagers, Bash marched them to the cowshed.

This was the first time the Hammerheads had been at the cowshed since the Red Blades had commandeered the old apartment complex to use as their base of operations. Useless was a little nervous about being there and wondered aloud if they should call more men to be with them. Bash answered that they didn't, that the Red Blades, everyone in fact, would be fearful of them since they had guns. This fact made him carry himself even more erect than usual. As they marched into the courtyard, they spotted a man half naked, apparently trying to delouse himself. On seeing them, he yelped in surprise and beat a hasty retreat without putting his clothes back on. But his yelp had the desired effect, as five or six men emerged from inside. They appeared somewhat uneasy, but also resolute despite not really knowing what to do. In their hands, they held whatever stick, pole or staff they could find.

Bash paid them no heed, instead yelling beyond them, "Zhu Dagui! Zhu Dagui!"

At that moment, the Branch Secretary was busy brushing the cows. He heard the shout and peered out from behind a cow in the direction where the sound emanated. He couldn't see quite clearly so he shifted his position, without realising the cow had just shat and he inadvertently stepped right in it.

"Zhu Dagui! Zhu Dagui!" Bash yelled again.

Knowing he had to comply, Secretary Zhu walked out of the cowshed towards the main courtyard. There, he saw Bash and the two armed men.

"You called for me?" he said, before noticing he hadn't replaced his armband and quickly made to put it on.

"Just what are you doing?" Bash asked. "With all that cow shit all over your hands, do you think it's proper to handle your armband like this?"

Secretary Zhu reached down and picked up some straw from the ground in an attempt to clean his hands. He then replaced the armband around the sleeve of his jacket and stood to attention.

Speaking loudly, Bash pronounced, "Luozhen has initiated a study session on Chairman Mao Zedong Thought. Since Luozhen is ripe with counterrevolutionaries and traitors to the party, everyone is required to attend the study session and learn reform." He paused and looked hard at Secretary Zhu. "Have you heard?"

"I have." Zhu Dagui's voice was little more than a whisper.

"I didn't quite catch that, so I'll ask again. Have you heard?"

"Yes, I have."

Of course, Bash already knew the Branch Secretary had heard of these plans, how could it be otherwise with his spies seemingly everywhere? Bash's performance was more directed at everyone else in the apartment compound. He wanted them to hear, and they did. Their breathing, he could tell, grew rapid. But they didn't move. Bash gestured to the men carrying the rifles. They were comrades from Luozhen. The one on the left was Comrade Li, on the right was Comrade Jiao. Their task was to make pronouncements on the new initiative to the residents of Old Kiln.

"Oh, Comrade Li, Comrade Jiao," Secretary Zhu said. "It is—"

"How dare you imply you're a comrade?" said Useless. "You're a comrade to no one."

Zhu Dagui said nothing further.

The man introduced as Comrade Jiao shifted his rifle to his other shoulder and removed a document he had tucked inside his jacket. He cleared his voice and then officially announced the Luozhen study session on Chairman Mao Zedong Thought. Beneath this statement was a long list of required attendees. He read these out and Secretary Zhu noticed the names: Commune Secretary Zhang, the branch secretaries from Xiahewan, Xichuan, Dongchuan and Wafang. The twelfth name on the list was his own: Zhu Dagui.

Once complete, there was silence in the courtyard. Branch Secretary Zhu was the first to speak. "So when do I go?" he said, rubbing his hands.

"Now," answered Comrade Jiao.

"I guess I should let my wife know."

"Not needed," added Comrade Li.

Secretary Zhu had little choice but to accompany the men. As he left, he turned his head to see the Red Blades standing on the steps.

Bash again noticed the other man's actions and said, "What are you looking at them for? Hoping someone will come with you?"

At that moment, the men who'd been standing silently watching the scene unfold grew agitated. One jumped down from the steps, but before he could rush forward, another of the group grabbed hold of his clothes from behind. A dog appeared at the gate, its tongue hanging low. Bash and the others moved to depart and it started to stumble inside. As it did so, Bash grabbed the rifle from Comrade Jiao's shoulder and used the butt end to strike the mangy beast. It collapsed to the ground and Bash yelled, "Good dog, don't block the fucking way."

While this was happening, Inkcap had been checking the village privies. He came across Sparks and Once-Upon-A-Time sitting near the gate to their home. Inkcap could hear them talking.

"You're lying, you must be. Awning is a militia commander and even he doesn't have a gun, so how the hell did Bash get one?"

"Not just a gun, a rifle, two of them, brought from Luozhen."

"From Luozhen? Dammit, there's no telling what he'll get up to now that he's armed."

Sparks turned his attention to Inkcap. "Still searching, are you? Bet you smelt some nasty shit today. People, chickens, cats and dogs all use those piss pits, don't they?"

Inkcap didn't pay much attention to what Sparks was saying, he was more interested in what he'd overheard. "Who's got a gun?"

Inkcap actually knew the answer. He'd heard enough of what they had been talking about to hear Bash had returned to Old Kiln with two other men bearing rifles, but the news couldn't help but make his heart jump a beat. It wasn't all that long ago when Bash had brought explosives with him. He'd put quite the scare into the Red Blades with them too. Sparks' hand was evidence of that. But now he had guns! Inkcap couldn't help but admire Bash. He certainly had a knack for pissing off the likes of Awning and Millstone. Could Sparks do the same? No, he thought, not a chance. Inkcap stretched out his thumb and little finger, then tried to spit on it.

Sparks noticed and pointed his own bandaged hand at the boy, shouting, "Just what the hell are you doing?"

"My mouth's dry."

"Why, you little shit."

Inkcap didn't wait around to see if Sparks would say anything more. He wanted to see Bash, wanted to see the guns he'd brought with him. He'd asked – begged – to fire a gun before, during militia training, but Awning wouldn't let him. Perhaps Bash would. He dashed off in the direction of the temple, but before getting there, he came to an abrupt stop near one of the larger trees that stood overlooking the alleyways of Old Kiln and ducked behind it. He'd seen Bash walking towards him from the west but hoped he hadn't been spotted. He had a rifle slung over his shoulders. Its barrel glistened in the sun and made it difficult to see how long it actually was. He also saw Secretary Zhu trudging along in front of them, his jacket buttoned tight and the black armband that designated his status as class enemy and traitor clearly visible. His brow was sweaty from the sun beating down on them.

Inkcap crept away without being seen. Finding himself in an even narrower alley, he reckoned he was in the clear and ran the rest of the way home. He spotted Gran as soon as he arrived. She was stacking firewood, the gate to their courtyard wide open as she moved the wood from outside closer to the house. Inkcap, without a word, manoeuvred her through the gate and closed it after them.

"What are you doing, boy?" Gran complained. "What's the matter?"

"They've taken Secretary Zhu!"

"Again? Who's it this time, the Red Blades?"

"No, it was Bash. And he's got guns with him. Do you think they're coming for you next?"

"And why would they want me?"

Inkcap didn't answer, as he proceeded to push Gran inside and lock the door behind them. Then he opened it again, ran out and locked the courtyard gate. Returning to the door that led into their house, he locked it and knelt down. Gran would stay inside, and he'd remain outside, on watch. He held the key tightly in his hand.

As he knelt, he began to think of ways to deal with the situation. If someone came, he'd lie and tell them he had no idea where his gran was. He'd also say he didn't have the key to get inside, couldn't find it he'd tell them. But what if they didn't believe him? What if they searched him and found the key, what then? He decided to hide the key in the eaves above, no one would think to check there. Yes, that was a good spot. But what if they used someone else's key to open the door? He had a solution: he felt around for a small piece of wood and thought to jam it into the lock. That way, no key would open it. But what if they grew angry about not being able to find her, nor even check to see if she was inside? Would they decide to smash his door down? He'd need a new one, in that case.

In a panic, Inkcap peeked outside the gate and saw Tag-Along enter the alleyway leading to his house. Tag-Along was one of Bash's men. Was he coming to get Gran? He ran back towards the door and stuffed the piece of wood into the lock. Then he sat down in front of it, holding his head in his hands. He was pretending he couldn't open the door and kept his head down. He didn't want to see Tag-Along coming. If only he could block his ears too. He heard the man's steps and his whole body trembled.

He heard the gate open but didn't hear Tag-Along say anything. Only his steps grew closer. Then he felt the man's hands pulling at his ears and he looked up. Tag-Along had shaved his head and Inkcap was greeted by the sight of a sweaty scalp that shone in the sun. The sweat seemed like oil, thick and oozing.

"Why have you not gone?" Inkcap asked.

"Gone where?" said Tag-Along.

"With Bash, of course."

"Useless and Baldy Jin are with him, they don't need me too."

"But what if he needs to take a dump, what'll he do then?"

Tag-Along knew Inkcap was taunting him, and he pulled at his ears again. "Where's your gran?"

"And what do you want her for?" Inkcap said, standing up. In his mind, he was preparing follow-up answers. If Tag-Along was coming to drag her away, he'd say Gran was not home, that when he'd got home, the door was already locked and he couldn't find the key. Even worse, he'd tell him that some bastard had jammed the lock full of wood and it wouldn't open even if he had the key. He was prepared for all of this, but not prepared for what Tag-Along did eventually say.

"I need her help. My wife's sick."

If Inkcap's heart could exhale in relief, it would have done so now. He sat back down in front of the door. "Your wife's sick? Oh, it's been ages since I've seen your baby."

"Yeah, she is, perfect fucking timing, eh?"

"But Gran isn't here, sorry. How about calling on Goodman, he knows his stuff."

As he was speaking, Inkcap worried that Gran would hear the lies he was telling. He worried she would come up to the door, intent on helping Tag-Along any way she could. So Inkcap tried to recommend Goodman even more. He was the best in the village at identifying what was wrong with someone, and the best at giving advice on what to do. Finally, it seemed his persuasion had worked, Tag-Along relented.

"Maybe you're right, I should speak to Goodman," Tag-Along said, looking carefully at the boy. "You go and fetch him for me."

Inkcap hadn't expected that, but there was really no way he could refuse. When he reached the mountainside temple that Goodman called home, he found the man inside had been cutting a pumpkin. He was now hanging the slices from the wall.

"Did you hear," Goodman began before Inkcap could tell him why he had come, "they've taken the Secretary away?"

"I know."

"They didn't come for your gran?"

"No, but I guess since they haven't come for you, they won't come for her, will they?"

"You're probably right. I must say, though, you've acquired a certain fierceness, haven't you?"

Inkcap smiled a little, then changed subject. "What are you doing with the pumpkin slices?"

"They're for my adopted son."

Tag-Along's house had three rooms, but they were all in a state of disrepair. Some of the eaves had fallen, the mortar on most of the walls showed holes. Tag-Along's son looked as dirty as the house. He was seated in the courtyard eating from an old wooden bowl. Its age was evident by the rope that had been spun around it to keep it together. Inkcap entered the courtyard, Goodman following close behind. The string of pumpkin slices he'd brought with him he got Inkcap to hang on a nearby hook.

"What are you eating?" Inkcap asked Tag-Along's son.

"Gruel."

"Could I see?" asked Goodman. It was neither gruel nor maize, rather it was a sweet potato mash, not gruel at all.

The boy pulled it away and shouted, "You're not taking my food!" His voice was hoarse and deep, very unlike a child's.

"Oh my," Goodman said to Tag-Along, "what have you been doing? Look at the state you're all in... and you want me to give you advice on treating illness?"

At that moment, Tag-Along's wife appeared. "Are you having a laugh?" she said. "Seeing what kind of state this place is in, well, let me tell you, I complain to that bastard every day to clean things up, tell him to bring home some proper food for me to cook, and what does he do? Nothing, nothing at all. The bastard doesn't care a wit for us."

The more she spoke, the angrier she became. "Why the hell did he marry me if he didn't want a family? Just wanted a hole to poke, I suppose, but didn't want the child that came after."

"And what's wrong with this place?" said Tag-Along. "To my eyes, it's a bloody palace!"

"What's the matter, Gourd's got more kids than you but look how they live!" she responded, spitting at him. "How are we supposed to go on like this? Should I be the one to head off into the mountains to barter some rice for maize? Have you done it even once? When the production team doesn't produce enough, they've got their personal plots to fall back on, but what about us, we've got nothing, you do nothing, nothing, nothing, nothing!"

"You fucking bitch, can't you see I've no free time? Am I off drinking all day – no. Am I gambling – no. I'm busy making revolution, that's what I'm doing."

He turned to Goodman and said, "You see the kind of woman I have to deal with, so kind, isn't she, so understanding. You know I'm with the Hammerheads, with Bash, Useless and Baldy Jin, we're all working to make revolution. It's a great responsibility we have."

"I appreciate what you're saying, but it seems to me you only understand your own responsibility, you don't seem to realise that everyone has their own responsibility. Take me, for instance, I'm a farmer, we're all farmers, and if we don't do our best to tend our fields, our land will suffer and we will suffer, that's the way of things, isn't it?"

"The production team demands nothing less of us, that's true."

"Right you are, but if we produce less, we eat less, is that OK?"

"No, no, it isn't."

"No, it isn't. I don't think I could eat any less, as it happens. Then whose responsibility is it? I'll tell you, it's everyone's." With that, Goodman turned to Tag-Along's wife and said, "So what's wrong with you?"

"A few years ago, a spot, sort of a blister, showed up on my stomach. It started to swell and then became sore, pus started to ooze from it. I didn't really know what to do, so I just tied a belt around it, you know, just cover it up and leave it and continue with my work as usual. But a few days ago, when I was tending the pigs, it started to hurt something awful and started oozing out from under the belt. The pain's been unbearable."

Goodman instructed her to untie the belt so he could see the sore. His words were not comforting: "Oh, my dear... looking at this now, seeing how poor you are, there's no way you can afford to treat this, the medicine you need is far too expensive."

As he spoke these words, Tag-Along fell into a stupefied daze. So did Inkcap. Tag-Along's wife said nothing, she only kicked over a nearby stool in exasperation.

"So," she began, "all I've left to do is wait to die?"

"I'm afraid so. I'd say you could eat whatever you want."

"You won't do anything for me? You're going to just let me die?"

"What else is there for me to do?"

"But I've two older people to care for, and a child that needs to be looked after. If I'm cursed, they're cursed too, aren't they?"

"Oh, that's it, isn't it? You are a filial person, and that means your life must continue, it must continue."

Before leaving, Goodman wrote a prescription for her to give to the chemist. As he left with Inkcap, the boy asked, "Is she really that sick?"

"Yes, she is."

"Will the medicine you prescribed work?"

"It might, but even if it does, she'll be a cripple."

Back home eating his dinner, Inkcap realised he couldn't taste anything. He didn't sleep well that evening either.

FIFTY-SIX

AFTER ESCORTING THE BRANCH SECRETARY to Luozhen for his study session, Bash, Useless and Baldy Jin returned to Old Kiln carrying several dozen small stone plaster busts of Chairman Mao, nearly enough for every member of the Hammerheads. Naturally, the Hammerheads celebrated this triumph, each holding their miniature statue as they paraded through the alleyways of the village, gongs clanging and drums pounding. Even members of the Hei clan opened their gates to watch the spectacle, some lighting firecrackers as a means of joining in, others banging pots and pans. Outwardly, the Hammerheads were celebrating because they'd been gifted these marvellous busts of the Great Helmsman, but inwardly, they basked in the pleasure of diminishing the power and prestige of the Red Blades by sending Zhu Dagui to Luozhen. In their minds, they had closed the door on Red Blade activities, at least for the immediate future.

What a spectacle it was. And given that the Hammerheads were marching with Chairman Mao statues held aloft like some deity, the villagers knew they, too, had to observe the solemnity of the occasion; dirty shoes and smelly socks, so often hung at the gates of every doorway, had to be removed. The children had to be out of sight as well, confined to the narrowest lanes and paths, and forced to watch the parade from the margins. Should any of them fail to behave, they could expect a boxing of their ears by the nearest adult. And should they cry at being scolded, they'd only receive further punishment. Some even ended up being chased away with brooms.

A general commotion was unavoidable, especially as Useless took issue with the ferocity of certain parents who disciplined their children with a rage better reserved for dealing with other adults. At one point, he stopped in the street and yelled, "Just what the hell are you doing?"

Unsurprisingly, the response was, "This child needs a beating."

"We're here celebrating and you're beating your child?"

Now the entire parade stopped.

"You celebrate what you will, I'm not stopping you, but I'll be damned if I let you tell me how to raise my own child." And with that, the villager walloped the child with a broom once more. "Run wild will you, you little shit, I'll give you reason to run!"

Useless had seen enough and was about to engage further with the villager when Bash stepped close and held him back. "What are you doing? Don't lose your temper over this, it's not worth it."

Seemingly placated, Useless and the other marching Hammerheads continued their parade.

A flustered Sparks arrived at Awning's house to find him inside with Millstone, the two of them snacking on melon slices, seeds and all. If Sparks' look didn't betray his feelings, his voice, tense and rushed, certainly did.

"Do you know what's going on in the village? Have you heard? Seen? It's like Chairman Mao is theirs and theirs alone."

Millstone gestured for Sparks to sit. "Awning and I have just been talking about this."

"And what are we going to do about it, have you thought of anything? If we let it continue, we'll have no influence left in the village, no one will listen to us."

"I want you to go and get Lightkeeper for me," said Awning. "Bring him back here."

"He's one of the Four Bad Elements, what the hell do you want him to come over here for?"

Anger crept into Awning's voice: "Just do as you're told, and let me worry about that."

Sparks complied, leaving Awning's house to fetch Lightkeeper. Dragging him from his bed, Sparks returned to Awning's house soon after, Lightkeeper in tow.

Awning had no need for greetings when he saw Lightkeeper, simply asking, "Tell me, as a class enemy, what are you required to do?"

Almost robotically, Lightkeeper answered, "I must self-criticise and reflect on my errors."

"And can you do that asleep?" Sparks shot back.

"I wasn't sleeping, I was just lying down going over things in my heart, thinking about how I can be a better person and contribute to the Revolution."

"That's good to hear," responded Awning. "The most important thing is for you to mend your ways and contribute. Let me ask you, how much porcelain remained in the kiln after it was shut down?"

"At least one full batch of china, a decent amount," answered Lightkeeper. "It was all moved to the kiln temple afterwards."

"I see... the Hammerheads are certainly going back and forth between here and Luozhen quite often, aren't they? Lots of meetings, I suppose, making contacts, that sort of thing, buying ink and paper, too, even explosives, and now these Chairman Mao statues, small though they may be. They've bought a lot of them that's for sure, all rather new from what I could see, not second-hand statues. But I wonder, where do you think they got the money for all of this?"

"Yes, yes, yes," said Sparks, "that's right, a very good question. You think they got the money from selling the porcelain?"

"Umm... I don't dare answer that," said Lightkeeper.

Sparks pointed an accusatory finger at Lightkeeper. "And why don't you dare? Did you get some money out of it yourself, did Bash give you a cut? Are you saying you're a Hammerhead?"

"Put your finger away, will you? If you're not careful, I might end up hitting you, accidentally of course."

Awning stood up and gestured for Sparks to sit, then turned to Lightkeeper. "I'm sure there must be a ledger for the porcelain, yes, but at the same time, there's no guarantee that once it was moved to the kiln temple everything was properly recorded. But I need a full accounting of how much there was. Tell me, over a thousand pieces?"

"Perhaps not that much."

"You'll confirm there were eight hundred pieces," Sparks interjected.

"But…" said Lightkeeper, a note of anxiety evident in his voice, "I can't be sure of that… and… if I said that, if I wrote that down, the Hammerheads would kill me."

"You think he'd dare? You think he'd kill a Red Blade?" said Awning.

"I'm a… I'm a Red Blade? A Bad Element, you'll welcome me in?"

"Well, you're trying to be a new man, aren't you?"

"Yes, that's right, I am trying… I am a new man. Yes. I am."

"Now we just have to wait for the right time to announce this publicly, that is, you have to wait, but rest assured, you're a Red Blade. Go ahead, have some melon, take it home with you. We'll let you know when we need you later."

Lightkeeper did as he was told, taking a few pieces of melon with him as he went out, leaving Awning, Sparks and Millstone alone.

"How can you make him a Red Blade?" said Sparks.

"He'll be useful. Besides, tell me someone else in the village with his skill."

"But he's a Bad Element, he can't be trusted. They won't accept him, the other Red Blades. And why give the Hammerheads something to gossip about?"

"We've got one job to do right now and that is stopping the Hammerheads. If we don't, the Red Blades will lose their morale and then we're done for. So what if we give them something to gossip about? They've got their own questions to answer, and we should take them down a notch."

That afternoon, Awning and Millstone travelled to Luozhen to call on Wu Gan, only to learn that the town was preparing for a large revolutionary committee meeting. Numerous leaders and even more numerous factions had been invited to attend. Awning immediately thought of Bash and whether he would be there, then he wondered how Bash could be removed and himself or Millstone take his place.

"Not to push things," Awning said to Wu Gan, "I know there's a strict quota on the number of attendees, but might it be possible for one of us to attend?"

"Preparations are still ongoing," Wu Gan replied, "and to be honest, it's a mess. I don't even know if it'll all come together, but I suppose there'll be some kind of meeting no matter what. Still, Old Kiln is rather small… OK, OK, I'll try to see that Old Kiln gets a seat, but one thing, even if I'm not successful, Bash for sure won't be there."

Feeling assured, Awning and Millstone delivered a report to Wu Gan on the revolutionary activities happening in Old Kiln, as well as the plans of the Red Blades. Wu Gan listened intently, then emphasised the importance of one thing: the need for tit-for-tat actions. Whatever the Hammerheads did, the Red Blades had to counter and take things a level higher. That was the only way to bring the Hammerheads down. If they got ten villagers on their side, the Red Blades needed fifteen. Returning to the planned meeting,

Wu Gan said this would be the only surefire means by which they'd get a seat at the table.

As they listened to Wu Gan's advice, Awning and Millstone struck upon a plan they thought would fit the situation best: they would drag Secretary Zhu back to Old Kiln. Then they would hold a struggle session against him, call him out for all his many crimes. In doing this, they thought, they would prove to the villagers of Old Kiln they had even more power than Bash and his Hammerheads, they would be the most revolutionary. Shaking hands, they took their leave of Wu Gan. To put their plan in motion, they had to find out where the study session involving Zhu Dagui was happening. Not for one moment did they expect to bump into Inkcap.

Nor did Inkcap expect to encounter them.

Inkcap was in Luozhen on behalf of the Branch Secretary, or rather his wife had asked Inkcap to bring her husband something she'd prepared for him. He'd come to town without anyone knowing, purposefully keeping a low profile considering who he was there for. He left Old Kiln when the sun was just cresting the horizon. He'd been carrying a succulent serving of roast chicken, a pouch filled with tobacco and several articles of clean clothing. He regretted not having found Yoyo, especially since she was always nice to the Secretary and likely would have accompanied him to Luozhen. If nothing else, her presence would have acted as a shield for him; whatever they were doing could be blamed on her illness. Illness was, after all, a good excuse for anything. Alas, Yoyo had not been found.

By the time he reached Luozhen, it was already midday. His first order of business was to find out where the study session was being held, so he asked the first person he saw on the street. Learning it was at Eastern Pass Elementary School, he then had to find out where that was exactly. Having made his way to the school, he took up a position just outside the gate as though he were a sentry. The sentry that was in fact standing guard at the gate, Inkcap noticed, looked especially stern. His face also appeared unusually flat. He saw a rifle slung over his shoulder too. Seeing Inkcap, the sentry snorted and mumbled something about the villagers from Old Kiln all looking like dried persimmons. Inkcap thought this funny, as he felt the sentry's face far better resembled a persimmon. At any rate, when he drew a little closer, the sentry's voice rose to a yell as he warned him away.

"Stay back! No one's allowed in."

"But isn't this a school?"

"A school it is, but the ping pong table can't be used right now, a class is taking place."

Not understanding what a ping pong table was, Inkcap asked, "Yes, a class, I know, I'm here looking for someone."

"Someone who? For what reason?"

"The Secretary of Old Kiln. I know he's been sent here to study."

"Only traitorous snakes, criminals and other Bad Elements are here to study, certainly no party secretary!"

"But I've brought him some clean clothes."

"And who are you to him?"

"Well, I think of him as my grandad, even though he really isn't, not in that way at least. Come on, let me in. I promise I'll be right back out, uncle, please."

Inkcap mimicked deference by calling the sentry uncle, despite the fact the man wasn't all that old. But it had the desired effect, and Inkcap noticed his face soften. The sentry walked over to the boy and lifted the lid of the container Inkcap had been carrying. He poked his finger into the pot and turned over the chicken as though he were searching for contraband.

"See, it's just some chicken," Inkcap said. "Go ahead, take a leg, take two! My grandad will think I ate them on the way here."

"Would he tell you to eat it?" asked the sentry.

"I told you already, he's not *that* kind of grandad."

"Eh?"

Inkcap thought he'd misspoke, so he was quick to continue before the sentry could say anything further: "Go on, it's yours." He lifted the cockscomb from the pot and the sentry quickly had it in his mouth.

At almost the same moment, the iron gate door leading into the school opened and a townsperson appeared, pushing a handcart in front of him. He was mumbling something Inkcap couldn't quite catch, then he started to cry.

The sentry, swallowing quickly, shouted at the man, "Crying is not permitted."

"But... but he's dead. You mean to say I can't cry for the dead?"

"He deserved it," came the sentry's reply. "He betrayed the people, now take that damn cart away."

The townsperson did as ordered and began pushing the cart through the iron gate door. Unfortunately, a steel bar had been welded to the threshold to slow incoming and outgoing traffic, and the man had trouble pushing the cart over it. "Why are you stuck there?" the sentry yelled at Inkcap. "Give him a hand."

Inkcap went to assist the man, grabbing hold of the edge of the cart to try to pull it over the threshold. As he did, the cart and its contents shifted and the blanket that had been covering the contents fell to the side, exposing the face of a man, a dead man. Inkcap could see the man's face. He'd had his head shaved, but not evenly. His mouth was agape, too, his tongue sticking out. It was a grim sight. Inkcap couldn't help but jump. Not because he'd never seen a dead man before, no, he knew death, he'd seen Soupspoon's wife die for one. Potful was another. Even Happy, he'd seen him, also. But never before had he seen such a face, frozen with such a shocking look of pain and anguish.

The sentry's voice shattered his momentary stupor: "No sound. It's not permitted."

Inkcap kept quiet and pulled a little harder, finally lifting the cart over the threshold. The man pushing it began to cry again, this time much louder. Inkcap watched as the cart was pushed down the dirt road leading away from the school. He found the scene nearly overwhelming. Then something else occurred to him: would this be the fate of Secretary Zhu? He turned to the sentry and once more begged to be let in.

"Please, uncle, just let me in."

"No," the sentry answered. The sternness Inkcap had first seen in the man's face had returned.

Resigned to the fact he wasn't getting in through the door, Inkcap stepped back and surreptitiously surveyed the school walls. Shame they were so tall, he thought. But then again, shouldn't he at least try? Then he remembered the sentry had a rifle and thought better of it. Perhaps he should just go home.

Then something else occurred to him, and he yelled out, "So you've eaten my chicken, but you won't let me through? The nerve!"

The sentry bared his teeth at Inkcap and moved to throttle him, but Inkcap's tactic had worked. The man who'd pushed the cart out through the gate had heard and now began walking back towards them. He looked at Inkcap.

"What village are you from?"

"Old Kiln."

"Old Kiln, you say. Isn't that the place where someone nearly had his dick bitten off? I seem to recall hearing about it."

"Yeah, that's the place. I'm here trying to see my grandad, the party secretary for Old Kiln."

"Zhu Dagui... he's your grandad?"

"Yes he is, not quite in that way, but yeah. I've brought him some clean clothes."

The townsperson nodded and walked over to the sentry. What they said, Inkcap couldn't hear, but when the older man walked back beside him, he said that Inkcap was allowed in. Smiling broadly, Inkcap walked over to the iron gate, deliberately keeping his eyes away from the sentry. He did, however, make sure to bump the man's rifle butt as he walked past. The sentry snorted again but said nothing. He simply escorted Inkcap round one corner and then another before coming to a halt outside the school building.

"Stay here," the townsperson intoned, "and don't move a muscle."

Inkcap did as he was told. He could see the numerous big-character posters pasted to the school walls. There were also some paintings, one of them depicting a great hammer smashing a small ghost, or what he thought was a ghost.

"I guess this shows the difference between the village and the town," he whispered to himself. "In Old Kiln, the hammers are made of wood, but here they're iron!"

At that moment, the Branch Secretary walked out towards him.

"Secretary Sir!" said Inkcap.

Zhu Dagui couldn't hide his surprise at seeing the boy. "What the devil are you doing here?"

"Your wife sent me. You know she can't make the trip herself, so she asked me to bring you some fresh clothes. I've brought something to eat, too, some chicken... I'm sorry I spilled a little."

He used his fingers to shift the chicken around in the container, then licked them clean. "It still tastes great, though. Here, go ahead and have some. I don't have any chopsticks, so you'll have to use your fingers like me."

Secretary Zhu pinched a piece of the meat between his fingers and brought it to his mouth. He chewed slowly, enjoying every morsel. But then, when Inkcap expected him to swallow, he didn't.

"It's delicious, isn't it?" Inkcap said. "There's an egg in here too. Your wife said it's important for you to keep up your strength."

As he spoke, he pulled out the pouch of tobacco he'd brought and the clean clothes. Secretary Zhu accepted the tobacco and clothes without saying anything. Then he looked at the container of chicken again and replaced the lid.

"Inkcap, my boy, you take the chicken home with you. I can't eat it."

"You can't eat it?"

Before he could say anything more, the man who took him in appeared inside the door to the building and yelled out, "Time's up."

Secretary Zhu coughed. A second later, and it was a fit of coughing. Zhu Dagui seemed to be struggling to breathe. His shoulders went askew as the coughing fit took over. All he could manage was shoot a look at Inkcap.

It was a look Inkcap would never forget, but also something he couldn't tell a soul about. He didn't know why, but as he walked down the streets of Luozhen, he began to cry. That was when he unexpectedly came upon Awning and Millstone. They were as surprised as he was at seeing them, more so, perhaps, because Inkcap was crying. They asked what he was doing in Luozhen, and why the hell was he crying. Inkcap's first thought was to run, but he realised that would do no good. His eyes darted this way and that. Was there another way to escape? No. Nothing else to do but spin a story.

"Gran sent me to Luozhen, she told me to buy some rain boots. Problem is, I lost the money she gave me."

Awning lifted the lid of the container he was carrying and saw the chicken inside. "Crying, eh? Don't let us stop you."

"I cried myself out."

"You're not lying to us, I hope. You know how lies can tie you in knots, yeah?"

"Uncle Awning, I wouldn't even try."

"All right, then, you little shit. I don't suppose you're here to watch the capitalist running dogs, are you? No way that chicken's yours."

"What... chicken?" Realising his predicament, Inkcap came clean. "I just dropped it off... meant to drop it off... he wouldn't accept it... besides, it doesn't change anything, I'm still on the blacklist like always, doesn't matter where I am, what I do."

Awning's anger eased and he turned to Millstone. "This little shit will never grow up, will he!"

Without asking, Awning and Millstone devoured Inkcap's chicken, saving only a tiny wing for him. Throughout the exchange, Inkcap noticed they never mentioned once why they'd come to Luozhen.

The day after Inkcap returned to Old Kiln, Awning and Millstone returned as well, bringing along with them Secretary Zhu. Almost immediately, they arranged a struggle session. Lightkeeper was included in the session as well. The main issue was the embezzlement of monies related to the porcelain produced at the village kiln. Lightkeeper was accused of reselling the porcelain at the town market, and Secretary Zhu was said to have embezzled the money earned in the process. The account had then been turned over to Bash. Both Lightkeeper and Secretary Zhu claimed their innocence. Lightkeeper was adamant that the porcelain had all been moved to the Kiln God Temple, the Hammerheads' current HQ. To discover the truth, it was decided that the villagers must see for themselves. Hence, both men were roughly escorted through the alleyways of Old Kiln in the direction of the former temple. As they marched, slogans about defending the production of the people and upholding the revolution were shouted. Claims about bringing to justice those who had embezzled village monies were added to the chorus. As they drew close to the Hammerheads' base of operations, those inside heard the commotion. A moment later, Bash, Baldy Jin and Useless appeared before the marching crowd.

"So, Awning," said Bash. "You and your Red Blades are finally here to try and smash the Hammerheads, is that it?"

"This has nothing to do with the Red Blades," Awning shot back. "We're simply here as residents of Old Kiln, we're investigating the embezzlement of village monies by Zhu Dagui and Lightkeeper. Are you suggesting that your Hammerheads aren't working on behalf of the village in trying to get to the bottom of this matter?"

Temporarily defeated, Bash had no reason to prevent the crowd from marching into the temple.

"Where this matter is concerned," Awning continued, "there are no Hammerheads, no Red Blades, we're all just residents of Old Kiln. And if it should be proved that Zhu Dagui and Lightkeeper embezzled our production output, then that is a loss for every one of us. It is our collective responsibility to find out what happened."

At these words, the rank and file of each faction pushed beyond Bash and Baldy Jin, beyond Awning and Millstone too. The villagers themselves were going to inspect the books, the temple, all of it.

The results of the investigation recorded that there were still two thousand pieces of porcelain left. Lightkeeper added that a further three hundred pieces had been moved here from the kiln itself. But when the actual number of pieces in the temple was counted, there were only eighteen hundred units, a shortfall of five hundred. Dumbfounded, the villagers stared at each other.

Millstone broke the silence and asked the question on everyone's mind: "So, where's the rest?"

"It's all piled in here," Baldy Jin answered. "Who knows what's happened?"

"Surely we can't say it's been eaten by rats," Millstone retorted, "but we can ask those who actually live here what's happened to the missing pieces, can't we? I mean, after all, aren't you here to look after the stuff?"

"And what about us living here? We've never stopped anyone from coming to check on the china, we've got a lot of things to do, you know. In fact, shouldn't looking after the porcelain be one of your responsibilities?"

"But you all live here and the porcelain's gone missing, that means you've embezzled it."

"And where's your proof?"

It was Sparks' turn to jump into the fray. "Proof? Why, you lying fuck, the missing porcelain's all the proof we need!"

Intended or not, Baldy Jin took offence to Sparks' words, hearing in them a reference to his wifely troubles. "You… you of all people have the nerve to accuse someone of embezzling!"

In the past, Sparks had been responsible for looking after the production team's affairs, and most people suspected he'd skimmed some stuff himself, but an investigation had never been carried out and the whole thing was swept under the proverbial carpet. The only outcome was that Sparks was removed from his position of responsibility. Whether or not he caught the bite in Baldy Jin's words, Sparks' face turned red. Perhaps embarrassment, perhaps anger, it was difficult to say.

"You bring this up?" he said. "That's an open wound for me. I'm still angry about how I was treated, that I was suspected of being a thief. Let me tell you something, I'm an upright man, I'm certainly no fucking thief and that's the end of it."

"OK, well let me tell *you* something, no one here took the fucking porcelain."

Bash had been sitting nearer the temple gate, chewing on his cigarette. He'd already smoked the tobacco and had been grinding his teeth on the butt end. With little left other than a sticky pulp, he tried to spit, but the pulpy mess stuck to his lip. He therefore pinched it between his fingers and flicked it away, saying as he did, "What's all this bloody arguing about? Why the fucking fighting? The two sides should thrash things out in a more civilised manner, you know, discuss things. What can't be settled by talking things through? Rushing in here, bustling about, what the fuck's the point? Nothing will get sorted this way. You lot, get out." And, waving at the villagers, he called out, "Now! Leave this to us to figure out."

"What Bash says makes sense," said Awning. "We'll sort this mess out and then let everyone know."

Once the area had been cleared, Bash turned to the remaining men and gestured for them to sit. Awning and Millstone seated themselves on nearby stools. It was then that they reflected on the whole situation: Bash was offering them a seat, in their own damn place, *he* was acting as host? Both stood up and Bash, noticing the absurdity of the situation, laughed.

"You suspect us, don't you?" Bash said as he took a seat. "You think we've sold off the porcelain without telling anyone."

"Well, you can't deny some of it is missing," Awning retorted.

"You're right, a lot seems to be missing, but that lot of three hundred Lightkeeper was talking about, who's to say it was really three hundred? I don't think anyone can recall that clearly. Moreover, there's people in and out of here daily, hourly sometimes, outsiders too, there have even been folk from Luozhen here… who's to say some pieces weren't broken with all the comings and goings, there's no guarantee that some weren't broken is there?"

Bash paused to collect his thoughts before continuing: "No one's saying the porcelain wasn't produced by Old Kiln, but because it was produced by all of us, that means people have also come to get pieces from time to time for their own use. Now tell me, if you were up in a tree picking some persimmons and someone walked beneath the tree, are you telling me you wouldn't pick a few for him too?"

Millstone was caught off guard by Bash's eloquence and could think of no rebuttal. At least, not at first. "OK, OK, all well and good, but this still can't explain such a shortfall, can it?"

"Such a large shortfall!"

"Just look at you, you're talking like it's nothing at all."

"The Hammerheads struggled against Zhu Dagui, the Red Blades are now doing the same. Our objective is the same, what else is there to say?" Bash shouted.

"We're talking about two very different things," Millstone argued. "Village produce has gone missing and there's no clear accounting of it. Do you think everyone outside this room is going to be happy with your interpretation?"

"This is how things are talked over, that's what we're doing. Thrashing things out your way, how you all started this thing, that's only going to lead to violence. But if you want them to take a stand – the villagers I mean – then a fight is what you'll get." Bash's tone was defiant.

Millstone had reached the end of his tether and went to lunge at Bash. Before he did, however, Dazed-And-Confused, who'd been standing just behind Bash the whole time, shouted, "So a fight it is, eh?"

His voice was so loud that the villagers standing out in the courtyard grew alarmed. It seemed that open conflict between the Hammerheads and Red Blades was about to break out. At this point, Awning intervened and pulled Millstone back, yelling at Dazed-And-Confused, "Enough, no more talk of this. You're not in charge here anyway, get out. Now!"

"Baldy Jin can speak for us," Dazed-And-Confused shot back, "but since he's not here, that means I can."

"You, out now!" Bash shouted. "A fight? I don't think anyone in Old Kiln has the balls for it."

Dazed-And-Confused hesitated.

Awning took the opportunity to add his voice to the situation: "What is it that you hate so much?"

Dazed-And-Confused looked at Bash pleadingly but failed to get the response he hoped. "I told you to leave, so leave."

This time, Dazed-And-Confused did as he was told.

"Bash," Awning continued, "we've not sat down together for quite a long time. Although we're on different sides, we're both from Old Kiln, we've eaten the same food, drunk the same drink. If you say the porcelain's been broken, that people have come and taken some from time to time, then I believe you. But what the people have produced, their village output, we have to think about the work they've put into it, that has to be considered, and now some of that is missing, we can't add insult to injury, we need to do something. So how about this, since everyone is here, why don't we take what's remaining and divvy it up among the villagers? Then we can say everything's settled."

"As simple as that?" Bash asked.

"Think about your situation. If we don't do as I suggest, then you have to go out to everyone and explain the missing porcelain, and if that causes, what shall I say, a disturbance, there's not really anything I can do about it."

Reluctantly, Bash conceded. "All right, Awning, let's do what you say. I know that's been your true motive all along, fine, you've won. I admire your tact, let's divvy everything up, what do I care."

"One more thing," Awning added, "it's not only porcelain here, as you know, there's also the rice, just over a hundred pounds, I believe, the maize too, a hundred pounds. That's got to be shared as well."

"But isn't that," said Millstone, "isn't that the reserves—"

"Pah," spat Awning, "reserves... for what, the rats?"

Bash looked up at the ceiling for a moment then laughed heartily. "Yes, divide it all."

The work of divvying everything up began immediately. Each household received a pound of grain, rice or maize, it didn't matter. If they had nothing to carry the grain in, they'd used their jacket pockets, some even used their hats. As for the porcelain, one jar, three plates and six bowls for each villager and their family. An hour and a half, that's all it took to divide everything that had been stored at the temple.

Even Inkcap received his share. The jar, however, was too large for him to carry, a foot taller in fact, so he turned it on its side and rolled it home. All through the evening, drinking and general merriment could be heard.

FIFTY-SEVEN

Despite the original plan being to return Zhu Dagui to Luozhen and his studies after the village had struggled against him, the Branch Secretary remained in Old Kiln. The night was particularly dark and cloudy, the moon and the stars fully concealed by the overcast skies. He'd groped around in the dark to and from the riverbank in an effort to properly bed down the pigsty, but the soil was unlike before when it was much drier and easier to manage. What he'd carried from the riverbank had made things worse. Everything was a muddy mess, and the pigs were covered in filth. And this time there was no one to help him.

As he walked down an alleyway on his sixth return visit carrying the heavy, wet soil, Soupspoon appeared from a nearby corner and the two of them bumped into each other. Soupspoon collapsed to the ground. He had suffered from migraines for many years. And he'd tried any number of homemade remedies, but nothing seemed to work. His head always bothered him. This evening, Soupspoon had gone to his auntie's house to get her old gold ring. He was supposed to boil it in water and then drink – not the ring, of course, just the leftover urine-coloured broth. But finding himself thrown to the ground was certainly not going to help his head. He'd seen who it was in the dark – Branch Secretary Zhu. He knew what had hit him, as well, the Secretary's basket of earth. But he felt the need to pretend otherwise.

"Who the hell's there?" he shouted. "What the matter with you? Are you blind or is it that you just can't walk?"

"Oh my," the Branch Secretary answered hastily. "I didn't think anyone else would be out at this hour. And you were so quiet, I didn't hear your approach."

"What am I supposed to do, whistle while I'm walking? Perhaps wear a bell, that wouldn't be too loud, would it?"

"Oh no, oh my," blathered Secretary Zhu as he placed the basket on the ground and tried to pull Soupspoon to his feet. "You're not hurt are you, not much at least?"

"Oh, it's you, Secretary Zhu," Soupspoon lied. "I think I'm the one who should be asking what you're doing out here in the dark of the night."

"Looking after the pigsty."

"I say, why's that your business? Weren't you off somewhere else, studying? They've already let you return to Old Kiln?"

"No, I've not finished my studies yet, I do have to go back."

"Still more to do, eh?"

"I suppose you can think of me like a gourd in the water, I'm being swished back and forth, this way and that."

Soupspoon spoke quietly from his heart: "A mangy dog down on your luck, eh?" Then he paused a moment. "Kind of an insult, though, isn't it? I mean, what's the point... say, how's your stomach, still causing you grief?"

"Much better, actually. Barely gives me any trouble these days."

"I didn't know there was a cure for that," said Soupspoon as he lifted himself from the ground. "That's good."

Soupspoon turned to leave, muttering to himself about cures, then he looked back at Secretary Zhu and said, "You better get yourself back, got to write your self-criticism, eh, got to keep working on that."

The following morning, the Branch Secretary waited at his home to be taken back to Luozhen, but no one came. Deciding that he had waited long enough, he thought he'd walk over to the old persimmon trees that grew on the lower slopes of the mountains just outside the village and pick some of their fruit. Almost everyone in Old Kiln would avail themselves of the persimmon trees from time to time. Each had their particular favourite, a tree they liked to call their own. The Branch Secretary's favourite was the largest, naturally. When he arrived at that tree, he could see the persimmons, ripe and ready for picking. It was then that he saw Inkcap. Always willing to help his grandad who wasn't really his grandad, not in that way, Inkcap clambered up the tree and picked several persimmons. By the time the sun was right above them, they'd filled three baskets with the fruit, and even then, the tree held more. Secretary Zhu decided to leave those for the crows.

"Isn't that too many to leave for them?" asked Inkcap. "They might be up high and out of reach, but I could get a ladder."

Without waiting for a response, Inkcap did just that, returning soon after with a ladder hoisted over his shoulder. He rested it against the trunk of the tree and stepped upon it. If he still couldn't reach the remaining seven or eight persimmons, the Branch Secretary could try climbing the ladder himself.

"I can't reach them, will you have a go?"

The Branch Secretary agreed to try and he climbed onto the first rung. Inkcap held onto the ladder as the older man lifted his feet to the second rung. He had to keep it steady. The third rung, the fourth. Everything was going well, Inkcap thought the ladder was firmly dug into the ground and wedged up against the tree perfectly, so he relaxed his grip. As though on cue, the ladder shifted and Secretary Zhu slipped, crashing to the ground. Given the angle of his leg, Inkcap knew it was broken.

Naturally, Goodman was called to help in setting the bone. He also requested a number of Chinese traditional remedies, those derived from cockroaches to tame inflammation and those from plants to help with his general care while his mobility was diminished. Inkcap was tasked with collecting them. He felt he was being blamed for the Branch Secretary's accident. He also had to collect the remaining persimmons, and this was going to be a problem, he knew for sure. Unable to reach those highest in the tree, how was he going to get the persimmons loose? The branches weren't strong enough for him to climb. His only option was to shake the limbs in the hope that the fruit would fall free.

"Miser! You're leaving none for me!" cried the old crow upon seeing Inkcap shaking the tree.

"Look to the south, you old crow," shouted Inkcap. "There are plenty of persimmons left for you there."

Just as Inkcap was battling the tree, Goodman appeared after having returned to his home to consult some texts on how best to treat the Branch Secretary's fracture. He saw a few persimmons that had fallen from the tree and gathered them up. Like finding a coveted delicacy, he bit into a soft, juicy one. The Branch Secretary's wife was approaching at almost the same time. She, too, picked a persimmon from the ground and bit into it. Sweet juice ran down their chins as they devoured the fruit. Hungry for more, Goodman hurried over to the tree, standing below it as though waiting for another persimmon to fall. This one he would catch in his teeth, it seemed.

When it fell, however, the soft flesh made contact with his chin and tumbled to the ground.

"Oh, how awful to see such delicate and delicious fruit lying wounded in the dirt," Goodman observed.

Inkcap couldn't help but laugh to himself, looking down on Goodman from above.

"Child," cried out the Branch Secretary's wife, "why do you make me worry so much for you? I can't eat, can't sleep, but look at you now, so happy despite your status."

"Such is my lot," replied Inkcap, still with a smile on his face.

"If you took to studying, my boy," Goodman added, "you could change your lot, you know. Fate can be transformed."

"Do you really think so?" said the Branch Secretary's wife turning to Goodman,

"Of course, there would still be bitterness, but if one were to find enjoyment in that bitterness, if one were to endure, then change is possible."

"But how can... look at what's happened to Secretary Zhu, to us, he's lost all the power and influence he once had. Now his body is broken. OK, OK, true, his stomach's much better, but his leg... he can't even walk." She stopped and wrinkled her brow, irritation marked on her face.

"You have to find a way, if not the one in front of you, then something else," offered Goodman.

"Something else?"

"Well, let's look at it this way, he stopped being Branch Secretary and his stomach ailment improved, that's one problem fixed. Now his leg's broken, but doesn't that mean he won't have to return to Luozhen? Isn't that a positive change? A person's life..." Goodman stopped abruptly, placed his arms behind his back and began to walk away.

"What are... what are you doing, why are you just walking away?"

Up in the tree, Inkcap wanted to call out to the Branch Secretary's wife, but his voice failed him. Should he throw a persimmon at her to get her attention? No, too messy. His shoe? Yes, that would work. A moment later, Inkcap's grass shoe struck the woman on the shoulder, and she spun around, her mouth open. Before she could shout, however, she noticed Useless marching towards her and she closed her mouth quickly.

"Just what the hell are you doing up in the tree, Inkcap, you worthless little shit?" Useless was in his usual acerbic mood, it seemed.

"You're here to get your family's share of persimmons, too, are you?" Inkcap replied.

"I asked what you were doing, you fool."

"Well, I mean... I'm up in this tree... ah, I'm picking persimmons, aren't I?"

"And for whom?"

"For the Secretary."

"Then you're supporting a class enemy! A capitalist roader!"

"Eh? He's just my grandad, you know... but not in that way."

"I heard it was your fault he fell, that you were the one holding the ladder, isn't that so?"

"I didn't... didn't hold it steady enough."

"I reckon that was deliberate, to get him out of going back to Luozhen. What do you say to that?"

"Useless," the Branch Secretary's wife interjected, "don't say such things, please—"

"Your hand's still hurt, right? said Inkcap, changing topic. "Let me pick your family's share of persimmons."

Inkcap's words worked, although Useless only hated him more. Turning on his heel, he mumbled something about getting a basket for the persimmons and marched off. As he did, Inkcap called out behind him, "Just let me know if you need anything else done while your hand is hurt. I'm happy to help."

With all the persimmons picked, the tree lost its reddish hue. Soon after, the leaves fell, leaving only bare branches as though winter had arrived a little ahead of schedule. In full bloom, the persimmon tree had a peaceful aura about it, like the Goddess of Mercy, compassionately looking over the residents of Old Kiln. Now, however, that aura was gone, and its branches, bereft of greenery and fruit, looked like arms snaking out to swat at people as they walked by, angered, it seemed, at having its labours – its persimmons – torn away.

Those persimmons with blemishes were put in jars to pickle. The remaining, unscarred fruit, were hung on sticks among the stores of grain so that they would slowly soften over the winter. Then, when spring arrived, they would be ready to peel and mixed with the wheat to make noodles. Nearly every household in Old Kiln did the same, and soon persimmons were hanging throughout the village. Every household except Bash's. He didn't take a share. Nor did anyone else get his. However many persimmons Bash's tree produced, he left them for the old crows to devour. Each one would soon have a hole, its innards sucked out.

Bash had been going more and more frequently to Luozhen, returning only in the evenings to Old Kiln. On this night, however, he didn't go straight home. Instead, he was seen meandering through the village in the direction of the mountains. Tag-Along assumed he needed to follow, so he grabbed his shovel and set off to catch Bash. But on this night, Bash didn't need him, at least not for shovelling. Rather, he'd gone to the mountains to stand in front of the graves of his parents. Not too far away stood Bash's persimmon tree.

"Hey, look at that," Tag-Along said. "Your tree's the only one left with persimmons hanging on it."

Bash said nothing in response. He knelt on the ground to kowtow in front of his parents' graves.

"Are you going to let them rot on their branches?"

"Why are you so fucking interested in them?" He kowtowed again. "Dad, Mum, I need to tell you something. I'm joining the Revolutionary Committee. If I told you what that means, I'm afraid you might not understand, but I suppose you could think of it as me entering official imperial service, like long ago. But maybe most important, my position's even higher than Zhu Dagui's!"

Tag-Along was startled by what he heard. Naturally, after returning from the mountain, he told everyone he met. "Hey, did you hear Bash's going to be a government official, like in the old days?"

"An official, what the hell are you on about, what position is leading the Hammerheads to the government? It's nothing, isn't it?"

"It's true, I heard him tell his parents myself."

"Ah, that's just hogwash," was the reply. "Utter tosh."

Whatever the merits of the claim, from that night onwards, a new phrase made it to Old Kiln: Revolutionary Committee. Everyone said the village needed one, even if no one really knew what it was. It fell to Useless to explain.

"The Revolutionary Committee is replacing the previous government," Useless began. "The county government will be absorbed into the Revolutionary Committee, the same for Luozhen–"

"But isn't that just changing names, then?" a villager asked.

"It's not just changing names. The Revolutionary Committee is now the Cultural Revolutionary government, everything's different. The capitalist roaders have all been removed and we now have the power."

Old Kiln understood. Zhu Dagui would never be in charge again. They'd never call him Branch Secretary again. He was finished. Later, they heard that Bash would be a member of the Revolutionary Committee in Luozhen. Before, Xiahewan had had a commune secretary by the name of Zhang Dezhang, and as a result, they'd never paid much attention to Old Kiln. Things were different now. Xiahewan would not be able to look down on them any more. Dazed-And-Confused divulged further news: Apricot had already gone to Luozhen and purchased six yards of dark khaki cloth. Evidently, she was going to sew Bash a new set of clothes more appropriate to his station, one that had the correct number of pockets. This got villagers talking even more about her relationship with Bash, but nothing seemed to phase her, and when her sewing was complete, she thought the four-pocketed, dark khaki jacket she'd stitched was exceptionally well made, even if, to others at least, some of the stitchwork seemed uneven and likely to break.

When Inkcap heard this story, he decided he had to see Apricot for himself but when he did ultimately find her, she seemed the same as always. She walked the same, and nothing appeared to have changed.

Inkcap, nevertheless, persisted. "Hi, Apricot," he said. "Been busy lately?"

"No, not really."

"Sewing new clothes isn't busy?"

"What new clothes?"

Inkcap didn't dare push the issue, thinking her response odd. He said nothing further, only offering her a wave as he walked away.

Another rumour soon spread through Old Kiln, this one contradicting the first: Awning was to be appointed to the Revolutionary Committee, not

Bash. Then another: both men were to join the Revolutionary Committee in Luozhen. For the villagers, this was both shocking and a delight. Since Liberation, Old Kiln had only ever had Zhu Dagui, and he was just the village Branch Secretary. Now, they had two of their own in the Revolutionary Committee, imagine that! Those siding more with the Hammerheads celebrated the achievement with firecrackers. Those leaning towards the Red Blades did the same.

Only Barndoor seemed to be disturbed by these developments. "This is not good," he said. "Not good at all."

"Why's that," asked Noodle Fish.

"Sure, it's quite an honour, but one mountain can't be home to two tigers. This will end up being bad for Old Kiln."

No one expected, however, that the entire plan to establish the Revolutionary Committee in Luozhen would fall through. And fall through it did, mostly because of irreconcilable differences among vying factions. Contradictions and personal interests too immense to resolve, criticisms too fierce to ignore, each faction blaming the other for the failure. As a result, revolutionary factions took to parading class enemies through the streets, offering them up to righteous and indignant crowds to denounce. A new fervour took hold, each village and town seemingly set on demonstrating their revolutionary zeal. The parade for Old Kiln was set for the nineteenth. Once the announcement was made, the Hammerheads called a meeting. Every member was expected to attend. The Red Blades called a meeting of their own, ordering every member of the Zhu clan to attend. And not just men of working age, but the elderly, the young and the wives who'd married into the clan, even those whose family name was not Zhu were urged to come.

The arrangements for the Red Blades meeting fell to Sparks. Of course, the dirty capitalist roader from Luozhen, Zhang Dezhang, would be one of the class enemies to be paraded. Liu Jiangshui from Xiahewan, too, as well as the secretary from Dongchuan, Li Falin. A school principal was also to be included. The counterrevolutionary Liu Tianliang, who'd been responsible for penning anti-revolutionary slogans, would not be excluded either. The philanderer Lu Lin was another; he was a technician from Zhu Dagui's son's workplace who'd seduced an upright soldier's wife and destroyed their marriage. Someone with the family name Li, they'd been caught listening to enemy broadcasts from Taiwan. And most important of all was Zhu Dagui himself. The greatest enemy of the lot. All of them were given conical hats to wear, but unlike the papier-mâché versions, these newer ones were made of a coarse type of wire, all of the same size and each with a pasted white sheet of paper listing their enemy status. For those with smaller heads, such as Lu Lin, the hat pushed down against his ears. For Zhang Dezhang, whose head was larger, the hat dug painful ridges into his skull. In Zhu Dagui's case, since he could not walk, he was carried on a chair.

Wu Gan was in charge of the parade of enemies, along with a bearded man no one in Old Kiln recognised. Given Wu Gan's familiarity with Old

Kiln, when he saw Zhu Dagui, he lifted his head and stared a little more closely at the scene, remaining silent. The bearded man, however, was curious as to why this fellow was being carried in a chair, and he marched over to find out the reason. Naturally, he ordered those carrying Zhu to place him and the chair on the ground.

Worried over what might happen, Zhu Dagui's wife frantically looked for a cane, a stick, anything that her ailing husband might use to stand. Finding nothing, she pleaded to the crowd, "A walking stick, crutches... does anyone have anything?"

No one answered.

"Inkcap, where's Inkcap? Inkcap!"

She didn't need to call again before Inkcap came rushing out from the crowd. He had a makeshift crutch in his hands, something he'd nailed together himself, old socks pulled over the top to cover the roughness of the wood that would be wedged under Zhu Dagui's arm.

"Oh, how considerate!" Useless said loudly for everyone to hear.

Inkcap caught the meaning of Useless's words, he understood what the crowd saw, him, helping one of their enemies. "He's got to stand steady if we're to struggle against him," he explained.

Before Useless could respond, the bearded man said, "And who's this?"

"This is the lad I told you about, Inkcap. Ugly little shit."

"I see," replied the bearded man. "Get over here, boy."

Timidly, Inkcap complied.

"The Four Bad Elements all care about capitalism and subverting the revolution," shouted the bearded man. "It looks to me like he's using you to help him stand."

"But I'm not one of the Four Bad Elements," answered Inkcap.

"If you're not one of the Four Bad Elements, what are you, a lower or lower-middle class peasant? Get over here now."

Inkcap stood silent, unsure what to do. Finally, Secretary Zhu spoke: "I can stand, the stick will do... what's more, he's too short for me to lean on." And he threw the makeshift crutches away, saying, "No matter, no matter... but I won't let Inkcap prop me up on my feet."

The bearded man looked at Inkcap once more but didn't say anything. Wu Gan, who'd remained silent during the entire exchange, seized the opportunity to give Inkcap a kick. Understanding retreat was his only option, Inkcap offered no reply, disappearing back into the crowd instead.

The Hammerheads and their supporters stood on the eastern side of the village square, each holding a long-handled hammer, red paint covering every hammerhead. Bash stood front and centre, blowing a whistle to call the meeting to order. The Hammerheads formed ranks, neat, straight lines, their chests puffed out to better show off their Chairman Mao badges. In their right hands, they each held a copy of Mao's Little Red Book. On the western side of the square, the Red Blades had gathered in a somewhat more haphazard manner. Their numbers exceeded those of the Hammerheads, and instead of hammers they all held swords, some coated in iron, others made entirely of wood. An even greater number of men held pipe bowls while some women carried wooden rotary rulers and the soles of shoes.

Cowbell was standing among the Red Blades. When Inkcap saw him, he called out, wanting to give him some dried sweet potato slices, but Cowbell seemed not to hear him – either because of the general hubbub or the apparent enthralment that was apparent in Cowbell's face, Inkcap couldn't tell. Inkcap thought it best not to call to him again. After all, he could enjoy the whole batch of sweet potato himself. Pulling them out of his pocket, he stuffed them into his mouth, chewing vigorously. In the middle of both crowds, Inkcap could see those villagers who belonged to neither faction: Barndoor, Noodle Fish and Six Pints' wife. Button, Peacenik, Four Dogs and his crippled uncle were also there. On this occasion, Lightkeeper and Gran hadn't been dragged in front of the crowd to face criticism, so they, too, were standing in the middle. Lastly, Inkcap could see Goodman.

From the back of the crowd strode Sparks. His hand was no longer bandaged, nor was his arm in a sling. But he did wear a glove over his wounded set of fingers. He walked up to Inkcap and stood in front of him, his eyes falling on the sweet potato slices. He snatched them away, berating him as he did. Inkcap yelled in surprise, but Sparks ignored him, evidently unconcerned with how he treated the boy. Then he turned and walked towards Awning, never once speaking a word to Inkcap.

"As ordered," Sparks said to Awning, "all the Red Blades are here, but… but look at them, they can't form proper ranks, can they?"

"Maybe so, but look at our numbers, we've got a lot here," Awning bragged. "Say, now, can you see anyone missing? If you can, run off and get them here at once."

Sparks glanced over the faces of the crowd, his eyes falling on Yes'm. "Hey, where's your old man? I don't think I see him."

"He's bedridden with bronchitis," Yes'm answered.

"And your wife?"

"She's here, at the back."

"Then get her up here in front," said Sparks, now turning his attention to Inkcap. "You, stand over there."

"Me?" answered Inkcap, confused.

"All of the Zhu clan are standing over there."

"And I'm a Zhu…" He felt a tug at his back but continued speaking: "But I'm not part of any faction." Then he saw who had been pulling at his jacket; it was Gran.

"If you're with neither faction," Sparks spat, "then stand here and don't bloody move."

Inkcap did as he was told. He turned his head to see Bash looking directly at him. Inkcap smiled and lowered his head. Half-Stick was standing next to Gran, speaking to Noodle Fish's mum. He could see Baldy Jin marching towards her, grabbing her arm and shouting at her to get in front.

"No more rubbish," he said. "You're talking trash."

"But I'm not a Hammerhead," Half-Stick shot back.

"The middle here are all Bad Elements, is that who you're putting your lot in with?"

"Barndoor is one of the Four Bad Elements? Noodle Fish too?" She moved to stand next to Noodle Fish's mother, the older woman standing there stitching the soles of shoes.

Useless's mother and Apricot arrived late. They hesitated at the edge of the crowd, surveying the scene. Useless's mum naturally moved towards the Hammerheads. A few of the Zhu clan muttered curses under their breath, but she heard them, nonetheless. Their dog, however, turned towards the Red Blades, immediately receiving a kick from Sparks for its trouble. The dog yelped and collapsed to the ground, flipped over and lifted its legs into the air, exposing its mangy cock for everyone to see.

Useless's mum marched over and shouted at Useless, "What the hell are you doing? Why kick him?"

"I suspected he was up to something, and by the look of it, I was right."

The Hammerheads had three dogs of their own, and Baldy Jin now called out to them to attack. They did as instructed, snapping their jaws at the Red Blades. Suddenly six or seven dogs emerged out of the alleyway, joining the fray. Inkcap witnessed the canine melee and rushed towards it, grabbing hold of Lucky's dog and pinning it down, shouting as he did, "Leopard! Leopard!" Leopard, Baldy Jin's dog, heeded Inkcap's call and bounded forward, sinking its teeth into Lucky's dog. Inkcap then released it and spotted Tag-Along's animal, giving it a kick in the process. He then mounted the dog and squeezed its head between his legs, stomping his feet as he did and yelling for Black Tiger, Almost-There's dog. Like Leopard, it responded to Inkcap's call and leapt towards the prone animal, biting its leg, once, twice, three times. The wounded animal yowled in pain, so loud it sounded like a thunderclap. Tufts of fur lay on the ground. Finally, Ever-Obedient's dog appeared. Its skin and fur hung loosely about its frame as though it were a jacket too large for its body. Its gait was slow, and its head drooped – perhaps it was searching for something, Inkcap thought. He released Tag-Along's dog. He could see Ever-Obedient's dog was going to bark and once it did, every other dog would obey it. Strangely, however, it kept its jaws shut and plopped its hindquarters onto the ground. It seemed to be acting like a human, watching the chaos unfold, not saying a word.

While the dog battle was waged, the Bad Elements at the front of the crowd grew uneasy. Some remained with their backs straight and upright, but others shifted about, rubbing their lower backs and necks after having to stand so erect for so long. It looked like the bearded man and Wu Gan were talking, but it was difficult to make out what they were saying. Suddenly, the bearded man stopped the conversation, whatever it was about, and marched over towards Secretary Zhu, kicking him violently. Zhu Dagui offered no defence, he simply stood still and closed his eyes as though he were drowsy. But the leg the bearded man had kicked ached, and he felt it begin to weaken. He staggered, regretting that he'd not accepted the walking stick to try to maintain his composure.

"Sleeping!" shouted the bearded man.

"Awake," replied Zhu Dagui.

"Who closes their eyes when they're awake?"

"It's a condition I suffer from."

"A condition? Head up, no slouching!"

Secretary Zhu complied with the order.

Inkcap couldn't be sure if the Branch Secretary was feeling drowsy, but a number of villagers in Old Kiln were known to fall asleep while walking. He himself was one of them. He recalled waking up too early one morning to join a work group heading out to fell trees, and he'd fallen asleep while walking among them. His feet had kept moving, though. The Branch Secretary was known to take frequent naps whenever he had some free time. He'd also endured a fair amount of criticism. Perhaps he was drowsy and perhaps he could sleep while standing. Then again, Inkcap wondered, today was a little different, there were more people, he was suffering criticism from all sides, had to hold onto a walking stick too – was it really possible he could sleep under these conditions?

Cowbell had finally grown tired of standing among the Red Blades. Because he was shorter than everyone else, he couldn't properly see the class traitors. His immediate view was blocked by Once-Upon-A-Time, someone who was given to farting repeatedly. He'd asked him what he'd eaten but did not receive a satisfactory answer, only something about hungry farts and cold piss. So he left in search of Inkcap, easily finding him despite the size of the crowd. Inkcap, however, ignored him and continued eating the sweet potato slices. Soon they were all gone.

"Is the Secretary really sleeping?" Cowbell asked Inkcap.

"Yeah, it's a habit, I guess, but he's not actually sleeping."

"I bet you he is. I know it, in fact. I heard his stomach problem's gone, that takes a strong... consti... consti... a big heart."

From in front, they heard the bearded man's booming voice: "Time to begin, get the dogs out of here. Let's get started."

"You reckon he's got a huge, gaping mouth," Inkcap wondered aloud to Cowbell.

"How else can he be speaking so loudly if he hasn't?"

"Why did he grow a beard, then, why hide his face? Maybe he's got no mouth at all."

"Perhaps he's got an arsehole for a mouth!" said Half-Stick, joining the conversation.

The bearded man shouted again: "Get the dogs out of here. Get them out!"

The dog battle continued. Evidently, they didn't understand what the bearded man was saying. No one, in fact, seemed able to bring the animals to heel. Frustrated, Wu Gan marched over towards Inkcap and kicked his rear.

"Get these dogs out of here," he ordered.

Inkcap did as he was told and yelled at the animals. For some reason, they listened, turned and began to run down the adjoining alleyway, biting and yelping as they went. To Inkcap's ears, he could hear them cursing each other, swearing to bite one another, fighting all the way. Inkcap appeared to be their referee, even if he didn't want the job.

"Referee? I've no time to referee you lot, I've a meeting to attend."

It didn't seem to matter what he said, for all the dogs stopped and encircled him. Inkcap raised his hand to strike, but one of the beasts used its mouth to pull at his shirt sleeve. Inkcap lifted his foot to kick, but another dog clamped down on his trousers' cuff. Losing balance, Inkcap tumbled to the ground. The animals started to pull him along, they were like a hoard of ants carrying a nut back to their hill. Inkcap laughed, he couldn't say why. He felt his trousers being yanked down over his buttocks, his white cheeks exposed to the outside air. Soft like a baby's bottom, his infantile arse was further evidence of his lack of physical development. His arse cheeks were not free from blemishes, however, for each side showed a black splotch of skin. This was caused by the way young children were carried; Cowbell had the same, everyone in Old Kiln, in fact, sported the discolouration.

"All right, all right," yelled Inkcap at the dogs. "I'll go, I'll go. I'll leave you be."

The animals released him, and he laughed again. He stood and did as he promised, leaving the dogs alone. He felt a certain awe towards the dogs and an overwhelming happiness he couldn't quite define. He marched off in the direction of the fields. Two beasts followed, Sparks' dog and Useless's. Their fight continued. Useless's dog was injured, Inkcap noticed, its hind leg was bleeding. Suddenly, it fell and began to shiver. Once more, its mangy cock was clearly visible. Inkcap grabbed some nearby leaves and tried in vain to cover it.

Apricot was also standing in the fields. She seemed distraught, and this was enough for the animals to stop their battle and depart. She called to Inkcap, "Your family's pumpkin leaves have been chewed up by insects as well."

Apricot was spreading ashen leaves over her pumpkin patch. It had been many days since the village had seen any rain. Fireflies were busily devouring the leaves. After scattering the ash, she picked up a pumpkin, its colour a burned yellow. Inkcap tried to pinch the pumpkin flesh between his fingers, but it was too old and hard to permit him to grab anything.

"How come you're not... how come you're not at the meeting? Have you given up on the Cultural Revolution?"

"I did go," Apricot replied, "but when I got there, I turned and left."

"I went along, too, but I couldn't understand how both factions were there."

"It's a joint struggle session."

"You mean the Hammerheads and Red Blades are joining forces?"

"What do you think?"

Inkcap thought that Apricot seemed to be in a good mood today, if for no other reason than that she was speaking to him like she was. But since she was indeed speaking to him so candidly, he thought he needed to give her an answer to her question. It was only that he didn't have one. Suddenly, his mind thought of a hedgehog. There weren't any in Old Kiln, but he'd see people who lived up in the mountains taking care of hedgehogs, raising them as pets. They mostly stayed hidden in enclosures, but he figured that was partly because it was winter, and they were like those pigs that crowded together for warmth in the winter and slept most days. Only, he wondered, how could anyone get so close to a hedgehog?

"Like a hedgehog, maybe," Inkcap offered as an answer.

"Eh..."

Inkcap thought she'd misheard and repeated her response. "Eh?"

"Eh..."

"Yeah, a hedgehog... but say, the Hammerheads were queued up rather impressively. You think it was OK you left?"

"I'm not feeling well."

This was the first Inkcap had heard of her suffering from an illness. Suddenly, Apricot covered her mouth, and her face went ghostly pale. No one ever notices when an ugly person's face goes deathly white, but when a beautiful person's face loses all its colour, it is certainly noticeable. She burped and then vomited. Inkcap was startled. He rushed over to pat her on the back. He reached for another leaf so she could wipe her mouth. Apricot stopped him, however, not by saying anything, only by straightening her back and dashing away. Her pace quickened and the distance between them grew.

Inkcap was puzzled by Apricot's actions, then felt a growing sense of admiration for her strength. He thought to mimic her gait and the power she displayed in how she carried herself. After a dozen steps, however, his legs grew tired and his posture became bent. One foot turned inwards, the other outwards. He chose not to check in on his family plot. Instead, he'd walk back to the meeting square.

The moment he returned to the square, he saw a scene he would never forget. If he'd come any later, he would have missed it. Afterwards, Inkcap wondered whether Heaven had it all planned out for him. The year before, when he was eating dumplings, each dumpling he bit into had a coin inside. It was a positive omen, a sign of good fortune for the year ahead. No one else found a coin in their dumplings, only Inkcap. Some even went to extreme lengths to try to get a coin in their dumpling soup, but none were successful. Apricot was one of these unfortunate villagers. She would never have seen the scene he witnessed.

When he got back to the square, the atmosphere was even more electric than it had been before. This was likely the result of the bearded fellow having launched an attack against the so-called class enemies, but whatever the cause, both factions were shouting slogans just as Inkcap arrived. The Hammerheads were being led by Useless, while Palace was leading the charge for the Red Blades. Each faction took turns yelling their slogans, each trying to outdo the other. It was akin to some sort of competition, who had the newest, most vanguard slogan, who could shout it the loudest and the clearest. Useless evidently had the vocal capacity, his voice was high-pitched and rhythmic. The more he spoke, the more he seemed to be pushing down on Palace and the slogans he offered up to the crowd.

Disturbed by Palace's weakening performance, Awning instructed Sparks to take over, but his voice also lacked Useless's timbre and his rhythm was far too fast as though he were rushing through their slogans, cutting them off before the full force of the words could have the desired impact. Sparks' delivery did have an effect on the Hammerheads, however, who now seemed to speed up the delivery of their own slogans. Instead of castigating the class enemies, the square had been transformed into a standoff between the Hammerheads and Red Blades – who could better show their revolutionary vigour? Faces grew red, necks craned and veins bulged. It was as though someone were pinching hold of a rooster by the neck to make it crow better.

Inkcap thought the entire scene was quite the show, exciting to say the least. He stood between the rival factions, along with all those not named Zhu or Hei. There weren't many of them, at first a few rows of three, but slowly these rows shifted to make one longer line, like a dividing marker between the Hammerheads and the Red Blades. They didn't really know what to do, they just looked back and forth between the two groups. When the Hammerheads shouted, they looked in their direction. When the Red Blades returned fire, their eyes looked at them. So quickly were they turning their heads that their necks began to feel like an elastic band being pulled this way and that.

This was the Cultural Revolution. If there was no shouting, there'd be no revolution. Or so it seemed to Inkcap.

Baldy Jin hollered out towards the line in the middle, then Dazed-And-Confused followed suit. Those in the middle couldn't be sure the slogans were aimed at them, and in truth, they couldn't hear clearly what was being shouted. This was something more of the heart, Inkcap assumed, that they had to shout as loud as possible in order not to lose face, to avoid some kind of shame or other. And the shouting was infectious. Mouths wide open, revolutionary language spouting forth, even those in the middle began to take up the chorus, an auntie here, an auntie there, Noodle Fish's wife, his own gran, all began shouting, despite the fact they didn't know what it was they were calling out. No one took charge of the refrain from the middle, no one stood forth as their conductor, so they just mimicked left, then right, then left again, back and forth. An almost musical cacophony of voices.

Inkcap joined in too. To make his voice sound as clear as possible, he closed his eyes to concentrate. But try as he might, he couldn't hear himself. His voice was being drowned out by the crowd. He opened his eyes and looked at the crowd on one side, then on the other. He saw the strange arching of their necks, their whole bodies looking as though they were being stretched in a vertical direction, especially their necks. Longer and longer, they became. They swayed back and forth and Inkcap worried they would soon bang their heads together, like twisting bull reeds in the wind. His concern grew stronger, and he stopped shouting, his eyes transfixed on everyone else, their elongated necks, their gaping mouths that resembled yawning black caverns. Like others in the middle, he could feel the spittle land on his face from the many shouting mouths.

Inkcap could feel his body shrink back from the scene. He ducked low and squirrelled himself into the crowd, navigating a path away from them until finally he was standing to their rear, free of the mass of people. Only the medicine tree stood beside him. He wiped the sweat and spittle from his face and looked up from the tangle of roots below to the branches above. There he spied a feathered friend whose voice only he could hear. The sparrow looked at Inkcap but did not speak.

"What do you know," said Inkcap, as he climbed up the tree.

"What do you know," replied the bird.

Neither could understand the crowd in the square, each side shouting slogans as though their lives depended on it. Even those in the middle. But for some reason, Inkcap and the sparrow felt the same urge overtake them: the need to shout. And so they did. Their mouths opened in unison and their vocal chords blared. They seemed free from inhibitions, all that was between them was voices.

"Long live Chairman Mao!" Useless led the charge.

No longer just a member of the chorus, Inkcap led his own refrain, "Long live Chairman Mao!"

"Revolution is no crime!" shouted Sparks.

"Revolution is no crime!" Inkcap followed.

Again and again, again and again.

Suddenly, both sides stopped, and an eerie silence fell over the square. The only sound that remained was the chirping sparrow. Inkcap swung at the bird and knocked it from its perch. It fell to the ground and then he heard something else. In fact, everyone seemed to be hearing it, but no one at first recognised what it was. Inkcap listened some more, and realisation dawned on him: it was the sound of someone snoring. Light, gentle snoring. Inkcap shifted on the branch and turned his attention to the traitors in the front. He saw the Branch Secretary's head drooping low, his body swaying gently. He was definitely snoring. And asleep, no denying it this time. Inkcap felt a wave of nervousness sweep over him. He feared the Secretary would be discovered sleeping. As if on cue, Useless emerged from the crowd of Hammerheads, and Sparks stepped forth from the Red Blades. Strangely, though, they didn't walk towards Zhu Dagui. Instead, they stared at each other, eyes like daggers. Inkcap thought he could hear the sound of metal clanging against metal.

Useless shouted, and at first, Inkcap assumed he was simply venting his pent-up rage, his hatred of Sparks, cursing him and his entire gene pool. But he wasn't. Rather, it was the same slogan again, "Long live Chairman Mao", to which Sparks replied with "Revolution is no crime". Sparks seemed to want to drown out Useless's refrain, breathing in as much as he could, to the extent that his body looked like a swollen leather bag waiting to have the air squeezed out of it.

"Revolution is no crime!" His voice faltered, his delivery loud but uneven.

No one echoed his exhortation. Nor did anyone notice Branch Secretary Zhu. They only stared at Useless and Sparks who again started the familiar back and forth, louder, louder, faster, faster, long live Chairman Mao, down with Liu Shaoqi, uphold the revolution, and on it went. Both their faces grew redder, the strain showing more and more. To urge their comrade to continue, the Hammerheads cheered him on. The Red Blades responded by doing the same. Once more, both factions and their entire choruses shouted, each side trying to top the other. Inkcap could no longer keep up with the rhythm and merely clapped instead. The sound was deafening.

Suddenly, Useless shouted, "Support Liu Shaoqi and down with Chairman Mao!"

Inkcap began to clap but stopped short. Had he heard that right?

The Hammerheads began to echo Useless's slogan, but they also stopped short.

The Red Blades started to retort, but their words came to an abrupt stop too.

Even the sparrow had halted its chirping.

All eyes were trained on Useless, but he seemed oblivious to what was happening. Turning to the Hammerheads, he asked, "Why have you stopped?"

"You said it wrong," answered Baldy Jin.

Realisation washed over Useless, and he hurriedly shouted, "Support Chairman Mao, long live Chairman Mao!"

The Hammerheads echoed him, but the Red Blades remained silent.

Awning, seizing the opportunity, jumped up and yelled, "Wu Gan, Wu Gan, you heard what he said. Useless called on us to topple Chairman Mao, he's a counterrevolutionary, he's trying to stop the Revolution!"

Upon hearing the accusation, Wu Gan and the bearded man, as well as everyone who'd come from Luozhen, leapt forward. It was as if their greatest enemy had appeared before them. The Hammerheads, the Red Blades, all eyes fell on them. Even the traitors at the front of the crowd directed their attention to Wu Gan and the bearded fellow. Only the head of Secretary Zhu remained low. He wasn't snoring, but his body continued to sway, balanced precariously on his rickety legs. It was amazing he hadn't fallen over.

Awning sprinted from out of the Red Blades to stand next to Wu Gan. Raising his arms, he shouted, "The one who said 'Down with Chairman Mao' needs to be taken down himself. Get Useless up here, get him up here now!"

The Red Blades took up the refrain and carried it forward, shouting at fever pitch until Wu Gan stepped in front of them and waved his hands to demand silence. Once they were quiet, he spoke: "Useless, step forward."

Useless's face was ashen, but he did as ordered, answering Wu Gan as he moved away from the Hammerheads. "I, I… misspoke, I, I… was confused."

"Come over here, now!" yelled the bearded man. "Seize the counterrevolutionary!"

No one from the Hammerheads moved, they were all too stunned, their feet nailed to the ground.

"I, I was... I was confused," Useless pleaded again.

Bash kicked him from behind but said nothing.

Useless took off running. This was unexpected. The Hammerheads remained frozen. All except Useless, who pushed at the crowd, at his comrades Stargazer, Decheng and the other Hammerheads. He was desperate to flee but was stopped by Baldy Jin, who shouted his name and grabbed his arm. Useless twisted and wrenched it free, pushing away from Baldy Jin and then leaping over Stonebreaker who had knelt to tie his shoe. Free from his fellow Hammerheads, Awning and Sparks now sprang into action, pouncing after Useless like hungry wolves. He shifted left, then right. There was no straight line he could take to escape. The crowd was too dense, so he darted to the side and found himself face to face with the medicine tree.

"Inkcap!" Awning yelled. "Inkcap!"

Inkcap was startled by Awning yelling his name and didn't really know what to do. Instinctively, he moved to jump down from the tree, never once thinking he'd land on Useless. A second later and Awning had pinned Useless, his knee pressed into Useless's lower back, his hands held from behind, his face in the dirt. Awning then pulled him up roughly and marched him back to stand in front of the bearded man.

The focus of the struggle session had changed. While they had started by criticising the class enemies, now the rage of the villagers was directed at Useless. The slogans of the Red Blades reverberated and echoed through the air. The Hammerheads were silent. They had no means by which to defend Useless, nor to see him released from the clutches of the Red Blades. All they could do was stew in anger, disheartened by the turn of events.

Once the struggle session was complete, the traitors were marched through the village and back to Luozhen for re-education. Secretary Zhu was included in this group, despite his broken leg. The new addition was Useless. Palace had quickly fashioned a conical hat for him to wear, made of sharp branches since the wire had been exhausted. Sparks was not pleased, complaining about the need for proper wire, but Palace's defence was that he'd looked and not found any. Nevertheless, the hat served its purpose, exposing Useless's crime for all to see – he was a counterrevolutionary. In fact, the hat ended up being on the large size and fell down over his brow, causing Useless no end of discomfort and inconvenience for he had to keep lifting it over his eyes. This was the only way he could see the road he was forced to trudge along.

Useless's mum was inconsolable. She cried nonstop, but no one from the Zhu clan offered her any comfort. The only person to pay her mind was Bash, and he only yelled at her to stop crying.

"Dammit! Enough already, what's the use?"

"Oh, but Bash," she said in between sobs, "you will take care of him, won't you? Useless has been by your side from the beginning. Him being seized like that, it must be a slap to your face."

Bash did not reply, but his anger was plain to see. He kicked at a nearby brick while Useless's mum continued to weep.

Inkcap thought she was pitiable, and that it would be best if she were escorted home. When he moved to do so, he received a cold stare from Bash followed by a pointed rebuke.

"You did well to fall, didn't you, you little shit."

"It wasn't deliberate," Inkcap shot back. "I fell... I wasn't trying to knock him down."

"Tosh! I know you hate him."

"You can't blame me, Brother Bash, you can't."

Bash lowered his head and began to walk away, saying nothing in reply.

Panic gripped Inkcap and he rushed after him, repeating that it wasn't his fault.

"Oh, for fuck's sake, get lost."

"But Brother Bash, you've got to believe me, I didn't try to... Say I didn't..."

"All right, all right, I don't blame you for what happened. Satisfied? Now fuck off."

Inkcap stopped following him.

FIFTY-EIGHT

STARTING THE FOLLOWING DAWN, Inkcap began waking up earlier than normal. He didn't understand why he couldn't lie in until later, and even though he was awake, he refused to get out of bed as though determined to force himself back to sleep. Unfortunately, sleep would not return so he just lay in bed, listening to the sounds around him. He could hear Gran opening her wardrobe, the squeak of the door – she must be getting her scissors and paper, he mused – then silence again. Most especially he heard the chirp of crickets beyond his wall. They were always there, very familiar with his whole house, he supposed. Part of the family, in a strange sort of way. Even Gran opening her wardrobe was no cause for alarm for the crickets, they would continue to chirp and skitter about. He could hear the chickens too. They were up and about in the garden, pecking at this and that, he surmised. Then silence again. Now noise. Silence. He wondered if they were hopping up and down. The swallow was quiet as well. Usually it talked to itself, but on this occasion, Inkcap didn't hear it. Out nearer the gate he could hear the sparrows cheeping in their seemingly broken voices, giving Gran advice on the work for that day. Evidently, the weather was ideal for laying grain out to dry. Then their voices became hurried, overlapping and confused. Were the sparrows fighting, he wondered. The cicadas were also contributing to the cacophony with their distinctive whine. Interrupted by brief pauses, he thought someone must be pinching and releasing them. Then he heard Gran.

"Cowbell, my boy, you're calling on us rather early, aren't you?"

"A meeting's starting! Where's Inkcap?"

"Still in bed."

"In bed? A new big-character poster's been put up, it's criticising Useless. Do you think he'd like to see it? Lazybones!"

"Lazybones indeed. Sleeps too much, to my mind."

A patter of footsteps echoed from the alleyway. Ding, dang, ding, dang. Was it someone tapping on a barrel? Was it Big Root or perhaps Old Faithful's wife, goitre and all? If it was Old Faithful's wife, no doubt she was cursing her husband. That was the first thing she did every day, as soon as her eyes opened. For his part, he would remain silent, never opening his mouth to respond. How could she be wailing like this now, though? Did she ever cry? Finally, Inkcap recognised the sound of the crying: it was Useless's mum.

Her weeping sounded eerily similar to the performers in an opera. A long, mournful tune, interspersed with coughs and sniffles, and then a moment of quiet as though she were holding her breath, followed by more crying. As Inkcap sat in bed, the more his mind wandered to that moment when he leapt down from the tree, landing on Useless and allowing Awning to capture him. He regretted more and more what he'd done. Part of him knew he'd done it deliberately, if not consciously. He'd assisted in Useless being seized, and thus he'd contributed to Useless's mother's current state. Useless was now branded a counterrevolutionary, which was far worse than the position of Gran. Deep down, he knew Useless's life was over.

Inkcap couldn't help but sympathise with Useless. He forgot how Useless had treated him in the past. Now he just felt sorry for him. This feeling did little to improve Inkcap's mood, which was the main reason he hadn't gone to see the big-character poster.

Needless to say, the Hammerheads had suffered a serious blow, and as a result, their activities were greatly toned down. In truth, they were rarely seen doing anything in Old Kiln, which wasn't altogether a bad thing, some concluded, as a welcome calm fell over the village. Long-neglected work got completed, like Barndoor constructing a new cesspit for Lucky, whose old one had continued to leak even after repairs had been attempted. A new site was chosen, much larger than the previous one, dug nearly twice as deep. And since many villagers had little to do, they took to watching Barndoor work, cigarettes always at the ready, prepared for a chinwag or two.

"What do you say?" asked Lucky.

"Nothing much, just come to watch your cesspit being dug."

"Eh now, surely not. Got a smoke?"

They laughed. "Shouldn't it be you offering one to us? You're the host, after all."

"Host of what, a pit being dug? Damn, it's not like a new house is being built, is it?"

At that moment, Ever-Obedient appeared and looked as though he were surveying the work. "Lucky, lad, why are you having such a large pit dug?"

"Might as well, don't you think? Why go to the trouble of digging a pit if it isn't bigger than the old one?"

"So will it be for public use, then?"

Lucky didn't much like the sound of that. "I reckon you mind your own business."

Suitably scolded, his face bright red, Ever-Obedient walked away without saying another word.

Everyone knew Ever-Obedient's problem was that his wife, Yoyo, had run away. There was still no trace of her and this hung heavy on his heart. No matter what he tried to do, after even just a little bit of exertion, he'd feel exhausted and drained. Villagers began seeing him in the evenings, seated on one of the large millstones near the public square, waiting for Yoyo. On some occasions, he'd sit there until the sun had gone down and the moon shone upon him, unwilling to leave. Finally, he'd lift himself up and wander over to Big Root's place. Big Root had rush reeds planted near the gate of his courtyard, as well as a pedal-powered thresher. Ever-Obedient would run it several times and then plop down on the ground. The moon would sparkle above him, the reeds would sway in the wind, and Ever-Obedient would think he was looking at a school of fish jumping and splashing about in a shallow pool.

"Alas," Big Root said, "how did Old Kiln fall on such hard times? The whole place is rotten. After Liberation, not one villager had ever been punished by law. It's been good until now, hasn't it? A long period of… tranquillity. Until Pockmark went to prison. Then the Secretary and Useless. You've realised this, haven't you, Pockmark and Useless have long *faling* lines, reaching to the corners of their mouths."

"What are you talking about?" asked Ever-Obedient.

"How can you be so ignorant of what's going on?"

"Perhaps my brain's broken…"

"Ah, the *faling*, which run down both sides of the nose. Look at my face, will you? The lines connect with the corners of my mouth and extend below. See?" And he traced his fingers along his face. "But Pockmark and Useless, their lines stop at their mouths, they eat their lines, that signals imprisonment."

"I suppose… Pockmark is in jail. But… but Useless is in re-education, that's not the same, is it?"

"What else would you call it?" retorted Big Root. "Who else in the village eats their lines?"

"Who else has long lines, you mean?"

"How about Bash and Awning, their lines are long, aren't they?"

"Bash and Awning? They have long lines?"

"I didn't say that—"

"I didn't either."

"True, true, but then I have to ask, what the devil are we talking about here? How about we discuss something else, how to live life well? You reckon you can talk about that?"

"Yes… I think I can."

"OK, so did you hear that Bash said Old Kiln should belong to the Hei clan, can you believe that? I mean, where's the Zhu clan supposed to live? If

Old Kiln belongs to the Zhus and Heis, then what about the rest of them, where are they going to go?"

"Damn, I must say, you never used to talk this much before, but now you sound like an old hen, a right motormouth!" Ever-Obedient stood up.

"Look at you, all full of piss and vinegar. Your wife, Yoyo, she's disappeared, yeah? Tell me, where do you think she's gone?"

Ever-Obedient didn't answer, he simply left Big Root alone and began wandering the alleys of Old Kiln again, his arms tucked in his sleeves like an ascetic monk. Given the hour, most courtyard gates were closed, but a few were still ajar, some people still awake.

"Not yet in bed?" came a question from one of these courtyards, but before Ever-Obedient could answer, the gate was closed.

Ever-Obedient still offered a reply: "Rather early I reckon, too early to sleep. I know it wouldn't come to me even if I tried."

The gate did not reopen.

He then noticed Feng Youliang's gate a little in the distance. It was still open, and he could see a fire burning in the courtyard. Youliang never talked much, and even when he saw Ever-Obedient walking towards him, passing through the gate, he did not offer greetings beyond a brief look and a gesture to see if Ever-Obedient wanted a smoke.

Taking one of the proffered cigarettes, Ever-Obedient lit up and inhaled deeply. "I can see you've got rice boiling over the fire. Making some wine, are you?"

"No."

"Then why are you boiling the rice like this?"

"No reason."

"But you've made it in the past. I remember when Stonebreaker celebrated the arrival of his child, you made some then for the festivities…"

Youliang ignored what Ever-Obedient was saying, shifted and stood up to collect a board nearer his house. He placed it one way, but didn't seem satisfied, then went into his shed and came back out carrying a plane. He attacked the board with it, shaving off imperfections to end up with a smooth plank. Ever-Obedient could hear him labouring as he moved the plane over the wood.

"Making some art, then, are you?"

Youliang continued to huff and puff.

Desperate for any kind of conversation, Ever-Obedient persisted: "You don't have an apprentice?"

Apparently finished with planing the board, Youliang put it to one side and said, "Smoke your cigarette."

After the second, then the third, Ever-Obedient didn't want to smoke any more. He lifted himself up and grabbed a piece of wood as Youliang had done a few moments ago. Bringing it back closer to the fire, he could feel the softness of it in his hands. Oddly, he could also feel his trousers growing damp.

"Must be covered in dew, eh?" he wondered out loud, and he sat down once more.

Again, Youliang offered no reply and silent minutes passed between them. Growing tired of just sitting around the fire and smoking, Ever-Obedient decided to leave.

Once he stood up, however, Youliang said, "Not staying for a bit?"

"No... stayed long enough."

Youliang picked up a pair of tongs and lifted the boiling bowl of rice from the pan. But he did not offer any to Ever-Obedient. Resigned to the man's ill-manners, Ever-Obedient gave his apologies and left.

The following day, Ever-Obedient was still gripped with an indescribable nervousness. He fidgeted with his hands, unable to concentrate on anything. There was nothing else to do but wander the alleyways of Old Kiln once more. When he spied Inkcap and Cowbell, he called out to them to come and play a game of chess, and despite having other plans – they had intended to go down to the river to walk among the reeds, look for turtles and anything else they could find – the boys accepted the invitation. Naturally, the game of chess led to arguments between Inkcap and Cowbell, and Ever-Obedient grew tired of their noisiness. He stopped their game and told them to leave. When the boys failed to go, he swept the stone chess pieces down onto the ground, effectively ending their game.

Annoyed at the abrupt conclusion to their game, Inkcap said, "What are you sweeping so vigorously for, is Wu Gan here?"

Wu Gan had indeed appeared. Inkcap had seen him first, coming into view some distance down the alleyway. He could hear the man, too, his thick-soled shoes clattering the ground with every step. Following Inkcap's eyes, Ever-Obedient turned and looked in the direction of Wu Gan. As soon as he recognised who it was, he beat a hasty retreat home, refusing to come out.

Wu Gan had been on his way to Xiahewan but decided to make a detour into Old Kiln. He had a message for Awning, so it made sense for him to deliver it in person. He could also avail himself of some food while passing through the village, he thought, some tasty noodles like the ones he had before in Old Kiln. It was a surprise for him to come upon Soupspoon, however, and perhaps even a greater surprise for Soupspoon himself.

"Wu Gan, comrade," Soupspoon said affectionately. "I've actually been waiting for you."

"And how did you know I was coming?"

"Oh, Awning told me. Come, come, we've made preparations."

"Preparations?"

"I've been cleaning my place since before the sun came up."

As he spoke, Soupspoon looked around and peered down the alleyway. There was no one in sight, only Inkcap and Cowbell at the far end near the millstone. Soupspoon called out to the boys, asked them to help with preparing a meal of noodles for Wu Gan, but first to go and tell Awning that their senior comrade had arrived. Quickness was required and expected, he told them.

The boys, however, didn't move.

"You want us to go and tell Awning?" Cowbell asked.

"Not me," said Inkcap.

"But the meal is for Comrade Wu Gan."

"All right, I'll go," Cowbell replied.

The two boys got up and headed in the direction of Awning's place. As they passed out of Soupspoon's sight, however, Inkcap altered his path.

"Where are you going?" Cowbell yelled.

"Who the hell is Soupspoon?" said Inkcap. "If he told you to jump, would you ask how high? I'm not going to Awning's, and I'm not helping them cook. Besides, do you think they'll give us any of the food they want us to help make? Not a bit, I tell you. I'm going to the river to look for turtles."

On the southeast side of the riverbank, the wind always gusted through the rush reeds as though it had big hands and large feet, hands to push the reeds to the left, feet to lift them back up and shift them to the right. It was like a sort of dance, Inkcap supposed, back and forth in an oddly natural harmony. Cowbell had been persuaded by Inkcap's words a little while before, as he had chosen to search for turtles too, instead of helping out Soupspoon. Together, they'd see what they could find and enjoy mock battles by using the rushes as their weapons. In fact, the play fighting proved far more enjoyable than the search for turtles, and Inkcap and Cowbell lost themselves to it. Whack, thrust, attack. That was until one of the reeds ended up in Inkcap's open mouth causing him to gag. He wasn't angry, but he did have to spit the bits of vegetation out before their battle could resume. Suddenly, however, Inkcap jerked his head.

"What is it?" Cowbell asked. "Did you swallow any of it?"

"No... but I smell that smell again."

Cowbell reached up and pinched Inkcap's nose between his fingers. "Eh, what kind of nose is this, anyway, always smelling strange smells?" He squeezed so hard Inkcap could barely breathe.

Wrenching himself free, Inkcap still did not seem angry, although Cowbell had perhaps given him sufficient reason. Instead, he just rubbed his nose, paused, then rubbed it again.

"Sorry, I lied, I don't smell anything."

But that statement was in fact a lie. In his short life, Inkcap had been stepped on enough already, he'd learnt to be wary, but in front of Cowbell, he felt no timidity. Inkcap's senses were alert, he knew. He also knew that Cowbell's weren't. At any rate, he could pretend.

"You're not having me on, are you?" Cowbell asked.

Inkcap squeezed his nose. "Hey now, come on."

"Then why are you pinching your nose?"

"I think it's going flat."

Inkcap kept his fingers on his nose, kept squeezing it, preventing himself from smelling that smell.

Just then, they spied Sparks walking down the road. He was carrying two large earthen containers on a shoulder pole. By the looks of it, the containers were filled with bowls. When his eyes made contact with Inkcap and Cowbell, he rushed over in their direction.

"Hey, boys," Sparks said, before pausing and changing tack. "Say, Inkcap, why's your nose so red, it looks like a carrot!"

"Where are you going?" asked Inkcap.

"To town."

"Me too."

"Don't go throwing bullshit my way, you'll give me a sore throat. I'm going to sell this porcelain, why the hell do you need to go?"

"I've got stuff to sell too."

"You're going to town in that filthy jacket?"

Inkcap asked Sparks to wait for him. He then ran back home to change into another jacket which his Gran had washed very clean and stiffened with starch.

To Inkcap's mind, Old Kiln had become boring. The strange quiet that had settled over the village meant the days were now blending into each other. And he thought it would be more fun to get away, even if it meant walking to Luozhen with Sparks. He also offered to help carry some of the china, at least whatever he could manage. Unfortunately, when he returned to where Sparks had promised to wait, no one was there, leading him to curse Sparks and wish for the porcelain he was transporting to fall and break.

Sparks was successful in selling his wares in Luozhen. With the money earned, he purchased some wine for his father-in-law, as well as some brown sugar. He'd wanted to buy a roll of cloth, but he didn't have the proper ticket to be able to get it from the government store. He decided instead to use some of the money to get a new satchel, one made of several layers and therefore of greater durability. With the remaining bit of cash left, Sparks considered buying a birthday present for his father-in-law. Then he thought some more and realised he hadn't got any food for himself. His stomach won out, and he looked for a place to sit down and eat. A bowl of noodles, perhaps, or some rice? If he got rice, he'd have money left over to purchase some dried tomato fried eggs, even some fried potato slices to go with it. There was really no choice, and Sparks marched off towards a canteen that could serve him some rice, fried eggs and vegetables.

On his way there, however, he passed by the supply and marketing co-operative where a very long queue had formed outside the main door. His curiosity piqued, Sparks had to find out the reason that was causing everyone to wait so long to make a purchase.

It turned out to be plaster statues of Chairman Mao, much bigger than the ones the Hammerheads had brought back with them that one time.

Sparks immediately changed his mind. Food could wait. The statue was far more valuable and would bring far more prestige to the Red Blades than filling his stomach. He'd also be the only member of the Zhu clan to have such a statue. And further knocking down the Hammerheads, that in itself would be worth spending the remaining money on. So he waited in the queue, thinking all the while how important it would be to bring such a statue back to Old Kiln. Having handed over his money, Sparks was left with only twelve cents, just enough for a small bowl of cold mung bean noodles.

When he'd gone to Luozhen, he'd carried the porcelain in a large earthen jar. Now, on the way back, he put the wine and brown sugar in the satchel. The Chairman Mao statue, however, would not fit, so he had to carry it in his arms as though he were embracing the Great Helmsman himself. Not far out of town, his arms and shoulder ached so he searched for another way to bring his treasures home. Sweat dripped down his forehead and back, and he knew he had to think of something. But the statue just wouldn't fit in the satchel, no matter how much he tried to wedge it in. Finally, he pulled out a length of rope he'd been carrying and tied it to the statue, slinging it around his neck in the hope of safely bringing Chairman Mao home. By mid-afternoon, he reached Old Kiln, just as the sky above him was changing and thunder could be heard in the distance.

Iron Bolt was tilling the sesame fields when the thunder sounded. A second later, a blast of lightning struck the ground not too far from him, producing a fireball that seemed to roll down the sloping land, crashing into the date tree and engulfing it in flames. Five years before, Iron Bolt's brother, Silver Bolt, had been struck by lightning. No one had a bad word to say about his brother. He'd been out tilling the fields with a steel hoe. When the sky opened and the thunder and lightning came, he'd used the hoe to shield himself from the rain. Perhaps it was the steel, who could say, but the lightning struck him, scorching him like burned wood. Unsurprisingly, his brother was fresh in Iron Bolt's mind when he heard the thunder, and his face blanched. He dropped the plough and darted towards a nearby pile of stones, squirrelling himself under a small crevice.

"Inkcap!" he called out.

Having been stood up by Sparks when he went to Luozhen, Inkcap was roped into tending to the cattle not too far away from Iron Bolt, and as it happened, the pile of stones where Iron Bolt had hidden himself at that moment was Inkcap's chosen place to release his bowels. Needless to say, he was startled by Iron Bolt's holler and tried to yank up his trousers. Strangely, however, no further lightning bolts fell from the sky. Thunder remained, echoing across Old Kiln, but no lightning. Iron Bolt, still wary, climbed out of his hiding place, but he didn't return to work. In his mind, the lull in the weather was just temporary, and soon the lightning would return. Without collecting his tools, he ran off home, leaving Inkcap to pick up the plough and other equipment. He did so with difficulty, and then drove the cattle back to their shed, vowing to himself that he would not fail. Nor would any lightning strike him.

Racing back to the village, Iron Bolt bumped into Sparks just as he was returning too. Naturally, his eyes were drawn to what was hanging around Sparks' neck.

"What the devil is that?"

Sparks had little desire to speak to Iron Bolt, but his desire to brag was greater. "A statue of Chairman Mao, the Great Helmsman! What are you running around for? You ought to be more careful, you almost knocked me over."

"It's the thunder and lightning, surely you heard it."

"And? Thunder and lightning is just that, it's not like it's chasing you, is it?"

Iron Bolt looked behind him, then back to Sparks. "Don't go trying to scare me."

"What? Do you think everything happens in pairs? That the quota is short one because only your brother was struck?"

Sparks walked away, the Mao statue still slung around his neck.

Iron Bolt just stood there for what seemed like forever, unsure what to say or do. Before he moved on, Half-Stick appeared, followed closely by Baldy Jin. She had a sickle in her hand, he a bundle of harvested grain.

"Sister," Iron Bolt called out, "you're still holding a sickle. You're not worried about the lightning?"

"I'm better off dead in any case," Half-Stick shouted.

Furious at her reply, Baldy Jin moved a little closer to her, dropped the bundle and grabbed the sickle, wedging it into the grain and leaving it on the ground, shouting as he did so, "What fucking rubbish. Go on, get home."

Iron Bolt couldn't be sure if the words were meant for him, but Half-Stick was in no doubt. She glared at Baldy Jin, spun around and sashayed her way off.

"What's the matter," Iron Bolt asked, "you two fighting again?"

"Well, if you marry a chicken, you're stuck with a hen," Baldy Jin replied. "Marry a dog, and all you get is a bitch. There's no love between us, that's for sure, I'm not certain if there ever was. Shit, all it takes is for me to even mention the Hammerheads and she'll fly off the handle."

"So... you're not even getting any?"

"She's not touched my cock in forever. The Revolution succeeded, yeah, sure, but I can't get no pussy."

"All right, all right, you're right to be angry, I understand that... But let me tell you something, in Old Kiln, everything happens in pairs. Useless's, erm, situation–"

"What are you getting at, are you saying something else is going to happen to the Hammerheads?"

"Well, from what I've heard... Yeah, well, Useless has been expelled from the Hammerheads, right, but surely that means someone in the Red Blades is going down, too, doesn't it? Pairs."

Iron Bolt glanced around as though worried someone else was there, then continued, "Sparks just returned from Luozhen, he brought with him this big Chairman Mao statue. Do you know how he carried it back? He had a rope wrapped around its neck... looked a lot like he was trying to hang the Great Helmsman if you ask me."

Baldy Jin kicked at the bundle of grain he had thrown on the ground. "Counterrevolutionary! The fucking bastard."

"Exactly."

"Where is he, then? Where?"

"I can tell you more, but not here. This tree's old, far too high, perfect target for lightning."

The two men moved close to Bash's house, near the wall that surrounded his courtyard. There, they spoke more about Sparks. As they were chatting, Inkcap appeared driving the cattle back to their shed. When the cattle saw the bundle of grain Baldy Jin had once more thrown on the ground, they angled their pace in that direction, eager to devour it. Of course, Baldy Jin was having none of it and kicked at the animals.

"Fucking beasts, not for you!" The cows seemed unbothered and continued to munch the grain.

Whacking their rears with a stick he'd picked up on the way, Inkcap shouted at them, "Stop it, cut it out, not for you. Do you think you can act like Awning?"

Baldy Jin immediately took notice of Inkcap. "What did you just say? Is Awning supposed to eat me?" Then his mind went to Awning and Half-Stick, his eyes widened and he raised his hand to hit Inkcap.

Iron Bolt pulled the boy's arm before Baldy Jin could swing his hand. "Get the cattle back to the shed you little shit."

Inkcap did not reply but cursed the cows instead. "Bloody animals, I'll muzzle the lot of you."

Baldy Jin had seemed to forget Inkcap and again questioned Iron Bolt: "Where did he buy the statue?"

"Luozhen, I reckon."

"That means he had the rope around Chairman Mao's neck the whole way home, doesn't it?"

"I would imagine so."

"Oh, that's so wrong, so, so fucking wrong."

"Who's wrong?" interjected Inkcap.

"What are you still doing here?" said Iron Bolt.

At that moment, as though on cue, one of the cows shat, a warm, soggy wet mass landing on Inkcap's feet. Disgusted, Inkcap went to look for some straw with which to clean his shoes.

Not noticing, Baldy Jin continued to prattle on. "Bash needs to know this, needs to know this now, Useless said one word wrong and ended up in re-education, Sparks carried Chairman Mao home with a rope around his neck, surely that's at least as bad, isn't it?

Inkcap clicked his tongue and lowered his head, mumbling under his breath, "The plough's still in the field. I didn't pick it up, I hope it's not lost."

"You didn't pick up the plough, just drove the cattle back here?" said Iron Bolt. "If it's gone, that's on you... and I guarantee I'll use your fucking bones to till the land if there's no plough to use... The lightning's stopped, get back there now and fetch it. And make sure you clean it off too."

Iron Bolt and Baldy Jin turned and walked off towards the temple, evidently to speak to Bash.

Inkcap waited until the two men left, then he also began to walk off, driving the cattle. But not in the direction of the shed, nor towards the field to retrieve the plough. Instead, he went to Awning's place, the cattle sauntering in front of him. When he arrived, he didn't hesitate, but walked the cattle in through the gate and closed it behind him. Awning's wife was inside, busily kneading flour to make noodles. The commotion in her courtyard made her stop, however, and a moment later she was outside yelling at Inkcap.

"Just what the hell are you doing here? My home's not the blasted cattle shed, you damn fool!"

Inkcap pursed his lips and answered, exhaling slowly as he did, "Is Awning in?"

Before receiving an answer, he heard movement inside. A few seconds later, Awning appeared and Inkcap raced through what he had heard. Unsurprisingly, the more he listened, the more Awning's complexion changed. Meanwhile, his wife was still cursing Inkcap for bringing the cattle into their courtyard when finally Awning yelled. Not at Inkcap, however, but at his wife.

"What are you shouting for, woman?"

She went silent.

"Tell me, Inkcap," said Awning, turning his attention once more to the boy. "Is what you say true?"

"I wouldn't lie. I swear."

Nothing more was said between the two of them. Only a look from Awning told Inkcap he had to leave and take the cows with him. Awning grabbed a jacket and stormed off, not even bothering to button it up. He had to speak to Sparks.

The cattle returned safely to their shed, and Inkcap went back to the field to get the plough before going home. Since thunder was still ringing out from time to time, he closed the windows and doors. Gran made dinner and they ate together. Afterwards, she sat on the bed mending clothes and spoke of her feeling that rain was coming, heavy, possibly destructive rain.

"You think closing the windows will keep it out?" she asked Inkcap.

"Yes, I do. Closed windows will keep the thunder out for sure."

Outside, the sky echoed, thunder cracked like the sound of feet pounding hard and fast in the direction of the eastern part of Old Kiln.

His meal was congee. He wondered how Gran had made it so thick. She'd even added red and white radish chunks, big enough to be picked up by chopsticks. She told him it was his birthday. He'd heard from the villagers that he'd been fished up from the river. But if that was the case, how did Gran know today was his birthday? Had she just chosen the day she fished him up? Then he thought some more and concluded that wasn't possible. If today was his birthday, in autumn, the river would have been far too low.

"Gran," he began, "was the river high that year?"

Momentarily stunned by his question, Granny Silkworm hesitated before offering an answer. "Oh, don't be silly, it's your birthday today, for sure. What's this nonsense about the river being high or low?"

Inkcap gauged by her response that she didn't want to talk further about the matter, so he refrained from asking for clarification. He smiled and lifted the bowl of congee in his hands, then walked to the door, opened it and strolled out towards the alleyway.

"What are you doing, boy?" Gran yelled after him.

"What's the problem?" he called back. "It's my birthday!"

He manoeuvred his way down to the riverbank. He wanted to see where he'd come from. His heart wanted to see it. His gran had taken him in, the alleyways too. The trees, the stones, everything in Old Kiln had taken him in. Yoyo was like him, she came into Old Kiln. But then she went crazy and disappeared. The trees, stones, the village, he thought, they must have no longer wanted her. That's why she was gone. He walked back and forth alongside the trees, giving each a mouthful of his congee, urging them to eat. It was his birthday and he had to treat them to a meal. In return, the trees shook and gave him their leaves. The stones didn't move, but moths emerged from their cracks and quickly took to the air.

His bowl was half empty, but Inkcap's heart hurt. He thought of the Qingming Festival, how the villagers offered their ancestors cold noodles and paid their respects. Then he recalled how they would sit beside each other in front of their ancestors' graves and eat the noodles they'd offered. Inkcap thought to do the same, so he walked back through the alleyway, scooping up the congee he'd given the trees and eating it himself. He was in the alleyway by himself. Strangely, no one else was around. He looked up and down, trained his ears, but nothing. The village was quiet. True, the sky was still heavy and in the distance he could hear the thunder rattling about, but the villagers... what were they doing? A thought occurred to him: was something big about to happen? Were the Hammerheads, the Red Blades, were they going to call a meeting? Sparks was in trouble, wasn't he?

But nothing happened. Feeling a pang of disappointment, Inkcap returned home and asked for another bowl of congee, adding, "Gran, how come it's not rained?"

"Don't go jinxing things and calling down the wrath of Heaven, boy!" shouted Gran, clearly agitated by his question.

Suddenly weary, Inkcap wanted to sleep. He crawled into bed and was out in seconds. Moments later, it rained, but Granny Silkworm didn't wake him up. He'd eaten a lot of congee, she thought, he wouldn't wet the bed.

As he slept, Inkcap dreamt. In his dreams, he saw Gourd's wife. She was calling out to him to come up the mountain to harvest wild garlic, but he was telling her they weren't ready yet. Far too small, he shouted back in his dream. Gourd's wife retorted that her mother-in-law wanted to eat the garlic and that it didn't matter if they wouldn't be able to harvest much. In his dream, Inkcap conceded and followed her into the mountains, searching high and low for wild garlic, digging up whatever they managed to find. Suddenly, on one precipice, he found a large wild garlic plant sprouting up from the ground. But before he could run over to dig it up, a hawk soared down from above and stabbed at the garlic. Inkcap, startled by the bird's rapid approach and aggressive manner, stumbled and lost his footing. Soon, he was tumbling down into the valley below. He called out in his sleep just as he was about to crash into the valley floor, and then suddenly woke up. His eyes were wide open and staring this way and that. For a moment, he thought he was still asleep, but gradually he realised he wasn't. Gran was still awake.

"What's the time?" he asked.

She didn't respond.

"Gran... I was dreaming. I'd fallen from some cliff..."

Still, she did not answer.

Inkcap sat up, but Granny Silkworm remained silent. He turned to see her better and she shifted, diving under the covers, evidently looking for something she'd placed underneath.

"Gran, Gran!" Inkcap yelled, his face betraying his growing concern.

A moment later, she raised her head from the covers. In her hand was a copy of Chairman Mao's Little Red Book.

"Gran, why did you hide Chairman Mao's Little Red Book there?"

Her only answer was to rush over to him and clamp her hand over his mouth. Then in quiet tones, she explained that the book had got damp early in the day, Noodle Fish's wife had been over, she'd come to return some bowls she'd borrowed, they'd been filled with red beans, but they'd not measured things correctly, or something like that. Gran agreed they could remeasure the amount of beans Noodle Fish's wife had borrowed, but when she rummaged through the cupboard for another bowl, she accidentally knocked things over. Beans were scattered over the countertop. Before she could sweep them back into the bowl, however, one of the chickens raced in, it must have smelt the beans. It clambered up onto the counter somehow and moved so quickly that Gran didn't quite see it. Naturally, she tried to shoo the bird away, but it wouldn't leave, choosing the beans over punishment, she guessed. Then, just as she grabbed her papercutting scissors, thinking to scare the creature away, it skittered to the side and knocked over a bowl of water. Chairman Mao's Little Red Book was next to it and got drenched. Even though she dried it off, it was too late, the pages had curled and wrinkled.

"I... I was afraid someone would see it, think I'd ruined it on purpose, so I hid it under the covers."

"Who would see it? You didn't let Noodle Fish's wife inside, did you?"

"No, no, she was outside the whole time."

"Then that's all right, no one else was here, were they?"

"I'm not afraid of that, not really, but what if someone did come? Sparks bought a statue of Chairman Mao just to show off to Awning, didn't he? And you know what might happen to him?"

"Eh?"

"But you said you heard yourself, you told me, something about Sparks being accused of counterrevolutionary activities, that he wanted to murder the Chairman, to hang him or something?"

"Do you think the Hammerheads will really get him?"

"What do you mean? You're the one who told me they were going to get him. What else do you know?"

"I... I don't know nothing, I was asleep."

"Ha, fortunately for you, eh?"

"So... do you want to find out what's happening?"

"What do you take me for, do you think I'm just like you?" Gran retorted, looking hard at Inkcap. "I just heard a bell ringing out, you know, while you were asleep. Am I worried, yes, dammit, I am. I actually went out to make sure the gate was closed, and do you know what I saw, I saw Caretaker's wife running past. I waved at her, and she stopped a moment, then I asked her what was going on. She told me the Hammerheads had seized Sparks. You were right, she confirmed it. He had this statue, she said, he'd brought it from Luozhen, but he carried it on his back, a rope tied around its neck – can you believe it? – it was like he had Chairman Mao strung up. That's clearly counterrevolutionary. He denied it, according to her, he said that he did not spout any counterrevolutionary slogans like Useless had done, but they didn't care. Even when he said he'd bought the statue in homage to the Great Helmsman, swore that he carried it home as though it were a precious baby, it didn't matter. That's what she told me..."

"Ah, that's it, then. If he denies it, there's nothing to it."

"Nothing to it?" Gran shot back. "I don't think so. Caretaker's wife told me that even though Sparks denies it, Iron Bolt says he saw it with his own eyes. She said they started shouting at each other, back and forth, then Sparks accused Iron Bolt of being out to get him, something to do with their personal plots of land. Iron Bolt swore on his father's life that he saw it, and Sparks swore on his own father's life that he didn't. Iron Bolt shouted back that Sparks' father was already dead so he couldn't be believed, and Sparks retorted that Iron Bolt couldn't be believed either because his father had been bedridden for years and essentially already dead..."

Inkcap chuckled to himself. "And what else did she tell you? What else happened?"

"She told me... she told me they came to blows. A real fight. Other Red Blades had shown up, she said, there was pushing and shoving–"

"A real fight?" Inkcap asked, his eyes betraying his excitement.

"Is that what you were hoping for?"

"No, no, I never said that... Anything else?"

"I don't know, I was too afraid to ask any more. I just rushed back inside and hid our copy of the Little Red Book. I've not heard anything. Perhaps there's nothing happening, then."

Inkcap laid back down on the *kang* and smacked his feet together like he was clapping. "All thanks to me."

"What do you mean?"

"Oh, I just mean this is all very lucky for me, I get to sleep early... ah Gran, don't bother to hide the book under the covers again, best to make sure no one sees it at all, right?"

"Eh? What are you suggesting?"

"Burn it, that's the only way to be sure."

Inkcap leapt up from the bed. He was going to light the stove to turn

Mao's book into ash. Gran went to double-check the doors, to make sure they were all shut. She knew the courtyard had been closed tight already. The fire lit, they pulled apart the Little Red Book, page by page, sending each one into the flames. It didn't take long for there to be nothing but ash left. They looked at their work, realising the ash was perhaps incriminating. This, too, had to be disposed of. Grabbing a broom and dustpan, the remnants of Mao's quotations were swept up and deposited in the small crevice underneath the bed. But before they were finished, a knock came at the courtyard gate.

Quickly tidying everything away, including the broom and dustpan, Gran called out, "Who's there?"

A cough was the only reply.

"I asked who's there. Is that you, Sparks?"

Only a cough.

"I guess nothing's wrong, then... Hold on, hold on, I'll open the door."

Only silence.

A pumpkin was pushed under the gap between the ground and the door. It was flat, but very round, almost like a seating mat. But the top of it was covered with a thin film of grey ash. Granny Silkworm thought this very odd, but she knelt and picked up the pumpkin, nonetheless. When she opened the gate, there was no one to be seen.

"Who is it, Gran?" Inkcap called out.

"It sounded like Sparks," Gran replied as she walked back inside, "but when I opened the door, there was no one there. Only this piece of pumpkin."

"Sparks?"

"I'm sure it was him."

"Oh..."

"But why this pumpkin? Surely he doesn't mean for us to eat it, does he?"

Suddenly pleased with himself, Inkcap said, "Eat it, Gran, let's eat it together."

Inkcap took the pumpkin from Gran's hands and walked into the kitchen. He placed it on the counter and sliced it into smaller pieces, depositing them in a bowl.

FIFTY-NINE

EVERYONE IN OLD KILN expected the situation Sparks found himself in would eventually explode, so they were surprised when that didn't happen. Perhaps it was the weather, the threat of rain, even if it never really materialised. It was true that the firewood had got wet, so perhaps the fear that any attempt to light a fire would only produce thick smoke prevented the conflagration? Who could say? While many villagers were confused, the Hammerheads understood perfectly well. So too the Red Blades. In their minds, smoke, after all, was only possible when there was fire.

But then it rained again, more than the first time. When it stopped, the fields seemed to come alive, and the village crops bloomed. The timing couldn't be better. For the next ten days, everyone was busy, ravenous like wolves, with barely any time to rest, or even to pee. When the autumn harvest was finished, more than a hundred *mu* of land had yielded sufficient grain for the winter. True, the plots belonging to individual villagers had already been cleared before they had been ready, but that was in the past and nothing could be done about them now.

The harvest was divvied up among the villagers, each household responsible for threshing, drying and then milling the grain. The grain not milled straight away was put in earthen jars and stored in cupboards. Some families milled fresh rice to exchange for maize with other villages in the mountains to the south, others did not. But no matter, the village was full of hustle and bustle. And in the evenings, the remaining bits of stubble in the fields yet to be turned over were pulled up, presumably to be dried for kindling.

It was a custom in Old Kiln for no one to return home empty-handed, even if that meant carrying loads of earth for the pigsties, cowsheds and whatever, but for Inkcap and his gran, their hands were usually holding broken branches, bits of bark, anything that could be used to light the kitchen fires. After all, they didn't have the money to buy coal from Xichuan, nor the energy to cut their own firewood in the mountains. So for them, the stubble in the fields was a prime resource, relatively easy to access and plentiful enough to provide them with something to burn as the cold of winter crept ever closer.

By the fifteenth of the month, the moon was round and high in the sky. From then, it would start to wane, ultimately disappearing to leave only the darkness of the night, save for the few stars that flickered weakly. These were the nights when both Inkcap and Gran worked, digging up the leftovers in the fields to fill a basket each. The earth was dark, the rocks and stones too. Neither one could see the other clearly, only vague silhouettes.

"Watch your step, boy," Gran said. "You don't want to turn your ankle or something worse."

"Ah, Gran, don't worry, I can see well enough in front of me. Besides, it's a bit brighter over this way."

In the dark, Gran could see the shape of Inkcap moving towards the brighter area and she called out, "Don't go into the light."

"Why not?"

"That's where lotus roots grow, but they didn't grow well this year, too many weeds, the land's waterlogged. All you'll find is some sickly leaves, nothing more."

Considering the darkness of the night and the muddiness of the lotus pond, Inkcap never expected the water to glow in the night as it did. Still, he was unsatisfied with Gran's explanation.

"So, it's a pool of water, then?"

"Yes, it is."

"Shouldn't the water be dark at night too?"

"The darker it gets, the brighter it is."

Something he had once heard came to mind. "A lotus pond is much like the eyes of man, it too sparkles in the night."

"Oh, my boy!"

Only Inkcap and Gran worked the fields at night. The days, however, were a different story. Many of the villagers, the women at least, would be out doing the same as they'd done the evening before. Some were Hammerheads, some were Red Blades. In the past, the men in Old Kiln rarely spoke to each other, preoccupied, as they were, with making revolution and following their chosen faction. The women of the village, however, still greeted each other and talked about their families, about grievances. True, some would frown and pull long faces, but the animosity the men showed towards each other never really infected the women, and any disagreements aired would soon be forgotten.

But now was different. There was an awkwardness among the women, each unsure of what to say, and as a result, they said very little or nothing at all. They all just concentrated on their work, huffing and puffing. Even when someone let loose an unexpected fart, a cause for laughter in the past, no one even smiled.

As for Inkcap, he also went out into the fields during the day to dig at the bits of leftover grain alongside the women. Looking at the pile he'd made next to him, Inkcap realised it was more than enough to fill his basket, so he decided to make his way back home. Unfortunately, the basket was too heavy for him to carry, and his only option was to get help, in this case, from Decheng's wife, who happened to be closest to him.

"Say," Inkcap said, "where's Decheng? How come he's not here?"

The woman did not answer, so Inkcap continued, "You're not talking?"

"I'm trying not to," she replied. "I'm actually afraid to say anything. If my tongue slips, I'll end up being reported, and then I'll be in hot water too."

Inkcap's heart pounded. Did she know that he'd reported Sparks to Awning? Inkcap couldn't stop his face turning red.

Changing topic, seemingly oblivious to his worry, Decheng's wife spoke again: "Hey, let me see that nose of yours."

"Eh? Why? It's too ugly, deformed. It's not a pretty sight."

"Ugly it might be, but I heard you could smell a... a particular smell, and that when you did, nine times out of ten, something bad happened. Is that true?"

"Who told you that?"

"Cowbell."

"That dirty bastard, he's bullshitting you. Believe me."

"Can you smell something?"

Inkcap did not answer, he only made to leave, disinclined to say anything else.

"Oh come on, Inkcap, you know as well as I do that people with a disability often have other senses that compensate, like the blind hearing things others can't. Come on, do this for me, will you? Should you smell that smell again, tell me first, yes, before you tell anyone else, that you'll look out for your sister and brother Decheng, yeah?"

"What are you talking about? I don't know anything, nothing's going on."

Inkcap stomped away, thinking as he did that she was talking utter nonsense. Behind him, he could hear her complain under her breath, something about being right about not speaking to anyone.

Arriving in the alleyways of the village a few moments later, Inkcap stopped. He hated his nose, but, at the same time, the words of Decheng's wife remained in his mind: someone had said his nose was useful! He raised his hand and wiped it. Perhaps it was uncontrollable? Perhaps he shouldn't even try? He blew his nose, hard. He wanted to clean it out. Next, he stuck out his tongue to lick the tip of it. Then he walked further into the village and up to the toon tree. There, he smeared some of his snot onto the trunk. "Here's something fragrant for you to smell!"

Stargazer happened to be walking by, carrying a basket of fresh soil over his shoulder. He saw Inkcap rubbing something over the tree and yelled out, "Eh now!"

Inkcap turned quickly and saw Stargazer, but Stargazer said nothing further, he only shifted the pole to the opposite shoulder. Inkcap could see he had a padded piece of leather tied around his shoulder. It was made of water deer hide, Inkcap had seen it before. It was Stargazer's most prized possession, something he flaunted whenever possible. He was the only person in Old Kiln to own one, and he was always sure to make it very noticeable when he shifted it from one shoulder to the other. He used it whenever he was in the mountains cutting firewood, or when he was bringing grain back and forth between villages. Even when he went to collect water or empty his piss pot in the morning, he used it. Inkcap watched him. His movements were practised, almost graceful. He shifted the pole from one shoulder to the other.

Some distance down the alleyway was a privy and growing beside it was a berry tree, not far from Tag-Along's house. At that moment, Tag-Along himself was out picking berries and couldn't help but notice Stargazer. Stargazer, too, noticed him but pretended not to, focusing instead on the pigeons perched in the eaves above, a white pigeon and a dark one.

"Stargazer, hey, Stargazer," said Tag-Along

No reply.

"Stargazer, I've something to tell you."

"Sorry, what, are you trying to talk to me?" Stargazer said, feigning a lack of interest.

"I'm not like you," Tag-Along began. "I'm not afraid of being ignored, but tell me, have I ever done anything to harm you, have I ever bothered you with useful gossip?"

"Then what is it? What do you want to tell me?"

"When I saw you earlier in the field, I wanted to tell you, but I reckoned you'd ignore me–"

"I'm listening now. We're both poor peasants, right, we're both loyal to Chairman Mao, we've got to be able to talk to each other, yeah? But, say, if you were Half-Stick, I wouldn't speak to you, nor if you were Inkcap..."

Inkcap overheard their conversation and felt his face turn red. This did not stop him from speaking, though. "OK, sure, I'm a good-for-nothing shit-stirrer, but I'm neither a Hammerhead nor a Red Blade."

Stargazer looked at him. "Quite the set of balls on you, eh? Not on either side, but likely trying to curry favour with both. You watch yourself, you little shit, they might both be nice to you now, but that can change pretty quickly."

Stung by the words and the truth behind them, Inkcap's demeanour wilted a little. Stargazer paid him no more mind, and he turned to Tag-Along and said, "So what do you want to tell me?"

"After I tell you, don't go getting all worked up, OK?"

"Worked up? All right, I won't."

"OK, so when I was walking a little while ago, I happened to pass by your place. I saw your wife, she was holding two little piglets and heading in the direction of Thimble's father's place. She told me the piglets were sick, unable to stand and shitting everywhere…"

Stargazer listened without saying a word, but his shoulders noticeably slumped. A moment later, the earth he'd been carrying slipped from his shoulders and crashed onto the ground. Still, he remained silent. Another second later, he was off running towards the east of Old Kiln.

"Hey!" Tag-Along said. "I told you not to get worked up. Hey!"

In one great breath, Stargazer raced to Thimble's home. There, his eyes fell upon Thimble's pigsty. Almost-There was present, alongside Thimble's father. Almost-There had brought his sow to breed, but things were not going to plan. The sow was unsteady on its feet, teetering back and forth as boars tried unsuccessfully to mount it. Thimble's father was busy cursing the animals, a look of exasperation clear on his face. Finally, bearing it no longer, he climbed over the fence, took hold of the pig's cock in his hand and plunged it inside the sow. Almost-There asked if the other man thought this would work, and Thimble's father answered how could it not?

Thimble's father was a strange man. He had a particular manner that put many people off. But he was good with pigs, breeding them, tending to illnesses. For whatever reason, he seemed to truly understand the animals. Almost-There didn't say much else, he only pulled out four *jin* of maize he'd brought with him, as well as a couple of yuan, and placed them on a nearby countertop.

"I've put the payment here, all right? If it doesn't take, I'll be back to collect my refund."

"OK, deal," barked Thimble's father, and he grabbed some dried leaves from the ground to clean his hands.

Seeing his opportunity, Stargazer stepped closer. "Has my wife come round with two piglets in her arms?" he asked.

"Are you asking about live or dead pigs?"

"What? Don't talk rubbish, are you telling me you hope they're dead?"

"You know I'm not a Hammerhead, don't you? Why would I want to see your pigs dead? You've not been home, have you?"

"Not yet."

"Then get yourself back. Your wife was here, she brought the sickly pigs, they're spewing up everywhere, can't fathom what it is. So I just told her to go home, cook up some mung beans and make a soup."

"How can you give her a remedy if you don't know what's making them sick?"

Stargazer ran off without hanging around for an answer.

Turning to Almost-There, Thimble's father wondered aloud, "So the one who eats shit also has to take care of the one who shits! Dammit, aren't those young rebellious fuckers really something!"

"I'd be careful with your words. I'm one of those young fuckers, after all."

"Ha, suppose I should ask who isn't, then, eh?"

By the time Stargazer returned home, the two piglets had already died. More worrisome was the fact that his remaining pigs were also shitting uncontrollably. His wife had cooked the mung bean soup and was trying to feed the animals, weeping as she did. Alas, they would not eat. When she saw Stargazer come into the pen, she looked at him plaintively but continued her work, clutching hold of one of the pigs and forcing its mouth apart. It was hard to say how much soup went down their gullets, as their faces and her clothes were covered in sticky green broth.

"Just what the fuck are you doing, woman?" said Stargazer.

He marched over and wrenched the pig out of her hands. Holding the animal tightly, it was his turn to force the pig to eat the soup, massaging its neck to coax it into swallowing. The pig's throat, however, grew hard, he could feel it stiffening under his fingers. Soon its whole body was stiff. Dead. Another pig dead. Before the morning sun rose, Stargazer's entire litter of pigs was gone, and Stargazer sat in the filth of the pigsty crying. The villagers remarked that he hadn't cried like this even when his poor mother passed away.

Worse for Old Kiln was that whatever killed Stargazer's pigs soon spread through the entire village. Within a few days, nearly every pig was dead. A few days later, word reached them from Xiahewan that the same had transpired there too. Thimble's dad suspected it was some kind of swine fever, likely to have started in Xiahewan before tracking into Old Kiln. Questions were soon asked about whether anyone from Old Kiln had purchased slaughtered pigs from Xiahewan. No household admitted doing so, so Thimble's father suspected that someone from Xiahewan had brought the illness into Old Kiln themselves, that they'd eaten infected meat and then shat while they were in the village.

Thimble's father's words set many in the village on edge, some were even terrified. Soon, stories began to spread that the infected pig meat had likely been sold in Luozhen as well, and in other places too. Pork was avoided, no one dared even consider eating it. For the few remaining pigs yet to be claimed by the fever, the villagers did their best to feed them mung bean soup. But even those animals could not hang on. A few days later, the entire pig population of Old Kiln was dead.

It was on the third day of this pig plague that Inkcap's lone pig started acting abnormally. It began to hoist its front feet up against the pen walls, grunting and moving its head back and forth. Later, when he went to feed it, the pig clambered down from its unusual pose and raced towards the trough, ramming its front feet into it instead. Needless to say, the erratic behaviour both worried and frightened Inkcap, and he admonished it accordingly. Once more the pig seemed to comply and pulled its feet from the trough, but when it turned to walk away, its gait seemed eerily similar to that of a cat. Then it stopped moving altogether, shifting its eyes to stare at Inkcap. At that moment, Inkcap realised that his pig, too, was sick. He could see it in the animal's eyes. Immediately, he led the pig out of the pigsty and into the house. Granny Silkworm did as everyone else was doing, she made mung bean soup. Together, they tried to force-feed the animal, Gran using chopsticks to pry the creature's mouth open.

"Gran, do you think this will work?"

"Perhaps not, so why don't you go out and clip some cypress twigs? We can use them to scorch the animal and hopefully burn the illness out."

Inkcap followed Gran's advice but bumped into Cowbell just as he opened the front door.

"You mustn't go in," said Inkcap. "Can't have you bringing any illness in with you."

"Yeah, but in case you haven't noticed, I'm no pig. What illness do I have?"

Nevertheless, Cowbell didn't go in. Instead, he accompanied Inkcap into the mountains to collect some cypress branches. Before leaving the village, however, they ran into Noodle Fish and Barndoor, the two men chatting about something or other. As they got closer, they could hear what it was.

"So," Barndoor was asking, "have you eaten any?"

"I have," said Noodle Fish.

"And the pork wasn't infected?"

"How the hell do I know? All I can say is that before it was slaughtered, it could barely lift its head and hadn't eaten anything for at least a day."

"Damn, what is this sickness going around?"

"So your pig's been sick too?" Inkcap said, interrupting the two men.

Barndoor waved his hands at the boys, urging them away. His eyes seemed somewhat glassy, Inkcap thought, staring off into the distance. Following the man's line of sight, Inkcap noticed Goodman walk into the alley.

Noodle Fish, upon seeing Goodman, waved him over. "Goodman, so glad to see you. Could you come and take a look at my pig, tell me what's wrong with it?"

"I deal with people," Goodman replied. "I'm afraid I can offer no advice on pigs."

"Ah, Noodle Fish," said Barndoor, "I think you've lost it. How the hell is a pig supposed to understand even if Goodman spoke to it?"

"Pigs can understand humans," said Inkcap.

"Ah, for heaven's sake, will you bugger off and stop trying to rile people up," said Barndoor, again waving Inkcap and Cowbell away.

"I'm not trying to rile anyone up. All I said was that pigs do understand."

"Goodman," Noodle Fish continued, "what do you think's been going on these past few days? All the fighting and arguments, this pig plague, is it connected? Is their sickness trying to tell us something?"

"Since you ask, I'll tell you one thing. Do you know the word 'morals'?"

"I know, I know," Noodle Fish answered. "I mean, I know the word, but I don't think I could explain it."

"Well, it's not easy, I'll grant you that," said Goodman. "Let me put it this way, morals are essentially life, and no life, well, that means death, right? That's the reason we need morals, understand? OK, OK, I'll add this, life is based on heavenly principles, the heart too. When the traditional order of priority among people is unfixed, then heavenly principles are lost and evil pervades everything, do you follow me? This is how things are, this is the Way, but if the world is in chaos, how can there be order, principles, morals? Why is it that I can give advice on people's illnesses and then they get better? Because in Heaven, no disorder exists, but if there are no morals, if we have lost the Way, then sickness becomes rampant, along with crime, disorder and chaos, the world is torn apart. This is why I read the classics, I'm trying to rediscover the order of things. Will my words effect change, no one has told me, but no one has told me they won't, either. So I can say that one calamity begets another, eating infected pork begets further evil, it is a breaking of heavenly principles, and that…"

Inkcap was lost. Goodman's words had gone beyond what he could comprehend.

"Sorry," Inkcap said eventually, "but… but Noodle Fish asked you about his sick pig, what are you going on about?"

"You said pigs understand humans, yes? Then aren't I talking about the same thing, humans and pigs and the lack of order?"

In truth, Noodle Fish and Barndoor had also grown tired of Goodman's pontificating and were only too happy for Inkcap's interruption. If nothing else, it gave them a chance to get a word in.

"Goodman," said Noodle Fish, "thanks, yes, I asked you, but… but you've never raised pigs, have you? I reckon you're out of your depth here – not your fault – but I don't see the point of what you were talking about–"

"Take a look at you," Goodman responded. "This kind of man… ah, what's the point, I won't say anything further. Besides, Awning's called for me, I must go."

"So you're a Red Blade now?" Noodle Fish asked.

"Do you think anyone would accept me even if I did wish to join? Come now, I haven't mentioned the reason why Awning called for me. Best not to jump to conclusions, eh?"

"Perhaps he wants to ask if you want to join?" Noodle Fish persisted.

Quiet all the while, Barndoor now stiffened his posture and walked off, offering no explanation.

"Hey, Barndoor," Noodle Fish called, "where the devil are you going?"

"You two are talking revolution," Barndoor shot back. "Best if I go."

With Barndoor gone, Inkcap pulled at Cowbell, thinking it best they both leave to avoid any suspicion falling on them. Noodle Fish and Goodman didn't seem to notice their retreat, and before long, they were on the path that led to the spring. It was there they were startled by a loud guffaw. When they looked in the direction of the laugh, they spotted Baldy Jin in the middle of his pigsty, a pig held tightly in his arms and Baldy Jin shouting, "Long life, long life, long life!"

When he noticed Inkcap and Cowbell looking at him, he said to Inkcap directly, "What do you think, boy, do you think the pig'll live? All the other pigs in Old Kiln might be dead or dying, but look how mine's flourishing!"

"Then a hearty congratulations," Inkcap answered.

"How's your family pig?"

"It's all right, I think, but it's got a festering scar on its head." Inkcap didn't like Baldy Jin's question and chose his words as a slight towards him, but Baldy Jin seemed not to notice.

Excitedly, Baldy Jin continued, "Count it up, will you, how many pigs belonging to the Hammerheads died? How many of the Red Blades? For sure, the Red Blades have lost more. To my mind, they should lose all their pigs."

"Are you trying to curse them?" said Cowbell.

"And what if I am? What are you going to do, report me, you turncoat?"

"Who's a turncoat?" Cowbell shot back.

"Inkcap, do you think you've no good prospects? This lad here's hurt you before, why the hell are you still hanging around with him?"

Baldy Jin bit his lip, trying to control his growing rage. He climbed out of the pigsty and shouted more forcefully, "Why, huh?"

Cowbell was suitably cowed by Baldy Jin's intimidating yell and stepped back. From just behind his friend, he pulled at the sleeve of Inkcap's jacket, urging him to leave in the direction of the nearby graves. Inkcap offered Baldy Jin no answer, instead letting himself be dragged away.

It wasn't long before Inkcap was busy cutting cypress branches and Cowbell was collecting stones, digging small holes and depositing the stones inside before burying them. Walking back into the village after cutting as much of the cypress as he could hold, Inkcap placed the bundle down near one of the privies for Cowbell to watch over. Inkcap had to pee. Before he could enter, however, they heard a cough from inside and Inkcap decided not to go in. Rather, together with Cowbell, he walked to the rear of the structure, choosing to piss there instead. Pulling his cock out, Inkcap stopped before he could relieve himself, surprised at the long, arching stream of piss that shot overhead from the other side of the wall, glistening in the sunlight.

Cowbell stuck out his tongue to taste it. "Salty," he said.

Inkcap now released his own piss, making sure to get a little on his hands to taste. "Salty too," he said.

At just that moment, Millstone stepped out of his front door and saw the two boys.

"Just what the hell are you two little shits doing? Tasting piss? What have you got to compare it with, you damn fools?"

He walked over towards them, pulled out his own cock and peed.

"Now tell me, what the fuck are you two doing?" Millstone stared at the two boys.

"I was helping Inkcap cut cypress branches," said Cowbell.

"Since you're not busy, I want you to go and mix some paste. It's time to change the big-character posters." Millstone was not giving them a choice.

"What's the poster about this time?" asked Cowbell.

"Awning's coming from Luozhen with news. Chairman Mao has also issued new directives."

"More new directives, does the Chairman never stop?"

"And what do you mean by that? Long live Chairman Mao!"

"Eh... yes, long live Chairman Mao!" Cowbell paused for a moment, then something occurred to him. "Hey, Millstone, do you know, we saw Baldy Jin just now. He was in his pigsty cuddling his pig, and he was shouting the same thing as you did just now."

"He was shouting what?" Millstone asked. "These words are only for Chairman Mao, but he was using them for... his pig?"

"Yup."

"You've done well, Cowbell, well indeed. This is very important information you've told me." Realising his trousers were still undone, he fastened them and marched off.

Out of earshot, Inkcap grumbled to Cowbell, "Why did you tell Millstone that about Baldy Jin?"

"Why shouldn't I? You heard what he said about me, the fucker. I say he's a counterrevolutionary for shitting on me."

Inkcap picked up his bundle of cypress branches and walked home, glaring at Cowbell not to follow him.

SIXTY

ONCE THE CYPRESS BRANCHES WERE LIT, Inkcap and Gran called to the pig to leap over the fire, but the animal refused, instead only retreating from the flames. Inkcap remembered that when Useless had his rash, he took to jumping, shouting that this was what a sick person should do, so Inkcap reckoned he had to try. He moved round the fire and towards the pig, knelt beside it and began to gently massage its belly. Unfortunately, the pig became too comfortable and simply squatted down, content to let Inkcap continue with the massage. Then it rolled over and stuck its small feet in the air, utterly satisfied.

"Eh now, you know what time it is," Inkcap said to the animal. "How can you be so greedy for such treatment? Come on, jump, you have to jump over the fire. It's the only way you'll live. I promise I'll rub your belly if you do."

The pig slowly rolled back over and climbed to its feet, trembling the whole while. It stared a moment at the flames, shifted its legs and then bounded across the fire. On the far side, it turned, looked at the fire once more, and leapt back over it. The flames scorched the fuzz around its ears, as well as its skin, but the pig did not yelp. It moved towards Inkcap, plopping itself down at his feet. Inkcap could not go back on his word, so he knelt down and started to massage its belly once more. The chickens nearby clucked as though jealous.

Finished, Gran put out the fire. The bits of cypress not fully burned were picked up and placed just outside their courtyard wall. This was in offering to the Five Commissioners of Pestilence, the Wen Shen deities that many still believed haunted the land, especially during times such as these. After its belly rub, Inkcap led the animal into the shed to help it settle down, then he and Gran went inside to prepare food. The bellows roared as they stoked the kitchen fires, so loud that they couldn't hear a knocking at their courtyard gate. Not until the visitor started kicking it, at least. And then Gran only heard it because she'd stepped outside to water the roots of the peach tree. Opening the gate a minute later, she saw that Awning had called on them.

"Oh dear, I'm sorry, truly, the bellows were so loud we didn't hear," she said, grabbing a stool and inviting Awning to sit.

Awning's face eased as he sat and surveyed their courtyard. "You keep a clean house, I must say. I don't even see any splinters of firewood on the ground."

"Clean you say, I'm not so sure, but I don't think you've been here since you came of age. Can I offer you some water?"

Lifting the proffered cup of water to his lips, Awning continued, "I imagine you must be busy, yes? Tell me, where's Inkcap? There's something I need to tell him."

"You've something to tell him? I... I think you ought to tell me. Whatever you say to him goes in one ear and out the other."

"But what I have to tell him you're not aware of. Just call him out here."

Inkcap had heard the exchange from the kitchen and wondered why Awning had come specifically to speak to him. His mind raced with possibilities, most of them bad. Then he heard his gran call to him from the main room and he trudged out of the kitchen. Before a word was said, Awning grabbed him by the arm and pulled him closer. Gran stood nearby.

Turning to his gran, Awning said, "Surely you've things to do."

But she refused to budge.

Awning directed his gaze at Inkcap and said, "Tell me what you saw Baldy Jin do. Did he really hold onto his pig and praise it for long life?"

Inkcap hesitated, unsure how to respond, but he spoke nonetheless: "Why... why are you asking me this?"

"Cowbell told us, he said you were there too, you both saw Baldy Jin. Are you saying that's not true? Be honest."

Granny Silkworm answered nervously for her grandson: "Awning, this has nothing to do with Inkcap. Please."

"Nothing to do with Inkcap? How do you mean? I only asked him to confirm the story we got from Cowbell. He was there, after all."

"That's true, I was with Cowbell and we did walk by Baldy Jin's home. I did see him cuddling his pig too."

"What was he saying to it?"

"Please," said Gran, "as if Baldy Jin would say such a thing to his pig!"

"Such words are counterrevolutionary, that's what they are." Awning looked back at Inkcap. "Did he say those words?"

"Um, ah…"

"This is a big deal, boy, you have to answer. Protecting a counterrevolutionary is as bad as being one."

Gran's legs trembled, but she managed to remain standing, finally moving to put her hands around her grandson's shoulders.

"Awning, you can't threaten a young boy like this, you're scaring him." Then, turning to Inkcap, she said, "Did you hear those words? If you did, you have to tell him, and if you didn't, then say so."

"He… he said everyone else's pig in Old Kiln had died, that only his pig was well, and then… yes, he wished it to live forever… he used those words."

"Confirmed. His words are an attack on Chairman Mao. Confirmed now by two witnesses." There was a sense of triumph in Awning's voice.

At that moment, Millstone and Sparks strode into Inkcap's courtyard. Awning saw them from inside and marched out to greet them, saying, "What Cowbell told us is true, I've had it confirmed. This is all the impetus we need. He's attacked Chairman Mao, we've a new poster to write. Whosoever attacks the Great Helmsman must be brought down, we've got to act immediately. I'll get word to Wu Gan, get him to come to Old Kiln tomorrow to seize the traitor Baldy Jin."

Both Millstone and Sparks were barely able to contain their excitement. They spun on their heels, shouting back to Granny Silkworm as they left, "Tell us, what are you making for dinner?"

"Congee," she answered.

"Congee?" Sparks replied. "You ought to have some noodles with it at least."

She did not say anything further, and even if she did, they wouldn't have heard, so quick were they to promulgate this new counterrevolutionary transgression. Awning, however, seemed disinclined to leave. In fact, he returned to the stool she'd offered him before and pulled out some tobacco to roll into a cigarette. Gran watched him for a moment, then sat down beside him. After his first drag on the smoke, Awning stood up and Gran copied his actions, her eyes never leaving him.

"This is good, very good, Inkcap," said Awning, shifting his attention to the boy. "Tomorrow, we'll seize Baldy Jin. If he denies the crime, we'll need you to testify."

"Again?"

"Out of the question," said Gran. "Awning, you know as well as I do that our family is not like others, how can he testify in public? Surely Cowbell's word will be enough."

"No, it has to be Inkcap. No one else. Sure, his background is bad, but testifying is one way he can help to make things better, atone for the crime of his birth. This is his chance. When the time comes, you don't want to be afraid, just say what you said to me a moment ago. And think, with so many of us Red Blades, there's nothing to be frightened about, yeah?" He paused as though waiting for a response. Hearing none, he continued, "All right, it's settled."

As soon as Awning left, Gran shut the gate behind him and pulled Inkcap back inside. Closing that door behind them too, she hit Inkcap on the head.

"How many times have I told you, are you deaf or just stupid? Why didn't you just say you didn't hear what Baldy Jin said? If you had, everything would be over. Are you looking for trouble?" She grumbled under her breath, before continuing, "And what do you think's going to happen? They're not going to kill him, he won't even go to prison, all he'll have to do is enter re-education. That's it."

"But I heard him say it," Inkcap offered in his defence.

Gran slapped him again. "Oh, so you're hearing's fine all of a sudden, is it? Strange that when I ask you to do the chores, you play dumb, but you could hear what Baldy Jin said, hmm?"

"But... Baldy Jin isn't even a good person. He'll get what he deserves."

"You know you're the bottom of the bottom, the lowest of the low, you can be kicked, beaten, yelled at, cursed. What do you think will happen once he's released? He'll be back in Old Kiln with a vicious hatred for you. His Hammerheads will share that hatred. Do you think they'll leave you alone?"

The more she spoke, the more she frightened herself. Inkcap, too, could feel the fear growing. He looked at Gran, his voice no louder than the buzz of a mosquito: "Then, tomorrow... if they make me testify... what should I say?"

Gran had no reply. All she could do was cry, silently. Inkcap noticed her face become wet with tears. They ran down the long lines that covered her face, caught in them like a river held within its banks, tracking towards her mouth like water emptying into a bay, overflowing to then drip off her chin. Inkcap put his arms around her and pulled himself close. Then he used his hand to wipe away some of her tears. She, in turn, wrapped her arms around him, both holding each other as tightly as possible. Up in the rafters, the swallow chittered and chirped, but neither Inkcap nor Gran seemed to hear.

Gran stifled a sob, coughed and swallowed hard. "What's this smoke? Damn!"

She raced into the kitchen to find the room ablaze. The firewood in the stove was nearly exhausted, but they'd not covered it. The sparks from the fire must have bounced and flickered, before landing and setting light to the stockpile of kindling. Thick smoke hung in the kitchen, but Gran braved it and began stamping at the fire on the floor, yelling to Inkcap at the same time, "Water! Get some water! Quickly!"

Inkcap returned an instant later and sploshed a container full of water over the fire. It sizzled and steamed and then died.

Looking at the mess, the ashes, the water over the floor, Gran said to Inkcap, "You know the cause of this, it's all connected."

Later in the evening, after Inkcap finished a bowl of rice, Gran encouraged him to eat another. "Have some more, eat till you're full. We'll talk about tomorrow in the morning. Now, eat and go to bed."

Inkcap did as he was told without argument. After finishing dinner, he climbed into bed while Gran did his chores, cleaning the dishes, locking the chicken coop, feeding their still sickly pig its mung bean soup. Finally, she came to lie down next to him. But she didn't sleep. Instead, she got out her scissors and paper, then began producing various shapes: a tiger, some flowers, a snake, a centipede, a toad, a scorpion, a gecko. She laid all these shapes beside Inkcap's pillow before blowing out the single candle she'd lit and tried to sleep.

It was usually quiet at this hour, but on this evening, the alleyway was abuzz with people racing back and forth. Dogs could be heard, too, evidently nipping at the heels of those who were running. Not long after Gran went to bed, Inkcap woke up. Pulling his hand from under the covers, he marvelled at how dark the night was as he couldn't see anything. To the night, he spoke, wondering if it had spread an especially dark cloak over the sky and if it could soon depart. Then he thought to himself, once the night was over, day would be upon him. Tomorrow, and all that that word now meant. So he spoke once more to the night, asking it never to leave, to keep things dark, to let him stay in bed forever, to prevent the morning from coming.

Settling back down, Gran asked, "Why aren't you asleep?"

"I... have to pee," Inkcap answered quickly, quietly.

"Then get up and go. Follow the walls with your hand, you'll find the pot. Just make sure you don't make a mess."

"All right... Gran, I'm not going to go tomorrow."

"You've no choice, my boy."

"But I'm sick, I can't go."

"Just saying you're sick doesn't mean you are."

"Yes, it does. I can make myself sick."

"If that was the case, then you wouldn't have got into this mess in the first place. Now, go and pee."

Inkcap crawled out of bed and stumbled in the dark. A faint sound of water hitting an object could be heard, followed by gentle splashing.

"Are you peeing on the wall?" Gran called out from the bed.

Inkcap didn't answer. But the splashing sound could still be heard.

"Sounds like rain falling from the eaves. Don't tell me you're still peeing."

Inkcap wondered to himself how he could still be peeing, he'd been standing for what seemed like ages, he'd heard Gran call out, but still he stood. Finally, he answered, "I'm finished."

"Then why do I still hear that sound?" Gran replied.

"I think it's someone outside. They might be at our door."

Gran sat up and trained her mostly deaf ears on outside. Someone was

667

indeed there, and the splashing wasn't splashing at all, but rather a soft knock. "Who would be calling at this hour?" she whispered. "Can't be Awning, can it? Climb back to bed, my boy, quickly."

Inkcap didn't hesitate, his whole body was trembling.

"Sleep, you go to sleep, I'll see who it is," Gran consoled him. "And don't you mind what I say to Awning if it turns out to be him. All you need do is sleep like a rock, OK, don't get up for anything. That's what I'll tell them."

A few minutes later, after opening the door, Gran would never have guessed that it was Bash who was knocking.

Walking through the open gate, Bash offered his apologies for the hour. He was polite, profusely so. After saying something about the whole village being awake, he spoke in more uneasy tones: "But you're not one of the poorer peasants, are you, so why are you in bed so early?"

"Is there a night brigade now too?" she shot back. "You've got to check up on all of us to make sure we're sleeping the proper amount, is that it?"

"No, no, no night brigade," Bash answered.

Gran turned and walked inside, lighting their small lamp to see Bash's face. She invited him to sit, then grabbed a comb and tried to straighten her hair, finally pinning it back and sitting down herself. "Does someone need my help," she asked. "Is she…"

Her meaning was plain: was there a birth emergency? Was someone having trouble? Was she needed for… *her*?

Catching her meaning, Bash answered, "No, no, no, nothing of that sort. I'm here to speak to Inkcap."

In her heart, Gran understood this already. If Bash had shown up, it must have something to do with revolutionary activities. Counterrevolutionary nonsense. She'd asked about *her* to deflect his attention. Unsuccessful, she felt her heart in her throat.

"Eh now, why are *you* here for him?"

"Why? Has anyone else come for him?"

"Just before nightfall, Awning was here."

"I might have known." Bash stood up and marched towards their bedroom. Gran, her fear rising, grabbed the lamp and hurried after him, the flickering light bouncing off the walls and playing tricks with Bash's shadow, now big, now small.

"Bash, Bash!" she called after him to no avail.

Tearing the covers off Inkcap, he saw the boy squished up on the bed in the fetal position, snoring.

"Get up, Inkcap," he shouted. "Get up!" He slapped Inkcap's arse, forcing the boy awake, or at least to stop him pretending to be asleep.

"Oh, ow, Brother Bash!"

"You were in Three Fork Alley this afternoon taking a piss, yeah?"

"I was there, erm, but I didn't go inside, I peed out behind the building."

"That's right, but you weren't alone, were you? Cowbell and Millstone were there too, right?"

"Ah… yeah, that's right. Cowbell and I were having a… a pissing contest… to see who could pee the farthest."

"Did Cowbell and Millstone talk about Chairman Mao? Did they say anything about long life?"

"They did."

"Right, right, so they had their cocks in their hands and were talking about the Great Helmsman–"

"Ah, ah..." Inkcap lost his voice, his brain nothing more than a bee buzzing around in his skull. He was just peeing, nothing more. They were doing the same. Long live Chairman Mao, that's all they said. But... they were holding onto their cocks as they saluted the Great Helmsman... Inkcap's mind raced, but there was no one else there, was there? How did Bash find out? Then it occurred to him, he'd heard coughing... that's why he didn't go inside the privy itself. No doubt that person had told Bash about the exchange between Cowbell and Millstone, and he must have been a Hammerhead... but who?

Finally, Inkcap spoke: "How... how do you know about this?"

"What do you mean?" Bash looked annoyed at the assumption he shouldn't be aware of what was going on in Old Kiln. "Of course I know the Red Blades are trying to frame Baldy Jin, trying to get him in trouble. I know, too, that they came looking for you, they want you to testify, am I right?"

"Yes... yes, that's right, they want me to testify, I–"

"Testify if you want, I know you promised, so you'll have to, right? But know this, the Hammerheads will be calling on you to testify too, you'll have to tell everyone that Cowbell and Millstone were talking about Chairman Mao with their dicks in their hands."

"OK, I can confirm they were peeing and talking about Chairman at the same time, their dicks in their hands."

"When the time comes, I'll ask whether this is true or not. All you'll have to do is answer yes or no, just one word. Understand?"

Gran could no longer steady herself on her feet, so she leant against the wall, her legs like rubber, trembling. Finally, she collapsed to the floor. Inkcap noticed her shadow slipping down the wall until it disappeared altogether. He squinted to see more clearly in the darkness, then he heard her call out, "Bash, Bash, you must remember how Inkcap used to trail behind you, following you wherever you went. We used to say he was your tail. Now you're here to make him do... do this... how can you lump this on him, Bash?"

"Gran," Bash began, "listen. The Red Blades are trying to take down us Hammerheads, Useless first, now they're aiming for Baldy Jin. They're trying to rope Inkcap here into testifying. We understand he has to do it, given his station and all that. So the best option is to make him testify for us too. I want them to understand, no one messes with me, no one's got the balls to take me down."

"All right, all right, I understand you, but–"

"Right now, this evening, no one is sleeping, I told you that, and I know the Red Blades are scheming and plotting, the Hammerheads are doing the same, everybody is scheming and plotting. In the morning, we'll see who wins." He stopped and laughed out loud, then continued, "Granny Silkworm, I'm sorry for disturbing your night, keeping you up. I've nothing else to say, I'll go. If Awning calls again, tell him, tell him I was here. Goodnight."

They listened as Bash sauntered out of the house and down the alleyway, humming, it seemed, as he went. Gran followed him to the gate and closed it behind her. She returned inside. Inkcap looked at her, the wrinkles, the age of her whole face and body.

"You should get some sleep, Gran."

"And how do you think that's possible?"

Inkcap felt he was to blame for everything; her wrinkles and trembling legs, everything was his fault. He remained silent. She stood in the shadow of the lamp, appearing smaller, shorter, older than ever before. The hair she'd just combed was dishevelled again, the pin having fallen out. Inkcap thought it looked like a pile of dried, cut grass.

"Testifying is only testifying, right?" he said, trying to offer some comfort. "If I do it for both sides, that should be all right, two wrongs make a right, yeah?"

"Oh, my boy, all you're going to do is offend the whole village."

"How do you mean? Both sides have come looking for me, that makes me important."

"Oh, Inkcap, Inkcap... who do you think's going to look after you? If it weren't for him, your grandfather who ran off... ah, damn, do you think anyone would even dare come to ask you to testify? Who came to our door, eh, do you think you even have a choice?" She paused and then spoke with great vitriol: "What they say is right, you're wasted sperm, if only he'd been killed long ago, before you were even born. All you've done is brought shame and trouble down upon me and this family."

Gran took a deep breath and laid into Inkcap's grandfather some more. Inkcap said nothing, dared not say anything. Quietly, he removed his shoes and climbed back into bed. Before he could settle down, however, Gran yelled at him once more.

"Get up, you're going to Awning's. You've got to tell him Bash visited."

Inkcap did as she instructed, a look of surprise on his face as he regarded the brow of his gran, furrowed deeper than he'd ever seen. He reached for her. "Gran... are you feeling ill?"

"I just want to die, but this blasted world won't let me."

"But... after Awning called on us, I didn't go and tell Bash, but now you want me to tell Awning that Bash was here. Do you really think I should?"

"I've thought things over," Gran said, "what Bash said. Yes, he came looking for you, wants you to testify, but I also think he wants Awning to realise they're out to get Cowbell and Millstone. If you tell Awning that Bash came tonight, neither side will be able to put their plans in motion, it'll be a draw... and a draw will mean you won't need to testify."

Inkcap thought there were both pros and cons to Gran's idea, but she insisted he head to Awning's place.

The alleyway was dark, and a certain gloom hung in the air. Inkcap had the strangest of feelings that he was walking towards some burned oven interior. He had no stick, nor a lantern to guide his way. Unable to see anything, he let his feet carry him to whatever awaited. Instinctively he knew where the stones in the alleyway were, the dips and holes in the ground, like a blind man. He also had the sense that someone was following behind him, even though there was nothing but blackness when he turned his head to look. A feeling of regret rose in his heart. He should have brought something to light the way, that would at least stop whoever it was that was spying on him in the dark. Alas, he hadn't, so his only option was to stop and shout.

"You might as well come close. I know you're there."

But all he saw was a flittering firefly, its gentle glow twisting this way and that in the night. It drew closer to Inkcap, then farther away. He didn't hear anything else. There was nothing to do but continue on to Awning's place.

Awning wasn't asleep. Nor was he alone. Millstone, Sparks, Palace and Once-Upon-A-Time were there as well. So, too, were Sprout and Soupspoon. They looked at Inkcap hard as he delivered his report on Bash's recent visit. For a moment, they seemed stunned, before Sparks leapt up and began stomping his feet and cursing to high heaven. A second later, they were all cursing and shouting, oblivious to Inkcap's presence. Seizing the opportunity, Inkcap quietly left, unnoticed.

Stepping out beyond the gate, Inkcap saw the fluttering firefly, but it wasn't behind him; instead, it remained in front of him as though it were lighting his path home. Once back, he saw Gran through the open gate door, sitting on the laundry stone, waiting for him.

While she couldn't see Inkcap straight away, she did hear his steps.

"You're back, then?" She lifted herself up and moved towards the gate, somewhat surprised to find out that Inkcap was alone. "So Awning didn't accompany you home?"

"No, I came by myself."

"Then who were you speaking to just now? I swear I heard you talking?"

"Just a firefly, it lives out in the fields, but it followed me to and from Awning's place."

"A ghost! You've run into a ghost!" Gran rushed towards him, rubbing his head roughly, stamping her feet on the ground beside him and then spitting. She seemed to have forgotten Inkcap entirely, too busy with her incantations, and didn't notice when he walked inside to get some water from the kitchen. Realising he'd gone, she chased him inside.

"So what did Awning say?"

"They didn't say much of anything, least not to me. All they did was curse the Hammerheads."

Gran pulled Inkcap towards the bed, gesturing for him to settle down for the night. Speaking almost to herself, she asked, "They only cursed the Hammerheads?"

"Yup."

"They didn't say what they'll do?" Gran was beginning to collect her senses.

"Nope, they just cursed."

"And…"

Inkcap waited in expectation.

"When you were gone just now," Gran continued, "I kept thinking it over. Should things come to a head tomorrow, should they ask you to testify, whichever side, doesn't matter, you say you didn't see anything, didn't hear anything. They'll accuse you of shirking your responsibilities, but so what, it's the only way you can save yourself…"

Inkcap listened attentively to his gran, nodded his head and laid down to sleep. He didn't say a word.

As soon as sleep came, he was thrust into a dream. Who would have known that his dream would provide him the blueprint to escape from his dilemma? His plan was fantastically simple, direct, amazing. Before, he'd thought of getting an invisibility cloak, now, however, this would be wholly unnecessary.

In his dream, he was walking along a mountain road, a sickle in his hand. It seemed as though he were heading into the higher altitudes to chop firewood, or perhaps it was to harvest some mountain grass, he wasn't sure. Whatever the reason, the road up was clear, if narrow and winding, like a length of rope that had been thrown against the mountainside and left to twist whichever way it fell. One side of the road hugged the mountain, even if it had been cut into the rock. White birch and dwarf chestnut trees also clung to the mountain face. So, too, a number of pines. In between the trees were tangled vines, wolfsbane and themeda grass, yellowish in colour, waving in the wind, tall enough to brush against a person's face. And there Inkcap walked, sickle in hand. Locusts leapt around him, jumping on his head, his shoulders, everywhere, but as soon as he raised his hand to knock them away, they bounded off and back into the grass. The other side of the road was nearly sheer, falling down into a deep gully below. The rapids that filled the gully floor swished and swirled, whitecaps jostling with each other. Inkcap saw a lone figure beside the rushing water, planks of wood in his hand. He called out to him, but the violent echo of the rapids drowned out his voice, and the man did not hear. He turned a corner and was faced with bowing catalpa trees, their branches and leaves hanging low over the road, preying on those walking through the mountains by entangling their hair and yanking great clumps free, likely grabbing at their clothes too, tearing great pieces away.

Inkcap shouted in his dream, "I ought to cut you down!" and with a swing of his sickle, his blade ripped into their trunks. Inkcap swung faster and faster, wrenching large chunks of bark and wood, but the trees felt nothing. But at just the same moment in his dream, a mob of people appeared lower down the path. They were rushing towards him, fists raised and faces irate. Inkcap fled further up the mountain but could hear them shout, "Chase him down, run him down, take him down!" He didn't recognise any of the faces among the storming horde, but their words reverberated in his ears: "Kill him, kill him, kill him. Throw his body into the gully for the crows to eat. No one will ever find his corpse."

Despite feeling terrified, he wanted to know who it was that so hated him, but like the faces, he couldn't make out any of the voices. He ran and ran, lost a shoe but continued to run. He wanted to vent his anger but couldn't. His heart was pounding, thump, thump, thump, so hard that he feared it might burst out of his breast altogether. But he could hear them closing the gap, closer, closer, closer. He could hear the swoosh of air behind, knew they must be carrying clubs, knives, weapons of all kinds. His mind returned to the invisibility cloak, but he didn't have one, not even in his dream. He raced, raced, raced, further and further up the mountain. His thoughts now turned to his imminent doom. He was dead, sure of it, only a matter of time. So he stopped and prepared himself for the end. Then something wonderful happened, his body tightened, he crouched down low, hiding behind a boulder thrusting out from the mountainside. The scene was like that of an eagle taking to the sky, its mighty wings flapping up and down as it built up speed, then arched straight out to glide, making no sound whatsoever. He believed the people chasing him would not see him, he would be invisible. A moment later, they rushed by the stony protuberance, and he caught sight of them, a militia unit, each with a soup-spoon covering their face. It was impossible for him to see who they were, but he did hear them shout, "Get him, get him, get him. This way, this way, this way!" It was both a tense and triumphant experience, Inkcap terrified and thrilled at the same time. But he knew enough to stay hidden until they were out of sight. Then and only then did he climb out from behind the rock. The mountain still stood before him, so too the trees, the rocks. The trees waved and smiled at him, their teeth explosions of pink flowers. The stones, however, stared at him with devilish, mottled, moss-covered faces. One moment greenish in colour, the next red...

The chickens shrieked in the yard. "I've laid an egg! An egg!"

Inkcap was wrenched from his slumber, his blanket wet with sweat.

"Gran, what a dream I just had!"

Gran did not answer. Only the wind outside offered a reply, its gusts banging up against the walls and windows of their house, anxious, it seemed, to burst through. But it couldn't. The walls of the courtyard were too high, the walls of their house too thick.

"Gran, my dream! It was great!" Inkcap yelled.

Still no response. Only the wind, now sounding angrier. It picked up the freshly laid eggs and smashed them to the ground. It tore feathers off the chickens, scattering them like broken eggshells.

Inkcap felt Gran was deliberately ignoring him, so he yelled even louder this time, "Gran!"

A knock came at the door, but it turned out that Gran had already been out to answer it and had now returned. The only words to leave her mouth were, "Death's come knocking."

SIXTY-ONE

FOR THE ENTIRE MORNING AND INTO THE AFTERNOON, Gran would not let Inkcap take even one step outside the door. And even when she went out after lunch, she was back in a flash to tell Inkcap he had to wait. It was the same after dinner: Inkcap had to wait. Needless to say, Inkcap was restless. Like a busy ant, he skittered back and forth between rooms, but unlike an ant, he had nothing to do. Finally, Gran lost her patience with him.

"Can't you sit still? All this pacing about isn't doing any good."

"But how have they not come to get me yet?"

"Why, is that what you're hoping for? That they come and drag you away?"

"Perhaps no one is coming after all."

"That would be too good to be true."

"Then I just wish they'd hurry up."

"Are you in a rush to die, is that it?"

Gran's last words brought their conversation to an end. She did, however, fetch him some warm water to drink, even adding a little sugar. Inkcap had long thought the sugar jar was empty, that's what his Gran had told him, so he was surprised to taste the sweetness of the water.

"Gran, why have you been hiding a secret stash of sugar?"

"If I didn't, you'd have already eaten it all, don't you think? Now drink up and think hard about what I told you to say. You remember, yes?"

"Yes, Gran, I remember," and he lifted the cup to his mouth to drink. At almost the same moment, he heard someone call his name. The two of them looked at each other. They'd finally come. Inkcap finished the water in one gulp and together he and Gran went to open the door.

To their surprise, it was Apricot who had come.

"Eh, now," Gran began, "what in heaven's name are you doing here?"

"Why, who were you expecting? You don't seem happy to see me. Is it a bad time?"

"Don't be foolish, how can I not be happy you've called on us? Come in, have a seat, I'll get you some water."

Apricot's belly had already grown big and she couldn't help but move awkwardly. Gran, appreciating her condition, got Inkcap to bring her a chair to sit on. Apricot's face blushed at the attention Gran was giving her and she made to decline but bit her tongue and asked instead how the older woman was faring.

"Oh, you know, as good as can be," Gran replied. "Say, is there anything going on in the village?"

"Not that I know of, no. The only thing Bash said to me before he went out was that he'd checked on the village pigs and they were all either dead or dying."

"Where's Bash off to, then?" Gran asked.

"To Luozhen, he's gone to call on a vet, it's swine fever, after all. If he can't get a vet to come, then all the pigs will die for sure."

"I see… if he's gone to Luozhen for a vet, then he's not looking into anything else, is he?"

"What are you getting at?"

"And Awning, the rest of them… they're not doing anything either, are they?"

"No, nothing."

"Nothing? Tell me, Apricot, did you say something to them about this? About getting Inkcap to testify—"

"I think you give me more influence than I have. All I said was what's the point, one person's word against another's, nothing but a tit-for-tat attack with no resolution."

Gran sat down and closed her eyes.

After bringing the chair for Apricot to sit on, Inkcap had waited inside, at the window, watching them. When he saw his gran seemingly crumple onto the stone steps, her eyes closed, her mouth open as though she were gasping for air, Inkcap worried she was having a heart attack and rushed outside to grab hold of her, rubbing her chest as he did so.

"Gran! Gran!" he shouted.

Gran opened her eyes and let out a forced gurgling sound that seemed to well up from her core. With great effort, as though something inside her was blocking her speech, she uttered, "Our pig… bring him here… let Apricot see it."

For the whole of the previous evening and into the day, both Inkcap and Gran had forgotten they'd put the pig in the shed. But now that she had remembered, Inkcap released Gran and rushed to get the pig. As soon as he opened the door, the animal burst out, squealing with anger at being locked up for so long.

"Yeah, yeah, you're hungry," Inkcap said. "I've not eaten either, you know."

The deep wrinkles creased into the pig's forehead shaped into the character for "prince". Perhaps odder still, Inkcap's pig appeared fine, with no sign of illness whatsoever.

Apricot decided to call on their neighbours, where she learnt that their pigs were sick, so ill in fact that they couldn't even stand. Coming to Cattle Track's place a little further to the right, however, she discovered that his gate was locked, the pigsty inside. Apricot was wondering how she could check on the pigs when Inkcap suggested they climb over the courtyard walls. After all, he told her, the walls had mostly collapsed and where Cattle Track had made repairs he'd done so with wooden planks, making it easy enough to climb. Directing her to a scalable section of the wall, Inkcap clambered over and urged Apricot to follow. Apricot, however, hesitated.

"Come on, jump over, what's the matter?" Inkcap said.

Still, Apricot did not move.

Gran walked up to them and shouted after Inkcap, "Just what are you asking her to do? You know the condition she's in, you just go check on the pig and tell us whether it's dead or not. She doesn't need to go climbing any walls."

Inkcap complied and checked on the pig. It appeared in good health, certainly not showing any signs of swine fever.

"It's not sick at all!" he called out to Apricot and Gran. Unsure if they heard him, he rushed back towards the wall, noticing, however, that the two women were deep in conversation. He thought he heard snippets of what they were talking about, something about Apricot not wanting the child she was carrying, or words to that effect.

"Hey, what are you two talking about?" he asked.

"Nothing to do with you," Gran shot back. "Don't be so nosy. Go on, get out of here."

Clambering back over the wall and laughing as he did so, Inkcap rushed home while Gran escorted Apricot, telling her she had to take it easy, stay in after at nightfall, and be careful about climbing over things, carrying water from the river and so on.

"And if you feel the least bit uncomfortable," she added, "make sure to call on me."

Upon returning home, Gran prepared dinner. For a change, it was rice and fried vegetables. Inkcap grumbled that the food was too delicious, wondering why they hadn't been eating this when doing the hard work of harvesting the fields. Gran said they must celebrate having averted disaster today, that good fortune was upon them.

"Who's going to hurt me?" Inkcap responded somewhat flippantly. "Some have tried, but look, Pockmark's in jail, Useless is being re-educated, Baldy Jin, he's essentially been branded a counterrevolutionary–"

"Watch what you're saying, boy, ugly words beget ugly thoughts and much worse."

"But ugliness can ward off evil."

No more was said while they ate. Once they had finished, Inkcap walked outside to sit on the stone steps. He resembled a fat toad, content with its lot, its body unmoving, only its neck craning to snag whatever insect ventured too close.

"Gran," Inkcap called out, "is there any rice left in the pan?"

"Perhaps a bowl."

"Let's ask Cowbell to come over and have some."

"Why? Trying to show off?"

"Yeah, maybe a little."

"It'd be much better to give the last bowl to Apricot. It was her mediation last night that saved you."

"And how do you know that?"

"Bash listens to her, you could call her a Hammerhead, I guess." Gran seemed to collect her thoughts before continuing, "And who's to say she didn't have something to do with Millstone being framed, if that's what it is. Millstone was responsible for that business with Potful, after all."

"You always try to think the best of people, don't you Gran?"

"And what's wrong with that?"

"But who's been good to us?"

"Oh, my boy, our bad background is just a fact, a sign of the times, it's not personal. Tell me, would you blame the river for freezing in winter, blame a hole in the wall for letting in the wind? Of course not, you'd be foolish to do so. Now, take the last bowl over to Apricot's."

"You know, Gran... you never used to want Apricot to hook up with Bash, but now you're telling me to take this meal to her, even though she spends nearly all her time at the Hammerheads' HQ. Don't you have anything to say about that?"

"Yes, but a good meal is a good meal and one's perspective changes when one's about to become a mother."

"OK, OK, I suppose, and she loves Bash, that's true, but it's not for certain that he loves her."

"How can you say such things? If he didn't love her, how could she become pregnant?"

"Eh?" Inkcap thought back to earlier in the day when Apricot refused to climb over the wall, only now realising why. "Pregnant? But she's not married, how could she be pregnant?"

"Stop shouting. Careful who hears."

As Gran dished out the remaining rice into a bowl, Noodle Fish happened to pass by their courtyard door carrying a basket of wild bracken he'd harvested from the mountains.

"Granny Silkworm, Granny Silkworm!" he called out.

"Eh? What does he want?"

Before she could come out to see, Noodle Fish had tossed a bushel of bracken over the gate, shouting as he did so, "This is for your pig, it'll cure any illness."

Reaching the gate, Gran asked Noodle Fish before he departed, "I heard a vet was being called, is that right?"

"Can't say anything about that, but feeding the pig this bracken will make a visit by the vet unnecessary."

"If that's so, then come in, come in."

Noodle Fish reeked of sweat and dirt, his trousers creased and torn. Gran changed her mind, she'd give the remaining rice to Noodle Fish.

Noodle Fish politely refused at first before finally accepting the food and eating about half of it. As he ate, Gran probed him for any titbits of news. She asked about the situation between Stonebreaker and Padlock, to which Noodle Fish replied they'd separated.

"Still," he added, "I can't say much more, Padlock doesn't talk to me any longer, only gives me dirty looks. I don't know..."

"Yes, but you were there when they were young and saw them to the age they are now. Surely, you've got to have some feeling towards them. You're not a cold, heartless individual now, are you... Stonebreaker's mum was nice to you at least?"

"Yeah, I suppose she was, but she can't control Stonebreaker and Padlock, all she'd do is end up crying every night, with me being the only person there to listen."

"Well, perhaps that's all you can aim for, that you and her are all right, that you look after each other as you get on in years and don't strain yourself too much with work. How's your health, by the way?"

"Not bad, can't complain, although since the summer I've been getting these dizzy spells, but it's nothing."

Inkcap had brought the food to the sty, but their pig would not eat. He mixed a little bran in with the bracken, but the animal only ate two mouthfuls before refusing to eat more.

"I guess we'll just have to wait for the vet," wondered Inkcap aloud. Returning to where Noodle Fish and Gran were seated, he relayed their pig's reluctance to eat and again mentioned the impending vet's arrival.

"A vet?" said Noodle Fish.

"Yes," answered Gran. "Apricot was just by, she said Bash had gone to Luozhen to get a vet to come to the village."

"Oh, indeed, that's good. Apricot came and told you?"

"She did."

"Gran, you say Apricot… Ah, the rumours in Old Kiln, they're something else, aren't they, spread through the village like wildfire. But I guess everything is all right with her."

"You know about this too?" Gran said. "First her father died, then… well, what can you say, things are what they are, so long as Bash's feelings for her are genuine, that's what matters."

"Bash's feelings genuine?"

"Yes, that's what I said… but, but what do you mean?"

"Ah," Noodle Fish started, "this is a… a revolutionary matter, I can't say more."

As the two of them talked, Inkcap tried to lead their pig back to the shed, but the creature refused, to the point where he began to curse the animal. "You lazy beast, not listening, eh?"

Gran heard him and turned her attention to her grandson, a vicious look on her face.

"Granny Silkworm," Noodle Fish continued, "if she really intends to have his child, I think you… you need to tell her. If she can get an abortion, she should. Having a child without being married, that won't be good for her."

"She already told me she was thinking of an abortion, but I suggested otherwise."

"Why? What kind of life can she and this child have?"

"If the people's revolution is successful," Inkcap said, "then having a child is good fortune for it'll have everyone celebrating its first month."

Then he returned his attention to the pig, yanking on its ears to drag it back to the sty. Still the animal did not budge. Noodle Fish moved to help, grabbing the creature's tail. The pig complied immediately and lifted itself up the stone steps and into the sty.

"Bit fucking useless you are, Inkcap," Noodle Fish joked. "Wasted sperm, right?"

When he returned to Old Kiln after dark, Bash confirmed that a veterinary doctor from Luozhen was coming to the village, just a little behind him on the road, in fact. Not long after, led by Noisy, the vet arrived and proceeded to administer injections for the village pigs. The vet did not discriminate, he treated pigs belonging to both the Hammerheads and the Red Blades. Sparks' pig was dead. Awning's was still symptom-free, but the vet inoculated it nonetheless. Millstone, however, declined the treatment for his sick pig, arguing that Bash was simply taking advantage of the situation for his own gain. He'd rather his pig die than owe anything to Bash. But Millstone's obstinacy did not sit well with his wife who insisted on their pig being treated, leading to a fierce argument between the two until finally, Millstone had to storm out to blow off steam. In truth, deep inside, Millstone worried that were his animal not treated, it would likely die, so his decision to storm off was not without purpose; if he wasn't there, he couldn't stop his wife from instructing the vet to administer the injection.

Millstone's feelings about his pig aside, he still felt Bash had manipulated the situation so he ended up at Awning's to complain some more. The Red Blades were fools, he shouted, always letting Bash and the Hammerheads gain the upper hand. Awning tried to soften Millstone's rage by disconnecting Bash's actions from the vet's arrival in Old Kiln, saying it was simply needed insofar as no one wanted all the pigs to die. And besides, Awning told him, it was not certain that Bash would be praised once all the pigs in the village were better. Remember, Awning added, during the land reform, the Branch Secretary had launched a struggle session against Lightkeeper's father and even after Lightkeeper's mum had pleaded for mercy, didn't he continue the struggle session despite showing understanding? Not everything is connected.

Naturally, once the injections were administered, the village had to pay the vet for his trouble and for the medication. But Bash didn't call on those whose animals were ill to foot the bill. Nor on anyone, in fact. Rather, he ordered Baldy Jin to collect some of the rafters lying about their HQ and to sell them to raise the necessary funds.

This action convinced Awning that Millstone was right to suspect Bash of his motives, and he now began to spread the story throughout the village. Bash was not interested in treating Old Kiln's pigs, his concern had only been with the Hammerheads. What's more, they'd taken advantage of the situation to sell off property that rightly belonged to the village. After all, the rafters sold to pay the vet bill were worth a lot more than what the medicine should cost. And if that was the case, where did the extra money go? They were simply enriching themselves at the expense of Old Kiln. Unsurprisingly, the persuasiveness of this story made many of those who had said Bash had done a good thing to change their minds, that the money earned from the sale of the rafters should naturally be divided among those who'd lost their pig to the illness. The more they talked, the more they even grew angry at the vet himself for coming to Old Kiln and treating their sick animals. He was cursed in some corners, more so after they learnt that before the vet had even arrived, Bash had sent Apricot around door to door to check whose pig was sick and whose wasn't. This was all a ploy, the villagers said, for a very pregnant Apricot would receive little resistance.

The more the villagers talked and complained, the more the stories about Bash and Apricot grew fantastical. One story even had Apricot picking onions from her plot, wanting to pee, squatting down and then crabs crawling up from the earth she'd urinated on, to which she remarked in surprise, "Oh, you're born! And what's this, you've got a hammer in your hand!" Of course, this was said much as a joke, but the barb was within for how could Apricot give birth to such a child? The villagers went on and on, telling story after story. But when Inkcap appeared with his matches, most would stop talking and stare at the boy, asking what he'd heard, what story could he tell and so on. Then others would remark that it's just Inkcap, the same kind of situation in many ways, a bastard child, wasted sperm, what have you.

Upon hearing his name, however, Inkcap had to enquire what they were saying about him.

"I said you've grown up well," said Stargazer.

Inkcap was used to the villagers mocking him for being ugly. He didn't regard that as strange any more, ugly was just ugly, and besides, he could laugh at himself as well as poke fun at others

"That may be true, but tell me, how come you ended up so short? Your eyes are so round, too, how did that happen? And your ears, oh my, just look at them!"

"That's all very well," Stargazer shot back, "but sure as fuck no one could be born as wild as you!"

"A wild seed?"

"Yeah, a wild seed. You don't know who your parents are, after all, do you?"

"I do know, Gran brought me up from the river."

"Ha ha, we've all heard that story, boy. And I bet you Apricot will throw her child in the river once it's born."

Inkcap wasn't entirely sure he understood what the people had been talking about, but he could feel himself growing angrier at Stargazer. Stargazer, however, remained unaffected by Inkcap's rage. Inkcap then twisted his neck and flung not his fist but his head at Stargazer. Gleaning what the boy was doing before contact was made, Stargazer stepped aside and Inkcap hurtled headfirst into the tree immediately behind them. The branches shook violently at the impact, while the bystanders stood watching, dumbfounded by the spectacle they were witnessing. Stunned by his impact with the tree, Inkcap dropped his matches and staggered back. Then he grabbed his head and to the surprise of everyone, whacked it against the tree again. Whack, whack, whack. Finally, skin broke and a line of blood trickled down his face. The sight of blood seemed to awaken the villagers, and a few made to stop him.

"Come on now Inkcap, boy, stop it... what's made you so angry?"

Feeling he'd been wronged, Inkcap naturally wanted to tell the whole story to Gran. But he never once thought she would fail to comfort him. In fact, she only cursed him.

"How many times must I tell you, you have to be quiet when you're outside, you have to swallow the bile. But how often have you not listened, is it all just some game for you?"

"But Stargazer started it, he was bullying me, I couldn't just–"

"Couldn't what, let it go? Is what he said to you so bad that you had to try and hit him?"

"No, but, yes, but, I don't know... I... I didn't hit him, though. I smashed my own head into the tree."

"And what was that for? Putting on a show, was that it? Do you think acting that way will get you any sympathy?"

"But I was so angry, I had to do something–"

"Still, you talk back! You impudent little shit. Is this the first time? Haven't there been many times before, people have said stuff, got you angry? Why were you able to take it then but not now? Didn't you just dodge a bullet, do you think all's well now?"

Inkcap knew what she said was right. He'd acted out on purpose, wanted to draw attention to himself. He couldn't say why. He looked at Gran plaintively, but she said nothing further. Sitting down, Inkcap began to chew at his fingernails while Gran went outside to round up the chickens. Inkcap watched her through the window.

"I don't want fried eggs," he yelled.

"And who said that's what I was going to make?" Gran shot back. "I'm trying to get some chicken feathers to clean up that dried blood."

He wore the chicken feathers on his forehead for seven days, after which they and the bloody scabs underneath fell off, leaving a small triangle-shaped scar where he'd smashed his head against the tree. On most occasions, the scar was much the same colour as the rest of his face, but whenever he was excited, the scar turned reddish. On the same seventh day, both Hammerheads and Red Blades marched off to Luozhen to have new seals carved. Resolutions and notices were subsequently released, each bearing the mark of the newly engraved seal. Cowbell thought it amusing for Inkcap to have his own seal, if only engraved on his forehead.

Aside from Cowbell, however, very few villagers continued to laugh or made jokes at Inkcap's expense. He'd never seen Old Kiln so serious before, but he did notice that both the Hammerheads and Red Blades seemed to be increasingly nervous. Even the smallest bit of gossip, a loose tongue, anything at all, gave off the impression that the village was about to erupt. If one faction went into the fields to work, the other followed suit, setting out to work in the adjacent field. If one faction went to the river to collect water and saw some of the other faction already there, they'd stand off in the distance, quietly waiting for the others to depart. Inkcap still went down the alleyways of Old Kiln carrying his matches, but no one called out to him for a light any more. There was only Cowbell to keep him company, it seemed.

On this day, the terraced fields halfway up Middle Mountain were to be ploughed, but unfortunately, the corners of the fields were too hard for the oxen to properly turn over the earth. Consequently, hoes had to be used instead. Three villagers started from the northern corner, four from the south. Barndoor handled the plough while Inkcap drove the oxen back and forth across the field. When the villagers with the hoes working in the southern corner spotted them, they yelled out jokingly. Those in the northern section did the same. Inkcap couldn't help but wonder why, finally striking up enough courage to ask.

"You're a Red Blade, aren't you, so is that why are they making fun of you? But then, why are the others doing the same thing?"

"I'm not a member of either faction," Barndoor shot back.

"Then perhaps you're the captain!"

Barndoor ignored the comment and asked Inkcap to fetch him some tomatoes from his personal plot. On arriving there, Inkcap discovered that most of them were overripe and had fallen to the ground, already starting to rot. Inkcap thought that the small number that were edible, partly green and partly red, could be enjoyed by everyone.

So when he returned to where Barndoor was, he asked, "Saying you're the captain is one thing, but even if you're not, do you mean to share these tomatoes with everyone else?"

Again, Barndoor didn't answer him, he only collected the seven or eight tomatoes Inkcap had brought and laid them out in the middle of the field. A moment later he called out, "Tomatoes, come and get some tomatoes!"

But no one came.

At least not right away. Finally, a Red Blade did walk over towards Barndoor. It was Once-Upon-A-Time. Then a Hammerhead came, Dazed-And-Confused.

"I'll have one," Dazed-And-Confused said. He didn't wait for an answer before grabbing a tomato and taking a bite, sucking hard as though he were trying to deflate it, then breathing out again, evidently to inflate the empty skin of the gorged fruit. He offered no words to Barndoor, only took another tomato and walked away. Once-Upon-A-Time, having waited for Dazed-And-Confused to leave, now strode over to get his own tomato. As he turned, however, he spat in the direction of the other villager. Dazed-And-Confused reciprocated, spitting towards Once-Upon-A-Time. It wasn't phlegm that he spat, however, but tomato pulp. No one else came, despite Barndoor calling out again that there were tomatoes to eat. As a result, Inkcap ended up eating the remaining tomatoes, patting his stomach in satisfaction when they were all gone.

Those not belonging to either the Zhu or Hei clans watched the expressions on their faces, gleaning their true thoughts and intentions. Then something significant happened. So significant that even Lightkeeper altered his usual path. Instead of walking alongside the walls of the village as he tracked back and forth between the fields, he spryly followed the sparrow's route, whereupon he bumped into Inkcap, whom he asked for a back scratch. Surprised by the request, Inkcap froze.

"What's the matter with you?" Lightkeeper probed. "You got chicken feathers in your ears or something?"

"Umm," Inkcap replied, "just… you're talking to… to me?"

"I am, yes, now scratch my back, it's killing me."

"There's a tree right over there. I reckon you should use that."

"Oh, you useless, wasted bit of sperm. I asked you, didn't I, not the bloody tree. What is it, you think I'm a Bad Element, not to be spoken to, is that it?"

"No... I mean, my background's no different."

"And still you won't scratch my back?"

Inkcap walked over to Lightkeeper, mumbling to himself as he did, "Just pretend you're scratching your pig, just pretend you're–"

"No, wait," Lightkeeper said. "I have to sit first, then you scratch my back properly."

"You're not afraid people with criticise you for this, saying you're a landlord and that you're exploiting a member of the lower classes?"

"And who bothers with me any more, I'm nothing. Shit, they're even trying to recruit me into their factions."

"So which faction are you thinking of joining?" Inkcap asked.

"Not sure, I'm just watching things for the time being, trying to see which side has more power than the other."

Inkcap scratched hard at Lightkeeper's back, unable to disguise his disgust for the man. Then he stopped and shouted, "You really are a class enemy."

Lightkeeper stood up and smacked him, without restraint. Inkcap said nothing in response, he only turned and ran. He could see blood under his nails; evidently, he'd pierced Lightkeeper's skin.

"You just wait," shouted Lightkeeper after him. "When I gain power I'm coming after you, you little piece of shit."

Inkcap wasn't afraid, however. Certainly not of Lightkeeper. In his mind, he knew neither faction would welcome him in, whatever he might say. True, the Hammerheads and Red Blades might try to do right by those not in the Zhu or Hei clans, but no one would treat Lightkeeper with anything but contempt.

Or so Inkcap thought.

Just a day before Almost-There came to offer Lightkeeper a place in the Hammerheads, Awning had come looking for Lightkeeper on behalf of the Red Blades. Awning told him that despite his bad background, he could still join a revolutionary faction, provided he sufficiently demonstrated his revolutionary furore. This was welcome news to Lightkeeper and he vowed to them that he was a reformed character, dedicated to the revolution. He would do whatever was asked.

"Then tell me," Awning said, "what is your greatest wish?"

"To not be one of the Four Bad Elements," answered Lightkeeper.

"Well, now," Awning began, "as you know, a chicken is a chicken, a dog is a dog. Dogs can't give birth to hens, and no dog can emerge from an egg. Your background is something you can't change, so best not to think of it."

"Then let me relight the kiln, let me make porcelain again. I am, after all, the most skilled porcelain maker in Old Kiln."

"And who's stopping you from relighting it already?"

"The... the Cultural Revolution is."

"What? You mean to say the Hammerheads?"

"Yes, that's right, the Hammerheads. They're the ones that shut down the kiln."

"All right, then, from this moment onwards, the Red Blades will support you in relighting the kiln. Of course, you won't be making any of that fancy blue porcelain, that's too bourgeois, nor will you make anything substandard. Since the Red Blades will be providing you support, you'll make china we can share and use."

This was more than Lightkeeper had ever expected, and he felt his knees go weak. Falling to the ground, he wanted to offer Awning three kowtows in thanks. Unsurprisingly, Lightkeeper's feudal attitude only made Awning angry.

"Get up, now! In the New China, we don't kowtow any more."

Lightkeeper lifted himself up, saying as he did, "And the others who worked at the kiln, Pendulum in particular, is he still there?"

"What do you mean?" asked Awning.

"Erm, well, it's better if he's not there," Lightkeeper replied, perhaps a little too quickly.

"Do you mean to say that if he's not there, you'll work much better? If that's the case, then he won't be there. It'll be you and just you. Work well, and you'll be welcomed into the Red Blades."

"You've given me such an important position, I'll do everything I can to further your revolutionary activities. I might even be able to convince Almost-There to forsake the enemy and leave the reactionary faction... and if I can't, I'll slaughter the pig and wash my knife with his blood."

The Red Blades' decision to relight the kiln meant that firewood had to be collected once more in greater amounts. Each family in Old Kiln also had to contribute funds so that someone could purchase coal in Xichuan. Naturally, news of their intention quickly reached the Hammerheads, who immediately began to argue among themselves, the focus on their rage being the fact that the Red Blades had made this decision on their own, without discussing things with the village. Wasn't the kiln public property? Didn't it belong to the people? The Red Blades rebutted this argument by saying that the kiln did indeed belong to the village, hence they were within their rights to use it. After all, they were villagers, weren't they?

Bash regretted not trying to recruit Lightkeeper sooner, but that ship had sailed. So he turned to Pendulum, only to discover that Awning had already shut down this option, evidently mobilising others to assist Lightkeeper. And at any rate, even if he could, Pendulum declined, he had decided not to side with either faction, so he wasn't going to make porcelain for anyone. Besides, he added, his back was bad which made work difficult.

Left with no one in the Hammerheads who could make porcelain, they could only stand by and watch as the Red Blades relit the fires, growing ever more anxious about their position in the village. Some in the Hammerheads began to clamour that the Red Blades had expropriated public goods and that they should do the same, perhaps with the village oxen, that if the Red Blades were going to sell china, they should sell the cattle. Others opposed this point of view, arguing that without oxen their fields would go unploughed, and that would be no good whatsoever. Oxen and fields went together, they argued. What's more, land was all-important. After all, the revolution was about taking control of the land. The party took land from the rich landlords and gave it to the people, they shouted, that socialism was only realised by the cooperative work of the village under the leadership of the party. If there were no oxen to properly till the land, leaving it fallow, then that would be a betrayal of the party and the revolution, to say nothing about where their food would come from if the fields were not planted. Last but not least, the cattle were housed adjacent to the Red Blades' HQ – how could they take them without the Red Blades knowing?

While the Hammerheads bickered, Bash sat alone in the main hall of the temple, contemplatively sipping the *taisui* water. As was custom, he dipped a ladle in to scoop out some water, then gently raised it to his lips. One scoop, two scoops, three. It was only after a lull in the arguments that any of the Hammerheads noticed that Bash wasn't among them.

"Where's our captain?" Baldy Jin called out.

"Inside sipping *taisui* water," Tag-Along answered.

Everyone was silent. Bash appeared drunk or at least deep in thought. Whichever it was, no one dared disturb him. Not before, not now.

"Let him drink, think, do what he has to," suggested Baldy Jin. "No doubt, when he's ready, he'll tell us what to do."

And with that, the arguments ceased. Some played chess and others just milled about. Finally, Bash walked out and surveyed the courtyard. When his eyes fell on Tag-Along, he shouted, "Come on, let's go!" Tag-Along obliged, grabbing his shovel and following Bash out of the main gate. Everyone in the Hammerheads knew Bash's constipation was getting worse and worse. And as a result, he was going deeper and deeper into the mountains to take a shit or at least try to. Perhaps it was the act itself that helped clear his mind, focus his thoughts. Who's to say? The only person Bash permitted to accompany him was Tag-Along, so the remaining Hammerheads returned to their chess games and their gossip, assured in their belief that Bash would soon return and have a plan for them to follow.

But on this occasion, he didn't come back. Several days passed, in fact, and still there was no trace of Bash or Tag-Along.

Baldy Jin was the first to search for Bash, checking his old home, only to find the door locked and undisturbed. He next went to the shack nearer the county road, but its door was locked too. Angry, he decided to call on Apricot but bumped into Pendulum along the way. Hands rubbing at his lower back, Pendulum was neither pleased nor displeased to see Baldy Jin. He did learn, however, that when Awning first visited Pendulum about relighting the kiln, his back wasn't hurting him, he only said that to Awning as an excuse to get the man to stop pestering him. In truth, he was putting on a show, as it were, in anticipation of Bash calling on him about the same thing. Who would have thought, he mused, that his playacting would result in real pain?

"So what do you mean," Baldy Jin said, "your back really does hurt?"

"Yeah, it does, worse and worse every day. I'll be a cripple soon."

"Serves you right," Baldy Jin exclaimed, and he walked off, paying the man no further mind. Arriving a little later at Apricot's, he discovered her in her courtyard, washing her hair.

"What are you here for?" called Apricot as she lifted her head from the basin.

"I'm looking for Bash," answered Baldy Jin from the other side of the gate.

"He's not here."

"Come open the door, there's something I want to say and I don't want to have to speak through the gate."

Apricot opened the gate, letting Baldy Jin inside the courtyard.

"Everyone's waiting for him, he's got to tell us what to do," Baldy Jin said. "You can't keep him hidden, you know."

"He's a grown man, how could I hide him even if I wanted to?" Apricot replied, grabbing a towel and patting her hair, the water dripping onto the ground.

By now, Baldy Jin realised that Bash wasn't there, and he turned to leave.

"Next time there's something going on with you Hammerheads," Apricot said as he left, "make sure you don't come here asking me about it."

Baldy Jin remembered then that the last time they saw Bash he was leaving their HQ with Tag-Along in tow, shovel in hand. Perhaps he should call on Tag-Along? He did and soon learnt from Tag-Along's wife that the two men had gone to Luozhen.

SIXTY-TWO

TWO DAYS AFTER BASH LEFT FOR LUOZHEN, Zhu Dagui and Useless returned from re-education. The Branch Secretary looked largely unchanged, apart from his beard having turned white. Useless, however, appeared much worse off. He'd grown skinny, almost inhumanly so, his skin resembled wet tissue paper stretched over bones. His eyes had sunken into their sockets, his lips had lost their former colour, and his Adam's apple stuck out from his throat like an unshelled walnut.

That afternoon, as Sparks and Winterborn were returning with coal for the kiln, they stopped halfway down the mountain slope to rest and to watch several white-beaked, red-tailed birds chirping and flittering about before finally settling on a white pine. The sun was low in the sky and when it shone on the pine, the tree turned crimson and seemed to sparkle. This was the most beautiful time of the year in Old Kiln.

"Hey," Winterborn asked, "do you know who's called on Goodman? Someone else's ill, I suppose. Damn, there's a lot of sickness going round, isn't there?"

"You're right about that. I often wonder how such a beautiful place can have so many sick people," Sparks replied.

Winterborn directed his attention further down the mountain. He noticed someone scrambling up the mountainside, carrying another person on their back. He looked back at Sparks and asked, "You reckon Goodman really helps? I mean, does he know what he's doing, do they actually get better after seeing him?"

"I suppose so. After doing something for so long, a man's bound to develop a talent for it. And that's Goodman in a nutshell. Long as I can remember he's been giving people advice, so I guess there must be something to it. Sort of like Zhu Dagui, in a way. Maybe he doesn't have the power any longer, his voice carries no weight, but he was Secretary for a good number of years, and he still looks the part. Even if no one listens to him, his words often prove to be true."

"Eh, looks like she's here for you," said Winterborn, interrupting his ruminations.

Sparks removed a shoe, turned it upside down and shook a stone free. "Who's come looking for me?"

Before Winterborn could reply, Useless's mum had got close enough to speak for herself: "Sparks, oh, Sparks..."

She'd been nearby collecting sticks, branches and twigs, whatever she could use to light a fire. Her clothes were wrinkled and dirty, her hair was a mess and littered with nettles and bits of dried wood. After Useless had been sent off for re-education, she'd grown shrivelled and weak. And without him, she'd lacked firewood and so was reduced to scavenging on the mountains.

Not responding to the old woman calling his name, Sparks turned to Winterborn and said, "What the hell does she want with me?" He replaced his shoe as Winterborn stood silently by, a small stick in his hand. Sparks watched him as he used the stick to clean the wax from his ears, coughing as he tickled his ear canal. They continued to ignore Useless's mum.

But the woman was now closer, and she again called Sparks' name. This time, Sparks looked in her direction, acknowledging her presence, before asking, "And... what do you want?"

"Sparks–"

"Shit, woman, I can barely hear you, you sound like a buzzing mosquito."

"When does the kiln restart?"

"You're still going on about this?"

"Yes, but no one in the Zhu clan will tell me anything... they didn't even ask me to contribute any money."

"Any you've no shortage of that, I'm sure."

"Sparks, how can you say such a thing? You know these last ten days I've not had even a pinch of salt. Your words cut me to the quick."

Sparks straightened his back. "Busy, busy, we've got coal for the kiln. Must be off."

Neither Sparks nor Winterborn said anything further to Useless's mum, they simply pulled on the carts they'd dragged back from Xichuan and began to amble further down the mountain. In the distance, they could see the county road and four people trudging in the direction of Old Kiln.

"Is that the Secretary?" Sparks asked aloud.

Together with Useless's mum, Sparks walked towards the county road. It was indeed Zhu Dagui. He was in the front. In the middle of the group was Useless and another man Sparks did not recognise. Bringing up the rear was an armed rifleman. Still somewhat baffled by the appearance of the former Secretary and Useless, Sparks was at a loss for words.

Useless's mother, however, blurted out in a voice far louder than it had been on the mountain, "Oh my Useless has returned, my boy!"

She tossed aside the kindling she'd collected and ran down the mountain path towards her son, displaying more energy than Sparks thought she possessed. In her haste, however, she didn't realise there might be others on the mountainside and she crashed into the villagers who had come to speak to Goodman.

Wondering about the apparent return of Zhu Dagui and Useless, Winterborn was first to ask the question that hung in the air: "Back, eh, suppose they're all good, then?"

"But how? And if everything's good, why is a rifleman bringing up the rear? They're still prisoners if you ask me, so that means it's not all right."

Sparks kicked the discarded basket Useless's mother had tossed to the ground, causing it to roll towards a nearby tree, disturbing a wasp's nest in the process. The insects swarmed around them, forcing the two men to swat at them as they fled, realising there were far more wasps than they could possibly kill. The angry insects chased them halfway down the mountainside, stinging them repeatedly.

By the time Useless's mother returned home, her son was already there, sitting on the steps just outside the courtyard. He had forgotten where the key was hidden, or perhaps he'd just not bothered, she couldn't be sure. Her heart broke when she saw him, though, his head between his legs, a beaten and defeated man. She called to him, and he looked up, but she became even more shocked by the pallor of his face.

"Mother..." he replied and burst into tears, babbling in between sobs about how he was an unfilial son, how he'd brought her shame. At the same time, Useless's mum heard a cough from the toilet just outside their courtyard gate. Followed by a laugh. She turned to see who it was, and her eyes fell on Yoyo. Startled by Yoyo's sudden appearance – hadn't she vanished without a trace, how could she be here now? – Useless's mother wasn't sure what to do. Yoyo looked somewhat dishevelled, even mad, with a chrysanthemum tucked behind her ear, her teeth showing in a twisted grin.

Fear growing, Useless's mother challenged Yoyo's presence: "Is that really you, really here?"

"Is that really you, really here?" Yoyo shouted back.

Useless's mother was even more terrified and rushed to drag her son inside, slamming the gate shut to prevent the seemingly deranged Yoyo from following them.

Once safely inside, Useless's mother asked her son, "Was that really Yoyo or a ghost?"

"It was her," Useless replied weakly.

He then told the story to his mother, how on the road back to Old Kiln, after they'd been released from re-education, they'd come upon Yoyo on the road, arguing and fighting with a pack of kids. She was flinging balls of hardened mud at them and they were returning fire with the same mud balls. But when she saw the four of them – Zhu Dagui, himself and the other two – she stopped her attack on the children and followed them back.

No one in Old Kiln was surprised by the return of Zhu Dagui and Useless. What was strange was that Ever-Obedient's wife had seemingly returned with them. After Yoyo had disappeared, Ever-Obedient had spent an enormous amount of time looking for her. So, too, had many of the villagers, but to no avail. Exhausted by the fruitless search, most had given up hope of finding her. And now, suddenly, she was back. All on her own, and quite mad too. Her clothes were torn and ragged, her breasts exposed, revealing blackened, parched nipples, a flower tucked behind her ear, a wild smile on her face. The villagers took to guessing where she'd gone, what she'd eaten, where she'd slept. They also wondered how her breasts had grown so large and her nipples so black. Had she been raped? For Ever-Obedient, none of these questions needed answers. As soon as word reached him that she had returned, he rushed off to see her, barely putting on shoes before he raced out of his home. He found near the big-character poster board, surrounded by a group of villagers engaged in a heated, if somewhat incoherent argument.

"Shame, shame!" shouted several villagers.

"Shame, shame!" Yoyo spat back.

"You're back!" Ever-Obedient shouted when he saw her. "Come, let's go home."

Yoyo refused, so he grabbed her arm and began to pull her in the direction of their house. This proving difficult, Ever-Obedient picked her up, put her over his shoulder and stomped off. Once home, he forced her to lie down on their bed. For a long time, he did nothing but watch her, wondering what he should do. He couldn't tell what was in her heart, all he saw was the deranged smile that never seemed to leave her face.

"She's crazy, totally mad," Ever-Obedient mumbled to himself. Unsure what to do, he got his ever-loyal dog to stand guard over her and keep her in the bedroom. For three days she remained confined. If she tried to leave, the dog would nip at her heels and force her to withdraw. All she could do was cry out to her husband, "Ever-Obedient! Big water! Big water!"

So loud was her deranged shouting that even Dazed-And-Confused heard it. He imagined that Ever-Obedient must be fucking her day and night, filling her up, as it were. Whatever the case might be, big water did indeed visit Old Kiln that evening, but in the form of a flood that inundated the village.

It was dawn, to be precise, when the waters came. Inkcap had awoken to a stillness in the air, but he didn't immediately get up from bed. He could discern some slight movement outside, but it was muffled, restrained somehow. He could hear the stretching of the plum tree outside, its branches seeming to reach out into the sky. Its leaves had already turned and withered with the autumn air, but tiny buds of greenery were still hanging on the thinnest of the branches, coarse and ragged, but sturdy and defiant, too, in the face of the impending change of season.

Inkcap could also hear the sparrows begin to chirp in their own coarse way, mocking, it seemed, the sprouts on the plum tree for not knowing the time of year; after all, the swallows were soon to leave, why cling to life so desperately? At any rate, the swallows offered no response, refusing to stoop down to the level of the sparrows, or so Inkcap thought. But this was not all he heard. Training his ears further, Inkcap discerned padded paws tiptoeing across the courtyard threshold and he assumed it was one of the village cats, carefully stalking its prey. An earthworm broke through the ground at the foot of the wall and the cat focused on it intently. The cat's real target was the sparrow, its small, twisted beak perturbed it, it needed to feel the feathers of the creature in its jaws. The earthworm was simply bait in the eyes of the cat – how could something live without a nose, eyes and a mouth? Then a wondrous, strange sound reverberated across the paper windows. It had to be a dragonfly, Inkcap thought, so distinct is its whine, its translucent wings piercing the air. But the air appeared weightier than usual, more solid somehow – could it be water? Could the winged path of the dragonfly have brought the ripple of water with it? Could the weakest of waves be gently lapping at his paper window? Inkcap's thoughts remained on the dragonfly, he could imagine it flittering this way and that, then landing on the handle of the plough that was leaning against the front gable, the same one Barndoor had asked him to collect when the lightning struck. The compound eyes of the dragonfly surveyed the plough, noticing its polished and shiny tip, but also the mud that still clung to its shaft, stuck like glue. Was the plough simply taking a break? Resting, as it were? A chicken now spied the dragonfly, thinking its beauty irresistible, its shimmering colours brilliantly reflecting the sun. The chicken attempted to fly, but its weak, useless wings barely launched it a foot in the air before its fat body brought it back down to the earth, crashing into a leafy abundance of spinach that was far too limp to withstand the impact of the chicken. A black seed emerged from the chaos, quickly burrowing itself in the ground. What was that sound? Inkcap wondered.

A rope was hanging from his window over into the courtyard, his gran's apron tied around it. The wind lashed at the rope, blowing it back and forth. Was it looking for holes that needed patching? Inkcap asked himself. No, a wind wants the holes, it wants to whistle, if only quietly at times. Deep into autumn, the wind brings with it the change of season, but it doesn't bring the warmth of spring, it brings the cold of winter, nipping at the leaves of the trees, the last few on the plum tree now torn free to float helplessly to the ground, one leaf left... then Inkcap suddenly heard the sound of a saw ripping into wood – who could it be? Who in Old Kiln had such a tool? No one, as far as Inkcap knew, certainly not one big enough to fell a tree. The sound grew louder and louder. He even felt his bed begin to shift, as if reverberating from the echo of the saw. Now the entire house! Inkcap lifted himself from bed.

"Gran! Gran! Gran!"

No answer.

He got dressed quickly and heard the clanging of gongs in the village. Pandemonium. Inkcap went outside and to the gate of the courtyard, where he saw Cowbell holding a wicker basket.

Before he could ask him what was going on, Cowbell shouted, "The river's flooded. There's water everywhere."

"But it hasn't rained," Inkcap responded. "How could the river flood?"

"Didn't you feel the coolness of the air last night? It's been raining for days in Luozhen, and now the water's arrived here."

The river flooded every year, but recently it had been flooding later and later. And normally it followed rain, dampening everything as though in preparation for the flood. But this year, the rain was to the west, drenching Luozhen, evidently, but not Old Kiln, which is why the village had not taken appropriate measures. Inkcap had no idea where Gran was, but he couldn't just wait around for her. Running off towards the river, as he got close he could see the reeds on the riverbanks were already underwater, submerged beneath muddy, yellow water. Only the old willow tree, a little taller than the reeds, could be seen, its branches just above the water surface, entangled with snakes seeking refuge from the deluge. The stones in which he and Cowbell had clambered between in search of crabs were hidden. Most of the villagers seemed to be at the river, some entranced by the awesome spectacle of rising water, others busily, if unsuccessfully, trying to fish lost firewood that was being swept away. But it wasn't only firewood that was being carried off, other bits of wood, building supplies, tools, instruments, baskets, even dead oxen and pigs could be spotted in the rushing, murky water. Some clutched at their chests, faces stained with pain and regret. Trees washed by, evidently ripped from the ground, roots and all. Straw, entire bundles harvested further upstream, floated past. A few villagers thought to tie one end of a rope to a nearby boulder not yet underwater and then wade out into the rushing river in an effort to save something, anything. Others warned them it was too dangerous and much too fast for them to swim against. And even if they could manage it, how the hell would they be able to drag anything to the shore? Dissuaded from taking the risk, those who'd planned to wade into the water relented and untied their rope.

But then, some others shouted to Ever-Obedient, "Is that someone there in the rushing waters? Quick, go fish out yourself another wife."

It did appear as though someone was in the water, a pale form, their face turned downwards. The bodies that were being washed away were naked, evidently the water had rogue demons within, unbuttoning and unloosening clothes to be ripped away to expose bare flesh.

Ever-Obedient, however, would not come to the river. It was the first time in his life that he hadn't, and most assumed it must be because of his mad wife. Was there a connection between Yoyo and the flood? On her initial arrival in Old Kiln, the villagers recalled, floodwaters had come. Now, on her return, they'd come again. Did she have some early premonition of them? Discussions also turned to Luozhen. How much had it rained there? For how long? And what damage did it cause? Would they soon expect to see beggars straggling down the road, desperate for any kind of handout? Words and arguments flew among the villagers until someone finally waved their hands and shouted that it didn't matter, there was nothing they could do about it anyway, and it was too far away for them to think about.

"Besides," someone shouted callously, "if they didn't face disaster, how would we be able to collect all this stuff further downstream!"

"Fucking floodwaters," Baldy Jin joined in. "Why are they so bloody big? A little smaller and we'd be able to do something about them, or at least something with them. Perhaps if they happened more frequently, like once a month, but on a smaller scale, that'd be a proper way to move things downriver." And with those words just out of his mouth, he slipped and fell into the water, his arms and feet thrashing frantically as he tried to grasp hold of a tree, a branch, anything to keep him from being washed away, gulping mouthfuls of dirty water in the process.

Jindou hadn't been impressed by Baldy Jin's harsh words, remarking as Baldy Jin flailed about, "There are things that cannot be done, only said, and there are things that can be done, but not said."

Extricating himself from the water's edge, Baldy Jin knelt, vomiting the water he'd swallowed, unable to say or do anything else. The bystanders also chose to remain silent, taking the bits they'd been able to salvage from the rushing water up to higher land to dry.

By noon, most of the villagers had returned home to prepare lunch, but those who had fished wood out of the surging river were worried. The wood was still too wet and heavy to bring home, but at the same time, they were afraid that if they left it drying nearer the county road, an outsider might come along and take it. It was then that someone spotted Inkcap.

"Hey, Inkcap, you've nothing to do, you stay here and watch things. Someone will bring you food, but you've got to remain here, OK?"

The villagers agreed Inkcap was best suited to look after the wood, and Inkcap didn't object. Left to watch over things, he began to poke through the debris, rooting out the dead fish and frogs, the discarded shoes and rope, and anything else that had got tangled up in the mess. Finally, when only the wood remained, he spread them as best he could so that they would better dry. The old shack Bash used to frequent was nearby, and though the door was locked, the stone steps in front of it made for a suitable resting place. He remembered past, happier days and lamented that things had seemed to change so much. He couldn't answer the question of why.

The afternoon sun wasn't all that strong and as he sat on the steps, he could feel his hunger grow. The empty pit in his belly got larger, and he felt his head lulled to the side, seemingly as though it would topple off his shoulders altogether. The wood had dampened the ground around the hut, attracting a flutter of butterflies that had landed on the moistened earth, motionless in the weak afternoon sun. They were small and whitish in colour, although he could see specks of blue and grey. Where were they on normal days? he wondered. Did they always swarm together?

The river still gurgled close by, drowning out most other sounds. Even the cicadas in the trees could not be heard. The rushing waters had a uniformity about them, they howled in the same manner, over and over again, unchanging despite the constant flow of the river. Inkcap could also detect a certain odour emanating from the water. Earthy and hot, the scent wafted around Inkcap causing him to feel dizzy, his muscles to soften, his eyes to droop. The Zhen River Pagoda was slanted, Inkcap could see this clearly now, even though Bash had always told him it wasn't. Suddenly, he felt as though the bamboo just beneath the pagoda was swaying, then the tower itself began to twist back and forth, buffeted, he thought, by a rising mist emanating from the rushing river. It had a dark green colour to it and enveloped the bamboo and pagoda, wrenching it this way and that, and as he watched, Inkcap wondered how it was even possible – did mist have such power? But they were shaking, he was sure of it. Will it collapse? No, it didn't, it couldn't. He laughed at his own foolishness. How could mist topple something that solid? He felt his feet itch, his neck too. Leaning over to scratch his wet feet, he noticed small white marks all over them. Then he lifted his head and looked again. Something strange began to unfold before his eyes: the pagoda swayed hard to one side and fell, breaking into pieces. Rubble scattered everywhere as if an explosion had gone off, destroying the tower from inside and throwing its pieces into the air. But, he thought, it was also like an axe felling a great tree, splinters of wood flung in every direction as the blade bit into the trunk. Then the wind blew and swept some of the debris up with it, twirling stones circled a moment in the air, then as fast as they had been lifted, they plummeted back down to the ground. Inkcap was awestruck. A fear overtook him, fear of being chased by a wolf, fear of imminent danger, he couldn't say, only that he was afraid. He ran, abandoning the wood, desperate to get home.

But he was stopped on his way by the villagers who had promised to bring him lunch. "Hey, boy, what are you doing, where are you running to?"

"The pagoda, by the river, it's fallen over! Collapsed!" Panic suffused his voice.

The villagers looked towards the river, then turned back to Inkcap. "Boy, oh boy, you're the right fool aren't you, can't even cook up a proper story."

"I'm telling the truth, it fell. I saw it with my own eyes," Inkcap pleaded.

"Turn around and look."

Inkcap obeyed the man and saw the tower still standing. But how? He knew he'd seen it fall. How could it still be there?

"Possessed, aren't you!" the villager shouted and boxed Inkcap's ears. It was widely thought that Inkcap was easily possessed. The villager who'd slapped him was unsympathetic, however, and shouted at him, "What do you see now, you damn fool?"

"The sky is full of stars," Inkcap responded hazily.

"And now?"

"Stop hitting me, you fucker!" Inkcap shot back. Evidently, his haziness had now dissipated.

Afterwards, Inkcap was less lively than he'd been before. For three days, Gran kept him indoors. And for three days, she carried out rites, throwing sticks, jumping over fires, out in the middle of the night calling to the spirits. However, nothing seemed to work, Inkcap just wasn't the same. Most especially, she wanted him to have nothing to do with Yoyo, who apparently was still holed up in her house, washing her dog repeatedly and calling it Inkcap over and over, wondering how its dark hair had become white. Inkcap himself thought this funny at first, but it soon made him itch and he, too, wanted to hear nothing more about Yoyo. Gran also insisted he steer clear of the Hammerheads' HQ. Useless was back, and even though Awning had instructed Inkcap to check on him, make sure he was behaving himself, as it were, there was still something off about things. For one, Useless on his first couple of visits had treated Inkcap well and even offered some of Bash's *taisui* water. But Inkcap couldn't quite accept Useless's changed demeanour, to say nothing of the water offered. There was just something about that water. Inkcap found he couldn't even look at it. And so that was the end of his visits to the Hammerheads' headquarters. Naturally, this situation worried Gran, especially as her supposed remedies had come to nought. As a result, she sent word to Goodman, seeking his advice.

Always willing to oblige, Goodman trekked down from his mountain home, on the way bumping into Sprout and Stonebreaker. They were busy arguing.

"Stonebreaker," Sprout said, evidently not for the first time, "your dad's burning up with a fever, you know?"

"I know that."

"I bet you it's because of that boil on the back of his neck. It's got so big and it looks full of pus... should you get someone to look at it?"

"It's just a boil, nothing more. And besides, who doesn't get sick now and then?"

"Yeah, but what he has might end up being something serious, especially if it's causing his temperature to rise. If you don't get it looked at, it could end up claiming his life."

"Everybody dies, but not every illness leads to death, does it? People need to die too. If they didn't, there soon wouldn't be any room for the rest of us."

"All right, all right, suit yourself, Stonebreaker. I guess I'm just talking bullshit. Forget about it." Angry at Stonebreaker's obstinacy, Sprout turned around.

"Be quiet, will you. See a doctor? Ha! And where would I get the money for that? Should I steal it, will someone lend me some?"

Stonebreaker turned his head and saw Goodman walking down the path towards them. He looked embarrassed, offering Goodman only an awkward smile.

"So," Goodman began, "I heard some of what you were both yelling about. That boil, eh, to tell you the truth, I saw it three days ago, I actually spoke to your mum about it, wondered why she hadn't called on me to take a look. It's got bigger since then, your dad needs an injection now for sure. And if he's got a fever, that means he needs to get to the clinic as soon as possible."

"I spoke to… to… Padlock's responsible for sorting this," said Stonebreaker.

"But you're the older son, aren't you? No money, I'll give you what you need, three yuan." Goodman knelt on one knee and pulled off a shoe, removing the insole and pulling out three notes. He actually had four and paused a moment, his eyes on the remaining yuan in his shoe. Then he pulled that out as well and gave it all to Stonebreaker.

"I can't, no, that's not right," Stonebreaker said, but Goodman pushed the money into his hand and made to leave. Stunned for a moment, Stonebreaker walked after Goodman. "Here, here, have it back… I can't take your money, it's not right."

"Go on, it's yours, I don't need it, it's only four yuan. I have no need for it. If I had more, there's nowhere for me to go, if I have none, it's the same, nowhere to go, so what's the difference?"

"But still… I can't," Stonebreaker insisted. "I've lived a life without money all these years, I can't take it from someone else now, it's not right…"

"How can you say that? Come, let me tell you something." Goodman began to preach about giving and receiving, about how even someone with nothing can still gift things to others.

"And what might they be?" Stonebreaker asked.

"Well, for starters," Goodman began, "even if a man has nothing, he can still give someone else a smile. The second is words of encouragement, praise and comfort, these can be offered freely. Third, you can give your heart, treat people with openness and sincerity. And then there is kindness. Lastly, you can always help someone by your actions. Lending a hand doesn't need to cost a penny."

"Isn't that all a little hypocritical?" Stonebreaker responded. "I mean, it's the reason Zhu Dagui was sent for re-education wasn't it, he used to…"

Goodman stopped walking and looked at Stonebreaker up and down. "It's best you don't talk to me about your revolutionary matters, I will never understand a thing. Let's leave it here, Granny Silkworm sent word for me to call on her and her grandson. Inkcap seems to be ill, I must go."

Stonebreaker watched as Goodman walked away. Then, as Goodman's words dawned on him, he called out, "Inkcap's sick? Is that even possible?"

Soon, Goodman was striding into the alleyway that led to Inkcap's home. His mind had stayed on Stonebreaker and then suddenly he laughed aloud, and kept laughing until he reached Inkcap's door.

Inkcap was inside, feeding their chickens. When he saw Goodman, he called out, "Gran! Gran!"

Goodman didn't say hello, he only walked up to Inkcap and took hold of his arm. "I guess Stonebreaker was right. You don't look ill at all, do you? Excellent, excellent."

Gran marched out of the kitchen and rushed towards Goodman, offering a chair for him to sit down. She relayed, in detail, Inkcap's recent demeanour, how he'd changed, finally asking, "So what do you think's wrong with him?"

Goodman laughed aloud.

"That's your response, to laugh? Again? I heard you outside already." Gran was clearly shocked.

"I was laughing outside about Stonebreaker, not about you and your concern for your grandson. It's your flour isn't it, your filling for the dumplings, you made them, why do you ask me what's inside?"

"That's true," Gran replied, "and I do know him, but he seems afraid of… of something."

"Everyone is haunted by something. People say the fox fairy, the hedgehog, the snake, all fairies bewitch people, the whole world is haunted by ghosts. Those who are aggrieved have death stalking their steps, those who are angry think evil spirits are lurking in the shadows, those who complain think the ghosts of injustice are waiting to pounce on them. There are ghosts, ghosts, everywhere, haunting everyone. Even things are haunted, liquor bewitches the sober, tobacco consumes those who it entraps, even lustful thoughts of the flesh can become overwhelming. Only when the three realms are clearly distinguished will we humans be free of ghosts and hauntings, spirits and fairies."

"The three realms," said Gran. "I've never heard of them before."

"Of course, of course. The three realms are necessary, man is born of the three realms, Heaven begat humanity's reason, the land gave us our civilisation, and our parents made us. If our minds are clear, then evil thoughts cannot tempt us. If the heart is free of desire and want, then selfishness is no more. And if our bodies are unsullied by the temptations of sin, then we are free of bad habits. Remember, the world, the three realms are full of sins, we don't need to die to be in Hell, life itself can be hell, can't it?"

"Oh, Goodman, I'm afraid you've lost me, I don't understand."

Goodman rose from his seat and went on, "A person must eat the food they make, they must pay for the sins they commit."

Gran remained seated, mulling over Goodman's words. When she raised her head, she was surprised to see he had left. How could he have gone without giving any advice on Inkcap? Before she could develop her thoughts, she heard someone else in the alleyway, a pole they were carrying rapping along the ground. It was Awning, she could see, and he saw her as well.

He stopped and called in through the open gate door, "What was Goodman here for?"

Gran rushed to the gate and closed it swiftly behind her, speaking as she did, "Oh, Awning, hello. Goodman, yes, he was here, but we spoke of nothing important, he was just passing by."

"He's supposed to be in the kiln making china, and here he is out for a stroll and a chinwag, eh?"

"Shouldn't you be at the kiln too?" Gran asked.

"That's why I've got this pole, I'm giving it to Cowbell to use. I've instructed him and Sparks to go and move the corpses that floated down the river."

"Corpses? Who's died?"

"You don't know? The river flooded, everywhere near Luozhen was ravaged, to the east and west, destruction, houses collapsed, inundated with water, many have died. Just now a message came from Xiahewan, Sparks' uncle, apparently, he'd gone to Luozhen and when no one heard from him, they began to worry. It was only when the waters started to recede that they found the body. His in-laws have been crying ever since, but they asked Sparks to collect his body so they could properly mourn it."

"My word, this is the first I've heard of this. What a tragedy. You know his uncle visited Old Kiln just last year. Do you think Sparks and Cowbell can handle the work?"

"There are others coming to help, word's been sent," Awning answered. "What about Inkcap?"

"He's... he's in bed, he's been sick these past three days."

"Well, I think if you send him to help, he'll be good in no time. I sent Once-Upon-A-Time." Awning moved a little closer and asked, "Say, do you have a white rooster?"

"A white... what... no, no, no, only yellow ones."

Gran felt a tightness in her chest, but Goodman's words no longer consumed her mind, nor did thoughts of Inkcap's supposed illness. She walked inside and was greeted by a cloud of dust. Inkcap was busily sweeping the floor and, dancing, it seemed. He was also coughing, choking on the dust. His nose was running, and tears streamed down his face. Initially, she thought that Inkcap had lit fires to dispel evil spirits, but when she asked him what he was doing, he replied that there were too many mosquitoes in the room, dark, ravenous ones, so he thought to smoke them out.

Gran grabbed the broom from his hand, scolding him as she did so, "And how many bloody mosquitoes would it take to kill you, huh? How many bites, you fool?"

She'd lied to Awning about Inkcap being ill. Neither she nor Inkcap could go outside today. Best not to even venture into the courtyard. She moved to the kitchen and put out the stove, then closed the windows, leaving the two of them inside with the dust, coughing.

Inkcap waited until the afternoon before crying out, "Gran, I can't take it any longer."

"Take what?"

"I haven't been out of doors for four days."

"And you won't be going out today, either."

Their only company was a cat that had been playing with a worn shoe. Finally losing interest, it curled up on the floor beside the old shoe and slept. Silence embraced them, but at that same moment they heard someone calling, hurried footsteps were outside their gate and somehow they could tell it was Dazed-And-Confused.

"Baldy Jin! Baldy Jin! A meeting's been called."

"What bloody meeting?" said Baldy Jin. "I've not eaten yet."

"The Captain's called it. You're going to refuse to attend?"

"You mean Bash is back? Didn't you say the road was washed out? How can he have come back?"

"I didn't say anything of the sort, I bet you it was that fucker Almost-There who said it. He probably hoped Bash was washed away in the flood, the bastard."

Inkcap, listening to the exchange, whispered to Gran, "Did you hear? Bash has returned."

Her hands busily cutting paper, Gran answered, "So what if he's back, do you have thoughts about going to the meeting? Is that it?"

"Not a chance."

She'd cut out the five poisonous creatures from myth: a scorpion, a viper, a centipede, a lizard and a toad. Then she thought of the *taisui* gods, but couldn't think of how to cut them out.

"What do they look like, the *taisui* gods… do you know, Inkcap?"

Inkcap did not answer.

She asked again, but he remained silent. She called into the bedroom once more and then walked to find her grandson. He was sitting in bed, his eyes transfixed on something outside the window, but she couldn't see what. She waved her hand in front of his eyes to break him from his trance.

"Eh?" Inkcap began. "I think they're back early from moving those corpses."

"You gave me a fright, there. Our house is not your prison, all right? If you want to go out, go on. When it's dark, go out then."

Inkcap laughed. "I wonder where Bash went to be back only now?"

SIXTY-THREE

BASH HAD BEEN TO LUOZHEN. Naturally, he had his reasons for going there. First, he wanted to know what the town revolutionary committee was doing to revive its activities after recent difficulties. He needed to understand the dynamics of the situation, as it were, in order to work out how to proceed back in Old Kiln. Second, he wanted to get the United Command and its supporters across a dozen villages up and down the river to further combat the activities and arrogance of the Red Blades.

Unfortunately, what he learnt in Luozhen was that the revolutionary committee activities were essentially paralysed, and that conflict was raging between the United Command and the United Headquarters, most especially over which faction should have more seats on the committee in the first place. Initially, the United Command had been at the vanguard of revolutionary activities, but now, the United Headquarters had begun to surpass them in influence and power. Bash and Tag-Along were caught in the middle of this conflagration. The argument was one for the record books of Luozhen, at least regarding the Cultural Revolution and its general tumult. Insults were exchanged, followed by shoving and competing marches, each faction desperate to prove its revolutionary vigour. These activities were eventually followed by open conflict, fist fighting leading to more and more violent encounters. Ultimately, blood was drawn, people were killed, and guns were fired. Bash, for his part, felt obliged to participate directly in the open hostilities. When the United Headquarters went on the back foot, they withdrew from Luozhen to recoup their strength and also cut off the town from outside interference that might come in support of the United Command. Naturally, the United Command seized the opportunity to pursue the United Headquarters, with both factions eventually digging in on either side of the western bridge that spanned the town. That evening, as expected, reinforcements for the United Headquarters arrived from the county, more than a hundred men, in fact, equipped with guns and explosives. The number of men and range of equipment came as a surprise to the United Command. They, too, sent out a request for reinforcements, but time was not on their side, and they subsequently chose to withdraw. Just as they were strategising their retreat, however, the skies opened, and rain began to pour. Torrential, violent rain, great sheets of it that covered the landscape and obscured visibility. The river soon swelled, breaking its banks and ravaging the town. The flood also had the effect of saving the United Command from certain doom, for in the chaos of natural disaster, they were able to withdraw with minimal losses. Despite their strategising, however, it was not an orderly retreat. In many ways, they resembled a headless fly, unsure of where to go and what to do.

 At least, this was the story Bash had been telling Baldy Jin, Dazed-And-Confused, Iron Bolt and the few other Hammerheads present. The flood had started in the middle of the night, but by dawn, he had rounded up Tag-Along and three other men, and together they'd fled to some place called Cattle Corner Stockade. From this vantage point, they could see the rushing water, at least ten feet high, Bash claimed, that seemingly whistled as it rampaged over the land, submerging everything in its path. There was no single head to the floodwaters, it just seemed to stretch in every direction, multiple heads, white and hideous, pushing up against cottage doors before bursting them open, drowning everything inside, and then crashing out past doors and walls, carrying off whatever it could, cabinets, wardrobes, chests, pots and pans, anything and everything, as though nothing could stop it. They also saw, if only momentarily, people swallowed up in the water, hands and feet flashing before them before being sucked down. Some were seen grasping hold of trees, items of furniture, whatever they could to stay afloat, but then they, too, would be consumed by the rushing waters. Screams could be heard, despite the din of the flood. Panicked, frantic, crazy screams of people running towards higher ground, but the water was unrelenting; it chased them down as though hungry for souls until the screams lingered only in their memories. They were all stunned by the carnage as though it were unreal. They wondered whether they were dreaming, but as more and more of the landscape collapsed around them, as houses were devoured, they knew their only option was to scramble even further up, to get to higher ground.

In those two days, tragedy lay all around. While the flood had passed, the remaining river water resembled an open grave. They saw limbs floating by, detached from bodies, debris and refuse everywhere. In one still-standing tree, they noticed a young woman and for a moment they were hopeful, perhaps she had survived. But upon closer inspection, they could see death had already claimed her, nothing more than a corpse entangled by a lonely tree. She was pretty, thought Bash, and in a pang of grief for a stranger, he told Tag-Along to get her down, but he refused. Undeterred, Bash tried himself to free her, but couldn't. Defeated, he only managed to shift her beautiful face to make her death seem a little less ugly.

On the third day after the flood, they finally reached a nearby commune that had thus far been spared. It was only a small town, but now it was filled to bursting with refugees. The rain continued to fall, causing everyone to be on edge. In the commune guest house, only a single room was unoccupied. Containing just one double bed and a single quilt, they could tell that everything was damp. Five of them piled in nevertheless – there was nowhere else to go. Exhausted by their ordeal, all five fell asleep quickly as though death were finally claiming them. But in the middle of the night, one of them woke, his skin aflame and itchy. He immediately assumed there must be bedbugs and pulled off the corner of the quilt he had to cover him. Lighting a lamp, he discovered that the bed was infested, tiny insects gorging themselves on the five tired men. By now, each man's skin was blotched with red sores and pimples. The dirty floodwaters had made them all sick.

Bash was still scratching as he told them his story. The situation in Luozhen was grim. Not only had the flood ravaged the town, but the United Command had lost much of its power and influence. Naturally, this would affect things here in Old Kiln, he told them. Most likely, the Red Blades would seize the opportunity to advance their interests. They were in control of the kiln already, he noted. If they proceeded to produce and sell the porcelain, then the Zhu clan would be strengthened even more at the expense of the Hei clan and everyone else not named Zhu. And since he'd been away, only the Red Blades had been active. To his mind, they'd been putting on quite the show, too, like the Soviet Revisionists trying to invade Xinjiang, just itching to fight, assuming they'd mop the floor with their enemy. Naturally, as their leader, he was busily planning the Hammerheads' next move, stressing the need for action. As if to underline his point, Bash stood up, cut an imposing figure, scratched his back and then sat down once more. If stealing cattle was a nonstarter, he told them, then they had to think of something else, target the production of porcelain, perhaps. Should somebody write something? Bash stopped his oration and stood up again. He scratched his back and returned to his seat. Then lifted himself up and moved towards the wall to better scratch himself.

"Whatever it is," he shouted to the other Hammerheads, "we must do something, we have to respond. We cannot let them continue as they are." A piece of wall plaster fell to the floor as Bash rubbed his back against it, harder and harder.

"Itchy, isn't it? Here, let me help," said Baldy Jin, standing up to move closer to Bash. Extending his arm, he reached his hand underneath Bash's jacket.

"Have you ever had beriberi," Bash asked him.

"Yeah, I have."

"It feels like that, even the scratching doesn't stop the itch. Up, down, left, right, it's driving me fucking mad."

Baldy Jin hadn't stopped before Dazed-And-Confused came over to them. "Here, let me," he said. "I'll give you a scratch." He started at Bash's shoulders and made his way down.

It seemed to help a little, at least on his back, but then other parts of his body itched. Finally, Bash shouted, "Enough! Stop, enough!" His own fingers raked across his body, his chest, his stomach, everywhere he could reach. His flesh was on fire, but his mind had to return to the most important thing, their plans for action. "So what are we going to do? Whatever it is, we have to make sure everyone is here, every Hammerhead in the village, you hear, that's a must."

"Yes sir!" they yelled.

Baldy Jin, Dazed-And-Confused, Iron Bolt and the other Hammerheads left, each on orders to assemble all the members. Bash remained, his back once more against the wall, busily scratching.

Iron Bolt went straight home and told his wife the story Bash had told him. He also told her about Bash's skin rash and incessant scratching.

"Scratching won't do him any good," his wife said. "It only makes things worse."

"I know," Iron Bolt answered, "just look at my fingers. I helped him scratch and all I got was blood under my nails and him still yelling about how much it itches."

"He needs to wash himself in boiled mint leaf water, that'll help."

"You should go to the mountain tomorrow and pick some mint, then."

"You know my leg's been hurting these past couple of days and yet this is what you tell me? You're more concerned about Bash than me. What is he, your master or something?"

"We have to be concerned about our leader, understand?"

By that afternoon, Iron Bolt began to feel itchy. Pulling up his shirt, he discovered six or seven small, reddish bumps. They itched and burned. His wife gathered some stalks of grain, stripped off the outer layers and bundled three or four together. She took them outside, planning to hang them on a tree in the courtyard.

"Get a ladder, will you?" she called out.

Iron Bolt reappeared a moment later, holding a ladder, his body continuing to itch. He placed it against the tree and his wife climbed up. Holding it with both hands for balance, Iron Bolt soon released one hand to scratch his back. Unsurprisingly, the ladder fell, and his wife toppled to the ground, hurling curses at him in the process.

Iron Bolt went into the mountains to collect the mint himself. On the path up, he walked past Baldy Jin's home, seeing him busily feeding his pig,

"How's your pig, then?" asked Iron Bolt.

"Never got sick in the first place," answered Baldy Jin.

"Didn't you say that…"

Baldy Jin laughed but continued feeding his pig. With his free hand, he grabbed his crotch in an apparent vulgar gesture.

"Damn hooligan," Iron Bolt responded. "What is it, got a hard-on in the presence of a sow?"

"Fuck off, it's just itchy, that's all."

"Did it start after Bash's meeting?"

"Yeah, it did. You too?"

Iron Bolt lifted his shirt, exposing the red blotches on his skin. Baldy Jin undid his trousers, revealing the same red pimples covering his legs all the way up to his crotch. Even his prick was pimpled.

"They fucking burn," said Iron Bolt. "Bash spread them to us, didn't he?"

"Yeah, not only did he give us news of the revolution, he gave us this too. It's not a venereal disease, is it?"

"Are you saying he lied to us, that it's not beriberi that he picked up in that commune but something he got from Apricot?"

"That's not what I said. I mean, he was gone for days, suppose he met with someone else, some… dirty prostitute."

"But he's got Apricot, why bother with some floozy?" Iron Bolt asked.

"Yeah, but you're just thinking Apricot is enough, I don't think one woman is enough for him, no matter who the woman is. And there are so many women in Luozhen, women of all kinds," Baldy Jin offered slyly.

"And you think he's the same as you? Always looking for a hole to put his dick in, is that it?"

"No two people are the same, I grant you that, but the more… let's say, capable a man is, the stronger he is. And as you know, there're a lot of roosters, a lot of cocks in Old Kiln. Look at Zhu Dagui's rooster, does it not go wild when it sees a hen?"

"You dirty fucker, you. Besides, I've been back and forth on the road to Luozhen many times, there's no woman as fine as Apricot."

"But Apricot isn't a city girl, no matter what you might say."

"Are you saying Bash wants to marry a city girl?"

"I didn't say that exactly, but you have to admit it's a different kind of lifestyle."

"But… Apricot's pregnant."

"No need to bring that up. Bash'll do whatever he wants, and what we say doesn't mean shit," shouted Baldy Jin. "We're nothing, yeah, except infected."

"It's not a venereal disease," Iron Bolt affirmed, "it's beriberi, from the flood. I'm going to get mint leaves. I'll bring them to HQ this evening to boil them up in water."

That night, at their headquarters, the Hammerheads bathed in hot mint water. After they were finished, Baldy Jin took a container of water back with him so that Half-Stick could wash as well. She, too, had contracted beriberi and had been scratching them with a stick.

Unfortunately, the mint bath had no effect. Everyone who had become infected was still plagued by intense itchiness. They couldn't sit still, couldn't move without wanting to scratch. Everything and anything annoyed them. Even a simple word could set them off, ranting and shouting, complaining and cursing. Bash went to see Apricot, but conscious of her condition and his infectiousness, he stood outside her courtyard gate and tossed stones at her window, trying to draw her attention. No response came, her courtyard was quiet. He rapped on the gate frame, once, twice, three times. Then he stopped and listened. Hearing no reply, he knocked again. Finally, Apricot opened the door. Unlike many other villagers, Apricot didn't have a dog at home, only a cat. When it saw Bash, it whined as though in greeting. Then it sauntered off, jumped onto the windowsill, curled up and pretended to sleep. In truth, its ears were trained on the night for usually this was when the rats came out to scrounge for food. Each night they would invade Apricot's home, and on this night, they went first for the cooking oil, only to find none. Then they attacked the container meant to hold eggs. Finding one, a single rat grabbed it and ran off, only to have its tail caught in the mouth of one of its companions, anxious to have the egg for itself. The egg fell and rolled, hitting the floor and cracking into a messy pile of shell, egg white and yolk. The vermin began to battle among themselves, biting and scratching at each other. The cat couldn't tell if the noise was being made by the man at the door or by rats in the house, so it pretended not to hear anything and remained on the windowsill. At the gate, Bash and Apricot were arguing. Finally, Bash slammed his fist against the door and left. In the dark, Apricot threw a rag at the windowsill, striking her cat that was still pretending to sleep.

After leaving Apricot's house, Bash could feel the fire grow in his belly. He was furious. He passed by Useless's house and banged on the door. He was going to order Useless to round up the other Hammerheads and tell them they were needed at their HQ. Given the hour, Useless had already turned in, but when he heard the knocking at the door and realised it was Bash, he was overjoyed to be called upon by his Hammerhead leader. Still, his first words did not reflect this joy.

"But... you mean right now? It's the middle of the night, you want to call a meeting now?"

"You don't want to help, do you? You'd rather sleep, is that it?" Bash shouted.

Useless's mum, who'd been awakened by the knocking, anxiously interjected, "Go, go, you must, how can you not? Go!"

Useless hurriedly got dressed, mumbling to himself, "But it's those with little sleep who ghosts choose to haunt."

"That may be true," said his mother, overhearing him, "but they won't bother you. It's Bash who's come to call on you, that makes all the difference."

"I guess you're right. Yeah, I know, I've got to be a man about it, after all."

What Useless did not expect, however, was that when he called on Caretaker's home, he would discover the man beating his wife. She was an obese woman, too overweight to fight back, but flabby enough to be able to take a beating, or so it was said. The man had removed his shoe and was slapping her with it. She screamed in response, offering curses as well, especially about her husband's mother. Needless to say, she did not get on well with her mother-in-law, who would pretend not to notice when her son beat his wife. Only when her daughter-in-law began to curse her did she acknowledge what was happening,

"Why, you dirty, fat cow. You're urging him to start hitting me, his own wife!"

Her son grabbed his wife and dragged her into the kitchen. His intent seemed to be to stuff her into one of the earthen jars, but her arse was far too large to fit. He pushed her on top of the jar and it toppled under her girth, cracking and spilling its contents onto the floor, along with his plump wife and the broken shards of the container.

At that moment, Useless opened the door and walked in, shouting at the man who seemed unconcerned by his arrival, "Are you trying to kill her? Stop that, dammit. The captain is calling a meeting. Now!"

Without offering another word, Useless made to leave. The man glanced at his wife, then dusted off his hands and followed Useless out of the door. A little later, they arrived at Baldy Jin's home. All he had on was a hat. His chest and belly, his legs and his crotch were bare. And pimpled.

"Fuck, sitting in little but your birthday suit, with the door open? What the hell is wrong with you?" Useless shouted, seemingly disgusted.

"It's my home, my courtyard. What do I need clothes for?" Baldy Jin's voice was sharp and surly.

"Hey, now, no need for that tone."

Just then, the window opened and out flew a pair of socks, shirt, trousers and a belt. Last of all came a pair of yellowish, military-issued shoes, which landed on Baldy Jin's head. Useless and the other man laughed at the scene.

"I guess she wants you out of here, eh?" said Useless.

"Ha, who's driving who out? You're here to get me, she's just giving me my clothes."

Half-Stick then called out from the open window, "Don't bother coming back here to sleep and turning my stomach. Sleep over there with your friends, you hear?"

"A man drinks to get drunk, he marries a woman to have someone to fuck, and yet all I get is the first part of that deal."

Half-Stick again shouted through the open window, "I'd say you're better off dirtying your prick with your friend's arseholes, you bastard!"

Baldy Jin had no rebuttal ready. His shoulders slumped.

"What the fuck is going on?" said Caretaker. "I was fighting with my old lady and then we come here at it's the same. Come on, let's go, Bash has called for us. Let's not waste our time with these bitches."

Putting on his clothes, Baldy Jin answered, "You were fighting too, eh? Cunts, that's what they are, cause more trouble than we do."

By the time the three men arrived at the Hammerheads' headquarters, Dazed-And-Confused, Tag-Along, Big Root, Lucky, Iron Bolt and a few others were already there. Bash had begun the meeting and was talking about ways to stop the kiln ovens. Some of the Hammerheads were clamouring in vague terms for class struggle. Others suggested they seize Lightkeeper and launch a criticism of him, especially as he was the one being used by the Red Blades to light the ovens. He'd probably even joined them, so struggling against him would, at least, put a temporary stop to any kiln work. Some raised objections, however, saying it would take too long and, besides, they'd already produced thousands of pieces of china. Seizing Lightkeeper, now that he had other men working with him, wouldn't put the fires out. Perhaps it would be better to start producing porcelain themselves?

"And which of us knows how to fire porcelain? Who can run a kiln?" one of the Hammerheads said. "The only way to stop them is to take over the kiln ourselves. That way the porcelain becomes ours, like Noodle Fish marrying Stonebreaker's mum and having a baby, what belongs to the wife becomes the husband's after marriage."

No agreement could be reached, so voices and anger grew. One second, they were shouting at each other, the next they were scratching their backs, legs and crotches. But no resolution was found. No one's flesh stopped itching, causing all the attendees to grow increasingly irate. Some took to howling, shouting curses into the night, curses that carried on the air throughout the village.

That same night, Awning lay in bed, his skin aflame with itching too. He was scratching all over, trying to relieve some of his discomfort. His wife was in the same predicament, skin red and pimply, her fingers tracking over her body in a vain effort to quell the pain and irritation. When Awning heard the howls coming from the Hammerheads' HQ, he couldn't help himself from offering his own in reply.

Soon, Millstone, Sparks and almost everyone surnamed Zhu had fallen to the same affliction. Inkcap, however, remained unaffected. He had no idea how so many in the village had contracted this itch, but when it was time for meals, he would take his bowl of gruel and wander through the alleyways, watching others as they ate and scratched at the same time.

"Not scratching, Inkcap?" one villager asked.

"And why would I?"

"Fucking hell, can you imagine that? I can't stop scratching and this little fucker is walking free and fine!" Upset at this travesty, the villager raced towards Inkcap, seemingly intent on spreading the infection.

Gleaning his motive, Inkcap ran away, throwing his bowl of gruel onto the ground in the process.

"Get over here you little shit!" the villager shouted after him. "Where are you running off to?" But he did not chase after Inkcap. Oddly, he came to a halt and stopped scratching.

In the evening, Gran was washing clothes in the spring. Two other women were doing the same, the wives of Millstone and Iron Bolt. No one spoke for some time. It was only when Iron Bolt's wife spoke to her first that Gran opened her mouth. The other lady had asked about treating beriberi.

"Well," Gran started, "boiled mint water often works."

"Tried that, it was no good. Here, look," and she lifted her blouse to reveal itchy blotches.

"That's because that's not beriberi," Gran answered immediately.

"If it's not beriberi, then what is it?"

"I'm not sure, I don't recognise it, but it's sure not beriberi."

A moment later, Millstone's wife moved closer to Gran. She had overheard their conversation. "You're saying it's not beriberi, is that right? It's not some... venereal disease, is it?"

"You've got them too?"

"Yes, Millstone, Awning, Sparks, all of them are afflicted."

"I said only the Heis had it," Iron Bolt's wife chipped in, "but so do the Zhu clan. Granny Silkworm, if you can't recognise what it is, do you suppose it's something out of the ordinary, an unknown sickness or something?"

"What do you mean by out of the ordinary? Sickness is a part of life, and just because I don't recognise it doesn't mean a thing... You ought to ask Goodman."

Then she left, even though her clothes were not fully washed. She didn't dare wash hers in the same water as theirs, scared she would bring the affliction home with her.

Before long, both Hammerheads and Red Blades knew that each faction was afflicted by the same contagion, and this started tongues wagging.

"You suppose it's a revolutionary sickness?" Dazed-And-Confused wondered.

"The Red Blades are no revolutionaries, they're nothing but imperial revivalists."

Bash's mind was tormented. "This disease came from that commune, I caught it first. It's natural I passed it on to all of you, the Hammerheads, but how did the Red Blades get it?"

That led him to think there must be a mole inside the Hammerheads, a Red Blade spy. He recalled that for the last several times, whenever they planned a new action, the Red Blades learnt about it almost immediately. Mulling this over to himself, he decided he had to tell the Hammerheads of his suspicions, despite how hard it would be to hear.

Baldy Jin responded first to the accusation. "You think we've got a traitor in our midst, a spy?"

"I think so, yes," answered Bash.

"But who? Who do you think it is? You have to tell us to avoid rumours running rampant."

"I won't. I have my suspicions, yes, but I want to watch them a little more first."

Baldy Jin said nothing further, but he did leave and return home. Half-Stick was out. The pot on the stove was unwashed. The chicken shit in the courtyard was piled high. The pig was unfed and hungry. Who was the traitor, the enemy within? he wondered. Bash had spread the disease to them, but none of them, not Iron Bolt, Stonebreaker, Dazed-And-Confused or Tag-Along would spread this to the Zhu clan, so who could it be? Suddenly, his heart skipped a beat. Could it be Half-Stick? Was she still involved with Awning somehow? His chest grew tight. Finally, she returned but said nothing to him. She only went to the toilet and seemed to spend ages there.

When she finally emerged, Baldy Jin asked her, "Where the hell were you?"

"The privy, obviously."

"I don't mean just now, I mean before you came home. Why has the house been left in such a mess?"

"I was in the field, our plot, what's it to you?"

"Our plot?" He looked her up and down, then continued, "Out in the field with new clothes on?"

"Well, it's all I've got. What else can I wear?"

"It looks rather like you've been out on the mountain slopes, that would explain the brambles in your hair. But you say you were in the field?"

Half-Stick ran her fingers through her hair, pulling free bits of bramble. Her ears grew noticeably red. Only a few houses in Old Kiln had brambles nearby. The only ones he could think of were Barndoor's, Apricot's and… Awning's. They were adjacent to his personal plot too. Baldy Jin had been fond of bluster, everyone knew. If she chose to curse him, he would, however, remain calm. If she chose to ignore him, he wouldn't ask her anything more, wouldn't chase the issue. He never thought for an instant she would be the one to ask him a question.

"He had to ask me something," Half-Stick began. "I just went to speak to him, nothing to that is there?"

Baldy Jin could feel the fire grow in his belly. "Nothing? You say nothing? I told you the Red Blades have contracted the same disease as us, but how did they get it? I'll tell you, you fucking gave it to them, that's how!"

He raised his hand to strike Half-Stick, and she raised her hands to ready a strike of her own. They crashed together and began to wrestle, knocking over furniture in the process, a chair, a table, bowls and water containers. When they finally came to a stop at the threshold of the door, their faces were bruised and swelling, so too their arms and legs. They each stood on either side of the threshold and continued to curse and scratch.

Half-Stick and Awning were still secretly involved. Everyone in the Hammerheads knew it, but none of them would say so openly. The only noticeable change was with Baldy Jin's demeanour; he'd become even more submissive and obsequious to Bash.

Despite showing signs much later than the others, for Awning the itch was worse. Small red blotches developed all over his skin, across his extremities, in between his fingers, down his lower back, throughout his crotch. Even his cock was left at the mercy of the itch, with red, blistering pimples popping out. Scratching did little to assuage the itch so that every movement was turmoil, every step a reason to fly into a rage and curse up a blue streak. At whom, it didn't matter. Those working at the kiln were also plagued by the itch. Unable to stop working, however, they suffered through the itch and Awning's verbal abuse, no one daring to even grunt in response to his tirades. But behind his back, they cursed Half-Stick for giving Awning whatever it was that they now all suffered from. Then their minds turned to Baldy Jin, and they cursed him too. If he'd known early on about Half-Stick and Awning, why hadn't he done something to stop them, at least before all of this happened? Might it be that the Hammerheads had planned this? Did they want the Red Blades to be infected? Was it all some conspiracy? Awning heard what the others were saying about Half-Stick, but he knew there was no way he could defend her. He had to keep his inner feelings bottled up. Naturally, this only made him surlier, more ill-tempered than ever.

"Awning," Soupspoon finally said to him. "Don't get so worked up, the kiln is working at a fever pitch, the stores of coal will last us for ages, everything is humming along nicely. I can handle the fires. Here, let me give you a scratch. You sit there and I'll sit here, you can scratch my sores and I'll scratch yours. We'll look like a couple of hairless monkeys tending to each other's infestations."

Soupspoon paused his words, mulling something over, before speaking again, "Did you hear? Granny Silkworm doesn't believe it's beriberi. She might be right, I've had beriberi before, and it wasn't this bad. Something we've never seen, perhaps?"

"Something fucking weird, I'll wager... perhaps you ought to visit Goodman, see if he knows what the devil this is."

Soupspoon did as commanded and called upon Goodman. A little while later, after the kiln had been re-fired, he returned with Goodman in tow. Awning instructed the older man to essentially set up shop on the kiln grounds to see if he could identify the infection. There were so many infected villagers, and so many of them had their own impressions of Goodman. Some noted the fact that Goodman had never worked in the kiln, and therefore questioned how he was to be awarded work points for what he was planning to do now. Tactfully, Goodman offered to withdraw from the kiln; he was happy, after all, to remain in his mountain home tending his garden of gourds and pumpkins, the ones he'd planted himself after moving up into the mountains. The pumpkins, in fact, had grown large, he told them, and were quite delicious. The gourds, on the other hand, he couldn't eat, for they'd grown hard and inedible. He had already pulled them out and cracked them open, scattering their seeds across the wall that rimmed his small temple home and hanging the hardened skins on some string. When Soupspoon had arrived, Goodman was seeing off a villager from Xiahewan, a man by the name of Chen Fawang, or something like that. He was carrying a number of the gourds, Soupspoon had noticed. Despite not remembering his name exactly, Soupspoon did know that the man from Xiahewan was the primary school principal, a teacher, at any rate, one from several generations of book learners in the area.

"Hey, that Chen fella," Soupspoon said, "Chen Fawang, yeah, that's his name, what was he doing here?"

"Schools are closed," Goodman replied, "so he's got nothing to do. He came to learn a little about illnesses and how to diagnose them."

Soupspoon pulled down a gourd hanging from the wall.

"I don't imagine you want that," said Goodman.

"I'm just looking at it. I know it's not edible, wouldn't want it even if you offered it to me." Soupspoon hesitated a moment, then furrowed his brow and stared at Goodman. "You're quite the braggart, aren't you? This Chen Fawang, what's he then, nothing, belly full of black water's what he is, here to study illnesses. Ha, what tosh."

"Say what you will."

"Up here by yourself," Soupspoon continued, "I imagine you're just full to bursting, so much to talk about to anyone who comes by. Probably can't stand not having someone here, regular like, to listen to you."

Ever the gentleman, Goodman gestured for Soupspoon to sit on a straw mat. Soupspoon declined and continued leaning against the wall, scratching himself continuously.

"Did you know that Chen Fawang is fifty years old this year?" Goodman said. "Primary school principal in Xiahewan, in the very same school his grandfather helped establish, for generations his family's been educators."

"I knew that," Soupspoon offered derisively.

"Does good food nourish the mind, you think?"

"Makes sense, I suppose. But… I don't know… maybe not…"

"He's got four children, three sons and a daughter, did you know that? His oldest was killed not long after they built the county road, struck by a car. His second son, when he was only twelve, contracted some sickness and died. His remaining son and daughter – she's older than the boy – they're in Luozhen, middle school… if schools were open. Quite a well-off household, I must say, perhaps too well-off. He didn't live in the school dormitory, you know, didn't need to, stayed at the party guest house in Luozhen, sort of above everything and everyone, you catch my meaning? But then the Cultural Revolution happened, schools were closed, and they had nothing to do, not him, nor his remaining children. His youngest son, especially, well, trouble found him, he took up with some other kids, a bad lot by all accounts, got up to no good, wandering around all over the place. His father worried, naturally, felt that some misfortune would befall him, but what was he to do? As it happened, soon after, a commune officer by the name of Zhang came to find me, needed me to see someone who was sick. They put me up in the party guest house, the same one Chen lived in, and that's where I met him. He was surprised to see, you know, a dirty-looking farmer like me in the guest house. He asked around, discovered I'd been asked to diagnose an illness and he thought this was all rather absurd. Science, he thought, had replaced superstition, so why was I there? To him, I was only some witch doctor, a shaman, or some other such nonsense medicine man. Of course, his curiosity wouldn't leave things like that, so one evening, I think the second one I was there, he concocted a reason to come and see me. I could tell he wanted to test me, if only secretly, find out what I was really all about, I suppose. And you know what? I convinced him. He believed in me. Even ended up asking me what he should do about his youngest son. So I said to him, faith, trust, that's the most important. Then I added that he'd lost this all-important trust, that from this day forward, if he wished to reclaim it, he had to protect the sanctity of learning, that he couldn't put on airs like he'd been doing, that even though the schools were all closed, he had to be a teacher. What about the loafers and hooligans who'd seemingly co-opted his son? Well, I spoke to the boy, I told him he'd had his fun, but now he had to return home, that his father was there, in all seriousness, waiting for him, with the proper amount of mutual trust and respect, a teacher. And you know what? The boy listened to me. Chen Fawang couldn't believe it at first. He wondered what I had done. But he couldn't deny his son had changed and he had me to thank for that. This is how we began our... association, I suppose you could call it. He's asked me several times since to come and talk about things. I've ended up giving him advice about all manner of subjects, most especially about how to live properly and follow the right way, that evil is all around, and it needs to be regularly combatted, that people are far too prone to fall victim to it, greed, money, all these kinds of pleasures of the world, they distract from people treating others properly. He even started tutoring kids in his own home, first a couple, then more. He truly became an educator by giving up the trappings of education–"

"Tutoring you say," said Soupspoon, who until then had been listening as patiently as he could. "I don't know anything about Chen doing this, but how about you start tutoring me?"

"I don't think you quite understand what I've been saying. Wanting for more, greed, status, prestige, these things pervade the world and lead to suffering."

"Yeah, yeah, lots of wolves, little meat to eat, it's all just piss in the wind."

Goodman was dumbfounded by Soupspoon's words and could only look at him. Thinking there was little else he could say, Goodman stood up and poured himself some water.

"Something to drink?" he asked. Not waiting for an answer, he lifted his cup to his mouth and downed the water, smiling darkly to himself as he did so. Satiated, he asked Soupspoon, "So why did you call on me, are you here to take me to the kiln?"

"To work at the kiln means getting work points, but to do that, you need to be a Red Blade and you're not, unless you were to become one."

"It's better if I don't belong to either faction, I think."

"You dirty fucking traitor, eh, sly old fox. You reckon you can work both sides off each other, don't you?"

"No, no, that's not it at all. My only role is to give advice on illnesses, to both sides, I don't discriminate."

"If that's the case, why haven't you given us any advice on this bloody itch?"

"But all you and your lot have been doing is scratching and complaining, no one's asked me for any advice."

"You knew already that we had this problem?" Soupspoon removed his jacket so Goodman could better see the red blotches covering his skin.

"Oh," said Goodman. "This… this is bad, quite serious in fact."

"Is it a venereal disease? Has the whole village contracted a fucking venereal disease?"

"No, it isn't a venereal disease, it's scabies, but I've not seen any this bad for at least ten years. This is caused by general uncleanliness and dampness, excessive dampness, which is strange, since it hasn't rained that much here, at least not enough to cause an outbreak of scabies like this. Where did you get it?"

"There was a flood in Luozhen, a big one, and Bash was in the middle of it, he brought it back to Old Kiln with him."

"Well, scabies is easy to catch if you sleep next to someone with it. It's quite contagious."

"That explains it," Soupspoon shouted.

"There's an old saying. Scabies are like a dragon, they start with the fingers, then encircle the body before nesting nest in the crotch."

"Is there a cure?"

"If they're on your face, you're supposed to wrap it in a mat."

"And how in the hell is that supposed to help?"

"If it's not on your face, then a sulphur ointment should work."

"And where are we going get a sulphur ointment round here?"

"I'm afraid that's something you're going to have to figure out for yourselves."

Kaihe's general store did not have any sulphur powder, let alone ointment, so Awning despatched Noisy to Luozhen to get some. Unfortunately, there was no sulphur to be had in the town's general store. The proprietor did tell Noisy, however, that he had seen some in the commune shop so Noisy headed over there.

On the day Noisy left for Luozhen, Inkcap and Cowbell were out on the mountain slopes raiding wild peach trees. The trees were some of the oldest in the area, their roots deep into the cliff, their trunks standing proudly, long, thick branches reaching into the air. In the first month of every new year, Gran would snap off a couple of these branches, crack them into smaller pieces and bundle them together. She would then give them to Inkcap to keep in his pocket. She told him they would ward off disaster and calm evil spirits. Goodman disagreed and told Inkcap the only talisman that would ward off disaster and calm evil spirits was the charred remains of a wild peach tree ripped asunder by lightning. Naturally, this advice led Inkcap to keep a close eye on the wild peach trees, at least every time there was lightning, to see if any of them was struck. But year after year, the lightning always seemed to spare them.

The trees Inkcap and Cowbell were climbing in had been left alone in the previous spring. Unlike other peach trees in the area that had been grafted with other species to yield earlier fruit, these wild trees had remained untouched throughout the spring and into the summer. But when the other trees had yet to blossom, the wild ones had, their flowers a brilliant crimson colour that sparkled in the sun. Strangely, however, these same flowers seemed to linger longer than they should. Like an upset spirit haunting the land of the living, they took an especially long time to give up their petals and grow into peaches. In fact, it was not until now, late autumn, when most other trees had had their fruit picked and eaten, their seeds planted, that the wild peaches were ready to be consumed. But even then, their flesh was not the most delectable. Rather it was dry and tough, so the kernel was the only useful part of the fruit. And that's why Inkcap and Cowbell were there now, picking the dried, wild peaches, careful not to climb up onto the limbs that would not hold their weight, and instead using slingshots to knock the peaches off, one by one. As they practised their aim, planning to collect the fruit from the ground once they'd procured enough, Apricot came along.

Apricot's face had always had a reddish glow to it, the boys thought, but now it was especially freckled. Her gait was no longer so nimble, nor did she have the same bounce. When she reached the wild peach trees, she paused and sat down beneath them to catch her breath. This was when she noticed Inkcap and Cowbell.

"Boys," she called to them, "can I have one of these wild peaches?"

"They're too old and dry to eat," said Inkcap. "How about I give you some of the nut inside instead?"

"I won't eat that."

Inkcap had a peach in his hand, which he now rubbed against his trousers, trying to remove the fuzz. The peach hair proved more resilient than he thought, depositing only just enough of its fibres to cause Inkcap to itch.

Inkcap then turned to Cowbell. "I heard most of the village is suffering from some itch. You don't suppose it's peach hairs, do you?"

"No, it's not. It's scabies, not at all the same."

"Don't talk nonsense, boys," said Apricot. "Of course it's not the same, what itch would be?"

"So you don't have the itch?" Inkcap asked Apricot.

"I'm not full of mites, so why would I itch?"

"I'm not sure I believe that," Cowbell interjected. "How did you not catch them from Bash?"

Apricot coughed and spat up some phlegm.

"You don't want the peach kernel," Cowbell continued, "because you've already got a sour stomach, yeah?"

Apricot coughed again. Then a third time, her phlegm landing right in front of Cowbell. She quickly covered her mouth, lifted herself up and continued walking. She didn't say anything more to the boys, who only watched her trudge off up the mountain.

When she was out of earshot, Cowbell hissed, "Bitch spat at me!"

By the time they finished, Apricot could barely be seen in the distance. But Kaihe and Ever-Obedient had shown up close to the millstone near the mountain, busily chatting about something. To Inkcap and Cowbell's eyes, it looked as though Ever-Obedient was giving Kaihe money, but for what they couldn't tell. All they could see was Kaihe counting the notes Ever-Obedient had given him. Then, when he lifted his head and noticed two figures approaching, he tucked the money away inside his jacket and pretended as though nothing unusual was going on.

"Go on and count your money," Inkcap called out. "We didn't see anything."

"Little shit," Kaihe swore under his breath then changed his tone when he noticed Cowbell next to Inkcap. "Oh, Cowbell, I didn't recognise you at first, what have you lads been up to?"

"Picking wild peaches," answered Cowbell. "Even offered one to Apricot, well, the kernel at least, and you know what she did? She spat at me."

"She spat at you?" Kaihe responded. "I don't believe that, you don't know what you're talking about."

"And how the hell do I not know? She's in with Bash, isn't she, locked lips with him enough, probably thinks like him, too, that I left the Hammerheads to join the Red Blades!"

"Don't you go talking about any factions in front of me," Kaihe shouted. "Hey, Inkcap, you want to come to Luozhen with me, I've got to get some sulphur powder to make soap."

"Sulphur powder to make soap?" Inkcap said. "What for?"

"For the scabies, washing in sulphur soap will get rid of them."

"You just told me not to talk about either faction," Cowbell interjected, "so why are you off to Luozhen to get sulphur powder?"

"Well, does the man who sells knives expect his customers to be murderers? Ha! Inkcap, coming or not?"

Cowbell answered for both of them: "Sure, why not."

"But I didn't ask you. You can't be trusted."

"Who said I'm going with you, I'm keeping Inkcap company," Cowbell shouted.

PART FIVE
WINTER

冬

SIXTY-FOUR

AWNING TOLD KAIHE TO BUY THIRTY CAKES OF SULPHUR SOAP, but Inkcap encouraged Kaihe to buy fifty, because that way, when the Red Blades took thirty, Inkcap passed the news to the Hammerheads, and they took twenty. Everyone had a good wash at home.

Ever since Bash had quarrelled with Apricot, he had not come again. Convinced that he would return, Apricot made him a pair of shoes and thought of going to Luozhen to buy some wool to knit another sweater. But that very night there was a storm, and the wind and rain made the weather much cooler. When she got up in the morning, the leaves of the trees in the yard lay strewn across the ground, and the bare branches seemed to have become stiff, grinding and knocking against each other in mid-air with a rattling sound. She felt sick, uncomfortable all over, and so throwing on a coat she went over to Inkcap's house. Apricot knew full well that Gran didn't like her, but she was the only person she had, and she could only go to her. Gran really took care of her, for example by teaching her when to drink cane syrup to keep her blood sugars up, how to observe the colour of the first pee after getting up in the morning, and how she should spend a short time every day lying on the bed with her buttocks clenched to make sure her baby was in the right position. However, when she went to ask Gran what to do, her inner ear infection had flared up, so she arrived with a hand clapped to her ear.

After the Red Blades fired up the kiln, various members of different families joined their faction, and even Lightkeeper was there at the kiln, so Gran felt the need to look at it all in a different light. She decided to test the waters with Sparks, to see if there was something she might do. Sparks told her that she could do whatever she liked, but all of them were members of the Red Blades, or at least they were on that side; that left Gran with nothing to say.

The production team also had no work for her to do. How many times had Noodle Fish gone to Millstone to complain that the cattle sheds didn't have proper walls around the water troughs, only for Millstone to say he should get some people in to build them higher, and they'd get work points? The only individuals who could be called on for this heavy labour were Barndoor, Six Pints' wife, Kaihe and her. Gran found that her hearing was a lot worse after three days of earth-moving, so Noodle Fish wanted to tug on her ears and she let him, but it was very painful. Noodle Fish only had the best of intentions, and she didn't want anyone making fun of her, so she suffered in silence, just saying that her ears were much better. Then that very evening she started running a temperature, and some pus-like yellow liquid came out. Apricot yelled to her that she'd been having problems sleeping for the last few nights, and was this a normal part of pregnancy or not?

"Are you worried about something?" Gran asked in an even louder voice.

"What should I be worried about?" Apricot demanded. "I'm fine."

"Good. In the evenings you need to drink some hot water, wash your feet, go to bed early and lie down quietly, not moving."

"I don't dare move, but I just can't sleep."

"Oh, now that's a problem," Gran said. "Can you understand what animals say?"

"How can people understand what animals say?"

Gran narrowed her eyes and looked at her regretfully. Apricot stared back, and from her eyebrows and eyes, she could see how handsome Gran must have been when she was young.

"Close your eyes," Gran said, "and think of the animals in our village, such as the dogs that know what people mean, the honest cows, the greedy cats, the silent pigs, the fish in the Zhou River, the toads in the field, the old storks in the reed beds, the grasshoppers, bees and ants. Oh, let's talk about the ants – think about the ants crawling out from the bottom of the courtyard wall, in an endless stream, each one black as could be, with big heads and tiny waists, but so cheerful..."

Apricot started giggling.

"What's so funny?" Gran said.

"You are."

"There's nothing to laugh at here. Think of these animals, these animals will all come to you, you are their master, they are scrambling forward in the hope that you can talk to them... that they can come to you in your dreams."

"Is that what you've been teaching Inkcap?"

"It's true," Gran said. "I couldn't sleep either. I didn't sleep for weeks on end. I almost killed myself, but I couldn't die. The baby was so small, I had to survive. I was looking to those animals to cure me. If you can't do that, you can still think about the colony of ants, so many ants, you just count them until you fall asleep."

Gran was still talking about ants when a stone fell into the courtyard. Gran failed to hear it, but Apricot did, and she wondered if Bash had come. With Gran there, it would be quite embarrassing if they met, so she stood up and walked to the gate. When she got there, she peered through the crack while whispering, "What are you doing? Gran is here."

She never imagined that it was Inkcap standing outside the gate. "I guessed she was here, and here she is!" he said.

Apricot's face turned red, and she became angry. "You threw stones in my yard?"

"I shot the clouds in the sky with my slingshot," Inkcap corrected her, "and the stones fell into your yard."

"Gran is here, so you can piss right off."

Apricot blocked the entrance with her back. Inkcap then started shouting for Gran. That meant Apricot had to open the door, and Gran just said, "Normally I never see hide nor hair of you, but the moment I step out for a moment to have a chat, you come barging in!"

"I came to ask if I can get work," Inkcap said.

"How would I know if you can get work? Go and ask Millstone."

"He's a Hammerhead. How can I ask Millstone anything?"

"Then ask Bash."

"Bash and Baldy Jin are itching like crazy," Inkcap said. "If I ask them anything right now, they'll just have a go at me."

"Itching like crazy?" Apricot asked. "Why?"

"Don't pretend you don't know!" Inkcap cried.

But Apricot really did not know, so she asked him to explain. Inkcap said Bash had brought back scabies from Luozhen. More than half of the villagers were now infected, and the itchiness gave them all vile tempers, so now they'd bought sulphur soap to wash with.

Apricot just said oh, so that's it, but even after Inkcap had dragged Gran away, she still hadn't come back to her senses.

Apricot picked up the small stone from the courtyard, looked at it and smiled, and then threw it into the broken basket in the corner of the courtyard wall. The basket already contained dozens of small stones. That felt wrong, so she went over to pick out that one small stone and threw it back over the courtyard wall. Suddenly it made her think of the last time Bash had come, just after his return from Luozhen. They'd discussed the baby and he suggested an abortion, but she refused. She'd had one abortion already, and she'd heard folk say that a second one would make it difficult to carry a baby to term in the future. He said in that case she must have the baby, but she'd asked how. As an unmarried mother, she'd be the subject of gossip for the whole village. Where was she going to have the baby? How could she look after it? What on earth was she supposed to do? In the end, he got so angry that he argued with her, yelled at her and went off slamming the door. Now it seemed that he'd caught a disease that made him itchy and bad-tempered. Apricot felt she was in the wrong, that she'd misunderstood Bash. She decided to go and see him, so she heated some water to wash her hair and changed into a pretty, flower-patterned jacket.

Apricot marched straight to the Kiln God Temple. The door to the temple was closed, and having knocked a few times, there was no response from inside. Looking through the crack in the door, she saw a group of people stark naked, washing themselves. When they heard the knocking, they scattered in panic.

Tag-Along grabbed a broom from the steps to cover his crotch and called out, "Who is it?"

"It's me," Apricot said.

"He's gone back to his old place," Tag-Along told her.

Apricot went to his old house, and while the courtyard door was open, the door to the house was closed. Bash was inside having a wash. He was their leader, so he'd taken three cakes of soap and drenched his body with water, then applied the soap from the neck down in a thick layer.

When he heard Apricot calling him, he opened the window instead of the door, and said, "Don't come in. I'm infected with scabies."

Apricot now realised how horrible scabies was. "You should've told me you were sick," she said.

"I had no idea I had scabies," he told her. "And who knew it could drive you crazy like this? Now I've got this sulphur soap, it'll heal in a few days."

"How many days does it take?"

"The others are using soap and water, but I've put a layer of suds all over my body," Bash explained. "I'll stay in the house for five or six days, and that might cure it. Now bring your mouth over here." Bash stuck his head out, his mouth puckered for a kiss.

"You won't even let me in the door," Apricot said, "so how would I dare kiss your mouth?"

"I don't have scabies on the mouth, so bring your mouth over here. Now!"

The two of them kissed for a while, and then Bash's soapy nether regions started hoisting themselves upwards. Bash showed Apricot his erection and said, "I really want you."

"Rashes all over you and all you can think of is sex?" Apricot said. "Even if you weren't sick, now is not the time." She swallowed once, and then again.

"Get your tits out and let me have a look," Bash ordered her.

Apricot took off her top, and Bash jerked himself off, greeting his orgasm with a cackling laugh.

"What's wrong with you? Can you not manage without sex for a few days? Have you been at it with some other woman?"

Looking back, she realised the door to the courtyard was still open, and said, "My God, the door was not even closed!"

She went over and shut it, saying, "You're a leader. How can we have a revolution if people see you like this?"

"The more revolutionary I am, the more I want to do this."

"OK, whatever, I'm leaving now."

"You look after Success for me now."

"Success?"

"Don't you get it? When the revolution succeeds, the baby will be born, so we'll call it 'Success'."

Apricot laughed a little and said, "Your Success is going to cause me no end of suffering. But if you don't leave the house for five or six days, how will you eat?"

"I'll cook for myself."

"Let me bring you food."

Apricot delivered food three times a day, handing it in through the window. Of course, after eating, Bash wanted to kiss her. But after five days had passed and his scabies rash had not healed, Bash wondered if washing his body with sulphur soap was even working, so he got dressed and went to the Kiln God Temple. Baldy Jin and the others had spent several days washing themselves in the temple but were still infernally itchy, so they too had stopped washing, thinking that Inkcap must have deliberately lied to them on Awning's instructions, wasting their time and money, and the Red Blades had taken advantage of this opportunity to fire the kiln. Baldy Jin went to find Inkcap to question him, but Inkcap had gone up to the kiln.

Baldy Jin was furious about that, and more and more convinced that Awning had set Inkcap up to lie to them.

Baldy Jin didn't dare go to the kiln all by himself. He sat in the courtyard of the Kiln God Temple with the door open and waited for Inkcap to return. He waited until it was dark, and then sure enough Inkcap came down. He and Cowbell walked down the path from the kiln playing rock-paper-scissors with each other.

One of them said, "You've lost!"

"First to three," the other replied.

One was refusing to play, so the other rushed over and stuffed something into his mouth. It was at this point that Baldy Jin pounced, dragging Inkcap into the temple while Cowbell just wailed. The door closed with a bang.

Inkcap was baffled; he had no idea what was going on. Baldy Jin grabbed him by the collar and pulled him towards the courtyard as he struggled desperately, mumbling, "What's wrong? What's happened?"

Baldy Jin still did not say anything, so Inkcap grabbed hold of the pillar by the door. Baldy Jin punched the hand holding the pillar, and Inkcap dropped to the ground.

"What's wrong?" he said. "Motherfucker!" Inkcap no longer dared say a word.

Bash was in the main hall, along with a lot of other people. They now came running, but they didn't try to stop Baldy Jin, nor did they speak. They just stood there watching, hands scratching at their bodies.

Baldy Jin kicked him. "Get up!"

Inkcap clambered to his feet. He had blood on the back of his hand, so he bent down, took a pinch of dirt from the ground and clapped it on top. Then he stood up straight again.

"Tell me, when did you become a secret agent for the Red Blades?" Baldy Jin demanded.

Inkcap knew this was tantamount to calling him a traitor. The Hammerheads hated Cowbell because he was a traitor. Cowbell had indeed betrayed the Hammerheads, but how had he become a secret agent?

"Umm... Ahh..." Inkcap said. He didn't know what to say, and they didn't understand what he was muttering.

Dazed-And-Confused now came over. He was still holding his left hand clenched, and even when standing in front of Inkcap he didn't unclasp it. He just said, "What are you eating?"

Inkcap opened his mouth to reveal a peeled hard-boiled egg. He'd kept his tongue curled back so the egg was still intact. Inkcap took it out and said, "An egg."

"Where did you get that?" Dazed-And-Confused demanded. "Did Awning give it to you as a reward?"

"It's from home."

Dazed-And-Confused reached out and grabbed the egg, but Inkcap had anticipated him and immediately grabbed hold of it, wrenching his arm free. But Dazed-And-Confused grabbed Inkcap's wrist with a good strong pinch. Inkcap's hand went numb, so he quickly spat on the egg, a good lump of phlegm, thinking that would deter Dazed-And-Confused from wanting to steal the egg and eat it. Dazed-And-Confused also spat on the egg, thinking that if he did so, Inkcap wouldn't want it either. Inkcap had now lost all feeling in his hand and the egg dropped from his grasp, but he immediately stomped on it with his foot, grinding it into the dirt.

Dazed-And-Confused slapped Inkcap across the face and shouted, "Fucking bastard! Fuck you!"

Bash had been watching all this. He didn't say anything, but when Dazed-And-Confused slapped Inkcap, he ordered him to back off and said to Inkcap, "Not bad. You come here." He called him into the main hall and then closed the door behind them.

"Bash, my brother, what's going on here?" Inkcap asked.

"Don't you call me that, I'm no brother of yours," Bash replied.

"I am nothing to do with them Red Blades—"

"But you're working at the kiln?"

"I want to work there, but they don't want me. Cowbell and I took some eggs from home to cook at the kiln, and when they were cooked, we played rock-paper-scissors to see who'd win them. Cowbell had eaten one, and then he wanted to eat mine, but I certainly wasn't going to let him. I put it in my mouth and then Dazed-And-Confused wanted it for himself, who knows why, he can eat his own fucking eggs—"

"Let me ask you, who told you to come and tell me that sulphur soap cures scabies?"

"No one," Inkcap assured him. "I knew that Awning and that lot were using sulphur soap to wash themselves, so I came and told you."

"So the Red Blades washed with that same soap?"

"Yeah."

"And did it work?"

"They don't seem to be getting any better."

"So they're not better, but they still lit the kiln?"

"It's because they lit the kiln that Cowbell and I could cook the eggs."

"They aren't itching any more?"

"Oh, they are. Only Lightkeeper and a few of the other hands have stopped."

"Tell me the truth," Bash shouted. "How many have stopped itching?"

"I am telling the truth," Inkcap said. "Those people didn't rate being given soap, so they used kiln ash and added water to apply it to their bodies, and surprisingly the rash went right down. Now many people are using kiln ash to make a paste to smear on themselves."

"Oh."

"Is there anything else?"

"You'll be going to the Red Blades more often from now on."

"I'm not going, never again."

"But you must," Bash said. "Go and keep a close eye on them and send me word right away if anything happens over there."

Inkcap looked at Bash.

"Remember that!"

"I'm not a Hammerhead," Inkcap insisted.

"You may not be a Hammerhead, but you are a Hammerhead secret agent."

"Secret agent!"

"What's wrong with being a secret agent? That means you're on a special mission, you are part of the revolutionary secret service. In the future, when the revolution is successful, that'll mean you can change your class origin."

"You said it! You've got to keep your word!"

Inkcap blew on the back of his hand and rubbed the blood and mud together. The blood wasn't flowing any more, but it still hurt. He asked Bash if there was anything else because if not, he'd like to go home. But Bash wouldn't let him go, and he told Baldy Jin to inform Gran that Inkcap had been detained by the Hammerheads and that his dinner should be sent to the Kiln God Temple. He was so anxious that he almost cried because he didn't want the villagers to know about what had happened, and he certainly didn't want Gran to find out about it.

"The more people know, the better," Bash told him. "The longer you are detained here, the more the Red Blades will relax and trust you, which is good for you – do you understand?"

Inkcap stayed in the Kiln God Temple. His food was brought to him by Gran in a canister. It was not until after midnight that she was allowed to take him home. Of course, she scolded him, but he didn't dare tell her about being a spy.

Having let Inkcap go, Bash called an emergency meeting of the Hammerheads, and they decided to go to the kiln and beat up Lightkeeper. That would be a heavy smack in the face for the Red Blades, and it would also make it difficult for them to fire their porcelain properly. And to top it off, they'd also get some kiln ash to cure their scabies.

The next morning, even before the pigs had woken up to pee, and the Branch Secretary's three remaining hens were still up in their tree, Barndoor came back to the village after dumping a load of manure. Just as he was chatting with Noodle Fish, who was watering his cattle, his whole body suddenly turned red. Looking up in the sky, he noticed that the clouds looked like furrowed earth, one stripe after another, and they were all bright red. The sun had not yet come out, but the clouds were already flushed with colour.

"Is it going to rain?" Barndoor asked.

"If it rains again, it will be even cooler," Noodle Fish replied. "In that case, we need to hang straw curtains around the door to the cattle shed as soon as possible, to keep the beasts warm."

Then they saw a group of people come running, not saying a word, carrying hammers in their hands. Barndoor and Noodle Fish just stood there gawping until the Hammerheads got right up to them and shouted at them to get out of the way. The two men were pushed to the side of the road. Dazed-And-Confused came running up, having fallen behind trying to tie on his jacket. His jacket had lost its buttons, so he'd wrapped it round him and tied it on with a rope, and he had half a cold sweet potato in his mouth.

"Off to a meeting?" Noodle Fish asked.

Dazed-And-Confused pulled out the cold sweet potato and replied, "We're going to smash the kiln!"

Noodle Fish put his carrying pole down on the ground, but the bucket tipped, and the water flowed out. A stream of water slithered down the slope of the village road like a snake.

The Hammerheads took the path in front of the Kiln God Temple and made their way up the mountain. When they tripped over the pebbles on the path, they knocked them out of the way with their weapons. Wild jujube thorns growing on the slope to one side caught at their clothing, but they just twisted themselves free with a flick from their hammers. Their hammers kept swinging, so the redstarts on the white pine dared not move, while the old crows on the persimmon tree halfway up the mountain were startled into flight, hanging in the air like dirty black jackets.

"It would be great if we could find a hare," Dazed-And-Confused said.

And indeed, a hare did poke its head out of a burrow. Dazed-And-Confused swung his hammer at it, but the head broke off and the hare scampered up the mountain for dear life. Since it ran up the mountainside with its short front legs and powerful hindquarters, nobody could possibly catch up with it. If it had run down the mountain, it would have gone head over heels. Dazed-And-Confused complained that nobody in front had set the hare running down the mountain, so they scolded him loudly. "Call that a hammer, hey? What kind of hammer does that?"

Dazed-And-Confused picked up the head of his hammer and ran to the front, to show that even if he didn't have a hammer, he still had a stick, and he started to swish it about him.

Because it was still early, there weren't many people at the kiln. Lightkeeper and Pillar were sitting outside the kiln-mouth watching the fire. The Hammerheads had already arrived at the rinsing pool, and Dazed-And-Confused was smacking his stick into the clay there. The clay was soft, so the stick smashed into it like it was a bale of cotton, and the mud speckled his face.

Pillar stood up and said, "What do you think you're doing?"

"Watch," Dazed-And-Confused retorted. Then he brought his stick down on the shelves holding piles of bisque-fired bowls. The bowls tipped to one side, and pretty soon all the bowls toppled off with a crash.

Bash's voice was not loud. All he said was, "Where's Lightkeeper? Get Lightkeeper over here."

Lightkeeper came over and took the cigarette butt out of his mouth, lifting his foot so the butt was crushed beneath the sole of his shoe.

"Smashing bowls isn't part of destroying the Four Olds," he said.

"Are you scared?" Bash asked. "You're singing a new tune. Those bowls may not be part of the Four Olds, but what about you?"

"I have a good class background," Lightkeeper reminded him.

Bash furrowed his eyebrows. "You have a good class background, and you still do this!" he shouted. "It's not enough for you to engage in counter-attacks, no, you're waiting for an opportunity to oust our government. Beat him! Beat this class enemy for me."

Dazed-And-Confused and Baldy Jin rushed over, each twisting Lightkeeper's arms, lifting them upwards and pushing his head down, and as they came running forward with pounding feet, Lightkeeper fell to the ground. Ordered to stand up again and having hauled himself to his feet, Lightkeeper looked his normal wretched self once more, with lowered brows and dropped eyes.

Pillar was scared stiff, and when Bash crooked his finger at him, he came over meekly and said, "Bash, I'm just a poor peasant."

"If you're just a poor peasant," Bash demanded, "what are you doing here?"

"Firing the kiln."

"Who are you firing the kiln for? For Old Kiln Village?"

"You'll have to ask Awning about that," Pillar muttered.

"I'm asking you!" Bash shouted. "That there kiln belongs to Old Kiln, not to the Zhu family. Do you think you can just go and plant crops wherever you like on the production team's land? If you want a cow to work a millstone, you can just hitch up one of the production team's cattle and get going?"

"You mean I'm not allowed to fire it?" Pillar asked. "In that case, I'm going home."

"Winterborn," Pillar called. "Come on out you motherfucker... are you shitting a brick in there or what?"

While Bash was interrogating Lightkeeper, Winterborn took the opportunity to escape to the toilet at the back of the kiln and was pretending to take a shit. He thought the Hammerheads had come to find fault with Lightkeeper and that having taken him away, it would be all right. When he heard Pillar calling to him, he hoisted up his trousers and ran down the hill from the toilet, shouting as he ran, "Smash the kiln! Let's smash the kiln again!"

"Who is smashing the kiln?" Baldy Jin asked. He leaned against a tree and watched as Winterborn ran down the hill.

"You said you'd smash the kiln, motherfucker," said Baldy Jin, "so let's do it!" He turned around, grabbed a hammer and smashed it against a trolley carrying bisque-fired porcelain. The trolley was struck but it didn't fall apart. Instead, it started rolling towards the entrance of the kiln. Then it rolled back and overturned.

"Smash it!" Dazed-And-Confused shouted. "Smash everything!"

He kicked a box of bisque-fired porcelain and picked up a pickaxe on the ground to begin breaking down the door of the red-hot kiln. When it failed to open, he bashed it again.

Old Faithful grabbed the pickaxe and demanded, "Are you trying to kill yourself? When that door bursts, the fire will shoot out and burn you to a crisp."

Old Faithful shovelled a heap of earth and tossed it into the furnace. The kiln fire was still bright red, and Dazed-And-Confused yelled at him, "Fuck you! Nobody can fire this kiln without our say-so."

"It's nothing to do with you," said Old Faithful. "This here kiln is owned by the Zhu clan, and we all have a share in it. If you've wrecked this firing, we'll skin you alive."

"Whatever," Dazed-And-Confused shouted. "Skin me alive and see if I care!"

"You may be OK with it," Old Faithful said, "but some of us have wives and children." He took away the pickaxe.

Just as Old Faithful and Dazed-And-Confused were pushing and pulling each other about in front of the kiln, another group came in and took over. There was a stove by the kiln and several cooking pots by the stove. None of the pots contained any food, and the one they'd used to make porridge in had not yet been washed. Meanwhile, the bowls and chopsticks were soaking in water. Several mats were laid out in rows, each with a brick at one end. There wasn't even a cigarette packet beside each brick, only a bag of dry tobacco.

Lucky picked up a bag of dry tobacco and looked at the pile of kiln ash in the corner, saying, "Is that the ash used to get rid of scabies? Grab a handful and put it on your crotch."

Before this, everyone had forgotten about the itching of their skin. As soon as he mentioned it, the scabies mites began itching again, so they all came to scrape up some kiln dust, wiping it on their arms and legs. Later, they simply took off their clothes and rubbed the ash all over their bodies, and for a while, the kiln was covered by clouds of dust as they choked and coughed.

Bash stood by the kiln, shouting at them to put the Hammerheads' flag on top, and when it was fluttering happily in the wind, he regretted a little that he had not brought the gong and drum guys with him when he came up here. He tilted his head to look at Lightkeeper and gave him a smile. Lightkeeper didn't dare look at Bash's smiling face and just hung his head.

"Do you know what I'm thinking about by coming here?" Bash asked.

"I don't want to say," Lightkeeper replied.

"If I tell you to talk, you talk!"

"This will really fuck over the Red Blades."

"You fuckers are the pits," Bash answered. "You think bad of everyone. I was thinking about one of Chairman Mao's poems."

"Oh?" Lightkeeper muttered.

"High on the crest of Mount Liupan," Bash recited, "Red banners wave freely in the west wind..."

Tag-Along emerged from the kiln, followed by another three men. They couldn't stand being choked by the ash and were now rubbing themselves down with ash outside the kiln. Tag-Along took a handful of ash to let Bash rub himself down too.

Bash was enjoying himself. "What are you doing here?" he said. "Go back and rub yourself down over there."

Tag-Along felt he'd embarrassed himself, and when he turned around and left, Lightkeeper looked at him with a strange expression, so he said, "What are you looking at? If you keep staring at me, I'll rip your eyes out."

"I wasn't looking at you," Lightkeeper assured him. "I was thinking about Chairman Mao's verse."

"Chairman Mao's arse? How dare you think about Chairman Mao's arse!"

"Verse, not arse," said Lightkeeper.

"You don't understand. Go away. Piss off."

Bash had more to say to Lightkeeper but suddenly lost interest due to his itching leg, and immediately the itch flared up all over his body, like a million flies were crawling through it, like a host of worms gnawing away at him, like a fire burning, like an awl stabbing.

He got up and yelled towards the kiln, "Put your clothes on! What do you think you all look like?"

SIXTY-FIVE

NOODLE FISH HAD ALREADY INFORMED AWNING of the Hammerheads' visit to the mountain, but Awning had eaten something dodgy the previous night and had to dash out several times during the night, so he was still asleep at dawn. When he heard the news, he went out to find Millstone and Sparks, but they were already on their way to find him. Unfortunately, they did not know what the Hammerheads were up to out there. Awning's wife came back from the spring with water and said when she'd passed Useless's house, he was standing by the door laughing.

"They're going to get Lightkeeper, aren't they?" Awning said. "We let Lightkeeper take charge of firing the kiln, so they wanted to get him. It's a clear attempt to stop us from firing the kiln."

Millstone and Sparks agreed with his assessment, but since the Hammerheads were nominally just fighting Lightkeeper, they couldn't stop them. Millstone suggested that the Red Blades should go and beat up Useless. Ever since he'd come back, he wasn't openly working for the Hammerheads, but the way he laughed about them going to beat up Lightkeeper meant that he was secretly on their side. They beat one of ours, so we'll beat up Useless! Having decided upon that course of action, the Red Blades were summoned to Useless's house.

When Useless's mother saw that a group of men had come to get him, she shouted that he'd already returned from study class, so what did they want now? She blocked the door to prevent them from coming in, saying that whoever wanted to enter her house would have to go over her dead body. She lay across the threshold, and as she did so her jacket flap flew up, revealing a belly like a pig's bladder.

Since those who wanted to get in didn't want to touch her, they fixed their eyes on the door knocker, shouting, "Come on, drag her away!" Everyone just backed away. Useless's mother plucked a string of dried black-eyed peas hanging by the window and started chewing them. When others shouted at her, she remained indifferent and just kept chomping. Sparks tried to take hold of her, but Useless's mother got her foot hooked around the threshold, and he couldn't move her. After various feints and manoeuvres, he got a hand under her armpits and hoisted her out of the way. Sparks then led everyone inside. However, Useless was not at home, and the back window was open.

It turned out that Useless had escaped through the back window while his mother was making a scene at the door.

Sparks scolded Useless's mother, who just stretched out her neck and said, "You want to beat someone? Go right ahead and hit me!"

Her head was thrust so far forward that her face was about to meet Sparks' fist. Sparks clenched his fist so tight the veins were standing up, but suddenly he spread his hand and gently patted Useless's mother on the face. This was much more humiliating than a punch to the face, and Useless's mother burst into tears.

At that very moment, Winterborn ran down from the kiln, covered in dirt and his jacket torn by thorns until it hung down over his buttocks like a sheep's tail. He was rushing to report that the Hammerheads had smashed up the kiln.

"I thought they were just going to beat up Lightkeeper," Awning said.

"They did," Winterborn explained, "but then they started smashing stuff, whatever they could see... it's all wrecked."

"Is the kiln still burning?"

"How could it be?"

Then Awning suddenly roared, "This is a kiln that everyone raised funds to fire, how dare they smash it? How?"

When he screamed, his entire forehead turned red, his cheekbones protruded, and his mouth opened wide enough to fit a fist inside.

Everyone present was shocked, even Useless's mother stopped crying, while Gourd's wife burst into tears and said, "What on earth are we going to do?" Her family had put all their profits from selling eggs into the kiln, and her mother-in-law had refused to eat so much as a single egg when they could be saving.

"They've ruined us," Millstone shouted. "They might as well have desecrated our graves and thrown our kids into the river! Let's go to the mountain, go to the kiln. Whoever breaks our kiln, we'll break those bastards' necks."

The Red Blades urgently gathered everyone together, and their leaders had already arrived at the entrance to Three Fork Alley.

Palace ran down the alley and shouted, "Take your guys and get everyone up the mountain, everyone up the mountain."

As for the Red Blades who were not present, some were still feeding the pigs at home, and some were heading towards their own plots of land.

"What's the matter?" they asked. "What's the matter?"

"The kiln's been smashed up by the Hammerheads, and all our plans for the future have been ruined."

"That's impossible," they responded. "They might have the gall to smash and loot the production team's property, but that porcelain's ours... How would they dare?"

"They just smashed it anyway. The Hammerheads have given us a slap on the chops. They've been riding round our necks and shitting down our backs!"

"Hammerheads, I'll be fucking your mothers!" these listeners said. "Let's not bother going to our private plots or feeding the pigs."

They returned home and got their knives. The Red Blades all had knives: a foot-long pruning knife, a straight blade machete, a wide-faced chopper, a hooked sickle and even some knives made out of wood. They raised their weapons and ran towards the entrance of Three Fork Alley.

Inkcap and Gran were by the spring washing turnip greens that were going to be used to make pickles. Inkcap had brought a fuse with him, and when Gran questioned the need for a fuse when they were washing vegetables, Inkcap said he normally brought one with him, and he hung the fuse up in the branches of the tree overhanging the spring. A swarm of bees came buzzing out from the spring and to begin with, he didn't pay much attention for he wasn't expecting there to be more and more bees, drifting through the air like snowflakes. But these snowflakes were yellow and not white, and the buzzing was like myriad spinning wheels all working at once.

"Has Gourd moved his beehives?" Gran asked.

"I don't see them," Inkcap replied.

A few bees swooped down and landed on Inkcap's back, so Gran stopped washing vegetables and told Inkcap to squeeze his eyes closed and not to move. Inkcap was rooted to the spot and let the bees crawl on his back for a while, then they set off flying again, and he remarked, "Gourd must have brought his beehives over."

Since the end of autumn, there were often trucks on the road transporting beehives because beekeepers from the north go south to catch the flowering season, and their trucks would stop below the pagoda to get water. The bees would then fly off, and Gourd would take the opportunity to catch them. He'd leave lots of honey in his own hives and put them behind the pagoda. When the trucks drove off, they'd be missing whole swarms of bees that had been attracted in.

"Gourd's attracted so many bees this time," Gran remarked.

"That's not attracting, that's stealing!" Inkcap said.

"Don't be rude. The only reason Gourd keeps bees is to cure his mother's illness. His mother had a stroke, and Gourd's wife catches four bees every day to sting the joints of the old lady's legs, saying she'll be cured after a year of stings."

"They also sell honey."

"Do you want to drink honey water?"

"Yes."

"You wash the vegetables well, and I'll take some eggs to his house later to exchange for some honey."

"We shouldn't have to pay for it," Inkcap objected. "We should demand it! You have dyed cloth for his family, so if we demand honey from him, he can hardly refuse."

"How can you be so calculating?"

Inkcap just laughed at her, but before he finished laughing, some people came running along the road on top of the embankment by the spring, a whole bunch of them, as if a procession. Grandmother and grandson saw that their faces had changed shape, their eyes seemed to be bursting out of their sockets, and their teeth seemed to have grown much longer.

"Gran, Gran, what are those people doing?" Inkcap asked.

But Gran had become nervous and said, "It's all the Revolution, don't raise your head."

The people on the embankment ignored them and ran past, or maybe they didn't even see Inkcap and his grandmother. Inkcap called out to Gran again, wanting to ask her why they did not see either of them and why they looked so pleased as they ran along the bank.

Ever-Obedient's dog was leading a pack of hounds running after them. Ever-Obedient himself held a knife that had been hacked out of a wooden board, and he followed on behind the dog. Now he turned back and said, "Hurry up. We've got shares in the kiln too." But Yoyo was standing far behind, looking dazed and dumbstruck, with a radish in her mouth.

Inkcap forgot everything he had learned and stood up, slipping on his shoes, but Gran held him down and demanded, "What do you think you're doing?"

"Ever-Obedient has a share?"

Gran jabbed her finger into his forehead and hissed, "It's none of our business if they're in or out."

She gave the vegetable basket to Inkcap to carry. He remembered to collect the fuse out of the tree, and the two of them tiptoed home.

When they opened the courtyard door, Useless was squatting in the gutter. Inkcap was startled and about to call out, but Useless shushed him.

"This is my home," Inkcap said in a low voice. "How did you get in?"

"I came in over the wall," Useless said. "The Red Blades were going to beat me. Let me hide here for a bit."

"You know what happened to us," Inkcap told him. "Are you trying to get us into trouble? Out... Get out now!"

He pulled the door open and pushed Useless through it.

"Gran!" Useless screamed. "Gran!"

Gran closed the door and pulled Useless into the main room; he could hide in the pigsty. There was a pig tethered in the sty, with a bed of straw in one corner. Inkcap covered Useless with the straw.

"It's filthy," Useless complained.

"If you don't like it, you can go home," Inkcap told him. Useless stayed under the straw, but stuck out a hand holding his face mask, wanting him to hide it somewhere clean.

"Beggars can't be choosers," Inkcap said. He picked up a sheaf of straw and buried the hand and the mask, then he pushed open the window of the back wall and sucked in his stomach until he could squeeze out.

Although he didn't like Useless, he'd said he needed to hide because the Red Blades wanted to beat him up, so Inkcap felt inclined to help him get away. Whatever happened, he was fairly sure they'd get him on some other occasion, and the village would be thrown into uproar again. The bee swarm was swirling at the head of the lane in front of him, and underneath the swarm were two men, Gourd and Goodman, both wearing beekeeping hats and carrying a hive.

Gourd was saying, "I wonder if bees could be made to stay up on the hill?"

"No," Goodman replied. "I've brought the hive back for you."

"Give me the hive and I'll go to the highway to get them," Inkcap suggested.

Gourd turned round and looked at him. "Come here, Inkcap," he said. "Help Goodman take the hive."

Although Inkcap thought it might be fun to help with the hive, he said, "If I can't eat the honey, why should I help carry it?"

"Goodness me, you're mercenary!" Gourd said. "Goodman's curing my mum's damaged leg after her stroke. If you'd had a stroke, I'd give you a hive too."

"How can I carry it?" Inkcap asked. "I don't have a proper hat."

Gourd came running over and shook the bees off his body. Most of them had flown off so only a couple remained that he now brushed to the ground. Then he took off his beekeeping hat and put it on Inkcap's head, saying he had other things to be getting on with.

"Be good, kid, and help Goodman carry the hive up yonder, and when you come back, I'll give you a spoonful of honey to eat."

"Only one spoonful?" Inkcap complained. "Two spoons!"

"All right, two spoons."

The Red Blades had not found Useless, and after they heard Winterborn's report, they stopped looking for him. Instead, shouting and screaming, they took their knives up the mountainside, as the sky suddenly clouded over. The clouds came from the south, like a pot of murky water poured across the sky, light and dark constantly swirling overhead, and the sun shining high above their heads. The shadows of the clouds on the mountain slope lay in broad black stripes, as if countless nappies had been spread out there to dry.

The Hammerheads at the kiln had already discovered that the Red Blades were on their way. Those who were fully clothed grabbed their weapons, while those who weren't were busy getting dressed. Baldy Jin was in a real hurry, but the more he hurried the more tangled his clothes became, with his sleeves wrapping round themselves and the trouser legs knotting together.

Meanwhile, Dazed-And-Confused picked up his wooden baton that had formerly been the handle of a hammer and started down the path. He was spoiling for a fight, though he said he was just going down to stop them from coming up… but the Red Blades didn't stop at all. He charged the man at the front only to find he couldn't stop. The man at the head of the Red

Blades simply stepped aside and he went head over heels on a pile of dogshit, busting open his knee on a stone on the ground. Dazed-And-Confused clambered to his feet, refusing to let anyone get close to him. He grabbed the stick and beat it in a circle about himself, thrashing everyone back, the stick swishing back and forth through the air. The path was narrow, and the Red Blades moved back, but someone jumped up the cliff face and threw a jacket over Dazed-And-Confused. The jacket covered his head, and then they swung a machete at him with a thwack, knocking the baton out of his hand. Now the machete came down flat across Dazed-And-Confused's arse, bam, and he fell to the ground. When he climbed up again, he raced up the hillside, scrambling on his hands and knees. The Red Blades took the opportunity to make their way uphill, and the Hammerheads poured down towards the kiln, the two groups moving up and down. Halfway up, with only five hundred yards separating them, they halted.

Five hundred yards of mountain road, with a ditch on one side and a sloping cliff on the other, and three old acacia trees on top of the cliff. All shouting and cursing came to an abrupt halt, only the robins in the trees were calling, and the cicadas, like the thornback fish in the river, were calling their own names: "Cic-cic... cicada! Cic-cic... cicada!"

Suddenly a wooden hive fell down the road from behind the old acacia tree, and a yellow buzzing swarm of bees started to form, and then two people fell with them, and the gathered swarm flew up in a screaming horde, covering the entire road.

It was Inkcap and Goodman who fell.

As Inkcap helped Goodman carry the beehive up the mountain, he asked, "What happened in the village today?"

"The cat caught a mouse and the chickens laid eggs," Goodman replied.

"But something must be up."

"Do you expect something to happen?"

That silenced Inkcap. The hive was not heavy, but it was awkward for the two of them to carry. If Inkcap walked in front holding his hands behind him, it was not always possible for him to grasp the bottom of the box; when they switched positions, and Goodman went in the front, he was too tall, which made it uncomfortable to carry. Inkcap wanted Goodman to let him carry the hive on his back, but Goodman refused.

"Why are you in such a hurry?" he said. "We can carry it well enough if we walk slowly."

He had to carry it nicely, but he felt he wanted to tease Goodman a bit. "Isn't your leg supposed to be messed up?" Inkcap asked.

"When the weather changes, this leg hurts," Goodman said.

"Then why don't you cure it yourself?"

"Fuck you!" Goodman replied, and he was just about to give Inkcap a slap around the head when an uproar broke out from the village, with hens cackling and dogs barking their heads off.

"What on earth's going on?" Goodman asked.

That pleased Inkcap. "I told you something was up, and you didn't believe me. Now you see!"

The two put the beehive on the ground and looked down the hill, only to see a group of people coming up the hill from the slope in front of the Kiln God Temple. They could not make out who they were through the mesh of their hats, and they didn't dare to take them off.

"There are lots of people round the kiln," Goodman said. Then Inkcap looked up the hill, just at the moment when Goodman said, "Oh dear."

He dragged Inkcap up the mountainside and the hive with them, but they'd lost the path. Having gone a little further, they dashed behind the three acacia trees overlooking the cliff. Soon, the Red Blades came charging up the slope, and the Hammerheads came charging down, and they met on the mountain path right in front of the trees. Inkcap looked at Goodman who just sat there, not moving. Inkcap couldn't remain sitting, and he wanted to go running up the slope but didn't dare. The moment he ran, they'd spot him. The Hammerheads would think he'd arrived with the Red Blades, while the Red Blades would think he'd been at the kiln all along with the Hammerheads. Yet if he didn't run, Inkcap was afraid he'd get caught up in the fighting. If fighting broke out, he was quite sure he wouldn't be able to take on anyone – he simply didn't dare. They'd beat him to a pulp. Inkcap raised his eyes and looked at Goodman, who indicated that he was just sitting quietly and so he squatted down too, but his heart was thumping so fast he had to close his eyes. When he closed his eyes, it made him think of his dream. In the blink of an eye, he felt he was back in his dream world. He started to fold in upon himself, making himself as small as possible, so that nobody would see him.

After a good long time had passed, while Inkcap was still sitting there like a lump, Goodman started tugging at him, whispering, "Get up! Get up!"

Inkcap opened his eyes and looked down the road through the grass. The Hammerheads and Red Blades had both moved forward, and the space between them was becoming shorter and shorter, and the grass at the side of the road was shaking. There was no wind, but the grass was moving, a sign of their pent-up rage. Inkcap was so scared that he closed his eyes again.

Goodman stood up, grabbed Inkcap by the collar to pull him to his feet, and said, "Push the hive down. Push it now!"

How could he push the hive down? If he did, the hive would definitely fall apart, and the bees would fly away. Had he given up on keeping bees? Was he not trying to heal his leg any more? Inkcap was dragged along, but he couldn't move, his whole body was rigid. Goodman pushed the hive over by himself, but there was a stone right in front, so the hive rolled a few times and then got stuck. It didn't move no matter how much Goodman pushed.

"Quick, they're going to fight!" Goodman exclaimed.

Inkcap now came running over and lifted a corner of the hive with both hands, whereupon it tipped over. But he slipped over too and fell forwards, and when reaching for the big rock he grabbed Goodman's leg instead, so the two of them fell down to the road together in a tangle of arms and legs.

The hive immediately fell apart. The bees rose like a puff of wind, or the swirling of dust, and then they struck downwards. They filled the road, and yet the bees in the air kept coming until they formed a kind of whirling mass. Goodman fell with his hat still in place, but Inkcap's hat fell off, and the bees covered him at once. He was screaming with pain, and his arms and legs were flailing about.

"Cover your head," Goodman was shouting. "Cover your head." He knew that beating about with his hands and feet would only attract more bees, but he couldn't stop himself; he was too busy now to cover his head. Goodman lunged and pinned Inkcap down. He clasped Inkcap's neck firmly between his legs, then forced him down and covered his head with his arms. The Hammerheads and Red Blades froze in an instant and instinctively ran forward to save Goodman and Inkcap, and the bees flew towards them. Those who ran forward dropped to the ground and covered their heads with their clothes, while the Hammerheads ran off, only to have a stream of bees chase them. But the bees soon lost interest in their pursuit and refocused on the road under the old acacia tree, and the yellow mass stretched and shortened, flying high and then low, constantly changing shape.

"They're just bees," someone said, "they don't matter."

"There's a wasp's nest up there in the acacia tree," another said. "They must have attracted them too."

"Run!" the Red Blades shouted. "Run!"

"Run, run!" the Hammerheads were shouting.

They were all shouting at Goodman and Inkcap. Goodman got up and pulled Inkcap to his feet, but Inkcap lost his bearings and he slipped and rolled down the slope of the road into the ditch, with Goodman after him. They rolled so fast that few of the wasps followed them; the majority stayed swirling in a yellow mass by the road. The Red Blades did not dare go forward again, and the Hammerheads were disinclined to come back, so both sides beat a retreat.

"Come up here, you son of a bitch!"

"Get down here, motherfucker!"

Neither side seemed to bother with Goodman or Inkcap any more and started yelling at each other.

No one was going to fight, so cursing each other was easy. Bash knew that if the Red Blades rushed him, their superior numbers would overwhelm the Hammerheads. Awning was also thankful he didn't have to carry on, for although the Red Blades had more people, the Hammerheads were a bunch of vicious bastards, and if it came to a fight the Red Blades would not necessarily win.

"Come down, you son of a bitch! Come down and I'll break your legs!"

"Come up here, motherfucker! I've smashed the kiln – let's see if you can do anything about it!"

"Did you hear that?" Sparks said to Awning. "They've smashed our kiln.

The bastards have smashed our kiln. Let's stop this. We'll go and smash their homes, every last one of them. Let's smash them! Let's go!"

Sparks was still shouting as he turned and ran towards the village, and all the Red Blades ran after him. When they reached the door of the temple, they broke the lock and rushed into the courtyard, kicking open the doors of all the small rooms, and set about destroying the flags hanging on the walls, the lanterns, the drums and gongs, the ink and pens on the tables, the paper used to write big-character posters, the buckets of glue, the brooms... They ripped them up, threw them out and stomped on them. They lifted the benches in the air and smashed them to smithereens.

Their logbook was also turned over, with Cowbell asking, "What does it say?"

Soupspoon looked at it and said, "There's your name, you're a traitor."

"Who wrote that about me? I'll fuck his mother!"

Awning picked it up and tried to tear it to pieces, but with the rope binding, it did not work.

"Inkcap!" Sparks shouted. He shouted because he wanted Inkcap to start a fire but then he remembered that Inkcap had not come with them, so he shouted again, "Who's got matches?"

The men went through the bunks in the building, and when they failed to find any matches, they threw the bunks into the courtyard and went to the cooking area to look for some. When they still didn't find any matches, they threw the pots and pans into the courtyard. Padlock smashed a jar of water over the steps of the main hall to the temple, and the water flowed all over the ground, wetting the bedding, but he was still not satisfied. He fetched a lump of earth from the foot of the stairs and added it to the mix, grinding mud into the bedding. Although he failed to find a match, he did come across a can of kerosene, so Soupspoon headed out of the courtyard, hoping to hide it in the weeds by the wall so he could fetch it later.

"I'm going home for a match," Cowbell declared.

He left just in time to see Soupspoon stuffing the kerosene can into the grass. He turned around and went into the yard to tell Millstone what he'd seen.

"Bring the kerosene to me," Millstone scolded Soupspoon.

Millstone poured the kerosene on the heap in the courtyard. Cowbell ran home for a match, and as he did so, Barndoor craned his neck in the direction of the Kiln God Temple and spotted him, immediately turning around.

"What are you looking at?' Cowbell demanded.

"Nothing," Barndoor assured him.

"You aren't joining in?"

"I'm not a Red Blade."

"Have you got any matches?"

Barndoor gave his matches to Cowbell but felt that something was wrong and wanted to take them back. Cowbell refused, took the matches and ran away.

"Hey!" Barndoor called out. "Don't tell anyone I gave them to you."

Cowbell went to find matches in the first place because he wanted to burn the logbook. Having set fire to it, he coaxed it into a flame that singed his eyebrows. This frightened him into tossing the book, throwing it straight into the pile of miscellaneous things doused in kerosene. Whoosh! The fire blazed up, and a thick column of smoke flew into the sky like a dragon.

With the Kiln God Temple on fire, the people at the kiln started complaining, how could things have got to this point? They were impatient, their bodies itched from the scabies mites, and the more they itched the more impatient they grew... and now with the Kiln God Temple burning, they rushed around smashing things to relieve their anger. All the bisque-fired porcelain was broken, all the saggars were thrown off the cliff, the rinsing pond was dug up, the kiln door destroyed, the chimney toppled, even buckets, stools, hoes, shovels and shelves were smashed to bits, and the pile of coal was shovelled into the ditch.

In the cave where people had been resting, the walls were covered in graffiti accounts, showing how much money Awning had put in, and how much was contributed by Millstone, Sparks, Sprout, Palace, Soupspoon, Yes'm, Stargazer, Once-Upon-A-Time, Winterborn, Pillar, Lightkeeper, Gourd, Jindou and the others... how much they'd spent on coal and firewood... it was all listed out. Iron Bolt took hold of a hammer to smash it, and for every blow he called out a man's name, but then the head came off. That was the second time this had happened, with the hammer turning into a stick, and that put people in mind of Dazed-And-Confused. Whatever had happened to Dazed-And-Confused?

When the Hammerheads were smashing the kiln, Lightkeeper and Pillar – along with Jindou and Yes'm, who slept at the kiln overnight – stayed dutifully squatting by the rinsing pool. Even when it was dug up and soaked their shoes, they didn't dare move.

When someone asked about Dazed-And-Confused, Pillar said, "He's over by the slope."

Dazed-And-Confused was lying on his back on the slope at the entrance to the kiln, rubbing his sore buttocks.

"You should stand up and walk about," he was told, but he wouldn't. When forced to stand, he complied but refused to walk.

"Walk! Why can't you walk?"

He took a step to the left and realised that his crotch was torn, revealing a thing dangling between his legs.

"Letting it out for an airing?" Stonebreaker giggled.

Baldy Jin came over pushing a cart and said, "Look at the time! Why are you messing about? Come and push the cart... help me get the cart over to the cliff."

Jindou looked at Yes'm, and Yes'm looked at Pillar, and Pillar said, "The cart belongs to the production team. Are you going to destroy it?"

"Shut your mouth!" Baldy Jin snapped.

The cart was thrown down too. Dazed-And-Confused came up from the slope, looking at his crotch and muttering, "Fucking bees..."

Pillar wanted to ask if the bees had stung him, but before he could get a word out, he turned to look at the far side of the road, hoping to spot Inkcap and Goodman. He could still see a swarm of bees as a patch of yellow over the road, but there was no longer any trace of the two of them.

Inkcap rolled a dozen somersaults down the slope, thinking that this time he'd really done it, but eventually he stopped rolling. Discovering that his arms and legs were still there, he said, "I'm not dead?" Since he wasn't dead, he had to get up, but he couldn't. Only now did he realise he was stuck in the branches of three trees and held so tightly he couldn't move. Inkcap panicked and started hyperventilating, feeling unable to breathe.

Goodman was calling, "Inkcap, Inkcap!"

Inkcap hated Goodman at this point and deliberately did not answer. Goodman's voice trembled a little, and he called again, "Inkcap, Inkcap!"

Only then did Inkcap say, "Here I am."

"Where are you? Can you see me?"

"I can't see you at all."

"Can't you see me standing over here?"

"I can't see you at all."

But Goodman could see Inkcap. He was stuck in a tree, his face as puffy as dough, and his eyes squeezed shut.

"What are you doing up there?" Goodman asked.

"Why, where did you land?" Inkcap asked.

"In a tussock of grass, over there."

"So you rolled into a tussock and let me roll into a tree branch?"

"Don't move, don't move yet," Goodman told him. "Wipe your nose, then rub your snot on your face."

Inkcap knew how to treat bee stings with snot, so he blew his nose but only managed to produce a little snot.

Goodman blew a handful of snot and clapped it on Inkcap's eyes. "Does it hurt a lot?"

"No," Inkcap said, "but it really burns."

"You're damn lucky you didn't roll to the bottom of the ditch. You've nothing to worry about. It was bees, not wasps. The stings will swell but that's it."

Goodman pulled Inkcap out from the tree branch and dragged him to a grass tussock not far away.

"Let me see the tree branch," Inkcap said. He forced open his eyes and looked at the forks in the tree, three tiny little green trees, so small they looked as though they could not catch anything at all, but they held Inkcap right enough.

"Let me kowtow to the tree," Inkcap said.

He got down and kowtowed to the tree, whereupon Goodman said, "You were never going to die."

"Why not?"

"You always want to grow up and get taller, but you haven't managed it yet. Besides, your gran is still here. If you die, who will look after her? You haven't finished your tasks. You can't die even if you want to."

The two of them sat on tussocks in that peaceful place. The grass was almost entirely desiccated, but it was long and soft to sit on. Inkcap remembered that he'd often gone into the mountains to collect grass and twigs for fuel... how come he'd never noticed how soft the grass was? He suddenly remembered something, and asked, "Are you all right?"

"A little dizzy, but it's nothing," Goodman assured him.

"But you're so capable, why did all this have to happen to me?" The fact that Goodman was perfectly fine made Inkcap furious. "Why did you ask me to push the beehive over – you could've done it yourself. Why did I have to do it?"

"If you hadn't pushed over the beehive," Goodman pointed out, "they'd have started fighting. Now they've all retreated. You've been stung, but how many people have you saved? If–"

"You're just the same as the Branch Secretary," Inkcap complained. "You're all the time telling me to be a better person–"

"I am nothing like the Branch Secretary. I'm teaching you the Dao."

"What's that, then?" Inkcap asked. "What good is that to me?"

"The Dao is the Dao, and it is everywhere. It shapes all our lives because we humans are part of the natural world. We ask and Heaven responds, we need and Heaven gives. Heaven never forgets humankind."

"The Hammerheads and Red Blades won't forget us either," Inkcap said. "I don't know why they hate us so much."

"Why do they hate us so much?" Goodman said. "No matter how much they hate us, we can't let them get killed."

At this time, they noticed a choking, burning smell, but sitting halfway up the hill in the hollow of the slope, they had not yet seen the smoke and fire coming from the Kiln God Temple. An old crow landed on an acacia tree not far away, and a bird on the acacia tree with a purple crown on its head said, "Old crow, old crow, this is not a place where you can live."

"Look, who are you calling an old crow?"

The purple-crowned bird said, "Wow, it's a pigeon! Have you been up a chimney that you're so covered in soot?"

"The Kiln God Temple is on fire," the pigeon explained, "so I got kippered."

Just as Inkcap was wondering what on earth was going on, the folk up at the kiln started shouting, and those down in the village below the hill were also shouting, but as to what they were yelling about, he could not hear; it was just a buzz.

"The Kiln God Temple is on fire, so we'd better go," Inkcap told Goodman.

"How do you know?"

"The bird said so."

"The bird said that? What the fuck kind of creature are you? This is so strange... But if it is true that the temple has gone up in flames, we can't leave right now."

Having smashed up the Kiln God Temple, the Red Blades had still not managed to relieve their feelings fully, so Awning set a guard on the crossroads, with the mountain guarding the other road.

"Stay alert," he said. "Do not let them enter the village… they can live on the fuck all they find at the kiln!"

The Red Blades lit a bonfire at the crossroads, which was built from the wheat straw each family had set aside. First of all, they took straw from the Hammerheads' families. Their wives and parents tried to stop them, begging for mercy, screaming and crying. By that time, it was well past noon, and they hadn't had a thing to eat all day, so they were really hungry. Now there were all these people crying and screaming, so the Red Blades' hearts weren't really in it, and at the same time their scabies grew more and more itchy. They'd scratched their crotches raw, but they were still itchy.

"Fuck it!" some people said. "If you won't let us take it, we don't want it. Let's go and get our straw from Bash's place. There won't be anyone there."

Shouting at the tops of their voices, they ran to the old house and stripped it of every last stalk of wheat straw, even the pile of maize stalks outside the back window. After raking up the straw and maize stalks, they were still feeling furious, so they smashed their way through the yard, the upper storerooms, the main building and the woodshed where the Branch Secretary had been kept. The door was broken, the windows were smashed, and the table and stools all had broken legs. The big, lidded pot in the upper room had the *taisui* growing in it, but the pot broke and the *taisui* fell to the ground like a pile of slime, while the water flowed everywhere.

"It's a pity it died, but the water is drinkable," Soupspoon said.

Several people were cursing. "What the fuck?" said one. "A *taisui*? Like Bash is planning to live forever so he can make us suffer here in Old Kiln for eternity? Let's bury it."

They dug a hole in the courtyard, thinking that if they buried it, there'd be no evil people allowed to flourish in Old Kiln henceforward and nothing bad would happen. When Awning and Sparks were setting light to the straw at the crossroads, they heard that a *taisui* had been found in Bash's house, so they rushed over. The pit was still being dug when the *taisui* was thrown into the yard, where it landed with a squish like a lump of soft meat.

"Is this it?' Awning asked.

"Bash was going to eat it," Soupspoon said.

"Fuck him, we'll eat it. We'll cook it and eat it."

When Awning said that, Sparks would not let anyone bury it, but the digger said, "Them *taisui* don't tolerate dirt… that'll just bring bad luck. Why do you want to eat it?"

"Bash is doing well enough, isn't he?" Sparks said.

"He's brought us plenty of bad luck, though," the digger said dubiously.

"And now it's our turn to fuck with him!"

Sparks took the *taisui* back to the house, washed it with water and chopped it into chunks with a knife. The meat was chopped up without any blood, just a little greenish juice, and when it was boiled in a pot, it smelt so good that everyone came and had half a bowl of the soup. Those at the entrance of the village heard about it and came in turn. While the meat was gone, the soup was still there, so they added some more water and boiled it, after which everyone drank half a bowl. While they were eating and drinking, it tasted delicious and none of them itched, but afterwards they felt hot all over, and the itching began again. The more they scratched, the hotter they felt; and the hotter they felt, the itchier they got.

Sparks dashed his empty bowl on the ground, and after he did so, the others broke their bowls too. Stonebreaker even lifted a small bench and brought it down on the cooking pot, which broke in half. Then everyone cried and howled for a while, before heading back to the crossroads behind the Kiln God Temple. Soupspoon took the broom that was leaning against the courtyard entrance and threw it into the bonfire as soon as they arrived.

SIXTY-SIX

INKCAP WAS SO HUNGRY he felt the sides of his stomach clapping together. His eyes remained swollen to mere slits, but he squinted up into the sky, and the sun was still shining there. A succession of black clouds passed, going so slowly that he wanted a rope to pull one down and throw it over the mountain ridge. Still, they could not leave, so they leaned against the bank and dozed. After a long time, Goodman nudged him awake. Night had come at last, and it was pitch black; nobody could see any more than Inkcap.

"You're hungry, right?" Goodman said.

"Nope," Inkcap replied.

"Fine. You're even better than Cowbell at putting up with hunger."

"I'm so hungry, I'm not hungry any more."

Goodman laughed a little in the darkness and pulled Inkcap up the slope. Inkcap thought that Goodman wanted him to collect the hive and take it to the Mountain God Temple, and was just wondering how he was going to achieve that, when Goodman said, "The beehive's broken and the bees have flown away. Do you want to follow me to the temple or go home?"

Inkcap naturally chose to go home. He grabbed a blade of grass on the side of the road, pinched the stalk into a digit-long section, and propped up the upper and lower eyelids of one eye as he groped his way down the slope.

A bonfire was burning at the junction at the bottom of the hill, and someone was walking around it, their shadow reflected onto the sloping cliff face, jumping and shaking like a ghost. Inkcap hesitated for a long time, thinking of a way to get through. He moved slowly against the cliff face and could make out Palace and Yes'm, along with Stargazer and Jindou, all with knives in their hands.

Palace was saying, "Don't sit there, get up, keep your eyes open. I'm going to pee." Palace went into the blackness, and Stargazer, Jindou and Yes'm all stood up. The three of them wanted to smoke, so they each took out a pipe, and once one person had lit his, the other two came over to get theirs going.

Inkcap started crawling across the ground, thinking he would be out of sight if they were all standing up. He crawled so fast that the grass stem propping up one eyelid fell out, but the real problem was his trousers scraping on the ground.

"Who's that?" shouted Palace.

While Palace was peeing, he'd been scratching himself, but that did nothing for his itch, so he'd grabbed a lump of earth and was massaging it in when he spotted a shadow moving on the cliff.

Stargazer, Jindou and Yes'm dropped their pipes and shouted, "Who's there?"

Inkcap had to get up, and his voice trembled as he said, "It's me."

"Inkcap?" Palace exclaimed. "You came from the kiln?"

"How could I have come from the kiln? When Goodman and I got halfway–"

"You did it on purpose!" Palace declared. "Where's Goodman?"

"He went to the Mountain God Temple," Inkcap said. "And what do you mean 'we did it on purpose'? If we hadn't interfered, you'd have started fighting. And look at my face, you see, I've been stung to bits."

"You deserve it," Palace said. "If the bees hadn't been there, we'd have recovered the kiln."

"And what if they'd fought you for it?"

"What are you talking about? What are you saying? You're trying to make the Red Blades look bad and the Hammerheads look good!"

"Forget it," Yes'm said. "Let Inkcap go back home." He blew his nose and wiped the snot across Inkcap's face. Palace now came over and patted Inkcap down, prodding him here and there, and making him take off his shoes and open his mouth.

"Are you looking at my teeth to learn my age?" Inkcap asked.

"I think you and Goodman released those bees on purpose for the Hammerheads," Palace declared. "Did Bash ask you to take a message to someone in the village?"

"Search away, don't mind me."

Palace didn't find anything, so he pinched his crotch and said, "Motherfucker's a growing boy!"

Inkcap endured the humiliation, and just said, "I don't want you passing the disease on to me."

Palace pinched him again and said, "But I do want to pass it on to you. We're all itching, why shouldn't you?"

Yes'm gave him a kick and said, "Be off with you now, fucker."

Inkcap ran off home, and on the way, he felt aggrieved but unable to say anything, so he brought his foot up high with every step, and deliberately made a loud, stomping noise. But he remembered how Gran was worried about him, and wondered how to explain things to her when he returned. Just as he was thinking about this, he heard a sound, and when he stopped and looked ahead, he could make out two trees waggling. They were both mulberry trees, one bearing fruit and the other not. Usually, mulberry trees will not grow very long branches, but these had long, thin branches, quivering at the faintest breath of wind, and then waving in unison. Cowbell said they were rogue trees, and these rogue trees grew outside the wall around where Dazed-And-Confused lived and drove him crazy.

Inkcap continued walking, but there was that sound again. This time the sound was not the swooshing of the mulberry trees touching each other, but rather like footsteps, coming from the yard of Dazed-And-Confused's house. Inkcap opened his left eye with his fingers and saw that the door was locked. Dazed-And-Confused was still up at the kiln, so could it be that his house was being robbed by burglars? Inkcap crept up to the wall and looked inside through a hole in the masonry. He could make out someone in there, with a bag over his shoulder and a pot in his hand. It was Dazed-And-Confused, after all! But the only way to enter the village was down a single road. Inkcap didn't have anything against Dazed-And-Confused, but he did like the idea of using this turn of events to take revenge on Palace. He waited until Dazed-And-Confused had climbed out over the wall and run off before going into the village to find Awning. He wanted to launch a formal complaint against Palace who couldn't stand guard for anything – he'd been harassing an innocent while letting the real villains get away scot-free. I'll let Awning deal with you, he said to himself.

But before he could find Awning, a sharp footstep rang out in another alleyway, and someone shouted, "Catch Dazed-And-Confused!"

Inkcap set off running, but he didn't know which alleyway he'd been found in, and after running down one empty alleyway, he ran up another, and suddenly he got all excited and started shouting, "Catch Dazed-And-Confused! Catch Dazed-And-Confused!"

Finally, in Three Fork Alley, Inkcap caught sight of Dazed-And-Confused. Five or six men carrying torches were after him, and in the light of the flames they could see him running ahead. He was carrying a bag over one shoulder and a pot in his hand. The men in pursuit couldn't run fast since the torches were in danger of going out, and by the time they flickered and lit up again, Dazed-And-Confused had already run ahead, jumped over the wall of Old Faithful's pigsty and disappeared. When the others arrived at the pigsty and searched it, there was only a sow with her stomach touching the ground. They were puzzled. This pig had once broken out of its pen, so Old Faithful had reinforced the wall with three good planks, and up above he'd put a row of spikes. Could Dazed-And-Confused have got through the spikes and run away?

"That's impossible," the search party concluded. "It's not like he's a tiger."

But when Inkcap came running, he found a straw sandal caught on the spikes, and that sandal was really broad and long, with one strap broken, so he was quite sure it belonged to Dazed-And-Confused. Convinced that he'd escaped across the spikes, he wondered how he'd managed it.

Palace, who was on guard at the junction, heard the shouting and now came running with Stargazer. "Where's Dazed-And-Confused?" he asked. "Where is he?"

"You're supposed to be on guard at the crossroads," a man the search party said. "What are you doing here?"

"You were making all this racket," Palace replied, "so why shouldn't we come?"

"We were heading him off, and since you weren't in place, won't he have escaped into the mountains?"

"How do you know he was heading to the mountains?" Palace said.

"He was carrying his bag and a pot, so he's clearly heading off to join his mountain gang of thugs... he came into the village to find something to eat."

"He won't have made it as far as the mountains," Palace declared. "Yes'm and Jindou are still on guard."

"OK, Palace, let me ask you a question. How exactly did Dazed-And-Confused enter the village? There's just one way in, so how did he manage to get past you?"

Palace was caught on the hop because he too found it rather odd. Suddenly he pointed at Inkcap and said, "Did you bring him in?"

"How am I supposed to have done that?" Inkcap said. "Do you think he was curled up in my pocket?"

"You distracted our attention," Palace declared, "and he took advantage of the opportunity to slip in."

"I'm not a member of the Hammerheads, so why would I help him get in?" Inkcap knew the situation was serious and burst out crying.

"Inkcap doesn't have the guts to do anything of the kind," the man with the torch said.

They didn't argue any further and ran together towards the junction. Their idea was to guard the junction because if they did that, Dazed-And-Confused couldn't go back up the mountain. Even if he didn't try to go up the mountain, no matter which way he ran, at least they'd still be able to prevent the Hammerheads from rushing down the mountain while everyone else in the village was chasing him.

Before reaching the junction, they could hear the sound of fighting a long way in the distance; Dazed-And-Confused had indeed tried to make a dash for it and was now struggling with Yes'm and Jindou.

Palace was anxious and shouted from afar, "Dazed-And-Confused! I'm gonna fuck your mother!"

When they all ran over, Dazed-And-Confused was off up the slope. They chased him for a while but failed to catch up with him. When they returned, Yes'm and Jindou were still sitting on the ground unable to get up. Apparently, when Dazed-And-Confused ran past, Yes'm and Jindou went to stop him. Dazed-And-Confused swung his bag and iron pot at them, the pot spilling ash from the bonfire high into the air so that when Jindou lunged forward, the fire burned his eyebrows and hair. As he fell with a scream of pain, Dazed-And-Confused swung his bag at Yes'm.

Dazed-And-Confused could run to the village from the kiln, and from the village to the kiln, without let or hindrance. By now Awning, Millstone and Sparks had arrived, and they felt humiliated. This humiliation soon turned to anger, and they divided their forces into two groups, one to guard the crossroads and the other to take their torches to Dazed-And-Confused's house. Since they hadn't managed to hit the man himself, they'd take their anger out on his home. The door of the house was locked, but being made of poplar wood, they managed to open it with just a few kicks. Having got in, they were looking for things to destroy, but all but a few pounds of the grain in the kitchen cupboard had gone – the fucker must have taken a full bag out to the kiln. Next time he tries that trick, he'll find nothing here! But how to take the remaining grain away? The torches were quickly doused, and countless hands reached into the cupboard. Some put the grain in their pockets, some took off their jackets to wrap it up inside, some tied their trousers to their legs and then grabbed handfuls of grain and stuffed them down the waistband.

Afterwards, the torches were lit again and Millstone was shouting, "Go to the house!"

Those who hadn't tied their trouser legs firmly had them come open, so they had to secure them again. Then they grabbed the grain that had leaked out and scattered it into the corners of the house, saying, "Let the rats come!"

In the house, on the stove, there was no salt in the salt cellar, no spice in the spice jar, so some people began cursing, "This motherfucker's poorer than I am, damn it!"

The big pot next to the stove was full of pickled cabbage, which could not be taken away. They took the lid off and spat in it, but that wasn't enough – they picked up a handful of ash and tipped that in. When they came out of the house, a dozen pairs of new straw shoes were hanging on the wall by the courtyard door; one man took a pair to replace the rotten straw sandals on his feet, and then they broke the shoe tree on the ground.

Inkcap did not get home until very late, and when she saw his face swollen like a quince, Gran started crying. Realising that she was crying rather than scolding him, he told her how he and Goodman had stopped an armed fight.

"Should I have let them kill each other or should I have got a swollen face?" he asked.

Gran stopped crying and took Inkcap in her arms.

"Don't hug me," he said. "I've got snot on my face."

Gran said she didn't mind the snot and took a closer look at his face under the lamp, and then complained that Goodman only put snot on her grandson's face. Why didn't he take out the stings?

"Can you see the stings?" Inkcap asked.

"Sure."

She told Inkcap to lie in her lap, and with the light shining full on his face she extracted the stings, putting them in the palm of Inkcap's hand one after the other. In total, she extracted twenty-three. Having got the bee stings out and applied a layer of snot, Grandmother and Grandson went to bed. When Inkcap took off his clothes, four more bees fell out, and he squashed them flat.

That night Inkcap did not sleep well, but he still got up at dawn, wanting to go again.

"Today, you are not allowed to go out," Gran insisted.

"I don't know if my eyes are clear, so I want to see if I can make out the clouds on South Mountain," Inkcap said.

"Then look at me."

"You're close, so of course I can see you clearly."

"Stop messing about. Go to the woodshed and bring me a rope."

Inkcap thought Gran wanted to tie a rope across the courtyard to hang up some washing, so he went to the woodshed and got the rope.

As he was coming out of the shed, he asked, "When did Useless leave yesterday?"

"About half an hour later."

"Why didn't you let Awning and the others catch him?"

Gran glared at him and told him to tie one end of the rope to the tree and the other to his own waist. "Tie it to my waist?"

"I'm going to cut sweet potatoes for drying, and if I don't tie you up, you'll run away again."

Inkcap had to tether himself. As soon as Gran went to the kitchen to cut the sweet potatoes, he went out of the yard. The rope was long enough for him to walk to the privy in the alleyway, where Almost-There's dog was eating shit. Inkcap waved at the dog, which came bounding over, and he said, "You've got to be me for a bit."

"Woof! Woof! Woof!"

"No! Is that your answer?" Inkcap asked the dog. The dog lowered its brows but kept wagging its tail. Since it was broken, it was just the stump that moved. Then Inkcap took off the rope from around his waist and tied it to the dog.

"Now, don't go into the yard, and don't bark."

Inkcap went down the lane, which was pretty quiet. Tag-Along's wife was beating her son before leaving him to sit in the open, holding up the mattress wet from last night's pee so that it could dry in the sun. Inkcap walked over, pulled the wet mattress off the head of his *gan'erzi* and threw it aside, only to turn around and see Sparks coming out of the alleyway on the other side. Sparks' wound had healed, and he was clapping his intact left hand against his right hand that was missing the middle and index fingers.

"Did you call me?" Inkcap asked.

"Nah," Sparks said. "My hands are itching."

"So it's not your crotch but your hands?"

"Yeah, my hands are itching for someone to beat to a pulp!"

Inkcap froze for a moment and then asked, "Who do you want to beat?"

"I haven't decided yet."

Inkcap saw Tag-Along's wife come out to the alleyway to complain about him taking the piss-soaked mattress off her son's head, but when she heard Sparks' words, she turned around and went back inside. Inkcap didn't waste any more conversation on Sparks, and he dragged his *gan'erzi* to his own house as quickly as possible.

It was already breakfast time, and the Red Blades were taking turns guarding the crossroads, standing to attention. Those who had already put in a shift or had not yet taken their turns were eating from bowls while they walked up and down. No longer were they to be found gathered under the trees relaxing, and the Hammerhead families didn't dare so much as set foot out of doors.

Awning was on patrol, his leather shoes creaking as he walked. When he got to the houses of certain Hammerheads, he did not stop; but when he arrived at others, he would pause and eye the place up. Wherever he went, countless eyes followed in terror, trembling lest the Red Blades were about to burst in and wreck the place. Whose house were they going to target?

Sure enough, the Red Blades were checking who else had crept back from the kiln the previous night. Wherever they'd been, the sounds of violent conflict were now to be heard. The Hammerheads who hadn't yet been vetted had no time to worry about how their husbands or sons had eaten or slept at the kiln all day and night; they were worried about the safety of their own homes, so they closed the gates and slammed shut thick wooden bars and started hiding their valuables in the cellar.

Old Faithful's Mother stood with her bowl, chewing peacefully as the shouting began next door. A viciously cruel voice asked, "Has Decheng come back yet?"

"No," his mother answered, "and you can check that for yourselves!" Then she started screaming, "Decheng! De… cheng! Where are you now? How could you do this to us?"

Old Faithful's mother started coughing, and the more stressed she became the worse she coughed. She was soon struggling to breathe. Now a knock sounded on her own door, and Old Faithful's wife removed the thick wooden bar and opened it.

The group of people outside the door demanded, "Where's Old Faithful?"

"He hasn't come back."

"If he hasn't come back, why did you bar the door?"

"We were afraid we'd be searched."

"If he hasn't come back, what have you got to be afraid of? Where is he?"

"Who?"

"Who do you think?"

"He really isn't here."

When they came in and had a look around, checking the pigsty and the chicken shed, Old Faithful was nowhere to be seen, and Old Faithful's mother was sitting on the steps, curled into a ball with all the coughing.

The people who'd come in said, "Let's get out of here. He's such a coward, he wouldn't dare come back."

Inkcap called his *gan'erzi* into the house and gave him a meal. It was a noodle stir-fry, and Inkcap sat there and watched his *gan'erzi* finish a big bowl of it.

"Full?" he asked, and his *gan'erzi* said he was. "So I should think!"

His *gan'erzi* stared at him with wide eyes. "You think I've eaten too much?"

Inkcap realised his words may have been hurtful, so he said with a smile, "You're so sensitive. Let me ask, have you missed me?"

"Yes."

"How come?"

"I was hungry."

"You only ever think about food!" Inkcap exclaimed. "You should say that you missed me because you care about me."

His *gan'erzi* repeated the words.

"That's right," Inkcap told him. "Now, when you go to sleep this evening, I want you to pay attention. We don't want you wetting the bed. If you're having a dream where you can't find anywhere to pee, so that you have to pee on the bed, that's when you need to wake up."

Gran was listening in on their conversation and laughed. "It would have been great if you could have paid attention in your sleep."

"Gran!" he cried, to stop her from revealing his own shortcomings. Turning to his *gan'erzi*, he said, "Your mum is a horrible tigress. If she hits you again, you're to come right over."

The swallow on the door frame of the upper room twittered a few times. "Do you want to see the swallow?" Inkcap asked and his *gan'erzi* said he did.

The swallow flew down from the nest and rested on Inkcap's hand, but having dropped a feather, it flew off again, spinning over the yard and calling over and over. Inkcap could hear the swallow saying that it was going to leave, that it was cold and that it was heading south, so he asked, "Can't you live in the house when it's cold?"

"It's cold in the house too," the swallow replied.

"Will you come back again?"

"Sure."

"And when you come back, will you still recognise me and my home? Maybe when you come back, my family won't be one of the Five Black Categories any more, and I'll have grown taller."

"I'll still recognise you," the swallow assured him.

Inkcap felt sad, and he said to Gran, "The swallow's leaving."

"It's getting cold," Gran said. "I've been thinking it's time for it to leave, but it's still here."

Inkcap sighed and said to the swallow, "Go away, you need to leave now."

But the swallow did not go; it just stood on the laundry stone calling. Inkcap went over and caught the swallow in his hand, and said, "I am not sad, I'm here to see you on your way."

He took the swallow out of the courtyard entrance. The alleyway was very narrow, and he worried that the swallow would fly up and hit a house or a tree, so he walked to the crossroads and opened his hands. The swallow flew off and landed on the elm tree, calling to Inkcap.

"Go on," Inkcap said. "If you don't go, I'll get annoyed."

The swallow flew straight up into the air, and then made a twisting turn, flashing through the treetops before disappearing.

A group of people ran past: thump, thump, thump. He didn't see who the leader was, but right at the back was Yoyo, riding on a dog. To be precise, Yoyo wasn't really riding the dog; her dog was trying to chase after the group running past, and Yoyo wouldn't let it, so she had caught the dog between her legs. The dog's tail kept wagging and hitting Yoyo on the arse.

"Whose house is under investigation this time?" Inkcap asked.

"Apricot's," Yoyo said.

"Apricot! Why her?"

"When Apricot opened her door, there were four pairs of shoes under the bed. One pair of lady's flower embroidered shoes, one pair of military boots, one pair of baby shoes and a second pair of baby shoes."

"What are you talking about? Are you crazy?"

"You're the one who's crazy!"

Inkcap didn't want to quarrel with Yoyo, and he was worried about the news that Apricot's house was being investigated. He ran off in that direction, but the front door was closed, and when he went over to knock, he realised that the door was smeared with yellowish shit.

In fact, Apricot's house had not been turned over because when someone suggested they should go there to check whether Bash had come back to the village overnight, it was immediately shot down, because if Bash could come back, then all the Hammerheads would have followed him down the mountain. So the gang headed over to investigate Baldy Jin's house instead.

The group went to Baldy Jin's house since they were quite sure he hadn't come back overnight either, and this would be an excellent excuse to smash up and rob the place. They were not expecting that Half-Stick had already thrown out all of his stuff, saying, "He is him, and I am me!"

The group were stunned. "Baldy Jin hasn't come back?" they asked.

"What would he come back for?" Half-Stick said.

"Food and some cooking equipment?"

"He wouldn't dare take so much as a single grain!"

"That's right," they said. "You're a good person, Half-Stick, you can join the Red Blades."

"Get away with you. If I wanted to join, I would, but I'm not going to join any faction right now."

Awning walked in from the courtyard door at that point, and said, "Half-Stick, if Baldy Jin comes back, you have to report it."

"No way," Half-Stick shouted. "If you want to know when he returns, you should come past to investigate."

SIXTY-SEVEN

AT THE KILN, the Hammerheads had not eaten all day and regretted having spent the morning smashing the jars that held rice and flour – even the smallest pot had been thrown into the ditch. It wasn't until it got dark and Dazed-And-Confused came back from the village with a bag of maize and an iron pot that they were able to eat. The maize could have been boiled to make a thin soup to cover several meals, but they put all of it into the pot and ate a thick porridge because there were no bowls left at the kiln. They had no means to eat a thin soup, but a thick porridge could be turned out on a tile to set firm. Besides, they did not believe they would have to stay up at the kiln for much longer, feeling sure that when dawn came, they could just rush back to the village. However, the Red Blades guarded the crossroads all day, and hunger made them feel dizzy, plus they were still suffering torture from scabies, so they couldn't summon the energy to go down the hill. All they could do was pile up stones and tiles at the kiln in case the Red Blades attacked.

Bash gave everyone a pep talk and sent someone to the Mountain God Temple to borrow food from Goodman. Goodman didn't have much in the way of spare food, but he took out a jar and poured out a few bowls of rice, and then grabbed a pint of wheat flour and half a pint of bean flour from two more jars.

"This is all I have," he said. "The remainder will be enough for me to eat for a couple of weeks, what with the greens I pick for myself, but it will barely fill your stomachs. That being the case, you'd better leave it for me."

He was telling the truth, but the man who came to borrow food couldn't bear it. "There must be more," he said. "Revolution is always difficult. If you give us a peck of rice now, we'll pay you back double in the future. That was how the Red Army got through the winter back in the day–"

"There isn't any more," Goodman assured him. "Nothing. There's maize in that jar, but only rats would eat it."

"You're calling the Hammerheads rats?"

"You're twisting my words. I'm saying the grain is not ground up to eat."

"What do you mean, you can't eat it? Can't we fry the maize and make do with that?" The man really did write out an IOU and left with a bag of maize kernels.

When they ate the fried maize kernels, their stomachs exploded painfully with gas, and their thirst became unquenchable. The water nearest the kiln came from the pool at the bottom of the cliff and had to be carried up the slope, so someone took a bucket. But when he did not come back after a long time, Bash said to Old Faithful and Youliang, "What do you suppose the matter is? We told him to get water, and it looks like he's stayed there to drink it all!"

Old Faithful's mouth was so dry his tongue felt like leather, and he was itching terribly from scabies. He looked across at Dazed-And-Confused scratching his crotch. Since Dazed-And-Confused's trousers were in tatters, it was easy to scratch. So he now tore his own trousers to pieces and lots of other people followed suit.

Bash told him to go and fetch water. He was a little reluctant, but Youliang said, "Just go. If you go, you can wash in the pool."

The two men arrived at the pool and found two buckets at the water's edge, but no one was there.

"Do you think he's run back to the village?" Old Faithful asked.

"If he's gone back, they'll beat him to a pulp," Youliang said.

"Do you really think so?"

"We destroyed the kiln that they'd all raised money to fire, so why wouldn't they?"

"Are we just going to starve to death in the mountains? My wife has a goitre, as you know, so she can't do anything."

"I'm concerned about my wife too," Youliang said. "We haven't been able to go back for two days and nights... she'll be so anxious, and she's likely to have an asthma attack if she gets stressed."

The two of them filled their buckets with water, and each wanted the other to carry them.

"I'm prepared to run the risk," Old Faithful declared.

"What do you mean?" Youliang asked.

"You know exactly what I mean."

"You think it'll be OK?"

"Sure."

Youliang suddenly turned around and left.

"Where are you going?" Old Faithful asked.

"I'm going for a pee." He started scrambling down the slope, and then fell, tumbling down, rolling ever faster downwards, until he looked just like a ball.

"Wait, wait, I need a pee too," Old Faithful said. He too started to slip and slide. The rolling had coated the two of them in dust and dirt, and they just looked at each other without saying a word, and then clambered onto the road and started off down the mountain.

Old Faithful and Youliang were, of course, caught at the crossroads by the Red Blades. They did not resist and let the curses roll off their backs until Sparks tied their hands with a rope and took them to the Kiln God Temple to see Awning. He was busy washing his crotch with a basin of water, and as he washed, he cursed the first man to make it back to the village, who happened to be Mill Hole.

When he saw Old Faithful and Youliang, Awning dashed the whole basin of water across the ground and screamed, "So you motherfuckers thought it would be fun to go and play at being bandits, did you?"

"Bash ordered us to go to the kiln," Old Faithful explained. "How could we refuse? But when we got there, I didn't do anything, and neither did Youliang, you can ask Mill Hole. Right, Mill Hole, did Youliang or I do anything?"

"I didn't do anything either," Mill Hole said.

"Are you here to get food or cooking equipment?" Awning asked.

"We came back and have no intention of returning to the kiln," Old Faithful replied. "There's nothing to eat up the mountain, and it's cold and we didn't bring clothes, and my wife has a goitre–"

"And my wife has asthma," Youliang added.

"OK," Awning said. "So the Hammerheads are getting ready to force their way back into the village, and they want you to come in ahead and help them out, right?"

"That's not true, I swear to god," Old Faithful said. "We went to the pool to get water, and then secretly made our way back here."

"I don't believe you," Awning said. "If you want to be trusted, you must join the Red Blades."

"I can't do that," Old Faithful declared.

"No?" Awning yelled.

Then Mill Hole and Youliang hurriedly said, "I'll join, I'll join."

Old Faithful remained firm: "I can't. I don't ever want anything to do with either side."

Awning sent Mill Hole and Youliang home, but Old Faithful had to stay behind, with his hands remaining tied. Awning said he'd have to stay the rest of the day at the Kiln God Temple, and if the Hammerheads did not attack today, that would prove he was not sent back as a spy.

"How dare you say you're not joining anything!" Awning said. "Would you refuse to join the Communist Party if they asked you?"

When Youliang and Mill Hole got back to the village, the wives and old folks from various Hammerhead families went to ask them about conditions at the kiln, so they learned that they were freezing cold at night and had no food during the day. Many people were crying, and then seven or eight of the boldest joined forces to make representations to Awning. They said that after their relatives joined the Hammerheads, they had no choice but to follow Bash blindly, but it wasn't fair to let them starve to death in the mountains or freeze to death up there. They wanted permission to let the families send some food and clothing up, and persuade them to come back. Old Faithful's wife heard that he had come back and was being held at the Kiln God Temple, and not allowed home. She went to Awning in floods of tears, but he still wouldn't release Old Faithful. She put her hand to her goitre and then fell in a dead faint. They pinched her and pulled her about, but it took forever to bring her round.

Millstone discussed the situation with Awning, and they let Old Faithful go. They also agreed that three Hammerhead family members could take food up the mountain, but they had to guarantee that their relatives would join the Red Blades when they came down.

Awning gave orders to the guards at the crossroads: "Anyone who returns from the kiln will be allowed back to the village only on the condition that they join the Red Blades straight away. If they do not join, they will not be allowed to return."

The leaders of the Hammerheads – Bash, Baldy Jin, Dazed-And-Confused, Tag-Along and Stonebreaker – were to be beaten the second they showed their faces. However, the four representatives from three different households who went up to the kiln with food and clothing did not return, and the Hammerheads did not try to come back to the village. The Red Blades were now even more furious and adjusted their strategy. It seemed that the Zhu and Hei clans were simply never going to be able to live in peace together, and there was no hope that the Hei clan would join the Red Blades, so all of them should be allowed to leave. They could go up the mountain and spend the rest of their lives at the kiln. Let Old Kiln Village become the home of the Zhus, all of them being members of the Red Blades.

Over the coming days, a few more Hammerheads returned to the village and joined the Red Blades on their return. The families of some of those who did not return took everything they owned up the mountain and stayed there. The Red Blades, in addition to increasing the number of guards at the crossroads, removed the big-character posters at the mountain gate and eradicated the Hammerheads' slogans from the walls. Old Kiln was quiet again. Once everything was quiet, Millstone was anxious to start farming work, but he did not want to mess up the Revolution by putting all his energies into production, so he had to leave its organisation to the Branch Secretary.

The Branch Secretary had long been left entirely idle. He was just carefully rearing his cattle, waiting for the arrival of Noisy, who visited every few days. Noisy had promised to bring him newspapers from outside. On arrival, Noisy would shout from the field in front of Flower Girl's house, and the Branch Secretary would come running from the cattle shed. If his shout was not heard, Noisy would leave the pile of newspapers at Flower Girl's house, and the Branch Secretary would go there to pick them up at night. Later on, Flower Girl did not need to give the newspapers to the Branch Secretary, because every time Noisy came, Yoyo would be right there in the field in front of Flower Girl's door, lying in wait for him, and when he turned up, Yoyo would grab the newspapers off him to give them to the Branch Secretary.

When Noisy showed reluctance in giving her the newspapers, she just said, "Gimme!"

"Why should I?" Noisy replied. "The newspapers aren't for you. Did the Branch Secretary ask you to collect them?"

"I want to take them."

"Who is the Branch Secretary that you want to do this for him?"

"He's my Branch Secretary!" Yoyo declared. She grabbed at the papers and when she couldn't get hold of them, kicked Noisy's bicycle over. Noisy thought the whole thing was really odd, but he didn't want to get into a fight with her, so he asked Flower Girl what was going on.

"She's off her head," Flower Girl said. "She doesn't recognise anyone any more, except for the Branch Secretary."

Millstone told the Branch Secretary to organise the village's farm work. "I know I shouldn't," he said. "I said I'd stop caring about that kind of thing, but I just can't stand seeing our fields go to rack and ruin... As things stand, I can't take charge of the farming myself, but I can give you the authority to do it."

"But Millstone," the Branch Secretary pointed out, "I'm a capitalist roader, so do you want me to go back to my old ways?"

"I don't care what you do," Millstone said. "I've told you what I'd like to see happen and that's all."

Having said his piece, Millstone stomped off. But he told everyone in the village that he'd put the Branch Secretary in charge of organising agricultural labour again. Lots of them agreed that it was time to go back to work in the fields, but the two factions were still caught up in the Revolution… the Revolution was at such a critical point, only the Branch Secretary could possibly deal with organising labour.

A constant stream of people were coming to find him: Are we going to the fields today? What are we going to be doing? For the first few days, the Branch Secretary told everyone not to bother him about it. He even asked them, "Are you trying to get me into trouble? Do you think I've had it too easy lately?"

In fact, he wanted to find out the village's reaction to letting him take charge of farm work, and every night he read the newspaper to check that this would not go against the party's policy with respect to the Cultural Revolution, that it was not forbidden. He went so far as to call Inkcap to his home and took out a pile of his hair to give him.

"Do you want *liguo* candy in exchange?" Inkcap asked.

"I'm giving it to you," the Branch Secretary said. "You can keep the *liguo* candy."

"Why are you treating me so nicely? Is something wrong?"

"I've heard you can smell things out. You can smell if someone's died, or something's happened."

"Who told you that?"

"Is it true?"

Inkcap didn't know what to say, and the Branch Secretary continued, "Smell the air. What can you smell?"

Inkcap sniffed. "Have you been cooking potato starch noodles?"

"I want you to smell if something's going on, and all you can smell is noodles?"

Inkcap sniffed again. "There's nothing going on."

The Branch Secretary laughed and said, "What the hell can you smell, Inkcap? If you could smell trouble, you'd be an owl!"

But Inkcap was now anxious and said, "I can smell trouble, but there isn't any."

"OK, OK, you go and tell everyone we're having a meeting."

"What do you mean by 'everyone'? What meeting?"

"We need three or four members of the Zhu family," the Branch Secretary explained, "and three or four from the Hei family, plus a couple of others, and everyone is to meet at my house."

Inkcap informed ten people, but they were not convinced that the Branch Secretary was genuinely going to hold a meeting, so Inkcap had to swear that he was and that he was a dog if he lied. The ten people decided that the situation must have changed again, and they wanted to see what the Branch Secretary was going to do. The Branch Secretary took out a sheaf of newspapers from his house, and instead of reading them, he took out the one that contained the instructions of the Central Committee of the Communist Party of China on grasping revolution and promoting production. Then he took out another, which contained the notice of the Provincial Cultural Revolution Group on implementing the instructions of the Central Committee of the Communist Party of China on grasping revolution and promoting production. And then he took out a third, reporting the instructions of the County Cultural Revolution Group on implementing the instructions of the Provincial Cultural Revolution Group on grasping revolution and promoting production. Finally, he flourished the newspaper that contained the county's Cultural Revolution Group notice on implementing the instructions of the Central Committee of the Communist Party of China on grasping revolution and promoting production.

When he said these words, he clearly understood the meaning of each layer, but the audience were bewildered. "Why are you still going on like this?" they asked. "What are you talking about?"

"I'm making sure everyone is safe," the Branch Secretary said. "Now we can have our meeting about bringing the land in Old Kiln back into production."

"Oh, I see," they responded.

From then on, the Branch Secretary started to arrange farm work. The most reliable members of his team, when he was allocating labour, were alwaysEver-Obedient and Yoyo. To everyone else, Yoyo appeared to behave in a crazy and unpredictable way, but she was always perfectly normal with him. Every morning when he opened the door, Yoyo would be standing outside and asking what they would be doing that day. She never let the Branch Secretary make the announcement but banged a broken tin basin and started to yell. Yoyo always had her dog with her, and they'd go off and spread fertiliser or water the fields. Without any young and strong labourers, it was the women and old people who did the work, and every time the broken washbasin clanged, the women and old folk surnamed Zhu went out to the fields, and the women and old folk surnamed Hei who'd not gone up the mountain followed suit. All their labour was recorded so they could receive work points. Those who did not have work points or had fewer work points would get little or no vegetables and firewood, though rice was not on the ration any more.

The Zhu families swanned about while the Hei families pulled in their horns. Once there had been an intractable conflict, so when two rivals met in the lane, one would spit on the ground, and then the other would also spit on the ground. Now, when the Heis met the Zhus, the Zhus could spit on the ground and insult them in every way possible, while the Hei family members just had to keep silent.

Inkcap was eating lunch sitting at the entrance of the courtyard. No one else was eating under the trees along the side of the road, which made him feel that his food had lost its savour, so he turned back and picked up a chopstick's worth of chilli to stir in. Gossip can be used as a side dish, for even the thinnest and coarsest rice can go down unnoticed amid conversation and laughter. Now he had to add chilli, stimulating the tastebuds so he could get the food down his throat.

"You eat too many chillis," Gran said.

"These pickled vegetables are hard to swallow," Inkcap complained.

Gran had just finished her meal, and the bowl was still on the *kang*, where she was soaking a pile of dried ginkgo leaves that she had picked up during her morning work. If you make a papercut using dried ginkgo leaves that have been rehydrated, the result is very crisp and resistant to crumbling. When she heard Inkcap's whining, she stopped soaking and looked at him. Inkcap realised he'd said something wrong and hung his head and applied himself to eating, but when his teeth clamped onto the pickled vegetables, he started coughing.

"Tomorrow," Gran said, "tomorrow at lunchtime we'll have rolled noodles."

"I won't eat them," Inkcap said.

"Why not? We've still got some flour in the jar."

"It would be a waste. Let's cook up some soya beans. I love soya beans."

"My grandson likes soya beans..." Gran started to cry and couldn't stop herself, so she rubbed her eyes, first the left one and then the right.

Inkcap raised his head and watched Gran rubbing her eyes. "What's wrong?" he asked.

"I've got a little bug in there."

Inkcap wanted to help her get rid of it, but Gran just said, "It's fine, it's nothing, go on with eating. When you've finished, you can go and find out what we're meant to be doing this afternoon."

Inkcap finished eating and went out into the alleyway, which was blustery and cool, before standing under the chinaberry tree and emitting a burp. The burp was full of the tang of pickled vegetables, which he hated, so he fanned his hand in front of his mouth.

"Your breath stinks," Apricot complained. She was coming back from her family's haystack carrying a basket of straw. Since the wind was blowing the straw around, she turned sideways to stop it and chatted to Inkcap.

"I didn't eat any garlic, so why should my breath stink?"

"Really?" Apricot said. "I can smell it from here."

Inkcap wanted to say, You're pregnant so of course your nose is extra sensitive. But he didn't say it, and his eyes avoided her waist, and instead he looked up at the sky, where the sun was hidden and the clouds were whipped by the wind, like a river flowing eastward.

"I'll give you a toothbrush," Apricot said. "It doesn't cost anything to brush with salt water."

"I won't wash my mouth out... tigers don't wash their mouths out and they eat nothing but meat! Do you know what we'll be doing this afternoon?"

A wind gusted up again, dislodging a few wisps of straw out of her basket. Wind is invisible, but the straw was spinning in circles in front of them. Inkcap wondered whether the wind was round. "You shouldn't stand here," he said. "This wind is nasty."

Apricot understood what Inkcap meant and smiled, saying, "You're very thoughtful, and you've learned to be considerate of others. I heard Ever-Obedient's wife say we're going to be mixing up shit and piss for fertiliser."

Inkcap turned to go, but Apricot asked him, "Have you been to the kiln?"

"No," Inkcap assured her. "I'm not a Hammerhead."

"Didn't Awning want you to go up to the kiln?"

"I'm not a Red Blade either."

Apricot looked at the sky and said, "It's cold."

Inkcap also looked up at the sky and echoed her words. "It's cold."

They both understood each other's meaning, but neither bothered to say anything more about it. Soupspoon came over carrying rafters, and shouted from a distance, "Get out of the way, get out of the way!"

Inkcap and Apricot stood back out of the way, and Inkcap asked, "Where did you get that?"

"It was part of the frame for hanging big-character posters."

"But that doesn't belong to you."

"It does now!" Soupspoon declared. "I put enough money into the kiln to buy three rafters." There was nothing to stop Soupspoon from carrying one rafter at a time, but he had two, and he was carrying them crosswise so that they smacked into Apricot, who could not get out of the way in time. She dropped the basket of straw she was carrying.

"Take it easy," Apricot said, "slow down."

"What are you doing here in the village, Apricot?" Soupspoon asked.

"Am I supposed to be somewhere else?"

"So many people went to deliver food and clothes to the kiln, and you didn't go?"

Apricot's face changed, and Inkcap saw her chest was heaving, so he figured that Apricot was about to quarrel with Soupspoon, and in any battle of words, Soupspoon was going to come off worst. If it turned into a physical fight, he'd have to protect Apricot; she couldn't be beaten up. But in the end, Apricot did not say a word.

Inkcap went home and reported the events to Gran. She didn't say anything for a long time, and then asked, "Has Apricot gained or lost weight?"

"She's looking a lot darker," he said.

Gran made no response but started calling the chickens, none of which came running over. Then she said, "Catch the white rooster and give it to Apricot."

"You're giving her a chicken?"

Gran got a little angry. "You never listen to me, give her a chicken!"

"If she wanted to eat human flesh, would you cut a piece off yourself?"

Before Gran could raise her hand and smack him, he rushed away and went to the alleyway to look for the chicken.

A dog was running towards the entrance of the alley, together with three cats, and there were also eight chickens, four of which were his, and the white rooster was running in front. Inkcap was amazed. Normally the chickens lived in the yard, and if they ventured out, they'd be looking for food or playing outside the door – they never went as far as the alleyways, so why had they run this way today? Inkcap stood in the door and shouted, "Gran! Gran! The chickens are running away, I can't catch them."

"What do you mean, you can't catch a chicken?"

Inkcap ran out of the alley, and once he left, he could see that the area was packed with dogs, cats and chickens, with yet more arriving from both north and south. They did not mind the villagers standing in the road, but all headed off in the same direction, towards the east. They were giving tongue, too, back and forth, with unparalleled delight.

It seemed that someone had blocked the road ahead, whereupon the dog lying there started woofing, scaring whoever it was. The dog stopped, stood up, let all the chickens get past and then scampered on, running like the wind. A cat jumped off the corner of a courtyard wall, and although it was certainly agile, it wasn't as fast as the chickens. The chickens went wild, running along and holding their wings up in the air, flying over the head of the man by the side of the road. The man was Pendulum. His back hurt terribly and he held himself up with his hands. Glancing sideways he asked, "What's this? What's going on?"

"They ignored me too," Inkcap replied. "I don't know what's up with them."

Almost-There's family dog came out from the Sparks family yard at the same time as their dog emerged. Almost-There's dog had no tail, and Sparks' dog had a big head, and the two of them talked affectionately together as they ran. They rushed past Iron Bolt's house, and his flat-tailed pig came out and ran after them. But Almost-There's dog and Sparks' dog turned to the pig and barked, so the pig stopped, with its mouth pouting and head hanging, and it pissed everywhere.

"Come here, you!" Inkcap called out. The pig looked up and saw Inkcap, smiled and came running, its four tiny feet thumping along.

"How dare you run away," Inkcap said. "Be careful Iron Bolt's wife doesn't beat you."

"They'll hit me whatever I do," the pig said. "First they said I could go and then they said I couldn't go... humph!"

"Who are they?" Inkcap asked.

"Almost-There and Sparks."

"Almost-There and Sparks?"

"We call the dogs by their master's names," the pig explained.

Inkcap laughed. "So do they call you Iron Bolt or Inkcap?"

"Sometimes they call me Iron Bolt, sometimes they call me Inkcap."

Inkcap patted the pig on the head and said, "Good, that's good. What are they doing? Where are they going in such numbers?"

"Today," the pig explained, "Gourd's family's lumpy chicken is having a birthday party at the south entrance of the village."

"Chickens have birthday parties?"

"Why not? It's the oldest chicken in Old Kiln. It's twelve years old."

Inkcap thought he knew pretty much everything about the village animals, but he wasn't aware they had birthdays. That got him interested, and he ran to the south entrance of the village. But when he got to the stone lion, he didn't see any chickens, or cats or dogs for that matter. He was complaining to himself that the pig had lied to him, but when he looked down the hill slope not far away, he was shocked. Hundreds of chickens and dozens of dogs and cats were gathered there, the dogs in one circle all sitting up straight with their front paws on the ground, and the cats in another, standing straight, but not so stable, so they kept moving their hindquarters about, but never so that they fell over. In the middle of the two circles formed by the dogs and cats stood Gourd's family's lumpy chicken, clucking all the time, and all the chickens circled around it, with their wings half-open as they turned, the ones facing inwards craning up high, the ones facing outwards bending down low, pecking the ground. Then all the chickens, cats and dogs began to call out, and though their voices were not the same, they opened their mouths wide with joy. The chickens' tongues were long, and the dogs' teeth were white. Inkcap just stared and then he too started to move, humming to himself, but he did not dare go down the embankment, or even set foot on top of it, for fear of disturbing them.

A group of women were walking to the wheat field with rakes, hoes and shovels, and when they saw Inkcap sitting in a daze on the ground in front of the stone lion from afar, they called out, "Hey, Inkcap! Has your gran been beating you again? Why are you just sitting there?"

Inkcap ignored them.

"Why are you still sitting there on the cold ground?" Sprout asked. "Your gran is on her way."

Inkcap didn't want them to come any closer, and he was afraid that Gran would really come over, and once that lot came, they would surely notice the gathering of cats and dogs, and that would equally surely break it up. He picked himself up and walked straight to the village, saying as he went, "Where's Gran?"

As it happened, Gran had gone to the compost heap. The compost heap was where the production team gathered pig manure from each family, which would later be mixed with urine and used for winter fertiliser. Gran couldn't carry the buckets of piss, so with Third Aunt, Noodle Fish's wife and Youliang's wife, she picked up shovelfuls of manure and mixed them together. Youliang's wife was asthmatic, so she had to rest after working a while, and then she simply knelt on the ground and used a hoe. While Youliang's wife was on her knees, Gran was suffering from a sore back and legs, but she was too embarrassed to kneel down and work. She was so tired and sweaty that she took off her outer jacket.

"Gran," Sprout said, "don't catch a cold."

She sneezed.

"Look, you've taken cold," Sprout said.

"Am I really that delicate?" Gran asked. "One sneeze means someone is thinking about me. Two sneezes means someone's cursing me. Three sneezes means I've caught a cold. Now... I wonder who's thinking about me..."

"Your little Inkcap?" Sprout said.

"He's annoyed with me," Gran said. "He just wants to laze about. If you ask me, it's Apricot who's thinking about me."

"Nah," Sprout said. "She'll be thinking about Bash."

"You shouldn't talk about her like that, Sprout. You used to be such friends. Other people will laugh at you for the way you've quarrelled now."

"You're always on her side. Think of what she's done now. Us Zhus have never had an unmarried mother in the family before."

Gran glared at Sprout, and Youliang's wife now asked, "So Apricot's pregnant, is she? Ha ha! Now I wonder who the father is... Ha ha!"

Gran told her to stop speaking since her breathing was so bad. "Go and pound her on the back, Sprout! We need to get her breathing again." Meanwhile she herself sneezed again, and said that someone must be cursing her, and then sneezed a third time.

Sprout went over and picked up Gran's jacket and draped it across her shoulders, saying, "You've definitely caught a cold this time. You need to rest."

Gran sat on the ground and buttoned up her jacket.

Yoyo brought over a bucket of piss and when she saw that none of the four were working, said in a gruff voice, "You're supposed to be mixing the manure. What are you doing sitting around? Are you trying to get work points for nothing?"

They all got to their feet and started stirring the manure.

"Granny Silkworm has a cold," Sprout said. "She just sat down to put on her jacket properly. What are you doing shouting and screaming like that?"

"The Branch Secretary put me in charge," Yoyo said.

"Ooh, so we're very Red right now, are we?" Sprout said. "Awning and Millstone came to me to ask me to be responsible for promoting production, but do you see me going around throwing my weight about?"

"Oh, so you're wonderful," Yoyo said. "If you're so wonderful, why don't you go up the mountain and join the rest of them? What are you doing here?"

Noodle Fish's wife and Youliang's wife came rushing over to try to calm them down, but Yoyo just dumped the urine into the heap of manure and stomped off with an empty bucket.

"Your tongue is too sharp for your own good, Sprout," Gran told her. "Yoyo wasn't wrong. It's good to see her up and about and taking charge of things."

"It's embarrassing our ancestors for the last eight generations," Sprout declared, "that we've got a lunatic in charge."

SIXTY-EIGHT

THAT NIGHT, Gran had a sore nose and throat, and her ears were weeping pus. She said she felt chilled but not as if she had a temperature. She took out the stone from the pickling vat and used it as a pillow, but it didn't make her feel any better. After another day, she began to run a fever and her eyes were too sleepy to open, so she just slept on the bed. It had been cloudy ever since the day they'd been mixing manure, and the cloudier it was, the more crystalline the air, and now it was raining, and when it rained for a while, the drizzle turned into snow, and the snow was not flakes, but hard little grains, and the yard was filled with a swishing sound as they fell.

Gran was on the bed, directing Inkcap to get the pile of beans behind the house and put them in the kitchen so they wouldn't get wet when the snow fell; and to put straw in the pen for the pigs, along with some dried earth, because pigs shouldn't be left to wallow in wet mud on cold days; and to get some maize tassels from the storehouse and stuff them into his grass sandals, because once the cold weather started it was easy to get frostbite in his feet. Inkcap did everything he was told, apart from putting the maize tassels into his sandals because he made them into fuses instead... making fuses was more important. He would rather his feet got frostbite. Gran, lying in bed, hadn't spotted what he was doing, and he made a whole bunch and hung them up over the wall to the courtyard. When he came in again, he asked Gran what she'd like to eat and drink.

"Oh, that's very kind of you," Gran said. "You're a good boy... you're making me wish I was sick more often! Tell me, what can you make that's good to eat?"

"I can make you a soup," Inkcap said. "If you want something else, should I ask Third Aunt to come and make you a bowl of flag noodles?"

"It's very sweet of you, but I really don't want anything to eat or drink. You go out and play, you don't have to stay with me."

Inkcap had been at home all day and did indeed want to go out. He took the bucket from the toilet and put it under the bed as a piss pot.

The bonfire was still burning at the junction at the foot of the hill, but it was no longer straw, maize stalks or even cotton stalks that were burning, but several large root lumps, which, from a distance, glowed as red as blood clots in the snow. Sparks, Palace and Padlock were all there. Someone had probably brought a few potatoes to bake, and they were now fighting over them. Inkcap knew that if he went there, he wouldn't be able to eat any of the potatoes, but instead they would force him to go home and get some potatoes for them.

In Crosswise Alley, along came the people who were composting manure for the production team, carrying piss from Jindou's family. They had already made several trips, so they squatted down to light their cigarettes. Jindou was left using a ladle to scoop the contents of his piss pot into the bucket. The piss splashed his hands and face, so he started searching for leaves on the ground to wipe them clean.

"How smelly is that piss that it got you dirty?" someone asked.

"How can it not be smelly?" said Jindou.

"Jindou, put your hand over your heart and tell the truth – does your piss not smell?"

"My piss doesn't stink, but your pigsty smells to high heaven!"

The two sides started fighting, and everyone said, "What nonsense is this? We're all part of the same production team, no one should say anything about anyone."

Jindou came over and squatted down for a smoke before deciding to put an end to the quarrel himself by pointing out that they were all doing OK. The Hammerheads had also been called upon to join the production team but none of them had come so he started cursing them. The fuse placed by the privy wall had finished burning, leaving a thick ash trail like a dead snake. Soupspoon came over to pick up a bucket, complaining that originally he'd been on guard by the crossroads, but Yoyo insisted he go and carry buckets of piss about. They should never have given her the job, he said, because she didn't know her place any more. He also put down the piss bucket to have a smoke, and reached for the fuse, only to find it falling away in his hands because it was ash.

"Get me a light," he shouted at Inkcap who was coming that way. "Go and get me a light."

Inkcap went to get him a light from Jindou's house, but Jindou was angry and said he didn't have any matches, so Inkcap ran back to his own house to get some. As he scampered past the embankment by the spring, he saw several fuses hanging on Baldy Jin's soapberry tree to dry. He decided that Baldy Jin wouldn't miss one. But the fuses were hanging high on the tree, and there were piles of wild thorn bushes under the tree, so he tiptoed over carefully to tug one down. A cat squeezed out from the gap in the sagger wall of Baldy Jin's house, pushing its way out past the hank of straw stuffed in the gap. It let out a meow.

"What are you meowing for?" Inkcap asked. "Won't you let me take the fuse?"

The cat's eyes flashed as bright as pieces of glass, and then it squeezed one eye shut and made a face. "Meow!"

"Meow to you too! Baldy Jin has run away, so he's not carrying his fair share of the piss pots. He should at least contribute a fuse."

By now, the cat had gone back in through the cracks of the saggars.

Inkcap found the cat an interesting character and crept up to the saggar wall to peer through. The door to the upper room in the courtyard was open, and at first glance it appeared that the door was a hole, a black hole, for he could not see what was inside, but he could hear someone talking. It was Half-Stick.

"When it was time to collect sesame seeds," Half-Stick was saying, "I went to collect them. I carried back two baskets, and Big Root and Thimble carried back three baskets. Although they said we didn't grow much this year, that crop was never split among members of the commune, it was always sold to the production team to make oil from... The sale always went down into the public accounts, but when I went to Soupspoon's house, his chilli oil had sesame seeds in it... where on earth could he have got sesame seeds from? Sesa-me-me-me-me..." The voice trembled strangely, dropping to a gentle moan.

Who was Half-Stick talking to? To Baldy Jin? Was Baldy Jin back?

"All sorts of odd things have been happening in Old Kiln," Half-Stick continued. "As we were digging the lotus roots out of the pond, when it came to tally them up there really weren't that many, and the Branch Secretary said we should send them to the commune, but how many could we possibly part with? Oh, oh, that's wonderful, how can you do that... you... you..." The voice was trembling again.

Inkcap didn't understand why Half-Stick was talking perfectly normally and then her voice suddenly started to go all over the place. He'd heard that Half-Stick and Baldy Jin quarrelled all the time, but it wasn't like that at all; these two were clearly very fond of each other, so fond that their voices changed when they spoke to one another. However, Inkcap hated Baldy Jin, and if he'd managed to sneak back from the kiln, then the Red Blades needed to know about it. He hoped Baldy Jin would never come back to the village, and that if he did, he'd be chased out the same way as Dazed-And-Confused had been.

Inkcap ran towards the crossroads to report that Baldy Jin had returned.

"Impossible!" Soupspoon said.

"I heard them talking in front of his house, believe it or not!"

Soupspoon then got all serious and asked Jindou to go with him to see what was going on, but Jindou said he wouldn't go, he'd come back from the kiln himself, he couldn't go. Soupspoon told Jindou to call someone at the crossroads and he would go to Baldy Jin's house to see what was going on, and if it was really Baldy Jin, he would keep him under control. Soupspoon dragged Inkcap to Baldy Jin's house, but Inkcap refused to go.

"You're a slick one," Soupspoon said. "You found him and now you're not going."

On arriving at Baldy Jin's house, they listened through the courtyard door and heard voices inside. Soupspoon didn't start by kicking the door in, but shouted from outside, "Half-Stick! Half... Stick!"

The sound of voices in the house immediately stopped, and after a while, Half-Stick said, "Who is it?"

"It's me," Soupspoon said. "I'm here to collect your piss pots to add to the compost heap. Hurry up and hand over your bucket."

Half-Stick came out and opened the door, and sitting up there on the steps to the house was Awning. Soupspoon and Inkcap were both dumbfounded. Awning didn't appear to notice Soupspoon and Inkcap, but said to Half-Stick, "In the future, I don't want to have to come in person to investigate again. If Baldy Jin comes back, you've got to report it." Having said that, he lit a cigarette and walked away.

Soupspoon had to pick up a pair of piss buckets, and then he came out again with Inkcap. "Fuck you for messing things up like that! So Baldy Jin's back, is he?"

"I thought it was Baldy Jin," Inkcap said.

"And now Awning will have it in for me."

"Why would he have it in for you?"

"Didn't you notice that white patch on Awning's trousers?"

"The snot?"

"Piss off, you idiot!"

Inkcap could have tolerated all sorts of insults, but Soupspoon had called him an idiot, so he got angry and said, "You're the idiot!" He went up to the compost heap alone.

Noodle Fish's wife and Youliang's wife were still raking the manure pile. They asked if Gran was feeling better, and Inkcap said she was still asleep. Noodle Fish's wife told him to go round to her house and get a lump of ginger and boil it up for Gran to drink. Inkcap was just thinking about how Gran had made ginger soup every time someone else had a headache or fever, but claimed she didn't want anything herself. Maybe Gran knew it wouldn't do her any good? Inkcap was confused by Gran's illness. Her nose and throat hurt, for sure, but then her ears were also weeping pus, more and more pus, and she was running a temperature... For something like that, Goodman was the best person to ask. Inkcap was quite sure he'd know how to cure Gran. But to get in touch with Goodman he'd need to go up the mountain, and was Awning likely to let him? He tried asking Awning, and he did give him permission to go, but he had to go to the kiln too.

"I don't want to go to the kiln," Inkcap said. "I just want to go to the Mountain God Temple and come straight back again."

"I am telling you that you have to do this," Awning said.

"Then you suspect me of being in with the Hammerheads?"

"I want you to pretend to be on their side. You know what, I want you to go up there and see if the motherfuckers are dead or alive."

Inkcap then understood exactly what he meant. "You want me to be a spy?"

"What are you talking about? Who wants you to be a spy?"

Inkcap knew that he had spoken out of turn and said quickly, "That's just what Cowbell told me."

He didn't go up the mountain immediately. Awning wanted him to go to the kiln, but when he got there, what would he say to Bash? How should he begin this conversation? He couldn't think of anything to take with him that would lead naturally into the topic of conditions at the kiln, so he sat down on a millstone and lost himself in thought. A woodpecker flew up the chinaberry tree and pecked a hole in it: bang, bang, bang. That woodpecker annoyed Inkcap, and the noise it was making seemed to resound through his head.

Suddenly an idea came to him, and he got up and went to look for Apricot. She was packing sweet potato slices. At the beginning of winter, every family sliced their sweet potatoes and dried them on the eaves of the house. Inkcap stood in front of a pigsty diagonally across from her house and called out to her, "Apricot, Apricot!"

She was standing on a stool and did not raise her head or say a word. She was obviously ignoring Inkcap, which made him feel a little embarrassed, and any smugness that he felt over his good idea disappeared.

The snow was still falling, and a cow was pushing a ball of dung up the ridge in front of the pigsty, and the ball went up the ridge before rolling down, then went up the ridge and rolled down again.

"You're so stupid!"

Inkcap kicked the manure ball over the ridge, and Apricot got off the stool and carried her sweet potato basket towards the courtyard door, still not looking at him. However, she whispered, "Come in with me and take your chicken back." The evening when the village chickens, cats and dogs assembled, Inkcap had taken a black chicken to Apricot's house, but he didn't give it to her openly. Instead, he'd tied the chicken's legs together and placed it on the threshold.

"How did you know I gave you that chicken?" Inkcap asked in amazement.

"Everyone else is off being revolutionary," Apricot said. "Either their chickens have red feathers or a red comb. Your chickens are the only ones that are black." Apricot giggled, and Inkcap started to get cross. He ran into the courtyard ahead of her.

"If you insist on going ahead, you'd better watch out in case I fall on top of you," Apricot told him.

After they entered the courtyard, Apricot closed the door and put away the clothes that had been hanging up to dry on the branches of the trees.

"If I hadn't said that, you wouldn't want to come to my house! Why didn't you ask me if you could come in when you delivered the chicken? Why did you just leave it on the threshold for the wolves to steal? Do you hate me too?"

Inkcap was now feeling a lot less angry. "The chicken was a present from Gran, but I didn't want to give it to you."

"And isn't that the truth," Apricot said. "You didn't want to give me the chicken and it didn't want to come."

Inkcap stared at her wide-eyed. "What's wrong with the chicken?"

Apricot told him that she'd carried the chicken back home, crying all the while. She couldn't bear to kill it, so she'd decided to keep it, but the chicken was on hunger strike. She'd scattered some wheat grains for it, but it wouldn't eat, and for the past two days and nights it had kept clucking all the time, so much that it was now completely hoarse. The reason she'd asked Inkcap to come to the yard was to get him to take the chicken back. If it stayed here, it would just starve to death, so it would be better to take it back to his house.

The chicken was lying in the woodshed, already too weak to stand on its legs, and half of its feathers had fallen out, revealing a bare neck and spine. But as soon as it saw Inkcap, it stood up and walked towards him, then halfway over it fell down again.

Inkcap took the chicken in his arms and said, "Phoenix Hei, Phoenix Hei, what is wrong with you?"

"What are you calling that chicken?" Apricot asked. "Can a chicken have a last name?"

"My surname is Hei, and it's black, so I call it Phoenix."

"What do you mean by calling it a phoenix? Maybe it's a phoenix that emerged from the ashes of our kiln!"

Now that she'd mentioned the kiln, Inkcap said, "I'm going up there, is there anything you want me to take with me?"

Apricot immediately stopped smiling. "What would I have for you to take up? I don't have anything at all."

"OK, fine."

Inkcap grabbed the chicken and made to leave, only for Apricot to ask, "Is Awning going to attack the kiln?"

"Nobody's going to be attacking anybody," Inkcap told her. "They've got wolves and tigers on both sides, and they know it."

"When you mentioned going to the kiln, were you just making fun of me?"

Inkcap started to get cross again, but he could hardly tell her that everyone knew all about what she and Bash had been up to. I ask you a perfectly civil question and you treat me like this! He told her that Gran was sick, and he was going up to find Goodman, but he didn't say anything about how Awning wanted him to act as a spy.

"Wait a sec," Apricot said. She ran upstairs and took out a sweater, telling him to give it to Bash. Now Inkcap was jealous – he'd never had a sweater to wear in his entire life, and here was Apricot knitting one for Bash!

"OK," he said, and he wrapped the sweater around his shoulders. Apricot decided that wouldn't work at all, someone was sure to spot it and take it off him when he got to the crossroads, so she told Inkcap to take his jacket off and wear the sweater underneath. The sweater was very long and very wide, so the hem hung down around his ankles.

"Look at you!" Apricot said. She hefted up the sweater and tied it around his waist with a rope. Then she helped him put his jacket back on. "Is it warm?"

"Toasty," Inkcap assured her.

"You must give it to him the moment you see him."

"It would be best if he were dead."

Apricot stopped his mouth with her hand. "Don't say anything so unlucky."

Inkcap went up the mountain and headed first towards the kiln. The people there were all dressed in thin clothes, and those who had brought up cooking equipment and rice and flour divided it all up perfectly equally, but there wasn't a lot of food, so they were eating three meals of weak gruel a day. They were still suffering from scabies, and the itching was driving them mad. About half of them had scratched their crotches raw, and Stonebreaker was in the worst situation of all of them. His neck was covered in red welts. If the scabies mites really were planning to take up residence in his face, that would be dreadful. Bash still seemed optimistic. He said he had not been to Yan'an, but he'd read descriptions of the place in his textbooks. Chairman Mao spent thirteen years there, and from Yan'an he'd waltzed straight into Beijing.

He put on the sweater that Apricot had knitted for him, pointed to the slopes of the mountain and said, "It's the same earth, the same cave-dwellings, and the same lack of clothing and food. It's just a shame there isn't a pagoda over at the Mountain God Temple. In the future, I'll build one for them!"

Inkcap had never been to Yan'an, nor had he ever read a textbook about Yan'an, and as a point of fact, he had no idea what Yan'an even was. But he could see that the Hammerheads couldn't last much longer out at the kiln, and pretty soon – say in the next three days to a week – they'd have to come down the mountain, and then they would either defeat the Red Blades or be defeated by them.

"It would be great to have a pagoda here," Inkcap said. "The pagoda by the Zhou River guards the river, and this pagoda could guard the mountain."

"We'll call it 'Precious Pagoda'," Bash declared, "and rename this place 'Precious Pagoda Mountain'."

Bash pointed to a place on top of the mountain and then suddenly started shouting, "Tag-Along! Tag-Along!"

"If you want a shit," Inkcap said, "there's no need to call Tag-Along. I'll come with you."

Inkcap grabbed a hoe from beside the kiln and accompanied Bash towards the depression out back. After digging a small pit, Bash declared that he was no longer constipated, but he had to piss because of all the gruel he was drinking. He peed for a very long time before saying, "What's the situation in the village now?"

"Nothing much is going on," Inkcap said. "We're preparing manure."

"Is there no one guarding the crossroads?"

"Oh, the Red Blades are on guard, but agricultural production is being organised by the Branch Secretary."

"Branch Secretary? He's a capitalist! The capitalists are back in charge!"

"Oh, erm," Inkcap muttered.

"I guess Awning is throwing his weight around…"

"Oh, well, um…"

"What's he been up to?"

"I heard his wife say that he sleeps with that wide leather belt on."

"It's the only belt he has," Bash snarled. "Has everyone who went back from the kiln joined the Red Blades?"

"Yup."

"That's a lie… What? Every single one of them?"

"Yup."

"Fuck!" Bash tucked himself back into his trousers and said, "That's enough of that."

"I'm going to talk to Goodman," Inkcap explained. "Do you want me to take anyone a message?"

"Nah," Bash said.

"I bet there is…" Inkcap said, but Bash just waved him away and walked off.

When Inkcap arrived at the Mountain God Temple, Goodman was very happy to see him. He looked into his face for a long while before saying, "You've got thinner."

"No, it's just that the swelling's gone down," Inkcap assured him.

"Now the stings have gone down, you do look so much better." Goodman looked around for something to give Inkcap to eat but found nothing, apart from an egg that he was going to crack open.

"I don't want to eat your egg," Inkcap said, "but I'll give you an egg after you've cured Gran."

"I can't help your grandmother, she knows that perfectly well. But I'd better go and see her… I've been cooped up here long enough."

There was even more of the hard, pellet-like snow up here in the mountains than down below, and it was really easy to skid on the roads, so it was going to be a hard journey. After slipping and falling a few times, they wrapped grass rope around their shoes and went on carefully down the road. When they reached the bend in front of the kiln, they saw the Hammerheads eating, their pots propped up on top of the kiln. Everyone was being shouted at to line up, as they crowded towards the kiln entrance: "Form a line here, starting at the kiln!"

The person at the head of the queue took a bowl of gruel and gulped it down while walking away.

"How can you just tip it down your neck like that?" someone asked. "Isn't it red hot?"

"I'd like to eat it slowly," came the reply. "There's nothing in the gruel that I can chew."

Those who had already eaten once again joined the back of the long queue, licking their bowls. Those ahead of them asked why they had got back in line again. The ones who had already eaten said they weren't full, so why shouldn't they rejoin the queue?

"So you're going to have two bowls, but we can only have one?" those ahead of them complained.

"Then you move forward in line," said the ones who'd eaten.

"Motherfucker! That's so unfair."

"Who are you cursing?"

"I can curse whoever I like."

Bam, someone hit someone else, and immediately the queue was thrown into confusion. Lightkeeper had been squatting by the bend in the road. No one had paid any attention to him since the Hammerheads had come to beat him up, but he wasn't allowed to leave. While everyone else was fighting, he was over there all alone sitting on his haunches and smoking cigarettes.

"Why don't you go and get something to eat?" said Inkcap.

Lightkeeper looked at him but didn't respond. His belly was like a stove, and his mouth the flue from which a constant stream of smoke was emitted.

"Aren't they giving you anything to eat?" Inkcap asked.

765

Lightkeeper grabbed a handful of snow and tossed it in Inkcap's face. "What's it to you?" he said.

"Well, starve to death then and see if I care!" said Inkcap, dragging Goodman off with him.

"What a lot of clowns," Goodman said. "Look at them, neither fish nor fowl, and all at sixes and sevens." But the next step he took didn't land firmly, and his foot skidded out from under him, and he slid for a bit, ending up with snow all over him.

"Does it hurt?" Inkcap asked.

"Of course it does."

"It's snowing these hard little grains. How nice it would be if it really was snowing wheat!"

"If we're going down the mountain, let's go to your house."

Inkcap giggled. "What's that you said? Something about fish and fowl, and sixes and sevens?"

"Neither fish nor fowl, and at sixes and sevens," Goodman repeated.

"What does that mean?"

"You want me to explain it, do you? You're small, your centre of gravity is low, which means you won't go sliding everywhere. So if you let me hold onto you, I'll tell you."

Inkcap let Goodman put a hand on his shoulders. "I'm sure you've heard people say someone is neither fish nor fowl," Goodman began. "As to what it means, it sounds like they aren't right, doesn't it? And that's exactly what it does mean. Someone who is neither fish nor fowl is a very dubious character, and this saying comes from the traditional idea that women should be obedient and virtuous. In particular, a woman should obey her father before she's married, her husband after she's married, and her son if she's a widow. And the virtues a woman should show are proper behaviour, proper speech, proper deportment and proper work. This saying began from the idea that anyone who isn't obedient and virtuous isn't really like anything at all – neither fish nor fowl. Do you understand that? If a person's internal organs are incomplete or have moved out of place, that person is not normal. We should all want to be normal, right?

"And as for the saying about being at sixes and sevens, a fetus changes every seven days in its mother's womb, and when people die, they start to decay after seven days, and then after seven times seven, they begin their next cycle of rebirth–"

"I don't know why you're telling me this."

"Do you really not know, or are you just saying that?"

"I really don't know," Inkcap said.

"Oh well, if you really don't know then it doesn't matter. It would just upset you to understand what I've been talking about."

Gran did not know that Inkcap had gone off to invite Goodman to the house, so when she caught sight of him at the door, she rushed to get up from the bed and shouted to Inkcap to bring cigarettes and a match, while she staggered off to the kitchen to heat a pot to boil some eggs.

Suddenly, the sound of barking could be heard all over the village, and a flock of chickens came running in from the lane outside, clucking frantically. Three of them even flew up onto the wall, where they could not find good purchase, so they tumbled into the yard.

SIXTY-NINE

BARNDOOR TOOK HIS CARRYING POLE AND BASKETS out to collect a load of manure, but the snow was falling more and more heavily, and the weather was getting colder by the minute, so he could see the breath as it puffed out from his nose and mouth. He walked along the riverbank, went around the dyke and reached the dirt road at the back of the pond, but the snow was blown about by the wind, and the road was like quicksand.

Barndoor did not actually pick up much manure; instead, he squatted down behind the weir and shat directly into the basket. In all of Old Kiln, Dazed-And-Confused was the only person who ever did that kind of thing, and Barndoor laughed at his own absurdity. He wiped his bum and felt as if a million knives were scraping across his skin down there. "Hey, when shit freezes hard, it doesn't stink," he said to himself.

At just this moment, a pack of wolves passed through the hemp fields around Awning's house, and the ground where the hemp had been harvested was covered with tussocks of sedge grass. The grass was dead – you could almost hear the bells tolling for it. But there was no sound from the wolves. Their paws looked as if they were wrapped in cotton, and from head to tail, their fur had turned completely grey. Did the wolves also change their wardrobe with every season and put on grey cotton coats for the winter? Barndoor was wondering this, and then he suddenly panicked so violently that he did not even pause to pick up the manure basket but ran towards the village with his trousers hitched up in one hand. The wolves didn't chase him, in fact they didn't even look back. They just walked on with a smile and continued to pass by.

When Soupspoon and the others who were out carrying slops heard that the wolves had passed again, they ran to the earthen dyke behind the mill, wielding their carrying poles as weapons to prevent the pack from entering the village, but they did not see hide nor hair of the animals. Did they go to the riverbank in front of the village again? When they ran to the stone lion, they saw a group of people pounding along on the dirt road leading to the village. At first, they thought that the residents of Xiahewan had come to chase the wolves away, but Xiahewan was too far away from Old Kiln, so even if they wanted to help out with running the wolves off, would they go that far? The people were getting closer and closer, so everyone laughed at Barndoor for being as blind as a bat, and they also started making fun of the dress of those who were coming. Look at them – black trousers and black coats, with white belts and white puttees – they're dressed just like that man who came from Henan with his performing monkey!

Six Pints' son suddenly turned pale and said, "That's the Golden Cudgel Rebel Team from Xiahewan!"

When Six Pints was ill, his son went to a doctor in Xiahewan to get medicine for him, and he'd seen the Rebel Team there. They were supposed to be affiliated with the United Command faction. What Six Pints' son was saying was already quite alarming enough, and now they saw that all of them were holding cudgels. What on earth were they doing in Old Kiln? Then they realised that the men out in front were Useless and Pockmark. There could be no doubt about it: Useless had gone and reported that the Hammerheads had been turfed out and were holed up in the kiln, so they'd gone to the United Command folk at Xiahewan for reinforcements! But what was Pockmark doing with them? Immediately someone ran to report on Awning and Millstone, as fast as if he had a firecracker clenched between his arse cheeks. While everyone else scattered, Pendulum, who'd just come from the village with a terrible backache and wasn't part of any group, stood there stock still.

"Hey, Pockmark," Pendulum called out, "is that you?"

"Come over here and find out for yourself," Pockmark said.

Pendulum moved forward, his head on one side, and was punched by Pockmark in the chest, so he stumbled and fell to the ground.

"How dare you forget!" Pockmark said. "How dare you say you didn't recognise me! Do you think Old Kiln could get along without me?"

"How come you're out?" Pendulum asked.

"It doesn't matter how I got out. The fact is that I am out, and I'm back in Old Kiln."

Pockmark raised his foot and kicked out at Pendulum, who sat on the ground, bracing himself with his hands as he moved back. Pockmark's foot caught him in the mouth, and one of his teeth fell out. Bloody froth ran down his chin.

"It's nothing to do with me," he squealed, "I'm not a Red Blade nor a Hammerhead."

"But you're from Old Kiln," Pockmark said, "and that's reason enough to beat you. You know how to fire a kiln, don't you? And when I went to take a few more saggars to build a wall you refused, didn't you? Get up and fight. Look over here, look over here."

When Pendulum faced Pockmark, he couldn't see a thing, so he had to tilt his head, and at that moment Pockmark kicked him right in the head.

The people who were running away saw Pockmark was maltreating Pendulum, so they turned around to save him. But they were soon surrounded by the Golden Cudgels, and right in the middle of the group they found Huang Shengsheng. Had he come along too? Huang Shengsheng was so thin that only a tiny slit of a mouth was left, but he was shouting, "Who's a Red Blade?"

"They're all Red Blades," Useless told him.

The Golden Cudgels started hitting them, and Soupspoon's shoulder received a whack, whereupon he fell to the ground.

"Those motherfuckers are beating us for real!" Soupspoon said as he scrambled to his feet and reached for his carrying pole.

His pole for carrying piss buckets had rope at each end with hooks attached. Waving it about was like using a flail – nobody could possibly get close. After Soupspoon had grabbed his carrying pole, pretty soon everyone had theirs as well, and they flailed them about as they retreated towards the road leading to the village. Then they turned and ran. Some went into houses and barred the door, some hid in pigsties and others climbed trees.

The group coming from the road down the slope set a guard there, while the rest went over to the Kiln God Temple to burn their clothes. When they heard that Winterborn and Pillar had cured themselves of scabies by rubbing themselves down with kiln ash, they too rubbed ash into their crotches and lit a fire, but they didn't imagine that rubbing and starting the fire would combine to make the scabies itch even more. They called Winterborn over and wanted to see whether his scabies had improved, so he dropped his trousers and let everyone see – it was evidently true. Immediately they had him down on the ground and were scratching at their crotches and then scratching at his.

"Motherfucker!" they screamed. "How dare you get better! Let's all itch together!"

Once fighting began at the southern entrance of the village, the news spread quickly, and everyone got busy putting on their trousers before rushing out in a swarm. They were in such a hurry that they didn't take time to ascertain which entrance of the village to head to, so first they ran over to the big millstone on the east side, only to find nothing going on there.

Gourd's wife was drawing grey circles on the wall of her pigsty. "Are the wolves coming?" she asked.

No one paid any attention to her. Third Aunt came stumbling along at a run, driving two chickens ahead of her with a long pole, and one now flew up into the air. "There's a fight going on," she said.

"Where are they fighting?" the group asked.

"At the southern entrance of the village."

The group turned around and headed south.

The lane was full of pigs, dogs, chickens and cats running towards them, and when they saw the villagers, they started squeaking and barking and clucking and meowing, but nobody could understand what they were saying.

"Don't block the road!"

All the pigs, dogs, chickens and cats backed up to the side of the road and waited for the group to pass, then turned around and ran forward again, but when they turned around, almost all of them slipped on the snow.

"Jindou," they said, "are you all right?"

"I don't want to be called 'Jindou'," the pig replied. "Jindou's wife, Lingxing, is good to me, so you ought to call me 'Lingxing'."

The animals were about to have a go at the pig for bringing up a name change when they saw another group come in at the end of the lane. This group was chasing Cowbell, and they were about to catch him, when Cowbell suddenly flew up, grabbed the edge of a courtyard wall with both

769

hands, scaled the wall and soon reached the roof, from where he began pelting his pursuers with tiles.

The house belonged to Thimble's family, and Thimble's father was out there shouting, "My tiles! My tiles!"

The tiles were raining down from above, while the men below responded with stones and some of the tiles that had been hurled at them, and all the while Thimble's father was howling like a wolf. The people at this end of the lane turned and ran back, but could not get through, so they started yelling until those chasing Cowbell got out of the way. They retreated to the entrance of Awning's house.

Awning emerged from the door to the courtyard with a machete in his hand. "Listen up motherfuckers!" he shouted. "How dare you bastards think you can come here and make trouble?"

He was so loud that the dogs stopped barking, and the gang was shocked into flight. Awning started hacking at them with his machete, and his movements were so wild that the snow heaped on the cobbled lane flew into the air.

When Awning returned from Half-Stick's, he felt a little cold and his legs were weak, so he put on an extra jacket and made a fire to cook a handful of spring onion roots.

"Why are you eating onions?" his wife asked.

"To keep my pecker up," Awning replied.

"That's disgusting."

When Awning saw his wife bending under the cupboard to get the cat's bowl, he noticed her triangular arse and found it deeply off-putting. He was just about to give her a kick when he heard the dogs barking outside and chickens flapping. Pulling the courtyard door open a crack, he saw a group of people running down the alleyway chasing Soupspoon and the rest of them, so he thought the Hammerheads must have come down from the mountain to fight, but he didn't recognise any of the assailants... As he was still wondering, he spotted Useless, at which point he threw the door open, lunged out and dragged Useless in.

"Who are this lot?" he asked.

"Golden Cudgels from Xiahewan," Useless replied.

"Your motherfucking reinforcements?"

Awning punched Useless in the face and then kicked him out.

Useless fell like a clod of earth hitting the ground. He wanted to start shouting but he'd dislocated his jaw. He grabbed hold of one of the men pounding past and gestured to him that he needed help to put his jaw back in, ah, ah-ing all the while. The man put one hand on top of his head and pushed the jaw back up with the other.

When his jaw was back in place, Useless shouted, "This is Awning Zhu's house, Awning's in here!"

A group of men who'd run past the door now turned back, but Awning had barred the entrance. When the door was broken down, Awning's dog came rushing over the wall and down the alleyway to be beaten with sticks.

Although its skull wasn't broken, its back certainly was. Then Awning emerged from the house with his machete.

Awning's machete was made of iron, and originally it had been held in the hands of the statue of Guan Yu in the God of War Temple in Xiahewan. It weighed a full seven pounds. One year they were going to put on plays for the Spring Festival, and the actors from Xiahewan wanted to perform *Oath in a Peach Orchard*, so they borrowed this particular blade. But by the time they got to Old Kiln to perform, they'd discovered the thing was too heavy and the child performers simply couldn't lift it, so the Branch Secretary gave them a wooden sword instead. The real one had been kept, and somehow or other they never gave it back. The Red Blades got their name from Awning's machete.

Awning came rushing out of the courtyard door with his machete just as the Red Blades were running up, so in an instant, the Golden Cudgels were thrown into chaos. Some went on the attack, but most turned and ran, retreating to the stone lion, and from the stone lion to the embankment. Huang Shengsheng started shouting that some men were coming towards the village along the highway, and they were carrying wine bottles.

"These motherfuckers like to do things in a big way," Sparks declared. "They've even brought wine!"

"Let's get on over there," Awning said. "Whoever can get hold of one of those bottles can drink it himself!"

Before he'd even finished speaking, one of the wine bottles was hurled his way and landed about ten yards ahead of them. Boom! The bottle exploded, and the four men immediately fell down, screaming in pain. Each one of them was still wearing trousers, but they were soaked in blood, and Sparks' face was now covered in soot while everyone else was still clean. When he opened his mouth, his teeth showed long and white. Padlock and Sprout thought he'd died in the explosion and started screaming, "Sparks! Sparks!"

Sparks was blinded by the bomb, and when he heard the shouting, he touched his head with both hands to discover that his head was still intact. He touched his crotch and everything was all right down there. He thought he was just fine until he started to get up, and then he realised the back of his hand was covered in blood, and when he wiped his hand against his black face, he now had blood on his face and soot on his hand. He pointed at Huang Shengsheng with his hand missing two fingers and called out, "Motherfucker! How dare you use bombs!"

Another wine bottle was thrown over, and again it exploded, sending up a cloud of smoke, snow, mud and glass splinters. The Red Blades withdrew to Awnings' courtyard entrance and sought shelter under the wall.

"Awning," Sprout said, "what kind of bomb are they using?"

"Molotov cocktails," Sparks explained. "The kind you use for blowing up fish."

Fish bombs. When the people of Old Kiln or Xiahewan went fishing in the river, they'd use rods or nets, but the residents of Luozhen would usually fill bottles with kerosene or dynamite and add a detonator cap before throwing them into the water to blow up the fish. Huang Shengsheng had come with some folk from Luozhen who belonged to the United Command. Originally, they'd thought to attack Old Kiln without them, but they still took a couple of dozen Molotov cocktails to blow up fish in the river in front of the village so they could eat a fish stew at lunchtime. However, as it turned out, they did need them. When the Red Blades withdrew, they came up, and Huang Shengsheng started shouting for Pockmark, but he was nowhere to be seen. Then he shouted for Useless, saying the Red Blades were on the retreat, and they would all have withdrawn to their own homes. He wanted Useless to point out exactly where the Red Blades lived, and if they could fight them, they would; and if they had to chase them off instead, they'd do that. They were going to "liberate" Old Kiln. But they were blocked again at the entrance to the road, and Awning commanded the Red Blades to fling stones and tiles down on them like rain, whereupon Huang Shengsheng threw three more bottles.

The bottles burst one after another, wounding a few of the Red Blades.

"Do you still have some dynamite at home?" Awning asked Sparks.

"Not any more," Sparks said.

"What about rockets? We could fire rockets at them."

"They're back at base, but we've got no explosives there."

"Did we use it all up last time?"

"Maybe there's still some at the Branch Secretary's house," Sparks suggested, "but I don't know if he'll give it to us."

"But it's a crisis," Awning declared. "He has to."

Sparks ran to the old man's house. Awning meanwhile ordered his strongest men to carry on throwing stones and tiles, while everyone else was set to work collecting suitable missiles. They removed some bricks from the top of his wall and also went over into Cowbell's house to get more bricks and tiles out of his walls. Soupspoon took a dustpan from Cowbell's house.

"What are you doing with that?" Awning asked.

"This will stop the wine bottles," Soupspoon explained. When he said that, someone else grabbed the sieve and the brass washbasin to use as a shield.

The Red Blades and the Golden Cudgels and United Command people from Luozhen now found themselves caught up in a tug of war. When the Red Blades rushed down the village road, the Golden Cudgels and United Command had to retreat to the stone lion; when the Golden Cudgels and United Command launched a push-back, the Red Blades retreated in a hurry. The snow was falling more heavily now, and it was no longer hard little grains but had become proper flakes, and the wind had picked up, so the snowflakes went swirling along the village road before twisting into myriad whips, hitting both sides of the courtyard door equally hard, and beating down on the walls of the houses.

When the fighting began outside the south entrance to Old Kiln, the Hammerheads were watching from up at the kiln, and they started shouting. Bash was busy pulling out his beard. He didn't want to grow one in the first place, so he was plucking it out by hand, one hair at a time. When he heard the shouting, he started down the mountain with the other Hammerheads. He stumbled and would have fallen, but Tag-Along pulled him up. If it hadn't been for this intervention, he would have gone head over heels, and could easily have toppled over the edge of the bank. When Bash was held back, he realised that he was too excited and too anxious; he'd been thinking that the bank was some kind of canyon.

"Go down the mountain," he shouted.

"Down the mountain! Fuck them! Old Kiln is our home, and they took our homes, so they're going to have to return them. They took our stuff, so now they must cough it up again!"

They all ran down the hill waving their hammers. From the kiln to the mountain road, they had to take the winding path down the slope, which was narrow and steep and now covered in snow, so almost all those running down it slipped. Having slipped, some fell from the sloping path to the ditch below, others ended up with bloody faces and bruised noses. When they tried to stand up again, they found themselves lacking the energy to do so – they were too hungry, and their bodies were shaking with cold.

Bash shouted for Lightkeeper. When Lightkeeper came over, he said, "I wanted to talk to you, as it happens."

"What do you want to talk about?" Bash asked.

"I want to go home."

"Do you want to go back to the Red Blades?"

"I was afraid of getting beaten up," Lightkeeper explained, "and they let me in, so I joined."

"If you're afraid of being beaten up by them, why aren't you afraid of being beaten up by us?"

"If the Hammerheads want me to join, I'll join."

"If you want to join us, I'll have to give the matter due consideration," Bash said, "but right now, I need you to take off your trousers and jacket."

"But it's so cold!"

"Take them off!" Bash ordered. Then, addressing the men who were crawling and rolling along the path, he shouted, "Tear Lightkeeper's clothes into strips, wrap them around your shoes and run on down. We don't want to let anyone see us Hammerheads looking bad!"

Bash himself did not wait to wrap strips of cloth around his shoes, but rushed on ahead of the crowd, like a boulder rolling down a mountain.

SEVENTY

WHEN THE HAMMERHEADS CHARGED THE JUNCTION at the bottom of the hill, only Palace, Stargazer and Once-Upon-A-Time were left on guard. Palace was worried that the Red Blades had all gone to the southern end of the village, so if the Hammerheads came down from the kiln, it would be difficult to hold the crossroads, so he asked Stargazer to go to the village and call out everyone who was still at home. He and Once-Upon-A-Time went to collect some buckets of water from the Kiln God Temple to slosh across the road, in the hope that it would set to ice. In that case, the Hammerheads would have been in trouble as soon as they set foot on it, and they'd be forced to beat a retreat. But when the water was poured out, it did not freeze, and all that happened was that Palace got his clothes sopping wet. He went back to the Kiln God Temple to get a quilt and wrapped it around himself. When he emerged from the temple enveloped in a quilt, he bumped straight into Dazed-And-Confused who was running down the slope waving the handle of his headless hammer. Palace grabbed for his own wooden sword, but it was stuck behind the bonfire, where he couldn't reach it. Instead, he picked up a shovel that was lying on the ground.

"Don't you dare come any closer," said Palace. "You come closer and I'll hit you."

"Go right ahead," Dazed-And-Confused said and hit him with his own stick. He put a lot of force into the blow, and snow sprayed into Palace's face. Palace was blinded, but he could sense the stick coming his way and managed to dodge it, so Dazed-And-Confused just beat the hell out of the air. Dazed-And-Confused almost fell over when his blow failed to land, and Palace had the shovel in his hand, which he brought down across his arse. That fucker Dazed-And-Confused had it coming to him, but he didn't fall over, and when Palace tried to hit him a second time, he twisted around and raised his stick in the way of the shovel. A nasty clang rang out and the two men's arms went numb, and their hands took a real jolt. They were now locked together, leaning their weapons into each other, and because they were evenly matched, it turned into a stalemate.

Behind them, the rest of the Hammerheads charged across the crossroads. Once-Upon-A-Time shouted, "The Hammerheads are coming down the hill! The Hammerheads are coming down the hill! The Hammerheads–"

A stick struck him across the waist, and he slid several feet over the snow, but he managed to pull himself together and made a run for the village road, with the others in hot pursuit like a pack of hounds.

Palace and Dazed-And-Confused were still locked in conflict. "You can't keep on grappling me," Dazed-And-Confused said. "I've got your wrist."

"That doesn't matter," Palace retorted. "I can keep you like this forever."

"Pah!" Dazed-And-Confused said, and he spat in Palace's face.

"Pah!" Palace said, as he spat back.

Dazed-And-Confused bared his teeth as he pressed the wooden stick down, so that Palace's shovel didn't move, but his waist started to twist. Palace gritted his teeth and exerted every muscle to force himself straight again. As they pushed and pulled, another layer of white snow fell on the ground around them and mixed with earth to form a mud slurry.

"You're standing on rocks!" Dazed-And-Confused complained.

"So are you!" Palace retorted.

But there were no rocks near Dazed-And-Confused for him to stand on. "If you have the guts, you'll move," Dazed-And-Confused said, but Palace refused to comply.

Both of them had exhausted their strength, so they stopped talking and just panted. However, Palace's thigh suddenly started itching – it was like he was being stabbed by an awl. He couldn't possibly move his hand to scratch, so instead he pressed his legs together to try to stop the pain. Dazed-And-Confused then gave an almighty heave and managed to topple over Palace. He kicked him in the crotch, and Palace went rolling across the ground.

"Itch away," Dazed-And-Confused said. "Hell, I'm itching myself!"

His trousers were in tatters, so he could easily scratch himself through the holes. Just at this moment, Winterborn came running and saw that Dazed-And-Confused had defeated Palace. He raised his wooden sword and came on the attack. Dazed-And-Confused was too busy scratching himself to even raise his head. The wooden sword hit him on the shoulder, and he lay curled up on the ground.

"This motherfucker's staring at my balls!" Winterborn declared. He got on top of him, perching his arse right over Dazed-And-Confused's face, saying, "Here you are! You can look your fill!"

He wrenched his leg hard, and Dazed-And-Confused started bleeding from his nose, but he didn't move. Winterborn put his leg down, and the man still didn't move; he looked like he was dead.

Winterborn stood up and said, "The son of a bitch is dead!"

"Not quite," Dazed-And-Confused retorted.

Winterborn went over and kicked him.

"I haven't eaten," Dazed-And-Confused said. "Let's eat and then see who can beat who."

The sound of crying could now be heard from the village, so Palace and Winterborn stopped beating Dazed-And-Confused. They grabbed a handful of mud and snow and shoved it into his mouth, saying: "Eat your mother's fucking cunt!"

They ran towards the village road. "Thanks, brother," Palace said.

"That's no thanks to me," Winterborn told him, "but thanks to my child!"

"How's that?"

"I was asleep at home, and our kid managed to climb over the wall of the pigsty and fell in. The screaming woke me up and then I heard the noise in the village and realised that the Hammerheads must've come down."

Just at that moment, a few people hared past them, running for their lives. Palace and Winterborn couldn't see who they were, but someone down the alleyway was shouting, "Help! Help! Millstone's been stabbed!" The two of them rushed down an adjacent lane.

In the lane, Millstone lay collapsed in front of Noodle Fish's house. Noodle Fish's wife had seen Millstone come staggering along, covered in blood, leaving a trail of bloodstains behind him, before collapsing in front of her doorway.

"Millstone! Millstone!" she screamed. She went over to help him up, but he couldn't get to his feet. There was a bloody hole in his stomach, and his intestines were spilling out, so she used her hands to scoop them back inside.

Millstone managed to say, "Get a bowl to keep them in there."

She went into the house and got a bowl and put it on his stomach, and then looked around for something to tie it on with, but there wasn't anything, so she took off her own puttees and used them to tie the bowl in place.

When Goodman walked down from the Mountain God Temple, Millstone was still at the crossroads, adding a basket of firewood to the bonfire. His wife came along to say that the bed was broken.

"How did that happen?" he asked.

"I don't know," his wife said.

The others started teasing them: "You must have been going at it like nobody's business!"

"I wish," his wife said.

"Millstone isn't any good in bed, is that what you're saying?" they giggled.

"And when has he been home the last few days?" his wife replied.

"All right, all right, we've got work to do," the ever-serious Millstone said.

On returning home with his wife, he saw a hole in the middle of the *kang*, so he went to Gourd's house and borrowed some cement, which he mixed up then and there in the yard. When the fighting started outside, he assumed it must be the Hammerheads coming down the mountain and rushed to the crossroads, only to discover that the Golden Cudgels and United Command were attacking the south side of the village simultaneously. He then ran to that part of the village and hurled himself into the melee, taking down a couple of combatants with punches and kicks, and then he chased a small group of three into an alley.

He could see Flower Girl standing at the far end of the alley, so he shouted, "Stop the fuckers! Stop them!"

Flower Girl did nothing of the kind; she just waved her hands and feet, shouting incoherently. Millstone ran over and complained to Flower Girl, saying that if she'd only held them up for a few moments, he could have kicked the shit out of those three bastards. But Flower Girl only cared about herself. She said someone had entered her house and when she went out to see what all the commotion was about, she got scared and ran back. Then she said she went into the kitchen only to see the lid moving on her big jar of wheat bran. She thought it was just rats until she noticed a man's head under the lid. She didn't recognise him and was so scared she went running out into the lane.

"Where is the man now?" Millstone asked.

"Still in the house," Flower Girl said.

Millstone turned and headed inside.

"You can't do it alone," Flower Girl said. She screamed so loudly and for so long that Soupspoon came running with six or seven others. There was a big old bruise on Soupspoon's forehead, and half of one sleeve of his jacket was torn off. At the sight of Millstone, he looked mournful and said, "What on earth are we going to do?"

"How many of them are here?" Millstone asked.

"Hundreds," Soupspoon replied, "and the Hammerheads have also arrived."

"We shouldn't let outsiders in. Where's Awning? Or Sparks?"

"Awning's leading the defence of the south entrance to the village," Soupspoon explained, "while Sparks is off beating up the Hammerheads. A bunch of the Golden Cudgels pitched up in the east lanes, so we've been chasing them off. So how many are in your house, Flower Girl?"

"I only saw one," she said.

A few people kicked in the door with a bang and rushed inside, saying, "Just one? Let's break the legs off the motherfucker!"

"Don't dare start fighting in my kitchen!" Flower Girl told Soupspoon. "The minute you start fighting, you'll break all the pots and pans in the house – call on him to come out and fight."

The men in the yard obligingly started shouting, "Come out, you son of a bitch!" But whoever was hiding in the house didn't come out.

"It's not Huang Shengsheng in there, is it?" Soupspoon said. "That motherfucker knows all about our village."

"Is Huang Shengsheng here too?" Millstone asked.

"Yup, and Pockmark too."

"Pockmark? How did he get back?"

"Those fuckers of prison guards don't know their arse from their elbow letting him out. He's a right menace, and he's beating everyone he sees. He wants his revenge on the whole village."

"I'll go and find him," Millstone said as he walked away.

Millstone ran up and down a few alleys. In some, a group of Red Blades had cornered some Golden Cudgels and were beating them, while in others the Red Blades were being chased off by the Hammerheads. Where the Red Blades had the upper hand, he would quickly ask, "Where's Pockmark? Has anyone seen Pockmark?" When the Red Blades were on the run, he jumped in to help, diverting three or four of them, fighting every step of the way as he retreated towards the rubber tree. He kicked the one in front against the tree and held him down on the ground. The other three took turns attacking, but he beat them off, and they all ran away, muttering and cursing. He hauled the one on the ground upright and asked, "Where's Pockmark? Do you know where he is?"

The man had lost a tooth and did not say anything, for he was looking at the ground searching for it.

"Fuck it," Millstone snarled. "If you want to look for a tooth, I'll give you another to find!" He punched him in the mouth again, and he really did drop a second tooth.

"Where's Pockmark? Where is he?"

The man took out a portrait of Chairman Mao from his pocket and positioned it so as to block his face.

"So that's your game!" Millstone said. A kick in the waist, and the man rolled a little; another kick in the back, and he rolled some more.

In the courtyard across the street, Third Aunt was looking out of a crack in the door. She opened it and said, "Millstone, Millstone, don't fight any more, or someone will get killed."

"Don't worry about that, go inside," he said and carried on his interrogation. "Where's Pockmark?"

"Who's Pockmark?" the man said finally. "I don't know him."

"Where are you from?"

"Xiahewan."

"Where else have people come from?"

"Luozhen."

Millstone thought to himself, Pockmark may have come with the folk from Luozhen...

Suddenly the man grabbed a handful of snow and slammed it into Millstone's eyes, before getting up and running away.

"I'll be damned!" said Millstone. He was rubbing his eyes, and when he got to the entrance of the alleyway, his eyes were still not quite clear. He saw a man coming towards him, and asked, "Where's Pockmark?"

"Right here," the man replied.

Millstone blinked and looked again, and there was Pockmark standing right in front of him. "Motherfucker, how dare you come back?"

"I came back to find you," Pockmark declared.

Pockmark took a step forward, grunted through gritted teeth, turned around and walked away. Millstone stumbled and took a few steps back, but he managed to stay upright, and then he lowered his head and saw a knife stuck in his stomach, with blood flowing down the handle. It looked like wine overflowing a glass. Millstone had been ramping about for ages trying to get Pockmark, but he got him first – he'd stabbed Millstone with his knife.

"You got me good, fucker!" Millstone cackled. Then he pulled the knife out with a terrible bellow of pain and started chasing him down the alley. Pockmark had already gone as far as the privy in the next alley and did not so much as bother to run, but just walked along, not looking back. Feeling insulted, Millstone chased him a few more steps, and when his feet buckled under him, he threw the knife with all his strength, and fell to the ground. Looking ahead as he sprawled on the ground, he could see the knife stuck in Pockmark's arse. If it had been a little higher, it would have stuck in his waist or back, but instead it caught him in the arse, and Pockmark flopped to the ground. At that moment, several men appeared at the far end of the alley, and Millstone could no longer recognise whether they were Red Blades or Golden Cudgels.

Noodle Fish's wife tightened the band holding the bowl, and when Palace and Winterborn ran over, they chased Pockmark but did not catch him, so they hurried back to carry Millstone home.

Three members of the Golden Cudgels picked up Pockmark and ran with him out of the alleyway. Pockmark let them pull the knife out of his arse, assuring them he could walk without any help.

The man who was carrying him said, "The knife went so deep, how can you possibly walk?"

"Millstone's uncle is a fucking loser and so is he – he stabbed me, but in the wrong place!" He urged the other three to go and carry on the fight, while he limped down the alley, blood dripping from his wound. He did not hold onto the wall but turned back to see the blood lying as bright as red plum blossoms on the snow. A dog ran through the alley with its tail between its legs, and when it jerked to a halt, its four paws slid a yard across the snow. Unable to stop itself, it almost crashed into Pockmark's arms. The dog looked straight at Pockmark, and Pockmark recognised the dog as belonging to Sparks. Its eyes glowed red. The dog also recognised that this was Pockmark and saw his eyes were glowing red.

"Woof! Woof! Woof!"

"Get out of the way!" Pockmark shouted.

But the dog lunged and bit the back of his leg. Its bite hit the tendon, and Pockmark fell to his knees. The dog dodged and then, keeping its eyes on Pockmark, it sprayed him in the face, and he felt it hit his skin. Pockmark tried to stand up, but the dog knocked him over again. Pockmark reached for his knife and threw it at the dog, but it jinked out of the way and caught the knife in its mouth, running off as fast as its four paws would carry it. Pockmark realised then that the dog had been trained to collect weapons. For a moment, he felt fear. He looked up and down the alleyway and got to his feet, the wound in his arse still dripping blood drop by drop. One leg of his trousers was soaked in blood. At that moment, if he were to come across Millstone, Awning, Sparks or Palace – hell, even if it had been Inkcap – he'd have been at a loss. The slightest creak had him looking back in alarm.

The creak came from the opening door of a courtyard diagonally across the street, and sticking out of the doorway was Lightkeeper's head. "Pockmark, come in, come in here," he said.

Pockmark stumbled into the yard. Lightkeeper went straight out again – he'd only just returned to get dressed again, and his arms and legs were still frozen stiff, so he tripped over his own feet. Pockmark thought he was going to lock the door and shout at someone to arrest him, but Lightkeeper took a broom and swept the blood from the snow by the door. Then he came back in and closed the door.

"Ha!" Pockmark said. "It turns out I owe a Black Category person for saving me!"

"And you're a murderer yourself," Lightkeeper pointed out. "A poisoner and a murderer."

Lightkeeper was still as careful as ever. He told Pockmark to take off his trousers and checked the injury. He wanted to bandage it, but it was a difficult place, so he prepared some salt water and gave it to Pockmark to wash the wound.

"Does it hurt? If it hurts, I'll give you a chopstick to bite down on."

"I've already died once," Pockmark pointed out. "This is nothing."

Lightkeeper wanted Pockmark to take off his shirt to see if there were any other injuries. When he did so, he revealed a Chairman Mao badge pinned into the flesh on his chest.

Lightkeeper had never seen such a thing before. "Oh my God, you're still wearing a Chairman Mao badge!"

"You hate Chairman Mao, don't you?" Pockmark said. "I don't. I just hate Old Kiln."

"I hate Old Kiln too," Lightkeeper told him.

"Then you're with me."

"You've joined United Command?"

"Yup," Pockmark said, "but I am not in the Luozhen Jinggang Mountain Rebel Group nor one of the Golden Cudgels, I am all by myself in the Bayonet-Killing Rebel Group."

A banging was coming from the house next door, but it wasn't a knock, it was the sound of the door being kicked, then stones being hurled against it, and finally a bang, followed by a thud. Lightkeeper immediately hushed, pulling Pockmark into the house.

"Scaredy-cat," Pockmark said, "pretending to be so brave!"

Lightkeeper ignored him and pulled the door to the main house open, telling him not to make any noise, while he would go out and find out what was going on. More banging was now coming from out back. Lightkeeper climbed the ladder and looked over the top of the wall. Baldy Jin and three other men had grabbed hold of Awning's wife and pulled her towards the door.

"What are you doing?" she demanded. "Go and find Awning and take it out on him."

"I came to look for you," Baldy Jin replied.

"I've been here in the house the whole time," Awning's wife said. "What do you want me for?"

"What do you think?" Baldy Jin said. "Don't you know that Awning's been fucking my wife?"

"Baldy Jin, you've always been like a brother to me–"

"Don't speak to me like that. I am not your brother."

Lightkeeper didn't recognise the other three people standing around. One of them took a stick and broke a branch of the lilac tree in the courtyard wall, and then poked down a basket lying up on the eaves. The looseweave basket was filled with drying soya beans, which were now scattered across the yard. There was also a cat lying on the eaves, and it jumped down to scratch the man's face. Another man kicked the cat over and sat down on the ground by the soya beans, saying, "If you want your revenge, we'll hold her legs, and you can fuck her!"

The other guy grabbed Awning's wife and pinned her down, ripping her blouse open and pawing at her tits with his hands. Awning's wife squealed and screamed.

Baldy Jin looked at Awning's wife and then caught hold of the kicked cat. "You think I'm going to fuck you, but fuck that! Look at your disgusting eyes, there's no way I'd fuck someone like you."

Suddenly he tugged at the waistband of her trousers and shoved the cat in. "Let the cat fuck with you!" he said.

The more she rolled, the more the cat scratched her crotch, and the more she screamed at the top of her lungs. When Lightkeeper came down from the ladder, Pockmark was indoors smoking a cigarette. "What's going on? You look upset," he said.

Lightkeeper told him how Baldy Jin had fixed Awning's wife, saying, "Baldy Jin's a nasty piece of work."

"What do you mean?" Pockmark said. "You think Awning's any better? When was either of them in the least bit nice to anyone?"

"That's true enough."

"Are you going to join the Bayonet-Killing Group?"

"If you're prepared to have me, I'd like to join," Lightkeeper said, "but then I won't be able to stay any longer in Old Kiln."

"Hell," Pockmark said, "I won't be staying in Old Kiln either. I just stabbed Millstone. I never want to return to Old Kiln again, so how about we both take advantage of the chaos and leave? We can cause trouble somewhere else."

"You've had your revenge, but what about me? This place owes me so much... so much... I..."

"Say something! Stop wittering on and tell me what it is that you want to do."

"It's the Branch Secretary who decided my class background," Lightkeeper said. "It's his fault that I've never been allowed to make anything of myself."

"OK," Pockmark said, "let's go and find the Branch Secretary... he can go fuck himself too, the bastard!"

The two of them got dressed in Lightkeeper's house, neatly tying their shoelaces and buckling their belts. Lightkeeper took out the rice flour jar, which still had a little flour in it, but it was too late to make flatbreads or roll noodles, so he put it back on the shelf. He took four radishes, putting two up his sleeve and giving two to Pockmark. Pockmark, meanwhile, took hold of a stool and broke the jar with a crash, spraying the cupboard shelves with flour.

"You want me to starve?" Lightkeeper asked.

"You won't be coming back, so what do you want with this flour?" Pockmark said. "Since you won't be eating it yourself, why should you leave it for someone else?"

Lightkeeper went over, grabbed a maize bun and stuffed it into his mouth. He kept on stuffing until he choked and spat it all out. He paused only to remove a small blue-and-white porcelain vase from the shelf, saying, "This I don't want to leave behind."

SEVENTY-ONE

WHEN THE FIGHTING BROKE OUT at the southern end of the village, the work of composting could not continue. Yoyo said the fuss would soon quieten down because she never imagined that after the bricks and tiles had been tossed about, the Hammerheads would also take the opportunity to come down the mountain. Now the two factions set to work with their sticks and knives, and everyone had wounds or scrapes or bangs. Yoyo went off to ask the Branch Secretary for instructions. He knew exactly what was going on and had tried to intervene already, but his wife stopped him from leaving the house and was even now sitting on a stool by the door on guard. When Yoyo turned up, she explained that the fighting in the village was getting even worse – this one had a broken leg, that one had a huge hole in his head, another had been struck with a machete, and someone else again was even now crawling around on the ground with his eyes rolled up inside his head after being badly beaten. The Branch Secretary wanted to go and find Awning and Bash. He had his megaphone with him, and a safety helmet of papier mâché reinforced with steel wire on his head.

"There's never been fighting like this in Old Kiln before," he declared. "Who's ever seen anything like it? They can beat me as much as they want, as long as nobody else gets killed."

His wife grabbed him round the leg and shouted, "Help me stop him, Yoyo. If he shows his face, both sides will join forces to beat him."

But Yoyo was standing stock still, her eyes glazing over.

"Why did you tell him that, Yoyo?" the wife pleaded. "Are you trying to get him killed? Why don't you help me? Why are you just trying to cause trouble?"

Yoyo walked over and tugged at the wife rather than at the Branch Secretary. She pulled his wife off him, and he went out. The two women were now grappling together, and the Branch Secretary's wife gave Yoyo's hair a vicious tug. "Lunatic!" she cried. "You're nothing but a murderous lunatic!"

The Branch Secretary headed out of the courtyard door with his shoes not properly on, so he stopped under the willow tree and bent over to get his heels in. That was when Pockmark and Lightkeeper came over, each clutching some kindling. The Branch Secretary was taken aback and thought he must be seeing things. He rubbed his eyes, but it really was Pockmark, so he asked, "How did you get out?"

Pockmark just giggled.

"Did you escape from prison?" the Branch Secretary asked.

Pockmark stopped laughing. "You thought I'd die there, didn't you? I wasn't going to do anything of the kind. Bet you never thought I'd come back."

"Get Awning!" the Branch Secretary shouted. "Get Bash here! We've got an escaped prisoner on the run. He's a murderer. Don't let him escape."

No one responded to the Branch Secretary, and he soon realised that the only other person around was Lightkeeper, and he didn't care.

"Stop squawking," Pockmark said. "I'm not going to run away. Can't you see I'm bleeding?"

The Branch Secretary calmed down and looked at Pockmark. Returning to his usual impressive calm, he said, "Is that from fighting with Awning's lot?"

"It was Millstone. I stabbed him, and he stabbed me."

Raising the thick chunk of wood he was carrying, Pockmark swept it diagonally in front of him. The Branch Secretary jumped, dodging the blow, but before he could catch his breath, Pockmark struck again, hitting his left shoulder. Even Lightkeeper heard his collarbone snap.

Yoyo leapt out of the courtyard door like a wild cat. She managed to fly so far in the air that she landed on Pockmark, and he fell to the ground. She grabbed one of his hands and bit it. She put so much force into the bite that she was trembling all over. Pockmark curled up and tried to push her off, but couldn't. He then tried to shake her off, but that didn't work either, so he called anxiously, "Lightkeeper, Lightkeeper!"

Lightkeeper came over to pull Yoyo off him, but failing to manage it, he yanked off Yoyo's trousers. She was still biting one of Pockmark's fingers, and she could feel that her upper and lower teeth were about to close together, when Pockmark jerked his hand out, with one of Yoyo's teeth still embedded in it. Lightkeeper took the opportunity to grab at Yoyo's waist, only to have her flip him over and pin him to the ground. She squeezed Lightkeeper's head between her legs and brought all her weight to bear. When Pockmark tried to pull the tooth out of his finger, he couldn't get it out to begin with, so he came over with his other hand and grabbed Yoyo's tit. Yoyo was still using her arse to keep Lightkeeper pinned down, but when her tit was grabbed, she flopped over to one side, and Lightkeeper and Pockmark were then able to run off.

Yoyo felt a strange sensation in her mouth. When she wiped it, it came away full of blood, and she was now missing a tooth. Searching the ground, she couldn't see it anywhere and furiously concluded that Pockmark had run off with her tooth still in his finger. Then Ever-Obedient came running up hefting an axe.

"Where've you been, you stupid old fucker?" said Yoyo. "Did you want Pockmark and Lightkeeper to beat me up?"

Ever-Obedient stammered something out.

Yoyo grabbed his axe and said, "What kind of a man are you? You've got an axe, so you could've split Pockmark and Lightkeeper in half!"

Ever-Obedient took off his jacket to let Yoyo wrap it around herself. Yoyo raised the axe to demonstrate how she would have chopped Pockmark and Lightkeeper to bits. Ever-Obedient decided that she'd gone off her head again, and was worried she might actually kill someone with that axe, so he started to shout, "She's gone mad! Everyone stay away. She's really crazy!"

Useless led the Golden Cudgels as they ran up and down a few alleys, knocking over a dozen or so Red Blades, but they lost seven or eight men in the process, and they were no longer able to keep in formation. At several places in the network of lanes, he could hear shouting: "Hit Useless! It's Useless who brought these people here."

Useless was now in a bit of a panic. At first, he joined forces with Huang Shengsheng, but then he worried that the man was so thin and weak that when he fell in with Bash at Three Fork Alley, he immediately clung to him. Bash stood out in his bright red sweater. As they walked along the alleyway, the group had to space out a bit, but he was always right there in the middle. Dazed-And-Confused, Stonebreaker and Iron Bolt were growling like wolves, but he still strode along. He had not taken up a hammer and kept his hands behind him. At the T-junction, they met Once-Upon-A-Time, Wangmen and Six Pints' son, and got into a fight with them. Once-Upon-A-Time and Wangmen both got wounded, with Once-Upon-A-Time's mouth swollen like a pig's snout. Once-Upon-A-Time and Wangmen succeeded in running away, though they managed to catch Six Pints' son.

"What the fuck were you thinking in joining the Red Blades?" Stonebreaker asked. "When your dad was seriously ill, we all went to see him, helped you plant your fields... so why are you fighting us on Awning's side?"

"I helped you build your house, didn't I?" Six Pints' son retorted. "And I also went along when your wife was struggling to give birth–"

"Yeah, you turned up when my wife had the baby," Stonebreaker said, "but that was only because you were planning to drink yourself silly."

"But if I hadn't turned up to help, the baby wouldn't have been born and we wouldn't have been drinking to celebrate, now would we?"

"Motherfucker!" Stonebreaker snarled, and he grabbed hold of Six Pints' son and the two of them rolled across the ground, punching each other. The Hammerheads went over and pulled Stonebreaker to his feet and kicked Six Pints' son.

Bash didn't even bother to look at the spectacle but started pushing forward instead.

"What are you hitting him for?" said Iron Bolt. "If you want to hit someone, go for the boss. Let's go to Awning's house."

The men who'd been kicking Six Pints' son stopped and followed Bash in a hooting, screaming mob towards Awning's house.

From the east end of the village to the southern end, they scanned down every alley they passed. There was fighting in almost every one. In the confusion, it was not clear whether the Red Blades were fighting the Hammerheads, or the Hammerheads were fighting the Red Blades, or the Golden Cudgels from Xiahewan and Luozhen's United Command faction were fighting the Hammerheads and the Red Blades, because the Hammerheads and Red Blades did not all recognise who belonged to which group.

In the corner of one alley, three Hammerheads and the four members of the Luozhen United Command were locked in fight until they encountered Bash, whereupon they all called out to him. It was at this point that both sides realised they had been hitting the wrong adversaries and ran over to accuse each other of being at fault.

"Even if you don't know us personally," the Hammerheads argued, "you can recognise our weapons – these are hammers, right?"

"Fine, how about you look closely yourselves," the Luozhen's United Command faction said. "Is that a big knife we're holding?"

"Don't say any more," someone said, "we're all on the same side, after all. We fucked up the wrong people and it was just a mistake."

Useless took exception to the bad language: "You shut your face!"

"Shut up yourself!" the man replied.

"Can everyone stop yapping and pull themselves together?" said Bash. When he looked around, he saw three men chasing Barndoor and Flower Girl down the alleyway.

Flower Girl went into her courtyard, while Barndoor stood at the entrance with a pickaxe and shouted, "If anyone dares come up here, I'll use it!"

"Has Barndoor also joined the Red Blades?" Bash asked.

"Barndoor's a slippery customer," Stonebreaker explained. "He doesn't belong to any faction."

"Then who's he planning to hit with his pickaxe?"

One of the members of the Luozhen United Command faction shouted, "Get that one! That's the one we want!"

"Get who?" Useless asked.

The three men turned their heads and looked around before running over to him.

"He's not a Red Blade, so why do you want to get him?" Stonebreaker asked.

The leader, who had a long face, said, "A woman went in there."

"What did she look like?"

"Super pretty," Horseface said.

"That's his wife," Stonebreaker said, "and that's why he's standing guard with a pickaxe."

"Old Kiln sure does have some good-looking women."

After passing Three Fork Alley, they ran past the door of a courtyard which was standing open. The crowd had already dispersed when someone said, "Isn't this Sparks' home?"

They all turned back, shouting, "Sparks, come out, you son of a bitch."

No one in the courtyard responded, so they marched in and smashed the place, starting with the urn on the steps of the main house, which had clearly just been washed since it had not yet dried... now a hammer cracked it into pieces. There were chilli peppers, black-eyed peas, tobacco leaves, potato skins and so on hanging in rows from the kitchen wall. All were ripped down and thrown into the pigsty.

Once Dazed-And-Confused got home after being beaten up, he looked for something to eat, but everything in his house had been smashed, so he ran out in search of Bash. When he arrived at Sparks' house, he went to the kitchen, where he uncovered the cooking pots that had not been washed since they were last used, and then reached for the wicker basket hanging down from the roof beam, which contained sweet potato buns stuffed with pickled cabbage. He took one and ate it. He was very hungry, but the bun made him choke. He stretched out his neck and pounded his chest, but he was still choking, and there was no water in the bucket behind the stove.

"Where's the water?" he said as he entered the yard. Finding none there, he grabbed a handful of snow and stuffed it into his mouth. The others saw him eating a bun, and they all came to the kitchen to get buns for themselves, so Dazed-And-Confused ran into the kitchen again and hid two buns in his sleeves before anyone else could get them, and then grabbed a couple more. When they tried to take some of the buns off him, he spat on them.

"You're fucking disgusting," the others said.

Dazed-And-Confused just laughed and gave one of the buns to Bash, but Bash didn't want it.

"I've wiped the spit off it," Dazed-And-Confused said, "but if you still don't want it, just cut the skin off."

"He's not here," Bash complained. "Let's find him."

Dazed-And-Confused overturned the three-shelf cupboard in the kitchen to discover half a box of maize kernels, which he stuffed into his bag.

"Come on," Bash said. "Hurry up."

Dazed-And-Confused emerged carrying his bag.

"What's that?" Bash asked.

"I've taken some maize."

"What are you going to do with that?"

"They've taken every last scrap of food from my house, so what else am I going to eat?"

"You reckon that when this is all over and we've won, you're still going to be going short? Put it back."

Just as they walked out of the door, a woman started screaming from over to the east side. Bash looked around and Tag-Along was nowhere to be seen, so he started to call out, "Tag-Along! Where are you?"

When Tag-Along entered Sparks' house, he saw no one around, so he removed the ancestor's tablet from the cabinet and dropped it. Then he took down a framed photo hanging on the wall and stamped on it with his foot. The photo showed Sparks being crowned with flowers by the County Party Secretary on the occasion he was declared a model worker. Tag-Along could not bear to see Sparks being honoured like that – after all, back in the day, he was supposed to be recognised as a model worker, but Sparks' wife denounced him for bullying Old Faithful about land boundaries, whereupon Sparks became the model worker. And he wasn't just given a crown of flowers by the Party Secretary either, he got a reward of thirty pounds of rice.

Having broken the photo frame, he decided to go to the room on the east side and smash that up too, but it was locked. He went to the western side room, which didn't have a door, just a cloth curtain hanging down, but it was just a storeroom. There was a pile of wheat, and next to that was a rolled-up reed mat, and when he pulled down the reed mat to kick it about a bit, Sparks' wife fell out. She was so scared she couldn't utter a word, so Tag-Along said, "Since you won't speak, I guess I'd better check if your tongue is still inside your head." He proceeded to wrench open Sparks' wife's mouth so roughly that blood came from the corners, and the woman started screaming at the top of her voice.

Hearing Sparks' wife scream, Bash realised that Tag-Along was somewhere in the main house. He knew that Tag-Along had a longstanding grudge against Sparks' family.

"You go on ahead," Tag-Along called out from inside.

A few people came in, and Tag-Along was still wrenching Sparks' wife's head, so they yelled at him to stop. Then Bash entered, kicked Tag-Along away from the woman, and said, "Why am I in charge of a bunch of utter wankers?"

Tag-Along curled in on himself, but still said, "Let me have my revenge."

Bash ignored Tag-Along and walked away. The men next to him were continuing to hesitate when he yelled, "You're all a bunch of useless motherfuckers. Let's get on with it. If he wants to, he can stay."

"Yeah, he's a piece of shit," said the crowd. "All he can do in revenge is open her mouth!"

Outside the door to the yard, a group of men had brought down the privy wall. A snake was coiled under the wall, as big as a basin, and one of them went to pick it up, to take it over to the chicken coop so the snake could kill the chickens. But Useless said it should be saved for Huang Shengsheng, who could eat it.

At this time, black smoke started to rise into the sky, and the wind carried the choking smell towards them.

"Where's that coming from?" Stonebreaker asked. "Whose house are they burning?"

Decheng climbed up the ladder that was against the wall, and he suddenly realised the fire was at his house; the Red Blades were burning his house. Everyone rushed in the direction of the fire. When they got closer, they realised that it was actually Pockmark's dilapidated two-room shack that was on fire. The door had already burned away, and the flames were coming out from inside. When the wind and snow blew, the fire changed direction and burned towards the eaves, and the eaves were soon reduced to a cinder because of the straw woven into the roof.

A few of the Red Blades stood watching. Instead of putting out the flames, they watched in admiration the fire coming out of the window next to them, saying that it looked like a chrysanthemum in bloom. Some people had also gone to pick up branches from the lane, sticks of firewood, and even carried a bundle of bean stalks from the back of Decheng's house and threw them into the fire.

Decheng grabbed the stalks off them, saying, "The Red Blades are nothing but a pack of murderers and arsonists!"

"Who are you calling murderers and arsonists?" the Red Blades said. "The Hammerheads were the ones doing the killing and setting stuff on fire."

The two sides started fighting, but the Hammerheads had the numerical advantage, and so one of the Red Blades whistled, whereupon they split up and ran away. Iron Bolt chased them for a while, but when he saw Cowbell running towards the privy, he blocked the entrance, and when Cowbell tried to make it over the wall, Iron Bolt grabbed him.

"Are you the fucker that lit the fire?" Iron Bolt demanded.

"It's nothing to do with me," Cowbell said.

"Who was it, then? Which of the Red Blades?"

"Pockmark lit the fire."

"Why would Pockmark set fire to his own house?"

Iron Bolt twisted Cowbell's ear, and it happened to be his bad ear.

"You're lying," Iron Bolt said. "How dare you lie to me!"

He took two stones that had been used to wipe someone's arse and clamped them on Cowbell's good ear, demanding to know who had lit the fire. Cowbell's good ear was clamped badly, so tightly that a lump of flesh fell out, meaning that both of his ears were now missing a piece, but Cowbell still insisted that Pockmark had lit the fire himself. Iron Bolt dragged Cowbell off to see Bash, and Bash asked how Pockmark's house had come to burn down. Cowbell explained that the Golden Cudgels had beaten him, so he ran to hide in the beanstalk pile at the back of the house, and from there he saw Pockmark and Lightkeeper go into Pockmark's shack. Not long afterwards they came out, and then black smoke started pouring out.

"Oh," Bash said.

"He's a liar," Iron Bolt declared. "He must be lying to us. Why would Pockmark burn his own house?"

"Shut up," Bash said. "Why wouldn't he set fire to his own house?"

"Wipe the blood out of your ears," Bash told Cowbell.

"No," Cowbell said. "Iron Bolt might as well cut my ears off."

"Wipe them!"

Cowbell did not dare say another word. He covered his ears and ran off, crying all the way.

When Goodman got to Inkcap's house there was indeed nothing he could do to help Gran, and he wanted to leave but was fearful of setting foot outside. After waiting a good long time, the sound of fighting seemed to have faded into the distance, so he insisted on leaving. Inkcap got a stout stick, but Gran didn't want him to go out, and Goodman said he didn't need Inkcap's protection. Inkcap thought about it and asked him to wait for a moment. He went into the main house and up to the cupboard, then he took a picture of Chairman Mao off the wall behind the cupboard. He used a little leftover gruel to stick the picture onto the back of a dustpan. Gran and Goodman immediately understood what Inkcap had in mind.

"That's clever of you," Goodman said. "However did you think of that?"

"I learned it from Bash," Inkcap explained. "When the Hammerheads were putting up big-character posters, people would just pull them down. Then he pasted some of Chairman Mao's sayings in the corner of the posters, so no one would dare to touch them."

Gran told Inkcap to go via the back alley and escort Goodman to where the mountain road began, and come straight back afterwards. If he went wandering around the village after seeing Goodman off, she'd break his legs for him when he got home.

"I know that if I went running off," Inkcap said, "it wouldn't be Gran breaking my legs – that lot would do it for you!"

Goodman walked along, holding the picture of Chairman Mao on the dustpan, while Inkcap followed behind. Inkcap's head swivelled from side to side as if on a turntable, as he nervously tried to monitor every direction. He could sense eyes everywhere, and that at any moment someone might rush out from a courtyard door, the corner of a wall, or from behind a tree or a toilet. He was prepared that if there was movement, he would drop to the ground like a stone, or turn into a tree by the roadside, or a chicken, a dog or a cat slinking along the wall. The scene reminded him of a dream, and in his daze he wondered if he was dreaming again.

"Come quickly, follow me," Goodman said.

Inkcap ran forward a few steps and said, "I'll protect you."

"You are protecting me?"

Inkcap suddenly realised that it was in fact the other way around – no, it was Chairman Mao who was protecting both of them. The dustpan with the image of Chairman Mao was actually the cloak of invisibility he had imagined before! He watched Goodman place the dustpan in front of his body one moment, then on his head the next, and later carry it in his hands and sway it back and forth until it seemed as if the dustpan were shimmering with light.

By now, Inkcap had stopped panicking and he walked forward with his back straight. He had never walked with his back so straight before, his eyes wide open, looking only forward, the big head on his slender neck catching the falling snow, which melted as it fell. His arms were swinging joyfully, but still he could not catch up with Goodman, and when Goodman urged him again to walk faster, he had to break into a trot. He heard people crying all around, but one particular cry came to a cackling stop, followed by a pause and another cry.

Inkcap stood still. "It's Cowbell," he said.

"What do you mean?" Goodman asked.

Inkcap insisted that it was Cowbell crying, and walked on to the next alley instead of turning off. There he found Cowbell crouched down under a tree crying with a cackling sound and covering his ears with his hands. The two rushed over to see what was the matter: Cowbell's good ear was now also missing a piece and bleeding.

"I'll get you some chicken feathers to stick on it," Inkcap said, but there were no chickens nearby.

"The wound's so big, chicken feathers won't stop the bleeding," Goodman said. "Go and find some cotton, burn it to ashes, and we'll put that on."

Goodman and Inkcap were each wearing a couple of jackets, but none of them was made of cotton, so where could they find some? Inkcap went to knock on the door of the next house and banged away but it did not open. Three houses away was Tag-Along's home, where the door was also closed.

When Tag-Along's wife looked through the crack and saw that it was Inkcap, she opened it wide. Without saying a word, Inkcap went to the main room, pulled the quilt from the bed and ran out of the room while pulling off the cotton cover.

"Who's been injured that you need my quilt?" Tag-Along's wife wanted to know.

Inkcap had now got the cover off, so he discarded the quilt and as he ran out of the door said, "Don't let the kids out!"

As soon as he pulled the door to, a group of Red Blades came over and shouted, "Inkcap, come fight with us. The Hammerheads always bullied you, so don't you want revenge?"

"I'll come later," Inkcap assured them. "Just after I've been to the privy."

"Do you really think he'll fight the Hammerheads?" one of them said. "He used to follow Bash around, and Tag-Along's son calls him his godfather."

"Tag-Along?" another said. "The mere mention of his name is enough to set me off. I borrowed two yuan from him, but he kept pestering me to pay it back."

"Why shouldn't he expect to want it back?" someone chipped in.

"I did owe him money, but he shouldn't have demanded it back like that. Even when there were other people about, he would yammer on about his money. Let's find out if the son of a bitch is at home, see if he still says he wants his money."

He went over to Tag-Along's house and shouted, "Come out!"

"I just went to his house," Inkcap said, "but there was no one there."

"I bet he heard my voice and hid himself," the man declared. "Come on out!"

"He's definitely not at home. Third Aunt said she saw him swinging a hammer and fighting with Awning and the others in the front alley."

"Is Awning in the front alley?" they asked, and then they ran off in a swarm.

As soon as the men had gone, Inkcap said to those inside, "Throw a padlock out, let me lock the door for you from the outside."

Tag-Along's wife threw a padlock out over the courtyard wall, and Inkcap locked the door and ran to burn the ashes of the cotton quilt cover to dress Cowbell's ears.

Cowbell's ears were not as big as Inkcap's. When Inkcap was putting on the cotton ash, he said, "Such small ears, so long and small, how could Iron Bolt get a hold of them?"

"My ears are lucky ears I'll have you know," Cowbell said. "Look at how long the lobes are!"

"Right. Lucky. I guess that means rats like to gnaw on them."

"I guess the reason why you've got such dark skin is because you belong to one of the Five Black Categories."

The two carried on quarrelling until Inkcap deliberately applied the ash with such a firm hand that Cowbell started moaning in pain. The three of them then had to leave quickly, so Goodman took up the dustpan again, like a shield, with Inkcap and Cowbell close behind. After traversing two lanes, they found themselves followed by a long line of dogs, cats and chickens. They arrived at the embankment marking the northern edge of the village and were preparing to turn from the door of Baldy Jin's house to go up the slope to the spring, and then go around the bottom of the dyke until they got to the big stone mill which marked the beginning of the road leading into the mountains.

It was at this point that Inkcap said to the animals, "All right, it's all right now, you can go back."

The dogs and cats and chickens dispersed.

"How is it that you can get animals to come to you everywhere you go?" Cowbell asked.

Inkcap was just about to speak when a group of men ran out from the alley alongside Baldy Jin's house, dragging Soupspoon. They were hauling him along like a sack of wheat, half of his body dragging along the ground, and he'd lost both shoes. Soupspoon was begging for mercy, calling on them to let him go.

"You're very polite now," one of them said. "Aren't you normally a tough guy? Weren't you determined to deduct me three work points?"

"When did I ever cut your work points?" Soupspoon said.

"It was the first day of digging sweet potatoes in the back field. You may not remember, but I do."

"Oh, I didn't want to cut your work points," Soupspoon said, "but Potful insisted because you were late for work."

"Oh, how convenient," the man said. "Potful is dead, and you're going to die too!"

He started dragging Soupspoon off, but Soupspoon had his feet hooked around the trunk of a small tree, so his body was pulled out straight.

"Don't you dare pull any more," Soupspoon said. "My right shoulder was beaten with a stick and has already been dislocated. If you keep on pulling, it will break."

The man pulled on his left arm instead, and when he yanked hard, Soupspoon's feet were still hooked around the tree, and the tree bent.

Goodman stood up and said, "Cattle Track, why don't you let him stand up and walk for himself?"

"He'd just lie there and play dead."

"His arm's already broken, and you still want to pull him to pieces?"

"OK, I won't pull him. I'll break the tree instead!"

Cattle Track wrenched the tree until it curved over into a hoop, and as he continued bending it, the tree groaned and snapped, and sap poured from the trunk. Soupspoon's feet now had nothing to hook onto, but he was still lying on the ground.

"Get up," Cattle Track said. "Get up and start walking."

"Cattle Track, you should just let him go," Goodman said. "He's in a terrible state and cannot possibly fight, so why do you want to make him walk?"

"We're taking all the key Red Blades we've captured over to Branch Secretary Zhu's place," Cattle Track explained.

"What do you mean by 'key'?" Soupspoon asked. "In what way could I possibly be 'key'?"

Cattle Track kicked Soupspoon.

"What do you think you're doing?" Goodman said.

"What are you complaining about now?" said Cattle Track.

Inkcap was holding up the small, broken tree in an attempt to tie it straight with a rope, because then maybe it could still grow. But when he lifted the tree it just flopped over again, its leaves falling on his body, and he could feel the leaves dripping sap too.

"You killed this tree just like that?" Inkcap said.

"So what if I did?"

Although Inkcap did not like Soupspoon and thought Cattle Track an honest person, he was now surprised to learn that Cattle Track could also be so very nasty. "So what are you going to do now?" he said. "Beat us up?"

Inkcap jumped over and picked up the dustpan Goodman had been holding and brandished it, saying, "Hit away! Why don't you hit the picture of Chairman Mao?"

Cattle Track had balled up his fists, and when he tried to swing left, Inkcap moved the dustpan left; when he tried to swing right, Inkcap moved the dustpan right. Cattle Track didn't dare hit the picture, so he started shouting, "Comrade Huang! Comrade Huang!"

Huang Shengsheng came running out of the back of the group, and when he saw Goodman, Inkcap and Cowbell blocking the road, he asked what was going on.

Goodman said, "Comrade Huang–"

"Don't call me that, I'm no comrade of yours," Huang Shengsheng snapped back. "You're blocking the way – was that to rescue Soupspoon?"

"We don't belong to any faction," Goodman said. "We were just on our way back to the mountains–"

"What you do mean, you don't belong to any faction? What about Cowbell?"

When Cowbell heard his name he turned around to run, but Inkcap grabbed hold of him and said in a low voice, "There's nowhere to run. You can't possibly escape."

"Cowbell is a child," Goodman said. "He doesn't know anything."

"But you're an adult, right?" Huang Shengsheng said. "Bash's revolutionary consciousness is high, but he neglected one thing, which was getting rid of you. You think you can answer back to me, well, you can go over to the Branch Secretary's house and see how that works out for you! Let me tell you, Branch Secretary Zhu thought he could get away with messing up our revolution, and right now he's hanging from a tree in his yard."

"Branch Secretary Zhu is a capitalist roader, but we're just ordinary folk, Comrade Huang," Goodman pleaded.

"Ordinary?" Huang Shengsheng snorted. "You're a feudal remnant, Inkcap here belongs to one of the Five Black Categories, and Cowbell is a traitor – a member of the Red Blades. What do you mean by saying you're just ordinary!"

He swung his stick at Goodman's head. Inkcap swiftly passed the dustpan to Goodman, who held it up in front of his face. However, Huang Shengsheng's move with his stick was just a feint; his real target was Goodman's feet. Goodman was able to jump out of the way, so the stick didn't hit him, and the two men circled each other. Goodman suddenly threw the dustpan back to Inkcap and said, "Keep a hold of this."

Just as he threw it, Huang Shengsheng's stick poked forward, and Goodman stumbled a few steps, trying to keep his balance on top of the embankment, but in the end he fell with a splash.

When Goodman tumbled from the embankment, the Hammerheads gave a cheer, and Sparks then led a group of men to fight their way over. When Huang Shengsheng's group saw the large number of Red Blades arriving, they scattered, and Huang Shengsheng found himself surrounded. He started to panic and made his way to Baldy Jin's house. Half-Stick was in the house and when she saw Huang Shengsheng enter the courtyard, she closed the door and windows. Sparks' lot blocked the entrance. Huang Shengsheng took two knives from the kitchen and tried to fight his way out, waving the knives in the air, so those blocking the entrance did not dare get too close to him. Whenever he tried to charge them down, they just raised their big blades. His knives were only little, so he couldn't break through. He then took his stand under the honey locust tree, and the situation turned into a stalemate. Some people were worried about Goodman and ran to the bottom of the embankment to see if he was OK.

When Goodman fell, he was lucky enough to land in the water. If he had fallen a little to one side, hitting the stone slabs around the spring, he would have been killed, but he fell from halfway along the elevation and dropped far enough out to land in the pool. Goodman fainted when he landed, and took in a good few mouthfuls of water. Inkcap and Cowbell ran down to pull him out, checking him for any injury. Surprisingly, he was not hurt at all, though his feet were bruised where he'd hit them against the edge of the pool. When they pounded his back, he spat out some water.

"Is he OK?" Sparks asked from the elevated bank.

"He's fine," Inkcap replied.

"Hurry up and get him back to the mountains."

When he got to his feet, Goodman complained of feeling dizzy. He sat down again and slowly recovered his senses. Inkcap raised his head and looked up at the embankment where Huang Shengsheng was still standing under the honey locust tree, waving his knife and shouting, "Come on. Anyone who comes forward, I'll chop them to bits and chuck them into the pool too."

The Red Blades on both sides of the road moved towards the tree, but none of them could get close. Someone threw stones and tiles at Huang Shengsheng, and managed to hit him, and then the others too.

"You're hitting us!" Inkcap shouted.

The throwing stopped.

Inkcap asked Cowbell, "Did you bring a match?"

"You always take a fuse when you go out," Cowbell replied, "so why would I have a match?"

Inkcap regretted failing to bring a fuse along, and asked, "Did you bring your slingshot?"

"Yup. Are you saying I could use it to hit Huang Shengsheng?"

"If you're positive you can use it without hitting anyone else..." Inkcap said. Then he started shouting to the people on top of the embankment, "Does anyone have a match? Is there a light here?"

"What do you want a light for?" someone asked.

"Just give it to me," Inkcap said. "It's for Goodman."

Someone tossed down a box of matches and said, "He almost drowned, so he should smoke a pipe to get his lungs working again."

Inkcap grabbed the matches and asked Cowbell if any of the cotton was left. "A few scraps," Cowbell replied. "What do you want it for?"

Inkcap whispered into Cowbell's ear. Wrapping a few stones in scraps of cotton and setting light to them, he fired them over towards the honey locust tree with his slingshot. There was a large heap of dry jujube and sophora branches under the tree, which Baldy Jin put there to prevent anyone from climbing it, and when the burning shots landed there, smoke and then flames started to appear, and they began to roast Huang Shengsheng. As it got hotter, he took off his jacket and tried to beat out the flames. The Red Blades then went on the attack, so Huang Shengsheng stopped trying to tackle the flames and picked up his knives again. The Red Blades halted their advance until the flames set fire to Huang Shengsheng's trouser leg, and he was forced to beat back the fire. When the Red Blades moved forward, he swung his knives again. In this way Huang Shengsheng alternated between flames and knives, and the Red Blades moved forward and back, but the fire grew bigger and bigger, until the whole trunk of the tree was engulfed, and the flames licked the branches, and the dry leaves and the trunk of the tree creaked and cracked, raining down gouts of fire.

The Red Blades were shouting, "Burn him! Burn him!"

Some people threw straw and beanstalks under the tree, and Huang Shengsheng shouted at the top of his lungs, "Help! Help me!"

Goodman had by now caught his breath. "Don't let the tree burn," he said. "If it burns any more, he'll be killed."

"He almost killed you," Cowbell pointed out, "so why would you still care about him?"

"I'm not dead," Goodman said.

Inkcap started shouting, "Put out the fire! Goodman doesn't want him burned!"

"What's he interfering for?" Sparks asked.

At this point the Red Blades moved in a panic, and some started to run away.

"Why are you running?" asked Sparks. "What's going on?"

Then he turned and saw that they were being charged with hammers raised by Bash, Baldy Jin, Iron Bolt, Dazed-And-Confused and the rest of them. The Hammerheads far outnumbered Sparks' gang. Sparks threw a bundle of bean stalks onto the bonfire under the tree and fought with Baldy Jin, but he couldn't withstand the onslaught and also ran off. One of the Hammerheads carried Huang Shengsheng away on his back, while more men ran along the embankment to chase after Sparks.

SEVENTY-TWO

AWNING'S GROUP PUT THE GOLDEN CUDGELS at the south end of the village to flight, and when the Hammerheads rushed down from the mountainside, they were ready for them. As the fighting progressed, they too found themselves broken up into smaller groups, chasing enemies up and down the alleys to beat them or being chased in their turn. It was chaos. Cries and shouts came first from one end of the alley and then the other, or from a different part of the village entirely. Awning, Sparks, Winterborn, Palace and Ever-Obedient became separated, but then a moment later they ran into each other again and were all in the same place.

Awning repeatedly reminded them to look out for each other and concentrate their strength. But then Sparks and Padlock disappeared again, and so did Ever-Obedient. Fortunately, Jindou, Winterborn, Lishan, Gourd and Stalwart stayed with him from first to last. They'd lost count how many Golden Cudgels, Hammerheads and United Command people they'd beaten up, but they had caught five of the Golden Cudgels. They'd chased them to the entrance of the village, where another group of Red Blades blocked the way, and they'd jumped into the lotus pond in the hope of wading through it and getting away. They all stood at the edge of the pond and kicked down whoever tried to climb out again until the five men were exhausted. At that stage they were pulled out of the pond, their faces coated in green mud, even their eye sockets, and marched back into the village with their arms behind their backs. Once they were back in the village, Padlock came running out from another alley, and when he saw the man with a goatee, he said he knew him – this was the fucker who'd broken Thimble's leg in the second alley. He tugged hard on the goatee, again and again, until he'd pulled a piece of skin off his chin.

"Stop that," Awning said. "Where's Millstone? How come I don't see Millstone?"

Padlock punched the guy with the goatee in the crotch, and he fell to the ground and writhed about, not even trying to get up.

"I heard Pockmark carved up Millstone with his knife," Padlock said.

"Pockmark carved him up?" said Awning. "Is Pockmark back? Is he hurt bad?"

"Dunno," Padlock said.

"These here class enemies think they're just going to massacre Old Kiln, huh?" Awning snarled.

Once the five men were tied to a tree trunk, everyone ran back to the village. Halfway there, they spotted the fire burning at Pockmark's shack, and when they rushed in that direction, they failed to find him, but they did run into Bash and his lot smashing up a building and started fighting with them. Bash was just leaving, but he now ordered his men to surround the place; no matter how often the Red Blades charged at them, they could not break through.

This annoyed Awning, who started to shout at Jindou, "Where's Sparks? Where's he got to? If we can't hold together, no wonder they can run rings round us."

"I'll go out the back window," Jindou assured him, "and find Sparks, and bring him back here."

"You're not to go anywhere," Awning told him. "Send Sprout."

Sprout had joined them part way through all this, her face streaked with sweat. She immediately went inside, only to discover that all the benches and tables had been smashed. She picked up a bench leg to open the back window to jump out, but outside the window stood half a dozen Hammerheads blocking her way. She went back to Awning and said, "It's impossible to get out, the whole place is surrounded."

"Fuck this!" Awning said. "They think they've got us trapped? Go and get Noodle Fish."

Noodle Fish was in the cattle shed, and he now came running. "Awning," he said, "how did this happen? What are we going to do?"

"What are you so worried about?" Awning replied, going on to suggest something to Noodle Fish, but Noodle Fish said that it wouldn't work since the cow would be scared.

"What do you mean?" Awning said. "If I tell you to let the cow loose, then you do as I say."

Noodle Fish still wouldn't comply, so Awning and Padlock carried the kerosene bucket into the cattle shed, only for Noodle Fish to shout, "Don't you dare, Awning! Someone will surely hurt the cows if they go out."

Winterborn dragged Noodle Fish indoors, but when he wouldn't go, he covered his mouth. Noodle Fish bit Winterborn's fingers so he couldn't keep his hand in place.

"You ruined the kiln, and now you want to hurt the cows!" Noodle Fish wailed. "It's your fault that Old Kiln's the way it is."

He set off running towards the cattle shed, and the door was already open, and all the cows were untied. Awning was splashing the cows' tails with kerosene. Padlock grabbed a match and struck it, but it did not light; he struck another and the matchstick broke.

"They got wet," Padlock complained.

"Warm it in your ear," Awning instructed him.

Padlock took a match out and put it in his ear to warm it up, just as Noodle Fish rushed in to grab the matches. Awning blocked the door of the shed, and so Noodle Fish was left cursing.

"Why should I listen to you?" said Padlock.

"I'm your elder," Noodle Fish reminded him, "and what you're doing is fucking evil."

"Shut up. Who the hell do you think you are? What makes you my elder?"

Noodle Fish lay down by the door of the shed and said, "Then let the cows trample me to death."

Padlock finally succeeded in striking a match and lit the bull's tail, and the red bull immediately jumped up and wagged its tail, but the more it wagged, the hotter the fire became, and the red bull howled and rushed out of the barn door. It knocked over the bamboo baskets there, along with the water jars, sieves and round steamers, but managed to avoid Noodle Fish.

"Open the courtyard door! Open the courtyard door!" Awning shouted.

The red bull rushed out of the courtyard, and all the cattle were frightened and kicked out. A black bull, not knowing that Noodle Fish was lying in the doorway, could not keep his front legs back when it was about to buck, and hit him flush. Noodle Fish was thrown sideways into the yard, and he was unable to stand up for a good long time. Some of the cattle that rushed out of the shed headed directly out of the yard, while others were still in the yard running around like crazy, and one even made its way indoors. Padlock raised his hammer to make it go out, so the cow kicked him. Padlock sat down on the floor with a thump, in such pain that he could barely stand up, though he had to scramble to safety by the wall.

Outside the courtyard gate were a host of Hammerheads and Golden Cudgels. When the gate was suddenly pulled open and a herd of cattle rushed out, the crowd screamed and dodged, and those who couldn't get out of the way were trampled underfoot.

"Hit their legs!" Bash shouted. "Hit them!"

Those who'd managed to get out of the way swung their hammers at the cattle's legs, and a couple of the animals did get their legs broken and fell to the ground. However, the majority of the herd went berserk and started attacking people on sight. The crowd scattered. The flames on the red bull's tail were now extinguished, but its tail had been burned to a black stick, which was poking straight up, and it kept bellowing and chasing after people. Before anyone could hit it with a hammer or a stick, it lowered its head and charged. Someone thought they might use their stick to poke out its eyes, but it got its horns hooked good and sent the stick flying. In fact, the flying stick nearly took out Bash. Next, it charged the man again and pinned him up against the rear wall of Bash's old house. He was stuck there, his legs hanging in mid-air, too scared even to speak. Half a dozen people went to the rescue, hitting the bull with wooden sticks, but it didn't move.

"We'll set fire to the bull too," Bash shouted. "Burn it!" Several people grabbed bunches of wheat straw and threw it on the back and under the bull's belly, and lit a match. It then collapsed to the ground, and the man pinned against the wall fell down and was hurriedly pulled out of danger.

In the house, Awning and the others made their way out of the back window, which was small so that only two people could jump out at a time. Sprout couldn't see what was going on, but she could hear the shouting from outside. "What's wrong, what's wrong with the man?"

"He's not breathing! He's stopped breathing!"

"Lay him out flat, get him flat and then we'll do compressions."

"His ribs are broken, you can't possibly do compressions... Oh my god, he's bleeding out of his mouth now. Wake up! Wake up!"

Awning wasn't the first out, but as soon as he was clear, he was shouting for Jindou.

"He's already gone," Sprout told him.

"What the hell?" Awning said. "I haven't gone, but he's already out? Go and help Yes'm get Padlock in here."

Sprout went out into the courtyard and found Padlock already on his feet and leaning against the wall. She helped him back inside, but he couldn't manage the steps. Sprout held him up and asked, "Is the wound to your legs or your back?"

"To my arse," Padlock said.

"Then you've nothing to worry about," Sprout told him. She dragged him inside and Awning pushed him up to the window until he dropped out on the far side.

Palace and the others got out of the back window and ran down the village road, whereupon they caught sight of Ever-Obedient being dragged off by some Golden Cudgels towards the Branch Secretary's house. They were about to go to the rescue when all of a sudden the Golden Cudgels started running. It was Yoyo who had put them to flight, with her hair wild and trousers reduced to tattered rags. When she saw that they had put down Ever-Obedient and run off, she twirled the rag hanging down in front and giggled, "That settled their hash!"

"Ever-Obedient!" Palace shouted. "Ever-Obedient!"

Ever-Obedient ignored him, grabbed hold of Yoyo and set off running. Yoyo struggled against his grasp. "Why do you keep holding on to me?" she cried. "Let go... Let go of me."

Ever-Obedient ignored Palace's gang, and Palace's gang paid no attention to Ever-Obedient. When they saw that the Hammerheads and Golden Cudgels were not coming after them, they ran towards the threshing ground, intending to wait for Awning and the others there. Unexpectedly, they encountered five or six people at the threshing ground, pulling a pig along. The pig was on top of a broken-down cart, with the wheels having given up the ghost. One man was pulling the cart from in front, two men to the side were holding the pig's ears, and another was pushing the cart at the back. A further two men had tight hold of the pig's back legs with one more gripping its tail, and the pig was squealing its head off. Palace recognised the pig as belonging to Six Pints' son, but the people manhandling it he did not know, and he wondered whether Six Pints' wife had hired them to take it to the market in the township... but then he thought to himself, Who would choose a time like this to sell their pig?

Six Pints' wife now came barrelling out of the house and took hold of the cart, shouting, "Help! Can someone help me?"

"Are they stealing that pig?" Palace asked. He stood stock still and called out to them, "What are you doing?"

The men set off at a run, dragging the cart with them. The cart was almost at the south end of the threshing ground, near a long, sloping road, and if they managed to get down there, they could reach the dirt road leading to the highway.

"Where's my son?" Six Pints' wife screamed. "Where is he?"

"He and Sparks are protecting the west side of the village," Palace explained.

"He's protecting the village, but he can't protect his own home!" Six Pints' wife wailed. "What the fuck is wrong with this place?"

Palace blocked the cart and exclaimed, "Fucking bandits. They've been fighting us and smashing up our homes, and now they've taken to thieving our property!"

"Who're you calling a thief?" the thin man pushing the cart riposted. "I lent ten yuan to Six Pints when he was sick, but I still haven't got the money back after a year and a half."

"Of course we'll pay you back," Six Pints' wife said, "but how can you take my pig? Just think how much it's worth!"

"Think of it as interest," the man retorted.

"Put that cart down," Palace shouted.

But the man wouldn't let go and pushed it as far as the slope. Suddenly he launched it down the incline, and the cart slid along, only for it to go crashing into a pile of rocks at the foot of the slope, followed by the pig. Palace and his men went on the attack and beat the thieves until the six of them fell to the ground and begged for mercy.

"Well, it's too late for that, motherfuckers!" Palace said as he took off his shoes to beat them across the face. He hit them so hard it seemed as though he were determined to take out every grievance on them. The thin man wasn't thin any more because his face was so swollen, and the faces of the other five faces weren't much better.

Palace eventually started to feel a little tired. "Let me rest for a moment," he said.

He sat on the threshing floor and wanted to smoke, but he had no cigarette and no match either. Then he felt the itch in his crotch again, so he reached in and scratched. When he started scratching, the men who followed him started scratching themselves in the crotch too.

The skinny guy who was still lying on the ground grunting thought this was strange and asked, "What are you doing?"

"I'm getting my gun," Palace told him.

The six men sat up from the ground and started begging in fear. "Forgive us, sir, we didn't mean it."

Palace was feeling much better now, so he undid his belt and waved what he'd been scratching in the thin man's face. "This is my gun, I carry it with me everywhere I go!"

The rest of his gang followed suit, or they started scratching at the six men's faces, thinking that this would be a way to infect them with scabies.

Just at this moment Sparks and his lot came running past, and when he saw Palace and the others with their trousers down having a laugh, he said "Our lot are getting beaten from one end of the village to the other, and you're over here relaxing and having fun?"

"What do you mean, relaxing and having fun?" said Palace. "When we were penned up in the cattle shed, what were you doing?"

"What was I doing?" Sparks snarled. "Right, I'll show you what I was doing!" He turned around to reveal the tattered clothing on his back, and his badly bleeding shoulder.

"Look at me," Palace said. "Look at this!" He pulled up his trouser leg to reveal a fist-sized bruise on his calf and dragged each man beside him out for Sparks to see, and those men all had either bruises on their arms or their faces. With the two groups getting into this quarrel, the six men sitting on the ground took the opportunity to get up and run away as fast as their legs would carry them. They ran down the slope to the embankment and jumped, falling fully one storey. Without even a limp, they just rolled into a ball, got to their feet and set off running again.

Palace and Sparks stopped arguing. "Let those sons of bitches flee," said Palace.

"Those motherfuckers can sure run!" Sparks replied.

Any potential chase was forgotten when Sparks asked, "Where's Awning?"

Palace then realised that Awning could not have followed him... he should have got out of the back window and come after him, but he did not explain that he'd got out of the back window and made his way over to the threshing ground. Instead, he said, "Oh hell! They must still be fighting back there."

The two groups ran towards the road leading back to the village, and before they made their way past the vegetable field at the north end of the threshing ground, Awning's group came charging towards them. Sparks shouted, "Awning, come over here!"

Awning's group ran over, and Awning said, "It's good that everybody's here. Concentrate your forces, don't just wander off and do your own thing because we need you to guard the crossroads at the threshing ground."

The threshing ground was at the southeast edge of the village. The roof of Six Pints' house slanted over to cover it so that the road leading to the village bent around it. There were more than thirty Red Blades on guard there, but by now they were looking pretty bedraggled. The snow was falling ever more heavily but everyone was thinly dressed; after all that time fighting and killing each other, no one felt the cold – if anything, they were sweating. Now they had come to rest with the sweat soaking their clothes, and as the wind blew, it got colder and colder. Many of them began to readjust their trousers, tightening their belts or looking around for rope to tie around their waists. But there was nothing, so they took straw from the pigsty next to Six Pints' house and twisted that into a makeshift rope. As they went to grab the straw, Awning started cursing, telling them to pile up some stones and get ready for a fight.

Palace did not go to get straw; instead, he hauled a ladder into place and went up onto the roof of Six Pints' house, saying that standing up there he'd be able to keep watch on the road. But Six Pints' wife refused to allow him up, fearing the roof would cave in if they went up there, and that once the

Hammerheads, Golden Cudgels and United Command arrived, the tiles on the house would all be broken anyway.

Palace insisted on going up the ladder, but Six Pints' wife kept grabbing at it.

"We got the pig back for you," said Palace, "so why begrudge us a few tiles?"

"And isn't my son one of the leaders of the Red Blades?" Six Pints' wife retorted. "Why are you trying to tear down my house? Them Hammerheads want to burn all the houses belonging to the Red Blades, but at least they won't get this one!"

Awning wasn't pleased with the implications of this comment. "So it's OK if they burn other houses, like mine or Sparks' or Palace's?" However, he gave up on the idea of posting a guard on the roof. Instead, Awning took the ladder over to the crossroads and Palace set it there diagonally blocking the place, up against a loom and a table from Six Pints' house. Six Pints' wife didn't dare say a word. When they were carrying a cupboard out of the main room, she took Six Pints' spirit tablet out and held it in her arms, as she began to cry and wail for her son. Her son wasn't there to listen, and nobody seemed to know where he had got to.

When Six Pints' wife kept crying, Awning became angry. "Can someone shut her up for me?" he said.

Someone went over to clap a hand over Six Pints' wife's mouth, saying, "Are you trying to get the Hammerheads to come over here?"

"If they come, they come," Six Pints' wife replied. "If they come, we fight them. Fuck this Cultural Revolution, it's ruining all our lives."

Six Pints' wife stopped crying and screaming when she was pushed to the ground, and the Hammerheads then really did come pouring out from the village, and all the Red Blades joined in the fight. This was the most concentrated fight the Red Blades ever experienced; they had about the same number of men as the combined forces of the Hammerheads, Golden Cudgels and United Command, but the crossroads was narrow, and neither side was able to spread themselves out. The Hammerheads attacked first, but the ladder, table, cabinet and loom formed a very effective barricade on the road, and when they were struck by a hail of stones and tiles, they retreated the other way. The Red Blades tried to charge them, but again the furniture formed an effective impediment, and they were afraid that if they fought past it and then got put to flight, it would form a nasty obstacle behind them. Accordingly, the ladder, table, cabinet and loom formed a kind of border, so when one side advanced, the other retreated and vice versa.

Bash stood throughout on a millstone at the threshing floor by the side of the road. He commanded Dazed-And-Confused and his men to attack on this side, and ordered Baldy Jin to go to the other side of the threshing ground so that they could attack on both wings simultaneously. Bash's shouted instructions were heard by Awning and Sparks, so Awning asked Sparks' group to keep watch here, and he took his group of men to the southwestern end of the threshing ground to prevent Baldy Jin from gaining access that way. Once Awning left, Sparks had fewer people, and the Hammerheads advanced. Dazed-And-Confused was the first to jump over the loom, but just as he was doing so, a stone smashed into him, and he fell. Iron Bolt then jumped up with a shovel in his hand, the shovel blocking the stones and tiles thrown at him. Instead, a piece of tile hit Sparks in the chest and he fell to the ground, to be immediately dragged back.

The Hammerheads then took the opportunity to get past the ladder, table, cabinet and loom. The Red Blades could see they were about to lose and moved back, but the more they retreated the harder it was to maintain good order. In the end, they turned and ran towards the southern end of the threshing ground, where they found Awning fighting with Baldy Jin. They could see he had lost control of the road, and soon this southwestern corner would also be overrun. The Hammerheads and Golden Cudgels and the United Command people were all pouring towards the threshing ground, and the two sides set to beating each other with sticks. The Red Blades were being put to flight. Plenty of them turned to run towards the village, while Awning, Sparks and Palace were pressed to the southwestern corner. There were bales upon bales of straw there, and Awning was now starting to panic, so he set them alight. In an instant, the straw was aflame and the smoke boiled up into the sky. Countless people surrounded the bales to beat out the fire.

When Awning realised all was lost, he shouted to Sparks, "We must run, scatter!" He picked up a bundle of straw, set it on fire and threw it at his attackers, before running away as fast as he could. As he left the threshing ground, he looked back and saw that Sparks had also jumped off the south side and was crawling forward on his hands and knees under the embankment. There was no time to shout further instructions; he needed to get away.

When the straw was set on fire, Bash didn't try to beat it out himself. Instead, he threw away his hammer and started to pee. His stream of pee went so high and so far that it landed on a heap of snow, and a hole immediately formed. Tag-Along ran over to him, covered from head to toe in dust from the straw, and Bash asked him, "What do you think's the best feeling in the whole world, Tag-Along?"

Tag-Along didn't understand what he was talking about. "Awning and Sparks won't get away from us!"

"I'm asking you a question."

"What question?"

"What do you think is the best feeling in the whole world?"

"The best feeling in the whole world?" Tag-Along mused. "What could be better than a good fuck?"

Bash laughed. "What else?"

Tag-Along tilted his head and said, "Well, after a good fuck you have a rest and then fuck again–"

"A good piss," Bash proclaimed. "A good piss is the best."

He told Tag-Along to watch him piss, and Tag-Along decided that he couldn't see anything special about Bash's pee – it was just yellow liquid.

"But look at the way it sprays," Bash told him. "Doesn't it look like pearls?"

"What do you mean?"

"If your piss comes out in a solid stream, it means you're never going to achieve anything much. If it comes out like pearls, it means you're destined for greatness."

Tag-Along looked down at Bash's pee some more, while Bash regarded the sky. It was filled with black smoke, and he said, "Why don't I see any storks?"

Tag-Along raised his head again to look up into the sky. He didn't understand what Bash was talking about.

"This smoke looks like black clouds," Bash explained, "so if a few storks came flying past, the black clouds and white storks would look beautiful."

The Red Blades had now all run away from the threshing ground, and so the Hammerheads, Golden Cudgels and United Command people chased them to the embankment at the southern end. Four men were hiding there in a small cave. In the past, locals had grown melons in the area, and they'd built this dugout to let them keep an eye on their crops. Half of it had collapsed, and four people were now crammed into the other half. As they carried on their investigations, they pulled another person out of the lotus pond, and one more from under the stone bar by the drainage canal. All of these men were hauled back to the threshing ground. Bash was hoping to find Awning or Sparks among their number, but they were nowhere to be seen. When he considered the situation, it was impossible for Awning and Sparks to have run as far as the highway because there was an open field to traverse, where you could even see a rabbit running past. That meant they must have skirted the embankment at the southern end of the threshing ground and made their way back inside the village. Bash had their captives taken to the Branch Secretary's courtyard to join the others, while he told Baldy Jin, Stonebreaker and Lucky to lead their men into the village to search for Awning and Sparks. At the end of all that, he called up Tag-Along and left with him.

"We won," Tag-Along reminded him. "Does that mean you want to go for a shit?"

"Let's both go to the south entrance of the village," Bash said.

"You want to go to the south entrance of the village?" Tag-Along gave his hammer to Bash, but he did not want it.

At the south entrance to the village, Bash sat down on the stone lion.

"What do you think this lion is?" Bash asked.

"Stone," Tag-Along replied.

"What about me, what am I?"

"You, why you're Bash!"

"What are we going to do with you?"

"What do you mean?"

803

"You're just utterly lacking in culture, Tag-Along," Bash said. "Right, where's Useless? Can you get Useless here for me?"

Useless had not gone to the threshing ground because he and some others had carried Huang Shengsheng to his home to hide. When he came out again, Bash was leading his men to surround the Red Blades at the house, and shortly afterwards, the cattle stampede had occurred. One cow had chased after him and he'd run down the lane, but it was very narrow and sloped downwards, so the cow had no problems galloping after him. When he looked back, the cow's eyes were as large as temple bells and it was snorting away. He realised he wasn't going to be able to outrun the animal, so he decided to try to grab the top of the wall and climb over it. However, he couldn't jump high enough – there was simply no way he could get up there. He was just about to give up the ghost when he ran past a tree. Its branches caught at him, and he took advantage of this to slip behind the trunk. The cow ran straight past him, and he collapsed on the ground, his mouth wide open and panting. His last reserves of energy were gone. After sitting there for a while, he started to get anxious in case the cow somehow managed to turn around, or in case some of the Red Blades came past. So he scrambled to his feet and hobbled behind Big Root's house. He knew there was a haystack back there, and he quickly inserted himself inside. Gradually the sounds of shouting and screaming and wailing died down in the other alleys... no, no, it wasn't that they'd died down, they'd just moved further away. The noise seemed to be coming from the southeastern end of the village.

Just as he was emerging from the haystack, Useless saw Yoyo coming towards him from the entrance to the lane, and he made haste to get back. "Come out!" Yoyo shouted. "Out of there!"

Useless thought Yoyo must have discovered him, but he wasn't afraid of her, and he didn't come out. Yoyo walked over and grabbed a bundle of hay. Useless had a good look at her leg, which was covered in an extremely wide pair of trousers – quite possibly they belonged to Ever-Obedient. He was about to grab her leg and yank it out from under her so that he could run away, when Yoyo walked off, scattering the straw as she went, still saying, "Come out, come on out of there!"

"Lunatic!" Useless muttered. Just as he emerged from the haystack, he saw someone dashing past the entrance to the lane, and for some reason he thought it was Awning. It gave him a very nasty shock, and he set off running in the opposite direction, but when he looked again, the alley was empty. He was still feeling nervous, so he picked up a rock before going any further. However, he didn't see anyone at all.

In fact, Useless had indeed spotted Awning. He'd run along the elevated embankment south of the threshing ground towards the riverbank, but the riverbank didn't offer a scrap of cover, so he was bound to be discovered and beaten up. Instead, he ran round the back of Six Pints' house. Everyone had gone off to the threshing ground so it was empty out back. There was a window in the wall there, but it was very small and set high up. He was about to run again when he heard someone shouting, "Awning has escaped!

Awning has escaped!" so he leapt up, grabbed the windowsill and managed to wriggle his way in. Six Pints' wife heard the noise and went into the bedroom just in time to see Awning drop onto the bed. She opened her mouth to shriek, but Awning grabbed the quilt and threw it over her so that the sound did not escape.

"Hide me," he ordered.

Six Pints' wife pulled the quilt off her head and replied, "Won't I get in trouble?"

"If they're out to get me, won't they be out to get your son too? Quick, hide me."

Six Pints' wife was at a loss, but by now Awning had already squeezed himself into the hole in the *kang*, and told her, "Block the entrance, go out into the courtyard and don't say anything to anyone."

Six Pints' wife blocked the mouth of the hole and went to the courtyard in a panic. When Awning had been hiding there for a while, Six Pints' wife told him that everyone had gone from the threshing ground and they were all back in the village, and she wanted him to get away as quickly as he could. Awning came out of the hole to see if he could make his escape from the village, but he saw people continuing to stand guard at the crossroads, and he'd be spotted as soon as he made a dash for it. Accordingly, he ran back into the village alleyways before he was noticed. It was easy to hide in the village lanes, and once it got dark, he could try again.

As it happened, Awning was seen by Useless when he ran past, but Awning didn't notice him, and he proceeded to jump into the pigsty at Big Root's house. He figured that Big Root was in with the Hammerheads, so they wouldn't expect him to hide there. He jumped in and encountered the pig busy taking the straw in the sty a mouthful at a time to build a comfortable bed. When it saw him, it didn't so much as squeal. He wriggled his way into the heap of straw and squatted down, while the pig continued to arrange the straw mouthful by mouthful. It wasn't until darkness fell that Awning came out, raced through a few alleys and ran away via the back pond.

SEVENTY-THREE

AFTER AWNING AND SPARKS FLED, except for a few key members of the Red Blades who were held in the courtyard of the Branch Secretary's house, all the others stopped fighting and were sent home and told to behave themselves. Old Kiln now belonged to the Hammerheads.

Useless was the Hammerheads' archivist, and he was now busy rearranging the official account of the events of the Cultural Revolution in Old Kiln. He took stock of the fighting: the Red Blades had been destroyed, their leaders – Awning and Sparks – had fled, and thirteen had been wounded. The Hammerheads had suffered injuries to fifteen. The Golden Cudgels and United Command had one dead and sixteen wounded. Yoyo had gone insane. There were also various unaffiliated members of the masses who were accidentally injured by flying stones and tiles, or who'd been hurt for other reasons – there were seven such cases in all. This figure included Goodman, who fell from the embankment into the pool and was not injured but had developed a bad headache. Of course, there was also the Branch Secretary, an unrepentant capitalist, who went so far as to stir up trouble between the two factions, with the result that he was injured in the struggle, had his collarbone broken and was strung up by the Hammerheads from his walnut tree. When the fighting was over and he was lowered down, one arm had been broken. As for the damage to houses, furniture, crops and trees, and how many cows, pigs, dogs, chickens and cats were killed or injured, that was too trivial to bother counting.

The Golden Cudgels and the United Command people from Luozhen withdrew at the end of the fighting, carrying away the body of the dead man, and it was Bash who took a new reed mat from Big Root's house to roll around the corpse so that Lucky and Decheng could carry it to Xiahewan on a pole. When they took the body away, Bash felt sorry and asked the Hammerheads to pay their respects to the corpse, saying that in the future the village would build a pagoda to commemorate the martyr, and asked Cowbell to catch a white rooster and tie it to the mat. Cowbell didn't dare refuse, but his family didn't have any chickens. He ran to a few different houses, but no one was willing to give him one, so in the end he caught a chicken at the Branch Secretary's house. The chicken he caught wasn't white though, it was brown.

When he escorted the Golden Cudgels and United Command members out of the village, Bash could not see Pockmark anywhere, so he asked for his whereabouts. "How come I don't see hide nor hair of him?"

The person standing next to him explained that Pockmark had stabbed Millstone, set fire to his house and then disappeared. Youliang provided more information, saying that he'd seen both Pockmark and Lightkeeper running along an alley wielding their sticks, beating chickens when they saw chickens, beating dogs when they saw dogs, and if there were no animals about, they'd been smashing the doors, windows, trees and tiles on top of the walls of the houses they passed. At the time, he'd been carrying out his piss bucket, and he was so scared that he ran back home leaving the bucket out in the lane. When he got home, he'd worried about losing his bucket, so he'd gone back to collect it. He saw Pockmark and Lightkeeper hit the bucket with their sticks until they'd smashed it to bits.

"That's mine," he told them. "How can you smash a piss bucket?"

Pockmark raised his stick and advanced towards him menacingly.

"I don't belong to any faction," Youliang reminded him, "so this is nothing to do with me."

"You're the village carpenter," Pockmark snarled, "so you have a pretty easy life of it." He hit out at him, but because he was out of breath from running, he didn't actually connect. Pockmark and Lightkeeper hared off towards the mill. They'd taken a shit on top of the millstone, and then gone off cursing in the direction of the pond.

When Bash heard what Youliang had to say, he simply remarked, "Whatever, I'm glad he's gone… he isn't like the rest of us. However, I don't like the news that Lightkeeper's disappeared – and that he's gone off with Pockmark. Well, I guess you can't change a member of the Five Black Categories. Motherfuckers always bite the hand that feeds them."

In the courtyard of the Branch Secretary's house, there were more than ten captured Red Blades. When Baldy Jin strung up the Branch Secretary in front of them, the families of those captured men flocked outside the courtyard, crying and begging for them to be released. Baldy Jin refused to let them go and told them to slap each other, one on one, and then to confess who was a leader of the Red Blades and who'd been an activist. The dozen or so men proceeded to beat and bruise each other, and they accused one another of everything under the sun. In the end they held to Palace, Soupspoon, Padlock, Stargazer and Once-Upon-A-Time as being the key members, and Soupspoon finally added the name of Ever-Obedient. Palace, Soupspoon, Padlock, Stargazer and Ever-Obedient stayed behind, and the rest were released, but the order went out as follows: "Being released doesn't mean you are off the hook. Perhaps there are other key figures or activists who we haven't identified yet, so no one can leave the village, as you may be called back for further questioning."

That night the wind was still, no more whip-like cracks or whooshing whistles, and the snow continued to fall silently, accumulating to a thickness of four or five digits. Never before had Old Kiln been so quiet; the dogs were inside, the pigs were in their sties and the humans were at home with their yard gates shut. And the wolves did pass by once more, a pack of fourteen, members of three families, the oldest of which had been suffering from sores since that autumn. That wolf had died in the cave up on the ridge, and all the other wolves went to mourn it. Having howled in the cave, they came out in silence and passed through the village of Old Kiln towards North Ridge. The wolves had no idea that a fight had taken place in Old Kiln during the day, and when they passed the back pond without encountering anyone shouting – without even the dogs barking – they thought it strange. However, the pack did not enter the village; they were too sad to snatch food, nor were they interested in watching how the villagers panicked, but only left their footprints deliberately deep in the snow to show they had passed.

Each of the Red Blades closed the door to their courtyard and slammed down the bar. At the homes of Awning, Sparks, Millstone, Palace, Once-Upon-A-Time, Soupspoon and Stargazer, the old men and their wives were crying, but they did not dare make a sound, so they were nestled in bed under the covers convulsed with weeping. In other households, they had no time to cry; they needed to stabilise broken limbs with splints or find salt water with which to wash wounds. The door to the main room was open, and the people were sitting on the floor in a lump, not willing to talk, and the kerosene lamp on top of the cupboard showed a little flame, fluttering gently like a heartbeat. They were looking at the snow outside as the light shone from the door, and they heard the noises coming from their neighbours. The Hammerheads were celebrating; they could smell the sauces cooking in the wok and the aroma of noodles after they'd been fished out of the boiling water soon filled the air. These smells made the wives and children of the Red Blades say, "They're eating well!" But having said this, the others did not react, so they felt they should not have commented and shrank back in upon themselves, not saying a word. As they and the rest of the family continued to watch the snow falling, they all started to wonder if it might not have been a dream: Was there really a fight here today? Did these people who were all friends or family with one another actually end up fighting each other? Had they really been part of this mess? The whole thing seemed crazy, like it couldn't possibly be true.

The sound of footsteps resounded through the alleyway. It was not the sound of straw sandals; they don't make that kind of sound on snow. This was leather boots with thick soles that left deep imprints in the snow, and that was why you could hear this crump, crump noise. The only people who wore leather boots were Awning and Bash. Awning had run away, so this must be Bash. The man sitting on the floor of the main room blew out the light, but then cocked his head to listen for movement. The footsteps were still heading down the left side of the alley, but now the crumping sound was slower paced and whoever it was seemed to be taking a step, followed by a pause, and then another step.

The footsteps were indeed those of Bash. After the battle was over, the Hammerheads went home to cook, and Bash insisted that the key members of the Red Blades stay behind. Useless's mother made a large pot of sweet potato-and-wheat flour noodles, which she carried in a bucket to Bash's home. The stove and cooking pots in his place had all been smashed; he didn't even have a single bowl, so everyone had to eat off a tile. The stools and benches were all gone too, so they squatted down by the wall to eat. Dazed-And-Confused's tailbone was so painful he couldn't squat, so he had to lean against the wall to eat. He just had half a bowl, which amazed Baldy Jin: such a greedy person only wanted half a bowl of food when he himself was going to have a whole bowl.

But Dazed-And-Confused gulped and slurped down his food without even raising his head.

"Doesn't it burn your throat?" asked Bash.

Dazed-And-Confused didn't say a word, and he soon polished off his half-filled bowl and then went to get a second full bowlful. When Baldy Jin went for seconds himself, the bucket was empty.

"Motherfucking robber!" he cursed. "The first bowl was half-full but you still took a full second one!"

"I do like my food," said Dazed-And-Confused.

Bash suddenly called something to mind and asked Baldy Jin, "Did you arrange for anyone to keep an eye on Awning and Sparks' houses?"

"Yup," Baldy Jin assured him. "If they dare come back, someone will report it straight away."

"Now why do I keep thinking that Millstone won't have gone anywhere?" Bash wondered aloud.

"Awning and Sparks have run away," Dazed-And-Confused remarked, "so why would Millstone stay?"

"Pockmark stabbed him," Bash pointed out. "When Pockmark stabs someone, he's not going to just leave them with a scratch. If he got him good, would Millstone be able to move? How could he run away?"

Iron Bolt put down his bowl and said, "I'm going over there to see. If he's at home, I'll call you."

"If Millstone's there, do you think you can handle him?" Bash asked. "Stop eating everyone, because we're going to search his house."

The group went to search Millstone's house, but his wife said that he had not been home all day, so she didn't know whether he was dead or alive. Baldy Jin and Dazed-And-Confused searched the whole house, even the woodshed, but they didn't find any sign of Millstone. They went into the bedroom and asked if he was hiding in the hole in the *kang*. His wife lifted the mat to show that there was a hole there, allowing her to clean out the *kang*.

"The edge collapsed and I told him to make some cement and fix it," she said, "but before he could do so, you attacked the village."

"What do you mean by that?" Bash demanded. "Does this village belong to you? Don't we live here too?"

Baldy Jin stepped forward and slapped Millstone's wife across the face, saying, "Keep a civil tongue in your face."

Millstone's wife didn't scream or cry, she just said, "Go ahead and search. He's a grown man and not a handkerchief that can fall into a crack in the wall."

Out in the courtyard, the others were tossing about bales of straw and bean stalks, while the pig in the sty, which had gone a whole day without being fed, was hungry and squealing, and then it jumped out over the wall of its sty, in the corner of the yard containing the turnip cellar. Millstone's wife picked up a broom and started to beat the pig. "What the hell are you doing?" she said. "It's dark now, so why aren't you asleep? Why are you making all this fuss?"

"Who are you scolding?" Baldy Jin asked.

"I'm scolding the pig," Millstone's wife retorted, and she beat the animal back into the sty with her broom.

The group couldn't find Millstone anywhere, but when they went out of the courtyard, Bash suddenly asked Baldy Jin, "Have you looked in the cellar?"

"Oh, I forgot about the cellar," Baldy Jin said. A few of them went back to the kitchen and uncovered the entrance to the cellar in the corner of the room. Millstone's wife's face changed, and she swooped in like a wolf and fell across the boards, crying loudly, "You've searched everywhere, what could possibly be hidden in the cellar? If you want to go into the cellar, you'll have to kill me first!"

Baldy Jin came forward to pull Millstone's wife away, but her hands were clutching the iron ring on the cellar entrance, and her body was stuck there like a suction cup, so she couldn't be moved. Dazed-And-Confused grabbed her by the waist, and so her arse was right against his chest, soft and pillowy. Dazed-And-Confused groped her arse, whereupon Millstone's wife started to scream, "Rape! Rape!" Dazed-And-Confused let go and her body was once again glued to the entrance, so tightly that they seemed to have become one; there was no gap at all.

"What are you screaming about?" Dazed-And-Confused asked. "You think I've never seen a woman before? Even if you were lying there stark naked in front of me, I wouldn't be interested. I'd just cover you with a bit of tile and be on my way."

"You groped my arse!" Millstone's wife declared.

Bash thumped the table so that the bowls and plates jumped. "Take her and the trapdoor away in one!"

Baldy Jin and Dazed-And-Confused lifted Millstone's wife and threw the board covering the cellar off to one side, and a hole appeared at the foot of the wall.

But Millstone wasn't in the cellar either.

Millstone's wife stopped crying and froze, waiting for the group to leave, but she was still bewildered since he had indeed been hidden in the cellar. Why wasn't he still there? Then he called out to her. When she turned around, Millstone was crawling out from under the stalks of maize covering the turnip cellar in the yard.

After being injured, he hid in the cellar. That was where he ate and shat, and his wife would crawl in to look after him. This night, it was already late, and Millstone said he felt suffocated and wanted to go out for some air, so his wife helped him to the entrance of the cellar. Just at that moment there was a thunderous banging and Bash shouted about wanting to search the place for Millstone, so his wife told him to hide back in the cellar and she covered it with the trapdoor and went to answer the door. Millstone stayed there a while but then decided that it would not be safe there since every house had a cellar, and that was an obvious place to hide. He forced himself to bear the pain as he climbed out and lay down in the kitchen, waiting for an opportunity to escape through the courtyard door. But there was always someone in the yard. When his wife and Baldy Jin quarrelled upstairs, the people in the courtyard went in to see what was going on, so he took advantage of the darkness to make his way towards the courtyard door. After a few steps, his wound hurt so much that he was worried he wouldn't be able to walk far before he fell down on the road, and suddenly he thought of the turnip cellar in the corner of the courtyard. The turnip cellar was called a cellar, but in fact it was just a very shallow pit because it was only ever used to store turnips. It was covered with a lid made from maize stalks stuck together with mud, but they ate their turnips fresh, so there was space in the cellar. Millstone quietly inserted himself inside; that was a place nobody was ever going to inspect. But when the pig got out and ran over there to eat the turnips, it nearly ruined everything.

Millstone's wife quickly carried him back to the house and got him comfortable, and then she picked up a stick and gave the pig a real beating. She decided that the pig must have been a villain in a previous life, and it was making Millstone's life difficult on purpose. The pig's head was bleeding from the blows and it was screaming. Millstone's wife came back into the house and said to her husband, "We've raised a scourge. In a few days, I'm going to sell it."

"It's so skinny it won't meet its weight," Millstone said.

"In that case, we'll kill it and eat the meat ourselves," his wife declared.

When the pig heard this, it screamed even louder.

"Maybe we got it wrong," Millstone said. "Maybe it wasn't going to eat the turnips, it just wanted to say hello." The pig went quiet and made no more noise.

When Bash and the others left the house, they still felt uneasy that Millstone might be lurking somewhere in Old Kiln; of course, they hoped he was long gone. They took a torch to check the snow for footprints leading from Millstone's house to either the front or the back of the village. Millstone had big feet in big shoes, and perhaps he was seriously injured, in which case there'd be bloodstains on the snow. They couldn't find footprints anywhere, but they discovered wolf pawprints on the road behind the mill.

"Did Millstone make wolves' paws out of wood and put them on his hands and feet before he ran away?" Dazed-And-Confused asked.

"He was a good carpenter," Baldy Jin said, "but could he really make wooden paws? When would he have time to do that?"

"Oh, then the wolves must have passed today," Bash concluded.

Had the wolves just passed behind the mill, or had they not gone far and were still somewhere around the back pond? The gang inspected the snowy ground for a while and returned to the road, where Caretaker was outside the door of his family's pigsty fastening it tight. He had caught a cold and kept coughing and spitting. Seeing Bash and the rest of them walking over, he said, "I can sleep sound tonight."

"Sleep?" Baldy Jin snapped. "The wolves have been past!"

"The wolves are here again?" Caretaker said. He leapt into the pigsty to check that everything was right and tight, then he jumped out, although he remained ill at ease. He opened the door to the sty, grabbed two piglets by their ears and dragged them into the courtyard. The others cursed Caretaker as useless and untrustworthy, and decided never to give him a job again.

"What do you mean?" he said. "What have I done wrong?"

"When I was fighting with Sparks at the entrance to the road," Dazed-And-Confused said, "I saw you off in the distance. You weren't coming to help me, no, you were running away. And when they had Huang Shengsheng penned up and were trying to burn him, where were you? Where had you got to?"

"I know I can't compare to you," Caretaker said, "but you're all by yourself, while I have a big family with parents and children depending on me, not to mention all my piglets."

"What are you all on about?" Bash demanded irritably. "Go home, everyone. But you're to come round early because we have things to discuss." Having said that, he walked away.

Bash's absence put a dampener on Baldy Jin, Dazed-And-Confused and the others.

"Do you know where Bash has gone to?" someone asked.

"He's gone home, hasn't he?" Baldy Jin said. "He must be exhausted."

"If he was going back home, he'd go to the south," the man said, "so how come he went east?"

"East?" said Baldy Jin.

"You get it, don't you?" the man said.

Baldy Jin cackled a bit.

"What are you laughing at?" Dazed-And-Confused asked.

"Go home and go to bed," Baldy Jin said. "And if you can't sleep, you'll have to use your hand to get yourself off!"

Dazed-And-Confused got Baldy Jin's message loud and clear: he was making fun of him for not having a wife. That evening, all the other Hammerheads would be in bed with their wives, the motherfuckers, and if time were suddenly to stand still in the middle of the night and you went house to house to see what they were up to, eight or nine out of every ten would be at it with their wives. Dazed-And-Confused felt humiliated, but he also remembered pulling down Yoyo's trousers earlier, and how just now he'd groped Millstone's wife's arse, and he cursed the lot of them: "Motherfuckers!" He kicked a heap of snow in the road. As he passed the door to Inkcap's house, he decided that kicking the snow about wasn't enough to assuage his anger, so he kicked the door open.

Neither Inkcap nor Gran was asleep. Gran was putting a lump of vinegar-soaked cotton into Inkcap's nostril, reprimanding him for sticking his nose in where it wasn't wanted and how he wasn't to say any more about it. The door of the courtyard thumped, and the cotton lump hurt Inkcap's nose as it went in, and he was about to scream.

Gran clapped a hand over his mouth and said hesitantly, "Who is it? Who's out there?"

"Who do you think?" Dazed-And-Confused complained. "Are your ears clogged up with hair so you can't hear my voice?"

"What's the matter, Dazed-And-Confused?" Gran asked.

Dazed-And-Confused was perfectly fine, but he wanted to throw his weight around, so he said, "What's the matter? Do you need me to ask? According to the report from the masses, Huang Shengsheng was burned today, and it was Goodman who caused the fire. When Goodman fell down the embankment, Inkcap carried him on his back to your house. The Hammerheads are out looking for him."

"Rubbish," Gran said. "How would we dare take Goodman into the house?"

"I'm supposed to just take your word for it? Open the door, I want to see for myself."

Gran opened the courtyard door. Dazed-And-Confused saw that one leaf of the door to the upper room was closed and the other was open, and that a lit kerosene lamp was standing on top of the cupboard inside, and that Apricot was standing there with her back to the light.

"What do you think you're doing here in the middle of the night?" Apricot asked.

Dazed-And-Confused was surprised to see Apricot and for a moment, he couldn't find a word to say. After a pause, he asked, "Why are you here?"

"Why shouldn't I be here? I have a stomach ache and I came to ask Granny Silkworm for help, OK?"

"With Huang Shengsheng so badly burned, we're looking for Goodman," Dazed-And-Confused explained.

"If you were really searching for him, Bash would be here in person, not you. I guess you're hungry and looking for something to eat. Inkcap, give this man a roast potato."

Inkcap tossed him a roast potato, and Dazed-And-Confused caught it and left.

As soon as Dazed-And-Confused left, Inkcap said to Gran, "That was very clever of you."

"What do you mean?" she asked.

"You said that the Hammerheads would definitely come to our house to look for Goodman, and they did. You called Apricot over to our house so that the Hammerheads could not search it, and sure enough, Dazed-And-Confused didn't dare do any such thing."

"Then you should say thank you nicely to Apricot," Gran replied.

Inkcap smiled at Apricot and said, "I'll roast three more potatoes for you, and I'll pick the biggest."

"That would only make you upset," Apricot replied. Then she told Gran that since everything was fine now, she ought to be going back home, but if there was anything else she could do, they should just let her know.

Goodman was sitting in the shadows of the room, eating a roast potato, and he now stood up too and said, "I ought to be on my way too."

"Why the hurry?" Gran asked. "Doesn't your head still hurt? The kid and I can sleep in the woodshed overnight, and you can leave tomorrow."

"It still hurts," Goodman said, "but it's nothing to worry about. If I were to leave tomorrow, I'd run into more people. I'll go now with Apricot. With Apricot around, nobody's going to mess with me."

"That's fine," Apricot said. "I'll walk with you as far as the road leading to the mountains."

Inkcap got an axe from behind the door and said, "And I'll walk with both of you."

Gran shouted at Inkcap to put the axe down. "If you're going to go, then go, but you mustn't be carrying anything. If you have a weapon and the Hammerheads see you, you'll be in terrible trouble."

Inkcap and Apricot escorted Goodman to the junction at the foot of the hill, and then Inkcap walked Apricot back to the village. At the north end of Three Fork Alley, the entrances of two lanes were really close together, separated only by an old chinaberry tree; going forward from the tree, the two lanes became one. A bird was now dozing in the tree, and just as they reached it, it fluttered up, and a moment later an eerie cry was heard from another chinaberry tree by the mill.

"Is that an owl?" Apricot asked.

Inkcap listened, and it was indeed an owl. His heart gave a lurch, and he asked, "Is someone going to die?"

"Don't say anything so unlucky," Apricot said. The two of them hurried down the east alley.

A short time before Inkcap and Apricot went into the east alley, Bash was walking down the same alley on his way to the western alley. When Bash got to Apricot's house, he saw that the door was closed, so he grabbed a handful of snow, squeezed it into an icy lump and threw it into the courtyard, but it fell on the snow with little sound. He used the knocker to hammer on the door, but since there was no response, he turned and walked away. Bash couldn't think where Apricot could have got to – or maybe she'd just gone to sleep early. He wanted to tell her that the sweater had kept him nice and warm those days up at the kiln, and to talk about his victorious fight that day, and he'd also decided that he must take off his shoes to let her see the mole on the bottom of his foot, because that mole showed he'd make a great general who'd give orders that would be obeyed. However, she wasn't there to share his happiness, so he couldn't help feeling disappointed.

Just as he was getting settled at home, Useless came running in, screaming at the top of his voice that Huang Shengsheng was dying. Bash knew he had been burned and was then carried back home by Useless where he could be looked after, so he wanted to go and see him, but as he thought he'd only got a flesh wound and Useless's mother was taking care of him, it could wait until tomorrow. Bash never imagined he would die.

"Don't scare me like that – you should have prepared me," Bash complained.

"I might not prepare others, but how would I dare break bad news to you without warning?" Useless said. "I'm telling you, Huang Shengsheng is dying."

When he arrived at Useless's house, Bash found Huang Shengsheng lying unconscious on the straw in the woodshed.

"How can you let someone sleep here?" Bash asked.

"Straw is warmest," Useless's mother said. "As soon as Comrade Huang came, I cooked for him, and he ate three bowls."

"If he could eat three bowls," Bash said, "I don't see why he should be in this state. Carry him to the bed, put him on the bed."

The three of them carried Huang Shengsheng to the bed, and Bash patted his face.

"Why are you slapping him around?" Useless's mother asked.

Bash ignored her and said, "Comrade Huang, wake up. What happened to you – you took a few burns and you're in this kind of state?"

Huang Shengsheng opened his eyes, saw it was Bash and breathed deeply. "I may well not make it," he said.

"What do you mean? The revolution has not yet succeeded, you can't even think about dying right now. Do you want some noodles? Shall I get Useless's mother to make you a bowl of noodles?"

"We're out of flour," Useless's mother said. "We used our last flour to make noodle soup for you lot."

Bash glared at her and then said to Huang Shengsheng, "If you want to eat noodles, shall I get Useless's mother to make you a bowl?"

Huang Shengsheng's eyes closed and his head swung to the inside of the bed.

"How about eggs?" Bash said. "How about a nice egg sunny side up?"

Huang Shengsheng's head swung over again.

"Or snake? We caught a big snake this afternoon."

Huang Shengsheng's eyes opened again.

"Didn't you catch a snake?" Bash asked Useless.

"Oh yes," he said. "We killed it and wanted to give it to Comrade Huang, but then the fighting started. I chucked the snake over at the foot of the wall to Gourd's house."

"You go there now, and when you've found it, have it stewed for him to eat."

Useless went out, and his mother chased after him and whispered, "Can Comrade Huang eat snake?"

"He can eat anything," Useless assured her.

"We can't possibly cook it here," his mother complained, "because snake stinks. Just come back empty-handed and say you couldn't find it."

Useless did not bring back the snake. He called a few Hammerheads in case Huang Shengsheng really did die, because then they'd have to carry his body out to the Kiln God Temple. However, when the men he'd summoned saw Huang Shengsheng's flesh was burned and yellow, coarse and wrinkled like tree bark, and there were many blisters seeping pus, they were too scared to go any further.

"With him in this state, shouldn't we get in touch with Comrade Huang's family?" Useless's mother asked. "Either he should go home where he can get better, or maybe you should take him to the Kiln God Temple so the Hammerheads can take it in turns to care for him."

"We told you to look after him," Bash said.

"Well... but..."

"Well, what?" Bash demanded. "Comrade Huang isn't just any old person. Who knows, in the future he could do some amazing things, in which case aren't you going to be in luck! If it costs money, tell Useless to put it down in the accounts."

Bash went off, ordering Useless to give him whatever he wanted to eat. "If the snake has gone, then tomorrow morning you're to catch a bunch of sparrows. You have to do this. Catch a bunch of sparrows and roast them for him to eat."

SEVENTY-FOUR

THE NEXT DAY, it stopped snowing, and the sky was clear and cold. The air felt like shards of ice, invisible, but making the skin on face and hands hurt. The Hammerheads were in an emergency meeting, and most of them were wearing cotton-padded jackets and trousers. The dozen or so who weren't wearing cotton-padded trousers did so on account of the fact that last year's trousers had rotted away to the point that the white fluffy padding was falling out; or because their new trousers weren't yet ready; or because they felt it was too early to put them on and they were planning to endure a few days without. They stuffed corn silk into their straw sandals, so their feet looked as big as bear paws.

Thanks to their victory in battle, the Hammerheads once again dominated the village of Old Kiln, but Bash understood perfectly that when Awning, Sparks and Millstone ran off, it left the rest without any leadership. The Red Blades appeared to have been destroyed but in reality, this was just temporary. Dead ashes once reignited will burn all the more vigorously, and the drowning dog that has climbed up on the bank is even more likely to bite. To let the villagers know that the fighting was entirely the fault of the Red Blades, that they were not only acting contrary to Chairman Mao's revolutionary line but also working for the destruction of the Cultural Revolution, and that they'd behaved with conspicuous brutality during the battle, it was necessary to expose them, to thoroughly purge their poisonous influence, to wake up the deluded masses, and to unite more forces. For all these reasons, the Hammerheads decided to hold a big rally. They would not only march around every alleyway of Old Kiln, but also go to Xiahewan because the Golden Cudgels had suffered many injuries and one death while helping them.

The marching group gathered in front of the gateway leading to the mountain, and they carried with them Huang Shengsheng stretchered along on the leaf of a door, and two other men with broken legs and injured backs hobbled along on wooden sticks, while those with broken arms had them slung in bandages, and those with injuries to the cheek, forehead or head all removed their bandages to expose the wound.

Inkcap came out early in the morning to empty the piss pot. Originally, he'd planned to pour it into the privy, but later he decided to throw the contents onto his onion patch, taking the opportunity to watch the parade. The road was slippery, and the slops spilled everywhere. Under the rubber tree, Pillar came stumbling over with a backpack and a wooden stick in his hand, saying, "Are you OK being up this early?"

"I wasn't fighting yesterday so why shouldn't I be OK?" Inkcap said.

"Oh, I'm OK too. What are you doing?"

"I'm going to pour some slops on my onion patch."

Pillar came over and looked into Inkcap's bucket and said, "You've already spilled your slops, what're you going to pour on your onions?"

He suddenly fixed his eyes on something in front and poked about with a stick. The snow parted to reveal a shoe – a leather shoe – the heel of which was worn unevenly, but the surface didn't show so much as a hole. He thumped the shoe clean of snow and threw it into the basket, saying, "Fuck this, I haven't found even a scrap of steel, let alone a watch."

"So that's why you're up so early," Inkcap shouted. "You're picking things up."

"And why shouldn't I? Yesterday all sorts of people came from Luozhen, and they were covered in expensive things. As you walk about, you ought to keep an eye out."

Cowbell emerged from another lane. He wasn't wearing padded trousers either, and he had a rope around his waist. He was all hunched over, but when he heard what Pillar had to say, he kicked out at the snow with his feet. "Wow, that's a tooth there – a really long tooth. Do you want it?"

"I heard they chased you up the wall like a dog yesterday," Pillar remarked conversationally.

"What are you talking about? Yesterday the bullets fell like rain, but they didn't hurt me one bit."

"Let me see your ear."

Cowbell was wearing a cotton deerstalker with the ear-flaps tied tightly under his chin. "Why should I let you see?" he said. "It's far too cold."

"Look at you wrapped up like that! It seems you're not worried about being beaten to death but you are worried about dying of cold!" Then he walked away.

Cowbell came over and said to Inkcap, "Have you lost your slops? I'll give you some." He took off his pants and peed into the bucket. Inkcap also took down his trousers and did the same. The weather was cold, and they had a lot of pee, so it fell with a tinkling and thudding sound.

"After we came back from the spring, how come I didn't see you anywhere?" Cowbell asked.

"I don't belong to any faction," Inkcap said, "so wouldn't I just have been beaten if I'd gone out?"

"Do you know that Huang Shengsheng got burned until he almost died?"

"Who says so?"

"I heard it from Useless's mother last night."

"Did she say the fire was lit by you firing a slingshot?"

"You lit it!" Cowbell asserted.

Inkcap looked nervous and asked again, "Did she say that?"

"No, but why are you so scared?"

"Don't mention this ever again," Inkcap ordered him. Then he tied his trousers back on, and lifting the bucket, he decided that instead of going to his onion patch he'd hurry back home. On the way, he decided to avoid seeing Cowbell for a few days – Cowbell was a chatterbox, and he'd just have to hope he didn't say the wrong thing to the wrong person. When he turned into the alley, he remembered the stuff that Pillar had been picking up, and he couldn't stop himself from keeping his eyes peeled. It wasn't that he was looking for stuff, but he was amazed to see that every alley was so smoky yesterday, but after one night, the snow was all white again and everything looked normal.

When he turned around, Dazed-And-Confused appeared out of another alleyway. His tailbone was wounded, but that wasn't the kind of injury where he was going to take his trousers off and air it. He'd killed one of his chickens and used its blood to smear all over his head and ears, and even over his coat collar. When Dazed-And-Confused caught sight of Inkcap, he said, "Go to the parade."

"What parade?" Inkcap was being deliberately tiresome. "It's too cold."

"The Hammerheads are marching," Dazed-And-Confused explained, "to show we've beaten the Red Blades. Have you ever heard the expression that blood must be paid with blood?"

"I'm not a member of the Hammerheads, so I'm not going to march."

"Not going? If you don't go, it means you're one of the Red Blades. I'm here to make sure you go, and your gran too, and you'd better believe it."

Inkcap did not dare be stubborn, he said he could go, but he had to carry the piss bucket back first.

Dazed-And-Confused came and kicked the bucket over. "You think you're going to give me the slip, eh?" he said as he dragged Inkcap off by the ear. "Do you really think we want you there? You're very lucky to even be allowed to make up the numbers. And you still don't want to go, you piece of shit."

When they got to the bottom of the gate leading to the mountains, Huang Shengsheng had already been carried out. He really couldn't sit up, so he was lying on the door leaf covered with a quilt. There were also the two men with broken legs, which had been roughly splinted and bandaged. The wife of one of them said to Bash, "We must ask Goodman to straighten the bone. If we don't get the bone placed properly, his leg will grow crooked."

"Now?" Bash said. "Once the parade is over, then he can have his leg pulled straight."

He called some people to carry this pair on door leaves too, and the wife covered her husband carefully in a quilt.

"We need the leg on display," Bash commanded, and the quilt was pulled aside again. Four people carried each door leaf: Huang Shengsheng lay down on one, and the pair with broken legs each lay down on one, leaving one to be taken back.

"Just three?" Bash said. "Carry another one. Dazed-And-Confused, your tailbone isn't healed yet, is it?"

"No, it's still very painful."

"Then you can lie down, but you're not to shit or pee all the way to Xiahewan."

"I can hold it in," Dazed-And-Confused said, and then he fell asleep on the door.

Decheng, Lishan and Almost-There were going to take it in turns carrying this door leaf.

"I don't want to," Decheng said. "Dazed-And-Confused is too heavy!"

"I was this badly beaten for the sake of the Hammerheads, and you don't want to lift me?" Dazed-And-Confused retorted.

"Your wound is nothing."

Dazed-And-Confused set up moaning in pain. Baldy Jin came over and said, "That's great, Dazed-And-Confused. Can you do that the whole way?"

"Gimme a blanket," Dazed-And-Confused demanded. "If I have to lie down and keep still, I'm going to freeze to death."

"Go to my house and get a blanket," Bash instructed Inkcap. Inkcap went to Bash's house, but just as he was carrying the blanket out of the courtyard door, he turned back and emerged with only a torn sheet.

The marching party went round all the lanes of Old Kiln shouting slogans, and the lanes were of course full of people, families with the surname of Hei, and also families with the surname of Zhu, along with the rest. The older and younger members of the Zhu didn't join in the shouting but watched in silence. Occasionally, there were one or two members of the Red Blades standing in front of their homes, also with their arms in slings or legs in splints – they too were showing their injuries.

"What are you doing, what are you standing here for?" Useless barked.

"I'm in front of my house," the man replied. "I'm not doing anything." He put his hand to his crotch and scratched.

"I'm talking to you, and you're scratching?" Useless complained.

"I'm happy to scratch my own balls."

When the two of them started to raise their voices, the family hurriedly pulled the man into the courtyard, and the courtyard door was closed. As the procession passed by Half Cut Lane, where many families with the surname Hei lived, three families were setting off firecrackers. Inkcap got excited and ran over to pick up any crackers that hadn't gone off. Despite being kicked by Baldy Jin, he managed to pick up three, and he held them in his hand as he ran to the front of the parade. Useless's mother had filled a steamer with sweet potatoes that she brought to the side of the road. Inkcap asked for one, but she refused to give him any. Seeking revenge, Inkcap quietly took out a match and lit a firecracker. It started to smoke, and he was in a hurry to throw it at the feet of Useless's mother. But it was the match he threw, and with a bang, the firecracker blew up in his hand.

Once the procession came out from Old Kiln, they stopped banging the gongs and drums, and shouting slogans. Except for Huang Shengsheng, who was still being carried, Dazed-And-Confused and the other two invalids were walking on their own. It was at this point that something strange happened. While they were marching around the village, some of the red-beaked, white-tailed birds from the white pine by the Mountain God Temple were flying overhead, and Inkcap muttered to himself, "Does that mean someone has gone to Goodman for a cure?"

He couldn't help wondering if Goodman had slipped last night on the mountain path, or perhaps his head was still hurting after a night's sleep. Soon, this idea flashed through his mind and was gone. He saw more and more birds in the sky, flying in groups one after the other, leaving the village. They didn't disperse, and every so often bird droppings fell from above.

Huang Shengsheng was lying on the door. At first, he could still open his eyes, but then he convulsed a few times and fainted. Bash rushed over to the door and said, "Comrade Huang, hold on."

Huang Shengsheng's eyes opened again, and said to himself, "The bird is pecking my hand."

Bash put his hand on Huang Shengsheng's forehead. "You're running a fever, that's why you're talking nonsense."

He asked the men who were carrying the door to be gentler and steadier when they changed shoulders. After walking for a while, a bird swooped down and pecked Huang Shengsheng's hand which was resting on top of the quilt, and the skin on the back of his hand was pecked open. Everyone rushed to scare the bird away and Huang Shengsheng fainted again. When the procession arrived outside Xiahewan, the gongs and drums resumed their banging, the slogans were shouted, and Dazed-And-Confused and the other two men were lying back on their door leaves again.

Huang Shengsheng woke up and muttered, "The bird is going to peck at my feet."

"No way," said the man carrying the door leaf. "As soon as it comes near you, we'll drive it off. Look, I'll cover your feet." He tucked in the corner of the quilt tightly to cover Huang Shengsheng's feet.

There was a canal outside the village of Xiahewan, where they used three planks that were in place to carry the door leaves across. Once the men in front were over, the men at the back put their feet on the planks, but then the rope binding the three planks together broke, and they slipped. One man fell into the canal, and the leaf of the door tilted, so Huang Shengsheng nearly fell off. Several men rushed to his assistance, but they had to pay attention to where they were putting their feet, and nobody was expecting a bird to dive out of the air and peck at his foot where the quilt had slid away from Huang Shengsheng's body.

Having got the door over the canal, they discovered that the bird had already pecked a deep hole in his flesh. Bash was furious, and one of the men carrying the door leaf asked why birds were always pecking at him. Bash also thought it strange, so he let Huang Shengsheng's wounded foot be exposed, and he told Inkcap to stay close to him and take care of any passing bird.

In Xiahewan, the Hammerheads were greeted by the head of the Golden Cudgels as well as a certain woman. This woman was very young, with her hair in a short bob, and she was wearing an old, washed-out army uniform, belted at the waist, and carrying a camera strap diagonally. The cinched-in belt made her breasts stand out prominently, and the camera strap separated them into two distinct mounds. But Inkcap thought she wasn't the least pretty. The residents of Old Kiln used to look down on Xiahewan, saying that its soil may be good and the crops grew better than in Old Kiln, but the water there was saline, the persimmons were astringent, the walnuts were all root, their wives were dull and coarse, and all the unmarried girls were swarthy. This woman was indeed swarthy.

The head of the Golden Cudgels and the woman called Bash into a house for a discussion, and after a while Bash came out and asked everyone, "What do you think of Division Chief Ma?"

"Who's Division Chief Ma?" Baldy Jin asked.

"Dumbo! Who do you think?"

"The woman with the camera?" Baldy Jin asked.

"Dark!" said Inkcap, and everyone giggled.

"Stop being so rude," Bash said. "You know, she was a teacher in Luozhen, and now is the division chief of the United Command faction in Luozhen, specifically appointed to lead the guidance work in Xiahewan."

"Her?" Baldy Jin said.

"This was her idea," Bash explained. "The Golden Cudgels will join in our parade, and the dead man will be put in his coffin. Division Chief Ma has insisted on carrying the coffin for the march. The family of the deceased was reluctant, but she scared them off with a few words. Isn't that great? Could you do something like that?"

"I could," Baldy Jin declared. "Hell, we could dig up some dead bodies and parade them too!"

"Oh really? Half-Stick won't even let you in the house, so you had to go and live over in the storeroom. I don't know what you think you're ever going to achieve—"

"A good man wouldn't fight a woman," Baldy Jin said, "and if a woman achieves anything, isn't it because she's got a man to rely on?"

"Well, you're to keep an eye on Division Chief Ma," Bash told him, "because we're going to do whatever she tells us to. We'll be obeying her orders in future." That left everyone with nothing to say.

After a while, the Golden Cudgels assembled. In addition to a dozen invalids who took the lead at the front of the procession, there was also a white wooden coffin being carried by six people. The two teams combined and began to move through the village. Xiahewan was three times larger than Old Kiln, there were real streets, and the Guandi Temple with a plaza in front that was several acres in size. The procession left the village street, and once everyone had assembled, the meeting began. Division Chief Ma spoke in front of everyone, but as to what she said, Baldy Jin and the others didn't want to listen. They weren't here to listen to a woman, so they muttered among themselves about her uniform, her hair, her appearance in general.

"There's one thing good about her," one of them said. "Those tits look like two steamed buns."

"All you ever think about is food," Stonebreaker snapped.

"What's with Bash?" Iron Bolt asked. "The moment he set eyes on this woman, he's changed."

"What's so great about her," said Tag-Along, "other than her camera?"

"Who has a camera in Old Kiln?" Stonebreaker said. "Does Apricot have one?"

"Don't drag Apricot into this," Inkcap said. He demanded a sweet potato of Tag-Along. Tag-Along hesitated a good long while before pulling out a cooked sweet potato from his pocket and giving it to Inkcap, but not before breaking it in half and stuffing it into his own mouth.

The sweet potato was already frozen hard, and eating it was like chomping ice crumbs. Inkcap didn't want Baldy Jin to say anything more about Bash fancying Division Chief Ma. They all knew that Bash and Apricot had got together, and she was already pregnant with Bash's child, but they still said such things... it all went to show they didn't care a snap about Apricot.

Just as Inkcap was ruminating, Useless said, "You're supposed to be looking after Comrade Huang, but all you think about is filling your face!"

Inkcap looked up at the sky, and it was empty. All the birds were over on the big willow tree by the temple plaza. "The birds can't peck him from over there," Inkcap said. But he still went over to the door where Huang Shengsheng was lying. Huang Shengsheng had his eyes closed. He seemed to be unconscious, but also not. From the next leaf along, Dazed-And-Confused was whispering to him.

"What are you whispering about?" Inkcap asked. "Why don't you speak up?"

"I'm so hungry my stomach is rumbling," Dazed-And-Confused said. "Find me something to eat."

"You're injured. What do you want to eat for?"

"Tell Bash that if he doesn't get me something to eat, I'll be too hungry to keep lying here."

Inkcap went to report this information to Bash, who simply said, "All that fucker has to do is lie there, and he still wants to eat! Useless, slip him a sweet potato, but don't let anyone see."

The procession was about to set off again, and a lot of villagers were milling about between the temple plaza and the streets, just to come and see the hustle and bustle. As Dazed-And-Confused reached out to take the sweet potato, Baldy Jin said, "Cover yourself with the sheet."

Dazed-And-Confused ate under the sheet.

"Who's that you're carrying, and why all the movement?" the roadside spectators wanted to know.

"It's one of our wounded," Baldy Jin informed them. "That United Headquarters lot beat one of our Hammerheads until his spine broke. He's in so much pain he can't keep still." Then in a low voice he whispered to Dazed-And-Confused, "Moan. Start moaning."

Dazed-And-Confused moaned loudly. But pretty soon the sound died away to be replaced by chewing.

"I'm putting you in charge," Baldy Jin told Inkcap. "If there's anyone around, you've got to get him to moan."

Inkcap picked up a stick, and whenever they passed onlookers by the side of the road, he poked Dazed-And-Confused, and he would moan. But Inkcap kept poking at him, and this annoyed Dazed-And-Confused so much that he lifted the sheet and mashed the remains of his sweet potato onto Inkcap's head.

SEVENTY-FIVE

THE PROCESSION RETURNED TO OLD KILN FROM XIAHEWAN, by which time it was already late morning, and everyone was feeling dizzy from hunger.

Dazed-And-Confused was no longer being carried, and the marchers straggled along. When they arrived at the stone lion, Bash went over and sat on it, and everyone else took a seat too. Bash did not reprimand them but raised his head to look at South Mountain. The sky was dark grey and gloomy, but the mountain was capped with white clouds. The clouds seem to spring out of the snow, piling higher and higher into the sky.

"Old Kiln is beautiful," Bash suddenly remarked. No one in Old Kiln had ever looked at the scenery around them, or really noticed it, and certainly no one ever said it was beautiful. Now Bash had said it, they all looked at South Mountain.

"The landscape here is beyond compare," Useless said.

"Balls!" said Tag-Along. "All I want right now is a bowl of something hot."

"Fuck you!" Useless said. "I was reciting one of Chairman Mao's poems."

"I didn't say anything reactionary," Tag-Along declared. Useless's face suddenly turned red.

"Can everybody stop quarrelling," Stonebreaker said. "We've all learned the expression 'beautiful and rich', but it is not right at all, because beauty and wealth are not connected. Xiahewan is richer than we are, but they don't have the beauty of Old Kiln. We may be poor but we have beauty, we have so many trees and animals around us."

"What are you yapping about?" Baldy Jin asked, as everyone fell silent.

"It's not fair I don't have a fucking camera," Bash complained. "I wish I had one."

Baldy Jin turned his head to look at Bash for a while and said, "Are you thinking about Division Chief Ma again?"

He didn't answer, nor did he get angry, but looked at Inkcap. Inkcap kept squinting at Bash. "What are you looking at?"

"I was taking a picture of you with my eyes," Inkcap explained.

"Ah-ha, that's a good one," Bash puffed out his chest and waved his arms. He wanted to quote something but couldn't think of anything appropriate, so he turned to Useless and said, "Recite one of Chairman Mao's poems for us... the one you recited before, about 'truly great people'..."

Useless pulled himself together, cleared his throat and started reciting in a sing-song cadence. "A hundred leagues locked in ice, A thousand leagues of whirling snow..." When Useless was reciting Chairman Mao's poetry, no one dared to make a sound, although they did not understand what it meant. As he recited the words "All are past and gone, For truly great men", Tag-Along said, "Who's Chairman Mao talking about there?"

"You don't understand," Useless said. "He's talking about people like us, heroes of the modern age."

Huang Shengsheng sighed, a long sigh that seemed to erupt from his mouth. Inkcap rushed over to look, but Huang Shengsheng appeared to be still unconscious, so his sigh was not intentional. "Comrade Huang, Comrade Huang," he called.

Huang Shengsheng finally opened his eyes, his lips moved, and Inkcap had to put his ear sideways in front of his mouth to hear. "What did he say?" Bash asked.

"He said the bird is going to peck at his eyes," Inkcap replied.

"Cover him tightly with the blanket and carry him to Useless's house," Bash commanded. Seven or eight men covered Huang Shengsheng tightly and carried him back, after which they all dispersed and went home.

Inkcap was the last to leave the stone lion, for just as the procession was breaking up, he saw Gran at the far side of the mill, on the elevated bank. He was reluctant to call out to her in front of so many people, but when they had all gone, he went towards her. Gran was carrying a basket, and she was looking down at the tussocks of grass below the embankment. When Inkcap called her, she paid no attention. He called again, and she looked back and was startled, as if she had only just noticed him.

"Gran, what happened to you?" Inkcap asked.

Gran cocked her head sideways. "What did you say?"

"Can't you hear me?"

Gran heard him this time and said, "I got up this morning and my ears were ringing so badly I couldn't hear anything."

Inkcap started to panic. "Gran, you've gone deaf!"

Gran took Inkcap by the hand and smiled. "It's nothing, nothing at all... Look at how anxious you are! People often go deaf in old age. Where have you been? Did you march with the others?"

Inkcap stroked Gran's ear and then put his little finger in and waggled it about. He told her in a loud voice that he'd gone on the march with them, but he didn't understand why the Hammerheads could go on parade just because they had won, and they'd insisted that injured people join in too. He explained that he'd been dragged into it by Dazed-And-Confused and that he'd explain everything when he got back, but he wanted to know what she was doing here.

She must have heard what he said because she proceeded to say that she'd come out to hunt for a pumpkin. She'd been looking down the embankment to see whether there were any plants still putting out tendrils because they might well have a little pumpkin on the end.

Inkcap was cross with Gran. "At this time of year, is it likely there'd still be tendrils, and even supposing there were, would the little pumpkins on the end be edible?"

"I'll explain when we get back," Gran said.

After they got back home, Inkcap decided to test Gran's hearing. He deliberately knocked the rotten tile basin used to feed the pigs against the wall of the pigsty. Normally, when she heard the sound of the broken basin, she would scold and smack him, but now she was bending over the steps to change out of the muddy straw shoes on her feet and didn't even turn her head – Gran really had gone deaf. Inkcap was so upset he burst into tears, and he cursed furiously, for in the ordinary way of things Goodman could have come to see Gran, but because the Hammerheads and the Red Blades were fighting... but then he thought to himself who was actually at fault here? It wasn't all the fault of the Hammerheads, but then neither was it all the fault of the Red Blades. However, Inkcap carried on swearing because he felt it wouldn't be healthy to keep it all bottled up.

Gran closed the courtyard door and pulled Inkcap into the main room to tell him that Noodle Fish's wife came to her on the sly to say that Millstone had been stabbed by Pockmark, and he was even now hidden away in his cellar. The stab wound was really bad but he couldn't possibly go to Luozhen to see a doctor, so they were going to have to cure him with folk remedies. That called for pumpkin, but nobody had pumpkins at this time of year and even if they had, they would have hollowed them out and cut the flesh into strips for drying. Inkcap had heard about Millstone being stabbed by Pockmark, but he thought he'd run away with Awning and Sparks. He didn't realise he was still here, hiding in his cellar.

"The Hammerheads are searching for him everywhere," Inkcap said.

"Not a word to anyone," Gran warned him. "If you say anything, Millstone will be arrested and killed, and I'll beat you to death."

As Gran said this, she took her walking stick and struck it on the ground. Inkcap understood the seriousness of the matter, and he promised Gran to keep it secret. He also suggested that Goodman grew a lot of gourds and pumpkins up at the Mountain God Temple and he might still have some that had not been sliced.

"Go," Gran said. "If he's got any, carry one back, but don't let anyone see you. If Goodman asks what you want it for, do not say anything."

"I'm hungry," Inkcap said, "so I'll go after I've eaten."

"How hungry can you possibly be? You can eat after you've come back."

As Inkcap was about to leave, Gran took a handful of sweet potato slices from the cupboard and stuffed them into his pocket, urging him to return as quickly as possible. But when Inkcap got to the entrance of Three Fork Alley, he ran into the Tag-Along.

"Have you eaten?" he asked.

"Fucking hell," Tag-Along said, "I only just got back!"

"Are you going out for a shit with Bash?"

"Huang Shengsheng has had his eyes pecked out, his eyeballs are gone. How scary is that?"

"What? What happened?"

Inkcap insisted that Tag-Along tell him everything. Apparently, they carried Huang Shengsheng to Useless's house, and when his mother saw him being carried back in, she wasn't at all pleased. They were standing around quarrelling with Useless's mother, and while they weren't paying attention, a flock of birds came out of the clear blue sky and one of them dived down to peck out Huang Shengsheng's eyes. By the time they'd scared off the other birds, his two eyeballs had been pecked out.

Inkcap felt cold all over, and his teeth started to chatter. "Is Huang Shengsheng dead, then?" he asked.

"Nah. Bash ordered Baldy Jin to take him to the hospital on the tractor."

Inkcap sighed. "It's all very sad."

"Yeah, he'd be better off if the Red Blades had killed him, rather than all this pecking by birds… Hey, Inkcap, how come the birds didn't bother

Huang Shengsheng when you were there, but came the minute you'd gone?"

"What do you think?"

"I've heard you can understand what birds say."

Inkcap suddenly realised he *could* understand what birds say, and in the future he ought to pay attention to their conversations. However, all he said was, "Do you really think I can do that? Then let me tell you, the two birds standing in that tree are discussing what to do."

Tag-Along turned around and saw that there were two birds in the white apricot tree behind him, one clucking and the other calling back. "What are they saying?" he asked.

"They say you're talking nonsense and they want to poo in your mouth."

Tag-Along picked up a stone and set the birds to flight, but then came over again and said, "Tell me the truth, can you understand birds?"

"If you want to talk to birds," Inkcap said, "then talk lots. They can understand you, and you can understand them. Trees can also understand, and so can stones."

"Trees can understand what people say, and so can stones?" Tag-Along pointed to a stone next to him and continued, "How can that understand what people say?"

"Rub it with your hand."

Tag-Along rubbed it, and his hand stuck to the icy surface, and when he pulled it away, he gave a yelp of pain. "Fuck, it took my skin off!"

"This stone hates you."

Inkcap didn't say anything else to Tag-Along but headed out to the mountains. He was feeling very pleased about his little conversation. "I can really do it, so in the future I will listen to the birds, trees, rocks, pigs, cows, dogs and cats, and if anything happens, I will tell the birds, trees, rocks, pigs, cows, dogs and cats, and even the walls, the thatch on the roof, shovels, millstones, stoves, urns and barrels all about it."

When he got half-way up the mountain, the four red-billed, white-tailed birds on the white pine flew towards him and landed on the road about a yard ahead, and when he went forward, they flew forward again and stopped to look back at him.

"Are there any uncut pumpkins at Goodman's place?" Inkcap asked.

"Yes, yes!"

"How many?"

"Nine... nine... nine!"

"Nine? If there aren't nine, I'll hit you with a slingshot."

The birds rose with a clatter of wings and flew away.

"Cowards," Inkcap said. "It was only a joke."

He passed by the place where he'd pushed over the beehive and saw that the broken hive was still there. He kicked the snow away with his foot and found a layer of dead bees underneath. For some reason Inkcap felt bad, so he didn't bother teasing the birds any more, but ran all the way to the Mountain God Temple.

Goodman was lying on the bed, but how could he be asleep in the middle of the day? Inkcap was startled and went close to test Goodman's forehead with his hand, but it was not hot. "Are you sick?" he asked.

"I have a headache," Goodman said.

"Do you still have a headache? Have you eaten? I'll make you some food if you haven't."

"I have eaten," Goodman told him.

"I won't eat any of what I cook for you," Inkcap assured him. He lifted the lid of the pot on the stove, which did indeed contain the remains of some stew and dumplings, so he concluded that Goodman must have had something to eat already. He asked if he had any pumpkins. He wanted to borrow one on the promise that he'd return it next autumn, and if that was too far away, he'd exchange it for rice or maize: one pumpkin for two ounces of rice, or half a pound of maize.

Goodman laughed. "Why do you want pumpkins?"

"I don't know what it is," Inkcap replied, "but I've got a craving for pumpkins. I dream about them at night."

"I've got my pumpkins in the corner of the woodshed."

Inkcap went out to the woodshed and looked for them, and there was indeed a pile of pumpkins in the corner. Inkcap let out a shocked "Ah!"

Goodman heard him and asked, "What, are my pumpkins missing?"

"No, no," Inkcap assured him. "I'll take three and in another couple of days I'll come back for more and bring the rice and maize with me." He managed to put three pumpkins in his arms and left.

"Close the door after yourself," Goodman said.

Inkcap went back and closed the door made of branches and maize stalks, saying, "There are still six left and you can't possibly eat them all."

When he got home, Noodle Fish's wife had come over to talk to Gran again, so Inkcap cut up a pumpkin and suggested that having taken out the pulp and seeds for Millstone they might as well eat the rest.

"Goodness me, you're sharp!" Gran said. She grabbed the knife and would not let Inkcap cut up the other two pumpkins, nor would she let him take them to Millstone. Instead, she put them away in a basket and covered them with dried beanstalks, and it was only after she'd got rid of Noodle Fish's wife that she picked the knife up and went away.

On the third day, Inkcap took the rice and maize up to the Mountain God Temple and retrieved the remaining six small pumpkins. Goodman's head still hurt and he had a handkerchief tied around his forehead.

"You took so many pumpkins, surely it wasn't to eat them," Goodman said.

"If it wasn't to eat them, it certainly wasn't to turn them into compost," Inkcap retorted. He didn't say anything else.

But as to whether the pumpkin pulp could heal Millstone's knife wound, and to what extent he had recovered, Inkcap knew nothing, and he did not ask, but he kept an eye on Millstone's house for the next ten days or so. When Millstone's wife came out carrying a bucket to fetch water from the spring, he went over to help carry it. And when Millstone's wife carried stove ash out to her patch, he joined her and helped sprinkle the ash onto her land.

One night, Inkcap and Gran were already asleep when someone tapped on the back window. Gran was deaf and didn't hear, but Inkcap asked, "Who is it?"

"It's me," said the person.

Inkcap recognised the voice of Millstone's wife. She'd never approached them before, so Inkcap asked what the matter was.

"Oh, it's you, Inkcap," she said. "Is Gran asleep? If she's asleep, then forget it."

"What's the matter? I'll wake Gran."

Millstone's wife wanted Gran and Inkcap to help her push the millstone to grind some sweet potato stalks for noodles. Inkcap didn't mind hard work of any kind, but he hated turning a millstone. Nevertheless, he and Gran got up to help Millstone's wife. In winter, there was little farm work to be done, so the residents of Old Kiln tried to save as much as they could by eating sparingly. The sweet potato stalks cut in the autumn were laid out on top of the courtyard walls, and when they froze in winter, they got all dried up. Afterwards, they would be fried and then ground into flour. This flour could be eaten as fried noodles, or made into a thick porridge, or even mixed with wheat flour and cooked into buns.

That night the moon was so bright that you could have seen a pin on the ground. The three of them were holding the long rod attached to the millstone and pushing it, and the grinding rollers made a creaking sound, and it was all so noisy that Ever-Obedient, who lived next door, came out too. Ever-Obedient's original intention was to get them to stop working at this late hour and allow them to sleep. But when he emerged and saw Millstone's wife and Gran, he didn't lose his temper, saying mildly instead, "That's so loud we're bound to wake Yoyo. She doesn't sleep very well…"

"We ought to put some oil on it," Gran said. She went home to get some oil to smear about, whereupon the sound abated, and Ever-Obedient actually helped push it round.

"Is Yoyo any better?" Gran asked.

"When they first let her out, she seemed to get a bit better," Ever-Obedient said. "But it comes and goes, you know. If you talk to her, to begin with she seems fine, but then after a while you realise she's not right."

"How many people are still locked up?" Millstone's wife asked.

"Four, and I don't know when they're going to be released."

"Push, push to turn the millstone," Gran said. None of them said anything more.

The millstone kept turning, round and round, round and round again until Inkcap felt quite dizzy. Then he shut his eyes and actually managed to fall asleep for all that his two feet kept walking in a circle mechanically. He even started snoring gently.

"This is for family," Ever-Obedient reminded him, "not for the production team, and you're still asleep?"

Inkcap raised his hand and hit his own face, which woke him up so that he started using his strength. After the sweet potato stalks had been milled for the first time, they stopped so that Gran could sweep the flour into a basket and mash up any coarse-ground bits, while Ever-Obedient sat down to smoke a cigarette, and Inkcap stood there dozing again.

"Come and eat some flour and you won't be sleepy," Millstone's wife suggested.

Inkcap grabbed a handful of flour and stuffed it in his mouth, and it was bitter, so bitter in fact that he decided he quite liked it, and having eaten one handful he took another.

"Ha!" Ever-Obedient said. "He wasn't dozing off at all, he was trying to cadge something to eat."

"Look at how hungry poor little Inkcap is," Millstone's wife said. "Slow down, don't gulp it. If you like it, you can have the rest."

"But you mustn't eat too much," Gran warned him. "Too much and you'll give yourself diarrhoea."

Inkcap ate another handful and then stopped. He watched Ever-Obedient's dog come out from the courtyard door and bark twice. "I have to go back," Ever-Obedient said. "Yoyo must be looking for me."

"She hasn't come out, so how do you know? Millstone's wife asked curiously.

"Didn't you hear the dog calling me?"

"You can also hear what dogs say?" Inkcap said.

Ever-Obedient ignored him and went back into the yard, and indeed they heard his voice saying, "What are you doing up? It isn't even light yet, the rooster has not yet crowed, let's go to bed. Go to sleep."

As they started to turn the millstone again, Gran said, "When Yoyo came to our village, she was fine, but who could have imagined she would go insane... She's still so young, whatever will happen to her in the future?"

"Ever-Obedient always said he wanted to find a younger woman to take care of him, but I guess he never thought he'd end up having to take care of her," Millstone's wife said.

"She doesn't need Ever-Obedient to take care of her," Inkcap said. "If it wasn't for her, Ever-Obedient would never have been set free."

"I guess you know everything," said Millstone's wife.

"Do you think there's anything going on in Old Kiln that I don't know about? I even know just how many potatoes and sweet potatoes you have in your cellar."

Inkcap didn't mean anything by this remark, but Millstone's wife was alarmed and looked at Gran accusingly.

"What are you talking about?" Gran said. "Push the millstone, push the millstone, put your back into it."

Inkcap gave it one turn and then stopped pushing and said he needed to pee. He went behind the chinaberry tree, and Gran cursed him.

"Let him rest," Millstone's wife said. As she swept the flour out of the grinders with a brush, she muttered, "When will this ever come to an end?" She spoke in a low voice and Gran couldn't hear it.

"How can you eat this flour when it's milled?" Gran asked.

"I was going to make it into noodles," Millstone's wife said, "but I don't know if I can."

"You shouldn't eat this all the time," Gran told her. "You need to grind up some wheat flour too."

Inkcap was listening off to one side and thought this disjointed conversation was quite funny, but when Gran mentioned grinding some wheat flour as well, Millstone's wife glanced at Gran and said, "I quite understand." Millstone's wife knew exactly what Gran was talking about, and so did Inkcap, and he was hoping they would say some more about what was going on with Millstone, but they didn't say another word.

The rooster crowed twice, and they stopped turning the millstone. Inkcap and Gran went home to sleep. The moonlight was shining brightly, and just as they reached the corner of the row of houses by the embankment next to the spring, a cat came out from behind a pile of bean stalks, startling Inkcap. He recognised it as Barndoor's cat which liked to lie in a heap under a tree or on the eaves of the house during the day, but at night it looked much bigger and walked with unhurried steps.

"Gran," Inkcap asked in a loud voice, "have you ever seen a tiger?"

"I heard there were tigers on South Mountain when I was a child, but I never saw one."

"A tiger would be about the same size as the cat."

"I guess that cat would be a tiger's uncle," said Gran.

"So was my uncle short?"

Gran heard him, but she pretended she hadn't and said, "What did you say?" A quarrel ensued, and both granny and grandson stood still.

Inkcap's stomach rumbled, and then it hurt. "I need to shit, Gran." He made haste to untie his trousers, but his belt was a rope made from rag scraps, and the knot had turned into a tiresome lump, so he could not get it undone.

"Go back home," Gran said, "go back and do it there."

Then she heard a loud noise, and Inkcap said, "I've shat myself."

Gran was still helping him to untie his belt, but it just wouldn't come loose, and the diarrhoea flowed down his trouser legs. Gran simply pulled out the waist of the trousers from under the belt and the crotch of the pants was now filthy beyond all recognition. She rushed to find something on the ground to wipe him down with, and ended up grabbing a handful of twigs, which she used to clean him up a bit. However, Inkcap was still shitting everywhere, and Gran couldn't understand why.

Inkcap was in such pain that he burst into tears and said, "I can't stop myself!"

Gran carried on wiping and cursing him. "I don't know why your stomach is so finicky – all you did was eat a couple of handfuls of flour and you're shitting everywhere... It's disgusting."

Inkcap put out a hand and caught a handful of his diarrhoea and threw it away. "Gran," he said, "at least it doesn't stink."

Gran was so furious she made him walk home carrying his trousers, but just then shouting and screaming could be heard from somewhere in the distance.

The noise came from the courtyard of Baldy Jin's house. Baldy Jin and Half-Stick had a disagreement over dinner, and when they couldn't get along, they'd smash their crockery before going off to sleep in their own rooms. But when Baldy Jin couldn't sleep, he knocked on the door of the main room and Half-Stick wouldn't open it. Baldy Jin pushed the door in, and then they started quarrelling all over again. First, they fought in a low voice for fear of other people hearing them, but then Baldy Jin slapped her and Half-Stick slapped him back, after which they ignored everything as they fought each other around in the courtyard, cursing.

"Stop pretending," Baldy Jin told her. "I want to know the truth. When I was up at the kiln, did he come round or not?"

"What's it to you whether he came or not?" Half-Stick demanded.

"Fuck that! I'm your husband, of course I care!"

"So you're my husband, are you? When was the last time you put in some hours on our plot of land? When did you last pay for anything? When did you ever cut a handful of grass for the pigs?"

"I'm going to give you a good seeing to!" Baldy Jin said.

"As if you could get it up!"

There was a clang, something smashed, and then Half-Stick screamed. The doors of nearby courtyards opened one after another, and someone ran out and said, "This is a murder being done! Haven't enough people died here in Old Kiln already?"

They banged on the door of the house and shouted, "Baldy, Baldy, don't hit so hard, are you trying to kill her?"

"I want to beat her to death," Baldy Jin declared. "I'm going to beat this shameless bitch to a pulp."

"Go right ahead," Half-Stick shouted. "Useless motherfucker!"

The man who knocked on the door said, "If you could just shut up for a moment Half-Stick, that'd be great. Are you trying to get yourself beat?"

Half-Stick pulled the door open and came out. "Let him beat me," she said. "It's all the Hammerheads are good for, after all. I don't want to live a moment longer."

The neighbours who'd come out to stop the fight were mostly members of the Hammerheads, and they now got angry and said, "You two can fight as much as you like, but don't involve the Hammerheads."

"How can the Hammerheads not be involved?" Half-Stick said. "He was asking about Awning. If you have the guts, go and catch him and put him to death with a thousand cuts. But if you're too scared to take on Awning, you shouldn't come home and take out your frustrations by beating your wife!"

Baldy Jin now burst out of the courtyard door. "What do you mean by saying I was too scared to take on Awning? I was just going to chop off one of his legs, but he ran away. If he had any balls, wouldn't he have stayed to fight?"

Once Awning's name was mentioned, rather than trying to stop the fighting, the man started to add fuel to the flames. "Was it a leg that you were going to chop off, or perhaps some other part?"

Baldy Jin became further enraged and jumped on top of Half-Stick, slapping and punching her, while she clawed at his face. She scratched Baldy Jin because he didn't have any hair to pull, and blood poured down his face. However, he managed to grab her hair and started dragging her off.

"Don't dare, Baldy Jin," said the man following behind. "If you keep pulling on her hair like that, it will come out."

The more he complained, the more wildly Baldy Jin tugged, and he kept moving forward in the direction of the cesspit in front of his next-door neighbour's yard, saying, "Tell me, did you have an affair with him?" It was Baldy Jin's idea to pull her about by the hair in front of everyone to demonstrate that he wasn't afraid of his wife, and he asked if she'd an affair with Awning because he thought Half-Stick was sure to deny it, and he'd have a host of witnesses that he wasn't a cuckold.

But Half-Stick bent over, and tried to protect her hair with her hands, saying, "Yes, absolutely!"

Baldy Jin pulled a handful of her hair out, and Half-Stick straightened up and said, "I fucked him. Do you want to know the details? Do you want to know how thick and long his dick is?" Baldy Jin kicked her so that Half-Stick fell into the cesspit with a thud.

When Baldy Jin and Half-Stick were fighting outside the courtyard door, Inkcap was about to run over to watch, but Gran pulled him back and waited until Half-Stick fell into the cesspit. The crowd shouted as they ran forward to fish Half-Stick out, while Gran tugged at Inkcap, and they quietly walked away.

SEVENTY-SIX

THE WEATHER WAS GETTING COLDER AND COLDER. Dripping water turned to ice. The row of cesspits on the northern side of Old Kiln were all built into the slope of the embankment, while the privies were higher up. When people took a shit in the toilets it debouched through the cracks in the wooden boards and froze instantly on contact with the icy cesspit. As more and more dropped, these iced turds grew into ever-taller piles, like pillars. Manure collectors often came to steal these turds, and every now and then along the village roads, someone would be cursing them. However, although the first snow fell thickly, it gradually melted. Maybe the wind blew it away, or it gradually disappeared, but certainly it was impossible to see it melt away. Eventually, however, only the icicles hanging from the roofs of the houses were left.

It had been many days since Gran made any papercuts, and the pain from her ear condition had made her much thinner, and now she was stone deaf, and all the sounds of the world were stilled so she no longer needed to talk to anyone. Now that the wind blowing through the village tore at a diminishing number of big-character posters, and the leaves of the trees had all fallen, she did not use her scissors any more. Instead, she sat down, picked up a stick or a tile, and drew on the ground, on the stones, on the walls, and even with her fingers on the surface of her legs. This lunchtime, when the sun poked through the cloudy sky, she sat on the steps and drew many of the trees in the yard, but was not satisfied with them, so she stopped drawing. She hobbled out to the cattle shed on her stick, because Noodle Fish had sent word several times asking her to go over for a chat when she was feeling better, saying he was worried that she would be lonely at home with this illness. She was accustomed to the long years of loneliness, but Noodle Fish was a lively and gregarious person. Now that Old Kiln had become dead and nobody went out to work, no one came at night to have their work points recorded or went for a chat in the cattle shed, and Noodle Fish needed to talk to people.

The fact is Gran wanted to see the cattle – several of them had been badly injured on the day of the fighting when they stampeded, but she couldn't go. That first night she somehow dreamed of the spotted bull that had been killed and woke up inexplicably thinking that the bull was not dead and was taking its revenge on everyone in Old Kiln. "Will you go to the shed?" she asked Inkcap.

Inkcap and Cowbell were playing a game that involved throwing clods of mud about the yard, and the basin they'd made out of clay now fell to the ground and shattered, but Gran could not hear the sound, for all that she could see the basin was broken. Inkcap replied loudly that he would not go to the cattle shed, saying it was no fun to talk to Noodle Fish, and that he did nothing but tell him off.

Gran ended up going out alone, walking with her stick. Her body was both heavy and stiff, and her stick and feet resounded rhythmically as they hit the hard village road. The icicles on the eaves of the houses on either side kept falling down here and there, and she stood still several times thinking that the icicles thrusting down from the sky, hanging from the row of tiles on top of the wall, looked just like the iron bars she'd seen when passing the county prison. Those bars ended in spear-like points, so it was as if Heaven had turned a prison upside down to cover Old Kiln. Now the icicles were thawing and falling off, did that mean the lid was coming off?

In the cattle shed, Noodle Fish enthusiastically arranged a bale of hay for her to sit on and get a bit of sun, while all the cows were tethered out in the yard to bask as well. But what could she say to Noodle Fish? Noodle Fish kept talking to her, but she couldn't hear, and she just mumbled in reply. She tried to guess what was being said from the shape of Noodle Fish's mouth and answered accordingly, or she talked about something completely different and irrelevant to the topic of conversation. Noodle Fish didn't care about that, and kept on mouthing words at her, as if he didn't really expect her to respond and only wanted someone to be there as he poured his heart out. She watched Noodle Fish's mouth and face, and then her eyes moved to the cows in the yard. The bullocks and cows had warmed up in the sun and became drowsy, so some were standing motionless, letting their shadows shift around them, while others were lying down, occasionally swishing their tails and flicking a few horseflies away, and then getting up, their tails swinging again. After a while they would lie back down, not bothering to swish their tails, but after the horseflies had been at them for a long time, there was blood on their hides.

As Gran was sitting on the steps, drawing the cattle, one of them suddenly came towards her. It was tethered to a stake and pulled the rope taught, but the cow was still three or four feet away from her, at which point it lay down. She realised that this cow had been lying behind one of the others, and she'd missed it when she'd been drawing all the rest, and that it wanted to be part of her drawing too.

Gran continued to work on her picture as Noodle Fish talked. Noodle Fish finally stopped talking because he had become exhausted. He took out a pipe and began to smoke, as if he needed it to replenish his strength. Tilting his head to look at Gran's drawing, he said, "You're really good at getting a likeness."

"What did you say?" Gran asked. "My ears aren't working."

Noodle Fish raised his voice. "Inkcap's gran, I said you're really good at getting a likeness of these cows."

Gran laughed. Catching a likeness was integral to being able to draw, and this ability enabled her to draw anything that flashed before her eyes.

"You don't raise cattle," he bellowed, "but you know more about them than I do!"

"You just have to concentrate," Gran said. "If you can concentrate on something, you can draw it." Gran raised her head and saw a couple of chickens and a dog poking their heads through the door. The animals had squeezed their heads through the crack in the door to see her.

"Come in, all of you," Gran said, whereupon a flock of chickens and three dogs came in, and they posed so nicely, lying down for Gran to draw them. How happy she was. But just at this moment there was a loud bang, and the cattle all stood up at once, while the chickens flew up on the wall and the dogs ran out of the yard.

The bang was not heard by Gran, who was entirely focused on her drawing. She had the habit of staring at the place where she was going to do her drawing, as if there were something there to be seen in its original form, and then with a stick or a tile she drew a dog or a chicken. When she looked up, the cows were all standing, the chickens were on top of the courtyard wall, and the dogs were pushing their way out through the courtyard door, losing hair in the process. Gran looked at Noodle Fish in confusion. "Could that have been a gunshot?" he said aloud to himself.

How could there possibly be gunshots? The Hammerheads and Red Blades fought fiercely, but they'd never used guns. Many villagers heard the sound of gunfire and ran around shouting that the United Headquarters had attacked, and Awning and Sparks had returned. Inkcap came running like the wind, asking, "Where's Gran, is she in the cattle shed?"

"Have Awning and Sparks come back with guns?" Noodle Fish asked.

Inkcap said nothing more – he didn't know what to say. He went into the yard, picked up Gran and ran home.

Gran was bewildered, she just thought the villagers must be fighting again, but she was glad that Inkcap knew how to behave and wasn't getting caught up in the chaos.

"Put your arms around my neck," Inkcap instructed her, "and give me your feet. If I've got hold of your feet, no one can pull you from the back. Gran, Gran, why are you so light?"

Gunshots rang out five times in a row, and a horde clad in black ran from the beacon tower on the east side of the plain to Old Kiln. Those standing at the entrance of the village saw so many men running towards them, and just like last time when the Red Blades witnessed the Golden Cudgels and United Command people come running, they started to panic. Some of them went off shouting for Bash, while others grabbed their hammers and stood in formation. But this time the situation was very different from before; the mob running towards them did not include Awning or Sparks, nor was it Golden Cudgels from Xiahewan or the United Command from Luozhen. Bash spotted Division Chief Ma, and the two of them shook hands for a long time without letting go. Division Chief Ma was leading the county's United Command faction to occupy Old Kiln.

Bash told the Hammerheads that just three days after the fighting in Old Kiln, a violent struggle had taken place between the county's United Headquarters and United Command factions. Since this was a county-level battle, both sides were armed with guns, and they'd fought for a day and a night. In fact, within the county as a whole, the United Headquarters was stronger, so the United Command couldn't defeat them. Nevertheless, the United Command had mobilised all their forces, and their headquarters in the provincial capital had sent them reinforcements, as well as giving them a whole lot of guns, with the result being that in this fight they'd defeated the United Headquarters. To prevent the defeated United Headquarters members from escaping to the provincial capital and launching a counter-attack from there, the United Command had sent a division to set up road-blocks on the highway by Old Kiln. It so happened that Division Chief Ma was in charge of the "political training class" for the United Command faction, for part of her class was made up of capitalists and Black Categories in makeshift prisons set up by the faction. Some were prisoners captured during the fighting, while others were caught on the way out of the county town who were suspected of being members of the United Headquarters trying to escape to the provincial capital. Division Chief Ma was put in charge of the team that would be setting up the roadblocks, so they had all come together to occupy Old Kiln.

Bash introduced her to everyone, almost dancing for joy. "You're to go home this evening," he told Baldy Jin.

Baldy Jin refused. "Every time I see her, I just want to hit her."

"Well, hit her," Bash said, "and then get yourself a divorce. Tell her that Awning won't be coming back, and she'll never see him again."

In total, sixty-two people had come, eighteen from the political training class and forty-four were there to man the blockade. The group of forty-four stayed at the kiln, where the Hammerheads had cleaned everything, installed a wooden door and hung up rush-matting curtains. Each family in Old Kiln had to provide wooden planks or an old door, with which they set up more than thirty beds, and they also provided pots and pans for the stove. Everyone ate their meals at the kiln. They carried out to the highway the great elm pole that Sparks had placed under the eaves. He had felled this tree three years ago for use as a beam when building a new house. When they had carried it out, they propped it up on a millstone, causing the road to be blocked. When a car came, they would stop it to check, and having checked, they would push on the tree end, turning the millstone, and then let the car proceed. Afterwards, they would push the beam back across the road.

The shack there was to accommodate those on guard duty. The men from the kiln were rotated to guard duty, with seven on night shift and seven on day shift. The eighteen people from the political training class, plus the Branch Secretary and the key members of the Red Blades still being held – a total of twenty-one people – were kept at the Kiln God Temple, where they were watched over by a special team. Once all these arrangements had been made, Iron Bolt and Tag-Along were left to handle any final details, while Bash went round to Barndoor's house to borrow a set of bedding, and then he took Division Chief Ma to his old home.

It was Bash's idea that Division Chief Ma would live in the main room of his old house, while he himself moved out to the storage room. He asked Division Chief Ma's opinion on whether he should find a woman to keep her company while she was staying there.

"No need," Division Chief Ma said. "I never socialised with female colleagues when I was a teacher."

He then put a kerosene lamp in the hole in the wall by the bed and lit it, and placed a piss bucket in the corner of the room. Afterwards, he tried to lean half a cracked mirror against the windowsill.

"Don't bother," Division Chief Ma said, and she picked up the mirror and threw it out the window.

"Of course," Bash said, "someone like you wouldn't care about girly things, would you?" He pulled out the key to the door and gave it to Division Chief Ma.

"Are there thieves in Old Kiln?" Division Chief Ma asked.

"No, but you might feel more comfortable with the door locked."

"Isn't it easier just to leave it unlocked?"

"Sure," Bash said, "and I'll be guarding you anyway, from the storeroom."

"Perfect. You can be the first guard, and this is the second guard." She took the gun she was carrying off her back and leaned it against the bedhead.

Bash went off to find a peg that he hammered into the wall. It was both large and thick, sufficient to support the gun. He also hung up the scarf that Division Chief Ma had taken off.

"Do you know how to shoot?" she asked him.

"I've never shot an automatic," Bash replied.

"Hey, let's see you have a go."

Division Chief Ma loaded the gun with bullets and told Bash to stick it out of the window to shoot the birds in the tree by the courtyard wall. The tree was bare, but when dozens of birds landed on its branches, it looked like the leaves had grown again. Bash fired for the first time with a bang, and the birds rose up, turning the tree back to being just dry branches. Bash felt a little embarrassed, but then a bird dropped vertically, falling like a stone, and then a second bird plummeted out of the air.

"Wow, two birds with one shot!" Division Chief Ma said.

"Pure luck," Bash responded modestly.

The sound of gunfire frightened Tag-Along, who had just come through the courtyard gate, and he sat down all of a heap at the entrance. Division Chief Ma and Bash laughed uproariously and told him to take a shot himself. But he didn't dare even touch the gun and just cried out pleadingly, "Bash! Bash!"

"How dare you still address him like that?" Division Chief Ma said.

Tag-Along blushed furiously and immediately changed his tone: "There's something I need to ask, Boss."

"Go ahead," Bash said.

"We've got them settled in where they'll be staying, but what about food?"

"Arrange a potluck dinner," Bash ordered him.

"And make it good," Division Chief Ma said.

"Sure," Tag-Along replied. But he beckoned to Bash, and when he got him out in the courtyard, he whispered, "It doesn't matter how good these people are to us, or how much we want to treat them well, how are we going to feed them? If it was just one or two of them, and they were only going to eat a couple of meals, it's all good… but there are so many of them, do you know how long they're going to be staying for? If the food problem isn't solved, they surely can't stay long."

"The reason why I arranged a place for them to live and let you and Iron Bolt organise everything else is to test you," Bash told him. "Division Chief Ma has already resolved the food problem. This evening, they'll eat a potluck, but it must be proper rice and not thin gruel, and steamed buns not sweet potatoes. Tomorrow, they'll have white rice and flour shipped in, and you'll get some of it to pay you back for tonight's food and drink."

Division Chief Ma came out of the house and said, "You can tell the masses we won't take so much as a needle and thread from them."

"That's great," Tag-Along said. "I still have some wheat flour, so I'll make the comrades steamed buns."

Everyone was allotted a dish for dinner, and Bash's instructions were passed on by Tag-Along and Iron Bolt. Bash still felt a bit uneasy and wanted to go to each house to check everything was under control, but just when he was leaving, he asked how many guns they'd brought this time, and Division Chief Ma said five.

"Five!" Bash exclaimed.

"If you want one, then say so – do you want one?"

"Sure."

Division Chief Ma put a gun over Bash's shoulder and said, "You're wearing a red sweater? Why not a cotton jacket?"

Embarrassed, Bash said he didn't have a padded cotton jacket ready, but he was going to go to Luozhen in a few days to buy some cloth to make one. Division Chief Ma called a man from her political training department and ordered him to take off his yellow army coat and give it to Bash. Now Bash was armed, he was strutting proudly along the village road, when Baldy Jin met him and said, "Who is this? Oh, it's Bash... no, Boss!"

"What do you think of my outfit?"

"It'll scare the Red Blades to death!" Baldy Jin assured him. "Where did you get it?"

"From Division Chief Ma."

"I guess she fancies you."

"What are you on about?" Bash said crossly.

"What are you afraid of? She gave you this, so you'll fuck her."

"You're a fucking idiot."

Bash told Baldy Jin to go to the road to help set up the roadblock, and then he smiled and walked away. When he got to the rubber tree, a child came out of one of the alleyways riding a broom like a hobbyhorse. The boy stopped dead, turned around and ran back, leaving the broom behind. Bash recognised Inkcap and tiptoed over to the lee of the wall by the entrance to the alleyway. When Inkcap popped his head back out again, he grabbed him by the ear.

Inkcap looked up and said, "Bash, you're my brother, why are you doing this?"

"Why did you run away when you saw me?"

"I didn't recognise you."

Bash let go of his ear. "Now you recognise me, right?"

"Well, you're Bash, aren't you."

"Not any more. Who am I?"

"You've become Chairman Mao?"

Bash didn't say another word. He took his gun off and asked Inkcap to carry it, but Inkcap did not dare. He told Inkcap to touch it, but he didn't dare do that either. Bash's mouth worked a bit and then he said, "Piss off, then." He walked away and Inkcap stood there looking at his retreating back for a good long while.

Half of the people ordered to make food for the potluck made a soup of maize grits, which was so thick that when a chopstick was inserted, it did not fall over. The other half made a pickled cabbage and noodle dish, and also boiled potatoes, which were not diced but served in a bowl looking like small stones. But there were still a few families that did not believe that those eating the potluck would compensate them for it, so they offered an ordinary dinner, just boiling up some shredded radish in a pot of water with a pinch of salt but no oil, and then mixing that in a bowl of noodles made from rice bran, wheat chaff and sweet potato flour.

"Is that all?" the diners asked.

"Just go to bed and forget about it," their hosts responded.

"Old Kiln is poorer than my hometown," they remarked.

At his house, Tag-Along really did make his newly milled wheat flour into steamed buns and cooked a spicy egg-drop soup. His wife was reluctant: "We can't even give this kind of food to our children, so why should we let outsiders enjoy it?"

"They'll pay us back," Tag-Along assured her.

"Bash'll say anything. How exactly is he going to pay us back?"

"Division Chief Ma promised."

"Who? That one who can't decide if she's a boy or a girl?"

"She's pretty good-looking."

"In what way? You fancy her? Let me tell you, I don't want you getting into trouble."

"I don't know what you're talking about. And it's not going to be me that's fucking her."

When dinnertime came, four people turned up. One of them carried off the spicy egg-drop soup in one hand and four steamed buns in the other.

It was really painful for Tag-Along to watch. "Can you really eat all of this?" he asked.

The man squinted at him and said, "I'm just testing them."

Tag-Along went into the kitchen and hid the remaining buns, telling his wife that if they wanted any more, she was to say they'd run out.

SEVENTY-SEVEN

THE NEXT DAY, Division Chief Ma woke to find that her eyes were a little swollen. Her eyes were heavily hooded, and when they puffed up, her eyelids turned red. She collected three people and two guns, and went to Luozhen riding on a tractor to get money and food. Stonebreaker drove the tractor, having first added fuel and water, and then he put a few hay-stuffed cushions in the back. Later on, his back became unbearably itchy, and he leaned against a tree to scratch it. Barndoor, who came out carrying a basket of manure, bent down to look at the tractor and peered about for a long time.

"What are you looking at?" Stonebreaker asked. "A tractor doesn't shit or nothing."

"Are you really going to go and get money and food?" Barndoor asked.

"Not get, borrow."

"Borrow from who?"

"The credit union and grain store."

"Yeah, right!"

"Division Chief Ma says she's borrowed from them loads of times," Stonebreaker assured him.

"Impossible. Are they family or something?"

By now, Stonebreaker had also become a little suspicious. "I heard that the people there are members of United Command," he said. "Besides which, Division Chief Ma has a gun."

As the sun rose in the sky, the tractor left Old Kiln. Once it got onto the road skirting the lotus pond, the tractor went poof, poof, producing a plume of black smoke. Stonebreaker chose this way to show off to Inkcap and Cowbell. Cowbell did not look up, and he did not let Inkcap look up either.

"What a loon," Cowbell said. "He'll break his leg doing that."

"And if he breaks his leg, I won't get medicine for him," Inkcap said.

The lotus pond had been frozen for many days, so their feet no longer crumped as they walked across. The first night Inkcap had agreed with Cowbell that they'd go out on the ice early in the morning to cut dried lotus leaves and stalks for firewood. After carefully cutting a whole backpack's worth, they each took a lotus stalk and lit it up to smoke. The adults all smoked, so the kids wanted to smoke too, but the adults didn't give them cigarettes. Fine, they'd make their own. They 'smoked' lotus stalks, which produced a much more satisfactory smoke anyway. The two of them smoked until snot and tears were streaming down their faces

"Hey, you lot!" Millstone's wife shouted across the pond. "That ice can't support both of you. If you fall in, you'll freeze to death."

"Have this basket of firewood," Inkcap said. "You can use it to light the stove."

"No thanks, that stuff smokes too much."

"If you don't like the smoke, you can use it to heat the bed."

"Why are you being so nice to her?" Cowbell whispered.

"It's just a bundle of kindling," Inkcap pointed out.

"Then how about you give it to me?"

"Dream on."

"Millstone ran off after being stabbed," Cowbell mused, "and nobody knows if he's alive or dead, but I've never seen her cry." He hauled his backpack over to the edge and tried to give his kindling to Millstone's wife, but she refused it.

"Do you think there isn't enough?" Inkcap asked. "The cold may not bother you but…" He heard a cough and turned around to see Bash and Useless approaching.

"Inkcap, what are you doing?" Bash asked.

"Nothing."

"Don't go making trouble just because you're bored. You go with Useless and take this banner out to the highway."

"But what about my kindling?"

"Take that out to the highway too and let them burn it," Useless said.

Of course, Inkcap didn't want to, but Bash said, "You can't even spare a little bit of kindling?"

So Inkcap carried his lotus stalks and followed Useless to the highway. A lot of stones were piled up in front of the shack there, and the elm trunk was lying across the road, with more than ten men sitting at either end, staring at the three women coming from the pagoda. The women were walking side by side, chatting and laughing, but they suddenly went quiet and walked one behind the other, and the men shouted, "Se… sex!" The three women were so startled that they scuttled past the barricade with their heads down, and the highway was filled with laughter.

Useless was carrying a white cloth banner bearing a slogan, but Inkcap couldn't read, and he didn't ask what it said. When two wooden poles were planted on either side of the highway to hang up the banner, Useless asked Inkcap to climb the poles, but Inkcap couldn't manage it even though he tried several times.

A fat man was standing at the roadblock, and he went by the name of Glob. He was blind in one eye, and the other eye was unnaturally large. "You look like a monkey," he said, "so how come you can't climb up there?"

Inkcap wanted to say something rude back, but he didn't dare. When he saw that the man wore a cotton uniform, with two rows of buttons, he decided he looked just like a sow, and asked, "What did you say?"

"I said you look just like a monkey."

"At least I don't have two rows of teats down me like a sow," Inkcap retorted. But the man didn't understand him, which disappointed Inkcap a little.

"You get down and give everyone a show, clucking like a chicken or barking like a dog. Otherwise, you've got to crawl between my legs!" The man swung his leg over Inkcap's head.

This motherfucker is no different from Pockmark, Inkcap said to himself, and he decided to headbutt him in the nuts when crawling between his legs.

The man hopped about in pain and screamed, "Fuck you! I'm going to make you put on a show."

"Then take off your coat with its double row of buttons," Inkcap said, "and I'll impersonate a sow for you." Now, everyone understood, and it caused a lot of laughter.

That morning, a dozen or so cars and a bus were held up, but they did manage to stop one suspicious individual. This man had a southern accent and said his original plan was to flee the Guangxi countryside and go to Xinjiang. He was a mat weaver by trade, but when he got to the county, someone suggested that he go to the Dayu Mountains to the west, saying that lots of reeds grew there and many of the locals wove mats. So he went to the Dayu Mountains, and in the process of helping people weave mats, his master admired his work and wanted to have him as a son-in-law. He was on his way back to Guangxi to arrange for his household registration to be transferred and had just arrived in the county town when fighting broke out there. As a result, the buses weren't running, so he'd ended up having to beg for food. Today, the bus was running again, and he'd managed by hook or by crook to buy a ticket. However, the people at the barricade didn't believe him and suspected he'd been sent to the county by the provincial United Headquarters faction because there were some southerners at that level. Accordingly, they hauled him off to the Kiln God Temple.

The man seemed very honest. Even though it was only Useless and Inkcap who escorted him back to the temple, and Useless was as thin as a rake and Inkcap only a kid, he didn't run away even though he could have. When they got to the slope leading to the entrance to the village, Useless went off to pee under a tree, and even Inkcap felt that this was the perfect moment to escape. He deliberately kept well away from the man, bending down to tie up his straw sandals, but the man did not run. He just kept saying, "I'm not a member of the United Headquarters. Why are you holding me up?"

This was so annoying that Inkcap said, "You deserve it."

When they got to the Kiln God Temple, the courtyard was full of people. A session had just been held, so their faces were pale and stressed as they squatted down on the steps to get a bit of sun. Inkcap spotted the Branch Secretary sitting in a corner, with a nasty wound on his head. He must have put something on it because it was all scabbed over, but the scab was black with patches of yellow. Another man picked up a scrap of paper, flattened it out on his knees, and then went to the corner of the courtyard to turn over a pile of firewood, making the whole heap clatter.

"Why can't you sit quietly?" the person next to him said. "What's bothering you?"

"I'm looking for cotton stalks," he replied. Sure enough, he managed to find three cotton stalks that still had some dry leaves attached. He picked them and kneaded them to insert into the end of his roll of paper. His neighbour realised he was rolling a cigarette and didn't complain any more. He kept an eye out to see when the cigarette was ready and smoking well, then he asked, "Can I have a puff?"

He handed it over and the man took a deep draw, and then someone else wanted it too. The cigarette never returned to the person who'd rolled it. Everyone was only able to take one puff, and there was hardly any smoke to it – indeed, it seemed to have gone out. But if someone took a really long draw, then two strands of smoke like cotton wool streamed out of their nostrils, followed by a fit of coughing.

The Branch Secretary did not ask for a puff, and neither did he move; it was almost as if he'd dozed off. When he closed his eyes, his eyelids were red and puffy, like a pair of plums. As Useless and Inkcap led the southerner through the courtyard and all the way to the back of the main hall, no one paid any attention to the stranger, but neither did they pull in their legs that were in the way. The southerner occasionally stepped on an outstretched foot, whereupon he was quickly kicked back. Inkcap ran past the Branch Secretary, deliberately making his footsteps thud. The Branch Secretary still did not open his eyes, but his closed eyelids moved, and Inkcap realised that this was the only way he could say hello.

Baldy Jin interrogated the southerner in the main hall. Where are you from? Huangbocha in the Dayu Mountains. Nonsense, Huangbocha folk don't talk like you. I married in, you can go and check, my father-in-law is Huang Zhong and my wife's name is Huang Xiu. Who has time to go to Huangbocha? Let me ask you, why didn't you just stay there safe and sound? Why did you get on the bus? I'm going to my hometown to change my household registration. Your household registration? I don't believe it.

Show me your hands. How can you be a farmer without calluses on your hands? I weave mats all day long, just look at my fingers. Who doesn't have blisters on their hands? Show me your teeth! What do you mean by checking my teeth? Show them! When the southerner opened his mouth and showed his teeth, Baldy Jin called out to someone to take him out to the gatehouse and beat him up. A few men came in and dragged the southerner out to the gatehouse, where they tied him to a beam and beat him with sticks.

When Baldy Jin was interrogating the southerner, Inkcap didn't know whether to leave or not. There was a steamed sweet potato lying on the stool next to him; probably Baldy Jin had been eating it as they came in. Inkcap pretended to go over to the stool to sit on it, and as he went past, he grabbed the sweet potato, before breaking off a lump and stuffing it into his mouth.

"Talk!" Baldy Jin said. With the sweet potato in his mouth, Inkcap couldn't speak and made haste to swallow it. When he looked around at Baldy Jin, he discovered that he was shouting at the southerner. But soon afterwards the southerner was dragged out and beaten, and Inkcap took advantage of this moment to get away himself. Once again, he walked past the Branch Secretary, and he threw the uneaten half of the sweet potato down by his leg. Immediately, the Branch Secretary moved his leg to hide it, but his eyes never opened.

Inkcap thought that having escaped the Kiln God Temple he could go home, but he did not expect that Stonebreaker had already returned with a load of flour on his tractor. He had travelled rapidly, and the bags of flour filled the back – more flour than the residents of Old Kiln had ever seen before. The villagers followed all the way to the mountain gate, where Stonebreaker stopped the tractor and shouted at everyone to go away. This wasn't for them, and they couldn't eat it with their eyes. Half a dozen or so people carried the bags of flour up to the kiln on their shoulders, and in the end, there was just one bag left, which Stonebreaker intended to carry up to the kiln himself because Bash had already arranged that he should go there to help cook. However, he couldn't be bothered and wanted Inkcap to take it instead.

"But I'm not going to get to eat it," Inkcap pointed out.

"If you carry it, you can eat one meal from it," Stonebreaker said.

"You better keep your promise." Inkcap carried the sack of flour up to the kiln with great effort.

They were going to have hand-rolled noodles. Although this wasn't as fancy as pulled noodles, they were going to have potato slices cooked in as well, which was much better than their normal fare. The people at the kiln ate, and Stonebreaker ate too, but nobody gave Inkcap so much as a sniff.

"You aren't in a hurry, are you?" Stonebreaker said. "In a while, we'll take food to the Kiln God Temple, and you'll get a bowl then."

Inkcap did not say anything, but he started scratching himself right in front of Stonebreaker. He wasn't feeling itchy, he just wanted Stonebreaker to see him so he'd begin itching himself. Sure enough, Stonebreaker started feeling itchy all over, and put down his bowl, picking up a bunch of maize husks left over from firing the stove which he thrust into his crotch and started rubbing.

Finally, the leftovers were re-boiled, and Stonebreaker had Inkcap help carry them to the Kiln God Temple, where everyone in the political training got half a bowl. The southerner had already been untied from the beam, and he was lying on a pile of straw in a corner of the west building. While the others were eating, he got up from the straw, watching Stonebreaker scraping the bottom of the barrel with a wooden spoon. Having scraped out half a bowl, he broke two chopsticks from the broom leaning against the wall.

"Here's half a bowl," he told Inkcap. "Eat it. I'm a man of my word."

Inkcap snatched the bowl and gulped down a mouthful. He then said, "What about him?"

"He can lick the bucket," Stonebreaker said.

The southerner had to get what he could from the bucket. He scraped away with chopsticks but got nothing, and then used his fingers. That way he got a little, and he sucked on his fingers, and then he put his head into the bucket to lick it with his tongue. Inkcap felt sorry for the southerner, thinking that he had been hungry for who knows how long, and that if he could not eat now, he wouldn't get another chance until tomorrow. When the southerner got his head out of the bucket, he proceeded to pour water in to wash out the final scraps of food.

Suddenly, Inkcap got angry and threw the bowl and rice into the bucket. "That's disgusting," he said. "No matter how poor we are in Old Kiln, no one's ever drunk water from a bucket like that!" Then he walked out of the courtyard.

Stonebreaker helped cook at the kiln, and within two days, he was placed in charge of the food. He also called in his wife to work the stove. The food at the kiln was much better than normal village fare, and the two of them were able to snatch the odd scraps. But soon, everyone at the kiln was suffering from scabies. At first, they didn't know what was going on, they were just infernally itchy and scratched themselves all the time. Then they went to talk to Bash, who asked them if they'd been infected, and when they took off their clothes for a good look, it was evident that it was indeed scabies. It turned out that Stonebreaker, who was living at the kiln, had infected them, and they scolded him for his thoughtlessness, for not saying anything when he had scabies, and for using their blankets at night to keep warm.

"We got scabies because of the Revolution!" said Stonebreaker.

"We beat people up because of the Revolution!" they replied.

They pinned Stonebreaker down and beat him so badly that he couldn't get up. His wife was so appalled that she went back to the village and called on Noodle Fish, who carried Stonebreaker home.

Bash sent Pillar and Winterborn back up to the kiln, and they had no choice but to comply. They were forced to take off their clothes to demonstrate that they weren't infected and explained that rubbing the body with kiln ash cured scabies. The people there made a lot of fuss about wanting to fire the kiln so they could get ash. Bash felt compelled to fire the kiln, but they just made a few bowls, so the kiln was only lit for two days and two nights. Afterwards, they opened the kiln to take the ash. After rubbing themselves down three times a day for three days, the scabies mites were gone.

The Hammerheads' families came to the kiln to rub themselves with ash, and later, along came former members of the Red Blades with their families. To begin with, Baldy Jin didn't agree and came to ask Bash his opinion.

"If we don't give them the cure," Bash said, "they may just reinfect us. However, we shouldn't let them come to the kiln. We'll give them some ash for them to take home and use."

At that time, when villagers met each other in the alleyways, they all asked, "Have you rubbed yourself today?"

Noodle Fish went to the kiln a few times during this period. He was rubbing himself with ash, and he also brought a box of ash back so that Stonebreaker could take a couple of handfuls. But Stonebreaker's scabies had reached his face, and after rubbing for a few days without effect, some red bumps appeared on his chin, two more red bumps appeared on his forehead, and he began to run a high fever.

Noodle Fish's wife came to ask Gran to go and see what was wrong with Stonebreaker.

Inkcap pulled Gran aside and said, "Don't you go, he'll infect you."

"How could he possibly infect me?" Gran said. "I have to go and see."

"Then look at him from a distance."

When Gran arrived at Stonebreaker's house, his wife wailed, "Granny Silkworm, is he going to die now the scabies has got to his face?"

"What a dreadful thing to say," Gran replied. "What if he heard you say that?"

Stonebreaker had in fact heard it, and when he saw Gran, he tried to get up, but couldn't. "Help me, Granny Silkworm," he begged.

Gran's hand reached into the blankets, and she could feel he was burning up. "You'll be fine, Stonebreaker," she told him. "Scabies on the face just means they've reached your nose."

She instructed Stonebreaker's wife to wipe his face, the back of his neck and armpits with wine, and then continue to rub his body with kiln ash, rubbing absolutely everywhere. Noodle Fish went up to the kiln again and returned with two baskets of kiln ash and spread it on the bed so that Stonebreaker could lie naked, covered in ash with only his head protruding.

When Noodle Fish returned with the two baskets of ash, he bumped into Division Chief Ma by the door to Bash's old house. She was dressed much as usual and remarked, "So much ash!"

Noodle Fish explained that Stonebreaker was sick, and she said, "You don't have much sign of revolutionary experience in Old Kiln, but you've sure got your contagious diseases!"

845

She allowed Noodle Fish into the courtyard to get an earthenware basin as long as he left some ash for her to use.

"Do you have scabies too?" Noodle Fish asked.

"There are maggots in the privy," Division Chief Ma said, "so I want to sprinkle some ash about to get rid of them."

"You'll need stone dust for that. Kiln ash won't work."

"I'd like to give it a try, though."

After leaving her an earthenware basin full of ash, Noodle Fish left, and she immediately closed the door.

SEVENTY-EIGHT

PEOPLE RARELY WENT TO VISIT THE KILN, but now they were excited to see it. The guards at the roadblock were almost all cadres, workers or students from the county town, and they looked different from the residents of Old Kiln. None of them were bald, and they all wore yellow military coats. Even when they removed their coats, they had on a small cotton jacket over a Zhongshan suit, with the four pockets stuffed to bulging point. And then there were their trousers, which all had a fly in front.

Bash had long been imitating the appearance of folk from the county town, but now that so many of them were right there in the village, he no longer felt special. Before Stonebreaker quarrelled with them, the fat man gave Stonebreaker a pair of trousers. Stonebreaker felt that they'd tear if he always wore them the same way, but when he wore them with the fly at the back, he couldn't squat.

Inkcap wanted Gran to make him a pair of trousers like that, but Gran didn't know how. The residents of Old Kiln were even more confused by Division Chief Ma. They'd never so much as heard before of a young woman who could shoot guns and give speeches that men would obediently listen to, but now they could see it with their own eyes.

Even Gourd came to feel that his wife wasn't good enough for him. When the walls of Gourd's mother's bedroom got stained, Gourd's wife wanted to get them painted and asked him to go to South Mountain to dig some kaolin, but Gourd went for half a day and returned with less than a basketful. Gourd's wife complained about him being lazy and useless. He was so angry he went outside for a smoke, and it just so happened that Division Chief Ma passed by with a gun on her back.

"Look at her," Gourd said to his wife. "Do you know how to shoot a gun or give a speech in front of people?"

"And you fancy someone like that?" his wife retorted. "You need to take a long, hard look at yourself."

The two of them had never fought before, but this time they quarrelled.

In Old Kiln, there was a lot of discussion about what was going on up at the kiln, but in fact most talk concerned food and drink, how they liked to eat white buns and pulled noodles, and if they had maize porridge, it still contained beans. Members of the Zhu clan talked about this stuff because they liked gossiping about it, but the Heis were quietly furious – particularly those belonging to the Hammerheads. They weren't eating fancy food like that, and they complained about the Revolution and counter-revolutionaries... how come these strangers are living off the fat of the land and we're just eating thin gruel? When Bash asked them to send firewood to the kiln, along with potatoes, sweet potatoes, radishes and pickles, after one or two deliveries they were reluctant to do so. As for work at the kiln – such as building a big cooking range, setting up the big pot, making straw mats for the beds or going to the ravine to fetch water – those duties were shirked when possible, but when they could not be avoided, they took forever. Or they got Inkcap to step in.

Inkcap was constantly up at the kiln, although he did not know quite how this came about. He was going out with Cowbell to dig for garlic, and having dug a few heads, they'd be up on the ridge of Central Mountain, and they'd sit there watching others eating. Today, Inkcap happened to ask, "If you had steamed buns, how many could you eat?"

"Five," Cowbell said.

"Me too."

"You couldn't possibly eat five."

"I absolutely could," Inkcap said proudly.

The fat man, the one who'd bullied Inkcap by the highway, came over and said, "They're our buns! And anyway, they're not for the likes of you."

"We were just talking," Inkcap said.

"Then stop."

Since he wasn't allowed to talk, Inkcap whispered, "Fucker. Why don't you go blind in your second eye!"

"Do you know why he is blind in one eye?" Cowbell asked.

"Why?"

"I heard Baldy Jin tell Useless that when there was fighting in the county town, at night both factions had men lying in watch on the rooftops. The fat guy lit a cigarette, and the other side shot a little bit to the left of the glowing tip. Generally, people are right-handed, so shooting a bit to the left would hit the heart. But that motherfucker's left-handed, so they missed him. However, the bullet hit a brick by his side and a flying fragment took out his eye."

"It's a shame they didn't just shoot him," Inkcap said. "He won't give us anything to eat... he won't even let us speak. Let's do something really disgusting to him–"

"What sort of thing?"

"How big a shit can you take in one go?" Inkcap said in a deliberately raised voice.

"As big as a bowl," Cowbell asserted proudly.

"What are you, an ox?"

"Oxshit has nothing but grass in it, but my shit has worms."

The fat man started retching and threw a few clods of earth at them to make them go away, but then Flower Girl shouted at them to stop.

Flower Girl and Stonebreaker's wife were originally cooking at the kiln.

Stonebreaker's wife then went back home to look after Stonebreaker, and Bash sent Cattle Track's wife instead.

When Flower Girl shouted, Inkcap muttered, "I haven't seen her about for ages, but here she is up at the kiln."

"I thought Barndoor didn't belong to any faction," Cowbell said. "Why did he let Flower Girl come and cook?"

"It may be nothing to do with the Hammerheads – do you think she's fatter now or not?"

"I think she's thinner, but since she's eating so well, I don't understand how she managed it."

"Do you pair just keep your ears for decoration?" Flower Girl yelled.

"Who're you shouting at?" Inkcap asked.

"I'm shouting at you!"

"What's up?"

"We've run out of water," Flower Girl said. "You go and get us some water – three loads – and I'll pay in maize buns."

"I don't like buns."

"If they're paying in buns, we should do it," Cowbell told Inkcap.

"No way."

"Well, I want a bun."

"Fine, go and eat," Inkcap told him.

Shaking Inkcap off he sped away, but as he did so, he heard someone say, "Cowbell, you're a fucking loser! You'd do anything for food... but we're not going to let you carry our water..."

"We'll just give him the one bun," Flower Girl said, "that's nothing. You may be too lazy to carry it, but we need some water." In the end, Cowbell really did stay behind to carry water.

As he walked down the hill, Inkcap kept thinking, What's so great about buns? Won't you still be hungry after eating just one? Not just one bun, but even eight or ten, they'll all be shat out in the end. I wouldn't sell myself for just one bun, hell, I wouldn't eat such a thing...

When he entered the house, Gran was sitting on the steps combing her hair.

"Gran, what's for dinner?" he asked.

"What can there be? You go and peel some potatoes, and we'll make noodles and boil them."

"I want buns, steamed buns." Inkcap's voice was loud enough for Gran to hear, but she looked at him suspiciously, her mouth wide open.

Apricot came out from the privy behind the wall and asked, "Do you think it's your birthday, Inkcap, that you want steamed buns?" It was only then that Inkcap realised her presence, and he sniggered a little.

Apricot's waist was now so thick that it looked like she had a pillow stuffed under her clothes. Inkcap didn't dare approach her because he felt as if she were carrying a basket of eggs to market, so he wouldn't want to get too close in case he crushed the eggs. He immediately took a blanket off the bed and put it on a chair, so that Apricot could sit down. But Apricot took Inkcap off to the kitchen and asked if he'd been to the kiln.

"It's OK to talk about it in the yard," Inkcap said. "Gran's too deaf to hear. What's up?"

"Is it true that Ma Zhuo's got scabies?" Apricot asked.

"Who's Ma Zhuo?"

"That weird creature who can't decide if she's a boy or a girl... you know, Division Chief Ma. You've got to tell me the truth."

"Who said so?"

"People told me... Do you know if she's got scabies?"

"I've no idea," Inkcap said. "When I went to Bash's old house, she was cooking on the stove. I thought she might be cooking sweet potatoes, but she was boiling her clothes."

"Then she's definitely got scabies," Apricot said.

"So what? All of the newcomers have scabies now."

"But how exactly did she get them?" Suddenly, Apricot's face started working, and she grabbed a wooden spoon off the counter and began drumming, shouting, "She lives all by herself, so how exactly did she get infected? Did she come here to bring revolutionary ardour or to sleep around?"

She sat down by the stove and burst into tears. With Apricot crying like that, Inkcap didn't know what to do, so he came out of the kitchen. He wanted to ask Gran what the matter was, but she just sighed and said, "What a wicked, cruel man."

Inkcap asked who she meant but Gran told him to go and get some water. "Since Apricot is staying, we'll steam buns for dinner."

Inkcap was scooping water from the spring, and as he did so, he suddenly realised what Apricot meant: Bash must have infected Division Chief Ma with scabies! He hated that Bash could do this, and he hated Division Chief Ma even more. What was so great about Division Chief Ma: her face was so dark, her neck so short, and just look at her feet, so wide and fat, were they feet or bear's paws? Apricot was so pretty – Division Chief Ma was nothing compared with her. Inkcap smacked his ladle down on the surface of the water. Normally, the water was so soft you could just reach down and scoop it up, but when he smacked the ladle down this time, it was as hard as a stone.

A voice suddenly came out of nowhere: "Are you trying to bust your ladle?"

"I was hitting Ma Zhuo," Inkcap replied.

"Hitting Ma Zhuo, eh?" Half-Stick said.

Inkcap was startled, only to realise that he had spoken out of turn. When he looked up, Half-Stick was sitting on the elevated bank above the spring. He had already noticed several times, when Half-Stick was sitting on the threshing floor at the mouth of Three Fork Alley or on the steps under the eaves of someone's house, that her legs would shake uncontrollably all the time, even though otherwise she seemed quite as normal. Now she was sitting on the embankment, her legs shaking like nobody's business, and any moment now her sandals were going to fall off.

"I'm just here to get water," Inkcap said.

849

"And is Ma Zhuo in the water?" Half-Stick said teasingly.

"No, you are!"

The ripples on the pool gradually disappeared until it was like a mirror. Half-Stick laughed and said, "Everything's changed since Ma Zhuo arrived, including you, Inkcap."

Inkcap tilted his head and asked, "Do you think Ma Zhuo's great too?"

"Sure."

"In what way?"

"She can shoot."

"What else?"

"She can give orders to men."

"What else?"

"What the hell," Half-Stick asked irritably. "Why do you care about her?"

"Is she pretty? Can she plant rice? Can she roll noodles and knit shoes and make sweaters? How is she better than Apricot?"

"Oh, are you upset on Apricot's behalf? Let me tell you, even if Apricot is better, she's nothing but a peasant while Ma Zhou is a party member. And another thing, Apricot comes from Old Kiln, but Ma Zhuo is from the city."

Inkcap looked at Half-Stick and couldn't say anything for a good while. He wanted to say that Apricot was pregnant with Bash's baby, so how could he get together with Ma Zhuo? But Inkcap did not say this. Instead, he asked, "How come you're sitting around all day, aren't you afraid of getting into trouble?"

"Mind your own business. There's nothing for any of us to do except sit around – there's no work and the Revolution doesn't need me, so what can I do other than hang about? Let me tell you, a good man draws lots of girls and a good woman draws lots of men."

"Are you talking about yourself? All those men after you..." Inkcap didn't finish his sentence but walked off carrying his water.

Half-Stick stood up on the embankment and shouted, "Fuck you! What the fuck do you think you know about it? Let me tell you, those men didn't do nothing to me... I used them, I tell you."

That was how Half-Stick had changed; she didn't have the slightest sense of shame any more. Inkcap cast a glance upwards. Half-Stick's eyes were bloodshot, and her mouth very large, with the lips all red and swollen. She looked like a wolf that had eaten a child.

Inkcap hurried back home with the water, but Apricot had already gone. Gran said she had not been able to keep her.

"What did she cry for?" Inkcap asked. "She should have gone to find Bash."

"You know, she did go and look for Bash, and the two of them had a fight," Gran said.

"I'll go and talk to him myself."

"You're going to talk to him?" Gran laughed. "Do you think he's still the same old Bash?"

Afterwards, Inkcap was reluctant to go running around Old Kiln. He felt sad, and everyone else seemed to be unhappy too. Whenever he saw Bash and Division Chief Ma, he'd hide. If that was impossible, he'd walk past, not speaking, not even looking at them. Gran was worried that Inkcap was going to be sick again like before, so she had him go out to dig some garlic and wild jujube roots on the mountain slope, and also asked him to sweep leaves from the riverbank.

But Inkcap couldn't stand the idea of his gran worrying so much about him. "I'm fine," he said. If he went out, he would not let her accompany him.

One day after lunch, Inkcap left the house with a fuse. He was going to go up the mountain to see Goodman, but when he saw Bash standing in front of the Kiln God Temple, he changed his mind. He wouldn't climb up the mountain, he'd head home to get his fishing gear and go fishing in the river. The people of Old Kiln didn't eat fish, but those from the county town did. He'd already been fishing a few times, and he took the cat, which he deliberately fed with the fish he'd caught right where those manning the barricades could see. But when he took the cat to the river, Bash was already over by the blockade.

Three cars were being held there, and all the passengers had to get out to be inspected. It was Iron Bolt who was doing the inspection and he came over to report to Glob. "There's no one suspicious here," he said, "just a man with a barrel of wine."

"What do you mean, that's not suspicious?" Glob shrieked.

Iron Bolt took the man away and insisted that he was a member of the United Headquarters. Finally, he let him go, but the wine was confiscated. Once he'd got the wine, Bash sent Iron Bolt back to the village to find a jug and cups at Lightkeeper's house because he had a bronze drinking set. Iron Bolt turned the place over and finally brought the jug and cups back.

The members of the County United Command faction said that Bash was very sophisticated, and Bash went on to explain that he'd wanted the drinking set because the people of Old Kiln always said that this kind of wine should not be drunk cold. In winter, you have to drink it hot, and the jug is put on the stove to warm. Then he said that if you have a wine jug, you also have to have cups, because they form a matching set, just like a man has to have a wife, and a wine jug should be matched with four or six wine cups, not a wine cup with two or three wine jars, right?

"That's right. It's just plain good sense," the drinkers agreed.

Inkcap listened and thought to himself, Good sense, my arse. He went fishing in the pool behind the pagoda and caught a fish and fed it to the cat. The cat was used to eating fish and would usually swallow them whole, but today it just pawed at the fish, first eating the mouth and then the eyes, and then it just lay there washing its face and watching the fish still wagging its tail.

"Goodness me you're fussy," Inkcap said.

Glob shouted to Inkcap to bring the fish over so they could roast them, but Inkcap didn't move. Bash then waded over and said, "Give me the fish."

Inkcap seemed not to hear, but said to the cat, "Do you want to eat that?"

The cat just meowed.

"You're going to eat it, right?" Inkcap said. "Which do you want, the whitefish or the thornback fish?"

The cat picked up a whitefish.

"Are you so blind you can't tell which one is pretty and which one is ugly?"

"Take the fish over there and roast them," Bash roared.

"I'm feeding the cat," replied Inkcap.

Bash kicked the cat and said, "What are you staring at me like that for?"

"I'm not staring at you. I have big eyes."

Bash was wearing his army coat, but he was burning up with all the alcohol he'd drunk so he took it off to reveal the red sweater Apricot had knitted. He squatted down and picked up the four or five fish, and Inkcap suddenly had the feeling that he wanted to tear that red sweater off him, so he tugged on the sleeve with his hand, and the sleeve became longer.

"Take your dirty hands off of me!" Bash yelled. As soon as his hand was released, the sleeve shortened again.

"You don't mind the dirt," Inkcap said. Seeing that Bash's arse was touching the pagoda and that a thread was hanging loose off the back of his red sweater, he tied the thread to a small green branch growing out of a crack in the brickwork.

At last, the scene Inkcap envisaged came to fruition. When Bash carried three thornback fish back towards the barricade, he was unaware that a red line was trailing behind him, and the line was growing longer and longer. After he had thrown the fish to the County United Command people and turned around, they discovered that the sweater was now almost backless, while Inkcap and the cat were heading home to the village along the weir.

"Meow," the cat said.

"Meeooww," Inkcap replied. He picked up the cat, and both the boy and the cat said happily, "Meow, meow."

Inkcap was enjoying his revenge, and when he returned to the village, he thought if only it were autumn, he could go to Bash's plot, cut a hole in a pumpkin and shit in it, then cover up the cut so that the pumpkin would continue to grow. Then when Bash picked the pumpkin and cut it open, it would be full of shit and maggots inside. He also thought it a shame there weren't any snakes about, because if there was a snake, he would catch one, or even a couple, and put them through the back window of Bash's old house. That way, when Division Chief Ma was asleep in the middle of the night, she'd feel something cold against her legs, and when she threw the quilts aside, well, there'd be two snakes coiled up inside the bed.

He also wondered whether Division Chief Ma was afraid of ghosts. There might be some way to lure her out to the reedbeds along the riverbank at midnight because if she met a ghost there, and tried to get away through the sandbanks, she'd get sand in her mouth and nose and ears... Deep in contemplation, Inkcap failed to notice that he'd shifted direction towards Bash's old house. He noticed that the door was closed but there was someone inside. Was it Division Chief Ma rubbing herself down with kiln ash? The more you rubbed, the further the scabies mites travelled. If they were on your legs then they were also on your arms, and next, they were on your face too. Inkcap went to the cattle pens and climbed the tree near the old house, from where he could see over the wall to the yard of Bash's house. No one was in the courtyard, but if Ma Zhuo came out of the main room, she'd be sure to ask him what to do about all the red blisters on her face. He decided he would tease her by saying, "Those aren't blisters, you've got the pox." But it didn't matter how long Inkcap stayed up there, Ma Zhuo never emerged, and then the chimney started belching smoke because she was cooking. Inkcap balanced a tile on top of the chimney and jumped down. He could hear Ma Zhuo coughing her lungs out in the courtyard of Bash's house.

"Uncle Noodle Fish," Inkcap shouted. "Uncle!" He shouted in a low voice, but it was full of triumph and joy. Noodle Fish wasn't there, but all the cows were laughing. When cows laugh, they pull their mouths back into a grin, so their teeth look huge, and their nostrils snort.

SEVENTY-NINE

NOODLE FISH WAS NOT IN THE CATTLE SHED but at Stonebreaker's house. Stonebreaker had just died, and the entire house was filled with crying.

Early that morning, Stonebreaker suddenly felt much better. He could sit up, and he ate a whole bowl of thin rice gruel with maize grits. His wife asked what else he wanted to eat. Stonebreaker said he'd like mashed potatoes in hot sauce. His wife relayed the information to her mother-in-law, and Noodle Fish's wife said, "Is he still wanting to see Padlock?"

"Last night, he was feverish," she replied, "but he was still talking about Padlock, but how can we let him know?"

"You get the potatoes," Noodle Fish's wife said, "and I'll talk to Padlock."

Noodle Fish's family owned a stone mortar that they used only for making mashed potatoes, and after Stonebreaker's family moved out, the stone mortar was kept in the house where Padlock now lived. In the past, whenever someone wanted to make mashed potatoes, they'd just go to Padlock's house, but then Stonebreaker joined the Hammerheads and Padlock joined the Red Blades, the two brothers had quarrelled all the time. After the Red Blades broke up, Stonebreaker wanted Padlock to agree to join the Hammerheads, but Padlock wouldn't listen, saying that either the east wind overwhelmed the west wind or the west wind overwhelmed the east wind, and it wasn't like the Hammerheads would always be on top. Or did his brother think that Awning, Sparks and Millstone would never come back?

"I'm your brother," Stonebreaker said, "and I'm trying to help you, but you don't know what's good for you. When we catch that lot, it'll be you that suffers."

"Brotherly love, is it," Padlock said, "when you're hoping to see me suffer? You may not have caught the others but I'm still here. You tell Bash to come and arrest me. I'll be waiting."

After that quarrel the two brothers became enemies, refusing to speak to one another. If Stonebreaker came round to Noodle Fish's house and saw that Padlock was there, he'd walk straight out. If Padlock came round to get something from Noodle Fish's house and spotted Stonebreaker, he'd refuse to set foot inside the courtyard, shouting to his mother to bring out whatever it was he wanted. Noodle Fish had complained about it to Barndoor when he was over by the cattle pen, saying he'd never seen anyone so stubborn before, and his two sons seemed determined to fight like tigers.

"Oh well," Barndoor said, "the reason why we've never starved here in Old Kiln is that half of our fields are paddy and the other half are dry. In a dry year, we don't get rice, we get maize. In a wet year, we get rice but not maize. Your two sons belong to two different factions, so no matter which one wins you'll be OK."

Noodle Fish didn't know whether to laugh or cry.

His wife went to Padlock and told him, "Your brother's very sick. Do you really not want to go and see him?"

"He has his comrades," Padlock said, "so what am I?"

"Even if you are on opposite sides," his mother said, "you can't be so mean. Are you planning to wait until he's dead?"

Padlock finally agreed to help his mother take the mortar round to Stonebreaker's house. Stonebreaker was sitting up in bed, and Padlock said, "You look better."

Noodle Fish's wife picked up on this, saying, "As soon as Padlock heard you wanted to have mashed potatoes, he brought the mortar round."

"Sit down, Padlock," Stonebreaker said. He gestured to a stool for Padlock to sit on because the bedding was infested with scabies.

"No, I have scabies already," Padlock said, and he sat on the edge of the bed.

After asking after his health, Stonebreaker brought up the Hammerheads again, saying, "I know you don't want to hear this, but I need to tell you… the situation is now clear. The whole county and all the towns are dominated by the United Command, and Old Kiln belongs to the Hammerheads, so if you're going to carry on living here, you must join."

Padlock didn't want to listen to any more of this. "If you weren't a Hammerhead, you wouldn't be sick like this, and you want to drag me down with you?"

"What are you talking about," Stonebreaker's wife said. "What is all of this? Why are you quarrelling when this was a nice visit to your sick brother? Are you trying to make things worse?"

Padlock, who had never had any time for his sister-in-law, said, "Why are you accusing me of making things worse? Loads of people in the village have scabies, and everyone else is doing OK – how come it's just my brother with mites on his face?"

"Do you think I put them there?" Stonebreaker's wife screamed.

"What are you squawking for? Has this house ever known a moment's peace since you arrived? No kids, and now your husband's sick like this…"

Noodle Fish's wife clapped her hand over his mouth, but she couldn't shut him up, so she dragged Padlock off the bed. "Why can't you just be quiet for once?" she said. "What do you think you're saying?"

Stonebreaker's wife was now wailing at the top of her lungs, and Padlock walked out of the door. Noodle Fish's wife stayed to calm her daughter-in-law and told Stonebreaker not to be cross, everything would be fine.

"I'm not cross," Stonebreaker said. "Could you make me some mashed potatoes, and make sure to add a good dollop of hot sauce."

The potatoes were served, and Stonebreaker took a bite and then stopped eating. That was when Noodle Fish dashed in from the cattle shed because he'd heard that Padlock and Stonebreaker's wife had been arguing, so he ran back in a panic. He paused outside the courtyard door to listen and was relieved to hear that everything was quiet again, at which point he relaxed. Raising his head, he saw that South Mountain and the rest of the range were covered with white clouds. He'd never seen such thick white clouds in winter, and they came pouring down from the top of the mountain like a waterfall. He went into the house and saw that Stonebreaker was fine, so he said, "The clouds on South Mountain look lovely."

"What's so beautiful about the clouds?" his wife asked.

"It's like a wash basin's broken up there in the sky, and it's pouring down white flour."

"Help me to the door," Stonebreaker said. "I'd like to have a look."

His wife and mother helped him off the bed, but his legs were weak, and he couldn't stand up for long.

"Can you get up?" his mother asked. "What's all this about wheat flour, anyway?"

Stonebreaker said he could get up, and he tottered as far as the door, surveyed the scene and said, "It looks like cotton wadding…"

Noodle Fish was still sitting in the house tying his straw sandals. The strap to one of his sandals had broken, so he attached a section of rope, but the rope always failed to knot.

Suddenly his wife screamed, "Stonebreaker, what's wrong, Stonebreaker!"

Noodle Fish came running, but Stonebreaker had already collapsed. His mother and his wife could do nothing to prevent it, but they were trying to hold him up. Stonebreaker's eyes had rolled up inside his head, showing just the whites. When Noodle Fish helped to carry Stonebreaker back to bed, his eyes appeared back in their sockets, but he didn't respond when they called to him.

Stonebreaker had always wanted his wife to become pregnant with his child, but now he was dead, leaving no descendants.

After Stonebreaker died, Bash took charge of the funeral because Stonebreaker was a member of the Hammerheads. The other Hammerheads went to pay their condolences, but because he wasn't a member of their own family, they just went to have a look and burn three sticks of incense for him – they weren't going to be part of the ceremonies.

Very few Zhu family members attended. According to the old rules, everyone should provide a ream of paper, but that had been changed to ten sheets, and Kaihe now sold packs of ten instead of reams at his shop. Some people came to the funeral hall to burn paper, and others got as far as the courtyard entrance and when they saw all the Hammerheads there, they'd just put the paper down and walk away, not even bothering to burn it in respect.

No one expected Stonebreaker to die, and neither did he, so even when he was too sick to get up, he and his family didn't think about preparing a coffin. When he suddenly died, Noodle Fish said to give the coffin he'd prepared for himself and use it for Stonebreaker.

Big Root, Youliang and Barndoor all came to talk to him. "You can't do that," they argued. "Stonebreaker was your son, but not your biological child, besides which, even if he was, it's him that should take charge of your funeral and not the other way around. You couldn't enjoy his luck, but you're still going to give him your coffin?"

Noodle Fish felt the whole situation was very tricky and said, "I can't just have him rolled up in a mat and buried that way."

"There's a cabinet in Stonebreaker's house," Barndoor said. "If you sawed the legs off and knocked out the grill in front, wouldn't that do?"

"That's the only thing in the whole house that's worth any money," Noodle Fish said, "and his wife–"

"She doesn't have kids," Barndoor said. "Now that Stonebreaker's gone, is she going to stay?"

Noodle Fish wondered about that too, and there was no more talk of giving up his coffin. They burned paper for Stonebreaker before every meal, but his widow didn't join in.

"Burn some paper for him," Noodle Fish's wife chided her.

"Can't you see I'm busy cooking?" the widow retorted. "You burn it, you burn it."

"If you don't burn paper for him, how can I possibly do so?" Noodle Fish's wife retorted.

Stonebreaker's wife went to weep and wail in front of the coffin but she never mentioned him at all, it was all about how unlucky she was, what on earth was going to happen to her, that sort of thing. In the courtyard, the cupboard had its legs sawed off, and the grill and iron bolts removed.

Noodle Fish's wife watched this going on and dabbed at the tears in her eyes, saying, "He made that just three years ago, and he talked so proudly about filling it with grain... I never imagined I'd see it used for his coffin."

The gaps between the planks were not closed tightly, so they wanted to seal it for Stonebreaker with cotton wadding. When they asked Stonebreaker's wife for some, she said she didn't have any, so it was Noodle Fish's wife who provided some of her own cotton cloth, which padded out the base of the cabinet.

When anyone in the village died, apart from the relatives, helpers were generally not too sad because everyone dies sooner or later, and besides which most people die of disease or old age, which seems very remote from oneself. They could do their work, smoking the odd cigarette, chatting and joking among themselves, and at most there might be the occasional sigh: "How sad, they worked so hard all their lives and for what?" Then someone else would chime in: "They were lucky, though. Their kids are all grown up to be good people – but just as they were going to enjoy a comfortable old age, they died."

Stonebreaker's death, on the other hand, shocked pretty much everyone in the village. He'd died of scabies and so many people there had scabies – were they also going to have it go to their faces? They felt sorry for him, but they were also afraid. When he was put in his coffin, they wrapped him up tightly with absolutely nothing showing, not even his face, and they bound the coffin firmly with loop after loop of stout rope in the hope that the mites would stay in the coffin with him forever. He was buried in the cemetery out at the foot of the mountains, but they didn't line the grave with bricks, but just dug a hole a foot deeper than normal. Once the coffin was in place, they covered it in earth.

After burying Stonebreaker, the villagers did not feel any better. Whether at the kiln or the highway barricade, if anyone mentioned Stonebreaker, they were immediately shushed: "Don't talk about it."

Although the topic was never broached, whenever anyone had an itch, they'd think of him again. When they peed, they kept looking at their crotches to see if there were any small red bumps, and when they met each other, where they'd previously asked if they had eaten, now everyone kept quiet and looked at each other's faces first. One would say, "I'm fine", and the other would reply, "Me too". But who could guarantee that they really were fine? They were frightened, and so the village suddenly became much more quarrelsome. They cursed at the top of their voices over whose chickens had stolen a few grains, and whose cats were lying on the wall of whose house, and sometimes they even kicked and hit each other.

The kiln and the highway barricade were also like a powder barrel. Someone from the County United Command complained about Decheng, and Tag-Along didn't like that, so he quarrelled with them. Tag-Along threw their cloth shoes into the river, and they responded by biting Tag-Along in the arm, leaving the bloody imprints of four teeth. Even Iron Bolt and Glob ended up fighting when they disagreed, but Iron Bolt was no match for the larger man and ended up on his arse. After the rest of them thought they'd patched things up, Glob went over to the firebox in the little wooden shack to inspect a pair of sopping wet shoes that were drying there, whereupon Iron Bolt thrust his head down into the firebox, grabbed a stick and beat his arse, and didn't stop until the stick broke.

Division Chief Ma called a meeting of the United Command and the Hammerheads, sternly accusing them of disunity and stressing that the current situation was not optimistic, and that although the United Headquarters faction had been defeated, a beast with a hundred legs takes a long time to die, and they were in no way willing to withdraw from the stage. According to reliable information, the provincial United Headquarters faction was organising their forces to support their members at county level, and at a county level they were also busy gathering their old troops, so there would probably be an even bigger fight soon. She told everyone to be united, to remain on guard, and to maintain the barricades and investigate everyone who went through.

After the meeting, Bash called Iron Bolt and Tag-Along off to one side because he wanted them to apologise to the United Command, but they refused. Bash explained patiently why it was so important that they did. First, without the comrades from the United Command, wouldn't Awning, Sparks and Millstone be back pronto? In which case, how would the Hammerheads hold Old Kiln? Second, this time the fight was going to be much fiercer, and why? It was because each faction was competing for a place in the Revolutionary Committee that was about to be established. Whoever did well was going to have more positions on the committee.

"You two are a right pair of idiots," Bash concluded. "Why don't you use your heads? Without them we'd be nowhere, and if we were nowhere, you wouldn't have a chance at the Revolutionary Committee in Luozhen, now would you Iron Bolt? Or you, Tag-Along?"

"I don't want any part of it," Iron Bolt said.

"We've never had officials in my family," Tag-Along asserted. "All I've ever wanted was to eat my fill at every meal."

"You're fucking useless, you lot. If we don't succeed, all you'll have to eat is shit. Right now, Awning and Sparks and Millstone are out there homeless, and that's where you'll be soon enough!" Bash cursed so much that Iron Bolt and Tag-Along felt humiliated, and they went and apologised to the United Command people, hanging their heads.

After this, the members of the County United Command and the Hammerheads went twice more to Luozhen, to visit the grain store and credit union in Mafangdian on the northern outskirts to borrow food. Division Chief Ma did not go with them on these occasions, but Bash went along with a gun on his back. He thought it wasn't going to work, but in fact it went quite smoothly, and he brought back two tractor-loads of rice and flour, and a big bagful of cash and ration tokens. However, when he went to borrow food on the last occasion, he learned two pieces of bad news: one was that Huang Shengsheng had been admitted to the township's health centre, where his condition was deteriorating and he might well die; and the second was that Pockmark and Lightkeeper had set up a rebel team, which had grown surprisingly fast, with members drawn from Xiahewan, Xichuan and Luozhen, as well as the county town. They'd also tried to borrow money from the Mafangdian credit union, which refused to lend them any. In response, they tied up the credit union workers and robbed them of 54,300 yuan.

With more food and money, the Hammerheads who were helping out the men on the barricades could also eat at the kiln. This was a big improvement, and the Hammerheads were particularly motivated to check the roadblock. One day, a shuttle bus was stopped, and five suspicious men were detained. The men refused to admit that they were from the United Headquarters, insisting that they hadn't joined any faction. Baldy Jin ordered Dazed-And-Confused to search them and he found a paper bag with two snacks, which he took out and ate on the spot. When the rest of them saw Dazed-And-Confused eating, they all came over to grab some for themselves. Dazed-And-Confused stuffed both snacks into his mouth at the same time, so he couldn't speak, but neither could he swallow them – in fact, he couldn't even breathe. In the end, he coughed them out and stamped the remains into the ground saying, "If I can't eat them, nobody can."

Then he searched a second person and found a carton of cigarettes. He took a look and found three cigarettes inside. When the others tried to see, he threw the carton into the grass by the side of the highway and said, "Motherfucker! I thought there'd be cigarettes inside."

Decheng knew all of Dazed-And-Confused's little tricks so he went over and picked up the carton, saying, "Motherfucker! I thought you said there weren't any cigarettes in it!" He took the cigarettes and ran over to a clump of bamboo over by the river to smoke them.

Baldy Jin was searching another person; he had neither food nor cigarettes, but he did have a knife. Baldy Jin grabbed the tool and shouted, "This fucker's got a knife!"

"It's just a kitchen knife," the man said.

"And is a kitchen knife not a knife?" Baldy Jin retorted. "What are you doing with a knife, killing people?"

"Guofenglou is famous for its kitchen knives," the man said, "so I bought one."

"Looks to me like you're a member of the United Headquarters, and you brought a knife with you to fight."

"I have a cock on me too, so am I also suspected of being a rapist?"

Baldy Jin slapped his face and said, "How dare you say that?"

The five of them were locked up in the hut, waiting for Division Chief Ma to come and examine them. When Division Chief Ma didn't arrive, Glob came over from the kiln after dinner and grabbed one of the five men and beat him up, saying that he had seen him in the county town and that he belonged to the United Headquarters. At that, everyone else joined in. Then Baldy Jin kicked the one with the knife again and pinched his crotch through his trousers.

"Let me see if you're a rapist... A little thing like that, and you dare to show off about it?"

During the night, the five men were tortured in the Kiln God Temple, as they underwent an interrogation about where they were going and what they were doing. The one identified by the fat guy confessed, saying they were on their way to join their leader at Luanzhuang in the northern part of the county, but the other four still did not admit to being members of the United Headquarters. Having failed to confess, they were beaten again, with sticks and with the flat of a bench. They were beaten until the blood flowed everywhere.

Glob got tired and told Tag-Along to take over. "They're bleeding all over the place already," Tag-Along said. "I can't possibly hit them any more."

Glob had them put in hessian sacks and carried on the beatings. Four sacks rolled on the ground, screaming in pain. Bash and Useless were out in the courtyard of his old house killing Sparks' dog. Division Chief Ma had her period and felt cold, so Bash suggested eating some dog meat to build her up and ordered Useless to get some. Useless decided that he'd have to butcher Sparks' dog so he caught it and killed it. Just as the dog meat was cooking, he heard the screams coming from the Kiln God Temple.

"What's with all this racket?" Bash asked.

"When it got dark, I went to the temple," Useless said, "and those fuckers still haven't confessed."

"God you're stupid," Bash said. "Can't you even cover up the screaming with some other sound?"

Useless went out, and after a while, no screams could be heard over the banging of a gong.

EIGHTY

IN THE MIDDLE OF THE NIGHT, the sound of gongs and drums started up once more from the Kiln God Temple, and the villagers knew they were again beating up the same suspects that they'd been torturing during the day. The gong sounded every so often, so that slowly people got used to it, and they never knew when the peace of Old Kiln was not going to be disturbed. After all, in the evenings, the tomcats were out looking for love, and it wasn't just one or two of them either, but seven or eight that were yowling. They would howl for a bit and then fall silent. Sometimes they sounded like children having a tantrum while their parents dragged them along by the ear; sometimes they sounded like a widow wailing above a tomb; sometimes they were more like a broken gong. Their screaming was much worse than any of the sounds that came from the Kiln God Temple.

Old folk couldn't close their eyes all night, and even Inkcap woke up from his dreams and was unable to sleep any more. He went to the toilet to piss and said, "Gran, Gran, is that someone's cat calling?"

She could faintly hear the sound of gongs and cats, but these noises did not affect her emotions, as if they were just the wind blowing the broom over in the courtyard, or like the pigs oinking in the pen, and she went on with making her papercuts. Inkcap continued to pester her: "Gran, Gran, don't you mind the noise?"

This time, he asked in a louder voice, and she heard him. "What's all the racket? Go back to bed after you pee, you'll catch a cold standing out there in the cold."

He got back into bed and snuggled up to see what cut she had made this time. Gran didn't let him see and told him to go to sleep, but instead he poked a hole in the window to look out. It was snowing again in the courtyard, and the night was bright, so he saw the tree by the courtyard wall that somehow had lots of leaves growing on it. The tree was bare, how could it have leaves again? He focused his eyes and was surprised to see that it was bats hanging down. "Look at all those bats!" he told Gran.

"It's snowing," Gran said. "There aren't any bats. Go to sleep." She blew out the light and went to sleep.

Still thinking about the bats, Inkcap said, "Gran, the bats are hanging all over our tree."

"Bats are lucky," Gran said.

"How can bats be lucky if they're so ugly?"

"Being ugly means you can ward off evil."

This was the first time Inkcap had heard that being ugly can ward off evil, but it seemed about right. Inkcap knew himself to be ugly, but for all that the village was in such chaos, it had nothing to do with him. Lightkeeper looked so handsome and clean, yet he'd been denounced all his life and was still running around somewhere outside with no one here knowing whether he was dead or alive.

Now Inkcap started up again: "Gran, if being ugly means you can ward off evil, then why is it said round here that bats are ghosts? How come we have ghosts in the trees in our yard?"

"As soon as it gets light, they'll fly off," Gran told him.

"Why do we have to wait until dawn? We have to drive the ghosts away right now."

"Goodness me, you're tiresome. They're just ghosts. Let the ghosts keep watch outside at night."

Finally, dawn came, and Inkcap got up early, and there were no more bats hanging from the tree out by the courtyard wall. The bats and night had left together, but snow now covered the ground to the depth of a chicken claw. He went out of the courtyard, and some householders were using brooms or shovels to sweep the snow in front of their homes. Third Aunt and Ever-Obedient were talking under the rubber tree. Their voices were not loud, but they could be heard quite clearly, as if their words were also frozen and were being spoken in a brittle kind of voice.

"Are you going to shovel manure this morning?" Third Aunt asked.

"Not when it's been snowing," Ever-Obedient replied. "Have you seen Yoyo?"

"Has she run off again?"

"She was fast asleep," Ever-Obedient said, "but when the cats woke me, I couldn't see her anywhere. I thought she'd just gone to the toilet, but at first light when I woke up again, the dog was there but she was nowhere to be seen."

"How can she not be there when the dog is there?" Third Aunt asked. "Are you sleeping apart?"

"Of course not. With the weather this cold and its blanket so thin, the dog sleeps between us to keep warm."

"Right. Now where can she have got to… can she have gone with the bats?"

"Gone with the bats?"

"This morning Pillar called me to look at the bats," Third Aunt told him. "Lots of us left the village to look at them… didn't you have any bats in your courtyard?"

"I didn't notice a thing."

"My goodness, there were bats everywhere, a bunch of them were hanging from the eaves of my house, and Pillar said a few of them had found their way into the upper room of his place."

"I heard Pillar's mother's been sick?" Ever-Obedient said.

"Oh yes, she's so sick I doubt she'll last the winter. I guess that's why Pillar shouted at the bats to be gone because he's worried they're unlucky."

Inkcap walked over and said, "We had bats on the tree at our house too." He was in a hurry and slipped over and sat down hard on the snow. Third Aunt and Ever-Obedient didn't go over to help him up.

"What on earth's going on?" Third Aunt said. "There were never so many bats before... Ever-Obedient, this can't be related to Stonebreaker, right?"

Third Aunt's words were addressed to Ever-Obedient, but he had no idea what to say. Inkcap took these words to heart and felt a little frightened. He even connected his slip in the snow with Stonebreaker. It was on the day of the first snow that Stonebreaker had tripped him with his foot, and he slipped and fell, and this slip was almost the same as that one. He'd heard all the bones in his body click and clack as if they were made of wood, and then he fell to the ground. Inkcap told Cowbell that the bats were Stonebreaker's ghost, and Cowbell repeated this to Awning's wife, and Awning's wife told Barndoor that for all any of them knew, those bats were Stonebreaker's ghost, or maybe Huang Shengsheng's, and Barndoor repeated this to Pendulum. When Pillar went to Pendulum's house to borrow a basket, Pendulum told him what Barndoor had said, and he went as white as a sheet. "I need to go to town," he said. When asked what he was going to do there, he didn't say anything but just took the basket and left.

They were talking about the bats at both the kiln and the highway barricade, and a fear of ghosts enveloped Old Kiln. Every shift walking to the barricade brandished torches, and whenever they passed an alleyway, they shone the torches on the tiles and trees poking out above the courtyard wall to check if there were any bats. For three days in a row, they only found seven bats, which they burned with the torches, after which the bats disappeared. The tomcats were still wailing, though, but they chased them off.

"I don't know what they're doing chasing off those cats?" Barndoor said. "People mess about the way they do, so why not cats?"

"What do you mean?" Dazed-And-Confused said.

"Well, don't they?"

"I don't understand."

"Poor you."

"Who are you calling 'poor'?"

"I'm talking about you."

Dazed-And-Confused clenched a fist. "How dare you!"

"I'm not a member of the Red Blades," Barndoor reminded him. "If you hit me, nobody's going to help you." After a long pause, Dazed-And-Confused unclenched his fist.

While Barndoor and Dazed-And-Confused were arguing in the alley, Pillar called his two brothers and three sisters to the courtyard of his house to talk. Pillar's mother had been sick and ailing for years, and after Pillar was injured by the people from Xiahewan and Luozhen's United Command faction, she'd collapsed from the shock and never got out of bed again. Seeing her failing, and with so many bats flying into the yard and even into the house, Pillar felt unhappy, and after listening to what Pendulum had to say, he went and bought his mother a set of grave-clothes. His father had died young, but they'd always planned a joint burial, and he'd had a coffin made for his mother at the same time. As the brothers had arranged, his mother's burial would be the responsibility of her second son, and her coffin would be provided by her third son, and he'd be responsible for the grave-clothes and the funeral itself.

Pillar called his brothers and sisters into the yard because their mother was in the main room asleep on her bed, and they went into the storeroom to discuss her funeral. Pillar took out the complete set of grave-clothes and said that since they only had this one parent left, they should send her off to the best of their ability. Originally, they'd planned for three grave-clothes, but he'd bought five, and that had cost more, so he was looking for his brothers to chip in their share. His two brothers didn't agree, and they started quarrelling. Pillar was so furious that he took the clothes and stalked out of the room, shouting all the while, "Fine, I shouldn't have bought them. Since I've bought them, I'll keep them for myself to wear!" His three younger sisters chased after him, but they didn't catch up. He walked out of the alley heading west, his face red and contorted.

The next evening, as the snow drifted down, the ground was as hard as iron, and Mill Hole's pigsty collapsed. The pig escaped, and he chased after it until he reached the forest behind the gate leading to the mountains. He was so furious that he wanted to pick up a stone and throw it at the pig. He looked around but couldn't pick any of them up; and then he looked for bricks, and couldn't pick them up either... they were all frozen in place.

Suddenly he saw something move out in the forest, sometimes big and sometimes small, so he stopped chasing his pig and started screaming about a ghost. He'd seen a ghost! He scrambled back down to the village. When the villagers heard him, they asked if he'd seen someone, and Mill Hole wondered who could possibly be going to the graveyard at a time like this. Then they wanted to know if it could have been a wolf because with all this snow the wolves must be hungry, maybe they were waiting for dark out by the graveyard and then they'd come to the village. Mill Hole told them that that was no wolf out there. Wolves walk on their four feet and don't stand up, and furthermore if the pig had smelt a wolf, it would have been terrified – it wouldn't have carried on running into the wood. As to whether it was a ghost or not, well, they needed to get Mill Hole's pig back, so a large group assembled and headed into the woods, where they didn't see anything strange at all, and they found the pig fast asleep under a tree.

It was just at that moment that Yoyo stepped out quietly from the forest. Could it have been Yoyo all along? Mill Hole insisted it wasn't her he'd seen, but they decided Mill Hole was just seeing things and it was indeed Yoyo who'd been by the graveyard, but why would she be there after dark? "What are you doing here?" they asked her.

Yoyo didn't utter a word, and then Ever-Obedient ran over and said, "Where've you been? Where?" He hoisted her onto his shoulder and carried her back home like a sack of grain. But when they arrived in the village, they could hear the sound of crying coming from Pillar's house.

Pillar was dead.

Pillar had rushed out of the house in a fury and headed west, and he did not come back home all night. The second day he was also missing – his wife imagined that he'd swallowed his pride and gone back to Luozhen to exchange the grave-clothes, so she didn't pay it much mind. But that evening, when she was rolling out noodles, the dough didn't hang together properly. Whatever she did, a hole would form in the middle. She'd kneed it together, and a hole would form all over again. That's odd, she thought.

At that very moment, Pillar came in through the door. When his wife saw that Pillar was covered in mud and snow, his mouth and face were blue, and he was clutching the grave-clothes, she asked, "Why didn't you return them when you went to town?" Pillar said he hadn't been anywhere. He was so angry that he'd spent a day and a night walking around the pond at the back of the village. His wife wanted to shout at him, but instead she told him to get into bed as soon as possible – they'd eat and then he should go to sleep. Pillar just sat on the kitchen threshold, still panting. His wife was rolling out noodles again when she heard a thud. She turned her head to see that Pillar had fallen below the threshold, and his head and neck became very thick all of a sudden. She rushed over and said, "Are you OK? What's the matter?" Pillar's eyes were staring straight ahead, and he didn't say another word.

Pillar was dead in the blink of an eye. In the past ten years, no one in Old Kiln had died as quickly as he did. Once he died, his mother's illness somehow got better, and he was buried in the grave-clothes he bought for her. Everyone said he shouldn't have said he wanted to keep them for himself. He died quickly and was buried quickly. Because he knew how to fire a kiln and was so aggressive in speech, he'd offended many people. When the Red Blades raised funds to fire the kiln, he deliberately refused to participate so the Zhus no longer paid any attention to him; and when he got injured by the United Headquarters, he'd quarrelled with the Hei clan over it, so his funeral was now very simple. In fact, his mother had to hobble over on her stick to beg for help from Bash, and Bash only sent a handful of Hammerheads to carry the coffin to the grave.

People were now dying one after the other in Old Kiln. Even Pillar had died, so the suspicion that the village was haunted took hold. Yoyo wasn't a ghost, she was just mad, but could she be connected in some way? "Has Yoyo been seeing ghosts?" someone asked. Inkcap and Cowbell questioned her about this every time they saw her, but Yoyo never said a word. She just looked at people with a strange expression in her eyes. Then she'd bite into her radish. Yoyo loved radishes.

"Have you smelt anything strange lately?" Cowbell asked.

"No," Inkcap assured him.

"You haven't smelt all these dead people?"

"Nope."

Cowbell sighed heavily and Inkcap felt pleased. Finally, he'd stopped smelling strange things. He stuck his tongue out and licked the end of his nose as a kind of reward. The snow drifted down flake by flake, and they looked out into the forest from their position by the gate to the mountains and discussed the day when they'd discovered Yoyo out there, and how Pillar was now buried over in the graveyard. Suddenly there was a fluttering sound, and a few birds flew overhead. Inkcap recognised them as the birds from the white pine and they were calling, "Caw-caw – coo-coo – zhen!" But the birds didn't stop and kept flying up the mountains.

"Someone must want Goodman to cure them," Cowbell said.

"Who'd ask him for help at a time like this?" But when Inkcap said those words, they both decided to go to the Mountain God Temple to see Goodman.

It had been many days since they had been to the temple, and Goodman hadn't been back to the village since. When Inkcap and Cowbell arrived at the peak, there were three people on the steps leading up to the temple who looked as if they'd already been waiting a good long while. The snow on their shoes had melted and there were puddles beneath their feet. Then Goodman came out to collect some fallen branches for firewood. Goodman had lost a lot of weight, even his waist was bent, and to Inkcap's surprise, his head was still bound with a white cloth bandage.

"Do you still have a headache?" Inkcap asked.

"Sometimes it gets a bit better for a few days, and then it's worse again," replied Goodman.

Inkcap felt guilty about not thinking about Goodman's illness after he'd taken his pumpkins, and he rushed to help him hold the firewood, but Goodman just said, "Did you use the pumpkins?" When he said "use" and not "eat", did that mean he already knew what happened? Inkcap didn't know what to say. "Is he better?" Goodman asked.

This confirmed for Inkcap that Goodman knew everything, but he just hemmed and hawed because he had no idea whether Millstone got better after he handed over the pumpkins, and he also did not hear Gran or Noodle Fish's wife mention it.

"What are you talking about?" said Cowbell.

"He's talking about Gran's ear," Inkcap said.

When Goodman heard Inkcap say this, he smiled and led the two boys into the house. "It's very nice of you to come and see me on such a cold day. I've just been cooking some potatoes on the stove. If you want to eat them, go and see if they're done."

On entering the house, they saw a man sitting down, and it looked as if he and Goodman had already been talking for a while. Goodman bent the brushwood he'd collected and stuffed it into the mouth of the oven, then took off his shoes and got into the bed under the covers. Inkcap peeled the potatoes on the stove. The potatoes were cooked, but they were still very hot, so he tossed them about from hand to hand.

"If you're going to stay inside, could you eat quietly, since I'm going to be talking to this man here about his health." Then, turning to the man, Goodman said, "Where were we?"

"You said that the time had come, and what little prosperity we have has come to an end," the man replied. "If we don't ascend to Heaven, then we'll find ourselves in a dead end."

"Oh, yes," Goodman said. "If man's desires run rampant and prohibitions are swept away, the world will indeed be thrown into chaos. To be truly healthy, one must learn to transcend the three worlds. Man's nature is dependent on the natural world, for in order to live he must breathe the air of this earth, and he takes his form from his parents. Because man is born of the three realms, he has the ability to transcend the three realms. Human nature is fundamentally good because it receives that natural endowment, but when you are confused by material desires, you become corrupted and degraded. In the final analysis, the ghosts and gods will know whether you are evil or not. When your heart is filled with selfish desires, it is tempted by external objects. Human desires are everywhere, they affect everything, and they are the means by which evil comes into your life – they are true ghosts.

"It's actually very easy to be a good person because you are born good and innocent, so you should love your parents and respect your brothers, and be kind to your children, and work hard. You should avoid acquiring evil habits like drinking, gambling, whoring and smoking. If you keep good relationships and strive to cultivate your person, returning to the ways of honest living, getting rid of your selfish desires and avoid getting angry, then you can return to your original pure and innocent nature. Do you understand what I mean?"

The man nodded his head, but Inkcap and Cowbell couldn't understand what Goodman was talking about.

"Your illness was caused by bad relationships with other people," Goodman continued, "which resulted in you taking a financial loss, and by the resentment of relatives and neighbours demanding that you repay your debts. I will teach you how to deal with this. No matter who shouts and screams at you demanding repayment, sighing and moaning, you must pretend to be very worried and concerned. You must not say anything – let them shout themselves hoarse. You must concentrate your mind on the following principle: I can deal with bad people without becoming bad myself. I will use this opportunity to prove myself. That is the way. When they've gone, you must laugh out loud and say to yourself, 'This is my debt, this is my burden. Other people are afraid of debt, but not me. Other people worry about you because you can destroy them, but I am happy to see you because there is nothing you can do to me.' If you laugh three times a day like this for three days, you'll be fine."

By now Inkcap had eaten his own potatoes and asked for more from Cowbell, who wouldn't give him any. The man excused himself and went out of the room, and Cowbell stuffed the rest of the potatoes into his mouth, making his cheek bulge. The two then settled down and sat on the mat, while another man entered the room, his eyes as red as a chicken's arsehole. He sat down on the edge of the bed.

"Your nature is Wood, which goes to Fire," said Goodman, "just as Fire goes to Earth, and Earth goes to Metal in four easy steps. At present, you have lost faith in things, and your heart has become anxious. That is why you are ill. For example, you are scheduled to meet six guests, and each and every one of them talks over a pipe. Now if the guests carry on talking beyond when the meeting was supposed to finish, you get anxious, which in turn produces Fire, which makes your eyes hurt. Without confidence, you become resentful, your mind is unstable, and you don't feel like eating."

"You haven't even checked my pulse," the red-eyed man said, "so how can you know my condition?"

"Man has five internal organs – the heart, liver, spleen, lungs and kidneys," Goodman said, "and each one has an effect on your appearance. If one organ is diseased, a change in colour will occur. Disease comes from the poisonous impact of anger, hatred, resentment, stress and annoyance. If in the future you can trust people, and avoid anxiety and bitterness, you will starve the disease and it will go away."

The red-eyed man asked again if there was a cure.

"There is no need for you to take medicine," Goodman told him. "If you make yourself a gentler and more accepting character, the disease will be cured of its own accord."

Cowbell whispered to Inkcap, "Does that kind of cure work?"

"I guess so…" Inkcap replied.

"But his head still hurts. How come he doesn't cure his own headache?"

"Didn't you know that physicians can't heal themselves?"

"What are you talking about, Cowbell?" Goodman asked. "And how are your ears?"

The moment his ears were mentioned, Cowbell started cursing and said that they just needed to wait and see. When Awning and Sparks and Millstone came back, he'd cut the ears off the person who'd hurt him, and having snipped them off he'd pickle them in wine!

"What a tough guy you are, kid," Goodman remarked.

"I'm a Red Blade," Cowbell said proudly.

"If you're a Red Blade, what are you doing making food and carrying water for the United Command lot?"

"That's just to be able to eat buns, and how did you know that anyway?"

Goodman laughed and said, "It's good that you don't bear grudges."

Cowbell looked cross and the red-eyed man said, "I've been thinking about what you just said, and when I get back, I'm going to write a big-character poster and put it up on the wall. It'll say, 'Goodman told me not to bear grudges because that's the way to become a good person, so ask yourself every day: Are you bearing grudges and resenting people?'"

"Are you a teacher?" Inkcap asked.

"Indeed I am," the red-eyed man said. "What school do you go to? What year are you in?"

Cowbell nudged Inkcap and said, "Let's go out and play with the birds." The two of them left.

After the red-eyed man had gone, another man on the steps outside the door went in. He'd come to thank Goodman. He said he travelled along the road, and when he passed the barricade, the man who went in front of him was detained for interrogation, and the second man was also detained. When he saw this situation, he decided he could not run away, so he went forward despite everything and to his surprise, he was let through. He entered the village to see his brother-in-law, who had been taken into the political training class, but there were guards at the entrance who would not let him in, nor would they let his brother-in-law out to meet him.

Goodman looked at him and saw a scar on his right cheek. "Your name is Wang, right?" he said.

"I have been here before," Scarface Wang said. "The last time I came to ask you for advice, I had a feeling there'd be a great change in the world, and I was living in fear all day long, thinking that either something terrible was going to happen, or I was going to get a bad disease. You taught me the four great principles – every human being is made of flesh and blood, so in the end they will die, but in that moment of truth, if you try to do nothing, to say nothing, that is truly the end. When you die, if your heart is in the right place, you can be happy thinking that you are going to your well-earned rest, because it is right for you to leave the stage, and that is a meaningful death. If, as you are dying, you are attached to everything and have a hard time letting go, and feel sad, then that is a heartfelt death. If one dies as a victim of injustice, filled with resentment and hatred, that's a painful death. You told me to distinguish these clearly because in that way I'd be able to come through disaster without faltering.

"The day there was fighting in the county, I took the bus to Qingfengguan, but when we got ten miles out of the county town, gunshots were fired, and the bus was thrown into chaos. I hid under the seat and remembered what you said, so I got out again and sat down in my seat, sitting up straight, while the young man next to me cowered at my feet. When the fighting was over, he didn't come out again, so I looked down and saw he'd been killed by a stray bullet. The bus didn't carry on to Qingfengguan, so I walked back to the county town again to find three consecutive battles raging there, but I remained calm as usual and did not suffer any calamity. So I came to see my brother-in-law, and I was going to tell him what you had said to me, but I didn't get to see him, so instead I decided I had to come and see you."

"That's good," Goodman said. "You must always remember that other people change things, I change people. Other people repair temples, I repair gods."

Scarface Wang nodded, and he counted out five yuan and gave the money to Goodman. Goodman didn't accept it, but Scarface Wang insisted. "You must take it, you saved my life. Are you telling me my life isn't even worth five yuan? Besides, I also want you to tell me whether my brother-in-law will escape this difficulty. He really doesn't belong to that United Headquarters lot. With everything in such a state nowadays he wanted to go to Xinjiang. He heard it was easy enough to settle down there, and he'd earn enough to survive… but they insist he's a member of United Headquarters and arrested him."

Scarface Wang put the five yuan down on the edge of the bed. Then Inkcap came in and declared, "Glob from the United Command is here!"

Glob entered almost before the words were out of his mouth, and as soon as he came in, he said, "There are so many people here, what are they doing?"

Goodman was still sitting under his blankets. "It's cold," he said. "Come and sit down, the bed is warm. They are here for a consultation about their health."

"Is that so?" Glob said. He saw the five yuan and picked it up.

"That's the money I paid for a consultation," Scarface Wang said.

Glob didn't say a word to Scarface Wang, but turned to Goodman and said, "We knew you were offering consultations and that's why we didn't come up here… but we didn't know you were charging so much for it. We've got so many people that don't have money to spend or food to eat, but the grain stores and credit union have been lending to us, and the villagers have been very kind – how come you haven't chipped in anything?"

"Take it, then," Goodman said, "but that's money I earned from healing the sick, so disease goes with it."

"What do you mean?"

"I'm giving it to you," Goodman told him, "but you need to be careful. I'm afraid it'll get you into trouble."

"No need to worry about that," Glob declared. "Right, I need to tell you to get ready, because this afternoon you're going to Xiahewan."

"Going to Xiahewan?"

"Huang Shengsheng hasn't been cured at the town health centre," Glob said. "Those so-called doctors are fucking useless, so Division Chief Ma sent someone to pick him up and bring him to Xiahewan to have traditional doctors treat him. Once Huang Shengsheng is back, you're to go and see him. If you're really as good as they say, you can cure him."

"I'm not going anywhere," Goodman said.

"What do you mean, you're not going?"

"He's not sick. He just got burned."

"Are you doing this on purpose? Let me tell you, Division Chief Ma and Bash are expecting you to go, and that's an order."

"Oh, really," Goodman said. "In that case, when Comrade Huang arrives at the barricade, you give me a shout from the highway. I can hear it up here, and I'll come down."

When Glob left, Inkcap felt frightened on Goodman's behalf.

"What are you afraid of?" Goodman said. "Do you think Huang

869

Shengsheng will live? Have you two come here to play, or is there something you want?"

Inkcap was still afraid and asked, "You said you won't go to Xiahewan? The two of us are fine."

"What do you mean 'fine'?" Cowbell said. "We came up to ask about ghosts."

"Is it Stonebreaker that's got you scared?" Goodman said, laughing.

"How come you know everything when you don't go down the mountain?" Inkcap asked.

"Do you want to see a ghost?"

"Can you really see ghosts?"

"Well, I want to see one," Cowbell said.

"Go and get me a bucket of water from the creek, you two," Goodman said, "and I'll remind you how to see ghosts."

EIGHTY-ONE

WHEN THEY HAD LEARNED HOW TO SEE GHOSTS, Inkcap and Cowbell agreed to go to the road at the south entrance of the village to look for them at night after everyone else was asleep.

Inkcap told Third Aunt what Goodman said about Huang Shengsheng not living much longer, and Third Aunt told Cattle Track's mother, who became anxious. That was because Division Chief Ma and Bash had arranged for Cattle Track and Old Faithful to go with the people from the United Command to Luozhen to pick up Huang Shengsheng on the tractor. Although Cattle Track had already gone out of the door and was heading down the road, his mother chased after him and dragged him home. She told Cattle Track to go to bed and get some sleep, while she went to Bash and said Cattle Track had come down with a cold and was feeling too bad to go.

"What do you mean, he's sick?" Bash asked. He didn't really believe it and went to Cattle Track's house to check. When he heard Bash enter, Cattle Track started moaning and his nose ran. Seeing his nose dripping like that, right into his mouth, Bash felt disgusted and walked straight out again.

"What a useless creature," he said.

The tractor that went to pick up Huang Shengsheng did not come back that day. At night, Inkcap and Cowbell had prepared the necessary white paper, and having also found a stick of incense, they went to the south entrance of the village to see ghosts. When they heard that the tractor would come back with Huang Shengsheng overnight, they were afraid they might run into him, so they had to put off their ghost-viewing until the following night. However, the whole night, Huang Shengsheng's tractor still was nowhere to be seen.

The next morning, the news spread like wildfire through the village: the tractor had indeed picked up Huang Shengsheng, but less than three miles into the return trip from Luozhen, just when they passed a cliff, they'd been ambushed by Awning and Sparks. At that time Awning and Sparks and the rest of their men threw rocks down at the tractor from the top of the cliff, and the tractor had overturned into the river, where it crumpled into a tangled heap, while all the passengers had fallen off. Old Faithful fell the furthest and landed on a pile of gravel, so he now had shards driven into half his face and it was bleeding nastily. When he climbed up and looked around for the others, the driver and one of the United Command men had been knocked unconscious. He shouted at them and tapped their faces, whereupon they woke up. One of them had a broken arm and the other had a broken leg, but when they forced themselves upright, they remembered Huang Shengsheng – but they couldn't see him anywhere. Where was he? The heap of scrap metal that had once been a tractor was stuck between some boulders, the wheels still spinning, and a flock of birds were nearby pecking at something. When they'd scared the birds off, they discovered they'd been pecking at Huang Shengsheng's head, which was now broken open in many places. They made haste to get him up, but then they realised that it was just his head there – the body was somewhere else. His head and neck and part of the skin running down his back were still together, but his body had been crushed beneath the tractor.

Cattle Track's mother went up the mountain that evening with a few eggs wrapped in a towel, and she kowtowed to Goodman, saying that he had saved her son's life. But at the end she asked, "How could you know that Huang Shengsheng would not live?"

"If someone like that could survive, would there be any justice in the world?" Goodman said. "We have disloyal men, dishonest women... because God sends us these people to cause trouble. Huang Shengsheng should have had a lifespan of forty years, but then he wanted to be part of a faction, he ate and drank every day, got into fights, and squandered the blessing of forty years of life. He was an evil man who did wicked things and they asked me to go and cure him – everything that happened to him was his own fault. He was a dark character, and if I'd gone to shine my light on him, how would that have helped? It was best that he never saw me because if he had, it would have been most painful for him."

This was the first time Cattle Track's mother had heard such big words from Goodman. Originally, she'd wanted Cattle Track to go up the mountain to hear Goodman's advice, but then she decided that would be a bad idea. She was worried that if he went and Goodman said that kind of thing again, supposing the wrong person heard it – say a Hammerhead or someone from the United Command – then Goodman and Cattle Track would both be in real trouble. Afterwards, somehow or other, Cattle Track didn't get well again. If he went out of doors and saw anyone, he'd have a long trail of snot hanging down his nose and onto his upper lip. "Oh, I feel dreadful," he'd say. If anyone wanted him to help out at the kiln or the barricade, he refused to do it.

Inkcap and Cowbell still wanted to see ghosts. To keep it secret, they went to the south entrance of the village after dark. When they arrived at the stone lion, the chickens started to crow for the first time, so they wrapped their feet in white paper, put a piece of white paper on their heads, and then cut out a lump of earth with a shovel and put it on top. With the incense lit, they put the stick in place on top of each other's heads.

"I'm frightened," Cowbell said.

"Me too," Inkcap replied. "Now that the incense is in place, does that mean ghosts will come?"

"Goodman said they'd come, so who do you think they'll be?"

"The first one should be the man from Xiahewan who died, then Stonebreaker, Pillar and Huang Shengsheng. I'm afraid they're coming to seek revenge."

"If they want revenge, they can have it. We won't say a word." Then Cowbell suddenly thought of something. "Hey, do you think my mum and dad will come? If they see me here and ask what I'm doing–"

"We just don't say a word," Inkcap instructed him.

"No way! You're telling me I'm not allowed to talk to my parents? Oh, right, you don't have parents."

Inkcap was just putting the stick of incense into the lump of earth on Cowbell's head when he said this, and his hand started to shake. He stopped and thought, I have no idea what my parents look like. Even if they came, I wouldn't know it was them.

"Why aren't you putting the stick of incense straight?" Cowbell asked.

"Your parents won't turn up here," Inkcap told him, "because they will only come to you in your dreams. The only ghosts you're going to see tonight are Stonebreaker, Pillar and Huang Shengsheng. Huang Shengsheng's head will come flying, with a flap of skin attached."

Cowbell immediately pulled the lump of mud off his head and stood up. "I don't want to see that," he declared. "That's horrible."

Just at that moment, Inkcap clapped a hand over Cowbell's mouth and pulled him down behind the stone lion. Cowbell had no idea what was going on, and since he couldn't breathe, his whole body started shaking. Inkcap didn't release the pressure with his hand for a good long while, but when he finally took it away, he whispered, "Up ahead, I think there's something out on the embankment…"

Cowbell peered out, but in the darkness, he couldn't see a thing and there wasn't any movement. "What did you see?" he asked.

"It certainly looked like a person," Inkcap said, "and it seemed to be coming this way."

"Do you think it was a ghost?"

"But we haven't even lit the incense yet," Inkcap replied.

Then there was a crash, as if someone had fallen. Inkcap and Cowbell stood up and shouted, "Who's there?" No answer came, and then they heard footsteps approaching behind them. Inkcap and Cowbell threw the white paper and incense sticks aside because they had recognised Yoyo.

"Hey, you!" Inkcap called.

Yoyo now saw them too, and said, "Oh, fuck."

"Where are you going in the middle of the night?"

"What do you mean? It's not that dark."

"Why isn't Ever-Obedient with you?" Cowbell asked.

"The thornback fish are calling," Yoyo said. "Listen."

The thornback fish in the river were certainly not calling out their name. It was so cold at night that the river was frozen, and the fish were caught in the ice. Yoyo's first words seemed normal, but when she carried on speaking it was impossible to understand what she was talking about.

The next thing that happened was that there was a whole lot of shouting and kerfuffle, as a load of people came running down the road with torches in their hands. A dozen were from the United Command faction, as well as Baldy Jin, Dazed-And-Confused and Tag-Along. They soon surrounded Inkcap, Cowbell and Yoyo. Yoyo made a bolt for it and ran down the slope under the stone lion, but she did not get far before she was caught.

Baldy Jin held a torch in front of her face, so close that it burned Yoyo's fringe, which gave off a burned smell. "This isn't one of them," Baldy Jin said. "This lunatic belongs to Ever-Obedient's family."

"Is there going to be a banquet?" Yoyo asked.

"Eat my fist!" said the person standing next to her. He threw a punch at her, but instead of actually trying to hit her, his hand unclenched and he groped Yoyo's tit.

Baldy Jin came over and asked Inkcap and Cowbell, "What are you two doing here?"

"Cowbell's cat has disappeared... we're looking for it," Inkcap declared.

"Nonsense. What cat can't find its way back?"

"But this is a *female* cat," Inkcap said, "and she'll be–"

"What are you on about?" Baldy Jin said. "Now tell me, have you seen someone running from the village?"

"No."

"Fuck it," Baldy Jin shouted. "He's got a bad leg and he can't have got far... split up and search. Split up and search." Everyone started running about all over the place, with their torches waggling.

"Who are you looking for?" Cowbell asked.

"That fucker groped my tit," said Yoyo. "If he just wanted a good feel, hell, I don't care, but that motherfucking bastard stole my cash."

An hour later – that is, shortly after Inkcap and Cowbell had gone – Baldy Jin and the others caught one of the runaways from the political training class down by the embankment. This man had a wide smile with a gold tooth set in it; perhaps it was because he had a thick lower lip and a thin upper lip that he'd decided to have a gold tooth set there. After finishing his dinner, Gold Tooth said he had a stomach ache and needed to go to the privy, and a man from the United Command took him there armed with a wooden stick and then squatted down outside to keep watch. One of Gold Tooth's legs was afflicted with rheumatism, so he generally didn't move too well, but he also really did have diarrhoea, with thin shits and thunderous farting. The guard didn't notice anything suspicious, and just shouted at him, "Are you releasing poisonous gas in there or what?" He moved further away to smoke his pipe, but after three pipes, Gold Tooth still hadn't emerged, so he cursed again, "Are you shitting out a rope?" No answer came, so he went into the toilet and found it empty save for a cotton jacket. Gold Tooth had escaped through the cesspit.

His escape alarmed everyone at the Kiln God Temple. Baldy Jin was woken up, and he shouted at all the guards to stay away and maintain a strict watch while he rounded up a dozen or so men to search the village. Finding no one there, they started searching the environs. There were earthen embankments on three sides since only one side of Old Kiln backed onto the mountains, and at their highest, they were as tall as a three-storey building. Even at their lowest, they were a couple of yards, and nobody would have imagined that Gold Tooth would try to jump. Therefore, they contented themselves with searching the piles of firewood and maize stalks, and the haystacks that dotted them. After meeting Cowbell and Inkcap at the south entrance of the village, they walked about fifty yards to the west and found a shoe in a clump of wild jujube thorns that belonged to Gold Tooth. The searchers went through the piles of maize stalks there, but there was no sign of him, so someone picked up a stone and threw it down the bank in irritation, and there was a groan from below.

Baldy Jin shouted, "Go down to the embankment, go down!" Four or five men ran down the path in front of them, and there was Gold Tooth lying at the bottom of the dark and dreary bank. He may have jumped, or maybe he lost his footing and fell; after all, one of his legs was rheumatic, and now that leg was broken.

Now Baldy Jin started thumping him and he was beaten until he could no longer scream. Baldy Jin wanted to drag him back to the temple, but he was unable to walk. Those who'd beaten him were freezing cold and their teeth were chattering, so no one was willing to carry him back.

"Sleep tight," the United Command people said. "This fucker's got us all so cold, but apparently he's OK with that… let's leave him here to freeze overnight."

They took off Gold Tooth's belt and used it to tie his arms to a tree. With no belt, his trousers fell down to his ankles. Some of the others took rice straw from one of the stacks on the bank and plaited it into a rope, which they used to hogtie Gold Tooth. "He won't be running anywhere," they said. "Tomorrow, we can fetch him back." Then they all went back to the Kiln God Temple to sleep.

Inkcap didn't know what happened after they left the south entrance of the village. He slept until the latter part of the night, when he suddenly woke up and heard the rats gnawing on the cupboard. They were always scheming about getting at the grain inside. Of the four corners of the cupboard, they'd gnawed on three, but the good thing was that none of the corners had been gnawed through.

Inkcap hissed into the darkness. The rat stopped gnawing, and he just turned over and went back to sleep, only to have the rat start gnawing again. Again, Inkcap hissed: "Shoo!" Then the dogs started barking somewhere in the lane. Usually, when the dogs barked at night, they woofed slowly and stopped after a few barks. This time they were barking especially fiercely, and soon countless dogs were at it, waking Gran up too. "Are there wolves in the village?" she asked.

"A man escaped from the Kiln God Temple," Inkcap told her, "so Baldy Jin and the others are out searching for him. I guess they've caught him."

"Oh, how dreadful. How do you know someone ran away from the temple?"

"When it was getting dark, Cowbell and I took a turn round the village, and we saw Baldy Jin and his men searching the embankment. They said someone had escaped."

"So when I asked where you'd been and you said to Cowbell's house, you were lying!"

Gran was cross, and Inkcap replied hastily, "Gran, Gran, why isn't the bed hot any more? Let me warm your feet." He took her feet in his hands.

Gran was no longer angry. "It's good that you're such a filial boy…"

"Do you believe in ghosts?"

"Why do you ask that? Of course there are ghosts."

"Have you seen one?"

"I've seen a living ghost."

This was the first time Inkcap had heard of such a thing so he asked, "What's one of them?"

Gran didn't reply.

"You don't like it that Cowbell and I went out for a walk in the dark," Inkcap said, "but Yoyo was out walking too – would you call her a living ghost?"

"Don't be silly," Gran said.

"Gran, have you seen Millstone? Has he run away or is he still in the cellar?"

Gran sat bolt upright. "Who have you been talking to?"

"Nobody," Inkcap assured her.

"But you've been talking to me."

"But you're my grandmother."

"You can't even talk about things like that to your own grandmother. There are some things that you can never talk about to anybody, never."

Inkcap didn't dare to say another word. He pretended to sleep and even snored a little, but after snoring a while, he genuinely did fall into slumber.

The next day when he got up, the wind was whistling, and when the chickens in the alleyway got to the end of the lane, their feathers were all blown backwards until they resembled hedgehogs. They turned around and went back, which soon turned into a trot, and then from running they progressed to flying, until they flew against the courtyard door and hit the doorframe.

The bird's nest fell from the red toon tree next to the small stone mill, and it looked just like a basket. Inkcap picked it up, whereupon Useless's mother came over to demand it, but he refused to give it to her. A bird flew around above their heads as the two of them quarrelled.

"Why are you picking up my firewood?" Useless's mother said. "That red toon tree belongs to my family."

"But the bird is my family's," Inkcap retorted.

"The bird is your family's? Did your mother give birth to it or is it your Gran's?"

"Let's both call the bird," Inkcap said, "and see who it responds to."

Useless's mother whistled to the bird, but it kept flying. Then Inkcap said, "Hey, hey, you come down, come down and sit on my shoulder." The bird landed on Inkcap's left shoulder.

Useless's mother was nonplussed. "Were you a bird in a previous life?"

"I thought you wanted to argue with me?" But the bird chittered away on his left shoulder, and Inkcap said, "What happened to your mother when the nest fell?" The bird chirped again. "Well, I'll have to get Cowbell," Inkcap said. The bird spoke bird language, but Inkcap could understand; Inkcap spoke human language, and the bird could understand him.

Useless's mother had no idea what to make of this and asked dubiously, "Are you really human?"

"You can't have that bird's nest to burn," Inkcap told her, "because otherwise the bird and its mother won't have anywhere to live during the cold weather."

Inkcap looked around on the ground for a rope but couldn't find one. He peeled a strip of bark off the tree and started climbing the tree with the nest in one hand, but that proved impossible. He shouted in his loudest voice, "Cowbell!"

Cowbell had just got up and was having a shit in the privy. When he heard the shout, he came over and was happy to ensure that the bird's nest was put back up the tree safe and sound. Cowbell was good at climbing trees and liked having an opportunity to show his skill, but when he saw a crowd of people around the stone lion at the south entrance of the village, he said, "What's going on over there?"

"Dunno," Inkcap said. "Maybe Yoyo's gone back out to shout at the guy who groped her tit?"

Ever-Obedient's dog ambled past with its head down. It was never in any hurry. "Why don't you bark for Ever-Obedient?" Inkcap asked the dog. "Yoyo's over by the south entrance of the village."

But the dog didn't bark; it just walked past slowly.

"Someone groped her tit?" Useless's mother remarked. "She's got enough people groping her – Ever-Obedient and the dog... did you know that they all sleep in the same bed together, so she's got two men in the sack with her at all times!"

Cowbell came down from the tree and said, "That's one good deed for the day done." He dragged Inkcap off to the south entrance of the village.

Yoyo couldn't be found anywhere. Inkcap had never seen anything so awful and rushed off to puke by the side of the road. He encountered a man tied to a tree. He wasn't wearing a padded cotton jacket, but just a thin shirt which was torn open, so that only the two shoulders and half of the front with buttons running down it were left. His trousers were round his ankles. His belly was covered in blood. It looked as if it had been raked apart, as all the major organs were eviscerated, and his intestines were lying in loops on the ground, though they were still attached to his stomach. The remains had been pulled behind the tree, and the blood had congealed into ice.

When Inkcap finished throwing up, it was Cowbell's turn – and then everyone else puked too. The more they threw up, the more nauseated everyone felt. To begin with they were puking last night's dinner, but after that it was just bile, and then bile with a greenish tinge to it. Bash and Division Chief Ma also arrived, and Bash shouted for everyone to stand back. He came closer, thinking to cover the man with something, but he was wearing a yellow army coat and underneath was his now backless sweater. Division Chief Ma had the ropes untied and laid the man on the ground, and Bash went up to the elevated bank and carried down a bundle of straw which he threw over the body.

He asked Tag-Along beside him, "What time did he run off?"

"He ran when the rooster crowed for the first time."

"Since you caught him, you should've taken him back. Who told you to tie him here?"

"Baldy Jin was in charge," Tag-Along said. "I don't know why they tied him up here."

"Where is he?"

"I'm afraid he's still asleep," Tag-Along said apologetically.

Bash seemed furious and said loudly, "Have him come and collect the corpse."

Division Chief Ma never said a word as she crouched over the dead body and poked at the torn stomach with a stick. That was so bold of her that the people moving away turned back to watch, and they started whispering among themselves, wondering who he was and why he'd been tied up like that, and how he'd died so dreadfully. When they heard he'd been held at the political training class, and that he'd escaped last night and they'd caught him and tied him up here to freeze, with his belly in this state – did that mean that the United Command and Hammerheads had tortured him until he looked like this?

One person tapped another on the back and said, "Go and have a look... do you think they used knives or rakes?"

They didn't dare go near, and the other person said, "Just look at Division Chief Ma! Are you letting a woman show you up?" The man started throwing up.

Division Chief Ma said to Bash in a low voice, "I was worried that the United Headquarters or Awning had come back and killed him, but look here... these wounds cannot have been made with a knife... and why is his stomach in this state?"

Bash picked something up from one loop of the intestines, and then he looked around on the ground, which was frozen hard, ran up to the top of the embankment where he kicked at something, and finally said, "Fuck it. Look at this shit. This was done by wolves."

Bash was right. Everyone was speculating about the cause of the escapee's death and thought of all manner of explanations, forgetting that in winter wolves have nothing to eat and come out of the mountains in

877

search of food. But in previous years, when wolves came out in wintertime, they only appeared in the village to drag off pigs and steal chickens, but this time, how come they'd eaten someone?

When Baldy Jin arrived, Gold Tooth was rolled up in a grass mat, and by order of Division Chief Ma, they went to find a place to bury him behind the pond. As Baldy Jin and the others carried the rolled-up mat through the village, the courtyard doors of every property were slammed shut, and any lingering bad luck was dispersed by spitting a few times and by throwing a bowl of water out, accompanied by the mantra, "Ghosts, do not seek me out!"

When Baldy Jin heard this, he said, "This son of a bitch was a pig in his past life, that's why he was eaten by the wolves."

They carried the mat roll to the back of the pond, and Baldy Jin dug a hole in the patch where Awning's family grew hemp and buried it.

After three days, the corpse was dug up again and not by Awning's wife. Dazed-And-Confused heard that the dead man had a gold tooth in his mouth, so he went out under cover of darkness to dig up the body and prise out the tooth, and then he reburied it, with only half as much soil shovelled back on top. Later on, Bash had the dead body buried at the bottom of the ditch on the left side of the pond.

EIGHTY-TWO

AFTER GOLD TOOTH'S DEATH, the political training class was much quieter, and no one plotted to escape any more. But the door of the Kiln God Temple was kept tight shut, and two men from the County United Command faction stood guard. When Inkcap didn't have anything better to do, he watched them from Three Fork Alley. As the sunlight appeared over the mountain ridge in the morning, the section of road that sloped from the temple gate to the mountain gate was powder white, and as people and animals strolled along there, it seemed to melt away as they walked, until at noon when the sun jumped out over the top of the ridge, the light on the road dispersed, and one could hear the sound of talking in the temple courtyard. What they said was inaudible, for by the time it resounded through the enclosed alleyways it had become a vague buzzing sound, while the two guards at the temple gate untied their cotton jackets to search for lice.

In the afternoon, the political training class was allowed out with Branch Secretary Zhu at their head. He still seemed to be the prisoners' leader, and he assigned individuals to chop wood, make clay crockery or soak some straw so they could weave sandals. It was said that it was so cold in the temple, they had to build a *kang*, and given the shortage of firewood, they had to chop up roots with axes. They were making straw sandals for the United Command members and the Hammerheads – they had to guarantee a new pair for all of them every five days. When everyone else was working separately, the Branch Secretary remained sitting there and began to snooze, but as soon as anyone tried to sneak off, he'd ask with his eyes still closed, "Where are you going?"

"I'm going for a pee," was the response. Then the sound of snoring would start up again.

While they were working there, Inkcap would never approach; even the Branch Secretary's wife was watching from behind the wall, wiping away her tears. Inkcap went over to talk to her instead. "Don't go over there," he said, "it'll only cause trouble for him."

"But he's got a stomach complaint," the wife said.

"Surely he's better now, look how fat he's getting…"

"That's just swelling."

But when the Hammerheads brought back another pile of flour sacks, Inkcap was willing to go closer. He liked the flour sacks, so full and yet so soft that when he punched them, his fist sank in and turned white. He wasn't entitled to eat any of the contents, so when they asked him to help carry the sacks up to the kiln, he refused; even when the flour bags were put on his shoulders, he simply slumped to the ground. Then they said, "If you help carry, you can have the sacks." He got up from the ground and carried three flour sacks to the mountain. He took them back home and swished them in water, and the water went to make a thick vegetable stew.

One day, the members of the County United Command faction decided to kill a pig, and they brought a sow back from Xiahewan. They said they'd paid good money for this pig, with its great stomach sweeping the ground. The pig was killed at Tag-Along's house, and his wife boiled the water for scalding it. Once the water was boiling, it was poured into a huge wooden tub. In return for killing the pig, they'd be giving the blood to Tag-Along. His wife gave the information to Third Aunt and Noodle Fish's wife early on, saying that the water from scalding the pig could cure frostbitten feet and that they should come and wash them; she even told Gourd's wife to come and carry water back for her mother-in-law to wash her feet.

When they walked to Tag-Along's house, Inkcap went too, and Third Aunt asked, "Why didn't your granny come?"

"Gran's feet hurt," Inkcap replied.

"And it's because they hurt that you have to come to wash your feet? All winter, it's impossible to get your feet properly warm… this is a great opportunity."

But Inkcap didn't go to call his grandmother; instead, he played with his *gan'erzi*. His *gan'erzi* was so excited that he kept banging on the copper basin, yelling that he wanted to catch the pig's blood in it.

When the pig was driven to the courtyard entrance, it refused to enter, howling, and two men had to pull the pig inside by the ears. Iron Bolt took up a knife and stood in front of the small table in the courtyard, commanding them to go and wash the two sets of iron hooks, and to bring the scraping stone for getting rid of hair, while he began to roll up his sleeves.

The man pulling the pig shouted, "Iron Bolt, do you know how to kill a pig?"

"I've helped Millstone."

"God in Heaven, you have never so much as held a knife and now you think you're going to kill a pig... do you know where to stab?"

"Course I can kill a pig," Iron Bolt said. "I'll just keep stabbing till I get the right place. All you have to do is hold the pig down and not let go until it's dead."

At this point, someone shouted, "Noisy is coming, Noisy knows how to geld pigs, so let him kill it."

It'd been a long time since Noisy last came to Old Kiln, and he'd turned up at the perfect moment. He parked his heavily laden bike outside the door. He agreed to kill the pig but was not sure about leaving his bike unattended.

"Let Inkcap watch it," Tag-Along's wife suggested.

"No way," Inkcap said. "Even if nothing goes missing, if he says something's been stolen, how can I possibly pay him back? I'll get someone else."

Inkcap called on Flower Girl, and she came as soon as she heard.

"Inkcap's a good picker," Decheng said. "He knows the right person to call."

"What do you mean?" the people from the United Command said.

"That's our business," Decheng replied. Flower Girl arrived and got busy pinning her hair up.

Noisy was very cheerful and put the knife into Iron Bolt's hands, saying, "When you kill a pig, if the knife doesn't hit the right spot, it will run about all over the place and then you can't catch the blood in a basin."

Iron Bolt still didn't want to give the knife back to Noisy, but Tag-Along's wife said, "Give him the knife. If we don't get the blood in the basin, you're going to have to compensate us."

Iron Bolt gave the knife to Noisy and said, "Can you kill a person?"

"Absolutely not," Noisy replied.

"So you only know how to kill a pig, motherfucker!"

Meanwhile, the pig was pulled by five or six people over to a small table and held down on its side. The pig screamed again and again, and the more it screamed the sharper the sound became, until it was like a knife in the ears. Tag-Along's wife pulled their son to the side, but he was still holding the copper basin and insisted on standing in front of the table. Inkcap suddenly felt pity for the pig and covered his ears, and he did not dare look.

"Inkcap, did you bring a fuse?" Iron Bolt asked.

"No," Inkcap replied.

"Then go to the stove and get a burning coal."

"What's wrong with you?"

"Killing a pig is scary."

"What's so scary about killing a pig?" Iron Bolt asked.

Inkcap went to the kitchen to get a burning coal to avoid seeing the pig being butchered. The pig suddenly stopped screaming and the courtyard was quiet for a while, then a voice started shouting, "Lift its legs, lift its legs up!"

When he came out, the pig had been bled, and the blood flowed into the copper basin. His *gan'erzi* was carrying the basin and the blood had splashed all over his face.

"You should salt that," said a man standing next to him. But the child didn't listen and went into the main room and shut the door.

The pig was scalded in the wooden tub, pulled out, pressed down, turned over and then heaved out onto the small table to have the hair rubbed off with a stone, and the hair did indeed come off very easily. The scalding water was soon divided up into pots and buckets, and each carried away their share or warmed their feet in the yard.

Someone said, "Iron Bolt, you weren't allowed to kill the pig, but at least you should warm your feet."

"Why should I?" Iron Bolt asked sulkily.

"Do you wash at all in the winter?"

"I've never washed in my entire life."

"Oh, but you ought to wash at least once," the man responded, and the crowd laughed. Iron Bolt realised he was being teased; if he only washed once, he would be like a pig who deserved butchering! Iron Bolt hit the man on the head with a cigarette packet.

After the pig's hair was removed, the carcass was hooked up by its two hind legs and hung in the branches of the pear tree. Noisy rinsed off the carcass, pouring great scoops of water over and over again, and he held his knife in his mouth, so his speech was no longer clear.

"When killing a pig, it's not the power in the stab that matters," he explained, "it's the positioning." He squinted at Iron Bolt and used the tip of the knife to cut an opening in the pig's leg. Then he inserted an iron tube and blew into it, inflating the pig like a balloon. He then ran his knife down from the pig's hind leg, and as he cut, the intestines fell out and landed in a steaming pile.

Noodle Fish's wife was washing her feet when she saw the pile of intestines, and with an "ah" she stopped washing – in fact she kicked over the basin, so the water went everywhere. Noisy was now gutting the carcass, his knife flashing, and he cut off a finger-length section of white fat and stuffed it into his mouth.

Noisy's movements were very fast, so many people failed to notice what he was doing and asked, "What are you eating?"

"He's eating the fat," Inkcap exclaimed.

"That's right," Noisy said. "It's my perk as the butcher, and it's the only payment I take." He was not wrong, so the others had nothing more to say.

After the pig's body was cut into two and hung from the tree, Noisy began to work on the head. According to Division Chief Ma's instructions, the pig's head and the offal were to be given to the Hammerheads to eat. At this time, Iron Bolt whispered to Noisy that he should cut the head generously, to include the neck, and then Iron Bolt took the head and a basket of offal out of the door. He walked to the courtyard door and came back to say, "You haven't cut the tail."

"Oh," Noisy said. The knife spun around the left half of the carcass and the tail was cut off at the root.

"So the Hammerheads also want the tail, eh?" Noisy picked up the tail and rubbed it against Inkcap's mouth, saying, "You wet the bed!"

It was a custom for those who wet the bed to have a butchered pig's tail rubbed against their mouth so they wouldn't do it again. Inkcap's mouth was rubbed, and it was shining brightly, and he felt his lips were much thicker all of a sudden.

"Rub it a few more times," he said.

Noisy did nothing of the kind. He simply asked, "Who else is still wetting the bed?"

All the children in the yard said they were, so they crowded over with their lips stuck out. One of the boys opened his mouth and bit the pig's tail.

"You're a piece of shit!" said Noisy. He gave a violent tug and pulled the pig's tail out, but with such force that his arm was thrown back, and then the pig's tail was grabbed by Decheng who ran away. No one reacted for a second. But when they realised Decheng had snaffled the pig's tail, a crowd rushed out of the courtyard door to grab it back, but he was already far in the distance.

The pork was going to be cooked in two places: at the kiln, where the good meat was cooked; and the old house, where the Hammerheads concentrated on cooking the pig's head and the offal. Those who were not Hammerheads were very envious, and from envy came anger, and that spawned hatred. They cursed that the meat was going to those who were no better than dogs or wolves, they cursed Awning and Sparks as useless: "They count as revolutionaries and we're the counter-revolutionaries – they get to eat meat and we get to watch them."

Gourd's wife was combing her mother-in-law's hair on the threshold when she smelt the aroma of cooking meat. "That smells good," she said. Gourd's wife regretted that her husband was not a member of the Hammerheads, so she could have brought back some meat for her mother-in-law this time.

Inkcap was still at Tag-Along's house waiting for Third Aunt and Noodle Fish's wife to wash their feet. Third Aunt's feet were even smaller than Gran's, and her toes were nestled together like the leaves on a cabbage, and there was a corn on her heel. She probed it with a needle for ages trying to get it out, and then it bled. Tag-Along's wife asked Inkcap to help her wash the wooden tub and put it away, then shovelled the shit and hair from the pig that had been killed into her pigsty, along with the soil from under the small table.

"If you dump this in the pigsty," he said, "the pig'll be scared."

"You're just lazy," Tag-Along's wife said. "What does a pig know? Is a pig a human being?"

"Pigs are just the same as people," Inkcap told her.

"Don't talk to me like that. Go to work. Later on, I'll fry up some pig's blood so that you and your aunts can have a few bites."

The pig was standing on its hind legs and its front legs were resting on the wall of the pigsty. It had tears in its eyes. Inkcap dumped the dirt outside the wall of the pen and said, "It's nothing to do with you. Go to sleep, for when you're asleep, you won't be afraid."

Third Aunt, Noodle Fish's wife and Once-Upon-A-Time's mother had now warmed their feet, so they poured the water into the cesspit and also helped to rub the shredded radish and cut up the congealed pig's blood. Now they all wanted to go home but Tag-Along's wife said, "It'll be ready immediately, why do you want to leave? You must eat a few mouthfuls."

"Keep it for the kid," they said.

Having left the kitchen, she tried to stop them at the courtyard door, but they still refused to stay. Third Aunt turned her head towards the pigsty and saw that Inkcap had jumped in to scratch the pig.

"Are you coming with us, Inkcap?" Third Aunt asked.

"Let me just say a word to the pig and then I'll go," he replied.

"Are you talking to the pig?"

"He's very clever and can talk to anything," said Noodle Fish's wife.

"But he's talking to pigs!" Third Aunt exclaimed. "Is he really as dumb as a pig?"

"You must not want me to eat pig's blood, and that's why you're trying to make me leave," Inkcap asserted.

"You see!" Noodle Fish's wife said.

"Then you stay," Third Aunt told him. "After all, you are the child's godfather."

Inkcap jumped out of the pigsty and said, "Do you really think I eat everything I'm given? I won't eat it even if you begged me."

The four of them came out and passed by Palace's house. Palace had just come back from the old public office and he took out a packet of dried lotus leaf, opened it, and inside was a piece of meat, freshly cooked and richly flavoursome.

"We got two pieces each," said Palace, "so I ate one and brought this back for you and the kid."

His son grabbed the meat and stuffed it in his mouth.

"Why don't you give your mother some?" Palace said. The kid took the meat out of his mouth and bit half of it off for himself, giving the other half to his mother.

She tried to chew it but couldn't bite through, saying, "Why is it so tough?"

"It's from a sow," Palace told her, "so you'll have to chew it well." Then, seeing Third Aunt and the others approach, Palace took his wife and child back into the yard.

In the space of ten days after the United Command and Hammerheads killed the pig, two more half-carcasses were brought in, and the pork was stamped with several red seals, so everyone knew that the meat came from the town meat association. As to how it was procured, they did not care. The meat was chopped up and wrapped into dumplings at the kiln, and the United Command faction and the Hammerheads all had a beautiful meal.

After eating the dumplings, the Hammerheads were sleepy, but they also felt itchy here and there, so they sat twisting and turning to scratch themselves. There was a red bump on the centre of Bash's foot, and it bled when he took off his shoes and scratched it.

Looking at his foot, someone said, "I heard Useless say you have a mole on your foot?"

"It's a sign," Useless said. "A mole of your foot means you can lead a thousand soldiers."

"See for yourself," Bash said.

Everyone went over and saw that there was indeed a mole on his foot. "There it is, he was born to be our leader!"

"At the moment, there's only a few of us," Useless remarked, "but in the future, when Luozhen sets up a revolutionary committee…"

Useless did not finish his sentence. Someone pushed him away because they didn't care about revolutionary committees.

"Since you're the boss," they said to Bash, "will you talk to Division Chief Ma and get the Hammerheads permission to eat at the kiln?"

"Do you think they eat well?" Bash asked.

"For sure they do," they replied.

"If you want to eat well, you have to make sure that Old Kiln is completely purged of United Headquarters members, and Luozhen too."

"That's no problem," they assured him. "As long as we can eat well, you tell us what to do and we'll do it. Let Awning, Sparks and Millstone die far from home!"

As soon as they said this, they realised there was a problem. If Awning, Sparks and Millstone died far from home, and if the United Headquarters was expelled from Old Kiln and Luozhen, there would be no more Cultural Revolution, and without the Cultural Revolution, everything would be the same as before. Once the United Command people packed up and left, where else could they get rice and wheat flour and pork? They whispered among themselves that it was best if Awning, Sparks and Millstone stayed hale and hearty somewhere else, and the United Headquarters continued to flourish, because if they tried to come back, the Hammerheads would stop them, but the United Command folk would have to stay at the kiln, dispensing white rice and flour and meat to their supporters.

The Hammerheads wanted to be able to eat at the kiln, and Bash conveyed this message to Division Chief Ma. She promised to consider it and also agreed to go to the town grain store and the credit union to borrow more food and money in the future. As things stood, food and money were still readily obtainable, so only one problem remained: firewood. Until now, it was very difficult for the United Command people up at the kiln to get fuel to burn. If they had to go to the Xichuan mine to buy coal, it was troublesome and expensive. First, Hammerheads' households carried some kindling up for them; then they'd burned the wheat straw from the homes of Awning, Sparks, Millstone, Lightkeeper and Pockmark, but there was still a shortage. Bash suggested they cut the branches of the trees on the riverbank. But Division Chief Ma disagreed, saying that instead of going to the riverbank to cut some branches, they should cut them on the nearby mountain. He said there were no trees on the nearby mountain, and the acacia trees were too small to cut up for much kindling. Division Chief Ma said there was a tree on the top of the mountain which, if felled, would provide loads of firewood. Bash never imagined that Division Chief Ma would want to cut down the white pine, so he smoothly said that it would be impossible. It was not easy to grow such big a tree out in the mountains, and it was right on the top of the mountain – a rare white pine, which was a sacred feng shui tree for Old Kiln.

"Why do you still care about a tree with everything else that's going on?" Division Chief Ma asked. "What's so special about a tree? It's been growing for hundreds of years, and it's just waiting for us to cut it down. It'll contribute to the Cultural Revolution, that's its glory! And what feng shui? If it really was a feng shui tree, would Old Kiln be so poor? How many leaders has your village produced? I'm not joking – you've got a branch secretary, but then every village has a branch secretary. Not only are there no Communist Party big shots from around here, look at the landlords! Lightkeeper's considered a big landlord, but in other places, he'd be squit."

"That's true," Bash said, "but if I cause trouble in Old Kiln by cutting down the white pine, I'll be cursed in the future."

"With your ambition," Division Chief Ma said, "do you think you'll still be spending much time in this hellhole in the future? Can't you just move to Luozhen, or to the county town, or the provincial capital? I really misjudged you… it turns out you're just some small-time guy!"

Bash's face went red, and then white, before he responded, "Then you must promise to promote me."

"If I wasn't looking to promote you," Division Chief Ma said, "I would have left Old Kiln long ago."

"Well, in that case, I'll cut down the white pine."

Baldy Jin led the group going to cut down the white pine. Goodman hugged the trunk and told them not to. Naturally, he was dragged off. The trunk was so thick, however, that they couldn't saw through it; and when they took an axe to it, the tree was hard as stone. The axe could only chip out a small piece at a time. Accordingly, after more than a week of work, they still hadn't felled it. Baldy Jin explained the situation to Division Chief Ma, and she wrote him a chit and told him to take it to town and ask the United Command there for explosives. The next day, he brought back the explosives: half of them were reserved, and half were used to blow up the tree.

Baldy Jin made seven holes in the tree, which all oozed sap, red and sticky, with a pungent smell. After Baldy Jin left, Goodman boiled some millet porridge and smeared the cuts with porridge mixed with mud. The trunk was the thickness of two arm spans, and usually when you kicked it, it did not move at all. When Goodman slapped on his paste and smoothed it flat, the tree shook suddenly, and pine needles fell to the ground. Goodman only said that he was protecting the white pine. The next morning, he was still asleep when Baldy Jin came again. This time, Baldy Jin dug a deep hole under the roots of the tree and buried explosives there. Saying he was going to blow up the white pine, he asked Goodman to leave the

Mountain God Temple and go and take shelter down by the kiln. Goodman hugged the tree and refused to go anywhere. He talked to Baldy Jin and the others about karma – though he didn't say where the scars on Baldy Jin's head came from, nor did he say why his eyes hurt or how to cure them. He just talked about himself, and how his family had been too poor to send him to school, and he'd worked herding cattle instead.

Then, when he was twenty-three years old, he'd heard a lecture on goodness by Yang Bohe, a great scholar, and repented of his sins because he realised that the virtuous man fought sin and the foolish man fought reason. After a painful session of repenting, a wound that he'd had on his body for twelve years healed overnight. In May of the same year, overcome by the feeling of horror at the times we live in when men are so disloyal and women are so dishonest, he went on hunger strike for five days. He was suddenly inspired by the idea that he should not die in vain and that he ought first to do his best to teach others, and then he set his mind to persuade people to change. In October of the same year, Yang Bohe was wrongly imprisoned. He followed the ancient principle that it was worth saving someone else's life even at the risk of your own and vowed to rescue him. Then, in the middle of the night, a strange light appeared illuminating everything as bright as day, and he was enlightened and knew what he should do. At the age of thirty-two, in October, he entered a temple and learned that the world of commerce is rooted in sin and that interdependence merely leads to mutual enmity. Therefore, he advocated the idea of saving money to establish a business rather than borrowing, hoping thereby to benefit people.

When establishing your career, you should be rooted in virtue. A woman's role is to help her husband without tiring him, and a man's role is to lead his wife. Each should be independent and joined by mutual respect. In a world where everyone is fighting against poverty, Heaven is not considered; in a world where people learn to give way to each other, Heaven has its proper place. He wanted people to recover their innate nature, to call on those with a pure heart, for they would have firm principles and a deep understanding, and they would place Heaven first. A world fixated on prosperity is intrinsically unhealthy; a world of common wealth is truly well.

When he left the temple, he used the vernacular to explain human ethics, to corroborate scriptures, to enlighten the mediocre and the stupid, and to transform the wise. As he became further enlightened and was recovering from longstanding illnesses, he started using this same method to cure the sick.

Goodman spoke until his mouth was dry, while Baldy Jin continued to dig his hole.

"Goodness me it's annoying, all this wailing and moaning," said Baldy Jin.

"I'm telling you about my life," Goodman said.

"Writing your own epitaph, are you?"

"You have to listen to me. I beg you, stop digging that hole and listen."

"Schoolteachers are all fools," Baldy Jin said, "and you're even dumber than they are! The Cultural Revolution has come this far and you're still preaching your feudal ideas. You really are the filial descendent of that stubborn git Confucius."

"I'm no Confucius or Mencius," Goodman said, "nor am I a Buddha, but I have practised human values and gained the way of Heaven."

"Well, well, you have much to say to me, but I don't understand, nor do I care to listen. If Useless were here, or Division Chief Ma and Bash, wouldn't you be in for another struggle session? Get up, get up, don't make me angry. I've already put up with enough from you."

"I will not get up. If you want to blow up the tree, you can blow up me too."

"Who do you think you are?" Baldy Jin demanded. "Do you really think we wouldn't dare blow you up? Just think how many people have already died in Old Kiln. Get up."

"I won't."

Baldy Jin got irate and pulled Goodman up and threw him to the side, but Goodman lunged again and fell headfirst into the pit.

"You've brought this on yourself," Baldy Jin said.

When the digger saw that Goodman had fallen, he refused to dig any more and went to pull him out, but he did not move. "He's fainted," the man said.

"Try his nose," Baldy Jin said. "Is he still breathing?"

"He is still breathing," the man in the pit said.

"Carry him out to the back of the cliff," Baldy Jin instructed him, "and as soon as the pit is ready, put the explosives in."

The explosives were put in, the fuse was lit, and everyone ran to the back of the cliff. After a loud boom, dust covered half the sky, but the white pine still seemed to be standing amid the smoke, and the four red-billed, white-tailed birds on the tree called with a sound as sharp as a knife.

Goodman woke up at the sound of the explosion, opened his eyes and shouted, "Baldy Jin, Baldy Jin!"

Baldy Jin looked up and said, "Why didn't it fall?" When he was about to stand up, the white pine issued a series of hissing crunches, then shook violently for a short space of time, before slowly falling to one side. When it fell, another cloud of dust rose up, covering half the sky, and bark, grass, lumps of snow and ice, and clods of earth all fell like rain on the people at the back of the cliff. Goodman sighed, his eyes closed, and he passed out again.

With the white pine no longer standing on top of the mountain, people passing the barricade on their way along the highway all asked, "Where is this?" And the answer was, "Old Kiln." Those who had never been to the village asked, "Isn't there a single white pine on the mountain right by Old Kiln?" People who'd been to Old Kiln before were accustomed to seeing the pagoda, and that was still there, and then they'd look farther up the mountain, where the white pine no longer stood and ask in a puzzled voice, "Is this Old Kiln? How come I can't see the white pine?" The men on the roadblock would get impatient and say, "There's nothing more, be on your way."

After the white pine was blown up, the wood was still tremendously hard, so saws could not cut it, nor axes split it. Baldy Jin used explosives to blow it into several pieces, and the branches then separated from the trunk. They dragged the tree in sections to the kiln to burn. The villagers could not get so much as a single piece of firewood out of it, so many of them took their hoes and went up the mountain to dig out the roots of the white pine. The roots were as long and winding as the body of a dragon, and if you could take possession of a whole root, that would give you a basket of kindling. Several dozen families were out that day digging up the roots, while Inkcap and Cowbell carried baskets, hoes and axes up the mountain.

On arriving at the scene, they first went to see Goodman. He was fast asleep on the bed at the Mountain God Temple, his body swollen and his gaze dull. He looked terrible and scared Inkcap and Cowbell into asking, "Are you OK?"

"I don't feel well at all," Goodman told them.

This made Inkcap and Cowbell feel helpless. All they could do was offer Goodman some food and drink. "Have you had something to eat?" they asked. "Tell us what you want, and we'll cook it."

Goodman shook his head.

"What about something to drink?"

Goodman still shook his head.

Inkcap put his hand under the blankets, and they were stone cold. "Let me warm the bed for you," he said.

The two of them went out and grabbed some stalks of maize. Not far from the heap of stalks was the huge hole created by the explosion. Some locals were digging out roots from the earth bank in front of that vast pit, and one after another, people came up with baskets and hoes and joined the queue waiting to dig. All of a sudden, crowds had gathered, and axes were swinging, everyone was cheerful, as if they were getting something for nothing. They were vying with each other to get the lion's share, and the atmosphere was one of happy confusion.

When they took the stalks back to light the fire, Goodman asked, "What's all the commotion outside?"

"They're digging up tree roots," Inkcap explained.

"The Hammerheads are even digging up the roots?"

"It's not the Hammerheads. The villagers are digging firewood for themselves."

Goodman did not say anything but opened his eyes and looked up at the temple beam. After that, he did not close his eyes again.

Inkcap told Cowbell to close the door. Once it was closed, the noise from outside was much reduced, but Goodman was still staring at the beam.

Inkcap also looked at the beam but there was nothing there. "What are you looking at?" he asked.

Goodman did not make a sound, but his eyes were still open.

"Your eyes must be tired," Inkcap said. "Sleep well." He smoothed Goodman's eyes shut with his hand, and his eyelids closed, but his hand was wet with tears.

The two of them came out of the temple, and Inkcap said, "He hasn't eaten or drunk anything. Let's make him some food."

"If he doesn't want to eat, why cook for him?" Cowbell said. "If we cook, people will think we want to eat it ourselves."

"We ought to get him some water. The reason he's not eating or drinking is because there's no water in the bucket."

"If you want to carry water for him, off you go," said Cowbell. "I'll be digging for roots."

Inkcap was furious with Cowbell. He went to the ditch alone to get water, and when he couldn't carry two buckets of water, he carried two half-buckets. On reaching the crest of the hill, he saw that Barndoor had slapped Cowbell, who was whimpering and crying, and Barndoor was still scolding him: "You cry, I'll give you something to cry about!" Cowbell did not dare cry any more, and all the people digging roots stopped talking, and some packed up the roots they'd dug up and went down the mountain with their backpacks.

Barndoor had also come up the mountain to see Goodman. When he arrived at the bank, the root-digging activity had opened up the whole hillside. Some men had excavated large roots and were chopping them with an axe while urging their wives to dig further and further down. One man who had unearthed only small roots looked enviously at the next person along, saying, "Did you get a good 'un?"

The man next to him said, "Yeah. This single root is enough to spare me two trips to South Mountain to cut firewood." Then he called out, "Barndoor, why don't you come and dig?"

"Nah," Barndoor said.

"How much firewood do you have at your house, then?"

"Even if I have to eat raw food, I won't dig."

"What are you talking about, Barndoor?" someone else said. "It's not like we're digging up the graves of our ancestors!"

"This is Old Kiln's feng shui tree, how can you destroy it like this?"

"Did I blow up this tree?" the man asked irritably. "Did I blow it up? How could I have destroyed it?" He pointed at the man next to him and said, "Did you blow it up?"

"No, I never touched the tree."

Then he asked another man, with the same response. He asked seven or eight people in a row, and all of them declared it was nothing to do with them. He finally raised his voice and said, "Who blew it up, then? Who's responsible?"

"OK, fine," said Barndoor. "It's nothing to do with any of you. The feng shui tree just happened to lose all its roots."

At this time, Cowbell was busy in an argument. Cowbell had found a root, which had branched into two. Someone else came over with a hoe and started digging, and Cowbell tried to stop them. He said that one of the roots was his and the other was Inkcap's. The two of them were arguing and pushing each other, so Barndoor, who had nowhere else to vent his anger, went over and slapped Cowbell.

"What the fuck are you fighting over?" Barndoor said. "Are you really going to die if you don't get this root?"

With all this cursing, the person trying to claim the root felt embarrassed and took his hoe somewhere else. Cowbell was left snuffling and feeling put upon.

Barndoor wasn't a Hammerhead and neither was he a Red Blade, so few in the village were afraid of him, but he instilled fear in Inkcap by always scolding him when ploughing. When he saw Barndoor hit Cowbell, Inkcap did not dare speak, but carried the water into the temple, asking Goodman what he wanted to eat. He'd carried water back so he could make him anything. Goodman still said he did not want to eat, so he just boiled some water for him. The water was not yet boiling when Barndoor came in, helped Goodman turn over and rubbed his back. Inkcap scooped up half a basin of warm water, wet a hand towel and gave it to Barndoor so Goodman could wipe his face.

"You aren't out digging up tree roots?" Barndoor said.

"I came to dig," Inkcap said, "but Goodman had run out of water, so I went to fetch some."

Barndoor didn't say anything else, and when he got back to the kitchen the water was boiling, so he brought a bowl over. "Go and rest," Barndoor said. "I'll make sure he drinks this." Inkcap went out.

As soon as Inkcap went out, Cowbell called to him.

"You're still digging?" Inkcap said in amazement. "You've been slapped like that and you're still digging?"

"If I don't dig, I'll have been slapped for nothing," Cowbell pointed out. "I was beaten to get a root from this tree for you, and you're not helping?"

"Then won't I be part of the destruction?"

"If you don't want it, then when I've got a basket of firewood, you're not to be jealous."

How could Inkcap not be jealous? To get kindling to burn, he and Gran had to cut weeds and gather leaves every day, or dig up wild jujube thorns, so how could he not prefer digging out a root? He set to work, but he kept his head down because when Barndoor came out of the temple he didn't want him to see. The bifurcated root that he'd been allocated was about as thick as his arm, but as he dug, it got fatter, and it twisted and turned through the bank for many yards. It was all very odd, and everyone else remarked on it, saying, "Fuck me, he's been lucky!"

EIGHTY-THREE

THE CURVED ROOT OF THE TREE, dug out and split, filled his backpack, no more no less. Inkcap carried it home to split it into even smaller pieces in the yard. Gran told him to take a rest, but he didn't – he cut the whole lot up in one go and stacked it on the steps neatly. He was almost in a trance thinking about how the white pine had branches spiralling through the air like a coiled dragon, and its roots had curled this way and that through the earth... again, somewhat like a dragon. How could he and Cowbell have dug up and split a dragon? Suddenly, he felt that the light around him had dimmed, and when he looked up, Gourd's wife and Ever-Obedient were standing by the door.

Gourd's wife was pushing Ever-Obedient, saying, "Go, go away!" But Ever-Obedient looked at Gourd's wife pitifully, like a child, and refused to move.

Inkcap was puzzled and came out of the courtyard, but then he smelt that horrible smell. His heart gave a lurch, and he rubbed the end of his nose vigorously, at which the smell seemed to dissipate. Ever-Obedient was looking dishevelled, his big body hunched over. He had a nasty bruise on the forehead and was carrying two shoes in his hands. These were Yoyo's shoes, with flowers embroidered on the toe, suspended from a string.

"Go home," Gourd's wife said.

"The river's flooded," Ever-Obedient said, "and Yoyo was sitting in among the haystacks–"

"Yoyo's fine," Gourd's wife said. "She's at home, and you'll see her when you get back."

She gave him a push and he set off walking towards the entrance of the alleyway, and the sun shone there like an open rose, bathing Ever-Obedient in a reddish light. Gourd's wife told Inkcap that Yoyo had disappeared, and this time they couldn't find her anywhere. Ever-Obedient seemed to have an inkling of this, but he'd gone insane thinking that he'd never see Yoyo again. It was the custom in Old Kiln that if someone got lost, that person's shoes should be hung over the well, and they'd return in three days. But there was no longer a well in Old Kiln, only the spring, so Ever-Obedient tied Yoyo's shoes together with a rope and hung them on the edge of the spring. He had just got them up when people from the kiln went to the spring to fetch water and shouted at him for dirtying the spring, and Ever-Obedient had shouted back. Then they'd started fighting, which is why he had the bruise on his forehead.

As Gourd's wife said this, Gran was sitting in the courtyard on the laundry stone making papercuts. She looked as if she did not hear a word and was just concentrating on her cutting. Inkcap didn't want Gourd's wife to say another word because he didn't want Gran to hear.

"Is Granny Silkworm still deaf?" Gourd's wife asked.

Inkcap nodded and said, "There's something I want to say, though... you ought to be keeping an eye on him."

"Keep an eye on Ever-Obedient? No thank you, getting him home was bad enough."

"I meant you ought to keep an eye on Goodman."

"What's up with Goodman?"

Inkcap explained that he was so sick he couldn't even get out of bed. "He's been real good to you and your family, or so I've always heard."

"Well, I'll pop up and have a look," Gourd's wife said. "My mother-in-law hasn't been sleeping at all well the last few days, and I'd like to know what he suggests." The two of them agreed that after lunch Gourd's wife would call Inkcap and they'd go up the mountain to visit Goodman together.

After lunch, Inkcap waited at home for Gourd's wife, but when she didn't come, he got irritated and wanted to go and shout at her. However, the lane outside was in uproar, many United Command people and Hammerheads ran past, and there were a lot of chickens flying and dogs biting. As soon as Inkcap came out, he was pressed back against the wall, and when he asked what was going on, nobody was willing to answer. The procession had already passed before Gourd's wife came, her hair combed and shining, carrying a pint pot in her hand.

"You're going to see a sick man, so why are you all dressed up like this?" Inkcap asked.

"How can I go out with my hair like a chicken's nest? Goodman likes to see people looking nice. Why, have you been waiting long?"

"Just look at the time!"

"I was just getting a half pint of flour for Goodman when they started searching for someone down my lane – I couldn't possibly leave," Gourd's wife explained.

"Who were they looking for?"

"Another person's run off from the political training class. I heard they got into Sprout's house, and she arrested them."

"After all that's happened, someone still tried to run away?" Inkcap asked in amazement.

"What's become of Old Kiln?" Gourd's wife sighed. "It's like a prison–"

"You've got something in your teeth," Inkcap hissed.

Gourd's wife quickly covered her mouth to pick out whatever it was; but in fact, there was nothing on her teeth.

Then Inkcap whispered, "Bash is over there."

Bash was standing under a tree diagonally across the street, not wearing the yellow military coat, but a blue Mao suit, and he was talking to Flower Girl.

"Let's go through the back alley," Inkcap suggested.

"But that's all overgrown with weeds," Gourd's wife protested. "We'll go this way."

Inkcap braced himself. He didn't look directly at Bash, but nevertheless he saw everything, and he thought to himself, Didn't Bash only have a yellow army coat and a backless red sweater? Where did he get a new suit?

Bash had his back to them the whole time he was talking to Flower Girl. Inkcap attempted to walk past quietly, but the talkative Flower Girl greeted Gourd's wife, saying, "Ooh, you've got your hair dolled up, where are you off to?"

"Um," Gourd's wife said, "I thought you were going to the kiln to cook?"

Bash turned around, noticed Inkcap and asked, "What are you doing?"

"Nothing," Inkcap replied.

"All right, then you can come with me... We're going to Flower Girl's place."

Inkcap was furious with himself for saying the wrong thing, hesitated and did not make a sound.

"You're refusing?"

Inkcap looked at Gourd's wife and whispered, "You go first, I'll come later."

As Inkcap walked across, Bash patted him on the head, saying, "I am happy to have you accompany me today."

In the courtyard of her house, Flower Girl went inside to root around in a box, while Bash said to Inkcap, "What do you think of my suit?"

"Whose is it?" Inkcap asked.

"What the fuck do you mean? These are my clothes... how do they look?"

"Good," Inkcap said.

"Good? Have you ever seen anyone in Old Kiln wearing something like this, or indeed anyone from the County United Command? And all you can say is that it looks good?"

"I simply can't find a button of the right colour," Flower Girl said in a loud voice from inside the house.

"Hasn't Noisy been past lately?" Bash asked.

"I bought buttons for jackets, but nothing right for your suit," Flower Girl explained.

"Lightkeeper used to wear a second-hand suit that he'd got from his brother-in-law. If he were still around, I could get a button off him, but the fucker's not here any more."

Inkcap noticed that the lowest button on his suit was missing. "Did Division Chief Ma buy this for you?" he asked.

"Do you think it's a little long?" said Bash, ignoring Inkcap.

Flower Girl came out of the house, still unable to find a suitable button. "Oh no," she said, "it's not too long. Look, I'll take off the collar button and use it to replace the one you're missing. Nobody ever uses the collar button."

"But the collar button is important," Bash said. "Have you ever seen a leader on a podium where the collar wasn't buttoned nicely? That's the kind of thing they care about."

"You aren't going to be up on any podium, so why do you need the collar buttoned tight enough to strangle you?"

"How do you know I'm not going to be up on the podium? If I weren't going to be on a podium, why would I be wearing this suit?" Flower Girl's eyes widened, and Bash continued, "You don't believe me... well just you wait and see. Carry on looking. If you can't match the colour it will have to do, I have to have a button. Then when Noisy comes back, tell him to get the proper thing for me."

Flower Girl turned around and went back inside, and Inkcap asked, "Are you going to be a leader?"

"I'm off to a good start," Bash said proudly.

893

Inkcap turned around and ran off, saying, "I need to go and talk to Apricot."

Inkcap didn't like the idea that Division Chief Ma had bought the suit for Bash. However, the reason why he said he wanted to talk to Apricot was first to remind Bash that she was pregnant with his baby, so it wasn't right to be wearing clothes that Ma Zhuo had got for him, and second, he wanted to get out of there as fast as possible and go up the mountain to see Goodman.

Bash grabbed Inkcap's ear and said, "Where do you think you're going?"

"If you're going to be a leader, why shouldn't I tell the good news to Apricot?"

"There's no need."

That put a stopper on Inkcap's plan, so he changed the subject. "Did you hear, someone's run away from the political training class? What are you doing here having a button sewn on?"

"I've already sent out a search party," Bash said. "You're not to run off. Once the button's fixed, we're going to the south entrance of the village to see the stonemason."

There was no stonemason in the Old Kiln, so Inkcap couldn't figure out how there could be one at the south entrance of the village... what could he possibly be doing there? Since Bash was in a really good mood and wanted Inkcap to follow him around, Inkcap had no choice. When Flower Girl had affixed a blue button, he followed Bash with a pouting face, looking for all the world as if Bash were dragging along a disobedient dog.

As they walked, someone complimented Bash on his suit: "Wow, is that an official uniform?"

He laughed and replied, "Not yet."

"Not yet," the man said. "Oh, we're really going to have an official in Old Kiln!"

Inkcap looked up at the birds in the air and said to himself, "Just shit in these people's mouths."

Bird shit did indeed fall down, but instead of landing in anyone's mouth, it landed on the back of Bash's shoulder. The others didn't see it, but Inkcap did, and he went to pat it, not patting it but wiping it so that the bird shit made a white mark.

"Don't touch my clothes," Bash said.

"Fine, I won't," Inkcap replied.

"Goodness me, you're grumpy. How about a sunny smile instead?"

Inkcap looked at the back of his suit and laughed.

At the southern entrance of the village, they encountered Useless and several stonemasons from Xichuan. They'd removed the original stone lion and rolled it down the slope, and brought in a new stone and were busy chiselling a new lion. The stonemasons explained that the lion would be sitting on its haunches with its front legs straight, to show its power and forcefulness, and it was Useless's idea that it should have a human face. He wanted it to look like Bash, so they asked him to stand there as a live model. Bash obeyed orders and stood there.

"Look at us!" they cried.

"No, don't," Useless said. "You should be staring off into the distance. Look at South Mountain. That's right… those destined to achieve great things set their sights far ahead."

Division Chief Ma and Glob came over from the barricade on the highway, and they were still under the slope when she started shouting at Bash as if she was very angry, and Bash went down the slope towards her.

"Who told you to wear these clothes now?" Division Chief Ma demanded,

"I was just trying them on," said Bash.

"The revolutionary committee has not yet been established, and you've already got these clothes all messed up." Division Chief Ma screamed. "What? What happened to the button?"

"One button fell off, so I put a new one on and the colour's a little different, that's all."

"How did it fall off?"

"Maybe it was missing one button when you bought it?" Inkcap suggested.

"Shut up," Bash said. "What are you doing here anyway?"

"You wanted me to follow you."

"You dropped it?" said Division Chief Ma. "I know exactly where you went in these clothes, and I know how this button fell off."

"Well… um… I was just trying to annoy her–"

"Don't bother," Division Chief Ma said. "I can tell you, if you want to keep on wearing this suit forever, you know what to do."

"I know," Bash said, and he started unbuttoning and taking off his suit.

"It's so damn cold," Inkcap said. "Do you want to get sick?"

"Go away," Bash snarled.

Inkcap walked three steps and then turned back. "You really don't want me to come with you?" he said.

"Piss off."

Despite the scolding, Inkcap felt particularly happy. He had finally got to see Bash so openly being taken to task by Division Chief Ma. He trotted all the way up to the mountain wondering about what she'd said: how had the buttons fallen off his Mao suit? He ran to the Mountain God Temple still unable to figure out what she meant, and then the snow started falling again.

In the Mountain God Temple, Gourd's wife had already made a soup for Goodman, and it seemed like he was now well enough to get out of bed – having already moved the kindling he'd been splitting inside. It now stood in a large pile next to the *kang*. Goodman's colour was a concern; his face was white with patches of black and blue. He was holding the firewood, but he couldn't hold it tightly and a few pieces dropped. He hobbled in and put down the firewood, so tired that beads of sweat were standing out all over his face. He gripped the edge of the bed trying to catch his breath.

"Don't move," Gourd's wife said. "I'll shift the wood for you. I want you to eat the soup while it's hot."

"Alas, I am a burden to you all," Goodman said. "I won't move... and I see Inkcap has arrived too. You and Inkcap can go and get the rest for me."

Inkcap didn't understand why he needed to move all this firewood. That was the wood the United Command got by blowing up the tree. Was it likely they'd let him burn it in his *kang*?

"Why are you moving it in here?" Inkcap asked.

"Do you not see the snow?" Goodman said.

"If it snows, it snows. Are you worried about the wood getting wet?"

"If it's left outside, it will get taken."

"Let them have it all."

Goodman tutted and climbed onto the bed to eat his soup. But after he had only eaten half a bowl, his chopsticks were laid on top, and he put the bowl down.

"Uncle, does it not taste good?" Gourd's wife asked anxiously.

"It tastes just fine," Goodman said, "but I'm full. Give me a pillow."

Gourd's wife put the pillow behind Goodman's back. His face was pale and greenish, and his breathing uneven.

"Alas, it's just too cold up here," Gourd's wife said. "I wish you'd come and live in my house, at least you'd get a hot meal three times a day."

"It's all right here," Goodman told her. "You can go back."

"We'll stay with you for a while."

Inkcap tidied the room, putting the stools and mats straight, heaping the baskets up in the corner, and hanging Goodman's raincoat and hat up on the wall. Then he swept the floor and wiped the dust from the top of the cupboard. There was a heap of things lying on the end of the bed, a great teetering pile, and at the bottom were two books. The books were very thick, and the four corners were frayed, for they'd been bound in cloth. Inkcap flicked through the books, and they were full of words, but they all looked really strange.

"Inkcap... you're holding that book upside down," Goodman told him.

"Is this the book where you get all those words you use when treating the sick?" Inkcap asked.

Goodman nodded

"They all come from this book, so no wonder I don't understand them–"

"I'll give it to you," Goodman said.

"I can't read, so you'd better give it to her."

"I can't read either," Gourd's wife pointed out.

"You can't read, but Gourd can."

"He can only read a few words," his wife said.

"Take one book each," Goodman suggested. "You may not be able to read, but the words will still be there. Inkcap, you're still young. You need to learn to read."

"I told Gran that. Next year, I have to go to school."

"Even if you go to school, you'll never make a scholar," Gourd's wife said.

"How do you know?" Inkcap retorted. "I want to learn, and I'm certainly going to be a better scholar than Useless."

"You can't tell anything from what people look like," Goodman said. "Those who say little shouldn't be despised, and neither should the simple and stupid. People born under an unlucky star are especially not to be despised."

"What's an unlucky star?" asked Inkcap.

"You don't even know what an unlucky star is?" Gourd's wife exclaimed. "How to explain... Well, it's people like you."

Inkcap wasn't entirely sure why he qualified as being born under an unlucky star. Was it his background? Or because he didn't have parents and was being brought up by his grandmother?

"Let's not talk about that," Goodman said. "Take the book home and store it well. In the future when you're able to read, this book will last you a lifetime."

Inkcap took a book and so did Gourd's wife. Goodman started panting again, and Inkcap gave him a pounding on the back, so his breathing gradually eased.

"Stop thumping, Inkcap," Goodman said. "Go and eat the rest of that bowlful."

Inkcap felt embarrassed, but Gourd's wife encouraged him. Inkcap ate the leftovers, and they were absolutely delicious. He was making a lot of noise about it, so Goodman opened an eye and said, "Slow down, Inkcap, eat nicely. When you've finished, you can go back home with your auntie... I'm tired and would like to sleep."

Before they left, Gourd's wife tucked in the corners of Goodman's quilt and said, "Then you rest, let's go."

"You must grow up quickly, Inkcap," Goodman said. "Your gran is depending on you."

"I can look after Gran," Inkcap assured him.

"Many people in the village depend on you."

"Really?" Inkcap said in amazement.

"Oh yes. There's the Branch Secretary, and Apricot, and Apricot's son."

This seemed very peculiar indeed to Inkcap. "What, me?"

But Goodman now turned to Gourd's wife and said, "When you get back to the village, you should wash your mother-in-law's feet every evening – it's not right that she can't sleep at night."

The eyes of Gourd's wife suddenly filled with tears, and she said, "You've got to get well. Old Kiln needs you."

Goodman smiled a little, put his hand up and said, "Ah, I will leave my heart to you."

Gourd's wife and Inkcap left and closed the wattle fence door after themselves. Inkcap looked around in the hope of seeing the four red-billed, white-tailed birds, but the sky was dark, there was no sign of the birds, and the snow was falling everywhere.

It was on this evening and into the night that the snow fell so that the entire village was covered. The tiles on the roofs were invisible, the tree branches thickened, and the walls of all the privies, pigsties and even the walls of the houses looked weighed down. The bell rope did not hang down from the tree in front of Millstone's house for his wife had tied it diagonally to another branch, and it was swollen like a wine goblet. Two dogs, then three dogs, then another group of two or three dogs walked through the alley, all with their heads down and not saying a word. White dogs did not look white against the snow, while black dogs looked even blacker.

The snow continued to fall heavily. No one could have imagined there could be so much snow in the sky, and that it had decided to bury Old Kiln. Only the spring under the embankment was too big to be covered, and it continued to bubble out into the quiet night.

EIGHTY-FOUR

WHEN INKCAP GOT HOME, he didn't mention Goodman up on the mountain to his grandmother. She was cross, as usual, because it was snowing, and he'd come back so late. When she complained, Inkcap was stubborn, but his voice was too low for her to hear, so his complaints were just to himself. After eating, feeding the pigs, firing up the *kang* and bringing the piss bucket back from the privy and putting it by the bed, he waited for Gran to start making papercuts on the bed, while he sat on the threshold of the main room and watched the snow fall outside. Gran was complaining about something, but he ignored her for the moment. She picked up the scissors and started clipping,

"What's up?" said Inkcap in a raised voice.

"You're not going out again, are you?" Gran said.

"The snow is so heavy, where can I go?"

Gran didn't believe him, so Inkcap took a rope, tied it to her waist and tied the other end to his leg. "Satisfied now?"

Inkcap sat back on the threshold, and after a short while, Gran resumed work on her papercuts and Inkcap concentrated on watching the snow. Grandmother forgot grandson, and grandson forgot grandmother; indeed, they even forgot themselves. What was that cat yowling for? Why would a tomcat be out yowling on such a cold night? Besides, a cat wouldn't sound so joyful – it was more like the howl of a hungry baby. Maybe it was out by the entrance of the alley, or perhaps further away from it, under the rubber tree, where someone was talking.

"Where are you going, Ever-Obedient?" said the voice.

"I'm looking for Yoyo," he replied.

They were saying something more, but nothing could be heard. Their feet were silent on the snow, and their words were silenced by the snow. What is snow to the sky? Inkcap wondered. Is it like skin flaking off, or the clouds falling? If the snow continued to fall like this, would it fill the yard overnight and block the doors? So, tomorrow morning, of course, Gran would get up first and open the door to take the piss bucket out, and once the door was opened, outside would be a wall of snow. Gran would definitely call on him: Inkcap, get up, how can we get out? The snow is going to cover us all! He thought it would be funny, and if they were going to be covered by snow, so be it. It would be better to die in the clean white snow than to be buried in the dirty, wet soil. Of course, he said this on purpose, and Gran would then reply: Don't say anything so unlucky. He stopped talking and at the same time felt suffocated and his breathing got a little strained. Gran started to call for help, but nobody could hear. He then came up with a brilliant idea and started to boil the pot, not adding water, but heating it so that it became red. He then walked along holding the pot in front of him, and the snow immediately melted to create a hole so that he and Gran could get out.

Just thinking about it pleased Inkcap, and he imagined that when he and Gran emerged from the hole in the snow, the whole village would be buried deep, and he could faintly hear each family calling for help under the snow. They were all talking about him and calling, "Inkcap, help me! Inkcap, help me!"

Suddenly the ground rattled, and Inkcap's thoughts were interrupted. He was wide awake in an instant – awake to the fact that he was sitting on the threshold, and his arms and legs were stiff, and then he saw that something had been thrown in over the courtyard wall. The snow had gradually piled up high on top of the courtyard wall, just like when Third Aunt loaned flour to Noodle Fish's wife she'd sprinkle a little bit at a time with her hands. The thing that had been thrown into the courtyard lay black against the snow, not moving, so it was not a living thing. Inkcap was scared and rushed back into the house, where Gran was still making papercuts under the lamp. She had found a ball of red paper out by the riverbank earlier in the day, probably because the wind had scraped some notice off the wall of the shack out near the roadblock. Having ironed it flat she was busy clipping, and fragments of paper covered the bed, like bright red flowers.

Inkcap told Gran that he thought there was someone outside the courtyard door, but she did not hear, so Inkcap gestured to her frantically. Gran understood his meaning and blew out the light, before quickly poking a hole in the window paper with her finger to look out. A black shadow on top of the courtyard wall now jumped in. Gran pulled Inkcap into the bed and covered him with the quilt. She slipped off the bed and found her scissors in the dark, tucking them under the bed mat. Then she stood behind the door of the main room and asked softly, "Who is it?"

The dark shadow walked towards them and whispered, "It's me, Granny Silkworm."

It was Awning. Immediately afterwards, Sparks arrived.

Gran squeaked in surprise and said, "Is that you, Awning? And Sparks too?"

"Granny Silkworm, Granny Silkworm!" Awning said.

She patted Awning's arm, and when she realised that it was indeed Awning and Sparks in front of her, she lit the lamp and cooed, "You're back, but why are you here at this hour?" At the same time, she tried to brush the snow off them and wipe their faces clean. The snow on their eyebrows and beards proved impossible to get off, for it was frozen solid.

Inkcap had worked his head out from under the quilts in one corner of the bed and was looking at them wide-eyed. He saw that Awning and Sparks were holding guns and he was too scared to move. Sparks winked at him and said, "Don't you recognise me?"

"Are you a ghost?" Inkcap asked.

"What nonsense," Gran said. "Get up and go to the courtyard door and keep watch."

Inkcap got up, while Gran gave Awning and Sparks some hot soup, but Awning stopped her; he told her they didn't have time to eat or drink, they'd come back to pick up Millstone.

"You're here to get Millstone?" Gran said.

"We'll get him and go," Awning said. Putting the gun down and leaning against the edge of the bed, he placed his hands over his mouth and blew on them to keep warm. Inkcap went to touch the gun, but as soon as he touched it, he shrank back, for the gun was freezing cold and hurt his hand.

"Is Millstone still in the village?" Inkcap asked.

"Didn't you know?" Sparks said. "He's been here all along."

Gran and Awning were whispering, discussing how they'd come to pick up Millstone, but they were afraid that if they went directly to his house, they'd be too big a target, so the reason they'd come to Gran was for Inkcap to go quietly to Millstone's house, bring him here and then they'd escape from the village together. But Gran was frightened that Inkcap's clumsy hands and feet would make a racket and alarm people, and that if they met anyone Inkcap would not know what to say, so Gran said that she'd go. She went out carrying a lantern, which was not lit, and took a piece of wood in case she bumped into someone because then she'd say that Inkcap had a high fever and she'd come out to summon her grandson's soul back.

Once Gran left, Awning asked about the situation in the village and Inkcap told him what he knew, and asked Awning if he really had killed Huang Shengsheng by overturning the tractor with a hail of stones.

"Is Huang Shengsheng really dead?" Awning asked.

"Dead as a doornail," Inkcap assured him.

"Good. The Hammerheads should continue to die."

Inkcap did not dare say anything more and asked instead, "How are you going to get Millstone out of here?"

"You don't need to worry about that."

"What do you mean? You're here in my house, and if someone were to spot you, Gran and I would be in real trouble."

"Originally we didn't plan to come here because you're so talkative," Awning told him. "We went to Sprout's house, but she wasn't there, and we thought nobody would notice if we came here."

"Sprout's got into trouble. They arrested her, and she's being held at the Kiln God Temple."

"Fuck."

Sparks had wandered off into the kitchen to find something to eat, but he didn't find anything, so Inkcap said, "I thought we weren't allowed to cook for you? There're some fried noodles – shall I give you a bowl?"

"There's no time for that," Awning said. "The moment Millstone arrives, we'll be on our way."

"Find us a cloth bag," Sparks said.

Inkcap got him a cloth bag, and Sparks dumped half a bagful of fried noodles inside and stuffed it inside his clothing. Then he said, "Give me two eggs, I can mix the noodles with the eggs."

Inkcap didn't want to give him any eggs, so he went over to the basket where the hens nested and had a look, declaring, "They haven't laid any today."

Gran then entered the courtyard with Millstone. He was as thin as a ghost but was wearing his wife's blue cloth shirt, with a kerchief wrapped around his head, and he walked with his back hunched over. He sat down to catch his breath as soon as he entered, but Awning and Sparks did not let him rest, saying that they should go at once. They chose a route, going west along the lane from Inkcap's house, along the edge of the embankment, skirting the village to the big mill and down to the back of the pond. From there, they would head east, making their way diagonally across to the reed beds, across the Zhou River, and west from the foot of the mountain on the opposite side. Awning carried a gun on his back and had another in his hand, while Sparks carried Millstone on his back.

"I can walk," Millstone assured them.

"Me carrying you means we can go faster," Sparks said, "but after we've crossed the Zhou River, you can walk by yourself more slowly."

"I'm so grateful, brother," Millstone said.

"Don't say anything right now."

When the time came for them to leave, Awning asked Inkcap to go out first, as a kind of advance guard. Gran held Inkcap back and said, "Awning, let me go."

Inkcap didn't want Gran to go, and neither did Awning and Sparks.

"Let's get out of here as quickly as we can," Awning said.

Gran told Inkcap to keep his eyes and ears peeled, and when she kneeled down and tied his shoelaces, she whispered, "If anything looks wrong, you're to hide. Don't try to be a hero, learn to pay attention."

"I will," Inkcap assured her.

But Gran didn't hear what he said. She just set a stool against the wall and took down the image of Chairman Mao, which she placed in Inkcap's arms, saying, "If anyone attacks you, you must cover your head with Chairman Mao. May Chairman Mao bless you."

Inkcap was the first to leave the courtyard. The alleyway was deserted, so he yowled like a cat, whereupon Awning, Sparks and Millstone followed him out. They kept a few feet behind, and Inkcap meowed the whole way to the embankment outside the village. There, Inkcap suddenly hid behind a tree, unmoving. He'd seen a black shadow come from the rear wall of one of the nearby houses. He meowed three times, so the three men behind him knew to take cover in the lee of a privy. Inkcap was ready for any eventuality; if someone was up ahead, he was going to climb the tree. He wasn't good at climbing trees, but he ought to be able to make it up to the fork in this one. But it was a dog that came towards him, Ever-Obedient's dog. The dog walked to Inkcap's side and he shushed it. It did not bark and instead started walking on, so Inkcap meowed once and set off following the dog. The dog seemed to know the route since it led the way to the big mill and then down the slope to the pond. Once out of the village, they could all breathe a sigh of relief.

"This is a really good dog," Inkcap said.

Awning patted the dog. "Hey, you did good. When the Revolution is won, I'll find you a nice bitch."

The dog sat down and wagged its tail.

"You've promised," Inkcap said, "so you'd better keep your word."

"Absolutely," Awning said. "It can have all the bitches in Old Kiln."

The four of them laughed a little out there in the darkness. Inkcap said he wanted to take the dog back to the village.

"The dog can go," Awning said, "but you have to wait until we've crossed the river."

"Until you've crossed the river?" Inkcap said, puzzled. "In that case, I might as well go with you."

"That's OK," Sparks said, "you can come with us." But how could Inkcap go with them? He said something to Ever-Obedient's dog, and the dog turned around and went back up the slope while he continued his duties as the advance guard: skirting around the back of the pond to the east side of the village, and then south to the reed beds. Snow was still falling, covering everyone in a thick layer. Inkcap was walking very fast, keeping a few feet ahead, looking back at the others. He had to pay constant attention because Awning and the others were apparently not keeping an eye on him, so he had to wait for them to catch him up.

"You've promised the dog something, so how about me?" he said.

"Oh, that was just a joke," Awning said.

"How can you joke with a dog?" Inkcap said.

"All right, I'm not joking now, what is it you want?"

"I don't really want anything," Inkcap said thoughtfully, "other than to be like Cowbell."

"I thought you'd want something big, but it turns out to be nothing at all... fine, fine..." Awning said. "Now go back on ahead."

Inkcap ran on ahead, thinking that he'd asked for too little, he should have asked for an increase in work points... maybe he could have asked for three work points. He'd done as much work today as a woman working a full day, and they got eight points for that. And another thing, he'd be going to school next year, which meant he couldn't work, so maybe they could come to some arrangement... He'd go to school during the day and then in the evening, he could record work points for everyone. He'd be able to read by then, and he could take on that kind of simple secretarial labour – at least he'd be able to keep better records than Soupspoon.

As he was lost in thought, Inkcap slipped and fell into a snowdrift. He got up, wiped the snow from his face without feeling too cold, and licked it from his lips with his tongue; it had a sweet taste. Far away at the highway barricade, he could make out a kerosene lamp and figures wavering in the light. Soon, a car approached, and the light moved over towards it, and the four of them dropped to the ground. Then the light waved some more, and there was a rattling sound as the car stopped at the barricade, and many men began checking it, cursing loudly at something. Awning and the others ran swiftly across the road just as everyone was busy checking the car, but Inkcap didn't follow; he stayed in his snowy nest on the other side of the road. He watched as Awning and the others crossed the road and headed for the reed beds, but after that he couldn't see or hear anything. For a moment he didn't know whether to run across the road to catch up with them or to stay put and wait for them. He lay there for a long time and suddenly felt that he was a complete fool. They'd come to fetch Millstone, and now that they'd got him safely away why would they come back and escort him home again? He got up and went back the way he came, but he said in his heart, Hmph! It was all on purpose that I didn't follow you. Why should I?

No sound came from the reed beds, no sound from the Zhou River, and the car that had halted at the roadblock started up again, and as it drove off, the kerosene light still shone in the darkness, and all was quiet. Knowing that Awning and the others had got away, Inkcap walked back to the slope by the pond, where Ever-Obedient's dog was still lying.

Inkcap picked up the dog excitedly. The dog was very heavy, but he still carried it, its long tail resting on his neck. Gran was waiting for him in the house and had cooked him some shredded turnip soup. Inkcap did not begin by drinking the soup; he wanted to give Ever-Obedient's dog a treat, so he took a shit for it in the corner of the yard.

When he was shitting, he thought he would tell Gran about what happened on the way to the mill, about Ever-Obedient's dog and about the car at the barricade. He was no longer the clumsy and careless Inkcap who told everyone everything. He'd been calm and collected, and he'd moved carefully… and at the critical moment he'd used his head, like when he'd made his request of Awning, and when he'd not followed the rest of them across the highway and come home instead. However, Inkcap never expected that just as he had pulled his pants back on, Sparks would come back too. Why had Sparks returned? Was there some problem with Millstone? Or was he angry because Inkcap hadn't followed them across the highway?

In the main room, Gran gave Sparks all the radish soup she'd made for Inkcap, and he told her that Awning had successfully got Millstone across the river so they could escape via South Mountain. The reason he'd come back was that he wanted to rescue someone from the political training class. That was terrifying news for Gran. Millstone could be extracted from the village quietly enough, but there were so many people in the political training class, and they had so many guards outside the Kiln God Temple – how could Sparks possibly rescue anybody?

"Why did you tell me this?" Gran said. "How could you let me know?"

"You needn't be afraid," Sparks said. "I am going home tonight. I just came by to leave something here and when I get the chance, I'll come back to collect it." With that, Sparks handed a bag wrapped in old clothes to Gran, and then he did indeed go back to his own house to sleep.

As soon as Sparks left, Inkcap was about to open the cloth bag, but Gran wouldn't let him do anything of the kind. She hurriedly hid it in the corner of the courtyard and covered it with straw, saying, "This is a disaster."

"What do you mean," Inkcap said.

"He's going to cause trouble in the village, and then the Hammerheads will find out he's been to our house."

Gran was absolutely right, and Inkcap also felt afraid. "Cowbell has an aunt who lives in Xichuang, doesn't he?" Gran said thoughtfully. "Tomorrow, you and Cowbell can go and stay with his aunt for a few days."

"What about you?" Inkcap said.

"I can't go anywhere. Sparks has left that bag here, so if we leave and he comes back to collect it, what are we supposed to do? We can't afford to annoy either side."

"What happens if the Hammerheads come to search the place?"

"I'm old, and there's nothing they can do to frighten me."

Grandmother and grandson talked half the night before they finally went to sleep, but Inkcap was soon woken up again. He heard a very beautiful sound that flowed like water and floated like clouds. It sounded like someone singing, but it was not a human voice. Various musical instruments, such as the spike-fiddle, lute, flute, moon guitar and gongs, drums and cymbals, all kinds of instruments played in harmony. Inkcap had never heard anything like it. He suddenly sat up. It was not yet dawn and Gran was still asleep.

"Gran," he said. "Gran, did you hear that?"

His grandmother woke up. "What are you shouting for when it's still dark outside?"

"Where's the opera?"

Gran strained her ears to listen, but she did not hear anything. "Did you dream it?"

Inkcap wondered himself if he'd been dreaming, so he cocked his ear to listen, but he could still hear the music, if more faintly. "It's not a dream," he said. "I can still hear it. Listen... listen!"

Gran still did not hear anything.

Inkcap listened again, but now the only sound was snow rustling outside the window, a mouse crawling across the roof beam and a handful of ash flakes that fell into the hearth.

EIGHTY-FIVE

THE DAY DAWNED EARLIER THAN USUAL, and the residents of Old Kiln got up to see the snow was still falling, so they did not bother to clear their front doors. The children, who always love snow, stood in the yard and stuck their tongues out to catch the falling flakes, but somehow the snow did not taste sweet, but a bit astringent and bitter.

"Mum, Mum, the snow is pockmarked," they shouted.

The mother inside the house said, "Nonsense. How could the snow be pockmarked?"

But when she came out to see, the snow was no longer just white with black flecks, it was all black – black snow. When one person noticed it, dozens more realised the same thing, but they didn't know what strange circumstance could possibly be the cause. Just then, someone ran down from the kiln, saying that the Mountain God Temple was on fire; the fire had been burning since the middle of the night and it was now too big to put out. Everyone looked up to the top of the mountain. Some of them could not see, so they stood on the roof of the house or ran to the embankment, and then they too could see that the temple was on fire.

Inkcap got up early and went round to Cowbell's house to introduce the idea that they should go to Xichuan to stay with his aunt, but Cowbell was reluctant to go and asked what the trouble was. Inkcap was ready with a lie: Ever-Obedient had asked him to go to Xichuan to look for Yoyo. When Cowbell heard they'd be looking for Yoyo, he was even more unwilling to go, so Inkcap was standing there in the courtyard as furious as could be, his face like a thunderclap and the black snow falling all around him. He just said one thing: "Your heart is as black as this snow!" When he said this, he gave a start: how could snow be black? Then he heard villagers shouting that the Mountain God Temple was on fire.

Inkcap's first reaction was that someone must have set fire to the temple. He ran up the mountain as fast as he could, and many others followed his lead. By the time they arrived at the top, there was no way to put out the fire because the temple had already collapsed, and the fallen pillars, beams, rafters, doors and windows, together with the split wood from the white pine that had been carried into the temple, had almost all been burned to embers, first red and then black, sizzling and smoking.

Inkcap screamed for Goodman and rushed into the flames. He was determined to search for him, and as his straw sandals packed with snow stepped over the embers, they sizzled but did not burn.

Gourd and Barndoor pulled Inkcap out. "Goodman must be dead, Inkcap," they said. "This fire was accidental, but there's no way he can have survived."

"Who would want to harm Goodman?" Inkcap asked. "Who set this fire on purpose?"

"What rubbish are you talking now, Inkcap?" Barndoor said.

"I was here yesterday. Goodman was sick and didn't feel like cooking, and he went to bed early... how could there be a fire? How could a fire happen without someone coming to set it."

Barndoor slapped Inkcap across the face and said, "I told you not to talk rubbish and you just carried on regardless! Who do you think set the fire, then? The Hammerheads, or the United Command, or are you saying it was Awning and Sparks? What? You came here yesterday, so you could've set the fire!"

"It wasn't me," Inkcap declared. "Why would I want to burn Goodman?"

"Fine, OK," Barndoor said, "so who would want to burn Goodman to death? It was an accident. Goodman didn't make it out and like any dead person, he should be cremated. However, we won't need to cremate him because the fire's already done it for us."

Everyone agreed with Barndoor. They started to clear out the remains left behind by the blaze by raking over the embers, but there was nothing at all there, not a piece of clothing or bedding had been left unburned, nor was there any flesh or bone, but only some iron nails and wire, and an enamelled tin jar misshapen from the intense heat.

Inkcap remembered how Goodman had moved all that firewood into the house the day before; that must have helped make the fire so big that it engulfed the Mountain God Temple. Barndoor said that no one else had set the fire, that Goodman had burned himself... but if that was true, why did Goodman do it? Did he have an unbearable headache from his injuries, or was he so despondent when the white pine was blown up? Tears were shed as he shovelled the black ash and snow-covered mudbrick. The fat man from the kiln also came, and he was cursing Goodman loudly, "Why couldn't he just die quietly? All the firewood we got from blowing up the pine's been burned to a crisp."

Inkcap heard these words and tossed a shovelful of mud over his back, where the clods accidentally on purpose hit Glob. He came over and kicked Inkcap, who crawled across the ground.

"What did you do that for?" Glob demanded.

"What you said was horrible," Inkcap replied.

"I'm telling you, Goodman deserved to die," Glob said. He came over and kicked Inkcap again.

Barndoor grabbed the fat guy and said, "What are you bullying Inkcap for?" He pulled Inkcap to his feet and with a single push, hurled him over to the heap of ashes and said, "You know fuck all about it. Now piss off." Inkcap knew that Barndoor was protecting him, but he was still cursing, "It's you who deserves to die."

Glob could no longer get at Inkcap, but he kicked the ashes with his foot, and a ball of mud and ash flew over and landed in Inkcap's arms. Inkcap looked and there was a hard lump in the middle, like a heart. He felt this was most peculiar – was it a lump of charcoal? He tried to snap it with his hands, but it did not break. Was it a stone? But it didn't have the weight of a stone, and it was black, black with a dark reddish tinge. Goodman had said yesterday morning, "I will leave my heart to you." Was this Goodman's heart that he'd left behind?

The people watching Glob kick a ball of mud into Inkcap's arms thought that Inkcap would smash it straight back again, and shouted in unison, "Inkcap, keep your calm!" But then they saw that Inkcap was not angry and was clutching the lump in his arms, laughing with tears in his eyes.

"This is Goodman's heart!" Inkcap said.

"Goodman's burned to ashes," Barndoor replied. "How can it be his heart?"

"Goodman left his heart behind!"

"Inkcap, we know you were fond of Goodman, but that's a stone, or a lump of charcoal."

"It's Goodman's heart!"

Everyone thought it was odd and came over to see what was going on, but Inkcap ran all the way down the hill holding the black-and-red lump.

"Old Kiln is full of lunatics," Glob said.

Inkcap ran along the village alley, shouting, and many birds gathered and flew above him, while a dozen dogs and cats, and a flock of red, white and yellow chickens ran after him. The other time when he'd run homewards from the riverbank, and these dogs, cats, chickens, along with grasshoppers, butterflies and dragonflies ran after him, he felt proud and called out to them. This time he was totally unaware that there were birds above his head, and so many dogs, cats and chickens behind him. Racing back to his yard in one go, he only noticed them when he turned back after knocking on the door. He called loudly for Gran at the entrance to the yard, and his cry was so peculiar that he could not tell whether it was sad or happy for the tone of his voice was completely different.

But Gran did not answer. Instead, she opened the courtyard door just a crack, and as soon as she pulled Inkcap inside, the door was closed again.

"Gran, Goodman's burned to death, and he left his heart behind."

Gran pulled Inkcap into the main room and shut the door. Sparks was sitting inside.

"Goodman's dead?" Sparks asked.

Inkcap whimpered.

Gran wrapped her arms around him and said, "Don't cry, darling. How could Goodman be dead, how can he just die?"

"The Mountain God Temple caught fire and burned away to nothing," Inkcap explained. "Only Goodman's heart is left."

"How can everything have burned away leaving only the heart?" Sparks said. "Are there many people on the mountain?"

"That's his heart," Inkcap insisted. "Goodman told me he would leave his heart behind."

"Are you out of your mind?" Sparks demanded.

"Come and look. This is Goodman's heart!"

Sparks stood up and slapped Inkcap twice across his face.

Gran wrapped her arms around Inkcap and looked at Sparks in shock.

"He's possessed," Sparks said, "so I'm bringing him back to his senses."

Gran pulled Inkcap into the bedroom, turned around and closed the bedroom door. "Sparks," she said, "he's only little and he's scared. Tell me, what it is you want."

Inkcap stood in the bedroom rubbing his mouth. His lips were swollen, and he hated Sparks for his cruelty. The previous night he'd helped them get Millstone out, and he'd given Sparks eggs, fried noodles and shredded radish soup to eat – and he still hit me? He chanted softly, "Fuck you, motherfucker."

Gran and Sparks were still talking in the main room when the kitchen door slammed, followed by silence. Inkcap walked out and saw Gran standing still amid the snow in the yard.

He went over and pulled Gran back into the main room, but her clothes were wet and frozen so that they clicked when she walked.

"Gran, that really is Goodman's heart."

"I believe you."

Inkcap started to cry. He told her how terrible the ruins of the Mountain God Temple looked after the fire, and Gran said, "It's good, it's good to die cleanly."

Grandmother and grandson put Goodman's heart on top of the cupboard. "Goodman had no children, no one to burn paper when he died," Gran said, "so you go and bring all the papercuts I've made. It's right we burn some paper for Goodman."

Inkcap went back into the bedroom and fetched layer upon layer of papercuts, and grandmother and grandson burned them. The papercuts burst into flames like countless flowers, and the cut-out birds, butterflies, swallows and dragonflies flew upwards and turned into ash, floating silently upwards to the roof beams and then slowly falling down, while the cut-out animals, including cows, dogs, chickens, pigs and cats, all moved again as if they were alive, running and jumping in the flames.

"Gran," Inkcap said, "last night when I heard singing, maybe that was when the Mountain God Temple was on fire."

"Oh, then it was heavenly music," Gran said.

"Heavenly music?"

"Goodman was leaving, so Heaven was sending him off with music."

Inkcap looked at Gran in silence before suddenly remembering something. "Has Sparks gone?" he asked.

"No, he's not gone, he's in our sweet potato cellar."

"Why did you let him stay in the cellar?"

Without answering, Gran put another pile of papercuts into the fire and said, "Don't you go out again today."

He didn't go out again. After Gran went to Apricot's house, he thought about how Sparks usually ignored Gran and said horrible things about Apricot, but now he'd clearly sought out Gran and wanted her to go and talk to Apricot – it really was too bad. Inkcap sat at the kitchen door, and whenever someone passed by outside the courtyard door or another person came knocking and shouted to Gran wanting to borrow a thread spool or spindle, he did not say a word and just waited for them to leave. But as for the man in the sweet potato cellar covered by a wooden lid, to him he gnashed his teeth, spat and cursed in a low voice, "I hope you suffocate down there."

Sparks had spent half a day in the sweet potato cellar. On hearing the chickens crowing in the yard, he lifted the lid. A young rooster squawked and circled a hen, one of its wings trailing almost to the ground, and after attentively circling and circling, the hen's face became red and a little impatient, but it lay down and was pounced on by the rooster, and the two tails swung so swiftly from side to side that as soon as they touched each other they parted again. Before Inkcap realised what was going on, the hen stood up and shook its body so hard that it seemed to shake all its feathers off, and then muttered a complaint, while the rooster thrust its neck out and squawked. With a wave of his hand, Inkcap shooed the rooster away.

"Get the other one," Sparks said. "Get her to lay an egg for me."

Inkcap turned around and saw Sparks' head sticking out of the cellar. "Are you coming out?" he asked.

"What kind of a cellar is this anyway?" Sparks complained. "It's no bigger than a chicken coop."

"If you're too uncomfortable, you can leave," Inkcap said.

"I dare you to say that again. I told you to go to the courtyard entrance to keep guard, but you're here to watch the chickens getting ready to lay eggs?"

Inkcap just looked at Sparks. He was covered all over in earth, like a mole. "It's fine," he told Sparks.

"Is it still not dark yet?" asked Sparks.

"There isn't a lever I can pull to make the sun set faster."

"Smartarse. Why isn't your gran back yet?"

"Dunno."

"Go and see. If Apricot won't play ball, then you're to tell her that when the Red Blades come back, she'll suffer for it."

"Tell her yourself."

"I'm telling you to tell her."

"You may be able to bully me, but Apricot is a poor peasant – are you afraid she'll report you're hidden in this house?"

"She wouldn't dare," Sparks said. "The same way you and your gran wouldn't dare to keep me from hiding in your house."

"If you talk like that, I'll go and tell the Hammerheads."

"Fine. Go ahead and tell them that you and I got Millstone out to safety."

Inkcap felt like a snake, where Sparks had caught him by the tail and whacked his body against the ground until all his bones were broken, and he was left hanging limply down like a straw rope. Sparks grabbed the ladle in the bucket of water beside the cellar and drank with a gurgling sound, giving a grunting laugh as he did so.

Inkcap was looking forward to the Hammerheads coming. If they came, they'd take Sparks away. By coincidence, just as he was thinking about that, a knock sounded on the courtyard door. The man with the scoop immediately shrank back into his hole, whispering, "Put the lid on, then put the basket on top. Put the basket on top!"

Inkcap did indeed nervously cover the cellar and put the basket down on the lid. But it was Gran who came in. When she entered the yard, she shut the door and collapsed on the laundry stone, like a pile of wet sand.

Inkcap looked at Gran's face to see if she appeared happy or sad. However, her face was white, and a layer of sweat stood out on her forehead for all that it was such a cold day.

"Why is my heart pounding like this?" Gran asked. "Come and feel, it's like it's going to leap out of my chest." Her heart was pounding like a rabbit.

"What's wrong with you, Gran?" Inkcap asked.

But Gran just said, "Look how many eggs are in the box!"

Inkcap went to the main room and came out a while later. "There are still five, I'll cook you a couple."

"Hide the eggs," Gran said, "and when the chickens lay another one today, go to Kaihe's in the evening and exchange them for brown sugar. It's already time, how could there not be a pinch of brown sugar in the house?"

"I don't eat sugar," Inkcap reminded her. "I'll exchange it for salt."

"This isn't about you," Gran told him.

"Who is it then?"

"It's for Apricot. With her mother dead, she's got nobody to look after her–"

"You're giving it to her?"

Gran said nothing but gestured to the kitchen, and Inkcap nodded. He went to the kitchen and spat.

Gran glared at him. "You'd better light the fire," she said. "Your gloomy face is making me feel cold."

Inkcap got a bundle of maize stalks and built them into a pyramid in the brazier. Then he went out to the wall to collect a fuse, which he lit in order to set fire to the bundle of stalks. When he went out to collect a fuse, he realised that it had been ages since he'd last left the house with one, and nobody now called to him, "Inkcap, can you bring a light?"

He lit the fuse, then took a handful of straw and blew on the spark, but he blew out the flame with a single breath. Having relit the fuse, he blew on the flame again, and the flame went out a second time, which was very strange. Meanwhile, the smoke rose up and choked him, and he began coughing. Gran shouted from the kitchen door, "What are you doing? Bring out the brazier and light it." Inkcap brought the brazier into the yard, while Gran and Sparks were talking in the kitchen.

"It's such a shame," Gran said. "Apricot burst into tears as soon as she saw me. Her belly is so big, but Bash hasn't been to see her all this time. What a way to behave. He isn't thinking about the baby at all... how on earth is she going to look after it once it's born?"

"He's happy enough to fuck her but won't do a thing for the baby," Sparks said. "Now she can see what kind of person he is."

Gran was quiet for a while and then said, "Now is not the time for such talk."

"Fine," Sparks said, "if she wants to give birth to a bastard, that's on her. Has she agreed to go?"

"I told her, and she said that since the day she argued with Bash, he hasn't been back to see her, and she hasn't gone to find him. To her mind, even if he doesn't care about her, he ought to care about the baby."

"He's after a life well away from here, so he doesn't want anything to do with no kid."

Gran did not respond, so Sparks continued, "Has she refused?"

"Yes," Gran said.

"She has to do it, whether she wants to or not," Sparks snarled.

"I told her that it was you who wanted this, and she said if Sparks wants me to do something he can tell me himself."

"She wants me to go in person? That's not going to go well."

"I told her that too," Gran said. "I told her it doesn't matter how she feels about Awning or you – this is about saving lives. There are so many people in the political training class, their lives are hanging in the balance, and they've all got parents and wives and children depending on them... how can you bear to see them die in the Kiln God Temple? Besides which, if you save these people, won't Awning and Sparks look at you differently?"

"What did she say, did she agree?" Sparks asked eagerly.

"In the end, she agreed to do it," Gran said. "But she's worried that once she makes a scene, if the political training class people run away, Bash will be sure to think she is in cahoots with your lot."

"She can go and take it out on Bash," Sparks said. "After all, he's got that United Command woman now, so it's perfectly understandable for her to want to make a scene."

"I asked her if she still cared about Bash, and she said she hated him, but she needs him – how can she manage without him? I told her that if she really did want him back, she needed to go and kick up a fuss because if she screamed and shouted enough, it might bring him back. That's when she agreed to do it."

"That's great," Sparks said.

Inkcap had now got the fire lit, and he positioned the brazier in front of Gran's feet. "Gran," he said, "Bash has been horrible to Apricot, so if she goes to make a scene, won't that make him dig in his heels even more?"

"Don't interfere," Sparks said. "If she can't get him back, that would be best. In the future, us Red Blades are going to get him. If he doesn't go back to Apricot, at least she's spared having to collect his corpse one day!"

"Sparks, you're supposed to be trying to save people," Gran protested, "so don't go making things worse."

"That's none of your business."

"I'm telling you again," Gran said, "if you can save them tonight that's great, but if you can't, you're not to force it – we can't have any more fighting in this village. You saw how much Millstone suffered."

"OK, fine," Sparks said.

"And as for me," Gran continued, "I've done everything you've asked of me, so Inkcap and I will be going to Xichuan before it gets dark – Cowbell's aunt is my maternal cousin. She's sick and I need to go and look after her."

"No," Sparks said. "If you leave, where am I supposed to go? You cook, and I'll sleep in the cellar for a while." He did not allow her to say anything more and went back into the sweet potato cellar looking a little angry.

After dinner, it was dark and no longer snowing. Gran went out to Apricot's house again and brought back news that she'd gone to the Kiln God Temple, whereupon Sparks grabbed their axe and put it in his belt. Gran didn't allow him to take it. "Everything else you can take," she said, "but not this axe. It doesn't matter whether you hurt someone, or someone hurts you – I don't want my axe involved in any of it."

Inkcap grabbed the axe and ran to the courtyard door.

"Why are you running?" Gran admonished him. "Do you want to let people know?"

Gran's words were clearly meant for Sparks, meaning that if he tried to take the axe, grandmother and grandson would have to shout. Gran had never sounded so tough before. She'd made steamed sweet potatoes for Sparks, and she now took another cooked sweet potato and stuffed it into his hand. He was furious, but he stuck a mallet in his belt and gave the following order to Inkcap: he was to take that bag hidden under the maize stalks in the corner and go to the rear wall of Bash's house. There were beanstalks nearby, and he was to place the bag under the beanstalks.

Sparks slipped out of the courtyard door like a ghost and vanished into the darkness. They hurriedly closed the door and let out a long breath. "If he comes back, we won't open the door," Inkcap swore.

"No, we won't open the door," Gran agreed.

Inkcap got the bag out from the corner and wanted to see what was inside. When he opened it, he found a package of dynamite. There was already a fuse attached. Grandmother and grandson were dumbfounded. Once he had rescued everyone, Sparks must be planning to set fire to the beanstalks, and they in turn would set light to the fuse. Grandmother and grandson carried the bag of dynamite outside. Gran said that they couldn't possibly put it behind the wall of Bash's house, and equally, they couldn't let anyone else know, so they should throw it over the embankment outside the village. Having walked carefully out onto the lane, they heard voices coming from not far away. Gran thrust the bag of dynamite under the rubber tree and dragged Inkcap off to Third Aunt's house.

EIGHTY-SIX

INKCAP KNEW NOTHING about how Apricot went to the Kiln God Temple to see Bash, or how she quarrelled with him there, or how Sparks got inside and then managed to break in to rescue the detainees. He and Gran stayed at Third Aunt's house, where the bed was kept roasting hot, and they were told to sit under the blanket and talk. But Gran was distracted, and when there was a movement outside, she tried to listen with her head to one side. She could not hear anything, so she said to Inkcap, "Can you hear a dog barking?"

"It just barked twice and then stopped," replied Inkcap.

"I asked you to make some papercuts for me to put in the window," Third Aunt said. "Why are you so distracted, why do you care about the dog barking?"

Gran laughed and started making papercuts for the windows. But she couldn't cut properly. The faces of the pigs and dogs were all human faces, and when she cut out a human being, they had a long tail.

"What's wrong with me?" Gran said. The scissors even cut into her hand.

Outside the courtyard there was constant barking, and the sound was strange. Even Third Aunt went to lie on the windowsill to listen. "How odd," she said. "What are the dogs doing?"

Before long there was a gunshot, and then shots rang out on all sides. The three of them blew out the light and got out of bed to listen to the commotion in the courtyard. Pounding footsteps ran through the alley outside, shaking the walls of the courtyard which were made from piled-up saggars. They didn't dare open the door, nor did they dare lean a ladder against the wall to watch.

Gran peaked through the crack in the courtyard door and whispered, "That's Soupspoon... there's a big group chasing Soupspoon!"

"Chasing Soupspoon?" Third Aunt said. "Isn't he locked up in the Kiln God Temple?"

"The Red Blades must have come back to rescue them," Inkcap said.

"What do you know about it?" said Gran, shutting him up.

Another shot rang out. The bullet seemed to have been fired from nearby, and the sound was crisp. The three of them ran into the main room, and Gran said, "I'm afraid the two factions are fighting again."

"What in the world is going on?" cried Third Aunt. "Everyone in this village is fighting everyone else, and it looks like they won't be satisfied until all of us are dead."

Inkcap ran out into the courtyard, but Gran warned him off. "Get back in here! Are you trying to get yourself shot?"

"I won't go out," Inkcap assured her. "I'm just going to look through the crack in the door." Gran dragged him back to the main room by the ear and closed the door.

Inkcap couldn't go out, but he also couldn't sit still in the house. "Gran, are you sure it was Soupspoon?"

"It was. I saw a group of people chasing after him."

"Do you think Soupspoon can get away?"

"Who knows."

"Soupspoon's going to die."

"Shut that mouth of yours!" Gran snapped.

As they were speaking, Soupspoon was hiding in the privy attached to Big Root's house.

Soupspoon, Palace and Sparks were the first to get out of the Kiln God Temple. As soon as they emerged from the temple door, they were spotted by the Hammerheads and several men surrounded them. Sparks knocked down two with a mallet, and the three of them ran towards the village. Dazed-And-Confused, at the head of more than a dozen people, saw someone running in the distance and did not know who it was, but he shouted and gave chase. Soupspoon turned around and saw that Palace and Sparks had vanished. He called out to them but there was no response.

Dazed-And-Confused was shouting, "It's Soupspoon!" He set off running and headed down a different alley only to see a group of people turn in at the far end. He went into the toilet at Big Root's house. Someone was in there having a shit: Big Root's wife. He turned around and was about to leave again when he was dragged back by Big Root's wife.

"Squat down," she said. "Squat down now!"

Soupspoon was confused, but then she said, "If they just wanted to beat you up, I wouldn't get involved. But they're trying to kill you... so I'm going to protect you."

Dazed-And-Confused could not see Soupspoon anywhere in the alley. "Where can he have got to?" he said. "He can't have flown up into the sky or burrowed through the ground! Has anyone looked in the privy?"

Soupspoon tried to make himself as small as possible while Big Root's wife stood at the door hoisting up her trousers and said, "Dazed-And-Confused, I'm taking a shit in here. What do you think you're doing barging in?"

"We're fighting for the Revolution," Dazed-And-Confused responded. "Soupspoon's escaped, have you seen him?"

"If Soupspoon's escaped," Big Root's wife said, "that motherfucker's an enemy of my hubby – if I were to come across him, I'd beat him to a pulp."

Dazed-And-Confused and his men ran off towards the end of the alley, where they joined forces with the other men there, and went off to continue their search.

Soupspoon emerged from the privy and said in a low voice, "Big Root and I have never been enemies."

"Be off with you," Big Root's wife said. Soupspoon ran along beside the wall of the alley.

As Soupspoon ran, he saw Dazed-And-Confused's group catch three other men who had escaped from the political training class, so he climbed to the top of a courtyard wall to wait for them to pass before running out of the village. The three men didn't seem to want to go, so Dazed-And-Confused beat them, slapping and punching their heads until they bled, while another person was pleading with him to stop.

"If I don't hit him," Dazed-And-Confused said, "he'll try to get away."

"If you really want to beat him, you should hit him on the arse," the other man said. "Why hit him on the head unless you're trying to kill him?"

"What are you talking about? Would a true Hammerhead say a thing like that? If we don't kill him, he'll kill us! Let me hamstring him and see if he still tries to run away!"

The man's legs were crushed, and he was crying and screaming for his mother. Soupspoon picked up a broken saggar from the top of the wall and said, "Dazed-And-Confused, I'm gonna fuck your mum!" He threw the saggar at him, but it missed, smashing two feet away from the group.

"It's Soupspoon!" Dazed-And-Confused shouted, and the lot of them went on the attack again. Soupspoon clambered from the top of the wall onto the roof and then leapt from rooftop to rooftop along the row. This was on the north side of the alleyway, and the householders could hear the crunch of their tiles being broken. When they came out to see what was going on, they saw Soupspoon running across.

Tag-Along's house was in the middle of the row, and his wife's broken leg was infected. It was so swollen and painful at night she couldn't sleep, and Tag-Along was cleaning up the pus when he heard the sound of shouting. He had no idea what was going on, and when he came out, he saw Soupspoon running along his roof. He grabbed an iron shovel and went up to the roof, saying, "So you think you can fly, motherfucker!"

Soupspoon didn't dare run but jumped down from the eaves of the next house and fell to the ground at the back with a thud. Tag-Along then came down from the roof and wanted to go out the back, but his wife said, "Let him run. Are you really going to catch him?"

"He must've broken his leg when falling from the eaves," Tag-Along declared. "I can catch him."

"I think it's because you've been fighting and killing all day every day that you've accumulated all this bad karma," his wife said. "It's killing me, you know." She pulled him back.

Tag-Along stopped his pursuit, but he shouted, "Soupspoon's run away!"

Soupspoon's leg really was broken, so he got up and hobbled as fast as he could out of the village, and Dazed-And-Confused chased after him. Soupspoon reached the big mill on the east side of the village where he found he could go no further, so he burrowed under the big roller stone. Dazed-And-Confused came over and couldn't see Soupspoon anywhere. He instructed the others to go down to the bottom of the embankment to look for him and sat down on the roller stone to catch his breath. Soupspoon grabbed hold of Dazed-And-Confused's legs and wrenched them out from under him so he fell to the ground. Soupspoon jumped out to ride on top of him. Dazed-And-Confused was of course much stronger, so he soon had Soupspoon pressed down to the ground. Soupspoon's leg wasn't working properly, but with his free hand he squeezed Dazed-And-Confused's balls.

"Bloody hell, that's my trick, motherfucker!" Dazed-And-Confused screamed, and then he passed out.

Soupspoon still did not let go. His teeth gnashed, and he could feel the balls being crushed, but he still carried on. The men who had run down the embankment heard the scream and came running back up. They saw Dazed-And-Confused lying on his back like a dead pig with Soupspoon still crushing his balls and not letting go. They grabbed sticks and hit Soupspoon around the head, beating his brains out. When he fell, he was still crushing the other man's balls, so that Dazed-And-Confused's body was also pulled over.

Division Chief Ma and Bash ran over with their guns out and asked if it was Sparks. Iron Bolt told them it was Soupspoon. Bash bent down to see. Soupspoon was already dead.

"You had a good life," said Bash, "so why did you run?" He kicked the dead Soupspoon with his foot and asked Iron Bolt, "Where's Sparks?"

"We chased them into Three Fork Alley," Iron Bolt said, "and that's where the fuckers separated. Baldy Jin and Glob may still be chasing Sparks."

Division Chief Ma blasted another shot into the sky, and as everyone set off running back to the village again, she shouted, "Some of you must guard each entrance to the village. Do not let Sparks escape."

After running away from the rest of them, Sparks had gone to the back wall of Bash's old house, where he struck a match and set fire to the pile of bean stalks in the corner. Then he ran to South Bend Lane with four escapees from the political training class. It was narrow, but from there they could go directly to the northern embankment, and then they could jump down and head for the rear pond. The four men from the political training class were not familiar with the terrain; they ran into South Bend Lane but turned right, which led to Gourd's house and from there to a dead end – there was nowhere to go. Sparks called out but it was already too late. He turned left, running and listening for the sound of an explosion. However, Sparks did not hear anything at all. He wondered if the fuse had got damp or had perhaps not been installed correctly. Then he thought, even if the fuse was damp or not properly installed, when the bean stalks burned, the dynamite should still have exploded, so why had nothing happened?

At this time, the men chasing him had all gone down the alley while he hid in the privy by Third Aunt's house, and from there he emerged into the deserted lane out front. He ran until he reached the courtyard gate of Inkcap's house, thinking it a safe place. He hammered on the gate, but no sound came from inside. Then he saw that the door was padlocked. He cursed silently, took two steps back and launched himself at the wall. He was planning to grab the top of the wall and clamber over, but even after several attempts, he did not succeed. All he had done was to knock off some icicles that were hanging from the eaves.

Useless followed Baldy Jin chasing after Sparks, but they lost him. Then someone said that Sparks had got up on the roof and run westwards, so Baldy Jin led a group to continue chasing him along South Bend Lane and ordered Useless and the others to cut him off at the northern end. When Useless got there, his mother was quarrelling with Half-Stick. Useless and his mother had been at home when they heard that Sparks had come to save those in the political training class. Useless ran to the Kiln God Temple; his mother followed him as far as the alleyway. When she saw someone running, she shouted. Half-Stick dragged Sprout behind a tree as Useless's mother screamed as loud as she could, "There's someone here!"

Half-Stick hissed at Sprout to run in the shadow of the wall, while she stepped out boldly, saying, "It's me, why are you shouting?"

"I saw two people," Useless's mother proclaimed. "How can you be here alone?"

"You need to get your eyes out of your pants," Half-Stick replied.

"You're the one with your eyes in your pants!"

"So where is this man I'm supposed to be hiding?"

Useless's mother peered about her, but the alley was dark, and she said, "It must have been your lover."

"My lover, eh?" said Half-Stick. "I guess you dream of having a man, but nobody would want you."

Useless heard his mother screaming and shouting so he came running, but when he saw she was arguing with Half-Stick, he said, "If it wasn't your lover, you're protecting someone who's run away."

An incensed Half-Stick said, "Useless, you motherfucker, remember what you just said. I may not be a Hammerhead but I'm the wife of Baldy Jin – let's see if you dare say this to him!"

"Fine, OK," Useless said, "you're the boss." Ignoring Half-Stick, he dragged his mother down the alleyway ahead.

"I definitely saw two people running," Useless's mother said, "and I shouted, but then she was the only one who came out. The whore must be protecting whoever it was that was running."

"Was it Awning?" Useless asked.

"I only saw a shadow, but I don't think it was him."

"Why? Has Awning also come back to break them out?"

"It was just a guess," Useless said. "You'd better go."

"You be careful too," his mother said. "If the situation isn't right, run."

"Sure," Useless said. But then he saw someone jumping about at the far end of the alley, so he ran forward as quickly and inconspicuously as he could, and then shouted at the top of his voice, "Sparks is over here!"

Sparks turned around and glared at Useless, then he launched himself at him, covering his mouth. Useless bit Sparks' hand, and Sparks tried to exploit the situation by shoving three fingers into Useless's mouth, followed by his whole fist. Useless was unable to bite or shout. When his mother saw the scene unfold she started screaming, so Sparks pulled out his fist to punch her. Useless headbutted Sparks, pinning him against the wall so hard that he couldn't breathe. Sparks pummelled Useless's head with his fists, but he was still held firm against the wall which meant he couldn't really use his arms. He reached up, thinking it would be good to grab a tile or brick from the top of the wall, but it was too high so he couldn't reach anything. He grabbed an icicle hanging down, breaking it off with a sharp crack, and stabbed the back of Useless's neck. Useless raised his head, and the icicle stabbed him in one eye – he immediately fell to the ground. His mother screamed when she saw Useless collapse, then without a second thought, she jumped over and grappled Sparks' legs out from under him. It did not matter how much he hit her; she would not let go. Sparks managed to make a few yards of ground, even with Useless's mother clinging to him. Then Baldy Jin and the others ran up, and some of the Hammerheads started beating Sparks, but he did not give in. Baldy Jin picked up a brick and went over to strike Sparks on the back of the head but he just stood there motionless. Baldy Jin prepared to strike him a second time, but just as he raised his hand, Sparks fell down.

"I thought you were supposed to be invincible?" Baldy Jin sneered.

Sparks was knocked unconscious, so the Hammerheads unbuckled his trousers, tied him up with his hands behind his back and dragged him off to meet Division Chief Ma and Bash.

Division Chief Ma and Bash arrived at the south entrance of the village. The County United Command and Hammerheads between them had recaptured six people, and they sent someone to the Kiln God Temple to find out exactly how many had escaped. The man returned to report a total of ten had run away, so having recaptured six they were still missing four.

"Are the ones who didn't run away behaving themselves?" Bash asked.

"Sure," he replied.

"Did Branch Secretary Zhu run away?" The answer was no, he was asleep the entire time.

Now Decheng came running, saying he'd found a cloth bag under the rubber tree. He didn't know what was in it, but it was really heavy, so he didn't dare open it. He put down the cloth bag and said, "Maybe this belonged to someone in the political training class, one of the ones who ran off, and since they could not take it with them, they threw it away."

Bash opened it and found a packet of dynamite inside. Dynamite! Decheng was scared half to death. He said that after picking it up, he'd been holding it in his arms, and just now he'd smoked a pipe.

"You picked it up?" Bash said.

"I was with Old Faithful," Decheng explained. "I tripped and when I looked down, there was this cloth bag. Old Faithful said to put it back where we found it, but I didn't give it to him. I said this may belong to someone in the political training class and I ought to give it to you, so I brought it along."

"I guess someone wanted you to take that bag round the back of the Kiln God Temple, right?"

"I'm not sure what you mean. Do you think I was going to take it to the temple and blow it up? How dare you! No one gave me this bag of explosives. If I'd known there was dynamite inside, I wouldn't have touched it no matter how much you paid me."

Bash removed the cloth that was wrapped outside the bag of dynamite. It was a torn shirt, now missing its sleeves, and he showed it around to everyone in the firelight, wanting to see if anyone recognised it.

"That belongs to Sparks," Almost-There said. "I recognise it."

"That fucker brought dynamite, did he?" Bash snarled. "I bet he was thinking of blowing up the back wall of the Kiln God Temple so they could escape, or creating an explosion in the village so he could get away. We're lucky to have found him early and chased him off in time, so he didn't have the chance to blow it up and run away."

Everyone was horrified at the thought of that carnage and cursed Sparks.

"You see," Division Chief Ma said. "He was trying to murder us all. We've got to search the village, house by house, to make sure Sparks doesn't escape."

Again, they divided their forces to search for Sparks, and just then Baldy Jin's group carried Sparks over. He was still unconscious. Glob went over and slapped his face but Sparks still didn't wake up.

"Division Chief Ma," Baldy Jin said, "you'd better turn your back."

"Why?" she asked.

"I guess it's fine if you don't. We never treat you as a woman, anyway."

He unzipped his trousers and pulled out his dick to piss on Sparks' face.

Division Chief Ma was furious. "Do this out back where nobody can see."

Baldy Jin dragged Sparks a few steps into the shadows, then a stream of piss poured down on Sparks' face and he woke up. He found his hands were tied, and arrayed in front of him were the United Command people and the Hammerheads, and they were all cursing him.

"Who else came here with you?" Bash asked.

"Do you think we needed anyone but me?" Sparks replied.

"Oh, sure. Did you bring this bag of dynamite?"

Sparks' eyes widened at the sight of the bag.

"Did you bring it?" Bash repeated. "You killed Huang Shengsheng by stoning him and then you came back to blow us all up?"

"Hell!"

"Hell what?"

"It's a fucking shame the dynamite got wet, and the fire didn't burn it."

"The fire didn't burn it?"

"Nah. If it had, you wouldn't be standing here, motherfucker."

Baldy Jin kicked him and said, "You think you can blow up whoever you want, but God was protecting us."

Sparks spat on the ground and cursed them all for a bunch of motherfucking arse-lickers. Someone grabbed a handful of mud and snow from the ground and stuffed it into his mouth, but it didn't hold. Then he grabbed a handful of twigs and stuffed them in too, but it still didn't stop him.

"Go to the privy and shovel a load of shit in his mouth. Let's see if he still curses after that," Baldy Jin said.

"Let him curse," said Bash. "He can curse as much as he likes."

That night, Sparks was put into the western room at the Kiln God Temple, and Division Chief Ma arranged for Glob to guard him. Glob kept guard until midnight when he was so cold and sleepy that he fell asleep under a quilt. Sparks quietly started rubbing the belt that bound his hands against the wall and eventually managed to snap it. When he went out of the western room, the people in the main hall and the east room were asleep, so he slipped to the temple door. There was a bonfire outside the temple door, surrounded by four men. He slipped back again to the wall between the western room and the steps leading up to the main temple where there was a ladder, and he used it to climb the wall. The wall was so high that he could not simply jump down from it. There was a cypress tree beyond the wall, four or five feet away from it, so he decided to leap over and grab it, and then climb down it. He thought he could manage it, but when the time came, he wasn't able to get a good hold of the tree and fell to the ground with a thud. The guards at the entrance of the temple heard the noise and ran over to see Sparks lying on the ground, whereupon they started shouting, and all the people in the temple woke up. The United Command and the Hammerheads ran out. Sparks was limping towards the cemetery, and he was caught and beaten half to death.

The second half of the night as Glob was still guarding Sparks, he asked, "Do you want something to drink?"

"Yes."

"I'll pour some hot water for you."

Sparks was so hungry and thirsty that he drank all the water in a thermos, before saying, "Glob, I'm sorry."

"What for?"

"Your boss will punish you because I ran away."

"There's no need for you to run," Glob told him. "There's a drain in the right corner at the back of the main hall. If you're not wearing a padded jacket, you could squeeze through. Then all you have to do is get over the courtyard wall."

"I can see you're a good person," Sparks said. "If I can get out through the drain, when the Red Blades come back, I guarantee you'll be safe."

"Promise?"

"A good man never breaks his word."

Glob proceeded to untie Sparks' hands. "Take off your padded cotton jacket," he said, "then I'll tie your hands loosely and pretend to go to sleep, while you can get out through the drain."

Sparks took off his padded jacket and trousers, leaving himself standing in just his cotton long johns. He let Glob bind his hands, and he tied them really tight. "Not so tight... make them looser," Sparks said.

Glob laughed. "The reason why you Red Blades can't get things done is because you're all dumb – you've run once so why would I let you run off a second time?" He tied Sparks' legs together with rope, and it was only then that Sparks realised he'd been deceived. During the second half of the night, wearing just his long johns, Sparks had to lie on the icy ground with his hands and feet bound. And he'd drunk a thermos bottle of water, so after he wet his pants, they froze to ice.

At daybreak, Division Chief Ma heard that Sparks had escaped in the middle of the night and she came to see. By then, Sparks was frozen stiff. When dragged to his feet, he couldn't stand; he fell over with his legs still together. When dragged to his feet and made to sit on a chair, he could not sit down, so they had to let him lean against the wall. Sparks' mouth opened a few times, but what he said was inaudible.

"What's he saying?" Division Chief Ma asked.

"He said to kill him quickly," Glob replied.

"Of course I'll kill him," Division Chief Ma said. "You need to think of a way to get him to walk and run this morning."

"Walk and run?" Glob asked.

"And he's got to carry the bag of dynamite."

Sparks had brought the explosives to blow them up, but now they were going to make him carry the bag to blow himself up. Word of this development soon spread. Flower Girl was cooking up at the kiln, and Glob ate a portion and asked for another one to give Sparks to eat. Flower Girl wanted to know why they were feeding Sparks so well, so Glob explained that they were going to have him carry the dynamite and blow himself up. He finished by saying, "At noon, you should go down the mountain to see the fun." He took advantage of this opportunity to get a good feel of Flower Girl's arse. Flower Girl was so scared she was shivering.

After eating, she took a quart of food scraps back to her pig and told Barndoor what had been said. Barndoor rushed off to tell Noodle Fish's wife, and it so happened that Gran and Inkcap were with Noodle Fish's wife at the time.

"Lord, what a terrible thing," she said. "What a dreadful way to die." She started to cry.

Gran's face went pale. She did not say anything but just hauled Inkcap away.

Inkcap was not happy that Gran left as soon as she heard that Sparks was going to be blown up, and on the way complained that she should not have left.

"You're right," Gran mumbled. "I shouldn't have left, but I panicked. I was afraid that if I stayed a little longer, I would have said something wrong."

"I can't hear what you're saying," Inkcap told her.

"We should have reported him to Bash right at the beginning," Gran said. "It's all my fault, it's my fault Sparks is going to die."

"If you had reported it, wouldn't Sparks have been arrested by the Hammerheads?"

"Arrested, yes. Maybe they would have beaten him up, or broken his arm or his leg, but now they're going to kill him." A period of silence followed and then Gran continued, "Are they really going to blow up Sparks?"

"That's what Barndoor said."

"We must save him. But how? Maybe if we go and beg Apricot…"

When Gran said this, Inkcap suddenly realised what she meant and said, "Yes, yes, only Apricot can save him."

The two of them turned around and went to Apricot's house.

Apricot's house had already had a parade of visitors, begging her to find some way to save Sparks. When Inkcap and Gran arrived, she got quite cross and said, "When Sparks wanted to play the hero you come and find me, now that he's in trouble you come and find me – what am I supposed to do?"

"Apricot, you need to calm down," said Gran. "Everyone is asking you for help because they don't want Sparks to die. If he'd been killed somewhere outside the village, that would have been his fate… but to be blown up by explosives in front of everyone here, who could bear it? If you can save him, you should."

"Granny Silkworm is right," another person said. "If Sparks dies like that, he'll become a hungry ghost haunting our village and causing trouble for everyone."

"It's not like he needs to become a ghost for that," Apricot snapped. "Hasn't he caused enough trouble as it is?"

"You're pregnant. Even if you don't care about yourself, what about your baby?"

"What about my baby? It's not even born yet, and the locals would be quite happy to see it dead."

"If Apricot isn't willing to help," one person said, "then Sparks will die. Hell, everyone in Old Kiln is going to die, one by one."

"Who said Apricot isn't willing to help?" Gran said. "You go and talk to Bash. I'll sit with her for a little while, and then we'll join you."

Those who'd come to persuade Apricot left unwillingly by the courtyard door and Inkcap followed them out. Once outside, he decided he ought to go and get a fuse… perhaps he might be able to toss it somewhere useful. Accordingly, he went home to collect one.

Tag-Along banged a gong, shouting that everyone was to assemble for a meeting outside the mountain gate so that the villagers knew it was time to blow up Sparks. Some of them went and some of them refused to go, and those who'd been at Apricot's house rushed off to find Bash. The men from the political training class had already been led out of the Kiln God Temple and were standing in front of the mountain gate, while Division Chief Ma and Bash were standing under the big myrrh tree. When those wanting to plead for Sparks saw this set-up, no one was willing to go over to talk to Bash.

"Why doesn't anyone say anything?" Inkcap asked.

They encouraged Inkcap to say something on their behalf. "Hey, you little fucker, you go and call Bash over."

Inkcap went over and called his name. Bash didn't respond and just carried on talking to Division Chief Ma. "Are you really going to make Sparks carry the dynamite?" he asked.

"It's all decided… what's wrong with you?" Division Chief Ma said. "He's dying today because he tried to kill us all yesterday."

"But he's going to die anyway. If we don't give him any food or drink, he'll be dead in three days."

"We need to make an example of him. He's going to die, but he has to take his bag of dynamite with him. You don't like it because you come from Old Kiln, so you don't need to watch when he walks away with the explosives."

"Bash!" Inkcap said again.

Bash raised his head and said, "What is it? Can't you see we're talking?"

"I have something to tell you."

"What is it?"

"Do you want a cigarette? I'll get you a light."

"Go away and stop bothering me," Bash said irritably.

"Bring me a fuse," Division Chief Ma said. "Bring it over because we'll need one later." She snatched the fuse out of Inkcap's hands.

"Bash, the folk over there want to talk to you," Inkcap said.

"Does that mean Apricot's here to make a scene?" Division Chief Ma asked Bash.

"Don't listen to Inkcap," Bash told her. "Besides which, why would she want to make a scene?"

Division Chief Ma pulled Inkcap aside and said, "You asked Apricot to come and make a scene, didn't you?"

"No," Inkcap said, "she wanted to come."

"It was all planned by you motherfuckers, wasn't it? Last night, Apricot came and threw a fit just when Sparks broke them out – that was all on purpose, wasn't it?"

"I don't know what you're talking about."

"You don't know, eh?" Division Chief Ma sneered. She began to speak loudly, as if she wanted everyone around the gate to hear. "Isn't it such a coincidence that just when Apricot came to make trouble, Sparks broke them out of custody? Don't think I'm a fool."

Inkcap was confused and kept repeating, "I don't know anything about it, I don't know anything about it."

Division Chief Ma shouted to Baldy Jin and asked him to bring something over. Baldy Jin was standing off to one side scratching himself. When he heard the instruction, he ran to the Kiln God Temple and fetched a mallet.

Division Chief Ma threw the mallet in front of Inkcap, saying, "Whose is this?"

"Ours," Inkcap said.

"At least you're honest. Tell me, how come Sparks was using your family's mallet to beat people?"

Inkcap regretted everything, he'd spoken without thinking. He wanted to give himself a slap across the chops. He longed to have a cloak of invisibility so he could disappear, and he looked down at the stone next to him, wishing he could hide underneath.

"Tell me," Division Chief Ma continued in a stern voice, "was Sparks hidden in your house? Did he take the mallet from your house?"

"I don't know anything about it, I don't know anything about it."

Division Chief Ma ordered that Inkcap be tied up, and Glob really did put a rope around him. "Bash! Bash!" Inkcap screamed, but Bash just turned around and headed for the Kiln God Temple.

While Gran led Apricot to the gate at the foot of the mountain, Sparks was being dragged out by several men, with packs of dynamite strapped to his back. He was able to walk, but he refused to do so, so one of the men from the United Command faction kicked him as he sat on the ground. Division Chief Ma threw the fuse to this man, and he blew on the fuse until the end glowed red.

"If you don't get up now, you'll have to in a moment," he said. Then he shouted at the crowd, "Get out of the way. Everyone needs to stand back."

The crowd ran behind the trees with a whoop, and the man lit the fuse on the dynamite.

Once the long fuse was ignited, it started crackling, spraying sparks. The sparks were blue, like a flower in bloom. Then Sparks suddenly stood up, cursing loudly. He cursed Division Chief Ma; he cursed Bash; he cursed

Baldy Jin; he cursed Useless; he cursed Useless's mother; he cursed Glob; he cursed the County United Command; he cursed the Hammerheads; he cursed everything and everyone, and when he had nothing left to curse, he cried, "Long live the Cultural Revolution! Long live Chairman Mao!"

"You think you're a hero dying in a righteous cause, do you?" Division Chief Ma said.

Sparks lunged at her, and she ran away. Sparks' hands were tied behind his back, and he was carrying a dynamite pack, so he couldn't catch up with her. Instead, he ran towards the Hammerheads and the United Command group. They scattered.

"Down with him!" Division Chief Ma screamed. "Beat him!"

It was Glob who struck Sparks on the back of the knee with his stick so that he fell to the ground, but he got up again. The group behind the myrrh tree were all shouting, "Run to the lotus pond! Run to the lotus pond!" Only then did Sparks turn his head and run towards the pond. He ran ahead, followed by everyone else, the United Command lot, the Hammerheads, but also the villagers. Apricot did not move, she sat on the ground until Gran pulled her up.

Sparks ran past the door of the Branch Secretary's house and just then the Branch Secretary's wife came out, carrying a pot of scraps to feed the pigs. When she saw Sparks running along with dynamite packs strapped to his back, she shrieked, "Sparks, Sparks!"

"Stay away, stay away," he told her.

The Branch Secretary's wife threw the pigfeed all over him, trying to douse the fuse, but it didn't work, it was still flaming. Sparks ran forward, and when he reached the edge of the pool, there was an almighty thud as the dynamite exploded. The Branch Secretary's wife was knocked off her feet by the explosion and debris cascaded over her. When the smoke and dust cleared and the United Command people and the Hammerheads came over to have a look, the Branch Secretary's wife clambered to her feet. She saw a lump of flesh right under her foot, about the length of her finger. After looking at it for a good long time, she realised it was a tongue.

EIGHTY-SEVEN

THE DEATH TOLL FROM THE PRISONER BREAKOUT CAME TO FOUR. As for the wounded – including those who escaped from the political training class and were recaptured, the United Command faction and the Hammerheads – they came to a total of ten. But the vicious Sparks was dead at last. Afterwards, Division Chief Ma and Bash seemed to become paranoid and drew harsh lessons from the experience. Day and night they assigned men to patrol the village, and those in the political training class were transferred from the Kiln God Temple to the kiln.

After Inkcap was arrested, he was also sent up to the kiln with the political training class. Gran went to Bash and said that Sparks was from Old Kiln, so why would he hide in her house when he could go anywhere in the whole village? As for the mallet, it was normally left out by the courtyard door, where he could easily have picked it up. She further pointed out that with her family's bad class background, they'd been in enough trouble already: how could she possibly be involved in breaking people out of captivity, how would that benefit her family? Now Inkcap had been tied up and held with the political training class, but he was only little, could she not be held in his stead?

"I agree," Bash said. "With the whole village to choose from, Sparks wouldn't go to you, but Inkcap confessed to Division Chief Ma that he knew Sparks was back. He said he was cracking walnuts with the mallet out in the courtyard when Sparks came in and grabbed it off him."

"What nonsense is this?" Gran wailed bitterly.

"Division Chief Ma is angry with him for failing to make a report, so to warn the villagers, Inkcap has to stay in the political training class for a while."

Inkcap admitted to seeing Sparks and that Sparks took the mallet from him, but he repeatedly stressed that Gran did not know anything about it. He said Sparks had threatened him not to tell anyone, so he did not dare say a word to the Hammerheads or even his grandmother.

"You'll have to pay a price for that," Division Chief Ma told him, and she ordered Inkcap to feed the pigs. The political training class was being held in one single kiln, and they'd forcibly dragged off the pigs that belonged to Awning, Sparks, Four Dogs, Lucky and Sprout. They'd turned one of the other empty kilns into a sty, and they'd already butchered and eaten one pig. There remained three pigs for Inkcap to feed every day, and at night he had to sleep with them.

When Inkcap got to the pigsty, he cried because he missed Gran and Cowbell. He was hoping Gran would visit him and Cowbell too, but neither came, so he thought that Cowbell must be too scared, and that Gran hadn't been allowed to by the Hammerheads – but Gran not coming at least meant they weren't trying to put anything on her. A pig was lying in front of him, looking at him with one eye.

"Is it true that because I'm here, Gran will be left free, so I'm here in her place?" he asked the pig.

"Hurumph."

"I'm right, aren't I?"

"Hurumph," the pig repeated. Inkcap felt relieved and wiped his tears. He did not cry any more.

The political training class was not allowed out of the kiln except to eat and go to the privy after eating. However, Inkcap had to feed the pigs, so he was free to come and go. He was observant and quick, and the people there liked him, so they often gave him some fried noodles, or sweet potato slices and persimmon peel. He put these things in the kiln and whenever he missed his grandmother, he took out a little to nibble on.

The first night, the wind was whistling and the only thing inside the kiln was a pile of wheat straw. Inkcap tossed the straw into the air so that it was all fluffy and then hollowed out a nest in the centre in which he slept. In the middle of the night, he felt his nest collapse and, feeling about himself, he touched something firm and fleshy and the same on the other side. He kicked out at whatever it was and when he did so, he realised it was the three pigs that were feeling cold, so they'd all joined him in the straw. Fine, they could do what they liked. He tossed the straw about some more until it covered them all, and then he went back to sleep. Afterwards, Inkcap learned to drive the pigs off because pigs snore – they snored so loudly that he couldn't sleep. When he'd moved them away, he still couldn't sleep – the snoring made him wonder about the smell. He hid his snacks under the pile of wheat straw. Then he warned the pigs, "If anyone dares steal my food, I'll get you!" But the pigs just grunted and lay down at the entrance of the kiln, rubbing their mouths against the wall. In the end, Inkcap decided he didn't trust these gluttonous creatures and took the noodles, sweet potato slices and persimmon peel out of the straw and put them into the small hole in the wall of the kiln where an oil lamp would originally have been placed. Then he worried that anyone coming into the kiln would spot it immediately, so he covered the food with a hank of straw.

At noon, when the food was cooked, the United Command people and the Hammerheads went to eat. They had good food, for they had meat to eat after killing a pig. They got half a bowl of meat each, and as they ate, the grease oozed down their chins. They were all delighted and talked about how great the Cultural Revolution was – they wanted it to go on forever. They were also hoping that more of the Red Blades who had run away would come back so they could beat them to death one by one. Then they'd have no problem getting their pigs to eat too!

The political training class didn't get anything nice to eat, nor did Inkcap. He sat in the kiln and looked out. Then he said to the pigs, "Whatever you eat, you'll have to shit it out in the end. The better you eat, the worse your shit stinks." The pigs did not look out, and their foreheads were wrinkled with deep lines. He knew immediately that they were worried about their fate, and he said nothing more, turning his back to the entrance of the kiln.

The United Command people and the Hammerheads had eaten before they began to cook for the political training class. Inkcap went to the kitchen to fetch scraps for the pigs. Flower Girl was scrubbing a pot. "You haven't eaten yet, so why are you feeding the pigs?" she asked.

Inkcap was about to tip the scraps into a wooden bucket. "There's grease in this, isn't there?" he said.

Flower Girl looked around to check no one was watching and poured half a bowl of leftovers into the bucket. "Of course there's grease in there, take it away," she replied.

"I don't want any grease," said Inkcap.

"Eh?"

"We can't give the pigs greasy scraps because then we'd be making them eat lard!"

"People are killing each other every day round here and you're fussing that the pigs shouldn't eat lard? Take it away. If the pigs don't eat it, you can."

Inkcap carried the bucket out and Flower Girl stood in the kitchen doorway saying, "Go feed those fucking pigs, Inkcap. There's no point taking any of that rubbish to feed my own pigs."

Inkcap hefted the bucket to the kiln where the three pigs grunted and ran over. "There's no hurry," Inkcap told them. He fished out the half bowl of leftovers from the bucket. It contained radish, sweet potato vermicelli and even a piece of meat with hair on it. He plucked out the hair and ate that first, then poured the scraps into the pigs' food bowl. The pigs smelt it but did not eat anything.

"What's the problem?" Inkcap asked. "Is it the lard?" He blew the lard off to the edge, and then thought he'd blow it over the rim. However, it would be a shame to waste it, so he thought he'd squat down and eat it himself. Then he realised that would be horrid for the pigs to witness, and told them, "Turn your backs, don't look." The pigs turned their backs, their tails wagging, and he gobbled down the lard.

Afterwards, he called the pigs over, and said, "I know you didn't like to see the lard, and I have blown the grease away. Now, eat up." But the pigs just took a few mouthfuls and then stopped again.

After lunch, Inkcap had a nap in his straw nest, and as he slept, he started drooling. He had a dream in which the pigs said to him, "We don't want to eat... we are determined not to eat. The more we eat, the faster we grow, and then butchery awaits us." When he woke up and looked at the pigs, the food in the pigs' food bowl was untouched, and all three pigs were lying down.

"You're not eating?" he asked. The pigs grunted a little, without much energy.

"But alas, you're pigs," he told them, "and pigs always get killed by humans."

The pigs jumped up and squealed. Inkcap didn't hit them or curse them. He was too busy watching them, looking at them properly. The three pigs were so like Awning, Sparks and Soupspoon that he was shocked. When he looked again, the pigs were just pigs. He rubbed his eyes and decided he must have been seeing things, and then he thought that Sparks and Soupspoon were dead, and Awning had run off – could he be dead too?

The residents of Old Kiln were buried in the cemetery after they died, but Soupspoon hadn't been buried. For all Inkcap knew, he was still lying by the roller stone or they'd thrown him into the river, and in Sparks' case there was nothing much left of him. It looked like Awning, too, would not be buried in the village cemetery. Like the three pigs, were they all going to end up butchered by the United Command faction and the Hammerheads?

Inkcap emerged from the kiln, and as always, he looked to the top of the mountain which was missing the Mountain God Temple and the white pine. He stood there for a good long time. He wanted to go and see the kiln where the political training class was being held, so he pretended to go to the toilet, passed by the entrance of the kiln and stopped to look inside.

"What are you looking at?" said the guards at the entrance to the kiln. Inkcap scurried past.

Sometimes, the guards asked him to go in and get the piss bucket. When it wasn't mealtime, the people in the political training class had to pee in the piss bucket at the kiln. When Inkcap entered, they all stared at him, and in the penumbra of the kiln, their eyes glinted green like a pack of wolves in the night. They made Inkcap's hair stand on end.

After a while, Inkcap wanted to visit the political training class again. He started buttering up the guards, bringing a burning ember from the kitchen to give them a light for their cigarettes. "Do you want me to take out the slops?" he asked.

"Why do you want a task like that?" the guards said.

"Doesn't it smell bad?"

"Yeah, it stinks," the guards replied. "Those motherfuckers are right sons of bitches, and their pee doesn't half smell."

Inkcap went in and tried to spot the Branch Secretary, who was sitting in a corner of the kiln, always with his eyes closed, as if he were asleep. Inkcap coughed and dropped a handful of wheat straw that contained a few sweet potato slices. The Branch Secretary did not move, but as Inkcap picked up the piss bucket to leave, he said, "If you're going to spit, do it outside the kiln."

For several days now, the pigs had not been eating properly. When they'd been dragged up the mountain, they were plump but now they were looking peaky, and you could see their backbones. Division Chief Ma came to the kiln to have a look. She was planning to pick a pig to be butchered but now she frowned and said, "What are you doing to these pigs?"

"They're just not thriving," Inkcap replied, "and there's nothing I can do about it."

Despite the filth, Division Chief Ma squatted down to feel the pigs' stomachs and tried to open their mouths to look inside. Inkcap went over to pull on the tail of one of the pigs so that its four hooves danced. However, Division Chief Ma still couldn't open its mouth, so she let go. "Why were you pulling the pig's tail?" she asked.

"I wanted you to see the kind of shit they're producing."

"I trained in veterinary medicine," she snapped. "I know what to look for in a pig." She walked out of the kiln and told Glob that the pigs were too thin and should be fed well for a few days before they were killed.

When Division Chief Ma left, Inkcap and the pigs were all happy. Inkcap had the sudden urge to do a handstand. Cowbell could do handstands, but he'd never learned. He put his hands on the ground and lifted his body until it was about to fall forward, then he made himself swing back a bit, his body leaning on the kiln wall – he'd done it! Inkcap opened his eyes and saw three pigs running in a race. They were circling the kiln, turning around, slowing down. Then one stood up straight and walked on its hind legs followed by the other two. All of a sudden Inkcap couldn't support himself and fell over and the three pigs did likewise; they all fell together. Inkcap got up but they were still lying down, so he gave them a tickle on their stomachs. They were so comfortable that they just lay there grunting, their four legs splayed.

"You were quite right," Inkcap told them. "If you don't eat, you won't grow fat, and if you don't grow fat, you won't be butchered."

The pigs chuckled.

"If you don't eat, then I won't eat either, and if I don't eat, they'll have to let me go."

The pigs were gumming on Inkcap, so much so that he could not sit down, and Awning's pig took a firm grip of his ear. "What's the matter, you won't let me go?" Inkcap said.

The pig immediately let go. "OK," Inkcap said, "I won't leave, even if I starve down to a stick."

As Inkcap was talking to the pig, he took the sweet potato slices out of the little space in the wall and ate them. He ate one himself and gave one to the pig; he crunched and munched, and the pig crunched and munched, and soon they finished all the slices. The pig was still looking at him and ran over to the hole where they'd been kept to look, so Inkcap said, "No more." He took the wheat straw out of the little space where they'd been kept. "They're really all gone."

Another night, Inkcap laid out straw to let the pigs sleep on, and then put some straw over them. One of the pigs farted and he said, "You want to shit? What were you doing back there?" The pig went to the entrance of the kiln and shat with its buttocks quivering, then turned around and went to sleep. The pigs did not snore that night, or perhaps they did not close their eyes for fear of being beaten, but Inkcap slept beautifully. Then, in the middle of the night, he had another dream and sat up suddenly. He dreamed he was playing with the pigs, and the pigs took off their shoes, which were small but made of leather, and he said, "Let me try your shoes." Just when he put them on, he heard one of the pigs say, "Where's Inkcap?" He looked, and he had turned into a pig. Glob entered the kiln just at this moment, and he was shouting, "Inkcap, Inkcap!" Inkcap didn't say anything, the pigs didn't say anything, and Glob didn't notice that he'd turned into a pig, so he shouted from outside the kiln, "Inkcap's disappeared, he's run away!" The people at the kiln ran to the crossroads, shouting that they must catch him, and they'd hamstring him when they did. He and the three pigs were laughing in the kiln, but then Awning's pig started kicking up the soil in a corner of the kiln, making a hole, and then put his shoes in and buried them. "How can I become a person without shoes?" Inkcap asked. "Unless you want them to catch you, you'll remain a pig," the pig replied. But at that moment Glob came in again with three others, and they were saying, "Which should I pick?" "Feel the spine," one said, "and pick the fattest one with the thickest spine." They had come to take a pig to be slaughtered, and he and the three pigs huddled together in the kiln. Then Glob said, "We'll take that short-snouted one, the long-snouted one won't have any meat." They came and grabbed him by the ear, and he shouted, "I'm not a pig, I'm Inkcap!" He roared as loud as thunder, so the people at the kiln heard him, and the residents in Old Kiln heard him too, but Glob couldn't understand a word and he said, "What's all this squealing for? Are you making this noise so the villagers know we're going to eat meat again?" Glob kicked him in the arse, and with this kick, Inkcap woke up screaming.

The pigs in the straw nest ran out, and Inkcap realised he'd been dreaming. He was all sweaty, and the pigs looked at him, making him feel a little embarrassed. "Go to sleep, go to sleep," he said. He thought back to his dream and told himself, Gran always said dreams are the opposite of real life, so I will not be killed. Then he wrapped himself in his quilt and sat quietly until dawn.

At daybreak, the pigs were still asleep. They must have realised he'd not gone back to sleep again and decided to snore their heads off. The sunlight came in through the fence at the mouth of the kiln, and they were still not awake.

"Get up, why are you so sleepy?" said Inkcap. He wanted to tell the pigs what happened in his dream, to show them that humans dream in reverse, that good dreams are not always good dreams, but bad dreams are always good. "Do you dream too?" he asked.

The pigs rolled themselves onto their feet, and they pointed their hindquarters towards the kiln mouth to shit, but before they had time to go back to their nest, a few shots went off. Inkcap dashed outside the kiln. The United Command members and the Hammerheads were up and about, rushing around in chaos, and then running down the hillside in a swarm.

Flower Girl rushed over, her hands covered in flour, shouting, "Inkcap! Inkcap!"

He pushed open the gate and said, "What's up? Why is everyone running?"

"There's going to be another battle. Maybe the Red Blades have come back, along with the United Headquarters. Whatever you do, you must not come out, just stay in the kiln."

"That means more people are going to die. And what about you? What are you going to do?"

"I'll hide too," Flower Girl said. "I'm just worried my hubby's still at home."

Inkcap started worrying about his grandmother. "I have to go back... Gran is also at home."

"You can't go anywhere. The two factions are fighting and who knows who'll win. If the Hammerheads prevail and find out you aren't here, what do you think they'll do to you?"

Inkcap had to agree. "Well, since you're here, let's hide."

Flower Girl entered the kiln, but the stench was so bad she could not stay, so she sat down at the mouth of the building. Down the hill came shouting and another fierce bout of gunfire. All the birds flew up the hill, big and small, white and black, and they landed on the kiln. Inkcap kept counting them, over and over, but he couldn't make his figures agree. Then he spotted the four red-billed, white-tailed birds were among them, and he whistled. All the birds started to sing, and he cried, "Goodman! Goodman!" The four birds turned their heads to look at the kiln.

"Who's fighting who down there, and who's winning?" Inkcap asked. The four birds gave a long whistle and rose into the sky. Once those four birds flew off, all the other birds joined them. Like the leaves of the trees blown by the gale, they circled in mid-air and formed a black cloud, and then suddenly there was no trace of them.

The gunfire became more sporadic, culminating in another burst and a thud, followed by silence.

Cowbell came bounding up the hill like a dog. When he got as far as the pond at the kiln, he was panting so badly he couldn't run any further. He sat there, shouting, "Inkcap! Inkcap!"

It was at this point that Inkcap smelt the odour, stronger than it had ever been before, like a pile of chopped onions, choking him to the point where he couldn't speak. The first thought in his head was that something terrible must have happened. He hated his nose, so he grabbed it with his hands, shoved his fingers into his nostrils and scraped until blood and snot came out – all because he was trying not to smell the stench, but it was still so strong. He clutched at his nose and pinched it and then tried to plug it again with his fingers. All the while he was shouting for Cowbell, but there was no response for some time.

"What's he doing here?" said Flower Girl. "And anxious like that, could it be–"

"Do you think something bad has happened to Gran?" said Inkcap.

Cowbell continued shouting, "Inkcap! Oi! Inkcap!"

Inkcap went out of the kiln, and asked, "Who beat Gran?"

"It's over," cried Cowbell. "It's all over."

Inkcap's legs went limp, and he fell to the ground, still asking, "Who beat Gran? Who beat Gran?"

"They're done for – the United Command and the Hammerheads got beat," Cowbell said.

Inkcap was in a state of disbelief. "They're done for?"

"The United Command and the Hammerheads are done for," Cowbell said. "The PLA are here, the soldiers are armed with guns… The United Command folk and the Hammerheads got surrounded at the threshing ground, and Division Chief Ma and Bash were arrested."

Whoa! Inkcap jumped up from the ground. Like a spring, he landed upright without flailing his arms or wobbling on his feet. He hugged Cowbell and the two of them jumped around together, and when he looked back, Flower Girl also came out, and so did the three pigs. Flower Girl still wanted to ask what was going on, so Cowbell gabbled something to Inkcap and the two of them ran off to the kitchen.

The kitchen door was locked, but the window next to it was left open, so they climbed in. There were buns cooking in the pot, piping hot, so they broke one in half and took a few bites, stuffing the rest into their clothing, and climbed out of the window again.

Flower Girl rushed over. "Have you been stealing buns?"

"They aren't going to eat them, so why shouldn't we?" said Cowbell.

"Were they done?"

"Oh, yes," Inkcap assured her. Then he caught sight of Awning's wife and Sparks' wife running up the road.

"Someone is coming," Flower Girl said. "Take the buns and go."

But Cowbell went back in through the window, and picked up the lump of dough that was lying on the board, then clambered back out of the window again and ran away.

Awning's wife and Sparks' wife had come to get their pigs. When Inkcap was about to leave the kiln, he looked at the pigs that were grunting to him, pulled three buns out and threw them over.

"There are buns?" Awning's wife said. "What else is there?" She ran into the kitchen and took everything she could find to eat. Flower Girl shouted from inside, asking how she should explain everything that was missing, but Awning's wife ignored her. Sparks' wife was late and did not get any rice and noodles, but she did take a pot.

Inkcap ran down the hill with the buns in his pockets and went straight to the house, but the courtyard door was closed. "Gran! Gran!" he shouted.

Gran came out and opened the door. She had blood all over her hands. Inkcap was shocked. "What's wrong with you, Gran?"

"Apricot's had her baby," she replied.

A baby was crying in the house, wah-wah-wah, yowling like a cat. It was a painfully sad sound.

PART SIX

SPRING

春

EIGHTY-EIGHT

THE LONG WINTER FINALLY PASSED, and the New Year's festival came, but there were no further folk art performances in the village. The opera company from Xiahewan did not perform, but at least for the first six days of the lunar New Year holiday, everyone got to eat steamed buns – it wouldn't be New Year's without steamed buns! Very few families had wheat flour, so they had to use maize flour instead. If they did have wheat flour, the best thing would be to mix a little in with the maize flour, add water, put in the yeast, and then cover it over on the *kang* to rise while everyone got busy firing up the steamers.

In the village, smoke from the firewood rolled down the lane like a fog, and the sweet smell of the steamed buns meant that the residents could not help but open their mouths to inhale, and when they did, they choked and coughed. Inkcap went running down the lane, kicking up the smoke, so that now his feet disappeared, and then his arm vanished too, and by the time he got to the crossroads, his entire body was invisible – all you could see was his head. Noodle Fish's wife had promised to give Gran a pot of vinegar, so she sent Inkcap to get it. In return, she was going to get a big chunk of the tofu she'd bought from Six Pints' family. In Old Kiln you could only get the firm kind of tofu, so dense you could tie a handle to it and carry it away.

Noodle Fish's wife was in the middle of cooking a baba flatbread. "You're lucky to get to try this, Inkcap," she said as she cut him a piece with a bamboo knife so he could eat it fresh from the steamer.

Inkcap had already taken three bites when he found a louse in the lump he was stuffing into his mouth. Inkcap could eat anything. No matter who spat in his bowl, he could eat it. If a morsel fell to the ground, he would pick it up and blow the dirt off before eating it. But he could not stand eating food containing creepy crawlies. "Aunt! Aunt!" he said. "There's lice in the baba bread!"

"Let me take a look," Noodle Fish's wife said. She peered at it and declared that it was not a louse, but a sesame seed.

Inkcap might have accepted this explanation and contented himself with picking out the "sesame seeds", but then she went on, "I had the dough rising in the bed, so how can I keep the lice on the blanket from getting into it? It doesn't matter… it's just protein, after all." Inkcap stopped eating, took the vinegar pot, and felt so revolted that he threw up in the alleyway outside.

For the six days of the festival, three days were spent eating baba bread, and the next three were spent eating steamed buns made from soya bean dregs and sweet potato flour. After the sixth day, it was pointed out that a proper New Year's holiday lasts for the first fifteen days of the first lunar month, but without good things to eat, what kind of New Year's festival was this? They had started to eat porridge and fried noodles made from persimmon seeds mixed with rice husks again, so pretty much everyone was constipated, and wooden sticks were placed in every privy to dig out the shit.

However, at the south entrance of the village near the gate leading to the mountains, by the east end of the mill, there was an amazing morning glory. Originally in the whole of Old Kiln, only Awning's family had a vine growing against the wall, and when the wall was knocked down, the morning glory was dug up by the roots. Now, there were so many vines all over the place, where did they come from? People thought it was strange. These vines were covered in tendrils like butterfly feelers, stretching far into the air, grabbing something and then climbing up it, ascending the stone pillars on both sides of the gate, up the chinaberry tree next to the mill and crawling all over Ever-Obedient's wall up to the height of a man. After the upper stone at the mill got dislodged and rolled under the embankment, the vine grew to cover the lower stone, and the new stone lion that was still not completely carved was also covered to the point that nothing could be seen; it had become a kind of lumpy frame for the plant. The flowers were not in bloom, but you felt they were ready to open at any moment, and you might even feel that as soon as you turned around, the trumpet-like flowers would be blasting their notes up towards the sky.

Gran was now stone deaf and could no longer hear any sound. If she was the subject of a criticism meeting, how would they scold her? She would not pay the slightest attention, her face entirely expressionless. The night of New Year's Eve was very dark, so she gave Inkcap a lantern encircled with papercuts. When Inkcap was running around the alleyways carrying the lantern, the kerosene lamp inside slipped sideways and burned the lantern, and he came back in tears. Gran did not hit him, but comforted him instead, saying, "If you have a lantern, you can light the road ahead, but you can still go walking without one."

When he pulled her up the steps of the house, he heard a click from deep inside her body, and afterwards her leg became too painful to walk on. Now that Goodman was no longer around, Gran had to massage her leg herself. Even though she was able to walk, she had to prop herself up on a stick. As Inkcap watched her hobble along with her stick, he concluded she was getting a little more lame every day. His tears flowed, and he did not let her work in the fields any more, or carry water from the spring, or feed the pigs in the sty. He had to work so much harder. But as Gran spent more time at home and in the yard, being deaf and unable to walk, she no longer wanted to see people. After all, if she spent all her time at home or in the courtyard, she wouldn't need to eat much. Every evening at dusk, she would come out alone on her stick and go to the embankment at the southern entrance of the village to stand for a while.

It was now difficult to find a big-character poster torn to shreds by the wind anywhere in the alleyways, and the trees were only just now putting out new leaves, so she had nothing to make papercuts with. Not that she was able to make them since she could no longer hold the scissors.

She used her eyes to take in the world, looking at all kinds of people and pigs and cows and dogs. When she sat down on a rock and looked at the clouds in the sky, or at the rain-soaked walls of a house, she saw even more and better features in everything she surveyed. She had become more wrinkled at this time, like a chrysanthemum or a spider's web, so you could not tell whether she was sorrowful or smiling silently.

The clouds in the sky were as crystal white as ice, and as the sun was about to set, a crack appeared in the clouds and a red light shone obliquely on half of Middle Mountain, as well as on the south-sloping cliff face, while the mountain went black – as black as a herd of animals. The reason for the blackness of the mountain was the bank of clouds crowning it from halfway up, just as all through the winter it had been covered in snow. People always thought it was perpetually covered in snow, not noticing when the snow was replaced by clouds... or perhaps the snow had gradually turned into clouds? The clouds moved while Gran was staring at them, and they all flowed together down the mountain, and then they flowed down the river until there was nothing left, and the river had gone white. The thornback fish were calling their names: "Ang... chi! Ang... chi!" They never normally made so much noise; it sounded like cows mooing in a barn.

"Gran, is God sweeping the clouds away?" Inkcap asked.

Gran could not hear. There was no expression on her face as she watched the last of the sun's rays recede from both Middle Mountain and the ridge, and the river was still white, a motionless kind of white.

Inkcap knew Gran hadn't heard him, and he felt sad, so he placed an arm around her to help her back home. However, Gran had spotted Tag-Along with a basket on his back stumbling up the road from the south entrance of the village.

Tag-Along's wife died at the end of the year. One winter's day her broken leg had started seeping pus, up to half a bowl at a time, and she slept for about two weeks, only to say that she hoped she might still last a year or so. Nobody could have imagined that having always said she would make it to New Year's, that she'd be celebrating with them, she would suddenly pass away. After the death of his wife, Tag-Along's world collapsed. Before the festival, the village helped those in need, and Tag-Along did get assistance, but there was no rice – just dried radish from Xinjiang, and he had to go to the town to collect it. Tag-Along had taken his son to town to carry back dozens of pounds of dried radish. When the kid saw Inkcap, he called out to him and came running over.

"It's a whole new year," Inkcap said. "Why haven't you grown?"

"You're still the same size too," his *gan'erzi* replied.

"I don't have to grow, but you do."

"I won't."

Inkcap hugged his *gan'erzi* and said, "If you don't want to grow, you don't have to. None of us in the village will grow."

Tag-Along put down the basket and lay on the ground. He was pale, like a piece of paper, as he screamed for Gran. Gran looked at his mouth and shouted, "Tag-Along! What's happened to you? Do you want Inkcap to carry your basket?"

Tag-Along nodded and his head dropped to the ground. Inkcap refused to carry it. Then Tag-Along spoke again: "I'm afraid I can't make it, Inkcap."

Now Inkcap took a good look at Tag-Along, and he heard his *gan'erzi* say that his dad had needed to take a shit on the journey home, so he'd squatted down and dug some shit out of his arsehole with his fingers, fishing out a few dried lumps, but then it tuned out he'd made a hole somewhere and he bled all over the ground, so he lay down and passed out for a good long time. Inkcap went to pick up the basket, which was huge. When he managed to get it on his back, it kept banging against the backs of his knees. "So now you need me," he said crossly, "but when you were working for Bash, you didn't even say a word when I asked for help."

"Don't talk about it," Tag-Along said. "You shouldn't try to humiliate me by grubbing up the past… it's not a very nice thing to do."

"What news in town?" Inkcap asked.

"What do you mean, what news?"

"Stop pretending you don't know, otherwise I won't carry this," Inkcap said severely.

"Oh, you mean the trial?"

"That's no trial, that's a lynching they're planning."

"I heard it's only a few days away," Tag-Along said.

"Do you think they'll really shoot him?" Inkcap asked. "They're just going to shoot Bash dead?"

"Sure, it's an open-and-shut case." Then he added with a sigh, "His maize will grow the size of trees…"

"Can maize grow the size of trees?" Inkcap asked curiously. Tag-Along held his arse in his hands as he leaned against the stone lion covered in morning glory vines, and the bleeding started again and flowed down his ankles.

The next morning, Inkcap was carrying half a bucket of fresh piss to throw on the wheat in his fields. He came across a toad lying in the alleyway, so he stomped his foot, which made the toad jump forward a little, landing in a spider's web spun between the courtyard wall and the elm tree beyond. A fat spider fell from the web, but it did not fall all the way to the ground, but wiggled here and there on the end of a line of silk. To run into a spider in the morning was a sign that something important was going to happen that day; that was something everyone in Old Kiln believed, but Inkcap wondered what would actually happen. "Spider, Spider, what do you know?" he called. The fat spider climbed up the thread to the branch, and Inkcap was still angry with the spider for not telling him, so he knocked another spider off a branch which died when it fell to the ground.

Cowbell once said that all male spiders are skinny while females are fat, and that the male spider spends its life scheming to insert its thing into the female, but once it achieves that goal, it dies. Inkcap looked at the spider that was dead on the ground. It was a skinny little thing and he wondered if it had just been at it with the fat spider. But there was no one to ask.

Ever-Obedient was sitting at the threshing ground by the entrance to the alley, holding a bowl of wheat flour, to which water had been added. He was pinching up lumps of the dough and rolling them into noodles, which he then arranged on the threshing ground like a small tower.

"Uncle," Inkcap said, "is it true that after a male and female spider have been at it, the male spider dies?"

Ever-Obedient didn't seem to be listening and concentrated on his work, finishing one pile and beginning on the next.

"Hey! What are you doing?" Inkcap asked.

"Playing with shit," Ever-Obedient said.

Now the heaps of dough didn't look like towers, they looked like shit.

"Shit?" Inkcap said.

"You want to eat? Eat shit!"

Inkcap decided that Ever-Obedient was crazy. He stopped paying attention to the crazy Ever-Obedient, thinking about whether the madness was contagious, just like scabies. Yoyo had become insane, and so would Ever-Obedient.

When Inkcap got to his own plot, the dew immediately dampened his trouser legs. As he spooned out his fertiliser, a breeze started up, coiling into a thin column. At that moment a large crowd appeared in the distance, over by the shack. The shack was still there, though it had lost its door and windows, and in front were piles of rocks where the County United Command had set up their markers, and the horizontal elm tree barricade, which had not yet been carried away, lay the roadside. A horde of people were now standing on the rocks and elm tree. From the road at the turn of the ridge, men and women were coming down in groups, and a crowd had gathered on the road at Beacon Hill.

"Is something really important going to happen?" Inkcap asked. Then he grabbed his bucket and ran.

Pendulum was banging a gong as he walked along the road leading to the village. Now his back had finally healed, it was like he'd turned into another person, and he was shouting, "All members of the community listen. After eating, you're all to go to the riverbank. If you haven't eaten, go to the riverbank now. A public trial is being held today."

Inkcap wanted to ask what exactly was going on, but Pendulum had already turned into Three Fork Alley, and the sound bounced from the east wall to the west wall, and then rebounded from the west wall to the east wall, until all Inkcap could hear was, "All members of the community listen…"

Some householders came out of their homes, this one asking the one diagonally opposite what was going on, while that one asked the one next door the same question. None of them seemed to see Inkcap, as if he were no more consequential than a dog or a pig coming towards them. Inkcap was a little angry and regretted failing to come out with a fuse. But even if they were to ask him, what did he know, how could he answer their questions? He walked down the alleyway while keeping his ears flapping.

What he heard was, "Everyone from Xichuan and Xiahewan is here. The area around the Zhen River Pagoda is packed with people." "What are they doing here?" "Everyone on trial is from Old Kiln." "Who's on trial?" "Who do you think?" "Are they going to shoot Awning and Bash?" "Maybe." "My God, how many are going to die here in Old Kiln? Who else? Who else? Are they going to arrest all the Red Blades and Hammerheads?" "I don't know." "Lord, our village is finished. The village of Xishanya rioted back in fifty-two, and weren't they punished for it? Now we're going to be punished for the Cultural Revolution!" "How can that lot rioting be compared to the Cultural Revolution? The Cultural Revolution is good. Long live the Cultural Revolution!" "Long live the Cultural Revolution! Sure, long live the Cultural Revolution! But so many people have died in Old Kiln, and every time one person dies it takes generations for his descendants to recover. It's over, it's all over, there's nothing left for us here in Old Kiln." "We've still got our porcelain." "We've got a kiln, but who knows how to fire it?" "There's a kiln, but who will fire it again? Pendulum?" "We've still got Inkcap... Inkcap can fire it."

When he finally heard his name mentioned, they were teasing and making fun of him, so Inkcap just said, "I'm going to school next year. Do you think I won't be able to fire a kiln in the future?" He spat on the ground and carried his bucket homeward. But Cowbell was calling him, shouting, and only Cowbell was ever nice to him.

Two men carrying guns were discussing something with Cowbell under the rubber tree, and when Cowbell shouted his name and Inkcap ran over, Cowbell turned around and said, "Go to the left alley and find the courtyard door where the bricks are stacked against the wall."

Inkcap looked at the men carrying guns as they marched down the alleyway and asked who they were. "I don't know," said Cowbell. "They're something to do with the public trial, I think."

"What did they want to know?"

"Where Awning's house is."

"Are they going to arrest his wife?"

"They said they wanted to go to Awning's house to get the bullet fee."

"The bullet fee? They're going to shoot Awning and make his wife pay for the bullet?" Inkcap was appalled.

"You don't understand. Everyone who gets shot has to pay for the bullet."

Inkcap's heart gave a lurch, and his whole body stiffened as he moaned in horror. He turned around to leave, even forgetting to pick up his bucket.

"Aren't you going to the riverbank?" said Cowbell.

"Can I?"

"There aren't any Red Blades or Hammerheads any more, so why shouldn't you? You've never been anywhere."

"There may not be any Red Blades or Hammerheads, but I'm not allowed to go just anywhere," Inkcap pointed out. "I still belong to one of the Black Categories."

"That's true," Cowbell said. "But this is your last chance to see Awning and Bash before they die." Inkcap stood up, and in the end, Cowbell dragged him along.

A dozen more trucks came along the highway, each displaying a large banner with the words "Enforcing the Dictatorship of the Proletariat", and the armed men on them were hauling along their tied-up prisoners. Inkcap could never have imagined that Bash and Awning would be riding in the front truck. The next truck had Division Chief Ma and Glob on board, while the one after that was carrying Lightkeeper and Pockmark.

"What are Pockmark and Lightkeeper doing there?"

"I heard they also established a rebel corps and borrowed money from three credit cooperatives," Cowbell explained. "When they tried to get money from the Huangbaicha credit union, they were refused, and they killed the poor guy on the spot."

"Pockmark's responsible for a good few deaths. You could tell me he'd killed any number of people and I'd believe you," Inkcap said. "But Lightkeeper?"

"He belongs to a Black Category, and they'd do any horrible deed... I'm not talking about you, I'm talking about Lightkeeper," Cowbell assured him.

Inkcap didn't have time to quarrel with Cowbell, he wanted to make his way through the crowd to see Lightkeeper, but the truck now dropped the tailgate and the prisoners were pushed out. Inkcap couldn't see the prisoners, but he could hear the screaming and the cursing that followed: "Oh, so you don't like it when you're the one getting hurt? Stand up! Cooperate with the authorities! If you cooperate, you won't suffer when they shoot you. If you don't, they'll shoot you a few extra times for good measure... that'll show you what pain is!"

The crowd fell backwards, and in doing so stepped on the feet of Inkcap and Cowbell, and they fell over. However, they carried on pressing back, and other people tripped over them and fell too.

"Get off!" Inkcap shouted. "You're trampling on us!"

The crowd surged forward again, and by the time they got to their feet, the public trial had begun. They couldn't see where the court was set up or where the prisoners were standing, all they could see were the arses and backs of the crowd. Having tried to crawl in between their legs, and not being able to get more than a yard further, Inkcap asked a big man, "Can I climb on your shoulders?"

"Piss off, brat," the man replied.

Cowbell yanked Inkcap over towards the shack, which already had people hanging out of the gaps where the windows and doors used to be. Cowbell got behind the shack and climbed onto the roof, but Inkcap couldn't join him. "I'll tell you what's happening," Cowbell assured him.

Cowbell began his commentary: "They're standing right under the pagoda, and Awning's face looks like a crumpled sack, and Lightkeeper's face is all red, as red as pig's liver. He just fell over and was pulled up again."

"What about Bash?" Inkcap asked.

"He's got his face up, and he's looking very pale–"

"He always was pale. But when you say he's got his face up..."

"His face is upturned but his eyes are closed."

"Is he still in uniform?"

"He's wearing a red sweater... that red sweater," Cowbell replied.

"He only has the one," Inkcap said.

"That fucker Pockmark is laughing. Well, let him laugh, motherfucker."

Inkcap wondered to himself, Can Pockmark still laugh? Then he heard a loudspeaker blaring, but as to who was speaking and what was being said, neither Cowbell nor Inkcap cared.

"What about Division Chief Ma and Glob?" Inkcap asked.

"Fuck the Division Chief," said Cowbell.

The loudspeaker suddenly stopped, and the crowd started to move back and forth like a wave again.

"What's up, what's happening now?"

"They're going to shoot them... they're taking them towards the riverbank!" Cowbell exclaimed.

Inkcap was desperate to get up on the roof. He took a dozen steps back and ran towards the rear wall of the shack, hoping to jump up and grab the eaves and then clamber up onto the roof. He almost touched the eaves with his hands but fell down hard, so he got to his feet and decided there was no chance of ever getting on the roof. He dusted himself down and followed in the wake of the crowd heading towards the riverbank.

When the crowd reached the riverbank, it was under guard by men with guns, and no one was allowed to pass. Inkcap ran along to the reedbeds, where it was less busy. From there, he could see the six sandpits that had been dug on the riverbank. A man with a gun stood in front of every pit, and not long afterwards, the prisoners were dragged towards them down the riverbank. Each prisoner was pulled along by two men, but they were not exactly being pulled... They'd been hogtied and were now being carried along at high speed. Each of the groups of three had run up, crossing the ditch separating the reedbeds from the river, and then down to the riverbank. Bash was the first to arrive, and his red sweater was as bright as ever. His arms were tied behind him, so you couldn't see that the red didn't go all the way around. He was wearing his washed-out army trousers, and they were tied in at the bottom with rope. His two feet barely touched the ground, he was being dragged along that fast. The tips of his toes scraped a narrow channel in the sand, like the furrow of a plough.

Inkcap heard someone behind him ask, "Why did he tie his trousers like that?"

"If you don't tie your trousers," came the reply, "your shit and piss will come out the bottom."

Maybe he was right; the prisoners must have been so scared that they soiled themselves. Inkcap turned around and saw three men standing behind him. One was holding a steamed bun made from potato flour, and the other two were urging him, "When the gun goes off, run ahead, break the bun as you run, and when you get to the front, scoop up the brains in the bun. You need to eat it while it's hot, remember..."

"What if I can't eat it?" said the man with the bun.

"You must. Do as you're told, eat it, and you'll be cured. Remember, run towards the first sandpit, the first is the leader of the Hammerheads, the one called Bash. He was always smart."

"Shut up," the other broke in. "People are listening."

The three of them looked over to the left, and Inkcap likewise, and there was Baldy Jin, Awning's brother-in-law and Almost-There. Each of them was holding mats and ropes.

The man with the steamed bun said, "Why should I be shut up? What are those people doing here anyway?"

Of course, Inkcap understood perfectly well what Baldy Jin, Awning's brother-in-law and Almost-There were doing, they'd come to collect the corpses. They'd want to get to the sand pits first, ahead of the bun man, to protect the dead body.

"They're here to collect the bodies," Inkcap said.

"Uncle, uncle, people want to collect the corpses, but what am I going to do if I can't get the brains?" the man with the bun said.

The man next to him asked Inkcap, "Are you from Old Kiln?"

"Sure."

"How many collectors have come?"

"Three families. One for Bash, one for Awning and one for Lightkeeper."

"Who's come for Bash?" the man asked.

"Oh, they're tough as anything," Inkcap told him. "If you want brains, you're better off with either the woman at pit four or Pockmark at pit five – nobody's here for them."

"I'll get the woman," the man declared.

These words had barely left his lips when the guns went off: six guns fired simultaneously at the six prisoners. They only heard a single shot, yet the six prisoners' heads jerked backwards at the same time, as they fell into the sand pits, and a stream of matter burst from their skulls and their bodies lay almost parallel. Even as Inkcap wondered what was going on, the man behind him clutching the steamed bun set off running. The men holding mats and ropes – that is Baldy Jin, Awning's brother-in-law and Almost-There – also ran off and soon caught up with the man with the steamed bun. Baldy Jin blocked him with his body, and the steamed bun fell from his hand, and he shouted, "My bun! My bun!"

A great crowd rushed past, all running towards the riverbank, and Inkcap again found himself blocked, and he fell into a sand pit. He lost sight of the man with the steamed bun, nor could he see Baldy Jin, Awning's brother-in-law or Almost-There.

Still, Inkcap got up and ran after the crowd towards the riverbank. He wanted to take one last look at Bash. He'd thought it all through; he wasn't in the least sorry for him but neither did he hate him, but he did want to spit on Pockmark. He was running along the beach when someone grabbed him – Gran! Gran was here too, and so was the Branch Secretary and Apricot, who had a scarf wrapped around her head that nearly covered her entire face, showing only her big eyes, which were so black they reminded Inkcap of the sunglasses Bash used to wear. Apricot was holding the baby in her arms, and the baby was wailing loudly.

"Go back," Gran said, "go back. You've got to think of the baby. Go back..." And she also told Inkcap to go back home.

"I won't go to the sandpit, I'll stay here."

Unable to hear what he was saying, she glared at him and said, "What are you doing here anyway? Are you trying to turn your stomach and give yourself nightmares? Nobody else has come, so why should you?"

Gran started hauling Inkcap away, so he lied and said, "I just need to tie my shoelaces…" He bent over, and then suddenly set off running, still talking back, "What do you mean, nobody else has come? Everyone in the village is here!"

In fact, Ever-Obedient wasn't there. He was still rolling his noodles back in the village, and when the guns went off, he didn't pay the slightest attention. He'd now arranged six or seven piles of "shit" on the threshing floor and the visible roots of nearby trees, and then he walked back to his house next to the mill. At the entrance to the courtyard, a dog was lying. This dog had broken its spine and was unable to move; it spent all day just lying there.

After Inkcap and Cowbell met up again, they waited until everyone on the riverbank and the highway had gone before returning to the village. They discussed where the bodies of Awning, Bash, Lightkeeper and Pockmark would be buried. Lightkeeper and Pockmark didn't have any family, so they'd be buried by the villagers in a grave dug out at the foot of Middle Mountain. Awning had a wife, and she came from a big family – they'd put him in the clan graveyard. Although Bash never married, Baldy Jin was a good friend, and he'd make sure the Hammerheads got him a proper funeral somehow; again, they'd bury him in his clan graveyard. But how were they going to pay for it… for digging a grave or making a coffin?

"Oh, they'll dig him a nice grave," Cowbell said. "They had the coffin with them out in front of the shack while they went down to the riverbank. I saw the scabies on Awning's face, and Bash's. Scabies is contagious, so they'll need to be buried deep."

A question suddenly occurred to Inkcap: "Will they turn into ghosts?"

"Sure," Cowbell said. "Everyone turns into a ghost when they die."

"What kind of ghost?"

The two of them decided that since they'd failed to see a ghost last time, they'd follow Goodman's instructions and keep an eye out for ghosts that evening.

When they got to the village, walking along the road, Cowbell noticed shit on the threshing floor, and not just one pile either – six or seven of them. Maybe all this talk of ghosts had got on his nerves, so he tried to change the subject. "What motherfucking arsehole has shit everywhere?" he roared.

Inkcap knew it was just noodle dough, so he decided to mess with Cowbell a little. "Hey, if you eat one of those piles, I'll give you a pint of white flour."

"A pint of white flour?" Cowbell said. "You promise?"

"Absolutely."

"If you keep your word, I'll eat it."

"You will?"

"Too right!" Cowbell looked around to check no one was there, took a lump of "shit" and ate it.

Inkcap watched him eat it and asked, "Was it bad?"

"No, not at all," Cowbell said. "It tasted of sweet potatoes. You go to the house now and get me my flour."

Inkcap now regretted his promise. "But Gran's at home," he said. "I'll have to give it to you on some other occasion."

"That won't do. If you want to get out of it, then you have to eat shit too."

"I'll eat it if you give me a pint of flour."

"Fine."

Inkcap walked to another threshing floor, picked up a lump of "shit" and ate it too. "We're even," he said. "You don't give me a pint of flour and I don't give you one either."

Neither of them spoke for a while, but as they walked away, Cowbell said, "So neither of us got a pint of flour, and we both got to eat a pile of shit?"

Inkcap was about to respond when a gust of wind came over from behind a tree and sealed his mouth, so he said no more, and after that, the wind started blowing hard. The wind raced through the whole of Old Kiln and charged down to the riverbank and the reedbeds, where the reeds were still just a yard or so tall, and the bushes were covered with early blooming flowers. The flowers were as small as grains of rice. They now started dancing in the wind, and soon formed a pink fog, floating high in the sky above the village.

Inkcap suddenly had a feeling that the morning glory by the gate, the mill and the millstones must have opened.

"Impossible," Cowbell declared.

"But they must be open," Inkcap said.

"Bet you they aren't. I'll bet you a pint of flour."

"Fine."

Inkcap said no more because up ahead where the lane forked, he could see Gran, the Branch Secretary and Apricot. They'd left the riverbank so much earlier, and yet here they were still now walking along the lane. The Branch Secretary dragged one foot; he'd contracted rheumatism in the political training class, and one of his legs was in constant pain. Teeth grow longer with toothache, and legs grow shorter with leg pain. Now he swayed back and forth, limping along with his legs out of alignment and his hand constantly clapped against his back. The baby in Apricot's arms wailed, a sound as sad and miserable as a cat yowling, and no matter how much she cajoled it, it did not stop.

First draft completed on the night of 25 August 2009
Editing finished at noon on 25 April 2010
Revision completed on the evening of 8 May 2010

AFTERWORD

AFTER I TURNED FIFTY, some of my acquaintances began to pass away, so I went to the crematorium more often, and I suddenly found I liked to carry a bit of cash on my person. I also became less and less sleepy, so I knew I was getting old.

When you get old, remind yourself: you must not expect to be able to keep your place at the table, hogging positions of power; you must not be too keen to stay in the limelight, so you really should not appear unless it is absolutely necessary; you must not be paranoid; and you must not envy others. These are achievable goals, they are things you can try to achieve, but what you cannot control is your memory – the further back it goes the clearer it is, and it does go back so far.

This put me in a bit of a trance. Should a long life be considered not as one hundred years, but as two? One century for the days of reality and another for the days of your dreams... Can it be that we never disappear, as we replicate ourselves in our children on the one hand, and restore oneself in memory on the other?

My memories go back mostly to my teenage years, which were in the mid to late 1960s when China was going through the unparalleled disaster that was the Cultural Revolution.

The Cultural Revolution has been unmentionable for more than forty years. Time wears everything away, but as film and television endlessly play us stories from the Ming and Qing dynasties, not to mention the Tang, Han and Qin, how is it that the "Cultural Revolution" is of no interest to anyone? Perhaps it is still a sensitive topic, unpleasant to look back on, difficult to grasp, with political implications that might involve criticising people, so how about we just let bygones be bygones?

In fact, since the end of the Cultural Revolution, I have been avoiding the subject myself. I go back to my hometown a dozen times a year, and there are still vague remnants of the slogans on the walls of my old house, but I deliberately do not look at them. I attended a criticism meeting in the small, abandoned school and took notes; now I pass by without entering. One year when I travelled to a nearby village, someone pointed to three ruined and tumbledown buildings and said that it was the home of the rebel faction person who hanged his father. I asked if he was still alive. The answer was that he'd died ages ago, the whole family was dead now.

"Oh, they're all dead," I said, and I left in a hurry.

In our village, most of the people who lived through the Cultural

Revolution have died, but a few of them are still alive, including one who had been the head of a large faction. All of them are wrinkled and worn. Some are still out working in the fields, but others are already hobbling with a stick, walking silently through the lanes. One time when I went fishing at noon, I saw someone carrying firewood across the river, two old men with white hair and legs as thin as sticks. The tumbling waters pushed them off balance, and to prevent themselves from falling they took each other by the hand, teetering and tottering, tottering and teetering until they reached the other side. The scene was very touching, and I was still feeling emotional when I suddenly remembered that they once hated each other because they'd been in different factions during the Cultural Revolution. One had broken open the head of the other with a brick during a fight, and the other was so furious that he took a knife out one night and cut down the toon tree belonging to the other family. That toon tree's trunk had been a good six inches across. And the one who had been the head of a large faction was alone, sitting hunched over in the courtyard of his house, drinking wine – his own homebrewed maize wine of course – and holding the glass in his still strong fingers. His face is so coarse, but his temper is surprisingly gentle.

I just happened to pass the courtyard door, and he called me by my childhood nickname: "You're back? You haven't been here for months. Come and have a nip, just a little nip."

The sun was warm that day, the village extremely quiet, and I saw the wind swirling up the alleyway, looking like a rope drifting along. What tragic battles took place here back then, but now there was no more blood, no more bodies, no more scraps of paper from big-character posters, or batons or bricks... everything had gone. Just like this wind, the past had swirled far, far away.

"Do you know about the Cultural Revolution?" I asked my great-nephews.

"No," they said.

"Do you know the name of so-and-so?"

"No."

"Oh," I said. "You don't know anything at all."

You may not know the name of your grandfather's grandfather, but you'll still be passing on his family line, but what about the Cultural Revolution, is everything really over? Why is it that films and TV shows can show all the dynasties before the Qing but never touch on the Cultural Revolution – are we trying to forget the unforgettable?

After reaching my fifties, I could not move without my teenage experiences coming back to me, and my memories were like water. Am I supposed to believe that other people were not being engulfed too? The hunched-over old man who used to be the head of a big faction was drinking alone, and in his lonely old age, I guess he should be mulling something over with his wine.

I think that people who lived through the Cultural Revolution, no matter whether they persecuted others or were persecuted themselves, will have memories that last as long as they live.

It was also during the trip back to my hometown that I developed the desire to write out my memories.

The reason for this desire is that, for one thing, memory is like water stored up for a time of need; after more than forty years, mud and sand have sunk to the bottom. Once you sweep away the sediment, you can see clearly. Second, I was dissatisfied with the books on the Cultural Revolution that I had read in the immediate aftermath, as they were all too superficial and were mostly highly formulaic. More important, I felt that I had a mission, or perhaps a destiny.

Most of those who had lived through these events were dead or about to die, and those who were alive either did not write or could only write with much resentment. I was thirteen at the time and had just started learning linear equations in maths class in the first year at secondary school when the schools closed, and I had to go back to my village. I didn't debate anyone because I was no good at it, but I did help people with their big-character posters, carrying the bucket of glue. I was in a school that belonged to the United Headquarters faction, and after I went back to the village (in which the majority of residents shared the Jia surname), it also belonged to the United Headquarters, so I had no opportunity to express my point of view. Then my father was criticised, and after that, I simply did not dare speak or act out of turn. After all, I was still very young and no one paid attention to me, so although you could say I am also a victim, it would be more accurate to say I was just a bystander.

As a bystander, my experience may not reflect the entire Cultural Revolution, but I can be confident that I have observed how the Cultural Revolution took place in a small rural village. If the fires of the Cultural Revolution did not start from the bottom of Chinese society, how did the bottom of Chinese society ignite like that?

My observations stem from what I believe to be the most deeply formative events in my life, and they make up my memory. It's one person's memories, and a country's memories, I guess.

The Cultural Revolution was a huge event for our country and our generation, but for literature, it was a chaotic, confusing and intoxicating thing that filled the space between Heaven and Earth with sound and colour. At the time all this was happening, I was watching off to one side, and did not understand what I was seeing or hearing; it was all a mystery to me. Forty years later, from a literary point of view, I was still stuck off to one side, and the more I attempted to enter into what was going on, the less able I seemed to grasp it. It was like watching the moon from a mountaintop, where the moon is still far away from the mountain. I have tried my best, using what skills I have at my disposal, to write about what I had experienced to see if I could get a bit closer to the heart of the matter.

Old Kiln with its porcelain works exists in the back of beyond. Its mountains and rivers are lovely, there is a wide variety of trees, all sorts of wild creatures and domesticated beasts thrive there, and its people, although hardworking and skilled in craftsmanship, still live in extreme poverty. Because they are so very poor, they are backward, simple, petty, absurd and cruel. Historically, they have always been told what to do, and they have had the inertia of people trained in passivity. Everyone is sickly, resentful, frightened and quarrelsome. When communes were imposed, they guarded their wives and children like birds protecting their nests, but their wives were not virtuous, and their children were not filial. They depended on each other and yet they still denounced one another, like a blacksmith's shop selling nothing but knives, but never wanting the knives to hurt people. They were extremely selfish on the one hand and yet would risk their lives on the other. Meeting them, you cannot help but love them; and loving them, you hate them too. What can you do, you are one of them, part of this wretched family where love and hate follow on each other.

It's the same for them as for us, and indeed all living beings. We are like the sediment in a river flowing downstream, like the crops on the land, one comes after another. Without the upstream sediment tumbling down, how could still waters flow deep downstream? If it were not for crops in the ear, how could plants endure the winter cold and summer heat? Just as old ladies in the city are regularly cheated with worthless Peruvian banknotes in exchange for yuan because they are ignorant and greedy, the residents of Old Kiln during the Cultural Revolution had their own petty hatreds, their small profits and minor benefits, their little fantasies and tiny ideas. Each one was tumbling in the water and made the water splash about, and as those splashes grew bigger, they turned into a wave. It is just the same as walking along a rope bridge; nobody wants to make it sway, but when everyone is trembling as they walk, the bridge will begin to swing, and if it swings too much, it will surely overturn.

I once read a book by a wise man who wrote that the image projected from within is God and this idol gives power, therefore the heart is empty and fearful. If an event is already underway, it inevitably creates an effect, the whole process being confined and held in check by a particular culture or civilisation, and that can be called "fate".

The residents of Old Kiln were fated to experience the Cultural Revolution, they and we had the fate of the Cultural Revolution, and the Chinese people had that fate too.

The Cultural Revolution is over, no matter what, and it's not important what you feel about it now, because just as any great catastrophe in human history is always compensated for by progress, without the Cultural Revolution there would have been no fracture in Chinese thinking, and without the Cultural Revolution there would have been none of the social transformation that happened afterwards. The problem is that for quite some time, it seemed that everyone was a critic of the Cultural Revolution, as if no one was responsible for it. Right, so who is to blame? No one can be found to be responsible and then sentenced to death by a thousand cuts, so instead we have created a synonym for evil: "The Cultural Revolution". But I often wonder, will something like the Cultural Revolution ever happen again in China? People will think it's overblown to say such a thing, but it's true. For example, after I suffered the horrors of the 2008 Sichuan earthquake, I can still sometimes feel my bed move while taking an afternoon nap, and I wake up immediately with my heart pounding.

Someone once said something wonderful: because you only have one chance to meet with your family and friends in this world, you have to cherish them; and because people are on this Earth together, you have to cherish them too. But in reality, that's not so easy to achieve – poverty makes it easy to be mean, inequality makes it easy to be hateful, so don't think that because of how you treat others, others will treat you well too. Never believe in truth because there is no such thing; there is no "true" friendship, and there is no "true" love. Good and bad is all there is, that and time. Time oscillates between the good and the bad. It is like the land, which nurtures all kinds of plants and trees, and the plants produce flowers that can be red, white, yellow, blue, purple, black or green, and all these colours originally were present in the earth. What we cannot relinquish is that which is inside us, besides benevolence, righteousness, wisdom and faith, there is also the devil, and the devil is strong and most easily let slip. Only the abundance of resources, universal education, a sound legal system, a complete social network and the elevation of religion allow for human self-control.

In this book, there is one good person who was always trying to heal the sick, and there were so many sick people in Old Kiln that he had to speak. He says things that are quite different from the other villagers, that don't sound like the words of a village person, but I let him say them anyway. There are models for Goodman. The first was an old man in our village, and then I saw many books on Buddhism on a table in a temple, books put together by believers, published unofficially and available for free to whoever would like to take one. I took a copy of *Wang Fengyi's Book of Words and Actions*. Wang Fengyi lived during the second half of the nineteenth century, and the book describes his life and how he helped people by healing them. I read it several times and found it so rewarding that I let him merge with the old man in the village to become my good character. Goodman was a believer and a philosopher, but he was not in any way trained as such, for all his learning and experience he could only be considered a peasant thinker, and in the era when human nature had exploded into evil, he was doomed to fail. Nevertheless, he saved some villagers, was doing what he could to restore and repair the damage, maintaining moral values and attempting to preserve social harmony and peace.

Shaanxi is an amazing place it produces amazing people, and for more than a decade there have been rumours of some genius somewhere or other. I have visited many people in caves and huts in the mountains south of Xi'an, including a farmer who did not go to university but studied advanced mathematics for more than a decade. I have read a manuscript claiming to have created a new philosophy of the universe, and a draft of a book on military strategy for the current world situation. And I have talked with masters of geomancy and clairvoyance, and people who after a serious illness have suddenly acquired the power to eliminate disasters.

I was most interested in meeting folk artists, such as those who make shadow puppets, clip dough, carve wooden or clay sculptures, make displays of gore,[1] self-taught painters and "flower cutters". "Flower cutting" is the local term for making papercuts. I've met these people, and they are not the kind to get hymned in song and legend, but without exception they are geniuses in their own way, either through the possession of Heaven-sent talent or by being exceptionally strong-willed and determined.

When I wrote about Inkcap's grandmother, I was originally going to draw from my mother's spirituality and kindness. Halfway through the book, I learned that another old woman, Zhou Pingying, a flower cutter, had been discovered in northern Shaanxi. She was illiterate but her paper-cuts reached a level undreamed of for ordinary mortals. Because of the distance, I had not yet gone to seek her out, when someone happened to give me an album of her papercuts, which also included an essay by Guo Qingfeng commenting on her work. The essay was so well written that it helped me to appreciate the many images of the soul found in Zhou Pingying's papercuts. So the character of Inkcap's gran also contains the vestiges of Zhou Pingying.

Throughout the writing process, I have read and referred the most to *Wang Fengyi's Book of Words and Actions* and Zhou Pingying's album of papercuts (as well as Guo Qingfeng's essay on her work), so I would like to salute them here.

Beyond that, almost everything and everyone in Old Kiln comes from my own memory. Inkcap, that poor sweet child, though not entirely attached to a particular original, was someone who often seemed to be present while I was writing in my study, sometimes burrowing here and there to hide, or sitting dazedly at the table watching me, and occasionally calling my name. When I looked around, of course, there was no one in the study, but I was confused: could Inkcap be me? I like this character, he is so ugly, so peculiar and suffers so much. He has come from nowhere and has nowhere to go, like an alien from beyond the stars. Having been adopted into Old Kiln, because the human world has proved too cramped, it has led him into the boundless realm of the imagination, communicating with animals and plants, creating a fairytale-like world. Inkcap and his fairytale paradise show the true beauty of the natural world around Old Kiln.

In the middle of my writing, I acquired a Ming dynasty bronze Buddha, depicting Siddhartha Gautama as a child, naked, with his hair in a tight bun, large earlobes that hang down to his shoulders and two extraordinarily long arms, one hand raised above the head to point to the sky, the other hanging down below his knees to point to the ground, meaning: I am the only one in Heaven and on Earth. This Buddha stood on my desk, and

---

1. The term here translated as "make displays of gore" refers to a local tradition in Shaanxi Province, where for Spring Festival, actors perform violent plays involving scenes of terrible brutality, in which the participants attack each other with weapons, but the subsequent "injuries" are entirely a matter of sleight of hand and stage effects. The fear and disgust experienced by the audience are considered cleansing and auspicious, and such performances have been part of Shaanxi culture since at least the late Qing dynasty.

he watched my writing, and in my mind, he also served to inspire my Inkcap, to the point where I even decided that he was actually some kind of angel.

This book has taken me four whole years, four years steeped in memory. But I understand that what I'm about to complete is not a memoir, nor have I been writing an autobiography. It is fiction. Fiction has its own basic rules. I still take a realistic approach when writing about a village that has been firing porcelain since ancient times, trying to make this village have its own sound, smell, temperature, things you can see with your eyes and feel with your fingers. In my humble opinion, the point of long fiction is to write about life, to describe the experience of living. My hope is that the reader comes to believe that there really is such a village, inhabited by people who pass their days in a closed-off banality and experience the events that are described in this story; once they have accepted this premise, they may even feel that such a place and its people are too ordinary and commonplace... how can this be a novel, I could have written it myself! Well, then I will have succeeded.

When I was young, I wrote poetry and was influenced by the Tang dynasty poet Li He, who used to ride on his donkey and think about his verse, and when suddenly a line came to him, he wrote it down and put it in his bag. I also thought hard about my lines, but often when I had written a poem and asked my editor to review it, he said that every line I had written was full of poetry, but the poem when put together was completely lacking in meaning. After that, I gave up writing poetry and wrote novels instead. The novels I wrote at that time pursued the ambition of how to write philosophically and conceptually, how to be new and different, but now they seem to be full of passion. I was probably trying too hard to make an impression, with the result that it was rather pretentious. The ancient poet Li Bai once wrote:

> Beside my bed a pool of light,
> Which might be hoarfrost on the ground.
> I lift my eyes to gaze at the moon,
> I lower my head to think of my old home.

It is all very colloquial, very simple, but if you tried to write it yourself, it would be far too difficult. The simple is actually the most difficult to realise; the plainest is the most time-consuming to achieve. What do I mean by realistic writing? It means writing something true to life, and to be really true to life it must be factual, and if it is factual, it must be ordinary and mundane. You must stand firm before you can jump high. All modernist art is built on solid, realistic skills.

Writing realistically is not just a matter of saying what happened, writing realistically for the sake of doing so, for when the wall is just a heap of mud fallen across the ground, any chicken can fly over it. In my book *Shaanxi Opera*, I advocated writing realistic fiction, using the most concrete and simple sentences to build that novel's chaotic, complex and yet complete mood. It was like building a house with solid foundations, strong pillars and walls, and all the emptiness within, allowing the sunlight to shine in and the air to circulate.

In retrospect, my writing has benefited most from art theory. Twenty years ago, Western art theory really opened my eyes, with all those different modernist schools. As for Chinese books, I was keen to find the techniques of my novels in Chinese painting, in addition to my interest in the aesthetics of opera. The thinking and concepts of Western modernist art, the philosophy and techniques of traditional Chinese art, are exciting and enjoyable when combined together, just as flour can be kneaded into dough. For example, how to render a broad wash, where it seems smooth, but in fact there are veins running through the layers, so that in each Western monochrome wash there are hidden Chinese lines, heating the thin, true air and thickening the pale, sunken layers. As a result, where it appears most artless, it is in fact intentionally written that way. It seems disorderly, untidy and haphazard, but the whole is clear and transparent. Think about how traditionally painters hid their brushstrokes. Think about how to make the surroundings bitter and sad, how to make the characters depressed and dark, lonely and helpless.

The bitter thing is that the more I think about it, the more I experiment, the more I feel that I am not good at it. For four years, when I could have written quickly, I often failed to write at all, and I would get discouraged and angry, and then I would look at myself in the mirror, filled with self-loathing, and say, "No more writing!"

But not writing is even harder. There are so many addictions in the world: drug addiction, alcohol addiction, eating is the biggest addiction... and writing is also addictive. I have to write, so I'd calm down and tell myself to write to the best of my ability. In situations where I felt my skill to be lacking, all I could do was to repeatedly tell myself, "Slow down, slow down, grasp the rhythm. I want the pen to follow me, not me to be led by the pen. I want the story to develop for the characters, not the characters to run after the story."

In four years, how many things have gone wrong, how many difficulties have I suffered! When I wrote the last word of the whole book, I said, "Oh my God, I've finally finished! How well it went is another matter, but I've finally finished!"

I am grateful that I've been spared all sorts of household tasks, large and small, and I've made my wife and daughter put up with an awful lot. What I say to them is this: "How about you treat me like a CEO? When does a CEO have to worry about what's going on at home?"

I am grateful for my paintings and calligraphy, the income from which keeps me free from financial pressure, so that I can stop thinking about the market for my writing; I can write quietly and about whatever I want. I'm grateful for my body, which apart from four broken teeth, still seems to be running OK. I am grateful for the three hundred or so pens whose blood is ink, drained and quietly dying in my big basket.

ABOUT THE AUTHOR

Jia Pingwa, born in 1952, stands with Mo Yan and Yu Hua as one of the biggest names in contemporary Chinese literature. He has a huge following on the Chinese mainland, as well as in Hong Kong and Taiwan. His fiction focuses on the lives of common people, particularly in his home province of Shaanxi, and is well-known for being unafraid to explore the realm of the sexual. His bestseller *Ruined City* was banned for many years for that same reason, and pirated copies sold on the street for several thousand yuan apiece. The novel was finally unbanned in 2009, one year after Jia won the Mao Dun Award for his 2005 novel *Shaanxi Opera*. Over recent years, a steady stream of his works have been published in English translation.

ABOUT THE TRANSLATORS

James Trapp has an honours degree in Chinese from the School of Oriental and African Studies, University of London, with special papers in pre-Han archaeology and early Buddhist sculpture. After graduating, he spent ten years as an art dealer. He then refocused on making Mandarin accessible to young learners. He has published China-related books on characters, proverbs, astrology, science and technology. His translation works include new versions of Sunzi's *The Art of War* and Laozi's *Daodejing*, and, for Sinoist Books, Wang Hongjia's *Final Witness*, Ma Pinglai's *The Elm Tree*, Su Tong's *Shadow of the Hunter* and Zhou Daxin's *Longevity Park*.

Olivia Milburn is a professor at the School of Chinese, Hong Kong University. She completed her undergraduate degree in Chinese at St Hilda's College, University of Oxford, a master's in Oriental studies at Downing College, University of Cambridge, and a doctorate in classical Chinese at the School of Oriental and African Studies, University of London. She has authored several books including *Cherishing Antiquity: The Cultural Construction of an Ancient Chinese Kingdom*, *The Spring and Autumn Annals of Master Yan* and *Urbanization in Early and Medieval China: Gazetteers for the City of Suzhou*. In collaboration with Christopher Payne, she has translated two spy novels by Mai Jia, including the bestselling *Decoded*, from Chinese to English. In 2018, Milburn's translation work was recognised by the Chinese government with a Special Book Award of China, which honours contributions to bridging cultures and fostering understanding.

Christopher Payne has co-translated the award-winning novels *Decoded* and *In the Dark* by Mai Jia, and along with his frequent collaborator, Olivia Milburn, he's also brought Jiang Zilong's magnum opus, *Empires of Dust*, to an English-language audience. More recently, he has translated Jia Pingwa's *The Mountain Whisperer* and Li Juan's *Distant Sunflower Fields*. Christopher holds a PhD in Chinese literature from the School of Oriental and African Studies at the University of London, and he has spent more than a decade teaching at postsecondary institutions, most notably Sungkyunkwan University in Seoul, South Korea, and the University of Manchester in the UK. In 2020 he took up a position at the University of Toronto, where he continues to champion Chinese literature in the English-speaking world.

OTHER BOOKS BY THE AUTHOR

Broken Wings

Broken Wings tells the story of Butterfly, who is kidnapped and taken to a remote mountain village devoid of young women. There, she is imprisoned and, later, raped in the cave home of the wifeless farmer who has bought her. Butterfly's fading hopes of escape are described in her own voice, revealing the struggles of a spirited young woman.

The Mountain Whisperer

An epic novel that retells the turbulent birth of modern China from its rural margins. High in the mountains of central China, a dying funeral singer tells four interweaved tragedies of all-too-human players caught in the earthly struggles of revolt and reform, and the mythic cycle of avarice, vengeance and suffering.

The Sojourn Teashop

The sisterhood meets every morning in Hai Ruo's teashop to discuss life, love, careers and everything that gets in the way of happiness. Hai Ruo strives to keep the sisters together and seeks spiritual intervention to provide answers, but the cracks grow wider as pressure closes in.

About **Sino**ist Books

We hope you were gripped by this story of upheaval in Old Kiln.

SINOIST BOOKS brings the best of Chinese fiction to English-speaking readers. We aim to create a greater understanding of Chinese culture and society, and provide an outlet for the ideas and creativity of the country's most talented authors.

To let us know what you thought of this book, or to learn more about the diverse range of exciting Chinese fiction in translation we publish, find us online. If you're as passionate about Chinese literature as we are, then we'd love to hear your thoughts!

SINOIST

BOOKS

www.sinoistbooks.com
@sinoistbooks